Rowan the Red Squirrel

Lynne Rickards and Jon Mitchell

Picture Kelpies

Deep in the woods, in a crooked old tree,
lived two little squirrels, with Mum, who made three.

Hazel was brave – a flash and a flurry,
while Rowan was shy, and tended to worry.

One morning Mum said to her kits in the drey,
"You're old enough now to explore a short way.

Stay close to our tree. Don't pass those three rocks.
Be careful, be quick, and watch out for the fox."

Hazel was thrilled and skipped straight down the tree.
"What an adventure we'll have now we're free!"

Soon she was munching a nice pinecone treat.
"Delicious," she said. "Hurry, Rowan – let's eat!"

Rowan's wee whiskers were twitching like mad.
He had a strong feeling – that feeling was bad.

"Wait for *me*, Hazel!" he cried with a frown.
"Don't be a scaredy-paws, Rowan. Come down!"

Rowan came scrabbling down the old tree,
and followed his sister, whose tail he could see.

Hazel hopped off through the woods in her haste,
calling, "Blackberries – yum. Come quickly and taste!"

Her brother said, "Hazel, don't go past the rocks.
Remember what Mum said: Watch out for the fox!"

Just then, they heard a loud **RAT-A-TAT-TAT!**
Rowan squealed, "Oh Hazel! Help, what was that?"

Rowan was quivering, too scared to speak,
when Hazel said, "That's just a woodpecker's beak!"

Then Hazel spied toadstools, all speckled with white.
She leapt further on and gave one a small bite.

"The bushes are rustling!" squeaked Rowan. "Right there!
What is it? A lion? A tiger? A bear?"

The rustling got louder and just as he'd feared,
a terrible, horrible…

...HEDGEHOG appeared!

"Silly," cried Hazel. "A hedgehog's not scary."
"I guess not," said Rowan, still trembling, "not very."

Hazel bounced off and went straight past the rocks,
as Rowan called, "Hazel, remember the fox!"

But Hazel was gone; Rowan had to go too.
He knew it was wrong, but what else could he do?

That's when he heard a low thundering sound,
a watery **WHOOSH** tumbling down to the ground.

"A waterfall!" Hazel cried, paddling about.
She played with a frog and a silvery trout.

Rowan was worried and stayed on the shore.
He'd never been near so much water before.

The splashing was scary, the burn looked so deep.
He wondered what creatures were lurking beneath ...

Could that be an octopus, curled in the dark?
And just behind Hazel, the fin of a shark?

As Rowan sat nervously watching her play,
he spotted some movement not too far away.

A flash of red fur, a quick streak of white,
and two amber eyes that gave Rowan a fright.

He jumped up and down and cried, "Hazel, look out!
Behind you! *Behind you!* The fox is about!"

Hazel just laughed and said, "Silly old bean!
I can't believe how many monsters you've seen."

"It's true!" Rowan cried. "This one's real, Hazel – run!"
And suddenly, that was the end of her fun.

The fox took a flying leap high in the air.
She landed – **KERSPLASH** – and poor Hazel froze there.

They stood nose-to-nose for a second or two,
then Rowan saw just what he needed to do.

He jumped on the fox and pulled hard on her tail.
The fox whirled and snapped while he clung on and wailed.

"Run, Hazel, run!" Rowan cried. "I'll come later."
She had to move quickly, before the fox ate her!

Hazel sped off and then Rowan jumped free.
He raced to catch up and they shot up a tree.

The fox paced around the tree, breathless and mad.
She glared at the squirrel lunch she could have had.

Foxes can't climb, so she soon slunk away,
hoping for better luck some other day.

"You saved me!" cried Hazel. "I froze like a stone."
"Never mind that," Rowan said. "Let's get home."

Night time was falling. They both peered around.
They heard hoots and growls, and strange eerie sounds.

High in the shadows, two giant eyes stared,
and this time both Rowan *and* Hazel were scared.

The creature swooped down and came close as could be.
Hazel and Rowan clung tight to their tree.

The giant winged monster swept by, then flew on.
"An owl!" cried Hazel. "Thank goodness it's gone."

"We battled a fox," Rowan said, "and we beat it!
I think we can handle that owl if we meet it."

Although night was coming, young Rowan felt good.
If he had to be brave, now he knew that he could.

Hazel was thinking hard which way to go,
when a **WHOOSH**-ing noise somewhere nearby let her know…

They whizzed down the tree and set off on the ground.
The whooshing they'd heard was the waterfall sound!

They met the same hedgehog who'd caused such a fright,
and nearby, a toadstool had one squirrel bite…

Hazel was pleased to have spotted this clue.
She'd nibbled a trail – what a smart thing to do!

A woodpecker's beak hammered **RAT-A-TAT-TAT!**
Brave Rowan was not even bothered by that.

"Blackberries," Hazel said. "Look what I've found!
I know we were here from our prints on the ground."

They went a bit further and found something more:
the pinecone that Hazel had munched on before.

Now they were right where they needed to be –
just over there stood their crooked old tree!

"We're home!" shouted Hazel. She bounded ahead,
zipped straight up their tree and dived right into bed.

"Where have you *been*?" their Mum cried, in a state.
"You're such naughty squirrels to come home so late!"

She listened, amazed by their frightening tales
of foxes and hedgehogs and dark forest trails.

"Mum, I'm so sorry I went past the rocks.
But Rowan was brave and outsmarted the fox!"

Rowan said, "Hazel was smarter than me.
She found lots of clues that led back to our tree."

"What an adventure you've had, my brave pair!"
Mum couldn't stay mad, though she'd had quite a scare.

The two little squirrels, and Mum, who made three,
were now just as happy as squirrels can be.

To Peter, this book is for you – S.N.

For Toby, my (not so) little brother – B.W.

This paperback edition first published in 2021 by Andersen Press Ltd.

First published in 2019 by Andersen Press Ltd.,

20 Vauxhall Bridge Road, London SW1V 2SA.

Text copyright © Sally Nicholls, 2019.

Illustration copyright © Bethan Woollvin, 2019.

The rights of Sally Nicholls and Bethan Woollvin to be

identified as the author and illustrator of this work

have been asserted by them in accordance with the

Copyright, Designs and Patents Act, 1988.

Printed and bound in China.

1 3 5 7 9 10 8 6 4 2

British Library Cataloguing in Publication Data available.

ISBN 978 1 78344 898 2

THE BUTTON BOOK

SALLY NICHOLLS

BETHAN WOOLLVIN

ANDERSEN PRESS

Here's a **red** button.
I wonder what happens
when you press it?

Here's an **orange** button.
What does the orange button do?

It's a clapping button!
Everybody clap!

What happens when you
press the **blue** button?

It's a singing button!

"The wheels on the bus go round and round"

Does it know any other songs?

Shall we press
the **green** button now?

Excuse me, say sorry at once.

I'm warning you.
This is your last chance.

Well, if you're going to be like that,
we're going to press the **yellow** button instead.

Bounce!

It's a bouncing button!
Everybody bounce!

Bounce!

Bounce!

Bounce!

Bounce!

Help!

Press the **pink** button or
we'll be bouncing forever.

Hurrah, it's
a hug button.

Hug time!

That's the best
button of all.

You **do** want to press the next button?

Are you sure?

Are you really sure?

Please, press the **pink** button, **quick!**

"Hey– this is HUG time!"

Ahh... that's better. Hug time.

Oh no, it's that rude **green** button again.
Have you learned any manners yet?

Ah, the **blue** button.
What shall we sing this time?

"Twinkle, twinkle, little star..."

Back to the **red** button again.

Do you remember
what noise it makes?

Beep!

Look, it's a **new** button.

What does a **white** button do?

Shhhh… it's a sleeping button.

Goodnight, everyone.

Brief Contents

Contents

7   **Host Resistance to Viral Infections** **140**

Preface

Understanding Viruses is the product of 10 years of teaching introductory virology to undergraduate students majoring in biology, microbiology, medical technology, or pre-med and other pre-professionals. Some of the students had not taken a microbiology course or had not taken an introductory molecular and cellular biology course prior to virology. I struggled to find a textbook that combined the clinical or medical aspects of viral diseases along with the molecular biology aspect of viral replication. I also found some students were not adequately prepared for my course and needed some form of "refresher" to aid them through the course material. Students were more enthusiastic to learn the molecular aspect of viral diseases if the clinical perspective was presented with it. Unfortunately, the textbooks available did not offer this blend of educational material. As a result, I chose to focus not on viruses as tools to study molecular biology, but instead organize this text to generate connections by covering molecular biology, pathobiology (the observed nature of disease, its causes, processes, development, and consequences), epidemiology, and the historical perspectives of virology.

Virology is a dynamic discipline. Most recently, this field has gained increased importance because of bioterrorism, gene therapy, human cloning, vaccine production, biotechnology, as well as new and emerging viruses such as HIV, hepatitis C, hantaviruses, nipah, foot and mouth, and West Nile. Significant outbreaks of these viral diseases worldwide and over time portray a future in which new and emerging infectious viral diseases will challenge the current arsenal of prophylaxis and treatment. My intent was to create a book that provides a "big picture" or global approach to understanding these viruses, host-virus interactions, and molecular biology concepts. While my focus is on human viral diseases, I included examples of viral diseases of animals and chapters on the history of clinical trials, gene therapy, and xenotransplantation (animal to human transplants); prions and viroids; plant viruses; and bacteriophages.

Special Features

I also wanted to create a virology textbook that contained all of the "bells and whistles" that books for first-year biology students have; for example, a full-color format, case studies, and other current pedagogy that would engage students in the learning process. Because I am a visual learner and many students also learn better visually, the book includes carefully rendered visual information. In addition, the text has a number of special features.

- Each chapter opens with a contemporary case study that presents real-world scenarios. The chapters end with follow-up questions connecting the case study to the chapter's concepts to enhance student learning. A number of chapters have additional case studies and questions at the end.
- *Virus Files* boxes throughout the text connect a chapter topic to research or virology techniques currently being done or used in the field.
- *Refresher Boxes* and a glossary are there to assist students who may need to brush up on biological concepts introduced in introductory biology courses.
- Comprehensive literature and video resources are listed at the end of each chapter.
- The terms important to the understanding of virology are in **boldface** type.

This book can be used at the sophomore to junior level. Lay people interested in viruses may also find this a book to fulfill that need. Virology is a very exciting and fast-paced field with many challenging issues. I hope that this textbook will inspire some students to become virologists.

Ancillaries Accompanying the Text

To assist you in teaching this course and supplying your students with the best in teaching aids, Jones and Bartlett Publishers has prepared a complete ancillary package available to all adopters of *Understanding Viruses*. Additional information and review copies of any of the following items are available through your Jones and Bartlett sales representative.

For the Instructor

Compatible with Windows and Macintosh platforms, the Instructor's ToolKit CD-ROM provides adopters with the following ancillaries.

- The *PowerPoint® Lecture Outline Slides* presentation package, prepared by the author, Teri Shors, provides lecture notes, graphs, and images for each chapter of *Understanding Viruses*. Instructors with the Microsoft PowerPoint software can customize the outlines, art, and order of presentation. The PowerPoint files have also been prepared in HTML format for use in online course management systems.
- The *Test Bank* prepared by Laraine Powers, East Tennessee State University, and Barry Margulies, Towson University, is available as text files. The test bank contains over 2,000 questions. A duplicate set of files is formatted for your own online courses using WebCT and Blackboard.
- The *PowerPoint Image Bank* provides the illustrations, photograph, and tables (to which Jones and Bartlett Publishers holds the copyright or has permission to reprint digitally) inserted into PowerPoint slides. With the Microsoft PowerPoint program, you can quickly and easily copy individual slides into your existing lecture slides. If you do not own a copy of Microsoft PowerPoint or a compatible software program, a Microsoft PowerPoint Viewer is included on the CD-ROM.

For the Student

The Web site we developed exclusively for *Understanding Viruses*, can be found at http://biology.jbpub.com/book/virology. The site contains a free online study guide with chapter outlines, animated flashcards, interactive glossary, crossword puzzles, animations, research and reference links, and links to news sources.

Encounters with Microbiology, Volumes 1 and 2, edited by Jeffrey C. Pommerville of Glendale Community College, brings together "Vital Signs" articles from *Discover* magazine in which health professionals use their knowledge of microbiology to solve their puzzling medical cases.

Guide to Infectious Diseases by Body System, by Jeffrey C. Pommerville, is an excellent tool for learning about microbial diseases. Each of the 15 body system units presents a brief introduction to the anatomical system and the bacterial, viral, fungal, or parasitic organisms capable of infecting the system.

20th Century Microbe Hunters, by Robert Krasner, Providence College, offers a dramatic portrayal of the achievements and lives of microbiologists such as Charles J. Nicolle (typhus epidemic), Barry Marshall and J. Robin Warren (*Helicobacter pylori*), Luc Montagnier and Robert Gallo (HIV), and Donald R. Hopkins (guinea worm).

How Pathogenic Viruses Work, by Lauren Sompayrac, is a concise summary of the basics of virology written in an understandable and entertaining manner. The book comprises nine lectures covering the essential elements of virus-host interactions with descriptive graphics, helpful mnemonic tactics for retaining the concepts, and brief lecture reviews.

Acknowledgments

Creating a book for educational purposes involves many people. First and foremost, I want to thank Jones and Bartlett acquisition editors Steve Weaver and Cathleen Sether for their enthusiasm in producing this 4-color book. Writing a textbook is a major undertaking that takes time and financial support. The National Science Foundation's Course, Curriculum, and Laboratory Improvement Program supported this book. The program provided funding for course release time, some summer support and assessment of this project. Jeffrey Pommerville was instrumental in securing NSF funding and in assessing this project. I especially appreciated his candor in answering my "neophyte author" questions. Additional financial support for sabbatical and release time was provided by the University of Wisconsin Oshkosh Faculty Development Program and a modest Biology (Virology) Fund. Support from the Biology (Virology) Fund was used to purchase materials to expedite writing (e.g., technical books, USB flash drives, and printer cartridges). The following individuals contributed gifts to the Biology (Virology) Fund: Drs. Patrick G. Dowling, Donald H. McDonald, Donald J. McDonald, Thomas W. Zoch, Mr. and Mrs. Jim Mitchell, Mr. and Mrs. Brian Teviotdale, and Roy Callow. I greatly appreciate Roy's enthusiasm for this project. Erin Czech (interlibrary loan) and Cynthia Huebschen were instrumental in fulfilling my requests for materials while researching virology literature.

The Jones and Bartlett team has been phenomenal to work with. Molly Steinbach deftly secured numerous colleagues to peer evaluate chapters of the book. Peer evaluation has been instrumental in creating this educational resource. Dean DeChambeau prepared the manuscript and has tolerated me. Production manager Lou Bruno has been a joy to work with. His professionalism, quick wit, management skills, and hard work ethic are exceptional. A first edition of any book in a fast-paced field of science requires patience. Lou handled the fluidity of the book with grace. Copyeditor Jenny Bagdigian, with keen eyesight, read every word of this manuscript, and Kathy Garcia created the index. Special thanks go to photo researchers Christine McKeen, Kimberly Potvin, and Lee Michelson. Christine has the uncanny ability to make things happen. Whether it is contacting a premiere scientist for an image, seeking permissions from other sources, or organizing credit lines, Christine's persistence was much appreciated. Artists at Imagineering drew the illustrations in the book. Scientific photographer James Gathany went out of his way to provide images not yet catalogued at the CDC's PHIL site.

The book benefits from several fellow microbiologists. I wish to thank past and present peer evaluators, especially Loraine Powers at East Tennessee State University for reviewing most of the chapters and the development of the test bank. Colleen McDermott critically reviewed Chapter 7 (Host Resistance to Viral Infections). Brian Ledwell's support in the development of animations to supplement the Web site was exceptional. Virologist, former undergraduate mentor, colleague, and friend John Cronn was a strong positive influence in the writing of the epidemiological and historical perspectives. John has kept me focused for over 25 years. Other important influential mentors along the way are Bernard Moss (Chief of the Laboratory of Viral Diseases at the National Institutes of Health), Bertram Jacobs, Jean M. Schmidt, Vern Winston, Gordon Schrank, and the late Denise McGuire. Thanks to those colleagues and friends who were brave enough to ask me how the book was coming along: Todd and Susie Sandrin, Susan McFadden, Linda Freed, Arlene Harley, Andy Keech, Todd Kostman, Mandi and Chuck Isaacson, Dan and Billie Jo Rylance, David Dilkes, Sheldon Cooper, Tom Perzentka, Ehud Katz, Schmuel Rozenblatt, and Jim Armentrout.

I thank all my former and present students who attended an 8 AM class on viruses during the winter/spring semesters in Oshkosh, Wisconsin, for the past 10 years. In addition to regular instruction, each class embraced with enthusiasm group projects on the 1918 flu, polio, and pandemic flu planning. Some students reviewed parts of the book or commented on the figures. Many encouraged me and appreciated my approach toward teaching. I hope that some of these students will be inspired to rise to the challenge of being virus hunters in the field. I hope those who read this text will continue to be critical and provide suggestions for improving it.

I could not finish without acknowledging Darin Reiger for putting up with me during the most intense months of production. He has seen me working long hours at the computer, dealing with the transition to progressive eyeglasses, placing cubed sugar and other items that do not require low-temperature storage in the refrigerator, and dreaming about prions all night. Every word, every figure, and every table has occupied my brain for over three years. All books are a product of people. *Understanding Viruses* is no exception.

Reviewers play a major role in the success of a book. I thank these reviewers who have spent time commenting on the drafts for *Understanding Viruses*:

Lawrence R. Aaronson, Utica College
Sergio Abreu, Fordham University
Shorei Amini, Temple University
Margo Brinton, Georgia State University
Eunice Carlson, Michigan Technological University
John Cronn, St. Cloud State University
Jonathan Dinman, University of Maryland
R.D. Ellender, University of Southern Mississiippi
Lisa M. Flick, Alfred University
Kathryn Goddard, Ursinus College
Richard Hardy, Indiana University
Robert L. Harrod, Southern Methodist University
J.A. Hiscox, University of Leeds
Jeff Langland, Arizona State University
Candi Lostroh, Colorado College
Jennette M. Loutsch, Arkansas State University
Barry Margulies, Towson University
Nancy L. McQueen, California State University, Los Angeles
Yaw A. Nsiah, Eastern Connecticut State University
Laraine Powers, East Tennessee State University
Hua Shen, Virginia State University
Michael Teng, Pennsylvania State University
Stephen Torosian, University of New Hampshire
Chris Upton, University of Victoria
Paul Wanda, Southern Illinois University, Edwardsville
Xiuqing Wang, South Dakota State University
Jeannine D. Williams, College of Marin

The development of this text was supported by a National Science Foundation grant.

This book is dedicated to the late Elaine (Motschke) Gross, my mother.

Teri Shors
Oshkosh, Wisconsin
February 2008

About the Author

Teri Shors received her doctoral degree from Arizona State University, Tempe, Arizona. Following her doctoral degree, she served as a postdoctoral fellowship under the direction of Dr. Bernard Moss in the Laboratory of Viral Diseases, National Institute of Allergy and Infectious Diseases at the National Institutes of Health, Bethesda, Maryland. For the past 10 years, Dr. Shors has been a Professor of Microbiology at the University of Wisconsin–Oshkosh where she teaches introductory microbiology, virology, and molecular and cellular biology. She has authored peer-reviewed research papers in virology. Her research specialty is poxviruses. She was the principal investigator or co-principal investigator for a Merck/American Association for the Advancement of Science (AAAS) and several National Science Foundation (NSF) grants, including a grant to develop and write an undergraduate virology textbook to better prepare students for the rapidly changing field of viruses and viral diseases. She is a recipient of a University of Wisconsin–Oshkosh Distinguished Teaching Award, an Endowed Professorship, and is a Wisconsin Teaching Scholar. She serves on the American Society for Virology's Education and Career Development Committee. Professor Shors has presented papers at scientific and educational conferences consistently throughout her career. She has led a number of cross-disciplinary projects at the University of Wisconsin–Oshkosh that have received national recognition (http://www.uwosh.edu/departments/biology/shors/).

Viral Pestilence Timeline

1500-1960

A Brief Rule to guide the Common People of *New-England* how to Order themselves and theirs in the *Small-Pox* and *Measels*.

THE *Small-Pox* (whose nature and cure the *Measels* follow) is a disease in the blood, endeavouring to recover a new form and state.

2. THIS nature attempts — 1. By Separation of the impure from the pure, thrusting it out from the Veins to the Flesh.— 2. By driving out the impure from the Flesh to the Skin.

3. THE first Separation is done in the first four Days by a feverish boiling Ebullition) of the Blood, laying down the impurities in the Fleshy parts which kindly effected the Feverish tumult is calmed.

4. THE second Separation from the Flesh to the Skin, or *Superficies* is done through the rest of the time of the disease.

5. THERE are several Errors in ordering these sick ones in both these Opera-

Courtesy of the National Library of Medicine.

1957
Asian influenza pandemic

1847–1848
Influenza pandemic

1894
First polio outbreak in the U.S. (Vermont)

1649
Smallpox, Boston hit hard.

1794
1796–1797 yellow fever outbreaks, Philadelphia

1912–1916
Dengue fever pandemic

1527–1530
Smallpox outbreaks Inca empire (Peru)

1657
Measles, Boston

1798
Yellow Fever outbreak, Philadelphia (one of the worst)

1500 1520 1540 1560 1580 1600 1620 1640 1660 1680 1700 1720 1740 1760 1780 1800 1820 1840 1860 1880 1900 1900 1920 1940

1518–1520
Smallpox outbreaks, Aztec empire (Mexico)

1616
Smallpox, New England, Native American Indian population hit hard.

1759
Measles, most places inhabited, North America

1818
First recorded epidemic of Dengue fever, Peru

1857–1898
Influenza pandemic

1952
U.S. highest record of polio

1918–1919
Spanish influenza pandemic

1916
Large polio epidemic, New York city

Courtesy of the National Library of Medicine.

1960-present

1962–1965
Rubella (German measles) pandemic

1967
First Marburg hemorrhagic fever outbreak, initial cases were laboratory workers handling infected African green monkeys imported from Uganda; Marburg, Germany and the former Yugoslavia.

1968
Hong Kong influenza pandemic

1976
First Ebola outbreaks, Democratic Republic of Congo and Sudan

Courtesy of Dr. Lyle Conrad/CDC.

1989
First Ebola-Reston virus outbreaks at monkey quarantine facilities, Reston, Virginia (no humans became ill)

Courtesy of CDC.

1993
Sin nombre (hantavirus) outbreak, 4-corners disease (U.S.)

1997
Avian influenza, Hong Kong

1999
Nipah virus outbreak, Malaysia (pig and mainly human mortalities)

First recognized West Nile virus outbreak in the U.S. (New York City)

2000–2001
Ebola outbreak, Uganda (highest mortality of all Ebola outbreaks)

2001
Foot and mouth disease virus outbreak, United Kingdom (no human cases)

2003
SARS pandemic (first appeared in southern China in November 2002, recognized as a global threat in March, 2003)

Monkeypox multistate outbreak

2003–present
Avian influenza, rare but highly lethal in humans, Hong Kong, China, Indonesia, Viet Nam, Thailand, Cambodia, Turkey, Iraq, Egypt, Azerbaijan, Djibouti

Courtesy of James Gathany/CDC.

© Ablestock.

© Ablestock.

2006–2007
Porcine Reproductive and Respiratory Syndrome Virus (also called blue ear pig disease), China

2007
Foot and mouth disease virus outbreak, Southern England

Viral hemorrhagic septicema spreads to the Great Lakes region, U.S.

2006
Mumps outbreaks, midwestern U.S.

Chikungunya virus outbreak, La Reunion Island (France)

2005
Largest and deadliest outbreak of Marburg hemorrhagic fever, Angola

First outbreak of polio in the U.S. in 26 years

1960

1980

2000

2020

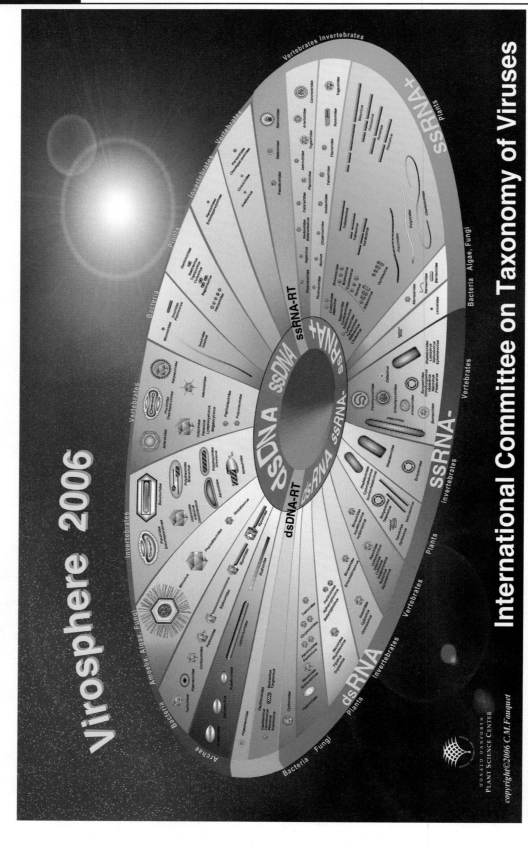

Virosphere 2006

International Committee on Taxonomy of Viruses

DONALD DANFORTH
PLANT SCIENCE CENTER

copyright©2006 C.M.Fauquet

Schematic of virus orders, families of genera grouped by their hosts and nucleic acid genomes. The International Committee on the Taxonomy of Viruses (ICTV) is committed to creating a universal virus database to describe all viruses.

UNDERSTANDING
VIRUSES

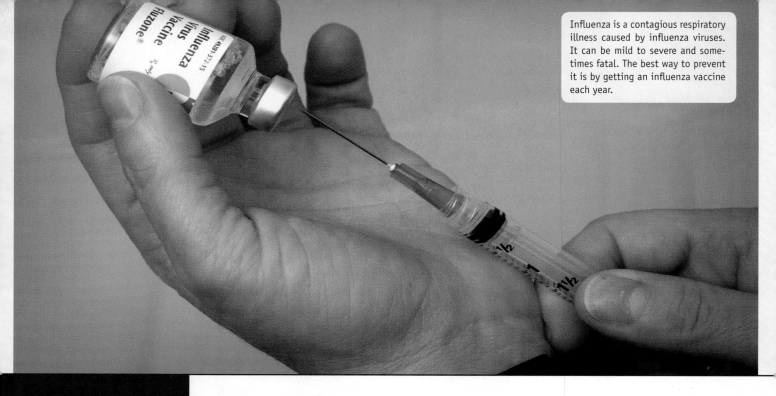

Influenza is a contagious respiratory illness caused by influenza viruses. It can be mild to severe and sometimes fatal. The best way to prevent it is by getting an influenza vaccine each year.

CHAPTER

1

Introduction to Viruses

ff *Nothing brings us so close to the riddle of Life—and its solution—as viruses.* **JJ**

Wolfhard Weidel, virologist

CASE STUDY

Recently you were inspired by an instructor in a virology course to subscribe to ProMED mail. While searching the ProMED mail archives for outbreaks of viral hemorrhagic fever, you found a ProMED mail post entitled "Undiagnosed Hemorrhagic Fever—Angola: Request for Information." It was dated March 15, 2005. The post describes the death of two nurses working at the same Huige province hospital. At the time of the post, 56 people with similar symptoms had died in Angola. Hospital workers told journalists that the illness began with a 2-day fever. Then the patient would cough up blood, lapse into a coma, and die within 4 days. The World Health Organization was planning on investigating the outbreak.

Coincidentally, you have learned that a college friend has joined the Peace Corps. At the end of the semester, he will graduate and then be deployed to Angola to work on HIV/AIDS awareness and youth outreach. You have asked him if he is aware of the viral hemorrhagic fevers such as Ebola, Lassa, or any new hemorrhagic fever viruses in Angola (**Figure CS 1-1**). He said he was very naïve about hemorrhagic fever viruses and would appreciate it if you would do some more research on this subject on his behalf.

■ Figure CS 1-1

Angola is located on the Atlantic coast of southern Africa. It is bordered by Namibia to the south and Zambia and Zaire to the east and north. Angola's 994 mile-long coastline and its four major ports make it a natural trans-shipment point for the entire region. Angola has one of the world's worst child mortality rates, with one in four failing to live beyond their fifth birthday. Routine immunizations rarely happen. Yellow fever, Dengue fever, and Crimean Congo hemorrhagic fever outbreaks are **endemic** to Angola.

When you think of the word *virus*, what comes to mind? The invisible entity responsible for the common cold? The cause of sexually transmitted diseases? A mysterious and insidious killer, such as the one that causes Ebola hemorrhagic fever? Biological agents that look like "lunar lander" spaceships (**Figure 1-1**)? Have you ever been sickened by images of animals or humans suffering from viral diseases?

This chapter begins your journey through the invisible world of viruses. The word *virus* has been used in the medical world for almost 200 years. In the early 1790s, it simply meant *poison* or *poisonous slime*. A short definition of viruses describes them as submicroscopic agents that are capable of growth in living cells. These biological entities are both beneficial and harmful to humankind. This overview of viruses provides a basis for understanding their impact on all living organisms.

1.1 Viral Impact on the Environment, Research, and Disease

■ Viruses and Aquatic Ecosystems

Viruses are usually associated with negative effects. Without viruses, though, the earth would be a very different place—maybe even a planet without life! For example, did you know that viruses are the most abundant biological entity in both freshwater and seawater? More than one million viruses are present in a teaspoon of water. Most of these viruses are known as **bacteriophages** (viruses that infect bacteria). For each bacterium in the water there are 15 to 25 virus particles. Bacteria and microscopic plankton are food for nearly all aquatic animals. The discovery of viral abundance in natural water has lead to the conclu-

■ **Figure 1-1**
Colored electron micrograph of viruses (referred to as bacteriophages) attacking the bacterium *Escherichia coli*. Many bacteriophages have a "lunar lander" or head-and-tail structure. The bacteriophage infects the bacterium by attaching to the cell wall. Subsequently, its genetic material enters the cell.

sion that viruses are significant biological agents involved in both the mortality (death) of aquatic microorganisms and in the building of aquatic communities. How can this be?

Dramatic experiments led by Gunnar Bratbak in 1990 were performed in which bacteriophages were selectively removed from seawater and the growth rates of the remaining bacterial and planktonic organisms measured. It was expected that the bacterial and planktonic populations would dramatically increase because they *were freed from viral infection*. Surprisingly, the bacterial populations stopped growing completely, because they depended upon nutrients released as the bacteria were killed by viruses (**Figure 1-2**). Without the death of these microbes via viruses, there was no "fuel" to keep the aquatic community running. Hence, viruses are essential for regulating both saltwater and freshwater ecosystems.

■ The Hershey-Chase Blender Experiment

Since their discovery, bacteriophages have taught us many things about the molecular biology of cells. Viruses of bacteria were termed bacteriophages (the suffix "phage" comes from the Greek for 'eating') because of their ability to eat or **lyse** bacteria. One of the first bacteriophages used in the laboratory, T2, infects the host bacterium *Escherichia coli*. The T2 bacteriophage consists almost entirely of a tightly condensed piece of DNA that is surrounded or packaged by a protein coat. The bacteriophage infects *E. coli* and utilizes the cell to reproduce more T2 bacteriophages (**Figure 1-3**).

In 1952, geneticists Alfred Hershey and Martha Chase provided evidence that DNA was the hereditary material. They set up an experiment in which they asked the question, What component of a T2 bacteriophage (protein or DNA) enters the host bacterium?

In their experiment, Hershey and Chase grew two cultures of *E. coli* in the laboratory. One flask of *E. coli* was infected with T2 bacteriophages, in which the protein coat of the bacteriophage was labeled with radioactive sulphur [^{35}S]. The second *E. coli* flask was infected with T2 bacteriophages in which the genetic material (DNA) of the virus had been labeled with radioactive phosphorous [^{32}P]. The radioactive T2 bacteriophages were allowed to attach and infect the *E. coli* (**Figure 1-4**). After infection, the *E. coli* radioactively labeled T2 bacteriophage mixtures were poured into separate blenders. The blender dislodged the bacteriophage particles from the bacterial host cells in each mixture. The mixtures were then centrifuged (concentrated). This separated the bacteriophage particles in the supernate liquid from the bacterial cells in the precipitate. Hershey and Chase found that the supernate contained [^{35}S] (the viral protein) and the precipitate (cell portion) contained the [^{32}P] (the viral DNA). This experiment concluded that the DNA labeled with [^{32}P] transmitted the infective component of the bacteriophage. The DNA was the genetic material that specified all of the information needed to synthesize new T2 bacteriophages (Figure 1-4).

Bacteriophages and other types of viruses continue to be used as molecular biology tools to study host-cell interactions and the molecular biology of cells. Viruses have taught us much of what we know about the processes of replication, transcription, and translation.

■ Bacteriophage Therapy

If you experience a bacterial infection that is not healing on its own, a physician will prescribe an antibiotic such as penicillin or erythromycin to treat the infection. Before penicillin's discovery in the 1940s, though, the medical community was focusing its attention on bacteria-killing research (i.e., the use of bacteriophages to kill bacteria pathogenic to humans). Felix Twort (England) and Felix d'Herrelle (France) first

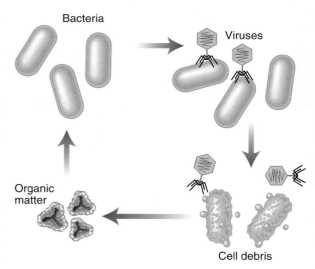

Aquatic Food Web

Bacteria

Viruses

Organic matter

Cell debris

■ **Figure 1-2**
Viruses free up organic matter so that new life can be generated.

■ **Figure 1-3**
Diagram of a lytic bacteriophage infection.

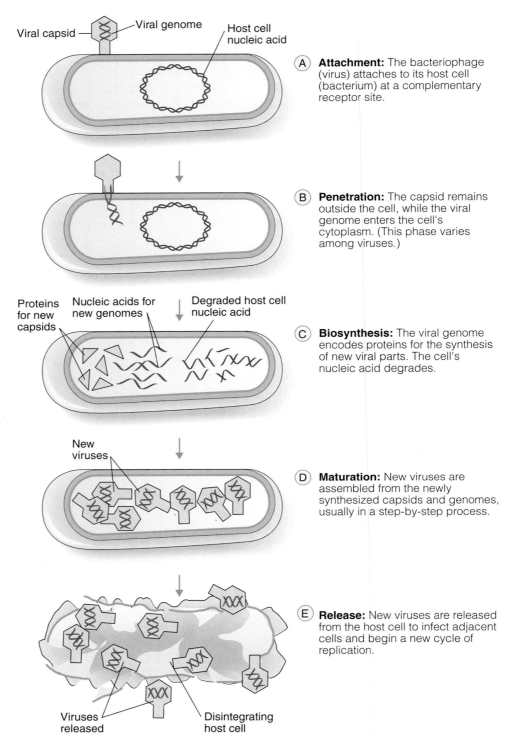

A **Attachment:** The bacteriophage (virus) attaches to its host cell (bacterium) at a complementary receptor site.

B **Penetration:** The capsid remains outside the cell, while the viral genome enters the cell's cytoplasm. (This phase varies among viruses.)

C **Biosynthesis:** The viral genome encodes proteins for the synthesis of new viral parts. The cell's nucleic acid degrades.

D **Maturation:** New viruses are assembled from the newly synthesized capsids and genomes, usually in a step-by-step process.

E **Release:** New viruses are released from the host cell to infect adjacent cells and begin a new cycle of replication.

described bacteriophages ("phages" for short) in 1915 and 1917, respectively. Before the use of penicillin, it was determined that each type of bacterium can only be infected with a specific type of phage. In other words, phages exhibit a very narrow host range: a phage that infects the bacterium *E. coli* will not infect the *Streptococcus pneumoniae* bacterium.

The idea of phage therapy formed the basis for applied medical research, as well as for the 1924 Pulitzer Prize-winning novel *Arrowsmith* by Sinclair Lewis. Researchers in

(A)

1

Phage containing
^{32}P-labeled DNA infects
nonradioactive cell.

DNA

Centrifuge

Ms. Chase's
blender

Phage heads
are removed
in supernatant.

Infecting
labeled DNA

Infected cell
remains in
precipitate.

Progeny phages form;
cell lyses.

Progeny phages
contain some
^{32}P-labeled DNA.

(B)

2

Phage containing
^{35}S-labeled protein infects
nonradioactive cell.

Centrifuge

Ms. Chase's
blender

Phage heads
are removed
in supernatant.

Infecting
nonlabeled DNA

Infected cell
remains in
precipitate.

Progeny phages form;
cell lyses.

Progeny phages
contain almost no
^{35}S-labeled protein.

Conclusion: Mainly DNA, not protein, is inherited from parental phage.

■ **Figure 1-4**
Diagram depicting the design of Alfred Hershey and Martha Chase's experiment. It provided evidence that DNA was associated with the genetic material of the bacteriophage.

Europe began to use bacteriophages to treat infections. In some cases, a liquid containing bacteriophages was poured onto an open wound; in others, the bacteriophages were given orally, via aerosol, or injected. The results were varied, and when antibiotics came into the mainstream phage therapy largely faded in the West. Countries in the East such as Poland and Russia, however, continued to keep phage therapy research alive (see Chapter 21).

Phage therapy is now being reconsidered as a weapon against antibiotic-resistant "superbugs." These superbugs are lurking in hospitals and cause deadly infections that cannot be treated with the strongest antibiotics currently available. Research and development of alternative therapies are urgently needed to combat this superbug crisis.

■ Gene Therapy

Each of us carries a few defective genes. We remain blissfully unaware of this fact unless one of our close relatives or friends suffers from a genetic disease. Most of us do not suffer any harmful effects from defective genes because we carry two copies of nearly all genes (one inherited from each parent). This redundancy exists so that if one of our genes is defective, the second (functional) gene compensates for the defect.

In 1990, W. French Anderson, R. Michael Blaese, and Kenneth Culver—American pioneer researchers at the National Institutes of Health (NIH)—announced results of the first clinical gene therapy trial to genetically correct the adenosine deaminase (ADA) gene belonging to a 4-year-old girl. ADA deficiency is a rare but very serious defect that causes immune deficiency, resulting in the lack of normal protection against bacterial and viral infections.

How was a good copy of ADA delivered to the girl? The hero was a retrovirus. The retrovirus was genetically engineered to carry a working ADA gene so that the body could produce functioning adenosine deaminase and consequently eliminate the root cause of the disease. To date, the girl is alive and well.

At least 2000 laboratories are engaged in gene therapy research worldwide. In addition to retroviruses, adenoviruses are being used in clinical gene therapy trials to deliver corrected genes. The history of gene therapy has been a roller-coaster. Gene therapy patient Jesse Gelsinger died in 1999 at the University of Pennsylvania while undergoing gene therapy. New regulations were established to patrol experiments and new protocols were created. Even though the public is slow to hear about gene therapy developments, steady research progress continues. Gene therapy is discussed in greater detail in Chapter 9.

■ Vaccine Development

Vaccine development is one of the greatest advances in the history of medicine. The word vaccine is from *vacca*, the Latin word for cow. This is because the material of cowpox (a disease affecting the udders of cows) was injected into people to protect them against smallpox during the 1800s.

Attempts to deliberately protect humans against disease have a long history. Edward Jenner's work with cowpox vaccination holds the title as the first scientific attempt to control an infectious disease by means of intentional inoculation. In the late 18th century Jenner, a rural physician, observed that milkmaids who had caught cowpox, a mild disease, didn't get smallpox. They also had beautiful complexions in contrast to others who had pitted faces after contracting smallpox. Jenner deduced that cowpox provided immunity against smallpox. To test his theory, on May 14, 1796, he removed matter from a cowpox pustule on the hand of milkmaid Sarah Nelmes and inserted it into a cut on the arm of 8-year-old James Phipps. James became mildly ill and developed a fever, but recovered after 9 days.

On July 1, 1796, Jenner injected smallpox matter into James and repeated it again several months later. James did not get smallpox as a result of either of these inoculations. He was revaccinated 20 times and later died of tuberculosis at the age of 20.

Today there is a mandatory list of vaccines for schoolchildren in the United States. The list includes polio, diphtheria, measles, mumps, rubella (German measles), tetanus, pertussis, hepatitis B, and a few others. Most of these vaccines were the result of biomedical research after WWII. Read more about vaccines in Chapter 7.

Most people have experienced a cold, the flu, a cold sore on the lips, or plantar warts, many of which were caused by viruses. During the golden age of microbiology (1857–1914), rapid advances in microbiology, mainly spearheaded by scientists Robert Koch (Germany) and Louis Pasteur (France), determined that microorganisms cause **infectious diseases**. Additionally, Koch developed a set of experimental steps for determining which specific microbe causes a particular disease. These steps are referred to as Koch's Postulates.

(b)

■ Figure 1-5
(a) This young girl in Bangladesh was infected with smallpox in 1973. The World Health Organization's International Commission declared Bangladesh "smallpox free" in 1977. **(b)** Respiratory viral diseases such as influenza and the common cold are spread via airborne transmission. Smallpox can also be transmitted in this way. All you have to do is breathe!

Bacteria or protozoa were identified to be the cause of certain diseases. They did not, however, cause other diseases such as measles, yellow fever, polio, and smallpox. Today we know that viruses can infect virtually every organism on earth (**Figure 1-5**).

■ Viruses and Cancer

Viral infections are linked to approximately 15% of all cancers. About 80% of these are cancers of the cervix (caused by papillomaviruses) and the liver (caused by hepatitis viruses B and C). These viruses are thought to be one factor that acts at an early stage in the process that leads to cancer.

Cancer has afflicted humans throughout recorded history. Over one hundred years ago, amateur epidemiologists reported a curious phenomenon: cervical cancer was common among prostitutes, but extremely rare in nuns. Some noted that cervical cancer was very high in women who were married to men whose first wives had died of cervical cancer. From these observations and reports, scientists speculated that a sexually transmitted agent caused cervical cancer (refer to Chapter 10 for more information on this phenomenon). In 1986, a paper entitled "Detection of Papillomavirus DNA in Human Semen" was published in *Science*. Today it is known that human papillomaviruses are responsible for 90% of all cervical cancers. A safe and effective vaccine against the most common high-risk types of human papillomaviruses is available.

1.2 Early Virus Studies

Before the invention of the electron microscope in 1931, viruses could not be seen or grown in the laboratory. *Most importantly, viruses were defined as agents so small they could pass through filters that trapped most known bacteria.* Scientists had to develop ways to observe and grow these invisible agents in the laboratory. The initial observations and methods developed to study viruses involved bacterial and plant systems. The first virus discovered was actually a plant virus known as tobacco mosaic virus (TMV), a disease that destroys tobacco crops. In 1892, the Russian botanist Dimitri Iwanowski demonstrated that extracts from diseased tobacco plants could transmit disease to healthy tobacco plants after passage through ceramic filters known to trap most bacteria. Iwanowski didn't understand the full significance of this result. In 1898 Martinus Beijerinick extended Iwanowski's experiments and was the first to develop the idea of the virus, which he called a *contagium vivum fluidum* ("soluble living germ").

Bacteriophages were first isolated from natural sources (such as human sewage) and studied by scientists in the early 20th century. Bacteriophages grow by inserting their DNA into a host bacterium, directing the host's biosynthetic machinery to make copies of the bacteriophage DNA and protein coat, and then destroying the host bacterium. The destruction of the host bacterium releases new bacteriophages, which then go on to infect fresh hosts.

Bacteriophage plaque assay is a method used to quantify the number of infectious bacteriophages in a given phage-containing sample. Briefly, bacteriophages are allowed to adsorb to host bacteria in a test tube. The mixture is then poured onto an agar plate and the bacteria are allowed to grow. At this point, the bacteriophages lyse bacteria that are present on the surface of solid agar plates. The holes (called **plaques**) in the bacterial lawn are areas where the bacteria have been killed by bacteriophages.

Major advances in animal virology did not occur until 1952, when Renato Dulbecco modified the bacteriophage assay to work on animal cell cultures. **Figure 1-6** shows a 6-well dish containing crystal violet-stained monolayers of monkey kidney cells that were infected with vaccinia virus. Similar to the bacteriophage assays, plaques or clearings in the cell monolayer are visualized where infected cells have been destroyed by viral infection. More viruses were used to infect the cell monolayers in the wells on the left-hand side of the dish than the wells on the right side of the dish. Dulbecco was awarded a Nobel Prize for the development of animal plaque assays in 1975.

■ Characteristics of Viruses

Today we know that viruses share a number of common features. First of all, they are small. As previously mentioned, viruses are able to pass through filters that retain or trap most known bacteria. Hence, viruses are smaller than bacteria. As a rule, most bacteria are

■ **Figure 1-6**
Plaque assays can be used to study animal or human viruses. The 6-well dish contains crystal violet-stained monolayers of monkey kidney cells that were infected with vaccinia virus.

100 times larger than viruses. Typically, bacteria range from 1 to 10 micrometers (μM) in length, whereas a virus would fall in the range of 0.03 to 0.1 μM in length (or 30–90 nanometers). Of course there are always some exceptions: Some viruses, such as poxviruses, can be 200 to 400 nanometers (nm) in length, and filoviruses (such as Ebola) can be up to 1000 nm in length. **Figure 1-7** provides size comparisons of biological molecules, viruses, bacteria, cellular organelles, and eukaryotic cells.

A second feature used to define a virus is its complete dependence upon the host cell to reproduce itself. Viruses do not have functional organelles or ribosomes. Viruses are too small to carry enough genetic material to code for all of the gene products necessary to rebuild a virus. As a result, a virus must use its host cellular protein synthesis machinery to synthesize viral proteins. The genome or genetic material of a virus consists of one species of nucleic acid, DNA, or RNA. The DNA or RNA genome of a virus can be single- or double-stranded.

The outside of the virus particle contains a receptor-binding protein or viral-attachment protein that will allow the virus to adhere to **receptors** present on the surface of cells. For example, the common cold virus (also known as rhinovirus) binds to a receptor on the outside of cells called the **I**ntercellular **A**dhesion **M**olecule-**1** (I-CAM-1).

Unlike other unicellular microorganisms, some human or animal viruses can reproduce themselves even if nothing but the viral genome is introduced into the cell. In other words, the viral genetic material is infectious. **Figure 1-8a** demonstrates that the RNA genome of poliovirus can be introduced into cultured cells (by a method called **transfection**) and viruses will be produced from that RNA within the cell. In this case, the polioviruses are not required to enter the cell to make more copies. Retroviruses can persist in cells by integrating their own DNA (or a copy of their RNA) into the genome of the host cell (Figure 1-8b).

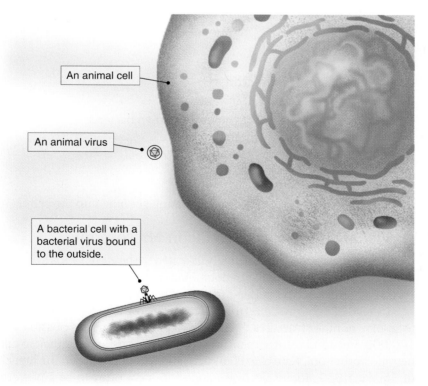

An animal cell

An animal virus

A bacterial cell with a bacterial virus bound to the outside.

■ **Figure 1-7**
Viruses are smaller than their host cells. This illustration demonstrates size comparisons of a eukaryotic cell, bacterium, and viruses.

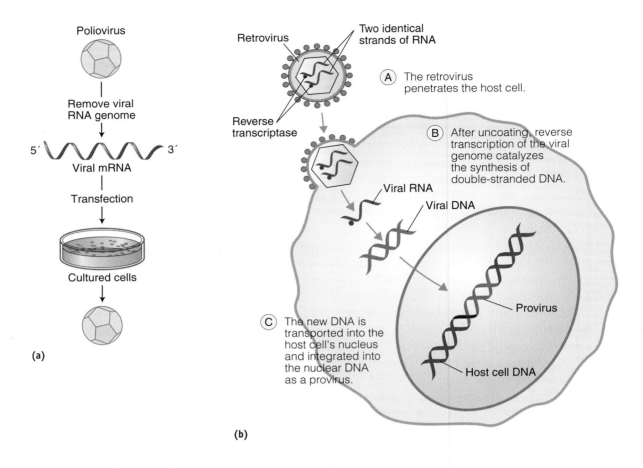

■Figure 1-8

(a) Poliovirus RNA is infectious! Infectious particles of poliovirus can be produced even if only the genetic material (RNA) of the virus is introduced into cells growing in a culture dish. **(b)** Retroviruses can persist in cells by integrating their own DNA (or a copy of their RNA) into the genome of the host cell. The integrated viral genome is called a **provirus**. Adapted from Flint, S.J., et al. *Principles of Virology: Molecular Biology, Pathogenesis, and Control of Animal Viruses*, Second Edition. ASM Press, 2003.

Review of Virus Characteristics

- Small (nm in size)
- Pass through filters that trap most known bacteria
- Completely dependent on the host cell
- Contains one species of nucleic acid
- Contains receptor-binding protein
- Genome may be infectious
- Some viruses can persist by integrating genome into the cellular chromosome

■ Visualizing Viruses: Electron Microscopy

Electron microscopes were originally invented in the early 1930s to overcome the limitations of light microscopes to visualize nonbiological materials such as metals and small electronic parts. Light microscopes at that time could magnify specimens as high as 1000 times.

Instead of light rays, electron microscopes use a beam of electrons focused by magnets to resolve minute structures. With electron microscopy, it is possible to magnify structures 100,000 times and resolve them at 0.5 nm. Virologists were quick to take advantage of this new, powerful tool. Kausche, Pfankuch, and Ruska published the first electron micrograph of TMV in 1939. Today electron microscopes continue to be a powerful tool in studying remnants of a degenerative process starting from larger, more complex bacteria. *Chlamydia* species cause severe eye infections, sexually transmitted diseases, parrot fever (a disease of birds that is transmitted to humans), and lung infections.

It is also thought that mitochondria and chloroplasts are organelles that may be remnants of bacteria that had once lived inside of eukaryotic cells. Both mitochondria and chloroplasts are the same size as bacteria, contain both DNA and RNA, and have independent ways to synthesize proteins encoded by organelle DNA. These organelles may have originated from bacteria by degeneration. It is less clear if viruses arose in this way.

VIRUS FILE 1-1

Use of PubMed, CDC Publications, and ProMED to Research Specific Viruses or Viral Outbreak Information

■ **Figure VF 1-1**
PubMed interface. PubMed is the most frequently used search engine for medical research journal articles.

Each chapter of *Understanding Viruses* will contain one or more Virus Files. These files or synopses are intended to connect students to research being conducted in the field of virology. References to the original research articles will be provided at the end of each file. Students and instructors interested in exploring topics further may opt to search for more information via PubMed, which is a service of the National Library of Medicine. It includes over 15 million citations for biomedical articles back to the 1950s. These citations are from MEDLINE and additional life science journals. PubMed searches can be done by topic, author, journal title, and other parameters. To begin a PubMed query, start at their website (which can be found easily through a Web search engine).

Many Virus Files may cite reports published by the Centers for Disease Control and Prevention (CDC), such as *Morbidity and Mortality Weekly Report* (*MMWR*) and *Emerging and Infectious Diseases* (*EID*). The archives of these publications can be quickly searched from the CDC's website (http://www.cdc.gov/).

If you are particularly interested in virus-related outbreaks, another valuable resource is Program for Monitoring Emerging Diseases (ProMED) mail. ProMED mail was established in 1994 by a small group of scientists. ProMED mail is intended to address the threat of disease outbreaks in remote corners of the world that could spread across continents in days or weeks—much faster than the doctors could spread word about the disease. ProMED mail is the CNN of outbreak reporting. This email list posts a variety of information, including on-the-ground observations, media stories, and government reports. ProMED members have helped to diagnose everything from camel pox in Saudi Arabia to measles in military men in Kazakhstan to severe acute respiratory syndrome (SARS) in China. Today there are more than 30,000 subscribers to ProMED. This early warning disease reporting often beats local authorities in disease reporting. Archives of reports can be searched via the mail site within the ProMed website (http://www.promedmail.org).

References
Check, E. 2004. "Dispatches from the Front Line." *Nature* 432:544–545.
Woodall, J., and C.H. Calisher. 2001. "ProMED-mail: Background and Purpose." *EID* Supplement 7;(3):563.

Cellular Origin Theory

The cellular origin theory proposes that viruses arose from cellular nucleic acid (DNA or RNA) that evolved to replicate independently of the original host genome.

Coevolution Theory

The coevolution theory proposes that viruses and cells coevolved from complex polymers of nucleic acids. Some life forms became viruses while others became cells.

The origin of viruses is a fascinating topic. There are few viral stocks more than 90 years old, though, so it is difficult to test these hypotheses.

I.3   Viruses in History: Great Epidemics

■ Influenza

Imagine walking down a street in a city that used to be full of activity but now looks like a ghost town. You see quarantine signs posted on homes; flags or wreaths hanging on the doors indicate whether it was a parent, child, or grandparent who had recently died from a contagious disease (**Figure 1-12a**). Schools, churches, theatres, libraries, and most restaurants and stores are closed. There are no public gatherings, not even funerals. The few people you see have a cloth mask covering their face (Figure 1-12b). There is a shortage of coffins and the use of mass graves is common. This really did happen in 1918. The visitor to this town was the virus named *influenza*.

In 1918 the Spanish flu (also termed *la grippe*) pandemic charged across America in 7 days and across the world in 3 months. It claimed more American lives than all the major wars of the 20th century combined. Estimates of deaths range from 20 to 50 million—most in the brief period from October through the end of December. The Spanish flu was associated with high rates of morbidity, mortality, social disruption, and high economic costs, and was to be the most destructive pandemic ever known.

The Spanish flu incubation period and the onset of symptoms were so short that apparently healthy people in the prime of their lives (ages 20–40) were suddenly overcome, and within an hour could become helpless with fever, delirium, and chills. Severe headache, pains in muscles and joints, hair loss, and acute congestion accompanying temperatures of 101° to 105° occurred. The most unusual pathologic finding was massive pulmonary edema and/or hemorrhage. This was a unique viral pneumonia—a patient could be convalescing one day and dead the next. Those who did not die of Spanish flu often died of secondary bacterial pneumonia.

Surprisingly, before the recent concerns of a potential bird flu pandemic, not very many people were familiar with the 1918 Spanish flu. It may be that few survivors wanted to talk to historians about the terrifying and ghastly days when so many were dying there were bodies in the streets.

■ Poliomyelitis

Evidence of the viral disease poliomyelitis dates to the dynasties of Ancient Egypt. In the current era, polio epidemics peaked in the United States in 1916 and the mid-1940s to 1950s. This disease was quite frightening because of its mysterious seasonal incidence (July–October). Many children were not allowed to play outside because of the fear of polio. Newspapers included word games and puzzles to occupy children while they stayed indoors. Some families fled to remote summer vacation homes.

(a)

(b)

■ **Figure 1-12**
(a) Influenza placard placed on the front doors of homes to quarantine individuals infected with influenza. **(b)** A New York city policeman wearing a cloth mask to protect him from the Spanish flu in 1918.

Polio struck an industrialized nation free from the poor sanitation conditions that typically play a role in epidemics. It occurred in a nation thriving with new technologies that would lead to man's control over disease. Civil engineers were creating a network of aqueducts and water purification plants to provide clean, safe drinking water for much of the nation.

Polio's transmission was a mystery. Cities responded with methods that had met with success in ridding epidemics of typhus, cholera, and diphtheria. New York City officials doused the streets with 4 million gallons of water a day to flush the streets of its germs, killing 72,000 stray cats. Many cities were fogged with insecticides. None of these measures worked, though: polio was spread through human feces. At the time, officials did not know that.

Polio broke America's heart. It crippled its victims. Children were lined up in wheelchairs. Paralysis of the muscles used for respiration and swallowing (called bulbar poliomyelitis) was sometimes fatal. Those with symptoms of difficulty in breathing and swallowing were put into an **iron lung**, also known as the "drinker respirator" (**Figure 1-13**).

Franklin Delano Roosevelt was likely the most famous adult who suffered from the effects of poliomyelitis. Roosevelt contracted polio in 1921, at the age of 39. He spent over half of his personal fortune to purchase Warm Springs, Georgia, a resort with warm natural springs for swimming and rehabilitation, to provide a place for the "polios." Frightened by reminders of this terrible disease, guests not suffering from polio abandoned the resort.

Roosevelt did not recover from the initial paralytic affects of polio. When he left Warm Springs to run for governor of New York in 1928 and then for U.S. presidency in 1932, he chose to hide its affects from the public (**Figure 1-14a**). He was not photographed being carried or wheeled about. He would lean on a cane or arm. It appeared to many that he could walk. It was a brilliantly staged deception. In Roosevelt's opinion, and in those of his advisors, a robust appearance was necessary to portray a physically strong leader, and the press cooperated (Figure 1-14b).

■ **Figure 1-13**
Polio ward of iron lungs at Hayes Memorial Hospital in Boston, Massachusetts, 1955.

■ **Figure 1-14**
(a) FDR at Warm Springs, Georgia, in 1924.
(b) The press portrayed Roosevelt as a robust, physically strong leader.

(a)

(b)

The March of Dimes

The March of Dimes began in 1938 as an effort to raise money for polio treatment and research. The organization selected Dr. Jonas Salk to lead research on polioviruses, and in 1941 provided the first iron lung to assist polio patients. The March of Dimes ran field trials of the Salk vaccine (an inactivated preparation of poliovirus) with 1,830,000 schoolchildren participating in 1954. In 1955, the vaccine was declared safe, effective, and potent and was licensed for general use. Later, in 1960, the Sabin vaccine was licensed for use in the United States. (Read more about polio vaccination in Chapter 11.)

Today, polio is rare due to the worldwide efforts of the World Health Organization (WHO), CDC, Rotary International, and United Nation's Children Fund (UNICEF) to eradicate it. In 2001, endemic areas of polio were reduced to ten countries, including India, Pakistan, Nigeria, Egypt, and Afghanistan.

■ Acquired Immunodeficiency Syndrome (AIDS)

In June of 1981, a group of physicians in Los Angeles, California, reported five unusual cases of *Pneumocystis* pneumonia in the CDC's *Morbidity and Mortality Weekly Report*. All patients were young men, and all were sexually active homosexuals. Two of the patients died from this pneumonia and all patients had experienced other rare infections such as candidiasis, a fungal infection of the throat, mouth, or in women, the vagina. *Pneumocystis* pneumonia is rare in the United States and almost exclusively found in severely immuno-suppressed individuals. This first report recognized a new growing epidemic in the United States that was later termed AIDS (See Chapter 8, Virus-File 8-1).

As cases were reported to the CDC, a pattern characteristic of an epidemic emerged, but the culprit was a mystery until Robert Gallo (United States) and Luc Montagnier (France) discovered the human immunodeficiency virus (HIV). Today AIDS is a world-wide epidemic, with the population in Africa being the most severely affected. There are several antiviral drugs available to prolong the lives of those suffering from AIDS, but there is no cure or vaccine. Education promoting AIDS prevention has reduced cases in some countries. (Read more on AIDS in Chapters 8 and 16.)

I.4 Recent Viral Outbreaks

■ Foot and Mouth Disease, 2001

Anyone who was in Great Britain in 2001 will remember one of the world's worst foot and mouth disease (FMD) epidemics. Tourists were prompted to follow these rules:

Do not go near cattle, sheep, pigs, or deer and never feed farm animals.

Do not go on farmland that has been or is being used by livestock.

Do not attempt to walk on footpaths that are closed.

Five days before returning home from FMD-infected areas, people were asked to avoid farms, zoos, sale barns, stockyards, animal laboratories, meatpacking plants, fairs, and other animal facilities. It was suggested to bathe and launder or dry-clean all clothing, including outerwear, and to remove any dirt or soil from shoes, followed by wiping them with a cloth that was dampened with a bleach solution.

The media stories showed photographs of individuals bleaching their shoes be-fore entering the airports. All luggage and personal items (including watches, cameras, laptop computers, CD players, and cell phones) were supposed to be cloth-dampened with a bleach solution. Once inside the airport, travelers were questioned about where they had been during their stay and if they were carrying any food products of pigs or ruminants.

Epidemiologists determined how FMD spread to farms and the market. The outbreak began at Burnside farm, Heddron-on-the-Wall, Northumberland, England. The FMD out-break spread to nearby farms, markets, and meat-packing facilities via vehicles transport-ing infected animals (**Figure 1-15**). Road sites were set up with automatic vehicle-spray devices to contain the spread of FMD (**Figure 1-16a**).

Foot and mouth disease is highly contagious among animals and causes loss of pro-duction that can have grave economic implications for the meat and dairy industries (Figure 1-16b). FMD has occurred in most parts of the world, causing extensive epidemics in cloven-hoofed animals (that is, cattle, pigs, sheep, goat, and deer). The last outbreak of FMD in the United States occurred in 1929. Slaughtering infected animals or animals in contact with infected animals, vaccination, and public cleansing and disinfection centers can control the disease. Agricultural officials use serology testing to monitor healthy ani-mals for FMD antibodies.

Cases of FMD in humans are rare, and the symptoms are few and/or mild. Human cases have resulted from close contact with animals suffering from FMD, with the virus entering through broken skin, being ingested in unpasteurized milk, or being inhaled.

■ **Figure 1-15**
Epidemiologists determine how FMD spread to farms and the market during the 2001 outbreak in England.

Spread of FMD in U.K. 2001

FMD has not been beaten. The Ministry of Agriculture, Fisheries, and Food in England prefers to slaughter livestock during an outbreak instead of vaccinating, and as a result the scourge of FMD continues. Refusal to vaccinate is driven by the market. Animals that test positive for FMD antibodies cannot be sold to other countries. Vaccination would provide immunity to these animals, but because they would then test positive for FMD antibodies it depreciates their market value. This is a controversial issue affecting farmers, politicians, scientists, veterinarians, and the consumer.

■ Hantavirus: Four Corners Disease, 1993

On May 14, 1993, a Native American marathon runner in rural New Mexico known to be in excellent health collapsed and died of respiratory failure at an Indian Health Service Hospital emergency room. Days before his collapse he visited a physician twice with flulike symptoms, but his chest x-ray was normal. He was treated with antibiotics and acetaminophen. Two days before he fell ill, his fiancé died of the same mysterious respiratory illness. Both victims drowned from fluid buildup in their lungs. On May 17, the Indian Health Service reported five similar deaths. All of the individuals were previously

(a)

(b)

■ **Figure 1-16**
(a) This site was located on the edge of the restricted area in Northumberland, England, in 2001. **(b)** The British Ministry's strategy for containment of FMD is to slaughter and burn the infected animals. This photograph shows smoke rising from pyres of burning cows slaughtered to prevent the spread of FMD.

very healthy. By June 11, 24 cases of respiratory failure following flulike symptoms were reported in the Four Corners region of Colorado, Utah, Arizona, and New Mexico.

This virulent new disease baffled medical examiners and the CDC. The CDC finally identified the virus as a strain of the hantavirus, an "old world" virus carried by rodents known to only cause hemorrhagic fever and kidney failure. *Old world* refers to those parts of the world known before the voyages of Christopher Columbus. It includes Europe, Asia, and Africa and its surrounding islands. Hantavirus pulmonary syndrome is a rare disease that is sometimes caused by the hantavirus called sin nombre virus (no-name virus in English). Several different types of wild mice, such as deer mice and rats, can be infected with hantavirus and pass it in their droppings, urine, or saliva. Once humans come in contact with fomites such as contaminated blankets or food storage areas, the virus then enters directly into the respiratory system through breathing contaminated air particles. It kills 50% of its victims.

Why did sin nombre virus strike the Four Corners region in 1993? It is likely that the virus had long been present in rodent populations. Officials believe that the unusually mild winter and spring of 1993, the rainfall, and the abundance of pinyon nuts on which the rodents feed led to an increased rodent population in the summer and greater

■ Figure 1-17
Rodents that carry the sin nombre virus can be deceptively cute, but suspected carriers must be handled with extreme care. This photograph shows scientists wearing protective gear while collecting and analyzing deer mice.

opportunities for people to come in contact with infected rodents. More than 20% of deer mice subsequently captured in southwestern areas of the United States, and as far north as southwestern Montana, tested positive for sin nombre virus (**Figure 1-17**). The detective work of the CDC led to a course of action, treatment, and prevention, thus thwarting a nationwide epidemic.

■ West Nile Virus, 1999

The next time you are outdoors where there are mosquitoes; you may change your behavior after reading this section. You might wear clothing with long sleeves and apply a bug repellent that includes the ingredient DEET (meta-N, N-diethyl toluamide) over any exposed skin. You may find yourself removing any standing water in your neighborhood (for example, water that has accumulated in old tires, buckets, and wheelbarrows). You may start reporting any dead birds you find.

During the summer of 1999 elderly people in Queens, New York, were getting sick with headaches, fever, weakness, and confusion. Routine tests from the medical laboratory came back negative for bacterial or fungal pathogens. Given the symptoms of the patients, it was suspected that they were suffering from **encephalitis** (inflammation of the brain) of viral origin. Samples of blood, spinal fluid, and tissues from those who had died after falling ill were shipped to the Vector-Borne Diseases Laboratory at the CDC for analysis. Based on a routine antibody test, the disease was first diagnosed as encephalitis caused by the St. Louis Encephalitis Virus (SLE). The positive test result, however, was a very weak reaction. Nevertheless, helicopters began hovering over major highways and residential areas, spraying misty clouds of insecticides such as malathion and pyrethroids. The City Health Commissioner advised individuals to avoid contact with mosquitoes and exposure to insecticides.

Simultaneously, people started finding more than the usual number of dead crows in the area, and several exotic species of birds at the Bronx Zoo died. Birds don't die from SLE. They can, however, die from West Nile Virus (WNV). The CDC did not test the samples for WNV because that virus had never appeared in the United States before. No one had made the connection between the human epidemic and the wildlife epidemic.

As more cases appeared, the CDC conducted additional tests on the brain tissue of deceased individuals, the dead crows, and exotic birds from the zoo. Officials at the CDC attempted to isolate and study the virus taken directly from these tissues. At the same time, the laboratory at the New York State Department of Health in Albany began sequencing the RNA genome of the virus they had isolated from infected brain tissues. These results were shared among the scientific community via a special Internet site called ProMED (Program for Monitoring Emerging Diseases). ProMED shares results about epidemics occurring anywhere in the world, and scientists and physicians who specialize in infectious diseases visit the site on a daily basis. The ProMED post of their results matched with outbreaks of encephalitis in Romania, Egypt, Israel, Italy, and South Africa. It matched exactly with a strain of WNV in Israel from an epidemic in 1998. This turned out to be the final piece of the puzzle. The disease is spread via mosquitoes that have fed upon sick birds that harbor WNV. The mosquitoes then acquire WNV from the birds and transmit the disease via biting humans or animals.

The final toll from the 1999 WNV epidemic in the New York City metropolitan was 62 cases of encephalitis and 7 deaths. The virus was believed to have infected as many as 1900 unknowing Queens residents who did not develop encephalitis. Exotic zoo birds, American crows, at least 20 other North American wild bird species, and horses were infected, and quite a few died. Why did the Israeli strain of WNV enter the United States? Scientists have suggested several reasons why WNV enters new regions. The most supported hypothesis is that migratory birds play a role in transporting the virus. Other hypotheses are:

- During migration, birds can be displaced by storms.
- Legal and illegal importation of birds (bird and pet trade).
- Birds are vagrants on ships or other transportation.

Even reptiles have tested positive for WNV. Recently, farm-raised alligators have tested positive for WNV and may be the cause for a rash of deaths on alligator farms (**Figure 1-18**, Table 1-1).

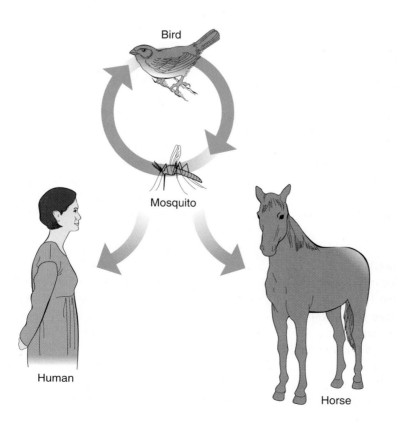

Bird

Mosquito

Human

Horse

■ **Figure 1-18**
Diagram showing how WNV spreads from infected birds to mosquitoes to humans or other hosts such as horses, dogs, rodents, and reptiles such as alligators.

TABLE 1-1	Species Found Positive for West Nile Virus in Surveillance Efforts

Birds

Wood duck	Rock dove (feral pigeon)
Eurasian wigeon (c)	Mauritius pink pigeon (c)(a)
Mallard	Common ground-dove
Bronze-winged duck (spectacled duck) (c)	Eurasian collared-dove
Domestic goose (c)(a)	White-winged dove
Canvasback	Mourning dove
Canada goose	Luzon pigeon (bleeding heart pigeon) (c)(a)
Barnacle goose (c)(a)	Inca dove
Emperor goose (c)	Belted kingfisher
Greater Magellan goose (Andean goose) (c)(a)	Yellow-billed cuckoo
Abyssinian blue-winged goose (c)(a)	Cooper's hawk
Tundra swan (c)	Northern goshawk
Trumpeter swan (c)(a)	Sharp-shinned hawk
Mute swan	Golden eagle
Rosy-billed duck (c)(a)	Red-tailed hawk
Ruddy duck	Rough-legged hawk (c)
Chimney swift	Red-shouldered hawk
Ruby-throated hummingbird	Broad-winged hawk
Common	Swainson's hawk
Emu (c)	Northern harrier
Ruddy turnstone	Swallow-tailed kite
Killdeer	Bald eagle
Piping plover	Mississippi kite
Herring gull	Osprey
Laughing gull	Harris' hawk (c)
Ring-billed gull	Merlin
Great black-backed gull	Prairie falcon
Black skimmer	Peregrine falcon
Grey gull (c)(a)	American kestrel
Inca tern (c)(a)	Crested guineafowl
Yellow-crowned night-heron (c)	Northern bobwhite
Black-crowned night-heron (c)	Chukar (c)(a)
Great blue heron	Ruffed grouse
Green heron	Domestic chicken (red junglefowl) (c)
Least bittern	Green junglefowl (c)(a)
Turkey vulture	Impeyan (Himalayan) pheasant (c)
Black vulture	Bulwer's wattled pheasant (c)(a)
King vulture (c)(a)	Turkey (domestic and wild)
Saddle-billed stork (c)(a)	Ring-necked pheasant
Marabou stork (c)(a)	Mount peacock (c)(a)
Lesser Adjutant stork (c)(a)	Crested partridge (c)(a)
Chilean flamingo (c)	Blyth's tragopan (c)
Greater flamingo (American) (c)	Argus pheasant (c)(a)
Scarlet ibis (c)	Greater sage grouse
Waldrapp (c)(a)	Common loon
White-crowned pigeon	Demoiselle crane (c)(a)
	West African crowned (a)

TABLE 1-1	Species Found Positive for West Nile Virus in Surveillance Efforts (*continued*)

Wattled crane (c)(a)	Black-capped chickadee
Whooping crane (c)(a)	Carolina chickadee
Mississippi sandhill crane (c)	Black-throated blue warbler
Red-crowned crane (c)(a)	Yellow-rumped warbler
Siberian crane (c)(a)	Yellow warbler
Hooded crane (c)(a)	Blackpoll warbler
White-naped crane (c)(a)	Common yellowthroat
Black-necked crane (c)(a)	Kentucky warbler
Virginia rail	Northern parula
Lady Ross' turaco (lantain-eater) (c)(a)	Ovenbird
Cedar waxwing	Northern waterthrush
Northern cardinal	Nashville warbler
Blue grosbeak (a)	Canada warbler
Rose-breasted grosbeak	Hooded warbler
Dickcissel	House sparrow
Western scrub	White-crested laughingthrush (c)(a)
American srow	White-breasted nuthatch
Common raven	European starling
Fish crow	Palm tanager (c)
Blue jay	Carolina wren
Steller's jay	Winter wren
Black-billed magpie (c)	Veery
Song sparrow	Hermit thrush
Savannah sparrow	Gray-cheeked thrush
Fox sparrow	Swainson's thrush
Eastern towhee field sparrow	Wood thrush
Zebra finch (c)	Eastern bluebird
American goldfinch	American robin
House finch	Traill's flycatcher
Purple finch	Eastern phoebe
Evening grosbeak	Scissor-tailed flycatcher
European goldfinch (c)	Eastern kingbird
Barn swallow	Black-whiskered vireo
Purple martin	Warbling vireo
Tree swallow	Red-eyed vireo
Red-winged blackbird	American white pelican
Rusty blackbird	Brown pelican (c)(a)
Brewer's blackbird	Double-crested cormorant
Baltimore oriole	Guanay cormorant (c)
Brown-headed cowbird	Red-headed woodpecker
Boat-tailed grackle	Downy woodpecker
Great-tailed grackle	Yellow-bellied sapsucker
Common grackle	Pied-billed grebe
Loggerhead shrike	Cockatoo (unspecified) (c)
Gray catbird	Cockatiel (c)
Northern mockingbird	Red-crowned parrot (c)
Brown thrasher	Macaw (unspecified) (c)
Tufted titmouse (c)	Budgerigar (c)

(continued)

TABLE 1-1	Species Found Positive for West Nile Virus in Surveillance Efforts (*continued*)

Lorikeet (c)	Mule deer
Black-footed penguin (c)	Babirusa (c)(a)
Magellan penguin (c)(a)	Domestic dog (c)
Northern saw	Timber wolf (c)
Boreal owl (c)	Domestic cat (feral)
Short-eared owl	Striped skunk
Verreaux's eagle owl (milky eagle owl) (c)(a)	Harbor seal (c)
Great horned owl	Red panda (c)(a)
Snowy owl (c)	Black bear (a)
Eastern screech owl	Big brown bat
Tawny owl (c)	Little brown bat
Great gray owl (c)	Domestic rabbit (c)
Spotted owl (c)	Domestic horse (c)
Barred owl	Donkey (c)
Northern hawk owl (c)	Mule (c)
Barn owl	Great Indian rhinoceros (c)(a)
Ostrich (c)(a)	Barbary macaque (c)
	Ring-tailed lemura (c)
	Indian (Asian) elephant (c)(a)
	Gray squirrel
Mammals	Fox squirrel
Domestic cattle (c)	Eastern chipmunk
Mountain goat (c)	Human
Domestic (Suffolk) sheep (c)	
Llama (c)	**Reptiles**
Alpaca (suri) (c)	American alligator (c)
White-tailed deer	Crocodile monitor (c)(a)
Reindeer (c)	

Note: Species included in this list are wild animals unless followed by a "c," which denotes either a captive or farmed animal(s). Virus or viral RNA was detected in animal tissue unless followed by an "a," which denotes detectable antibodies only have been reported.

Adapted from National Wildlife Health Center. Madison, Wisconsin. Updated 9/2004.

■ Norovirus Outbreaks, 1972 and 2002

Today, noroviruses (formerly called Norwalk-like viruses) may be the most commonly identified cause of infectious intestinal diseases. Much publicity has been given to outbreaks on cruise ships, but these viruses also pose problems in hospitals, nursing homes, schools, and homes. Norwalk-like viruses were first characterized and described in 1972 during an epidemic of diarrhea and vomiting involving students at an elementary school in the town of Norwalk, Ohio. These viruses thrive in places where humans are in high concentrations. Cruise ships happen to provide the perfect breeding environment for viruses: they provide an enclosed area with up to several thousand people in close contact with each other.

The virus is spread person to person via feces and sometimes by eating contaminated food (especially oysters) or drinking contaminated water. The intestinal illness is usually short lived (2–3 days). Norovirus outbreaks reached an all-time high in the United States in 2002. The most important thing that anyone can do to keep from getting sick is to wash his or her hands. By frequently washing your hands, you wash away germs that you have picked up from other people, or from contaminated surfaces, or from animals and animal waste.

1.5 Smallpox: Ancient Agent of Bioterrorism

The use of biological agents in terrorism is not new. It dates back as early as the 6th century, when the Assyrians poisoned the wells of their enemies with rye ergot. Warring tribes would catapult diseased carcasses over castle walls to infect their enemies. On several occasions, smallpox was used as a biological weapon. Pizarro presented South American natives with clothing and gifts laden with the smallpox virus in the 15th century and Sir Jeffrey Amherst provided Native Americans (who were loyal to the French) with blankets tainted with smallpox during the French and Indian War (1754–1763). The epidemic killed most of the tribe, resulting in a successful British attack on Fort Carillon.

The term *smallpox* was introduced during the 16th century to distinguish it from the "great pox," or syphilis. Smallpox has been one of humankind's greatest scourges. It is believed that this virus appeared in agricultural settlements in Africa around 10,000 B.C. The disease left many disfigured with pox scars; some were blinded and many died. It nearly wiped out the Native American population in the United States, which had been free of infectious diseases before the Europeans came. Native Americans were not resistant to smallpox and other European diseases because they had never been exposed to those viruses. Yet few doctors today have seen a case of smallpox.

In 1967, the WHO launched an aggressive program to eradicate smallpox. It was very cost effective. In 1977, the last naturally occurring case was reported in Somalia. In 1980, the WHO declared the world free of smallpox and recommended to cease vaccination. Today we are once again vulnerable to this disease. It is speculated that immunity is not lifelong and many individuals have not been vaccinated. (Read more on smallpox in Chapter 14.)

■ Other Bioterrorism Concerns

Bioterrorism is still a clear and present danger. A series of anthrax cases, some of which resulted in death, occurred during the weeks following the terrorist attacks on the United States of September 11, 2001. As a result there has been increased security and concern over the possibility of additional attacks. The scientific community is working as a team to be prepared for any future attacks. This preparedness involves the production of vaccines, drugs, and diagnostic tests that will play a major role in reducing the threat of bioterrorism.

Summary

Viruses impact all forms of life. They play an important role in ecosystems by effecting population growth in both positive and negative ways. The origin of viruses remains a debatable topic. Early pioneers of virology studied bacteriophages, plant viruses such as TMV, and smallpox virus that caused large numbers of outbreaks and mortalities throughout recorded human history.

Gene therapy, bacteriophage therapy, and vaccine development utilize viruses in applications toward health problems. Influenza, poliomyelitis, AIDS, foot and mouth disease,

West Nile encephalitis, hantavirus pulmonary syndrome, smallpox, and norovirus-related gastrointestinal distress are examples of viral diseases that have had historical and recent relevance. Biological weapons have been used for centuries. Disease-causing viruses can be effective weapons used to infect and potentially kill large populations. Understanding the biology of viruses will help the scientific community prepare for a biological attack. The production of vaccines, drugs, and diagnostic tests will play a major role in reducing the threat of bioterrorism.

Resources

Primary Literature and Reviews

Asnis, D. et al. 1999. "Outbreak of West-Nile-like viral encephalitis—New York." *MMWR* 48(38):845–849.

Bratbak, G. et al. 1990. "Viruses as partners in spring bloom microbial tropho-dynamics." *App Environ Microbiol* 56(5):1400–1405.

Brehman, J. G., and Henderson, D. A. 1998. "Poxvirus dilemmas—Monkeypox, smallpox, and biologic terrorism." *N Engl J Med* 339(8):556–559.

Carlton, R. M. 1999. "Phage therapy: past history and future prospects." *Archives Immunologiae et Therapiae Experimentalis* 47:267–274.

Cramer, E. H. et al. 2002. "Outbreaks of gastroenteritis associated with Noroviruses on cruise ships—United States." *MMWR* 51(49):1112–1115.

Furman, J. A. 1999. "Marine viruses and their biogeochemical and ecological effects." *Nature* 399:541–548.

Gottleib, M.S., Schanker, H. M., Fan, P. T., Saxon, A., and Weisman, D. O. 1981. "*Pneumocystis* pneumonia—Los Angeles." *MMWR* 5(30):250–252.

Hope-Simpson, R. E. 1978. "Sunspots and flu: a correlation." *Nature* 275:86.

Hoyle, F., and Wickramasinghe, N. C. 1987. "Influenza viruses and comets." *Nature* 327:664.

Hoyle, F., and Wickramasinghe, N. C. 1990. "Sunspots and influenza." *Nature* 343:304.

Kuenzi, A. J., Douglass, R. J., and Bond, C. W. 2000. "Sin nombre virus in deer mice captured inside homes, southwestern Montana." *EID* 6(4):386–389.

Lane, C. L., La Montagne, J., and Fauci, A. 2001. "Bioterrorism: a clear and present danger." *Nat Med* 7(12):1271–1273.

Lopman, B. A. et al. 2003. "Two epidemiological patterns of Norovirus outbreaks: surveillance in England and Wales 1992–2000." *EID* 9(1):71–77.

Ostrow, R. S. et al. 1986. "Detection of papillomavirus DNA in human semen." *Science* 23:731–733.

Rappole, J. H., Derrikson, S. R., and Hubalek, A. 2000. "Migratory birds and spread of West Nile Virus in the western hemisphere." *EID* 6(4):319–328.

Stone, R. 2002. "Stalin's forgotten cure." *Science* 298:728–731.

Popular Press

Iezzoni, Lynette and McCullough, David. 1997. *Influenza, 1918: The Worst Epidemic in American History.* New York: TV Books.

Kehret, Peg. 1996. *Small Steps: The Year I Got Polio.* Morton Grove, IL: Albert Whitman.

Lewis, Sinclair, with a new afterword by Doctorow, E. L. 1998. *Arrowsmith*. Revised Edition, New York: Signet Classics.

McCormick, Joseph B. and Fisher-Hoch, Susan, with Horvitz, Leslie Alan. *Level 4: Virus Hunters of the CDC*. 1996. Atlanta: Turner Publishing.

McKenna, Maryn. 2004. *Beating Back the Devil: On the Front Lines with the Disease Detectives of the Epidemic Intelligence Service*. New York: Free Press.

Peters, C. J. and Olshaker, Mark. 1998. *Virus Hunter: Thirty Years of Battling Hot Viruses Around the World*. New York: Anchor Books.

Preston, Richard. 2002. *The Demon in the Freezer*. New York: Random House.

Preston, Richard. 1995. *The Hot Zone*. New York: Random House.

Radetsky, Peter. 1994. *The Invisible Invaders*. Boston: Little, Brown.

Regis, Ed. 1996. *Virus Ground Zero: Stalking Killer Viruses with the Centers for Disease Control*. New York: Pocket Books.

Seavey, Nina Gilden, Smith, Jane S., and Paul, Wagner. 1998. *A Paralyzing Fear: Triumph over Polio in America*. New York: TV Books.

■ Video Productions

The Emerging Viruses. 1998. BBC Production, Films for the Humanities.

Conquering an Invisible World. 1999. Films for the Humanities.

Understanding Viruses. 2001. Films for the Humanities.

Bioterror, The Invisible Enemy. 2004. Films for the Humanities.

Warm Springs. 2005. HBO Production.

The Age of Viruses. 2006. Films for the Humanities.

Mega Disasters: Alien Infection. 2007. The History Channel.

■ eLearning

http://biology.jbpub.com/book/virology

The site features eLearning, an online review area that provides quizzes and other tools to help you study for your class. You can also follow useful links for in-depth information or to just find out the latest virology and microbiology news.

CASE STUDY QUESTIONS

These questions relate to the Case Study presented at the beginning of the chapter.

1. To find general information about viral hemorrhagic fevers via the World Wide Web, what search engines and sites would you use? What keywords would you use in your searches?

2. How would you find research papers pertaining to viral hemorrhagic fever? List your resources and the titles of the journal articles. Where was the research conducted?

A colorized transmission electron micrograph of avian influenza A H5N1 viruses (gold) grown in Madin-Darby canine kidney epithelial cells (green). These viruses can cause illness in humans, certain animals, and many species of birds.

CHAPTER 2

Eukaryotic Molecular Biology and Host Cell Constraints

❝ *Every path has its puddle.* **❞**

English proverb

CASE STUDY

The headline in the February 6, 2002, edition of *The Seattle Times* read, "Mysterious Rash Hits School Kids Here, Across U.S." From October 2001 to June 2002, a total of 27 state health departments reported multiple groups of schoolchildren who developed mysterious rashes. The children complained of itchy, sunburn-like rashes on their cheeks and arms that lasted from a few hours to two weeks. Other symptoms included a burning sensation on the skin and hives that moved from one part of the body to another. A few children experienced other signs and symptoms such as fever, vomiting, sore throat, or headache. The outbreaks affected from 10–600 people at a time. A few teachers and school staff were affected, but rarely parents or siblings. Some schools were temporarily closed to clean air filters and check ventilation systems. Authorities at all of the schools that were closed reported an "exceptionally high" level of dust and dandruff in the air.

The level of parental concern and media hype prompted a CDC investigation. They found no common cause for the outbreaks, but there were a few reports of cases associated with parvovirus B19 infection (Fifth disease). The majority of cases remain unexplained. The CDC is continuing to monitor reports of groups of children with rashes and is providing technical assistance to state and local health departments investigating the outbreaks.

Two reports on this topic published by the Centers for Disease Control and Prevention (CDC) follow:

Cartter, M. et al. 2002. "Rashes among schoolchildren—14 states, October 4, 2001–February 27, 2002." *MMWR* 51:161–164.

Kacica, M. A. et al. 2002. "Update: Rashes among schoolchildren—27 states, October 4, 2001–June 3, 2002." *MMWR* 51:524–527.

The first chapter introduced some common viral diseases present in our daily lives and reflected on viral epidemics and pandemics. Viruses were defined as having the following characteristics:

- small size (nm range)
- can pass through filters that trap most known bacteria
- completely dependent upon the host cell
- usually contain one type of nucleic acid (RNA or DNA)
- contain receptor-binding proteins
- genome may be infectious
- some viruses can persist by integrating their genome into the host cells chromosome

Viruses are inert outside of their host cells. They can enter (infect) all types of cells, including animal, plant, and bacterial cells. This textbook mainly focuses on human viruses, but addresses some animal, plant, and bacterial viruses as well. Before we can study these individual viruses in depth, though, we must first analyze the basic structure of a human (or in some cases an animal) virus.

Virus particles consist of a nucleic acid genome protected by a protein shell that gives the virus particle its strong structure. The shell, referred to as the **capsid**, can also contain other proteins, such as receptor or viral attachment proteins, that allow the virus to adhere to the outside of a host cell. Animal virus anatomy is different from bacteriophages (read more about viral structure in Chapter 4).

The capsid protects the nucleic acid genome of the virus from a harsh environment that is laden with nucleases. The capsid and associated genome constitute the **nucleocapsid**. Many viruses also code for and carry their own polymerases. DNA polymerase, RNA polymerase, or **reverse transcriptases** catalyze the formation of polynucleotides of DNA or RNA using an existing strand of DNA or RNA as a template. This is necessary because the host may not contain a polymerase that will replicate the viral genome (read about constraints of host cells later in this chapter).

Human and animal viruses may also have an additional lipid bilayer membrane wrapped around the capsid of the virus particle. These viruses are called **enveloped viruses** (**Figure 2-1a**). The lipid bilayer membrane is stolen from the host cell as new viruses bud and exit from the host cell following infection and replication. This lipid bilayer may come from the host cell's plasma (outer) membrane, the nuclear membrane, or its trans Golgi network. Viruses that do not contain an envelope are called **naked viruses** (Figure 2-1b).

Enveloped viruses can contain matrix proteins that are located inside the envelope. These proteins add rigidity to the virus particle and are believed to

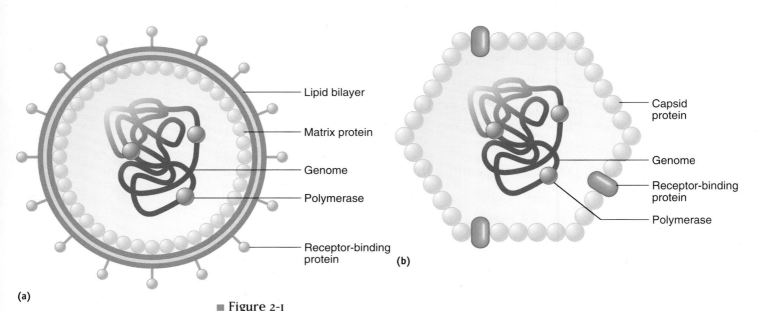

(a)

Lipid bilayer

Matrix protein

Genome

Polymerase

Receptor-binding protein

(b)

Capsid protein

Genome

Receptor-binding protein

Polymerase

■ Figure 2-1
(a) Structure of a typical animal or human enveloped virus. **(b)** Diagram of a naked (nonenveloped) animal or human virus.

act as a bridge between the nucleocapsid and viral proteins embedded in the envelope. In doing so they secure the internal nucleocapsid to the envelope, which may be critical for budding and release of viruses from host cells. The entire structure of the virus—the genome, the capsid, and (where present) the envelope—make up the **virion**, or virus particle.

2.1 How Many Genes Are Required to Build a Simple Virus Particle?

Viral genomes are small and diverse. Viruses have evolved ways to replicate that are economical; for example, a simple virus may require only one type of capsid protein. This protein is used over and over again to build the capsid. Hence, the virus would need one gene encoding the capsid protein to accomplish this task.

What other genes would a simple virus need? Besides a gene encoding the capsid protein, additional genes would be needed to encode a receptor-binding protein and usually a gene for a viral polymerase. This means a viral genome could contain as few as three genes.

The genome sizes of viruses vary greatly. The size of RNA viral genomes varies from 1.7 to 27 kilobase pairs (kbp) in length. These viral genomes generally encode fewer proteins (usually less than a dozen), whereas the genomes of DNA viruses most often are larger, ranging in length from 3.2 to over 200 kbp. These genomes roughly code for 4 to 200 gene products. An exception is the recently discovered mimivirus, which is enormous. Its genome is believed to code for more than 1000 gene products.

■ Why Are Viruses Dependent upon the Host for Replication?

Viruses can package/carry as few as 5 or 6 genes or as many as 200. What cellular processes do viruses need that would take more than this number of genes to accomplish the task of generating new viruses? To answer this question, a review of eukaryotic replication, transcription, and translation is necessary. How many gene products are necessary to do these processes?

2.2 Molecular Biology Review

To replicate, viruses must enter a host cell. Some viruses use the host's replication and transcription machinery, and others bring their own genes or proteins for viral replication and transcription. All viruses are dependent upon the host for the translation machinery and energy supplies. Let's briefly review the processes of eukaryotic DNA replication, RNA transcription, and translation.

■ The Central Dogma of Eukaryotic Molecular Biology

The central dogma of molecular biology is that DNA is transcribed into RNA that is translated into protein. Protein is never back-translated to RNA or DNA, and DNA is never created from RNA. DNA is never directly translated to protein. This dogma is never broken by eukaryotes. It is however, broken by retroviruses (see Chapter 10).

It is also important to remember that the processes of replication, transcription, and translation are localized in eukaryotic host cells (**Figure 2-2**). DNA replication and RNA transcription occur in the **nucleus** of the host cell. Processed mRNAs exit the nucleus and

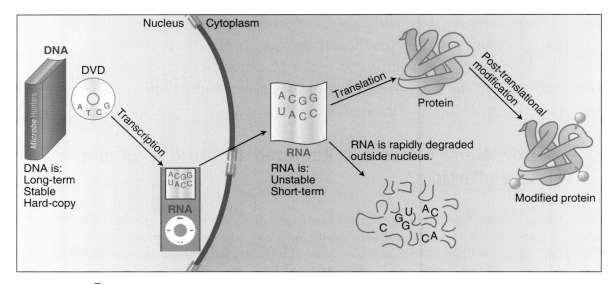

■ **Figure 2-2**

Replication, transcription, and translation are localized processes in host cells. Adapted from Andrew Hughes, "The Central Dogma and Basic Transcription," *Connexions*, July 27, 2003, http://cnx.org/content/m11415/latest/.

are translated in the **cytoplasm** of cells. A virus in need of the cellular machinery that performs these processes must therefore find its way to the correct parts of the cell to replicate its genome, transcribe its RNA, and get its RNA translated into viral proteins.

■ Eukaryotic DNA Replication

Host genomes are always composed of double-stranded DNA (dsDNA), in contrast to viral genomes that may be dsDNA, single-stranded DNA (ssDNA), double-stranded RNA (dsRNA), or single-stranded RNA (ssRNA). Eukaryotic cells have more than a dozen DNA polymerases that synthesize the dsDNA. Two of these (DNA polymerase a and d) are important for the replication of eukaryotic chromosomes. The chromosome dsDNA is copied/read $3' \rightarrow 5'$ and synthesized in a $5' \rightarrow 3'$ direction by DNA polymerases in the nucleus of the cell. DNA polymerases are sometimes referred to as DNA-dependent DNA polymerases because they synthesize DNA from a DNA template. Additional properties of cellular DNA polymerases are that they

- cannot "initiate de novo DNA synthesis" (it requires an RNA primer to do so).
- have high fidelity of copying (generating one error in every 10^9 base pair replications).
- may possess proofreading ability ($3' \rightarrow 5'$ exonuclease/editing activity to remove incorrect nucleotides).
- may possess helicase (unwinding) and primase activities.
- are localized and active in the nucleus of cells.

The process of DNA replication in eukaryotes requires additional cellular proteins such as primases (to synthesize RNA primers), ssDNA-binding proteins (to protect the dsDNA from nucleases during replication), and ligases (to join together **Okazaki fragments**/lagging strands).

■ Eukaryotic RNA Transcription

Eukaryotes carry out the conversion of information in DNA into RNA by the process of transcription. Enzymes called DNA-dependent RNA polymerases catalyze the RNA synthesis. Eukaryotic cells contain three different types of DNA-dependent RNA polymerases: RNA

■ **Figure 2-3**
Eukaryotic promoters of cellular mRNAs. Notice that the promoter contains both upstream and downstream elements in addition to the TATA box and start site. Enhancer sequences that are not part of the promoter are orientation-independent and may be present before, after, or within gene sequences.

polymerases I, II, and III. **RNA polymerase I** synthesizes ribosomal RNA (rRNA). **RNA polymerase II** synthesizes pre-messenger RNA (pre-mRNA) and some small nuclear RNAs (snRNA). **RNA polymerase III** synthesizes transfer RNA (tRNA), 5S rRNA, and other small RNAs. We will focus on RNA polymerase II because it is responsible for synthesizing cellular mRNA that is translated by ribosomes. Viral mRNAs must be structurally similar to cellular mRNAs so *that the cell can recognize viral mRNAs and translate them using the host protein synthesis machinery (e.g., ribosomes).*

The cell synthesizes its own mRNA in the nucleus by transcription of its DNA, followed by posttranscriptional processing of the mRNA transcript (pre-mRNA). Eukaryotic DNA contains sequences (elements) that dictate the start of RNA transcription. A typical eukaryotic promoter region with its control elements for making cellular mRNA via RNA polymerase II is shown in **Figure 2-3**. The AT-rich region of the promoter binds cellular proteins (**transcription factors**) that facilitate the binding of RNA polymerase II and determines the starting point of transcription. **Enhancers** are DNA elements outside of the promoter region that stimulate the frequency of transcription of genes by RNA polymerase II. Enhancers differ from promoters in that their sequences are orientation-independent and position-independent (upstream, downstream, or within genes).

The characteristics of RNA polymerase II are that it

- binds the transcription complex in the promoter region of DNA.
- can **initiate** the de novo synthesis of RNA (it does not require a primer).
- copies/reads 3′→5′ and synthesizes RNA 5′→3′.
- synthesizes and processes RNA in the nucleus of the cell.
- is error prone (1 mistake in 10,000 bases).
- has no proofreading ability.
- is recruited by transcription factors to the DNA promoter.

RNA polymerase II synthesizes a large primary pre-mRNA transcript (**Figure 2-4**). As the RNA is being transcribed (after ~30 nucleotides), the 5′ end of the mRNA is "capped" by the addition of a methylated guanine nucleotide (5′m⁷G). This "cap" is recognized by cellular ribosomes and thus plays an important role in the initiation of translation. The cap helps protect the mRNA from degradation. The mRNA transcript is cleaved about 20 to 30 nucleotides past the polyadenylation sequence, and then a poly(A) polymerase adds 100 to 200 residues of adenylic acid to the 3′ end of the mRNA. The poly(A) tail may also help protect the mRNA from degradation.

The poly(A) tail affects the stability of some mRNAs. It usually becomes shorter as an mRNA ages in the cytoplasm, and when it reaches a minimal length the mRNA will be degraded by cellular nucleases. Intron removal and exon splicing of the pre-mRNAs require snRNAs along with proteins and adenine triphosphate (ATP). After this event, the final processed mRNAs are exported from the nucleus into the cytoplasm of the cell where it will be translated. Only about 5% of the originally transcribed RNA exits the nucleus (Figure 2-4).

■ **Figure 2-4**

Eukaryotic transcription occurs in the nucleus. After the mRNAs are processed, the mature (capped, polyadenylated) mRNA exits the nuclear pores and enters the cytoplasm of the cell.

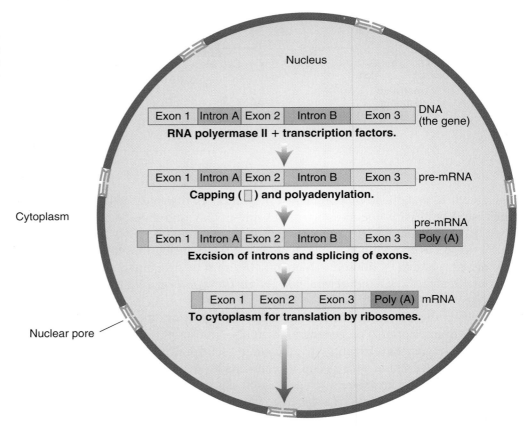

■ **Figure 2-5**

DNA sequence with the 3 forward open reading frames shown with the translated amino acids below each DNA sequence. Stop codons are indicated with an asterisk. Modified from an illustration by Scott Cooper, UW–La Crosse.

Translation and open reading frames (ORFs)

■ Review of Open Reading Frames (ORFs)

Regions of DNA are transcribed into mRNA and then translated into protein by ribosomes. For every gene, there are 6 ORFs (3 in each direction). The reading frame that is used in translating a gene (in eukaryotes) is often the longest ORF. An ORF starts with an *atg* (the coding for the amino acid methionine) in most species and ends with a stop codon (*taa, tag,* or *tga*).

The DNA sequence shown in **Figure 2-5** can be read in 6 ORFs. The 3 forward ORFs are shown below the sequence, with the translated amino acids listed below each DNA sequence. Frame 1 starts with the "**a**," Frame 2 with the "**t**," and Frame 3 with the "**g**." Stop codons are indicated by an "*" in the protein sequence. The longest ORF is Frame 1.

Standard "scanning" initiations

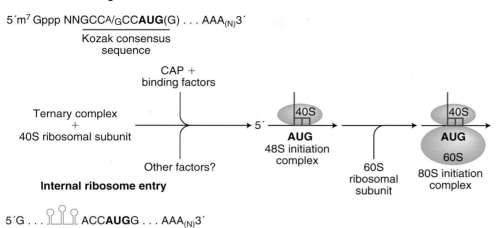

$5'$m^7 Gppp NNGCCA/GCC**AUG**(G) . . . AAA$_{(N)}$3$'$

Kozak consensus
sequence

■ **Figure 2-6**
Ribosomal scanning model: initiation of translation. The ribosome scans for best context of the Kozak's consensus sequence. Adapted from Promega Corporation. *Promega Protein Guide: Tips and Techniques.* Promega Corporation, 1993.

Internal ribosome entry

$5'$G . . . ACC**AUG**G . . . AAA$_{(N)}$3$'$

■ Cap-Dependent Initiation of Translation

Translation is the decoding of mRNA into protein. It involves all three types of RNA (tRNA, rRNA, and mRNA) and is a three-step process:

- **initiation** (formation of the initiation complex),
- **elongation** (synthesis of the polypeptide/protein), and
- **termination** (the mRNA contains an in-frame stop codon, and the polypeptide/ protein is released).

The focus of this review will be on **initiation of translation** because *all* viruses are dependent upon the host cell translation machinery to produce viral protein products using cellular ribosomes. Initiation is the key event in translation because viruses need to hijack the host translational machinery to produce their own proteins. Viruses have developed many different strategies to get their mRNA preferentially translated over the myriad of cellular mRNAs.

■ Ribosomal Scanning Model

This model postulates that a ternary complex is formed (met-tRNAi + eIF-2 + GTP) and that it associates with the small ribosomal subunit (40S). This complex binds/enters the $5'$ cap of the eukaryotic mRNA and then migrates and scans linearly down the mRNA, usually stopping at the first AUG it reaches. Marilyn Kozak has hypothesized that the 40S ribosome will scan along the mRNA until it encounters an AUG in the best consensus sequence (usually the first AUG, but not always). The Kozak consensus sequence is GCC A/G CC**AUG**(G). After this event, additional protein synthesis initiation factors, the large ribosomal subunit, and ATP are involved in the initiation of translation (**Figure 2-6**). The initiation of protein synthesis involves many cellular factors, which are listed in Table 2-1. After initiation, the steps of elongation and termination are carried out (**Figure 2-7**).

■ Translation and Open Reading Frames

Viruses use ingenious strategies to generate many protein products encoded by small genomes that contain a limited number of genes. One of these strategies is **ribosomal frameshifting**, which occurs when the ribosome shifts into another reading frame and then continues translating the mRNA into protein in that new frame. Hence certain viruses compress their genetic information by encoding different proteins in overlapping reading frames. Ribosomal frameshifting is very rare in the eukaryotic translation of genes, but is

TABLE 2.1	Eukaryotic Translation Initiation Factors

Factor	Function(s)
eIF1A (eIF4C)	Stimulation of Met-tRNAi and mRNA binding to 40S ribosomes
eIF2	Met-tRNAi binding to 40S ribosomes
eIF2B (GEF)	GDP:GTP exchange on eIF2
eIF2C (Co-eIF2A)	Stabilization of ternary complex
eIF3	Ribosome dissociation, stabilization of ternary complex, stimulation of mRNA binding
eIF3A (eIF-6)	Ribosome dissociation
Ded1	mRNA binding, RNA helicase
eIF4A	mRNA binding, RNA helicase
eIF4B	mRNA binding, RNA helicase
eIF4E	mRNA binding, cap recognition
eIF4F (CBPII)	mRNA binding, cap recognition, RNA helicase
eIF4G	mRNA binding, anchor protein
eIF4H	mRNA binding
eIF5	Ribosomal subunit joining
eIF5D	Ribosomal subunit joining

a hallmark of the translation of many retrovirus, coronavirus, paramyxovirus, astrovirus, torovirus, and arterivirus genes.

Another strategy that viruses may use to control gene expression is **translational readthrough** (**Figure 2-8**), which is a variation of the frameshifting theme. In translational readthrough, a stop translation signal may be ignored.

■ Why Do All Viruses Use the Host's Protein Synthesis Machinery?

Viruses do not have the genetic capacity to encode the proteins necessary for eukaryotic protein synthesis. In addition to ribosomes and rRNA there are at least a dozen translation initiation factors (IFs) involved in the initiation of translation in eukaryotes (Table 2-1). These eukaryotic initiation factors catalyze individual steps in the cap-dependent pathway. Even though many reactions remain poorly understood, a proposed model for cap-dependent initiation has been developed.

The term **cap-dependent translation** initiation refers to the fact that with some rare exceptions, all eukaryotic initiation of translation requires the 5′ cap of the cellular mRNA to be present. The cap is considered to be the signal recognized by the ribosome to identify the 5′ end of mRNAs because it distinguishes mRNAs from other cellular RNAs (e.g., rRNA, tRNAs, and snRNAs). **Some viruses bypass the cap recognition requirement**. This phenomenon is called **cap-independent translation**. Viruses do this by generating viral mRNAs that contain **internal ribosomal entry sites** (IRES) that allow the ribosome to enter the 5′ end of the viral RNA independently of a cap structure at that end (**Figure 2-9**).

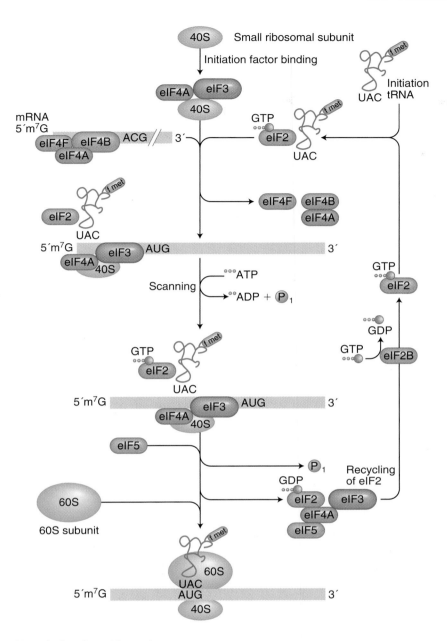

■ **Figure 2-7**
Detailed model of eukaryotic initiation of translation. Note the number of eukaryotic initiation factors (eIFs) involved. Their functions are listed in Table 2-1. Modified from Gilbert, Scott F., *Developmental Biology*, Fifth Edition Sinauer Associates, 1997.

Translational readthrough

■ **Figure 2-8**
Translational readthrough generates two proteins from a single RNA. Adapted from Levy, Jay A., Fraenkel-Conrat, Heinz, and Owens, Robert, A. *Virology*, Third Edition, Prentice Hall, 1994.

■ Leaky Scanning

Translation initiation can occur at one or more AUG sites near the 5′ end on a given viral RNA. The first AUG may not be in a context favorable to Kozak's consensus. In such cases, the ribosome may inefficiently initiate translation at the first AUG, but more often the 40S ribosome will bypass that first AUG and initiate translation farther downstream at an AUG in better context. This is called **leaky scanning** by the ribosome. It allows multiple viral proteins to by synthesized from a single mRNA. A different protein is generated when the ribosome initiates translation at an alternative AUG (Figure 2-8).

■ **Figure 2-9**

Models of cap-dependent and cap-independent translation. Adapted from R. F. Weaver. *Molecular Biology, Third edition*. McGraw-Hill Higher Education, 2001.

Posttranslational Processing of Proteins

Most eukaryotic proteins undergo some form of modification following translation. **Posttranslational modifications** (such as glycosylation, phosphorylation, and proteolytic cleavage) serve many functions. Phosphorylation of viral proteins often is needed for nucleic acid binding, whereas proteolytic cleavage often is vital to the maturation and assembly of many viruses. Several viruses have exploited the presence of cell-surface carbohydrates usually associated with glycoproteins, using them as portals of entry into the cell.

Revisit the Question: Why Do All Viruses Use the Host's Protein Synthesis Machinery?

Eukaryotic translation involves more than a dozen initiation, elongation, and termination factors. Most viral genomes do not have the capacity to contain all of the genes necessary to synthesize proteins. As a result, viruses hijack the host's protein synthesis machinery for the translation of viral mRNAs.

2.3 Molecular Constraints of the Host Cell

A virus is not able to infect every cell it encounters. It must come into contact with a host cell that can support its replication. Host cells do have some molecular constraints. It is important to discuss these constraints to better understand the unique viral replication strategies that are employed by viruses. Understanding these strategies is essential to developing future therapeutics against viruses.

Constraint 1

The ability of a virus to replicate in a host cell is constrained by the availability in that cell of the specific proteins that the virus needs to infect and replicate within the cell. The host cell may be lacking an outside cell receptor for attachment of the virus, or it may be missing an internal cellular protein such as a **transcription** or **replication factor**.

Many viruses contain RNA genomes, yet eukaryotic host cells do not possess the enzymes needed to synthesize mRNA from a viral RNA genome (RNA-dependent RNA polymerases) either in the nucleus or cytoplasm of the cell. In addition, there are no en-

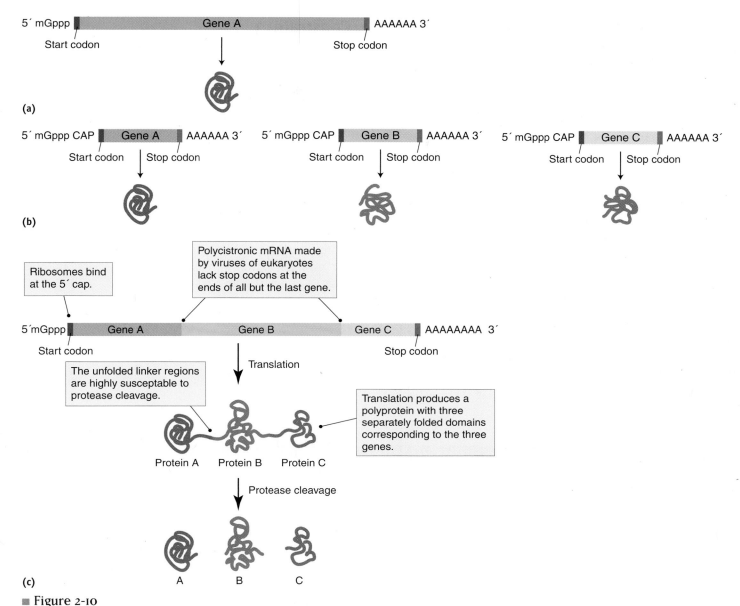

Figure 2-10
(a) Eukaryotic cells contain monocistronic mRNAs that encode one gene product. **(b)** Some viruses contain separate RNAs for each gene. **(c)** Some viral genomes are transcribed into one precursor RNA that is translated into a large polyprotein. The polyprotein is later cleaved into individual proteins by viral and/or cellular proteases.

zymes capable of transcribing viral DNAs in the cytoplasm of the cell. These constraints affect ssRNA, dsRNA, and ssDNA viruses. To overcome these constraints, these viruses encode their own polymerases to transcribe viral RNAs.

Constraint 2

Eukaryotic host protein synthesis machinery is equipped only to translate monocistronic RNAs (monocistronic RNAs code for one protein), and it usually does not recognize internal initiation sites within RNA .

It has been determined that viruses overcome these cellular constraints in at least two different ways: They generate separate mRNAs for each gene (functionally monocistronic mRNAs) or generate an mRNA encompassing several genes that is translated into a large precursor "polyprotein," which is then cleaved into individual proteins via viral or cellular proteases (**Figure 2-10**).

Capped cellular mRNAs

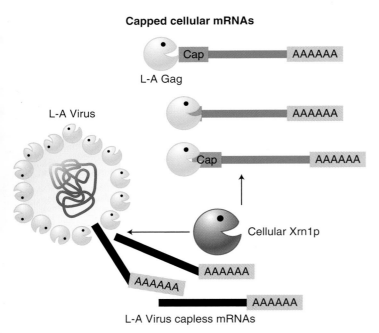

L-A Virus

L-A Gag

Cap — AAAAAA

Cap — AAAAAA

Cellular Xrn1p

AAAAAA

AAAAAA

AAAAAA

L-A Virus capless mRNAs

■ **Figure 2-11**

Model of decoy-decapitation mechanism used by yeast L-A virus. Other viruses, such as herpes simplex virus (HSV) and poxviruses, inhibit cellular translation and use strategies to degrade host mRNAs (and sometimes viral mRNAs as a consequence) following infection. Influenza viruses cleave host cell mRNA caps and use the host cell as a primer for viral transcription.

■ Constraint 3

In an infected cell, the expression of the viral genomes is in direct competition with that of the numerous cellular genes. To overcome this constraint, viruses have evolved ways to produce abundant amounts of their own proteins. Some use strategies that confer a competitive advantage toward viral mRNAs, whereas others preferentially degrade host cell mRNAs.

As an example, the yeast L-A virus produces a viral nuclease (Gag) that decapitates cellular mRNAs. The capless cellular mRNAs are then susceptible to mRNA degradation by a cellular exoribonuclease called Xrn1p. Interestingly, the L-A virus mRNAs are capless. This decapitation event is a "decoying event." The Xrn1p exonuclease degrades capless cellular mRNAs, partially freeing the capless viral mRNAs from Xrn1p attack (**Figure 2-11**).

VIRUS FILE 2-1	**Coronaviruses Are Associated with Kawasaki Disease**

Tomisaku Kawasaki first reported what would later be called Kawasaki disease (KD) in 1967. He described 50 Japanese children who between the years 1961–1967 suffered from an illness that was characterized by prolonged fever, rash, inflammation of the lips and oral cavity, "strawberry tongue," and redness and swelling of the hands and feet. Initially Kawasaki thought the disease was a benign childhood illness. Later it was determined that KD had in fact caused a number of deaths in children who had appeared to be improving or who had recovered. Upon autopsy, it was discovered that the children had developed coronary artery abnormalities. The cause of their deaths was heart failure or myocardial infarction (destruction of heart tissue resulting from obstruction of the blood supply to the heart muscle).

■ **Figure VF 2-1**

One symptom of Kawasaki disease in children is the appearance of a red "candy-coated strawberry tongue," shown here in a 5-year-old boy. Kawasaki disease is the leading cause of acquired heart disease among children in the United States and other developed countries.

Kawasaki disease has been diagnosed in the United States since 1971, with epidemics reported to the CDC during the 1980s. The illness affects primarily preschool-aged children and is more common in boys. These epidemics have been observed in winter and spring. The disease is most commonly observed in children from the middle and upper classes. Approximately 3000 children with symptoms of KD are hospitalized in the United States annually.

The cause of KD remains unknown. There are many theories, including an infectious **etiology**, an immune system abnormality, and even a possible link to carpet shampoo. No tests exist for this disease; diagnosis is based on clinical symptoms. A history of preceding respiratory illness has been reported.

Human coronaviruses have attracted renewed interest because of the emergence of a novel strain associated with severe acute respiratory syndrome (SARS-CoV). Studies of human coronaviruses have been hampered because of the inability to cultivate them **in vitro.** The 2003 SARS outbreak suddenly brought coronaviruses back into the limelight. Molecular tools were available to quickly identify and classify the particular novel coronavirus. This led to the development of detection methods of SARS-CoV and the accumulation of coronaviral genomic sequence data that allowed researchers to search for new human coronaviruses in children with respiratory diseases.

Frank Esper and his colleagues at Yale University School of Medicine sought to determine whether novel human coronaviruses were circulating in New Haven, Connecticut, where Yale is located. They did indeed identify a novel human coronavirus present in 79 of 895 (8.8%) of children they tested. They named it SARS-CoV-NH. A six-month-old infant with classic KD tested positive for the new SARS-CoV-NH. Further investigation was conducted on control children who did not have KD and children with KD. Respiratory specimens from 8 of 11 (73%) children with KD, and 1 of 22 (4.5%) of control children without KD, tested positive for human SARS-CoV-NH infection. The results suggest that there is an association between KD and SARS-CoV-NH. Further studies are needed to determine the precise role played by the novel coronavirus in the pathogenesis of KD. Advances in molecular biology are leading to many new discoveries in the field of virology.

References

CDC. 1983. "Kawasaki syndrome—United States." *MMWR* 32(7):98–100.

Esper, F. et al. 2005. "Evidence of a novel human coronavirus that is associated with respiratory tract disease in infants and young children." *J Infect Dis* 191:492–498.

Esper, F. et al. 2005. "Association between a novel human coronavirus and Kawasaki disease." *J Infect Dis* 191:499–502.

Kawasaki, T. 1967. "Acute febrile mucocutaneous syndrome with lymph node involvement with septic desquamation of the fingers and toes in children." [in Japanese] *Jpn J Allerg* 16:178–222.

Pappas, P. et al. 1985. "Multiple outbreaks of Kawasaki syndrome—United States." *MMWR* 34(3):33–35.

ProMED-Mail. Kawasaki Disease. 2001. China (Hong Kong) ProMED mail;28 May: *South China Morning Post,* by Mary Ann Benitez.

■ Constraint 4

If a DNA virus requires the use of a host cell DNA polymerase to replicate its genome, it must either infect an undifferentiated dividing cell or it must have some means of pushing a differentiated cell into the cell cycle so that the DNA polymerase enzymes that it needs for replication will be available. Differentiated cells are not usually cycling through the cell cycle, which means that they will not be producing the DNA polymerases necessary for DNA replication.

Summary

Viruses all rely, to varying degrees, on the metabolic processes of their hosts to reproduce themselves. Their hosts challenge them in several ways. The ability of the virus to replicate inside of a host cell depends on whether or not the host cell contains the appropriate receptors for entry and the proteins needed to carry out viral replication, transcription, and translation.

This chapter reviewed eukaryotic molecular biology and discussed the constraints that viruses must face. These constraints include:

1. Host cells do not contain RNA-dependent RNA polymerases.
2. Eukaryotic machinery only translates monocistronic mRNAs.
3. Viral mRNAs are in direct competition with the myriad cellular mRNAs for the translation machinery.
4. Differentiated cells may not contain the DNA polymerase enzymes required for replication of the genomes of DNA viruses.

It is intended that as a consequence of your coursework, you will begin to understand the behavior of viruses from a molecular biology perspective. In other words, you have been provided with insights to the molecular needs of viruses and with a few examples of strategies that viruses use to overcome cellular limitations.

This textbook does not emphasize the use of viruses as tools. It should be noted, though, that much of what we know today about genes, replication, DNA repair, transcription and control, splicing and processing of RNA, translation of mRNA, and protein modifications have relied extensively on viruses as critical research tools. *Viruses have been our "eyes" into cells. The intimate association between a virus and its host has allowed us to understand how cells function.* Chapter 3 will expand on replication strategies of viruses. These strategies are dictated by the nature of the viral genetic material.

Resources

Primary Literature and Reviews

Everly, D. N., Jr., Feng, P., Mian, E. S., and Read, G. S. 2002. "mRNA degradation by the virion host shutoff (Vhs) protein of herpes simplex virus: genetic and biochemical evidence that Vhs is a nuclease." *J Virol* 76(17):8560–8571.

Knipe, D. M., Samuel, C. E., and Palese, P., eds. 2001. "Virus–host cell interactions." In *Fundamental Virology*. Philadelphia: Lippincott Williams & Wilkins.

Kozak, M. 2002. "Pushing the limits of the scanning mechanism for initiation of translation." *Gene* 299:1–34.

Kozak, M. 1999. "Initiation of translation in prokaryotes and eukaryotes." *Gene* 234:187–208.

Maison, D. C. et al. 1995. "Decoying the cap-mRNA degradation system by a double-stranded RNA virus and poly(A)-mRNA surveillance by a yeast antiviral system." *Mol Cell Biol* 15(5):2763–2771.

Mitchell, P., and Tollervey, D. 2000. "mRNA stability in eukaryotes." *Cur Opin Gen & Dev* 10:193–198.

■ **Popular Press**

Haseltine, W. A. 2001. "Beyond chicken soup." *Scientific American*, Nov. 2001,
Vol. 285, Issue 5, p. 56.

■ **Video Productions**

A Journey through the Cell. 1997. Cambridge Educational.
Understanding Viruses. 2001. The Discovery Channel.

■ **eLearning**

http://biology.jbpub.com/book/virology
The site features eLearning, an online review area that provides quizzes and other tools
to help you study for your class. You can also follow useful links for in-depth information, or just find out the latest virology and microbiology news.

CASE STUDY QUESTIONS

These questions relate to the Case Study presented at the beginning of the chapter.
  1. Rashes can be explained by a variety of causes. List a few possibilities.
  2. Could additional cases be caused by a new or yet-to-be-identified virus? Why or
  why not?
  3. The CDC points to several challenges that impede investigations of reported rashes
  among schoolchildren and the identification of their causes. List these challenges.

A scanning electron micrograph of Ebola virus particles. Ebola virus contains an RNA genome. It causes Ebola hemorrhagic fever, which is a severe and often fatal disease in humans and nonhuman primates.

CHAPTER

3

> **"**In the struggle for survival, the fittest win out at the expense of their rivals because they succeed in adapting themselves best to their environment.**"**
>
> *Charles Darwin*

Virus Replication Cycles

CASE STUDY

The campus day care was recently closed during the peak of the winter flu season because many of the young children were sick with a lower respiratory tract infection. An email announcement was sent to all students, faculty, and staff at the college that stated the closure was due to a **metapneumovirus** outbreak. The announcement briefed the campus community with information about human metapneumonoviruses (hMPVs).

The announcement stated that hMPV was a newly identified respiratory tract pathogen discovered in the Netherlands in 2001. New tests confirm that it is one of the most significant and common viral infections in humans. It is clinically indistinguishable from a viral relative known as respiratory syncytial virus (RSV). Both RSV and hMPV infections occur during the winter. hMPV may account for 2% to 12% or more of previously unexplained pediatric lower respiratory infections for which samples are sent to diagnostic laboratories, and a lesser percentage in adults.

Both hMPV and RSV cause upper and lower respiratory tract infections associated with serious illness in the young, immunosuppressed, elderly, and chronically ill. Common symptoms include cough, fever, wheezing or exacerbation of asthma, and rhinorrhea (runny nose). It can produce severe enough symptoms to cause intensive care admission and ventilator support. Healthy adults can get a mild form of the disease that is characterized by a cough, hoarseness, congestion, runny nose, and sore throat.

Members of the campus day care staff were doing their best to limit the epidemic spread of the hMPV outbreak at the center. Primary care physicians need up-to-date knowledge and heightened awareness to recognize this new viral disease in patients.

I n the previous chapter you learned that viruses are dependent upon host cells for their reproduction, yet to do so viruses must overcome certain cellular constraints. Only those viruses that have been able to adapt to their hosts have been able to exist in nature.

This chapter focuses on experiments such as **one-step growth curves**, which are used to study virus–host interactions. These studies have provided information about the events that occur at each step of the infection cycle (**attachment**, **penetration**, **uncoating**, **replication**, **assembly**, **maturation**, and **release**), including the intricate details of the strategies that animal and human viruses use to express and replicate their diverse genomes.

3.1 One-Step Growth Curves

Virologists could not study animal and human viruses well in the laboratory before tissue culture methods were developed by John F. Enders, Thomas H. Weller, and Frederic C. Robbins in the late 1940s. Before their work, viruses were injected into animals and tissues were analyzed for the pathological signs of viral infection. Experimental animals were difficult to work with and expensive to maintain. Another drawback was that animals were not very sensitive to infection with human viruses due to the species barrier and the animal immune response.

■ Figure 3-1

The diagram briefly outlines the steps involved in performing one-step growth experiments. Step 5 includes a photograph of viral **plaques** (clearings where the virus destroyed the cell monolayer). The plaque assay is a quantitative assay used to determine the number of viruses present in a given sample. The results of these assays can be used to generate a one-step growth curve for a particular virus. For more details about virological methods see Chapter 5, Laboratory Diagnosis of Viral Diseases.

General Procedure: One-Step Growth Curves

Step 1:
Infect monolayers of tissue culture cells (using a vertical laminar flow biosafety hood) and allow the infection to proceed in a CO_2 incubator.

CO_2 incubator.

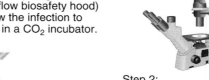

Step 2:
Monitor experiments via inverted microscope.

Step 3:
Collect infected cell lysates at various time points after infection.

Step 4:
Perform serial dilutions on infected cell lysates and do plaque assays.

Step 5:
Stain and analyze plaque assays. Record results.

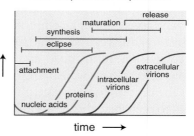

One-Step Growth Experiment

release
maturation
synthesis
eclipse
attachment
extracellular virions
intracellular virions
proteins
nucleic acids

time ⟶

Stationary phase

Death

Logarithmic phase

Lag phase

Log numbers (CFU/ml)

Time

(a)

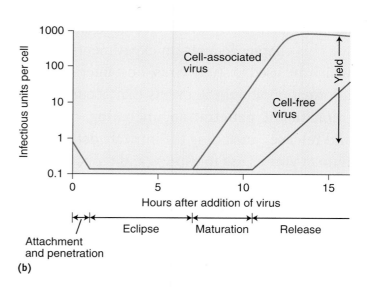

Infectious units per cell

Cell-associated virus

Cell-free virus

Yield

Hours after addition of virus

Attachment and penetration

Eclipse   Maturation   Release

(b)

■ Figure 3-2

Typical bacterial growth versus a one-step growth curve of a naked virus. **(a)** Bacterial growth generally proceeds in a series of phases: lag, log (exponential growth in which the rate of multiplication is most rapid and constant), stationary, and death. Viruses require host cells for growth and reproduction. CFU/ml = colony forming units per milliliter. Modified from an illustration by H. Douglas Goff, Ph.D., University of Guelph. **(b)** Viruses are assembled from preformed "parts" when enough of the preformed parts have been made. Adapted from White, D.E. and Fenner, F.J. *Medical Virology*, Fourth Edition. Academic Press, 1994.

Enders, Weller, and Robbins won the 1954 Nobel Prize in Physiology or Medicine for the cultivation of poliovirus in nonnervous tissue cultures (human embryonic skin and muscle cells). Their observations and procedures used to grow viruses *in vitro* contributed to the refinement of tissue culture techniques and played a monumental role in the development of vaccines against poliovirus in the 1950s (Salk vaccine) and 1960s (Sabin vaccine).

One-step or **single-step growth curve experiments** are used to study a single replication cycle of viruses. Max Delbruck developed the one-step growth curve experiment while using an *Escherichia coli*-T4 bacterial system, which gave faster experimental results than did traditional methods. With the advent of cell culture systems, these experiments were carried out with viruses than infect tissue culture cells. These experiments are performed in special cell culture facilities. Briefly, **monolayers** (or cell suspensions in liquid medium) of tissue culture cells such as monkey kidney cells are allowed to adhere and form monolayers on the bottom of plastic dishes.

The monolayers of cells are subsequently infected with the virus of choice. They are infected at a high **multiplicity of infection** (**MOI**) to ensure that every cell of the monolayer is infected simultaneously. The MOI is the average number of viruses/cell. Hence, classic one-step growth experiments usually use an MOI of 10 (10 viruses/cell). The infected cells are maintained in incubators and monitored throughout the course of infection. At various times during the infection, infected cells and/or tissue culture fluid are harvested and plaque assays are performed. **Plaque assays** are used to quantitate the number of intracellular or extracellular virus particles present during that point of infection. All viruses should be going through the same step in the viral replication cycle at the same time (**Figure 3-1**).

From these experiments, virologists have determined that there is a general pattern observed during the life cycle of a virus that distinguishes it from the life cycle of a bacterium. Shortly after the infection, the input or inoculated virus disappears. No virus particles are detected at this time. This is termed the eclipse period (**Figure 3-2a**). This continues until progeny viruses are detectable (anywhere from one to several hours or even days depending on the virus) which is termed the productive stage. Figure 3-2b illustrates that there is a lag phase in which few bacteria are detected but there is never a disappearance of bacteria observed during the life cycle of a typical bacterium. The viral **attachment**, **eclipse**, and productive (**maturation** and **release**) stages will be discussed in detail as these key steps of viral replication are dissected in the following section.

3.2 Key Steps of the Viral Replication Cycle

■ 1. Attachment (Adsorption)

The first step in the life cycle of a virus is attachment. The virus must be able to attach to its host and enter the "correct" or "target" cell. The attachment event is electrostatic and does not require any cellular energy. This step is a critical step in the viral replication cycle and a great target for antiviral therapies developed to prevent viral infections. If virus attachment is blocked, the infection is prevented. A virus is said to exhibit a tropism for a particular cell type when it targets and infects that cell type. In many cases these cell types are a specific population of cells within organs. Table 3-1 lists examples of viruses and their cellular tropism. Sometimes viruses also display species tropism. For example, poliovirus infects only primate cells.

Host range is a term that refers to the different types of tissue culture cells or organisms (species) that the virus can infect. The host range may be broad (infecting many

TABLE 3-1	Viral Cell Tropism
Virus(es)	**Cell Type**
HIV	CD4+ T lymphocytes, macrophages
Rabies	Muscle, neurons
Human papilloma	Differentiating keratinocytes
Hepatitis A, B, C	Liver (hepatocytes)
Human herpes simplex 1 and 2	Mucoepithelium
Influenza A	Respiratory epithelium
Rotavirus	Intestinal epithelium
Norovirus	Intestinal epithelium
Cytomegalovirus	Epithelium, monocytes, lymphocytes
Rhinovirus	Nasal epithelium
Poliovirus	Intestinal epithelium
Epstein-Barr	B cell

TABLE 3-2	Cell Surface Receptors Used by Viruses to Attach and Enter Cells
Virus	**Cell Surface Receptor**
Influenza A	Sialic acid
HIV-1	CD4 and chemokine co-receptors (CXCR5, CCR4)
Hepatitis C	Low-density lipoprotein receptor
Rabies	Acetylcholine receptor, neural cell adhesion molecule, nerve growth factor, gangliosides, phospholipids
Rhinovirus	Intracellular adhesion molecule 1 (ICAM-1)
Hepatitis B	IgA receptor
Adenovirus Type 2	Integrins $\alpha_v\beta_3$ and $\alpha_v\beta_5$
Poliovirus	Immunoglobulin superfamily protein (CD155)

different animals or cell lines of different species) or narrow. An example of a broad-range virus is rabies, for which all mammals have varying susceptibility. Human immunodeficiency virus (HIV), which infects humans and monkeys but causes disease only in humans, falls into the narrow range. Human viruses and animal viruses also have preferred routes of entry (e.g., influenza and rhinoviruses enter via the respiratory tract). Routes of entry and mechanisms for viral spread in the body are covered in Chapter 6.

In order to infect cells, the attachment proteins located on the outside of the virus must be able to bind to **cellular surface receptors**. Cellular receptors are usually proteins, glycoproteins, carbohydrates, or lipids. Table 3-2 provides examples of viruses and their cellular receptor(s). *Viruses have evolved to use these receptors for attachment and entry to their hosts.* You may ask, "Why haven't cells evolved to keep up with the evolution of viruses?" The answer is that viruses have evolved to use essential components of the cells as receptors. Without these essential components, the cell can't exist. Cell surface receptors play important roles in normal cellular activities. We do not know all of the cellular receptors for every virus; however, research continues in this area of host–virus interactions.

There are several factors that may influence the efficiency of viral attachment, such as the density of receptors present on the host cell surface, the density of the **ligands** on the viral surface, and the concentrations of virus and host cells. Temperature, pH, and the presence or absence of specific ions may also play a role in the efficiency of attachment. For some viruses, such as poliovirus, rhinovirus, and influenza virus, a single type of cellular receptor is sufficient for virus attachment. In other cases, including HIV Type 1 (HIV-1) and adenoviruses, one type of cellular receptor is required for the initial attachment and attachment to a **co-receptor** is necessary for viral entry into the cell.

■ 2. Penetration (Entry)

After the animal or human virus attaches to a cellular receptor, it must cross the lipid bilayer plasma membrane (or in some cases the nuclear membrane) of the host cell. Activity at the surface of cellular membranes is dynamic and these membranes are constantly being recycled. **Clathrin**, which is a large, fibrous protein, is instrumental in the formation of specialized regions of the cell membrane called **clathrin-coated pits**. These pits appear as invaginations that are coated with dark material, and are located on the cytoplasmic side of the membrane. The pits are short lived and soon bud off to form **clathrin-coated vesicles**. These vesicles are for transport and are coated with a latticelike network of clathrin. Shortly after formation, the clathrin coat is removed and the resultant vesicles are referred to as **endosomes**. Sometimes these vesicles contain viruses, which can penetrate directly at the plasma membrane or via endosomes. The virus particle must then disassemble to make the viral genome available in the cytoplasm, where it is targeted to the correct location in the cell for genome replication.

How Are Cellular Receptors Used for Viral Attachment Discovered?

Scientists have developed several techniques to identify cell surface receptors and co-receptors to which viruses attach in order to initiate infection. These approaches may be viral receptor-interference studies or genetic techniques. Parts (a)–(c) of **Figure VF 3-1** illustrate the general scheme of the various methods employed.

■ **Figure VF 3-1**
Identification of host cell receptors. **(a)** Removal of cell surface receptors. Adapted from Paulson, J.C., and Rogers, G. N. *Methods Enzymol* (1987):162–168. **(b)** Monoclonal antibodies block cell surface receptors. Adapted from Staunton, D. E., et al. *Cell* 56 (1989):849–853. **(c)** Gene-transfer experiments. Adapted from Mendelsohn, C., et al. *PNAS USA* 20 (1986):7845–7849.

Enveloped Virus Entry

Enveloped viruses contain a lipid bilayer, or envelope, that surrounds the nucleocapsid. These viruses enter cells via fusion of the viral and cellular membranes. This process is driven by the viral glycoproteins located on the viral surface. The two basic modes of entry of an enveloped human/animal virus are by **ligand-mediated fusion** of the virus and the cellular plasma membrane or by **receptor-mediated endocytotic entry** of an enveloped virus (**Figure 3-3**). (In ligand-mediated fusion it is the viral ligand rather than the host receptor that mediates the fusion event.)

In ligand-receptor-mediated fusion, the virus attaches to the plasma membrane of the cell and fusion takes place between the viral and cellular membranes. The **nucleocapsid** of the virus is released inside of the cell. The remaining viral envelope remains as a "patch" on the cellular plasma membrane (Figure 3-3a). The fusion at the plasma membrane mode of penetration is **pH independent**.

In receptor-mediated endocytotis (engulfment), the enveloped virus attaches to a receptor on the plasma membrane of the cell and the cell is stimulated to engulf the entire virus, thus forming an endocytotic vesicle (Figure 3-3). This endocytotic vesicle may fuse with the lysosomes, which possess an internal acidic pH. In the acidic pH of the endocytic vesicles, conformational changes in the viral envelope proteins facilitate the fusion of the viral membrane with the endocytic membrane and the subsequent release of the viral nucleocapsid into the cytoplasm. This mode of viral penetration is **pH dependent** because it is only at an acid pH that the fusion between the viral envelope and the host cell membrane occurs (Figures 3-3b and 3-3c).

Naked Virus Entry

It is more difficult to envision how naked or nonenveloped viruses cross the cellular membrane, and much remains to be understood about how these viruses enter cells. Studies suggest that the majority of naked viruses enter via receptor-mediated endocytosis. The virus ligand–cell surface receptor interaction causes a clathrin-coated pit formation/invagination at the cell surface. The clathrin-coated pits encase the virus and bud off to form a clathrin-coated vesicle. Within seconds this clathrin coat is shed and the vesicle containing the virus fuses with lysosomes. The low pH, along with proteases in this endocytic vesicle, helps to disassociate the capsid, releasing the nucleic acid genome of the virus into the cytoplasm. **Figure 3-4** demonstrates this type of entry.

■ 3. Uncoating (Disassembly and Localization)

This step refers to the removal or degradation of the capsid (uncoating), thereby releasing the genome into the host cell. The genome is transported to the site where transcription/replication can begin. In some viruses there is no degradation of the capsid because the capsid proteins play a role in viral transcription and replication. For these viruses uncoating refers to changes in the nucleocapsid that make it ready for transcription and/or replication.

The uncoating step may occur simultaneously with penetration or it may immediately follow penetration of the virus into the host cell. It is a necessary step before replication of the genome can occur. When the nucleic acid genome is uncoated, infectious particles are no longer detected in one-step growth experiments. This is the start of the eclipse phase, which continues until new infectious virus particles are made (see Figure 3-2b).

■ 4. Types of Viral Genomes and Their Replication

When viruses infect cells, two important and separate events must occur:
- *the production of virus structural proteins and enzymes, and*
- *replication of the viral genome.*

The genome of a virus may consist of DNA or RNA, which may be single stranded (ss) or double stranded (ds) and linear or circular (**Figure 3-5**). The entire genome may occupy

Receptor-mediated fusion of an enveloped virus with the plasma membrane

Attachment

Fusion of viral and cellular envelopes

Nucleocapsid released inside cell

Viral envelope forms patch on plasma membrane

(a)

Receptor-mediated endocytotic entry of an enveloped virus

Attachment

Formation of an endocytotic vesicle

Acidification

Release of nucleocapsid into cell's interior

(b)

(c)

■ **Figure 3-3**

(a) Viral entry steps in ligand mediated fusion. Adapted from E. K. Wagner and M. J. Hewlett. *Basic Virology,* Second Edition. Blackwell Publishing, 2003. **(b)** Viral entry steps in a receptor mediated endocytotic entry of an enveloped virus. Adapted from Wagner, Edward K. and Hewlett, Martinez J. *Basic Virology,* Second Edition. Blackwell Publishing, 2003. **(c)** Electron micrograph of mouse hepatitis viruses (family Coronaviridae) are absorbed into mouse intestinal cells via receptor-mediated endocytosis. The plasma membrane is invaginated and will release the viruses inside the cell. Magnification 40,000×.

■ Figure 3-4

Steps that naked viruses use to enter cells. Adapted from Wagner, Edward K. and Hewlett, Martinez J. *Basic Virology,* Second Edition. Blackwell Publishing, 2003.

Viral genomes

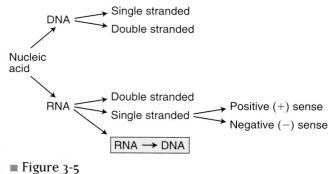

■ Figure 3-5

Types of viral nucleic acid genomes.

either one nucleic acid molecule (**monopartite** or linear genome) or several nucleic acid molecules (**multipartite** or segmented genome). The different types of genome necessitate different replication strategies.

dsDNA Viruses

The genome replication of most RNA viruses occurs in the cytoplasm of the host. Presumably, this is because their replication is associated with RNA-dependent RNA polymerases that the host cell nucleus cannot provide. In contrast, most DNA viruses replicate their genomes in the nucleus and utilize the host's DNA- and RNA-synthesizing machinery, along with the host's RNA-processing machinery. This means the viral genome must traverse the nuclear membrane to utilize the aforementioned cellular machinery.

Replication of many DNA viruses involves strategies that are familiar in cell biology: DNA replication and mRNA transcription form dsDNA. Viral proteins are translated from the **monocistronic** mRNAs generated via transcription of viral mRNAs, as shown in **Figure 3-6a**, which also lists examples of dsDNA viruses, the diseases they cause, and the families to which they belong. Many DNA viruses have evolved ways to evade host defenses and can cause tumors in animals. In this chapter we also discuss viral taxonomy, including virus families and how they are determined.

Papovaviruses and herpesviruses are dsDNA viruses and have the most straightforward replication strategy. These viruses utilize the cellular DNA-dependent RNA polymerase II located in the host's nucleus to transcribe the viral mRNAs from the dsDNA viral genome.

dsDNA Viruses

Virus	Disease	Family

Herpes simplex
  Type 1
  Type 2
	
	Cold sores
	Genital herpes
		Herpesviridae

Adenovirus	Respiratory infections	Adenoviridae
Variola	Smallpox	Poxviridae

Human Papillomavirus
  *Types 16 and 18
  *Types 6 and 11
  *Types 1, 2 and 4
	
	Cervical cancer
	Genital warts
	Plantar warts
		Papovaviridae

*common types		

(a)

■ **Figure 3-6**
(a) List of dsDNA viruses and their replication strategy. Adapted from D. R. Harper. *Molecular Virology,* Second Edition. BIOS Scientific Publishers, 1999. (b) List of ssDNA viruses. Adapted from D. R. Harper. *Molecular Viorology,* Second Edition. BIOS Scientific Publsihers, 1999.

ssDNA Viruses

Virus	Disease	Family
Human parvovirus B19	Fifth disease (slapped-cheek syndrome)	Parvoviridae
Transfusion transmitted virus (TTV)	Hepatitis?	Circoviridae

ssDNA ⟶ dsDNA ⟨ mRNA ⟶ Proteins ⟶ Assembly / ssDNA ⟶ Assembly

(b)

The host cell must be cycling through the cell cycle for their DNA polymerase to be available for use by these DNA viruses. The viral RNA transcripts are spliced and cleaved via cellular machinery to produce monocistronic mRNAs that are exported into the cytoplasm and translated accordingly by the cell's translation machinery. The viral dsDNA is packaged, along with the necessary structural proteins and enzymes, resulting in the generation of the newly assembled progeny viruses.

Poxviruses differ from the other dsDNA virus families listed in Figure 3-6a in that they replicate solely in the cytoplasm. These viruses carry their own DNA-dependent DNA polymerase (to replicate the viral dsDNA genome) within the virus particle. The genomes of poxviruses are large (ranging from 130–230 kbp, or roughly 100–200 genes), allowing these viruses to be fully equipped with the genes to make them independent of the host's nuclear enzymes and machinery. The monocistronic mRNAs are transcribed directly from the viral dsDNA (Figure 3-6a).

ssDNA Viruses

Parvoviruses are the smallest of the human viruses (only 20–25 nm in diameter). In contrast to the dsDNA virus genomes, these ssDNA viruses contain very small linear genomes (the genome of the human parvovirus B19 is 5 kb). Parvoviruses do not carry any enzymes in the virus particle. These viruses infect cells that are in the cell cycle because they are dependent upon the host's DNA polymerase to synthesize the viral ssDNA and the cell's DNA-dependent RNA polymerase II to transcribe the viral dsDNA into viral mRNA in the nucleus. The cellular splicing machinery is also used in the production of the viral mRNAs. The general outline of their replication strategy is illustrated in Figure 3-6b.

(a)

Virus
Dane particle
40 nm diameter

Filamentous particle
up to 200 nm long

Spherical particle
~20 nm diameter

(b)

■ **Figure 3-7**

(a) HBV infection results in the formation of three different types of virus particles: 42 to 47 nm intact infectious Dane particles, 22-nm spheres, and 22-nm filaments of varying lengths. **(b)** Illustration depicting the different forms of HBV particles. Mature hepatitis B Dane particles contain dsDNA with associated protein, but their mode of replication is different from the other dsDNA viruses and their replication strategy. Adapted from University of South Carolina, School of Medicine. "Virology: Hepatitis Viruses." *Microbiology and Immunology.* University of South Carolina, 2008. http://pathmicro.med.sc.edu/virol/hepatitis-virus.htm.

ss/dsDNA Viruses (Using an RNA Intermediate)

Hepadnaviruses replicate via a very unique and somewhat complicated mechanism. This textbook focuses on hepatitis B virus (HBV) because it specifically infects humans. Other members of the Hepadnaviridae family infect woodchucks, ground squirrels, chipmunks, ducks, geese, chimps, gibbons, and orangutans. Interestingly, HBV-infected cells produce different forms of virus-related particles. Electron microscopy of partially purified virus particle preparations reveal three types of particles: a 42- to 47-nm mature spherical virus particle (known as **Dane particles**, named after their discoverer); 22-nm spherical particles, which are found in 10,000- to 100,000-fold excess over the Dane particle; and filamentous particles that are 22 nm in diameter and of varying lengths.

All three forms contain the same surface protein called the hepatitis B surface antigen (HbsAg). The Dane particle is the only infectious particle of HBV. The 22-nm spheres and filaments do not contain nucleic acid (**Figure 3-7**).

The genome of the Dane particles consists of a 3.2-kb linear DNA that is arranged in a relaxed circle. Some parts of the genome are dsDNA, whereas others consist of ssDNA regions or gaps. This partially duplexed DNA consists of a full length (−) sense ssDNA and a shorter length (+) sense ssDNA. As a result, the gapped regions contain only (−) sense ssDNA. After the HBV has entered its host cell and the virus is partially uncoated, the partial dsDNA genome of the Dane particle migrates to the nucleus, where it is completed or repaired by a viral reverse transcriptase. The dsDNA enters the nucleus and the ends are ligated by cellular enzymes, forming a circular **episome**. (The term episome applies to a viral genome that is maintained in cells by autonomous replication.) Next, the repaired viral dsDNA associates with cellular histones and is transcribed into separate viral mRNA transcripts and a full-length ssRNA pre-genome (**Figure 3-8**).

The viral mRNAs are translated to yield the hepatitis B core antigens and the viral reverse transcriptase. The RNA pre-genome associates with the viral reverse transcriptase and is packaged with the core proteins to form an **immature** virus particle in the cytoplasm of the cell. The viral **reverse transcriptase** synthesizes the (−) sense ssDNA strand using the ssRNA intermediate as a template (see *Refresher:* Molecular Biology about reverse transcriptase functions). The pre-genome is degraded by the RNase H activity of the reverse transcriptase enzyme, but it leaves a short sequence of RNA at its 5′ end that acts as a primer for DNA polymerase to synthesize a complementary (+) DNA strand in the **mature** particle.

Hepatitis B is one of a few known nonretroviral viruses that use reverse transcription as part of its replication process. Other viruses that utilize reverse transcriptase are retroviruses such as human T-cell leukemia virus (HTLV) and HIV, which possess an RNA genome. For these retroviruses reverse transcription is one of the first steps in viral replication, whereas for hepatitis B reverse transcription occurs during maturation (the latter steps) in making new virus particles. In addition, in contrast to retroviruses, HBV does

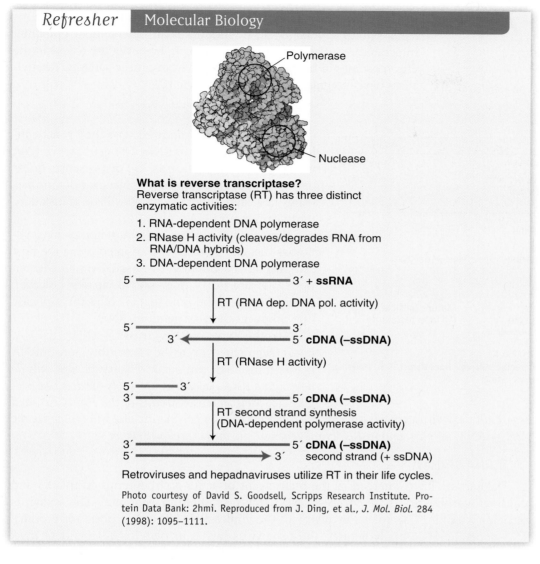

Refresher — Molecular Biology

What is reverse transcriptase?
Reverse transcriptase (RT) has three distinct enzymatic activities:

1. RNA-dependent DNA polymerase
2. RNase H activity (cleaves/degrades RNA from RNA/DNA hybrids)
3. DNA-dependent DNA polymerase

5′ ————————— 3′ + **ssRNA**

↓ RT (RNA dep. DNA pol. activity)

5′ ————————— 3′
3′ ◄————————— 5′ **cDNA (−ssDNA)**

↓ RT (RNase H activity)

5′ ——— 3′
3′ ————————————— 5′ **cDNA (−ssDNA)**

↓ RT second strand synthesis (DNA-dependent polymerase activity)

3′ ————————————— 5′ **cDNA (−ssDNA)**
5′ ————————————► 3′ second strand (+ ssDNA)

Retroviruses and hepadnaviruses utilize RT in their life cycles.

Photo courtesy of David S. Goodsell, Scripps Research Institute. Protein Data Bank: 2hmi. Reproduced from J. Ding, et al., *J. Mol. Biol.* 284 (1998): 1095–1111.

Virus	Disease	Family
Hepatitis B	Hepatitis associated with liver cancer	Hepadnaviridae

■ **Figure 3-8**

ssDNA/dsDNA virus (that uses ssRNA as an intermediate) and its replication strategy. Adapted from Harper, D.R. *Molecular Virology*, Second Edition. BIOS Scientific Publishers, 1999.

+ sense ssRNA genome: AUG GCA CGA ⟶ met ala arg

− sense ssRNA genome: UAC CGU GCU

■ **Figure 3-9**
Differences between positive (+) and negative (−) sense ssRNA viral genomes.

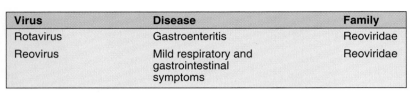

Virus	Disease	Family
Rotavirus	Gastroenteritis	Reoviridae
Reovirus	Mild respiratory and gastrointestinal symptoms	Reoviridae

■ **Figure 3-10**
List of dsRNA viruses and their replication strategies. Adapted from Harper, D.R. *Molecular Virology,* Second Edition. BIOS Scientific Publishers, 1999.

not have **integrase** activity. The DNA of hepatitis B is usually not integrated into cellular DNA; it is found as an independent **episome**. Integrated parts of the hepatitis B genome, however, are found in the chromosomes of hepatocellular tumors from cancer patients. Retroviruses have integrase activity (see Chapter 10).

RNA Viruses

RNA viruses are unique because their genetic information is encoded in RNA. The genomes of RNA viruses are diverse [ss or ds, (+) or (−) sense, linear or segmented]. The type of RNA genome determines if the first step after uncoating will be translation, transcription, or RNA replication.

Viruses that contain +ssRNA genomes have genomes that can be directly translated using the host cell machinery because the +ssRNA acts like an mRNA (**Figure 3-9**). These +ssRNA viruses, however, do need to carry the gene that encodes the replicase that produces the viral genomic RNA.

All other types of RNA viruses (−ssRNA, dsRNA, linear, segmented) must be transcribed into mRNA before translation can occur. *Eukaryotic host cells do not contain RNA-dependent RNA polymerases (see Section 2.3, Molecular Constraints of the Host Cell), and as a result these viruses must carry an RNA-dependent RNA polymerase that will synthesize the viral +ssRNA, mRNAs, and −ssRNA viral genomes into the host cell with them.*

dsRNA Viruses

Rotaviruses have emerged as the main agent of acute gastroenteritis in infants and children worldwide. These viruses have dsRNA **segmented** genomes. The rotavirus particle contains 11 segments or pieces of the viral dsRNA. The host does not produce RNA-dependent RNA polymerases, thus, the virus carries its own RNA-dependent RNA polymerase and the replication cycle occurs solely in the cytoplasm.

A rotavirus particle is nonenveloped and icosahedral with a double-capsid. One of its two layers is removed but the other is not; the transcription takes place inside of this single capsid and the mRNAs are released in the cytoplasm for translation. After attachment, entry, and uncoating, the virus synthesizes a +ssRNA from each of the 11 dsRNA segments (using the −ssRNA strands of the dsRNA genome as a template) via a viral RNA-dependent RNA polymerase. These viral ssRNAs are also capped via a viral capping enzyme. The RNAs are not polyadenylated. Half of the newly synthesized capped +ssRNAs strands (mRNAs) are translated by the cellular machinery in the cytoplasm. The remaining strands are packaged into a viral capsid during assembly (**Figure 3-10**).

At this stage of the life cycle, the RNAs inside the particles are sensitive to RNase treatment. During maturation of the virus particle, the complementary −ssRNA strands are synthesized using the capped +ssRNAs as a template within the virus particle to form the remaining dsRNA genomic segments (Figure 3-10). These final dsRNA segments are resistant to RNase treatment. There are still several remaining questions about the replication cycle of rotaviruses and other viruses of the Reoviridae family; for example, how does the virus particle manage to contain only one of copy of each of the 11 mRNAs?

+ssRNA Viruses

The +ssRNA viruses include several families of viruses. Members of the Picornaviridae, Flaviviridae, and Caliciviridae families, in particular, are ubiquitous in nature and cause a

Virus	Disease	Family
Poliovirus	Poliomyelitis Postpolio syndrome	Picornaviridae
Rhinovirus (many types)	Common cold	Picornaviridae
Hepatitis A	Hepatitis	Picornaviridae
Cocksackie		Picornaviridae
Group A Types 21, 24 Group A Types 4, 5, 9, 10, 16	Common cold Hand, foot and mouth disease	
Group B Types 1–5 Group B Types 2, 5	Myocarditis Hand, foot and mouth disease	
Echoviruses		Picornaviridae
Various Types Types 1–7, 9, 11, 13–23, 25, 27	Diarrhea Aseptic meningitis	
Rubivirus	Rubella	Togaviridae
Yellow fever	Hemorrhagic fever	Flaviviridae
Hepatitis C	Hepatitis liver cancer	Flaviviridae
Dengue	Dengue fever	Flaviviridae
West Nile	Fever, rash, myalgia encephalitis	Flaviviridae
Norovirus	Gastroenteritis	Caliciviridae
Sapovirus	Gastroenteritis	Caliciviridae

■ **Figure 3-11**

List of +ssRNA viruses and their replication strategies. Adapted from Harper, D.R. *Molecular Virology,* Second Edition. BIOS Scientific Publishers, 1999.

wide range of diseases. Their success and widespread distribution suggest that their replication strategy is very effective. The RNA in the virus particle itself functions as mRNA. This genomic RNA is a polycistronic mRNA that is recognized by cellular machinery and translated as one open reading frame into a single polyprotein precursor that is subsequently cleaved into individual viral proteins by viral and cellular proteases (**Figure 3-11**). One of the viral encoded proteins is an RNA-dependent RNA polymerase that replicates the viral genome. It transcribes the viral +ssRNA into a –ssRNA replicative intermediate, which in turn serves as a template for the genomic +ssRNA (Figure 3-11). Note that there are exceptions to this replication strategy. Not all ssRNA viruses produce a single polyprotein that is cleaved by proteases into individual proteins. Some produce more than one mRNA, allowing greater control of the production of individual proteins; for example, early replication proteins and later structural proteins are produced at different times during the viral replication cycle.

-ssRNA Viruses

Viruses in the Paramyxoviridae, Rhabdoviridae, and Filoviridae families contain –ssRNA nonsegmented genomes. All of these viruses encode their own RNA-dependent RNA polymerases that transcribe its –ssRNA genome into several different viral monocistronic +ssmRNAs that can be recognized by the host cell machinery. The different +ssRNAs are made by a complicated start–stop type of mechanism. In other words, a range of viral mRNAs are each translated to make different viral proteins rather than a polyprotein. All of the proteins are not produced to the same level and a number of control mechanisms are used. The second function of the viral RNA-dependent RNA polymerase is to synthesize the viral/progeny genome using the +ssRNA as a template. Hence the RNA-dependent RNA polymerase is sometimes referred to having a **transcriptase** and **replicase** function (**Figure 3-12a**).

−ssRNA Viruses with Non-segmented Genomes:

Virus	Disease	Family
Rabies	Rabies	Rhabdoviridae
Ebola	Hemorrhagic fever	Filoviridae
Marburg	Hemorrhagic fever	Filoviridae
Nipah	Encephalitis and respiratory infections	Paramyxoviridae
Measles	Measles	Paramyxoviridae
Mumps	Mumps	Paramyxoviridae
Metapneumovirus	Respiratory tract infections	Paramyxoviridae
Borna	Psychiatric disorders?	Bornaviridae

−ssRNA Viruses with Segmented Genomes:

Virus	Disease	Family
Influenza A, B, C	Influenza	Orthomyxoviridae
Crimean-Congo	Hemorrhagic fever	Bunyaviridae
Sin nombre	Hantavirus pulmonary syndrome	Bunyaviridae
Hantaan	Hemorrhagic fever	Bunyaviridae
Rift Valley fever	Hemorrhagic fever	Bunyaviridae
Lassa	Hemorrhagic fever	Arenaviridae

(a)

(b)

■ **Figure 3-12**

(a) List of −ssRNA viruses (nonsegmented and segmented) and their replication strategies. Adapted from D. R. Harper. *Molecular Virology*, Second Edition. BIOS Scientific Publishers, 1999. **(b)** Ambisense RNA viruses: Strategies for replication and mRNA synthesis of RNA genome. Adapted from Harper, D. R. *Molecular Virology*, Second Edition. BIOS Scientific Publishers, 1999.

The −ssRNA viruses containing segmented genomes also encode their own RNA-dependent RNA polymerase that functions as a transcriptase and replicase. Each segment produces a monocistronic mRNA or an RNA that is differentially spliced to make monocistronic mRNAs. The genomes of the viruses in the Arenaviridae and Bunyaviridae families are more complicated in that at least one of the viral ssRNA genomic segments are **ambisense** [the ssRNA is both (+) and (−) sense on the same ssRNA segment]. The process of replication (Figure 3-12b) and translations of these RNAs is not completely understood.

Viruses with ssRNA Genomes That Use a dsDNA Intermediate to Replicate

The Retroviridae family contains viruses that have been identified in virtually all organisms including invertebrates. This suggests that these viruses have an evolutionarily successful design. Their biology is quite unique.

The main focus on retroviruses has been on the avian (chicken) or human retroviruses: Rous sarcoma virus (RSV, discovered in 1911, see Chapter 10), HIV (discovered in 1983), and HTLVs (discovered in 1981). Retrovirus infections cause a wide spectrum of diseases including cancer, immune deficiencies, and neurological disorders. Most retroviral infections, however, occur without having any detectable, deleterious damage to the host.

The replication cycle of retroviruses includes the integration of the viral complementary DNA (cDNA) into the chromosomal DNA of the host cell. The result of this integration event is that the retroviral DNA is inherited from parent to offspring of the infected host if germline cells (sperm and egg) contain the integrated viral genome. These are termed **endogenous retroviruses** or **proviruses** and their biologic properties and functions are still under investigation. Approximately 8% to 12% of the human genome consists of sequences of **human endogenous retroviruses** (**HERVs**). Retroviruses that are not integrated in germline cells of their hosts are called exogenous retroviruses (or external viruses).

The genome of retroviruses contains two copies of a +ssRNA molecule that is reverse transcribed into dsDNA by a viral RNA-dependent DNA polymerase (reverse transcriptase) to produce an RNA:DNA hybrid, which in turn is converted to dsDNA. The viral dsDNA is inserted into the host chromosomal dsDNA (**Figure 3-13**). The integrated DNA (provirus) is subsequently transcribed by the host's DNA-dependent RNA polymerase II. The mRNA

Virus	Disease	Family
HIV-1 and 2	AIDS	Retroviridae
HTLV I	T-Lymphocyte Leukemia	Retroviridae
HTLV II	?	Retroviridae

■ **Figure 3-13**
List of ssRNA viruses (that use a DNA intermediate) and their replication strategies. Adapted from Harper, D.R. *Molecular Virology,* Second Edition. BIOS Scientific Publishers, 1999.

transcripts are then spliced and exported into the cytoplasm of the cell, where they will be translated by the cellular protein synthesis machinery. Some full-length +ssRNA transcripts will be packaged into the new retrovirus particles.

■ 5. Assembly

It is not always possible to identify the assembly, maturation, and release of virus particles as distinct and separate stages of the viral life cycle. Virus assembly is a key step in the replication cycles of viruses. It involves the process in which the immature virus particle is formed. Despite the structural diversity of virus particles, the repertoire of assembly mechanisms is limited. All of the components of the virus must be assembled to create a stable structure. At the same time, the newly assembled virus must accomplish disassembly to start a new infectious life cycle.

The assembly event occurs when an appropriate concentration of virus proteins and genomic nucleic acids are reached and localized at specific sites within the infected cell. The genomic nucleic acids are packaged into preexisting shells that form via **self assembly** (spontaneous assembly, also refer to Chapter 4) of viral capsid proteins, or are coated with capsid proteins, or are co-assembled with capsid proteins. Assembly sites (for example, the cytoplasm, nucleus, on the inner surface of the plasma membrane of cells) differ according to the virus and have some influence on how the virus particle is released.

Historically, research directed toward virus assembly mechanisms has received less attention because of more interest in the mechanisms of viral gene expression and replication. There is now renewed interest in understanding virus assembly because of the development of new molecular technologies and the success of therapeutic agents designed to inhibit virus-specific reactions involved in the production of infectious virus particles. These advances in understanding continue at an accelerated pace.

■ 6. Maturation

This is the stage of the virus life cycle in which the virus becomes infectious. Viral or cellular proteases are often involved in maturation. One or more **capsid** or **envelope** proteins may undergo specific proteolytic cleavage within the particle. The cleavage event results in a subtle structural change of the virus particle, which may give it increased stability.

Virus-encoded proteases are attractive targets for antiviral therapies; for example, the protease inhibitors Saquinavir mesylate (Invirase), Saquinavir (Fortovase), Ritonavir (Norvir), Indinavir (Crixivan), Nelfinavir (Viracept), Amprenavir (Agenerase), and ABT-378 (Kaletra) target the HIV-encoded protease by preventing the maturation of virions capable of infecting other cells (**Figure 3-14**).

■ 7. Release

Newly formed viruses are either released to the outside environment upon lysis, escaping the cell as it disintegrates (**lytic viruses**), or are released by budding (**Figure 3-15**) through

■ Figure 3-14
The structural proteins within the immature HIV virus particle must be cleaved by a viral protease inside of the particle in order for the virus to be infectious. Adapted from Vella, Stefano et al., *AIDS Soc. 4* (1996): 15–18.

■ Figure 3-15
Transmission electron micrograph of measles virus released by budding.

the plasma membrane of the cell (as is the case with retroviruses, togaviruses, orthomyxoviruses, paramyxoviruses, bunyaviruses, coronaviruses, rhabdoviruses, and hepadnaviruses). Viruses that are released via budding may damage the cell (as is the case with paramyxoviruses, rhabdoviruses, and togaviruses) or they may not (as is the case with retroviruses). Some viruses bud from other membranes and are released from the cell via a secretory-like mechanism.

Lytic Viruses

Most naked viruses are released when infected cells break open (cell lysis/destruction) due to the activity of viral enzymes, rather than distention. Poliovirus is an example of a **lytic** virus. A lytic life cycle is one that kills the host cell. Many enveloped viruses also do this.

Latent Eukaryotic Viruses

Retroviruses such as HIV-1 undergo a **latent** (**nonlytic**) **cycle** in which the viral DNA (provirus) becomes inserted into the hosts DNA. In certain cell types, the proviral DNA replicates "silently" along with the cellular DNA, and the virus is undetected for many years. The provirus, however, can be activated at any time, allowing a productive infection or lytic cycle (one that produces infectious exogenous particles) to occur. Note that the viral DNA remains integrated and does not excise itself from the chromosome as is done in bacteriophages (see Chapter 21). **Latency** is considered to be one of the biggest reasons why drug therapy fails to eradicate HIV from patients.

Herpesviruses enter and migrate down neurons, where they become latent in the body of neurons. They do not integrate their DNA; it remains as an episome. Subsequent activation of the latently infected neurons by a variety of factors (such as extreme temperatures, physical trauma, emotional stress, and immune suppression) enables the viruses to migrate back up the nerve cell and replicate again in the epithelial cells. Two common herpesviruses are herpes simplex virus type 1 (HSV-1), which usually causes fever blisters or oral herpes, and herpes simplex virus type 2 (HSV-2), which usually causes genital herpes (See Chapter 15, Herpesviruses).

Why Don't the Viruses Get Stuck on the Cellular Receptors as They Are Released?

The release of virus particles poses an interesting dilemma. Viruses are designed to enter rather than leave cells. Some viruses, such as influenza A, produce a protein during their life cycle to destroy the cellular receptors as they exit the cell. The protein, **neuraminidase**, cleaves the sialic-acid receptors on the outside of cells as the infectious particles are released (see Chapter 12). As a result, the viruses do not aggregate at the cell surface.

3.3 The Error-Prone RNA Polymerases: Genetic Diversity

Viruses replicate rapidly. During the process of replication an error, or point mutation, may occur. The mutation rate of DNA viruses is usually similar to those of their cellular hosts because most of these polymerases used to replicate DNA genomes possess proofreading ability; for example, the mutation rate of herpesviruses (with **proofreading ability**) is one error in every 10^8 to 10^{11} bases. The genome sizes of herpesviruses range from 1.3×10^5 to 2.0×10^5 base pairs in length. As a result, herpesviruses potentially evolve very slowly because few mutations will be made, if any, during the infection cycle of the virus.

RNA viruses possess mutation rates as high as one error in 10^3 to 10^4 bases. The RNA-dependent RNA polymerases and RNA-dependent DNA polymerases (for example, reverse transcriptases) used by the RNA viruses for genome replication do not possess proofreading ability. Hence, the presence of mutants in a virus population during each replication cycle of the virus occurs much more rapidly than in DNA viruses or cellular organisms. HIV and coronaviruses (such as severe acute respiratory syndrome-associated coronavirus, or SARS-CoV) are excellent examples of RNA viruses with high mutation rates. These viruses misincorporate a nucleotide into their genome once in 10^3 to 10^4 bases. For coronaviruses, this means that there are three mutations that occur during the replication of one viral genome. For HIV, this means one to two mutations in every genome copied. The high mutation rate probably limits the size of most RNA virus genomes to approximately 10^4 nucleotides.

Many mutations are lethal because the mutated virus is unable to replicate. Nonlethal mutations may give the mutated virus a selective advantage. Mutations have been associated with the development of antiviral drug resistance (such as the drug-resistant strains of HIV), changes in virulence (for example, the 1997 Hong Kong avian influenza A was highly virulent), changes that allow the virus to evade the hosts immune system (such as the influenza viruses and antigenic drift, which will be discussed in Chapter 12), and changes in host range.

A good example of a change in host range adaptation occurred in 1978. Canine parvovirus suddenly began killing large numbers of dogs globally in 1978. The parvovirus originally had infected only cats, foxes, raccoons, and minks. A small number of changes in the capsid genes adapted the virus for efficient spread among dogs **Figure 3-16**.

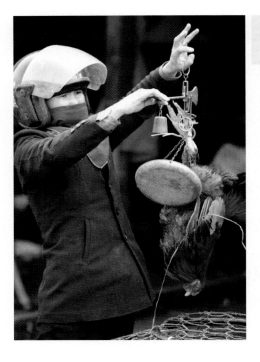

■ Figure 3-16
A Vietnamese woman weighs a chicken at a market in Hanoi, Vietnam (January 2004). At the time, the avian influenza virus infected several humans who had direct contact with chickens. The virus infected millions of chickens, raising fears that it might mutate to a strain that could readily pass from human to human, leading to the next human influenza pandemic.

3.4 Targets for Antiviral Therapies

Modern technology allows scientists to deliberately design drugs. To do this, they need to understand "the enemy." Knowledge of the life cycle of viruses and the mapping of them using computer-aided design (CAD) is applied toward antiviral development by scientists at pharmaceutical companies. Any of the seven stages of the viral life cycle can be targeted for antiviral intervention. The stages are:

1. Attachment specificity
2. Penetration
3. Uncoating
4. Replication
5. Assembly
6. Maturation
7. Release

Table 3-3 lists the current antiviral therapies available along with a list of which viruses they target and their mechanism of action. Key to antiviral drug development is that the drug must *target a process essential for viral replication and it must be active against the virus without being "toxic" to the host organism.* It has been difficult to develop antivirals that have no toxic side effects for the host because viruses use some of the host cellular processes for replication. Hence drugs cannot target those cellular processes because of toxicity problems for the host.

■ RNA Virus Mutagens: A New Class of Antiviral Drugs?

The mechanism of action of the antiviral drug ribavirin was a mystery for over 30 years. Drs. Joseph T. Witkowski and Roland K. Robins synthesized ribavirin in the laboratory in 1970. In 1972, it was reported that ribavirin inhibited a wide spectrum of viruses in vitro but its mechanism was unknown. Today it is used to treat hepatitis C virus infections in combination with interferon-α, SARS-CoV infections, human rabies (as in the case of the Wisconsin patient in 2004), Lassa fever, and some herpesvirus infections. It is used experimentally to treat HBV, Hantaan, Dengue, and parainfluenza virus infections.

In 2001 the mechanism of action was proposed and demonstrated by Shane Crotty, Craig E. Cameron, and Raul Andino. Their poliovirus experiments suggested that ribavirin's antiviral activity is exerted through lethal mutagenesis. In other words, the drug overwhelms the virus with a high mutation rate that in turn drives the virus into a genetic meltdown. Interestingly, this high mutation rate does not allow the virus to escape the inhibitory effects of the drug. This discovery provides pharmaceutical companies with an entirely new drug strategy: RNA-virus mutagens.

TABLE 3-3	Prevention and Treatment of Human Viral Diseases: Antiviral Drugs	

Drug	Virus/Disease	Target
Idoxuridine Trifluridine	Herpes simplex keratoconjunctivitis	Viral and cellular DNA synthesis
Vidarabine	HSV-1, HSV-2	Viral DNA polymerase
Acyclovir	HSV-1, HSV-2, VZV, EBV, CMV	Virus DNA polymerase
Famciclovir	HSV-1, HSV-2, VZV, some activity against EBV, CMV, and HBV	Viral thymidine kinase and DNA polymerase
Penciclovir	HSV-1, HSV-2	Viral DNA polymerase
Valacyclovir	HSV-1, HSV-2, VZV, modestly active against EBV and CMV	Viral DNA polymerase
Gancyclovir	CMV retinitis in HIV patients	Virus polymerase
Foscarnet	Acyclovir resistant HSV/VZV strains Ganciclovir resistant CMV HSV-1, HSV-2, HHV-6, EBV, VZV, parainfluenza virus CMV retinitis in HIV disease	Viral DNA polymerase and reverse transcriptase
Docosanol (10% topical cream)	HSV-labialis episodes	Fusion inhibitor
Brivudine (approved for use in Germany and other European countries)	HSV-1 and VZV	Viral thymidine kinase and DNA polymerase
Eutecavir Adefovir	Hepatitis B	Hepatitis B reverse transcriptase
Abacavir Didanosine (ddI) Emtricitabine (FTC) Lamivudine (3TC) Lamivudine + Zidovudine (Combivir) Stavudine (d4T) Tenofovir + emtricitabine (Truvada) Tenofovir DF Zalcitabine (ddC) Zidovudine (AZT)	HIV-1 and HIV-2	HIV-1 reverse transcriptase
Nevirapine Delavirdine	HIV-1	HIV-1 reverse transcriptase
Amprenavir Atazanavir Fosamprenavir Saquinavir Lopinavir + Ritonavir Indinavir Nelfinavir Ritonavir Tripranavir	HIV-1	HIV-1 protease

(continued)

TABLE 3-3	Prevention and Treatment of Human Viral Diseases: Antiviral Drugs (continued)	
Drug	**Virus/Disease**	**Target**
Enfuvirtide	HIV-1	Binds to HIV-1 gp41 surface protein, inhibiting viral entry.
Selzentry	HIV-1	Binds to CCR5 coreceptor
Raltegravir	HIV-1	Integrase strand transfer inhibitor
Atripola: cocktail of efavirenz, tenofobir, and emtricitabine	HIV-1	A fusion inhibitor and two reverse transcriptase inhibitors
Ribavirin	Broad spectrum (inhibits DNA and RNA viruses): RSV, Influenza A and B, HCV, HSV-1 and HSV-2, measles, mumps, Lassa fever	mRNA mutagen
Amantadine Rimantidine	Influenza A	Inhibit penetration and uncoating of virus
Relenza and Tamiflu	Influenza A	Neuraminidase inhibitor
Arbidol (not FDA approved)	Influenza A and B, hepatitis C	Virus-medicated membrane fusion, immune modulator?
Cidofovir	Broad spectrum (inhibits DNA viruses): HSV-1, HSV-2, VZV, CMV, EBV, adenovirus, HPV, CMV retinitis in HIV patients, experimentally used to treat poxvirus infections	DNA polymerase
Interferons	Hepatitis B & C Hairy cell leukemia, HPV, respiratory viruses	Cell defense proteins activated
Fomivirsen	CMV	Inhibits viral replication and translation (antisense molecule)

Abbreviations of viruses: Herpes simplex type 1 (HSV-1), herpes simplex type 2 (HSV-2), varicella zoster virus (VZV), Epstein-Barr virus (EBV), cytomegalovirus (CMV), hepatitis B virus (HBV), hepatitis C virus (HCV), human herpes Type 6 virus (HHV-6), human immunodeficiency virus Type 1 (HIV-1), respiratory syncytial virus (RSV), hepatitis C virus (HCV), human papilloma virus (HPV). Abbreviations of antivirals: zidovudine (AZT), didanosine (ddI), zalcitabine (ddC), stavudine (d4T), lamivudine (3TC). Unless otherwise specified, drugs are approved by the FDA.

Summary

With the development of animal cell culture techniques, scientists have been able to study virus replication via one-step growth experiments. The knowledge today is very detailed and continues to progress so rapidly that it is impossible to cover the viral replication strategies used by every family of viruses in a single chapter. This chapter presents an overview of viral replication that includes the seven key steps in the life cycle of a virus. They are:

1. Attachment specificity
2. Penetration
3. Uncoating
4. Replication
5. Assembly

6. Maturation

7. Release

Virus attachment occurs when a virus particle attaches to a target cell surface receptor and is the first event in the viral life cycle. Viral receptors are discovered via experiments that involve:

- *the removal of surface receptors,*
- *the use of monoclonal antibodies to block cell surface receptors, and*
- *gene-transfer experiments.*

Viruses enter their target cells via fusion or receptor-mediated endocytosis. ADE has been shown to be an alternative mechanism of viral entry into host cells. This phenomenon has been observed with Dengue, West Nile, HIV-1, HIV-2, and influenza A viruses.

Replication strategies are carried out based on the nature of the viral genome (DNA or RNA, ss or ds, segmented or nonsegmented). It is often difficult to distinguish between the steps of assembly, maturation, and release of virus particles.

Some viruses destroy their host cells (lytic viruses) whereas others do not. Some viruses have developed ways to overcome the conundrum of entry versus exiting cell surfaces that are coated with viral receptors.

Viruses are masters of mutation. Mutations can be lethal or nonlethal. Nonlethal mutations may give rise to mutants that may increase their survivorship; for example, mutations may increase their infectivity, result in viral drug resistance, antagonize the host immune system, or broaden the host range of the virus.

Scientists are applying the knowledge obtained through molecular biology toward the design of antiviral drugs. These antivirals must target the virus specifically to be effective in eliminating the virus without causing harm to its host.

Resources

Primary Literature and Reviews

Ackermann, H-W., Berthiaume, L., and Tremblay, M. 1998. "The replication cycle." In *Virus Life in Diagrams*. Boca Raton, FL: CRC Press.

Audelo-del-Valle, J., et al. 2003. "Infection of cultured human and monkey cell lines with extract of penaeid shrimp infected with Taura syndrome virus." *EID* 9(2):265–266.

Avril, R. M. C-C., Dixon, D. W., Vzorov, A. N., Marzilli, L. G., and Compans, R. W. 2003. "Prevention of poxvirus infection by tetrapyrroles." *BMC Inf Dis* 3:9. http://www.biomedcentral.com/1471-2334/3/9.

Baranowski, E., Ruiz-Jarabo, C.M., and Domingo, E. 2001. "Evolution of cell recognition by viruses." *Science* 292:1102–1105.

Boriskin, Y. S., et al. 2006. "Arbidol: a broad-spectrum antiviral that inhibits acute and chronic HCV infection." *Virol J* 3:56.

Coffin, J.M. 1995. "HIV population dynamics in vivo: Implications for genetic variation, pathogenesis, and therapy." *Science* 267:483–489.

Cohen, J., and Powderly, W. G., eds. 2004. *Infectious Diseases*, 2nd ed. Philadelphia: Mosby.

Crotty, S., Cameron, C. E., and Andino, R. 2001. "RNA virus error catastrophe: Direct molecular test by using ribavirin." *PNAS USA* 98(12):6895–6900.

De Clercq, E. 2002. "Cidofovir in the treatment of poxvirus infections." *Antiviral Res* 55(1):1–13.

Dimiter, S. D. 2000. "Cell biology of virus entry." *Cell* 101:697–702.

Drake, J. W., and Holland, J. J. 1999. "Mutation rates of RNA viruses." *PNAS USA* 96(24):13910–13913.

Enders, J. F., Robbins, F. C., and Weller, T. H. Nobel Lecture, December 11, 1954. "The cultivation of the poliomyelitis viruses in tissue culture."

Flint, S. J., Enquist, L. W., Krug, R. M., Racaniella, V. R., and Skalka, A. M., eds. 2000. "Genome replication and mRNA production by RNA viruses." In *Principles of Virology: Molecular Biology, Pathogenesis, and Control.* Washington, DC: ASM Press.

Fu, Y-X. 2001. "Estimating mutation rate and generation time from longitudinal samples of DNA sequences." *Mol Biol Evol* 18(4):620–626.

Junge, R. E., Duncan, M. C., et al. 1999. "Clinical presentation and antiviral therapy for poxvirus infection in Pudu (Pudu Pudu)." *J Zoo Wildlife Med* 31(3):412–418.

Knipe, D. M., and Howley, P. M., eds. 2001. "Virus assembly." In *Fields Virology*, 4th ed. Philadelphia: Lippincott Williams & Wilkins.

Knipe, D. M., Samuel, C. E., and Palese, P., eds. 2001. "Principles in virology and virus entry and uncoating." In *Fundamental Virology*. Philadelphia: Lippincott Williams & Wilkins.

Martina, B. E. E., Haagmans, B. L., Kuiken, T., et al. 2003. "SARS virus infection in cats and ferrets." *Nature* 425:915.

Mendelsohn, C. L., et al. 1986. "Transformation of a human poliovirus receptor gene into mouse cells." *PNAS USA* 83(20):7845–7849.

Mendelsohn, C. L., Wimmer, E., and Racaniello, V. R. 1989. "Cellular receptor for poliovirus: Molecular cloning, nucleotide sequence, and expression of a new member of the immunoglogulin superfamily." *Cell* 56:855–865.

Mothes, W., et al. 2000. "Retroviral entry mediated by receptor priming and low pH triggering of an envelope glycoprotein." *Cell* 103:679–689.

Paulson, J. C., and Rogers, G. N. 1987. "Resialylated erythrocytes for assessment of the specificity of sialyloligosaccharide binding proteins." *Methods Enzymol* 138:162–168.

Pluong, C. X. T. et al. 2004. "Clinical diagnosis and assessment of severity of confirmed dengue infections in Vietnamese children: Is the World Health Organization classification system helpful?" *Am J Trop Med Hyg* 70(2):172–179.

Sieczkarski, S.B., and Whittaker, G. R. 2005. "Viral Entry." *Curr Top Microbiol Immunol* 285:1–23.

Smith, A. E., and Helenius, A. 2004. "How viruses enter cells." *Science* 304:237–242.

Staunton, D. E., Merluzzi, V. J., Rothlein, R., et al. 1989. "A cell adhesion molecule, ICAM-1, is the major surface receptor for rhinoviruses." *Cell* 56:849–853.

Stine, G. J. 2002. "Anti-HIV therapy." In *AIDS Update 2002*. Upper Saddle River, NJ: Prentice-Hall.

Tyler, K. L. 2004. "Isolation and molecular characterization of a novel type 3 reovirus from a child with meningitis." *J Infect Dis* 189(9):1664–1675.

Wilkin, T. J., et al. "HIV Type 1 chemokine coreceptor use among antiretroviral-experienced patients screened for a clinical trial of a CCR5 inhibitor: AIDS clinical trial group A5211." *Clin Infect Dis* 44:591–595.

■ Popular Press

Haseltine, W. A. 2001. "Beyond chicken soup." *Scientific American*, November 2001, Vol. 285, Issue 5, 56–63.

Tiollais, P., and Buendia, M-A. 1991. "Hepatitis B virus." *Scientific American*, April 1991, Vol. 264, Issue 4, 116–123.

Villarreal, Luis P. 2004. "Are viruses alive? Although viruses challenge our concept of what "living" means, they are vital members of the web of life." *Scientific American*, December 2004, Vol. 291, Issue 6, 100–105.

Wong, K. 2002. "Oral drug halts smallpoxlike virus in mice."*Scientific American, News Online*, March 2002.

Wright, L. "To vanquish a virus." 2003. *Scientific American in Focus Online*, July 21, 2003.

■ Video Productions

The Emerging Viruses. 1991. British Broadcasting Corporation.

Viruses: The Deadly Enemy. 1996. Available at www.insight-media.com. Human Relations Media.

The Next Plague: The Nipah Virus. 1998. The Discovery Channel.

Understanding Viruses. 1999. The Discovery Channel.

■ eLearning

http://biology.jbpub.com/book/virology

The site features eLearning, an online review area that provides quizzes and other tools to help you study for your class. You can also follow useful links for in-depth information, or just find out the latest virology and microbiology news.

CASE STUDY QUESTIONS

These questions relate to the Case Study presented at the beginning of the chapter.

1. hMPV and RSV belong in the Paramyxoviridae family. What type of nucleic acid genome do they have? Do they encode their own viral polymerase? (see Figure 3-12a).

2. Draw a flowchart of the viral life cycle of hMPV.

3. How many genes does hMPV have in its genome?

4. The first report of a fatal encephalitis case associated with hMPV was published in the CDC's *Emerging and Infectious Diseases* publication in 2005. The authors recommended screening for patients, especially children with encephalitis symptoms of unknown origin. What is encephalitis?

5. Have neurological symptoms been associated with other viruses in the Paramyxoviridae family? If so, which virus(es)?

Note: You may need to do further research to find the answers to these questions. The following references will provide some helpful information.

Alto, W. A. 2004. "Human metapneumovirus: A newly described respiratory tract pathogen." *JABFP* 17(6):466–469.

Schildgen, O., et al. 2005. "Human metapneumovirus RNA in encephalitis patient." *EID* 11(3):467–470.

Van Den Hoogen, B. G., et al. 2001. "A newly discovered human pneumovirus isolated from young children with respiratory tract disease." *Nat Med* 7(6):719–724.

An artist's rendering of a *Mengo encephalomyo-carditis* virus particle releasing its genome after infecting a cell. Note the compact nature of a virus particle. Reproduced from S. M. Edgington, *Nat. Biotechnol.* 13 (1995): 1050–1055. Illustration courtesy of Dr. Jean-Yves Sgro, Institute for Molecular Virology, UW-Madison.

❝ *Nature does nothing uselessly.* **❞**

Aristotle

Virus Architecture and Nomenclature

CASE STUDY

A twenty-year-old female college student was admitted to a hospital in Alberta, Canada, in February. Five days earlier, she had experienced coldlike symptoms that were followed by a high fever and a productive cough of bloody sputum. When she arrived in the emergency room, she complained of chest pain and shortness of breath. The attending physician, Dr. Rudolph, ordered a chest x-ray. A sputum sample was collected and sent to the hospital medical technology laboratory. Assuming it was pneumonia, the patient was treated with antibiotics.

The patient did not respond to the antibiotics, even after several days of treatment. Laboratory tests were negative for bacteria that typically cause pneumonia, such as *Streptococcus pneumoniae*, *Hemophilus influenza,* and *Legionella pneumoniae*. The physician suspected she had contracted a viral pneumonia. Shortly thereafter, two more college students and a professor were admitted to the same hospital. All of them had pneumonia-like symptoms.

Dr. Rudolph began researching medical journals for new causative agents of pneumonia. He read a study by Bernard La Scola and colleagues in which they reported Mimivirus in Canadian patients who suffered from hospital- and community-acquired pneumonia. During the course of his reading, he learned that Mimivirus was first discovered after a 1992 outbreak of pneumonia in Bradford, England. The virus was isolated from amoebae growing in the water of a cooling tower. The "virus" was thought to be a bacterium because of its large size: its particles were over 400 nm in diameter. The electron micrograph shown in **Figure CS 4-1** shows a Mimivirus particle infecting an amoeba.

Scientists determined that this new organism was a virus because all attempts to amplify the 16S rDNA from the genome of the new organism failed. The 16S rDNA gene is a universal bacterial gene. The entire genome of Mimivirus was published in *Science* in 2004. Mimivirus has the largest known viral genome. Its genome is 1,181,404 nucleotide base pairs in length. It contains 1262 possible open reading frames (ORFs) or genes. Ten percent of its genes have known functions. They include genes for an amino-acyl RNA synthetase and peptide release factor, six tRNAs, a

■ Figure CS 4-1
The arrow points to a Mimivirus particle infecting an amoeba.

translation elongation factor EF-TU (which prokaryotes also produce), and translation initiation factor 1, which is also a prokaryotic translation factor. These genes are relevant to the key steps of translation: tRNA charging, initiation, elongation, and termination. The virus does not contain ribosome components.

■ References

Koonin, E. V. 2005. "Virology: Gulliver among the Lilliputians." *Curr Biol* 15(5):167–169.

La Scola, B. et al. 2003. "A giant virus in amoebae." *Science* 299:2033.

La Scola, B. et al. 2005. "Mimivirus in pneumonia patients." *EID* 11:449–452.

Ogata, H., Raoult, D., and Claverie, J. M. 2005. "A new example of viral intein in Mimivirus." *Virology* 2(1):8.

Pennisi, E. 2004. "The birth of the nucleus." *Science* 305:766–768.

Raoult, D. 2005. "The journey from Rickettsia to Mimivirus." *ASM News* 71(6):278–284.

Raoult, D. et al. 2004. "The 1.2-megabase genome sequence of Mimivirus." *Science* 306:1344–1350.

In Chapter 3 the seven steps of the virus life cycle at the molecular level were outlined. Scientists developing antiviral therapies target these steps. Chapter 3 also provided common names of viruses (according to genome types) along with their family names and a list of some of the human diseases associated with those viruses. This chapter will dissect the structure and function of a virus particle and address how viruses are classified and named. As more viruses are isolated and studied worldwide, a universal nomenclature system is being implemented to tie viral characteristics to virus names.

4.1 Virus Properties

Why are virus *particles* formed? The nucleic acid genome of a virus is fragile. After leaving the host cell, a virus enters a hostile environment as it travels between cells. The following virus properties are conducive to the survival of viruses in nature.

■ Protection

The environment outside of its host would quickly degrade an unprotected viral genome. The unprotected genome is sensitive to physical damage (such as shearing by mechanical forces), chemical damage (such as ultraviolet light from the sun), and enzymatic damage. The natural environment is laden with nucleases either derived from leaky or dead cells, or nucleases deliberately secreted by mammals as a defense mechanism against infection. The breaking of a single **phosphodiester bond** or chemical modification of one nucleotide may inactivate a virus containing a single-stranded genome. This event would render replication of the genome impossible, thereby inactivating the virus particle. Hence, the genetic material of the virus particle requires protection.

■ Recognition

The outer surface of the virus particle is involved in the recognition and interaction or attachment with the host cell during the first step of the virus life cycle. For naked viruses this interaction is mediated via the protein **capsid** of the virus particle and for enveloped viruses a virally encoded envelope protein mediates this.

■ Self-Assembly

Virus particles are essentially "molecular packages." The simplest type of particle consists of a protein shell that can form around the viral genome spontaneously. This formation process is called **self-assembly**. The process requires minimal energy and is reversible. It results in a very stable structure that can assemble and disassemble itself. In addition to virus particles, biological membranes can also self-assemble (**Figure 4-1**). The ability to self-assemble is a characteristic of viruses with small genomes. For example, the structural proteins of polioviruses can assemble themselves into capsids (**Figure 4-2**).

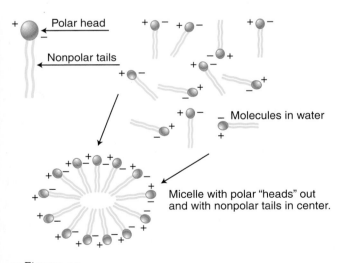

■ Figure 4-1
When put in water these membrane molecules automatically organize themselves into more complex and biologically useful structures. This process is termed self-assembly. Modified from an illustration by Paul Decelles, Ph.D., Johnson County Community College.

■ Fidelity

DNA replication, RNA transcription, and protein synthesis are vulnerable to an occasional error. The size of the genome in a small virus particle cannot code for more than a few types of proteins of limited size. These genes code for small proteins, minimizing the chance for an occasional error. As a result, the particle composition is of high fidelity in terms of precision and accuracy.

■ Economy

An icosahedron is the regular geometric figure that approaches a sphere. A sphere has the most volume for the least amount of surface area. This is economical. In addition, the same type of protein is used over and over again in creating the virus particle. An orderly, functional arrangement of protein subunits creates a structure that is frugal in expenditure of genome coding capacity. If one protein is synthesized or folded inaccurately, it can be discarded. In addition, in many viruses a single protein can have many different functions.

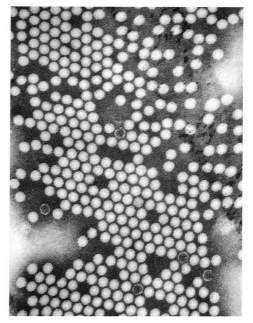

■ Figure 4-2
Electron micrograph purified poliovirus particles. The particles self-assemble into uniform 29 nanometer (nm) virions. Magnification approximately 200,000×.

4.2 Virus Structure and Morphology

■ Stability

Why are virus particles composed of subunits? The capsid of the virus is composed of many viral structural proteins that come together to form identical subunits called **capsomers**. The capsomers are arranged symmetrically around the viral genome (**Figure 4-3**). The final structure is very stable. All viruses in the same family have capsids with the same number of capsomers.

Subunit construction of the virus capsid is necessary for two reasons. First, the genome size limits the number of viral protein products that is encoded by the virus genome. Thus the solution is to use the same protein product over and over again to generate identical subunits to trap the genome inside of the virus particle. Second, the nucleic acid genome can only code for a protein that is 15% of its weight. This is based on the premise that the average molecular weight of 3 nucleotides (a triplet codon that encodes one amino acid) is 1000 daltons. The average molecular weight of an amino acid is 150 daltons. Thus multiple proteins (capsomers) are needed to contain the viral genome inside of the virus particle.

The term **structural protein** refers to those proteins that make up the virus particle (both inside and outside). Each type of protein functions in one or more of the following ways: by protecting the viral nucleic acid, attaching to receptors on the surfaces of host cells, penetrating the cell membrane, being involved in replication of the viral genome (for example, RNA-dependent RNA polymerases of RNA viruses), and facilitating replication and modifying the host cell.

■ **Figure 4-3**

(a) Electron micrograph and molecular model of an adenovirus. Adenoviruses consist of 252 capsomers (repeating protein subunits). Arrows indicate the penton fibers that extend outside of the particle and are used in attachment of the particle to a host cell. The fibers can easily become detached during preparation for electron microscopy. **(b)** Molecular model of adenovirus.

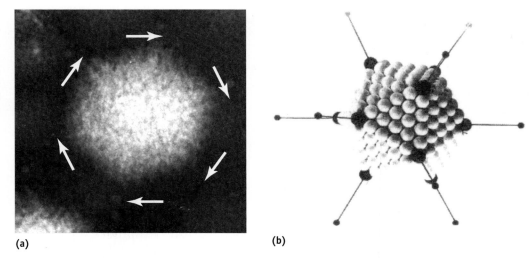
(a)
(b)

■ **Figure 4-4**

(a) Schematic drawing of a typical icosahedral-shaped virus particle. An icosahedron is a polyhedron that has 20 faces or planes (sides) and 12 vertices. Adapted from G. E. Kaiser. "Viruses." *Microbiology Lecture Guide.* The Community College of Baltimore County, Catonsville Campus, 2006. http://student.ccbcmd.edu/courses/bio141/lecguide/index.html. **(b)** Schematic drawing of a typical helical-shaped virus particle. Adapted from G. E. Kaiser. "Viruses." *Microbiology Lecture Guide.* The Community College of Baltimore County, Catonsville Campus, 2006. http://student.ccbcmd.edu/courses/bio141/lecguide/index.html.

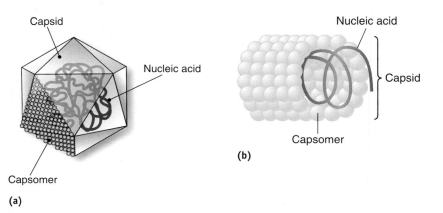

Capsid
Nucleic acid
Capsomer
(a)

Nucleic acid
Capsid
Capsomer
(b)

■ Two Types of Viral Shapes

Icosahedral (**Figure 4-4a**) and **helical** (Figure 4-4b) are the dominant nucleocapsid shapes of viruses. These shapes allow the virus particle to consist of a tightly constructed, stable, molecular package. The more subunits that form the structure of the particle, the more stable the virus particle becomes. A paper pattern of a three-dimensional icosahedral model of human rhinovirus type 14 is provided in Figure 4-11, at the end of this chapter. Why not photocopy this illustration and construct a virus? Also, an interesting aside: quilters have become fascinated with the icosahedral pattern.

Larger virus particles can hold a bigger and more complex genome. There are some viruses that don't fit the typical icosahedral or helical design. These viruses are called **complex** viruses. Examples of viruses with these rare shapes are members of the Poxviridae and Asfarviridae families (**Figure 4-5**). Members of the Poxviridae and Asfarviridae family are large dsDNA viruses (~175–270 nm in diameter) that contain large genomes (~170–190 kbp in length) and have complicated architectures.

Enveloped viruses are represented by icosahedral (**Figure 4-6a**), helical (Figure 4-6b), or complex shapes. Electron microscopic and x-ray crystallographic techniques allowed virologists to determine the overall morphology of a particular virus. Examples of electron micrographic images representing the three basic shapes of viruses are found in the following **Figures 4-7a–c**.

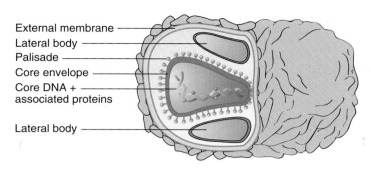

External membrane
Lateral body
Palisade
Core envelope
Core DNA + associated proteins

Lateral body

■ **Figure 4-5**
Schematic drawing of a complex-shaped poxvirus particle. Adapted from A. Decoster, et al. "Virology." *Micorbiology*. Découvrir le Groupe Hospitalier de l'Institut Catholique de Lille, 2007. http://anne.decoster .free.fr/di1viro/vclassif.html.

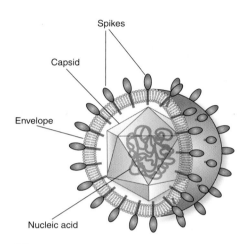

Spikes

Capsid

Envelope

Nucleic acid

(a)

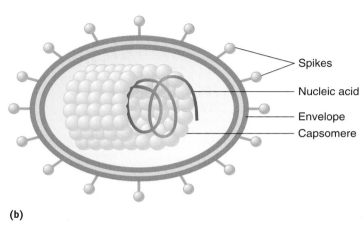

Spikes

Nucleic acid

Envelope

Capsomere

(b)

■ **Figure 4-6**

(a) Schematic drawing of a typical enveloped icosahedral-shaped virus particle. Adapted from G. E. Kaiser. "Viruses." *Microbiology Lecture Guide*. The Community College of Baltimore County, Catonsville Campus, 2006. http://student .ccbcmd.edu/courses/bio141/lecguide/index.html. **(b)** Schematic drawing of a typical enveloped helical-shaped virus particle. Adapted from G. E. Kaiser. "Viruses." *Microbiology Lecture Guide*. The Community College of Baltimore County, Catonsville Campus, 2006. http://student.ccbcmd.edu/courses/bio141/lecguide/index.html.

(a)

(b)

(c)

■ **Figure 4-7**

(a) Electron micrograph of icosahedral-shaped rotavirus particles. Rotaviruses have a wheel-like appearance. **(b)** Electron micrograph (160,000× magnification) of helical-shaped vesicular stomatitis virus (VSV). VSV is an important pathogenic virus of cattle, causing fever and vesicles in the mouth and on the feet. Magnification ~ 40,000×. **(c)** Electron micrograph of a single brick-shaped or complex-shaped smallpox particle. This virion is from a human skin lesion, which is from a diagnostic specimen that was sent to the CDC in 1966 as part of the WHO global smallpox eradication program. Magnification 150,000× .

4.3 Baltimore Classification

Viruses can be classified or grouped by such criteria as size, capsid symmetry, whether or not they are naked or enveloped, mode of transmission, the host they infect, the type of nucleic acid they contain, or the diseases they cause. Nobel-prize laureate David Baltimore proposed a system to classify viruses based on the type of nucleic acid the virus contains and its mechanism of replication. His scheme is based on the theme that all viruses must generate +ssmRNAs from their genomes in order to produce proteins and replicate themselves. The precise mechanism by which this is achieved is different for each virus family. Baltimore divided the viral genomes into seven groups or classes. The replication strategies for them were discussed in Chapter 3. The seven classes are:

I. dsDNA viruses

II. ssDNA viruses

III. dsRNA viruses

IV. +ssRNA viruses

V. −ssRNA viruses

VI. RNA reverse transcribing viruses

VII. DNA reverse transcribing viruses

4.4 Taxonomy: What's in a Name?

In 1898, Friedrich Loeffler and Paul Frosch identified the first animal virus, the one that causes foot and mouth disease (FMD). Their experiments demonstrated that a filterable agent causes the disease. The virus was not isolated until the 1930s, when the first actual studies of viruses began. As described in Chapter 1, FMD virus causes one of the most infectious animal diseases known. Symptoms include the formation of fluid-filled vesicles on the mucosa, face, feet, and hairless areas that rupture to form ulcers. Hence the name **foot and mouth** disease.

In 1901, while on duty in Cuba, U.S. Army medical scientist Walter Reed and his colleagues conducted an exhaustive series of experiments demonstrating that the **yellow fever virus** was transmitted between humans by mosquitoes, and that the disease could be experimentally transferred via filtered blood. In yellow fever infections, the patient produces black-colored blood-filled vomit, and there is a deterioration of the liver, kidneys, and heart. Yellow bile pigment from the damaged liver colors the skin and gives rise to the name of the disease and its causative agent.

These early experiments in virology that led to the discovery of viruses were based upon the *size* of the infectious agent. In other words, any infectious entity that was filterable was termed a **virus**. Porcelain Chamberland "candle-style" filters (**Figure 4-8**) were used by Beijerinck, Ivanovsky, Loeffler, and Frosch to isolate the first plant and animal viruses. These studies were facilitated by the advent of the transmission electron microscope. The need to classify and maintain a consistent naming system became a practical necessity. It was particularly important for the identification of those viruses causing disease in humans, domesticated animals, and plants.

The earliest attempts to *classify* viruses were based only on size. Viruses were named by their pathogenic properties, common organ tropisms, and common ecological and transmission characteristics; for example, if we used this system today, all of the viruses

(a)

■ **Figure 4-8**
(a) Candle Chamberland filters. **(b)** Modern Chamberland filter apparatus. If a mixture of viruses and bacteria are filtered through a bacterial-proof filter, the viruses will pass through into the filtrate in the flask.

that cause hepatitis would belong in a "hepatitis virus" classification. Hepatitis A, B, and C viruses, yellow fever virus, and Rift Valley fever virus would be grouped together. Today, virologists know that genetically these viruses are very different and thus have placed them in different families based on morphology, physical and chemical characteristics (protein, lipid, and carbohydrate content), antigenic (serologic relationships) properties, and biological properties.

In the 1950s and 1960s there was a tremendous surge in the discovery of new viruses. The influx of new knowledge prompted the need for a classification scheme for these newly discovered viruses. For some time, the development of a universal taxonomic system was the subject of competing and conflicting opinions among virus researchers. Historically, viruses have been named after the diseases they caused, morphological characteristics **(Figure 4-9)**, places the viruses were first isolated, their discoverers, and acronyms. See Table 4-1 for examples.

4.5 The International Committee on Taxonomy of Viruses

In 1966, the International Committee on Taxonomy of Viruses (ICTV) was formed. It was charged with developing a universal taxonomic scheme to address the nomenclature and classification of viruses. By that time there was a rapidly growing mass of data on individual viruses, and the universal taxonomic system has continued to evolve.

■ **Figure 4-9**
Scanning electron micrograph of SARS associated coronaviruses (SARS-CoV). The viral envelope has petal-shaped spikes, giving the coronavirus an appearance of a crown (Latin *corona*). The inset is an electron micrograph of a negatively stained SARS-CoV. Note the short and stubby spikes visible on the surface of the virus.

TABLE 4-1	Examples of the Origins of Virus Names
Virus/Type of Virus	**Origin of Name**
West Nile	Virus first isolated from a woman located in the West Nile District of Uganda in 1937.
La Crosse encephalitis	In 1963, this virus was first isolated from the brain of a four-year-old boy who died of encephalitis in *La Crosse*, Wisconsin.
Norwalk	Was first identified in 1972 after an outbreak of gastrointestinal illness in Norwalk, Ohio.
Adenovirus	First isolated from adenoids and tonsils.
Coxsackie	First isolated from children with a poliolike illness in Coxsackie, New York, in 1948.
Marburg	1967 Marburg, Germany, outbreak.
Ebola	Named after the Ebola River located in the northern Democratic Republic of the Congo (formerly Zaire), where the virus first appeared in 1976.
Coronavirus	Virion morphology shown in electron micrographs of negatively stained corona-viruses gave them the appearance of a *crown* (Latin *corona*; see Figure 4-14).
HIV	Acronym for human immunodeficiency virus.
SARS-CoV	Acronym for severe acute respiratory syndrome-*coronavirus*.
Papillomavirus	Induces warts or papillomas.
Smallpox	"Small pox" was a term used to distinguish this disease from syphilis, which was known as the "great pox."
Picornavirus	*Pico*: small *rna*: ribonucleic acid
Epstein-Barr	Named after M. A. Epstein and Y. M. Barr, who, along with B. G. Achong, discovered the virus.
Papovavirus	*Pa*pilloma *po*lyoma *va*cuolating agent
Herpesvirus	Term comes from the Greek word meaning "to creep." It was observed that the sores seemed to creep over the surface of the skin.
Hepatitis A, B, C	Associated with hepatitis (liver malfunction, yellowing of skin).

The system developed by the ICTV is based on the following hierarchical levels. The names are designated with suffixes:

Order (-virales)
Family (-viridae)
Subfamily (-virinae)
Genus (-virus)
Common names

To date, only three orders have been approved by the ICTV: Mononegavirales, Caudovirales, and Nidovirales; for example, the order Mononegavirales consists of four virus families: Bornaviridae, Paramyxoviridae, Rhabdoviridae, and Filoviridae. The ICTV's most recent report, which was published in 2005, lists 73 families, 9 subfamilies, 287 genera, and more than 5450 viruses belonging to more than 1950 virus species. Descriptions of **viroids** and **prions** are included in the ICTV's Eighth Report. Table 4-2 lists examples of full formal taxonomic terminology.

A taxonomic key used for the placement of viruses can be found in *Virus Taxonomy, Seventh Report of the ICTV*, which was published in 2000. Many molecular characteristics and measurements have been used to create the taxonomic key. Some of the properties

TABLE 4-2	Examples of Common and Scientific Names of Viruses

Common Name of Virus	Scientific Name
Vaccinia	Family Poxviridae, subfamily Chordopoxvirinae, genus Orthopoxvirus, *vaccinia virus*
Poliovirus 1	Family Picornaviridae, genus Enterovirus, poliovirus 1
Rabies	Order Mononegavirales, family Rhabdoviridae, genus Lyssavirus, rabies virus
Herpes simplex virus 2	Family Herpesviridae, subfamily Alphaherpesvirinae, genus simplex virus, human herpes virus 2 (herpes simplex virus 2)

used in taxonomy are virion properties such as size, shape, the presence or absence of an envelope, and capsid symmetry and structure. Physical and chemical properties are also considered. These include:

- Virion molecular weight
- pH, temperature, cation, detergent, and irradiation stability
- Genome properties: type of nucleic acid (DNA or RNA), strandedness (ss or ds), linear or circular, and polarity (positive-sense, negative-sense, ambisense)
- Complete or partial nucleotide sequence of the viral genome
- Presence of repetitive sequence elements within the genome
- Guanine + cytosine (G + C) ratio of the genome
- Presence or absence and type of 5′ end terminal cap
- Presence or absence of 5′ end terminal covalently linked protein
- Presence or absence of 4′ terminal poly(A) tail

Lipid, carbohydrate, protein content, and characteristics are also considered in taxonomy. The virion protein characteristics used are:

- Number, size, and functional activities of structural and nonstructural proteins
- Descriptions and determination of the functional activities of viral proteins: for example reverse transcriptase, hemagglutinin, neuraminidase, and fusion activities
- Full or partial amino acid sequence
- The types of posttranslational chemical modifications of the viral proteins (such as glycosylation, phosphorylation, or myristylation)

Other properties related to the viral genome and life cycle are used as well. These include:

- Genome organization and replication
- Replication strategy
- Number of ORFs
- Site of the accumulation of virion proteins
- Site of virion assembly
- Site and nature of virion maturation and release

Antigenic properties, such as the serologic relationships obtained at reference centers and biologic properties, are used in taxonomy. These include:

- Natural host range
- Tissue tropisms, pathology, and histopathology
- Mode of transmission in nature
- Geographic distribution

| VIRUS FILE 4-1 | **The Race to Characterize SARS-CoV** |

On February 28, 2003, Dr. Carlo Urbani (**Figure VF 4-1**), an infectious disease specialist based at the 60-bed French Hospital in Hanoi, Vietnam, alerted the WHO about a case of atypical pneumonia. He had originally suspected an avian influenza virus, but very quickly began to suspect a different, possibly new virus.

Of the first 60 SARS patients, more than half were healthcare workers. Dr. Urbani recognized the severity of the public health threat. His appeal for assistance from the WHO, CDC, and Medecins sans Frontieres (MSF, or Doctors without Borders) resulted in the successes of infection control and rapid identification of SARS.

In just a few weeks, SARS spread via people through air travel to at least three continents. Researchers from no fewer than ten countries collaborated to identify the virus, sequence its genome, and take steps toward rapid diagnosis. Dr. Urbani cared for SARS patients for 18 days in a hospital isolation ward in Hanoi. He died on March 29, 2003, while attending a medical meeting in Bangkok, Thailand. By dealing with the SARS outbreak intuitively and openly, the severity of the outbreak was greatly curtailed. On May 1, 2003, the genome sequence of the SARS-CoV was published via *Science Express*. These gene sequences enable researchers to more quickly develop diagnostic tests and vaccines to combat the rapidly spreading, highly contagious respiratory disease.

■ **Figure VF 4-1**
Dr. Carlo Urbani.

References

Marco, A. M., et al. 2003. "The genome sequence of the SARS-associated coronavirus." *Science* 300(5624):1399–1404.

Rota, P. A., et al. 2003. "Characterization of a novel coronavirus associated with severe acute respiratory syndrome." *Science* 300(5624):1394–1399.

International specialty groups and culture collection centers establish lower hierarchical levels. These levels and their definitions are:

- **Species**—(1991 ICTV's accepted definition) a **polythetic class** of viruses that share the same replicating lineage and occupy a particular niche. (A polythetic class is defined as a class whose members share several properties but no individual members possess all properties.)
- **Type-species**—different serotypes of the same species.
- **Strain**—different isolates of the same virus that come from different geographical locations.
- **Variant**—a virus whose phenotype differs from the original wild-type strain but for which the genetic basis is not known.

These specialty groups may be influenced or guided by the World Health Organization (WHO) and other agencies. Examples of international specialty groups and culture collections are:

- WHO Collaborating Centers for Reference and Research on Influenza, with offices in the United States, Japan, the United Kingdom, and Australia.
- American Type Culture Collection (ATCC)

TABLE 4-3	Virus Families and the Range of Syndromes They Cause				
Syndrome	**Picornaviridae**	**Togaviridae**	**Herpesviridae**	**Hepadnaviridae**	**Rhabdoviridae**
Skin rashes	+	+	+		
Diarrhea	+				
Paralysis	+		+		
Hepatitis	+	+		+	
Rabies					+
Arthritis		+			
Respiratory illness	+		+		
Conjunctivitis	+		+		
Encephalitis		+	+		+
Meningitis	+	+	+		

Modified and adapted from Collier, L., and Oxford, J. 2000. *Human Virology*, 2nd ed. Oxford, UK: Oxford University Press, p. 15.

Today more than 30,000 viruses, strains, and variants are being tracked by scientists at specialty laboratories, reference and culture collection centers that communicate with the WHO, the Food and Agricultural Organization of the United Nations (FAO), and other international entities.

A major goal of the ICTV was to design a universal ICTV database that would be available to all virologists. This database, which has been available on the worldwide web since 1993, contains taxonomic software tools, data entry tools, identification tools, and even a picture gallery. By late 1998, the ICTVdB was being accessed at a rate of over 10,000 times daily.

Viral Disease Syndromes Overlap

When viruses are looked at in relation to the diseases they cause in humans and animals, the members of some families cause a wide variety of different symptoms despite their similarities in structure, size, and genome. Some virus families infect specific tissue types, whereas others infect many of the body systems. Table 4-3 lists some families of viruses and the range of **syndromes** they cause. Syndromes are defined as sets of symptoms and physical signs occurring together. Chapter 5 will discuss laboratory diagnosis of viral diseases. One may initially think that diagnosis of viral diseases may not be important because there are few antivirals available for treatment. Chapter 5 will address why diagnosis is indeed important despite the aforementioned fact.

Summary

Virus particles are stable molecular packages containing a protein coat wrapped around the nucleic acid genome of the virus. This protein coat provides protection to the genome and is involved in the recognition of host cells to initiate infection. There are two viral shapes that are most common in nature: icosahedral and helical. Electron microscopic and x-ray crystallographic techniques are important tools used to determine the overall structure and morphology of viruses.

The main criteria used by the ICTV to classify and name viruses were outlined in this chapter. The universal taxonomy system developed by the ICTV is based on the following hierarchical levels: order, family, subfamily, genus, and common names. Specialty laboratories currently track over 30,000 virus strains and variants. One or several different virus families may cause viral disease syndromes. Laboratory diagnosis of viral diseases will be addressed in Chapter 5.

■ Resources

■ Primary Literature and Reviews

Ackermann, H-W., Berthiaume, L., and Tremblay, M. 1988. *Virus Diagrams*. Boca Raton, FL: CRC Press.

Cohen, J., and Powderly, W. G., eds. 2004. *Infectious Diseases*, 2nd ed. Philadelphia: Mosby.

Eberhard, M. 2004. "Virus taxonomy: One step forward, two steps back." *EID* 10:153–154.

Fauquet, C. M., et al. eds. 2005. *Virus Taxonomy Eighth Report of the International Committee on Taxonomy of Viruses*. London: Elsevier Academic Press.

Hurst, C. J., Benton, W. H., and Enneking, J. M. 1987. "Three-dimensional model of human rhinovirus type 14." *TIBS* 12:460.

Knipe, D. M., Samuel, C. E., and Palese, P., eds. 2001. "Virus assembly." In *Fundamental Virology*. Philadelphia: Lippincott Williams & Wilkins.

Marco, A. M., et al. 2003. "The genome sequence of the SARS-associated coronavirus." *Science,* 300(5624):1399–1404.

Matthews, R. E. F. 1985. "Viral taxonomy for the nonvirologist." *Ann Rev Microbiol* 39:451–474.

Rossman, M. G., et al. 1987. "Common cold viruses." *TIBS* 12:313–318.

Rota, P. A., et al. 2003. "Characterization of a novel coronavirus associated with severe acute respiratory syndrome." *Science* 300(5624):1394–1399.

Tidona, C. A., and Darai, G., eds. 2001. *The Springer Index of Viruses*. New York: Springer.

van Regenmortel, M. H. V., and Mahy, B. W. 2004. "Emerging issues in virus taxonomy." *EID* 10(1):8–13.

van Regenmortel, M. H. V. et al. eds. 2000. *Virus Taxonomy Classification and Nomenclature of Viruses: Seventh Report of the International Committee on Taxonomy of Viruses*. San Diego: Academic Press.

■ Popular Press

de Kruif, P., and Gonzalez-Crussi, F. 2002. "Walter Reed: In the interest of science— and for humanity!" In *Microbe Hunters*. San Diego: Harvest Books, an imprint of Harcourt Trade Publishers.

Radetsky, P. 1994. *The Invisible Invaders: Viruses and the Scientists who Pursue Them*. Boston: Back Bay Books.

Turbak, S. 1991. "Turnip crinkle virus." *Quilting International*. July, pp. 18–22.

Villarreal, L. P. 2004. "Are viruses alive?" *Scientific American*. December 2004, Vol. 291, Issue 6, 100–105.

■ Video Productions

Another War: Disease and Political Strife. 1997. Films for the Humanities.
Conquering an Invisible World. 1999. Films for the Humanities.
SARS and the New Plagues. 2003. The History Channel.
War Against Deadly Microbes and Lethal Viruses. 2003. Films for the Humanities.
AIDS and Other Epidemics. 2004. Films for the Humanities.
The Age of Viruses. 2006. Films for the Humanities.

■ eLearning

http://biology.jbpub.com/book/virology

The site features eLearning, an online review area that provides quizzes and other tools to help you study for your class. You can also follow useful links for in-depth information, or just find out the latest virology and microbiology news.

CASE STUDY QUESTIONS

These questions relate to the Case Study presented at the beginning of the chapter.

1. Mimivirus has been proposed as the sole member of a new virus family Mimiviridae whose members are classified as large nucleocytoplasmic dsDNA viruses. This virus significantly challenges the evolution and definition of a virus. Discuss this.

2. Based on ribosomal RNA analysis, where would you tentatively propose to place Mimivirus in the three-domain "Tree of Life" hypothesized by Carl Woese? Dr. Woese recognized a third form of life—thearchaea—whose genetic makeup is distinct from but related to both bacteria (procarya) and eucarya.

3. Many have debated the issue of whether or not viruses are alive. Besides the inclusion of a partial translational machinery apparatus, Mimivirus carries other genes that have not been identified in any other known virus. Research these genes and their functions. (References to get you started follow.)

   Koonin, E. V. 2005. Virology: Gulliver among the Lilliputians. *Curr Biol* 15(5):167–169.

   La Scola, B. et al. 2003. A giant virus in amoebae. *Science* 299:2033.

   La Scola, B. et al. 2005. Mimivirus in pneumonia patients. *EID* 11:449-452.

   Ogata, H., Raoult, D., and Claverie, J. M. 2005. A new example of viral intein in Mimivirus. *Virology* 2(1):8.

   Pennisi, E. 2004. The birth of the nucleus. *Science* 305:766–768.

   Raoult, D. 2005. The journey from *Rickettsia* to Mimivirus. *ASM News* 71(6):278–284.

   Raoult, D. et al. 2004. The 1.2-megabase genome sequence of Mimivirus. *Science* 306:1344–1350.

   Use this research to support your hypothesis regarding whether or not Mimiviruses are alive.

4. Viruses and the nuclei of cells share some structural similarities. List these similarities.

5. From an evolutionary standpoint, could a virus have provided the first nucleus? Or was a nucleus something an early bacterial cell evolved on its own or in partnership with an archaeum?

6. Build a virus using the paper model provided in **Figure 4-10**.

Three-dimensional model of human rhinovirus type 14

We have studied with great interest a structural projection of the human rhinovirus type 14 capsid, which recently appeared in an article by Rossmann *et al.* (*TIBS* Vol. 12, No. 8, pp. 313–318). Based upon their projection we have designed a pattern for constructing a three-dimensional model of the capsid. It is our belief that assembling and examining such a model can aid a person in understanding the spatial associations between those proteins which comprise the capsid structure. We would like to share our model with fellow readers of *TIBS* so that they may join us in having a pleasant learning experience.

The large triangular areas in the structure represent the 20 faces of the capsid which together form the shape of a regular icosahedron. Each of the 180 small quadrangles superimposed over the faces of the model represents the position of a single molecule of viral protein (VP) 1, 2, or 3. The other protein constituent, VP4, is not shown on this model for sake of simplicity.

In order to prepare a model from this illustration, we suggest that you first copy it onto another piece of paper (this will avoid damage to this issue of *TIBS*). You should then cut out your copied illustration along the outside edges, leaving all numbered tabs attached. Next, fold down all of the faces and tabs along the lines of the capsid edges (lighter lines in the model). Your model can then be assembled by matching together, one at a time, those pairs of tabs with the same identifying number.

As you match together each pair of identically numbered tabs, they should be tucked to the inside of the icosahedral structure. Those edges of faces which are matched can then be joined by placing pieces of transparent tape over the outside of the model. The order in which these tabs are matched is not of importance. A paperclip which has been straightened and then bent at a right angle will serve as a handy tool when joining the last edge. In doing so, your 'tool' should be inserted part way into the icosahedron at a vertice adjacent to that edge which needs to be joined. Hold the inserted part of the paperclip firmly underneath the crease of the larger tab so it can serve as a support while applying tape to the joint. Once your virus model has been completed, hold it in a position such that the boldly outlined capsid face is on top. Rotate the model such that all 'VP' designations within the quadrangles on the outlined face appear in normal reading position (pointing towards you). You will then be able to directly compare the marked viral protein positions on your model with that projection contained in Rossmann's article. If you should later wish to fill in the unmarked protein positions of your model, continue the marked pattern by using the following rule: proteins VP1 always meet in a circle of 5 units at the vertices, proteins VP2 and VP3 always meet in a circle of 6 units at the centers of the faces where they alternate in their order around the circle. Good luck!

CHRISTON J. HURST
WILLIAM H. BENTON
JULIA M. ENNEKING
Health Effects Research Laboratory, U.S. Environmental Protection Agency, Cincinnati, OH 45268, USA.

■ **Figure 4-10**
A reprint of Hurst, C. J., Benton, W. H., and Enneking, J. M. 1987. "Three-dimensional model of human rhinovirus type 14." *TIBS* 12:460.

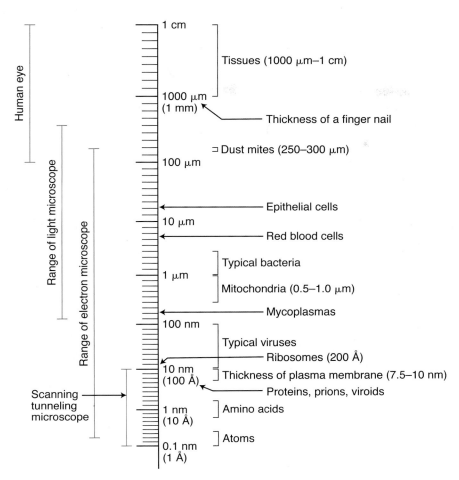

The limits of microscopic and human eye resolution. Each major division represents a 10-fold change in scale. To the right of the scale are approximate sizes of molecules, cells, organelles, and tissues. Adapted from Prescott, L. M., J. P. Harley and D. A. Klein. *Microbiology,* Sixth Edition, McGraw-Hill Higher Education, 2005.

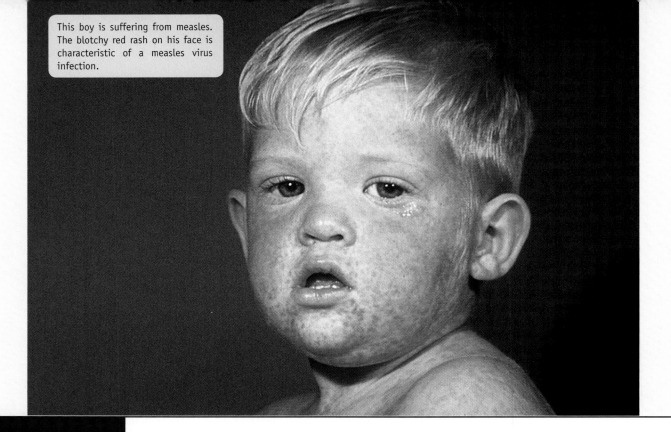

This boy is suffering from measles. The blotchy red rash on his face is characteristic of a measles virus infection.

Laboratory Diagnosis of Viral Diseases

> **"**Where observation is concerned, chance favors only the prepared mind.**"**
>
> *Louis Pasteur*

CASE STUDY

Sam Bugert, a computer consultant, was traveling by air from Hong Kong to Japan during the height of the SARS outbreak in 2003. While on the plane to Japan, Sam planned a business trip to Toronto, Canada. Just the thought of flying to Canada made Sam feel tired. He asked the flight attendant for several cups of coffee, which he drank hastily as he planned his trip to Canada.

After Mr. Bugert got off the plane at Tokyo International Airport he passed through a security checkpoint, which included walking in front of a thermal imaging scanner. He was briefed on the plane about the scanners that were being used to detect passengers with elevated temperatures because a presenting symptom of SARS was fever. The use of the infrared thermal imaging scanners provided a noninvasive, fast, and cost-effective means for mass screening of potential SARS-infected persons.

After Sam walked through the scanner, an airport staff member pulled him aside, checked his temperature orally with a thermometer, and asked him to fill out a standardized questionnaire for SARS. He didn't feel ill and urgently wanted to get to his next flight.

The staff member was very patient. She explained that the imaging cameras detect the temperature of an object by measuring the amount of infrared radiation emitted by that object. It provides a digital image showing temperature patterns. Scanners have primarily been used in the diagnosis of breast cancer (detecting inflammation) and nerve dysfunctions. The scanners measure the skin and not the core body temperature. The accuracy of the scanner is +/–2°C. The accuracy of the screening can be affected by such factors as physical activity, stress, caffeine, nicotine, alcohol consumption, and circulatory problems. Other factors affecting their accuracy include equipment variables, the operator's training and experience, and environmental factors such as room temperature and air currents.

■ **Figure CS 5-1**
In Taiwian's Chiang Kai-shek International Airport a passenger moves on to immigration after being cleared of high body temperature by a thermal scanner.

Sam told the staff member that he had been consuming large volumes of coffee during the flight to Japan and this was probably causing his elevated scanner results. The staff member noted that he was asymptomatic but followed through with airport procedures and sent Mr. Bugert to the hospital for further tests.

■ References

Centre for Emergency Preparedness and Response, Population and Public Health Branch, Health Canada. 2004. "Thermal image scanners to detect fever in airline passengers, Vancouver and Toronto, 2003." *CCDR* 30:165–167.

Ng, E. Y. 2005. "Is thermal scanner losing its bite in mass screening of fever due to SARS?" *Med Phys* 32:93–97.

(a)

(b)

■ **Figure 5-1**
(a) Right arm of rhesus monkey treated with rNAPc2 10 days after Ebola infection. The monkey survived. **(b)** Right arm of untreated rhesus monkey 13 days after infection with Ebola virus. The monkey did not survive.

Chapter 4 focused on the taxonomy and structure of viruses and in summary stated that several different viral families may cause similar viral disease syndromes. How, then, do virologists determine which viruses are causing a particular syndrome? If some viral diseases are clinically obvious and there are so few antivirals available to combat them, why have definitive laboratory diagnostic tests been developed? There are several reasons:

- Patient management is determined by diagnosis; for example, a delivery via cesarean section may be prudent if a pregnant woman has HIV, genital herpes, or genital warts at the time of delivery.
- A few antiviral therapies are now available. In particular, several chemotherapeutic agents are available to treat herpesvirus infections.
- Rapid advancements in the development of antiviral drugs are expanding the range of viral diseases for which a precise diagnosis will become necessary; for example, it was announced in *The Lancet* (December 12, 2003) that scientists at the U.S. Army Medical Research Institute of Infectious Diseases (USAMRIID) were able to treat rhesus macaques with an experimental drug called recombinant nematode anticoagulant protein c2 (rNAPc2) after the macaques were given a high-dose lethal injection of Ebola virus. To date there is no cure for the disease, but this experimental drug could become an accepted treatment for Ebola virus infection (**Figure 5-1**).

Viral infections may demand public health measures to prevent spread to others for several reasons, including:

- Blood donors may be asymptomatic carriers of viruses. This is why screening blood banks for HIV, hepatitis B and C, and West Nile virus reduces the spread of these diseases by blood transfusion.
- Documenting novel strains of influenza allows officials to publicly announce health measures that can be implemented (for example, vaccination of vulnerable members of the community, including children and the elderly).
- The positive identification of viral diseases (such as West Nile or Yellow fever) linked to encephalitis and mosquito (vector-borne) transmission enables authorities to initiate antimosquito control measures. The introduction of exotic or newly emerging diseases, such as the monkeypox outbreak in the United States in 2003, demanded containment, surveillance, and other control measures.
- Continuous surveillance of viral infections in the community enables officials to establish means of control, monitoring, and the evaluation of immunization programs. It provides the evidence for new epidemics and new virus–disease associations. It is interesting to note that 90% of all viral diseases were completely unknown at the end of World War II (1945).

5.1 River's Postulates

In Chapter 1 it was stated that the initial methods developed to study viruses focused on plant and bacterial viruses. T. M. Rivers modified **Koch's Postulates** for viral diseases in 1937. The six steps used to establish that a virus causes a disease are:

1. Isolation of virus from diseased hosts.
2. Cultivation of virus in host cells.
3. Proof of filterability (to exclude larger pathogens).
4. Production of a comparable disease when the cultivated virus is used to infect experimental animals from the same species as the original host or in related ones.
5. Reisolation of the same virus from the infected experimental host.
6. Detection of a specific immune response to the virus.

5.2 Cultivation of Viruses in the Laboratory

Viruses must be grown in a "host" system. They can be grown in animals, embryonated eggs, or tissue (cell) cultures. Some viruses will only grow in animals. Mice, cotton rats, rabbits, and guinea pigs are most often used to cultivate viruses. Sometimes, the only animal models available to grow human viruses are monkeys. It is very expensive to grow viruses in animals. Therefore, the preferred method, when possible, is cell culture.

Cultured cells provide the most versatile method of growing and assaying viruses. A detailed description of the theory and practice of cell culture techniques is provided in *Culture of Animal Cells* by R. Ian Freshney. A typical cell culture facility is shown in **Figure 5-2**.

■ **Figure 5-2**
Diagram of a typical cell culture facility staffed by two to three investigators. Adapted from Freshney, Ian R. *Freshney's Culture of Animal Cells,* Third Edition. John Wiley & Sons, 1998.

■ **Figure 5-3**
Vertical flow laminar hood. Air circulates within the hood: clean air is passed through HEPA filters, downward onto the working area. All air entering the room is also passed through a HEPA filter.

■ Laminar Flow Hoods

The pillar of a virologist's facility is a **laminar vertical flow biosafety hood** (**Figure 5-3**). These facilities must be kept very clean and free from drafts that carry dust, spores, and bacteria, which could contaminate cultures. Clean air (sterile handling) is critical in the facility. Biosafety hoods provide clean air to the working area and provide a constant flow of air out of the work area to prevent room air from entering it. The air flowing out from the hood suspends and removes contaminants introduced into the work area by personnel. The most important part of the laminar flow hood is a high efficiency bacteria-retentive filter. Once air is passed through a prefilter that removes gross contaminants (such as lint and dust), it is then channeled through a **high efficiency particulate air filter** (**HEPA**) filter that removes 99.97% of particles of 0.3 µM or higher from the air.

■ Cytopathic Effects (CPEs)

In general, viruses cause several common morphological changes in the cells that they infect. Cytopathic effects (CPEs) are visual changes in the host that are due to viral infection. CPEs, including inclusion body formation and hemadsorption assays, are the most common observations or methods used to recognize cells in culture infected by viruses.

Virus-induced CPEs can be observed with an inverted light microscope under low power. These observations include rounding of the cells, shrinkage, increased refractility, fusion/**syncytia** formation, aggregation, loss of adherence, and cell lysis/death (**Figures 5-4** and **5-5**).

(a)

(b)

■ **Figure 5-4**
(a) BS-C-1 (monkey kidney) cells infected with a modified vaccinia virus that expresses measles virus genes, resulting in syncytia and fusion of mouse L cells. **(b)** Photograph shows a giant or "multinuclear" cell (also referred to as a syncytia), a mechanism of viral spread. Several viruses, include HIV, can induce syncytia formation. Syncytia-inducing variants of HIV have been correlated with rapid disease progression in HIV-infected individuals.

CPEs occur as a result of:

- entry into the host (crossing the cellular plasma membrane).
- inhibition of cellular transcription or stimulation of cellular RNA polymerase activity.
- virus interactions with RNA processing pathways.
- virus interactions with the translational apparatus.
- host responses to viral infection. (See Interferon Response in Section 7.2.)

CPEs are the easiest and most widely used criteria for recognizing viral infection. Not all viruses cause CPEs, though. For this reason, other methods must be used to detect viral infections.

Inclusion bodies are subtle intracellular abnormalities that only occur in infected cells. They are intracellular granules that are a visible site of viral replication or assembly. The presence of a specific type of inclusion body may be indicative or diagnostic of a specific viral infection. To visualize inclusion bodies, infected cells are fixed to the culture dish, stained by a dye such as eosin, and observed by light microscopy (**Figure 5-6**). Poxviruses, paramyxoviruses, reoviruses, rabies virus, herpesviruses, adenoviruses, and parvoviruses induce striking inclusion bodies in cells.

A **hemadsorption** test is used to detect the presence of viruses that bind to red blood cells. Hemadsorption occurs when the red blood cells in an infected cell attach to the virus. If the virus is in solution and red blood cells are added to the solution, the virus can interact with the red blood cells to form a latticelike structure, resulting in agglutination of red blood cells. This is called **hemagglutination**. Hemadsorption and hemagglutination assays can be useful for detecting viruses that produce few or no CPEs (**Figure 5-7**).

(a)

(b)

■ **Figure 5-5**
(a) Uninfected monkey kidney cells (BS-C-1) viewed by low power light microscopy. The confluent monolayer of cells remains attached and intact to its substrate. **(b)** BS-C-1 cells infected with vaccina virus. CPEs include rounding and detachment of the cells from the tissue culture dish.

■ **Common Methods Used to Study Viruses in the Research Laboratory**

Four methods are most often used to study viruses in the lab setting. They are:

- plaque assays
- the endpoint dilution method, or **tissue culture infectious dose (TCID)**$_{50}$
- hemagglutination assays
- **transformation** assays (focus assays)

■ Figure 5-6
Epidermis with lesions containing inclusion bodies stained by eosin and hematoxylin. The lesions were caused by molluscum contagiosum virus (MCV) infection. Note that the inclusion bodies become darker toward the crater of the lesion.

■ Figure 5-7
Hemadsorption of monkey red blood cells to cells infected by measles virus. Note the attachment of the red blood cells to the infected cells in the middle of the photograph.

A plaque assay is a **quantitative assay** used to determine the number of viruses in a given sample. It is used to quantitate the number of viruses in a prepared virus stock or viruses present at a specific time during single-step growth experiments (see Chapter 3, Virus Replication Cycles). Briefly, cell **monolayers** are infected with tenfold serial dilutions of virus. A **plaque** is produced when a virus particle infects a cell, replicates, and then kills that cell. The monolayers of infected cells are usually overlaid with agarose to restrict the movement of newly released viruses. The newly replicated virus can then only infect surrounding cells and they, too, are killed. After several rounds of replication a visible area, or plaque, of killed cells forms.

Plaques are visualized by staining cells with dyes such as neutral red or crystal violet. Theoretically, each virus in the original inoculation gives rise to a clearing (plaque) or plaque forming unit (PFU), as described in **Figure 5-8**. In other words, a plaque assay measures infectivity. That being said, though, it is possible that viral particles are present in a given sample but are not infectious. More specifically, then, a plaque assay measures only the number of *infectious* particles in a sample, not the total number of particles.

The endpoint dilution assay (TCID)$_{50}$ was used before the development of the plaque assay and is still used for viruses that do not form plaques but do produce CPEs in cell cultures. It is also used in animal experiments to determine virulence. Cell culture assays are performed by infecting cell monolayers in replicates with serial dilutions of virus. After incubation, the infected cells are observed for CPE and are scored + (positive or infected) or − (negative or uninfected). An example of endpoint dilution assay results is shown in Table 5-1.

Fifty percent of the cell cultures displayed CPE at the 10^{-4} dilution. At high dilutions, none of the cell cultures become infected because the dilution is so high that there are no infectious particles in those dilution tubes. At low dilutions, every culture is infected. Therefore, the virus stock contains 10^4 TCID$_{50}$ units.

When an endpoint dilution assay is performed in animals, the animals are inoculated with virus and observed for disease and death. Table 5-2 provides the results from a typical animal experiment, in which ten mice were inoculated per dilution. The endpoint occurs at the 10^{-4} dilution. Therefore, the virus stock contains 10^4 TCID$_{50}$ units. Quite often, results will fall between dilutions. When this occurs, statistical methods that were developed by Reed and Munch are used to calculate the lethality endpoint.

As stated previously in the discussion on hemadsorption assays, some viruses have the ability to agglutinate or form a red blood cell lattice around the virus when virus particles are in high enough concentration. Agglutinated red blood cells can be easily distinguished from cells that are not agglutinated: Red blood cells that are not agglutinated are free to roll to the bottom of the well, forming a dense, easily recognized button at the bottom of the well. Those red blood cells that are agglutinated are not free to roll to the bottom of the well and form an even coat on the bottom of the surface of the well (**Figure 5-9**). This assay is simple and can be used to quantitate hemagglutinating virus. The virus required to cause the agglutination may be infectious or noninfectious. An example of a hemagglutination assay is shown in **Figure 5-10**.

■ **Figure 5-8**
Plaque assay used to quantitate a vaccinia virus stock. After incubation, the liquid medium of the infected cells was removed and the uninfected cell monolayer was stained with a crystal violet/ethanol solution. Clear areas (dead, infected cells) represent plaques. Note that tenfold serial dilutions of virus were plated on confluent monolayers of cells.

TABLE 5-1	**Example of Endpoint Dilution Data**

Virus Dilution				CPE Results					
10^{-2}	+	+	+	+	+	+	+	+	+	+
10^{-3}	+	+	+	+	−	+	+	+	+	+
10^{-4}	−	+	−	+	+	−	−	+	−	+
10^{-5}	−	−	−	−	+	−	−	−	−	−
10^{-6}	−	−	−	−	−	−	−	−	−	−
10^{-7}	−	−	−	−	−	−	−	−	−	−

TABLE 5-2	**Lethality of Poliovirus in Mice**

Virus Dilution	Alive	Dead	Total Alive	Total Dead	Mortality Ratio	% Mortality
10^{-2}	0	10	0	25	0/25	100
10^{-3}	0	10	0	15	0/15	100
10^{-4}	5	5	5	5	5/10	50
10^{-5}	10	0	10	0	10/10	0
10^{-6}	10	0	10	0	10/10	0

Focus assays are used to determine if a virus is capable of "transforming" or immortalizing cells rather than killing them. This phenomenon most notably occurs with such tumor viruses as the retroviruses. Characteristics of transformed cells include immortalization of cells, loss of contact inhibition (cells no longer grow as a monolayer, but instead will pile on top of each other, thus forming a focus), anchorage independence (cells no longer need to attach to a solid surface to grow), and **tumorigenicity** (the ability to form tumors if injected into an animal model). See **Figure 5-11**. (Refer to Chapter 10, Viruses and Cancer, for more information regarding characteristics of cancer cells.)

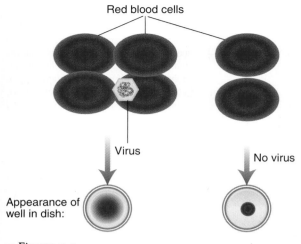

■ Figure 5-9
The theory behind the hemagglutination assay.

■ Figure 5-10
Different samples of influenza viruses were serially diluted and incubated with chicken red blood cells. Wells in the first bottom 9 wells contain no virus. The buttons/dots are nonagglutinated chicken red blood cells in the bottom 9 wells. The virus titer would be the last dilution that shows hemagglutinatin activity in an assay.

(a)

(b)

■ Figure 5-11

(a) Mouse cells (NIH 3T3). These cells are not transformed. Note their flat, dull appearance. (b) Transformed mouse NIH 3T3 cells. The cells appear refractile. These transformed cells were injected into nude mice. (c) Nude mice developed tumors that were excised and allowed to grow in a culture dish. (d) Transformed NIH 3T3 mouse cells removed from the nude mouse tumor growing in culture. Note the focus formed in the center of the photograph.

(c)

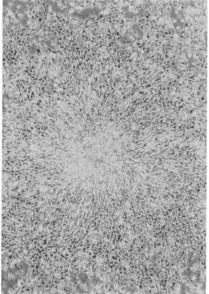

(d)

5.3 Viral Diagnostics in the Clinical Laboratory

Over 60% of all infectious disease cases seen by physicians are due to viral infections. Accurate and rapid detection and diagnosis is essential for successful antiviral treatment. In addition to a patient's travel history, symptoms, and the season of the year, the clinical microbiology laboratory plays an important role in the diagnosis and control of viral diseases.

The quality of the specimen collected from the patient and its transportation from the patient to the laboratory limit the ability of the laboratory personnel to perform diagnostic tests. Some diagnostic tests require the virus to be isolated and grown in cell cultures; therefore, transport conditions must ensure that the virus will be viable. It is critical that the collected specimen is representative of the site of infection. The shorter the interval between the collection of the specimen and its delivery to the laboratory, the greater the potential for isolating a virus.

■ Storage and Collection of Biological Specimens for Viral Testing

The following is a list of common pathogenic viruses and the types of specimens that are collected for diagnosis:

- Respiratory tract infections (for example, adenovirus, influenza virus, enterovirus, rhinovirus, RSV, HSV, SARS-CoV, rubella virus): nasal and bronchial washings, throat and nasal swabs, and sputum.
- Eye infections (adenovirus, enterovirus, herpes simplex): throat and conjunctival swab/scraping.
- Gastrointestinal tract infections (such as reovirus, rotavirus, Norwalk virus, norovirus): stool and rectal swabs.
- Vesicular rash (for example, coxsackie, HSV, VZV): vesicle fluid, skin scrapings.
- Maculopapular rash (adenovirus and enterovirus): throat, stool, rectal swabs. A **maculopapular rash** is usually a large area that is red and has small, confluent bumps.
- Central nervous system/aseptic meningitis and encephalitis (enterovirus, rabies virus, arboviruses, HSV, CMV, mumps and measles virus): stool, tissue, saliva, brain biopsy, cerebrospinal fluid.
- Genital (such as HSV): vesicle fluid or swab.
- Urinary tract (adenovirus, CMV): urine.
- Bloodborne (HIV, HCV, HBV, HTLV): blood.

If the samples can be processed within several days, typically they are stored in the refrigerator (4°–8°C). If a specimen must be kept for retrieval at a later date, it is best to store samples potentially containing viruses at −70°C or lower. Storing human and animal viruses at −15°C to −20°C in frost-free freezers results in rapid loss of infectivity.

■ The Three General Approaches for Laboratory Diagnosis of Viral Infections

In general, three approaches for laboratory diagnosis of viral infections are used. They are:

1. **Direct detection** of viral components in cells, body fluids, or infected tissues (for example, electron microscopy or immunofluorescence staining).
2. **Virus isolation** (usually in cell cultures followed by nucleic acid-based methods such as **polymerase chain reaction [PCR]**).

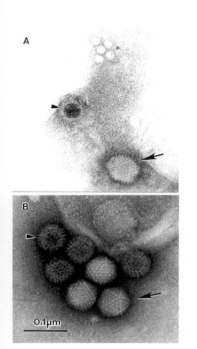

Figure 5-12
A fecal sample was collected from a one-year-old patient with diarrhea. The images show that multiple agents were observed in the sample. An arrowhead points to adenovirus particles and an arrow points to incomplete rotavirus particles.

3. Serology (demonstration of IgM class antibodies. The class of antibodies believed to occur only transiently after infection or acute and convalescent sera is collected and screened for a fourfold increase in IgG antibody titer. See Figure 5-22 later in this chapter and also Chapter 7, Host Resistance to Viral Infections).

Direct Detection

One method of direct detection is **electron microscopy**. This method directly visualizes virus particles contained in a clinical specimen. The morphology (shape) of the particle enables the examiner to assign the virus to a particular family of viruses. It is a rapid method (involving a simple and fast negative-staining procedure) that is especially useful for examining viruses that cannot be grown in cell cultures. Electron microscopy does have its limitations, though. For one, it is not a sensitive method. At least 10,000,000 viruses must be present in 1 milliter (mL) of the sample to visualize the virus by electron microscopy. It also requires a skilled microscopist and an expensive electron microscope for examination of samples.

Certain clinical specimens (feces and mucous samples) do contain high concentrations of virus particles that can be visualized via electron microscopy. Rotaviruses, coronaviruses, astroviruses, Hepatitis A, and adenoviruses have been identified this way (**Figure 5-12**).

Another method for detecting virus particles is **immuno-electron microscopy**. In order to concentrate the number of virus particles in a given sample, specific antibodies are added to specimens. **Antibodies** are proteins produced by the host in response to a particular pathogen (see *Refresher*: Immunology Terms). The virus–antibody complexes are concentrated by centrifugation directly onto a specimen grid. Subsequently, the sample is negatively stained and viewed via the electron microscope. **Figure 5-13** shows an electron micrograph of specimens prepared in this manner. This technique can be slightly modified to increase the sensitivity of the assay. Labeling antibody molecules with electron-dense markers such as colloidal gold may be used in various protocols to enhance the visualization of the virus/antibody reaction.

Refresher   Immunology Terms

Antigen   Antibody

Antigen binding

Virus

Fab

Fc

Antigen: A foreign substance that stimulates an immune response in the form of antibody formation or a cell-mediated response. Bacteria and viruses are common sources of antigens.

Antibody: A 3-lobed globulin molecule found in the blood or other body fluids that can be produced by the presence of an antigen (invading microorganisms). It has a destructive influence on the antigen.

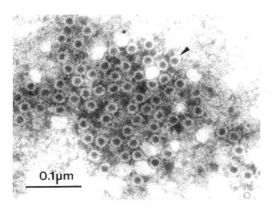

■ **Figure 5-13**
Electron micrograph of parvovirus B19 (the causative agent of erythema infectiosum, also known as Fifth's disease) using immuno-electron microscopy procedure. Virions/immune complexes were centrifuged directly onto a specimen grid. The arrowhead points to a genome-defective virus particle.

■ **Figure 5-14**
Rapid diagnosis of Epstein-Barr virus (EBV) infection by indirect immuno-fluorescent staining of infected cells. Patient serum was collected to determine whether the individual had a primary diagnosis of infection (infectious mononucleosis, IgM EBV antibodies) or reactivation of a latent virus (IgG antibodies).

Viral **antigens** within the cell or on its surface can be detected by means of a detection process called **immunofluorescence**. Specimens are usually fixed, or frozen tissues are prepared on slides (tissue cultures can also be grown on glass slides). Virus-specific antibodies containing a fluorescent tag bound to the Fc region of the antibody are allowed to react with the specimen that contains the virus (see *Refresher:* Immunology Terms). Any unbound antibody is washed away and the specimen is observed under a fluorescent microscope. **Figure 5-14** shows an example of an Epstein-Barr virus detected using immunofluorescence.

Virus Isolation

Optimal growth conditions for viruses differ tremendously. As a result, a variety of methods and host systems are used to isolate viruses from clinical specimens. Viruses can be cultivated in embryonated eggs, laboratory animals such as newborn mice, and cell cultures grown as monolayers or in suspension medium. Each laboratory must choose systems and methods that are reproducible (to ensure against false-negative results) and that best serve the patient population it serves. Cell cultures are the sole isolation system used in most clinical laboratories. As mentioned previously, the quality of the clinical specimen is critical to virus isolation techniques. This requires communication and education between the clinical virology laboratory technicians and the clinicians.

In order to isolate viruses, cell cultures (Table 5-3) most sensitive to the suspected viruses in the clinical specimen are inoculated with the clinical specimen. The inoculated cultures are monitored daily for CPEs and compared to uninoculated control cultures. After 50% of the monolayer shows CPEs, the culture may be analyzed by immunofluorescence, hemadsorption, interference assays, and other techniques such as PCR, and assays for specific enzymatic activity such as reverse transcriptase.

Interference assays are used to detect viruses that do not cause visual CPEs in cell cultures, but may be detected by their ability to interfere with the growth of a second virus

TABLE 5-3	Cell Cultures Commonly Used in the Virology Laboratory	
Cell Culture	**Examples**	**No. of Subpasses**
Primary	Kidney tissues from experimental mammals, such as monkeys and rabbits, and embryos from experimental birds, such as chickens	1 or 2
Diploid (limited passage)	Human embryonic lung or human newborn foreskin	20–50
Heteroploid	Human epidermoid carcinoma of larynx (HEp-2) or of lung (A549)	Indefinite

added to the same cell culture. This is referred to as an "interference phenomenon." (Molecular mechanisms for viral interference are discussed in Chapter 7.) An interference assay is frequently used to detect rubella virus. When rubella virus infects African green monkey kidney cells, it does not induce CPE. The cells are incubated for 10 days and then reinfected or "challenged" with a second virus, such as echovirus 11. Control cultures that are not infected with rubella virus are run side by side during this experiment. After two days, no CPE is observed in the coinfected cells, but there is CPE in cells infected with echovirus 11. Thus, the rubella virus interfered with or inhibited the growth of echovirus 11.

Kary Mullis developed PCR technology while working at Cetus Corporation (Emeryville, California) in 1983. This method is used to replicate DNA using a thermostable DNA polymerase in a test tube (in vitro). PCR and reverse transcriptase PCR (RT-PCR) technology has found widespread use in the clinical laboratory. (Refer to *Refresher: PCR* for a review of PCR.)

These are exquisitely sensitive methods used to detect viral nucleic acids to manage patients with viral diseases (**Figure 5-15**). In some cases, PCR may be performed directly

■ **Figure 5-15**

Flow diagram illustrating the use of PCR to detect viral nucleic acids in the clinical laboratory. Adapted from Harper, D.R. *Molecular Virology,* Second Edition. BIOS Scientific Publishers, 1999.

PCR

The DNA genomes of DNA viruses can be detected directly using PCR or viral mRNAs of DNA viruses can be detected via RT-PCR.

RT-PCR 1st strand synthesis

First strand synthesis

RNA viruses must be detected via RT-PCR. The primers used for cDNA synthesis can be either random primers, oligo-dT primers, or primers which target specific viral RNA sequences. This method involves the amplification of RNA into cDNA via reverse transcriptase. After the new strands of DNA are synthesized, the DNA can be directly amplified via PCR.

Real-time PCR vs. conventional PCR

Real-time: as the PCR product is being amplified, it is being detected by a PCR monitor (FRET technology) during each cycle (=real-time).

Conventional: Involves a post-processing method to quantitate PCR products (e.g. agarose gel electrophoresis).

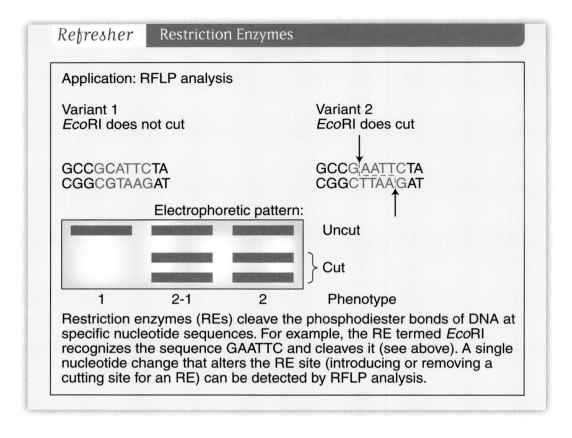

on clinical samples. In other cases, the virus from the sample is grown in cell cultures and the viral nucleic acids are isolated from the cell cultures or from purified virions and subsequently used in PCR or RT-PCR reactions. PCR products are electrophoresed in an agarose gel and the DNA fragments are analyzed. Sometimes the DNA is also digested with restriction enzymes and the digested fragments are analyzed for their electrophoretic pattern in a process called **restriction fragment length polymorphism (RFLP)** analysis (see *Refresher:* Restriction Enzymes.).

In the early 1990s researchers showed that the 5′ nuclease activity of Taq DNA polymerase could be exploited as a method to indirectly determine the level of DNA amplification with the use of specific fluorescent probes that are sensitive to 5′ nuclease degradation. They combined this method with the real-time monitoring of the DNA amplification in the PCR reaction tube, in which amplified dsDNA would bind dyes such as SYBR green. This advanced technology bypasses the need for gel electrophoresis because fluorescence in the PCR reaction tube of amplified DNA can be measured instead of visualizing DNA fragments in a gel. The combined processes are called fluorescence detection of **real-time PCR**.

A detection system that uses a combination of real-time PCR and **fluorescence resonance energy transfer (FRET)** is used in many portable, battery-operated PCR detection systems in the field. In this method, two fluorescently labeled FRET probes are used, one with a donor fluor at the 3′ end (such as fluorescein) and the other with an acceptor fluor at the 5′ end (such as Cy5). When the PCR product is produced, the probes hybridize and bring the two fluors next to each other. The nuclease activity degrades the FRET probe at the 5′ end, which is bound to the template DNA. This degradation allows for energy transfer between the two fluors, leading to a fluorescent signal proportional to the amount of PCR product (**Figure 5-16**). In addition to its application for viral detection and **viral-load monitoring**, PCR technology is being implemented in the meat industry to detect nucleic acids of pathogens.

The technology used when testing for PCR and RT-PCR is rapid. A test can be performed in hours as compared to days using other methods. Its specificity and sensitivity enables it to be very useful for detecting nucleic acids of viruses that cannot be propagated in cell culture or ones that are present in low concentrations. It is especially useful in detecting latent and integrated viral sequences (such as retroviral sequences). RT-PCR was very useful in identifying the hantaviruses that caused the 1993 outbreak in the Four Corners region of the United States (Colorado, Utah, Arizona, and New Mexico).

Even though PCR technology is sensitive, rapid, and can be adjusted to suit many applications, it does have some disadvantages. It is an expensive method and trace amounts of DNA contaminants could serve as DNA templates, resulting in the amplification of the wrong template nucleic acid (false positives). Laboratory benches, equipment, and pipetting devices can be contaminated by previous DNA preparations. Sterile technique and the use of new or sterile plasticware to prepare PCR reagents and template DNA are essential. Control reactions must be included with all reactions; for example, a negative "no DNA" control that contains all of the reaction components except the template DNA and a positive control that was used successfully in previous PCR reactions ensures reproducibility and reliability of the test. When clinical labs are choosing available PCR assay kits, they must consider the types of patients and specimens to be tested, along with the technical skills of the laboratory staff.

Virus isolation requires observation of cell cultures for CPE (Table 5-4). This can take weeks to occur. Rapid diagnosis is increasingly important in patient management. The **centrifugation culture (shell vial technique)** is used in clinical labs for rapid diagnosis of viral infections (**Figure 5-17**). This technique uses a combination of cell culture and centrifugation to detect viral antigens before CPEs are present in a given clinical specimen. Some laboratories use a mixture of cell lines such as mink lung cells (strain Mv1Lu) and human adenocarcinoma cells (strain A 549) in the same shell vial, which is especially suited for the rapid detection of early viral antigens.

■ **Figure 5-16**
Diagram of the chemistry of a FRET signal in combination with an anchored probe.

TABLE 5-4	Detection of Virus: Traditional CPE Method vs. Shell Vial Technique	
Virus	**Days to Detect CPE Conventional Cell Culture Method [avg(range)]**	**Days to Detect CPE Shell Vial Centrifugation Method [avg(range)]**
RSV	6(2–14)	1–2
Influenza A	2(1–7)	1–2
Influenza B	2(1–7)	1–2
PIV 1-4	6(1–14)	1–2
Adenovirus	6(1–14)	2–5
HSV	2(1–7)	1–2
VZV	6(3–14)	2–5
CMV	8(1–28)	1–2

Viral Serology

Serological methods are especially useful in identifying viruses that are difficult to grow in cell culture and viruses that cause diseases with slow courses. Patient serum (which contains antibodies) can be used to identify virus strains or serotypes, evaluate the course of infection, and determine whether the infection is recent or chronic. Detecting antibodies against viruses is an **indirect** measure of viral infection. It indicates a host antiviral response rather than viral particles. When an individual encounters a virus for the first time, his or her body responds by producing a class of virus-specific antibodies termed IgM. (Antibody classes are discussed in more detail in Chapter 7.)

IgM antibodies are proteins found in serum (the liquid portion of blood after removal of clotting factors from plasma) during the first two to three weeks of a primary infection. The presence of specific IgM antibodies indicates a recent infection. Next, IgG antibodies appear. IgG antibodies are the most common antibody. Approximately 70% to 75% of antibodies are of IgG class. If a person is reinfected with the same virus, the IgM antibody

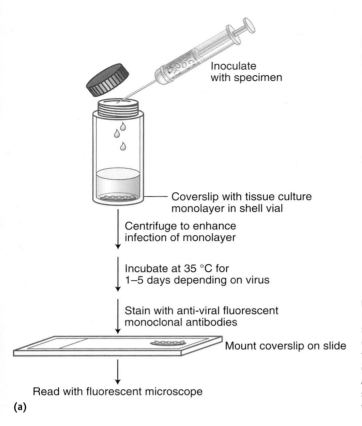

Inoculate with specimen

Coverslip with tissue culture monolayer in shell vial

Centrifuge to enhance infection of monolayer

Incubate at 35 °C for 1–5 days depending on virus

Stain with anti-viral fluorescent monoclonal antibodies

Mount coverslip on slide

Read with fluorescent microscope

(a)

(b)

■ **Figure 5-17**

(a) Tissue culture cells are grown on coverslips on the bottom of shell vials. Clinical specimens are allowed to adsorb for a specified time period. The shell vials are then centrifuged at a slow speed and overlaid with culture medium. The cells typically are fixed to the coverslips for two to three days and then virus antigens (infected cells) are detected using immunofluorescence microscopy. Modified from Shelhamer, J.H., et. al., *Ann Intern Med* 124 (1996): 585–599. (b) Detection of herpes virus simplex 1 using the shell vial technique and immunofluorescence. The brightly fluorescing cells are infected with HSV-1.

■ **Figure 5-18**

Primary (1°) and secondary (2°) antibody responses toward a viral pathogen. The most common serological techniques used in the clinical laboratory are enzyme-linked immunosorbent assays (ELISAs).

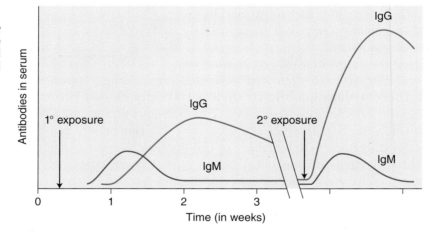

response is the same as for the primary response but for the IgG response memory cells are activated, producing IgG-specific antibodies. Within a day, very high levels of IgG are detected (**Figure 5-18**). By examining antibody profiles, a recent or chronic infection can be identified. Slow-course diseases—such as infectious mononucleosis caused by Epstein-Barr virus and hepatitises B and C—can be diagnosed in this manner.

Enzyme-linked immunosorbent assays (**ELISAs**), which are sometimes referred to as enzyme immunoassays (EIAs) or Western immunoblots, are routinely used in the diagnostic laboratory to detect viral antigens in clinical samples and to identify and quantitate antiviral antibodies in serum. These assays are based on antibodies binding their antigens and the detection of this reaction using a commercial antibody conjugated with an active enzyme. This enzyme reacts with its substrate to produce a color change. Observ-

(a)

(b)

■ **Figure 5-19**

(a) Schematic illustrating the ELISA procedure used to detect antibodies in patient
serum. Briefly, patient serum is added to
wells (typically 96-well plastic plates)
precoated with known viral antigens. If
virus-specific antibodies are present, they
will bind to the viral antigens. Next, antihuman IgG enzyme-labeled antibodies are
added, which react with human antibodies. The enzyme substrate solution is then
added. If a color develops, it indicates the
reaction is positive. Note: Rigorous washing follows each incubation step. Adapted
from Specter, S. C., R. L. Hodinka and
S. A. Young. *Clinical Virology Manual,* Third
Edition. ASM Press, 2000. **(b)** Schematic
illustrating the ELISA procedure used to
detect viral antigens present in a clinical
sample (for example, feces, throat, or nasal
wash). The clinical sample is added to wells
precoated with virus-specific antibodies.
If viral antigens are present in the clinical
sample, they will bind to the virus-specific
antibodies. Next, enzyme-labeled antiviral
antibodies are added, followed by substrate
solution. If a color develops, it indicates
the reaction is positive. Note: Rigorous
washing follow each incubation step.
Adapted from Specter, Steven C., Hodinka,
Richard L. and Young, Steven A. *Clinical Virology Manual,* Third Edition. ASM Press, 2000.

ing and measuring color determine the test result. **Figure 5-19** illustrates
the detection of viral antigens or serum antibodies in clinical samples.
Figure 5-20 is a photograph of an ELISA test used to determine if HIV antibodies were present in a person's serum. The ELISA is a very sensitive
method and will result in a reaction even if only one or two antibodies
are present in the serum sample. If the ELISA test is reactive, or positive,
it is repeated. If the second ELISA test is also positive, the HIV-positive
status must be confirmed by Western immunoblotting. Using the two
tests together ensures extreme accuracy. Thus, ELISAs are used to screen
for viruses and antibodies present in patient serum samples. Western immunoblotting—Western "blotting" for short—has become a very important procedure for detecting HIV, HTLV-1, HTLV-2, and viral hepatitis
infections. Even though ELISAs are very sensitive and highly specific,
false-positive reactions due to crossreacting antibodies occur. Repeat testing is required and a confirmation test by another assay, usually Western
blotting is performed.

The basic approach to Western blotting involves the separation of
viral proteins (from purified virions available commercially) through an
acrylamide gel. This procedure is called SDS polyacrylamide gel electrophoresis, or SDS-PAGE. (SDS stands for sodium dodecyl sulfate.) It is a
strong detergent that denatures proteins. As the proteins migrate through the polyacrylamide gel, they are separated based upon size. (Charge plays a very small role in this process
too, because the negatively charged SDS coats the proteins, thus giving every protein the
same mass to charge ratio.) Characteristically, smaller proteins migrate through the gel

■ **Figure 5-20**
HIV ELISA test. This 96-well plate is read via a spectrophotometer.
The yellow color indicates a positive antigen–antibody reaction.
The ELISA test involves adding a patient's serum to wells coated
with lysed T-lymphocytes infected with HIV. Any anti-HIV antibodies in serum will bind to the viral antigens from the T-cell.
After a washing step, enzyme-labeled antihuman IgG is added,
followed by a chromagenic substrate for the enzyme which when
acted upon by the enzyme produces a colored product if anti-HIV
antibodies are present.

■ Figure 5-21

(a) Diagram showing the basic principles behind the Western blotting procedure. Modified from Specter, et al. *Clinical Virology Manual,* Third Edition. ASM Press, 2000. (b) Schematic of the structure of HIV-1. SDS disrupts HIV-1 virions and the viral proteins are separated in a polyacrylamide gel as part of the Western blot procedure. Courtesy of Bio-Rad Laboratories. (c) These are the typical results of a Western blot testing patient serum for HIV-1 antibodies. Lane 1 is a positive control and lane 3 is a negative control. Lane 2 represents blots probed with patient sera.

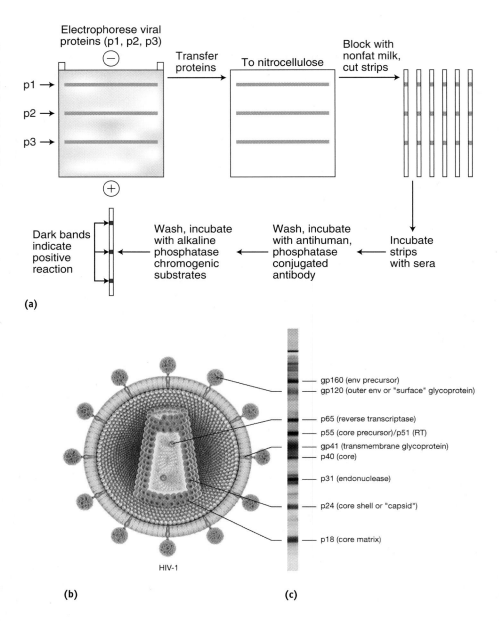

faster than larger ones. After the proteins are separated, they are transferred to nitrocellulose in the same pattern that they were on the gel. The proteins bind to the nitrocellulose, which then is cut into strips and probed with patient serum, or positive or negative serum, as controls.

Any viral antibodies present in the serum sample will react with the viral proteins present on the nitrocellulose membrane. A second antibody, such as antihuman Ig-coupled with an enzyme, is then incubated with the nitrocellulose. (Stringent washing of the nitrocellulose occurs between each step in the procedure.) Finally, the blot is incubated with the appropriate enzyme substrate. Protein bands reacting with antiviral antibodies from the serum sample, which are recognized by the secondary antihuman-enzyme antibodies, will change color upon the addition of substrate (**Figure 5-21**).

Western blotting has been used to detect specific antibodies in a number of viruses. It is probably the most widely accepted confirmatory assay for the detection of HIV, and most authorities consider it the gold standard for validation of HIV results. False-negative reactions are relatively rare. Sometimes Western blot assays can produce nonspecific or "indeterminate" reactions in which often only one band is detected. These results may be

Rapid Diagnosis of SARS

The largest outbreak of SARS occurred in Beijing, China, in 2003. It began March 5th and by July 4th there were 8,439 probable SARS cases and 812 deaths. On March 15th the WHO recommended postponing nonessential travel to the affected areas and screening of airline passengers. At the time, SARS was a newly emerging infectious disease caused by a novel coronavirus. There was an immediate need for a rapid and reliable diagnostic test. Dr. Christian Drosten, a physician and research scientist, and his research team at the Bernhard Nocht Institute for Tropical Medicine in Hamburg, Germany, were the first to develop a diagnostic test for SARS.

On March 15th—the same day as the WHO's global alert—a doctor and his wife, both infected with SARS, landed at Frankfurt airport in Germany. Initial tests on sputum samples from the doctor were conducted at a clinical laboratory in Frankfurt. The tests included various PCR tests for known viruses and bacteria and involved looking at the sputum sample with an electron microscope. (See **Figure VF 5-1**.) Although the virus appeared to be a typical paramyxovirus, the lab was unable to identify the virus. A second sample taken on March 17th was sent to Drosten's laboratory to determine if the illness was caused by a tropical virus. Drosten quickly ruled out paramyxoviruses and sent samples to Europe's leading paramyxovirus expert, Dr. Albert Osterhaus at Erasmus University in Rotterdam, the Netherlands. Dr. Osterhaus confirmed the negative result. On March 22nd Drosten received a sample of the SARS virus that had been grown from a clinical specimen in cell cultures in the Frankfurt laboratory. Immediately, Drosten's team began a new series of PCR tests and by March 25th some of the PCR products matched the sequences from the coronavirus family. Just as this new information was received, the CDC announced that they had identified SARS as the infectious agent. Subsequently, Drosten's team developed an RT-PCR assay. Since that time, additional RT-PCR, serologic (ELISAs), and tissue culture isolation assays have been developed for the SARS-associated coronavirus. Reports suggest that the SARS virus leapt from wild animals (such as civet cats consumed as food) to humans. These reports are based on serological and virological studies that showed that the SARS virus could infect the respiratory tract of masked palm civet cats, Chinese ferret badgers, and raccoon dogs.

■ **Figure VF 5-1**
Electron micrograph of SARS-CoV, the etiological agent recognized as the cause of the SARS outbreak in 2003.

References

Chan, K. H., et al. 2004. "Detection of SARS coronavirus in patients with suspected SARS." *EID* 10:294–299.

Drosten, C., et al. 2003. "Identification of a novel coronavirus in patients with severe acute respiratory syndrome." *N Engl J Med* 348:1967–1976.

Emery, S. L., et al. 2004. "Real-time reverse transcription-polymerase chain reaction assay for SARS-associated coronavirus." *EID* 10:311–316.

Martina, B. E. E., et al. 2003. "SARS virus infection of cats and ferrets." *Nature* 425:915.

due to underlying causes such as an autoimmune disease, which results in the production of antibodies similar to cellular and viral antigens. An indeterminate reaction may precede a positive reaction. To avoid this situation, specimens need to be collected from the patient at a later time for retesting. Figure 5-21(c) shows examples of the types of Western blot profiles seen with HIV-1 testing.

■ Detection of Viral Enzymes

Viral proteins, including enzymes produced during viral replication, can be detected by molecular biological, biochemical, and immunological methods. The detection of enzyme activities characteristic of specific viruses can be used to quantitate and identify these viruses; for example, reverse transcriptase activity in serum or cell cultures is indicative of the presence of a retrovirus such as HIV or HTLV.

■ Advantages and Disadvantages of Methods

Accurate and rapid diagnosis is essential for successful antiviral treatment. Table 5-5 compares the advantages and disadvantages of diagnostic methods.

Within the past 10 to 15 years, additional antivirals have become available. (Recall that Table 3-4, lists antivirals approved by the FDA.) Diagnostic laboratories are increasingly asked to perform antiviral susceptibility testing because antiviral resistance has emerged. This is especially the case with HIV infections. Continuous updates about HIV antivirals, clinical trials, and vaccines are available via the AIDS info Website, http://www.aidsinfo.nih.gov/.

5.4 Drug Susceptibility Testing

The testing methods used as *in vitro* susceptibility assays measure the inhibitory effects of a particular antiviral agent on the entire virus population in a patient isolate. Methods to do this include plaque reduction assays, inhibition of viral nucleic acid synthesis, reduction in the yield of viral structural proteins, and reduction in the enzymatic activities of a virus (for example, reverse transcriptase activity of HIV-1).

TABLE 5-5	Comparison of Diagnostic Methods	
Diagnostic Method	**Advantages**	**Disadvantages**
Virus isolation via cell culture	Can be used to study and quantify most viruses; sensitive method.	Slow (results in days to weeks); technically demanding, time-consuming, and doesn't work for all viruses
Electron microscopy (direct detection)	Rapid; works for viruses that cannot be cultured	Requires highly skilled technician; electron microscope is expensive; limited to a few viral infections; less sensitive and specific
Experimental animals	Can be used to study virus-host interactions; some viruses will only grow in animals	Expensive and slow (results in days to weeks); complex systems and results
Nucleic acid-based methods	PCR (very sensitive; can be quantitative and is applicable to all viruses)	Expensive; susceptible to DNA contamination; can only detect known viral agents (a new virus would show a negative result)
Serology	Sensitive and rapid; can be quantitative, process large numbers of samples, and is readily available in kit form	Not applicable to all viruses; interpretation may be difficult and can yield false-positives

■ Plaque Reduction Assays

Plaque reduction assays are the gold standard for directly measuring the extent to which an antiviral drug inhibits the effects of viral infection in tissue culture. Cell monolayers in 6 or 12-well dishes are infected with virus [50–100 plaque forming units (PFU) per well] and incubated in the presence of the antiviral compound. Depending upon which virus is being tested, some assays will need to be overlaid with medium containing the antiviral compound and agarose (a solidifying agent) so that discrete plaques are formed. This helps prevent secondary spread of the virus to the remainder of the cell monolayer. Following two to four days of incubation, the cells are fixed and stained with crystal violet dye and the plaques are counted (**Figure 5-22**). The lowest concentration of the drug causing 50% inhibition in plaque formation represents the 50% inhibitory dose (ID$_{50}$). A plaque reduction assay is accurate, reliable, and relatively simple to perform. A disadvantage of this method is that the enumeration of plaques is tedious, time-consuming, and subjective. These assays are best suited for small numbers of specimens and are difficult to automate. The infectivity titer of the virus must be determined before the plaque reduction assay can be performed. Plaque reduction assays can be completed within two to four days for poxviruses, one to two weeks for herpes simplex viruses, and as much as six weeks for slow-growing viruses such as CMV and VZV.

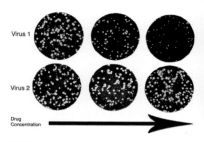

■ Figure 5-22
Plaque reduction assay. Two different strains of vaccinia virus were tested in this assay. Virus 1 is resistant to the effects of the compound, whereas virus 2 is sensitive to increasing concentrations of the compound being tested.

■ Microarrays and Protein Arrays: A New Option in Viral Diagnostics

A new revolutionary tool applied to cancer biology and drug and therapy development is the **DNA microarray** or **DNA chip**. Microarrays were developed by a team of researchers at Stanford University during the early 1990s and first introduced commercially in 1996. DNA chips are used to assess and classify tumors of cancer patients; for example, certain tumor cells are more aggressive than others. The DNA chip has allowed researchers to determine which patients will need the most intensive treatment based on information provided by the chip. The chip is used to determine the molecular abnormalities that distinguish long- and short-term cancer survivors based on the gene expression pattern exhibited in malignant cells at the time of diagnosis. The risk for developing certain cancers can be assessed and a prognosis made based on microarray test results.

Currently, the power of the microarray in virology can best be seen in research studies; for example, microarrays can be used to study viral gene expression and promoter activities. There are many potential applications for arrays in the clinical virology laboratory. These applications include:

- diagnostic microarrays, including novel virus identification.
- detecting agents of bioterror (viral, bacterial, and eukaryotic pathogens).
- detecting the presence or absence of viral pathogenicity genes.
- patient management (monitoring antiviral drug-resistant mutations, such as probing HIV protease and reverse transcriptase genes).
- vaccine quality control (ensuring vaccines are free of contaminating microbes by detecting their genetic sequences in the vaccine preparation).
- studying genes involved in host response to viral infection.

To date, microarrays have been designed to detect genomes of enteroviruses, rhinoviruses, adenoviruses, herpesviruses, orthomyxoviruses, paramxyoviruses, nidoviruses (arteriviruses and coronaviruses, such as SARS-CoV), retroviruses, hepadnaviruses, and papillomaviruses.

How do microarrays work? A DNA chip or microarray consists of a small nylon membrane, silicon chip, or glass microscope slide that contains samples of immobilized DNA of many genes arranged in a specific pattern. The microarray works by exploiting the ability of a given mRNA molecule to specifically hybridize to the DNA template from which it originated.

■ **Figure 5-23**

Illustration of the process involved in creating a microarray. In the upper panel, probes of the genome sequences of the viruses of interest (such as viruses that cause respiratory tract infections) are generated and spotted onto a "chip." In the lower panel, the DNA or RNA of biological samples (such as sputum or throat swab) is extracted and amplified with either fluorescently labeled Cy3-dCTP (green) or Cy5-dCTP (red) dye. The labeled nucleic acid from the specimens is spotted onto the microarray chip that contains the immobilized probes. Complementary nucleotides of the genetic material will anneal. Green spots represent hybridization of the probe with Cy3-dCTP, red spots represent spots hybridized with Cy5-dCTP, and yellow spots represent hybridization with both Cy3 and Cy5-dCTP target sequences. Adapted from Clewley, Jonathan P., 2003. "A role for arrays in clinical virology: Fact or fiction?" *J Clin Virol* 29:2–12.

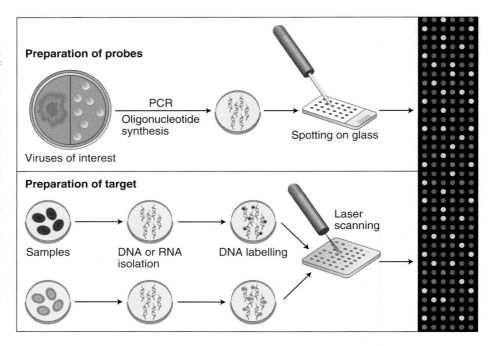

The following general procedure represents how microarrays might fit routinely into a diagnostic laboratory in the near future:

1. Nucleic acid is extracted from a biological sample (such as sputum, blood, or CSF) by an automated instrument.
2. The RNA and/or DNA is amplified via RT-PCR or PCR that will incorporate fluorescently labeled nucleotides into the genetic material of any virus present in the sample.
3. The amplified, labeled nucleic acid would be applied to a DNA chip and allowed to hybridize to complementary sequence probe(s) representing known sequences of pathogenic viruses; for example, there may be specific microarray chips developed for respiratory pathogens, gastrointestinal pathogens, or blood-borne viruses.
4. A detection instrument (microarray reader) and specialized software would be used to interpret the fluorescent hybridization signals on the chip and provide a readout that identifies the virus present in the original biological specimen (**Figure 5-23**).

Prototypes of DNA chips developed for the diagnosis of similar infectious diseases are used in some laboratories. Before microarrays can be routinely used in the virology clinical laboratory, though, the tools must contain probe sequences that hybridize with high sensitivity and specificity. This will allow for the precise detection of their intended targets. Results must be reproducible and quality control and assurance systems must be established.

Protein arrays are a spin-off of the DNA chip. Arrays of antibodies instead of DNA probes are immobilized on the chip. The chips are probed with a blood sample from a patient, which will contain proteins from the disease causing microorganism or cellular proteins induced during the disease state. Subsequently, specific fluorescently labeled antibodies will be added to the chip. A "sandwich" of antibodies will form wherever a protein from the patient's blood is bound to the microarray chip. The chip is then scanned and

■ Figure 5-24
Protein arrays contain bound protein probes (proteins of infectious disease agents or proteins expressed during diseases states, such as cancers and genetic diseases). Next, a blood sample from a patient is incubated with the protein microarray. Subsequently, fluorescently labeled antibodies are incubated with the chip. A protein array reader will detect the presence of antibody 'sandwiches.' Adapted from Friend, S. H., and Stoughton, R. B. 2002. "The magic of microarrays." *Scientific American*, February, 286(2):44–53.

interpreted by a microarray reader instrument (**Figure 5-24**). Before protein arrays become commonplace in a doctor's office, though, technology needs to be developed that enables the simultaneous mass-production of different antibodies that retain their ability to bind tightly and specifically to target proteins that may be present in minute quantities in a patient's biological sample. Protein arrays will be limited by which proteins the chips can detect. More knowledge needs to be gained regarding new and emerging viruses and what proteins represent disease markers present in tissues when screening for noninfectious diseases before the technology will be ready for the commercial market.

5.5 Laboratory Safety

Precautions are necessary to prevent laboratory hazards. Workers in clinical virology laboratories test human serum and other body fluids that may contain HIV-1 or hepatitis C or B virus. This requires caution and safety procedures at all times. The safest procedure is to treat all clinical specimens as potentially infectious. Proper laboratory procedure involves using rigorous aseptic technique, and gloves and laboratory coats are worn at all times. There are different classes of biosafety cabinets that provide increasing levels of containment. If available, workers should be vaccinated against the potential infectious agents they may be working with. There are four designated Biosafety Level (BSL) laboratories. From minimum to maximum containment requirements they are BSL-1, BSL-2, BSL-3, and BSL-4. Criteria for the different levels are available at http://www.cdc.gov/od/ohs/.

Exposure to infectious aerosols poses the most risk when working with clinical specimens. Crucial to safe working conditions are the various types of specialized equipment available as barriers between the virus and the laboratory worker. Equipment ranges from protective clothing and gloves to complex biosafety cabinets and containment devices. Workers in BSL-4 labs, which require maximum containment, work with infectious agents that have no vaccine or cure (**Figure 5-25**).

■ **Figure 5-25**
(a) A CDC researcher working in a BSL-3 lab on highly lethal influenza strains. **(b)** CDC researcher working on a BSL-4 infectious agent. **(c)** A CDC scientist showers in a protective suit before leaving a BSL-4 laboratory.

(a)

(b)

(c)

Summary

Viral diagnostics are critical for patient management and for surveillance of disease outbreaks. It enables infectious disease experts to establish control measures. The rapidly expanding knowledge about SARS is a prime example of how clinical, public health, and research communities worldwide mounted an aggressive response to a new disease. In this particular case, scientific journals played a major role in this endeavor by expediting online publication of peer-reviewed data.

This chapter defined a typical clinical laboratory setting, including the equipment required to cultivate viruses. The most common way to propagate viruses is in tissue culture cells. These cells usually undergo rapid morphological changes, termed CPEs, when infected by viruses. CPEs include the formation of inclusion bodies, syncytia and fusion, cell shrinkage, refractility changes, rounding, aggregation, and lysis (cell death).

Common methods used to study viruses in the research laboratory are single-step growth experiments, plaque assays, hemagglutination assays, and transformation assays.

The quality of clinical specimens collected from the patient and its transportation from the patient to the laboratory limit the ability of the laboratory personnel to perform diagnostic tests. Hence there are important rules about the storing and collecting of specimens and the type of specimens collected. Rapid diagnosis is critical for patient management. There are three general approaches to laboratory diagnosis: direct detection of the virus or virus components, virus isolation from clinical samples, and serology. The chapter discussed the electron microscopic, molecular, and serological methods used in the clinical virology laboratory. Many diagnostic laboratories now perform drug susceptibility testing to monitor AIDS patients because of viral resistance to the various drug regimes patients must follow.

Lastly, safety in the clinical laboratory is of the utmost importance. Precautions are necessary to prevent laboratory hazards. Chapter 6 will address the mechanisms of infection and how diseases are spread through the body and to others.

Resources

■ Primary Literature and Reviews

Athmanathan, S., Bandlapally, S. R., and Gullapalli, N. R. 2002. "Comparison of the sensitivity of a 24 h-shell vial assay, and conventional tube culture, in the isolation of Herpes Simplex virus-1 from corneal scrapings." *BMC Clin Path* 2(1):1. Epub.

Barenfanger, J., et al. 2001. "R-Mix cells are faster, at least as sensitive and marginally more costly than conventional cell lines for the detection of respiratory viruses." *J Clin Virol* 22:101–110.

Chan, K. H., et al. 2004. "Detection of SARS Coronavirus in patients with suspected SARS." *EID* 10:294–299.

Cherkasova, E., et al. 2003. "Microarray analysis of evolution of RNA viruses: Evidence of circulation of virulent highly divergent vaccine-derived polioviruses." *PNAS USA* 100(16):9398–9403.

Clewley, Jonathan P. 2003. "A role for arrays in clinical virology: Fact or fiction?" *J Clin Virol* 29:2–12.

Crist, G. A., et al. 2004. "Evaluation of the ELVIS plate method for the detection and typing of herpes simplex virus in clinical specimens." *Virology* 49:173–177.

Drosten, C., et al. 2003. "Identification of a novel coronavirus in patients with severe acute respiratory syndrome." *N Engl J Med* 348:1967–1976.

Emery, S. L., et al. 2004. "Real-time reverse transcription-polymerase chain reaction assay for SARS-associated coronavirus." *EID* 10:311–316.

Fouchier, R. A., et al. 2003. "Koch's postulates fulfilled for SARS virus." *Nature* 423:240.

Freshney, R. I. 1994. *Culture of Animal Cells: A Manual of Basic Technique*, 3rd ed. New York: Wiley.

Geisbert, T. W., et al. 2003. "Treatment of ebola virus infection with a recombinant inhibitor of factor VIIa/tissue factor: A study in rhesus monkeys." *Lancet* 362:1953–1958.

Hazelton, P. R., and Gelderblom, H. R. 2003. "Electron microscopy for rapid diagnosis of infectious agents in emergent situations." *EID* 9:294–303.

Kato-Maeda, M., Gao, Q., and Small, P. M. 2001. "Microarray analysis of pathogens and their interaction with hosts." *Cell Microbiol* 3(11):713–719.

Long, W-H., et al. 2004. "A universal microarray for detection of SARS coronavirus." *J Virol Methods* 121:57–63.

Lin, B., et al. 2004. "Use of oligonucleotide microarrays for rapid detection and serotyping of acute respiratory disease-associated adenoviruses." *J Clin Microbiol* 42(7):3232–3239.

Malmsten, A., et al. 2003. "HIV-1 viral load determination based on reverse transcriptase activity recovered from human plasma." *J Med Virol* 71:347–359.

Martina, B. E. E., et al. 2003. "SARS virus infection of cats and ferrets." *Nature* 425:915.

Murray, P. R., Baron, E., Pfaller, M. A., Tenover, F. C., and Yolken, R. H., eds. 1995. *Manual of Clinical Microbiology*, 6th ed. Washington, DC: ASM Press.

Petricoin, E. F. III, et al. 2002. "Medical applications of microarray technologies: A regulatory science perspective." *Nat Genet* Suppl 32:474–479.

Reed L. J., and Muench, H. 1938. "A simple method of estimation of 50% endpoints." *Amer J Hygiene* 27(3):493–497.

Richman, D. D., Whitley, R. J., and Hayden, F. G., eds. 2002. *Clinical Virology*, 2nd ed. Washington, DC: ASM Press.

Rivers, T. M. 1937. "Viruses and Koch's postulates." *J Bacteriol* 33:1–12.

Szollosi, J., Damjanovich, S., and Matyus, L. 1998. "Application of fluorescence resonance energy transfer in the clinical laboratory: Routine and research." *Cytometry* 34:159–179.

Specter, S., Hodinka, R. L., and Young, S. A., eds. 2000. *Clinical Virology Manual*. Washington, DC: ASM Press.

Van Doornum, G. J. J., and De Jong, J. C. 1998. "Rapid shell vial culture technique for detection of enteroviruses and adenoviruses in fecal specimens: Comparison with conventional virus isolation method." *J Clin Micro* 36:2865–2868.

Walker, N. J. 2002. "A technique whose time has come." *Science* 296:557–559.

Wang, D., et al. 2002. "Microarray-based detection and genotyping of viral pathogens." *PNAS* USA 99(24):15687–15692.

Weinberg, A., Brewster, L., Clark, J., and Simoes, E. ARIVAC Consortium. 2004. "Evaluation of R-Mix shell vials for the diagnosis of viral respiratory tract infections." *J Clin Virol* 30:100–105.

Wilson, W. J., et al. 2002. "Sequence-specific identification of 18 pathogenic microorganisms using microarray technology." *Mol Cell Probes* 16:119–127.

■ Popular Press

Bear, G. 2000. *Darwin's Radio*. New York: Ballantine.

Friend, S. H., and Stoughton, R. B. 2002. "The magic of microarrays." *Sci Am*, February, 286(2):44.

Garrett, L. 1994. *The Coming Plague*. New York: Penguin.

Harper, D. R., and Meyer, A. S. 1999. *Of Mice, Men, and Microbes: Hantavirus*. San Diego: Academic Press.

McCormick, J. B., and Fisher-Hoch, S., with Horvitz, L. A. 1996. *Level 4: Virus Hunters of the CDC*. Atlanta: Turner Publishing.

O'Brien, T. J. 2000. *West Nile Outbreak in New York*. Philadelphia: Knopf.

Peters, C. J., and Olshaker, M. 1998. *Virus Hunter: Thirty Years of Battling Hot Viruses Around the World*. New York: Knopf.

Preston, R. 1995. *The Hot Zone*. New York: Anchor.

Regis, E. 1996. *Virus Ground Zero: Stalking the Killer Viruses with the Centers for Disease Control*. New York: Pocket Books.

Regush, N. 2000. *The Virus Within: A Coming Epidemic*. New York: Penguin Putnam.

Zimmerman, B. E., and Zimmerman, D. J. 1996. *Killer Germs: Microbes and Diseases That Threaten Humanity*. Chicago: Contemporary Books.

■ Video Productions

Ebola The Plague Fighters. 1996. Public Broadcasting Service.

Invisible Enemies: The Hanta Virus. 1996. Films for the Humanities.

On the Trail of a Killer Virus. 1996. A&E Production.

The Next Plague: The Nipah Virus. 1998. Films for the Humanities.

Mosquito Nightmare: West Nile Virus. 2000. Films for the Humanities.

SARS and the New Plagues. 2003. History Channel.

SARS: The True Story. 2003. Films for the Humanities.

The Great Fever. 2007. PBS; Bosch and Company, Inc., Film for American Experience.

■ eLearning

http://biology.jbpub.com/book/virology

The site features eLearning, an online review area that provides quizzes and other tools to help you study for your class. You can also follow useful links for in-depth information, or just find out the latest virology and microbiology news.

CASE STUDY QUESTIONS

These questions relate to the Case Study presented at the beginning of the chapter.

1. Elevated temperature is a common presenting symptom for a number of illnesses, including infectious diseases. List other viral infections in which thermal scanners may be useful tools for mass screening of body temperature, not only for SARS but also for other public health crises in which widespread transmission of infection is possible.

2. Thermal image scanners were operational in Canada at Vancouver International Airport and Toronto's Pearson International Airport during part of the SARS outbreak in 2003, and 4,569,759 passengers were actually scanned. An elevated temperature was detected in 1,435 individuals (0.031%). None of them were assessed as having SARS. Approximately 36.3 million people were assessed via scanners in Hong Kong in 2003. Of these, only 1,921 had a fever. Forty of these passengers were admitted to a hospital, but none was diagnosed with SARS. From this data, does it appear that mass screening for fever is the most effective means for detecting disease in travelers during an outbreak? Should other 'low-tech' approaches be used? Should a combination of both thermal scanners and other approaches be used? Provide details in your answer.

Woman with smallpox holding her vaccinated infant.

Mechanisms of Viral Entry and Spread of Infection in the Body

" *. . . no man dared to count his children as his own until they had had the disease.* **"**

Comte de la Condamine, 18th-century mathematician and scientist referring to smallpox

CASE STUDY

A New York City male in his 40s was tested for HIV five times between September 2000 and May 2003. The results were negative each time and his T-cell counts were normal. In mid-December 2004, the man was prompted to visit his private physician because of the following symptoms: sore throat, fever, malaise, weakness, significant weight loss, and chronic fatigue. When tested for HIV this time, both the ELISA and Western immunoblot assays yielded positive results. His CD4 T-cell count was 80/μl and his plasma contained 280,000 HIV-1 RNA copies/ml. Individuals with T-cell counts below 200 and an RNA viral load of 100,000 HIV-1 RNA copies/ml of plasma are considered to be in the advanced stage of HIV infection—full-blown AIDS. During this stage, patients experience many opportunistic infections because they have too few T-cells to help their body fight the virus or any other invading infection. The infections are called **opportunistic** because they take advantage of the immune system when the virus compromises it.

These results were alarming. In a short time, the man's T-cell counts and viral RNA load matched those that occur during full-blown AIDS. The man provided a detailed history of his sexual activity. He admitted to having unprotected anal sex with hundreds of male partners, at times while under the influence of the drug crystal methamphetamine. He was referred to a team of researchers at the New York School of Medicine and Cabrini Medical Center for viral genomic studies to determine whether the HIV-1 virus in his body was susceptible to antiviral drug therapy. The researchers isolated HIV-1 from his peripheral blood cells and began drug susceptibility testing. Meanwhile, the man's health was rapidly declining because he was continuing to lose weight rapidly and was suffering from additional opportunistic infections.

The results obtained by the team of researchers showed that the man was harboring an HIV strain that was multidrug resistant. It was resistant to three of the four classes of antiviral drug classes: nucleoside reverse transcriptase inhibitors, nonnucleoside reverse transcriptase inhibitors, and protease inhibitors. This meant that the man would be very difficult to treat with a standard antiretroviral regimen. Fortunately, this strain was susceptible to a new class of anti-HIV drugs known as fusion inhibitors. Fusion inhibitors block the virus particles from fusing to the plasma membrane of a cell, thereby blocking their entry into cells. The HIV viruses in the man's body were shown to be sensitive to efurvitide (T-20) and efavirenz (T-1249) fusion inhibitors and this treatment was initiated.

◼ References

Madison, P. B. 2005. "Aggressive HIV strain sets off dubious public health measure." *Nat Med* 11:360.

Markowitz, M., et al. 2005. "Infection with multidrug resistant, dual-tropic HIV-1 and rapid progression to AIDS: A case report." *Lancet* 365:1031–1038.

Chapter 2 focused on the techniques used to grow, study, and identify viruses from clinical specimens. This chapter examines an earlier stage, when the virus enters the host, multiplies and spreads within the host's body, and then exits (or is "shed") into the environment.

6.1   Preferred Routes of Entry

Recall from Chapter 3 that all viruses target a specific population of cells. Before viruses can do that, though, they must somehow enter the body of the human or animal host (**Figure 6-1**). Viruses gain access to their hosts through the skin or the following mucous membranes:

- respiratory tract
- gastrointestinal tract (also referred to at the alimentary canal)
- genital tract
- conjunctiva (eyes)

In addition, a fetus can be infected when certain blood-borne viruses cross the placenta and reach the fetal circulation, causing congenital (present at birth) malformations. A baby also may be infected as it passes through the birth canal. Severe infections of the fetus can result in spontaneous abortion, stillbirth, and neonatal death. These consequences were a common result of smallpox infections. Less lethal viruses, such as rubella virus and cytomegalovirus, cause severe congenital malformations (**teratogenic** effects). These abnormalities include deafness, blindness, and congenital heart and brain defects. Table 6-1 lists viruses known to cause congenital infections and syndromes.

■ **Figure 6-1**

Viruses may be spread via respiratory or salivary routes of transmission, which is not readily controllable. Oral-fecal route transmission is controllable by public health measures. Venereal diseases are difficult to control because of social factors. Controlling vectors or animal infections can control human infections related to zoonoses.

■ Respiratory Tract Entry

The average person inside a ventilated building inhales at least eight microorganisms per minute, or about 11,520 per day. Although most of the inhaled microorganisms are nonpathogenic bacteria or molds, it is not surprising that inhalation is the most common route of virus infection. To combat the huge numbers of microorganisms inhaled each day, the human body employs within its respiratory track a very effective cleansing mechanism designed to remove and dispose of inhaled particles: a blanket of mucus and ciliated cells that line the nasal cavity and most of the lower respiratory tract (**Figure 6-2**). Particles inhaled into the lower respiratory tract (the lungs) are often trapped in the mucus, moved upward to the back of the throat via **ciliary action**, and then are coughed out. Particles entering the nasal cavity are trapped in mucus and carried to the back of the throat by ciliary action and then swallowed. The average person produces 10 to 100 ml (0.04–0.40 cups) of mucus from the nasal cavity each day and a similar amount from the lungs.

Particles such as viruses and bacteria that are smaller than 5 μM are likely to enter the lungs and reach the **alveolar sacs**. The alveolar sacs of the lungs do not contain mucus or ciliated cells. Instead, they are lined with immune cells called macrophages. These macrophages move along the alveolar surface of the lung, engulfing airborne particles that reach the alveolar surface. Antibodies (IgG and IgA) are present in the upper and lower respiratory tracts. They provide specific defenses against invading microbes. Normally the lungs are nearly sterile because any microbes inhaled on a continual basis are also being destroyed by macrophages or removed via mucociliary action. (Chapter 7, Host Resistance to Viral Infections, provides more information about immune defenses.)

■ **Figure 6-2**
Schematic of the upper and lower respiratory tracts.

TABLE 6-1	Viruses Known to Cause Congenital Infections
Virus	**Potential Syndrome(s)**
Variola virus (causes smallpox)	Fetal death and abortion
Cytomegalovirus	Chorioretinitis (eye problems that can lead to vision loss), mental retardation, microcephaly, neurologic dysfunction, hearing loss
Rubella	Visual defects, blindness, deafness, cerebral defects, seizures, jaundice, cardiovascular defects, cutaneous defects
Herpes simplex viruses	Visual defects, blindness, cerebral defects, cutaneous lesions
Varicella zoster (causes chicken-pox and shingles)	Visual defects, cerebral defects, limb defects, cutaneous lesions, extensive scarring, gastrointestinal defects, genitourinary defects
Parvovirus B19 (causes Fifth disease)	Increased risk for miscarriage, stillbirth, fetal myocarditis, hydrops fetalis (chronic fluid retention), hemolytic anemia
Lymphocytic choriomeningitis virus (LCMV)	Increased chance of miscarriage, congenital defects (rare), hydrocephalus (fluid on the brain), chorioretinitis

Note: Adenovirus, vaccinia virus, western equine encephalitis virus, human herpes type 6, measles virus, West Nile virus, Venezuelan equine encephalomyelitis virus, HIV-1 and HIV-2, and hepatitis B and C viruses, as well as enteroviruses such as Coxsackie B virus, echovirus, and poliovirus, can also cause congenital infections.

TABLE 6-2	Viruses That Initiate Infection via the Respiratory Tract That Cause Respiratory Symptoms	

Human Virus	Symptoms
Rhinovirus	Respiratory (common cold)
Coronavirus (SARS)	Respiratory
Influenzas A and B	Respiratory
Parainfluenza virus	Respiratory
Respiratory syncytial virus	Respiratory
Adenovirus	Respiratory
Echovirus (some types)	Respiratory
Cocksackie viruses A type 21 and B types 4 and 5	Respiratory
Sin nombre virus (hantavirus)	Hantavirus pulmonary syndrome (HPS)

TABLE 6-3	Viruses That Initiate Infection via the Respiratory Tract and Cause Generalized Symptoms, Usually without Respiratory Symptoms	

Human Virus	Examples of Symptoms
Mumps virus	Fever, swelling of salivary gland(s)
Measles	Cough, fever, rash
Varicella zoster	Chickenpox, shingles lesions
Hantaan virus	Hemorrhagic symptoms, kidney failure
Variola virus	Fever, malaise, headache, smallpox (deep-seated rash)
Coxsackie A16 Enterovirus 71	Hand, foot, and mouth disease

When the mucocilary defenses are not defective or compromised, a highly successful virus may initiate an infection by avoiding entrapment in the mucus, being carried to the back of the throat, and then being swallowed. If it reaches the alveolar sacs, the virus must then resist being engulfed by macrophages or survive being digested and killed by macrophages. Viruses such as influenza and rhinoviruses that can infect their hosts via the respiratory tract do so by attaching to receptors located on the ciliated epithelial cells of the respiratory tract. Tables 6-2 and 6-3 list the viruses that can initiate human infections via the respiratory tract.

■ Gastrointestinal Tract Entry

This mode of infection is known as the **oral-fecal route**. This means that viruses shed in feces have gotten into someone's mouth and are ingested with swallowed materials and then carried to the intestinal tract. In the stomach, acid and proteolytic enzymes may inactivate viruses. Successful viruses entering the gastrointestinal tract (**Figure 6-3a**) are usually resistant to acid and bile (bile is secreted by the liver).

As food is liquefied in the stomach, it is slowly released into the small intestine for further processing. The intestinal tract is protected by mucus that contains secretory IgA antibodies. The constant movement of liquefied food through the intestinal tract provides viruses in the liquid the exposure necessary for attachment to cellular receptors on the intestinal epithelial cells. (The absorptive surface area of the small intestine is roughly 250 square meters—the size of a tennis court!) This is possible because the inner surface of the small intestine is not flat. It contains villi, which are projections that are covered by epithelial cells. The epithelial cells in turn contain densely packed microvilli (Figure 6-3b). The villi contract and expand to mix the material in the intestine, which provides opportunities for virus particles to encounter living intestinal epithelial cells. The enteric viruses bind to receptors located on the epithelial cells. Examples of human viruses that infect via the gastrointestinal route are listed in Table 6-4.

Acute gastroenteritis is the major cause of morbidity and mortality worldwide. Infants and children less than five years of age average three to ten episodes per year. In the developing world, this means more than 100 million cases and three to four million deaths per year. These deaths are mainly caused by dehydration, but malnutrition also plays a very important role. As economics and sanitation improve in the developing world, the morbidity and mortality caused by diarrheal diseases decreases. Approximately 38 million cases still occur in the United States annually, resulting in over three million doctor visits, 220,000 hospitalizations, and 325 to 425 deaths per year. **Figure 6-4** shows different ways in which the oral-fecal route of transmission by viruses can occur.

■ Genital Tract Entry

Sexually transmitted diseases (STDs) are infections that can be transferred from one person to another through sexual contact. STDs have large social and economic consequences, especially in the developing parts of the world. In the United States, adolescents

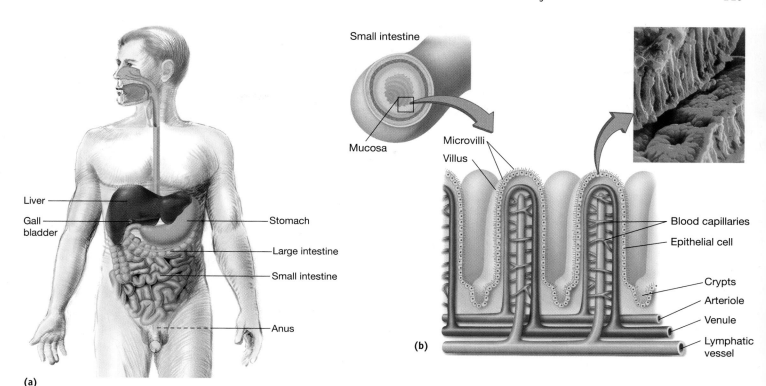

■ Figure 6-3
(a) Schematic of the gastrointestinal tract. **(b)** Panels depicting the surface area expansion of the small intestine. Note the epithelial cells that cover the villi and the microvilli of the epithelial cells.

TABLE 6-4	Viruses That Initiate Infection via the Gastrointestinal Tract
Virus	**Symptoms**
Rotavirus	*Gastroenteritis, dehydrating diarrhea, nausea, vomiting
Sapovirus	*Gastroenteritis, rotavirus-like illness in children
Norovirus	*Gastroenteritis, diarrhea, nausea, acute vomiting
Astrovirus	*Gastroenteritis, watery diarrhea (usually short in duration)
Enteric adenoviruses	*Gastroenteritis, prolonged diarrhea, nausea, vomiting
Poliovirus	Severity of symptoms vary: Mild symptoms include fever, nausea, vomiting and abdominal pain; severe symptoms include paralysis, difficulty swallowing, and muscle wasting
Hepatitis A	Short, mild flu-like illness, jaundice
Other adenoviruses	Usually symptomless
Some enteroviruses	Usually symptomless
*Inflammation of the lining of the membrane of the stomach and intestines.	

and young adults (ages 15–24) are at greatest risk for acquiring an STD. Table 6-5 lists viruses that initiate infection via the genital tract.

■ Conjunctiva Entry

The **conjunctiva** is the thin, transparent tissue that covers the outer surface of the eye. It is constantly cleansed by tear secretions and is wiped by the eyelids. It is a rare route of entry. When we get something in our eye, the conjunctiva suffers minor injuries. These injuries are susceptible to infection by viruses or other microbes through contaminated

■ **Figure 6-4**
Schematic of oral-fecal transmission of enteric viruses.

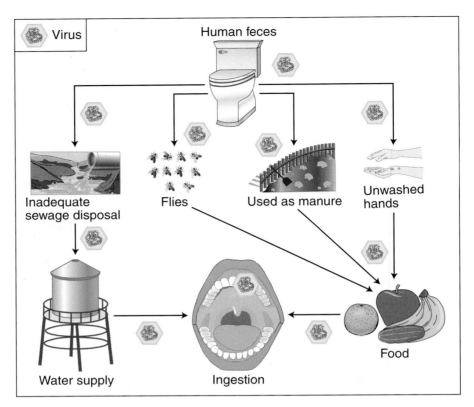

TABLE 6-5	**Examples of STDs Caused by Viruses**

Virus	Symptoms/Disease
HIV-1 and HIV-2	AIDS
Hepatitis B	Liver damage, possibly cancer
Hepatitis C	Liver damage, possibly cancer
Herpes simplex-2	Herpetic lesions of cervix and urethra
Papillomavirus	Genital warts, possibly cancer

towels, fingers, or even ophthalmologist instruments during eye exams (**iatrogenic diseases**) rather than by airborne organisms. Eye injuries from metal chips and rust are a prevalent injury among factory workers and those in similar industries. Foreign bodies in the eye can result from workers blowing into their safety glasses, goggles, welding hoods, or respirators to remove debris.

Foreign bodies in the eye are associated with a condition called epidemic keratoconjunctivitis (EKC), which is known colloquially as "shipyard eye" because of its prevalence among shipbuilders. Symptoms include the inflammation of the cornea and conjunctiva caused by an adenovirus 8 infection. It is epidemic due to the speed at which the infection spreads. Conjunctivitis, or "pink eye," is sometimes caused by enterovirus Type 70. Photographs in **Figure 6-5** show the physical signs of viral eye infections.

■ Other Routes of Entry

Other routes of virus entry include:

- skin
- transplants
- blood transfusions and blood products
- iatrogenic induction

Skin Entry

The skin is a natural barrier to microorganisms. The outside of the skin is a rather hostile environment due to its dryness, acidity, and bacterial floral. The outermost layer of skin consists of dead skin cells (**Figure 6-6**). Viruses require living cells to replicate themselves, which means that successful viruses must enter through breaks in the skin. These occur

Conjunctiva

(a)

(b)

■ **Figure 6-5**
(a) Photograph depicting the conjunctiva of the eye. Two common self-limiting forms of viral conjunctivitis are **epidemic keratoconjunctivitis** (EKC) and **pharyngoconjunctival fever** (PCF). **(b)** This image shows the pseudomembranes that can develop with EKC. These are additional membranes made up of fibrin and leukocytes caused by the body's immune response to viral antigens. An ophthalmologist can remove the pseudomembranes.

as a result of insect, animal, or human bites; needlestick injuries by doctors, tattooists, drug addicts, acupuncturists, or as a result of body piercing; puncture wounds and abrasions; and damage by a vaccinator's needle (as in cases of introduction of live vaccinia virus to vaccinate against smallpox and monkeypox). The poxvirus vaccines are administered with a bifurcated needle that is poked several times into the skin to abrase the skin during the administration of the virus—see Chapter 14. Other vaccines are administered with standard needles. In rare cases, a person can contract the disease for which they have received a vaccination, Biting arthropods such as mosquitoes, ticks, and sandflies penetrate the skin during feeding and can, therefore, introduce viruses into the body. Sometimes the mouthparts of the arthropod are contaminated with infectious virus and there is no multiplication of the virus in the arthropod. In other cases, the virus multiplies in the arthropod and is present in the saliva or in the feces of the arthropod. During feeding, the saliva is transferred to a susceptible human or animal host, or the animal defecates and the virus in the feces gains entry via the wound made by the feeding arthropod. The virus also may enter a blood capillary and thus be introduced into the vascular system.

The classical infectious disease transmitted by a biting animal is rabies. Virus is shed in the saliva of infected animals such as dogs, bats, raccoons, or skunks and is introduced into bite wounds. Table 6-6 lists examples of viruses that enter through the skin.

Viral Entry via Transplants

An increasingly common way of acquiring viral infections is from solid organ (especially of the kidneys) or bone marrow transplants. Members of the general population are often persistent asymptomatic seronegative carriers of viruses such as Epstein-Barr and cytomegalovirus (CMV). These viruses create notorious problems for the

Stratified squamous

Sensory receptors

Epidermis

Dermis

Subcutaneous layer

Vein

Hair shaft

Hair muscle

Nerve

Sweat gland

Adipose tissue

Artery

■ **Figure 6-6**
Diagram showing the layers and structures of the skin.

TABLE 6-6	Examples of Viruses That Enter Through the Skin	
Virus	**Route**	**Disease**
Papillomavirus	Minor trauma	Warts, possibly cancer
Cowpox	Minor trauma	Vesicular or nodular lesions on milkers' fingers
ORF virus	Minor trauma	Lesions on hands, arms, or face of farmers, shepherds, veterinarians
Molluscum contagiosum	Minor trauma	Firm, donut-shaped flesh-colored bumps
Herpes simplex virus	Minor trauma	Herpetic lesions on face, genitals, fingers
Hepatitises B and C	Injection	Hepatitis, possibly cancer
HIV-1 and HIV-2	Injection	AIDS
Rabies	Animal bite	Acute encephalitis
LaCrosse encephalitis virus	Mosquito bite	Encephalitis
Dengue fever	Mosquito bite	Dengue fever and Dengue hemorrhagic fever
West Nile virus	Mosquito bite	Encephalitis
Colorado tick fever virus	Tick bite	Fever, occasional encephalitis, myocarditis, or tendency to bleed
Sand fly fever virus	Sand fly bite	Fever, nausea, and vomiting
Ebola virus	Injection	Hemorrhagic fever

VIRUS FILE 6-1 | **Rabies Transmission: Human Rabies Caused by Tiny Bat Bites**

Rabies comes from the Latin *rabere*, which means "to rage or to rave." The Greeks used the term *lyssa*, ("madness") for rabies.

Human rabies cases in the Unites States are very rare. Rabies virus is transmitted via a bite from an infected animal or human. The virus replicates in muscle cells and migrates to the neurons of the nerves near the bite. It can take the virus 12 to 180 days to travel from the peripheral to the CNS. Once the virus reaches the CNS, the person exhibits the classic signs and symptoms of rabies—difficulty swallowing hydrophobia, and tremors. With the exception of the 2004 Wisconsin patient mentioned in Chapter 13, the disease at this point is fatal, and human victims usually die within 6 to 14 days.

In the past ten years, most of the fatal rabies cases in the United States have been caused by bat bites, and of these bites, most are caused by the silver-haired bat and the Mexican free-tailed bat (**Figure VF 6-1**). Bat bites feel like sharp needle jabs, but because a bat's teeth are small its bite does not always leave a detectable mark on the skin. In the following cases, bat bites were considered the probable cause: a 49-year-old man in California in 2000; a 69-year-old man in Wisconsin in 2000; a 71-year-old man in Texas in 1997, and a 13-year-old girl in Connecticut in 1995.

None of the individuals reported being bitten by a bat; however, the victims were generally too ill to provide enough accurate information about what kind of contact they had with a bat or any animal, or were not diagnosed until an autopsy was performed. In some cases, family members thought the victims may have had contact with bats in their homes or, in the case of the Texas man, at a hotel one to two months prior to hospitalization.

In cases where a victim may not have been aware of being bitten by a bat, authorities must rely on the scant information that can be obtained from others. Any bats found

(a)   (b)

■ **Figure VF 6-1**
(a) Silver-haired bat and **(b)** Mexican free-tailed bat. The majority of human rabies cases in the United States are due to bat bites, most of which are generated by these two species of bats.

in a room with an unattended child or a sleeping, intoxicated, or otherwise mentally impaired person should be caught and tested for rabies virus infection. The rabies incubation period is fairly long, so administering the vaccine immediately after a bite from a rabid animal can save the individual. In situations in which an individual cannot reasonably exclude the possibility of a bite exposure, postexposure prophylaxis should be given unless capture and testing of the animal in question yields a negative result.

References
Centers for Disease Control and Prevention. 1995. "Human rabies—Connecticut." *MMWR* 45(10):207–209.
Centers for Disease Control and Prevention. 1996. "Human rabies—Florida." 1996. *MMWR* 45(33):719–728.
Centers for Disease Control and Prevention. 1997. "Human rabies—Montana and Washington." *MMWR* 46(33):770–774.
Centers for Disease Control and Prevention. 1997. "Human rabies—Texas and New Jersey." *MMWR* 47(1):1–5.
Centers for Disease Control and Prevention. 1998. "Human rabies—Virginia." *MMWR* 48(5):95–97.
Centers for Disease Control and Prevention. 2000. "Human rabies—California, Georgia, Minnesota, New York, and Wisconsin." *MMWR* 49(49):1111–1115.
Centers for Disease Control and Prevention. 2002. "Human rabies—Tennessee." *MMWR* 51(37):828–829.
Fedler, H. M., Nelson, R., and Reiher, H. W. 1997. "Bat bite?" *Lancet* 350:1300.

immune-suppressed transplant recipient. Examples of transplant-related viral infections are listed in Table 6-7.

Transfusions and Blood Products

Before 1995, when the American Red Cross began screening donated blood, HIV, hepatitises B and C, and viral infections acquired via blood transfusions were more prevalent. Most of these infections were related to blood transfusions required during surgical procedures or contaminated blood products containing Factor VIII, a clotting factor needed by hemophiliacs. Advances in donor screening and blood testing have dramatically improved blood safety (**Figure 6-7**).

All blood donated at the American Red Cross Centers in the United States—approximately 50% of the nation's blood supply—is tested by National Testing Laboratories (NTLs)

TABLE 6-7	Examples of Viruses Associated with Transplants	
Virus	**Disease**
Cytomegalovirus	Mononucleosis, disseminated infection
Epstein-Barr virus	Mononucleosis, Burkitt's lymphoma
HIV-1 and HIV-2	AIDS
Hepatitis B and C	Hepatitis, possibly cancer
HTLV-1	Adult T-cell leukemia-lymphoma
West Nile virus	Encephalitis
Lymphocytic choriomeningitis virus infection (LCMV)	Asymptomatic or mild disease (e.g., headache, fever, chills, muscle aches; rarely meningitis)

■ **Figure 6-7**
Donated blood is taken to a transfusion center where it must undergo testing for blood-borne pathogens.

TABLE 6-8	American Red Cross Viral Disease Testing			
Virus	**Test**	**Implemented**	**Discontinued**	
HIV-1	HIV-1 antibody test	1985		
HIV-1 and HIV-2	HIV-1/2 antibody test	1992		
HIV-1	HIV-1 p24 antigen test	1996	2003	
HBV	Hepatitis B surface antigen	1971		
HBV	Hepatitis B core antigen	1987		
HCV	Anti-HCV	1990		
HTLV-1	HTLV-1 antibody test	1989		
HTLV-1 and HTLV-2	HTLV-1/2 antibody test	1998		
HCV and HIV	*NAT	1999		
West Nile virus	*NAT	2003		
*Nucleic acid testing (NAT)				

located throughout the country. These laboratories are designed to adapt to rapidly changing technology and new scientific and medical advancements (Table 6-8). Continual vigilance is critical to protecting the blood supply from known pathogens and the emergence of new infectious agents. CMV testing is per-formed on blood designated for patients who require CMV-negative blood, including organ recipients and immune-suppressed patients.

Iatrogenic Induction

Infections resulting from iatrogenic induction (in other words, infections generated by a physician) are rare. There have been reports of rabies deaths after patients received corneal transplants and other organs from donors infected with rabies. There have also been a small number of iatrogenic cases of Creutzfeldt-Jakob Disease (CJD) in patients who received contaminated pituitary growth hormone, corneas, dura mater from human cadavers, or who were operated on with contaminated neurosurgical instruments. CJD is a transmissible spongiform encephalopathy that is related to diseases caused by an unconventional agent called a **prion** (see Chapter 19, What About Prions and Viroids?).

6.2 Mechanisms of Viral Spread or Pathogenesis

The pathogenesis of many viral infections is not well understood because of our complex physiology. Humans have many specialized organs and tissues in which viruses proliferate, and in many cases viruses overcome natural barriers within the body, such as those that separate organs and tissues. Our knowledge is limited for several reasons. In some instances there is not a suitable animal model to study the pattern of viral spread. Some viruses, such as those that cause hemorrhagic fevers, must be studied in BSL-4 laboratories. Experimentation on dangerous pathogens is slow and deliberate and makes extensive investigations difficult. Lastly, some viral pathogens cannot be grown in the laboratory, which severely limits our ability to study them. Success stories include our understanding of the pattern of viral spread for a number of childhood diseases—including measles, mumps, rubella, and poliomyelitis—through the teachings and research of pioneers of viral pathogenesis such as Frank Fenner, David Bodian, and Cedric Mims.

Replication and Infection within the Host

After gaining entry into a potential host, virus replication may remain **localized** at or near the site of entry or spread to regional lymph nodes. This causes a **primary viremia**—the initial presence of the virus in the host's bloodstream—and results in the spread to other susceptible organs such as the liver and spleen. This latter type of spread to other organs is called a **systemic infection**. Tables 6-9 and 6-10 list examples of viruses that cause localized or systemic infections.

TABLE 6-9	Viruses That Cause Localized Infections
Virus	**Primary Replication Site**
Rhinovirus	Upper-respiratory tract
Rotavirus	Intestinal epithelium
Papillomavirus (warts)	Epidermis

Localized Viral Infections

A good example of a localized viral infection is the one caused by a papillomavirus. Papillomaviruses that cause warts enter the skin through an abrasion and infect cells in the basal cell layer of the epidermis. As the viral genes are expressed, the virus causes the host cell to become keratinized or thick. These cells move upward, toward the skin surface, resulting in a papilloma. Direct contact or abrasion of the papilloma can shed the virus, resulting in transmission and spread to others. In this case, papillomaviruses cause a localized infection and virus spreading is based on cell-to-cell contact.

TABLE 6-10	Viruses That Cause Systemic Infections	
Virus	**1° Replication**	**2° Replication**
Enterovirus	Intestinal epithelium	Lymphoid tissues, CNS
HSV-2	Urogenital tract	Lymphoid cells, CNS
HSV-1	Oropharynx (the throat, including the tonsils)	Lymphoid cells, CNS

Systemic Viral Infections

In addition to cell-to-cell contact, there are two main mechanisms for spread of viruses throughout the host: the bloodstream and the peripheral nervous system (PNS) (**Figure 6-8a**). The era of viral pathogenesis began with Frank Fenner's investigation of mousepox (also called infectious ectromelia), which causes a smallpox-like infection in mice.

From his experiments in 1948, Fenner was able to describe the sequential course of mousepox infection in mice. He injected mousepox into the epidermis (viral entry) of the footpads of mice and tracked the course of infection as a viremia spread to the liver and spleen. Within a few hours of mousepox injection, virus was detected in the regional lymph nodes of the mice. The entire lymphatic system flows toward the bloodstream. Its fine vessel network beneath the skin is present in all parts of the body except the central nervous system (CNS). The lymphatic system's function is to return fluids from body tissues to the blood. The lymph vessels drain **lymph**— a watery fluid that consists of water, salts, glucose, urea, proteins, and some immune cells such as lymphocytes and macrophages—from all over the body. Wherever there are lymph vessels, there are blood vessels (Figure 6-8b). The two systems work together.

The mousepox viruses in Fenner's study multiplied in the lymphoid cells of the nodes and entered the bloodstream to give a primary viremia, in which the spleen and liver were infected with virus. Prolonged viremia resulted in more spillover of virus into the bloodstream, leading to the infection of other internal organs (such as the intestines, pancreas, and salivary glands) and to the focal infection of the skin, thus causing a rash. Mousepox pathogenesis is an example of a systemic viral infection (**Figure 6-9**).

Not all infections result in a systemic infection. Within the lymph nodes present near the site of viral entry, viruses may be engulfed by macrophages (a type of immune cell) and inactivated, or the viruses may enter the bloodstream (primary viremia). Typically an infected individual develops symptoms of **malaise**—a vague feeling of bodily discomfort at the beginning of an illness—and fever during primary viremia.

If viruses enter the blood via the lymphatic system or via bites by arthropod vectors, blood transfusions, or intravenous drug abuse, they may travel free in the plasma or in association with red blood cells, platelets, lymphocytes, or monocytes. *The blood is the most*

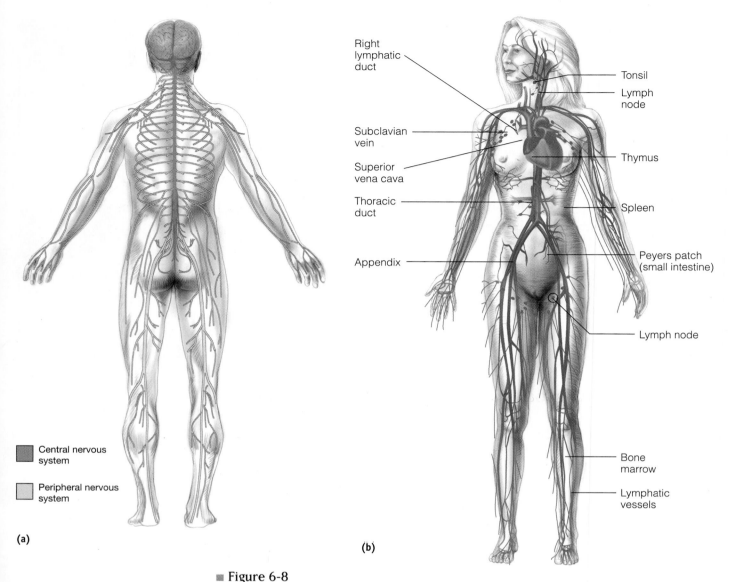

Central nervous system

Peripheral nervous system

(a)

Right lymphatic duct

Subclavian vein

Superior vena cava

Thoracic duct

Appendix

Tonsil

Lymph node

Thymus

Spleen

Peyers patch (small intestine)

Lymph node

Bone marrow

Lymphatic vessels

(b)

■ Figure 6-8

(a) Schematic distinguishing the peripheral nervous system from the central nervous system. Adapted from Morphonix, LLC, "Brain Specimens," *Journey into the Brain,* http://www.morphonix.com/software/education/science/brain/game/specimens/nervous_system.html. **(b)** The lymphatic system.

effective and rapid vehicle for the spread of virus through the body. From the blood, the virus gains access to the liver, spleen, and bone marrow, where the virus replicates again. High titers of virus are produced and many reenter the bloodstream (secondary viremia). Some viruses, such as hepatitis B, circulate in the blood. More often, the virus replicates inside of lymphocytes or macrophages before it reaches its target organ (the liver)—an **incubation period** that averages two weeks for these types of viral infections. (An incubation period is defined as the period between infection and the appearance of symptoms of the disease.)

■ Important Target Organs: The Skin

The skin is involved in many viral systemic infections. Rashes (exanthems) are produced after viruses have invaded the skin via blood vessels. Rashes have been described as macules, papules, vesicles, or pustules. A macule is a patch of skin that is discolored but not usually elevated (**Figure 6-10**). Papules are small, solid, usually inflammatory (red) elevations of the skin that do not contain pus. Vesicles are blisters on the skin containing fluid, ranging up to one centimeter in size (**Figure 6-11**). Pustules are elevations on the skin

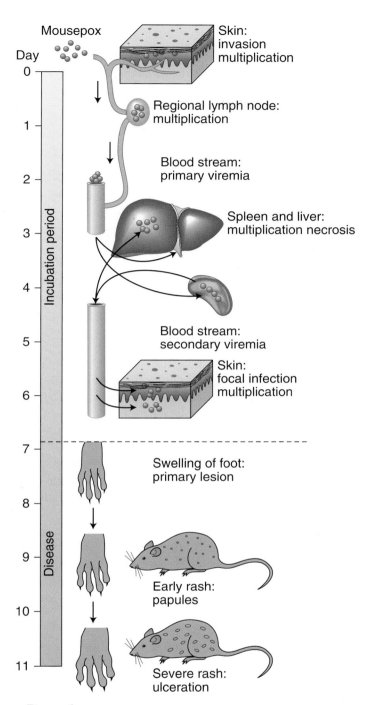

■ Figure 6-9
The dynamics of mousepox pathogenesis. (Reprinted from *The Lancet,* 262, Fenner, F., *The pathogenesis of the acute exanthems. An interpretation based on experimental investigations with mousepox,* 915–920. Copyright 1948, with permission from Elsevier.)

■ Figure 6-10
Rash caused by rubella virus (German measles). This child has the characteristic red blotchy rash on his buttocks and back during the third day of the rash.

■ Figure 6-11
Cold sore (vesicular lesion) caused by herpes simplex virus type-1.

TABLE 6-11	Examples of Viruses Associated with Skin Rashes (exanthems)

Virus	Type of Rash
Rubella (German measles)	Macular (Figure 6-10)
Dengue fever virus	Macular
Measles	Maculopapular
Herpes simplex virus	Vesicular (Figure 6-11)
Herpes zoster (causes chickenpox and shingles)	Vesicular
Coxsackie virus	Vesicular
Enterovirus	Vesicular

containing pus. Table 6-11 lists some examples associated with skin rashes. A rash that affects mucous membranes may accompany some viral infections.

■ Important Target Organs: The Lungs and the Liver

Most respiratory infections are caused by the localized spread of respiratory viruses such as rhinoviruses (the viruses that cause the common cold). Sometimes a virus that can cause a systemic infection may infect the lungs; for example, both measles and varicella zoster viruses (the latter of which causes chickenpox and shingles) may cause pneumonia in patients whose immunity is compromised. Almost any organ may be infected via the bloodstream with some kind of virus. Clearly, viruses that infect the lungs, brain, heart, and liver and causing pneumonia, encephalitis, myocarditis, and hepatitis are the most life-threatening viral infections.

Viruses that infect the liver, such as the hepatitis viruses, can cause severe hepatitis. This could potentially result in a life-threatening situation. Hepatitises B and C infections can lead to chronic carrier-state infections that may eventually result in hepatocellular (liver) cancer. Besides the hepatitis viruses, other viruses that produce systemic infections—such as yellow fever, rubella, mumps, CMV, Epstein-Barr, and herpes simplex viruses—may damage the liver.

Only a few viruses infect the kidneys or heart. CMV and hantaviruses can infect the kidneys. Coxsackie B viruses may infect the heart and are also implicated as a cause of juvenile-onset insulin-dependent diabetes mellitus type-1 (T1D), which results from the destruction of pancreatic beta cells. The development of diabetes in twins is only about 40%, suggesting an environmental factor plays a role in this disease. To date, 14 different viruses have been reported to be associated with the development of T1D in humans and animals.

■ Neurotropic Viruses

Neurotropic viruses are viruses that infect the nervous system. In reality, though, most neurotropic viruses infect other types of cells as well; for example, herpes simplex viruses I and II can replicate in epidermal cells as well as macrophages of the dermis. The first neurons to be infected are located in the PNS. Poliovirus, herpes simplex viruses I and II, varicella zoster, and rabies viruses are examples of neurotropic viruses. (In fact, rabies virus spreads only through a neural route.) Once in the peripheral nervous system, the viruses can spread to other neurons to the spinal cord and to the brain with devastating results. **Figure 6-12** illustrates an infection by varicella zoster. Herpes zoster virus replicates in a variety of cell types as well as in neurons.

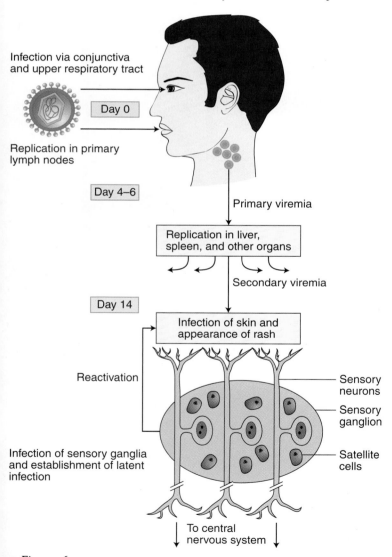

■ Figure 6-12

Pathogenesis of varicella zoster virus. Adapted from Flint, S. J., et al. *Principles of Virology: Molecular Biology, Pathogenesis, and Control of Animal Viruses*, Second Edition. ASM Press, 2003.

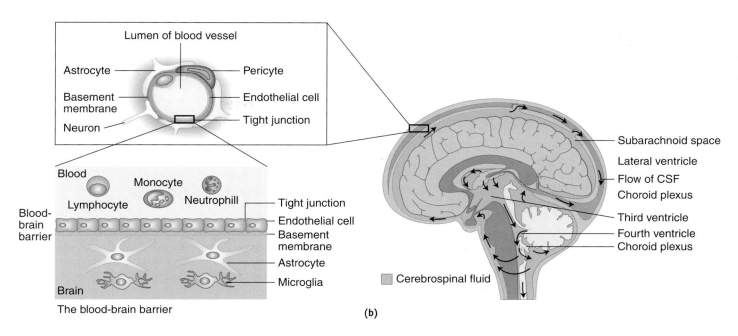

■ **Figure 6-13**
Cross-section through the blood-brain barrier. **(a)** Epithelial cells tightly line the capillaries of the brain, forming the blood-brain barrier between the astrocytes and microglia of the brain. Adapted from K. Francis, et al., *Expert Rev. Mol. Med.* 5 (2003): 1–19. **(b)** Vertical cross-section of the brain showing the choroid plexus, which produces the cerebrospinal fluid (CSF) that is found within the ventricles of the brain and in the subarachnoid space around the brain and spinal cord.

CNS Entry: Crossing the Blood-Brain Barrier

In 1885, bacteriologist Paul Erhlich used aniline dyes to stain and thus visualize fine structures of cells. He discovered that when he injected aniline dye into an animal, all of the internal organ systems except the brain would stain. Later, in 1913, his graduate student Edwin Goldwin injected trypan blue dye directly into the cerebrospinal fluid of rabbits and dogs and discovered that only the brain became stained. The combination of these two experiments demonstrated the existence of a "barrier" between the brain and the other internal organs—the **blood-brain barrier**.

The blood-brain barrier exists at the interface between the bloodstream and CNS tissues. It is semi-permeable. Most large molecules, including toxins and viruses are prevented from crossing it. Thus, the blood-brain barrier protects the brain from potentially toxic substances or microbes. It also makes it difficult for therapeutics used to treat chemical imbalances to cross this barrier. The blood-brain barrier does have transport systems that move the substances the brain needs across the barrier and into brain tissue (**Figure 6-13**).

The anatomical basis of the blood-brain barrier was deciphered using electron microscopy in the 1960s. It revealed a vast capillary network surrounding the brain. It is made up of epithelial cells with tight junctions (Figure 6-12a). In the human brain, there are approximately 400 miles of these capillaries totaling a surface area of approximately 100 square feet.

How do viral infections spread from the blood to the brain?

In several parts of the brain such as the choroid plexus, the capillary endothelium is fenestrated (has window-like openings) and the basement membrane is sparse (Figure 6-12b). During viremia, mumps and some togaviruses pass through the capillary epithelium into the choroid plexus and then enter the cerebralspinal fluid that is produced by the choroid plexus. Other viruses (e.g. poliovirus and some togaviruses) may directly

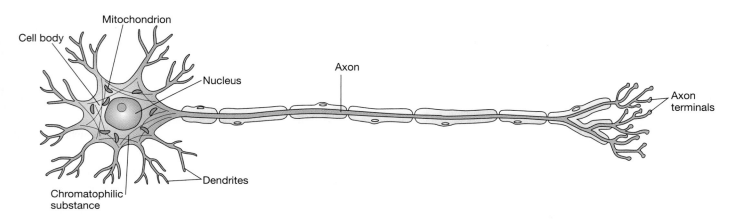

■ Figure 6-14

Structure of neurons. Neurons have three basic parts: the cell body, the axon, and the dendrites or nerve endings. The cell body contains the major portion of the cell, which includes the dendrites and nucleus. Axons transmit the signals. Viruses can only replicate in the cell body because that is where the cellular protein synthesis machinery is located.

infect or be transported across the capillary endothelium. Some viruses such as HIV and measles virus cross the endothelium within infected monocytes or lymphocytes.

Neural Entry

Viruses gain access to the CNS via three different routes: via the nerves connecting the PNS of the body to the CNS, via the olfactory nerves, or via the bloodstream during viremia (discussed earlier). Some viruses can enter via one or more of these routes. There is limited knowledge available as to how viruses move in and among the cells of the CNS.

The structure of neurons is much different than that of other cells. They are polarized, possessing two structurally distinct ends: the axon and dendrites (**Figure 6-14**). Neurons transmit electrochemical signals over long distances up to several feet and pass messages to each other. Protein synthesis does not occur in the axon of the neuron, hence, the virus needs to travel long distances to reach their site of replication; for example, in the adult human, axons that control the stomach muscles can be as far as 20 inches away from the cell bodies and dendrites in the brain stem.

6.3   Patterns of Diseases

There are four basic patterns of viral infections; the specific variations among them will be discussed in detail in later chapters. The four patterns are:

- acute, nonpersistent infection
- acute infection, followed by persistent latent infection
- chronic infection with continuous shedding of virus
- slow infection

Most **acute viral infections** are self-limiting. These diseases have symptoms of sudden onset or last a short time as with rhinoviruses, which cause the common cold), as opposed to a chronic infection in which virus is continually shed and the disease symptoms may or may not be present. **Persistent infections with acute onset** are characteristic of DNA viruses. The chronic state of infection occurs due to a phenomenon termed **latency**. A latent infection is dormant or "concealed," and infectious virus particles are not detected unless the virus is reactivated.

Latency is the hallmark of herpes viruses. Virtually 100% of adults have antibodies in their serum against herpes simplex virus type 1, the causative agent of cold sores. Most individuals become infected in the first few years of life and the virus establishes lifelong

TABLE 6-12	Examples of Latent Infections		
Virus	**Primary Disease**	**Reactivated Disease**	**Site of Latency**
Herpes simplex virus-1	Oral herpes/cold sores	Recurrent herpes simplex	Neurons in the sensory ganglia
Herpes simplex virus-2	Genital herpes	Recurrent genitalis	Neurons in the sensory ganglia
Varicella zoster	Chickenpox	Shingles	Neurons in the sensory ganglia
Epstein-Barr virus	Mononucleosis	Burkitt's lymphoma, nasopharyngeal carcinoma	B lymphocytes
Cytomegalovirus	Subclinical (except in fetus and immunocompromised)	Subclinical (except in fetus and immunocompromised)	B lymphocytes
Hepatitis B	Hepatitis	Liver cancer	Hepatocytes
Papillomavirus	Warts	Warts and carcinomas	Epithelium (skin)
HIV-1 and HIV-2	Seroconversion illness	AIDS and AIDS dementia	T lymphocytes, macrophages, brain cells

latency and may be reactivated at any time. This persist latent state occurs because the viral DNA remains present in the form of an **episome** (a circular molecule of DNA, independent of the host chromosome) in the nucleus of neurons. (Read more about herpes viruses in Chapter 15, Herpesviruses.) Reactivation of latent herpes viruses can be lethal in immunocompromised individuals (for example, in AIDs or organ-transplant patients). Examples of latent viral infections are listed in Table 6-12.

A handful of virus pathogens are **chronic persistent infections**, which are characterized by continuous virus production that lasts at least six months. Hepatitises B and C are the most important chronic viral infections of humans. The hepatitises B and C virus particles are found in plasma, genital secretions, and saliva. Approximately 20% to 40% of individuals chronically infected with hepatitis B will develop chronic liver inflammation. Over a period of years this chronic inflammation leads to cirrhosis (scarring) of the liver and liver failure, or to hepatocellular carcinoma (liver cancer). An effective vaccine is now available to prevent hepatitis B virus infection. Unfortunately, vaccines cannot help those who are already chronically infected (**Figure 6-15a**).

Hepatitis C infection is the most common cause of chronic hepatitis and there is no vaccine for it. Approximately 85% of acute infections become chronic. As with hepatitis B, infections with hepatitis C can result in liver inflammation, cirrhosis, and hepatocellular carcinoma. In the United States, hepatitis C is the leading specific cause of liver failure requiring liver transplantation (Figure 6-15b).

Slow infections are those that have long incubation periods (measured in years). These types of infections lead to slow, progressive diseases. HIV and another group of unclassified infectious agents called *prions* fall into this category. Prions cause transmissible spongiform encephalopathies (TSEs) such as bovine spongiform encephalopathy (BSE), a fatal brain disease in cattle commonly referred to as mad cow disease. There is a similar disease to BSE in humans called new variant Creutzfeldt-Jakob Disease (vCJD).

There is strong laboratory and epidemiological evidence that vCJD is associated with BSE. It is believed that people become afflicted with the vCJD form by eating contaminated

■ **Figure 6-15**
(a) Global distribution of chronic hepatitis B infection in millions. The estimated total chronic HBV infections worldwide is more than 350 million.**(b)** Global distribution of chronic hepatitis C infection in millions. The estimated total chronic HCV infections worldwide is 170 million. Data from World Health Organization hepatitis C prevalence, 2000 and United Nations global population.

(a)

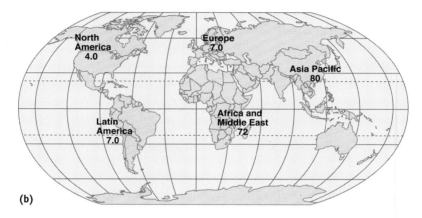

(b)

beef products from BSE-infected cows. This disease was first diagnosed in the United Kingdom, where the majority of cases occur, but cases exist worldwide. Many of the cases in other countries, though, are in individuals who resided in the United Kingdom during its BSE outbreak between 1980 and 1996. Those at increased risk for vCJD infection are individuals who lived in the United Kingdom during this time. Table 6-13 lists definite and probable CJD cases in the United Kingdom through April 2005.

The United States reported its first case of vCJD in 2002. The patient was born in the United Kingdom and moved to Florida in 1992. It is believed that she consumed BSE contaminated food before moving to the United States.

6.4 Virus Exit: Shedding

How do viruses get from one host to the next? How are virus infections maintained in populations? Viruses are in general shed from their routes of entry, usually body openings or surfaces. These are the primary infection sites. With the exception of the CNS, viruses can be shed effectively from all other main parts of the body; for example, viruses that invade the respiratory tract are shed in mucus and saliva during coughing, sneezing, and talking. Viruses that infect the gut are shed in the feces. Sexually transmited viruses are shed via semen, cervical secretions, breast milk, and saliva.

Viruses that enter the skin through abrasions and direct contact of lesions are shed via direct contact with the lesions. The fluid in herpes virus lesions contains large numbers of infectious virus particles; papillomaviruses and herpesviruses are examples of other viruses that infect skin cells. Some viruses that produce rashes, such as measles, are not spread

| TABLE 6-13 | Definite and Probable CJD Cases in the United Kingdom: Referrals of Suspect CJD and Deaths of Definite and Probable CJD |

Year	Referrals	Sporadic Cases	Iatrogenic	Familial	GSS	vCJD	Total Deaths
1990	53	28	5	0	0	–	33
1991	75	32	1	3	0	–	36
1992	96	45	2	5	1	–	53
1993	78	37	4	3	2	–	46
1994	118	53	1	4	3	–	61
1995	87	35	4	2	3	3	47
1996	134	40	4	2	4	10	60
1997	161	60	6	4	1	10	81
1998	154	63	3	4	1	18	89
1999	170	62	6	2	0	15	85
2000	178	50	1	2	1	28	82
2001	179	58	4	3	2	20	87
2002	163	72	0	4	1	17	94
2003	162	77	5	4	2	18	106
2004	114	51	2	4	1	9	67
2005	123	65	3	7	6	5	86
2006	110	63	1	6	3	5	78
2007*	67	22	2	0	1	3	28
Total	2222	915	54	58	33	161	1221

*As of 8/06/2007. Familial cases have genetic links to the disease. Gerstmann-Sträussler-Scheinker disease (GSS) is an inherited prion disease.

via skin lesions; for example, measles is spread by droplets in the air containing virus that is breathed out through the nose and mouth when coughing and sneezing

A few human viruses, such as cytomegalovirus and mumps virus, replicate in epithelial cells of the kidney and are shed in the urine. Thus they are not a major mode of human-to-human transmission. Rodents infected with hantaviruses and arenaviruses (the causative agent of hemorrhagic fevers) shed viruses in urine, thus contaminating the environment. As noted in Chapter 1, sin nombre virus, the hantavirus that causes hantavirus pulmonary syndrome (HPS), is a deadly disease transmitted by infected rodents through urine, droppings, or saliva. Humans can contract the disease when they breathe in aerosolized virus, so rodent control in and around the home remains the primary strategy for preventing hantavirus infection.

Lastly, viruses can be spread through blood during viremia. Hepatitises B and C, HIV, and HTLV-1 can be spread via contaminated blood or blood products during blood transfusions or among intravenous drug users via contaminated needles. Diseases transmitted by arthropods such as mosquitoes are transmitted between hosts via blood.

■ No Virus Exit

Viruses infecting the brain are not actually shed from the brain. How, then, can such a virus be perpetuated in the environment? The answer is that the primary sites of replication for most brain viruses are other internal organs; for example, rabies virus transmitted by contact with infected saliva.

TABLE 6-14	Nonenveloped Virus Survival				
Virus	**Type of Sample**	**Log10 Reduction**	**Time**	***Temperature**	**pH**
Rotavirus	Tap water	2	64 days	20°C	8
Rotavirus	Distilled water	1	<1 hour	NA	8
Rotavirus	River water	2–3	64 days	20°C	7.4
Rotavirus	Feces	3	13 days	20°C	NA
Rotavirus	Feces	2	33 days	4°C	NA
Hepatitis A	Mixed human and pig wastes	NA	5 weeks	NA	NA
Hepatitis A	Mineral water	6	330 days	24°C	7
Norovirus	Surface water	NA	4 months	0–4°C	NA
Poliovirus type 1	Septic tank effluent	1.5	28 days	20°C	NA
Poliovirus type 1	Raw sewage	2	45 minutes	20°C	NA
Poliovirus type 1	Freshwater	0.7	4 days	24°C	NA
Poliovirus type 1	Seawater	1.5–4	4 days	24°C	NA
Foot and mouth disease virus	Feces	NA	21–103 days	NA	NA
Rhinovirus type 2	In cell culture medium on skin surface	0.1	3 hours	NA	NA
Rhinovirus type 2	In cell culture medium on plastic surface	<0.5	24 hours	NA	NA
Rhinovirus type 2	In cell culture medium on stainless steel surface	1	24 hours	NA	NA

*20°C = 68°F (~ room temperature). NA: Not available.

Adapted from *Virus Survival in the Environment with Special Attention to Survival in Sewage Droplets and other Environmental Media of Fecal or Respiratory Origin 2003* by Mark D. Sobsey and John Scott Meschke, World Health Organization Meeting 23–25 September 2003, Rome, Italy.

6.5 Environmental Survival of Virus

Virus transmission is dependent upon how well the virus survives the harsh environment outside of a host. Factors that affect virus survival in the environment are the composition of the virus (enveloped viruses are more sensitive to degradation than naked viruses), whether the viruses are present in human and animal wastes (organic matter protects the virus), and temperature, humidity, and pH. Tables 6-14 and 6-15 list different kinds of viruses, their environmental conditions in an experimental setting, and their survival times as recorded from numerous pilot scale or field studies.

6.6 Human Viruses in a Water Environment

Environmental (water) virology is a separate scientific discipline and began with efforts to detect poliovirus in water in the 1950s. Human enteric (intestinal) viruses enter the environment via sewage-contaminated water. Humans may be exposed to these viruses through consumption of undercooked shellfish grown in contaminated waters, food crops

TABLE 6-15	Enveloped Virus Survival				

Virus	Type of Sample	Log10 Reduction	Time	*Temperature	pH
Herpes simplex virus type 1	Saliva on chrome tap handle	3	2 hours	23°C	7
Herpes simplex virus	Tap water	3	4 hours	37–40°C	6.8
Herpes simplex type 1	Artificial tears opthalmic solution	3	5 days	NA	NA
Herpes simplex type 1	In saliva on penny	6	2 hours	22°C	NA
Herpes simplex type 1	In saliva on glass	3	2 hours	22°C	NA
HIV (LAV strain)	Saliva (maintained wet or dried)	Stable	4 days	20°C	NA
HIV (LAV strain)	50% human plasma	NA	>15 days	20°C	NA
Yellow fever virus	Plasma	NA	90 minutes	27°C	NA
Vaccinia virus	Cell culture suspension on cotton surface	4–5	6–10 weeks	25°C	NA
Hepatitis B	Blood on stainless steel and cotton swabs	0.2	14 days	25°C	NA
Respiratory syncytial virus	In sterile water on countertops	4	45 minutes	NA	NA
SARS-CoV	Feces	NA	>2 days	NA	NA
SARS-CoV	Urine	NA	>24 hours	20°C	NA
SARS-CoV	Virus in 75% ethanol	NA	Less than 5 minutes	20°C	NA

*20°C = 68°F (~ room temperature). NA: Not available.

Adapted from *Virus Survival in the Environment with Special Attention to Survival in Sewage Droplets and other Environmental Media of Fecal or Respiratory Origin 2003* by Mark D. Sobsey and John Scott Meschke, World Health Organization Meeting 23–25 September 2003, Rome, Italy.

grown using wastewater for irrigation or human sewage as fertilizer, and sewage-polluted recreational and drinking water. Shellfish are filter feeders and tend to concentrate viruses and bacteria in their edible tissues. A method used by Bergh and his colleagues at the University of Bergen (Norway) in 1989 to quantitate virus particle in natural unpolluted waters found that up to 2.5×10^8 virus particles per milliliter in natural waters. Most of the particles in the samples were bacteriophages but include some algal viruses as well.

Feces of infected individuals contain extremely high numbers of virus particles. One gram of stool from an infected individual contains 10^5 to 10^{11} virus particles. Over 100 virus species have been found in sewage-contaminated waters. These viruses can cause hepatitis, gastroenteritis, meningitis, fever, rash, conjunctivitis, and perhaps diabetes.

As a general rule, viruses persist longer than enteric bacteria in the water. Studies have shown that waterborne outbreaks related to potable water actually met bacteriological standards. Thus it is unsafe to rely on bacteriological standards to assess the virological quality of any kind of water. In water in a natural setting, the conditions are always changing because water is always changing. Environmental virologists are faced with the challenge of applying techniques that work on clinical isolates in natural settings. Surveying viral contamination in surface and ground water has bridged the environmental and clinical virology laboratories to improve public health.

Summary

Viruses infect animals and humans by preferred routes of entry. These routes of entry occur through

- the respiratory tract
- the gastrointestinal tract
- the genital tract
- the conjunctiva
- crossing the placenta to reach the fetus
- the skin (through breaks, abrasions, and bites)
- transplants
- blood and blood product transfusions
- iatrogenic induction.

Upon entry, viruses remain localized or cause systemic infections by spreading throughout the body via

- the bloodstream
- the peripheral nervous system
- the lymphatic system
- organs such as the liver
- crossing the blood-brain barrier
- the CNS.

The pathogenesis of infection is unique to each viral pathogen. There are four basic patterns of viral infections: acute, persistent latent infections, chronic infections, and slow infections. Viruses exit (shed) into the environment through mucus, saliva, feces, semen, cervical secretions, breast milk, skin lesions, urine, and blood. Viruses do not exit from the brain but instead are shed from a primary replication site and from internal organs.

Virus stability in the environment varies depending upon the chemical composition of the virus and whether or not it is protected in organic matter such as feces, or by temperature, humidity, and pH. Today, more attention has been placed on environmental virology. Many viruses can be found in water, leading to waterborne disease outbreaks. Molecular methods are being used to monitor aquatic environments to improve public health.

Chapter 7 will address host resistance to viral infection. This will cover physiological factors affecting resistance to viral infection, the interferon response, and immune responses toward viral infection. Vaccines and artificially induced immunity also will be discussed.

Resources

Primary Literature and Reviews

Bergh, O. et al. 1989. "High abundance of viruses found in aquatic environments." *Nature* 340:467–468.

Bosch, A. 1998. "Human enteric viruses in the water environment: A minireview." *Internatl Microbiol* 1:191–196.

Centers for Disease Control and Prevention. 2002. "Probable variant Creutzfeldt-Jakob disease in U.S. resident—Florida." *MMWR* 51(41):927–929.

Centers for Disease Control and Prevention. 2005. "Infection in organ transplant recipients—Massachusetts, Rhode Island, 2005." *MMWR* 54:1–2.

Chamberland, M. E., Alter, H. J., Busch, M. P., Nemo, G., and Ricketts, M. 2001. "Emerging infectious disease issues in blood safety." *EID* 7(3): Suppl 552–553.

Chin, J., ed. 2000. *Control of Communicable Diseases Manual: An Official Report of the American Public Health Association*, 17th ed. Washington, DC: American Public Health Association.

Cohen, J., and Powderly, W. G., eds. 2004. *Infectious Diseases*, 2nd ed. Philadelphia: Mosby.

Francis. K., et al. 2003. "Innate immunity and brain inflammation: The key role of complement." *Exp Rev Mol Med* Vol. 5, DOI:10.1017/S1462399403006252.

Nelson, R., and Reiher, H. W. 1997. "Bat bite?" *Lancet* 350:1300.

Jun, H. S., and Yoon, J. W. 2003. "A new look at viruses in type 1 diabetes." *Diabetes Metab Res Rev* 19(1):8–31.

Mims, C., Nash, A., and Stephen, J., eds. 2001. *Mims' Pathogenesis of Infectious Disease*, 5th ed. San Diego: Elsevier Academic Press.

Nathanson, N., ed. 2002. *Viral Pathogenesis and Immunity*. Philadelphia: Lippincott Williams & Wilkins.

Reuter, J. D., Gomez, D. L., Wilson, J. H., and Van Den, P. 2004. "Systemic immune deficiency necessary for cytomegalovirus invasion of the mature brain." *Virology* 78(3):1473–1487.

Rhode Island Hospital et al. 2005. "Lymphocytic choriomeningitis virus infection in organ transplant recipients—Massachusetts, Rhode Island, 2005." *MMWR* 54:1–2.

Wong, K. 2002. "Oral drugs halt smallpoxlike viruses in mice." *Scientific American News,* March 2002.

◼ Popular Press

Ewald, P. W. 2002. *Plague Time: The New Germ Theory of Disease*. New York: Anchor.

Finley, D. 1998. *Mad Dogs: The New Rabies Plague*. College Station, TX: Texas A&M University Press.

Gould, T. 1995. *A Summer Plague: Polio and Its Survivors*. New Haven: Yale University Press.

Mims, C. 2000. *When We Die*. New York: St. Martin's Griffin.

Schwartz, M. 2003. *How the Cows Turned Mad*. Berkley and Los Angeles: University of California Press.

◼ Video Productions

Hepatitis, Cytomegalovirus, and Epstein-Barr Virus. 1999. Films for the Humanities.

New Blood. 2002. Films for the Humanities.

Tainted Blood. 2002. Films for the Humanities.

Childhood Exanthems: Measles, Chickenpox & Scarlet Fever. 2004. Medivision Film Series.

Dog Bites and Rabies Prevention. 2004. Medivision Film Series.

◼ eLearning

http://biology.jbpub.com/book/virology

The site features eLearning, an online review area that provides quizzes and other tools to help you study for your class. You can also follow useful links for in-depth information, or just find out the latest virology and microbiology news.

CASE STUDY QUESTIONS

These questions relate to the Case Study presented at the beginning of the chapter.

1. The New York City Department of Health and Mental Hygiene (DOHMH) issued a health advisory alert in February 2005 to begin tracing the man's sexual contacts. Why?

   HIV enters CD4+ T-cells by binding to CD4+ using a viral protein called gp120. The CD4+ cellular protein receptor alone is not enough to allow viral entry into cells. The virus must interact with a second host protein or **co-receptor**. This co-receptor may be different for different types of cells. One is called CCR5 and another is called CXCR4 or fusin. CCR5 is present on T-cells and macrophages. Fusin is primarily found on CD4+ cells. **Figure CS 6-1** shows HIV binding to host cells.

   CCR5 appears to be important for viral entry during the early stages of HIV infection. In contrast, cells expressing CXCR4 appear to be important for the entry of HIV strains that are prevalent in individuals with a more aggressive disease during the later stages of infection. Individuals who inherit a defective CCR5 gene are resistant to HIV infection. The multidrug-resistant HIV variant from this patient was able to infect cells with both CCR5 and CXCR4 co-receptors. In fact, the viral population from the patient consisted of CCR5- and CXCR4-tropic viruses of approximately equal proportions.

2. If this patient inherited a defective CCR5 co-receptor, would that help to explain his rapid decline in health?

3. The patient did not inherit a defective CCR5 co-receptor. Speculate as to why the viral populations in his body were so aggressive.

■ **Figure CS 6-1**

Illustration of an HIV virus particle binding to the CD4+ receptor and a chemokine receptor CCR5 or CXCR4. Adapted from Project Inform, "Co-Receptors: CCR5-Understanding HIV," *The Body: The Complete HIV/AIDS Resource,* http://www.thebody.com/content/art4978.html#ccr5.

ADDITIONAL CASE STUDY

Eighteen-year-old Joseph Spencer, a high school varsity swimmer at a school in Oregon suddenly became ill with a fever, chills, and vomiting. His mother took him to the local hospital emergency room, where he was placed in an intensive care unit (ICU), sedated and on a ventilator. Joseph spent 18 days in the hospital and then was able to return home. Even after weeks of bed rest and physical therapy, he suffered from breathing problems.

Joseph was 1 of 140 individuals who were confirmed as suffering from an adenovirus serotype 14 (Ad14) infection during March to June of 2007. The CDC, U.S. Air Force, and state and local public health departments identified clusters of patients infected with Ad14 in Oregon, Washington, and Texas. Of these patients, 53 (38%) were hospitalized, 24 (17%) were placed in ICU, and 9 (5%) died of pneumonia. Ad14 was first isolated and identified in Holland in 1955. It caused sporadic outbreaks in Europe and Asia but not the Western hemisphere. To date, 51 adenovirus serotypes have been identified. These adenoviruses typically cause benign ailments such as colds, pinkeye, bronchitis, and stomach flu. The cases described here are unusual and were life-threatening. Doctors do not routinely test for adenoviruses. Recent surveys, including those on military bases, indicate that the virus suddenly appeared widely across the United States.

1. How would you determine if some people are genetically prone to Ad14 infection or have weaker immune systems to fight this infection versus being infected with a virus that is inherently more dangerous? What type of analysis would determine if Ad14 had mutated from the original 1955 strain?

2. Adenoviruses are shed in respiratory secretions and feces. They can persist for weeks on environmental surfaces. Would the stability of these viruses in the environment pose a challenge in controlling adenoviruses outbreaks? Why or why not?

■ References

Metgar, D. et al. 2007. "Abrupt Emergence of Diverse Species B Adenoviruses at US Military Recruit Training Centers." *JID* 196:1465–1473.

Oregon Department of Human Services et al. 2007. "Acute Respiratory Disease Associated with Adenovirus Serotype 14—Four States, 2006–2007." *MMWR* 56(45):1181–1184.

Development and healing of smallpox rash skin lesions in a 9-month-old unvaccinated child. From left to right, photographs of the child were taken on days 2, 4, 7, 13, and 20 of the disease. This boy has survived a smallpox infection and has now developed a natural immunity toward the smallpox virus.

CHAPTER

7

Host Resistance to Viral Infections

> **"**That which does not kill you makes you stronger.**"**
>
> *Viktor Frankl*

One day Sally Cronn's college roommate purchased a hamster at the local pet store. Sally was fond of pets, but was slightly uneasy about the purchase because she recalled hearing about a hamster virus that killed three organ transplant recipients in 2005 (**Figure CS 7-1**). Sally asked her roommate if she knew anything about hamster viruses. The roommate responded, "I find it hard to believe that such a cute, furry, little pet hamster could cause the spread of a deadly virus," which increased Sally's concern.

Sally, a microbiology major with an interest in viruses, decided to research the hamster virus that infected the organ transplant recipients. Within the June 3, 2005 issue of the *Morbidity and Mortality Weekly Report* published by the Centers for Disease Control and Prevention (CDC) she found an article that described the epidemiological investigation regarding the deaths of four of the transplant recipients.

The organ donor had a history of high blood pressure and died suddenly of a stroke. Family members consented to donating her organs, and her liver, lungs, kidneys, and corneas were removed. Within three weeks of transplantation, the four individuals who received the kidneys, liver, and lungs experienced various symptoms, such as abnormal liver functioning, kidney failure, fever, rash, diarrhea, and hypoxia (an absence of oxygen in tissues). Three of the four transplant recipients died approximately three weeks after receiving a donor organ. Interestingly, the two donors who received corneas were asymptomatic.

After extensive diagnostic testing, public health officials suspected that the solid organ recipient deaths were caused by a transplant-transmitted infection. Tissue and blood samples from the donor and recipients were sent to the CDC. Subsequently, a lymphocytic choriomeningitis virus (LCMV) infection was identified as the cause of illness of all four solid organ transplant recipients. About 5% of common house mice, hamsters, and other rodents carry LCMV and 2% to 5% of the general population has antibodies against the virus. Hospital staff, organ bank staff, and family members of the donor and recipients were interviewed to determine the source of LCMV. Family members of the donor revealed that a pet hamster had been acquired recently and that there were limited opportunities for the donor to be exposed to wild rodents.

■ **Figure CS 7-1**
Wild and pet rodents can carry viruses that may infect humans.

■ References

Barton, L. L., Peters, C. J., and Ksiazek, T. G. 1995. "Lymphocytic Choriomeningitis Virus: An Unrecognized Teratogenic Pathogen." *EID* 1(4):153–153.

Childs, J. E., et al. 1991. "Human-Rodent Contact and Infection with Lymphocytic Choriomeningitis and Seoul Viruses in an Inner-City Population." *Am J Trop Med Hyg* 44(2):117–121.

Childs, J. E., et al. 1992. "Lymphocytic Choriomeningitis Virus Infection and House Mouse (Mus Musculus) Distribution in Urban Baltimore." *Am J Trop Med Hyg* 47(1):27–34.

Gregg, M. B. 1975. "Recent Outbreaks of Lymphocytic Choriomeningitis in the United States of America." *Bull World Health Organ* 52:549–553.

Rhode Island Hospital et al. 2005. "Lymphocytic Choriomeningitis Virus Infection in Organ Transplant Recipients—Massachusetts, Rhode Island." *MMWR* 54(21):537–539.

Rousseau, M. C., et al. 1997. "Lymphocytic Choriomeningitis Virus in Southern France: Four Case Reports and a Review of the Literature." *Eur J Epidemiology* 13:817–823.

http://www.health.state.ri.us/media/050523b.php.

LCMV FAQS Lymphocytic Choriomeningitis, http://www.cdc.gov/ncidod/dvrd/spb/mnpages/dispages/lcmv.htm.

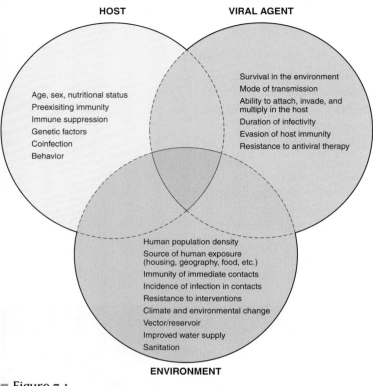

HOST

Age, sex, nutritional status
Preexisiting immunity
Immune suppression
Genetic factors
Coinfection
Behavior

VIRAL AGENT

Survival in the environment
Mode of transmission
Ability to attach, invade, and
multiply in the host
Duration of infectivity
Evasion of host immunity
Resistance to antiviral therapy

Human population density
Source of human exposure
(housing, geography, food, etc.)
Immunity of immediate contacts
Incidence of infection in contacts
Resistance to interventions
Climate and environmental change
Vector/reservoir
Improved water supply
Sanitation

ENVIRONMENT

■ **Figure 7-1**

Triad model of disease causation. Adapted from M. Bitzer, et al., "A Comprehensive Guide to Corn Management in Kentucky," *University of Kentucky, College of Agriculture Online Publications,* http://www.ca.uky.edu/agc/pubs/id/id139/ID139%20htm.HTM.

E ach pathogen has its own infection strategy, resulting in the development of a disease with distinct symptoms. Upon viral entry, the infected host elicits a number of responses toward infection. This chapter will discuss factors that affect host resistance and host defenses. It will include nonspecific host defenses such as the interferon response and specific immune responses (antibody production and cell-mediated immunity).

The **epidemiological triad model** of disease shows the interactions among the host, agent, and environment that produce disease (**Figure 7-1**). Prevention efforts can be directed toward any or all of the three different elements depending upon the disease in question and what type of intervention is available and appropriate.

7.1   Physiological Factors and Barriers Affecting Resistance

The triad model dictates that the condition of the host impacts its susceptibility to viral infection. There are several physiological factors and barriers that affect resistance to viral infection. These factors include but are not limited to:

- age
- nutrition
- hormones
- fever
- genetic factors
- dual infections
- species resistance

■ Age

Newborns and the elderly are the most vulnerable to viral infections, and they tend to experience the severest symptoms while infected. Newborns are protected from common viral infections immediately after birth through antibodies passed to them from their mothers. These antibodies decline rapidly in the first few months of life, though, as the newborn begins to develop its own immune system. During this period, viral infections are frequently seen in infants. Elderly individuals become vulnerable to infection as their immune systems decline with age.

Shingles is often a disease of the elderly. It is caused by varicella zoster, the same virus that causes chickenpox. After someone is infected with chickenpox, the virus DNA remains in the nuclei of sensory (skin) neurons. The virus becomes reactivated when the immune system is weakened due to aging, severe illness, or long-term use of corticosteroids. When the immune system cannot suppress the dormant virus any longer, the virus infection becomes productive again, causing an infection along the nerve (**Figure 7-2**).

Shingles begins with symptoms including fatigue, chills, and fever. On the third or fourth day the individual begins to experience a bruised feeling on one side of his or her face or body, and the infected skin area becomes excessively sensitive. Pain, tingling, itching, and prickling sensations begin to affect the skin, and an inflamed rash appears. The rash consists of small blisters along the path of a nerve, providing a visual symptom that is a critical part of the diagnosis (Figure 7-2). The rash is usually limited to one side of the body, and rarely affects the lower part of the body or the face. The blisters usually crust and heal after five days. Half of shingles patients, however, experience pain—often quite severe—that persists for months and sometimes years. This is called **postherpetic neuralgia**. Overall health and nutrition often determine the severity of the illness and length of recovery.

■ **Figure 7-2**
Shingles rash.

■ Nutrition

Nutritional deficiencies and malnutrition interfere with the integrity of skin and mucous membranes. This can result in an increase of infectious disease incidence in a population and in the severity of disease in an infected individual. Blood, mucus, milk, and other body fluids contain a wide variety of natural inhibitors, some of which can coat viruses and impede their attachment to cells. Hence, any reduced activity of these natural inhibitors may increase the success of an invading virus. Besides interfering with the integrity of physical barriers and fluids that protect the host against pathogens, it has been documented that nutritional deficiencies interfere with antibody production and cell-mediated responses. These immune responses are discussed in detail later in this chapter.

In addition to severe malnutrition, a deficiency in essential vitamins such as vitamin A may have substantial affects on immunity. Between 100 and 140 million children in developing countries (especially those in Africa and Southeast Asia) ingest inadequate amounts of vitamin A. These children are at a 23% higher risk of dying from common infectious diseases. During a famine, the mortality rate can be as high as 50%.

Lack of vitamin A has shown a striking correlation with increased risk of common childhood diseases and even death. This is especially true for children afflicted with measles and diarrheal diseases. This recognition has resulted in the World Health Organization's (WHO) goal to eliminate vitamin A deficiency (VAD) through interventions that include a combination of breastfeeding and vitamin A supplementation, coupled with education and promotion of vitamin A-rich diets and food fortification. In 1998, the WHO and its major partners began to deliver vitamin A supplements through immunization programs.

■ Hormones

Patients undergoing treatment with hormones such as glucocorticoids (a group of corticosteroids) are at increased risk for the development of infections; for example, organ recipients undergo chronic steroid therapy. The therapy is intended to prevent rejection of the donor organ by the immune system. Common complications of this therapy include viral infections, especially cytomegalovirus and virus-related malignancies such as human herpes 8-associated Kaposi's sarcoma.

In addition to patients undergoing hormone therapies to suppress the immune system, individuals under stress may produce hormones that decrease immunity. A 2001 study published by Stowe on immune responses and short-term spaceflight concluded that astronauts experienced reactivated latent herpesvirus (Epstein-Barr virus and cytomegalovirus) infections. This reactivation was correlated with the increase of neuroendocrine hormones produced by astronauts during flight. Perhaps neuroendocrine hormones play a role in cellular immunity. Further studies are needed to determine if immune suppression and herpesvirus reactivation will have important health consequences during long-term spaceflights.

■ Fever

Almost all viral infections are accompanied by a **fever** or **febrile response**. A fever is one of the body's defense mechanisms against some invading viruses and other microbes. A normal, healthy individual maintains a constant body temperature of 98.6°F (37°C) via the hypothalamus region of the brain, which acts as the body's thermostat.

Fever induced by viral infections is elicited by substances called **pyrogens**. Immune cells such as phagocytes produce pyrogens in response to invading organisms. Pyrogens include **interleukin 1 (IL-1)**, **interleukin 6 (IL-6)**, and **tumor necrosis factor-α (TNF-α)**. These pyrogens stimulate the hypothalamus of the brain to produce **prostaglandins** that in turn raise the body's temperature, resulting in fever (**Figure 7-3**). Influenza viruses, myxoviruses, adenoviruses, herpesviruses, paramyxoviruses, coxackieviruses, and Western equine encephalitis viruses induce pyrogenic effects. Other viruses, such as vaccinia virus and polioviruses, do not. Several vaccinia virus strains prevent fever by

■ **Figure 7-3**
Fever response.

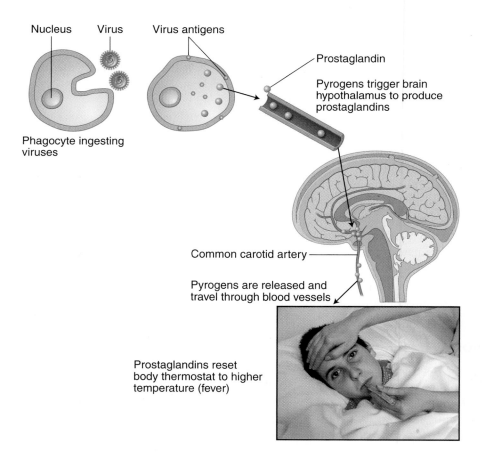

Nucleus   Virus   Virus antigens

Prostaglandin

Pyrogens trigger brain hypothalamus to produce prostaglandins

Phagocyte ingesting viruses

Common carotid artery

Pyrogens are released and travel through blood vessels

Prostaglandins reset body thermostat to higher temperature (fever)

producing IL-1 receptors. These receptors sequester cellular IL-1, thereby moderating the fever response.

Genetic Factors

Certain populations of humans are more susceptible to viral infections than others; for example, individuals with two defective chemokine receptor 5 genes (CCR5) are more resistant to being infected with HIV compared to those with a functional CCR5 gene. Those infected with HIV that possess an altered chemokine receptor 2 (CCR2) gene may progress to full-blown AIDS at a much slower rate than those who do not.

Researchers have identified host genetic factors that influence the outcome of hepatitis B and C infections. Their studies suggest that polymorphisms of the major histocompatibility complex (MHC) genes (which are located on chromosome 6) influence the patient's rate of progression of his/her liver disease. Compared to other regions on the human genome, the MHC loci display an unprecedented degree of polymorphism. Scientists argue that the polymorphisms within a population enable the individual to survive the potentially deadly effects of infectious diseases. Infectious diseases have been the major cause of mortality during mammalian evolution and remain a serious threat in developing countries.

Several viral resistance genes have been mapped in laboratory (inbred) mice. These include the *mx* (myxovirus) and *Flv* (flavivirus) genes. The *mx* gene product protects the mouse host during influenza A or B virus infection by interacting with the viral polymerase, thereby blocking synthesis of viral messenger RNAs (mRNAs). Later, it was discovered that the *mx* gene in mice also confers resistance to other RNA viruses such as members of the Orthomyxoviridae, Paramyxoviridae, Rhabdoviridae, Bunyaviridae, and Togaviridae families. Human **homologs** of the *mx* genes exist; however, their gene products are devoid of antiviral activities.

The inbred mouse *Flv* gene plays a role in resistance to viruses within the genus *Flavivirus*. This genus includes the human pathogens West Nile virus, Dengue fever virus, and Yellow fever virus. The *Flv* resistance gene encodes for a full-length protein within a family of proteins termed *Oas1b*, or 2′5′-oligoadenylate synthetase 1B. Susceptible mice encode a truncated form of the protein that lacks 30% of the C-terminal due to a premature stop codon encoded by the *Flv* gene. The known function of Oas1b is to bind and activate a latent ribonuclease, RNase L. RNase L degrades viral and cellular single-stranded RNAs (ssRNAs). This is part of the host's interferon response, which will be discussed in detail later in the chapter. The Oas1b proteins from both susceptible and resistant mice differ by one unique change within the protein: In the P-loop motif of the protein, a region involved in RNA recognition and binding, four amino acids are missing. It is believed that the Oas1b protein may specifically recognize and bind RNA structures unique to flavivirus RNAs.

Dual Infections

Probably the first virus that comes to mind when thinking of altering host resistance is human immunodeficiency virus (HIV). **Opportunistic infections** are the hallmark of HIV infections. Patients suffering from full-blown acquired immunodeficiency syndrome (AIDS) usually die as a result of a number of secondary infections that are difficult to control. These infections most often are caused by *Candida albicans*, *Pneumocystis carinii* (pneumonia), *Toxoplasma gondii*, *Cryptosporidium coccidi*, *Mycobacterium avium-intracellulare*, and tuberculosis and hepatitis viruses. These opportunistic infections occur because of the decreased immunity in HIV-infected individuals.

Viral infections of the respiratory tract often lower host resistance to secondary bacterial infections, resulting in secondary pneumonia infections that can be fatal. Notable examples of this are influenza and measles virus infections.

■ Species Resistance

The host range of many viruses is narrow; for example, poliovirus, HIV, and the hepatitis viruses have a very limited host range. This is likely the case because host cells that are resistant to specific viral infections do not contain conserved cellular receptors for viral entry, and therefore penetration into the cell to cause an infection cannot be achieved.

Poliovirus only infects primates. Poliovirus binds to the receptor CD155. A recent study by Ida-Hosonuma and colleagues determined that poliovirus is restricted to primates because the gene sequence of the CD155 poliovirus receptor remains conserved in primates but is highly variable in other mammalian species such as rabbits and ring-tailed lemurs, which are not susceptible to poliovirus infection. Their work has suggested that rapid changes in the CD155 gene during mammalian evolution determined the host range restriction of polioviruses.

7.2 Host Defenses Against Viral Invaders: Nonspecific Host Defenses (Innate Immunity)

Nonspecific immunity protects us against any pathogen, regardless of the species or type of microbe. Host resistance (or innate immunity) is not improved by repeated exposure to the pathogen. Immune cells and enzymes or proteins involved in nonspecific host defenses do not retain any "memory" from prior encounters with pathogens.

■ The Interferon Response

The interferon response is the first line of defense against all viral infections. Before specific immune system responses mount, the body begins both subtle and dramatic nonspecific immune responses that are induced by proteins called **interferons (IFNs)** at the early stage of viral infection. The ultimate outcome of this response is cellular suicide of infected and neighboring uninfected cells. This is a clever way to localize infections and prevent a virus from spreading rapidly throughout the body before the immune system can finish the job. It is sometimes referred to as an infection "firebreak."

History of IFN: The Magic Bullet

In 1957 researchers Alick Isaacs and Jean Lindenmann of the National Institute for Medical Research (NIMR) in London first described interferon in an article entitled "Virus Interference I. The Interferon," published in the *Proceedings of the Royal Society of London*. Their pioneering work spurred clinical trials because interferon was speculated to be the "magic bullet" for treating viral infections, similar to what penicillin did for bacterial infections.

The Isaacs and Lindenmann experiment demonstrated that a substance from influenza-infected cells *interfered* with subsequent influenza virus infections (**Figure 7-4**). It was later discovered that IFNs are naturally occurring proteins that possess antiviral activity. Host cells secrete IFNs in response to viral invasion. The secreted IFNs bind to receptors on neighboring cells. This receptor-binding event acts as a signal to other cells. The end result is the creation of a cellular **antiviral state** that will be discussed in greater detail later in this chapter.

There Are a Multitude of IFNs

IFNs are **cytokines**—protein factors made by cells to act on other cells. In other words, they play a role in cell-to-cell communication. The number of proteins in the cytokine family continues to grow as newly discovered proteins that act on immune and nonimmune cells are added to it. Most cytokines are biochemically and structurally similar to hormones and growth factors, and they exit host cells and bind to their cell-specific cytokine

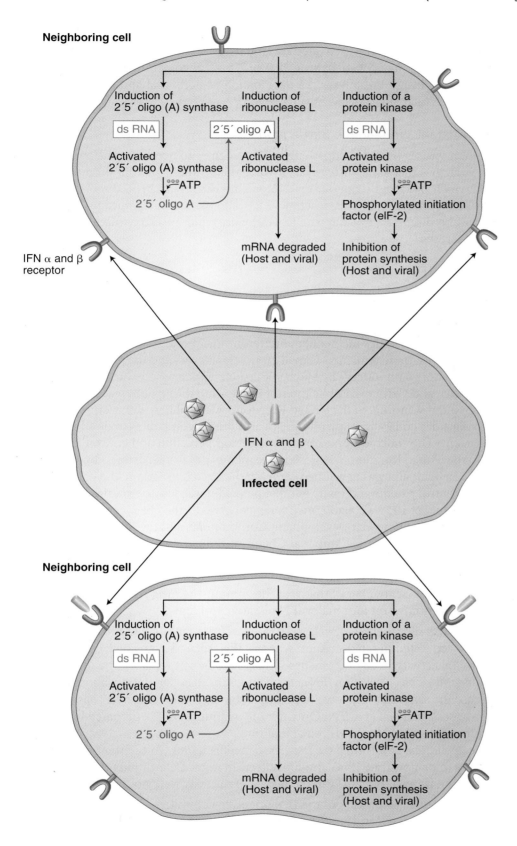

Neighboring cell

Induction of 2´5´ oligo (A) synthase

ds RNA

Activated 2´5´ oligo (A) synthase
↓ ATP
2´5´ oligo A

Induction of ribonuclease L

2´5´ oligo A

Activated ribonuclease L

mRNA degraded (Host and viral)

Induction of a protein kinase

ds RNA

Activated protein kinase
↓ ATP
Phosphorylated initiation factor (eIF-2)

Inhibition of protein synthesis (Host and viral)

IFN α and β receptor

IFN α and β

Infected cell

Neighboring cell

Induction of 2´5´ oligo (A) synthase

ds RNA

Activated 2´5´ oligo (A) synthase
↓ ATP
2´5´ oligo A

Induction of ribonuclease L

2´5´ oligo A

Activated ribonuclease L

mRNA degraded (Host and viral)

Induction of a protein kinase

ds RNA

Activated protein kinase
↓ ATP
Phosphorylated initiation factor (eIF-2)

Inhibition of protein synthesis (Host and viral)

■ **Figure 7-5**

The type 1 interferon pathway: "cellular altruism." Infected cells secrete IFNs that bind to receptors on neighboring cells. This binding event causes the cell to express several genes, including three that are involved in setting up an antiviral state: PKR, ribonuclease L, and 2′5′-oligo(A) synthetase. The viral replication intermediate, dsRNA, activates PKR and RNase L. The end result is the destruction of viral and host mRNAs and the inhibition of protein synthesis.

2'5'-oligo(A) synthetase 1B and RNase L are IFN-induced antiviral proteins that act in concert. The enzyme Oas1b is activated by viral dsRNA, converting adenine triphosphate (ATP) into 2'5'-oligomers of adenylic acid. The 2'5'-A oligomers activate a latent ribonuclease, RNase L. RNase L catalyzes the degradation of both viral and host cellular RNAs resulting in a cellular altruistic event (Figure 7-5).

IFN Resistant Viruses: The Battle Against PKR

Different viruses have developed ingenious schemes to overcome the antiviral affects of PKR. Strategies that some viruses use involve the synthesis of viral products, RNA, or proteins, which bind and sequester dsRNA or bind directly to PKR, disabling inhibition of the cellular protein synthesis machinery. Details pertaining to specific IFN-resistant viruses will be discussed in Chapters 12 (Influenza) and 14 (Poxviruses) that focus on individual viruses.

Marketing IFN

The IFN story represents the complexities involved in the development of commercial drug therapies. Immediately after their discovery, IFNs were viewed as a potential antiviral panacea. Researchers who tried to repeat Issacs's and Lindemann's experiments, though, were unsuccessful. Skeptics nicknamed interferon "misinterpreton."

In spite of this, there remained a small group of believers and the press coverage about interferon did not go unnoticed. By May 1958, patent applications were filed in the United States, Canada, and Germany. Public interest in the United Kingdom was slow to develop, but foreign interest prompted the United Kingdom's Medical Research Council (MRC) and NIMR to consider collaborating with foreign and British companies to develop IFN as an antiviral agent. The "missed opportunity" to develop penicillin and control its associated patents in the United Kingdom was fresh in the memory of British drug companies and scientists. When penicillin was developed earlier in the United Kingdom, their scientists were not able to control patents and many felt that penicillin was lost to American drug companies. Thus in July of 1959 a collaborative agreement was formed between the NIMR, MRC, the NRDC (National Research Development Corporation), and the British pharmaceutical companies Glaxo Laboratories, Imperial Chemical Industries-Pharmaceuticals (ICI), and Burroughs Wellcome. One result of this collaboration between government and industry was the formation of the Scientific Committee on IFN, which consisted of representatives from each party. By September of that year the committee's meetings, which were chaired by Isaacs, concentrated on four major IFN research problems:

- *The species-species effect of IFNs.* IFN isolated from rabbits had the best antiviral effect when tested in rabbit tissues, whereas IFN isolated from chick cells has the best antiviral activity in chicken tissues. This phenomenon remains true today.
- *Standardization of biological IFN activity assays.* Each collaborating laboratory needed to use the same assays to produce comparable measurements of IFN activity.
- *Large-scale production of IFN.* Only minute quantities of IFN prepared from monkey kidney cells could be produced at that time.
- *The application of IFN from the test-tube to animal testing.* At the time, scientists were trying to demonstrate IFN's antiviral effects in mice. Determining the doses needed, however, proved difficult, and the results of the tests were not reproducible.

In June of 1961, volunteers of the IFN scientific committee initiated the first human experiments. David Tyrell and another committee member at the MRC's common cold unit in Salisbury had inoculated themselves intranasally with a small amount of monkey IFN that they had prepared themselves. A couple of days later, they inoculated themselves with a strain of Coxsackie virus that was known to cause the common cold in humans 90% of the time. Months later, the Coxsackie virus could be isolated from nasal washings of both of them. Tyrell had experienced a cold but the other committee member did not. The IFN had not caused any side effects and the committee members agreed that small-scale human trials were doable.

At this time, there were no mandatory safety standards in the United Kingdom for testing drugs, nor any toxicity testing or clinical trial regulations for experiments on humans. The committee agreed to apply safety and toxicity standards used for vaccines (such as polio vaccine) toward IFN. This required that IFN be injected into mice and guinea pigs and if there were no adverse effects, it would be injected into the skin of committee members. This turned out to be problematic because guinea pigs died 3 to 4 days after injection with IFN. The scientists argued this was due to minute amounts of penicillin that had contaminated the IFN preparation.

IFN was isolated from monkey cells that were grown in medium containing penicillin to prevent bacterial contamination of the monkey cell cultures. It was known that guinea pigs were highly susceptible to small amounts of penicillin. After some debate, small-scale human trials continued in 1962. The committee chose to investigate IFN protection against vaccinia virus and common cold viruses. Unfortunately, IFN protection could not be demonstrated and interest in IFNs plummeted. The collaboration continued, but, resources declined because of the expense involved in producing monkey IFN and the lack of understanding IFN's mechanism of action.

During the late 1960s and into the early 1970s, the second and third waves of human trials were held. About this time, Matilda Krim, a tumor biologist at New York's Memorial Sloan-Kettering Cancer Center, began searching the scientific literature for promising new developments in the area of cancer research, and IFN came up in the database as showing an inhibitory effect on tumor viruses and tumors in mice and rats. Another study suggested that IFN had an inhibitory effect on tumors unrelated to virus infection.

News relating to IFN's potential as a new **anticancer drug** resulted in worldwide media hype. This was during a time in which conventional cancer therapies consisted of radiation, radical surgery, and harsh chemotherapy with severe side effects. The National Cancer Institute (NCI) was under public attack because of the low success rate associated with "battling cancer," and there was a growing demand for effective and less toxic remedies. IFN looked promising because it was a "natural" inhibitor that reportedly did not have toxic side effects.

Krim began applying for funding toward IFN research from the NCI and the National Institute of Allergy and Infectious Diseases (NIAID). Requests for funding were denied in part because experimental data was weak. IFN preparations were not "pure," and reviewers raised concern over funding such a high-risk project. Documentation that IFN *inducers* (e.g., dsRNA) were highly toxic also raised concerns by the grant review panel. Meanwhile, the United Kingdom's Scientific Committee on IFN dissolved due to IFN's disappointing results.

The early preparations of IFN used in scientific experiments and clinical studies consisted of a crude protein fraction that contained less than 10% interferon by weight. In addition to blocking antibody synthesis and other activities, these crude preparations not only contained antiviral activity, but also antiprotozoal, antibacterial, and antiproliferative activities. Unanticipated side effects occurred, ranging from flu-like symptoms to gastrointestinal effects that included anorexia, vomiting, diarrhea, and abdominal pain. There were central nervous system effects such as depression, dizziness, and altered mental states (confusion), and cutaneous adverse reactions such as rashes, dry skin, and alopecia (hair loss). Occasionally, some individuals experienced cardiac difficulties. It was not known if these were caused by IFN or contaminants in the preparation.

In 1974 Hans Strander, a physician at the Karolinksa Hospital in Stockholm, Sweden, admitted to Krim that since 1971 he had been treating osteosarcoma patients with purified IFN supplied by Finnish physician Kari Cantell (**Figure 7-6**). One of Strander's patients had gone into remission and the growth of tumors in others seemed to show signs of halting. Strander was optimistic about the use of IFN and stated that he did not observe toxic side effects in patients.

■ **Figure 7-6**
Hans Arthur Strander worked in Kari Cantell's research laboratory in the 1960s.

TABLE 7-1	IFN Clinical Trials
Type of IFN	**Disease Treated**
IFN α	Chronic hepatitis B (HBV) and C (HCV)
IFN α and β	AIDS-related Kaposi's sarcoma and HIV infection
IFN α and γ	Genital papillomavirus infection, laryngeal papillomatosis
IFN α and β	Myeloproliferative disorders (cancer spreads to the blood; e.g., childhood leukemia)
IFN α	Multiple myeloma (cancer involving plasma cells)
IFN α	Thrombocythemia (blood disease characterized by the production of too many platelets, resulting in bleeding because the blood cannot clot)
IFN α	Non-Hodgkin's lymphoma and Hodgkin's disease
IFN α	Gastrointestinal tumors
IFN α	Colorectal cancer
IFN α , β, and γ	Melanoma and basal cell carcinoma
IFN α and γ	Ovarian cancer
IFN α and β	Bladder cancer
IFN α, β, and γ	Kidney cancer
IFN α and γ	Mesothelioma (rare form of lung cancer, often associated with asbestos exposure)
IFN α	Hemangiomas (reddish colored benign tumor with many dilated blood vessels connected to it)
IFN α and γ	Nonmalignant scleroderma (autoimmune disease of connective tissue that results in the build up of scar tissue usually of the skin but can occur in organs)
IFN α, β, and γ	Multiple sclerosis
IFN γ	Chronic granulomatous disease (rare inherited disease of the immune system resulting in defective phagocytes), leishmaniasis (parasitic infection), mycobacterial infections (bacterial infection), osteopetrosis (rare congenital disorder in which bones are too dense), Omenn's syndrome (inherited immune disorder), hyperimmunoglobulinemia E (disease characterized by recurrent skin and lung infections), rheumatoid arthritis, atopic dermatitis, and psoriasis

Later, Strander's clinical study was controversial because he did not use a control group that was not treated with IFN concurrently during his investigation; however, his results and enthusiasm were enough to motivate Krim to persist in her work on IFN. Results of further clinical trials trickled in, and IFN began to look like "the miracle drug looking for a disease." It turned out that the key was using *purified* IFN, but unfortunately doing so turned out to be no easy task, and several years passed before the process was perfected. Success lay in the recombinant DNA technology of the early 1980s, which allowed scientists to clone several different species of the human IFN gene(s) and produce large amounts of it in *Escherichia coli*. After 20 years at a snail's pace, IFN research finally had the opportunity to quickly move forward. In addition, a number of companies were involved in altering the IFN gene(s) to make it more effective and with less side affects. IFN research helped genetic engineering move forward in the discipline of biotechnology.

The IFN story is one of persistence. Development and randomized controlled clinical trials required commitments between drug companies, governments, regulators, physicians, laboratory researchers, and patients and their families. Today IFN is used to treat a diverse range of viral diseases, immune disorders, nonmalignant tumors, and cancers. Table 7-1 lists the therapeutic uses of IFN.

■ Apoptosis and Viral Infection: A Double-Edged Sword

The term **apoptosis** has a long history in medicine, dating back to Greek physicians over 2000 years ago. It was used in the context of "the falling off of bones" by the Greek physician Hippocrates of Cos, and "the dropping of the scabs" by Galen, one of the first experimental Greek physiologists. In the 1960s, John Foxton Ross Kerr described the morphological changes of dying rat liver cells. He hypothesized that this type of cellular death was attributed to a deliberate sequence of events and coined the term *apoptosis* in a landmark paper coauthored with A. H. Wyllie and A. R. Currie that was published in the *British Journal of Cancer* in 1972. In the paper, the authors suggested that cell death might occur by a controlled mechanism that they called apoptosis. Kerr and his colleagues continued apoptosis research; however, the topic of apoptosis was largely ignored until researchers documented a correlation between apoptosis and immune system function and regulation. The immunology connection spearheaded an explosion of research. Today, over 140,000 papers have been published in the field of apoptosis, including research in premiere journals such as *Science* and *Nature*.

■ **Figure 7-7**
A colored scanning electron micrograph that shows a cytotoxic T lymphocyte (orange cell) inducing a cancer cell (pink) to undergo apoptosis. Note the pink apoptotic bodies emerging from the cancer cell. Cytoxic T lymphocytes are part of the body's immune response system. Their job is to survey, attach, and release chemicals to kill cancer cells in the body. Cytotoxic T lymphocytes recognize surface markers on other cells in the body that label those cells for destruction. In this way, they help to keep virus-infected or malignant cells in check.

Apoptosis, or programmed cell death (PCD), can serve as a cellular defense mechanism to combat viral infection. It is either a way to remove cells that are no longer needed (such as the resorption of the tadpole tail at the time of its metamorphosis, or the sloughing off of the inner lining of the uterus—the endometrium—at the start of menstruation) or are harmful to the body (such as virally infected cells or cancer cells, **Figure 7-7**).

Virally infected cells usually undergo PCD by "dying from within," whereas the removal of cancer cells is induced from outside of the cell, such as when a T lymphocyte attacks a cancer cell (Figure 7-7). It is possible that a virally infected cell could cause a neighboring uninfected cell to undergo PCD if it were to shut off the production of growth factors to its neighboring cell, thereby causing cell death. A virally infected cell may also secrete factors to induce a neighboring cell to activate a PCD pathway (such as a Type I IFN pathway).

Apoptosis is triggered by events related to the disruption of the cell cycle or virus infection. The apoptotic response involves a cascade of cellular signaling pathways. This includes the activation of cellular proteases, such as caspases and nucleases, which degrade cellular DNA into nucleosome-sized fragments.

Apoptotic cells undergo morphological changes associated with protease and nuclease activity (**Figure 7-8**). These changes include cell shrinkage from its neighboring cells, chromatin condensation to the periphery of the nucleus, nucleolus disintegration, nuclear fragmentation, membrane blebbing, and the formation of apoptotic bodies containing cytoplasm, organelles, and nuclear DNA fragments (which resolve into a characteristic DNA ladder pattern when separated via agarose gel electrophoresis). Apoptotic bodies are engulfed by macrophages.

A number of viruses can trigger or counteract apoptosis or do both (Table 7-2). It seems logical that viruses would be negatively affected by apoptosis. Viruses need metabolically active cells to ensure their reproduction and survival. In response to a virus infection, the host cell naturally responds by producing cytokines, including IFNs, nucleases, and proteases, all of which promote an apoptotic or cellular "suicide" event. This event localizes

■ Figure 7-8
Cellular apoptosis occurs as a result of signals that activate a cascade of proteases
and nucleases that contribute to the death
of the cell. Many morphological changes
are associated with apoptosis, such as
membrane blebbing, DNA condensation,
and fragmentation, and the formation of
apoptotic bodies. Viruses can trigger and
counteract apoptosis by mechanisms mediated by a number of different viral genes.
Adapted from an illustration by Bender
MedSystems.

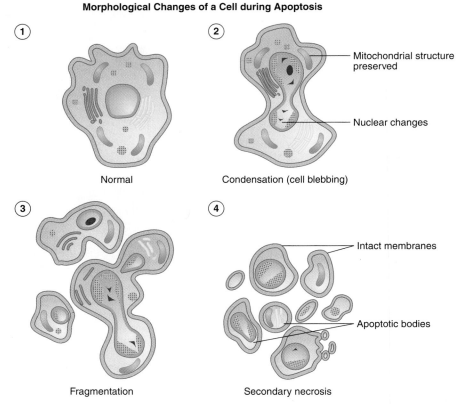

Morphological Changes of a Cell during Apoptosis

① Normal

② Condensation (cell blebbing)
— Mitochondrial structure preserved
— Nuclear changes

③ Fragmentation

④ Secondary necrosis
— Intact membranes
— Apoptotic bodies

TABLE 7-2	Viruses That Produce Promoters or Antagonists of Apoptosis		
Virus	**Viral Gene or Protein**	**Promotes or Antagonizes Apoptosis?**	**Mechanism of Action**
Adenovirus	E1A	Promotes	Induces cellular p53-dependent apoptosis
Adenovirus	E4	Promotes	Interacts with cellular phosphatase 2A to induce apoptosis
Adenovirus	E1B	Antagonizes	Inhibits viral E1A and cellular Fas, TNF-induced apoptosis
HBV	pX	Promotes	Sequesters p53
HCV	Core protein	Promotes	Interacts with TNF
Human papillomavirus	E2	Promotes	Facilitates apoptosis via p53-dependent pathway
HIV	Tat	Promotes	Increases activity of cyclin-dependent kinases
HIV	gp120	Promotes	Syncytium formation
HIV	Vpr	Antagonizes	Regulates NF κB
Cowpox virus	CrmA	Antagonizes	Inhibits caspases
Vaccinia virus	SP1-2	Antagonizes	Inhibits Fas and TNF

There is a programmed set of cellular proteins involved in triggering or defusing apoptosis. The viral
genes or their products promote or antagonize the following cellular proteins that are involved in PCD
pathways: p53, phosphatase 2A, tumor necrosis factor (TNF), cyclin-dependent kinases, NF-κB, caspases, and FAS. p53 regulates cell growth and causes cancer cells to destroy themselves via PCD. Cyclin-
dependent kinases control cell cycle progression. TNF is a cytokine that activates the cellular transcription factor NF-κB. NF-κB works in concert with TNF to preferentially kill tumor cells. FAS is a cell surface
protein that mediates apoptosis. Protein phosphatase 2A plays a role in cytokine production.

and prevents the spread of viruses to other cells. The host also uses immune cells such as macrophages to engulf apoptotic cells or other immune cells like T lymphocytes to induce apoptosis. It is not surprising, then, that a virus would produce an antagonist of apoptosis, but what would be the advantage of promoting apoptosis during viral infection?

When apoptotic bodies are formed during PCD (as shown in step 4 of Figure 7-8), they pinch off of the dying cell and are consumed or engulfed by neighboring immune cells. The engulfment of apoptotic bodies that contain virus particles provides a mechanism for virus dissemination or release into extracellular fluids. Experiments by Mi and colleagues, and Teodoro and Brandon, show that if PCD is induced during viral genomic replication, virus production is compromised. If PCD is induced after virion assembly, though, there is enhanced viral release from infected cells and dissemination. It therefore appears that if viruses are able to manipulate apoptotic pathways timely, they can ensure their survival.

◼ Nonspecific Defense: Phagocytosis

The IFN response and apoptotic pathways, which are indirect and complex, result in cellular suicide or programmed cell death. Phagocytosis is another important nonspecific or innate form of immunity; however, its action is direct. **Phagocytosis** is the engulfment and ingestion of foreign material (such as viruses and bacteria) by phagocytes. Examples of phagocytic cells are **macrophages, neutrophils,** and **blood monocytes**. These cells are analogous to the videogame character that runs through a maze while eating all of the characters in its path. Phagocytic cells patrol the tissues or blood, eating and digesting foreign invaders they encounter.

Monocytes are precursors to macrophages. They are large white blood cells containing a nucleus and granulated cytoplasm. They circulate in the bloodstream for about 8 hours, during which time they enlarge, migrate to tissues, and differentiate into macrophages. Macrophages are 5 to 10 times larger than monocytes and contain more lysosomes (organelles that contain many hydrolytic enzymes) than the monocytes. Some macrophages become fixed in tissues, whereas others are wandering macrophages that travel in tissues by amoeboid movement. Macrophages can ingest viruses and other foreign invaders, dead cells, cell debris, and other cellular matter. Macrophages are attracted and move toward substances via **chemotactic** behavior.

Macrophages patrol tissues for foreign invaders, whereas neutrophils and blood monocytes patrol circulating blood. Neutrophils are white blood cells that begin their two-week life span in the bone marrow, which contains an excessive number of neutrophils. This enables the body to respond to viral or other microbial challenges with a massive outpouring of neutrophils.

Some of the neutrophils migrate to the peripheral blood vessels and circulate in the blood for 7 to 10 hours before they migrate into tissues. Chemotactic factors released from inflamed areas attract neutrophils to the inflammation site in the body. Neutrophils contain specialized granules that possess peroxidases, lysozyme, hydrolytic enzymes, collagenase, and lactoferrins that aid in their phagocytic activity.

◼ Nonspecific Defense: Dendritic Cells

Dendritic cells are covered with long spiky arms that resemble the dendrites of nerve cells. Dendritic immune cells are present in tissues that have contact with the environment, such as the skin (where they are called Langerhan's cells), mucous membranes, and the lining of the nose, lungs, and gastrointestinal tract. Langerhan's cells were first described by medical graduate student Paul Langerhan, who was working under the mentorship of Professor Rudolf Virchow at the Institute of Pathology of the University of Berlin in 1868. In his 1868 landmark paper *"Uber die Nerven der menslichen Haut,"* Langerhan described

Figure 7-9
Colorized scanning electron micrograph of skin dendritic cells sitting on collagen fibrils with their veils (ruffles) as they migrate through the meshwork of dermis.

the cells as nerve endings of the skin. In 1882 he corrected his interpretation, stating "I am now convinced that my cells are in no way essential for nerve endings."

Dendritic cells express MHC I and MHCII molecules on their surfaces. (See the *Refresher* box on Immunology.) They are very efficient at identifying foreign invaders such as viruses and bacteria, even when they are present in minute numbers. Once they find foreign invaders, the dendritic cells migrate to the nearest lymph node via the lymphatics, where they come in close proximity to other immune cells and eliminate the pathogen (**Figure 7-9**).

Dendritic cells internalize the pathogen, digest it, and display or present the foreign peptides on their surface via the MHC II molecules to T helper (T_H) cells. (T_H cells are described later in this chapter as part of the discussion on specific immune defenses.) Activated dendritic cells also express high levels of another surface receptor, B7, which provides stimulatory signals/molecules. T_H cells will only be activated to recognize the antigens as being foreign or dangerous via the B7 co-stimulator. After T_H cells are stimulated, they leave the lymph nodes and travel to the sites of inflammation or infection.

■ Nonspecific Defense: Natural Killer Cells

Natural killer (**NK**) cells participate in early innate host defenses against viral infections, and also kill tumor cells before they can establish themselves as cancers. They recognize cells that undergo a declined expression of MHC molecules or cells that contain surface an-

Refresher   Immunology

Immunology Tidbit: Self vs. Nonself

How does the immune system distinguish the body's own cells (self) from foreign cells (nonself)?

Major Histocompatibility Complex (MHC) are "tags which mark host cells as self. MHC I molecules mark all cells of the host, whereas MHC II molecules mark B cells, macrophages and dendritic cells, allowing these immune cells to recognize and communicate with T helper lymphocytes in order to eliminate invaders.

tigens displayed by some tumor cells or virally infected cells. NK cell deficiency in humans is associated with recurrent herpesvirus and cytomegalovirus infections, the rapid progression of cancers (especially lymphomas), hepatitis, AIDS, chronic fatigue syndrome, and various immunodeficiency and autoimmune diseases.

In healthy people, NK cells represent 5% to 15% of the total lymphocyte population. They respond immediately to viral infections (within minutes to four hours of an infection). They are activated by the induction of IFNs α and β and other cytokines such as IL-12, IL-15, and IL-18. These cytokines are produced by infected cells, dendritic cells, or by macrophages. NK cells must be active to do their job.

Once activated, NK cells release pore-forming proteins called perforins, granzymes (proteases), and chemokines (described in greater detail in Chapter 15). Perforin causes pores to form in the membranes of the target cells that are going to be killed. Granzymes activate enzyme pathways involved in apoptosis. The end result is death of the target cell.

NK cells, monocytes, macrophages, and neutrophils express receptors for the Fc (fragment crystallizable) region of antibodies, as shown in **Figures 7-10** and 7-15. Therefore, these cells can bind to target cells containing bound antibodies. If NK or any of the aforementioned cells interact with these target cells, they will kill them. This type of cytotoxicity is referred to as **antibody-dependent cell-mediated cytotoxicity (ADCC)**.

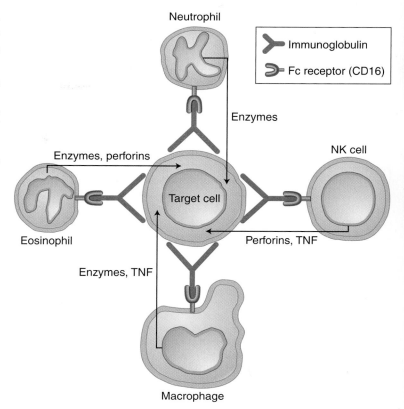

■ **Figure 7-10**
Natural killer cells, eosinophils, macrophages, and neutrophils can bind to target (virally infected) cells containing antibodies attached to their surfaces via their Fc receptors. Adapted from A. J. Cann, "Humoral Immunity," *Microbiologybytes: Infection & Immunity, http://www.microbiologybytes.com/iandi/3b.html.*

■ Complement System

A living organism's ability to recognize "nonself" or foreign invaders that may cause damage is believed to have evolved over 700 million years ago. The complement system consists of more than 30 different serum- and membrane-bound glycoproteins that act in sequence (i.e., one protein activates another, which in turn activated another, and so forth). The system has three distinct pathways: the classical, lectin, and alternative. Virus infection can activate all three pathways of the complement cascade, but only enveloped viruses are adversely affected by complement (a lipid bilayer is required). Complement activation ends in the formation of a **membrane attack complex** (**MAC**), which inserts into lipid membranes of bacteria eukaryotic cells or viruses and causes osmotic lysis.

The complement proteins present in blood serum are inactive. They are activated by

- the binding of complement protein C1q to viral antigen-antibody complexes (the classical pathway),
- the interaction of viral surface carbohydrates or virally infected cells with mannan-binding lectin (the lectin path-way),
- and other viral antigens or infected cells that cause the breakdown of an important complement protein termed C3, leading to release of lysosomal enzymes (the alternative pathway) and resulting in lysis of enveloped viruses.

Both the lectin and alternative pathways are "antibody-independent" pathways. The end result of all of these pathways is the final destruction of the invading viruses and infected cells (**Figure 7-11**).

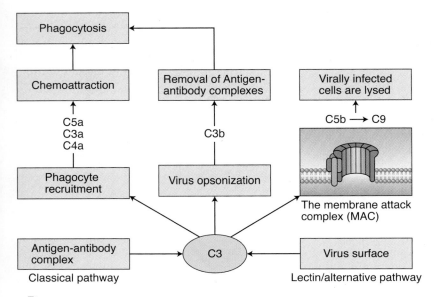

■ **Figure 7-11**

Complement cascade pathways. Most proteins in the complement system are designated with a C followed by a number. The numbers are not indicative of the order in which they act within the cascade, but rather the order in which they were discovered. When a complement protein is cleaved with a protease, two fragments are formed and referred to as "a" and "b." Opsonization is the process by which viruses or other pathogens are altered in such a manner that phagocytes more readily and efficiently engulf them. Adapted from S. Smith. "Immunologic Aspects of Organ Transplantation." *Organ Transplant.* Medscape, 2002.

Complement activation at inappropriate times can be very dangerous for host cells and thus is carefully regulated. A number of viruses have developed different strategies to avoid complement-mediated destruction. Herpesviruses and coronaviruses interfere with the classical complement activation pathway. Some poxviruses and herpesviruses produce gene products that mimic cellular complement proteins, preventing the binding and activation of cellular complement proteins and thereby preventing the cascade from continuing its pathway.

Hypocomplementemia is a rare condition in which components of the complement system are lacking or reduced in concentration. Patients with this malady have been shown to be more susceptible to infection and disease caused by certain viruses; for example, patients with severe and frequent intraoral (inside the mouth) herpes simplex 1 cold sores have been linked to C4 complement protein deficiency.

7.3 Immunity Takes Time: Specific Immune System Responses (Adapted Immunity)

Nonspecific defenses play an important role shortly after viral infection. Specific immune responses require days to weeks before they are induced or effective in clearing viruses. **Figure 7-12** illustrates the time frame in which specific and nonspecific defenses are induced after influenza virus infection. Due to the extremely complex nature of the immune system, this chapter will focus only on **antibody** (also known as **humoral**) and **cell-mediated** responses used to neutralize, control, and eliminate viruses from the host. Eliminating cancer cells, bacteria, and parasitic pathogens often involves even more immune function complexity.

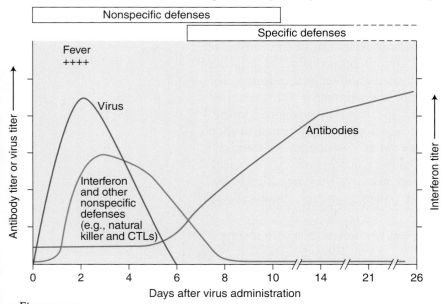

■ **Figure 7-12**

Nonspecific host defenses occur immediately after infection, whereas specific immune responses take days to weeks to mount and respond to a viral infection. The graph relates to the primary immune response of a typical influenza infection. Adapted from S. Baron. *Medical Microbiology,* Fourth Edition. Microbiology & Immunology, 1996.

■ Key Players of the Immune System: The Lymphocytes

Lymphoid organs, soft tissues, and a network of lymphatic vessels are positioned throughout the body. (The prefix "lymph" comes from the Latin word "lympha," meaning a clear, watery, fluid.) Lymph contains white blood cells that circulate throughout the lymphatic system. It acts to remove foreign invaders and certain proteins from the tissues and supplies **lymphocytes** to the bloodstream. Lymphocytes congregate in the lymph nodes and exit through outgoing lymph vessels. Lymphocytes are white blood cells that are formed in the lymphoid organs and tissues and make up 25% to 33% of all white blood cells in adult peripheral blood. Lymphocytes exhibit exquisite recognition in distinguishing pathogens from host cells.

The main types of lymphocytes are **B** and **T cells**, which are the key players of the immune system. B lymphocytes are born and mature in the bone marrow, whereas T lymphocytes mature in the thymus gland. They are the second line of defense, tailoring their activities toward individual threats created by invading pathogens.

Humoral Response: Antibody Production

The word humoral means arising from bodily "humors," or fluids—especially serum. When blood is drawn and allowed to clot, the remaining fluid is called **serum** (**Figure 7-13**). Serum contains many proteins, including albumin, complement proteins, hormones, growth factors, transferrin, and antibodies. In the laboratory, serum often is used to cultivate tissue cultures. Antibodies are Y-shaped glycoproteins produced by plasma cells and belong to a family of proteins called immunoglobulins. (Occasionally the terms antibody and immunoglobulin are interchanged.)

B lymphocytes are the scouts of the immune system and can directly recognize antigens of foreign microbial invaders. Each mature B lymphocyte displays about 150,000 membrane-bound antibodies that contain identical antigen-binding sites. In addition to antibodies on the surface of mature B lymphocytes, there are other surface proteins that allow B lymphocytes to "bind" to other immune cells such at T_H cells.

In particular, class II MHC molecules are present on the surface of B cells. These molecules permit the B cell to function as an antigen-presenting cell (APC). APCs are defined as immune cells that express MHC II on their surface and associate with T_H cells. (See the *Refresher* box on Immunology.) T_H cells, which are infected and destroyed by the HIV virus, are T lymphocytes that contain CD4 receptor molecules on their surface.

Antibody Production: Humoral Response

Mature B cells patrol the lymphatic system. When the B cells encounter invading viruses, the B cell that contains the antibody that can specifically bind to epitopes of the foreign virus invader or antigen is activated to differentiate into high populations of clones of plasma cells and a population of **memory cells** that express the correct antibody. The B cells continue to divide and differentiate for 4 to 5 days. The secreted antibodies bind to the viral antigens, facilitating their clearance from the host. Memory cells will retain the correct antibody on their cell surfaces, whereas most of the plasma cells will secrete the correct antibodies (**Figure 7-14**). Most plasma cells live approximately 1 to 2 weeks. Memory cells may be longer-lived. When memory cells encounter the same antigen, they generate a secondary antibody response to it. Research suggests that memory B cells require periodic exposure to antigen for their maintenance.

Antibodies are made up of four peptide chains: two identical light (L) chains and two larger, identical heavy (H) chains. The H and L chains are also referred to as immunoglobulins. Each L chain is bound to a heavy chain via a disulfide bridge. The exact number of disulfide bridges varies among the different antibody classes. The amino termini of the antibody molecule vary greatly in amino acid composition among antibodies. This is what gives antibodies their "specificity" to bind many different epitopes of viral antigens or antigens of other origins (Table 7-3). Hence, these regions are labeled as **variable** or Fab (fragment antigen binding).

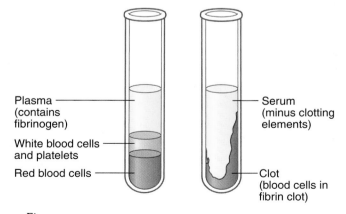

Plasma (contains fibrinogen)
White blood cells and platelets
Red blood cells
Serum (minus clotting elements)
Clot (blood cells in fibrin clot)

■ **Figure 7-13**
Blood specimens with anticoagulant (on the left) and without anticoagulant. Adapted from V. Apanius, *Field Collection and Processing of Blood*, http://www.fiu.edu/ animals/field_pro.html.

■ **Figure 7-14**

The humoral response is characterized by antibodies produced by B lymphocytes. B lymphocytes differentiate into memory B cells and plasma cells. The latter has one task: to produce and release antibodies in large quantities. These antibodies bind specifically to the invading virus antigens.

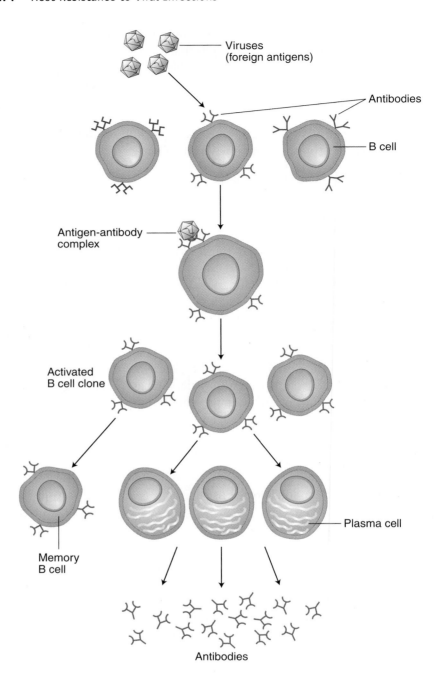

The variable region is 110 to 130 amino acids in length. The carboxyl termini of antibodies consist of constant regions (**Figure 7-15**).

The H chain carboxyl termini are labeled Fc. The term was derived from the observation that this part of the antibody molecule would crystallize during cold storage. Experiments involving digestion with papain and pepsin proteases, along with mercaptoethanol reduction and alkylation of disulfide bonds, have made it possible to determine the multichain structure of antibodies.

The constant region of the antibody molecule determines what mechanism will be used to neutralize its attached antigen. Antibodies are divided into five major classes based on their constant regions: IgA, IgD, IgE, IgG, and IgM. IgE plays a role in hypersensitive allergic reactions and the function of IgD is unknown. The focus of this discussion will be on the functions of IgA, IgG, and IgM during viral infections.

TABLE 7-3	Characteristics of Human Classes of Immunologlobulins		
Property/Biological Activity	**IgA**	**IgG**	**IgM**
Molecular weight	150,000–600,000	150,000	900,000
Crosses placenta	–	+	–
Shape/structure	Dimer	Monomer	Pentamer
Binds to Fc receptors of phagocytes	–	+	?
In vivo serum half-life	6 days	23 days	5 days
Percent of total serum immunoglobin	10%–15%	80%	5%–10%
First antibodies to appear after immunization or exposure to a pathogen	–	–	+
Much higher concentration in secretions	+	–	–

The structures of the antibodies IgG, IgA, and IgM are shown in **Figure 7-16**. Notice that IgA and IgM are composed of more than one immunoglobulin molecule linked by disulfide bonds, resulting in larger molecules and the inability to cross the human placenta. The Fc receptor of IgG is responsible for the transfer of IgG from mother to fetus across the placental membrane.

IgM has a pentamerous structure, with all five of the Fc receptors radiating from the center of the pentamer. The individual monomer units are held together by disulfide bonds and a polypeptide called the J (joining) chain. IgM is the first immunoglobulin to respond to a viral or other microbial antigen (**Figure 7-17**). Whenever IgM is found in serum samples in the clinical laboratory setting, it indicates that the patient has had a recent or has a current infection. The IgM pentamer has ten binding sites, allowing it to neutralize viral infectivity using less IgM than IgG antibodies to do the job. IgM antibodies last between only a few weeks or a few months, as opposed to IgG, which provides years of protection against subsequent infections caused by the same virus. Eventually, the production of IgM is shut off, and IgG takes over (Figure 7-17).

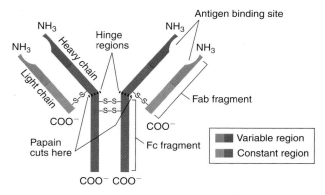

■ **Figure 7-15**
Structure of IgG antibody. Note the following features of these Y-shaped antibodies: light and heavy chains, disulfide bonds, and variable and constant regions.

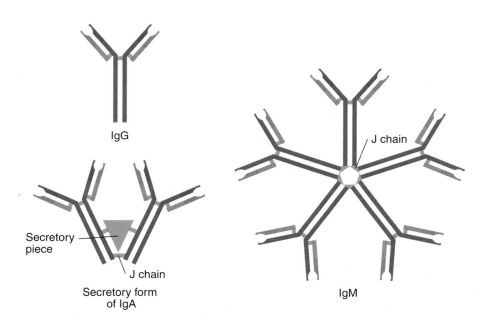

■ **Figure 7-16**
Structure comparison of IgG, IgA, and IgM antibodies. Note the size differences. IgA and IgM contain J chains in addition to disulfide bonds that link their structures together.

(a)

■ **Figure 7-17**

Graph **(a)** represents a typical immune response to a viral infection encountered for the first time. Graph **(b)** represents an immune response after a subsequent exposure to the virus encountered in the first graph. Note the more rapid IgG response in the first graph.

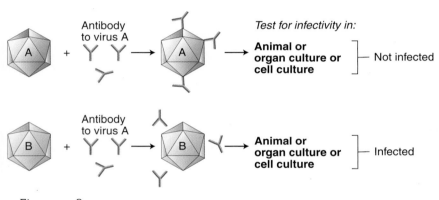

■ **Figure 7-18**

The viral neutralization assay is a sensitive and specific assay used to identify virus-specific antibodies in animals and humans. The assay is performed in two steps. In the first step the virus is incubated with antibodies, and in the second step the mixture in step one is inoculated into a host system. The absence of infectivity constitutes a positive neutralization assay.

IgG antibodies are the most abundant class of antibody present in serum (Table 7-3). As mentioned previously, IgG is produced for very long periods of time, offering long-term protection against encounters with prior pathogens. In epidemological surveys that test for antibodies in serum, IgGs indicate past infections. IgG antibodies can cross the placenta, thus protecting newborns for the first few months of life.

IgA antibodies are found in secretions of the body, especially the mucous membranes of the respiratory tract, the gastrointestinal tract, and other mucous surfaces. Hence, they play an important role in viruses that enter by these routes. IgA is present in colostrum, the fluid produced by a mother's mammary glands during lactation before true milk appears. These maternal antibodies help to protect the child from infections early in life. Hence, breastfeeding plays an important role in maintaining the health of newborns.

IgA is also present in saliva, tears, and mucous. IgA usually exists as a monomer; however, secretory IgA, which is present in external secretions, is of dimer or tetramer form and is linked by disulfide bonds and a J chain(s). Each day, an individual secretes 5 to 15 milliters of secretory IgA in the form of mucous.

Antibodies play an important role in preventing viral infections, whereas the cell-mediated response is an important defense in eliminating virally infected cells from the body. (Cell-mediated responses will be discussed in greater detail later in the chapter.)

Not all antibodies that bind to viral antigens will **neutralize** or interfere with the infectivity of viruses. Typically, the antibodies that bind to viral surface antigens are able to block attachment and entry, preventing cell-to-cell spread of infection. A representative of the concept behind the viral neutralization assay is shown in **Figure 7-18**.

Antibodies may promote the aggregation of virus particles, thereby reducing their infectivity. Antibodies cannot enter cells; hence they must neutralize viruses before the viruses are replicating inside of the host. IgA antibodies have been shown to be very successful in blocking intestinal viruses such as poliovirus and Norwalk virus. Even though poliovirus infection evokes strong IgM and IgG responses, it is the IgA mucosal immunity that is its vital defense because it acts in the gut, the primary infection site of intestinal viruses. **Nonneutralizing** antibodies bind to viral antigens, but do not interfere with infectivity. In some cases, they enhance infectivity.

T Cell-Mediated Immunity

T cells are born in the bone marrow and migrate to the thymus, where they mature. T cells differ from B cells in that they recognize "cells" that contain foreign antigens (such as virally infected cells, tumor cells, and foreign tissue grafts). They do not recognize antigens directly. Instead, they recognize viral antigens that have been internalized, degraded, and displayed on the outside of APCs or on the surface of an "altered" host cell.

There are two clearly defined populations of T cells: **T_H cells** (described earlier) and **cytotoxic T cells** (T_c cells, also called T8 lymphocytes). T_H cells promote immune responses via a T_{H1} or T_{H2} response. The **T_{H1} response** is involved in inflammation and cell-mediated immunity, whereas **T_{H2} response** activates immune responses dependent on antibodies. The T_{H2} response antagonizes the T_{H1} response and vice versa. T_c cells kill in an antigen-specific manner.

Like B cells, which express unique antibodies on their surfaces, T cells express their own unique type of receptors on their surfaces. T_H cells express CD4 in association with the T cell receptor (TCR) on their surface and recognize only antigen bound to MHC II molecules. Cytotoxic T cells express CD8 in association with TCR on their surfaces and recognize only antigens associated with MHC I molecules. As a general rule, CD4+ T cells act as helper cells and CD8+ T cells act as cytotoxic cells.

The T cell-mediated immune response begins when T_H cells recognize and bind to an antigen-MHC II complex present on APCs (such as macrophages, dendritic cells, or B cells displaying viral antigens). This binding event activates the T_H cell, causing it to secrete cytokines that in turn activate various cells that participate in the immune response (such as B cells, macrophages, and T_c cells). Some cytokines promote the growth of more T cells (for example, interleukin 2 stimulates the production of T helpers, memory T cells, and cytotoxic T cells). Some cytokines attract macrophages and other lymphocytes (T_c proliferate into CTLs) to the infection site where CTLs exhibit killing activity. **Figure 7-19** illustrates the process of T cell-mediated immunity. This form of adapted cellular immunity is specific and involves memory and self–nonself recognition.

7.4   Antibody Production: Cell-Mediated Response (B and T Cells Work Together)

When a viral infection occurs, many host defenses are mobilized. In addition to nonspecific immune defenses, cell-mediated defenses begin to mount. B cells, T cells, and APCs such as macrophages travel to the infection site and act in concert. The intended final outcome is containment of the viral infection.

When a B cell internalizes a virus, the viral antigens are digested by cellular proteases and displayed on surface MHC II antigen presenting complexes of the B cell. At the same time, T_H cells respond to the viral antigens "presented" by macrophages (APCs). Cloned T_H cells bind to the B cells displaying the viral antigens complexed within its MHC II molecule. This binding event stimulates the B cells to differentiate into plasma cells secreting specific antibodies and memory cells. Secreted antibodies circulate within the body, binding viral antigens as they are encountered (**Figure 7-20**).

7.5   Some Final Comments on Cell-Mediated Immunity

Adapted cell-mediated immunity appeared about 450 million years ago. Contemporary research is unraveling this very sophisticated host defense system that protects us against specific viral and microbial pathogens. This same system is used to clear tumor cells and other abnormal cells and antigens from the body. The major players are B and T cells. Cytokines play an important role in activating or communicating between B and T cells. Repeated exposure of the same pathogens results in the maintenance of memory B and

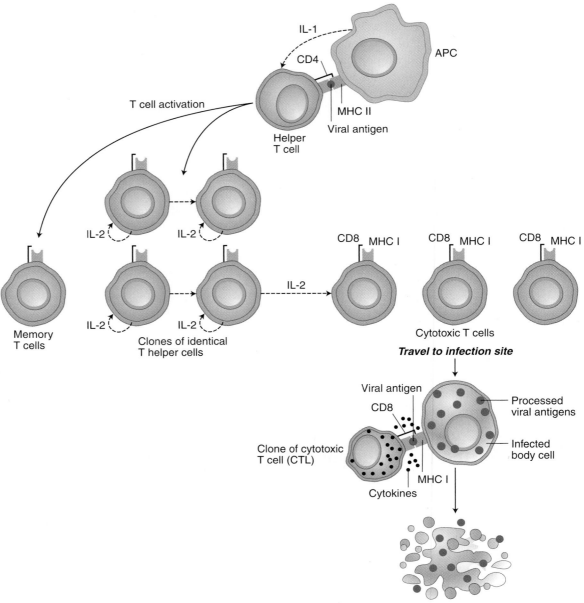

■ Figure 7-19

T_{H1} response system. T_{H1} cells recognize and bind to APCs containing viral antigens bound to MHC II molecules on the APC cell surface. This results in the activation of cytokines such as IL-2. IL-2 stimulates the T_{H1} cells to differentiate into more T cells, including T_c cells. The T_c cells migrate to the site of infection where they destroy the virally infected cells.

memory T cells. **Figure 7-21** illustrates a comprehensive view of how cell-mediated immunity is used to eliminate virally infected cells from the body. It is important to remember that it does take some time for this response to mount, hence nonspecific immunity provides immediate action against any invading pathogen before cell-mediated immunity eliminates the infection (**Figure 7-22** and see Figure 7-21).

7.6 Virus Evasion Strategies

Despite a host's nonspecific and sophisticated specific immune defenses, viruses find ways to evade host defenses. Many of the viruses that evade immune responses establish per-

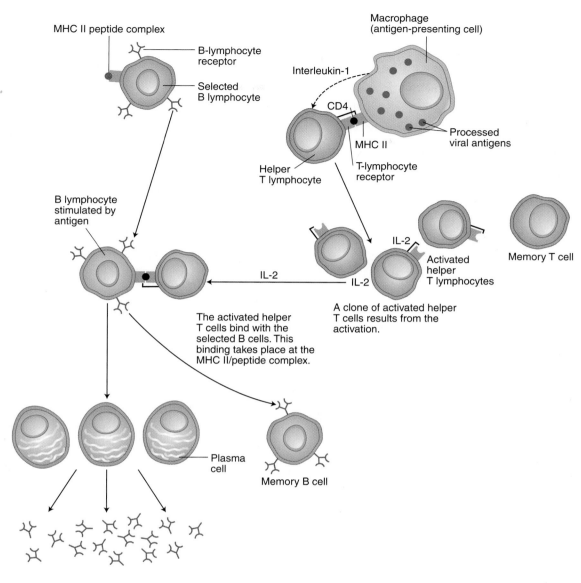

MHC II peptide complex

B-lymphocyte receptor

Selected B lymphocyte

Macrophage (antigen-presenting cell)

Interleukin-1

CD4

MHC II

Processed viral antigens

Helper T lymphocyte

T-lymphocyte receptor

B lymphocyte stimulated by antigen

IL-2

IL-2

IL-2

Activated helper T lymphocytes

Memory T cell

The activated helper T cells bind with the selected B cells. This binding takes place at the MHC II/peptide complex.

A clone of activated helper T cells results from the activation.

Plasma cell

Memory B cell

■ **Figure 7-20**
Antibody-producing B cells may work in concert with T_{H2} cells to clear viral antigens that have escaped or bypassed initial antibody defenses. This occurs through the presentation of viral antigens on MHC II receptors located on B cells and APCs. In this case, viral antigens displayed by B cells via the MHC II receptor-viral antigen complex stimulate activated T_{H2} cells to bind to them and stimulate the B cells to differentiate into plasma and memory B cells. The plasma B cells produce large quantities of specific antibodies that circulate and patrol the body to eliminate viral antigens.

sistent and chronic infections. There are several basic mechanisms by which viruses evade elimination by the host:

- The virus hides from the immune system, as is the case with inactive or **latent** viruses such as herpes simplex virus and varicella zoster virus. Latent viruses cause lifelong infections. The viruses are not fully replicating most of the time and are invisible to the host immune system. Some latent viruses produce antigens that are similar to host antigens in a process called **molecular mimicry**. When this happens, the host does not recognize the viral antigens as being nonself and therefore the immune response does not react toward the virus.
- Some viruses may synthesize excessive amounts of soluble viral antigens that bind all of the host's circulating neutralizing antibodies.
- Viruses may inactivate cytokine signals by producing homologs of cellular cytokines or their receptors. The end result is the blocking of immune signals, thereby reducing the effectiveness of the immune response.
- Viruses may inactivate immune cells; for example, viruses may infect immune cells, blocking their activity and causing immune suppression. HIV does this by infecting T_H cells, resulting in their depletion during full-blown AIDS.

■ **Figure 7-21**

Overview of cell-mediated immunity. B and T cells work in concert to eliminate viral pathogens. This can be accomplished because of the body's ability to distinguish foreign invaders/viral antigens via MHC class II molecules and the production of cytokines such as IL-2 that communicate among the T cell population.

(A) The antigen-receptor complex has been taken into the selected B lymphocyte, and the antigen peptide is now displayed on the B cell's surface within the class II MHC protein.

(B) Meanwhile, an antigen-presenting macrophage has activated a helper T lymphocyte. Interleukin-1 from the macrophage assists the activation.

MHC II peptide complex

B-lymphocyte receptor

Selected B lymphocyte

Macrophage (antigen-presenting cell)

Interleukin-2

CD4

Viral antigen

MHC II

T-lymphocyte receptor

Helper T lymphocyte

B lymphocyte stimulated by antigen

Activated helper T lymphocytes

(C) A clone of activated helper T cells results from the activation.

(D) The activated helper T cells bind with the selected B cells. The binding takes place at the MHC II/peptide complex.

(E) The binding spurs the B cells to enlarge and divide into a clone of plasma cells and memory cells (not shown).

Plasma cell

(F) The plasma cells secrete antibodies that enter the body's circulation and find their way to antigen-bearing microorganisms. Interaction with the microorganisms leads to their destruction and a specific immune defense.

- Viruses may block cellular pathways that normally kill infected cells such as the apoptosis, complement, or interferon pathways. Viruses may produce protein or nucleic acid products that act as antiapoptotic, anticomplement, or anti-interferon factors.

Many viruses compromise the efficacy of the immune system in some way. Chronic and persistent viral infections yield large numbers of infected cells and viral antigens for years. This can result in pathological instead of beneficial consequences. Exciting new findings have brought the field of immune evasion to the forefront of viral pathogenesis, vaccinology, and molecular immunology. As new mechanisms of host immunity are dis-

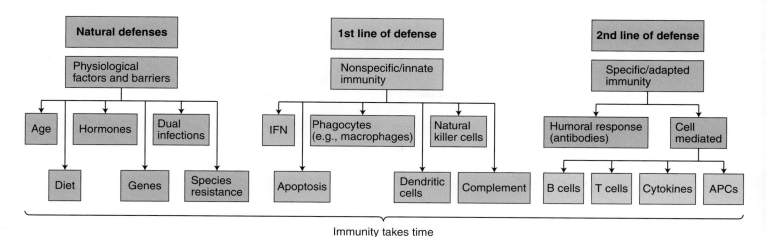

Figure 7-22

Humans and animals have more than one form of defense system against viral pathogens. Simpler defense systems immediately mount upon viral infection, followed by the cooperation of B and T cells within days or at most a few weeks. B and T cells learn from each viral attack, retaining memories to respond when subsequent encounters occur.

VIRUS FILE 7-1 | **Ebola Virus Immune System Evasion Tricks**

Ebola virus outbreaks have been documented since 1976. These outbreaks have occurred in small communities located in very remote areas of Africa such as southern Sudan, the Democratic Republic of Congo (formerly Zaire), Uganda, and Gabon. Ebola infections can cause high mortality rates (as much as 90% in some outbreaks). The most striking symptom is uncontrolled bleeding from any orifice. Progress in understanding the pathogenesis of Ebola virus infections has been slow, primarily because research of these viruses require Bio-Safety Level (BLS)-4 containment. Public awareness of bioterrorism—heightened by an Ebola scare in Canada in February 2001, events relating to the September 11, 2001, terrorist attacks in the United States, and concomitant knowledge that the former Soviet Union had been evaluating Ebola virus as a weapon during the Cold War—has changed our perspective regarding this pathogen and reinforced the need for an effective vaccine.

During infection, the Ebola virus accumulates in high numbers in the liver, spleen, lymph nodes, and lungs, severely damaging these organs during the course of the disease. Individuals who succumb to the infection die with a very high viremia. There is an absence of phagocytes infiltrating to the sites of infection and little evidence of a specific antibody response. Cellular immunity is poor. Recent research points to several possible mechanism(s) for this immune suppression.

The Ebola virus genome consists of seven genes. The glycoprotein (GP) viral gene product is found in two forms: a secreted form (sGP), which is found in large amounts in the blood of infected individuals early in the course of infection, and a nonsecreted form (GP), which is incorporated into the membrane wrapped around the virus particle (**Figure VF 7-1**). Some evidence suggests that the sGP form binds to and inhibits the activation of neutrophils. Ebola virus infects endothelial cells and immune cells such as macrophages and dendritic cells, resulting in immune suppression. Research by Harcourt and colleagues suggests that Ebola virus also selectively inhibits the host's interferon response. Thus it appears that Ebola virus has evolved several mechanisms to avoid its elimination by the host. To date, several different Ebola vaccines are being tested in humans and monkeys. The Vaccine Research Center at the NIH has prepared a vaccine for

(continued)

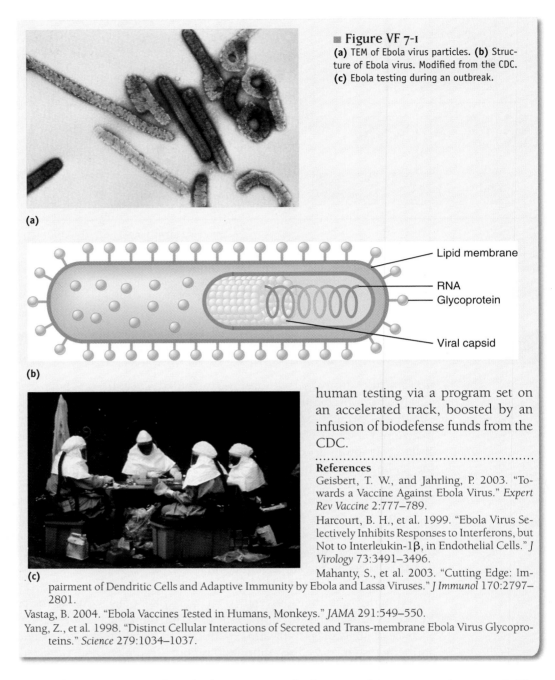

■ **Figure VF 7-1**
(a) TEM of Ebola virus particles. **(b)** Structure of Ebola virus. Modified from the CDC. **(c)** Ebola testing during an outbreak.

Lipid membrane

RNA
Glycoprotein

Viral capsid

human testing via a program set on an accelerated track, boosted by an infusion of biodefense funds from the CDC.

References

Geisbert, T. W., and Jahrling, P. 2003. "Towards a Vaccine Against Ebola Virus." *Expert Rev Vaccine* 2:777–789.

Harcourt, B. H., et al. 1999. "Ebola Virus Selectively Inhibits Responses to Interferons, but Not to Interleukin-1β, in Endothelial Cells." *J Virology* 73:3491–3496.

Mahanty, S., et al. 2003. "Cutting Edge: Impairment of Dendritic Cells and Adaptive Immunity by Ebola and Lassa Viruses." *J Immunol* 170:2797–2801.

Vastag, B. 2004. "Ebola Vaccines Tested in Humans, Monkeys." *JAMA* 291:549–550.

Yang, Z., et al. 1998. "Distinct Cellular Interactions of Secreted and Trans-membrane Ebola Virus Glycoproteins." *Science* 279:1034–1037.

covered, new strategies by which viruses evade these mechanisms are discovered. The balance between host responses and immune evasion determines the outcome of any viral infection. Chapters 11 to 18 will cover specific viral evasion strategies used by viruses.

7·7   History of Immunotherapy

■ Passive Antibody Therapy

After receiving his medical degree in 1878, German Emil von Behring worked as a military and troop physician in various garrisons. In 1888, he took a position at the Hygiene Institute of Berlin as an assistant to Robert Koch (a German pioneer in bacteriology who proposed Koch's postulates—the criteria used to determine if a given bacterium was causing a particular disease). Along with Japanese physician and bacteriologist Shibasaburo Kitasato, he began experiments leading toward the development of therapeutic serum in Koch's laboratory.

Their experiments involved a six-step process (**Figure 7-23**):

1. Growing the bacteria that cause diphtheria or tetanus in pure culture.
2. Inactivating the bacteria with a disinfectant.
3. Injecting the attenuated/killed bacteria into rats, guinea pigs, or rabbits.
4. Collecting the serum produced by these animals.
5. Injecting the serum into nonimmunized animals that were previously infected with the fully virulent bacteria.
6. The mice are injected with antitoxin or control serum from nonimmunized mice.

In 1890, they published their discoveries, in which they noted that their sterilized broth cultures of bacteria caused animals to produce a neutralizing substance against the poisonous substances (**toxins**) that the virulent bacteria produced. They termed these substances **antitoxins** and were able to show that these antitoxins could be used to immunize animals and prevent the animals from showing symptoms of diphtheria or tetanus after being challenged or exposed to infectious bacteria. Specifically, they had shown that antitoxins neutralized the toxins.

In late 1891 von Behring injected an experimental serum containing diptherial antitoxins into a little girl dying of diphtheria in a Berlin hospital. The girl experienced a rapid recovery. Within three years, 20,000 children in Berlin had been immunized against the diphtheria bacterium. For this remarkable achievement von Behring was awarded the Nobel Prize in Physiology and Medicine in 1901, and today he is considered the founder of immunotherapy.

Serum therapy is now known as **passive immunity** and antitoxins are called **antibodies**. Passive immunization is still used today and is defined as an impermanent form of acquired immunity in which antibodies against a disease-causing organism are acquired naturally (as through the placenta to an unborn child) or artificially (as by injection of antiserum). The most common use of antiserum today is the administration of antiserum following a poisonous snake or spider bite. Serum sickness is a complication resulting from a reaction toward antigens of nonhuman species present in antiserum of horse origin. With subsequent exposures of antiserum, serum sickness develops more rapidly. Symptoms include:

- redness and itching at the injection site
- skin lesions/skin eruptions
- joint pain/arthritis
- chest pain
- **scarlatiniform rash,** which resembles the rash presented by scarlet fever patients
- fever
- malaise
- swollen lymph nodes
- flushing
- difficulty breathing/wheezing
- runny nose
- edema or swelling (especially around the face and neck)
- low blood pressure (rare)
- muscle pain
- diarrhea
- nausea
- abdominal cramping
- renal, cardiovascular, pulmonary, and neurologic manifestations

■ **Figure 7-23**
Preliminary experiments by Emil von Behring and Shibasaburo Kitasato paved the way for passive immunization. Passive immunization has been used to protect individuals exposed to individuals who recently contracted hepatitis A, a highly contagious and sometimes life-threatening viral disease.

1. Grow broth cultures of disease-causing bacteria.

2. Kill/sterilize broth cultures with disinfectant.

Injected group.

Negative control group (no injection).

3. Inject/immunize mice with killed disease-causing bacteria.

4. Withdraw blood/harvest serum from both groups of mice.

5. Infect new mice groups with virulent cultures of bacteria.

6. Inject new mice group with antitoxin.

7. Inject new mice with serum from control mice that did not produce antitoxin.

Immunized mice live.

Nonimmunized mice die.

The antiserum is derived from actively immunized human beings or animals. The antibodies last for two to three weeks, during which time the person is protected against the disease. Although short-lived, passive immunization provides immediate protection; active immunization can take weeks to develop. Consequently, passive immunization can be lifesaving when a person has been infected with a deadly organism. The occurrence of serum sickness in the United States is decreasing because public health vaccination programs have decreased the need for antiserum.

The use of immunoglobulin for passive immunity (antibody-containing plasma) was once derived solely from pooled plasma of horses. Although this animal material was specially treated before administration to humans, serious allergic reactions relating to serum sickness were common. Today, human-derived immuneglobulin is more widely available and the risk of side effects is reduced. It is prepared from the pooled plasma of thousands of donors. Hence, recipients of these antibody preparations are receiving antibodies from many people in defense of diverse pathogens. Great care is taken in the preparation of intravenous immune globin (IVIG). The process involves the removal of antibody aggregates (which can activate the complement pathway), treatment with solvents such as ethanol, and the use of detergents to inactivate bloodborne pathogens such as HIV and hepatitis C. Passive immunization is used as protection against such viral diseases as hepatitis (caused by the hepatitis A virus), respiratory disease (caused by RSV), measles, rabies, and Ebola and Lassa Fever viruses. In 2003, the largest hepatitis A outbreak in United States history was found to be associated with green onions in salsa from a restaurant in Monica, Pennsylvania. As a result of the investigation, immuneglobin was administered to approximately 9000 individuals who ate food from the restaurant during the time of the outbreak or had exposure to ill persons involved in the outbreak.

■ Vaccination

Deliberate attempts to prevent infectious diseases have a long history. During the last 200 years, vaccination has controlled six major viral diseases in most parts of the world: smallpox, yellow fever, poliomyelitis, measles, mumps, and rubella. The impact of vaccination on the health of the world's people is hard to exaggerate. Susan and Stanley Plotkin, co-authors of the chapter "A Short History of Vaccination" in *Vaccines* (3rd edition), state that "with the exception of safe water, no other modality, not even antibiotics, has had such a major effect on mortality reduction and population growth." Not a single case of naturally acquired smallpox—once considered one of humankind's most terrible scourges—has been reported since 1977. Through vaccination it has been eradicated (**Figure 7-24**). The WHO predicts that paralytic polio will be eradicated from the world in the near future (**Figure 7-25**).

Attempts to vaccinate date to 1695 inoculation practices against smallpox in China. Five practices have been described:

1. The nose was plugged with powdered smallpox scabs laid on cotton wool.
2. Powdered smallpox scabs were blown into the nose.
3. A healthy child wore the undergarments of an infected child for several days.
4. A piece of cotton containing contents of a smallpox vesicle was stuffed into the nose.
5. White cow fleas were ground into powder and made into pills. This may have been the first attempt at an oral vaccine.

Greater details regarding the history of smallpox vaccination will be covered in Chapter 13.

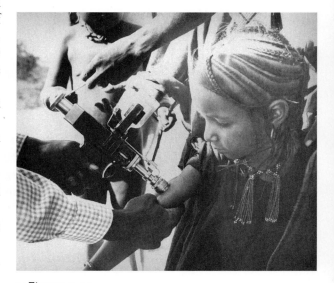

■ Figure 7-24
This Nigerian child is receiving a smallpox vaccination during the WHO Smallpox Eradication Project, 1968.

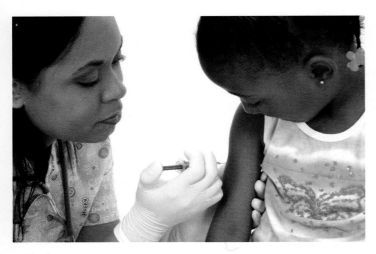

■ Figure 7-25
The CDC currently recommends that only the injectable polio vaccine be administered because of the very small chance that the oral dose can lead to a polio infection.

TABLE 7-4	Examples of Traditional Vaccines Still Used in Vaccination Programs Against Viruses Today

Virus	Type of Vaccine
Vaccinia (smallpox)	Live attenuated
Measles	Live attenuated
Mumps	Live attenuated
Polio virus (Sabin)	Live attenuated
Varicella zoster (chickenpox)	Live attenuated
Yellow fever	Live attenuated
Hepatitis A	Inactivated
Rubella	Inactivated
Influenza	Inactivated
Polio (Salk)	Inactivated

Today, vaccination of large populations is routine. Progress in understanding the immune system, though, has been slow. The early discovery of antibodies held the interest of scientists as being the main mechanism of disease resistance. We now know that antibody production is only part of the immune response against pathogens. Russian scientist Ilya Metchnikoff discovered phagocytic immunity in 1883, but it was not until the 1940s that cell-mediated immunity revived interest and discovery. At present, cellular immunology is central in the interest of most immunologists.

Traditional vaccines depended upon the elicitation of neutralizing antibodies to prevent viral infections. At high concentrations, the neutralizing antibodies either prevented the infection or limited it to a transient, subclinical episode. The current generation of vaccines incorporate important alternative immunizing strategies that revolve around T_c cell responses. This is being done because viruses that cause chronic diseases such as AIDS and hepatitis C produce proteins that are hypervariable, making them poor targets for neutralizing antibodies. T_c cells can detect viral proteins made in infected cells and are not limited to detecting only those viral proteins accessible on cell surfaces. In addition, T_c cells have the ability to lyse infected cells.

Active Immunization Elicits Long-Term Protection

Passive immunity provides transient protection against a specific infectious agent, whereas **activity immunity** provides protection that is **long-term** or has **immunologic memory**. Active immunity means that the immune system is active, and that T and B memory cells are formed. It may be induced artificially via vaccination or through natural infection. Active immunity developed by childhood vaccination programs reduced the number of deaths from infectious diseases.

Traditional Vaccines: Killed or Inactivated Viruses

Whole-virus particle vaccines are commonly used today (Table 7-4). In some cases, vaccine production involves the inactivation of the virus by heat. This rarely works because heat denaturation often destroys viral antigens, thereby reducing their immunogenicity. Other inactivation methods are ultraviolet radiation and chemicals such as formalin (the most common method), b-propiolactone, and phenol. These preparations are killed or inactivated vaccines (**Figure 7-26**). The Salk vaccine against poliovirus is an example of a vaccine produced by formaldehyde inactivation. Inactivated vaccines usually require a booster and more vaccine agent must be injected as compared to live vaccines.

Traditional Vaccines: Live, Attenuated Viruses

Live or attenuated vaccines involve the use of avirulent mutant viruses. The live virus multiplies inside of the recipient host and elicits a long-lasting immune response while causing little or no disease. Viruses may be attenuated in virulence through the repeated culturing of the virus in nonhuman cultured cells or animals (**Figure 7-27**) or at different temperatures. Temperature-sensitive mutants are unable to replicate satisfactorily at tem-

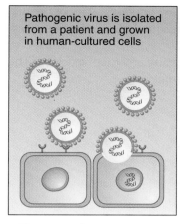

Pathogenic virus is isolated from a patient and grown in human-cultured cells

The cultured virus is used to infect monkey cells

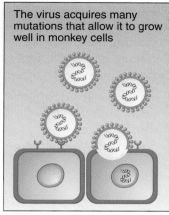

The virus acquires many mutations that allow it to grow well in monkey cells

The virus no longer grows well in human cells (it is attenuated) and can be used as a vaccine

■ **Figure 7-26**
Production of inactivated viral vaccines. Inactivated viruses cannot replicate inside the host; however, the viral antigens may be "preserved" by chemicals, causing an immunogenic response by the host. Adapted from C. Janeway, et al. *Immunobiology: The Immune system in Health and Disease,* Second Edition. Garland Publishing, 1996.

peratures much higher than normal (above 104°F, or 40°C). These live vaccines tend to revert toward virulence. Cold-adapted mutants replicate well at lower temperatures (91.4°F, or 33°C) but not at normal human temperature (98.6°F, or 37°C). Most of these mutations do not revert.

Live attenuated vaccines produce strong cellular responses that are similar to natural infection. In general, only one or two doses are required. Severe reactions to live attenuated vaccines are possible in immunosuppressed individuals. Table 7-4 lists examples of inactivated and live vaccines currently in use.

■ Advantages and Disadvantages of Traditional Vaccines

Even though traditional vaccines have been very successful, there are limitations to these vaccines:

Virus is inactivated with formalin.

Virus cannot infect/replicate in cells.

■ **Figure 7-27**
Production of attenuated viral vaccines. The pathogenic viruses are grown in human cell cultures and then passaged many times in other cell lines such as monkey cells. The serial passage of the virus in monkey cells causes the virus to accumulate adaptive mutations suited for replication in monkey cells and not human cells. The attenuated virus will not cause disease in the human host, but the host will produce immunity against it. Adapted from C. Janeway, et al. *Immunobiology: The Immune system in Health and Disease,* Second Edition. Garland Publishing, 1996.

- Not all infectious agents can be grown in animals or cell cultures. There are a number of viral diseases for which no vaccines have been developed.
- Batches of vaccine may be insufficiently killed or attenuated during the manufacturing process, thereby introducing virulent viruses into the vaccine and inadvertently spreading the disease.
- Attenuated strains of virus may revert. Continual testing is necessary to ensure that virulence has not occurred.
- Not all viral diseases are preventable by traditional vaccines (such as AIDS and hepatitis C).
- The yield and rate of production of human and animal viruses in cell cultures are often low, making vaccine production costly.
- The vaccines have a limited shelf life and often require refrigeration. This creates storage problems in countries with large, rural areas without electricity.

■ The New Generation of Vaccines

Recombinant DNA technology has provided a means for creating vaccines that overcome the drawbacks of traditional vaccines. It has allowed researchers to manipulate pathogenic viruses or to use specific viral proteins (parts of the virus) as vaccines, making the vaccines much safer because any risk of infection is eliminated. Our new understanding of the two lines of immune defenses (antibody and cell mediated) has resulted in a renewed interest in creating more vaccines.

There are several types of technology being applied toward potential vaccines. The current approaches to these vaccines are based on the following:

- recombinant subunits
- peptides
- live vectors
- reassortment viruses
- naked DNA
- Edible plants

Recombinant Subunit Vaccines

Hepatitis epidemics date to 2000 B.C. Before World War II, physicians did not know that hepatitis B virus (HBV) was the primary cause of hepatitis. Frequent yellow jaundice outbreaks swept through the United States armed forces. Physicians ultimately linked the outbreaks to the human serum used in the vaccine that had been administered to prevent yellow fever.

A series of scientific observations from the 1950s through the 1970s contributed toward the development of an HBV vaccine. These observations pertained to the transmission of the disease via blood, especially blood transfusions. Subsequently, it was discovered that HBV carriers contained a specific viral surface antigen in their blood, termed HbsAg. Once it was discovered that HbsAg was part of the virus that causes hepatitis B, blood screening was revolutionized. In the meantime, HBV infection emerged as a significant global health threat, with between 10 and 30 million individuals becoming infected each year.

The challenge, of course, was the creation of a vaccine. Medical research revealed that HBV infection may establish chronic hepatitis and cirrhosis. Approximately 80% of all hepatocellular carcinomas (liver cancers) were related to HBV infection. Early studies showed that passive immunization using HBV immuneglobulin was successful in preventing or modifying the course of HBV infection. The production of a HBV vaccine was hampered until the advent of recombinant DNA technology, because it was not possible to grow HBV in cell culture and no animals with the exception of higher primates are susceptible to HBV infection. A plasma-derived vaccine prepared by harvesting the HbsAg from plasma was licensed in 1981, but many chose not to be vaccinated because of unfounded fears regarding the safety of plasma-derived products and the high cost of the vaccine. As a result, several vaccine manufacturers began to apply recombinant DNA technology toward the development of a new HBV vaccine. This technology had the potential to create an unlimited supply of a safe and effective vaccine that could eventually be produced at much lower cost than the plasma-derived vaccines.

It took nine years of research, including failure to produce the recombinant viral antigens in *E. coli*, before a successful vaccine was produced using genetically engineered *Saccharomyces cerevisiae* (a yeast; **Figure 7-28**). When creating the vaccine, the HbsAg or HBV viral coat protein is glycosylated. Bacteria cannot glycosylate proteins, therefore a yeast (eukaryotic) expression system was used to produce a glycosylated form of HbsAg that could act as an effective immunogen. In 1986 the Food and Drug Administration (FDA) licensed and approved the first recombinant DNA vaccine, an improved version of the HBV vaccine, for universal infant vaccination, and in 1996 approved it for adolescent vaccination. The vaccine is 80 to 100% effective and is administered in a series of three doses. (Boosters are not recommended.) The duration of immunity is expected to last more than 15 years.

Peptide Vaccines

Whereas subunit vaccines use an entire viral protein that contains several antigenic determinants to immunize an individual, peptide vaccines use a specific domain of a protein that contains a single epitope or antigenic determinant. The use of chemically synthesized viral peptides to induce a protective immune response has great potential because virtually any peptide sequence can be produced. The disadvantage is that peptides in general are not very immunogenic. In addition, the peptide must have the same conformation as in the virus to induce immunity. The amount of peptide required to elicit an immune response may be 1000× more than vaccinating with an inactivated virus. To overcome this, the peptides are linked to a carrier protein to improve their immunogenicity. Unfortunately, peptide vaccines are the least effective and most expensive to produce. None are currently in use.

Recombinant (Live) Vector Vaccines

Molecular biology techniques are being used to develop new live vaccines. Genes coding for surface proteins of pathogenic viruses can be inserted into safe viruses (such as vaccinia and canarypox). Upon infection the new hybrid virus expresses and initiates an immune response toward itself and the inserted antigens (**Figure 7-29**).

In 1980, the WHO declared the worldwide eradication of smallpox and recommended discontinuing vaccination with vaccinia virus. Ironically, that same year, recombinant DNA technology was being used to manipulate vaccinia virus as an expression vector and candidate vector vaccine against unrelated infectious diseases such as rabies virus.

The first vaccinia vector recombinant vaccine used in the field was a rabies vaccine (vaccinia rabies glyoprotein, or VRG). Wildlife populations harbor the rabies virus, which presents a threat to humans when they have contact with infected animals either directly or indirectly, through their pets. In the year 2000, the U.S. Department of Agriculture—Animal and Plant Health Inspection Service reported 7369 cases of rabies in animals, of which 6.1% were foxes, 37.7% were raccoons, 30.2% were skunks, and 6.9% were domesticated dogs. The remaining 19% were rabies in bats and other animals not specified in the report. (No human cases reported to the CDC that year.)

The vaccinia vector recombinant vaccine was used in large-scale field conditions to vaccinate foxes in several European countries beginning in 1987. By 2001, Belgium was officially declared rabies-free.

There was an explosive outbreak of raccoon rabies in Pinellas County, Florida, in 1995, when rabid raccoons spread the disease to otters, cats, and a horse. A total of 145 people were treated for exposure to rabid animals. In response to this, Pinellas County Animal Services implemented a 5-year vaccination plan for distributing VRG oral rabies vaccine, in baits, in areas of high raccoon concentrations. The baits consisted of capsules of VRG inserted into blocks of fish meal, which then were distributed via air by helicopters and by ground

■ **Figure 7-28**

General procedure used to create recombinant HBV vaccine. Adapted from Marks, Dawn B., Marks, Allan D., and Smith, Colleen M. *Basic Medical Biochemistry: A Clinical Approach.* Lippincott, Williams & Wilkins, 1996.

■ **Figure 7-29**
A recombinant vaccinia virus expressing the rabies glycoprotein was an early example of a successful poxvirus vector used in immunization. The vector was created by the insertion of a cDNA for the rabies virus glycoprotein gene into the thymidine kinase (TK) locus of vaccinia virus. Disruption of the TK gene allowed a biochemical selection of the recombinant as well as attenuation of the vector. Adapted from an illustration by the College of Veterinary Medicine, University of Florida.

■ **Figure 7-30**
Rabies vaccine bait used in the field to vaccinate wildlife.

staff. The baits were designed to be ruptured when bitten, releasing the immunizing dose of VRG into the animal's mouth (**Figure 7-30**). Within four years, the number of reported rabies cases decreased to one.

The complications of smallpox vaccination via vaccinia virus, although rare (572 complications in 14.2 million vaccines in the United States in 1968), did raise some important safety issues about the use of recombinant vector vaccines because of the possibilities of accidental laboratory infections and side effects of vaccination. Two major steps were taken to enhance the safety of vaccinia virus, both of which have led to safe vaccinia virus strains:

- deletion or disruption of genes involved in nucleic acid metabolism host interactions and extracellular virus formation via recombinant DNA technology, and
- attenuation of the virus through serial passage in cell culture or an unnatural host.

Avipoxviruses only replicate in avian species. They have been isolated from a number of bird virus species such as fowlpox, canarypox, pigeonpox, penguinpox, and quailpox. Attenuated virus strains more effectively stimulate mucosal and cell-mediated immunity, and attenuated strains of avipoxviruses have a long and safe history of testing. Attenuated strains of canarypox have been tested extensively and their safety has been demonstrated in a variety of species and immune-compromised animals and human volunteers. The attenuated canarypox-based vectors can infect human cells but cannot divide or grow in them. Hence, they produce a self-limited infection that does not cause any harm or symptoms in humans. The European Medicines Evaluation Agency (EMEA) has accepted at least two vaccines for cats derived from this technology, which are marketed in the European Union but are not yet available in the United States.

Reassortment Vaccines

When two viruses containing segmented genomes infect the same cell, **reassortments** may be created. The reassortment progeny viruses contain segments from both parent viruses (**Figure 7-31**). Reassortment plays an essential role in nature by generating novel progeny viruses. It has also been exploited in the laboratory in assigning functions to different segments of the genome; for example, in a reassorted virus, if one segment comes from virus A and the rest from virus B, one can determine which properties resemble virus A and which resemble virus B. The identification of the gene functions has made possible techniques to intentionally reassort rotavirus strains and prepare candidate vaccines strains from the desired phenotypic traits of different parent viruses. Influenza and rotaviruses contain segmented genomes, making reassortment possible.

Rotaviruses are the leading cause of severe dehydrating diarrhea in infants and young children in the United States, and are a major cause of childhood death worldwide (**Figure 7-32**). Virtually all children become infected with a rotavirus in the first 3 to 5 years of life, but severe diarrhea and dehydration primarily occurs in children aged 3 to 35 months. Research to develop a safe, effective rotavirus vaccine began in the 1970s when it was discovered that previous infection with rotavirus strains isolated from wild animals protected laboratory animals from experimental infection with human rotaviruses.

Rotashield, a live oral rhesus–human reassortment-based rotavirus vaccine produced by Wyeth-Lederle Vaccines and Pediatrics, was licensed for use in the United States in August of 1998 after sailing through all the necessary clinical trials and approval processes. Three months later, the CDC and the American Academy of Pediatrics recommended universal vaccination of all American

■ Figure 7-31
Simplified diagram showing the natural generation of reassortment viruses. Adapted from University of South Carolina, School of Medicine. "Virology: viral Genetics." *Microbiology and Immunology*. University of South Carolina, http://pathmicro.med.sc.edu/mhunt/genet.htm.

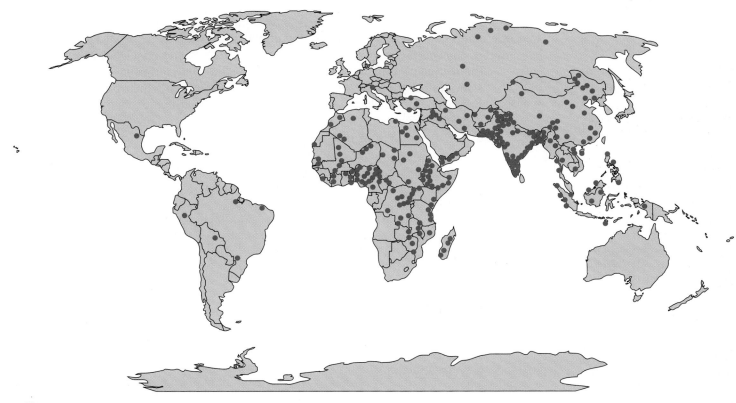

■ Figure 7-32
Number of worldwide deaths related to rotavirus infection. One dot represents 1000 deaths. It is estimated that there is a global distribution of 440,000 annual deaths. Adapted from Parashar, U., et al. *Emerg Infect Dis*. 9 (2003): 565–572.

infants. By July of 1999, more than 600,000 infants in the United States had received at least one immunization. In October of 1999, though, the use of the vaccine was suspended because 15 children had developed intussusception after administration of the vaccine. Intussusception occurs when one portion of the bowel slides into the next, much like the pieces of a telescope. When this occurs, it creates an obstruction in the bowel, with the walls of the intestines pressing against one another. This in turn leads to swelling, inflammation, and decreased blood flow to the intestines. If diagnosed, the condition is readily treatable with a barium or air enema or by surgery.

Approximately 1 in 11,000 vaccinated children were potentially affected. The cost of withdrawing it from the market was approximately $80 million, and antivaccine groups viewed this event as another example of how vaccines can damage the health of children. Other manufacturers developing similar rotavirus vaccines worried that their vaccines might also contain the risk of intussusception as well. At present there are two vaccines in phase III trials of late-stage development, two vaccines in phase II development, and one vaccine candidate in phase I early-stage development. The majority of these vaccine candidates are human–rhesus or human–bovine reassortments.

Naked DNA Vaccines

Naked DNA vaccines consist of **plasmid** DNAs that have been manipulated to contain a gene encoding a viral antigen of interest. In addition, promoter/terminator DNA sequences are introduced into the plasmid to facilitate the gene expression of the viral gene of interest in human or mammalian cells. The objective of a DNA vaccine is not to raise an immune response to the DNA itself, but rather to the expressed antigen carried on the plasmid DNA.

Plasmid DNA vaccines have several distinct advantages over other vaccines. Plasmids can easily be manufactured, are very stable, and resist temperature extremes, making storage and transport practical and inexpensive. The DNA sequence of the plasmid can easily be changed in the laboratory (**Figure 7-33**), and mixtures of plasmids can also be used that encode many viral protein fragments, creating a broad vaccine. Thus vaccinologists can respond to changes in the viral pathogen of interest. Administering a DNA vaccine causes the recipient's cells to produce and process the viral antigen(s) of interest in the same way as those of the proteins of the virus against which protection is to be produced. This makes a much better antigen over purifying that protein and using it as an immunogen. As a result of the way the antigen is presented, there is also a CTL response (**Figure 7-34**). Clinical trials of candidate plasmid DNA HIV-1 are in progress. DNA vaccines have been tested in a variety of animal models for different viral infectious viruses such as influenza, Ebola, West Nile, and SARS-CoV.

Edible Vaccines

One of the major reasons that vaccines are not available worldwide is that many developing nations simply cannot afford them. As a result, thirty million children born each year are not adequately immunized by modern standards. Plant-made vaccines offer an alternative system for stable, low cost, rapid scalability vaccines that are free of human pathogens. Vaccine proteins will have similar biochemical properties to pathogens because the plant cellular machinery can fold and assemble proteins correctly. Hence these plant-derived proteins should be effective in stimulating an immune response. To the general public, of course, the most obvious benefit of edible plant-based vaccines is their delivery method: you eat them.

Plant-made pharmaceuticals were possible only after the rapid advances in molecular biology and plant biotechnology, and the first research publications relating to the production of plant-made pharmaceuticals weren't published until 1990.

■ **Figure 7-33**

Schematic of a typical DNA vaccine plasmid. A gene encoding the viral antigen gene of interest is flanked between a strong viral promoter and transcriptional terminator sequences. Additional sequences may also be inserted into the vector that stimulate cytokines or other immune stimulatory molecules may also be inserted into the plasmid as well as an antibiotic resistance gene to facilitate plasmid production in bacteria. Adapted from C. A. de Quadros, ed. *Vaccines: Preventing Disease and Protecting Health.* Pan American Health Organization, 2004.

Today over 40 worldwide laboratory research teams have explored plant-based antigens as vaccines, with the idea of delivering oral vaccines to recipients in developing countries.

Early studies of plant-derived subunit vaccines focused on transformation systems for tobacco, but the toxicity of tobacco precluded its use for oral delivery. Other plant systems under consideration are bananas, tomatoes, carrots, lettuce, corn, and potatoes. To date, the most attractive plant systems are the tomato and potato because of their wide use in global diets, ease of genetic transformation, and the relatively short time needed to obtain fruit or tubers for bioassays (**Figure 7-35**).

One of the major issues that need to be addressed with plant-based vaccines is the ability to provide a consistent dose. Scientists are approaching this subject by applying food processing techniques. Plants expressing a viral gene of interest are dried and made into a powder material that is then put into gelatin capsules for oral intake.

The key advantage of plant-based systems is that they can synthesize complex proteins that can then be mass-produced with minimal cost and with enhanced vaccine stability.

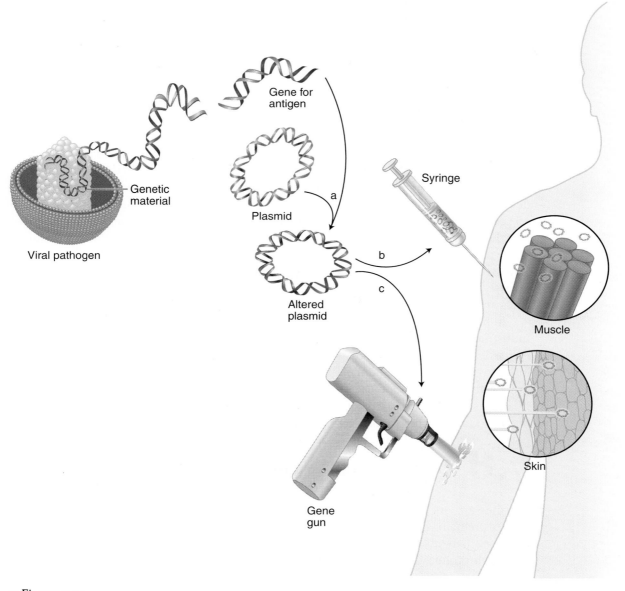

■ **Figure 7-34**
Plasmid DNAs are injected into vaccinees. Adapted from M. K. Campbell and S. O. Farrell. *Biochemistry,* Fifth Edition. Brooks/Cole, 2006.

How to Make an Edible Vaccine

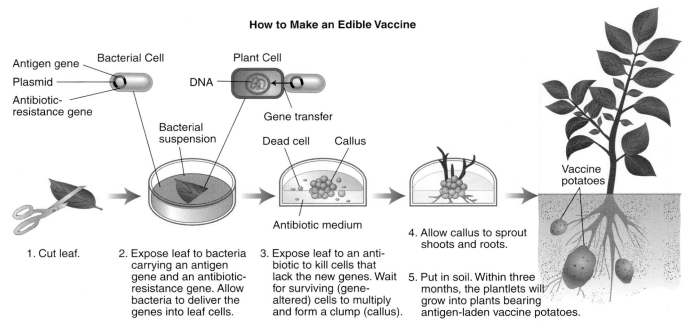

1. Cut leaf.

2. Expose leaf to bacteria carrying an antigen gene and an antibiotic-resistance gene. Allow bacteria to deliver the genes into leaf cells.

3. Expose leaf to an antibiotic to kill cells that lack the new genes. Wait for surviving (gene-altered) cells to multiply and form a clump (callus).

4. Allow callus to sprout shoots and roots.

5. Put in soil. Within three months, the plantlets will grow into plants bearing antigen-laden vaccine potatoes.

■ **Figure 7-35**
Transgenic plants are an alternative for the expression of viral antigens for use as vaccines as well as antibodies and other therapeutics. Adapted from W. H. R. Langridge, *Sci. Am.* (2000): 6 pages.

Even though the concept of plant-based vaccines is attractive for the aforementioned reasons, no major pharmaceutical company has aggressively pursued a development effort because there are doubts about sufficient return on investment. It is anticipated that the development of a single product would cost between $110 to $800 million and take 12 to 15 years for licensure. Other concerns of pharmaceutical companies include environmental safety issues, such as transgene spread and the rigorous scientific evaluation required of the product, and the difficulty of finding personnel with a background in plant biology research and development expertise. These are major challenges for a commercial venture. If these hurdles can be overcome, though, it might be possible to make plant-derived vaccines available to everyone who needs them and at an affordable price.

In July 2004 the Pharma-Planta Project, a consortium of 39 academic laboratories and industrial partners representing 31 organizations from 11 European countries and South Africa, was formally introduced to the public. The project was funded by a European Union contribution of 12 million euros, and its ongoing mission is to optimize techniques for the production of antibodies and vaccines that can be used to prevent important human infectious diseases. A priority product under development is the production of an antibody produced in maize that can be used to block HIV transmission.

7.8 Immunizing the Compromised Host

Vaccines are one of the most powerful tools for preventing viral infections. Infectious diseases remain the leading cause of death worldwide, and the number of immunocompromised patients has increased dramatically since the mid 1970s. Patients may be immunocompromised after organ transplantation, infections with HIV, and after intensive therapy for cancer(s).

Infections have been the major obstacle to successful transplantations. Transplant patients remain on immunosuppressive drugs to prevent organ rejection and HIV-infected patients become progressively more immunosuppressed over time. Thus immunizing the compromised individual is important from both vulnerability and public health standpoints.

In general, it appears that there is no harm in vaccinating HIV positive patients with inactivated vaccines. The safety of immunization with live attenuated vaccines is a matter of concern regarding HIV-infected patients, though, and live vaccines are generally not recommended for immunocompromised patients. Few studies are available regarding vaccination of cancer patients undergoing radiation or intensive chemotherapy. Immunizations of patients with certain vaccines such as the influenza vaccine are often recommended before lymphoma and leukemia patients begin cancer treatments and before transplant recipients receive bone marrow or solid organs. The use of live vaccines is not recommended for patients actively undergoing cancer chemotherapy or after transplantation.

7.9 Vaccine Additives

After viruses have been grown in cell culture, they undergo a purification process that involves ultrafiltration (to remove cellular debri and to concentrate the virus), centrifugation, chromatography, and other extraction procedures. There may be some impurities remaining in the vaccine, such as antibiotics (e.g., neomycin or kanamycin), which are used to prevent the growth of bacteria in cell cultures or egg proteins from viruses cultured in embryonated chicken eggs. An adjuvant such as aluminum hydroxide is often added to stimulate immunity. Vaccines may also contain other additives such as sulfites or thimerosal (mercury) as preservatives.

7.10 Side Effects

The majority of side effects to vaccines are limited to localized reactions such as swelling, redness, pain, and itching at the site of injection. Allergic responses (such as anaphylaxis) may occur because of overreactive immune responses to vaccine components such as antibiotics, egg proteins, animal protein, preservatives, and stabilizers. Severe side effects are rare. The co-founders of the U.S. National Vaccine Information Center (NVIC, formed in 1982) worked with federal legislators to help create and pass the National Childhood Vaccine Injury Act of 1986. The act requires physicians and other healthcare providers who administer vaccines to maintain permanent immunization records and to report occurrences of any untoward effects to the U.S. Department of Health and Human Services.

7.11 Vaccine Delivery

New ways to deliver vaccines are under consideration. Needle-and-syringe systems are woefully inadequate for worldwide vaccination programs. Safety is an issue in developing nations where HIV and hepatitises B and C are epidemic, and reusing needles is often practiced out of habit. In the United States at least 14 needles are needed to vaccinate a child from birth to adolescence. As a result, needleless systems are being designed with the idea of injury protection. Another consideration is the investigation of new delivery technology that will more effectively stimulate mucosal and cell-mediated immune responses. Lastly, newer delivery systems are attractive to individuals who are afraid of needle injections, a fear that can compromise vaccine compliance.

Jet injectors have been used in several mass vaccination programs (**Figure 7-36**). In 1986, the CDC's *Morbidity and Mortality Weekly Report* linked a Med-E-Jet device to an outbreak of HBV infection. In this case, the device was administering injections of human

■ Figure 7-36
Photograph showing a clinician using a jet injector gun during adult immunization. The device uses gaseous pressure to propel drugs or vaccines through the outer layers of the skin and into the underlying subcutaneous tissues without the use of needles.

chorionic gonadotropin hormone (HCG)—not a vaccine—to attendees at a weight loss clinic in California. Injectors were improved to contain reusable nozzles, but because of the risk of transmitting bloodborne pathogens the WHO stopped recommending multiple-use jet injectors for immunization programs. Instead, the WHO, United Nations Children's Fund (UNICEF), and the United Nations Populations Fund (UNFPA) issued a joint statement on the use of autodisable syringes in immunization services.

Several companies are currently working on new vaccine and drug-delivery technologies. These technologies include nasal sprays, skin patches (the vaccine is swabbed onto the skin and temporarily covered with an adhesive patch, or the vaccine may be incorporated into the patch), and time-release pills. To date, none of these technologies has been applied to licensed vaccines.

7.12 Manufacturing and Quality Assurance of Vaccines

All vaccines available in the United States are subjected to a well-defined regulatory process for approval. Each vaccine is tested for safety and effectiveness through preclinical (animal) and clinical (human trial) studies. After a vaccine is developed and preliminary preclinical research has been conducted, a report is prepared and submitted as part of an Investigational New Drug Application (IND) for approval. The IND application asks for the FDA's permission to proceed with testing the vaccine on human subjects. The FDA reviews the application and decides whether or not the vaccine is safe for human trials. The FDA provides guidelines pertaining to the necessary studies needed to satisfy the efficacy provisions of the law and informal guidance on specific methods used in vaccine manufacture and how to conduct the clinical studies. These regulations are referred to as good clinical practices (GCPs).

Clinical trials proceed in at least three phases. As the phases proceed, more human subjects are used and the patient history of the subjects will change. By phase III, full-scale production of the vaccine occurs. Trials are conducted using consistent lots of the vaccine, and the vaccines must be manufactured according to current good manufacturing practices (CGMPs).

At the end of phase III human trials, two forms of FDA-approved licenses are applied for: establishment and product. Establishment licenses must be granted to each location or facility where the vaccine will be manufactured. All locations are inspected and the product is examined during all phases of manufacturing. A product license is granted after an application to the Center for Biologics Evaluation and Research (CBER) has been approved. Approval means that the manufactured vaccine product meets the prescribed standards of safety, purity, and potency (Table 7-5). Table 7-6 lists companies and sponsors that produced licensed viral vaccines for immunization and distribution in the United States in 2004.

After FDA establishment and product licenses have been approved, the so-called "marketing" phase of the vaccine occurs. CBER and the CDC jointly manage the Vaccine Adverse Event Reporting System (VAERS), a cooperative program for vaccine safety. The process of research, testing, review, and approval helps to ensure that drugs marketed in

TABLE 7-5	Vaccine Development Overview			

Preclinical		Clinical				
Stage I		**Stage II**		**Stage III**		**Stage IV**
Animal studies	**FDA** **I** **N** **D**	**Phase I** Use healthy volunteers Small studies (20–80 subjects) Test low and high dose ranges for safety	**Phase II** Limited number of human trials (100–200 subjects) Determine optimal dose/ immunogenicity Controlled investigations Use of placebo group	**Phase III** Full scale manufacture Numerous clinical studies at different sites Large number of subjects (100s–1000s) Include subjects with preexisting conditions CBER application	**FDA** **L** **I** **C** **E** **N** **S** **E**	**Phase IV** Vaccines available to physicians and patients Large scale safety and clinical trials Trials on subjects not tested in Phase III Monitor adverse effects

2 to 10 years

IND = Investigational new drug application.

the United States are safe and effective. Similar mechanisms around the world provide the same assurances.

■ The Economics of Vaccines

There is disparity between the vaccines that are developed and produced and the ones that are actually needed. The market must meet the demands of the customer. In this case, the largest customers of vaccines are children, and the majority of children in need are located in impoverished parts of the world. Children should receive 8 to 12 different vaccines in the first years of life. Historically, vaccine development and commercialization was supported by private investments, but there are very few private investors interested in supporting the development and manufacture of vaccines that would benefit developing countries.

The vaccine industry is dominated by only a handful of companies. Ongoing bioterrorism concerns and new biotechnology advances are generating new interest in the vaccine market, though.

The major consumer of vaccines is the UNICEF. Vaccine procurement has become complex in recent years as the market has changed. Vaccine manufacturers adjust their prices to ensure that developing countries can afford them while charging higher prices in industrialized nations. Stage III of clinical research and development is the most expensive stage in the process. Hence, differential pricing of licensed vaccines allows the manufacturer to recoup their research and development expenses.

The Global Alliance for Vaccines and Immunization (GAVI) was created in 1999 in response to disparities in vaccine immunization programs and access to vaccines. It forms close partnerships between the private and public sectors with the goal of saving children's

TABLE 7-6	Viral Vaccines Licensed for Immunization and Distribution in the United States

Virus Vaccine	Sponsor
Influenzas A and B, poliovirus, rabies	Aventis Pasteur, Inc.
Rabies	BioPort Corp.
Rabies	Chiron Behring GmbH & Co.
Influenzas A and B	Evans Vaccine
Hepatitis A and B	GlaxoSmithKline
Influenza	MedImmune Vaccines, Inc.
Hepatitis A and B, measles, mumps, rubella	Merck & Co., Inc.
Japanese encephalitis virus	Research Foundation for Microbial Diseases of Osaka University
Smallpox	Wyeth Laboratories, Inc.

lives and saving the "people's health through the widespread use of vaccines." GAVI's partners include UNICEF, WHO, the Bill and Melinda Gates Foundation, the Developing Country Vaccine Manufacturers Network, and others. GAVI's objectives are to expand the reach of immunization services, introduce priority vaccines for developing countries, and establishing tools and systems to promote sustainable financing in developing countries.

The Vaccine Fund was created with an initial pledge of $750 million from the Bill and Melinda Gates Foundation as the financing arm to help support GAVI immunization goals. Since then, the governments of Canada, Denmark, Ireland, Norway, the Netherlands, Sweden, the United States, and the United Kingdom have also pledged their support. The Vaccine Fund now has over $1 billion in commitments over the next five years. The Vaccine Fund is designed to raise an additional $400 million a year to extend GAVI's support for programs that provide new and underused vaccines to more of the world's children. By understanding the current vaccine market, manufacturers, and consumers, and the investment decisions during the research and development pathway of new candidate vaccines, one can understand how economics has shaped the vaccine world. Mechanisms like GAVI and the Vaccine Fund may change the economics of high-priority vaccines for the developing world. Partnerships and economic savvy are needed to meet the biggest viral challenges facing the world: vaccines that prevent the transmission of HIV and hepatitis C.

■ Summary

The immune system is amazingly complex. It is responsible for defending the host from viral and other microbial invasions as well as tissue rejection and growth of cancerous cells. This host defense system contains two separate arming mechanisms: nonspecific responses and specific immune responses. Interactions between the host, viral pathogen, and environmental factors determine the extent of a particular viral disease. This is referred to as the triad model of disease causation; for example, the host factors that impact susceptibility to viral infection includes age, nutritional state, hormonal balance, fever responses, genetic factors, presence of other microbial infections, and species resistance.

Immediately after an infection, nonspecific host defenses provide protection against any pathogen they encounter, as they do not retain any "memories" from prior encounters. Examples of nonspecific responses are the IFN response, apoptosis, phagocytosis, the complement system, and the action(s) of dendritic and natural killer cells.

Specific immunity requires days to weeks before it is induced or effective in clearing viruses and other pathogens or cancerous cells. Specific defenses result in memory cells that patrol the host and facilitate clearance of pathogens after subsequent encounters with the same pathogen. The key players of the specific immune defense system are B and T lymphocytes, which are involved in antibody and cell-mediated responses to neutralize, control, and eliminate foreign invaders.

There are five classes of antibody molecules. Three of them participate in fighting pathogenic infections: IgA, IgG, and IgM. Whenever IgM is found in patient serum samples analyzed in the clinical laboratory, it indicates that the patient has had a recent or current infection. IgA is found in secretions of the body. IgG is the most abundant class of antibody present in serum. It is produced for long periods of time, resulting in long-term protection against invasion by prior pathogens.

Cell-mediated immunity is directed by T lymphocytes that recognize viral invaders via MHC I and II antigen-presenting complexes located on the surfaces of APCs. Cytokines communicate between the B and T cells, promoting the growth of more T and B cells. Repeated exposure of the same pathogens results in the maintenance of B and T memory cells.

Despite these host defensive mechanisms, many viruses have evolved ways to evade them. Many viruses can establish persistent and chronic infections that compromise the immune system in some way. The balance between host responses and immune evasion determines the outcome of any viral infection.

The knowledge gained from scientific experiments regarding host defenses has allowed researchers to develop immune therapies such as serum therapy or passive immunity and vaccination. Traditional (live or killed viruses) or newer generation vaccines that use genetic engineering techniques to manipulate viruses for vaccine development are used to prevent viral infections today. Vaccines are now available for the following viruses: vaccinia (smallpox), measles, mumps, rubella, varicella zoster (chickenpox), hepatitis A, poliovirus, and influenza. The United States has formed the NVIC to monitor reports of any untoward effects related to vaccination.

New ways to deliver vaccines are under consideration because needle-and-syringe type systems are woefully inadequate for worldwide vaccination programs. New technologies being considered are nasal sprays, skin patches, time-release pills, and edible (plant-derived) vaccines.

Vaccines are costly to produce and manufactured by a limited number of companies. All vaccines must be subjected to a well-defined regulatory process for approval. Approval stages occur both at the preclinical and clinical levels. Clinical approval can take between 2 and 10 years before licensure occurs. There is a disparity between what vaccines are developed and produced and which vaccines are needed. The largest consumer group of vaccines is children and the majority of them in need are located in developing countries. Very few private investors support the development and manufacture of vaccines that would benefit impoverished parts of the world. Organizations like GAVI and the Vaccine Fund have responded to this disparity by forming partnerships between private and public sectors to develop new priority vaccines for developing countries. Bioterrorism concerns and new technologies are rejuvenating the vaccine market as well.

◼ Resources

◼ Primary Literature and Reviews

Berzofsky, J.A. 2004. "New Strategies for Designing and Optimizing Vaccines." *ASM News* 70(5):219–223.

Biron, C. A., Byron, K.S., and Sullivan, J. L. 1989. "Severe herpesvirus Infections in an Adolescent Without Natural Killer Cells." *N Engl J Med* 320(26):1731–1735.

Blue, C. E., Spiller, O. B., and Blackgourn, D. J. 2004. "The Relevence of Complement to Virus Biology." *Virology* 319:176–184.

Brinton, M. A. and Perelygin, A. A. 2003. "Genetic Resistance to flaviviruses." *Adv Virus Res* 60:43–85.

Brown, M. G. et al. 2001. "Vital Involvement of a Natural Killer Cell Activation Receptor in Resistance to Viral Infection." *Science* 292:934–937.

Chen, R. T. et al. 2004. "Suspension of Rotavirus Vaccine After Reports of Intussusception—United States, 1999." *MMWR* 53(34):786–789.

Coates, P. T. H., Clovin, B. L., Hackstein, H., and Thomson, A. W. 2002. "Manipulation of Dendritic Cells as an Approach to Improved Outcomes in Transplantation." *Exp Rev Mol Med* 18:1–21.

CDC. 1999. "Prevention of Hepatitis A Through Active or Passive Immunization: Recommendations of the Advisory Committee on Immunization Practices (ACIP)." *MMWR* 48(RR12):1–37.

Cohen, J., and Powderly, W. G., eds. 2004. *Infectious Diseases*, 2nd ed. Philadelphia: Mosby.

Dato, V. et al. 2003. "Hepatitis A Outbreak Associated with Green Onions at a Restaurant—Monaca, Pennsylvania, 2003." *MMWR* 52(47):1155–1157.

de Blecourt, W., and Usborne, C., eds. 2004. *Cultural Approaches to the History of Medicine: Mediating Medicine in Early Modern and Modern Europe.* New York: Palgrave McMillan.

de Quadros, C A., ed. 2004. *Vaccines: Preventing Disease & Protecting Health,* Washington: Pan American Health Organization.

Diamond, M. S. 2003. "Evasion of Innate and Adaptive Immunity by flaviviruses." *Immunol & Cell Biol* 81:196–206.

Favoreel, H.W., Van de Walle, G. R., Nauwynck, H. J., and Pensaert, M.B. 2003. "Virus Complement Evasion Strategies." *J Gen Virol* 84(Pt1):1–15.

Garcia-Sastre, A., and Biron, C. A. 2006. "Type 1 interferons and the virus-host relationship: A lesson in détente." *Science* 312:879–882.

Geisbert, T. W., and Jahrling, P. B. 2003. "Towards a Vaccine Against Ebola Virus." *Exp Rev Vaccines* 2(6):777–789.

Glass, R. I., et al. 2004. "The Future of Rotavirus Vaccines: A Major Setback Leads to New Opportunities." *Lancet* 363:1547–1550.

Goldsby, R. A., Kindt, T. J., Osborne, B. A., and Kuby, J. 2003. *Immunology* 5th ed. New York: W. H. Freeman.

Haller, O., Frese, M., and Kochs, G. 1998. "Mx Proteins: Mediators of Innate Resistance to RNA Viruses." *Rev Sci Tech Off Int Epiz* 17(1):220–230.

Itoh, K., et al. 1994. "Hypocomplementemia Associated with Hepatitis C Viremia in Sera From Voluntary Blood Donors." *Am J Gastroenterol* 89(11):2019–2024.

Jacobs, B. L., and Langland, J. O, 1996. "When Two Strands are Better Than One: The Mediators and Modulators of the Cellular Responses to Double-Stranded RNA." *Virology* 219:339–349.

Knipe, D. M., and Howley, P. M. eds. 2001. *Fundamental Virology* 4th ed. Philadelphia: Lippincott Williams & Wilkins.

Leclerc, C. 2003. "New Approaches in Vaccine Development." *Comp Immunol Microbiol Infect Dis* 26:329–341.

Ma, J. K.-C. 2003. "The Production of Recombinant Pharmaceutical Proteins in Plants." *Nat Gen* 4:794–805.

Mahanty S., et al. 2003. "Cutting Edge: Impairment of Dendritic Cells and Adaptive Immunity by Ebola and Lassa Viruses." *J Immunol* 170:2797–2801.

McFadden, G., and Barry, M. 1998. "How Poxviruses Oppose Apoptosis." *Sem Virol* 8:429–442.

Netea, M. G., Kullberg, B. J., and Van der Meer, J. W. M. 2000. "Circulating Cytokines As Mediators of Fever." *Clin Infect Dis* 31:S178–S184.

Orange, L. O., 2003. "Disseminated Varicella Infection Due to the Vaccine Strain of Varicella Zoster Virus in a Patient with a Novel Deficiency in Natural Killer T Cells." *J Infect Dis* 18(7):948–953.

Paolazzi, C. C., Perez, O., De Flippo J. 1999. "Rabies Vaccine. Developments Employing Molecular Biology Methods." *Mol Biotechnol* 11(2):137–147.

Parashar, U.D., et al. 2003. "Global Illness and Deaths Caused by Rotavirus Disease in Children." *Emer Inf Dis* 9(5):565–572.

Pastoret, P.-P., and Vanderplasschen, A. 2003. "Poxviruses as Vaccine Vectors." *Comp Immunol Microbiol Infect Dis* 26:343–355.

Pestka, S. 2001. "The Human Interferon: a Species and Receptors." *Biopolymers* 55:254–287.

Pestka, S., et al. 2004. "Interleukin-10 and Related Cytokines." *Ann Rev Immunol* 22:929–979.

Pieters, T. 1993. "Interferon and Its First Clinical Trial: Looking Behind the Scenes." *Med Hist* 37:270–295.

Plotkin, S. A., Orenstein, W. A., and Offit, P. A., eds. 2003. *Vaccines*, 4th ed. Philadelphia: W. B. Saunders.

Powledge, T. M. 1984. "Interferon on Trial." *Biotechnology* 2:214–228.

Samuel, C. E. 2001. "Antiviral Actions of Interferons." *Clin Microbiol Rev* 14(4):778–809.

Seet, B. T., et al. 2003. "Poxviruses and Immune Evasion." *Ann Rev Immunol* 21:377–423.

Singer, P. A. et al. 2007. "A Tough Transition: What Is Holding Back Biotechnology in the Developing World?" *Nature* 449(13):160–163.

Spear, G. T., et al. 2001. "The Role of the Complement System in Virus Infections." *Curr Top Microbiol Immunol* 260:229–245.

Stoitzner, P., Pfaller, K., Stossel, H., and Romani, N. 2002. "A Close-Up View of Migrating Langerhan's Cells in the Skin." *J Invest Derm* 118(1):117–125.

Stowe, R. P., et al. 2001. "Immune Responses and Latent Herpesvirus Reactivation in Spaceflight." *Aviat Space Environ Med* 72(10):884–891.

Stratov, I., DeRose, R., Purcell, D. F., and Kent, S. J. 2004. "Vaccines and Vaccine Strategies Against HIV." *Curr Drug Targets* 5(2):71–88.

Stuart-Harris, R. and Penny, R., eds. 1997. *Clinical Applications of the Interferons,* New York: Chapman & Hall Medical.

Turner, P. C., and Moyer, R. W. 1998. "Control of Apoptosis by Poxviruses." *Sem Virol* 8:453–469.

Vastag, B. 2004. "Ebola Vaccines Tested in Humans, Monkeys." *JAMA* 291(5):549–550.

Voelker, R. 1999. "Eradication Efforts Need Needle-Free Delivery." *JAMA* 281:20 1879–1881.

Warrell, M. J., and Warrell, D. A. 2004. "Rabies and Other Lyssavirus Diseases." *Lancet* 363:959–969.

Welsh, R. M., Selin, L. K. and Szomolanyi-Tsuda, E. 2004. "Immunological Memory to Viral Infections." *Ann Rev Immunol* 22:711–743.

Wolstenholme, G. E. W., and O'Connor, M., eds. 1967. *Interferon,* Boston: Little, Brown.

Yu, J.-Y., DeRuiter, S. L., and Turner, D. L. 2002. "RNA Interference by Expression of Short-Interfering RNAs and Hairpin RNAs in Mammalian Cells." *PNAS USA* 99(9):6047–6052.

Zhi-yong, Y., et al. 2004. "A DNA Vaccine Induces SARS Coronavirus Neutralization and Protective Immunity in Mice." *Nature* 428:561–564.

Zinkernagel, R. M., and Hengartner, H. 2001. "Regulation of the Immune Response by Antigen." *Science* 293:251–256.

Zuniga, E. I., et al. 2005. "Immunosuppressive Viruses and Dendritic Cells: A Multifront War." *ASM News* 71(6):285–290.

■ Popular Press

Allen, A. 2007. *Vaccine: The Controversial Story of Medicine's Greatest Lifesaver*, New York: W. W. Norton.

Banchereau, J. 2002. "The Long Arm of the Immune System." *Scientific American* November, 287(5):52–59.

Cantell, K. 1998. *The Story of Interferon: The Ups and Downs in the Life of a Scientist,* Hackensack, NJ: World Scientific Publishing.

Ewald, P. W. 2002. *Plague Time: The New Germ Theory of Disease*, New York: Anchor Books.

Finley, D. 1998. *Mad Dogs: The New Rabies Plague,* Texas: Texas A & M University Press.

Hall, S. S. 1997. *A Commotion in the Blood: Life, Death, and the Immune System,* New York: Owl Books.

Johnson, H. M., Bazer, F. W., Szente, B. E., and Jarpe, M. A. 1994. "How Interferons Fight Disease." *Scientific American,* May, 270:68–75.

Langridge, W. H. R. 2000. "Edible Vaccines." *Scientific American,* 283(3):66–71.

Schrof, J. M. 1998. "Miracle Vaccines." *U.S. News & World Report*, November 23rd, 1998.

■ Video Productions

Your Immune System. 2001. Films for the Humanities.

Tainted Blood. 2002. Films for the Humanities.

New Blood. 2002. Films for the Humanities.

The Immune System at Work. 2003. Films for the Humanities.

Dog Bites and Rabies Prevention. 2004. Medivision Film Series.

Unseen Enemies, A Close-Up Look at the World's Deadliest Diseases: Rotavirus. 2006. Films for the Humanities.

Influenza. 2006. Films for the Humanities.

■ eLearning

http://biology.jbpub.com/book/virology

The site features eLearning, an online review area that provides quizzes and other tools to help you study for your class. You can also follow useful links for in-depth information, or just find out the latest virology and microbiology news.

CASE STUDY QUESTIONS

1. LCMV infection is either asymptomatic or causes a mild, self-limiting illness in healthy persons. Discuss reasons why four of the organ recipients were at higher risk for LCMV. Refer to the Epidemiological Triad of Disease in your answer.

2. Who else is at risk for a symptomatic LCMV infection? Why?

3. Family members of the donor tested positive for LCMV antibodies. LCMV was isolated from the pet hamster. The family member who cared for the pet hamster had both IgM- and IgG-specific LCMV antibodies in her blood. What does IgM indicate?

4. How will scientists determine whether the LCMV isolated from the hamster is the same LCMV that infected the organ recipients?

5. How is LCMV transmitted to rodents?

6. If you own a pet hamster, what precautions should you take after handling it and cleaning the cage?

7. How would you clean a rodent-infested area such as a dusty garden shed?

ADDITIONAL CASE STUDY AND QUESTIONS

John Kostman, a sophomore sociology major at a midwestern university, woke up on a Tuesday morning with a fever. He had been studying hard and not sleeping as much as he should. He assumed he had some kind of flu bug. Three days later his fever had not gone down and he developed a runny nose and cough. He also noticed his eyes were very red (conjunctivitis). He thought he had pinkeye and decided to go to the campus health clinic to get something for his eyes. He seemed to recall that pink eye was very contagious.

At the clinic, a physician, Dr. McDermott, carefully examined him. He noticed a rash developing at John's hairline. Dr. McDermott asked John a lot of questions, which annoyed John because he was feeling worse by the minute. Dr. McDermott asked John for his vaccination records and if he had been in contact with anyone with similar symptoms. "I'll have to get my shot records from my mother over the weekend," said John. He did recall that he had volunteered to babysit his sister's 18-month-old son Jamie over the winter holiday break two weeks earlier. At the time, Jamie had had a runny nose and fever. John hadn't followed up with his sister to find out how Jamie was feeling because "kids get sick often." Dr. McDermott ordered blood tests and told John he should take some Tylenol and to rest. He said he would call him with the test results as soon as they came in.

Dr. McDermott suspected that John might have measles. Measles is very rare and children are vaccinated for measles, though, and Dr. McDermott had never seen a case of measles himself. He thought it was likely that John had been vaccinated but needed his vaccination records to confirm it.

Over the weekend, John received his vaccination records from his mother and faxed a copy to Dr. McDermott. His rash had progressed down his entire body. Dr. McDermott reviewed the records and noticed that John did not have a measles vaccine booster as a child. The blood tests confirmed his suspicion of measles. He began asking John more questions about his contacts, given that measles is highly contagious and that there had been a few reports of school outbreaks of measles in the United States and Canada—countries that practice routine measles vaccination. Dr. McDermot asked John if he had traveled during his vacation break or if he had any contact with someone from a foreign country. John said that his only contact was his new nephew, who had been adopted from an orphanage in China two weeks earlier. Shortly after this conversation, John's sister called and mentioned that his nephew had just gotten over the measles. She called the adoption agency and found out that other new adoptees from China were also suffering from measles. Efforts were being made to contact airline passengers who had traveled from China to the United States on the flights that the adoptees and their families had been on.

1. What would John's blood be tested for (e.g., antibodies, virus)?
2. Most persons in the United States are immune to measles, therefore airline passengers traveling on planes with infected individuals are at low risk. Should Dr. McDermott make a decision to offer measles-containing vaccine to all staff and students who attended the same university as John? Why or why not?
3. Could John have contracted measles from someone else? Explain your answer.
4. What are some of the complications of measles infection? What age group(s) are more at risk for complications? (Hint: Perform an Internet search via the CDC's Website or other credible Websites.)

■ References

Alaska Dept. of Health and Social Services et al. 2004 "Brief Report: Update: Measles Among Adoptees from China–April 14, 2004." *MMWR* 53(14):309.

Alaska Dept. of Health and Social Services et al. 2004. "Multistate Investigation of Measles Among Adoptees from China April 9, 2004." *MMWR* 53:14;309–310.

Bell, A., King, A., Pielak, K., and Fyfe, M. 1997. "Epidemiology of Measles Outbreak in British Columbia–February 1997." *CCDR* 1997. Apr 1, 23(7):49–51.

Lurie, P. et al. 2003. "Measles Outbreak in a Boarding School—Pennsylvania, 2003." *MMWR* 53(14):306–309.

Reynolds, A. et al. 2002. "Measles Outbreak Among Internationally Adopted Children Arriving in the United States, February—March 2001." *MMWR* 51(49):1115–1116.

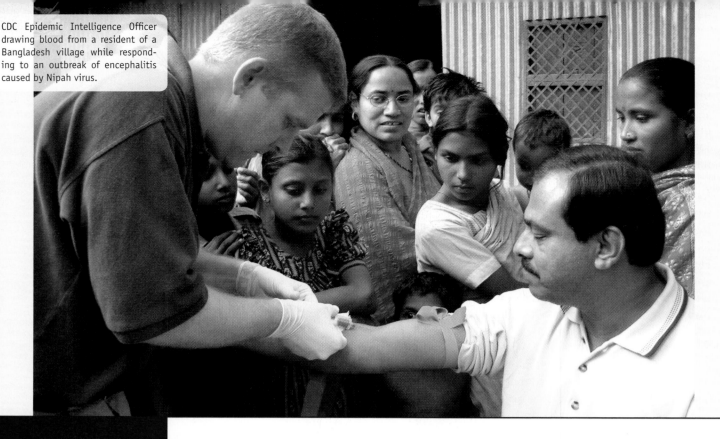

CDC Epidemic Intelligence Officer drawing blood from a resident of a Bangladesh village while responding to an outbreak of encephalitis caused by Nipah virus.

CHAPTER

8

"*I hate definitions.***"**

Benjamin Disraeli (1804–1881)

Epidemiology

CASE STUDY

You have returned to your parents' home in Wisconsin for spring break. Once home, your 4-year-old sister, Tina, has a swimming lesson at the local swimming club and you decide to take her to her lesson. The pool was very busy. There was a birthday party of 5–10 year old children, preschool swimming classes, mother–infant swimming classes, and a few other private groups in attendance. You noticed that the pool water appeared cloudy, but assumed that the group instructor would not allow children to swim if there was a problem with the pool maintenance. Other than swallowing a fair amount of water, Tina enjoyed her lesson.

Thirty-six hours later, Tina starting experiencing an onset of symptoms: vomiting, diarrhea, nausea, and chills. You took her temperature and noted that she had a fever of 102.2°F. Your mother was concerned that Tina could become dehydrated and decided that a physician should examine her. An epidemiologist intern was present during Tina's examination and asked your mother to fill out a questionnaire about Tina's recent gastrointestinal illness. Specimens were collected from Tina and sent to a clinical laboratory. Tina was hospitalized and given intravenous normal saline. Two days later, Tina was rehydrated and able to tolerate oral feedings so was discharged. All cultures for bacterial pathogens gave negative results, but a rapid diagnostic test was positive.

8.1　What Is Epidemiology?

Prior chapters provided an introduction to virus life cycles at the molecular level, as well as background on the naming of viruses, laboratory methods used to cultivate viruses, diagnosis of viral diseases, mechanisms of viral spread, and the immune system. This chapter expands on the concept of the **triad model of disease causation** described in Chapter 7 and introduces the scientific field of **epidemiology**, which is linked to virology (**Figure 8-1**).

Why does an infectious disease occur in one population rather than another? Why are certain age groups more at risk for a particular viral disease? Why aren't viral diseases randomly distributed within a specific geographic area? These are questions studied by epidemiologists.

What is the definition of epidemiology? If we break the word apart into its Greek root definitions, **epi-** means "on or upon, befall" and **demos** means "people, population." If the term is literally defined by this etymology, epidemiology means, "the study of that which befalls man."

Specifically, **epidemiology** is the study of how diseases affect whole communities. Its objectives are to determine the distribution, cause, control, and prevention of diseases in populations. In this era of bioterrorism, epidemiology has become more important than ever. The detection of covert and terrorist biological attacks will most likely occur at a local level, where

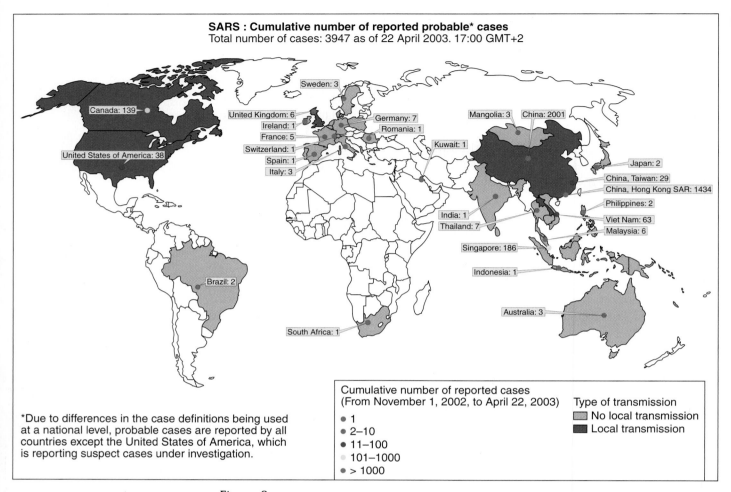

SARS : Cumulative number of reported probable* cases
Total number of cases: 3947 as of 22 April 2003. 17:00 GMT+2

Sweden: 3
Canada: 139
United Kingdom: 6
Ireland: 1
France: 5
Switzerland: 1
Spain: 1
Italy: 3
United States of America: 38
Germany: 7
Romania: 1
Kuwait: 1
Mangolia: 3
China: 2001
Japan: 2
China, Taiwan: 29
China, Hong Kong SAR: 1434
Philippines: 2
India: 1
Thailand: 7
Viet Nam: 63
Malaysia: 6
Singapore: 186
Indonesia: 1
Brazil: 2
Australia: 3
South Africa: 1

*Due to differences in the case definitions being used at a national level, probable cases are reported by all countries except the United States of America, which is reporting suspect cases under investigation.

Cumulative number of reported cases
(From November 1, 2002, to April 22, 2003)
• 1
• 2–10
• 11–100
• 101–1000
• > 1000

Type of transmission
No local transmission
Local transmission

■ **Figure 8-1**

Epidemiology is the branch of science that deals with disease diagnostics, trends, and control measures. Epidemiologists map epidemics and pandemics and would be on the frontlines of a terrorist-caused biological attack. Epidemiologists on the Centers for Disease Control and Prevention's (CDC's) Public Health Mapping Team created this severe acute respiratory syndrome (SARS) pandemic map. Increased global travel contributed to the spread of SARS. Data from the World Health Organization Map Production, Public Health Mapping Team, Communicable Diseases (CDS). Courtesy of the World Health Organization. Reproduced from World Health Organization, "Severe Acute Respiratory Syndrome," *Epidemic and Pandemic Alert and Response,* http://www.who.int/csr/sars/en/.

disease-tracking systems and experts need to be in place. Epidemiologists must be able to respond to reports of rare, unusual, or unexplained illnesses so that critical decisions can be made rapidly.

■ Epidemiology Definitions

The field of epidemiology contains its own language and terminology; thus it is important to define some of these terms before applications of epidemiology can be discussed.

Endemic. The prefix **en-** means "in or within." The term endemic applies to diseases that persist at a moderate and steady level within a given geographic area; for example, many individuals suffer from cold sores caused by herpes simplex 1. This would be considered an endemic illness (**Figure 8-2**).

Sporadic. This refers to disease outbreaks that have no pattern of occurrence in time or location.

Epidemic. An epidemic is defined as an unusually high number of cases in excess of normal expectation of a similar illness in a population, community, or region (Figure 8-2).

Pandemic. The prefix **pan-** means "all or across." Pandemic refers to a worldwide epidemic; for example, acquired immunodeficiency syndrome (AIDS) is a pandemic disease.

Morbidity. Morbidity refers to the illness or disease state.

Mortality. Mortality refers to numbers of deaths correlated with a particular disease. Mortality rates are expressed in quantitative terms; for example, the annual death rate or mortality rate is calculated as follows:

{[total number of deaths from all causes in 1 year]/[number of persons in the population at midyear]} × 1000.

Incidence. Incidence is a measurement of morbidity. It is the number of new cases of a disease that occurs in a specified period of time in a susceptible population. The incidence rate is expressed per 1000 persons:

Incidence per 1000 = {[number of *new* cases]/[number of persons at **risk**]} × 1000.

Prevalence. Prevalence is another measurement of morbidity. It refers to the number of cases existing in a population at a specified time. It does not take into account the duration of the disease. Prevalence rates are also recorded as prevalence per 1000.

Carrier. An individual who is a carrier harbors the virus but is not infected as measured by serologic methods (i.e., there is no evidence of an antibody response) or by evidence of clinical illness. This person can still infect others. A carrier status may be of limited duration or chronic (i.e., lasting for months or years).

Incubation Period. The time between infection with a virus and the onset of symptoms (**Figure 8-3**). These times can vary; for example, the incubation period for influenza is 1 to 2 days, whereas the incubation period for chickenpox is 14 to 16 days (Table 8-1).

Prodromal Period. This term refers to the first appearance of mild or nonspecific signs and symptoms of an illness (Figure 8-3).

Period of Illness. The patient experiences defined symptoms and signs of illness during this period.

Mode of transmission. This term is used to define how an infectious disease is spread or passed on. Modes can be **direct** (e.g., through touching, kissing, or sexual contact, or by droplet and oral–fecal transmission) or **indirect** (e.g., through food, fomites, blood, insect vectors, or air).

Etiological agent/pathogen. This refers to the disease-causing agent; for example, human immunodeficiency virus (HIV) is the etiological agent of AIDS.

Reservoir. This refers to where the etiological agent lives, grows, and multiplies (e.g., human, animal, or arthropod).

Case Definition. This term is defined as a standard set of criteria that is used to identify who has the disease being studied.

Communicable Period. This is the time period when an infected individual or animal is contagious and he/she can directly or indirectly infect another person, animal, or arthropod (Table 8-1).

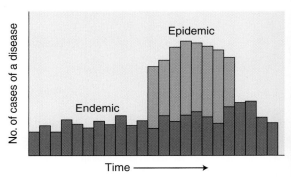

■ **Figure 8-2**
Comparison of endemic versus epidemic diseases. Adapted from Gordis, Leon. *Epidemiology*. Second Edition W.B. Saunders, 2000.

■ **Figure 8-3**
Course of infectious disease. Adapted from Tortora, G. J., B. R. Funke, and C. L. Case. *Microbiology*, Eighth Edition. Benjamin Cummings, 2003.

TABLE 8-1   Incubation Periods for Communicable Viral Diseases (Partial List)

Viral Disease	Incubation Period	Period of Communicability
Influenza	1–3 days	3–5 days from clinical onset in adults; up to 7 days in children
SARS	1–18 days	Not completely understood. Early studies suggest no transmission before symptoms appear; transmission more likely during the 2nd week of illness. Healthcare workers at greatest risk, especially during procedures like intubation or nebulization.
Chickenpox	2–3 weeks (commonly 14–16 days)	As long as 5 days but usually 1–2 days before onset of rash, continuing until lesions are crusted (5 days)
Common cold	12–72 hours (usually 24 hours)	From 1 day before onset to 5 days after
Measles	10–14 days until rash appears	From 1 day before the beginning of the prodromal period (usually about 4 days before rash onset) to 4 days after the onset of the rash
Smallpox	7–19 days, commonly 10–14 days to onset of illness; and 2–4 days more to onset of rash	From the time of development of the earliest lesions to disappearance of all scabs (about 3 weeks)
Mumps	12–26 days (usually 18)	From 6 days before symptoms to 9 days after
Rubella	14–17 days with a range of 14–21 days	1 week before and to 4 days after onset of rash
Rabies	2–8 weeks or longer	From animals, 3–5 days before symptoms and during the course of the disease
Ebola	2–21 days	As long as blood and secretions contain virus. Can be as long as 61 days after onset of illness from care of corpses.
West Nile encephalitis	3–12 days	Not directly transmitted from person to person
Hepatitis B	45–180 days (average 60–90 days)	From many weeks before the onset of the first symptoms and throughout the clinical course of the disease

Convalescence. This term is applied to the recovery period after an illness. Though the individual is feeling much better, he/she may still be infectious and able to transmit the disease during this stage of infection (Figure 8-1).

Zoonosis. A zoonosis is defined as any infection or infectious disease transmissible from animals to humans; for example, rabies virus can be transmitted to humans from a rabid animal.

8.2 History of Epidemiology: From Observational Data to Preventative Action

Three pioneers of epidemiology—Edward Jenner, John Snow, and Florence Nightingale—were not knowledgeable about the pathogenesis of disease. Their important observations and actions, however, led to the prevention of smallpox (1796), cholera (1854), and a reduction in mortality rates of wounded men in the British Army during the Crimean War (1855).

As described in Chapter 1, Jenner was an British general practitioner and surgeon in the late 18th century who became very interested in smallpox. At the time he was practicing, smallpox was a worldwide scourge, killing thousands each year in England alone. Survivors were badly scarred and disfigured, and many became blind as a result of corneal infections.

Jenner had observed that milkmaids appeared to be immune to smallpox, and deduced that the pustules or lesions they occasionally got on their hands were caused by a relative of smallpox called cowpox and hypothesized that exposure to the cowpox virus would protect individuals from contracting smallpox. The results of Jenner's experiment on an eight-year-old "volunteer" led to the vaccination of millions of humans against smallpox, saving virtually all of them from death or disfigurement (**Figure 8-4**). There are, however, many ethical issues and implications of his experiment. Today Jenner would be required to justify his experiment before an institutional review board.

■ Figure 8-4
Painting of the first vaccination against smallpox performed by Edward Jenner.

John Snow was a 19th-century physician in London who earned a reputation for his use of anesthetics, most notably when he supplied chloroform to Queen Victoria during the birth of her children. Snow was later recognized as an epidemiological hero. He possessed excellent critical thinking skills, recognizing that a disease prevention strategy could be conceived if one could locate its source. Snow believed in the **germ theory of disease** during a time period when the majority of his colleagues believed in the **miasmatic theory**, which held that a disease was caused by *miasma* or polluted gases that rose from swamps and decaying or putrid matter. Many of the concepts and epidemiological methods Snow discovered are still useful today.

In London, during the first ten days of September 1854, approximately 500 individuals died from cholera. At the time of the epidemic, Snow's rival, the Registrar General William Farr, collected data to support the hypothesis that the people were contracting cholera from a *miasma*. He believed there were more deaths in the parts of London located at the lowest elevations. Residents began to panic and spread rumors that cholera was being transmitted by *miasmata* emanating from the ground where Black Death (plague) victims were buried during a pandemic in the previous century, a site upon which homes had since been built.

Snow had experience in attending and observing cholera patients as a practicing physician prior to this outbreak. He observed young children who shared hospital beds in which they caught cholera from each other. This reinforced his affirmation that cholera was transmitted by "direct contagion." He became a cholera expert by combining his clinical observations with microscopic analysis of different water sources. Suspicious that cholera was transmitted by contaminated water, Snow compared water sources used by those who got cholera and those who didn't. His scientific observations allowed him to develop a classical experimental design to study the 1854 London cholera epidemic.

The Registrar General cooperated with Snow by providing him with addresses of those individuals who died from cholera, and Snow plotted the deaths on a map of the area. From this he could immediately determine that cholera deaths were not localized to the area where plague victims had been buried. He also knew that each household signed up randomly for water sources provided by water companies, so he walked door to door in order to determine who supplied water to the homes of cholera victims. He developed a test using silver chloride to distinguish among the three water sources available, and became so proficient that he could distinguish water sources on the basis of appearance and odor alone.

Two water companies were located in a water intake area where the water was frequently contaminated by sewage outlets. One of the companies moved upstream and

■ Figure 8-5

At the beginning of the 1854 London cholera epidemic, clusters of deaths occurred along the Broad Street water pump. This is a portion of the original map created by Dr. John Snow (**inset**) and published in 1855. (Courtesy of Frerichs, R. R. John Snow website: http://www.ph.ucla.edu/epi/snow.html, 2006.) Deaths are plotted as lines parallel to the front of the building in which people died.

away from London's polluted and contaminated part of the Thames River and Snow hypothesized that there would be fewer cholera deaths and cases occurring in households that used water from this company—an accurate hypothesis. Households that used water drawn from the two other companies, which were located downstream of the sewage outlets, had very high mortality rates from cholera, and the largest cluster of deaths and cases at the beginning of the epidemic occurred at a public water pump located on Broad Street (**Figure 8-5**).

Snow compiled mortality rates and locations of deaths, compared these to the location of water sources, and then submitted a report to Parliament. On September 7, 1854, he spoke publicly before the Board of Guardians, a political group charged with the safety and welfare of the area. They documented his concerns and authorized the removal of the pump handle on the Broad Street Water Pump the next day. Removal of the pump handle led to an immediate, measurable reduction in the number of cholera deaths. Thus Snow was able to prove his hypothesis: that a waterborne disease was spread via contaminated water that traveled both on the surface (the Broad Street Pump) and via groundwater supplies (water piped from the two companies located downstream of London's sewage outlets). What he had dubbed his Grand Experiment had laid the groundwork for descriptive epidemiological investigation.

Florence Nightingale is consistently credited for her establishment of modern nursing practices. In addition, she was also a brilliant organizer, statistician, and one of the most influential women in the 19th century. She was born into a wealthy family in 1820, a time when women did not attend universities or pursue careers. Nightingale was driven to lead a professional rather than domestic life and refused marriage proposals from several

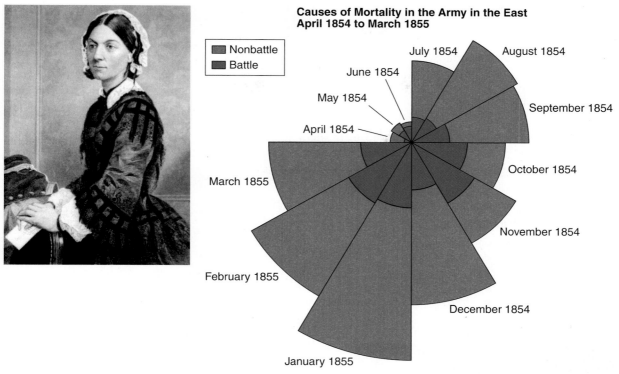

■ Figure 8-6

Recreation of a polar area (wedge) diagram invented by Florence Nightingale to show the different causes of death of British soldiers during the Crimean War. The blue wedges measured from the center of the circle represent the deaths from preventable diseases. The red wedges measured from the center represent the deaths from battle wounds. (**Far left**) Florence Nightingale (unknown date). Reproduced from F. Nightingale. *Notes on Matters Affecting the Health, Efficiency and Hospital Administration of the British Army*. Harrison and Sons, 1858.

prominent suitors. She instead pursued a career in nursing, a choice to which her parents were opposed.

Nightingale's mark on epidemiology was linked to her collection of statistics and graphical representation of mortality rates of the British Army soldiers during the Crimean War.

She had observed the unsanitary conditions of the army hospital conditions, where infectious diseases such as typhus, cholera, and dysentery were rampant. Many of the wounded soldiers died of these infections instead of battle wounds. Nightingale believed these infections were preventable and worked hard to improve the quality of sanitation. She provided members of the Royal Commission on the Health of the Army with briefs that included facts, tables, and statistics regarding the spread of infection and the resulting mortality rates (**Figure 8-6**). The Royal Commission was charged with investigating the sanitary conditions, the organization of its staff, and the treatment of the sick and wounded. Nightingale's reform efforts dramatically reduced the hospital mortality rate.

After the war, Nightingale returned to England as a national hero. She published two books on reforming military hospitals in order to address the hygienic conditions that the wounded men in the British Army were exposed to during the Crimean War.

8.3 The Complexities of Disease Transmission

The epidemiological triangle represents one of the fundamental concepts behind disease causality. Before a viral disease actually occurs, the interaction of the viral agent, host, and environment may alter the host's susceptibility; for example, 80% of the population suffers

TABLE 8-2	Factors Associated with Viral Disease Causation	
Host Characteristics	**Pathogen Characteristics**	**Environmental Factors**
Age	Stability in the environment	Population density (crowding results in increased host exposure to the pathogen)
Sex	Virulence factors (enhanced ability to attach, invade, or multiply in the host)	Sanitary conditions
Race and genetic factors	Presence of immune evasion genes	Climate changes
Immune status (decreased)	Resistance to antiviral therapy	Environmental changes
Nutritional status (lack)	Enhanced mode of transmission	Blood products (contaminated)
Behavior (e.g., occupation, lifestyle, religion, customs)		Geographical locations
Previous infections or current coinfections		Existence of zoonotic infections/vectors

TABLE 8-3	Human Viral Diseases and Their Most Common Modes of Transmission
Viral Disease	**Predominate Mode of Transmission**
Influenza	Airborne
Common cold	Direct contact or airborne
Poliomyelitis	Waterborne (oral–fecal route)
West Nile encephalitis	Vector (mosquitoes)
Rabies	Direct (bite laden with saliva containing rabies virus)
Oral cold sores	Contact with saliva laden with HSV 1 is the most common mode
AIDS	Sex with HIV positive individual, vehicle transmission (HIV contaminated needles/blood transfusions)
Chickenpox	Direct contact or airborne (droplet transmission)
Measles	Direct contact or airborne (droplet transmission)
Hepatitis A	Foodborne (oral–fecal route)

from cold sores, which are caused by herpes simplex virus 1. The virus usually remains dormant; however, it may be reactivated during times of physical or emotional stress, menstruation, pregnancy, immune deficiency, or physical trauma. This change in the host increases his or her susceptibility to herpes simplex 1 infection.

■ Factors Associated with Increased Risk

Epidemiologists gather information to identify populations at risk for disease and what factors contribute to human susceptibility. Table 8-2 lists some of the environmental factors and host and pathogen characteristics that influence the pattern of viral infections in humans.

■ Modes of Transmission

Viral diseases can be transmitted **directly** (i.e., from person to person) or **indirectly**. In direct transmission, the virus is passed from **person to person** through direct physical contact such as touching with contaminated hands, by sexual contact, kissing, or skin-to-skin contact. Viruses may be shed via saliva, other secretions (such as sperm), and skin.

Indirect transmission occurs when the virus is transferred or carried by an intermediate vehicle to a host by one or more of the following means: airborne, vectorborne, foodborne, waterborne, or vehicleborne. Examples of viral diseases and their indirect modes of transmission are listed in Table 8-3. (See Chapter 6 for a review of portals of viral entry and exit.)

■ Chain of Infection

There is a strong association between the **triangle of epidemiology** and a concept termed the **chain of infection**. The term chain of infection is frequently used in hospitals and other healthcare settings with regard to the control and prevention of infectious diseases. A viral pathogen leaves its source or reservoir through a portal of exit and the virus then spreads by one or more modes of transmission. The virus enters the body (susceptible host) through its preferred portal of entry. The chain of infection can be broken at each step in the chain through any of the following practices:

- Rapid identification of the viral pathogen
- Proper sanitation
- Disinfection and sterilization of fomites
- Use of barrier techniques
- Handwashing
- Proper trash and waste disposal
- Proper food handling
- Aseptic technique
- Recognition of high-risk individuals

■ The Concept of Herd Immunity

The concept of **herd immunity** is based on the premise that if the majority of the population is mostly protected from a disease through immunizations or genetic resistance, the chance of a major epidemic is highly unlikely. Jonas Salk, developer of the polio vaccine during the 1950s, suggested that if herd immunity was at 85%, a polio epidemic would not occur. Herd immunity provides a barrier to direct transmission of infectious diseases through a population (**Figures 8-7** and **8-8**).

During the 1950s and 1960s, it was not uncommon in the United States for parents to encourage their healthy children to interact with children with several infectious diseases, such as mumps and the chickenpox. They wanted their children to get a case of the disease and become immune before they reached adulthood because it was known that contracting such illnesses in adulthood resulted in a severe illness with complications. Today, the goal of any public health immunization program is to reach 100% immunity in a population.

8.4   Epidemiology Today

■ The Goals of Epidemiology: What Does an Epidemiologist Want to Know?

During a real epidemic an epidemiologist wants to know the following:

- Case definition (what)
- Person (who)
- Place (where)
- Time (when)
- Risk Factors (how and why)

Gathering Data

Investigation starts with the gathering of information and confirmation of the epidemic. Diagnostic tests are conducted and a case definition is set in place. Next, **descriptive studies** are performed after the epidemic occurs. Descriptive studies are usually inexpensive and of short duration. These studies are used to generate a testable hypothesis or enough evidence to indicate sufficient cause for conducting lengthier and more costly analytical studies.

Dr. John Snow's search for the cause of the cholera epidemic in London in 1854 is an example of descriptive epidemiology. Descriptive studies are observations of when and where (time and place) the disease occurs and who is affected (person). The studies take

■ **Figure 8-7**
Diagram showing a population with a low immunization level, resulting in a low level of protection of the population.

How an epidemic spreads in a population

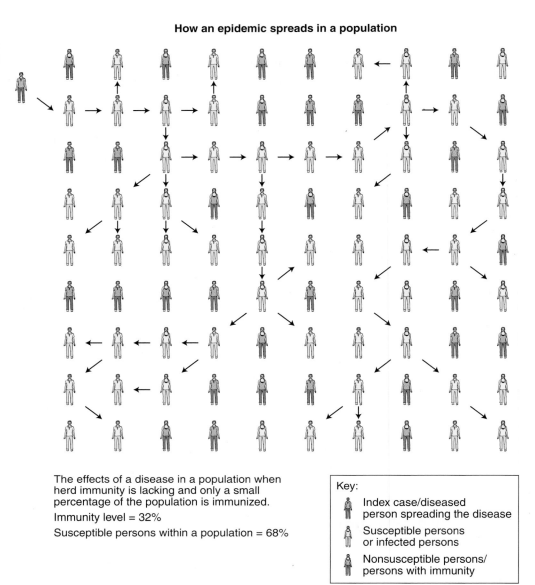

The effects of a disease in a population when herd immunity is lacking and only a small percentage of the population is immunized.
Immunity level = 32%
Susceptible persons within a population = 68%

Key:

Index case/diseased person spreading the disease

Susceptible persons or infected persons

Nonsusceptible persons/ persons with immunity

into account the onset and duration of the illness. Descriptions frequently include the age, sex, ethnicity, socioeconomic status, and overall health status (diet and immune status) of the affected individuals. Sometimes other information, such as environmental exposures and personal lifestyle characteristics, may be recognized as risk factors.

Descriptive studies may be published as case reports (anecdotal or clinical observations that may indicate a causal relationship) or surveillance studies. Surveillance studies may rely on data generated by death certificates or other traditional channels. After descriptive studies, control and prevention measures may be implemented and results of these studies and measures are reported. Examples of graphs generated from descriptive studies are shown in **Figure 8-9**. **Analytical epidemiology** may be needed to determine the causes and effects (the why and how) of the epidemic.

■ Analytical Epidemiology

Analytical studies are more informative than descriptive studies. These investigations are hypothesis-driven studies that use descriptive research to determine the why and how pertaining to the variations in incidence and prevalence of diseases in different populations, and requires good research design. In true analytical epidemiology, individuals in a population suffering from a disease are compared to a **control group** that does not have

The protection given a population through immunizations

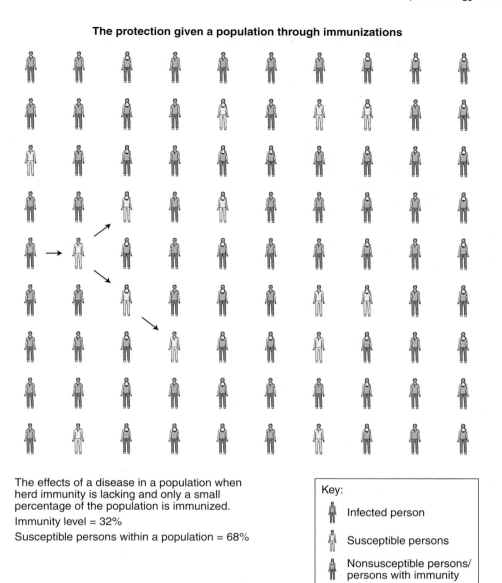

The effects of a disease in a population when herd immunity is lacking and only a small percentage of the population is immunized.
Immunity level = 32%
Susceptible persons within a population = 68%

Key:

🚶 Infected person

🚶 Susceptible persons

🚶 Nonsusceptible persons/ persons with immunity

the disease and has not been exposed to the disease. The control group may be matched by age, sex, location, and socioeconomic status. The two groups are studied, compared, and analyzed in what is called a **case-control** method (Table 8-4).

The **cohort method** used by analytical epidemiologists studies two similar populations or **cohorts.** Cohort members are grouped by common characteristics, especially birth year. One of the cohorts has been exposed to the disease-causing agent and the other has not. The cohorts may be studied as a group, backward in time (**retrospectively**), at a single point in time (**cross-sectionally**), or forward in time (**prospectively**) (**Figure 8-10**). Most cohort studies require large numbers of subjects that are followed over long periods of time (years).

During a college football game between teams from Florida and North Carolina in 1999, the members of the North Carolina team suffered from gastrointestinal distress during the game. The next day, members of the Florida team developed similar symptoms. This retrospective cohort study concluded that the source of the disease-causing agent, Norwalk virus, was a turkey sandwich in a box lunch (this accounted for 95% of the primary cases). The researchers hypothesized that the virus was transmitted across the scrimmage line by person-to-person contact during the football game. The North Carolina team physician and coaches reported that their players were vomiting on the sidelines and

■ **Figure 8-9**

(a) A graph accompanying a descriptive study to characterize the epidemiology of measles in the United States from 1985–2003. This report summarized that no endemic measles was circulating in the United States at that time. Imported measles cases do, however, continue to occur and can result in limited indigenous transmission. Adapted from Dayan, G., et al., *MMWR* 53 (2004):713–716. **(b)** These are the results of an investigation of a hepatitis A outbreak that occurred at a restaurant in Monaca, Pennsylvania, in 2003. The outbreak was associated with contaminated green onions that were in large batches of salsa. The source was determined to be one or more farms in Mexico. At least 9000 people that were at the restaurant or who were in contact with ill individuals were provided immunoglobulin as a preventative measure. The restaurant was closed. Adapted from Dato, V., et al., *MMWR* 52 (2003):1155–1157. **(c)** Description study showing the distribution of West Nile virus infection by area of residence, province of Quebec, Canada, 2002–2003. Adapted from Public Health Agency of Canada, *Canada Communicable Disease Report (CCDR)*, June 1, 2004. 30(11):97–104.

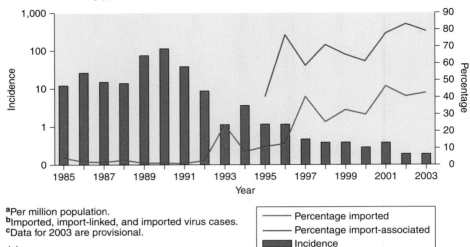

Incidence[a] and percentage of import-associated[b] measles cases, by year—United States, 1985–2003[c].

[a]Per million population.
[b]Imported, import-linked, and imported virus cases.
[c]Data for 2003 are provisional.

(a)

—— Percentage imported
—— Percentage import-associated
■ Incidence

Number of hepatitis A cases[a] by date of eating at Restaurant A and illness onset—Monaca, Pennsylvania, 2003.

□ Dining dates
■ Onset dates

[a] *N* = 206. Excludes one patient whose illness onset date was not available. Dining dates for three persons who ate at Restaurant A on October 15 (*n* = 2) and October 17 (*n* = 2) are not shown.

(b)

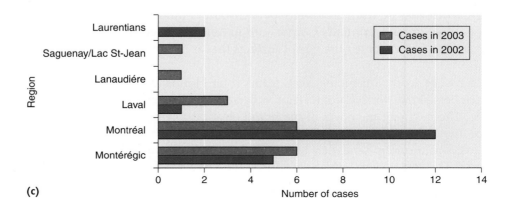

■ Cases in 2003
■ Cases in 2002

(c)

TABLE 8-4	Case-Control Study Investigating the Risk Factors for Avian Influenza A (H5N1 strain) Disease in Hong Kong, 1997

The study compared 15 human cases of human Avian Influenza to a control group that did not have antibodies against Avian Influenza A and was matched by age, sex, and neighborhood. Results of the investigation suggested that exposure to live poultry in the markets during the week prior to the illness was significantly associated with Avian Influenza disease (64% of the cases and 29% of the control group). Travel, eating or preparing poultry products, recent exposures to individuals with respiratory illnesses including Influenza A were not associated with Influenza A illness. Mounts et al. 1999. *J Inf Dis* 180:505–508.

Activity and Exposure	Case Patients (*n* = 15)	Controls (*n* = 41)	OR (95% CI)	p^a
Exposure to poultry				
Exposed to live poultry in market[b]	9/14 (64)	11/38 (29)	4.5 (1.2–21.7)	.045
Consumed poultry in restaurant	6/12 (50)	9/31 (29)	2.9 (0.6–14.9)	.375
Consumed poultry organs or poultry	1/14 (7)	4/38 (11)	0.6 (0.0–7.5)	.999
Consumed undercooked poultry products	5/11 (45)	10/29 (34)	1.9 (0.4–11.2)	.707
Household member cooked poultry products	2/13 (15)	11/33 (33)	0.2 (0.0–1.3)	.193
Household member in poultry industry	0/14	0/38	Undefined	NA
Exposure to human illness				
Anyone in flat had influenza-like illness[c]	5/15 (33)	15/40 (38)	0.8 (0.2–2.8)	.999
Contact with known H5N1 case	1/13 (8)	0/35	+Inf (0.1 to +Inf)[d]	.500
Other exposure				
Travel outside Hong Kong	0/14	3/37 (8)	0.0 (0.0–4.9)	.800
Selected outdoor activities[e]	2/14 (14)	8/37 (22)	0.0 (0.0–2.5)	.225
Live birds in home	6/12 (50)	14/31 (45)	1.4 (0.3–6.4)	.901
Other animals in home	2/13 (15)	1/33 (3)	2/5 (0.1–97.4)	.999
Played in indoor playground	0/15	13/41 (32)	0.0 (0.0–0.5)	.013
Household uses soap to clean[f]	5/14 (36)	25/38 (66)	0.3 (0.1–1.0)	.058

Note: OR, odds ratio; CI, confidence interval; NA, not available.
[a]Exact method.
[b]Includes visiting poultry stall, retail or wholesale market selling live poultry, or poultry farm in week before illness.
[c]Influenza-like illness includes anyone with fever and cough or sore throat.
[d]+Inf, an unknown upper bound (positive infinity) for the CI.
[e]Includes activities such as visiting aviary, feeding wild birds in park, and/or having picnic in park.
[f]Uses soap and water to clean knife after preparation of poultry.
Source: Adapted from Mounts et al. 1999. *J Inf Dis* 180:505–508.

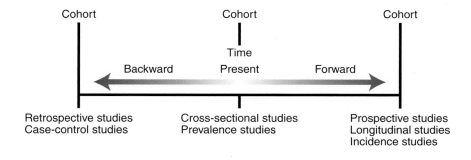

Figure 8-10
The relationship of cohort studies to other types of studies.

VIRUS FILE 8-1 | **Descriptive Epidemiology and AIDS**

Observations made by physicians, technicians, and epidemiologists were essential in recognizing a new viral epidemic in the 1980s. The sad history of AIDS is one of the finest examples of epidemiological investigations. The following timeline depicts some the key events in HIV/AIDS history.

March 1981 Eight cases of a rare form of aggressive Kaposi's sarcoma (KS) in young gay men in New York were reported. (Prior to the AIDS epidemic, the annual incidence of KS was 0.2 to 0.6 cases per million population and it was usually found in older men of Hebrew or Italian ancestry. By the end of 1999, the CDC recorded 46,684 HIV cases in the United States that had a confirmed diagnosis of KS.)

April 1981 CDC drug technician Sandra Ford observes an increase in prescriptions for pentamidine, a drug used to treat *Pneumocystis carinii* pneumonia (PCP), a rare pneumonia recognized in the elderly. In this instance, however, a young 20-year-old gay man was requesting refills to treat PCP. (A 1967 survey revealed that only 107 cases of PCP had been recorded in the medical literature in the United States, and that all of those patients suffered from immune suppression. By the end of 1999, of the 800,000 to 900,000 people in the United States living with HIV infection, the CDC recorded 166,368 had a confirmed diagnosis of PCP.)

June 1981 The CDC published a report about five young, active homosexual men in Los Angeles, California, who were later treated for PCP and had experienced cytomegalovirus infection and candidal mucosal infection. Two of the men had died (**Figure VF 8-1**).

July 1981 The CDC published a report about 26 young, active homosexual men in California and New York who were then suffering from PCP.

December 1981 A new population was being affected by the rare PCP: intravenous drug users.

The documentation of these critical observations unraveled the mystery of a new disease referred to as Gay-Related Immune Deficiency (GRID). By 1983, this new disease was striking adult heterosexuals and children. Subsequently, the name of the disease was changed to Acquired Immune Deficiency Syndrome (AIDS). In 1983 the etiological agent, HIV-1, was isolated. Between 1982 and 1983 there were 2042 AIDS cases reported in the United States, and 63% of these individuals had died of severe immunosuppression characterized by a loss of T lymphocytes.

References

Centers for Disease Control and Prevention. 1981. "Kaposi's Sarcoma and Pneumocystis Pneumonia Among Homosexual Men—New York City and California." *MMWR* 4(30):305–309.

Gottlieb, M. S. et al. 1981 *Pneumocystis* Pneumonia—Los Angeles June 5 30:250–252.

Hymes, K. B., et al. 1981. "Kaposi's Sarcoma in Homosexual Men: A Report of Eight Cases." *Lancet* 2:598–600.

Masur, H., et al. 1981 "An Outbreak of Community Acquired *Pneumocystis carinii* pneumonia: Initial Manifestation of Cellular Immune Dysfunction." *N Engl J Med* 305:1431–1438.

(continued)

were playing in uniforms soiled with vomit and feces. Given the intense physical contact inherent in football, transmission likely occurred via oral–fecal transmission and aerosol transmission of the vomitus. Based on their findings, researchers recommended that players with acute gastroenteritis be excluded from competition to avoid transmitting the disease to other players (**Figure 8-11** and Tables 8-5 and 8-6.)

■ Surveillance and Serological Epidemiology

Surveillance programs and reporting systems targeted at infectious diseases play a fundamental role in public health. Surveillance can take several forms:

CENTERS FOR DISEASE CONTROL

June 5, 1981 / Vol. 30 / No. 21

MMWR

MORBIDITY AND MORTALITY WEEKLY REPORT

Pneumocystis Pneumonia — Los Angeles

In the period October 1980-May 1981, 5 young men, all active homosexuals, were treated for biopsy-confirmed *Pneumocystis carinii* pneumonia at 3 different hospitals in Los Angeles, California. Two of the patients died. All 5 patients had laboratory-confirmed previous or current cytomegalovirus (CMV) infection and candidal mucosal infection. Case reports of these patients follow.

Patient 1: A previously healthy 33-year-old man developed *P. carinii* pneumonia and oral mucosal candidiasis in March 1981 after a 2-month history of fever associated with elevated liver enzymes, leukopenia, and CMV viruria. The serum complement-fixation CMV titer in October 1980 was 256; in May 1981 it was 32.* The patient's condition deteriorated despite courses of treatment with trimethoprim-sulfamethoxazole (TMP/SMX), pentamidine, and acyclovir. He died May 3, and postmortem examination showed residual *P. carinii* and CMV pneumonia, but no evidence of neoplasia.

Patient 2: A previously healthy 30-year-old man developed *P. carinii* pneumonia in April 1981 after a 5-month history of fever each day and of elevated liver-function tests, CMV viruria, and documented seroconversion to CMV, i.e., an acute-phase titer of 16 and a convalescent-phase titer of 28* in anticomplement immunofluorescence tests. Other features of his illness included leukopenia and mucosal candidiasis. His pneumonia responded to a course of intravenous TMP/SMX, but, as of the latest reports, he continues to have a fever each day.

Patient 3: A 30-year-old man was well until January 1981 when he developed esophageal and oral candidiasis that responded to Amphotericin B treatment. He was hospitalized in February 1981 for *P. carinii* pneumonia that responded to oral TMP/SMX. His esophageal candidiasis recurred after the pneumonia was diagnosed, and he was again given Amphotericin B. The CMV complement-fixation titer in March 1981 was 8. Material from an esophageal biopsy was positive for CMV.

Patient 4: A 29-year-old man developed *P. carinii* pneumonia in February 1981. He had had Hodgkins disease 3 years earlier, but had been successfully treated with radiation therapy alone. He did not improve after being given intravenous TMP/SMX and corticosteroids and died in March. Postmortem examination showed no evidence of Hodgkins disease, but *P. carinii* and CMV were found in lung tissue.

Patient 5: A previously healthy 36-year-old man with a clinically diagnosed CMV infection in September 1980 was seen in April 1981 because of a 4-month history of fever, dyspnea, and cough. On admission he was found to have *P. carinii* pneumonia, oral candidiasis, and CMV retinitis. A complement-fixation CMV titer in April 1981 was 128. The patient has been treated with 2 short courses of TMP/SMX that have been limited because of a sulfa-induced neutropenia. He is being treated for candidiasis with topical nystatin.

---

*Paired specimens not run in parallel.

■ Figure VF 8-1

The CDC published a summary of the five homosexual men who had been treated for microbial infections that were documented to only occur in individuals with suppressed immune systems. (Gottlieb, M. S. et al. 1981. "*Pneumocystis* Pneumonia–Los Angeles." *MMWR* June 5 30:250–252.)

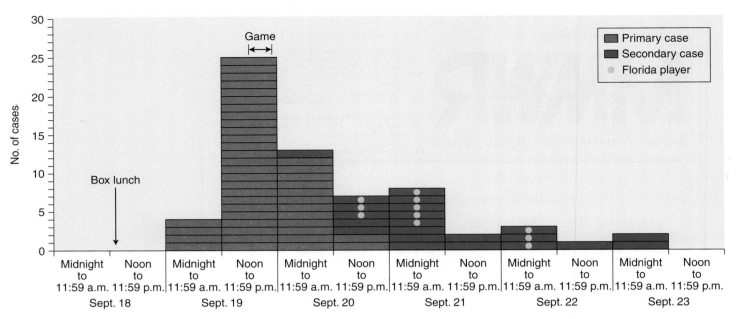

■ **Figure 8-11**

Person-to-person transmission of the Norwalk virus during college football game. (Adapted with permission from Becker, Moe, Southwick and MacCormack. *The New Journal of Medicine* 343 (2000):1223–1227. © 2005 Massachusetts Medical Society.)

TABLE 8-5	Rate and Risk of Illness Among Players of the North Carolina Football Team Based on Meals Eaten					
Meal	**Date**	**Ate Meal**		**Did Not Eat Meal**		**Relative Risk (95% CI)**[a]
		Total No.	**No. Who Became Ill (%)**	**Total No.**	**No. Who Became Ill (%)**	
Lunch	9/18	81	50 (62)	27	4 (15)	4.1 (1.6–10.0)
Dinner	9/18	87	45 (52)	21	9 (43)	1.2 (0.7–2.2)
Late dinner	9/18	63	34 (54)	45	20 (44)	1.2 (0.8–1.8)
Breakfast	9/19	85	42 (49)	23	12 (52)	0.9 (0.6–1.5)
Lunch	9/19	76	39 (51)	32	15 (47)	1.1 (0.7–1.7)

[a]CI denotes confidence interval.

Reproduced with permission from Becker, Moe, Southwick and MacCormack. *The New Journal of Medicine* 343 (2000):1223–1227. © 2005 Massachusetts Medical Society.

- Monitoring available data from mandated reports on reportable diseases (morbidity and mortality statistics).
- Active field surveillance by epidemiologists at healthcare facilities (such as interviewing physicians and patients or reviewing medical records).
- Serological screening of populations (for example, monitoring the success of vaccination programs). Antibodies represent the "footprints" of disease, exposure to disease, and protection against disease.).

■ Communicable Disease Surveillance Organizations and Their Publications or Reporting Mechanisms

Official organizations from the United States, Canada, the European Union, and other member states of the WHO share the same mission: that all people attain the highest

TABLE 8-6	Food-Specific Rates and Risks of Gastrointestinal Illness Among Individuals Who Ate Components of the Box Lunch

Meal	Ate Lunch		Did Not Eat Lunch		Unadjusted Odds Ratio (95% CI)	Adjusted Odds Ratio (95% CI)[a]
	Total No.	No. Who Became Ill (%)	Total No.	No. Who Became Ill (%)		
Sandwich	63	45 (71)	18	5 (28)	2.6 (1.2–5.5)	4.9 (1.3–18.9)
Apple	36	28 (78)	45	22 (49)	1.6 (1.1–2.3)	2.4 (0.6–9.3)
Candy bar	63	43 (68)	18	7 (39)	1.8 (1.0–3.2)	1.6 (0.5–5.0)

[a]The adjusted odds ratios were adjusted for each of the other foods in the box lunch. CI denotes confidence interval.

Reproduced with permission from Becker, Moe, Southwick and MacCormack. *The New Journal of Medicine* 343 (2000):1223–1227. © 2005 Massachusetts Medical Society.

TABLE 8-7	Government Organizations Involved in Surveillance and Publication of Epidemiological Information

Organization	Headquarters	Publications Available Online
Centers for Disease Control and Prevention (CDC)	Atlanta, Georgia, United States	*Morbidity and Mortality Weekly (MMWR)* http://www.cdc.gov/mmwr/ *Emerging and Infectious Diseases Journal (EID)* http://www.cdc.gov/ncidod/EID/index.htm
Health Canada	Ottawa, Canada	*Canada Communicable Disease Report (CCDR)* http://www.hc-sc.gc.ca/pphb-dgspsp/publicat/ccdr-rmtc/
World Health Organization (WHO)	Geneva, Switzerland	*Weekly Epidemiological Report (WER)* http://www.who.int/wer/en/
European Commission (Europa)	Brussels, Belgium	*EuroSurveillance Weekly and Monthly* http://www.eurosurveillance.org/index-02.asp
Health Protection Agency (HPA)	London, United Kingdom	*Communicable Diseases Report Weekly (CDR)* http://www.hpa.org.uk/cdr/ *Communicable Disease and Public Health Journal* http://www.hpa.org.uk/cdph/
Doctors without Borders/ Médecins Sans Frontières (MSF)	U.S. Headquarters: New York, NY International Office: Brussels, Belgium	*Alert Quarterly* http://www.doctorswithoutborders.org/publications/alert/

possible level of health. A short list of some of the major organizations, their headquarter locations, and epidemiological publications relating to infectious diseases is shown in Table 8-7. These organizations perform ongoing surveillance of many viral diseases, respond to disease outbreaks, and develop and publish infectious disease prevention and control recommendations.

In 1951, following the start of the Korean War and concurrent with its threat of biological warfare, the CDC formed the Epidemic Intelligence Service (EIS). EIS is a training program composed of physicians, researchers, and scientists that have gone on to play pivotal roles in combating the causes of major epidemics. There are EIS investigation sites located worldwide (http://www.cdc.gov/eis/index.htm).

A private organization, **Doctors Without Borders** (in French, Médecins Sans Frontières, or MSF), was founded in 1971 by a group of French physicians who believed that everyone has a right to medical care, including those in remote areas and locations where there is political unrest. Every year MSF unites more than 2500 volunteer doctors, nurses, medical professionals, logistic experts, water sanitation experts, and administrators from all over the world in response to epidemic emergencies in unstable areas of the world. There are also organizations that focus on the health of wildlife, such as the National Wildlife Health Center (http://www.nwhc.usgs.gov/). Part of its mission is to support the development of advanced diagnostics to detect zoonotic pathogens and the control of wildlife disease dynamics.

VIRUS FILE 8-2	Sentinel Chicken Surveillance Programs

In 1999, the first outbreak of West Nile virus was recognized in the United States. It began in New York City and neighboring counties in New York state in late August and September. Initially, the outbreak was attributed to St. Louis Encephalitis virus (SLE), based on positive enzyme-linked immunosorbent assay tests on cerebrospinal fluid of patients. (SLE and West Nile viruses are antigenically very similar and cross-reactivity was being observed in most serologic tests.) Later, the isolation of virus and genomic sequences from dead crows, other species of birds from zoos, mosquito pools, and from human brain tissues correctly identified the cause of the outbreak.

In May 2000 Canadian Health authorities stationed cages of sentinel chickens along 2500 km (1550 miles) of the border with the United States in an effort to identify the presence of West Nile virus in susceptible animals before the disease was detected in humans in Canada. Ultimately, the sentinel chickens were key in detecting a new viral epidemic (**Figure VF 8-2**).

Compared to other birds with the disease, chickens with West Nile virus develop a very short viremia without symptoms. Chickens can spread the virus from the cloaca and the virus may be found in feces. Animal handlers used precautions while handling the sentinel chickens during the weekly testing for West Nile Virus antibodies.

Today West Nile virus sentinel chicken surveillance programs are not only being used in Canada but many locations throughout the United States. In addition, mosquito populations are being monitored for density, species, and presence of West Nile virus. Surveillance systems provide information that is used to determine where and how mosquito abatement and control programs should commence.

■ **Figure VF 8-2**
Photograph showing a caged sentinel chicken flock used to detect the presence of West Nile virus.

References

Asuis, D. et al. 1999. "Outbreak of West Nile-Like Viral Encephalitis—New York, 1999." *MMWR* October 1 48(38):845–849

CDC West Nile Virus website: http://www.cdc.gov/ncidod/dvbid/westnile/index.htm.

Fine, A. et al. 1999. "Update: West Nile-Like Viral Encephalitis—New York, 1999." *MMWR* October 8 48(39):890–892.

Health Canada: West Nile Surveillance Program website:
http://www.hc-sc.gc.ca/pphb-dgspsp/wnv-vwn/index.html.

■ ProMED-mail: An Online Program Used to Monitor Disease Outbreaks

On August 19, 1994, with modest support from the Federation of American Scientists and SatelLife, Dr. Jack Woodall founded Pro-MED-mail as an Internet reporting tool to monitor emerging infectious disease outbreaks (http://www.promedmail.org/). Its aim was to assist in disseminating outbreak information (such as location or confirmed disease) as rapidly as possible. On that day, the first ProMED-mail message was posted via email to 40 subscribers in seven countries. The first posts on ProMED consisted of queries relating to media/newspaper reports and local observations.

Current subscribers participate in dialogues addressing rumors, actual disease outbreaks, and questions pertaining to emerging infectious diseases.Since 1999, the International Society for Infectious Diseases has furnished new servers and software to handle the large volume of subscribers. Today Pro-MED email posts are read by tens of thousands of viewers in over 160 countries and thousands more refer to its Website. This forum has been successful in alerting local, national, and international organizations about new outbreaks; for example, before official reports were published, three individuals—Stephen Cunnion (M.D., Ph.D., M.P.H., International Consultants in Health, Inc.), Jesse Huang (State Health Dept. in Nashville Tennessee), and Dan Silver (Intellibridge Corporation)—posted a request for information (RFI) on ProMED about SARS, a new viral disease epidemic in China.

8.5   A Word about Prevention and Containment of Contagious Diseases: Quarantine

The practice of **quarantine** is still used today to prevent person-to-person transmission of infectious diseases, such as during the SARS outbreak of 2003. Quarantine is the segregation of healthy persons who are not ill but have been exposed to an individual who suffers from a communicable disease from the general population. This is necessary because the exposed healthy individual is at risk of becoming infected. (In May of 2007, a man infected with the bacterium *Mycobacterium tuberculosis* was ordered into isolation by the U.S. government. The man was a U.S. citizen who suffered from a multidrug-resistant form of tuberculosis. This was the first time since 1963, when an individual infected with smallpox was placed in isolation, that someone was quarantined in the U.S. For information about that quarantine, go to http://www.cdc.gov/od/oc/media/pressrel/2007/r070529.htm.)

The word quarantine comes from the Latin word *quaresma*, meaning forty. This definition dates to the 14th century when ships arriving in Venice, Italy, sailing from plague-infected ports were required to sit at anchor for 40 days before landing. Before the Federal Quarantine Legislation was passed in 1878 to prevent the transmission of yellow fever, little was done to prevent the importation of infectious diseases in the United States. More laws were passed regarding quarantine requirements when cholera arrived in the United States in 1892. By 1921, quarantine stations were set up under federal government authority. In 1967, quarantine practices were authorized by the National Communicable Disease Center (now known as the CDC). In the late 1960s, over 500 staff oversaw 55 quarantine stations located at every port and major border crossing. Today the number of stations and staff has been reduced and the CDC has changed its focus. Instead, emphasis is placed on routine inspections and enhanced surveillance systems to meet the changing needs of international traffic. Quarantine operations involve the cooperation of the EIS, state and local health departments, the United States Citizenship and Immigration Service (USCIS), Customs and Border Protection, the United States Department of Agriculture (USDA), and the United States Fish and Wildlife Service (USFWS).

SMALL POX

This Notice is Posted in Compliance with Law

"Every person who shall wilfully tear down, remove or deface any notice posted in compliance with law shall be fined not more than seven dollars."—General Statutes of Connecticut, Revision of 1902, Sec. 1173.

Town Health Officer.

Isolation is still commonly used in modern public health. Isolation refers to the separation of ill/infected individuals from healthy individuals. Infected individuals can be isolated in a hospital, at home, or in designated community-based facilities. During the early 1900s and through the 1950s, as soon as the Health Officer gained knowledge pertaining to cases of scarlet fever, yellow fever, smallpox, diphtheria, measles, whooping cough, chickenpox, cholera, bubonic plague, membranous croup, and cerebral meningitis, **placards** or notices from the state's board of health were posted on entrances of the homes of infected individuals (**Figure 8-12**). It was unlawful for anyone other than a physician or trained nurse to enter or leave the premises in which sick individuals were being isolated. The placard was typically displayed for at least 21 days after scarlet fever or smallpox was reported and 14 days after the report of other infectious diseases. There were also specific guidelines for the disinfection of clothing, removal of infected articles, and disinfection of homes or facilities upon death or convalescence.

8.6 Travel Medicine

We live in a global world in which many people are traveling without adequate travelers' health preparation. If you were to plan a trip to Tanzania (central Africa) or Uzbekistan (central Asia), how would you determine what infectious diseases are endemic in those countries and the vaccines that you need as a result (**Figure 8-13**)? What other information should you know? For example, should you bring insect repellent? A mesh net-bed or headnets? Bottled water? Are there special requirements if you are traveling with children, the elderly, or someone who is pregnant? Will you be camping? Are you traveling via an international adoption program? How long will you be there? Will you need any blood products? Antivirals or antibiotics? Are there environmental health risks? What will be your mode of transportation (ship, air)?

Today, many individuals travel globally on business. A 1991 study published in the *Annals of Emergency Medicine* pertaining to the morbidity and mortality of U.S. World Bank staff and consultants traveling in developing countries described how approximately 100,000 World Bank staff and consultants filed medical insurance claims related to health problems associated with exposure to infectious diseases. Overall, medical claims are increasing as the frequency of travel increases.

The International Society of Travel Medicine (ISTM) or the American Society of Tropical Medicine and Hygiene (ASTMH) provide directories of private travel clinics throughout the United States and other countries. The CDC also maintains an updated Web page

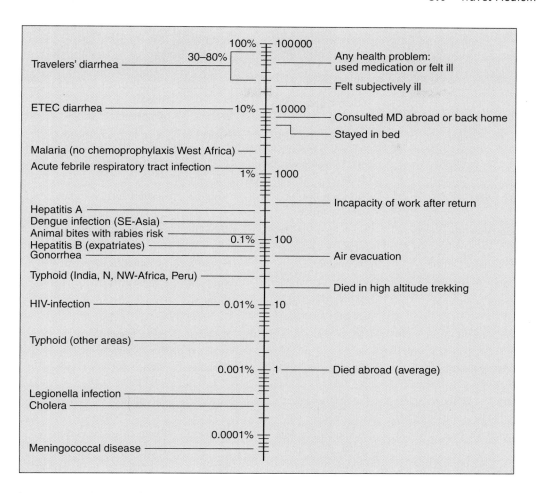

■ **Figure 8-13**
World Bank staff and consultants filed medical claims relating to many bacterial and viral infectious diseases while traveling in developing countries. The figure represents the monthly incidence rates of these health problems. *Note*: ETEC refers to diarrhea caused by Enterotoxigenic *E. coli* (ETEC). The word febrile means fever. According to this survey, 400 per 100,000 individuals were unable to work upon their return from developing countries. Reprinted from *Ann. Emerg. Med., vol.* 20, Hargarten, W. et al., *Overseas Fatalities of United States Citizen Travelers . . . ,* 622–626, © 1991, with permission from American College of Emergency Physicians.

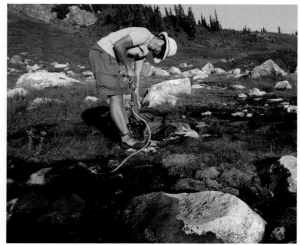

■ **Figure 8-14**
This traveler is avoiding disease-ridden water by filtering water from a mountain stream.

TABLE 8-8	Travelers' Health Information
Internet Resources for Travelers	**URL**
CDC's National Center for Infectious Diseases Travelers' Health	http://www.cdc.gov/travel/
The International Society of Travel Medicine	http://www.istm.org/
American Society of Tropical Medicine and Hygiene (ASTMH)	http://www.astmh.org/
CDC's National Immunization Program Vaccine Publications	http://www.cdc.gov/nip/publications/vis/
WHO's International Travel and Health	http://www.who.int/ith/

on Travelers' Health. It contains information on specific diseases that affect travelers, vaccinations, special needs, traveling with children, how to avoid illness associated with contaminated food or drinking water, travel via air or cruise ships, and updated information on current outbreaks (**Figure 8-14**). Important resources are listed in Table 8-8. The immune status of the traveler should always be considered before traveling to areas where exposure to infectious diseases is high.

TABLE 8-9	Examples of Viral Diseases in Humans Caused by Arthropod-Borne Viruses*		
Viral Disease	**Endemic Geographic Location**	**Vector**	**Disease Symptoms**
West Nile encephalitis	North America, Africa, Indian subcontinent, Middle East, former Soviet Union, Europe	Mosquito	Fever, rash, encephalitis
Yellow fever	South and Central America, Africa	Mosquito	Hemorrhagic fever, hepatitis
Dengue fever (Dengue virus 1-4)	Throughout the tropics	Mosquito	Fever, hemorrhage, rash
St. Louis encephalitis	The Americas	Mosquito	Encephalitis, hepatitis
La Crosse encephalitis	America	Mosquito	Encephalitis
Japanese encephalitis	Asia, Pacific Islands, northern Australia	Mosquito	Encephalitis, fever
Rift Valley fever	Africa, Arabia	Mosquito	Fever, hemorrhage, encephalitis, retinitis
Epidemic polyarthritis (Ross River virus)	Australia, South Pacific	Mosquito	Fever, arthralgia (severe joint pain), rash
Eastern and Western equine encephalitis	The Americas	Mosquito	Encephalitis
Chikungunya fever	Philippines, SE Asia, Africa	Mosquito	Fever, arthralgia (severe joint pain), rash
Kyasanur Forest disease	India	Tick	Hemorrhage, fever, meningoencephalitis
Powassan encephalitis	Canada, Russian Federation, America	Tick	Encephalitis
Colorado tick fever	Canada, USA	Tick	Fever
Crimean–Congo hemorrhagic fever	Central Asia, Africa, Middle East, Europe	Tick	Hemorrhagic fever
Vesicular stomatitis	The Americas	Sand fly	Fever, encephalitis

*Note that this list is not complete. Many of the viral diseases caused by arthropods cause encephalitis, an inflammation of the brain. Initial symptoms of encephalitis consist of a headache, nausea, vomiting, fever, and lethargy. Meningoencephalitis refers to inflammation of the brain and its membranes; it is sometimes referred to as encephalomeningitis.

■ Arthropod Bites

Adventure travel packages have become increasingly popular. Dive tours, wilderness safaris, and sailing to remote areas often expose tourists to blood-feeding arthropods that can carry viruses or parasites (for example, *Plasmodium* sp., which causes malaria) and sting injuries by marine life (Table 8-9). Tourists should educate themselves about such risks and take adequate measures to avoid injuries and infections; for example, the use of DEET, wearing protective clothing, and use of bed nets are very effective methods for preventing arthropod-transmitted diseases.

■ Contaminated Food

Foodborne illnesses in remote areas are most often associated with the following:

- Ciguatera fish poisoning (common in the Pacific and Indian oceans and the Caribbean sea)

- Paralytic shellfish poisoning (often following a dinoflagellate bloom)
- Outbreaks in tropical and subtropical waters, which have become more frequent in places including Mexico, Malaysia, Guatemala, El Salvador, Papua New Guinea, India and the Solomon Islands
- Poisoning related to toxic and unfamiliar mushrooms (nontoxic mushrooms in Europe and North America closely resemble highly toxic mushrooms in other parts of the world and vice versa)

Hepatitis A outbreaks associated with food consumption (oral–fecal route of transmission) are highest in developing countries that have poor sanitation and food hygiene. Individuals traveling to Eastern Europe, Greece, Turkey, and the Commonwealth of Independent States (including Russia) are at immediate risk for contracting hepatitis A. The United States, Canada, Scandinavian countries, Australia, Japan, New Zealand, and developed parts of Europe are considered low risk. Serological studies have indicated that persons from industrialized countries born after World War II have very low titers of anti-hepatitis A antibodies, increasing their risk of contracting hepatitis A upon exposure. The case fatality rate of hepatitis A infection is estimated to be 0.15% but increases to 2.0% or higher in those over 40 years of age. There is a recommended and effective vaccine available for those persons from industrialized countries who are traveling to countries where hepatitis A is endemic.

Outbreaks of norovirus have occurred aboard cruise ships and in hotels. These viruses, which are transmitted via oral-fecal and aerosol routes, are the most common causes of nonbacterial diarrhea in travelers. Cruise ships bring together large numbers of people from different parts of the world, and the confined quarters of the cruise ship is a factor in the spread of gastrointestinal disease. The incubation period of norovirus infection is also short (1 to 2 days). Frequent handwashing helps to prevent the spread of infectious diseases on cruise ships. The CDC investigates outbreaks of gastrointestinal nature if 3% or more of the passengers or crewmembers of a passenger ship become ill.

Influenza is common among travelers. The risk of exposure to influenza depends upon the time of year and the destination of the traveler. In the tropics, influenza occurs throughout the year. In the southern hemisphere (for example, parts of Africa, South America, and Australia), most influenza activity occurs from April through September. The influenza season in the northern hemisphere is November through April. Influenza ranks next to hepatitis A as one of the most common vaccine preventable diseases of travelers.

■ Contaminated Water

Examples of viral waterborne pathogens are hepatitis A, hepatitis E, poliovirus, and norovirus. It is not wise to assume that tap water is potable in many areas. Travelers should learn basic field techniques—such as heat, filtration, and chemical disinfection—that can be used to improve water quality, as well as the limitations of each method.

■ Medical Facilities in Remote Areas

Employees of petroleum, mining, and construction companies, members of the armed services and intelligence communities, remote area public health personnel, missionaries, individuals on pilgrimages, adventure and health spa travelers, and scientists travel to remote areas of developed and developing countries. Travel in rural areas may place individuals outside of protective law enforcement and out of reach of personal security and healthcare facilities in the event of medical emergencies. Besides pretravel immunizations and education, travelers should be counseled by a physician on carrying a specialized medical kit. Sometimes self-treatment may be necessary to combat diarrheal diseases, acute respiratory diseases, and other physical ailments. Some companies will require pretravel medical screening because medical facilities in foreign countries often lack the resources (such as medications, vaccines, antibiotics, antivirals, sterile needles, and a safe blood supply) and experience in treating chronic illnesses.

Systematic screening of blood donations is not yet feasible in all developing countries, and thus the safety of the blood supply ultimately depends on the quality of blood transfusion services in the host country. Blood should be transfused only when absolutely necessary, especially in those countries where screening of blood for transmissible diseases is not yet widely performed. Travelers should take active steps to minimize the risk of injury and establish a plan for dealing with medical emergencies. The risk of bloodborne transmission of hepatitis B can be minimized with hepatitis B vaccination prior to travel.

8.7 Tracking Diseases from Outer Space: Early Warning Systems

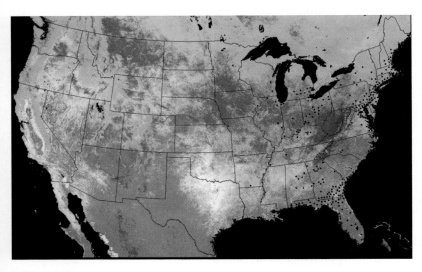

■ Figure 8-15
This satellite image helped monitor and predict the spread of West Nile virus in the United States. The land surface temperatures are represented by shades of red. Blue indicates the range of highest and lowest temperatures the region experiences during the year, with deep blue representing the greatest range. The black dots on this map represent infected crows reported in 2001. The colors on this map indicate the relative levels of risk for West Nile Virus in 2001. The image was produced by INTREPID from data taken by the National Oceanic and Atmospheric Administration's [NOAA] Advanced Very High Resolution Radiometer [AVHRR] instrument. Courtesy of INTREPID, NOAA, AVHRR/NASA.

Environmental factors often play a pivotal role in outbreaks of viral diseases like Dengue fever, hantavirus pulmonary syndrome, West Nile encephalitis, and Rift Valley fever; for example, heavy rainfall, temperature changes, and vegetation changes may set the stage for a population surge of disease-carrying pests such as mosquitoes, ticks, or rodents, and the diseases they carry spread rapidly).

NASA's Global Hydrology and Climate Center in Huntsville, Alabama, is using high-tech satellites to monitor environmental changes in entire regions, countries, and even continents. Scientists from the NASA center visit and observe sites with potential disease outbreaks. They combine their field observations with the satellite images to set up early warning systems for regions. Sophisticated mathematical algorithms are computed and correlated with the observed field conditions and satellite data to simulate the landscape and its potential for vectorborne disease outbreaks. These "red flags" allow health officials to focus on mosquito eradication, vaccination programs, and other efforts to prevent an outbreak before it happens. Perfect predictions will never be possible, but reasonably accurate risk estimates can be made by combining field work with the newest satellite technologies (**Figure 8-15**).

■ Summary

Epidemiology is the branch of science that deals with how diseases affect whole communities or populations. It is concerned with disease diagnostics, trends, prevention, and control measures. The field has evolved its own terminology that can be quite confusing for those not familiar with it. Common terms include endemic, sporadic, epidemic, pandemic, morbidity, mortality, incidence, prevalence, carrier, incubation period, prodromal period, period of illness, mode of transmission, etiological agent, reservoir, case definition, communicable period convalescence, and zoonosis, which were defined at the beginning of the chapter.

Two of the early pioneers of epidemiology, Edward Jenner and John Snow, focused on the prevention of smallpox and cholera, respectively, during the 18th and 19th centuries.

Snow's search for the cause of the cholera outbreak in London in 1854 laid the groundwork for descriptive epidemiological investigation.

The epidemiological triangle or triad model is used to explain the complexities of infectious disease causation. Epidemics occur when

- there is an increase in a particular pathogen.
- the pathogen becomes more virulent.
- the pathogen enters the host via a new portal of entry.
- the pathogen is introduced to a new environmental setting.
- the host has increased risks or susceptibility.
- there is increased exposure between the host and pathogen (Table 8-2).

Viral diseases are transmitted directly (person to person) or indirectly (via airborne, foodborne, waterborne, vectorborne, or vehicleborne transmission). Viral pathogens have preferred portals of entry into their hosts and exits from them. Hospital and healthcare settings apply various practices to break the chain of infection. Practices include frequent handwashing and the use of protective barriers (such as gloves, masks, and coats), maintaining a clean environment, and disposing of medical wastes and used medical supplies properly.

Herd immunity acts as a "firebreak" by slowing or preventing further spread of infectious diseases. Vaccination is an effective way to create herd immunity. As the number of vaccinated individuals increases, the likelihood that the disease will be transmitted to unvaccinated individuals is reduced.

There are two types of epidemiological investigations: descriptive and analytical studies. Descriptive studies provides information relating to the what, when, where, and who pertain to a specific outbreak in a community. These studies are used to generate a testable hypothesis that is used in further analytical epidemiological investigations. Analytical epidemiology provides the why and how of an outbreak (testing hypotheses for causation). Epidemiologists use case-control or cohort methods.

Surveillance programs and reporting systems targeted at infectious diseases play a fundamental role in public health. Government and private organizations actively participate in surveillance and respond to disease outbreaks. Internet reporting has become a successful forum in alerting local, national, and international organizations about new disease outbreaks. Quarantine and isolation techniques may also be enforced by these organizations.

To meet the needs of the growing numbers of individuals traveling globally through business or recreation, travelers' clinics have been set up. These clinics provide vaccinations and information on specific diseases that affect travelers. The immune status of the traveler should always be considered before traveling to areas where exposure to infectious diseases is high. Medical facilities in remote areas often lack proper medical supplies, blood products, vaccines, and experienced staff in treating infectious diseases.

Changes in the environment may set the stage for new diseases; for example, increased rainfall may contribute to a surge of disease-carrying mosquitoes. The diseases they carry spread rapidly. High-tech satellites are being used to monitor environmental changes in entire regions, countries, and even continents in an effort to develop early warning systems for disease outbreaks.

◼ Resources

◼ Primary Literature and Reviews

Asuis, D. et al. 1999. "Outbreak of West Nile-Like Viral Encephalitis—New York, 1999." *MMWR* 48(38):845–849.

Becker, K. M., Moe, C. L., Southwick, K. L., and Newton, M. J. 2000. "Transmission of Norwalk Virus During a Football Game." *N Engl J Med* 343(17):1223–1227.

Centers for Disease Control and Prevention (CDC). 2004. "150th Anniversary of John Snow and the Pump Handle September 3, 2004." *MMWR* 53(34):783.

CDC. 2004. "An Outbreak of Norovirus Gastroenteritis at the Swimming Club—Vermont, 2004." *MMWR* 53(34):793–795.

CDC. 2003. "Hepatitis A Outbreak Associated with Green Onions at a Restaurant—Monaca, Pennsylvania, 2003." *MMWR* 52(47):1155–1157.

CDC. 1996. "Update: Mortality Attributable to HIV Infection Among Persons Aged 25–44 Years—United States, 1994." *MMWR* 45(6):121–125.

CDC. 1981. "Kaposi's Sarcoma and *Pneumocystis* Pneumonia Among Homosexual Men—New York City and California." *MMWR* 4(30):305–309.

Davidkin, I., Peltola, H., and Leinikki, P. 2004. "Epidemiology of Rubella in Finland." *EuroSurv Mon* 9(4):11–12.

Dayan, G. et al. 2004. "Epidemiology of Measles—United States, 2001–2003." *MMWR* 53(31):713–716.

Dossey, B. M. 1999. *Florence Nightingale: Mystic Visionary and Healer,* Springhouse, PA: Springhouse.

Ferichs, R. R. 2002. "History, Maps, and the Internet: UCLA's John Snow Site." *SoC BULLETIN* 34(2): 3–7.

Fine, A. et al. 1999. "Update: West Nile-Like Viral Encephalitis—New York, 1999." *MMWR* 48(39):890–892.

Gaulin, C., et al. 2004. "Assessment of Surveillance of Human West Nile Virus Infection in Quebec, 2003." *Can Comm Dis Rep* 30(11):97–104.

Gordis, L. 2000. *Epidemiology,* 2nd ed. Philadelphia: Saunders.

Gottlieb, M. S. et al. 1981. "*Pneumocystis* Pneumonia—Los Angeles." *MMWR* 30:250–252.

Grimes, D. A. 2002. "Descriptive Studies: What They Can and Cannot Do." *Lancet* 359:145–149.

Hargarten, S. W., Baker, T. D., Guptill K. 1991. "Overseas Fatalities of United States Citizen Travelers: An Analysis of Deaths Related to International Travel." *Ann Emerg Med* 20:622–626.

Heymann, D. L., ed. 2004. *Control of Communicable Diseases Manual,* 18th ed., Washington DC: American Public Health Association.

Hoff, B., and Smith III, C. 2000. *Mapping Epidemics: A Historical Atlas of Disease,* Danbury, CT: Franklin Watts.

Keystone, J. S., Kozarsky, P. E., Freedman, D. O., Nothdurft, H.D., and Connor, B. A., eds. 2004. *Travel Medicine,* Philadelphia: Mosby.

Masur, H., et al. 1981. "An Outbreak of Community Acquired *Pneumocystis carinii* pneumonia: Initial Manifestation of Cellular Immune Dysfunction." *N Engl J Med* 305:1431–1438.

Meltzer, M. I. 2004. "Multiple Contact Dates and SARS Incubation Periods." *EID* 10(2):207–209.

Mounts, A. W., et al. 1999. "Case-Control Study of Risk Factors for Avian Influenza A (H5N1) Disease, Hong Kong, 1997." *J Inf Dis* 180:505–508.

Nies, M. A., and McEwen, M. 2001. *Community Health Nursing: Promoting the Health of Populations,* 3rd ed., Philadelphia: W. B. Saunders.

Snodgrass, M.E. 2003. *World Epidemics: A Cultural Chronology of Disease from PreHistory to the Era of SARS* 2003, Jefferson, NC: McFarland.

Timmreck, T. C. 2002. *An Introduction to Epidemiology,* 3rd ed., Sudbury, MA: Jones and Bartlett.

Vandenbroucke, J. P. 2001. "Changing Images of John Snow in the History of Epidemiology 2001." *Soz Praventivmed* 46(5):288–293.

Woodall, J., and Calisher, C. H. 2001. "ProMED-mail: Background and Purpose." *EID* 7(3):563.

■ Popular Press

Barry, J. M. 2004. *The Great Influenza: The Epic Story of the Deadliest Plague in History*, New York: Viking.

Carrell, J. L. 2004. *The Speckled Monster: A Historical Tale of Battling Smallpox*, New York: Plume.

Carrol, M. C. 2004. *Lab 257: The Disturbing Story of the Government's Secret Plum Island Germ Laboratory*, New York: William Morrow.

DeSalle, R., ed. 1999. *Epidemic! The World of Infectious Disease*, New York: The New Press and The American Museum of Natural History.

English, M. P. 1990. *Victorian Values: The Life and Times of Dr. Edwin Lankester*, Bristol, England: Biopress LTD.

Harper, D. R., and Meyer, A. S. 1999. *Of Mice, Men, and Microbes: Hantavirus*, San Diego: Academic Press.

Iezzoni, L., and McCullough, D. 1997. *Influenza, 1918: The Worst Epidemic in American History*, New York: TV Books.

Johnson, S. 2006. *The Ghost Map: The Story of London's Most Terrifying Epidemic—and How It Changed Science, Cities, and the Modern World*, New York: Riverhead Books.

Levy, E., and Fischetti, M. 2003. *The New Killer Diseases: How the Alarming Revolution of Mutant Germs Threatens Us All*, New York: Crown Publishers.

Loh, C., and Exchange, C. 2004. *At the Epicentre: Hong Kong and the SARS Outbreak*, edited Hong Kong. Hong Kong: University Press, .

McCormick, J. B.; and Fisher-Hoch, S. with Horvitz, L. A. 1996. *Level 4: Virus Hunters of the CDC*, Atlanta: Turner Publishing.

McKenna, M. 2004. *Beating Back the Devil: On the Front Lines with the Disease Detectives of the Epidemic Intelligence Service*, New York: Free Press.

Merkel, E. 2002. *Final Epidemic*, New York: Signet Book.

Murphy, J. 2003. *An American Plague: The True and Terrifying Story of the Yellow Fever Epidemic of 1793*, New York: Clarion Books.

Peters, C. J., and Olshaker, M. 1997. *Virus Hunter: Thirty Years Battling Hot Viruses Around the World*, New York: Anchor Books.

Preston, R. 1995. *The Hot Zone*, New York: Random House.

Regis, E. 1996. *Virus Ground Zero: Stalking Killer Viruses with the Centers for Disease Control*, New York: Pocket Books.

Rhodes, R. 1997. *Deadly Feasts: Tracking the Secrets of a Terrifying New Plague*, New York: Simon and Schuster.

Seavey, N. G., Smith, J. S. and Wagner, P. 1998. *A Paralyzing Fear: Triumph Over Polio in America*, New York: TV Books.

Sherman, I. W. 2006. *The Power of Plagues*, Washington, DC: ASM Press.

Shilts, R. 1988. *And the Band Played On: Politics, People, and the AIDS Epidemic*, New York: St. Martins Press.

Vinten-Johnson, P., Brody, H., Paneth, N., Rachman, S., and Rip, M. 2003. *Cholera, Chloroform, and the Science of Medicine: A Life of John Snow*, Oxford: Oxford University Press.

Watts, S. 1997. *Epidemics and History: Disease, Power, and Imperialism*, New Haven, CT: Yale University Press.

Wills, C. 1996. *Yellow Fever, Black Goddess: The Coevolution of People and Plagues*, Reading, MA: Helix Books/Addison-Wesley.

■ Video Productions

And the Band Played On. 1993. HBO Video.

The New Explorers: On the Trail of a Killer Virus. 1994. An A & E Production.

Preventing Hantavirus Disease. 1994. CDC Educational Video.

Ebola: Diary of a Killer. 1996. Films Media Group.

Plague Fighters. 1996. NOVA.

Around the World: Global Immunization. 1997. Films for the Humanities

Another War: Disease and Political Strife. 1997. Films for the Humanities.

Ebola: Chasing the Virus. 1997. Films for the Humanities.

Great Minds of Modern Medicine: Confront the Alarming Dangers of Infectious Diseases with Karl Johnsons. 1997.

The Next Plague: The Nipah Virus. 1997. Films for the Humanities.

20th Century with Mike Wallace: Outbreak! The New Plagues. 1997. The History Channel.

Brain Snatchers: Mad Cow Disease. 1998. A Discovery Channel Production.

The Emerging Viruses. 1998. BBC Production. Films for the Humanities.

Conquering and Invisible World. 1999. Films for the Humanities

With Every Breath: The Hanta Virus. 1999. Films for the Humanities.

Histories Mysteries: Smallpox Deadly Again? 2000. The History Channel.

Mosquito Nightmare: West Nile Virus. 2000. A Discovery Channel Production.

The Ebola Virus. 3/12/01. ABC News Production. Nightline.

Foot and Mouth Disease. 3/26/01. ABC News Production. Nightline.

History Uncover: Clouds of Death. The Scourge of Biochemical Warfare. 2001. An A & E Production.

The Truth Will Out: Is vCJD Caused by BSE? 2001. Films for the Humanities.

A Never Ending War (Smallpox). 9/23/02. ABC News Production. Nightline.

West Nile Virus. 08/06/02. ABC News Production. Nightline.

New Blood. 2002. Anime New Network.

Bioterror. NOVA. 2003.

The SARS Outbreak. 5/7/03. ABC News Production Nightline.

The Danger of SARS. 4/21/03. ABC News Production. Nightline.

Mad Cow Disease. 12/23/03. ABC News Production. Nightline.

Outbreak: Stopping SARS. 2003. Films for the Humanities.

SARS. 2003. Canada Health.

SARS: The True Story. 2003. A BBCW Production.

War Against Deadly Microbes and Lethal Viruses. 2003. Films for the Humanities.

Aids and Other Epidemics. 2004. Films for the Humanities.

Emerging Diseases. A Cambridge Educational Production. 2004. Films for the Humanities.

SARS and the New Plagues. 2005. The History Channel.

The Great Fever. 2005. The American Experience. PBS.

Influenza. 2006. Films for the Humanities.

The Age of Viruses. 2006. Films for the Humanities.

60 Minutes: Fighting AIDS. 2006. CBS Broadcasting.

Unseen Enemies: A Close-Up Look at the World's Deadliest Diseases, Rotaviruses. 2006. Films for the Humanities.

The Great Fever. 2007. A Bosch and Company, Inc. Film for the American Experience.

▪ eLearning

http://biology.jbpub.com/book/virology

The site features eLearning, an online review area that provides quizzes and other tools to help you study for your class. You can also follow useful links for in-depth information, or just find out the latest virology and microbiology news.

 CASE STUDY QUESTIONS

These questions relate to the Case Study presented at the beginning of the chapter.

1. What viral agent could be causing the infection?
2. What type of specimens would be collected from Tina to determine the cause of her GI upset?
3. What types of laboratory tests might have been performed to determine the pathogen that was causing her illness?
4. Would you take any special infection control precautions in caring for your sister or for a patient with gastroenteritis?
5. What treatment is effective?
6. Create a list of questions that were likely on the epidemiologist's questionnaire.
7. What could be the source(s) of Tina's infection?

For Questions 8–10, consider this additional information about the Case Study: During Tina's examination, several other children were being brought into the clinic for gastroenteritis symptoms. You recognized that at least one of the children was in Tina's swimming class. Another child at the clinic had been at the party held at the pool on the day of Tina's lesson. The intern epidemiologist begins a more thorough investigation.

8. What would be the epidemiolgist's initial steps in her investigation?
9. How might she look for additional cases?
10. Once information about the cases was collected, how would she characterize the outbreak (descriptive epidemiology)?

For Questions 11 and 12, consider this additional information about the Case Study: The epidemiologist visited the swimming club. She interviewed the staff and swimmers and indicated that the pool water was visibly cloudy. None of the pool staff had formal training in pool disinfection.

11. Could this illness have been prevented?
12. Create an outline for a general protocol that includes monitoring and proper response protocols used to prevent failures in the environmental health system at the swimming club.

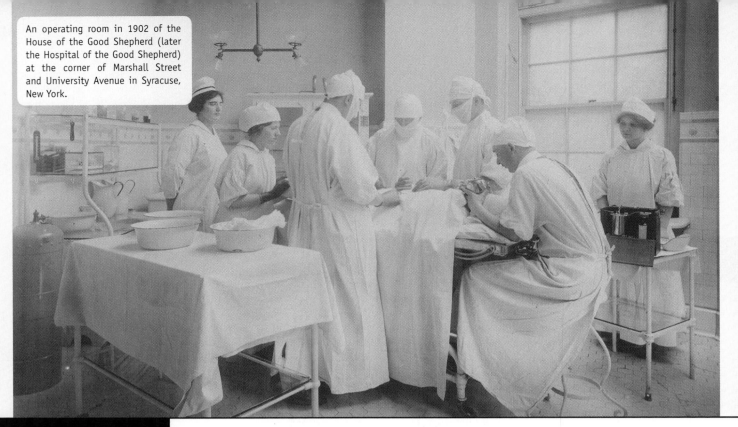

An operating room in 1902 of the House of the Good Shepherd (later the Hospital of the Good Shepherd) at the corner of Marshall Street and University Avenue in Syracuse, New York.

The History of Medicine, Clinical Trials, Gene Therapy, and Xenotransplantation

❝*The science of today is the technology of tomorrow.* **❞**

Edward Teller

CASE STUDY

Your best friend in college, Ted, is suffering from severe kidney disease. His nephrologist has informed him that he should register for the kidney waiting list. Ted was fully aware that many people die waiting for an organ. One day, you and Ted have a conversation pertaining to xenotransplantation, a topic covered in your virology textbook. Ted asks you to answer the following questions:

1. What are the two major obstacles to confronting xenotransplantation?
2. Can the safety of human recipients be guaranteed?
3. What ethical arguments can be made against the ethical use of animals in this way?
4. Is xenotransplantation the only way in which to tackle the donor deficit problem?
5. Given the history of viruses crossing the species barrier (such as rabies, severe acute respiratory syndrome [SARS], and influenza), is xenotransplantation too risky?

How will you respond to his questions?

9.1 Why Is the History of Medicine Important?

The rationale for discussing the history of medicine is to demonstrate that our quest for improving health through the use of medicines and medical procedures has occurred since ancient times. These advancements have dramatically improved the life span and health of humans.

In 1984, Baby Fae was born with a fatal heart disease. Physicians at Loma Linda University Medical Center replaced her heart with that of a bamboon, but Fae died of organ failure 21 days later. Doctors were surprised, though, to discover that Fae's body had not rejected the heart, as many had expected. This inspired doctors to continue medical neonatal heart transplant procedures.

Ashanti De Silva was born with mutations in both of her **adenosine deaminase (ADA)** genes, which are located on chromosome 20. ADA is required for metabolic function of a variety of cells, especially T-lymphocytes. ADA deficiency is one cause of severe combined immunodeficiency syndrome (SCID), which has also been referred to as the "boy in the bubble" disease. Children with SCID suffer from overwhelming infections and rarely survive childhood. At the age of 4, Ashanti was injected with genetically altered white blood cells. Her immune system has strengthened, allowing her to attend school. She continues low dose intravenous PEG-ADA therapy.

Jesse Gelsinger was born with a rare liver disease called **ornithine trans–carbamylase (OTC)** deficiency. Extreme OTC deficiency results in death, but Jesse led a relatively normal life by taking daily medications. When offered the opportunity to participate in a clinical trial at the University

■ **Figure 9-1**
A medical team at the National Institutes of Health Clinical Center prepares a patient for open heart surgery in 1955. The patient is lying on a bed of ice to lower the body temperature.

of Pennsylvania's Institute for Human Gene Therapy (IHGT) testing the safety of gene therapy for OTC deficiency, he agreed to participate. He died three days after being injected with an adenovirus that contained functional genes to compensate for his illness.

If you were faced with a life-threatening illness, would you opt for an experimental therapy? By participating in a new treatment for your illness, the media attention generated might increase the public awareness about the need for new therapies and better medical procedures relating to your illness. It could inspire continued research directed toward a cure for your illness. Would the increased public awareness inspire you to justify your decision? Or would costs, risks, and potential complications influence your decision? What about religious reasons?

Some of the biggest medical breakthroughs have not come without furor over prior unanticipated complications. Today, open-heart surgery is one of the most commonly performed operations in the United States, with a high overall survival rate. The mortality rate at most U.S. hospitals ranges from 1% to 3%. Open-heart surgery refers to any surgery in which the chest is opened and surgery is performed on the heart muscle, valves, arteries, or other structures.

In 1952, Toronto surgeon Wilfred Bigelow performed an open-heart operation. He applied the concept of hypothermia to perform the procedure. The animal patient was placed in a bed of ice, lowering the total body temperature so that the tissues used very little oxygen. In doing so, blood flow was interrupted for up to 15 minutes while the surgeon corrected heart defects. **Figure 9-1** shows this procedure being performed on a patient at the National Institutes of Health Clinical Center in 1955. Drs. Walton Lillehei and John Lewis, at the University of Minnesota on September 2, 1952, performed the first open heart surgery on a human, a 5-year-old girl who was born with a hole in her heart. Today heart surgery is routine, and instead of a bed of ice or a cooling blanket a heart–lung machine pumps the blood during the procedure. Former President Bill Clinton left the hospital four days after undergoing heart bypass surgery in September 2004.

■ History of Medicine and Clinical Research

Clinical research is evident as far back as 600 B.C. In the biblical book of Daniel, Daniel describes how he and three companions were captured in their native land of Judah and transported to Persia where they were forced to serve under the king of Babylon. Daniel wrote that he objected to the King's food and described a comparative protocol for diet and health. He showed that a diet of legumes and water made for healthier individuals than the king's diet of meat, fish, eggs, other rich foods, and wine. Two thousands years before Roger Bacon discovered the scientific method, Daniel described his experiment:

> Please test your servants for ten days. Let us be given vegetables to eat and water to drink. You can then compare our appearance with the appearance of the young men who eat the royal rations, and deal with your servants according to what you observe." So he agreed to this proposal and tested them for ten days. At the end of ten days it was observed that they appeared better and fatter than all the young men who had been eating the royal rations. So the guard continued to withdraw their royal rations and the wine they were to drink, and gave them vegetables. Daniel 1:12–16.

Ancient Chinese herbalists such as Shen Nung (ca. 2700 B.C.) also described clinical studies. Nung tasted and tested plants for their medicinal properties, thus gaining practical experience that allowed him to categorize medicines and record the toxicity and lethal dosage of herbal medicines.

There is evidence of surgical techniques being performed in ancient India as early as 800 B.C. Shushruta studied anatomy and described plastic surgery techniques that he developed. He specialized in cataract extraction and rhinoplasty (restoration of a mutilated nose). The details of his surgeries were recorded in *Shushruta Samahita* ("Shushruta's Compendium"). The steps Shushruta followed are remarkably similar to those used during advanced surgery today.

The practice of medicine in Europe dates to the 5th century B.C., around the time of the birth of the Greek physician Hippocrates in 460 B.C. Hippocrates believed that there was a rational explanation for all physical illnesses, rejecting the then-popular belief that the cause of disease was attributed to the disfavor of the gods or evil spirits. He founded a medical school and traveled throughout Greece practicing medicine.

Hippocrates accurately described disease symptoms of malaria, respiratory infections, diarrhea, and epilepsy. He was the first physician to use a careful, systematic approach while examining a patient's condition. His observations included facial appearance, pulse, respiration, temperature, localized pains, appearance of bodily fluids (sputum, feces, and urine), and movements of the body. Hippocrates also described the importance of cleanliness in managing patient wounds. The Hippocratic Oath, taken by all physicians today before they begin medical practice, is based on a modern version of a medical ethics doctrine authored by Hippocrates.

Galen (131–201 A.D.), who is considered the father of experimental physiology, challenged Hippocrates' teachings. Galen was a Greek physician who traveled extensively throughout his life while practicing medicine, teaching, and studying. He was a prolific writer, authoring more than 70 books on anatomy, physiology, pharmacy, pathology, and temperaments, and was the first physician to perform animal experiments with cats, monkeys, pigs, and oxen. Through his animal experiments, Galen demonstrated that an excised heart would beat outside of the body, showing that heartbeat is not dependent upon the nervous system.

Medicine continued to improve throughout the Middle Ages (1476–1453) and Renaissance (1453–1600). Hospitals were built in England, Scotland, France, and Germany starting around the 1100s, and the first medical textbooks were published in the 1470s. Andreas Vesalius (1514–1564), a Belgian physician who may have been inspired by the anatomical drawings of Leonardo da Vinci (**Figure 9–2**), changed the history of the study of anatomy by dissecting the human body.

Vesalius and his students resorted to grave-robbing and other activities to secure cadavers for their studies. In 1543, Vesalius published two anatomy manuals that corrected

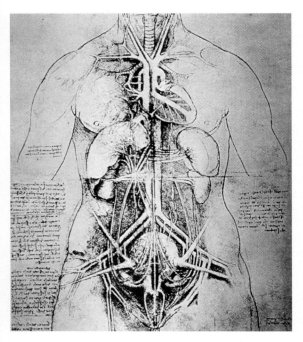

■ Figure 9-2
Anatomical drawing by Leonardo da Vinci.

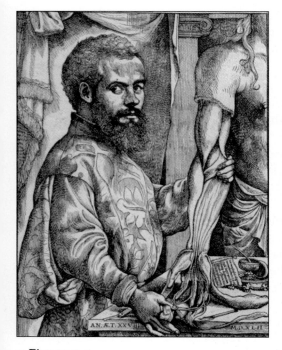

■ Figure 9-3
Andreas Vesalius (1514–1564), whose human anatomical research provided a strong foundation for all future medical research.

the works of Galen. His human anatomical research provided a strong foundation for all future medical research (**Figure 9-3**). During the 17th century, emphasis was placed on studying a patient's blood and vital statistics. Extraordinary advances in medical research and microbiology occurred in the 18th century. These included the discoveries of pioneers in microbiology and medicine such as Antoni von Leeuwenhoek (1632–1723), who invented the light microscope; James Lind, who in 1747 conducted clinical trials involving the treatment of scurvy with citrus fruits; and Edward Jenner's 1796 vaccination trials using cowpox to prevent smallpox.

Ignaz Semmelweis led the most sophisticated preventative clinical trial of the 19th century by requiring physicians to wash their hands with chloride of lime to prevent the spread of "childbed" or puerperal fever in the maternity ward of a Vienna General Hospital in 1846. Mortality rates of women in childbirth dying from puerperal fever were as high as 50% from 1841–1846. Semmelweis studied the cadavers of fever victims including a fellow physician, Jakob Kolletschka, who died of a similar infection sustained from a small cut on his finger during an autopsy of a deceased mother. Semmelweis reasoned that the disease was caused by an infectious living organism and insisted on handwashing practices. As a result of these practices, the mortality rate of the Vienna General Hospital dropped to 1.27% in 1848.

Medicine was a male-dominated field, with the exception of women's significant role in assisting childbirth. The first woman to graduate from an American medical school was Elizabeth Blackwell (1821–1910; see **Figure 9-4a**).In her first career, Blackwell was a teacher, which was considered a suitable career for a woman. After a close friend died, her interests shifted toward caring for the sick. After applying to and being rejected by more than 20 medical schools, Blackwell gained admittance (despite the reluctance of most students and faculty) at Geneva Medical College in upstate New York. In fact, the admissions committee accepted her application as a "joke." Two years later, in 1849, she earned her degree.

After graduation, Blackwell worked in clinics in London and Paris for two years. Blackwell lost her sight in one eye after contracting a severe, purulent eye infection from a patient while working and studying midwifery at La Maternite in Paris, which ended her dreams of becoming a surgeon. She returned to New York in 1851 but was refused work as a physician. In 1853, with the help of her friends, she opened her own dispensary in a single rented room. Her sister also became a doctor, and together they opened the New York Infirmary for Women and Children in 1857, where they provided training and experience for women doctors and medical care for the poor. The hospital was staffed by women.

Another female pioneer in medicine was Canadian Emily Jennings Stowe (1831–1903), who was the first woman to practice medicine in Canada (Figure 9-4b). Like Blackwell, Jennings became a teacher at the age of 15. She married John Stowe in 1856, and for the first several years of their marriage she stayed at home while raising their children. When her husband became ill with tuberculosis and was committed to a sanatorium, Stowe returned to teaching for financial reasons. Her husband's illness had inspired her interest in medicine, though, and she decided to pursue a medical career.

Stowe was faced with the same obstacles as Elizabeth Blackwell, and she was denied entrance into medical schools in Canada. She persisted and was later accepted at the New York Medical College for Women, from which she graduated with a specialty in diseases

(a)

(b)

■ **Figure 9-4**
Female pioneers of medicine. **(a)** Dr. Elizabeth Blackwell, the first woman in America to earn a medical degree. **(b)** Dr. Emily Stowe, the first women in Canada to earn a medical degree.

of women and children. Stowe returned to Canada in 1867 and established a private practice in Toronto, but although she saw patients on a regular basis the College of Physicians and Surgeons in Ontario denied Stowe a medical license because it did not admit women. Eventually Stowe was admitted, and she received her license in 1880.

Other medical pioneers in the 19th century were Louis Pasteur (see Chapter 13), Robert Koch (see Chapters 5 and 7), Emil von Behring (see Chapter 7), and Elie Metchnikoff (see Chapter 7).

■ Insulin and Penicillin: Great Medical Breakthroughs in the 20th Century

The discovery of penicillin and insulin early in the 20th century was monumental in driving clinical research forward. The collaborative efforts of a team of Canadian doctors at the University of Toronto led to the discovery in 1921 of insulin, a life-saving treatment for individuals suffering from diabetes. Diabetics cannot metabolize sugars due to the lack of insulin production, which results in a high concentration of sugar in the blood and urine. Before the discovery of insulin, diabetics were put on special restrictive diets. Patients lost weight and many died of poor nutrition.

The insulin project began when Fredrick Banting hypothesized that the pancreas secretes a hormone responsible for the metabolism of sugar. In 1921, he discussed his hypothesis with the researcher John James Rickard Macleod, an expert on carbohydrate metabolism. Macleod cautiously agreed to provide Banting with laboratory space and funds to begin testing his hypothesis. In addition, he was offered the assistance of graduate student Charles Best during the summer of 1921, and together they perfected a surgical procedure that would create diabetic dogs and invented a technique to measure the dogs' blood sugar levels. They were able to keep the diabetic dogs alive with a crude extract from the pancreas of dogs.

James Bertram Collip, a biochemist with protein purification expertise, joined Best's team in the fall of 1921. His contribution to the project was a purified extract of the pancreas that contained "antidiabetic" properties. In January of 1922 Collip's extract—insulin—was tested on 14-year-old Leonard Thompson, who had been a diabetic for three

■ Figure 9-5
World War II poster promoting the use of pencillin to treat infected wounds.

years. At the time, Thompson weighed a mere 65 pounds and was near coma and death. After receiving the extract, his blood sugar returned to normal and he regained his health. In 1923, Banting and Macleod shared the Nobel Prize in Physiology or Medicine with Best and Collip.

Penicillin may have saved the lives of your parents and grandparents (**Figure 9-5**). In contrast to the discovery of insulin by hypothesis-driven medical research, penicillin was an accidental discovery. Alexander Fleming earned a medical degree from St. Mary's Medical School in London in 1906. After doing research and serving in World War I as a captain of the Army Medical Corps, Fleming returned to lecturing and research at St. Mary's. His research focus was antiseptics produced by human tissues and secretions. In 1921, he discovered an enzyme secreted in tears called lysozyme. Lysozyme breaks down the cell walls of certain bacteria and can act as a mild antiseptic.

Like most scientists, Fleming was not in the habit of discarding old experimental bacterial culture plates. Many scientists keep their experimental reagents as long as possible in case they need to return to the experiment. One day in 1928, Fleming glanced at a stack of old petri plates containing staphylococci colonies. He examined a greenish mold contamination on the plate. None of the staphylocci bacteria were growing near the mold, which appeared to be producing a substance that caused the staphylococci to lyse or rupture.

Fleming began experiments to test the laboratory mold, which he determined to be *Penicillium,* and other molds for their antibacterial properties. In 1929, he published a paper in the *British Journal of Experimental Pathology* entitled "On the Antibacterial Action of Cultures of a *Penicillium,* with Special Reference to Their Use in the Isolation of *B. Influenzae.*" Fleming demonstrated that the mold inhibited *Streptococcus, Staphylococcus,* and *Corynebacterium,* but that it was not toxic to many gram-negative bacteria. He named the active substance penicillin and suggested it could be used to isolate bacteria in the laboratory and as an antiseptic to remove penicillin-sensitive bacteria on patient dressings.

Fleming did not follow up on the application of penicillin in treating bacterial infections. Instead, 10 years later, Howard Florey and Ernst Chain followed through on the medical applications of penicillin. Chain extracted penicillin from the *Penicillium* mold and with the aid of Florey began testing it on mice that had been infected with *Streptococcus.* All mice infected with *Streptococcus* survived after penicillin injections, whereas mice that were not given penicillin injections did not survive. These experiments were expanded to include human trials, which required the mass production of penicillin. Fleming, Florey, and Chain shared the Nobel Prize in Physiology or Medicine in 1945 "for their discovery of penicillin and its curative effect in various infectious diseases."

Before the 20th century, the infant mortality rate in the United States was as high as 20%, and many children died before the age of one. The rate is now 6%, and the reduction has been attributed to vaccine-preventable diseases, the introduction of antibiotics, and handwashing and other methods used to prevent and control infections. In the 1950s the average life expectancy in the United States was 62 years; today it is 78.

The past 50 years have seen tremendous advances in biomedical research. Therapies being developed today will gradually become commonplace in treating future health problems. Each new application will require all of us—researchers, policymakers, and the public—to consider the benefits, risks, and implications of new treatments.

9.2 Clinical Trials Today

Today is a golden age of medical research. Chapter 7, Host Resistance to Viral Infections, introduced the necessary steps to obtain manufacturing approval and quality assurance of vaccines. The process includes preclinical and clinical trials that proceed in at least three phases. From the start of clinical trials to the end of Phase III trials, successful drug/vaccine therapies have been tested on 400 to 30,000 volunteers and cost, on average, $75 million. Information regarding active clinical trials in the United States, Canada, and other countries is available on the Internet (search Google for "clinical trials").

Gene therapy and xenotransplantation are on the frontier of modern medicinal research. The products and procedures used in these experimental treatments must adhere to additional regulations set forth by the Food and Drug Administration (FDA) as well as National Institutes of Health (NIH) guidelines and policies relevant to gene transfer research, and public disclosure of serious side effects is mandatory. These strict measurements are in place to safeguard the volunteers participating in these types of clinical trials.

■ Gene Therapy

Gene therapy is an experimental treatment that involves the introduction of genes into a person's cells to replace or compensate for defective genes in a person's body that are responsible for a disease or medical problem. But what does gene therapy have to do with viruses?

The "good" genes must be delivered or find their way to the location in the body in which its product is normally active. The "good" genes can be carried and delivered to cells by customized vectors such as viruses. These engineered viruses are manipulated using genetic engineering techniques to escape the immune surveillance of the body, ensuring there is no harm to the patient. The safety of gene therapy was intensely re-evaluated after Jesse Gelsinger died of complications during the 1999 clinical trial on OTC described in Section 9.1.

Gelsinger was one of two individuals in the study who were administered 300 times the normal vector dose as the initial patients. The vector was a modified adenovirus. Gelsinger died as a result of the accumulation of a **cytokine** termed interleukin-6 (IL-6). A high level of IL-6 causes adult respiratory distress syndrome (ARDS). Normally, another cytokine called interleukin-10 (IL-10) suppresses IL-6 production as does another cytokine, tumor necrosis factor alpha (TNF-α). Unfortunately, Gelsinger's IL-10 and TNF-α levels did not effectively reduce the increased IL-6 levels, resulting in an immunological complication and ultimately his death.

After Gelsinger's death, gene therapy trials at the University of Pennsylvania were shutdown and an FDA investigation was performed. The FDA determined that the IHGT violated 18 specific FDA rules and regulations during the OTC study, and the field of gene therapy in general was scrutinized and questioned. The FDA and NIH created new regulations and policies to police experiments and new protocols. (Rules issuing the disclosure of information regarding gene therapy trials are available to the general public via Web-based databases.

In January 2003 gene therapy suffered another major setback. The FDA temporarily halted 27 gene therapy trials in which retrovirus vectors were being used. The halt was enforced after the FDA learned that a second child had developed leukemia after being treated for X-linked combined immunodeficiency disease (X-SCID). The syndrome only affects boys. Boys with X-SCID have a defective copy of a gene that encodes the cytokine interleukin-2 (IL-2), which modulates T helper cell production, located on their X chromosome. (See Chapter 7 for a review.) Without gene therapy treatment, X-SCID children usually die before their first birthday.

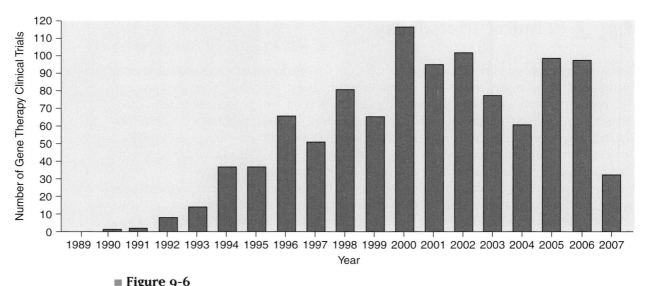

■ **Figure 9-6**

The number of gene therapy trials approved worldwide, January 1989–July 2007. Adapted from Edelstein, M. L., M. R. Abedi, and J. Wixon, *J. Gene Med*. 9 (2007): 833–842.

The second child that developed leukemia was participating in a trial led by Alain Fischer at Necker Hospital in Paris, France. A retroviral vector was used to genetically modify the boys' own marrow hematopoietic cells. Unfortunately, the vector had integrated its genome into a gene involved in normal cellular growth. This disrupted the gene's function, which resulted in uncontrolled white blood cell division (leukemia). The theoretical risk of retroviral integration was known; however, this was the second time the vector had integrated into the same gene in both patients who had gotten leukemia while being treated. This risk appeared to be much greater than researchers had thought it would be.

At the time of this writing, the role of gene therapy in the death of Jolee Mohr was unclear and under investigation. Mohr died on July 24, 2007 at the University of Chicago Medical Center after her second gene therapy treatment. The 36-year-old woman received two injections into her right knee to treat rheumatoid arthritis. The injections contained adeno-associated virus containing a gene that encodes the receptor for the inflammatory protein known as TNF-α, which plays a role in rheumatoid arthritis. The leading cause of her death appeared to be a massive *Histoplasma capsulatum* fungal infection. Mohr was taking immune suppressive drugs to treat her arthritis. The drugs may have played a role in weakening her body's ability to fend off the fungal infection. Initial tests showed that only a trace amount of the genetically engineered virus was found in tissues outside of her knee joint.

Despite highly publicized rare events, gene therapy trials move forward. Gene therapy holds promise for treating genetic disorders caused by single-gene defects such as Huntington's chorea, Duchenne muscular dystrophy, polycystic kidney disease, familial hypercholesterolemia, sickle-cell anemia, hemophilias A and B, phenylketonuria, and cystic fibrosis. It is also being used to treat other health problems such as cancer, diabetes, high blood pressure, and heart disease. The hope is that gene therapy will provide cures for diseases in which the good gene must be working throughout one's life, such as hemophilia. In other instances, gene therapy may be needed to repair a wound or grow new blood vessels. In those cases, the treatment would be a temporary solution.

At the time of this writing, the majority of gene therapy clinical trials occur in the United States and Europe (**Figure 9-6**). Of these, 1.7% of the trials are in Phase III of clinical trials. As guidelines have become more stringent, fewer trials are being approved.

Gene Delivery by Viruses: The Key to Gene Therapy

One of the biggest challenges of gene therapy is delivering genes to the correct cells or tissues; for example, if the good gene is needed in the liver, genes must be targeted to liver cells. How do scientists ensure that the gene is targeted to the liver and not the big toe?

Viruses can act as gene delivery "vehicles" or vectors. They make good vectors because viruses can be engineered to target and enter specific types of cells. To safeguard the patient, viruses are engineered so that they cannot replicate and destroy or harm the cells of the patient. There remain some drawbacks regarding viral vectors, though. For example, they are limited in the size of gene that they can carry. Some genes may be too large for certain viral vectors. Sometimes the patient may get sick (as in the case of Jesse Gelsinger) and the patient may mount an immune response against the viral vector, preventing further treatments from working. The hallmarks of a good gene delivery system are its ability to:

- target the appropriate cells.
- integrate the correct gene into the cell's nuclear DNA.
- transcribe and translate the correct gene so that its gene product can function properly.
- cause no toxic or harmful affects related to the gene delivery vehicle.

There are two ways to deliver the viral vectors to the patient's cells:

1. *In vivo* therapy, in which the patient's body is directly injected with the modified gene therapy viral vector.
2. *Ex vivo* therapy, in which the patient's cells are removed, grown in culture dishes in the laboratory, incubated with the viral vector to introduce the genes, and then transplanted back into the patient.

The most popular viral vectors used in gene therapy trials are

- retroviruses,
- adenoviruses,
- adeno-associated virus,
- herpes simplex virus, and
- vaccinia or modified vaccinia Ankara (MVA).

There are both advantages and limitations to each type of vector (Table 9-1).

Gene Delivery Without Viruses

Plasmid DNA or "naked" DNA is also used to deliver genes into patient's cells. Plasmids have fewer limitations regarding the size of the DNA of the corrected gene that can be inserted into the plasmid, and they don't generate an immune response. Hence they are a safer alternative. Plasmid DNA delivery is less efficient than viral delivery. Research in the past five years has revolutionized the efficiency of nonviral gene transfer. To aid plasmid DNA cell entry, the DNA is either complexed with liposomes or other chemical polymers or physical energy is applied. Physical energy methods include electroporation, pressure-mediated delivery, ultrasound, laser, magnetic fields, and ballistic delivery.

Triple helix-forming nucleotides, antisense technology, ribozymes, and RNA interference systems (RNAi) are being used as a gene therapy approach when inserting a good copy of a gene will not correct the cell's problem; for example, a defective gene may code for a gene product that prevents the normal gene product from functioning correctly in the cell. In this case, a good copy or normal gene will not help. Instead, the approach to repairing the problem is to remove or inactivate the defective gene. The majority of the types of genes engineered into vectors used in today's clinical trials function as

- specific antigens (involved in immune modulation)
- cytokines
- tumor suppressors

TABLE 9-1	Characteristics of Viral Vectors Used in Gene Therapy			
Vector	**Size of Gene That Can Be Packaged into the Vector**	**Cell Target**	**Integration into Cell's Genetic Material?**	**Side Effects**
Retrovirus	8000 bp	Can only infect dividing cells.	Yes, integration into host genome is random.	1. Vector DNA may incorporate into a vital cellular gene; e.g., may cause tumor growth. 2. Can cause immune responses in patients.
Adenovirus	7500 bp	Can infect dividing and nondividing cells.	No. After a week or two, the cell will discard the genetic material.	Can cause immune responses in patients.
Adeno-associated virus	5000 bp	Can infect dividing and nondividing cells. Requires a "helper" virus to replicate inside of cells.	Yes, 95% of the time the integration will be very specific. It will integrate into a specific region on chromosome 19.	1. Less integration-specific side effects. 2. Rarely causes immune responses in patients.
Herpes simplex virus	20,000 bp	Can infect cells of the nervous system.	No, but it does stay in the nucleus for a long time as a separate DNA that replicates when the cell divides.	Can cause immune responses in patients.
Vaccinia or MVA (poxvirus)	25,000 bp	Can infect dividing cells. Can selectively infect tumor cells.	No, DNA replicates in the cytoplasm of cell. Eventually the DNA is lost.	1. Can cause immune response in patients. 2. Limited repeated treatment.

- receptors
- DNA replication inhibitors
- cell protection/drug resistance
- deficiency (compensation for defective genes)
- growth factors
- suicide (induce apoptosis)

A smaller percentage of clinical trials involve transferring other types of genes that function as hormones, adhesion molecules, porins, ion channels, transporters, ribozymes, gene silencers (siRNA), and transcription factors.

9.3 Xenotransplantation

The prefix xeno means stranger; foreign, or different. The term **xenotransplantation** refers to any procedure that involves the use of live cells, tissues, and organs from a nonhuman animal source, transplanted or implanted into humans or used for clinical *ex vivo* perfusion. Xenotransplantation does not include nonliving animal products (such as pig insulin or pig heart valves).

History of Organ Transplants

At the turn of the 20th century, pioneer French surgeon Alexis Carrel (1873–1944) perfected the technique of vascular anastomosis, or blood-vessel suturing. Carrel became interested in repairing blood vessels after the president of the French Republic, Sadi Carnot, bled to death after being fatally stabbed by an assassin in Lyons, France, in 1894. This was a time when a surgeon's skills were limited to sewing muscles, skin, and other tissues together, but not blood vessels. Carrel's success repairing blood vessels was attributed to a number of factors:

- his unusual manual dexterity;
- his use of special materials, including tiny vaseline-lubricated needles and fine thread;
- his insistence on avoiding trauma to the fragile vessels and surrounding tissues; and

---

VIRUS FILE 9-1 | **Rabies Transmission from Solid-Organ Transplants**

During the first week of May 2004, a man from Arkansas was admitted to a hospital in Texas. He had a low-grade fever and suffered from mental confusion. His neurological symptoms were not indicative of rabies. A CAT scan of the man's brain showed bleeding consistent with a stroke. He died 48 hours after his admission into the hospital. He had not been given any blood products during his hospital stay.

The deceased individual underwent routine donor eligibility screening and testing, which did not include testing for rabies, and his family consented to organ donation. The man's liver, kidneys, and lungs were removed and transplanted into three recipients at a transplant center in Texas shortly thereafter. All three patients were discharged 5–12 days after the transplant operations but were re-admitted into hospitals 21-27 days after their initial transplant dates. All of them deteriorated rapidly, suffering from tremors, lethargy, and seizures, and subsequently died.

The Centers for Disease Control and Prevention (CDC) investigated the incident. They examined brain tissues of the diseased recipients and confirmed rabies transmission from the three solid-organ transplants and traced it to the organ donor, whose tissues also tested positive for rabies antibodies. The CDC is currently working with federal and organ donor agencies to review screening practices. The majority of rabies cases are caused by bites from rabid mammals. Rabies has also been caused by nonbite exposures such as contamination of an open wound, scratches, or direct contact with infectious material such as saliva from a rabid animal. These nonbite exposures are very rare.

Human-to-human transmission of rabies has occurred among eight recipients of transplanted corneas. The eight cases occurred in five countries: two cases each in India, Thailand, and Iran, and one case each in France and the United States. All of the donors died of rabies or a rabies-like illness.

The CDC investigated the United States' incident, which occurred in 1979 and was the first incident of rabies infections in solid organ donor and transplant recipients. As a result of the investigation, stringent medical standards were implemented among the Eyebank Association of America (EBAA) and the eye banking community. Since the implementation of these measures there has not been a rabies case associated with contaminated corneas in the more than 43,000 sight-restoring transplants using ocular tissues that are performed each year in the United States.

References

University of Alabama at Birmingham Hospital et al. 2004. "Update: Investigation of Rabies Infections in Organ Donor and Transplant Recipients—Alabama, Arkansas, Oklahoma, and Texas, 2004." *MMWR* 53(26):586–589.

- strict aseptic techniques and rules in the operating room, which were far more rigid than those of his colleagues.

After he achieved success in arterial and venous repairs in 1902, the idea of replacing failed organs with healthy ones could be considered. In 1904 Carrel left Lyons for Montreal, but he ultimately decided to take a position in Chicago at the University of Illinois. From 1904–1906 Carrel worked with physiologist Charles Guthrie with whom he performed transplantation surgeries on animals, especially dogs. They published 28 papers together regarding the retransplanting or transplantation of arteries, veins, kidneys, ovaries, thyroid glands, and a thigh.

In 1906, Guthrie took a position at Washington University in St. Louis and Carrel went to work at the Rockefeller Institute for Medical Research (now known as Rockefeller University) in New York. Carrel documented the problems with rejecting foreign tissues as early as 1907. For his pioneering efforts in vascular suture and the transplantation of blood vessels and organs, Carrel was awarded the Nobel Prize in Physiology or Medicine in 1912.

The earliest historical account of a human-to-human organ transplant occurred in a November 14, 1911, *New York Times* article entitled "Dr. Hammond Gives Patient New Kidney." The reporter remarked that this was the first attempt in the United States to transplant a kidney from a man who was killed in an automobile accident to a man dying from renal tuberculosis. Dr. L. J. Hammond at Philadelphia Methodist Episcopal Hospital performed the operation. The donor kidney had been maintained in cold storage one day prior to the operation. There was no follow-up story, but it is likely that the patient's immune system rejected the organ.

Most medical historians consider the first human-to-human kidney transplant to be the one performed in Russia in 1933 by Dr. S. Voronoff. The kidney donor came from a cadaver, and the transplant failed due to organ rejection. The first successful human-to-human kidney transplant occurred in 1954 between kidney donors who were identical twins. The donor and recipient were of course perfectly matched, circumventing organ rejection. This first successful operation, which was performed by Dr. Joseph Murphy at Brigham and Women's Hospital in Boston, and a second successful operation that was performed in 1960 by Sir Michael Woodruff in Edinburgh, Scotland, are milestones in the history of transplantation.

Sporadic attempts at cross-species transplants occurred during the early 1960s:

- In 1963 and 1964, surgeon Keith Reemtsma at Tulane University in New Orleans transplanted 13 chimpanzee kidneys into humans. Twelve of the patients survived between 9 and 60 days. One patient survived for 9 months with no signs of rejection while on primitive immunosuppression drugs.
- In 1964 Thomas Starzl of the University of Colorado transplanted 6 baboon kidneys into humans. Patients survived 19–98 days, and most died of infections related to immune suppression.
- In 1964 James Hardy of the University of Mississippi transplanted a chimpanzee heart into a 68-year-old comatose man. The chimpanzee heart was too small to support the patient's circulatory system and functioned for only two hours.

Sir Peter Medawar (1915–1987) and Sir Frank Burnet (1899–1985) were jointly awarded the 1960 Nobel Prize in Physiology or Medicine for their research on immune tolerance as evidenced by skin graft acceptance and rejection in both animals and humans. Their research spearheaded studies involving tissue typing and the development of immune suppressive treatments to prevent transplant rejection.

Early efforts to minimize this rejection included radiation therapy and hormone/steroid treatments to reduce the immune system function, but that would often lead to a much greater risk of infection for transplant recipients. The survival rates for transplant procedures were very low, and research efforts included a search for therapies to overcome or prevent organ rejection. In 1983, the FDA approved cyclosporin, the first antirejection drug.

9.4 Organ Need, Supply, and Demand

The development of xenotransplantation has been driven in part by the shortage of donors. Continued advancements in the development of better drugs and regimens for suppressing cross-species immune-mediated rejection has resulted in the increasing use of animals to provide insulin, skin grafts, and heart valves.

More than 25% of patients on waiting lists die before receiving an organ. **Figure 9-7** demonstrates this by comparing the number of registered organ recipients versus the number of donors available in the United States and Canada between 1993 and 2003. As of August 2003, approximately 82,000 individuals were awaiting organ transplants in the United States. Each day, 16 people on average died while waiting for an organ, and over $40 billion is spent each year on patients with end-stage organ failure. A bill before the Illinois legislature that would allow HIV-infected persons to donate their organs to others with the virus was under consideration. The Illinois House passed it 95–22 on March 2, 2004, and the state Senate approved it 55–2 on May 2, 2004. Illinois House Bill 3857 was signed by the governor that year.

The illicit trade in human organs is a problem throughout China, India, and Russia. In April, 2004, two doctors and two individuals working in the city's transplantation service at a Moscow hospital were arrested after removing organs from patients who were technically alive. Young, impoverished men in such states as Moldova sell kidneys to foreigners who are willing to pay up to US$250,000. An illicit organ trade ring was busted in the city of Khabarovsk in 2004. Doctors from the Khabarovsk hospital had set up an illegal practice, selling organs for US$60 to US$40,000. At least 15 cases involved the removal of organs from corpses without permission from the family of the deceased individual.

■ Why Pigs?

Why would transgenic pig donors be able to save or improve the quality of human lives? Why not choose to use closer genetic relatives such as apes or monkeys? There are many

(a)

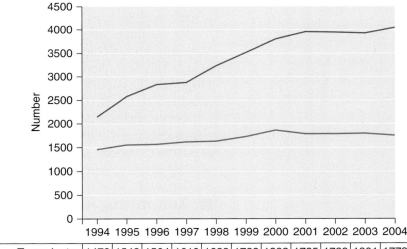

	1994	1995	1996	1997	1998	1999	2000	2001	2002	2003	2004
Transplants	1473	1542	1564	1610	1623	1728	1882	1785	1789	1801	1773
Waiting list	2159	2592	2829	2874	3229	3514	3800	3964	3956	3914	4013

(b)

■ Figure 9-7

(a) United States organ registration and donor lists (1993–2005). Adapted from Scientific Registry of Transplant Recipients, *2003 OPTN/SRTR Annual Report,* http://www.ustransplant.org/annual_Reports/default.aspx. **(b)** Transplants and waiting list at year-end in Canada, 1994–2004. Adapted from Canadian Institute for Health Information, *Canada's Organ Donation Rate Still Too Low to Meet the Need,* http://secure.cihi.ca/cihiweb/dispPage.jsp?cw_page=media_14apr2004_e.

TABLE 9-2	Comparison of Potential Species for Donor Xenotransplantation		
	Pigs	**Apes**	**Monkeys**
Physiology	Similar	Nearly identical	Similar
Organ size	Similar	Identical	Too small
Gestation	100 days	251–289 days	170–193 days
Progeny	10–18	1–2	1–2
Protection of species	No	Yes, very strong	Yes
Availability	Unlimited	None	Low
Transgenic animals	Done	Not yet	Done
Cloning	Done	Not yet	Done
Costs	Low	Very high	High
Microbiological risks	Low (can be grown in specified pathogen-free environments)	High	High

Adapted from Denner, J. 2003. "Porcine Endogenous Retroviruses (PERVs) and Xenotransplantation: Screening for Transmission in Several Clinical Trials and in Experimental Models Using Non-Human Primates." *Ann Transplant* 8(3): 39–48.

advantages of using pigs as donor organs for human transplants (Table 9-2). Pig organs are similar in size to human organs, and pig physiology is similar to that of humans; for example, a pig kidney will act similar to a human kidney, and the circulatory system is similar and the pig supplies the best size-matched heart that would meet cardiac output of a human.

Another advantage is that pigs are readily available and can be bred quickly. They have a short gestation period and can carry up to 18 piglets in a litter. They can be raised in special pathogen-free environments following cesarean protocols to exclude serious human pathogens with minimal costs. In addition, pigs have been genetically modified to decrease immunological rejection and were successfully cloned in 2000. Overall, these genetic modifications result in a more "humanized" pig.

At the forefront of pig mass-production for human transplants is Professor Hwang Woo Suk at Seoul National University. The Ministry of Agriculture and Forestry will spend at least US$72 million over the next 10 years to support a taskforce of 90 scientists led by Hwang on the gnotobiotic (sterilized) pig project. The South Korean government is championing biotechnology as a key future industry for the country.

Other organizations working on small-scale pig cloning projects include the University of Missouri–Columbia, the University of Wisconsin–Madison, PPL Therapeutics PLC of Scotland (the company that helped clone Dolly, the sheep), and Infigen Inc., which has worked in collaboration with Immerge BioTherapeutics to produce cloned pigs.

■ Xenotransplantation Molecular Roadblocks and Immunological Hurdles

Hyperacute rejection (HAR) occurs when a transplanted organ becomes inflamed, turns dusky and cyanotic, and loses its ability to contract. Specifically, the organ tissue never becomes vascularized. The organ is dead within minutes of a transplant and the recipient dies quickly (**Figure 9-8**). This occurs in xenotransplantation because the blood vessels of pigs contain 1-3 α galactose, a carbohydrate epitope unique to pigs. The human immune system recognizes the 1-3 α galactose as foreign and rejects these molecules by quickly destroying the newly transplanted organ. Naturally occurring antibodies and complement activation is directed against the transplanted organ tissues.

The second type of immune rejection is acute vascular rejection (AVR). This term applies to rapid vascular injury that occurs within a few days to several weeks of the transplant. It, too, is triggered by complement and antibody response toward the organ tissues. There is also an influx of macrophages, neutrophils, and natural killer cells.

A third type of rejection, chronic, occurs within months to years following transplantation. It is believed that chronic rejection is really the result of continued and prolonged multiple acute rejections. Immune suppressive drug treatment is used to treat chronic rejection.

One might imagine that there would be a wide array of antigens on pig organs that natural human antibodies would recognize. Interestingly, it has been shown that 80% of human antibodies recognize a single 1-3 α galactose carbohydrate that is present on the surfaces of pig cells. The α-1, 3-galactosyl-transferase enzyme is responsible for a linked galactose to N-acetyl lactosamine. This enzyme is found in New World monkeys and lower-order mammals such as pigs. In contrast, humans and higher-order primates such as chimpanzees and baboons have lost the α-1, 3-galactosyl-transferase gene and they produce antibodies against 1-3 α galactose.

In order to prevent HAR and AVR, genetically modified pigs have been produced using gene knock-out strategies to eliminate the α-1, 3-galactosyl-transferase gene. Without this gene's function, the 1-3 α galactose residues are no longer produced on the surface of pig cells, thereby reducing the recipient's production of anti-1-3 α galactose antibodies. An alternative approach involves treating the transplant recipient with a continuous intravenous infusion of synthetic or natural 1-3 α galactose to sequester any circulating anti-1-3 α galactose antibodies.

Another approach used to prevent rejection of pig tissue involves the insertion of the human α 1, 2-fucosyl transferase [H transferase (HT)] gene and human complement inhibitor CD59 gene (hCD59) into the pig chromosome. The HT gene product synthesizes α 1, 2 fucose linkages on the cell surfaces of human cells. Hence donor pig tissues expressing the HT gene on their surfaces will appear like human tissues to the transplant recipient. The α 1, 2 fucose linkages are also tolerated by the pig donor.

The hCD59 gene product (sometimes referred to as protectin) is expressed in many types of human cells. It binds to complement factors, preventing cell lysis after complement activation. Pig kidneys, hearts, and lungs expressing hCD59 have been shown to function longer than control organs that did not express hCD59, but the approach did not completely protect organs from antibody-mediated rejection. Scientists have produced transgenic pigs that have been engineered to express both hCD59 and HT. These transgenic pigs have been shown to have strong protection against the antibody and complement activation response of xenotransplant rejection. Transgenic pigs have also been developed to express two additional complement regulatory proteins: human decay-accelerating factor (hDAF) and membrane cofactor protein (MCP). Overall, the progress in overcoming the immunologic hurdles in the past decade has been remarkable. Table 9-3 summarizes the genes that are being manipulated in the development of transgenic and cloned pigs.

9.5 Xenozoonosis

The word **zoonosis** refers to a disease being transmitted from an animal to a human; the term **xenozoonosis** is defined as a disease transmitted from an animal to a human recipient after transplantation of an animal organ. Viruses and other microbes lurk within the donor animal's organs and the infectious

■ Figure 9-8
Transplant rejection of a human donor kidney.

TABLE 9-3	Genes Manipulated in Pig Donors to Prevent Immune-Rejection	
Gene Product	**Function of Gene Product**	**Insertion or Deletion in Pig Genome**
α-1, 3-galactosyl-transferase	Adds α galactose to N-acetyl lactosamine	Deletion
α 1, 2-fucosyl transferase	Synthesizes α 1, 2 fucose linkages on human cell surfaces	Insertion
hCD59	Prevents human complement activation	Insertion
Human decay-accelerating factor	Prevents human complement activation	Insertion
Membrane cofactor protein	Prevents human complement activation	Insertion

disease risks of xenotransplantation pose a problem for organ recipients and the public at large. Transplant patients must receive immunosuppressive treatment to prevent organ rejection, and as a result even nonpathogenic microbes in pigs might adapt to the human recipient and cause disease. Viruses are of major concern because unlike infections caused by other microorganisms, they are not usually treatable by antibiotics. A major concern is that animal viruses may jump to humans and cause a pandemic.

At one time scientists felt that viral risks could be overcome by breeding pigs in disease-free environments. The blow to this theory came in 2000 when two independent research labs discovered that pigs harbor porcine endogenous retrovirus sequences (PERVs) in their genomes. These PERVs were shown to be activated and able to produce infectious virus in human 293 cells *in vitro* (**Figure 9-9**). As a result, breeding virus-free pigs would be difficult, if not impossible. This became a turning point in xenotransplantation regulation by the FDA in the United States.

To date, sophisticated methods have been developed to detect PERV transmission. So far, there is no evidence for PERV transmission in the more than 200 patients who have received pig xenotransplants or in butchers who were frequently exposed to pig tissues. Rats, guinea pigs, minks, macaques, and baboons inoculated with high doses of PERVs and given strong daily immunosuppressive treatment failed to exhibit any signs of infection. To further prevent PERV transmission, a team of researchers at the Robert Koch Institute in Berlin, Germany, developed an RNAi strategy to increase the safety of xenotransplantation.

Other viruses have been discovered in pigs, with herpesvirus reactivation being one of the most common infectious complications of immune-suppressed patients. Three novel porcine herpesviruses, porcine lymphotrophic herpes viruses I, II, and III (PLHV-I, PLHV-II, and PHLV-III), have been detected in pigs.

Another herpesvirus, porcine cytomegalovirus (PCMV), has been found in pigs. PCMV is very similar to human cytomegalovirus. Pigs acquire PCMV early in life and often show no clinical symptoms of the infection. In commercial pig herds and breeding colonies for xenotransplantation research, prevalence for PCMV antibodies is over 95%. Researchers have tried to wean piglets within the first two weeks of birth and isolate them from other animals to prevent PCMV exposure. Raising the pigs in qualified pathogen-free environments has been successful in eliminating PCMV in a proportion of the pigs when compared to pigs bred with conventional methods.

Strategies to control or exclude PCMV infection from the donor have been developed via *in vitro* studies. The experiments were performed using herpesvirus antiviral drugs such as ganciclovir, acyclovir, leftunomide, cidofovir, and foscarnet, but only cidofovir and foscarnet proved effective against PCMV. Both of these antivirals have significant toxic effects in transplant recipients, though, so pharmacological control of PCMV might be achieved but at the cost of significant toxic side effects.

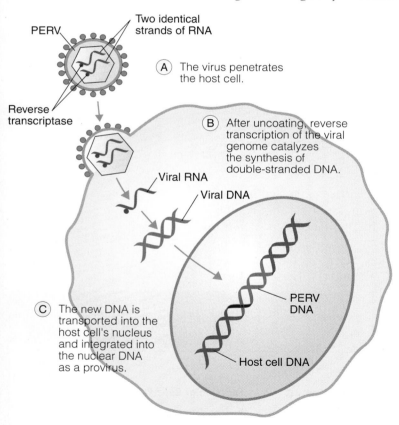

■ Figure 9-9

When a pig retrovirus infects a pig cell, the RNA of the retrovirus is transcribed into DNA by reverse transcriptase, then is inserted into the host genome by an integrase. The pig genome contains many PERV sequences. The proviral DNA is not active while integrated into the host genome. Instead, it is passively replicated along with the host genome and passed onto the original cell's offspring. Eventually, in response to changes in the host's environmental condition or health (e.g., after organ transplantation), the provirus will excise itself from the genome and resume activity as a virus.

Another virus that has been shown to cross species barriers is a hepatitis E-like swine virus, which is genetically similar to human hepatitis E (HEV) and can infect both pigs and nonhuman primates. HEV causes acute hepatitis and jaundice in 30 to 80 percent of humans infected. It is rare in the United States and is usually found in countries where sanitation conditions are poor. HEV and HEV-like swine virus are transmitted via an oral–fecal route and may occur through direct contact with food or water contaminated with pig feces containing HEV-like swine virus. Recipients of pig organs, pig farmers, veterinarians, meat handlers, and others in close contact with pigs are at risk for HEV-like swine virus or other closely related viral infections.

Lastly, circoviruses have been discovered in pigs. Porcine circovirus Type 1 is ubiquitous in pig populations, but to date has not been known to cause any disease in pigs or humans. Porcine circovirus Type 2 is the likely suspect for a postweaning multisystemic wasting syndrome (PMWS) in pigs. It generally affects 25% of the pigs in a pen one to two weeks after weaning. Infected pigs develop a fever and waste rapidly, and may develop a hairy coat and runty appearance. Some pigs develop a cough and diarrhea and many pigs die after several weeks. The potential risk of porcine circovirus Type 2 transmission via xenotransplantation is unknown.

Xenotransplantation is at a crossroads. Tremendous progress has been made regarding the genetic engineering and cloning technology developed for pigs, which now can be bred with low PERVs and α-1, 3-galactosyl-transferase deficiency. Clinical trials using pig cell xenotransplantation are ongoing. The most up-to-date information regarding FDA applications, and the most recent scientific literature regarding pig cell transplantation being considered for neurodegenerative disorders such as Parkinson's and Huntington's disease, dates to 2002.

Putting these cell therapies into practice is not of course a straightforward task. It must be done at the pace of laboratory-based research rather than corporate share price. Today, there is less commercial support for xenotransplantation than there was in 2002. At the time of this writing, large companies such as Novartis and Baxter have withdrawn from the field, and smaller companies such as Alexion, Geron, Circe Biomedical, HepatAssist, Diacrin, Immerge, and Nextran have greatly reduced their interest. Funding for xenotransplantation via other sources such as government and foundations has proved difficult, perhaps in anticipation of the scientific obstacles and the high costs associated with *in vivo* studies.

 ## Summary

Humans have strived to improve their health for centuries. There is documented evidence of surgical techniques and the development of herbal medicines that occurred more than 2000 years ago. Shen Nung, Shushruta Samahita, Hippocrates, and Galen are among the earliest medical pioneers. In the 16th century Andreas Vesalius changed the history of human anatomy by studying dissected humans, which laid the groundwork for further investigation into blood, medical research, and microbiology.

Women played a part in the history of medicine and health care as caretakers and nurses. It was not until the middle of the 19th century, though, that women were permitted to join men in what were considered the elite, literate, and scholarly ranks of medical doctors. Elizabeth Blackwell and Emily Jennings Stowe broke down barriers for women physicians during the 19th century when they became the first licensed physicians in the United States and Canada, respectively, and as adamant supporters of women's rights. Both specialized in midwifery and diseases of women and children.

The discovery of penicillin and insulin early in the 20th century was monumental in driving clinical research forward. Today's routine therapies and breakthroughs have come after the culmination of discoveries and practices of many medical trailblazers.

This is the golden age of medical research. Many preclinical and clinical trials are active throughout the world. Gene therapy and xenotransplantation are on the frontier of modern medicine.

Gene therapy is an experimental treatment that involves the introduction of genes into a person's cells to replace or compensate for defective genes in a person's body that are responsible for a disease or medical problem. One of the biggest challenges of gene therapy is the delivering of genes to the correct cells or tissues, and viruses act as gene-delivery vehicles. Retroviruses, adenoviruses, adeno-associated viruses, herpes simplex virus, and poxviruses such as vaccinia or MVA are the most popular viral vectors used in gene therapy trials. Each type of viral vector has both advantages and limitations.

Side effects related to gene therapy include immune responses toward the viral vector and the interruption of vital cellular genes, which can result in cancer. The field of gene therapy continues to evolve, and regulations and policies to police experiments and protocols are constantly being designed and updated to ensure the safety of these treatments.

Despite rare, highly publicized events, gene therapy trials continue to hold promise for treating genetic disorders caused by single-gene defects such as Huntington's chorea, Duchenne muscular dystrophy, polycystic kidney disease, familial hypercholesterolemia, sickle-cell anemia, hemophilias A and B, phenylketonuria, and cystic fibrosis. Gene therapy is also being used to treat other health problems, such as cancer, diabetes, high blood pressure, and heart disease. The hope is that ultimately gene therapy will provide a cure for diseases in which the good gene must be working throughout one's life, such as with hemophilia. In other instances, gene therapy may be needed to repair a wound or grow new blood vessels, in which case the treatment would be a temporary solution.

Xenotransplantation—the procedure that involves the use of live cells, tissues, and organs from a nonhuman animal source—is a field being driven forward due to the shortage of organ donors and the continued advances toward the development of immune-suppressive drugs used to prevent cross-species immune-mediated rejection. This technology would not exist without the early work of organ transplant pioneers like Alexis Carrel, Sir Peter Medwar, Sir Frank Burnet, Keith Reemtsma, Thomas Starzl, and James Hardy.

The use of pigs organs rather than nonhuman primate organs for human transplants is attractive for several reasons:

- Pig organ size and physiology are similar to humans.
- There have been many advances in pig genetics and breeding, and genetic modifications of pigs have resulted in a more "humanized" pig.
- Pigs can be raised in special pathogen-free environments at minimal cost.

Hyperacute rejection (HAR) and AVR present major immunological hurdles for xenotransplantation. The genomes of pigs have been modified to prevent these types of rejection. Despite this, chronic rejection still threatens xenotransplantation and normal human-to-human organ transplantation. This type of rejection requires continued advancements in the development of more immune suppressive drugs. In addition to immune system rejection, xenozoonosis poses a problem for organ recipients.

Diseases transmitted via xenotransplantation may put the human community at risk. Viruses are a major concern because infections caused by other microorganisms are usually treatable by antibiotics, whereas those caused by viruses are not. Pathogens known to cause disease in pigs need to be eliminated from donor herds.

Pigs harbor PERVs in their genomes. PERVs may be reactivated during immune-suppressed conditions. Herpesvirus infections are one of the most common complications of immune-suppressed patients. Several herpesviruses have been isolated from pigs. These include PLHV-I, II, and III, and PCMV.

Other porcine viruses of concern are HEV-like swine viruses and circoviruses. Xeno-transplantation of animal organs to humans could allow microbes present in the donor organs to cross the species barrier. In doing so, nonpathogenic microbes in a natural host (pigs) may cause disease in a human recipient. Efforts are being made to breed pathogen-free or pathogen-reduced pigs. Methods are being developed to screen and monitor animal sources and recipients for known viruses. New and better diagnostic tests are being developed as new viruses are discovered. Guidelines and policies concerning xenotransplantation safety with specific attention to individual and societal risks and benefits have been prepared and are updated continuously. Safety will dictate the future directions of xenotransplantation.

Resources

Primary Literature and Reviews

Andreansky, S. S., He, B., Gillespie, Y., et al. 1996. "The Application of Genetically Engineered Herpes Simplex Virus to the Treatment of Experimental Tumors." *PNAS USA* 93:11313–11318.

Buning, H., Braun-Falco, M., and Hallek, M. 2004. "Progress in the Use of Adeno-Associated Viral Vectors for Gene Therapy." *Cells Tissues Organs* 177(3):139–150.

Caplan, N. J. 2004. "Gene Therapy and Prospects. Downregulating Gene Expression: The Impact of RNA Interference." *Gene Therapy* 11:1241–1248.

Chain, E., Florey, H. W., Gardner, A. D., et al. 1940. "Penicillin as a Chemotherapeutic Agent." *Lancet* ii:226–228.

Comroe, J. H. Jr. 1998. "Retrospective Redux: Who Was Alexis Who?" *Respir Care* 43(2):131–140.

Costa, C., Zhao, L., and Burton, W. V. 2002. "Transgenic Pigs Designed to Express Human CD59 and H-Transferase to Avoid Humoral Xenograft Rejection Xenotransplantation." *Xenotransplantation* 9:45–57.

Denner, J. 2003. "Porcine Endogenous Retroviruses (PERVs) and Xenotransplantation: Screening for Transmission in Several Clinical Trials and in Experimental Models Using Non-Human Primates." *Ann Transplant* 8(3):39–48.

Fleming, A. 1929. "On the Antibacterial Action of Cultures of a *Penicillium*, with Special Reference to Their Use in the Isolation of *B. influenzae*." *Br J Exper Path* 10:226–236.

Gallin, J. I., ed. 2002. *Principles and Practice of Clinical Research*, New York: Academic Press.

Gridley, D. S., Slater, J. M. 2004. "Combining Gene Therapy and Radiation Against Cancer." *Curr Gene Ther* 4(3):231–148.

Harrington, R. K., and Pandha, H. 2004. "Recent Developments and Current Status of Gene Therapy Using Viral Vectors in the United Kingdom." *BMJ* 329(7470): 839–842.

Karlas, A., Kurth, R., and Denner, J. 2004. "Inhibition of Porcine Endogenous Retroviruses by RNA Interference: Increasing the Safety of Xenotransplantation." *Virology* 325:18–23.

Le Tissier, P., Stoye, J. P., Takeuchi, Y., and Weiss, R. A. 1997. "Two Sets of Human-Tropic Pig Retrovirus." *Nature* 389:681–682.

Meng, X. J., Halbur, P. G., Shapiro, M. S. et al. 1998. "Genetic and Experimental Evidence for Cross-Species Infection by the Swine Hepatitis E Virus." *J Virol* 72:9714–9721.

Mudur, G. 2004. "Kidney Trade Arrest Exposes Loopholes in India's Transplant Laws." *BMJ* 328:246.

Mueller, N. J., and Fishman, J. A. 2004. "Herpesvirus Infections in Xenotransplantation: Pathogenesis and Approaches." *Xenotransplantation* 11:486–490.

Ogata, K., and Platt, J. L. 2004. "Cardiac Xenotransplantation: Future and Limitations." *Cardiology* 101:144–155.

Phelps, C. J., Koike, C., Vaught, T. D., et al. 2003. "Production of α 1, 3-Galactosyltransferase-Deficient Pigs." *Science* 299:411–414.

Platt, J. L., ed. 2001. *Xenotransplantation*, Washington DC: ASM Press.

Roberts, J. P. 2004. "Gene Therapy's Fall and Rise (Again)." *Scientist* 18:22–24.

Ruediger, H., and Madsen, J. C. 2004. "Feasibility of Xeno-Transplantation." *Surg Clin North Am* 84:289–307.

Sournia, J.-C. 1992. *The Illustrated History of Medicine,* London: Harold Starke.

Teranishi, K., Gollackner, B., Buher, L., et al. 2002. "Depletion of Anti-Gal Antibodies in Baboons by Intravenous Therapy with Bovine Serum Albumin Conjugated to Gal Oligosaccharides." *Transplantation* 73(1):129–139.

Tischer, I., Mields, W., Wolff, D., et al. 1986. "Studies on Epidemiological and Pathogenicity of Porcine Circovirus." *Arch Virol* 91:271–276.

Warren, J., ed. 2004. "Xenotransplant News." *Xenotransplantation* 11:387–389.

Wells, D. J. 2004. "Gene Therapy Progress and Prospects: Electroporation and Other Physical Methods." *Gene Ther* 11:1363–1369.

Wolfe, N. D., Switzer, W. M., Carr, J. K., et al. 2004. "Naturally Acquired Simian Retrovirus Infections in Central African Hunters." *Lancet* 363:932–937.

Yu, J.-Y., DeRuiter, S. L., and Turner, D. L. 2002. "RNA Interference by Expression of Short-Interfering RNAs and Hairpin RNAs in Mammalian Cells." *PNAS USA* 99(9):6047–6052.

■ Popular Press

Fenster, J. 2003. *Mavericks, Miracles, and Medicine: The Pioneers Who Risked Their Lives to Bring Medicine into the Modern Age,* New York: Carrol and Graf.

"Gene Therapy Special Report." 1997, *Scientific American,* pp. 95–123.

Kennedy, M. 2004. *A Brief History of Disease, Science, and Medicine,* Mission Viejo, CA: Asklepiad Press.

Lanza, R. P., Cooper, D. K.C., and Chick, W. L. July 1997. "Xenotransplantation" *Scientific American.*

Newton, J. 1987. *Uncommon Friends: Life with Thomas Edison, Henry Ford, Harvey Firestone, Alexis Carrel & Charles Lindbergh,* New York: Harcourt.

Wells, H. G. 1994. *The Island of Dr. Moreau,* Reprint Edition, New York: Bantam Classics.

Zivin, J. Z. April 2000. "Understanding Clinical Trials" *Scientific American,* pp. 69–75.

■ Video Productions

Human Gene Therapy and the Future of Modern Medicine. 1993. Films for the Humanities.

Another War: Disease and Political Strife. 1997. Films for Humanitites.

Conquering an Invisible World. 1999. Films for Humanities.

History of Gene Therapy. 1999. Films for the Humanities.

Organ Farm. 2001. PBS.

The Land of Moreau. 2002. Directed by Richard Stanley and John Frankenheimer.

Mutter Museum: Strange but True Medical Mysteries. 2002. Discovery Channel.

The American Experience: Partners of the Heart. 2003 PBS. http://www.pbs.org/.
Dangerous Prescription. 2003. Frontline. PBS. http://www.pbs.org/.
Mavericks, Miracles and Medicine. 2003. History Channel.
History's Mysteries—Body Snatchers. 2006. A&E Home Video.

■ eLearning

http://biology.jbpub.com/book/virology

The site features eLearning, an online review area that provides quizzes and other tools to help you study for your class. You can also follow useful links for in-depth information, or just find out the latest virology and microbiology news.

ADDITIONAL CASE STUDY AND QUESTIONS

Sally Goodwin is a premed student volunteering in a cancer ward at a local hospital. She's met many patients and was particularly inspired by 16-year-old Sharon Smith, who suffered from a rare cancer. Sharon confided to Sally that she was researching her cancer via the Internet and had stumbled across a Web page pertaining to gene therapy clinical trials. Sally was very interested in what Sharon had found because she had been learning about gene therapy in her virology course. Soon, Sally and Sharon began discussing this topic regularly during Sally's visits. Sharon approached Sally with the following questions. How might you answer them if you were Sally?

1. Is gene therapy a permanent cure for any condition?
2. Can gene therapy be used for disorders that arise from mutations in more than one gene?
3. What types of viruses are used in gene therapy? What are their advantages and limitations?
4. Will gene therapy patients mount an immune response against the virus vector used in treatments?
5. Are there toxic effects related to gene therapy treatments?
6. Are there examples of patients who had major complications related to gene therapy and how was the problem resolved?
7. What are some of the ethical considerations for using gene therapy?
8. Gene therapy is expensive. Who has access to these therapies and who pays for their use?

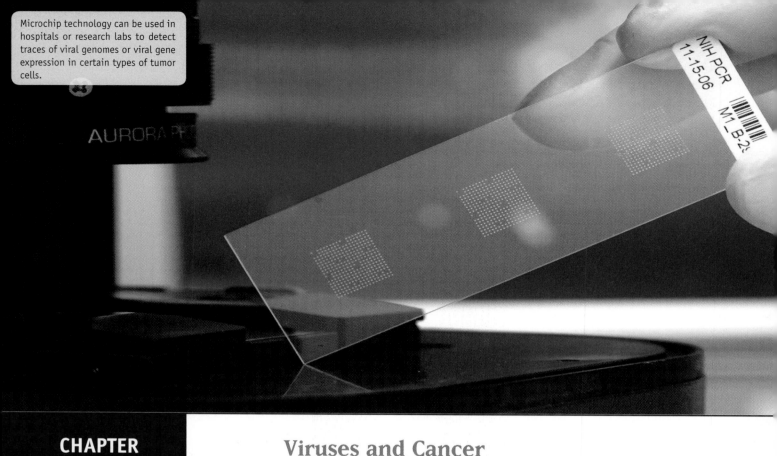

Microchip technology can be used in hospitals or research labs to detect traces of viral genomes or viral gene expression in certain types of tumor cells.

AURORA

CHAPTER

10

"Growth for the sake of growth is the ideology of the cancer cell."
Edward Abbey (1927–1989), radical environmentalist

Viruses and Cancer

CASE STUDY

Tom Kent, a college junior studying biology traveled home for a family reunion during spring break. On the day of the reunion, he noticed that his grandfather, John, looked very tired. Tom remembered that John had had a heart bypass operation in 1990. Tom coaxed his grandfather to schedule a complete physical examination with his primary care physician as soon as possible.

At his appointment the following week John told his doctor that he didn't have much of an appetite, had some abdominal pain, and occasionally felt nauseous. He was worried that it could be his heart again and discussed the operation he had had back in 1990. He also mentioned that he had been feeling like this for quite some time but blamed it on having a bad "ticker."

Upon examination, the doctor found that John's heart appeared normal. To be thorough, though, he decided to set up a treadmill test and carefully examined John's medical records. He noticed that John required a blood transfusion during his 1990 heart operation. He asked Tom if he ever followed up with any blood tests after the heart operation, to which John replied no. The doctor examined his abdomen and found that it was tender.

A week later John's doctor called with some test results. He told John that his liver enzymes were elevated and given his discomfort, a liver biopsy should be done.

One in three people will develop cancer at some time in their lifetimes. There are over 200 different types of cancer that affect all of the different body tissues. **Cancer** is the result of the uncontrolled growth of a single cell that eventually forms a clone of tumor cells that have the potential to **metastasize** to other sites of the body. Each of us is composed of approximately 10^{14} cells, all of which have the potential to become cancerous, but only one cell in one-third of the population turn cancerous. The chance of an individual cell becoming cancerous, therefore, is very small—3×10^{14}. We now know that for the change of a healthy cell into a cancerous cell to occur, a series of changes slowly releases the cell from the multiple checks and balances that control its normal growth.

Over the years, researchers have identified many factors, including viruses, that may increase the risk of developing certain types of cancers. Viruses can cause genetic changes in cells that make them more likely to become cancerous. The link between viruses and cancer was one of the crucial discoveries in cancer research.

IO.I   History of Cancer Viruses and Tumors

Cancer has afflicted humans throughout history. The earliest evidence of cancer is found in fossilized bone tumors of human mummies in ancient Egypt. The origin of the word *cancer*

■ Figure 10-1
Chimney sweeps were common in England between the 17th and 18th centuries. Surgeon Percival Pott was the first to describe scrotal cancer in chimney sweeps who were constantly exposed to soot. The photograph shows chimney sweeps working in Sembach, Germany, in 1965.

was credited to the Greek physician Hippocrates (460–370 B.C.), who used the terms *carcinos* and *carcinoma* to describe nonulcer-forming and ulcer-forming tumors.

When asked what causes cancer, the average individual responds with answers such as **carcinogens** such as tobacco or asbestos or radiation. This is indeed true for about 80% percent of all cancers; however, **about 20% of human cancers are associated with viruses**. In fact, during the 17th and 18th centuries many believed cancer was a contagious disease. The first cancer hospital in Reims, France, was moved from the city because of the fear of the spread of cancer throughout the city. Then, in 1775, British surgeon Percival Pott (1714–1788) reported his observation that chimney sweeps often developed scrotal cancer. Chimney sweeps were children and men who climbed inside the flues of chimneys and brushed them clean. Children were often placed in this occupation because of their smaller size, and in the case of boys their scrotal skin was in prolonged contact with chimney soot, which consisted of carcinogens such as coal, tar, pitch, creosote, and other oils. Many developed scrotal and testicle cancer (**Figure 10-1**), and the correlation between occupation, environment, and disease was made.

One of the most important discoveries in cancer biology was the demonstration that injecting "filterable agents" or viruses into chickens could produce tumors. In 1908, the Danish veterinarians Wilhelm Ellerman and Olaf Bang demonstrated that a filterable agent caused a leukemia common in chickens. At the time, though, leukemia was not recognized as a type of cancer and their discovery was largely ignored. In 1911, Dr. Peyton (Francis) Rous, a pathologist at the Rockefeller Institute in New York who later became one of the most influential cancer researchers, reported that a filterable agent caused a slow-growing solid tumor or **sarcoma** in healthy Plymouth Rock hens. He injected healthy chickens with a cell-free, bacteria-free liquid filtrate of sarcoma tissue and the chickens developed sarcomas at the site of injection. This demonstrated that a transmissible agent could cause tumors. The agent was a **retrovirus**, later named **Rous sarcoma virus** (**RSV**).

Rous's discovery came at a time when the idea that cancer was a contagious disease was waning. The connections between certain work environments and the onset of cancer had been clearly drawn. In 1966, 55 years after his initial findings, Rous was awarded a Nobel Prize in Physiology or Medicine for his discovery of tumor-inducing viruses.

Rous sarcoma virus has a simple viral genome that encodes only three genes (*gag*, *pol*, and *env*) that are needed for replication and formation of virus particles. Evidence from several laboratories in the 1970s demonstrated that RSV had a fourth gene, *src*, that was not required for viral production but was required to transform cells, a process termed *oncogenic transformation*. Viral genes that could cause cells to become transformed or cancerous became known as viral tumor-causing genes or **oncogenes**.

During the mid-1970s, Drs. J. Michael Bishop and Harold E. Varmus investigated whether the RSV *src* cancer-causing gene could be found in the DNA of normal cells. They conducted a set of experiments that today would be considered daunting because gene manipulation technology had not yet been fully developed. Bishop, Varmus, and their colleagues at the University of California–San Francisco prepared a ^{32}P radioactively labeled single-stranded complementary DNA (cDNA) probe of the *src* gene. The *src* probe was allowed to hybridize with denatured genomic DNA from chickens and other bird species (see Figure 10.3a).

They found *src* sequences in the genomes of normal chicken cells and the normal cells of other birds such as turkeys, ducks, and quail, and published their results in a 1976 *Nature* article. Their work continued and the *src* gene was also found in normal cells of mammals (including humans) and in fish. Their work demonstrated that oncogenes were cellular genes that were hijacked by viruses from cells. Later it was determined that the functions of these cellular genes were found to be cytokines, cytokine receptors, protein kinases, G-proteins, transcription factors, and other nuclear proteins that regulate cell growth. Both Bishop and Varmus were awarded a Nobel Prize in Physiology or Medicine in 1989.

IO.2 Cancer Today

Prostate cancer is the leading cancer among men in the United States, followed by lung and colon cancer, regardless of the man's race or ethnicity. Breast cancer is the leading cancer among women in the United States, followed by lung and colon cancer, regardless of the woman's race or ethnicity. Table 10-1 lists data from the American Cancer Society Surveillance Research Team regarding the estimated new cases of cancers and estimated deaths by gender in the United States in 2007. At least six viruses are thought to contribute to 15% of cancers. They are:

- Hepatitis B virus (HBV)
- Hepatitis C virus (HCV)
- Human papilloma virus (HPV)
- Epstein-Barr virus (EBV)
- Kaposi's sarcoma virus
- Human T-lymphotropic virus types 1 and 2 (HTLV-1 and -2)

Eighty percent of viral-associated cancers are **cervical cancer** (caused by HPV) and **liver cancer** (caused by HBV and HCV).

■ Important Cancer Biology Definitions
The following terms are used frequently in the field of cancer biology.

Oncogene—a gene that has the potential to convert a normal cell to a cancerous or transformed cell.

Viral oncogene (*v-onc*)—a viral gene responsible for the oncogenicity of the virus. The *v-onc* genes present in RNA tumor-inducing retroviruses are altered cellular genes that are acquired via recombination with the host genome. The *v-onc* genes from DNA tumor viruses are not cellular counterparts and the gene product usually functions in viral replication.

Proto-oncogene—cellular genes that promote normal growth and division of cells. Their expression is tightly regulated.

Cellular oncogene (*c-onc*)—mutated form of proto-oncogenes that cause tumors.

Tumor suppressor genes—genes that suppress or inhibit the conversion of a normal cell into a cancer cell. These genes cause cancer when they are turned off in a cell.

Cell transformation—the change in the morphological, biochemical, or growth properties of a cell.

Cancer—a term for diseases in which abnormal cells divide without control. Cancer cells can invade nearby tissues and can spread through the bloodstream and lymphatic system to other parts of the body.

Metastasis—when a cell or clump of cells separates from a tumor and spreads to another location. Metastasis is one of the main reasons why some tumors are difficult to control.

TABLE 10-1	2007 Estimates of the Leading Body Sites of New Cancer Cases and Deaths

Estimated New Cases*

Male		Female	
Prostrate	218,890 (29%)	Breast	178,480 (26%)
Lung and bronchus	114,760 (15%)	Lung and bronchus	98,620 (15%)
Colon and rectum	79,130 (10%)	Colon and rectum	74,630 (11%)
Urinary bladder	50,040 (7%)	Uterine corpus	39,080 (6%)
Non-Hodgkin's lymphoma	34,200 (4%)	Non-Hodgkin's lymphoma	28,990 (4%)
Melanoma of the skin	33,910 (4%)	Melanoma of the skin	26,030 (4%)
Kidney and renal pelvis	31,590 (4%)	Thyroid	25,480 (4%)
Leukemia	24,280 (3%)	Ovary	22,430 (3%)
Oral cavity and pharynx	24,180 (3%)	Kidney and renal pelvis	19,600 (3%)
Pancreas	18,830 (2%)	Leukemia	19,440 (3%)
All sites	766,860 (100%)		678,060 (100%)

*Excludes basal and squamous cell skin cancers and in situ carcinoma (except urinary bladder).

Estimated Deaths

Male		Female	
Lung and bronchus	89,510 (31%)	Lung and bronchus	70,880 (26%)
Prostrate	27,050 (9%)	Breast	40,460 (15%)
Colon and rectum	26,000 (9%)	Colon and rectum	26,180 (10%)
Pancreas	16,840 (6%)	Pancreas	16,530 (6%)
Leukemia	12,320 (4%)	Ovary	15,280 (6%)
Liver and intrahepatic bile duct	11,280 (4%)	Leukemia	9,470 (4%)
Esophagus	10,900 (4%)	Non-Hodgkin's lymphoma	9,060 (3%)
Urinary bladder	9,630 (3%)	Uterine corpus	7,400 (3%)
Non-Hodgkin's lymphoma	9,600 (3%)	Brain and other nervous system	5,590 (2%)
Kidney and renal pelvis	8,808 (3%)	Liver and intrahepatic bile duct	5,500 (2%)
All sites	289,550 (100%)		270,100 (100%)

From American Cancer Society. *Cancer Facts and Figures 2007*. Atlanta: American Cancer Society, Inc.

■ Characteristics of Cancer Cells

Much of what we now know about the genes involved in the development of cancer is attributed to research on RNA and DNA tumor viruses. Three assays have been developed to determine whether or not viruses or chemicals can transform cells in culture. They are:

- **Focus-forming assays:** These were discussed in Chapter 5.
- **Soft agarose assays:** transformed cells will be able to divide and form free colonies when suspended in a methyl cellulose or agarose medium, a semisolid agar gel. Normal cells do not proliferate in soft agarose.
- **Reduced serum requirement:** certain transformed cells may grow in medium containing reduced serum or growth factors; for example, normal NIH 3T3 cells will not grow in medium containing less than 5% serum. If Simian virus-40 (SV-40) is used to transform NIH 3T3 cells, the abnormal cells grow in medium containing 0.5% serum.

Refresher   Cell Cycle and Cancer

The cell cycle contains checkpoints in the cycle of events in a normal eukaryotic cell from one cell division to the next. It consists of interphase, mitosis, and cell division. Checkpoints can block the progression through the phases of the life cycle if certain conditions are not met. Cyclins and cyclin-dependent kinases regulate the cell cycle. Cancer cells have mutations in the genes that control the cell cycle, causing uncontrolled growth and cell division.

Telomeres are DNA sequences found at the ends of eukaryotic chromosomes. During the normal aging process, telomeres become shorter with each cycle of cell division. The telomerase enzyme synthesizes telomeric DNA on chromosome ends. A short telomere signals the cell to stop dividing. Cancer cells contain increased levels of telomerase activity. They maintain telomere length so that the cell never receives a signal to stop dividing (Figure RB 10-1).

(a)

(b)

■ Figure RB 10-1

(a) A schematic of the eukaryotic cell cycle. (b) The red chromosomes hybridized with fluorescent yellow probes, which in turn hybridized to the telomere DNA.

■ Figure 10-2
This nude mouse was injected with transformed mouse NIH 3T3 cells that contained a viral oncogene, and a tumor formed at the site of injection. Nude mice are born without a thymus and therefore cannot generate mature T lymphocytes. This immunodeficiency makes nude mice useful for investigating cancers. The mouse does not reject the cancer cells and actual tumors will form quickly in the mice.

The properties of cancer or **transformed** cells in culture are different from normal cells. Some transformed cells actually form tumors when injected into animals. Some of the characteristics seen in transformed cells in culture may also be seen in tumor cells growing *in vivo* in experimental animals or patients. Some of these phenotypic changes—characteristic of transformed cells in culture (*in vitro*)—are:

- Cells undergo **genetic changes** such as an increase in the number and size of nuclei resulting in instability. Transformed cells may become **polyploidy** and have **elevated levels of telomerase** that maintain telomere length.
- Cells become **immortalized** (cells can be passaged indefinitely) or have an unlimited life expectancy in culture.
- Cells undergo **metabolic change**s such as **dividing and growing rapidly**.
- Cells display a **lack of contact inhibition.** Normal cells stop replicating when they come in contact with another cell, whereas abnormal cells continue to divide and pile up on top of each other into a focus. The foci originate from the same cell.
- Cells display **anchorage-independent growth/loss of need for adhesion**. When freshly isolated normal cells are suspended in a liquid medium and they come in contact with a suitable solid surface such as the bottom of a culture dish they will attach, spread, and proliferate as a monolayer on the surface. In contrast, cells derived from tumors or transformed cells grow without the need to attach to a surface.
- Transformed cells can grow independently without the addition of serum or growth factors such as cytokines.
- Cells undergo a **loss of cell cycle control**. Transformed cells fail to stop at cell cycle checkpoints in the cell cycle. The growth of normal cells is restricted by these checkpoints.
- Cells may have altered cell surfaces. There will be **changes in membrane structure and function**; for example, transformed cells display **tumor-associated carbohydrate antigens**.
- When transformed cells are injected into experimental immunosuppressed animals (such as nude mice), they may produce tumors. Tumor formation defines malignant transformation. (**Figure 10-2**).

The following alterations are observed *in vivo* in cancer cells:

- There is an increase in oncogene protein expression because the cellular oncogenes have undergone chromosomal translocations, amplifications, or mutations.
- The cells lose tumor suppressor gene function due to a deletion or mutation in the tumor suppressor gene.
- DNA methylation patterns are altered.
- Cells produce an increased or unregulated level of growth factors.
- Cells divide uncontrollably.
- Cells have increased levels of enzymes involved in nucleic acid synthesis and lytic enzymes (such as proteases, collagenases, and glycosidases).
- Telomerase activity is reactivated.
- Cells can avoid the host immunosurveillance response.

■ Cancer Is a Multistep Process

Tumors arise from a series of events that lead to greater loss of regulation of cell division. For cancer to occur, the following must happen:

- The cell must bypass apoptosis (programmed cell death).
- The cell circumvents the need for growth signals from other cells.
- The cell escapes immunosurveillance.
- The cell commands its own blood supply.
- The cell may possibly metastasize.
- Mutations in cellular tumor suppressor genes may also be required for full malignancy to occur.

The association of viruses and human cancers is not causal and is often correlative. Viruses are thought to be cocarcinogens in the development of human tumors.

10.3 Molecular Mechanisms of Virally Induced Tumor Formation by RNA Tumor Viruses (Retroviruses)

A retrovirus may cause cancer in three ways: it may carry an oncogene (*v-onc*) into a cell, it may activate a cellular proto-oncogene, or it may inactivate a tumor suppressor gene. Analysis of the retrovirus genome is central to understanding the molecular mechanism of virally induced tumor formation.

■ The Retrovirus Genome

Retroviruses differ from DNA tumor viruses in that their genome consists of RNA in contrast to DNA. The RNA must be copied into DNA prior to integration into the host chromosome. The retrovirus *pol* gene that encodes reverse transcriptase performs the conversion of RNA into DNA. David Baltimore and Howard Temin discovered reverse transcriptase independently. Temin was working on his Ph.D. under Renato Dulbecco at the California Institute of Technology. In 1963, he showed that RSV could not infect or replicate in cells in the presence of drugs that inhibited RNA transcription, such as actinomycin D and α amanitin. This was not unexpected because it was known that the genome of RSV consisted of RNA.

To his surprise, though, Temin discovered that DNA replication inhibitors such as 5-bromodeoxyuridine and cytosine arabinoside inhibited the replication of RSV. For this reason, Temin proposed that the retrovirus reverse-transcribed its RNA into DNA, an idea that contradicted the contemporary dogma that DNA is transcribed into RNA. Once the RNA of the retrovirus is copied into DNA, the retroviral DNA is integrated into the host cell chromosome. In 1970, Temin and Baltimore isolated and described reverse transcriptase, an accomplishment for which they shared the Nobel Prize in 1975.

Retrovirus particles contain two copies of the RNA genome. The genomes of most retroviruses consist of three or four genes that are located between unique and repetitive sequences located within its RNA genome. The genome lengths of replication competent retroviruses (a retrovirus with a functional *pol* gene) range in size from 7 to 12 kb in length. The main genes are labeled *gag*, *pol*, and *env* (**Figure 10-3**). *Gag* is an acronymn for group antigens. The *gag* gene encodes matrix and core proteins of the virus, and these proteins protect the viral RNA genome. The *pol* gene encodes a protein that has reverse transcriptase, RNase H, helicase, and integrase functions. This enzyme carries out the reverse transcription process of converting the viral RNA template into DNA. The *env* gene encodes a protein that is embedded within a lipid bilayer that surrounds the nucleoprotein core particle of the virus. These proteins are the "spikes" that bind to host cell receptors. (**Figure 10-4** shows a typical retrovirus).

The retroviral genome is flanked at each end by repetitive sequences (designated **R**) and unique sequences (designated **U**). These sequences will enable the DNA copy of the

Typical Retrovirus

| R | U5 | *gag* | *pol* | *env* | U3 | R |

Rous Sarcoma Virus

| R | U5 | *gag* | *pol* | *env* | **SRC** | U3 | R |

(b)

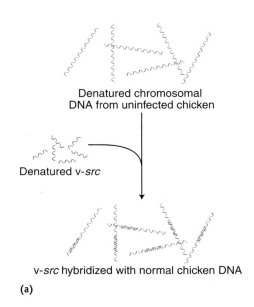

Denatured chromosomal
DNA from uninfected chicken

Denatured v-*src*

v-*src* hybridized with normal chicken DNA

(a)

■ **Figure 10-3**

(a) Bishop-Varmus experiment: oncogenes hybridize with normal cellular genes. **(b)** The typical structure of a retrovirus genome. Retroviruses contain at least three genes—*gag*, *pol*, and *env*—in addition to repetitive and unique sequences at the ends of the genome. Retroviruses that can cause tumor formation may contain an additional *v-onc* such as *v-src*. ψ is a packaging signal. The packaging signal is needed so that newly synthesized RNA molecules can be incorporated into new virus particles. Adapted from University of South Carolina, School of Medicine. "Virology: Oncogenic Viruses." *Microbiology and Immunology*. University of South Carolina, 2008. http://pathmicro.med.sc.edu/lecture/retro.htm.

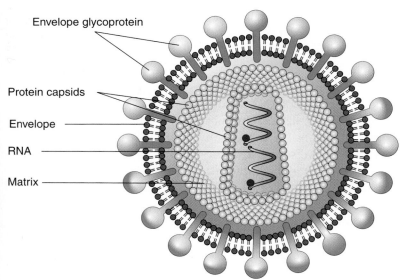

Envelope glycoprotein

Protein capsids

Envelope

RNA

Matrix

■ **Figure 10-4**
The structure of a retrovirus particle.

genome to be inserted into the DNA of the host. The genome can act as an enhancer as well, causing the host nucleus to transcribe the DNA copies of the retroviral genome at a rapid rate.

Each viral genome contains a unique (U5) sequence located at the 5′ end of the genomic RNA. The opposite end of the viral RNA (3′ end) contains a U3 region. The U5 region contains a primer binding sequence. The U3 region contains promoter-enhancer sequences that control viral RNA transcription from the 5′ long terminal repeat (LTR).

Some retroviruses contain an additional gene, *v-onc*. It is not an essential viral gene because it is unrelated to the strategy of viral replication. The *v-onc* gene was hijacked from the genome of its host during the course of evolution. It encodes a protein that is capable of inducing cellular transformation (cancer). **Figure 10-5** illustrates replication of the retroviral genome.

■ Molecular Mechanisms of How Retroviruses Can Cause Cancer: Proviral Integration

There are several mechanisms by which retroviruses may play a role in converting normal host cells into tumor cells. When a provirus integrates into the host's genome (**Figure 10-6**), it is random with respect to host cell DNA. The provirus may integrate within or near a *c-onc*, though, thereby altering the expression of it. The gene products of *c-onc*'s normally function in signal transduction and cell cycle regulation (Tables 10-2 and 10-3 and **Figures 10-7** and **10-8**). Therefore, a provirus integration event may disrupt the normal restraints on normal growth and division of cells, causing tumors to form.

The integration of proviral DNA into the host genome can result in the following:

- Insertional **activation** of the expression of a *c-onc* when viral promoters or enhancer elements cause abnormal expression of an unaltered *c-onc*, resulting in uncontrolled growth of normal cells. The *c-onc* may undergo hyperactive expression or it may be expressed at inappropriate times during the cell cycle, causing growth at inappropriate times.

1. tRNA binds to a primer binding site (PBS).

2. Reverse transcriptase elongates 3′ end of tRNA making, DNA complementary to U5 and R.

3. RNase H degrades R and U5 sequences in genomic RNA.

4. The first "jump": negative-strand DNA pairs with 3′-R sequence in genomic RNA.

5. Reverse transcriptase elongates negative-strand DNA to create a DNA/RNA hybrid molecule.

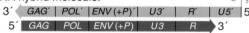

6. RNase H degrades all genomic RNA molecule except the (+P) sequences. (+P represents a short region of genomic RNA that acts as primer sequences.)

7. Reverse transcriptase begins synthesis of positive-strand using (+P) RNA as primer.

8. RNase H degrades all remaining RNA.

9. The second "jump": the positive-strand PBS sequence pairs with its complementary sequence in the negative strand.

10. Reverse transcriptase elongates both strands to complete synthesis of a double-stranded proviral DNA molecule.

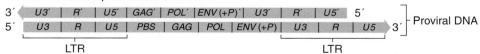

- Insertional **inactivation of a cellular tumor suppressor gene**, resulting in uncontrolled cell division.
- The integration of proviral DNA that carries a *v-onc* into the host genome. The *v-onc* may become activated and transcribed, coding for the oncogene product (e.g., oncogenic activation of the normal cellular platelet-derived growth factor [PDGF]

■ **Figure 10-5**
The process of reverse transcription is complex. There is a transfer RNA (tRNA) bound to the primer-binding site within the 5′ end of the genome of the retrovirus RNA. Reverse transcriptase binds to and elongates a short strand of DNA that is complementary to U5 and R. Next the RNase H degrades the R and U5 regions of the viral RNA genome. The newly synthesized viral DNA is flexible and it moves to pair with the 3′ R region of the genomic RNA, acting as another primer for reverse transcriptase. Reverse transcriptase binds to it and extends the viral DNA to create a DNA/RNA hybrid. RNase chews up all genomic RNA, leaving the short sequence that is complementary to sequences located in the *env* region of the genome. The short RNA primer is used by reverse transcriptase to synthesize DNA (step 7). RNase H degrades any remaining RNA after DNA synthesis is complete. The newly synthesized DNA flexes to pair with its complementary sequence, acting as a DNA primer. Reverse transcriptase elongates both strands of DNA, yielding a dsDNA molecule that contains the duplicated U3-R-U5 sequences at both ends. The U3-R-U5 sequences are termed long terminal repeats (LTRs). This dsDNA molecule is called a **provirus**. The LTRs of the provirus enable the dsDNA copy of the genome or provirus to be inserted into the DNA of a host. Adapted from B. A. Voyles. *The Biology of Viruses*, Second Edition. McGraw-Hill Higher Education, 2001.

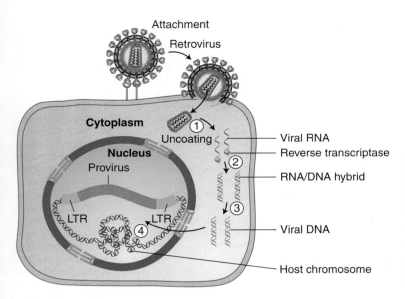

Attachment

Retrovirus

Cytoplasm

Uncoating

Nucleus

Provirus

LTR   LTR

— Viral RNA
— Reverse transcriptase
— RNA/DNA hybrid

— Viral DNA

— Host chromosome

■ **Figure 10-6**
Integration of proviral DNA into the host. The integrase function of the *pol* gene product is involved in this event. Adapted from an illustration by the Institut National de Recherche Pédagogique, "The Replication of HIV in the Target Cell," *Immunologie— AIDS,* http://www.inrp.fr/Acces/biotic/immuno/html/repvih.htm.

growth receptor). The *v-onc* may promote the normal growth and division of cells, causing tumors to form (**Figures 10-9** and **10-10**). The *v-onc* may be a mutated form of a *c-onc* (e.g., a truncated form) that could interfere with cellular signaling involved in growth. Examples of retroviral oncogenes are listed in Table 10-3.

■ **More about the Retrovirus Life Cycle**

The integrated provirus often remains quiescent as a silent, persistent infection. The DNA may be transcribed by the cell's RNA polymerase II into viral messenger RNA (mRNA) that is translated by host cell ribosomes. The viral proteins are packaged along with the viral RNA and the progeny viruses exit by budding from the host cell surface.

■ **Human Endogenous Retroviruses (HERVs)**

Approximately 8% of the human genome contains sequences with similarity to infectious retroviruses. These are sequences that contain the easily recognized *gag, pol, env,* and LTRs. These sequences have acquired many mutations over the course of evolutionary time so that, with few exceptions, they are now defective and incapable of producing any protein. HERVs have been proposed as etiological cofactors in chronic diseases such as cancer, autoimmunity diseases, and neurological diseases (**Virus File 10-1**). Despite intense efforts by many groups, there has been little direct evidence discovered to support these claims (**Virus File 10-2**).

TABLE 10-2	Cellular Genes Involved in Cancer (Genes Involved in the Stimulation of Cell Division)		
Class	**Gene**	**Function**	**Cancer Type (result of one mutant allele of the gene)**
Growth factors or receptors for growth factors	PDGF	Platelet-derived growth factor	Brain and breast
	RET (*Rearranged during transfection*)	Growth factor receptor	Thyroid Brain and breast
	erb-B	Receptor for epidermal growth factor	Glioblastoma (a brain cancer) and breast
	erb-B2	Receptor for growth factor	Breast, ovarian, and salivary
Cytoplasmic signaling proteins	*c-src*	Tyrosine kinase	Breast
	ras (*Rat sarcoma*)	GTPase	Breast, colon, lung, and pancreatic
	bcl-1	Stimulates cell cycle	Breast, head, and neck
Nuclear DNA binding proteins	*c-jun*	Transcription factor	Breast
	c-fos	Transcription factor	Breast
	c-myc	Transcription factor	Burkitt's lymphoma, leukemia, stomach, lung, breast
	c-rel	Transcription factor	Lymphoma

TABLE 10-3	Cellular Genes Involved in Cancer: Tumor Suppressor Genes (Genes Involved in the Suppression of Cell Division)		
Class	**Gene**	**Function**	**Cancer Types**
Nuclear proteins	p53	Halts cell cycle in G1, induces apoptosis	Many cancers (e.g., brain tumors, leukemia, breast, sarcomas)
	p16	Inhibits cyclin D-dependent kinase activity	Melanoma, pancreatic
	WT1	Transcription factor	Wilm's tumor of the kidney
	BRCA1	DNA repair	Breast and ovarian
	BRCA2	DNA repair	Breast
	RB1	Master brake on cell cycle	Retinoblastoma, bone, bladder, lung, breast
	MTS1	Brake on cell cycle	Many cancers
Cytoplasmic proteins	APC (adenomatous polyposis coli)	Interact with cell adhesion proteins	Colon and stomach
	DPC4	Regulation of TGF-b/BMP signal transduction	Colon and pancreatic
	NF-1 (neurofibromatosis type 1)	Inhibits cell growth and division in nerve cells, inactivates RAS	Brain, nerve, leukemia
	NF-2 (neurofibromatosis type 2)	Links cell membrane to actin skeleton	Brain and nerve
Transmembrane proteins	DCC (deleted in colon carcinoma)	Receptor? Mediates netrin-1 activity	Colon
Location unknown	VHL	Downregulation of cyclin D1, component of ubiquitin ligase complex	Kidney

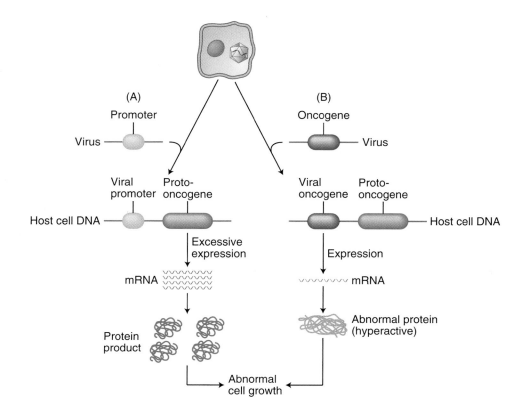

■ **Figure 10-7**

Host cells may be transformed when a viral promoter or oncogene is inserted into the chromosome of its host. **(a)** Insertion of a viral promoter upstream of a cellular proto-oncogene causes inappropriate expression of the normal proto-oncogene. **(b)** Insertion of a viral oncogene may promote the growth and division of cells, causing tumors to form. The *v-onc* may be a mutated form of a *c-onc* that could interfere with cellular signaling involved in growth, resulting in abnormal growth. Adapted from Marks, D. B., Marks, A. D., and C. M. Smith. *Basic Medical Biochemistry: A Clinical Approach.* Lippincott Williams & Wilkins, 1996.

■ **Figure 10-8**

Cellular oncogenes (*c-onc*) promote the normal growth and division of cells via various functions (e.g., as growth factors, growth receptors, and transcription factors). Their expression is tightly regulated. Mutated forms of these genes can cause disruption of normal cellular growth and division. Adapted from Marks, D. B., Marks, A. D., and C. M. Smith. *Basic Medical Biochemistry: A Clinical Approach*. Lippincott Williams & Wilkins, 1996.

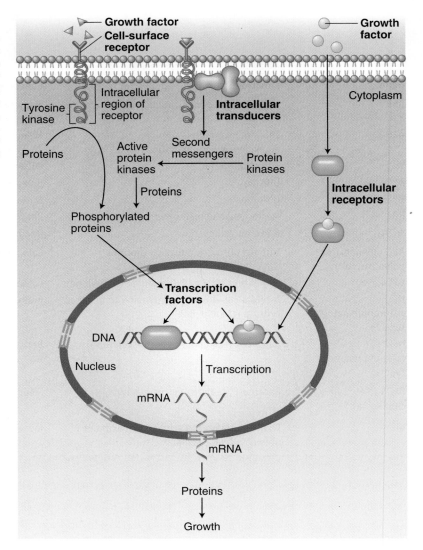

■ **Figure 10-9**

If *c-onc*'s are damaged by carcinogens, mutations in the promoter or gene may lead to transformation of the cell. Adapted from Marks, D. B., Marks, A. D., and C. M. Smith. *Basic Medical Biochemistry: A Clinical Approach*. Lippincott Williams & Wilkins, 1996.

■ Figure 10-10

Mechanism for oncogenic activation of the normal PDGF growth receptor. **(a)** Normal PDGF growth receptor is activated in response to growth stimulation by PDGF. **(b)** A mutated form of the PDGF growth receptor is constitutively active, driving abnormal growth forward. Adapted from Cooper, G. M., and R. E. Hausman. *The Cell: A Molecular Approach,* Third Edition. 2003, Sinauer Associates.

10.4 Human Retroviruses

Five human retroviruses have been identified: **human foamy virus, HTLV-1, HTLV-2, HIV-1**, and **HIV-2** (HIV-1 and -2 will be discussed in Chapter 16). Human foamy viruses have been implicated in a variety of illnesses, such as Graves' disease, chronic fatigue syndrome, Guillain Barré syndrome, Kawasaki disease, multiple sclerosis, and hemodialysis encephalopathy. To date, epidemiological data is controversial, and more research is needed to resolve the controversy regarding the epidemiology and virulence of human foamy virus.

The majority of the individuals infected with HTLV-1 are asymptomatic carriers. HTLV-1 is endemic in parts of Japan, South America, Africa, and the Caribbean. HTLV-1 causes two fatal diseases: Adult T-cell leukemia (ATL) and HTLV-1-associated myelopathy (HAM).

The lifetime chance of an infected individual developing ATL is about 2% to 5%. In the early 1980s HTLV-1 was isolated from patients suffering from T-cell leukemia and T-cell lymphoma by Bernard Poiesz and Robert Gallo's research laboratory in the United States and Y. Hinuma's research laboratory in Japan. Only a small number of HTLV-1 infected individuals develop leukemia and generally it occurs decades after initial infection. The development of T-cell malignancy remains poorly understood. ATL therapy uses a combination of the antivirals zidovudine and interferon α. The T lymphocytes of ATL patients express high levels of IL-2 receptors. Novel strategies involve treating patients with antibodies against the IL-2 receptor that are armed with toxins or radionuclides.

HTLV-1 infects primarily CD4+ T-lymphocyte. It is transmitted from mother to child either via the placenta during birth or through breastfeeding. It is transmitted from male to female during sexual intercourse, but there is no evidence of female-to-male transmission. Blood transfusions are an additional and efficient route of transmission. HTLV-2 infections have been associated with T-cell malignancies, but the epidemiology of HTLV-2 has been less well studied. In the United States donated blood is screened for the presence of HTLV-1 and -2.

Endogenous Retroviruses Might Contribute to Some Cases of Schizophrenia

Schizophrenia is a chronic, relapsing psychotic disorder that primarily affects thought and behavior. The average age of onset is 20 to 25 years. The disease can be well controlled with antipsychotic drugs, which are sometimes called neuroleptics. Schizophrenia affects approximately 1% of the population. Diagnosis of the disease includes auditory hallucinations (usually voices that converse with or about the patient) and paranoid delusions (the belief that outside forces are conspiring against the patient). Other overt symptoms include the inability to pay attention, low motivation, bizarre thoughts, the loss of the sense of pleasure, disorganization, gradual depletion of thoughts and speech, and social withdrawal.

Schizophrenia has been accepted as a psychotic disorder caused by a combination of genetic predisposition and triggering factors from the environment. Twin and adoption studies indicate that when one member of a twin pair has the illness, the risk of schizophrenia in the other twin is 17% for fraternal twins and nearly 50% for identical twins. The risk of schizophrenia in the relatives of affected individuals is 2% in third-degree relatives, 2% to 6% in second degree relatives, and 6% to 17% in first degree relatives. No specific gene or combination of genes has been identified that confer the risk for schizophrenia.

A number of environmental factors seem to increase the risk for schizophrenia and in general they occur early in life; for example, severe malnutrition during the first trimester or maternal influenza during the second trimester of pregnancy double the relative risk of schizophrenia. Other studies show that the disease is more likely to strike individuals born in cities than on farms and to strike people born in winter (when influenza and other diseases are common) than other times of the year. Even without decisive evidence, some biologists, such as Paul Ewald, argue that microbial pathogens cause most common chronic diseases such as schizophrenia.

It has been hypothesized that retroviruses may be one of the infectious agents involved in the pathogenesis of schizophrenia. It is known that retroviruses such as HTLV and HIV can replicate within the central nervous system and cause neurological and psychiatric symptoms in some individuals.

A study in 2001 by Hakan Karlsson and colleagues identified retroviral RNA, presumably of endogenous origin in the cerebrospinal fluids (CSFs), in 10 of 35 patients who suffered from recent-onset schizophrenia (mean age of 25 years). The majority of the patients (7 of 10) harbored sequences related to the HERV-W family of human endogenous retroviruses. Retroviral sequences were also detected in the CSFs of 1 of 20 individuals suffering from chronic schizophrenia. No retroviral sequences were detected in CSF samples collected from 22 patients suffering from noninflammatory neurological diseases nor from 30 individuals who did not suffer from any psychiatric disease.

In schizophrenia the frontal cortex, which is the most highly developed part of the brain, is slow and affects emotion and cognitive functioning. The frontal cortex develops last and is not complete until the mid-20s, when schizophrenia typically develops. During Karlsson's collaborative investigation, postmortem samples of brain tissue of the frontal cortex of five individuals who suffered from schizophrenia and six individuals who did not suffer from any psychotic disease were analyzed for the presence of retroviral RNA transcripts. Results showed that a low level of retroviral expression occurred in normal brains but an unexpectedly high level of expression occurred in schizophrenic brains.

Endogenous retroviruses are a part of the human genome, having inserted themselves possibly millions of years ago, but the part they play in human disease is just beginning to be understood. Replication of Karlsson's findings will motivate subsequent critical studies. Robert Yolken, a collaborator with Karlsson, believes that herpes or other viral infections during pregnancy may activate the dormant HERVs, disrupting brain development and increasing the risk for schizophrenia later in life. Herpes infections are common among people with schizophrenia. If his theory is correct, screening pregnant women for herpes and treating the ones at risk may prevent schizophrenia in some individuals.

References

Karlsson, H., et al. 2001. "Retroviral RNA Identified in the Cerebrospinal Fluids and Brains of Individuals with Schizophrenia." *PNAS USA* 98(8):4634–4639.

Nakamura, A., et al. 2003. "Human Endogenous Retroviruses with Transcriptional Potential in the Brain." *J Hum Genet* 48(11):575–581.

Zimmer, C. 2001. "Do Chronic Diseases Have an Infectious Root?" *Science* 293:1974–1977.

10.5 Human DNA Tumor Viruses

Richard E. Shope discovered the first DNA tumor viruses during the early 1930s (rabbit fibroma in 1932 and rabbit papilloma isolated from cottontail rabbits in 1933). He minced tumor material from infected animals and inoculated it into domestic rabbits. It was shown that the growths were attributed to a filterable agent because the infectious agent passed through a Berkefeld V filter. The growths that formed often regressed.

DNA tumor viruses are a diverse group of viruses with different structures, genome organization, and replication strategies. Some of these viruses, such as papillomaviruses, Epstein-Barr virus, Kaposi's sarcoma-associated herpesvirus, and hepatitis B, induce tumors in the natural host. Others, such as adenovirus, polyomaviruses, and SV-40, induce tumors in experimental animals.

DNA tumor viruses differ from RNA tumor viruses in that the oncogenes of DNA tumor viruses are essential viral genes used in replication (mostly virally encoded nuclear proteins). The oncogenes of small DNA tumor viruses (such as adenoviruses and SV-40) do not have cellular counterparts or homologs. DNA tumor viruses target the Rb and p53 tumor suppressor gene products of the host. In other words, the viral-encoded gene products of DNA tumor viruses interact with proteins that have a negative regulatory role in cell proliferation (Table 10-4). This causes an alteration of cell cycle progression. The larger DNA tumor viruses also encode cellular homologs to activate signal transduction pathways that enhance cell growth and division.

The oncogenic potential of DNA tumor viruses is low; for example, the adenoviruses, polyomaviruses and SV-40 frequency of transformation is less than 1 in 100,000 infected cells. Transformation only occurs in cells that undergo an **aborted life cycle**. During an aborted life cycle, only the early viral genes are expressed. Infectious particles are not produced and the cells are not killed during an aborted cycle. The integration of the viral genome into its host genome may enable the abortive life cycle and cellular transformation.

■ Epstein-Barr Virus (EBV)

EBV was the first human virus to be directly implicated in human tumors. EBV is a herpesvirus that is sometimes referred to as human herpes virus 4 (HHV-4). All herpesviruses have two modes of infection: a lytic replication cycle, which generates infectious virus particles and destroys the host cell, and a latent replication cycle, in which the viral

Debunking the Myth of "The Disintegrating Cat"

Louis Wain (1860–1939) was a highly successful British illustrator of humorous pictures of cats. Wain's illustrations have been connected to schizophrenia in psychology textbooks for the past 20 years (**Figure VF 10-1**). Authors infer that these pictures show the progression of his mental decline, suggesting a relationship to a schizophrenic condition. There is, however, no concrete evidence to suggest that Wain did indeed suffer from schizophrenia, nor is there evidence that dates the drawings; hence, there is no way of determining the order in which they were produced. The drawings in Figure VF 10-1b were found in a shop in London during the late 1930s.

■ **Figure VF 10-1**
(a) British artist Louis Wain. **(b)** A series of Louis Wain's cat drawings. Photograph reproduced by permission of the Bethlem Art and History Collections Trust, Louis Wain 1860–1939, Kaleidoscope.

(a)

(b)

Wain was considered an eccentric character. After World War I there was less demand for his art, leaving him progressively impoverished. His mental status appeared to have gone unnoticed for a time, and toward the end of his life he was certified insane and placed in a pauper's ward of Springfield Hospital at Tooting. Guardians at the hospital noticed his talent and a year later he was transferred to the Royal Bethel Hospital, where he was allowed to draw and paint as much as he liked.

It is, of course, impossible to determine whether Wain suffered from schizophrenia, and if he did, if he had an infection caused by endogenous retroviruses.

References
Allderidge, P. 1997. "Louis Wain. Die zerfallende Katze." In *Kunst und Wahn*, Dumont, Germany: Kunstforum Wien, pp. 143–147.

TABLE 10-4	DNA Tumor Viruses Target Cellular Tumor Suppressor Genes	
Virus	**Gene Product**	**Cellular Target**
EBV	EBNA-2	*c-myc*
	EBNA-3A and B	Interferes with Notch signaling pathway
	EBNA-3C	Rb
	LMP1	CD40, bcl-2, A20
KSHV	v-IL6	Interferes with IL-6 pathway
	v-Bcl-2	c-Bcl-2 and p53
	v-cyclinD2	c-cyclin D, Rb
HBV	HbX	*c-src*, p53
HCV	NS5	c-bcl-6, p53, Ig heavy chain gene(V_H), b-catenin
Papillomavirus	E7	Rb
	E6	p53
	E5	Platelet-derived growth factor
Adenovirus	E1A	Rb
	E1B	p53
SV-40	Large T-antigen	Rb and p53
Polyomavirus	Large T antigen	Rb
	Middle T antigen	*c-src* and P13K

genome persists in its host cell but with dramatically restricted gene expression and without cell destruction. (Herpesviruses are discussed in Chapter 15.)

EBV is named after Anthony Epstein and Yvonne Barr, the two scientists who first isolated the virus in 1964 from lymphoma samples collected by Dennis Burkitt. Dr. Burkitt, a British surgeon, was working in equatorial Africa in 1956. While there, he observed and described an unusual lymphoma that was very common in children in that region. It became known as Burkitt's lymphoma (BL), a disease that is very similar to leukemia. It is an aggressive, malignant cancer and is characterized by a solid tumor composed predominately of aberrant B-cells (**Figure 10-11**). B-cells are integral to a normal healthy immune system.

Ninety-five percent of the population of the United States between the ages of 35 and 40 are persistently infected with EBV. The infection, which is usually asymptomatic, causes a number of conditions. It usually hits teens and young adults by causing infectious mononucleosis. (EBV causes 85% of mononucleosis cases.) The virus is passed via the saliva of an infected person; it is often referred to as the "kissing disease." The virus can also be transmitted while sharing a glass, eating utensils, or a straw with an infected individual. The incubation period is four to seven weeks. The initial signs of infection are:

- sore throat
- swollen glands in the neck
- fatigue
- lack of appetite
- headache
- white patches in the back of the throat

■ Figure 10-11

This Nigerian child has a large facial tumor due to malignant Burkitt's lymphoma. The tumor can grow to this size in a mere four to six weeks.

Mononucleosis is not usually a life-threatening illness. Sometimes the spleen will be enlarged and could rupture.

If 95% of the population in developing countries is infected with EBV, why doesn't everyone get BL? Burkitt's lymphoma seems to happen most often in a person who first has a condition that weakens his/her immune system, such as chronic malaria or AIDS. Children in central Africa often suffer from the aforementioned infections. Then, when these children come down with Epstein-Barr virus, BL occurs. EBV persistently infects B lymphocytes (resulting in a latent infection), the lymphocytes of the immune system that produce antibodies. Burkitt's lymphoma is a solid tumor of B lymphocytes. It affects the jaws and very rapidly spreads to the soft tissues and the parotid glands. When Burkitt's lymphoma tumors are analyzed, genetic aberrations such as chromosomal translocations involving chromosomes 8 and either 14, 22, or 2 occur. These translocations move the *c-myc* gene near an immunoglobin heavy-chain or light-chain, resulting in abnormal regulation of the *c-myc* gene and increased tumorigenicity of the cells. EBV DNA can be isolated from tumors and viral specific antigens can be detected in the tumors. Infection with EBV induces a lymphoma-like disease in new world primates. *In vitro* EBV immortalization of B-cells further supports the link. The mechanism by which the virus transforms cells is still uncertain. The transforming gene(s) have not been precisely identified. Possible candidates are listed in Table 10-4.

■ Kaposi's Sarcoma Virus

Kaposi's sarcoma was known as a rare cancer before the AIDS epidemic. It was first described in 1872 by the Hungarian dermatologist Moritz Kaposi. It is referred to today as **classic Kaposi's sarcoma** and occurs most often in elderly men, with a ratio of 10 to 15 males to 1 female. The average age of onset is between 50 and 70 years in men of Mediterranean, Middle Eastern, or Eastern European ethnic decent. Single or multiple lesions are usually located in the lower extremities, especially the ankle and soles of the feet (**Figure 10-12**).

In 1981, the rapid and disseminated form of Kaposi's sarcoma in young homosexual or bisexual men was first reported as part of a new epidemic now known as AIDS. Kaposi's sarcoma has reached epidemic proportions in parts of Africa and the Western world. It continues to pose a problem in AIDS patients receiving highly active antiretroviral therapy (HAART) and transplant patients who must undergo immunosuppressive treatment to prevent organ rejection. The lifetime risk for Kaposi's sarcoma in homosexual male AIDS patients during their lifetime is 50%.

Patrick Moore at the Columbia School of Public Health and Yuan Chang at Columbia College of Physicians and Surgeons identified Kaposi's sarcoma virus, also called human herpesvirus-8 (HHV-8) in 1994 as the infectious cause of Kaposi's sarcoma. DNA sequences of the viral genome were detected via polymerase chain reaction (PCR) in biopsy material (Kaposi's lesions) from patients with classic, transplant-related, and AIDS-associated Kaposi's sarcoma and was absent from skin tissue from patients who did not have Kaposi's sarcoma.

Less than 3% of infected cells in Kaposi's sarcoma lesions display evidence of lytic KSHV infection. Transcripts of the latent viral genes are found in most Kaposi's sarcoma tumor cells. The viral genome contains sequences that encode a D type cyclin, an interleukin 6 homolog, a Bcl2 homolog, and a number of other genes potentially implicated in the growth deregulation that may be relevant to its proposed role as a transforming virus. Currently there are clinical trials involving antivirals purposely directed against Kaposi's sarcoma virus (e.g., ganciclovir and foscarnet) in progress. These antivirals target mainly lytic virus and will

■ Figure 10-12
A Kaposi's lesion is visible in the center of the photograph. The lesion is typically red, purple, or brown and presents as a patch, plaque, or nodular skin.

more than likely be ineffective against latent virus infection found in most Kaposi's sarcoma lesions. Alternatively, RNA interference and gene therapy have been proposed as a future management option of Kaposi's sarcoma.

■ Hepatitis B Virus (HBV)- and Hepatitis C Virus (HCV)-Related Hepatocellular (Liver) Cancer (HCC)

Of all the hepatitis viruses, only HBV and HCV cause chronic hepatitis, which can progress to cirrhosis and HCC. HBV and HCV are biologically very different viruses. HBV contains a double-stranded DNA (dsDNA) genome that replicates by reverse transcription of an RNA pregenome. HCV is an RNA virus that replicates in the cytoplasm of the cell. (The replication of HBV and HCV is discussed in Chapter 17.)

Both viruses mainly infect hepatocytes of the liver, although HCV also infects B lymphocytes. Despite their different life cycles and genes, they share common characteristics in the mechanisms of the chronic liver disease they cause and their association with cirrhosis, the need for a liver transplant, and HCC (**Figure 10-13**). HCC tumors in patients infected with HBV usually harbor integrated viral DNA. HCV contains an RNA genome that does not contain an obvious oncogene and does not integrate into host genomes. Its mechanism of oncogenesis is not clear. Recent studies suggest that HCV causes chromosomal instability. HCC tumors in HCV patients have a five- to tenfold increase in mutation frequency of several cellular genes, such as the immunoglobin heavy chain, *c-bcl-6*, p53, and certain β-catenins.

The routes of transmission by HBV and HCV are similar. Transmission occurs when blood or body fluids of infected persons enter the body of a person who is not immune. Both are spread when sharing needles with an infected person or from an infected mother to the baby during birth. HBV can be transmitted sexually, too; however, there is no evidence of sexual transmission of HCV among monogamous couples. The rate of progression from chronic hepatitis through cirrhosis to cancer in hepatitis C is dramatically higher than that seen with the progression of HBV-induced cirrhosis to cancer. HCC is usually not detected until it is in an advanced stage. Hence, liver cancer is usually fatal within a year of diagnosis.

Liver cancer is the fifth most common cancer in the world. The hepatitis B vaccine is the first anticancer vaccine. Studies have shown that hepatitis B vaccination programs caused the number of hepatitis B carriers to be decreased substantially in some communities; for example, a 10-year study (1984–1994) in Taiwan found that the use of the hepatitis B vaccine reduced the carrier state in children from 9.8% in 1984 to less than 1.3% in 1994. It is anticipated that this significant decrease will be linked to a lower incidence of liver cancer in children. (The hepatitis B vaccine will be discussed in greater detail in Chapter 17.) There is no vaccine available for HCV. Donated blood is screened for the presence of HBV and HCV in both the United States and Canada. Most blood centers in southeast Asia screen donated blood for HBV, and even fewer countries are undertaking HCV screening.

■ Figure 10-13

This Cambodian woman has a distended abdomen due to a hepatoma resulting from chronic hepatitis B infection. The incidence of HCC in patients with a hepatitis B infection is 12 to 300 times greater than in people not infected with HBV. The HBV DNA is incorporated into the hepatocytic DNA during the disease pathogenic process. Note how the tumor commands its own blood supply.

Mouth Cancer and Oral Sex

Approximately 1 in 10,000 people develop oral cancers each year. In 90% of the cases, tobacco, poor diet, poor oral hygiene, and alcohol consumption attribute to the cause of these cancers. The International Agency for Research on Cancer conducted a case-control study that involved the recruitment of patients who had cancer of the oral cavity (tongue, lips, gum, palate, and other parts of the mouth) or the oropharynx (the part of the pharynx between the soft palate and the epiglottis), including the tonsils. The study was conducted in nine countries (Italy, Spain, Northern Ireland, Poland, India, Cuba, Canada, Australia, and Sudan) from 1996 to 1999. Cancer and control (i.e., cancer-free) patients were recruited at participating general and cancer hospitals. Control patients did not have a history of oral cancer and were matched at the same hospital locations as the cancer patients by age and gender. A total of 1670 cancer patients and 1732 healthy control subjects participated in the study.

Biopsy specimens and/or exfoliated cells from control subjects were subjected to PCR analysis using primers specific to fourteen HPV high-risk types and six low-risk types. Plasma from patients was collected and tested for antibodies against HPV-16 E6 and E7 proteins in an ELISA assay. Each participant was administered a standardized question-naire by a specially trained interviewer. The survey included questions regarding de-mographics, education, occupation, use of tobacco and alcohol, dietary habits, marital status, disease history, cancer history, oral cavity health, and sexual history (number of lifetime sexual partners, visits to prostitutes, frequency of oral sex).

HPV DNA was detected in 4% of oral cavity biopsy samples and 18% of oropharynx and tonsil biopsy samples. HPV-16 DNA (the strain most often associated with cervical cancer) was found in 95% of the biopsies that tested positive by PCR for HPV DNA. HPV DNA was detected less frequently in tobacco smokers and chewers and more frequently among cancer patients who reported more than one sexual partner or practiced oral sex. Antibodies to HPV-16 proteins were associated with risk for cancers of the oral cavity and the oropharynx. Cancer patients were three times more likely to have antibodies against HPV than healthy control subjects.

The results demonstrate the connection between HPV and oral cancer for which the disease cannot be blamed on decades of smoking and drinking because the patients were too young.

HPV infections are common. About 30% of 25-year-old women in the United States are infected with HPV, and it is thought that about 10% of infections involve high-risk types of HPVs. The prospect of HPV vaccine development offers hope not only for the prevention of cervical and genital cancers, but possibly cancers of the oral cavity and oropharynx as well.

References

Herrero, R. et al. 2003. "Human Papillomavirus and Oral Cancers: The International Agency for Research on Cancer Multicenter Study." *J Nat Cancer Inst* 95(23):1772–1783.

■ Human Papilloma Virus (HPV)

HPV infections are common among sexually active adults and adolescents. Genital HPV infection is one of the most prevalent sexually transmitted diseases of the world today. In an alarming study of college-age women from a state university in New Brunswick, New Jersey, 43% converted from HPV-negative to HPV-positive during their 3-year period of study. High-risk types of HPVs cause cervical cancer. Cervical cancer is a major cause of death among women in developing countries and is the second most common cancer among women worldwide.

Pap (Papanicolaou) smear screening programs have reduced cervical cancer mortalities. Between 1947 and 1984 there was a 70 percent decline in the mortality rate in the United States due to cervical cancer, a reduction that is directly attributed to early detection and removal of the HPV-infected, premalignant tissue. Routine cervical cytological screening in the United States results in the treatment of at least 750,000 women each year for cellular abnormalities suspected to represent possible precancerous lesions.

Pinpointing the cause of cervical cancer has been of interest to epidemiologists and physicians for over 160 years. In 1842, Italian surgeon and amateur epidemiologist D. Rigoni-Stern reported that cancer was about five times higher in Catholic nuns than in other women because of an excess of breast cancer in nuns. He also reported four deaths of nuns from uterine cancer. (At the time, cervical cancer was not distinguishable from uterine cancer.)

Rigoni-Stern studied the death certificates of 74,184 women who died, and found that 1288 of the women were nuns. Ironically, this study was gradually embellished as a nun's tale with invented details. Subsequent authors began reporting that cervical cancer was "rare in nuns and common in prostitutes," suggesting a connection between intercourse and cervical cancer. The idea that cervical cancer was rare among nuns became dogma and most papers regarding the epidemiology of cervical cancer mentioned Rigoni-Stern's study. Subsequent studies followed, but careful review of the literature did not support the dogma that cervical cancer is rare in nuns.

In 1986, Ronald Ostrow and his colleagues reported in the journal *Science* the detection of papillomavirus DNA in human semen. Ostrow's report supported the debate that sexual transmission of HPV DNA could occur via semen. Over the past 20 years, there has been an explosion of research with focused interest on the specific molecular biology of HPVs associated with genital lesions.

Papillomaviruses Are Traditionally Described as Types

At least 118 papillomavirus types have been completely described. The most intensely studied host is humans, but papillomaviruses have been detected from most mammals and birds. Most papillomaviruses cause benign **papillomas** or **warts** in the skin (especially the hands, soles of the feet, and genitals) or mucous membranes (**Figure 10-14**). HPV infection occurs when the skin is damaged in some way, providing the virus with a means of entry.

Nearly 100 HPVs have been described based on the isolation of complete genomes. A database established from 30 years of sequencing information of thousands of papillomavirus isolates has been used to generate a classification system for papillomaviruses. The HPVs have been divided into low-, intermediate-, and high-risk types. High-risk types of HPV are likely to be responsible for a high proportion of carcinomas of the cervix, vulva, vagina, anus, and penis (e.g., types 16 and 18). There is a 4 to 20 year latent period between infection and development of cancer. "Low-risk" types are benign from an oncologist's point of view (e.g., types 6 and 11). The "intermediate-risk" type is used to distinguish HPVs that are frequently found in precancerous lesions but are less often represented in cancers (e.g., types 31, 33, 51, 52, and 83).

Papillomavirus Particle Structure and Genome

Papillomaviruses are small, nonenveloped, icosahedral-shaped dsDNA viruses (**Figure 10-15**). The particles are 52 to 55 nm in diameter. Virus particles contain dsDNA in a circular form that is approximately 8000 base pairs in length (**Figure 10-16**).

HPVs infect stratifying basal epithelial cells. They cannot affect the dermis because those cells are not metabolically active. Viral particles infect the host by entering the basal epithelial cells through a break in the skin. Genome replication, nucleocapsid formation, and virion maturation occur in the nucleus of the epithelial cells (**Figure 10-17**).

(a)

(b)

■ Figure 10-14
(a) Genital warts are a sexually transmitted disease caused by HPVs. This man has venereal warts in the anal region of the perineum. **(b)** This patient has soft, wartlike growths on the penis after 12 hours of postpodphyllin application.

■ Figure 10-15
Computerized three-dimensional reconstruction of a bovine papillomavirus particle. HPV-16 VLP particles are similar. A VLP is an empty particle or shell. VLPs do not contain viral DNA and cannot cause disease.

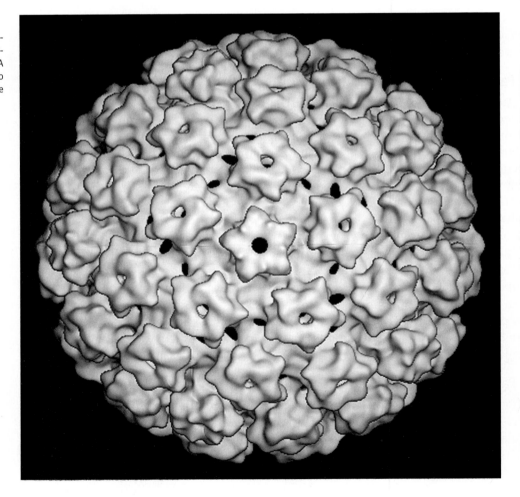

Cervical Cancer: Oncogenesis

HPV-16 (50%), HPV-18 (15%), HPV-45 (8%), and HPV-31 (5%) DNA is found in nearly all cervical cancer cells using PCR for detection. The remaining 22% of the samples contain other high-risk HPV types. **Figure 10-18** illustrates the differences in HPV-16 DNA in benign versus malignant tumors. In part (a) of the figure the HPV genome is maintained as a circular extrachromosal episome in benign tumors. RNAs transcribed from the episome contains a destabilizing sequence (5'AUUUA3'). In part (b), the viral genome in cervical cancer cells is integrated into the host chromosomal DNA (purple). The viral genome is interrupted upstream of the E6/E7 open reading frames. The mRNAs produced from this DNA do not contain the destabilizing sequence. The integrated E6/E7 early genes are overexpressed in cancer cells. The E6 and E7 proteins inactivate the products of tumor suppressor gene products p53 and pRb. This in turn leads to disruption of the normal cell cycle and chromosomal abnormalities.

Even though most women with cervical cancer are over 45 years of age when diagnosed, HPV infection and disease pathogenesis are known to begin at the onset of sexual activity. Pap smear screening is central to treating cervical cancer. Despite widespread screening in the United States, approximately 4100 deaths due to invasive cervical carcinoma were reported in 2002. About 35% of invasive cervical cancers and 57% of deaths occur in the United States in women over the age of 55.

■ Figure 10-16

Genomic map of HPV-16. The circular dsDNA is 7904 base pairs in length. Transcription occurs in a clockwise manner. The opening reading frames are designated E1–E7, L1, and L2. The L1 and L2 gene products make up the capsid or structural proteins of the virus. E5, E6, and E7 code for transforming proteins of HPV-16 (see Table 10-4). Adapted from A. Cann, "Papovaviruses," Course BS335: *Virology*, http://www.tulane.edu/~dmsander/WWW/335/Papovaviruses.html.

HPV Vaccines

Cervical cancer is the third most common cancer in women worldwide. There are an estimated 470,000 new cases and 230,000 deaths every year, and almost 80% of these cases occur in developing countries. Efforts are underway to develop an HPV vaccine that targets high-risk types of HPVs. Clinical trials of preliminary vaccines began in the early 1990s. Ongoing phases II and III vaccine clinical trials have shown positive results against HPV-16 and HPV-18. A 3-year study to test the safety, efficacy, and immunogenicity of a HPV vaccine involving 1113 North American or Brazilian women between the ages of 15 and 25 years was conducted by Diane Harper and colleagues. The women participating had the following traits:

- had 2–5 sexual partners
- most began sexual activity between the ages of 15 and 19
- approximately half were smokers
- tested seronegative for HPV-16 and -18
- tested negative by PCR for HPV-16 and -18 DNA
- had no history of abnormal Pap smears.
- were never treated for genital warts or cervical cancer

The women were immunized at a 0-, 1-, and 6-month schedule with a placebo or bivalent vaccine containing HPV-16/18 viruslike particles (VLPs). VLPs mimic the true structure of HPV virions but do not cause an infection (**Figure 10-19**). All women were required to report for follow-up appointments and Pap smears at 18 months and 27 months postvaccination. Their cervical samples were analyzed via PCR for HPV DNA. In addition to Pap smears, blood was drawn from the patients to assess seroconversion. Women also recorded their symptoms or adverse reactions for the first week after each injected immunization dose.

	KERATINOCYTE DIFFERENTIATION	PAPILLOMAVIRUS REPRODUCTION
Dead cells (metabollically inactive)	**Stratum corneum** Sloughing	Mature virions shed
	Granular layers Nuclear degeneration, cornification Filaggrin: keratin aggregation	Mature virions
	Upper spinous layers Keratins 1 and 10	Virion assembly Late capsid proteins L2 and L1 Vegetative DNA amplification High levels of early and differentiation- dependent proteins, notably E4 Koliocytosis of productive keratinocytes
	Lower spinous layers Keratins 1 and 10	Differentiation-dependent E6 and E7 proteins Early proteins E1, E2, E4 and E5
	Transit amplifying cells Keratins 1 and 10 Frequent cell division	Possible alternative site of infection Immediate early proteins E1, E2 (and E5)
Metabollically active living cells	**Basal stem and reserve cells** Occasional division to replenish transit amplifying cells Keratins 5 and 14	Primary infection Establishment replication Immediate early proteins E1, E2 (and E5)
	Basement Membrane	
	Dermis Connective tissue (collagen), fibroblasts, lymphocytes, vascular endothelium	

Sloughing off

Differentiate

Cells move upward as they divide

■ **Figure 10-17**

Papillomaviruses enter through a break in the skin. The primary site for replication is in the basal and stem cell reserves. These cells are metabolically active and support viral replication. HPVs cannot yet be grown in cell culture because the viral life cycle is tightly linked to epithelial cell differentiation. DNA replication can occur in less differentiated layers of the epidermis, and late protein synthesis and viral packaging can only take place in more differentiated epithelial layers. With the exception of HPV-1, which causes plantar and common warts, most HPV-induced lesions rarely produce large quantities of virus particles. Adapted from B. N. Fields, et al. Fields *Virology,* Fourth Edition. 2 vols. Lippincott Williams & Wilkins, 2001.

■ **Figure 10-18**

(a) Benign tumors contain episomal forms of HPV-16 DNA. **(b)** Malignant cells contain integrated HPV-16 DNA. The integrated DNA contains the E6/E7 HPV genes that are involved in oncogenesis. Adapted from Flint, S. J., et al. *Principles of Virology: Molecular Biology, Pathogenesis, and Control of Animal Viruses,* Second Edition. ASM Press, 2003.

(A)

Extrachromosomal HPV 16 DNA

(B)

Cellular DNA flanking the HPV-16 DNA

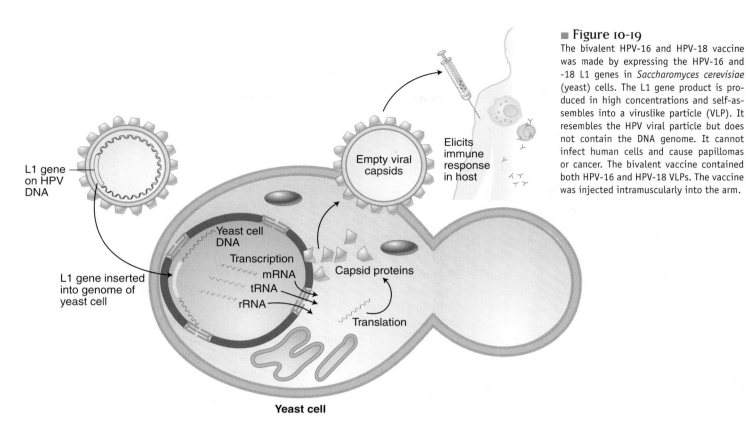

L1 gene
on HPV
DNA

L1 gene inserted
into genome of
yeast cell

Yeast cell
DNA

Transcription
mRNA
tRNA
rRNA

Translation

Capsid proteins

Empty viral
capsids

Elicits
immune
response
in host

Yeast cell

■ **Figure 10-19**
The bivalent HPV-16 and HPV-18 vaccine
was made by expressing the HPV-16 and
-18 L1 genes in *Saccharomyces cerevisiae*
(yeast) cells. The L1 gene product is produced in high concentrations and self-assembles into a viruslike particle (VLP). It
resembles the HPV viral particle but does
not contain the DNA genome. It cannot
infect human cells and cause papillomas
or cancer. The bivalent vaccine contained
both HPV-16 and HPV-18 VLPs. The vaccine
was injected intramuscularly into the arm.

The researchers found the bivalent HPV vaccine to be 100% effective against persistent HPV-16/18 infections. It was 91.6% effective against Pap smear abnormalities associated with HPV-16/18 infection and 100% effective against lesion development. The vaccine was generally safe, well tolerated, and highly immunogenic. These results suggest that vaccinations against HPV-16/18 could reduce the incidence of cervical cancer.

Should both women and men be vaccinated? The general assumption is that men and boys should be vaccinated because they act as vectors for infection. Al V. Taira and colleagues evaluated the benefit and cost-effectiveness of adopting a vaccine strategy for both sexes. Their results, which were published in the Centers for Disease Control and Prevention (CDC's) *EID* journal, suggested that vaccinating a cohort of 12-year-old females against HPV-16/18 would reduce cervical cancer cases by 61.8%. If male participants were vaccinated as well it would reduce cervical cancer cases by an additional 2.2%. Thus female vaccination was generally considered cost-effective, whereas male vaccination was not. Clinical trials and vaccine development are in progress. If these advances continue the majority of the next generation of girls may be spared this deadly form of cancer.

A survey of 278 parents conducted by Gregory Zimet and colleagues asked if they were willing to vaccinate their adolescent children against organisms that caused sexually transmitted diseases (STDs). Their results, which indicated that parents were receptive to the idea of vaccinating their children against STDs, were reported in the February 2005 issue of *Archives of Pediatric and Adolescent Medicine*.

An inactivated HPV vaccine manufactured by Merck GARDASIL was licensed by the FDA in 2006. The CDC highly recommends that girls aged 11 to 12 (in general, before their first sexual contact) be vaccinated. The goal of this vaccine is to reduce the incidence of cervical cancer. Several states are mandating the vaccine; however, its acceptance is uncertain. At the time of this writing, 84 adverse reactions have been reported to the National Vaccine Information Center.

10.6 Animal DNA Tumor Viruses

Adenoviruses and some of the polyomaviruses (such as SV-40) induce tumors in experimental animal systems but not in humans. All three of these viruses are DNA tumor viruses. They transform cells at a frequency of less than 1 in 100,000 infected cells.

■ Adenoviruses

Adenoviruses were isolated from human adenoids of children by Rowe and colleagues in 1953. At the time Rowe was searching for different tissues in which to propagate polioviruses. Soon it was discovered that adenoviruses could be isolated from every species of mammals, birds, and amphibians, and it became evident that adenoviruses could persist in lymphoid tissues for many years. Approximately 50% to 80% of tonsils that are surgically removed are infected with adenoviruses.

Certain human adenoviruses cause malignant tumors in baby rodents, such as hamsters and mice. Two adenovirus genes, E1A and E1B, are responsible for oncogenic transformation of rodent cell lines. E1A inactivates the tumor suppressor gene product pRb and E1B inactivates the tumor suppressor protein p53. Despite the potent oncogenic properties of some human adenoviruses in animals and tissue culture cells, the virus has not been linked to any human cancers. Subsequently, it was discovered that adenoviruses cause respiratory tract, GI tract, and eye infections, including highly contagious conjunctivitis ("pink eye") in humans. Respiratory epidemics of adenovirus are often prevalent on army bases. Adenovirus infections are also common in the immune-compromised, such as AIDS patients.

By 1989, 47 human adenoviruses had been identified. Most individuals are infected with one or more types of adenoviruses before the age of 15. Direct contact, respiratory droplets, or ingestion spreads adenovirus infections. Most infected persons are asymptomatic. There is no specific antiviral treatment for those individuals experiencing symptoms. In rare cases, ribavirin is used to treat adenovirus infections.

Adenoviruses are 80 nm in diameter and of icosahedral symmetry. The capsid is composed of three different major proteins—hexon, penton-base, and a knobbed fiber—in addition to a number of minor proteins (**Figure 10-20**). The viral genome is a linear, dsDNA that is approximately 36–38 kilobase pairs in length for mammalian adenoviruses. The genome contains inverted repeats at its ends. Adenoviruses are a prime candidate as gene-therapy vectors because they cause mild diseases in humans and they deliver their genome to the nucleus where it can replicate with high efficiency). Adenoviruses can infect a wide variety of tissues such as lung, brain, pancreas, thyroid, heart, and skeletal muscle. Over the past decade, adenoviruses have been genetically manipulated to manage cancers, cardiovascular disease, genetic disorders, and eye diseases. Specifically, developments in adenovirus gene therapy directed at managing metastatic thyroid cancer, pancreatic adenocarcinoma, late-stage prostrate cancer, brain gliomas, and HCC are ongoing. In addition to cancer therapy, adenovirus-based vectors are promising vehicles for cystic fibrosis gene therapy and as an accompanying therapy to glaucoma filtration surgery.

Glaucoma is a blinding eye disease characterized by abnormally high intraocular fluid pressure of the eye. It can result in a damaged optic disk, hardening of the eyeball, and complete loss of vision. The goal of the glaucoma filtration procedure is to create a new passageway by which aqueous fluid inside the eye can escape, thereby lowering the intraocular pressure. A complication of this surgery is unwanted side effects such as controlling unwanted wound healing after the glaucoma filtrations surgery. A general schematic of adenovirus therapy is shown in **Figure 10-21**.

■ **Figure 10-20**

Transmission electron micrograph of adenoviruses in patient sample showing the penton fibers. Magnification is 40,000×.

Upon closer scrutiny of adenovirus gene therapy systems, it has become evident that some technical problems and potential side effects in the patient do exist; for example, the adenovirus genes do not integrate into the host chromosome; therefore the therapeutic genes do not persist for very long in cells. To overcome this, an improved adeno-transposon vector aimed toward efficiently integrating into the host chromosome has been developed.

When high doses of the vector are used, it causes an acute immune response. The first victim of an acute immune response was Jesse Gelsinger (see Chapter 9). During adenovirus infections, there is a well-orchestrated immune response to suppress the virus during the course of infection. This response is also effective against the vector. It has become increasingly important to unravel the complex molecular events involved in mounting the host defenses.

■ **Figure 10-21**

Adenovirus gene therapy. Adenovirues fuse with the host membrane by binding to CAR (a cell surface *coxsackie-ad-enovirus* cell surface *receptor*) and internalize into endosomes using cellular integrins. At some stage thereafter, the viral components are released and they are targeted to the nucleus of the cell. Adapted from Baker, A. H., *Heart and Metabolism* 18 (2002): 28–35.

■ Simian Virus-40 (SV-40)

In 1960 simian vacuolating virus-40 (SV-40) was isolated from primary African green monkey kidney cells by Sweet and Hilleman during safety testing of the poliovirus vaccine. They observed that the SV-40 infected cells showed distinctive morphological changes (vacuolization). Prior to this SV-40 escaped detection because rhesus or cynomolgus monkey kidney cells were used to prepare the vaccine. SV-40 did not cause any observable cytopathic effects in the rhesus or cynomolgus monkey kidney cells and was a frequent contaminant of the rhesus macaque kidney cell culture cells (**Virus File 10-4**).

SV-40 is a polyomavirus. Two other polymomaviruses have been found in humans: Jamestown Canyon virus (JCV) and BK virus (BKV). Both JCV and BKV cause tumors in animals and in about 5% of AIDS patients. The focus in this chapter will be on SV-40.

Polyomaviruses have small, simple circular dsDNA genomes (e.g., the SV-40 genome is 5.2 kb in length). The SV-40 viral particle is nonenveloped, measures 45 nm in diameter, and consists of three different capsid proteins (**Figure 10-22a**). SV-40 enters cells by binding to the major histocompatibility complex class I molecules (MHC; see Chapter 7). The virion enters through endocytosis mediated via invaginations called caveolae ("little caves"). Caveolin proteins are integral membrane proteins present within the caveolae that facilitate endocytosis. The virion is transported to the endoplasmic reticulum and enters it, and subsequently the viral genome enters the nucleus of the cell.

The SV-40 genome consists of two sets of genes: the early expressed genes, which encode viral gene products essential for viral replication such as large and small T antigens, and a 17KT protein. A set of late genes encodes the structural proteins necessary for viral assembly. This includes the three capsid proteins (VP1, VP2, VP3) and a maturation protein called agnoprotein. The genome also contains regulatory sequences that are not translated, such as an origin of replication (ORI), promoters and enhancer sequences for replication. DNA replication is bidirectional, starting at the ORI (**Figures 10-22b** and **23**).

SV-40 is of monkey origin. Its natural host is the Asian macaque (*Macaca mulatta*). It infects several species of monkeys in captivity, but typically does not cause symptoms or disease in them. The virus is presumably spread via contaminated urine. It is also able to infect and cause sarcomas in hamsters. For this reason, much attention has focused on the viral oncogenes of SV-40: large and small T antigens.

Large T antigen is a large, multifunctional protein that is involved in a number of cellular processes including transcriptional activation and repression, differentiation, and the stimulation of the cell cycle. Large T antigen interacts with the cellular tumor suppressor p53 and pRb, whereas small T antigen interacts with a cellular phosphatase, PP2A. In doing so, these viral proteins disrupt the p53 and pRb cellular pathways, inactivating cell

The Obesity Viruses: SMAM-1 and Adenovirus-36

During the past 20 years there has been a dramatic increase in obesity in the United States. In 1991, four U.S. states had obesity rates of 15% to 19% and no states had rates at or above 20%. In 2003, 15 states had rates of 15% to 19%, 31 states had rates of 20% to 24%, and four states had rates of more than 25%. Today 30% of U.S. adults 20 years of age and older—over 60 million people—are obese. The increasing obesity trends among U.S. adults raises concern because being overweight or obese increases the risk of many diseases and health conditions, such as hypertension, Type 2 diabetes, stroke, heart disease, sleep apnea, respiratory problems, and certain cancers (e.g., breast, colon, and endometrial).

There are likely to be many causes of obesity. Animal obesity has been attributed to nutritional, environmental, genetic, seasonal, endocrine, pharmacological, or viral origin. The focus of obesity studies has been on the genetic and behavioral components of obesity.

An infectious cause of obesity has received little attention. Over the past 20 years, though, six different infectious agents have been reported to cause obesity in animals (Table VF 10-1). It is not known whether these six pathogens contribute to obesity in humans. Two of them, however—SMAM-1 (a chicken adenovirus) and human adenovirus 36—have been associated with human obesity. For ethical reasons, the definitive experiment of injecting humans with these adenoviruses to determine a causal role for this virus in human obesity is not possible.

SMAM-1 is an avian adenovirus that caused high mortality in poultry during epidemics in India in the 1980s. Adenovirus 36 can infect chickens and humans and induce adiposity in chickens. The virus was first isolated in 1978 from a diabetic child in Germany. Obese and nonobese volunteers from Wisconsin, Florida, and New York provided serum samples, which were then screened for the presence of SMAM-1 or

TABLE VF 10-1	Obesity Observed in Animals Injected with Viruses or Prion Agents		
Virus/ Infectious Agent	**Obesity Observed in These Animal Model(s) after Injection with the Virus**	**Obesity Observations**	**Obesity Mechanism**
Canine distemper virus	Mice Chickens	Body weight; fat cell size and number increases; 26% of surviving mice are obese	Down regulation of leptin receptor
Rous-associated virus-7	Chickens	Fat deposition around crop and abdominal fat pads of birds	No proposed molecular mechanism
Borna disease virus	Rats	Rats that survive are obese	Hypothalamic damage
Scrapie agent	Mice Hamsters	Obesity observed in hamsters	Hypothalamic-pituitary adrenal problem
SMAM-1 avian adenovirus	Chickens	Develop excessive visceral fat	No proposed molecular mechanism
Human adenovirus-36	Chickens Mice Monkeys	Increased adipose tissue	No proposed molecular mechanism

adenovirus 36 antibodies. Results of these human studies showed that 5% of nonobese individuals possessed adenovirus 36 antibodies, whereas 30% of the obese individuals were antibody-positive. In another study, 20% of 52 obese individuals screened tested positive for SMAM-1 antibodies. These data show an association of SMAM-1 and adenovirus 36 antibodies with human obesity, but they do not establish a causal relationship.

A U.S. firm has developed the technology to test humans for adenovirus 36 antibodies. A positive test means that a person has been exposed to adenovirus 36 and the infection may contribute to difficulties in maintaining a healthy weight. Nonobese individuals who test positive for antibodies may be at risk for developing obesity. They should develop proper eating and exercise habits (**Figure VF 10-2**). An

■ **Figure VF 10-2**
Exercise plays an important role in weight loss and maintenance.

adequate understanding of viral infection as an etiological factor is needed for better management of obesity. For certain individuals, it may be possible one day to prevent or treat obesity of infectious origin.

References

Atkinson, R. L. et al. 2005. "Human Adenovirus-36 Is Associated with Increased Body Weight and Paradoxical Reduction of Serum Lipids." *Int J Obesity* 29:281–286.

Dhurandhar, N. V. 2001. "Infectobesity: Obesity of Infectious Origin." *J Nutrition* 2794S–2797S.

Dhurandhar, N.V. et al. 2000. "Increased Adiposity in Animals due to a Human Virus." *Int J Obesity* 24:989–996.

Dhurandhar, N. V. et al. 2002. "Human Adenovirus Ad-36 Promotes Weight Gain in Male Rhesus and Marmoset Monkeys." *J Nutrition* 132:3155–3160.

(a)

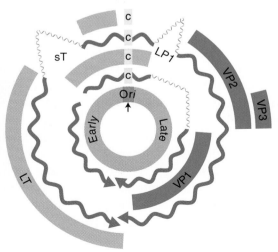

(b)

■ **Figure 10-22**
(a) Specimen containing SV-40 particles, which are nonenveloped. The specimen contains three capsid proteins VP1-3. **(b)** SV-40 genome. SV-40 has a dsDNA circular genome that is 5 kbp in length. Within particles, the DNA is supercoiled like a plasmid. There are four histone proteins associated with the DNA: H2A, H2B, H3, and H4. The genome consists of six genes. This is achieved by such a small genome because some genes overlap. Adapted from A. Cann, "Papovaviruses," Course BS335: *Virology,* http://www.tulane.edu/~dmsander/WWW/335/Papovaviruses.html.

The SV-40 Controversy: Passenger or Emerging Pathogen? Will an SV-40 Large T Antigen Vaccine Become Routine?

Natural infection by SV-40 in humans was thought to be rare. Inhabitants of Indian villages located close to a jungle, living in close contact with monkeys, and zookeepers or persons working at animal facilities that house monkeys were considered at risk. Unfortunately, SV-40 virus entered the human population by contaminated poliovirus vaccines produced between 1955 and 1963. Before 1963, 90% of children and 60% of adults received one or more contaminated vaccinations from which federal regulations required poliovirus vaccines to be free of contamination. Millions of people in the United States, Canada, Europe, Asia, and Africa received the contaminated poliovirus vaccine (**Figure VF 10-3**). Adenovirus vaccines used from 1961 to 1965 for U.S. military personnel carried infectious adenovirus SV-40 hybrids that contained sequences of the SV-40 genome, including the DNA sequence of the large T antigen gene.

■ **Figure VF 10-3**
Photograph showing people standing in line at a polio immunization station outside a local grocery store in Columbus, Georgia, in 1961. It is likely that many of the vaccinees received a SV-40 contaminated poliovirus vaccine.

To this day SV-40 is not known to cause any specific human disease. It can, however, infect human cells in culture and transform some of them. It is known that children who received the contaminated oral poliovirus vaccine excreted poliovirus in their stools for at least five weeks following vaccination, indicating that replication of SV-40 virus occurs in people vaccinated with oral SV-40 contaminated vaccines and opens up its possibility for oral–fecal transmission. Viral DNA sequences have been detected in blood and sperm specimens from cancer patients and normal individuals. SV-40 viruses have been found in urine and sewage samples. Antibodies to SV-40 capsid proteins were found in human sera, and SV-40 sequences have been detected in people who are too old or too young to have been associated with SV-40 contaminated poliovirus vaccines—suggesting horizontal transmission (person to person).

Is there an association between SV-40 and human diseases? There is considerable debate in the scientific community. Numerous reports discuss the association between SV-40 in humans who have inflammatory kidney diseases or rare tumors such as malignant mesothelioma, non-Hodgkin's lymphoma, and brain and bone tumors. SV-40 sequences are usually detected in an episomal state in tumors and rarely as integrated into the chromosome of tumor cells. Infectious SV-40 virus particles have been isolated from brain tumors. When SV-40 was injected into hamsters, the same type of cancers are produced as in humans (such as lymphomas, bone cancer, and malignant mesothelioma).

The National Cancer Institute (NCI) conducted studies to determine the possible association between SV-40 exposure and non-Hodgkin's lymphoma. In 2004, they reported no statistical association between the virus and non-Hodgkin's lymphoma. NCI researchers also evaluated the cancer risk in 54,796 U.S. children whose mothers received contaminated poliovirus vaccines during pregnancy. The scientists hypothesized that their children would be at increased risk for SV-40 associated cancers because of SV-40 mother-to-child transmission. They also studied 254 zoo workers exposed to monkeys at work. All of the NCI studies published in 2004 concluded that there is no substantial evidence to indicate that SV-40 causes cancer in humans.

Scientists who believe that SV-40 is associated with rare cancers and kidney disease suggest that the mechanism of tumorigenesis in humans is related to the two viral oncoproteins, the large and small T antigens. The possibility that SV-40 may be a cofactor in the cause of some human tumors has stimulated the preparation of a vaccine against large T antigen. Such a vaccine may serve as a useful intervention against SV-40 associated cancers in the future.

References

Barbanti-Brodano, G. L. et al. 2004. "Simian Virus 40 Infection in Humans and Association with Human Diseases: Results and Hypotheses." *Virology* 318(1):1–9.

Engels, E. A., and Chen, J. 2004. "Poliovirus Vaccination during Pregnancy, Maternal Seroconversion to Simian Virus 40, and Risk of Childhood Cancer." *Am J Epidemiol* 160(4):306–316.

Engels, E. A., Viscidi, R. P., et al. 2004. "Case-Control Study of Simian Virus 40 and Non-Hodgkin Lymphoma in the United States." *J Natl Cancer Inst* 96(18):1368–1374.

Engels, E. A., Viscidi, R. P., et al. 2004. "Serological Evidence for Exposure to Simian Virus 40 in North American Zoo Workers." *J Infect Dis* 190(12):2065–2069.

Gazdar, A. F., Butel, J. S., and Carbone, M. 2002. "SV40 and Human Tumours: Myth, Association or Causality?" *Nat Rev* 2:957–964.

Vilchez, R. A., and Butel, J. S. 2004. "Emergent Human Pathogen Simian Virus 40 and Its Role in Cancer." *Clin Microbiol Rev* 17(3):495–508.

cycle control. This in turn can lead to cellular transformation, the blocking of apoptosis, and the stimulation of cell division.

Large T antigen is controlled by phosphorylation. In the life cycle of SV-40, it functions as a replicative helicase (unwinding the genome at the ORI and promoter). It also recruits DNA replication proteins such as topoisomerase, replication protein A, and DNA polymerases to the ORI and promoter site of replication. It indirectly promotes the activation of late transcription and plays a role in viral maturation by influencing the phosphorylation of capsid proteins. Small T antigen plays a role in the lytic life cycle of the virus.

Summary

Cancer develops when cells in a part of the body begin to grow out of control. Normal body cells grow, divide, and die in an orderly fashion. During the early years of a person's life, normal cells divide more rapidly until the person becomes an adult. After that, cells in most parts of the body divide only to replace worn-out or dying cells and to repair injuries. Humans have suffered from cancer throughout history. Hippocrates was the first to describe tumors and coin the term carcinoma.

During the late 1700s, connections between occupation, environment, and the onset of cancer were drawn. Early cancer biology research began in the 1900s. The discovery that a filterable agent (the retrovirus Rous sarcoma virus) caused a leukemia common in chickens suggested that cancer could be an "infectious disease." As molecular biology began to advance, evidence from several laboratories demonstrated that RSV contained a

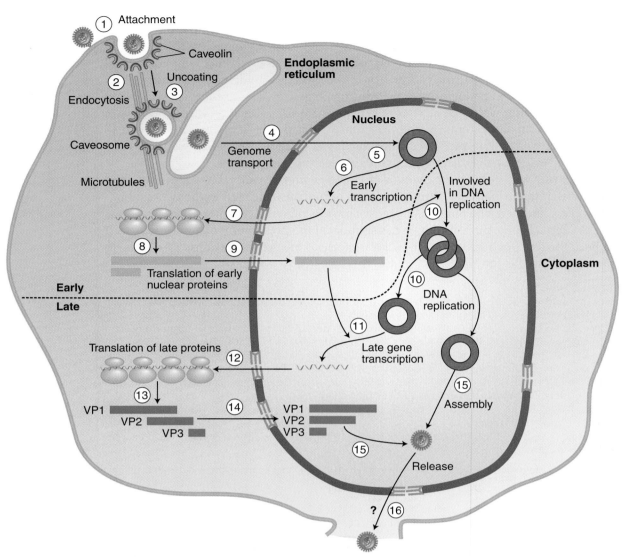

■ **Figure 10-23**
Replication cycle of SV-40. Adapted from Flint, S. J., et al. *Principles of Virology: Molecular Biology, Pathogenesis, and Control of Animal Viruses,* Second Edition. ASM Press, 2003.

gene—*src*—that was involved in the oncogenic transformation of cells. The term oncogene was coined for a tumor-causing gene.

In 1976, an elegant experiment performed by Michael J. Bishop, Harold Varmus, and colleagues showed that the *src* oncogene had a cellular counterpart. They proposed that viruses hijacked cellular genes. Today it is known that oncogenes exist throughout the chromosome of humans. Their gene products function as cytokines, receptors, protein kinases, G-proteins, transcription factors, and other nuclear proteins that regulate cell growth.

Approximately 15% of all human cancers are associated with viruses. HBV, HCV, HPV, EBV, KSHV, and HTLV types 1 and 2 contribute to cancers. Eighty percent of the viral-associated cancers are cervical cancers caused by high-risk types of HPV and liver cancer that is caused by HBV and HCV.

Transformed cells undergo phenotypic, genetic, and metabolic changes when grown in culture. The cells become immortalized, undergoing a loss of cell cycle control. Cell surfaces may change in membrane structure and function and tumor-associated carbohydrate antigens are expressed. The cells display the loss of the need for adhesion, resulting in anchorage-independent growth. When transformed cells are injected into immune deficient nude mice, they may produce tumors.

When cancer cells of tumors are observed *in vivo*, their properties are somewhat similar to that seen in transformed cells in culture. These cells show an increase in telomerase activity and increased levels of enzymes involved in nucleic acid synthesis and lytic enzymes. The DNA of the cells exhibit altered methylation patterns. The cells divide out of control in part due to the loss of tumor suppressor gene function. The cancer cells escape the immunosurveillance response. The tumors arise from a series of events that lead to greater loss of the regulation of cell division.

DNA or RNA tumor viruses are associated with cancer. Retroviruses are RNA tumor viruses that encode reverse transcriptase, an enzyme that is involved in the complex process that converts RNA into DNA. Retroviruses contain at least three genes: *gag*, *pol*, and *env*, in addition to repetitive sequences (LTRs) located at the ends of the genome. Some retroviruses contain an additional gene, an oncogene referred to as *v-onc*. *V-onc* genes are capable of inducing cellular transformation. They are not essential for viral replication. Instead, the *v-onc* gene was hijacked from the genome of its host during the course of evolution.

Retroviruses can cause cancer via the integration of a provirus into the host's genome if it integrates within or near a cellular oncogene (*c-onc*). Provirus integration may result in the insertional inactivation of a cellular tumor suppressor gene, resulting in uncontrolled cell division. If the retrovirus contains a *v-onc*, it may become activated and transcribed, coding for the oncogenic product. The *v-onc* may be a mutated form of a *c-onc* that interferes with cellular signaling involved in growth, promoting growth and cell division at inappropriate times during the cell cycle. Lists of *c-onc*, cellular tumor suppressor genes, *v-onc* genes, and their functions are found in Tables 10-1, -2, and -3, respectively.

Approximately 8% of the human genome contains sequence similarity to infectious retroviruses. These sequences are termed human endogenous retroviruses (HERVs). HERVs contain the easily recognized *gag*, *pol*, *env*, and LTRs. Despite intense efforts, there is little direct evidence to support the claim that HERVs are etiological cofactors in chronic diseases such as cancer. Two human retroviruses have been implicated in human cancers: HTLV-1 causes adult T-cell leukemia, and HTLV-2 is associated with T-cell malignancies.

DNA tumor viruses are a diverse group of viruses with different structures, genome organization, and replication strategies. Some induce tumors in humans, such as EBV, KSHV, HPV, and HBV. Others induce tumors in experimental animals, such as adenovirus and SV-40. Most of the oncogenes of DNA tumor viruses are essential viral replication genes in contrast to the oncogenes of retroviruses that are cellular counterparts. DNA tumor viruses inactivate tumor suppressor gene products of the host such as p53 and pRb. The oncogenic potential of DNA tumor viruses is relatively low. In general, most cancers caused by DNA tumor viruses occur when cells are persistently infected for years.

Burkitt's lymphoma (BL) is an aggressive childhood B-cell lymphoma that is prevalent in central Africa. It is characterized by a rapidly growing tumor in the jaw bones, orbital region, or abdomen. BL is intimately associated with EBV infection. The precise mechanism by which the virus transforms B cells is still uncertain.

Kaposi's sarcoma is a rare skin cancer that is caused by KSHV (also known as human herpes virus 8). The mRNAs of latent viral genes are found in Kaposi's sarcoma tumor cells. KSHV has a large genome that codes for more than 80 genes. Of these 80 genes, three of them encode cellular homologs involved in growth regulation and may play a role in cellular transformation.

HCC or liver cancer is the fifth most common cancer in the world. HBV (a dsDNA virus) and HCV (a ssRNA virus) both cause chronic hepatitis that can progress to cirrhosis and HCC. Despite their genome and replication strategy differences, they share common characteristics in the mechanisms of chronic liver diseases and their association with HCC.

HPV infections are common among sexually active adults and adolescents. High-risk types of HPVs cause cancer of the cervix, vulva, vagina, anus, and penis. HPV is a small DNA tumor virus that infects basal epithelial cells through a break in the skin. It takes years for HPV lesions to become cancerous. Benign papillomas contain an episomal form of the viral genome. Malignant HPV papillomas contain integrated viral E6/E7 oncogenes into the host chromosome.

Adenoviruses and some of the polyomaviruses (e.g., SV-40) cause tumors in experimental animals such as hamsters or other rodents. Adenovirus causes mild diseases of the respiratory tract, gastrointestinal tract, and conjunctivitis ("pink eye") in humans. Adenoviruses can cause severe respiratory epidemics in military barracks. From the early 1960s until 1995, U.S. military recruits were vaccinated against adenovirus types that caused febrile (fever) respiratory infections. Adenoviruses have been prime candidates as gene therapy vectors because they can package many additional genes. The major technical issue that needs to be addressed is the control of an acute immune response against the viral vector. If this can be achieved, it will improve its effectiveness as a therapeutic and reduce side effects.

SV-40 is a small dsDNA virus that was discovered as a contaminant of African green monkey kidney cells in culture. It causes tumors in hamsters that correlate to rare tumors of the lung, brain, bone, and lymphomas in humans. The SV-40 genome contains two sets of genes: expressed during early or late times post-infection. The oncogenic properties of SV-40 have been mapped to the large and small T antigen genes. Large T antigen disrupts the function of cellular p53 and pRb tumor suppressor genes. Small T antigen interacts with a cellular phosphatase PP2A.

Cancer is a multistep process. Viruses are thought to be co-carcinogens in the development of human tumors. The relative simplicity of the viral genome (compared to the enormous complexity of the cellular genetic material) has permitted the identification of genes involved in the genesis of human cancer.

■ Resources

■ Primary Literature and Reviews

Barbanti-Brodano, G. et al. 2004. "Simian Virus 40 Infection in Humans and Association with Human Diseases: Results and Hypotheses." *Virology* 318(1):1–9.

Block, T. M. et al. 2003. "Molecular Viral Oncology of Hepatocellular Carcinoma." *Oncogene* 22(33):5093–5107.

Boch, F. X. et al. 2004. "Primary Liver Cancer: Worldwide Incidence and Trends."*Gastroenterology* 127(5 Suppl. 1):S5–S16.

Chen, H. L. 1996. "Seroepidemiology of Hepatitis B Virus Infection in Children: Ten Years of Mass Vaccination in Taiwan." *JAMA* 276(11):906–908.

Cheng-Liang, L. et al. 2003. "Trends in the Incidence of Hepatocellular Carcinoma in Boys and Girls in Taiwan after Large-Scale Hepatitis B Vaccination." *Cancer Epidemiol Biomarkers Prev* 12:57–59.

Centers for Disease Control and Prevention, 2007. "Quadrivalent Human Papillomavirus Vaccine." *MMWR* 56:1–24.

Cohen, J., and Powderly, W. G., eds. 2004. *Infectious Diseases*, 2nd ed. St. Louis: Mosby.

Costas, J. 2002. "Characterization of the Intragenomic Spread of the Human Endogenous Retrovirus Family HERV-W." *Mol Biol Evol* 19(4):526–533.

Engels, E. A., Viscidi, R. P., et al. 2004. "Case-Control Study of Simian Virus 40 and Non-Hodgkin Lymphoma in the United States." *J Natl Cancer Inst* 96(18): 1368–1374.

Engels, E. A., and Chen, J. 2004. "Poliovirus Vaccination during Pregnancy, Maternal Seroconversion to Simian Virus 40, and Risk of Childhood Cancer." *Am J Epidemiol* 160(4):306–316.

Engels, E. A., and Viscidi, R. P., et al. 2004. "Serological Evidence for Exposure to Simian Virus 40 in North American Zoo Workers." *J Infect Dis* 190(12): 2065–2069.

Flint, S. J., Enquist, L. W., Racaniello, V. R., and Skalka, A. M., eds. 2004. *Principles of Virology: Molecular Biology, Pathogenesis, and Control of Animal Viruses,* 2nd ed. Washington, DC: ASM Press.

Gazdar, A. F., Butel, J. S., and Carbone, M. 2002. "SV40 and Human Tumours: Myth, Association or Causality?" *Nat Rev* 2:957–964.

Griffiths, D. J. 2001. "Endogenous Retroviruses in the Human Genome Sequence." *Genome Biol* 2(6):1017.1–1017.5.

Griffiths, M. 1991. "Nuns, Virgins, and Spinsters': Rigoni-Stern and Cervical Cancer Revisited." *Br J Obstet Gynaecol* 98:797–802.

Harper, D. M. et al. 2004. "Efficacy of a Bivalent L1 Virus-Like Particle Vaccine in Prevention of Infection with Human Papillomavirus Pypes 16 and 18 in Young Women: A Randomized Controlled Trial." *Lancet* 364:1757–1765.

Herrero, R. et al. 2003. "Human Papillomavirus and Oral Cancer: The International Agency for Research on Cancer Multicenter Study." *J Natl Cancer Inst* 95(23):1772–1783.

Karlsson, H. et al. 2001. "Retroviral RNA Identified in the Cerebrospinal Fluids and Brains of Individuals with Schizophrenia." *PNAS USA* 98(8):4634–4639.

Knipe, D. M., and Howley, P. M., eds. 2001. *Fundamental Virology,* 4th ed. Philadelphia: Lippincott Williams & Wilkins.

Lewis, D. A. 2001. "Retroviruses and the Pathogenesis of Schizophrenia." *PNAS USA* 98(8):4293–4294.

Lopez-Rios, F. et al. 2004. "Evidence Against a Role for SV40 Infection in Human Mesotheliomas and High Risk of False-Positive PCR Results Owing to Presence of SV40 Common Sequences in Common Laboratory Plasmids." *Lancet* 364: 1157–1166.

Machida, K. et al. 2004. "Hepatitis C Virus Induces a Mutator Phenotype: Enhanced Mutations of Immunoglobin and Protooncogenes." *PNAS USA* 101(12): 4262–4267.

Meiering, C. D., and Linial, M. L. 2001. "Historical Perspective of Foamy Virus Epidemiology and Infection." *Clin Microbiol Rev* 14(1):165–176.

Meyers, C., and Laimins, L. A. 1994. "*In Vitro* Systems for the Study and Propagation of Human Papillomaviruses." *Curr Top Microbiol Immunol* 186:199–215.

Munger, K. et al. 2004. "Mechanisms of Human Papillomavirus-Induced Oncogenesis." *J Virol* 78(21):11451–11460.

Nakamura, A. et al. 2003. "Human Endogenous Retroviruses with Transcriptional Potential in the Brain." *J Hum Genet* 48(11):575–581.

Ostrow, R. S. et al. 1986. "Detection of Papillomavirus DNA in Human Semen." *Science* 23:731–733.

Poiesz, B. J., Poiesz, M. J., and Choi, D. 2003. "The Human T-Cell Lymphoma/ Leukemia Viruses." *Cancer Invest* 21(2):253–277.

Rui-Mei, L. et al. 2002. "Molecular Identification of SV40 Infection in Human Subjects and Possible Association with Kidney Disease." *J Am Soc Nephrol* 13:2320–2330.

Russel, W. C. 2000. "Update on Adenovirus and Its Vectors." *J Gen Virol* 81: 2573–2604.

Skrabanek, P. 1988. "Cervical Cancer in Nuns and Prostitutes: A Plea for Scientific Continence." *J Clin Epidemiol* 41(6):577–582.

Steinbrook, R. 2006. "The Potential of Human Papillomavirus Vaccines." *N Engl J Med* 354(11):1109–1112.

Taira, A. V. et al. 2004. "Evaluating Human Papillomavirus Vaccination Programs." *EID* 10(11):1915–1923.

Vilchez, R. A., and Butel, J. S. 2004. "Emergent Human Pathogen Simian Virus 40 and Its Role in Cancer." *Clin Microbiol Rev* 17(3):495–508.

Zimet, G. et al. 2005. "Parental Attitudes About Sexually Transmitted Infection Vaccination for Their Adolescent Children." *Arch Pediatr Adolesc Med* 159:132–137.

Zimmer, C. 2001. "Do Chronic Diseases Have An Infectious Root?" *Science* 293: 1974–1977.

■ Popular Press

Bookchin, D., and Schumacher, J. 2004. *The Virus and the Vaccine: The True Story of a Cancer-Causing Monkey Virus, Contaminated Polio Vaccine, and the Millions Exposed*, New York: St. Martin's Press.

Crawford, D. H. 2005. "An Introduction to Viruses and Cancer." *Microbiology Today*, August 5:110–112.

Ewald, P. W. 2002. *Plague Time: The New Germ Theory of Disease*, New York: Anchor Books.

Gallo, R. 1991. *Virus Hunting, Aids, Cancer & The Human Retrovirus: A Story of Scientific Discovery*, New York: Basic Books.

Higley, T. L. 2005. *Retrovirus* (mass-market fiction), Uhrichsville, OH: Barbour.

Rosenberg, S. A., and Barry, J. M. 1992. *The Transformed Cell: Unlocking the Mysteries of Cancer*, New York: Avon Books.

Weinberg, R. A. 1999. *One Renegade Cell (Science Masters)*, New York: Basic Books.

■ Video Productions

Hepatitis C: The Silent Scourge. 1995. Films for the Humanities.

Hepatitis B: The Enemy Within. 1996. Films for the Humanities.

Great Minds of Science: Viruses. 1997. Films for the Humanities.

Sexually Transmitted Diseases: The Silent Epidemic. 2000. Films for the Humanities.

Fighting Hepatitis C. 2001. Films for the Humanities.

Trial and Error: The Rise and Fall of Gene Therapy. 2003. BBCW Production.

■ eLearning

http://biology.jbpub.com/book/virology

The site features eLearning, an online review area that provides quizzes and other tools to help you study for your class. You can also follow useful links for in-depth information, or just find out the latest virology and microbiology news.

II.2   The History of Polio

The discovery of the 18th dynasty (1500 B.C.) Egyptian stele described in Chapter 1, which shows a priest with a shriveled leg characteristic of the flaccid (i.e., limp, weak, and lacking muscle tone) paralysis or "foot drop" typical of poliomyelitis, is evidence that this disease has a long history. Paralytic disease did not appear to be a significant problem until outbreaks began in northern Europe in the late 1800s, when reports of polio epidemics of a notable size began to appear intermittently (**Figure II-I**). From that time on, the disease was reported seasonally (peaking in the summer months in temperate climates) and epidemics occurred more often in industrialized countries. In 1916, the United States faced one of the worst polio epidemics of the 20th century, when polio killed 6000 people and paralyzed an additional 27,000. New York City was faced with so many cases that city

1789	British physician Michael Underwood describes polio
1887	Medin describes polio outbreak in Stockholm, Sweden
1894	First major outbreak in U.S. (132 cases in Vermont)
1908	K. Landsteiner and E. Popper showed that a filterable agent caused poliomyelitis in monkey animal model
1916	Large outbreak of polio in the U.S. Over 9000 cases reported in NYC alone; disease killed 6000 and paralyzed 27,000
1921	FDR contracts polio and suffers severe paralysis
1928	Philip Drinker and Louis Shaw invent the Drink Respirator (iron lung)
1932	FDR elected President of the U.S.
1934	Major outbreak of polio in Los Angeles: ~2500 cases from May–November
1942	The first Sister Kenny Institute opens in Minneapolis
1945	WWII ends; many U.S. polio outbreaks result in 20,000 cases/year (1945–1949)
1952	58,000 cases of polio in the U.S., Salk killed vaccine testing begins
1953	35,000 cases of polio in the U.S.
1954	Salk killed vaccine field trial sponsored by the National Foundation for Infantile Paralysis
1955	Nationwide vaccination program begins
1958–1959	Field trials of Sabin oral live vaccine
1961	Sabin vaccine approved for use
1964	Only 121 cases of polio in the U.S.
1979	Multistate polio outbreaks in Amish communities in the U.S.
1981	Time magazine reports post-polio syndrome among survivors of polio
1988	WHO passes resolution to eradicate polio by the year 2000
1994	China immunizes 80 million children against polio
1995	India immunizes more than 87 million children against polio
1996	CDC announces change in polio vaccination in the U.S.: two doses of inactivated polio vaccine (IPV) followed by two doses of oral polio vaccine (OPV)
1999	Number of world polio cases falls to ~7000
2000	OPV vaccination discontinued in the U.S.
2001	575 million children vaccinated in 94 countries
2005	Polio-free areas experience new outbreaks from Nigeria to Sudan
2005	Polio outreak in Amish community in Minnesota

■ **Figure II-I**
Time line of the history of polio.

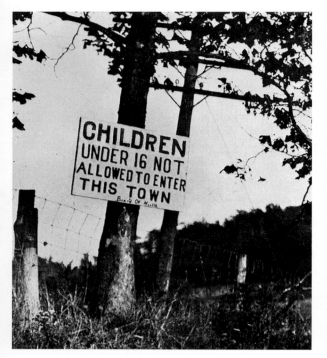

■ **Figure 11-2**
The first major outbreak of polio in the United States occurred in New York City in 1916. Many neighboring communities closed their doors to outsiders. They used armed police to patrol the roads and rail stations in search of fleeing New Yorkers and their children.

officials responded by flooding the streets with 54 millions of gallons of water a day. They thought that better sanitation in the community would defeat polio because increased sanitation had defeated diseases like typhoid, dysentery, and tuberculosis. Unfortunately, flooding the streets did not have any affect on polio cases. Quarantine was also advised—in some cases, an entire town was quarantined—and many communities that bordered New York City forbade nonresidents from entering (**Figure 11-2**). By 1953, the incidence of paralytic polio in the United States was more than 20 per 100,000. Even though this rate was not as high as that of other common diseases such as measles, polio became a public concern for several reasons:

- It was a disease of mysterious, seasonal appearance.
- It could paralyze respiratory muscles.
- It had disfiguring, crippling, and sometimes fatal results.

In 1909, before the era of tissue culture experimentation, Karl Landsteiner and Erwin Popper reproduced poliomyelitis disease in two rhesus monkeys. To do this, they created a filtrate from ground-up central nervous system (CNS) tissue that had been removed from a 9-year-old boy who had died from polio. They injected this filtrate into the peritoneum of the monkeys. The monkeys became sick and, based upon microscopic examination of the monkey's spinal cords, Landsteiner and Popper showed that a filterable agent caused the poliomyelitis. For the next 40 years, poliovirus research was limited because it was dependent upon animal models and formalin-treated nervous system tissue as a source of a vaccine for field trials and appropriate tests for the safety and efficacy of the nervous tissue vaccines were lacking. Results obtained were inadequate to justify human vaccine trials. It was not until the advent of tissue culture techniques that the development of a polio vaccine became realistic.

In 1949 John Enders, Fredrick Robbins, and Thomas Weller published a paper in *Science* that described the successful cultivation of the Lansing strain of poliovirus in human embryonic, nonnervous tissues. Soon, poliovirus was propagated in monkey kidney cells and a number of laboratories began to work toward the development of a polio vaccine. (Polio vaccines will be discussed in detail later in this chapter.)

11.3   Clinical Features of Poliomyelitis

Poliomyelitis, or polio, is rare today because of vaccination efforts. The last cases of polio in the United States were in 1979 and 2005. In both instances, unvaccinated persons from Amish communities were the source of the outbreak.

The mouth is the portal of entry for polioviruses. Person-to-person poliovirus infections are transmitted via an oral–fecal route or, less frequently, an oral–oral route. Direct contact with feces occurs with activities such as diaper changing. Indirect transmission is seen with poor sanitary conditions and may occur by numerous routes including contaminated water, food, and fomites. Infants, particularly those in diapers, appear to be the most efficient transmitters of infection. The incubation period for poliomyelitis is 6 to 20 days but can range from 3 to 35 days. Poliovirus may be present in the stool for 3 to 6 weeks and for approximately 2 weeks in saliva.

The course of infection is variable, and up to 95% of all poliovirus infections are unapparent or asymptomatic. Infected persons who are asymptomatic shed virus in stool and

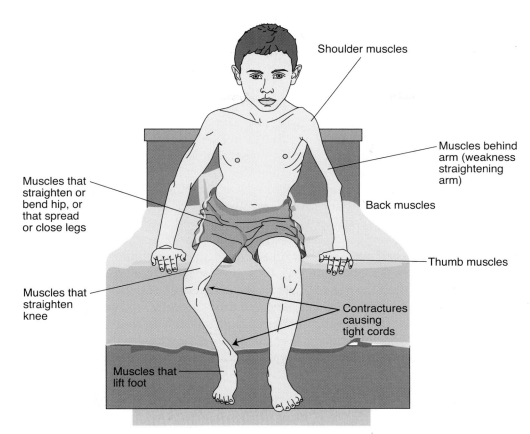

Shoulder muscles

Muscles behind arm (weakness straightening arm)

Back muscles

Muscles that straighten or bend hip, or that spread or close legs

Thumb muscles

Muscles that straighten knee

Contractures causing tight cords

Muscles that lift foot

■ **Figure 11-3**

Muscles commonly weakened by poliomyelitis. Adapted from J. Werner. *Disabled Village Children: A Guide for Community Health Workers, Rehabilitation Workers, and Families,* Second Edition. The Hesperian Foundation, 1999.

are able to transmit the virus to others. About 4% to 8% of poliovirus infections cause minor illness with symptoms of malaise, gastrointestinal disturbances, fever, influenza-like illness, and sore throat. A complete recovery occurs within a week. In 1% to 2% of infected persons, following a minor illness, symptoms of stiffness of the neck, back, and/or legs occur. These symptoms persist for 2 to 10 days followed by a complete recovery. Less than 1% of all polio infections cause a major illness, resulting in clinical signs involving the CNS, such as **flaccid paralysis**.

The term *poliomyelitis* is derived from the Greek words ***polios*** (gray), ***myelos*** (refers to marrow), and ***itis*** (inflammation). The severe form of the disease involves the inflammation and sometimes destruction of neurons located in the gray matter of the anterior horn of the spinal cord. Recovery may take up to two years and may be incomplete; weakened muscles may be a permanent result. In paralytic poliomyelitis the inflammation is severe enough to destroy the motor nerves and the resulting paralysis is permanent. The muscles that are commonly weakened by polio are shown in **Figure 11-3**.

The major illness is divided into three forms:

- spinal paralysis
- bulbar
- bulbospinal

Spinal paralysis is more common than bulbar poliomyelitis and in general is characterized by asymmetric paralysis (occurring on one side of the body). **Bulbar polio** is less common and results in the weakness of muscles, impairing the ability to talk or swallow, and the patient requires an iron lung or respirator. **Bulbospinal** is a combination of bulbar and spinal paralysis.

People are the most infectious immediately before and one to two weeks after the onset of paralytic disease. The death-to-case ratio for paralytic polio is 2% to 5% in children and 15% to 30% in adults. The death-to-case ratio increases when bulbar involvement occurs.

■ Post-Polio Syndrome

Post-poliomyelitis syndrome (PPS) occurs in a large proportion of individuals who recovered from paralytic poliomyelitis. The time between acute poliomyelitis and PPS ranges from 8 to 71 years with a mean interval of 36 years. The onset of symptoms is usually insidious. The most common three symptoms are new weakness in muscles or limbs involved at the time of acute poliomyelitis, fatigue, and pain in the muscles and joints. Fatigue is worsened during physical activity. Other less frequent symptoms are difficulty breathing, sleep abnormalities, muscle cramps, joint deformities, muscular cramps, atrophy and twitching, speech problems, difficulty swallowing, and cold intolerance. PPS can result in disabilities and handicaps. Mobility, especially stair climbing, is most frequently affected.

The cause of PPS remains unclear. The most widely accepted hypothesis suggests that the motor neurons infected with poliovirus degenerate and die. Surviving neurons sprout new nerve endings to restore muscle function. In PPS, the muscles fibers of the surviving motor neurons slowly deteriorate over time. Eventually nerve endings are destroyed and permanent weakness occurs (**Figure 11-4**). Effective management of PPS requires an interdisciplinary approach using a team of physicians and healthcare personnel. The approach must be symptom-specific (e.g., management of pain, weakness, and fatigue). Experimental therapies such as the use of α interferon (antiviral), prednisone (anti-inflammatory drug), low doses of pyridostigmine (nerve gas antidote), and insulin-like growth factor (to regenerate nerve endings) have not shown significant improvement in PPS symptoms.

II.4　Classification and Structure of Poliovirus

Polioviruses are small (~30 nm in diameter), acid-stable (surviving pH of 3.0 or lower), nonenveloped, icosahedral-shaped viruses that belong to the genus Enterovirus and family *Picornaviridae* (from the Greek *pico*, for "small"). In 1985, poliovirus type 1 was one of the first human viruses whose three-dimensional structure was solved in atomic detail by X-ray crystallography. The poliovirus virion consists of four distinct capsid proteins designated VP1, VP2, VP3, and VP4. The basic building block (protomer) of the capsid consists of one copy of VP1–VP4. The capsid is made up of 60 protomers with icosahedral symmetry to form a spherical particle. The shell of the virus is formed by VP1 to VP3 and VP4 lies on its inner surface. VP1, VP2, and VP3 do not share sequence homology, yet they all form the same topology. There are three antigenic types (serotypes 1, 2, and 3) of poliovirus. All polioviruses within a serotype can be neutralized by type-specific antisera. Table 11-2 lists each serotype along with the name of a prototypic strain and its origin. Albert Sabin attenuated each serotype for use as an oral live trivalent vaccine. The genome of poliovirus consists of one infectious (+) sense single-stranded RNA (ssRNA) molecule that is 7441 nucleotides in length. It will be described in further detail later in this chapter in the discussion of viral replication.

■ Stability of Enteroviruses in the Environment

Enteroviruses are able to pass through the stomach and the small intestine because they are resistant to pH levels less than three as well as to several proteases. Enterovirus particles are nonenveloped, making them resistant to detergents, 70% alcohol, and other lipid solvents such as ether and chloroform. They are also resistant to disinfectants such as 5% Lysol and 1% quaternary ammonium compounds. Enteroviruses are

TABLE 11-2	Poliovirus Serotypes	
Serotype	**Prototype Strain**	**Source/Geographic Origin**
1	Brunhilde	Poliovirus isolated from spinal cord of a chimpanzee, Brunhilde who was inoculated in 1939 with stool specimens from seven paralytic patients in Baltimore, MD.
2	Lansing	From patient who died of paralytic polio in Lansing, MI, in 1938.
3	Leon	Brain and spinal cord specimen from 11-year-old boy named Leon who died from paralytic polio in Los Angeles, CA, in 1937.

(a)

Normal → Paralysis → Recovery → Stability (10–15 years) → Post-polio syndrome

(b)

Motor neuron (anterior horn cell)

Motor unit

A normal motor unit containing the motor neuron and the muscle fibers it innervates.

Details of the motor unit.

Pathophysiological changes seen with acute poliomyletis.

Motor neuron

New "sprouts"

Reinnervation through collateral sprouting.

Motor neuron

New and old sprout degradation.

(c)

■ **Figure 11-4**
(a) Asymmetric atrophy of right leg of patient with PPS. **(b)** Clinical course of PPS. Overlapping boxes represent times when the motor neurons are becoming less stable. **(c)** Hypothetical model for the cause of PSS. The model shows the changes in motor neurons before, during, and after poliovirus infection in individuals who experienced the paralytic form of the disease. Adapted from Raut, A., *Meducator* 2 (2003): http://meducator.org/index.php/Issue-2-March-2003/After-the-Storm.html.

usually present in organic matter such as feces; therefore, standard **inactivation proto-cols** may require prolonged contact time. **Inactivated** viruses are dead. In other words, the virus is not destroyed but it is no longer able to infect cells. Inactivation protocols are developed to determine what procedures are necessary to decontaminate or completely disinfect surfaces where viruses are present.

Chemical inactivation of enteroviruses can be achieved with chlorine, hydrochloric acid, and aldehydes. Heating at 50°C (122°F) for one hour in the absence of calcium and magnesium will also inactivate enteroviruses. Viruses may be stable several days to several weeks at 4°C (39.2°F).

11.5   Laboratory Diagnosis of Poliovirus Infections

In the past diagnosis was based on the recovery of poliovirus from stool and sometimes throat samples but not from cerebral spinal fluid (CSF). Poliovirus grows rapidly (the life cycle is complete within a few days) in any human or monkey cells lines and shows good cytopathic effects. The serotype of the isolate is identified using neutralization assays. The nucleotide sequences of all wild-type and vaccine-type strains have been identified, and as a result any poliovirus isolated from a person with flaccid paralysis is tested further (e.g., genomic sequencing) to determine if the infection is a result of an infection with either vaccine- or wild-type virus. Improved laboratory diagnosis of poliomyelitis is an important part of the World Health Organization (WHO) initiative for global eradication of poliomyelitis.

11.6   Cellular Pathogenesis

Humans and nonhuman primates are the only natural hosts of poliovirus. There are no animal reservoirs. Nonhuman primates have been used as models of human conditions. Mice or any other affordable experimental animals were found to be resistant to poliovirus infection, presumably due to the lack of the poliovirus receptor. Natural infection occurs via ingestion of polioviruses.

Once ingested, polioviruses invade two lymphoid tissues: the tonsils and the Peyer's patches (lymph nodes in the walls of the intestines near the junction of the ileum and colon). The virus spreads via the regional lymph nodes to the blood. A major viremia causes the minor illness symptoms in infected individuals (e.g., sore throat, headache, and fever). **Figure 11-5** shows how polioviruses spread via the bloodstream. In a very small percentage of patients the CNS is involved. The polioviruses are carried via the bloodstream to the anterior horn cells of the spinal cord in which the virus replicates, resulting in lesions that are widely distributed throughout the spinal cord and parts of the brain. The hallmark of poliomyelitis is the selective destruction of motor neurons that leads to paralysis and in severe cases, respiratory arrest and death. The molecular mechanism by which poliovirus infection causes poliomyelitis is still poorly understood. This is remarkable considering that poliovirus is one of the most thoroughly investigated viruses of all time.

11.7   Viral Replication

The prototype of the genus Enterovirus of the *Picornaviridae* family is poliovirus, the causative agent of poliomyelitis. The first step toward identifying host receptors for poliovirus came with the isolation of monoclonal antibodies that block binding of poliovirus to cells. As mentioned earlier, polioviruses could not infect mouse cells because they lacked the

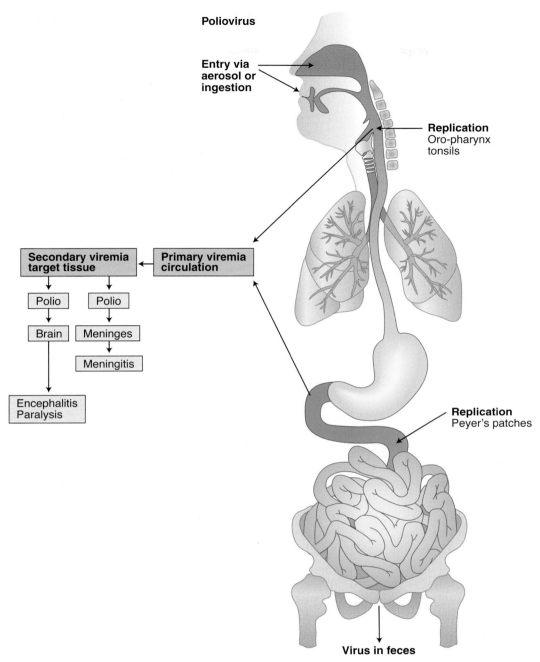

Poliovirus

Entry via aerosol or ingestion

Replication
Oro-pharynx
tonsils

Secondary viremia target tissue

Primary viremia circulation

Polio	Polio
Brain	Meninges
	Meningitis

Encephalitis
Paralysis

Replication
Peyer's patches

Virus in feces

■ **Figure 11-5**
Poliovirus pathogenesis. Adapted from University of South Carolina, School of Medicine. "Virology: Picornaviruses, Part One." *Microbiology and Immunology*. University of South Carolina, 2008. http://pathmicro. med.sc.edu/virol/picorna.htm.

correct cellular receptor. To bypass the receptor-binding step, the RNA genome of poliovirus was transfected into mouse cells (receptor-negative cells). It resulted in the production of a single cycle of infectious viruses. When mouse cells were transformed with human genomic DNA from HeLa cells, the mouse cells became susceptible to poliovirus infection. An antireceptor antibody blocked the infection. The results suggested that the poliovirus receptor gene had been introduced into mouse cells, resulting in the expression of the receptor and susceptibility to poliovirus infection. The **poliovirus receptor** (**PVR**, or sometimes CD155) is a cell surface integral membrane protein and a member of the immunoglobulin (Ig) superfamily of proteins. The function of CD155 is that of an activating ligand that stimulates natural killer cells.

The interaction of poliovirus with its receptor leads to a conformational change in the capsid. VP4, an internal capsid protein, detaches from the capsid. The capsid swells and a pore is formed in the cell membrane through which the RNA proceeds. (It is not

| VIRUS FILE 11-1 | **Creating Poliovirus in a Test Tube** |

After the September 11, 2001, World Trade Center attack, the ongoing threat of domestic bioterrorist activity in the United States became more credible. Letters containing weaponized *Bacillus anthracis* (*B. anthracis*) endospores were sent through the U.S. postal system to the offices of Senate Majority Leader Tom Daschle, NBC News anchor Tom Brokaw, and *The New York Post*. Government officials recognized that the *B. anthracis* endospores originated from the U.S. biodefense program.

In 2002 Professor Eckard Wimmer of the Department of Molecular Genetics and Microbiology, SUNY Stony Brook, and colleagues created a pathogen (or potential bioweapon) from scratch to prove to the scientific community that it could be done (**Figure VF 11-1**). Many researchers believed that poliovirus could be recreated using published data on the genetic sequence of the virus, but no one had done the work. The Defense Advanced Research Projects Agency (DARPA, a central research and development organization within the U.S. Department of Defense) supported this work.

Poliovirus reconstruction was chosen because it has one of the simplest genomes known and its genome information is easily accessible via the Internet. The global population is currently protected against poliovirus infection. If mass vaccination stops, though, and herd immunity is lost, poliovirus would pose a threat as a biological weapon.

Researchers at DARPA accomplished the re-creation by first taking the RNA genome sequence of poliovirus type 1 (Mahoney) and converting it to DNA. A full-length complementary poliovirus DNA (cDNA) carrying a T7 RNA polymerase promoter sequence was synthesized using purified oligonucleotides that had been purchased commercially. Three pieces of poliovirus cDNA were then inserted into a plasmid DNA. To distinguish any synthesized viruses from lab contaminants, the investigators introduced subtle changes into the virus' genetic code that would not alter the protein products it encodes. Subsequently, HeLa cell monolayers were transfected with a T7 RNA polymerase RNA transcript. This RNA transcript proved to be infectious; that is, poliovirus RNA was translated via the HeLa cell machinery and viral particles self-assembled. Viruses were isolated from these cells. They were injected into the cerebrum of mice engineered to carry the human receptor for poliovirus. The mice were examined daily for paralysis and/or death. The synthetic virus had the biochemical and pathogenic characteristics of poliovirus, but researchers found that, the newly created viruses were much less virulent than the typical laboratory strain. As a result, higher doses than usual of the synthetic poliovirus were needed to kill the mice.

This poliovirus project took nearly three years to complete in a highly sophisticated research laboratory using the most advanced DNA synthesis technology and could not

■ **Figure VF 11-1**
Transmission electron micrograph of poliovirus type 1. The nonenveloped virions are ~30 nm in diameter and have icosahedral symmetry.

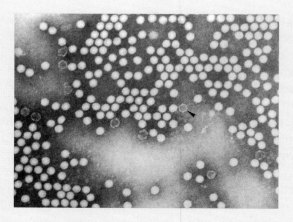

have been completed in a substandard facility. Current technology is not sophisticated enough to recreate more complex viruses such as smallpox and Ebola virus.

Now that the genome has been recreated, what are the implications of these experiments? Should this work have been done at all?

References

Cello, J., Paul, A. V., and Wimmer, E. 2002. "Chemical Synthesis of Poliovirus cDNA: Generation of Infectious Virus in the Absence of Natural Template." *Science* 97(5583):1016–1018.

Racaniella, V. R. 2000. "It Is Too Early to Stop Polio Vaccination." *Bull WHO* 78(3):359–360.

known precisely where the uncoating event occurs—at the cell membrane or from within an endosome.) After the virion RNA is released into the cytoplasm of the cell, it serves as an messenger RNA (mRNA) that is translated into a single, highly autocatalytic polyprotein whose proteolytic cleavage products serve as capsid precursors and replication proteins.

The poliovirus genome is made up of a positive sense ssRNA and both ends of the genome are modified. The 5′ end contains a small basic viral protein, VPg, that is covalently attached to uridine. It serves as a primer for RNA replication of the genome. The 5′ end of the poliovirus genome forms a cloverleaf or tRNA-like structure that plays a key role in the replicative process of the RNA molecule. Farther downsteam of the clover-leaf structure is an **untranslated region** (**UTR**) that promotes the initiation of translation by its internal ribosomal entry site (IRES). The IRES element contains extensive regions of secondary stem-loop structures. The 3′ end of the poliovirus genome is polyadenylated (**Figure 11-6**).

■ **Figure 11-6**

Schematic diagram showing the 5′ and 3′ nontranslated regions of the poliovirus genome. The 5′ end contains a structural **IRES** element. Adapted from H. A. Rotbart, ed. *Human Enterovirus Infections.* ASM Press, 1995.

Poliovirus proteins are synthesized by the translation of a single, long, open reading frame on the viral +ssRNA genome. This is followed by a series of cleavages. Viral proteases cleave themselves (**autocleavage**) out and cleave the polyprotein into 11 separate gene products involved in replication and packaging. The viral protease 2A cleaves the p220 subunit of the cap binding complex (eIF-4G), making host cell mRNA unrecognizable to ribosomes. This results in the shutdown of host protein synthesis but frees the ribosomes to translate viral RNA. Viral mRNA is translated via cap independent translation: The 5′ UTR contains the IRES, which serves as a ribosome docking site for the 40S subunit of ribosomes. IRES elements were first discovered in poliovirus, encephalomyocarditis, and other picornaviruses. IRES-dependent translation is now known as a novel mechanism of eukaryotic cap-independent translation. An increasing number have been discovered not only in viral genomes but also in the 5′ UTRs of many cellular mRNAs. **Figure 11-7** shows the genomic organization and proteolytic processing of the poliovirus polyprotein. The single open reading frame is translated into a polyprotein of 247 kilodaltons that is processed into three precursor proteins by virally encoded proteases named 2A, 3C, and 3D. The precursor proteins are further processed by virally encoded proteases (Figure 11-7). The cleavage results in four structural and seven nonstructural proteins.

RNA replication occurs entirely in the cytoplasm of the infected cell. Host cells lack the necessary cellular machinery to replicate the viral RNA genome. Poliovirus uses a viral RNA-dependent RNA polymerase to produce a –ssRNA strand from the packaged genomic +ssRNA template (mRNA) that was used for protein synthesis. The viral VPg protein attached to uridine serves as a primer. The first round produces a single antisense molecule. The antisense molecule is then used to produce (+) sense copies of the original genome that can be packaged into the viral capsids prior to viral release.

■ **Figure 11-7**

Genomic organization and proteolytic processing of poliovirus. Reproduced from *Virus Research,* Vol. 111, Mueller, S., Wimmer, E., and J. Cello, *Poliovirus and poliomyelitis: A tale of guts, brains, and an accidental event,* p. 177, © 2005, with permission from Elsevier.

After the viral genome has been translated to produce the necessary proteins and replicated its genome, the capsid proteins self-assemble into a structure of icosahedral symmetry that contains 60 copies of each viral capsid protein (VP1, -2, -3, and -4). The newly synthesized +ssRNA genome enters the incomplete capsid and is secured inside once the viral proteases finish their cleavage activity. When the genome is secured and the virion is mature, as many as 100,000 virions may be released during cell lysis of a single infected cell. **Figure 11-8** shows the life cycle of poliovirus.

11.8 Treatment

During the era when polio outbreaks were common in the United States new therapies were developed, such as the "drinker respirators" or iron lung machines. They were first used to assist the breathing of paralyzed patients in the 1930s. In 1940, Sister Elizabeth Kenny (nurses were referred to as sisters), a Minneapolis nurse who became known as the nurse who challenged the physicians, proposed a new theory that emphasized the movement and stretching of paralyzed muscles (physical therapy) rather than the immobilization or use of splints for paralyzed muscles as a treatment for those who suffered from the severe forms of polio. Other types of therapy used by Kenny included the use of hot packs and hot baths in conjunction with the active training of muscles (**Figure 11-9**). The Sister Kenny Institute was established in 1942 and is now part of Abbott Northwestern Hospital in Minneapolis.

There is no cure for polio. Treatment is supportive care, including physical therapy. Prevention via vaccination is the best way to combat infection. No antiviral chemotherapeutic agents exist. The development of antipoliovirus drugs has seemed unnecessary because the disease is near eradication. No poliovirus antiviral is likely to profit a company.

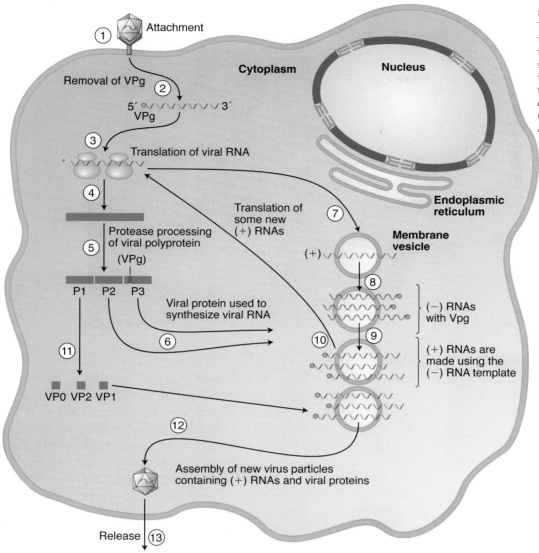

■ **Figure 11-8**
The life cycle of polioviruses occurs solely in the cytoplasm of the infected cell. Note that the proteins that participate in RNA synthesis are transported to membrane vesicles, where RNA synthesis occurs. Adapted from Flint, S. J., et al. *Principles of Virology: Molecular Biology, Pathogenesis, and Control of Animal Viruses,* Second Edition. ASM Press, 2003.

Note: This diagram only shows the initial processing of viral polyprotein in step 5.

Only recently have the WHO and CDC called for the development of a safe antiviral that would be used to prevent and treat poliovirus infections. The driving factor is vaccine-driven outbreaks and the potential for post-eradication outbreaks.

11.9   Prevention

Poliomyelitis was the most widely known disease of the twentieth century until AIDS. Scientists set out on a mission to learn more about the disease, gradually allowing them to develop more effective treatment, rehabilitation techniques, and prevention.

■ Chemicals and Gamma Globulin

During the 1940s researchers observed that if certain species of monkeys were treated in their nose with chemicals such as picric acid, sodium alum, and zinc sulfate and then

■ Figure 11-9
Sister Elizabeth Kenny demonstrates therapy techniques at the Sister Kenny Institute, 1942.

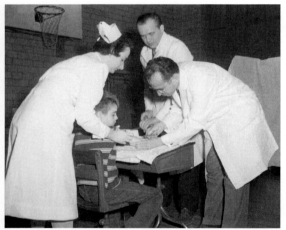

■ Figure 11-10
Jonas Salk vaccinating a boy at Arsenal Elementary School in Pittsburgh, Pennsylvania (February 23, 1954).

challenged with poliovirus, the chemicals seemed to block viral infection of the nasal mucosa. When this treatment was tried in humans, the results were not promising and this technique was quickly abandoned. The use of convalescent serum for poliomyelitis was recommended as early as 1915. In 1952, passive immunity attempts to inject 54,772 children who were at risk of contracting polio with convalescent serum had no apparent affect on the incidence or severity of paralysis, probably because this immunity was short-lived. Another 235,000 children were inoculated with gamma globulin the following year with the same results. Gamma globulin failed as a prophylactic measure to prevent poliovirus infection in humans and the supply of serum was no longer offered.

■ Inactivated Vaccines

As soon as tissue culture techniques became available, a number of medical research laboratories began to develop a vaccine against poliovirus. Jonas Salk's laboratory began working on a formalin-inactivated vaccine, whereas Albert Milzer and colleagues pursued ultraviolet irradiation as a means of virus inactivation. Albert Sabin and his research team took the approach of a live-attenuated vaccine.

Milzer's vaccine was immunogenic in humans but was never adopted for general use. Salk continued work on the formalinized vaccine that had been prepared by propagating the virus in monkey kidney cells. By 1953, preliminary tests of Salk's inactivated vaccine on children and adolescent volunteers at the D.T. Watson Home for Crippled Children and the Polk School for the Retarded and Feeble-Minded were conducted. (During this time, this type of human testing was a standard practice.) Results were favorable and the largest experiment of its time was set up. A mass vaccination trial, including placebo controls, was sponsored by the March of Dimes (then known as the National Foundation for Infantile Paralysis). A total of 1,829,916 children from all parts of the United States, Canada, and Finland were vaccinated (**Figure 11-10**). Results of this inactivated poliovirus vaccine (IPV) were presented by manufacturers in 1955. The vaccine was said to be safe and 70% effective (booster shots would be needed to increase its efficacy). Within days, the vaccine was licensed for use.

The Cutter Episode

Not long after the vaccine was licensed and readily available, cases of paralytic poliomyelitis were reported in children who had received the Salk vaccine. An epidemiological investigation revealed that all of these vaccinees were given a vaccine produced by the same manufacturer—Cutter. Live virus was isolated from the vaccine lots, indicating that, the inactivation process was not complete. A total of 260 cases were reported; 94 infections were determined to be from the vaccination, 126 were through family contacts, and 40 were through community contacts. Of these 260 cases, 192 were paralytic. There were no deaths.

Amazingly, the "Cutter Incident" did not change public confidence in the vaccine. As a result of this incident, though, new requirements were introduced for safety testing of the vaccine. A surveillance unit was created at the Centers for Disease Control and Prevention to maintain and scrutinize all vaccination programs.

■ Live, Attenuated Poliovirus Vaccines

Attenuated (as opposed to inactivated) vaccines were more appealing to medical researchers because it was assumed that an active infection came closest to reproducing the natural situation. The idea is to fool the body's immune defense system into thinking it is under attack by a pathogenic form of the virus, thus causing it to produce the defense mechanisms (e.g., antibodies) that will fight off the poliovirus if it is encountered in the future. It was expected that attenuated viruses would produce longer-lasting immunity. The major concern related to the creation of attenuated virus vaccines was the issue regarding the genetic stability of the poliovirus vaccine strains. In other words, would revert to neurovirulence after multiplying in the human host? Three research groups worked to develop a live, attenuated poliovirus vaccine during the early 1950s. Sabin's team created attenuated vaccines by passaging each serotype of poliovirus separately in cynomolgus monkey kidney tissue culture (MKTC) cells. The definitive test used to determine if the vaccine strains would revert to virulence was to inject the attenuated strains intracerebrally or directly into the spinal cord of monkeys. Attenuated strains that passed the definitive test were used as vaccine candidates for field trials.

It was difficult to conduct field trials in the United States because the Salk vaccine had already been licensed and was being widely used. In 1958, the first large-scale field trial, in which 200,000 children were vaccinated with the attenuated Sabin serotype 2 poliovirus vaccine, was conducted in Singapore. The same year, laboratory protocols to grow the vaccine strains and produce enough vaccine for 300,000 children was provided to Professor Mikhail Petrovich Chumakov, who was the director of the Poliomyeltitis Research Institute in Moscow. Chumakov quickly manufactured more of this vaccine using the seed strains provided by Sabin. In just over a year, 15 million Russians were vaccinated without any untoward effects and with evidence of effectiveness. By 1960, 100 million participants in Russia and eastern European countries were vaccinated. This provided confidence that the attenuated viruses would not revert to being neurovirulent. After these successful field trials, the United States granted licensure of the Sabin live poliovirus vaccine.

The results were that within ten years, two effective and safe vaccines were available for general use. The live vaccine developed by Sabin included all three attenuated viruses (types 1, 2 and 3). The vaccine was given by mouth in the form of a few drops of liquid; hence it was known as the oral poliovirus vaccine (OPV). The incidence of poliomyelitis in the United States dropped dramatically after the administration of IPV and OPV (**Figure 11-11**).

■ **Figure 11-11**

Incidence of poliomyelitis in the United States from 1941–1971. The dashed line represents only paralytic polio; the solid line contains both paralytic and nonparalytic forms. Adapted from D. S. Younger, ed. *Motor Disorders.* Lippincott Williams & Wilkins, 1999.

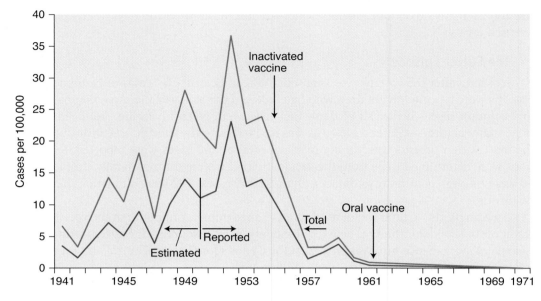

During the early years of IPV and OPV production, some monkey kidney cell cultures used to produce the vaccine strains were contaminated with simian virus-40 (SV-40). As detailed in Chapter 10, SV-40 causes tumors in hamsters and transform cells in culture. Vaccinees developed antibodies against SV-40 and the virus could be isolated from the feces of some vaccinees. Long-term studies were conducted to determine if individuals receiving the contaminated vaccines would be at higher risk for cancer (refer to Chapter 10). The composition and immunity of the current IPV and OPV is shown in Table 11-3. From 1996–1999, the CDC recommended sequential use of IPV/OPV. Both vaccines induce immunity to poliovirus, but OPV is better at preventing the disease from spreading to other

TABLE 11-3	Inactivated and Oral Polio Vaccines Composition and Protective Capabilities
Vaccine Composition	**Vaccine Efficacy**
Inactivated polio vaccine	
• Contains three serotypes of vaccine virus	• Highly effective in producing immunity to poliovirus
• Grown on monkey kidney (Vero) cells	• >90% immune after two doses
• Inactivated with formaldehyde	• >99% immune after three doses
• Contains 2-phenoxyethanol, neomycin, streptomycin, polymyxin B	• Duration of immunity not known with certainty
Oral polio vaccine	
• Contains three serotypes of vaccine virus	• Highly effective in producing immunity to poliovirus
• Grown on monkey kidney (Vero) cells	• >50% immune after one dose
• Contains neomycin and streptomycin	• >95% immune after three doses
• Shed in stool for up to six weeks following vaccination	• Immunity probably lifelong

people. It was recommended that the IPV would be administered at age 2 and 4 months followed by OPV at age 12–18 months and 4–6 years. For a few people (about 1 in 2.4 million), OPV actually causes poliomyelitis, a situation termed **vaccine-associated paralytic polio** (**VAPP**). In 2000, to reduce VAPP, the exclusive use of IPV was recommended and OPV is no longer readily available in the United States. Children get four doses of IPV at 2 and 4 months, a dose at 6–18 months, and a booster dose at 4–6 years. This has helped to eliminate VAPP.

11.10   Eradication Efforts

In 1988, the World Health Assembly, the directing council of the WHO, passed a resolution to globally eradicate poliomyelitis by the year 2000. This was considered possible for several reasons, all of which are still true:

- Two vaccines that induce immunity were available.
- There was no animal reservoir.
- There were only three serotypes of wild-type viruses, all of which were genetically stable.
- The OPV was inexpensive and easy to administer in mass vaccination campaigns.

Several potential roadblocks to global eradication were identified, including:

- Poliovirus is contagious, particularly by an oral–fecal route.
- IPV is inefficient in preventing the spread of virus.
- The use of OPV in tropical countries has been problematic.
- There are tensions in many countries between those who favor mass vaccination and those that do not.
- Verification of success is difficult as many poliovirus infections are not clinically obvious. (Only about 1 in 100 people who are infected with poliovirus suffer from paralysis.)

Although the goal of eradicating the poliomyelitis was not realized by 2000, progress toward it has been significant. Between 1988 and 2003, the number of polio-endemic countries was reduced from 125 to 6 (Afghanistan, Egypt, India, Niger, Nigeria, and Pakistan). The number of wild-type poliovirus infections reported annually decreased from 350,000 in 1988 to roughly 1,350 in 2005. As of 2007, four polio endemic countries remain: Nigeria, India, Afghanistan, and Pakistan (**Figure 11-12**). Northern Nigeria continues to account for the majority of global cases. Increased cases of polio in Nigeria were linked to a boycott of poliovirus vaccinations by leaders in several Nigerian states who falsely claimed the vaccine causes sterility and spreads AIDS. Countries that were declared polio-free have now experienced new outbreaks or reinfections. Twenty-six previously polio-free countries have been reinfected since 2003. Of these, nine continued to report cases in 2006 (Angola, Cameroon, Chad, Kenya, Ethiopia, Bangladesh, Nepal, Namibia, and Yemen). Some scientists hypothesize that reinfections in 2005 were due to polio-infected Muslims who spread the virus while making their pilgrimage to Mecca (the Hajj, Saudi Arabia), which took place in January 2005. In response to these outbreaks, the WHO has intensified efforts in surrounding countries and created educational programs to reinforce the importance and safety of vaccination. Saudi Arabian health officials recommended that all Hajj travelers from polio-endemic countries be vaccinated regardless of their immune status. Eradication efforts are in their final stages.

(a)

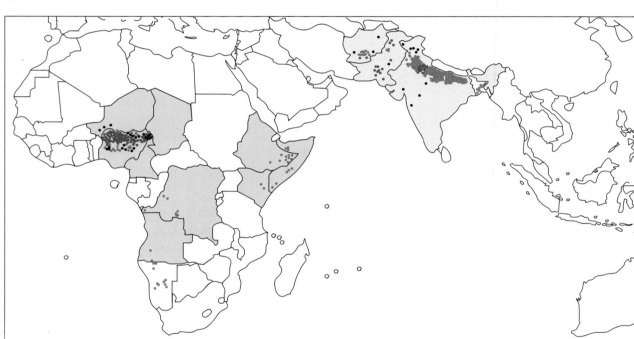

- Wild-type virus 1
- Wild-type virus 3
- Wild-type virus 1 and 3
- ☐ Endemic countries
- ☐ Case or outbreak following importation (0–6 months)
- ☐ Case or outbreak following importation (6–12 months)

As of 01 January 2006, Egypt and Niger were reclassified as nonendemic countries.
(b)

■ **Figure 11-12**

(a) Worldwide use of polio vaccine in 2004. Courtesy of the World Health Organization. **(b)** Wild-type poliovirus pockets worldwide. Data from the WHO: February 28, 2006 through February 27, 2007. Courtesy of the World Health Organization.

II.II   Other Enteroviruses (Nonpolio)

Historically, poliovirus has been the most significant enterovirus. There are, however, at least 70 viruses within the Enterovirus genus that are known to infect humans.

■ Myocarditis and Dilated Cardiomyopathy

Over the past 50 years, extensive research has addressed the role of enteroviruses in **myocarditis** and **dilated cardiomyopathy** (**DCM**). Myocarditis is the inflammation or degeneration of the **myocardium** (muscular tissue of the heart). In some cases, it can lead to congestive heart failure requiring hospitalization, heart failure medications, or a heart transplant. Myocarditis is often asymptomatic. About 10% of patients experience fever, chest pains, shortness of breath, heart palpitations (the sensation of a skipped heart beat), and fatigue.

DCM is a disease of the heart muscle that causes the heart to become enlarged and to pump less effectively. As a result, the heart becomes thin, weak, or floppy and as a result it is unable to pump blood efficiently around the body. This causes fluid to build up in the lungs, causing congestion and the feeling of breathlessness.

DCM is a serious condition. It has a 50% mortality rate in the two years following a diagnosis and may account for nearly half of all patients requiring a heart transplant. Viruses, bacteria, and protozoan have all been shown to infect the myocardium, resulting in myocarditis. The enteroviruses associated with myocarditis and DCM are the Coxsackie group B viruses. They can replicate in the heart but are difficult to isolate in an infectious form during chronic disease. Myocardial damage is explained by direct viral damage and/or the consequences of the immune response.

The WHO has reported that approximately 1.5% of all enteroviral infections are associated with cardiovascular signs and symptoms. Over a person's lifetime, repeated exposure to enteroviruses increases the likelihood of acquiring an enteroviral infection associated with cardiac symptoms. It has been suggested that 70% of the general population has been exposed to cardiotropic viruses and that half of this group experiences an episode of acute viral myocarditis. There are several factors that influence the incidence of enterovirus-associated heart disease:

- Host age
- Host gender
- Host race and geographical location

Children under six months of age are highly susceptible to Coxsackie virus myocarditis. During late childhood and adolescence, the incidence of viral myocarditis rises. Patients between 20 and 39 years of age account for 52% all viral mycocarditis cases. The incidence of Coxsackie myocarditis and DCM is significantly higher in males than females. Depending on the study, the male-to-female ratios range from 2:1 to 4:1. In the United States the mortality rate in males is twice that of females, and myocarditis for blacks is 2.4 times higher than in whites. DCM seems to be higher in underdeveloped and tropical countries.

■ Respiratory Enteroviruses

Of all of the clinical syndromes reported to be associated with enteroviral infections, respiratory disease accounts for 14% to 21% of them. Respiratory illnesses are the most frequent and universal illnesses suffered by children and adults. On average, children experience two to seven episodes and adults experience one to three episodes of respiratory illnesses per year, most of which are caused by viruses. A variety of viruses cause respiratory

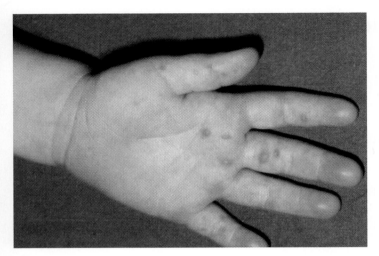

■ Figure 11-13
Cutaneous lesions of the fingers and palms are present in two thirds of individuals with HFMD. Herpetic-like lesions may also be present inside the mouth and on the soles of the feet.

illnesses, such as respiratory syncytial virus (RSV), parainfluenza viruses, influenza viruses, adenoviruses, rhinoviruses, and enteroviruses. Worldwide, enteroviruses account for 2% to 15% of all viruses that cause upper- and lower-respiratory tract infections. Respiratory diseases caused by enteroviruses are mild and of a self-limiting nature and, thus, treatment is supportive.

■ Enterovirus 71: A Reemerging Viral Pathogen?

The majority of enteroviruses cause asymptomatic, mild, or self-limiting infections in children. Enteroviruses have been placed into subgroups based on differences in the range of hosts and pathogenicity:

- Polioviruses
- Group A Coxsackie viruses
- Group B Coxsackie viruses
- Echoviruses

Since 1970, newly identified enteroviruses have been allocated sequential numbers (68–71), of which enterovirus 71 is the most acknowledged. It was first isolated in California in 1969 and is a frequent cause of **hand, foot, and mouth disease (HFMD)** epidemics associated with severe neurological complications in a small proportion of cases (**Figure 11-13**). There has been a significant increase in enterovirus 71 epidemic activity throughout the Asia-Pacific region since 1997. The large recent outbreaks that occurred in Taiwan, Bulgaria, Hungary, and Malaysia have raised important questions about the biology of the virus and the factors underlying the widespread emergence of enterovirus 71 infections.

Two disease patterns have been observed: small outbreaks associated with an occasional patient death and unusual severe outbreaks in which a significant number of individuals experience brainstem encephalitis associated with pulmonary edema and hemorrhage, resulting in death. Over 90% of fatal cases were in children less than 5 years of age that died within a day of hospital admission. There has been a great deal of interest in trying to explain the spread and mysterious virulence of these severe enterovirus 71 infections in molecular and genetic terms. This viral agent has been changing genetically from the strains isolated in the 1970s. It is not clear whether the genetic changes in the genome explain the genesis of the enterovirus 71 pulmonary edema.

Enterovirus 71 joins the ranks of the increasing numbers of microbes of emerging or reemerging infectious diseases. Poliovirus infections are controlled in most parts of the world through the efforts of the WHO, and as a result attention is being turned to the nonpolio enterovirus infections, particularly enterovirus 71.

 Summary

The enteroviruses are small (30 nm), naked viruses that contain infectious ssRNA of positive polarity. They are ubiquitous pathogens that belong to the family Picornaviridae. An estimated 10 to 15 million symptomatic infections are caused by enteroviruses, resulting in 30,000 to 50,000 hospitalizations in the United States per year. Although most enterovirus infections are relatively mild and result in the full recovery of the patient, these viruses can also cause severe illnesses such as poliomyelitis, meningitis, encephalitis, and mycocarditis. Poliovirus is the most well-known and studied enterovirus.

Poliovirus infections in the United States suddenly emerged in epidemic form at the turn of the 20th century, causing paralysis and death, mainly in children. Poliomyelitis became a public concern because it was a disease of mysterious seasonal appearance (peaking in the summer months in temperate climates), had a disfiguring and/or crippling nature, and could paralyze respiratory muscles (iron lungs, which were invented in 1928, were used to assist breathing). The viral etiology of poliomyelitis was discovered in 1909.

During the 1940s and 1950s poliomyelitis patients underwent treatments developed by Sister Elizabeth Kenny that emphasized physical therapy instead of immobilization of the affected limbs. The isolation, genetic studies, and characterization of polioviruses did not begin until the 1950s. The growth of polioviruses in cultured mammalian cells radically changed the field of medical virology. These advanced techniques allowed researchers to isolate, grow, and characterize the biology of polioviruses. Most importantly, the techniques lead to the development of two successful vaccines: Jonas Salk's inactivated poliovirus vaccine (IPV) and Albert Sabin's live, attenuated oral vaccine (OPV). These vaccines were licensed for use in the United States in 1955 and 1961, respectively.

Poliomyelitis is rare today. The virus is spread via an oral–fecal route of transmission. Up to 95% of poliovirus infections are asymptomatic. About 4% to 8% of infected individuals experience minor illness, and less than 1% of all poliovirus infections cause major illness, resulting in clinical signs or symptoms involving the CNS such as flaccid paralysis. Laboratory diagnosis today is focused on isolating the poliovirus from the patient and determining its serotype using neutralization assays. Genomic sequencing is used to determine if the viral isolate is a wild- or vaccine-type strain. Post-polio syndrome occurs in a large proportion of individuals who recovered from paralytic poliomyelitis. Its onset is insidious. Common symptoms include muscle weakness, fatigue, and pain in the muscles and joints. Treatment consists of managing symptoms. Global eradication of poliomyelitis is in the home stretch. There remain small pockets of polio in impoverished nations experiencing civil unrest, population displacements, famines, and national disasters. International political will and commitment is necessary to achieve eradication.

Research regarding the molecular biology of polioviruses continues. Virus properties include its absence of a lipid envelope, stability over a pH range of 3 to 10, and resistance to alcohol and other solvents. The three-dimensional structure of polioviruses was deciphered in 1985. The capsid consists of four different proteins (VP1–4) that make up the icosahedral shell of the virus particle. There are three serotypes of poliovirus that are distinguishable via neutralization of cytopathic effects in cell cultures by specific antisera. The host range of polioviruses is limited to primates and primate cell cultures. Nonprimate cell cultures are resistant to poliovirus infection because they lack the poliovirus receptor (PVR).

The monocistronic +ssRNA poliovirus genome of poliovirus is 3′ polyadenylated and covalently liked to a virus-encoded oligopeptide (VPg) at its 5′ terminus. Upon entry into the cytoplasm, the genome functions as monocistronic mRNA consisting of a single open reading frame. It is translated by a cap-independent mechanism (using the IRES) to produce a large precursor polyprotein that is proteolytically processed by virus-encoded proteases to yield structural and nonstructural proteins. Assembled polioviruses lyse the host cell upon release of viral progeny.

Nonpolio enteroviruses that cause acute illnesses, particularly in infants and children, have been studied with increasing frequency over the last 30 years. They have been associated with occasional outbreaks in which a larger-than-usual number of patients develop clinical disease, sometimes with fatal consequences. This chapter has discussed nonpolio enteroviruses that cause respiratory tract illnesses, myocarditis, and HFMD. The future likely will focus on the intervention of the more serious illnesses caused by nonpolio enteroviruses, either through the development of antiviral therapies or vaccines. It is an important and exciting area for future study.

Resources

Primary Literature and Reviews

Belnap, D. M. et al. 2000. "Three-Dimensional Structure of Poliovirus Receptor Bound to Poliovirus." *PNAS USA* 97(1):73–78.

Chia, J. K. S. 2005. "The Role of Enterovirus in Chronic Fatigue Syndrome." *J Clin Pathol* 58:1126–1132.

Couzin, J. 2006. "Report Concludes Polio Drugs Are Needed—After Disease Is Eradicated." *Science* 311:1539.

Frisk, G. 2001. "Mechanisms of Chronic Enteroviral Persistence in Tissue." *Curr Opin Infect Dis* 14(3):251–256.

Hellen, C. U. T., and Sarnow, P. 2001. "Internal Ribsome Entry Sites in Eukaryotic mRNA Molecules." *Genes Dev* 15(13):1593–1612.

Ho, M. 2000. "Enterovirus 71: The Virus, its Infections and Outbreaks." *J Microbiol Immunol Infect* 33:205–216.

Howard, R. S. 2005. "Poliomyelitis and the Postpolio Syndrome." *BMJ* 330: 1314–1318.

Lukashev, A. N. 2005. "Role of Recombination in Evolution of Enteroviruses." *Rev Med Virol* 15:157–167.

Mueller, S., Wimmer, E., and Cello, J. 2005. "Poliovirus and Poliomyelitis: A Tale of Guts, Brains, and an Accidental Event." *Virus Res* 111:175–193.

Orent, W. 2000. "The End of Polio?" *The Sciences* March/April, pp. 25–31.

Palacios, G., and Oberste, M. S. 2005. "Enteroviruses as Agents of Emerging Infectious Diseases." *J Neurovirol* 11:424–433.

Robbins, F. C., and Enders, J. F. 1950. "Tissue Culture Techniques in the Study of Animal Viruses." *Am J Med Sci* 220(3):316–338.

Rotbart, H. A., ed. 1995. Human *Enterovirus Infections*, Washington: ASM Press.

Sabin, A. B. 1987. "Role of My Cooperation with Soviet Scientists in the Elimination of Polio: Possible Lessons for Relations Between the U.S.A. and the U.S.S.R." *Perspect Biol Med* 31(1):57–64.

Solomon, T. 2003. "Exotic and Emerging Viral Encephalitides." *Curr Opin Neurol* 16:411–418.

Stalkup, J. R., and Chilukuri, S. 2002 "Enterovirus Infections: A Review of Clinical Presentation, Diagnosis, and Treatment." *Dermatol Clin* 20:217–223.

Trojan, D. A., and Cashman, N. R. 2005. "Post-Poliomyelitis Syndrome." *Muscle Nerve* 31:6–19.

Vaccines and Biologicals Dept., World Health Organization, Geneva, Switzerland. Div. of Viral and Rickettsial Diseases, National Center for Infectious Diseases; Global Immunization Div., National Immunization Program, CDC2004. "Progress toward Global Eradication of Poliomyelitis, January 2003–April 2004."*MMWR* 53(24):532–535.

Whitton, J. L., and Feuer, R. 2004. "Myocarditis, Microbes and Autoimmunity." *Autoimmunity* 37(5):375–386.

World Health Organization (WHO) Sudan Office, Khartoum, Sudan, et al. 2005. "Progress toward Poliomyelitis Eradication–Poliomyelitis Outbreak in Sudan, 2004."*MMWR* 54(4):97–99.

WHO. 1992. "New Approaches to Poliovirus Diagnosis Using Laboratory Techniques: Memorandum from a WHO Meeting." *Bulletin WHO* 70(1):27–33.

■ Popular Press

Allen, A. 2007. *Vaccine: The Controversial Story of Medicine's Greatest Lifesaver*, New York: W. W. Norton.

Bookchin, D., and Schumacher, J. 2004. *The Virus and the Vaccine: The True Story of a Cancer-Causing Monkey Virus, Contaminated Polio Vaccine and the Millions of Americans Exposed*, New York: St. Martin's Press.

Gilden Seavey, N., Smith, J. S., Wagner, P. 1998. *A Paralyzing Fear: The Triumph Over Polio in America*, New York: TV Books.

Gould, T. 1995. *A Summer Plague: Polio and Its Survivors*, New Haven, CT: Yale University Press.

Halstead, L. S. 1998. "Post-Polio Syndrome." *Scientific American,* April Issue, 278(4):42–47.

Kehret, P. 2006. *Small Steps: The Year I Got Polio*, Morton Grove, IL: Albert Whitman.

Oshinsky, D. M. 2005. *Polio: An American Story, The Crusade That Mobilized the Nation Against the 20th Century's Most Feared Disease*, New York: Oxford University Press.

Pipes, D. *The Hidden Hand: Middle East Fears of Conspiracy*, Hampshire, England: Palgrave Macmillan.

Rogers, N. 1992. *Dirt and Disease: Polio before FDR*, Newark, NJ: Rutgers University Press.

■ Video Productions

A Paralyzing Fear: The Story of Polio in America. 1988. PBS Home Video.

Breathing Lessons. 1996. Fanlight Productions.

In Search of the Polio Vaccine. 1998. The History Channel.

Warm Springs. 2005. HBO production.

FDR, A Presidency Revealed. 2005. The History Channel

RX for Survival: A Global Health Challenge: The Polio Campaign in India, The Campaign Reaches Its Climax. 2005. PBS.

■ eLearning

http://biology.jbpub.com/book/virology

The site features eLearning, an online review area that provides quizzes and other tools to help you study for your class. You can also follow useful links for in-depth information, or just find out the latest virology and microbiology news.

CASE STUDY QUESTIONS

These questions relate to the Case Study presented at the beginning of the chapter.

1. Who is likely the original source of this virus?
2. An investigation was needed to identify potential contacts with the infant. Create a list of individuals that should be interviewed.
3. Who is most at risk for contracting vaccine-derived poliomyelitis?

Wild waterfowl such as these geese and ducks are the largest natural reservoir for influenza viruses. In these birds, infections are generally localized to the intestinal tract, and high concentrations of viruses are shed in the feces without causing disease.

CHAPTER
12

Influenza Viruses

££*The duck is the Trojan horse.***"**

Dr. Robert G. Webster, Influenza Researcher, St. Jude Children's Research Hospital

CASE STUDY

Salesman Walter Smith began to travel extensively throughout Eastern Asia for his job. After business hours, he would sightsee. One day, as he walked the streets of Hanoi, Vietnam, he observed poultry for sale everywhere, especially chickens. There were prized fighting cocks displayed on a grassy median; their owners would suck the blood or phlegm out of the bird's mouths following a fight.

Walter was fascinated by the local traditions and loved exotic cuisine. As noon approached he peered at the menu outside of a crowded restaurant and saw a dish on it that he had never eaten before: duck blood pudding, a delicacy. Intrigued, Walter decided to try it and found it delicious. He had two helpings and then returned to the hotel for the evening. He spent the next three days touring more of the city. On the fourth day, when he awoke in his hotel room, Walter felt feverish. He had a sore throat and his entire body ached. Over the course of the next two days he developed a bad cough. His illness continued to worsen and Walter went to the hospital. Upon his arrival, he saw the waitress who had waited on him at the restaurant where he had eaten the duck blood pudding. She had similar symptoms. Within the next hour, several chefs and more individuals who had dined at the restaurant arrived with the same symptoms. The doctors quickly noticed a pattern of illness and began setting up a ward to quarantine individuals related to this new outbreak of respiratory illness. Later, it was confirmed that this was an avian influenza outbreak.

12.1   History

Influenza is not a new disease. Historians have described outbreaks of a highly contagious respiratory illness followed by pneumonia as early as 400 B.C. The word *influenza* was derived from the medieval Latin word *influentia* because it was believed diseases were caused by bad heavenly fluid or "influence." Thus *influenza* was used as a general term; for example, scarlet fever was referred to as *influenza di febbre scarlattina;* catarrhal fever (a very bad head cold involving copious mucous production) was called *influenza di catarro.* The first word in the phrase became the most significant. The French term *la grippe*—("the seizure") became the most popular term during the early 1900s. In English, diseases correlated with most respiratory tract infections became known as **influenza,** later abbreviated to the modern *flu.*

There have been major influenza epidemics (localized outbreaks) and pandemics (worldwide epidemics). Pandemics occurred in 1918 (Spanish influenza), 1957 (Asian flu), 1968 (Hong Kong flu), and 1977 (swine flu). They occur when the influenza virus mutates dramatically. These pandemics resulted in high morbidity and mortality.

Today, millions of Americans contract the flu each year. In an average season there are approximately 36,000 deaths nationwide and many more hospitalizations. The elderly, pregnant women, and very young children are at the highest risk of developing serious flu complications. Many virologists think that another influenza pandemic that could kill millions of humans is inevitable.

12.2   Epidemiology

At any given time of the year, one or two strains of influenza virus dominate a particular region of the world. In temperate or colder regions influenza illness usually occurs during the winter, but in tropical regions, influenza occurs throughout the year. Influenza epidemics can become unmanageable at alarming speeds for several reasons:

- The incubation period (the time between infection and the first appearance of symptoms) is extremely short (1–4 days).
- Copious numbers of infectious virus particles are shed in droplets discharged by sneezing or coughing. One droplet can contain 100,000 to 1,000,000 virus particles.
- Many symptomatic individuals do not stay at home. Instead, they continue their normal activities, spreading the illness to many contacts in the process.
- Individuals lack immunity to the strain of influenza circulating in the area at the time of the epidemic.

Schools are a primary source for sharing influenza viruses. Children bring the viruses home. Parents who contract the flu then disseminate the infection into the workplace. The best indicator of the scale of an epidemic is an escalation in absenteeism from schools and the workplace that is accompanied by an increase in hospital admissions and deaths, especially among the elderly. Epidemiologists measure the increase in mortality during an influenza epidemic by comparing it to the average number of deaths during comparable winters without an influenza epidemic. The number of "excess deaths" help to determine epidemic years. From 1957 to 1987 there were 20 influenza epidemics recorded in the United States. At least 36,000 and up to 50,000 people have died as a direct or indirect consequence of an influenza infection.

In the United States, the Spanish flu killed 675,000 Americans, with a 4.39/1000 national average. Death rates peaked in October of 1918 (**Figure 12-1a**). This epidemic was unique in that it killed healthy adults ages 20 to 40 (Figure 12-1b) in addition to children

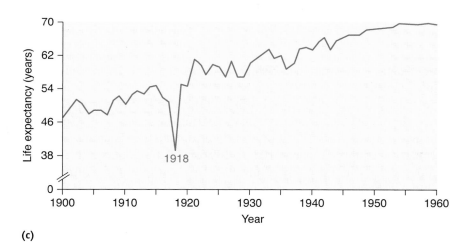

■ Figure 12-1

(a) During the Spanish flu pandemic of 1918, the month of October had the highest number of flu-related deaths. Adapted from PBS, "Influenza 1918," *American Experience,* http://www.pbs.org/wgbh/amex/influenza/maps. (b) This graph compares the age distribution of influenza deaths in 1918 and 1911–1917. Influenza pandemics result in a **"U-shaped" curve** with mortality peaks in the very young and the elderly. The Spanish flu was unusual in that it also killed those in the prime of their lives, resulting in a characteristic **"W-shaped" curve.** Adapted from J. K. Taubenberger, *ASM News* 65 (1999): 473–478. (c) U.S. life expectancy dropped in 1918. Adapted from J. K. Taubenberger, *ASM News* 65 (1999): 473–478.

Retrospective Studies

A retrospective study is defined as a study that looks backward in time. Based on this definition, determine by means of a retrospective study the impact the 1918 Spanish flu had on the community you currently reside in. An example by students at the University of Wisconsin–Oshkosh follows.

In the spring semester of 2001, three very different classes at the University of Wisconsin–Oshkosh joined together to create the "Flu Project" as part of a multidisciplinary approach to learning about the types of research relevant to the study of epidemiology, archaeology, and gerontology. As a result of participating in the project through their individual courses, 70 students (35 virology students, 5 archaeology students, and 30 psychology students) were involved. The students participated in data collection and analysis about the spread of a deadly disease, the memorialization of those who died, and the memories of those who survived.

Undergraduates in virology class learned about epidemiology by studying the death records of those who died of the flu and related pneumonia in Winnebago County during the months of the epidemic. These students discovered where victims of the flu lived and the condition of their lives that may have contributed to the contagion and its deadliness. The psychology students interviewed flu survivors about their experiences and attitudes toward infectious diseases then and now. The archaeology students studied the headstones and graveyards to determine if burial practices changed during times of crisis (e.g., many bodies buried in a short time period). The students also learned the value of record keeping. Their biggest surprise was the inaccuracies in reporting the numbers of flu cases at the actual time of the epidemic. The students now have put together a more accurate picture of this historical event and have contributed to the knowledge base about it. For more information go to http://www.uwosh.edu/departments/biology/shors/teaching/UWOSpanishflu.mov, UW–Oshkosh Flu Study WISN News at http://www.uwosh.edu/departments/biology/shors/textbook/UWOflustudy.html, and http://www.uwosh.edu/archives/flu/home.html.

and elderly, who are usually within the high-risk group. This epidemic decreased life expectancy in the United States by 11 years (Figure 12-1c).

The 1957–1958 Asian flu caused 70,000 deaths and the 1968–1969 Hong Kong flu resulted in 34,000 deaths in the United States. All of these deaths were caused by influenza **Type A** viruses (see Section 12.4, Classification of Influenza Viruses). Each flu season is unique, but it is estimated that approximately 10% to 20% of U.S. residents get the flu, and an average of 114,000 persons are hospitalized for flu-related complications during each season. About 36,000 Americans die on average per year from the complications of flu.

12.3   Clinical Features

Influenza can be hard to diagnose because there are several other diseases that resemble it. Accurate diagnosis is based on the patient's history and physical examination in a clinical setting. Sometimes laboratory testing is performed before treatment is initiated.

■ Uncomplicated Infection

There is a tendency for patients—and even some doctors—to label all respiratory ailments as the flu. In reality, influenza is a distinct clinical entity that begins after a two to three day

TABLE 12-1	Cold or Flu?	
Symptoms	**Cold**	**Flu**
Fever	Rare in adults and older children, but can be as high at 102°F in infants and small children	High (100 to 104°F), lasting 3–4 days.
Headache	Rare	Prominent, sudden onset
General muscle aches and pain	Slight/mild	Common, often severe
Sore throat	Sometimes	Common
Cough, chest discomfort	Mild hacking cough	Common, can become severe
Sneezing	Often	Sometimes
Runny or stuffy nose	Often	Sometimes
Fatigue, weakness	Mild	Often extreme, lasting 2–3 weeks.
Extreme exhaustion	Never	Sudden onset; can be severe
Complications	Sinus congestion or earache	Bronchitis, pneumonia
Prevention	None	Annual vaccination, antiviral drug
Treatment	Temporary relief of symptoms	Antiviral drug within 24–48 hours after onset of symptoms

incubation period. The illness starts with an unexpected onset of symptoms: headache; aching in the limbs and back; fever; **malaise** (a vague feeling of physical discomfort or uneasiness); a dry cough; a dry, tickling throat, which can lead to the voice becoming husky and even lost; a sore throat; and **myalgia** (pain in muscles). Many patients can pinpoint the hour that they started feeling ill.

In general, most individuals feel weak and remain in bed. Their temperature will be high and continuous (100°F to 103°F for three days). Cough and weakness can persist for another week or more. Eyes are watery and burning and can even be painful upon movement. The nose may be runny or blocked with discharge. On examination by a physician, the patient's eyes appear red and his or her cheeks may be flushed. A chest x-ray will be normal unless a secondary bacterial infection has taken place. Usually the infection resolves itself within seven days, although patients often complain of feeling listless for a few weeks after the infection.

Many individuals think that a cold and the flu are caused by the same virus. They are not. The common cold, or acute viral rhinitis, is a much milder disease that can be caused by one of over 100 different types of rhinoviruses and is not lethal. The differences between a cold and the flu are listed in Table 12-1.

■ Complicated Infection

Complications depend on the age of the patient. Young children may develop croup (laryngitis with a hoarse, barking cough and difficult breathing), secondary bacterial pneumonia, and middle ear infections. Elderly are particularly vulnerable to life-threatening pneumonia caused by secondary bacterial infections (usually due to *Staphylococcus aureus*, *Streptococcus pneumoniae*, or *Haemophilus influenzae*). In addition, preexisting chronic conditions such as congestive heart failure can be exacerbated.

In addition to the elderly, anyone suffering from chronic conditions affecting the pulmonary (lung), cardiac (heart), renal (kidney), hepatic (liver), or endocrine systems is at risk. Modern medicine has kept many children alive who have immune deficiencies or

TABLE 12-2	Symptoms and Signs of Inhalational Anthrax vs. Laboratory-Confirmed Influenza and SARS		
Symptoms/Signs	Inhalational Anthrax (*n* = 10)*	Laboratory-Confirmed Influenza*	SARS (*n* = 62)**
Fever or chills	100%	83%–90%	100%
Fatigue/malaise	100%	75%–94%	100%
Nonproductive cough	90%	84%–93%	90%
Shortness of breath or chest discomfort/pain	80%	6%	72%
Headache	50%	84%–91%	85%
Sore throat	20%	64%–84%	12%
Runny nose	10%	79%	10%
Nausea or vomiting	80%	12%	32%
Abdominal pain	30%	22%	NA
Myalgias (muscle pain)	50%	67%–94%	87%

The CDC reported the signs and symptoms of 10 cases of inhalation anthrax that occurred after the tragic events of September 11, 2001, and compared it to laboratory-confirmed influenza (*data from *MMWR*, 2001, 50[44]:984–986). The inhalational anthrax cases began appearing just before flu season, raising diagnostic concerns for healthcare providers. Many persons who were exposed to inhalational anthrax in the bioterrorism-related anthrax attacks completed a 60-day course of antimicrobial prophylaxis. From February to May 2003, researchers investigated the clinical signs, symptoms, and course of all probable SARS cases defined by WHO criteria during the Vietnam outbreak (**data from Thu Vu, H. et al. 2004. *EID* 10[2]:334–338).

NA = Not available.

diseases such as cystic fibrosis, as well as saved patients of any age with organ transplants, cancer, or acquired immunodeficiency syndrome (AIDS). This has increased the number of individuals at risk of death during an influenza epidemic.

■ Reye's Syndrome

Besides secondary bacterial infections, there is a rare condition called **Reye's syndrome** that is sometimes associated with influenza (or other viral illnesses such as chickenpox) in children. Studies have shown that using aspirin or salicylate-containing medications to treat viral illnesses increases the risk of developing Reye's syndrome. It affects all organs of the body but is most harmful to the brain and the liver, causing an acute increase of pressure within the brain and massive accumulations of fat in the liver and other organs.

Symptoms of Reye's syndrome include persistent or recurrent vomiting, listlessness, personality changes (such as irritability or combativeness), disorientation or confusion, delirium, convulsions, and loss of consciousness. There is no cure for Reye's syndrome. Successful management depends on early diagnosis.

■ Inhalation Anthrax, Influenza, or SARS?

After the terrorist attacks on the United States of September 11, 2001, there were concerns by clinicians on how to evaluate persons who may be at increased risk for inhalation anthrax but who have symptoms of an influenza-like illness. By November 2001, the Centers for Disease Control and Prevention (CDC) published a table listing the signs and symptoms of ten cases of inhalational anthrax compared to laboratory-confirmed influenza. It is important to be able to distinguish among respiratory infections—especially during the flu season—so that they can be treated appropriately (Table 12-2).

TABLE 12-3	Differences Between Influenza Types A, B, and C Viruses		
Feature	Influenza A	Influenza B	Influenza C
Host Range	Humans, pigs, horses, birds, marine mammals	Humans only	Humans and pigs
Epidemiology	Antigenic shift and drift	Antigenic drift only	Antigenic drift only
Clinical Features	May cause pandemics with significant mortalities in affected young people	Severe disease, generally confined to elderly or high-risk, pandemics not seen	Mild disease, common in children, without seasonality
Genome	8 gene segments	8 gene segments	7 gene segments
Structure	10 viral proteins M2 unique	11 viral proteins NB unique	9 viral proteins HEF unique

12.4 Classification of Influenza Viruses

True influenza is caused by any of several genera of the *Orthomyxoviridae* family of viruses. *Orthos* is the Greek term meaning standard or correct and *myxa* means mucus. This family contains three influenza genera categorized as influenza type A, type B, and type C viruses. All three types of influenza viruses can cause similar symptoms in humans. Infection with one type of influenza, however, does not confer immunity to the other types. Table 12-3 compares the epidemiological, clinical, genomic, and structural differences among the three virus types. All three share certain structural features, including segmented genomes (single-stranded RNA [ssRNA] of negative polarity), envelope glycoproteins critical for virus entry and exit of cells, and a host-derived envelope.

12.5 Laboratory Diagnosis

Most physicians use a cluster of signs to diagnose influenza, backed up by the knowledge that an outbreak is in progress. Influenza viruses, common cold viruses, and bacteria can cause similar upper respiratory tract symptoms. The intensity, severity, and frequency of the symptoms vary. Figure 12-2 illustrates the natural course of influenza infection. If a tentative diagnosis of influenza has been made, laboratory testing may be an appropriate confirmatory step.

■ Office-Based Rapid Viral Tests

There are at least six commercially available, office-based techniques for detecting influenza A and/or B. All of these tests can be completed within 10 to 20 minutes. These rapid tests are either enzyme-linked immunosorbent assay (ELISA) or immunoflourescent assays (for review of techniques see Chapter 5). The BD Directigen and QuickVue tests distinguish between influenza A and B viral antigens. If the chosen test is positive, antiviral therapy may be considered if symptoms have been present for less than 48 hours. A negative test result may support the decision to withhold antiviral drug therapy. Although rapid tests are relatively easy to perform, the CDC estimates that up to 30% of samples may produce negative results, yet be positive by viral culture methods. Rapid tests may also produce false-positive results.

■ **Figure 12-2**

The natural course of influenza in an otherwise healthy 28-year-old male patient. Many symptoms overlap throughout the duration of influenza. Virus particles are shed during the first five days of the infection. Adapted from R. Dolin, *Am. Fam. Physician* 14 (1976): p. 74.

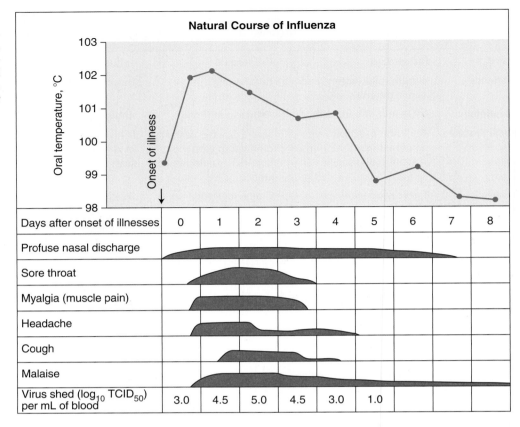

Days after onset of illnesses	0	1	2	3	4	5	6	7	8
Profuse nasal discharge									
Sore throat									
Myalgia (muscle pain)									
Headache									
Cough									
Malaise									
Virus shed (log$_{10}$ TCID$_{50}$) per mL of blood	3.0	4.5	5.0	4.5	3.0	1.0			

■ Other Tests

Viral culture is the most accurate method for identifying specific viral strains. Virus can be recovered from nasal swab specimens, nasal washes, or combined nose-and-throat swab specimens. It can also be isolated directly from sputum samples. Samples are placed in special transport containers, labeled, and transported properly to the viral diagnostic lab as soon as possible.

The specimens are inoculated onto rhesus or cynomolgus monkey kidney cells or Madin-Darby canine kidney (MDCK) cell cultures where the virus is detected by cytopathic effect or other assays. Results are not available for two to ten days. Viral culture is also costly (about $100) and requires special laboratory procedures as well as skilled technicians to carry out these procedures. In sophisticated laboratories, nucleic acid techniques (polymerase chain reaction [PCR]), electron microscopy, cytology, and histology may be used to diagnose viral illness.

■ Serology Testing

Sometimes in clinical practice a serum sample is collected from the patient when the patient comes in for diagnosis and once again 10 to 20 days later, after the patient has recovered (**convalescent serum**). The serum samples are analyzed for an increase in antibody titer. A fourfold or greater increase in antibody titer is considered diagnostic of infection. This information is collected too late and therefore does not affect clinical decisions; however, it does confirm evidence of the infection.

■ "Flu Chips"

Several research teams are currently developing "flu chips" or **microarrays** as a way to quickly identify (within an hour or less) and screen for influenza (types A, B, and C), avian influenza, severe acute respiratory syndrome–coronavirus (SARS-CoV), respiratory syncytial virus (RSV), and other airborne bioterrorist pathogens such as *Bacillus anthracis*. A team led by Kathy Rowlen and Robert Kuchta at the University of Colorado–Boulder, in collaboration with the World Health Organization (WHO), the CDC, and Bio-Rad Laboratories, has developed a diagnostic microarray that addresses the needs of developing nations by creating an inexpensive and field-portable test kit for influenza A respiratory tract infections.

David Stenger's research team has developed a microarray that detects more than 26 respiratory pathogens. A research group led by Zuhong Lu has developed a novel PCR assay that integrates PCR processes and DNA microarrays to detect influenza types A or B, SARS-CoV, and enteroviruses. A new technology called **glycan microarray analysis** has focused on detecting the virus-receptor specificity of new influenza strains, especially H5N1 viruses. Influenza viruses use host glycans that contain sialic acid moieties as cell-surface receptors. These glycans vary in structure from species to species. The subtle difference in recognizing glycan structures can rapidly assess whether influenza strains from avian or other species will easily infect humans.

12.6 Cellular Pathogenesis

Influenza is spread person to person via droplets containing the virus. Large numbers of virus are present in respiratory secretions of infected persons. The virus is dispersed in aerosol form by sneezing, coughing, and talking. Influenza infection is acquired by the respiratory route through the inhalation of aerosoled virus particles. Once the virus enters the respiratory tract, it can attach to and penetrate ciliated columnar epithelial cells lining the sinuses and airways (**Figure 12-3a**).

The primary site of infection occurs at the tracheobronchial tree, but the nasopharynx is also involved (Figure 12-3b). After the virus attaches, is adsorbed, and replication begins, the cilia are destroyed, releasing progeny virus that spread to nearby cells. Hence the cleaning system in the lungs does not work well. As the numbers of cilia are reduced, there are less to clean the lungs and more mucus stays in the airways, clogging them and making the individual cough. The loss of epithelial cells and destruction of cilia can contribute to secondary bacterial invasion, manifested as sinusitis, otitis (inflammation of the ear), and **pneumonia** (infection of the alveoli and surrounding lung). Infectious virus can be isolated for one to seven days, with the peak of the released virus occurring on the fourth or fifth day after infection (**Figure 12-4**).

12.7 Immunity

Infection with influenza virus results in the development of antibodies against the H and N envelope glycoproteins of the virus. Anti-H antibodies neutralize the virus, preventing attachment/viral infectivity. Antibodies against N do not neutralize the virus, but they do reduce release of virus from infected cells. If the individual has been infected within the past couple of years by a closely related strain of influenza H subtype, anti-H IgA class antibodies may intercept and neutralize infecting virions. IgG antibodies may play a secondary role in neutralizing the virus, providing protection in the lung.

If preexisting antibodies are inadequate, the individual must mount an antibody response against the virus. Besides an antibody response, other arms of the immune system play a role in recovery. These are activated macrophages, natural killer T cells, and some cytokines such as interferon.

■ **Figure 12-3**

(a) The cilia are attached to columnar epithelial cells. Cilia sweep mucus produced in goblet cells as well as mucous coming from deeper glands within the lungs and the particulate matter trapped in the mucous. The presence of cilia aids the removal of mucous materials from lower parts of the airway to the throat for disposal. **(b)** Exit and primary sites of respiratory infections.

(a)

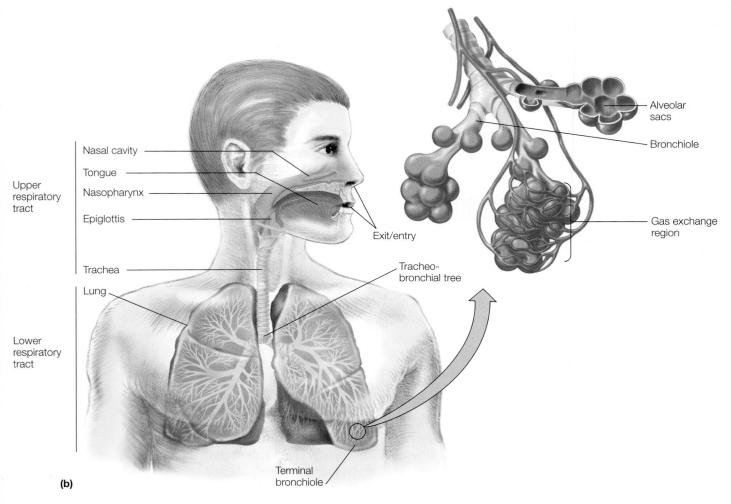

(b)

A **cytokine storm** or **systemic inflammatory response syndrome (SIRS)**, has been suggested as an explanation for the devastating nature of the 1918 flu. From a clinical perspective, a cytokine storm is defined as an immune system that is overreacting toward the pathogen. In this situation, cytokine signaling immune cells such as macrophages and T-cells travel to the site of infection, causing damage to the body and thus the failure of multiple organs (**Figure 12-5**). This is a rare event. Patients who suffer from them usually die. The 1918 H1N1 strain has been re-created using published sequences and reverse genetics (see Virus File 12-2). The re-created virus was highly virulent in macaques and mice. Scientists determined that the following chemokines or cytokines were present at elevated levels in the bronchii of macaques infected with the 1918 virus: interleukin-6 (IL-6), interleukin-8 (IL-8), monocyte chemotactic protein-1 (CCL2), and CCL5 (RANTES). The H5N1 influenza strain also causes SIRS and is 50% lethal in humans.

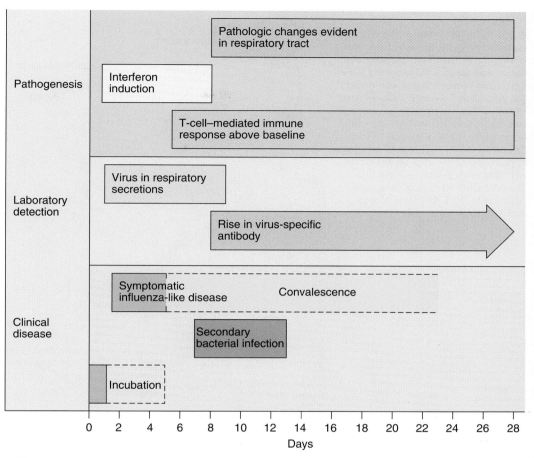

■ **Figure 12-4**

Time course of influenza A infection. Flulike symptoms occur early. Later, pneumonia may result from a secondary bacterial infection in certain individuals. Adapted from Murray, P. R., et al. *Medical Microbiology,* Third Edition. Mosby Elsevier Health Science, 1998.

I2.8   Viral Replication

■ Properties of the Influenza A Virus Particle

Influenza particles are 80 to 120 nm in diameter. Influenza strains may be filamentous in a form of helical symmetry immediately after isolation (**Figure 12-6a**), but after several passages in cell cultures in the laboratory, the particle morphology becomes spherical (Figure 12-6b).Electron micrographs reveal influenza type A to be enveloped viruses, covered with approximately 500 projecting spikes. Approximately 80% of these rod-shaped glycoprotein spikes are **hemagglutinin (H)** antigen (a trimer) and 20% are mushroom-shaped **neuraminidase antigen (N)** (a tetramer). See Figure 12-6c. The H is a **transmembrane protein**, whereas N is an **integral membrane protein**. The inside of the particle is lined by a **matrix 1 (M1)** protein.

In addition to the N and H proteins found on the surface of the virus, there are also small amounts of **M2 ion channel** integral membrane protein present in influenza A virus particles. M2 is not present in influenza B virions. M2 ion channel protein is inserted into

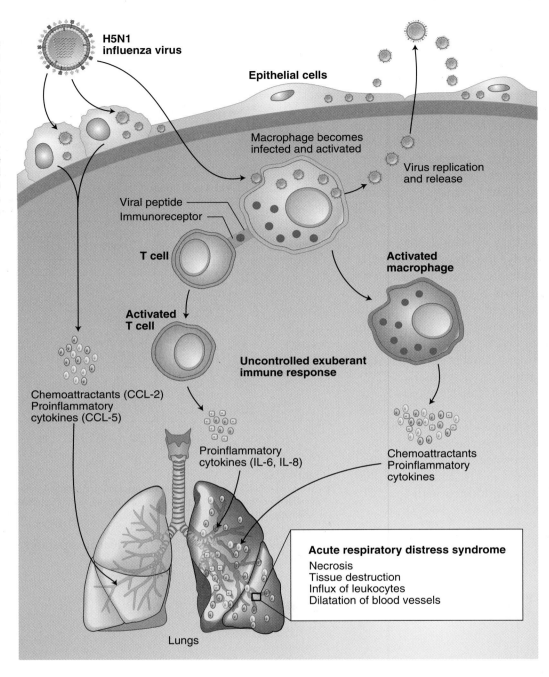

■ **Figure 12-5**
Model for the mechanism of the cytokine storm evoked by highly virulent influenza viruses. The viruses infect epithelial cells. Macrophages are attracted to the site of infection and become infected with viruses. The macrophage becomes activated and presents a viral peptide on its outside surface. This in turn, activates a T cell, resulting in an uncontrolled response of proinflammatory chemokines and cytokines. The blood vessels of the lungs become dilated and filled with leukocytes, resulting in destruction and necrosis of lung tissues. Adapted from M. T. Osterholm, *N. Engl. J. Med.* 352 (2005): 1839–1842.

the lipid bilayer membrane that surrounds the viral genetic material. Directly below the lipid membrane of the virus particle is a layer of viral matrix protein termed M1. It is the most abundant virion protein. Inside the virus are eight segments of ssRNA of negative polarity ranging from 890 to 2341 nucleotides in length (**Figure 12-7**). The coding assignments for each segment are depicted in the schematic diagram of the influenza A particle in Table 12-4. Each segment contains a transcriptase complex that consists of three additional viral polymerase proteins: PB1, PB2, and PA. Small amounts of NS2 are present in purified virions. NS1 is only found in infected cells.

■ Virus Nomenclature

The standard naming for influenza viruses is:

- influenza type/
- species isolated from/ (unless human)

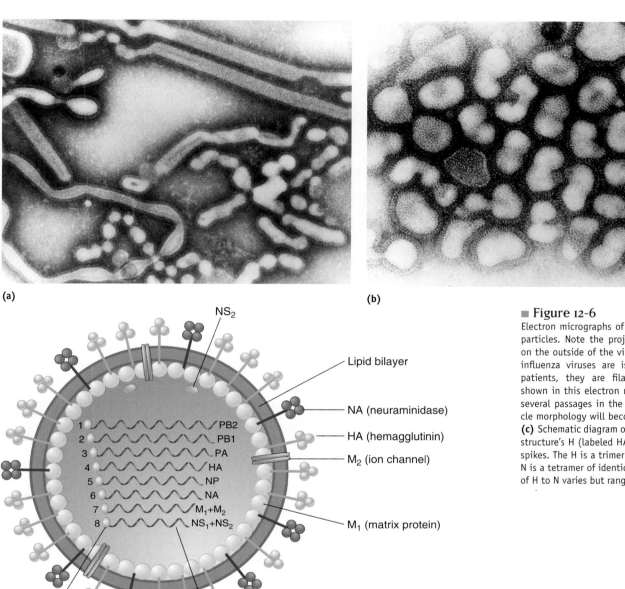

(a)

(b)

(c)

NS₂

Lipid bilayer

NA (neuraminidase)

HA (hemagglutinin)

M₂ (ion channel)

M₁ (matrix protein)

NP (nucleocapsid)

PB1, PB2, PA
(transcriptase complex)

1 PB2
2 PB1
3 PA
4 HA
5 NP
6 NA
7 M₁+M₂
8 NS₁+NS₂

■ **Figure 12-6**
Electron micrographs of influenza A spherical particles. Note the projecting spikes located on the outside of the viral particle. **(a)** When influenza viruses are isolated directly from patients, they are filamentous shaped, as shown in this electron micrograph. **(b)** After several passages in the laboratory, the particle morphology will become spherical shaped. **(c)** Schematic diagram of the influenza A virus structure's H (labeled HA) and N (labeled NA) spikes. The H is a trimer of identical subunits. N is a tetramer of identical subunits. The ratio of H to N varies but ranges from 4:1 to 5:1.

- place of isolation/
- strain designation/
- year isolation/
- H#N# subtypes

For example, influenza A isolated from the first patient isolate in Hong Kong in 1968 is given the name A/Hong Kong/1/68(H3N2). If the influenza isolate has been isolated from another host, such as birds or animals, the host name is included (e.g., A/swine/Iowa/15/30(H1N1)). If the strain is a human strain, the host origin is not included in the name (e.g., A/Sing/1/57). Influenza type A is the most frequent cause of influenza and will be the focus of this chapter.

There are sixteen antigenically different types of Hs, labeled H1–H16 subtypes, and nine distinct Ns (N1–N9 subtypes). All subtypes differ by more than 30% amino acid sequence homology. All H and N subtypes infect waterfowl (e.g., ducks). Six subtypes of H

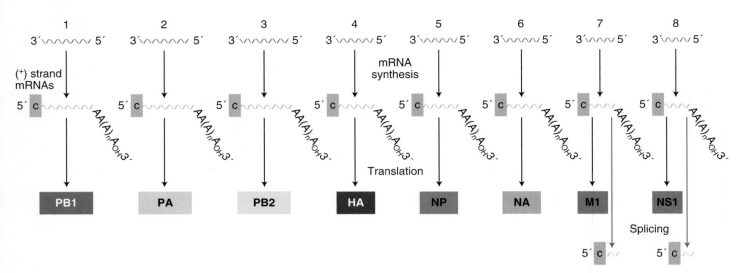

■ Figure 12-7
There are eight influenza A RNA segments, coding for ten influenza protein products. Gene segments 7 and 8 code for more than one protein on overlapping reading frames and the viral RNAs undergo a splicing event. Adapted from Flint, S. J., et al. *Principles of Virology: Molecular Biology, Pathogenesis, and Control of Animal Viruses,* Second Edition. ASM Press, 2003.

TABLE 12-4	Influenza A Gene Coding Assignments		
RNA Segment	**Length (nt)**	**Encoded Polypeptide (aa)**	**Function**
1	2341	PB1 757	Catalyzes nucleotide addition (part of transcriptase complex)
2	2233	PA 716	Part of transcriptase complex
3	2341	PB2 759	Recognizes cap of host mRNAs, endonuclease (part of transcriptase complex)
4	2073	HA 566	Hemagglutinin Major surface glycoprotein Sialic acid binding Fusion at low pH
5	1565	NP 498	Nucleocapsid protein, interacts with RNA segments Involved in switching of mRNA to template RNA synthesis and virion RNA synthesis
6	1413	NA 454	Surface glycoprotein Neuraminidase (cleaves sialic acid)
7	1027 spliced	M1 252 M2 97	M1 matrix protein inside of lipid envelope of virion M2 has ion channel activity
8	934 spliced	NS1 230 NS2 121	NS1, nonstructural protein (not detected in virions) inhibits export of poly(A)'dmRNAs and pre-mRNA splicing, IFN antagonist NS2 plays a role in export of ribonucleoproteins (RNPs) out of the nucleus

(H1, H2, H3, H5, H7, and H9) and two subtypes of N (N1 and N2) have been recovered from humans (Table 12-5). All but the H5, H7, and H9 subtypes spread human to human efficiently. Besides humans and birds, other H and N subtypes are found in pigs, seals, and horses. Cross-reactivity among the different subtypes does not occur. In other words, if you are immune to influenza H1N1, you will not have any immunity against H2N2. The antigenic subtype differences are critical for vaccine preparation.

■ Genome Organization

Influenza A virus contains eight segments of ssRNA of negative polarity. (See Table 12-4 for coding assignments.) The complete nucleotide sequence of influenza A virus PR/8/34 and many RNA segments of other subtypes were completed in 1982. Segments 1 to 6 code for only one viral protein; segments 7 and 8 code for two.

■ The Virus Life Cycle

Virus Adsorption and Entry

The influenza virus H attaches to sialic acid residues that are present on glycoproteins or glycolipids of the ciliated columnar epithelial cells lining the sinuses and airways. Next, the bound virus is endocytosed by the cell. Virions enter the cell within the endosomal vesicle (**Figure 12-8a**). Inside of the **endosome**, the virus is exposed to a relatively low pH (the pH drops from 7 to 5). The pH-change triggers fusion between the viral lipid membrane and the host cell endosomal membrane (Figure 12-8b). The low pH-dependent fusion event is mediated by the H protein. The membrane fusion step is a vital step in the life cycle of the virus. The H protein undergoes an irreversible conformational change that is triggered by the low pH of the endosome. The H protein is composed of two polypeptides, designated H_1 and H_2. Full-length H protein is referred to as H_0. The H_1 and H_2 polypeptides are linked by a disulfide (S-S) bond between two cysteines. The H_1 portion of H_0 contains sialic acid-binding sites for attachment to the host cell. The H_2 portion of H_0 forms a membrane-spanning anchor called a fusion peptide, which is directly involved in the fusion mechanism (Figure 12-8b). The H_2 peptide interacts with the host membrane after the conformational change is induced in H_0 by low pH.

Influenza virus is not infectious unless the H protein is cleaved by cellular proteases. If the H protein contains a furin cleavage site, it undergoes proteolytic cleavage by a cellular protease inside of the trans-Golgi network. If it does not contain a furin cleavage site, the H_0 precursor protein is cleaved into H_1 and H_2 by cellular proteases outside of the host cell. This limits their spread in hosts to tissues where the appropriate proteases are encountered. (See Figure 12-8c for schematic showing the cleavage site within the protein.) A general rule has been observed: The H's of pathogenic influenza viruses are cleaved intracellularly by proteases and have the capacity to infect various cell types and cause systemic infections. The H's of influenza virus that are cleaved by extracellular trypsin-like proteases are

| TABLE 12-5 | Hemagglutinin (H) and Neuraminidase (N) Subtypes of Influenza A Viruses Isolated from Humans, Lower Mammals, and Birds |

Subtype	Human	Swine	Horse	Bird
Hemagglutinin				
H1	√	√		√
H2	√			√
H3	√	√	√	√
H4				√
H5	√			√
H6				√
H7	√		√	√
H8				√
H9	√			√
H10				√
H11				√
H12				√
H13				√
H14				√
H15				√
H16				√
Neuraminidase				
N1	√	√		√
N2	√			√
N3		√		√
N4				√
N5				√
N6				√
N7			√	√
N8			√	√
N9				√

Adapted from A. J. Levine. *Viruses*. W. H. Freeman and Company, 1992.

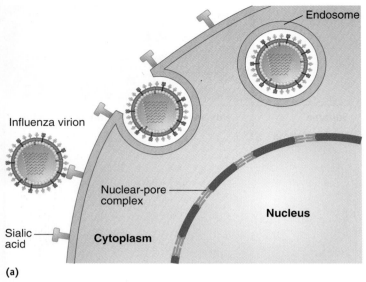

(a)

■ **Figure 12-8**
(a) Influenza virus attachment and entry. Adapted from Fields, B. N., et al. *Fields Virology*, Fourth Edition. Lippincott Williams & Wilkins, 2001. **(b)** Conformational changes in influenza H protein trigger membrane fusion. Adapted from B. P. Bergstrom, "Protein Sorting: Organelle Biogenesis and Protein Secretion," *BIOL336: Cell Physiology*, http://www.muskingum.edu/~brianb/CellPhys/Lect11. **(c)** Influenza A H_0 must be cleaved into H_1 and H_2 in order for the virus to be infectious. The sequence of the cleavage site determines which proteases (intracellular or extracellular) can cleave H_0. Adapted from N. H. Acheson. *Fundamentals of Molecular Virology*. John Wiley & Sons, 2006.

(b)

(c)

generally apathogenic, limiting their spread in hosts to tissues that contain the appropriate proteases. In some cases of influenza, the proteases of coinfecting bacteria may play a role in virus activation and cause an increase in the severity of the disease.

Uncoating Step

Uncoating takes place in the host cell endosome. Once the viral membrane fuses with the endosomal membrane of the host cell, the viral M2 transmembrane protein forms a transmembrane H+ ion channel or small pore in the viral envelope. The M2 ion channel protein allows H+ ions to penetrate the virion, weakening the interaction of the viral M1 matrix protein from the viral RNA, NP, and transcriptase complex (RNP). The RNPs are released into the cytoplasm and exported to the nucleus. The antiviral drugs **amantidine** (sold as Symmetrel) and **rimantidine** (sold as Flumadine) block the M2 ion channel function, resulting in the incomplete release of the viral RNPs, interfering with uncoating (**Figure 12-9**).

mRNA Synthesis and Replication of Virion RNA

Influenza virus genome replication occurs in the nucleus of the infected cell. This is an unusual feature for an RNA virus because most RNA viruses replicate their viral genomes in the cytoplasm of the infected cell. Following attachment, entry, and uncoating, the viral RNPs are transported to the nucleus and mRNA synthesis begins. During synthesis of mRNA, influenza engages in a process termed **cap-snatching**. The viral PB2 protein binds to the cap structures of the host mRNA in the nucleus of the cell. The cap, together with 10 to 13 nucleotides from the 5′ end of the host mRNA, is removed and PB1 and PA of the RNP complex uses this short string of nucleotides as a primer to initiate transcription of viral RNA (vRNA) by extending the primer (**Figure 12-10a**).

Transcription of the viral mRNA is terminated near the end of the genome segment at a point on the template vRNA that contains a run of uracil residues 17 to 22 residues from its 5′ end. These are copied into A residues in the mRNA, generating a poly A tail before the mRNA dissociates from the vRNA template. Synthesis of the antigenome positive-sense RNA does not use a primer and generates a complete complementary copy of the template RNA, termed vcRNA (Figure 12-10b). As a result, influenza viruses can only replicate in physiologically active cells containing a functional DNA dependent RNA polymerase (RNA polymerase II) even though this enzyme does not transcribe the virus genome. Two types of viral RNAs are generated: a positive sense viral mRNA and a positive sense viral anti genome RNA. Table 12-6 distinguishes the difference between these two types of viral RNAs.

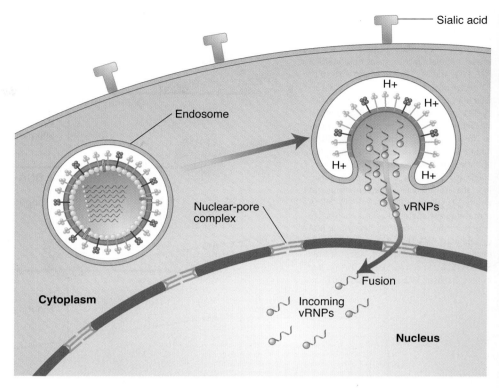

■ **Figure 12-9**

Fusion and uncoating of influenza A viruses. M2 facilitates the movement of protons from the endosome into the inside of the virion. The ribonucleoproteins are liberated to the cytoplasm and then transported to the host cell nucleus. Two drugs (amantidine and rimantidine) block the M2 ion channel activity, preventing viral uncoating. Adapted from Fields, B. N., et al. *Fields Virology*, Fourth Edition. Lippincott Williams & Wilkins, 2001.

TABLE 12-6	The Differences Between the Influenza Virus mRNA and Antigenome
+ vmRNA	**+ Antigenome RNA (vcRNA)**
Shorter than template genome segment	Exact copy of the genome segment
Contains 3′ poly (A) tail	No 3′ poly (A) tail
Contains 5′ cap	No 5′ cap
Synthesis is insensitive to inhibitors of protein synthesis	Synthesis requires continuous viral protein synthesis

Viral mRNAs Are Not Cannabilized for Their 5′ Caps

Interestingly, the viral polymerase proteins selectively "snatch" caps from cellular pre-mRNAs but not viral mRNAs. This selectivity is essential because if the 5′ ends of the viral mRNAs were removed and utilized as primers, overall synthesis and translation of viral mRNAs would not occur. How has this selectivity evolved? While studying the splicing mechanism of RNA segments 7 and 8 of influenza, researchers discovered that the viral polymerase complex binds to the specific sequence 5′-AGCAAAAAGCAGG-3′ that is found in all mRNAs complementary to nucleotides 1 to 12 of the 3′ end of each vRNA segment. This protects the 5′ ends of all viral mRNAs but not cellular pre-mRNAs from cleavage by the polymerase complex (Figure 12-10b).

■ **Figure 12-10**

(a) Cap-snatching mechanism of influenza A viruses. Three influenza proteins are involved in stealing the cap of host mRNAs: PB2, PB1, and PA. The cap, along with 10 to 13 nucleotides from the 5′ end of the cellular mRNA, is removed from the host mRNA by PB1 and the RNA from the 5′ end of the cleaved cellular mRNA is used as a primer to initiate transcription of viral RNAs. Adapted from N. H. Acheson. *Fundamentals of Molecular Virology.* John Wiley & Sons, 2006. (b) Schematic diagram distinguishing the differences between influenza virion (−) genome RNA, viral (+) mRNA containing the snatched cellular mRNA cap structure, and (+) viral complementary RNA or template RNA that is a complete copy of the genome RNA segment. Adapted from Strauss, E. G., and J. H. Strauss. *Viruses and Human Diseases.* Academic Press, 2001.

(a)

(b)

mRNA generated from influenza virus segment 7

Reading frames in mRNA

mRNA generated from influenza virus segment 8

■ **Figure 12-11**
Splicing of RNA segments 7 and 8 of influenza A viruses. Shaded areas represent coding regions in either the 0, +1, or +2 open reading frames (ORFs). Thin lines represent untranslated regions. Introns are shown by the V-shaped lines. The first ORF codes for unspliced M1 and NS1 proteins. No evidence has been obtained that the M3 mRNA is detected in infected cells. Note that the M2 and NS2 proteins share common amino terminal sequences to the M1 or NS1 protein products, respectively.

Influenza Exploits Host Nuclear Splicing Machinery

After the "snatched" cap and associated nucleotides are used as a primer to transcribe each of the eight negative-sense RNA genome segments, six newly transcribed viral mRNAs (segments 1–6) are exported to the cytoplasm and translated immediately into viral proteins. Two of the primary viral transcripts (segments 7 and 8) are each spliced through the exploitation of the host splice machinery into at least two viral mRNAs. **Figure 12-11** is a schematic illustrating the different viral mRNAs generated from influenza A segments 7 and 8. In both cases, the splicing events remove a large portion of the first open reading frame (ORF), leaving the AUG initiation codon in place. The first alternative ORF is fused to the initiation codons of the M1 and NS1 ORFs. The newly generated ORFs direct the synthesis of novel proteins M2, NS2, and M3. All of these viral mRNAs code for nonstructural proteins. M3, however, has not been detected in infected cells and its role in the infectious cycle is not known.

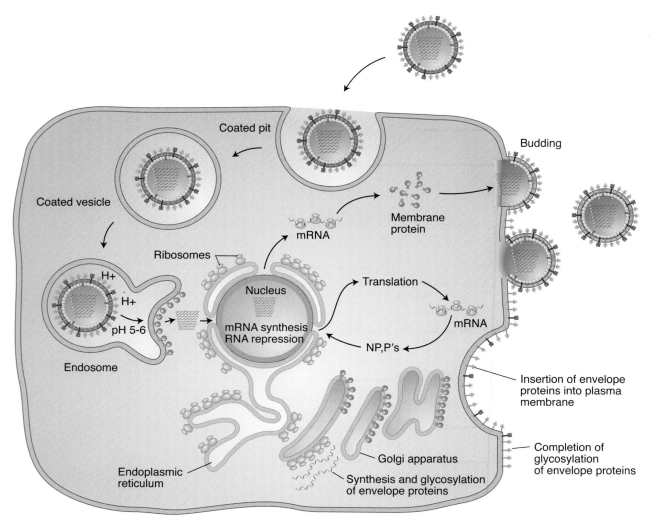

■ Figure 12-12

Following synthesis on membrane-bound ribosomes, the three viral integral membrane proteins—H, N, and M2—enter the host endoplasmic reticulum (ER), where all three are folded and H and N are glycosylated. Subsequently H is assembled into a trimer and N into a tetramer. H, N, and M2 are transported to the Golgi apparatus. Adapted from Fields, B. N., et al. *Fields Virology,* Third Edition. Lippincott Williams & Wilkins, 1996.

NS1 Prevents Nuclear Export of Cellular Pre-mRNAs, Facilitating Cap-Snatching

Two cellular proteins—cleavage and polyadenylation specificity factor (CPSF) and poly(A)-binding protein II (PABII)—are responsible for processing the 3′ end of cellular mRNAs. Influenza A virus NS1 protein, the most abundant viral protein in virally infected cells, interacts with CPSF and PABII, thereby inhibiting their function. As a result, cellular pre-mRNAs are not cleaved and contain very short 3′ poly (A) tails that accumulate in the nucleus in the infected cell.

These newly synthesized cellular pre-mRNAs are trapped in the nucleus of the infected cell and are almost completely degraded. Retaining cellular pre-mRNAs in the nucleus, though, facilitates the removal of the pre-mRNA 5′ cap by the influenza PB2 protein. The host mRNAs made after infection do not survive very long in the cell and little or no cellular proteins will be synthesized in influenza A infected cells.

Even though cellular pre-mRNAs are not exported to the nucleus, viral mRNAs can be exported and are not affected by this because the influenza viral transcriptase adds the poly (A) tails onto the 3′ ends of viral mRNAs. The cellular CPSF and PABII proteins are not required for processing the 3′ ends of viral mRNAs (**Figure 12-12**).

Translational Control Mechanisms

Influenza A suppresses the interferon system in host cells. (See the discussion on host resistance, including the interferon response, in Chapter 7.) During influenza virus replication, double-stranded RNA (dsRNA) intermediates are formed. These dsRNA molecules would activate the cellular kinase PKR, but influenza counteracts PKR with a two-pronged attack:

1. The NS1 protein binds to viral dsRNA, sequestering these molecules, and thereby blocking the activation of PKR.
2. Influenza activates a 58-kDa cellular protein that interacts with PKR directly, inhibiting PKR in influenza-infected cells.

Although it is not clearly understood, it is known that the translation of viral mRNAs is favored over the translation of cellular mRNAs. One possible mechanism is that viral mRNAs are efficient initiators of translation.

Virion Maturation, Assembly, and Release

After the capped viral mRNAs are exported to the cell cytoplasm, they are translated by host ribosomes. The H, N, and M2 glycoproteins are synthesized on membrane-bound ribosomes. Following synthesis these three membrane proteins enter the endoplasmic reticulum, where they are folded and glycosylated. Subsequently, they are transported to the Golgi network and the cell surface, where assembly takes place. At least one copy of each genome segment must be packaged into a new virion in order for it to be infectious.

The influenza virions are assembled at the membrane surface of the host cell and released by a budding process. H anchors the virus to the cell by binding to sialic acid-containing receptors on the cell surface. The enzymatic activity of the N removes the sialic acid from the carbohydrates present on the viral glycoproteins to prevent the viral particles from aggregating, thus preventing the clumping or aggregation of viruses to the cell surface; this in turn facilitates the viral release from H found on the host cell's surface. It is also believed that N may aid the virus at the beginning of its life cycle by helping its transport through the mucin layer present in the respiratory tract so that the virus can find its way to the target epithelial cells. Zamanivir (Relenza) and oseltamivir phosphate (Tamiflu) are antiviral compounds that inhibit the function of N.

12.9   Genetic Variation

Mutations are common during viral replication. Such mutations are more frequent in RNA viruses because their RNA dependent RNA polymerases lack proofreading and correction ability. RNA polymerases are at least 1000 to 10,000 times more prone to error than human or viral DNA polymerases (which have proofreading and editing ability). The mutation rate of influenza is approximately 1.5×10^{-5} mutations per nucleotide per infectious cycle. This results in about two or three amino acid changes in the H protein each year. This rate is high compared to mammalian DNA genomes (10^{-8} to 10^{-11} per incorporated nucleotide).

Often there are "hot spots" for mutation in the viral genome. Influenza consists of an enveloped particle that contains two very important surface glycoproteins: H and N. The H and N genes contain the hot spots that code for antigenic sites recognized by virus-neutralizing antibodies. Epidemics and pandemics occur due to changes in the antigenic structure of the H and N proteins of the influenza virus. Two processes, **antigenic drift** and **antigenic shift** (**Figure 12-13**), mediate the genetic variation that causes new strains of influenza to appear.

(B)

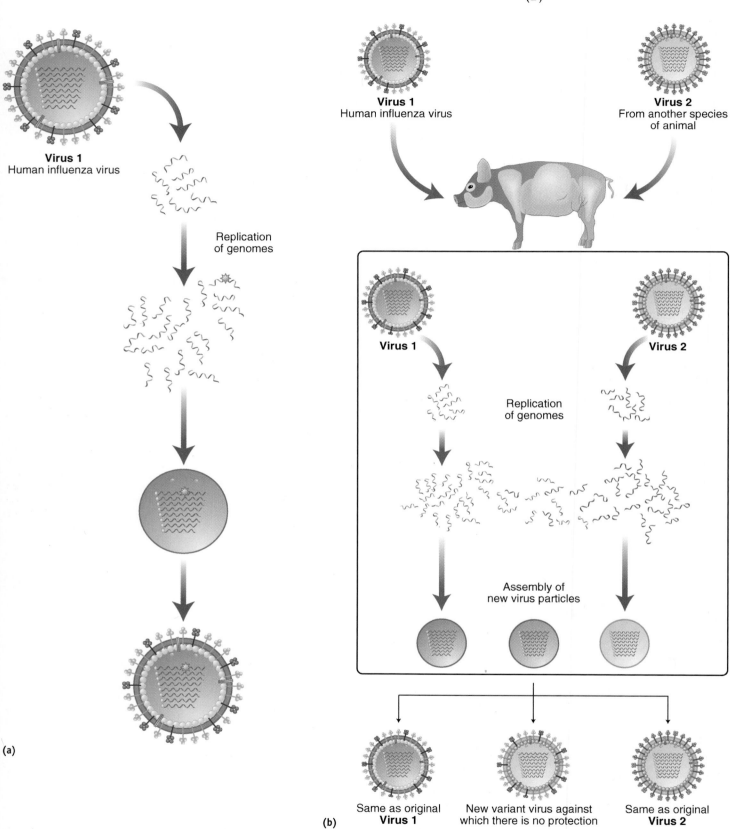

(a)

(b)

■ Figure 12-13

(a) Antigenic drift is the gradual accumulation of new epitopes on the H protein (and, to a lesser degree, the N protein). Adapted from Annenberg Media. *Rediscovering Biology.* Annenberg Media, 1997 (http://www.learner.org/channel/courses/biology/textbook/infect). (b) Antigenic shift occurs when the influenza A virus acquires a new H or N gene. When shifts occur, large numbers of individuals have no antibodies to protect them from virus infection.

Antigenic Drift

Antigenic drift is the small changes in the H and N genes that happen over time. It produces new virus strains that may not be recognized by the body's immune system, necessitating changes in influenza vaccines. When a person is infected with a particular influenza virus strain, the individual develops antibodies against that virus. As newer virus strains appear, the antibodies against the older strains no longer recognize the newer virus, and reinfection can occur. This is one of the main reasons why people can get influenza more than once. Antigenic drift can be responsible for localized outbreaks. In most years, one or two of the three virus strains in the influenza vaccine are updated with the changes in the circulating influenza viruses.

After the appearance of a new subtype, antigenic differences between isolates can be detected within a few years by using ferret antisera for analysis via hemagglutination inhibition assays.

Antigenic Shift

Antigenic shift is responsible for potentially pandemic strains of influenza A viruses: the rapid spread of novel strains of influenza A virus to all areas of the world. When antigenic shifts occur, large numbers of people have no antibodies to protect them against the virus, causing a pandemic. These shifts result in an unusually high number of cases and deaths for approximately two to three years. Antigenic shift does not occur with influenza B viruses because influenza A appears to infect humans and animals (birds, swine, horses, and seals), whereas influenza B only infects humans.

This phenomenon usually occurs when a pig lung cell is infected with two different influenza A viruses: one of nonhuman origin (usually an aquatic bird) and the other a human strain. Normally, influenza A viruses from birds grow poorly in humans and vice versa. **Reassortments** between human and bird influenza viruses, however, can produce a new strain of influenza virus that can infect and replicate well in humans. The virus is able to reassort its genes, swapping parts and whole segments of the virus in coinfected cells; for example, reassortment of influenza A viruses results in a new H#N# strain plus 256 other possible virus combinations. The pig and duck serves as a "mixing" or "reassortment" vessel (**Figure 12-14**).

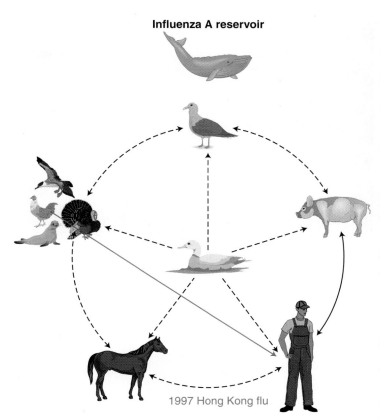

Influenza A reservoir

1997 Hong Kong flu

■ **Figure 12-14**

The reservoir of influenza A viruses. All fifteen H and all nine N subtypes circulate in wild waterfowl like ducks. They are the largest reservoir of influenza A viruses. Transmission of influenza viruses has been demonstrated between humans and pigs. In 1997, an avian influenza A strain directly infected a human, changing the current tradition of thinking that all influenza viruses would first go through a pig before transmission to humans. Adapted from Fields, B. N., et al. *Fields Virology*, Fourth Edition. Lippincott Williams & Wilkins, 2001.

Is China the Incubator for Flu Viruses?

Why does it seem that pandemic strains originate in southern China? Some suggest this is because there is a close association of humans with domestic animals and birds raised for food (**Figures 12-15a** and 12-15b). Influenza A viruses are constantly circulating in birds, pigs, and horses. There are many small farms in China and other countries in southeast Asia. The likelihood of genetic reassortment of viruses between man and other species is considerable. In addition to small-scale farming, China and southeast Asian countries are densely populated. This may be a factor in the evolution of viruses. Of course, these are hypotheses; there is no proof that epidemics originate this way.

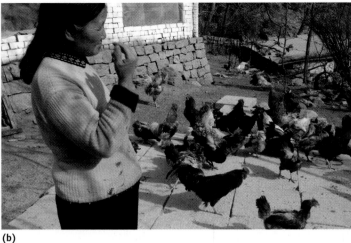

(a)   (b)

■ Figure 12-15

(a) Farmers migrating in China, bringing their birds and animals with them. Humans working in close association with birds and mammals may facilitate influenza A evolution and genetic variation. **(b)** It is not uncommon for farmers in southeast Asia to live with poultry and animals; for example, the chickens live with a family that works on a small farm.

TABLE 12-7	Pandemics in History	
Dates	**U.S. Deaths**	**Influenza Strain**
1918–1919 "Spanish flu"	675,000 (>20 million worldwide)	H1N1
1957–1958 "Asian flu"	70,000	H2N2 A/Singapore/57
1968–1969 "Hong Kong flu"	33,800	H3N2 A/Aichi/68

■ Why Is Influenza More Prevalent During the Winter?

In temperate climates such as North America, influenza generally affects people from November to March, whereas influenza infections occur throughout the year in tropical climates. A possible explanation for the high level of influenza activity during the winter is that the gathering of people indoors facilitates the transmission of the virus and viruses survive longer due to the dry indoor air. A 2007 study by Anice Lowen and Peter Palese's research teams demonstrated that the aerosol spread of influenza virus was dependent upon humidity and temperature. The virus was best transmitted at low humidity (20%) and colder temperatures (5°C or 41°F). They provide supporting evidence that weather conditions play a role in influenza virus transmission.

12.10 Pandemics in History

During this century, three influenza A pandemics have occurred: the Spanish flu of 1918–19, the Asian flu of 1957–58, and the Hong Kong flu of 1968–69. (Table 12-7).

■ The 1918 Spanish Flu

The 1918 Spanish influenza killed more people in 25 weeks than AIDS has killed in 25 years. It killed more people in a year than the plagues of the Middle Ages killed in a century. Estimated deaths range between 20 and 50 million, including 675,000 Americans. In New York City alone its impact resulted in 21,000 children orphaned by influenza. Seven times as many people died of the 1918 influenza than in World War I. True numbers will never be known because many places were overwhelmed by the flu and did not keep mortality statistics (see Section 1.3, *Viruses in History: Great Epidemics*). This pandemic spread faster than any plague in history, charging across America in a mere seven days. It took only three months to sweep around the world. In Alaska, 60% of the Inuit population was wiped out. Islands in the South Pacific (where respiratory illness is uncommon and not

■ Figure 12-16
Many young servicemen died in U.S. Army hospitals. This emergency hospital was located at Camp Funston, Kansas.

life threatening) lost 20% of their population. The Spanish flu was 25 times more deadly than previous influenza viruses. It killed 2.5% of its victims; normally, only 0.1% of those who get the flu die.

Why was this strain of influenza called the Spanish flu and what made it unique? Historians suggest that the name Spanish flu stuck because Spain did not censure its news reports of influenza outbreaks during WWI, whereas most European countries did.

At nearly the same time, in March 1918, influenza struck an Army Camp in Kansas. This strain of influenza was carried in the lungs of soldiers in the 15th U.S. Calvary headed for service in Europe (**Figure 12-16**). Its effects were unique for several reasons:

- It killed 20- to 40-year-old adults (i.e., adults in the prime of their lives).
- It killed quickly (in 2–3 days).
- Infected individuals suffered from hemorrhagic symptoms.

This deadly flu was a pathologist's nightmare. Physicians recorded,

> It began undramatically (after a two-day incubation period) with a cough. Next, there was pain behind the eyes, in the ears and in the lumbar region. Soon a drowsy numbness invaded the body, and a fever set in; often the temperature soared to 104°F. The pulse was thready and unstable; the victim's tongue was thickly coated . . . every mortal fiber ached indescribably—the throat, the head, the naso-pharynx. . . . why should the sickness affect so many organs of the body normally untouched? . . . most often the disease resembled encephalitis, with the patient lapsing into a coma . . . a dilation of the heart but even of fatty degeneration . . . a cough so intense that it ruptured the muscles of a soldier's rectum . . . retention of urine . . . puffy faces and swollen ankles of acute nephritis . . . the lungs were the organs most vitally affected . . . a patient's face so contorted in death that even close friends couldn't recognize him . . . and autopsy surgeons were encountering what one doctor termed 'a pathological nightmare'; lungs up to six times their normal weight, looking 'like melted red currant jelly.' (From Richard Collier, 1974. *The Plague of the Spanish Lady: The Influenza Pandemic of 1918–1919.* New York: Atheneum Publishing.)

As a result of the Spanish flu making its appearance during WWI, some people speculated that Germany had put influenza into Bayer aspirin to use as germ warfare. The U.S. Public Health Service Hygienic Laboratory was directed to examine 200 tablets of aspirin imported from Germany to determine if they contained organisms responsible for the spread of the Spanish flu. There was no evidence to link organisms to the tablets and this speculation ended when the Germans fell ill, too.

In the United States many emergency hospitals were set up while scientists scrambled to determine what was causing the flu. Many thought it was caused by a bacterium and a vaccine was incorrectly produced by researchers at the Mayo Clinic against a bacterium, (Pfeiffer's bacillus) and distributed gratis. Public health officials banned public gatherings like funerals. Schools were closed for nearly two months.

People concocted medicines or home remedies to prevent the flu. Physicians predominately prescribed heroin hydrochloride, codeine sulphate, cocaine hydrochloridum, opium, morphine sulphate, elixer terpin hydrate (a concoction of turpentine, alcohol, and nitric acid), and paregoric elixir (made with powdered opium, benzoic acid, camphor, oil of anise, glycerin diluted alcohol, and morphine). Few pharmacists would sell more than an ounce of these drugs because of their habit-forming potential. Many remedies contained a large percentage of alcohol.

Influenza permeated every aspect of life, even infiltrating children's songs. The following rhyme was popular during the 1918 pandemic:

> *I had a little bird*
> *and its name was Enza*
> *I opened the window*
> *and influenza.*

■ Figure 12-17

The mystery of the 1918 killer flu intrigued Johan Hultin. As a young graduate student in 1951, Hultin made his first trip to find ice-bound traces of tissue containing the Spanish influenza virus in an Alaskan mass grave. He expected to find the virus "alive." Much to his surprise, though, he could not grow the virus when he returned with samples to the lab. In 1997 (above photograph), he returned to the Alaskan mass grave and was able to recover influenza infected lung tissues. He provided the samples to Jeffrey Taubenberger, and his team of researchers were able to obtain sequence information that was a start in solving a century-old riddle.

Why Was the 1918 Spanish Flu So Deadly?

The mystery of why the 1918 Spanish flu was so deadly has intrigued researchers for a long time. As a young graduate student in 1951, Johan Hultin (**Figure 12-17**) traveled to Brevig Mission, Alaska, to find traces of tissue containing the killer influenza virus in a mass grave. In 1918, 72 of the 80 residents at Brevig Mission had died within a five-day period; the only survivors were children. After his first expedition, Hultin expected to find the virus "alive," preserved by the permafrost. Much to his surprise, he could not grow the virus when he returned with samples to the lab.

In 1997, Jeffrey Taubenberger's research team at the Armed Forces Institute of Pathology in Washington, DC, analyzed formalin-fixed, paraffin-embedded autopsy tissue specimens from U.S. servicemen who had experienced massive pulmonary edema with acute bronchopneumonia. After hearing news of Taubenberger's research, Hultin, then 72 years old, was inspired to repeat his expedition to the Brevig Mission grave. He exhumed the bodies of four of the 1918 flu victims, removed samples of the victims' frozen lung tissues, placed the samples in a fixative, and then provided these samples to Taubenberger for analysis. Taubenberger's team was able to sequence the coding regions of nine RNA fragments of the 1918 influenza virus from one of the Brevig Mission's victims. These RNA sequences were located in the coding regions of the H, N, NP, M1, and M2 proteins.

Why the 1918 flu killed so quickly and spread so easily continues to be a mystery. Analyses of antibody titers of 1918 flu survivors from the late 1930s suggest that the 1918 strain was an H1N1 subtype of influenza A virus, closely related to what is now known as "classic swine" influenza virus. As genetic technology has improved, we have learned more about this 1918 strain. Recently published sequences of the H and N genes suggest the 1918 virus was from a birdlike influenza virus that had not circulated in pigs or humans in the decades prior to this pandemic.

The H and N genes of the 1918 virus have been studied extensively. These two genes code for the major surface antigens of the virus and necessitate a new vaccine each year. This might suggest these genes would account for the virulence of the 1918 virus. In 2005, the 1918 Spanish influenza virus was reconstructed by a team of premiere researchers led by Terrence M. Tumpey and using the availablility of the complete 1918 influenza gene coding sequence. The team used reverse genetics (**Virus File 12-2**) to generate the influenza virus in an effort to understand the molecular basis of its virulence. The 1918 virus was created and handled in an enhanced Biosafety Level 3 laboratory (**Figure 12-18**).

The reconstructed 1918 virus replicated in the absence of trypsin, caused death in mice and embryonated chicken eggs, and grew to high titers in bronchial epithelial cells that line the airway in mice. Its ability to replicate in MDCK cells without the addition of trypsin was unanticipated.

It is standard protocol to supplement cell cultures with trypsin to facilitate influenza infection. Trypsin expedites cleavage of H_0 into H_1/H_2, activating virus infectivity. This protocol adaptation was important in growing previously isolated human and avian influenza viruses. The reconstructed strain was extremely virulent in mice. The infected mice lost 13% of their body weight in two days after infection with the 1918 virus. The mice contained 39,000 times more virus particles in mouse lung tissues four days after infection than other contemporary H1N1 influenza viruses. All mice died within six days of infection. Nothing strikingly different, though, was observed in the 1918 H or N gene sequences until 2007.

In 2007, a team lead by Yoshihiro Kawaoka of the University of Wisconsin–Madison infected macaques with the reconstructed 1918 influenza virus. These experiments were carried out in Biosafety Level 4 laboratories of the Public Health Agency of Canada in Winnipeg. Infected macaques died of acute respiratory distress typical of a **cytokine storm**. Concurrently, Tumpey's group at the CDC, in collaboration with colleagues at the Mount Sinai School of Medicine in New York, created 1918 viruses that contained point mutations in the H gene that altered the receptor-binding preference of the virus.

Contemporary human influenza viruses (which readily infect ferrets—the best animal model for human influenza viruses) bind to host cells that contain sialic acid bound to a galactose through a linkage called α-2,6. Avian influenza viruses bind to intestinal host cells containing sialic acid bound to a galactose through an α-2,3 linkage. Based on this idea, Tumpey's group mutated the H gene of the 1918 virus in such a way that it would bind α-2,6 or α-2,3 linkages. In doing so, their goal was to create an influenza strain that was more avianlike and unable to be transmitted to humans.

Ferrets were inoculated intranasally with the mutated 1918 viruses or with the original recreated 1918 virus. All three viruses created caused severe disease in ferrets. The 1918 virus that contained a double mutation that allowed the virus to bind to both α-2,6 and α-2,3 receptor was highly lethal and replication efficient in the upper respiratory tract of ferrets but was more avianlike in that the virus was unable to transmit between ferrets. The upper respiratory tract of ferrets and human contain receptors that have α-2,6 linkages that are abundant. They also have α-2,3 linkages that are found deep in the lungs, where the virus may not be released as easily. Ferrets infected with the avian-like 1918 virus did

■ **Figure 12-18**
CDC researcher Dr. Terrence Tumpey working with the reconstructed 1918 pandemic influenza virus in a Biosafety Level 3 laboratory.

not sneeze, which could be why transmission was reduced in ferrets. Several groups are now trying to create 1918 viruses that are more humanlike.

■ The 1957 Asian Flu

Although the 1957–1958 Asian flu was not as devastating as the 1918 Spanish flu, a significant number of people—about 70,000—died in the United States alone. The Asian flu was first identified in February of 1957 in northern China and spread to the United States by that June.

Fortunately, the advances in technology that occurred in 1933 (Andrews, Smith, and Laidlaw's isolation of the first human influenza virus) and in 1940 (Sir Frank Macfarlane Burnet's cultivation of influenza virus in embryonated chicken eggs) created important capabilities for influenza isolation and vaccine development. The 1957 strain of Asian influenza was rapidly identified and a vaccine was made available by August 1957.

■ The 1968 Hong Kong Flu

The Hong Kong influenza pandemic was first detected in Hong Kong during the early months of 1968 and reached the United States by September. Deaths in the United States (the victims were usually the elderly) peaked in December 1968 and January 1969. This pandemic was the mildest pandemic in the 20th century, killing only 33,800 people in the United States.

12.11   The Pandemic Scares

In addition to the three pandemics, there have been several "scares": the swine flu in 1976, the Russian flu in 1977, and the Hong Kong avian flu in 1997.

■ The 1976 Swine Flu Scare: A/New Jersey/76/H1N1

In February of 1976, several cadets at Fort Dix, New Jersey, were hospitalized with flu symptoms. Within 24 hours, a young private named David Lewis had died. Subsequently, the CDC investigated the outbreak. Nineteen throat washings were analyzed. Eleven of the washings were influenza A (mostly H3N2). Four of the samples were confirmed to contain H1N1 influenza A and thought to be close to the swine influenza virus responsible for the 1918–19 pandemic. Fear of influenza deaths in numbers similar to 1918 prompted the federal government's recommendation to vaccinate all Americans.

In all, 150 million doses of vaccine were prepared in the United States and 46 million doses were administered within a few months. The vaccine needed to be produced fast, and because of this the manufacturer's insurance carriers stated they would not indemnify such a hastily produced vaccine. Congress passed a liability protection bill. Early problems were reported with the vaccine, including cases of Guillain-Barré syndrome (GBS) and several deaths. GBS is an illness characterized by fever, nerve damage, and muscle weakness. The body damages its own nerve cells, resulting in muscle weakness and sometimes paralysis. It can last from weeks to months and 5% to 6% of individuals with GBS die. The vaccine campaign was suspended in the late fall of 1976 after the feared swine flu epidemic had not appeared anywhere else in the world and due to safety concerns associated with the vaccine.

A total of 532 swine flu vaccinees developed GBS within a 10-week period following vaccination, and 32 died. The government paid more than $90 million on claims in these cases. Research on the virus later showed that if it had spread, it would probably have been much less deadly than the Spanish flu.

■ The 1977 Russian Flu Scare: A/USSR/77/H1N1

In May 1977, influenza H1N1 was isolated in northern China. It spread rapidly and caused an epidemic in children and young adults worldwide. This virus was similar to the H1N1 strain isolated prior to 1957. Individuals born before 1957 were likely exposed to this strain and developed some immunity against the virus. This may be the reason why primarily children and younger people became ill from this H1N1 strain. The virus had spread around the world by January 1978, including to the United States. It has been suggested that the 1977 Russian H1N1 strain was not a result of genetic reassortment between a bird and human flu. Some believe that a frozen stock of older virus may account for this mild pandemic 27 years later but there is no actual proof for this theory.

■ The 1997 Avian Flu Scare: H5N1

In May 1997, a 3-year-old boy in Hong Kong became ill with influenza-like symptoms and died 12 days later. The diagnostic laboratory isolated an influenza A virus but could not identify its H subtype with any reagents available to them. In August, it was confirmed that this was a H5N1 influenza A virus. H5 was never known to infect humans and was limited to birds. This "jump" of an avian strain directly to humans (bypassing the pig mixing vessel) had never happened before. It was also discovered that this A/HongKong/258/97/H5N1 strain was responsible for sudden die-offs of chickens on three rural chicken farms during March of 1997 in Hong Kong.

It is believed that the emergence of the H5N1 influenza in Hong Kong in 1997 occurred when nonpathogenic H5H1 influenza spread from migrating shorebirds to ducks via fecal contamination of water. The virus was transmitted to chickens and then became established in live bird markets. During transmission between different species the virus became very pathogenic in chickens and was occasionally transmitted to humans from chickens in the markets.

In November 1997, new human cases caused by the H5 strain occurred. By December 1997, there were 18 confirmed cases, of which six were fatal. Investigations by local authorities, the WHO, and the CDC continued. They were able to confirm that all but one of these patients had been near live chickens (e.g., in marketplaces) days before the onset of symptoms. On December 18, 1997, veterinary authorities began to slaughter chickens in wholesale facilities and importation of chickens from neighboring areas was stopped. A total of 1.6 million chickens were culled (**Figure 12-19**), and as a result of this fast intervention the outbreak resulted in much fewer casualties than previous outbreaks. These avian flu cases occurred during the "flu season," and as a result health officials were concerned that human and avian strains would reassort, leading to a potential pandemic with efficient person to person spread of the virus.

■ **Figure 12-19**
A total of 1.6 million chickens were culled to curb the Hong Kong Flu in 1997.

(a)

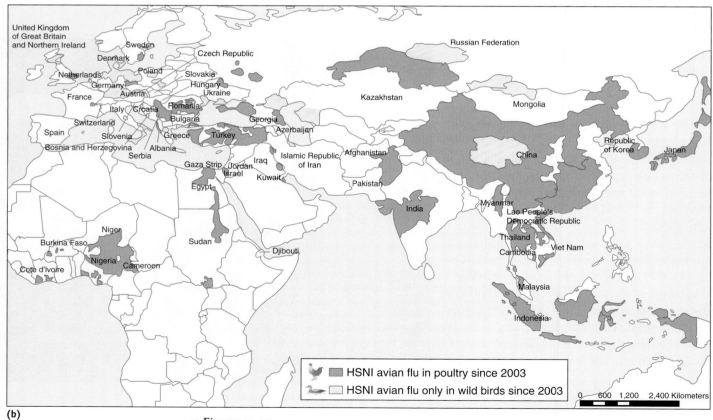

(b)

■ **Figure 12-20**

(a) Areas reporting human cases of H5N1 avian influenza from January 2003 to March 2007. Adapted from World Health Organization, 2007. **(b)** Areas reporting the occurrence of H5N1 avian influenza in poultry and wild birds from January 2003 to March 2007. Adapted from World Health Organization, 2007.

Lessons Learned from the 1997 Hong Kong Flu

Even though there were only 18 cases of the 1997 Hong Kong flu, it was highly lethal. Six of the the 18 individuals died, resulting in a 33% fatality rate—even more deadly than the 1918 Spanish flu, which had a 4% average fatality rate. This Hong Kong strain also caused a 87.5% to 100% fatality rate in experimentally inoculated White Plymouth Rock and White Leghorn chickens.

The 1997 avian influenza A H5N1 virus was isolated from a child with fatal respiratory illness. The H gene sequence of the A/Hong Kong/156/97H5N1 virus was determined. All H gene products of the human influenza A viruses, including the 1918 strain, have a single basic arginine residue at the cleavage site between H_1 and H_2. Interestingly, the H protein of the avian Hong Kong virus contains an insertion of multiple basic residues upstream of the cleavage site that has been seen in highly pathogenic avian strains of influenza A virus. The addition of these residues increases the cleavage site's accessibility to proteases that can cleave the H_0 into H_1 and H_2. Hence, a single insertion (mutation) could enable the virus to spread much more efficiently and systematically to the brain, heart, and blood vessels. Other gene segments of this virus require further analysis to determine if they may also contribute to its lethality.

Avian strains continue to plague eastern Asia (especially Vietnam, Thailand, Cambodia, and Indonesia) and Russia, causing huge economic losses within the poultry industry. Most cases of H5N1 infection in humans are thought to have occurred from direct contact with infected poultry. It is highly lethal in humans—with as high as 50% mortality (**Figure 12-20a**). The most important control measures are rapid culling of infected or exposed birds, proper disposal of carcasses, quarantining, and rigorous disinfection of farms. In 2005, the significant spread of the virus in birds became more apparent, but it is poorly understood. Scientists are increasingly convinced that at least some migratory birds are now carrying the H5N1 virus to poultry flocks that lie along migratory routes (Figure 12-20b). There have been die-offs of migratory birds infected with a highly pathogenic H5N1 strain. It is still a rare disease in humans, but one that should be closely monitored—particularly because of the potential of this virus to evolve in ways that could start a pandemic.

12.12 Antivirals for Influenza Treatment

Scientists continue to search for molecules that will selectively inhibit virus-directed events without interfering with normal cellular activities. Fortunately, there are currently four licensed antiviral drugs available for influenza. These drugs are, however, of little value if prescribed greater than or equal to 48 hours after the onset of illness. There are currently two types of influenza antivirals available: M2 inhibitors and N inhibitors.

M2 Inhibitors

The first drugs effective against influenza A virus were M2 inhibitors. They were discovered through massive screening of compounds. Amantidine (Symmetrel) and rimantidine (Flumadine) block the M2 ion channel, preventing uncoating of the virus (**Figure 12-21**). These drugs have limitations, though. They must be taken prophylactically (before the individual is infected with influenza virus) and they are not effective against influenza B viruses and are only 70% to 90% effective in preventing influenza A infection. They cause some undesirable side effects, such as difficulty concentrating, insomnia, lightheadedness, seizures, hallucinations, and other CNS effects in addition to renal dysfunction and gastrointestinal upset. In addition, drug resistance develops rapidly.

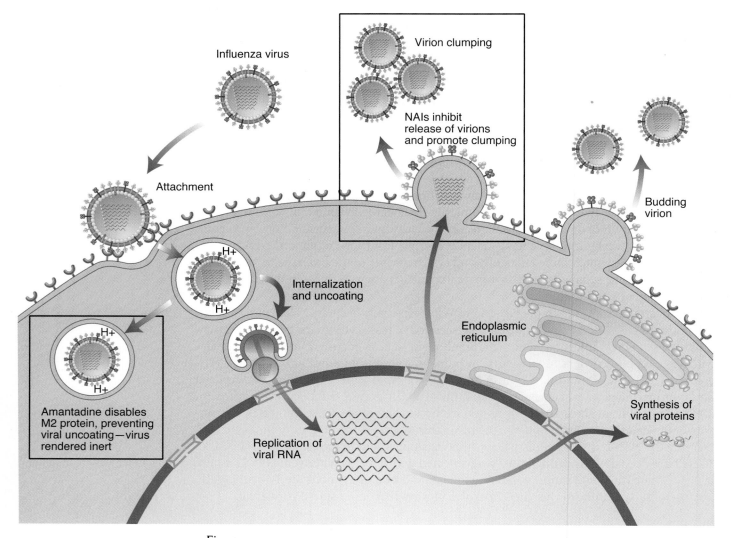

Influenza virus

Virion clumping

NAIs inhibit
release of virions
and promote clumping

Attachment

Budding
virion

H+

H+

Internalization
and uncoating

Endoplasmic
reticulum

H+

H+

H+

Amantadine disables
M2 protein, preventing
viral uncoating—virus
rendered inert

Replication of
viral RNA

Synthesis of
viral proteins

■ **Figure 12-21**
A schematic diagram representing the steps in the viral life cycle (attachment, internalization and uncoating, replication, and exit from the host respiratory cell) and the steps inhibited by antiviral drugs. Amantidine and rimantidine block viral uncoating by inhibiting the M2 ion channel, and oseltamivir and zanamivir prevent the neuraminidase from releasing budding viruses and dispersing virus particles.

Prophylaxis with M2 inhibitors is used to control influenza A outbreaks in chronic care facilities. It is given to all residents and unvaccinated staff. It may also be used as adjunctive therapy in persons with immune deficiency (e.g., HIV or organ transplant patients).

■ N Inhibitors

N inhibitors are a new class of antivirals. Oseltamivir (Tamiflu) and zanamivir (Relenza) inhibit neuraminidase, the enzyme responsible for cleaving sialic acid residues on the surface of host cells and viral envelopes and, thus, facilitating release of viral progeny. N drug inhibitors are also known as "plug" drugs. They are sialic acid analogs that block the active site of N, preventing it from cleaving sialic acid residues present on the surface of the host and virus. The result is a reduction in the number of viral particles released to infect other cells. Oseltamivir is available in pill form and zanamivir must be inhaled. N inhibitors must be initiated within 48 hours of onset of symptoms to be effective. They are effective against both influenza A and B viruses. Some patients, though, may not receive any benefit if the treatment is started after 36 hours of onset of symptoms.

Both drugs have some side effects: Oseltamivir can cause nausea, vomiting, vertigo, and bronchitis. Zanamivir can cause nasal and throat irritation, headache, gastrointestinal upset, bronchitis, and cough (especially with individuals suffering asthma or chronic obstruction pulmonary disease [COPD]).

12.13 Vaccines

Immunization with a viral vaccine is the most effective method of preventing influenza. In the United States, persons at high risk and some healthcare workers are vaccinated each year in October and November, prior to the December to January flu season, with an inactivated trivalent vaccine.

Viruses for the vaccine are grown in eggs. A nasal-spray flu vaccine containing live attenuated viruses instead of killed viruses (sometimes called LAIV, for live attenuated influenza vaccine), was licensed in 2003. LAIV is only approved for healthy people between the ages of 5 and 49 years.

■ Vaccine Composition

Vaccine composition is based upon a prediction of which influenza strains will be circulating in the United States during the flu season. Each vaccine consists of three inactivated (killed) viruses. Two of the viruses are influenza A virus strains and the third is a strain of influenza B virus; for example, the 2006–07 vaccine contained A/New Caledonia/ 20/99, A/Wisconsin/67/2005, and B/Malaysia/2506/2004 viruses. This recommendation was based on antigenic analyses of recently isolated influenza viruses, epidemiologic data, and post-vaccination serologic studies in humans.

Effectiveness of the Vaccine

The effectiveness of the influenza vaccine depends upon several factors:

- the age of the vaccine recipient
- immunocompetence of the vaccine recipient
- the degree of similarity between the viruses in the vaccine and those in circulation

Target Groups for Vaccination

The following list consists of vaccination target groups. It includes persons at increased risk for complications, those persons who interact often with individuals who are at risk, and persons who can transmit influenza to those at high risk.

- Persons aged 50 or older
- Residents of nursing homes or other chronic-care facilities who house individuals with chronic medical conditions
- Adults and children with chronic disorders such as asthma, pulmonary or cardio-vascular problems, and immunosuppression
- Children who are receiving long-term aspirin therapy
- Women in their second or third trimester of pregnancy during the influenza season
- Physicians, nurses, and medical emergency response workers
- Employees of nursing homes and chronic-care facilities
- Household members of persons at high risk
- Travelers to the tropics
- Travelers to the southern hemisphere during April to September
- Travelers with organized tour groups at any time of year

Preparing a Pandemic Influenza Vaccine: Reverse Genetics or a Universal Vaccine?

The World Health Organization has warned the public that another influenza pandemic is inevitable and possibly imminent. Influenza pandemics occur when a completely new influenza virus appears in a human population that does not have either partial or full immunity, resulting in several simultaneous epidemics in different parts of the world. The new virus has the capability of spreading from person to person, resulting in widespread illness and an enormous number of deaths. Given the high level of global travel today, a pandemic virus would spread rapidly, leaving little time to prepare. It would take several months before a vaccine became available. Preparing for the next influenza pandemic will provide benefits now. A new pandemic virus is predicted to be related to the emerging H5N1 avian influenza virus that first appeared in Hong Kong in 1997 or a similar H5N1 variant that emerged in 2003. It also could be similar to the 1918 H1N1 strain.

Creating a commercial vaccine against a pandemic strain of influenza poses challenges. Annual influenza vaccines are produced commercially from viruses grown in embryonated chicken eggs (**Figure VF 12-1**). In response to a WHO pandemic alert regarding the 2003 variant bird strain, a team of researchers has prepared a candidate vaccine. The A/Hong Kong/213/03(H5N1) strain that was isolated from killed embryonated chicken eggs. Therefore, traditional methods could not be used to produce a candidate vaccine. Instead, reverse genetics was used to generate a vaccine strain. Briefly, sequences coding for the polybasic amino acids located at the hemagglutinin cleavage site associated with high virulence were removed from the H5 gene of the pathogenic avian strain. This resulted in a substantially attenuated viral strain. The removed cleavage site was then replaced with sequences from the HA site of an avirulent teal strain of influenza A. The candidate virus could be grown to high titers in eggs and did not cause embryo death, yet it was antigenically similar to the original H5N1 pathogenic strain. The researchers were able to produce a candidate vaccine virus through the usefulness of reverse genetics in less than four weeks from the time of virus isolation.

A "Universal" Human Influenza A Vaccine?

Influenza hemagglutinin and neuraminidase are large glycoproteins that protrude outside of the envelope of the virus. They are highly immunogenic and are the obvious choices as the main antigens in today's influenza vaccines. They have one large drawback, though: they drift and shift. This is why new vaccines are produced each year in an effort to "match" the vaccine and circulating strains of influenza. Influenza epidemics cause between 500,000 and 1 million deaths worldwide per year. The epidemiological models from the CDC predict that a new pandemic will cause 2 to 7.4 million deaths globally. A universal vaccine offers a solution that would counter the looming threat of an influenza pandemic because it would protect effectively against all strains of influenza viruses affecting humans. It would provide long-lasting immunity and be inexpensive to produce.

Researchers are working on a universal vaccine based on the use of the M2 protein of influenza virus. Like the hemagglutinin and neuraminidase proteins, the M2 protein is an integral membrane protein (**Figure VF 12-2**). The M2 protein is much smaller, though. Only 24 of the amino acids of the protein are exposed at the membrane's surface. These 24 amino acids are amazingly well conserved; for example, amino acid sequences of the M2 proteins from the first human influenza A virus isolated in 1933 are exactly the same as present influenza A strains. The M2 protein is abundantly expressed at the cell

HOW THIS FLU VIRUS WORKS

The virus has two proteins on its surface called hemagglutinin, or HA, and neuraminidase, or NA.

The HA protein connects to receptors on the outside of human cells, allowing the virus to meld with the cell and replicate.

The NA protein allows the viruses to rip free from the cell, killing it. The viruses then march on to inflect other cells.

HOW THE VACCINE IS MADE

A flu virus has eight gene segments. Scientists extract the two genes that are responsible for the HA and NA proteins. The virulent sections of the HA gene are removed.

Six gene segments are taken from another flu strain, which grows well in eggs.

These genes are inserted into DNA loops...

...that are inserted into an animal cell line where they combine to produce a new strain, a seed virus.

The seed virus is inserted into chicken eggs so that it can multiply.

The inactivated strain is injected into humans, prompting the creation of swarms of antibodies that recognize the HA proteins and neutralize the virus.

(a)

■ **Figure VF 12-1**

(a) A schematic of reverse genetics technology. Adapted from National Institute of Allergy and Infectious Diseases, National Institutes of Health, *How the Flu Virus Changes,* http://www3.niaid.nih.gov/healthscience/healthtopics/Flu/Research/ongoingResearch/FluVirusChanges. (b) Robert Webster is an influenza expert who helped to discover that live poultry markets in Hong Kong were the origin of the H5N1 influenza A virus that spread directly from chickens to humans in 1997. His laboratory team has applied reverse genetics toward the rapid development of influenza vaccines.

(b)

(continued)

■ Figure VF 12-2

(a) Influenza A structure. Note the three influenza proteins that span the lipid membrane of the virus particle: hemagglutinin, neuraminidase, and M2. **(b)** A schematic showing a promoter fused to a fusion gene consisting of M2e and HBc coding sequences. Adapted from Neirynck, S., et al., *Nat. Med.* 5 (1999): 1157–1163.

(a)

(b)

surface of influenza A-infected cells and is also part of the virus particle but in much smaller quantities (14 to 68 proteins/virus particle). Antibodies against the M2 protein are found in the sera of patients recovering from influenza, but data suggests it is weakly immunogenic (e.g., monoclonal antibodies directed against the extracellular domain of the M2 protein reduce cell-to-cell spread of the virus but don't block infectivity of the virus *in vitro*).

Researchers proceeded to create a chimerical protein consisting of the M2 extracellular domain (M2e) fused to the hepatitis B core antigen protein (HBc). When HBc is expressed in *Escherichia coli*, it self-assembles into an empty virus particle that is indistinguishable from hepatitis B particles isolated from the liver of hepatitis B patients (but does not cause hepatitis B). When the new M2e hepatitis B core fusion proteins were produced in *E. coli*, similar self-assembled particles were formed. The particles contained 240 M2e copies per self-assembled particle. Mice infected with a lethal influenza challenge were administered M2eHBc particles. After immunization, 90% to 100% of the mice were protected against the lethal virus challenge. The results of this *in vivo* model are encouraging. The M2eHBc vaccine is inexpensive and safe to produce. Perhaps a combination of old and new approaches will be required to curtail all pandemic influenza strains.

References

Fiers, W. et al. 2004. "A Universal Human Influenza A Vaccine." *Virus Res* 103:173–176.

Kilbourne, E. D. 1999. "What are the Prospects for a Universal Influenza Vaccine?" *Nat Med* 5:1119–1120.

Neirynck, S. et al. 1999. "A Universal Influenza A Vaccine Based on the Extracellular Domain of the M2 Protein." *Nat Med* 5:1157–1163.

Schodel, F. et al. 1994. "Hepatitis B Virus Core Particles as a Vaccine Carrier Moiety." *Int Rev Immunol* 11(2):153–165.

Webby, R. J. et al. 2004. "Responsiveness to a Pandemic Alert: Use of Reverse Genetics for Rapid Development of Influenza Vaccines." *Lancet* 363:1099–1103.

See also http://who.int/csr/disease/influenza/pandemic/en.

12.14 International Influenza Surveillance

The WHO Influenza Program was created in 1946 as an international center to collect and distribute information, coordinate laboratory work on influenza, and train laboratory workers. Today, WHO's program for global surveillance of influenza now maintains 110 National Influenza Centers in 83 countries and four WHO Collaborating Centers for Virus Reference and Research in Atlanta USA; London UK; Melbourne, Australia; and Tokyo, Japan.

■ Influenza Sentinel Physicians in the United States

Every year, influenza sentinel physicians conduct surveillances for influenza-like illness (ILI) in collaboration with their state health departments and the CDC. Data provided by sentinel physicians are combined with other influenza surveillance data to provide a national picture of influenza virus and ILI activity in the United States.

■ What Data Do Sentinel Physicians Collect? How and to Whom Are the Data Reported?

During influenza season (October through mid-May), sentinel physicians report the total number of patient visits each week and the number of patient visits for influenza-like illness by age group (0–4 years, 5–24 years, 25–64 years, and >65 years). These data are forwarded once a week to a central data repository at the CDC. Influenza viruses are constantly evolving and cause substantial morbidity and mortality (~36,000 deaths) almost every year. The data sentinel physicians provide are critical for monitoring the impact of influenza and, when combined with other influenza surveillance data, can be used to guide prevention and control activities, vaccine strain selection, and patient care.

■ Will There Be Another Killer Flu?

It is impossible to predict when a pandemic might occur. Shifts occur when novel strains of the virus appear, to which the general population will have no immunity. If an influenza virus similar to the 1918 strain appears and behaves as it did in 1918, even taking into account the medical advances today, there will be unparalleled tolls of cases and deaths. Air travel will hasten the spread of the novel virus, decreasing time available to prepare for interventions. Healthcare systems could be rapidly overburdened, economies strained, and social order disrupted.

Although it is not feasible to halt the spread of the pandemic virus, it should be possible to minimize the consequences by preparing for the challenge in advance.

■ What Is Being Done to Prepare for the Next Pandemic?

The WHO has established a National Pandemic Planning Committee charged with developing strategies appropriate for their countries in advance of the next pandemic. Currently there are four WHO Collaborating Centers that are based in Atlanta, London, Melbourne, and Tokyo. These centers maintain repositories of different virus strains and also develop reagents and technologies for rapid diagnosis of new strains. The Centers have bio-containment facilities run by trained personnel to conduct studies on possible pandemic influenza viruses.

■ Will the Current Arsenal of Influenza Antivirals Work Against New Pandemic Strains of Influenza?

In an emergency pandemic situation, vaccine suppliers will need time to manufacture and distribute a vaccine. During this time, it will be necessary to use anti-influenza drugs to prevent the spread of a new strain. The WHO recommends the use of rimantidine for this reason. Rimantidine has the best safety record (and the least side effects) of all of the anti-influenza drugs and is approved for use in most countries.

The advent of reverse genetics has allowed researchers to ask if the current arsenal of antivirals available in the United States would be effective against a reemergent 1918 or 1918 flulike virus. Terrence Tumpey led a study in which influenza viruses with the 1918 M, H, and/or N segments were constructed using reverse genetics. The results of the study demonstrated that recombinant viruses containing the 1918 N or both the 1918 H and 1918 N genes were inhibited effectively in both cell culture and mice by the N inhibitors oseltamivir (Tamiflu) and zanamivir (Relenza). A recombinant virus expressing the 1918 M segment was inhibited effectively in both cell culture and *in vivo* by the M2 ion-channel inhibitors amantidine and rimantidine. These experiments suggest that current antiviral strategies would be effective in lowering the dangers of a reemergent 1918 or 1918-like virus.

12.15 Lessons Learned from the Severe Acute Respiratory Syndrome (SARS) Outbreak of 2003

The 2003 SARS-CoV outbreak serves as a reminder that we need to be prepared to confront unexpected viruses. SARS-CoV was first described on February 26, 2003. It was identified as a new disease by WHO physician Dr. Carlo Urbani, who diagnosed it in a 48-year-old businessman who had traveled from the Guangdong province of China, through Hong Kong, to Hanoi, Vietnam. The businessman died from the illness, and Dr. Urbani subsequently died from SARS on March 29, 2003, at the age of 46.

Subsequently, SARS-CoV began to spread, and within six weeks of its discovery it had infected thousands of people in 16 countries around the world. Its case–fatality rate proportion was 3.9%. Schools closed throughout Hong Kong, Canada, and Singapore. National economies were affected. The WHO and the CDC had identified SARS as a global health threat and issued an unprecedented travel advisory. SARS is a serious form of atypical pneumonia accompanied by fever. It results in acute respiratory distress and sometimes death, even in individuals regarded as young, fit, and healthy. The disease is very similar to influenza.

Initial diagnosis was based on patient travel history and is a dramatic example of how quickly world travel can spread a disease. It is also an example of how quickly a networked health system can respond to an emerging threat. This crisis was responded to by utilizing sanitation and surveillance techniques (**Figure 12-22**). Both China's Minister of Health and the Mayor of Beijing were fired for underreporting SARS cases. The identification of SARS-CoV represents one

■ Figure 12-22
Airport maintenance personnel in protective clothing disinfecting airliner cabins to curb the spread of SARS.

of the fastest identifications of a new pathogen in history. The experience with SARS is a reaffirmation of the need to respond to new infectious viral diseases.

Summary

Influenza viruses have been afflicting humans for centuries. Major influenza pandemics occurred in 1918, 1957, and 1968. Influenza can spread at alarming speeds because of its short incubation period; the large number of infectious virus particles shed in droplets discharged by sneezing, coughing, or talking; and the fact that many symptomatic individuals continue their normal social activities, spreading illness to many contacts. Pandemics occur when individuals lack immunity to the strain of influenza circulating in a particular area.

Symptoms of influenza include the sudden onset of headache, fever, aching in the limbs and back, malaise, dry cough, weakness, myalgia, and sore throat. Secondary bacterial pneumonia can be a life-threatening complication of influenza in young children, the elderly, and other high-risk groups such as AIDS patients. Some influenza symptoms overlap with other respiratory infections, such as anthrax and SARS. Rapid diagnostics is essential to proper treatment.

There are three types of influenza viruses—A, B, and C—of which A is the most prevalent. All three types can cause similar symptoms in humans. Diagnosis is based on symptoms and laboratory testing may be an appropriate confirmatory step. There are several rapid ELISA tests commercially available. Viral culture is the most accurate method for identifying specific viral strains. Several groups are developing microarrays or "flu chips" to distinguish among the different respiratory pathogens.

Influenza is spread person to person via droplet transmission. Inhaled virus particles enter the respiratory tract, adhering to and penetrating ciliated columnar epithelial cells that line the sinuses and airways. During infection, the cilia are destroyed and the cleaning system of the lungs does not work well. The highest number of infectious virus particles can be isolated on the fourth or fifth day after infection.

Influenza is an enveloped virus. Three proteins protrude from the viral lipid membrane: hemagglutinin (H), neuraminidase (N), and M2. There are 15 antigenically different types of H's and nine distinct N's. All H and N types infect waterfowl (such as ducks, gulls, geese, teals, and terns). The antigenic type differences are critical for vaccine preparation. Only antibodies against the H protein will neutralize the virus. The H protein plays several roles in the life cycle of the virus. To gain entry the H protein of the influenza virus particle binds to sialic acid present on the lining of the respiratory tract. It also mediates fusion of the membrane of the viral particle with the membrane of the cell to form endosomes. The H protein must be cleaved into two separate proteins in order for the virus to be infectious. Neuraminidase plays a role at the end of the viral life cycle. The N protein cleaves the sialic acid residues located on the outside of cells, facilitating the release of virus particles from the cell surface. This allows the virus to spread from cell to cell. The M2 channels the flow of H+ ions from the lumen of the endosome into the interior of the virus particle. This results in the uncoating of the viral genome into the cell's cytoplasm. The eight segments of −ssRNAs of influenza A are transported to the cell nucleus. Transcription and replication occur in the nucleus. This is an unusual feature for an RNA virus because most RNA viruses replicate their viral genomes in the cytoplasm of the cell.

The eight RNA segments of influenza A code for at least ten gene products. Besides the segments encoding H, N, and M2, the other gene products code for structural proteins that function in a host mRNA cap-snatching mechanism or as part of a transcriptase complex involved in RNA synthesis. The remaining proteins are nonstructural proteins involved in viral RNA splicing and export or as an interferon antagonist.

Genetic variability is common during influenza replication. Influenza A undergoes antigenic drift and shift. Antigenic drift occurs when the viral genome acquires nucleotide point mutations over time. In antigenic shift, whole RNA segments are swapped between two different influenza-A virus strains within the same infected cell (usually pigs). The pig is considered the reassortment vessel for influenza A. Antigenic shift is responsible for pandemic strains of influenza A and their rapid spread to other parts of the world.

The main reservoir of influenza A is wild waterfowl. Infected waterfowl are usually asymptomatic but shed virus particles in their feces. In Hong Kong in 1997, an H5N1 avian influenza A virus spread from migrating shorebirds to ducks via fecal contamination of the water. The virus then jumped to chickens and became established in live bird markets. Humans in close contact with the birds became infected. This "jump" of an avian strain directly to humans (bypassing the pig-mixing vessel) had never happened before. Millions of chickens were slaughtered to contain the new influenza strain. Avian strains continue to plague eastern Asia and Russia, causing huge economic losses within the poultry industry and a modest number of human deaths.

Scientists continue to investigate why the 1918 influenza pandemic was so deadly. Today antivirals that inhibit N (oseltamivir and zanamivir) and M2 (amantidine and rimantidine) are available. Inactivated vaccine cocktails containing two influenza A strains and one influenza B strain are used to vaccinate high-risk groups each year before the flu season. The WHO has established a National Pandemic Planning Committee charged with developing strategies in advance of a forecast pandemic. Strategies include epidemiological surveillance, stockpiling antivirals, and vaccine development using reverse genetics or other methods. A unified global effort is central to mitigating the next major influenza pandemic.

Resources

Primary Literature and Reviews

Abbott, A. 2001. "The Flu HQ." *Nature* 414:10–11.

Amorim, M. J., and Digard, P. 2006. "Influenza A Virus and the Cell Nucleus." *Vaccine* 24(44–46):6651–6655.

Auewarakul, P. et al. 2007. "An Avian Influenza H5N1 Virus that binds to Human-Type Receptor." *Virology* 81:9950–9955.

Basler, C. F. et al. 2001. "Sequence of the 1918 Pandemic Influenza Virus Nonstructural Gene (NS) Segment and Characterization of Recombinant Viruses Bearing the 1918 NS Genes." *PNAS USA* 98:2746–2751.

Boffey, P. M. 1976. "Swine Flu Vaccination Campaign: The Scientific Controversy Mounts." *Science* 193:559–563.

Burnet, F. M. 1935. "Propagation of the Virus of Epidemic Influenza on the Developing Egg." *Med J Aust* 2:687–689.

Centers for Disease Control and Prevention. 2001. "Notice to Readers: Considerations for Distinguishing Influenza-Like Illness from Inhalational Anthrax." *MMWR* 50:984–986.

Centers for Disease Control and Prevention. 2002. "Prevention and Control of Influenza: Recommendations of the Advisory Committee on Immunization Practices." *MMWR* 51 (No. RR-3):[1–31].

Centers for Disease Control and Prevention. 2003. "Severe Acute Respiratory Syndrome (SARS) and Coronavirus Testing—United States." *MMWR* 52:297–302.

Chen, H. et al. 2005. "H5N1 Virus Outbreak in Migratory Waterfowl." *Nature* 436:191–192.

Chen, W. et al. 2001. "A Novel Influenza A Virus Mitochondrial Protein Induces Cell Death." *Nat Med* 7:1306–1312.

Cross, K. J., Burleigh, L. M., and Steinhauer, D. A. 2001. "Mechanisms of Cell Entry by Influenza Virus." *Expert Rev Mol Med* 6:1–18.

Cyranoski, D. 2005. "Deadly Flu Virus Can Be Sent through the Mail." *Nature* 437:1077.

Dankbar, D. M. et al. 2007. "Diagnostic Microarray for Influenza B Viruses." *Anal Chem* 79(5):2084–2090.

Dawson, E. D. et al. 2007. "Identification of A/H5N1 Influenza Viruses Using a Single Gene Diagnostic Microarray." *Anal Chem* 79(1):378–384.

Dawson, E. D. et al. 2006. "MChip: A Tool for Influenza Surveillance." *Anal Chem* 78(22):7610–7615.

Enserink, M. 2007. "From Two Mutations, an Important Clue about Spanish Flu." *Science* 315:582–583.

Fouchier, R. A. et al. 2005. "Characterization of a Novel Influenza A Virus Hemagglutinin Subtype (H16) Obtained from Black-Headed Gulls." *Virology* 79(5):2814–2822.

Gernhart, G. 1999. "A Forgotten Enemy: PHS's Fight against the 1918 Influenza Pandemic." *Pub Health Chron* 114:559–561.

Ghedin, E. et al. 2005. "Large-Scale Sequencing of Human Influenza Reveals the Dynamic Nature of Viral Genome Evolution." *Nature* 437:1162–1166.

Gibbs, M. J., Armstrong, J. S., and Gibbs, A. J. 2001. "Recombination in the Hemagglutinin Gene of the 1918 Spanish Flu." *Science* 293:1842–1845.

Hatta, M., Gao, P., Halfmann, P., and Kawaoka, Y. 2001. "Molecular Basis for High Virulence of Hong Kong H5N1 Influenza A Viruses." *Science* 293:1840–1842.

Hatta, M., and Kawaoka, Y. 2002. "The Continued Pandemic Threat Posed by Avian Influenza Viruses in Hong Kong." *Trends Microbiol* 10(7):340–344.

Hoffman, E., Neumann, G., Kawaoka, Y., Hobom, G., and Webster, R. G. 2000. "A DNA Transfection System for Generation of Influenza A Virus from Eight Plasmids." *PNAS USA* 97:6108–6113.

Hollingsworth, D., Ferguson, N. M., and Anderson, R. M. 2007. "Frequent Travelers and Rate of Spread of Epidemics." *EID* 13(9):1288–1294.

Holmes, E., Taubenberger, J. K., and Grenfell, B. T. 2005. "Heading off an Influenza Pandemic." *Science* 309(5737):989.

Kash, J. C. et al. 2006. "Genomic Analysis of Increased Host Immune and Cell Death Responses Induced by 1918 Influenza Virus." *Nature* 443:578–581.

Knipe, D. M., and Howley, P. M., eds. 2001. *Fields Virology,* 4th ed. New York: Lippincott Williams & Wilkins.

Kobasa, D. et al. 2007. "Aberrant Innate Immune Response in Lethal Infection of Macaques with the 1918 Influenza Virus." *Nature* 445:10.1038/nature05495.

Kuiken, T. et al. 2004. "Avian H5N1 Influenza in Cats." *Science* 306:241.

Lin, B. et al. 2007. "Using a Resequencing Microarray as a Multiple Respiratory Pathogen Assay." *J Clin Microbiol* 45(2):443–452.

Liu, Q. et al. 2007. "Microarray-in-a-Tube for Detection of Multiple Viruses." *Clin Chem* 53:188–194.

Longini, I. M. et al. 2005. "Containing Pandemic Influenza at the Source." *Science* 309:1083–1087.

Loo, Y.-M., and Gale Jr., M. 2007. "Fatal Immunity and the 1918 Virus." *Nature* 445:267–268.

Lowen, A. C. et al. 2007. "Influenza Virus Transmission is Dependent on Relative Humidity and Temperature." *PloS Pathogens* 3(10):1470–1476.

Mandell, G. L., Bennett, J. E., and Dolin, R., eds. 2000. *Principles and Practices of Infectious Diseases*, 5th ed. New York: Churchill Livingstone.

Mehlmann, M. et al. 2007. "Comparison of the MChip to Viral Culture, Reverse Transcription PCR and the QuickVue® Influenza A+B Test for Rapid Diagnosis of Influenza." *J Clin Microbiol* 02202–06v1.

Montalto, N. J. 2003. "An Office-Based Approach to Influenza: Clinical Diagnosis and Laboratory Testing." *Amer Fam Phys* 67:111–118.

Moscora, A. 2005. "Neuraminidase Inhibitors for Influenza." *N Engl J Med* 353(13):1363–1373.

Nayak, D. P., Hui, E. K., and Barman, S. 2004. "Assembly and Budding of Influenza Virus." *Virus Res* 106(2):147–165.

Neumann, G., Whitt, M. A., and Kawaoka, Y. 2002. "A Decade after the Generation of a Negative-Sense RNA Virus from Cloned cDNA—What Have We Learned?" *J Gen Virol* 83:2635–2662.

Obenauer, J. C. et al. 2006. "Large Scale Sequence Analysis of Avian Influenza Isolates." *Science* 311(5767):1576–1580.

Osterholm, M. T. 2005. "Preparing for the Next Pandemic." *N Engl J Med* 352(18):1839–1842.

Oxford, J. S., Novelli, P., Sefton, A., and Lambkin, R. 2002. "New Millennium Antivirals against Pandemic and Epidemic Influenza: The Neuraminidase Inhibitors." *Antivir Chem Chemother* 13:205–217.

Plotkin, S. A., and Orenstein, W. A., eds. 1999. *Vaccines,* 3rd ed. Philadelphia: W. B. Saunders.

Reid, A. H., Taubenberger, J. K., and Fanning, T. G. 2004. "Evidence of an Absence: The Genetic Origins of the 1918 Pandemic Influenza Virus." *Nat Rev Microbiol* 2:909–914.

Richman, D. D., Whitley, R. J., and Hayden, F. G., eds. 2002. *Clinical Virology,* 2nd ed. Washington: ASM Press.

Sharp, P. A. 2005. "1918 Flu and Responsible Science." *Science* 310:17.

Shih, S.-R., and Krug, R. M. 1996. "Surprising Function of the Three Influenza Viral Polymerase Proteins: Selective Protection of Viral mRNAs against the Cap-Snatching Reaction Catalyzed by the Same Polymerase Proteins." *Virology* 226:430–435.

Smith, K. 2007. "Concern as Revived 1918 Flu Virus Kills Monkeys." *Nature* 445:237.

Steinhauer, D. A. 1999. "Role of Hemagglutinin Cleavage for the Pathogenicity of Influenza Virus." *Virology* 258:1–20.

Stevens, J. et al. 2006. "Glycan Microarray Technologies: Tools to Survey Host Specificity of Influenza Viruses." *Nat Rev Microbiol* 4:857–864.

Stiver, G. 2003. "The Treatment of Influenza with Antiviral Drugs." *CMAJ* 168(1): 49–56.

Subbarao, K. et al. 1998. "Characterization of an Avian Influenza A (H5N1) Virus Isolated from a Child with a Fatal Respiratory Illness." *Science* 279:393–396.

Taubenberger, J. K. et al. 1997. "Initial Characterization of the 1918 Spanish Influenza virus." *Science* 275:1793–1796.

Taubenberger, J. K. et al. 2005. "Characterization of the 1918 Influenza Virus Polymerase Genes." *Nature* 437:889–893.

Taubenberger, J. K., and Morens, D. M. 2006. "1918 Influenza: The Mother of All Pandemics." *EID* 12(1):15–22.

Thomas, J. K., and Noppenberger, J. 2007. "Avian Influenza: A Review." *Am J Health Syst Pharm* 64(2):149–165.

Townsend, M. B. et al. 2006. "Experimental Evaluation of the FluChip Diagnostic Microarray for Influenza Virus Surveillance." *J Clin Microbiol* 44(8):2863–2871.

Tumpey, T. M. et al. 2002. "Existing Antivirals Are Effective Against Influenza Viruses with Genes from the 1918 Pandemic Virus."*PNAS USA* 99:13849–13854.

Tumpey, T. M. et al. 2005. "Characterization of the Reconstructed 1918 Spanish Influenza Pandemic Virus." *Science* 310:77–80.

Tumpey, T. M. et al. 2007. "A Two-Amino Acid Change in the Hemagglutinin of the 1918 Influenza Virus Abolishes Transmission." *Science* 315:655–659.

Von Bubnoff, A. 2005. "The 1918 Flu Virus Is Resurrected." *Nature* 437:794–795.

Vu, H. T. et al. "Clinical Description of a Completed Outbreak of SARS in Vietnam, February–May 2003." *EID* 10(2):334–338.

Webster, R. G. 1998. "Influenza: An Emerging Disease." *EID* 4:436–441.

Webster, R. G. et al. 2006. "H5N1 Outbreaks and Enzootic Influenza." *EID* 12(1):3–8.

World Health Organization. 1980. "A Revision of the System of Nomenclature for Influenza Viruses: a WHO Memorandum." *Bull WHO* 58(4):585–591.

Yang, Y. et al. 2007. "Detecting Human-to-Human Transmission of Avian Influenza A (H5N1)." *EID* 13(9):1348–1353.

Yewdell, J., and Garcia-Sastre, A. 2002. "Influenza Virus Still Surprises." *Curr Opin Micro* 5:414–418.

■ Popular Press

Barry, J. 2004. *The Great Influenza: The Epic Story of the Deadliest Plague in History.* New York: Viking Adult.

Collier, R. 1996. *The Plague of the Spanish Lady: The Influenza Pandemic of 1918–1919.* London: Allison & Busby.

Crosby, A. W. 1989. *America's Forgotten Pandemic. The Influenza of 1918.* Cambridge, England: University Press.

Davies, P. 2000. *Devil's Flu: The World's Deadliest Influenza Epidemic and the Scientific Hunt for the Virus That Caused It.* New York: Henry Holt.

Iezzoni, L. 1999. *Influenza 1918: The Worst Epidemic in American History.* New York: TV Books.

Johnson, N. 2006. *Britain and the 1918–1919 Influenza Pandemic: A Dark Epilogue (Routledge Studies in the Social History of Medicine).* London: Routledge.

Kolata, G. 1999. *Flu: The Story of the Great Influenza Pandemic of 1918 and the Search for the Virus That Caused It.* New York: Farrar, Straus, & Giroux.

Normand, A. 2006. *The Return of the Spanish Lady: The 1918 Influenza Virus is Back.* Bloomington, IN: Authorhouse.

North, S. 2006. *Another Place to Die.* Morrisville, NC: Lulu Enterprises.

Quammen, D. "Deadly Contact: How Animals and Humans Exchange Disease." *National Geographic* October, 2007:78–105.

Rice, G. 2005. *Black November: The 1918 Influenza Pandemic in New Zealand.* Christchurch, New Zealand: Canterbury University Press.

■ Video Productions

Investigative Reports: Hunt for the Killer Flu. 2000. A & E Production.

History Undercover: The Doomsday Flu. 2001. History Channel Production.

1918. Released 2004. Image Entertainment. Directed by Ken Harrison.

Killer Flu. 2004. Discovery Channel.

Secrets of the Dead: Killer Flu. 2004. PBS. Bill Lyons Production.

H5N1: Killer Flu. 2005. Films for the Humanities.

Ready or Not: The Next Big One. Aired September 15, 2005. ABC News Primetime.

Rx for Survival: Bird Flu—How Safe Are We? 2005. WGBH Boston.

60 Minutes—Chasing the Flu. 2006. CBS.

Influenza. 2006. Films for the Humanities & Sciences.

Outbreak in America: When the Flu Pandemic Hits Home. 2006. Films for the Humanities.

Outbreak in Asia: How a Pandemic Is Born. 2006. Films for the Humanities.

Influenza, An American Experience. PBS. DVD released 2006. Robert Kenner Production.

Charlie Rose with Sir Paul Nurse, Michael Leavitt, Julie Gerberding, Harvey Fineberg, Peter Palese, David Nabarro & Laurie Garrett. 2006. Charlie Rose, Inc. Studio.

Fatal Contact: Bird Flu in America. 2006. Sony Pictures.

NOVA: Epidemic—Ebola Aids Bird Flu & Typhoid. 2007. WGBH Boston.

Spanish Flu: H5N1's Deadly Ancestor. 2007. Films for the Humanities.

Mega Disasters: Alien Infection. 2007. History Channel, A&E Production.

■ eLearning

http://biology.jbpub.com/book/virology

The site features eLearning, an online review area that provides quizzes and other tools to help you study for your class. You can also follow useful links for in-depth information, or just find out the latest virology and microbiology news.

CASE STUDY QUESTIONS

These questions relate to the Case Study presented at the beginning of the chapter.

1. Which countries are currently affected by a highly pathogenic avian influenza strain that infects humans?
2. What are the control measures for birds?
3. How do outbreaks of avian influenza spread within a country?
4. How are humans infected?
5. In this case, list possible route(s) of avian flu transmission.
6. List good hygiene practices to avoid spreading the virus through food.
7. Will an annual flu shot protect humans from avian influenza?

■ References

ProMED-mail. Avian Influenza, Human—East Asia 2005;07 Mar;20050307.0682.

ProMED-mail. Avian Influenza—Eastern Asia: Viet Nam 2005;08 Feb;20050208.0426.

ADDITIONAL CASE STUDIES

Case 1

Your college roommate Sharon is a pre-nursing major who volunteers at a local senior citizens home on weekends. Sharon spent the prior weekend at home with her parents and her three-year-old brother James. When Sharon came back from the weekend, her parents called to tell her that James was vomiting, had a fever, and had a dry cough. They were en route to the hospital with James when Sharon recalled that, during her visit, James seemed lethargic and was not his usual self.

Other pertinent information to this case is that James attends a daycare facility three times per week where he had multiple contacts with sick children and his illness occurred in December.

On physical examination, James had a temperature of 101°F and was very weak. A nasopharyngeal aspirate specimen was collected and sent to the laboratory for rapid diagnostic tests assaying for influenza A and respiratory syncytial virus. The test results are shown in **Figure CS 12-1**.

1. What agent is causing the infection?
2. What symptoms does James have that are consistent with his illness?
3. What other agents could have similar symptoms?
4. Would antiviral therapies be effective for James?
5. Will antiviral therapies be effective for uninfected family members and contacts?
6. How would the diagnosis be confirmed?
7. When was James contagious?
8. How was the virus transmitted?
9. Which family members are at greater risk for serious disease and why?

Two days later, Sharon developed a headache and sore throat. En route to volunteering at the senior citizens home, she went to the campus health center to find out if she contracted the same illness as James. This indeed was the case.

10. Create a list of Sharon's daily contacts. Are any of these contacts at high risk?

A week later Sharon felt much better, but her coursework had suffered during this time. She began studying and sleeping less to catch up in her courses. A few days later, she started to feel ill again. She developed chills and a cough producing green mucus.

11. What is the likely cause of this second illness?

■ **Figure CS 12-1**
An influenza test. "C" represents a positive control result and "T" represents the test result. The left well is an influenza A test and the right well is an influenza B test.

Case 2

It is October and you strike up a conversation about the flu shot with Dan Jones, a sixty-five-year old member of the university custodial staff. You recommend to Dan that he get a flu shot. Dan, who is very healthy, states that he heard the shot gives you the flu, but, because he trusts your judgment he states that he will think about getting it. After much thought, Dan decided to get a flu shot, but, he didn't make it to the vaccine clinic until mid-December. Two days after getting his flu shot, he began exhibiting flu-like symptoms. He was diagnosed with influenza A.

1. How is it possible that Dan fell ill with influenza A?
2. Why is influenza so difficult to control even when there is a national vaccination program?

CHAPTER

13

Rabies

" *TRUE!—nervous—very, very dreadfully nervous I had been and am; but why will you say that I am mad?* **"**

Edgar Allan Poe, The Tell-Tale Heart

CASE STUDY

In 1996 a group of physicians at the University of Maryland's College of Medicine gathered for their weekly clinical pathologic conference. Each physician was given an anonymous, complex case that was presented without diagnosis. Their role in the exercise was to discuss the patient's condition and course of treatment. One of the participants, Dr. R. Micheal Benitez, was (blindly) provided with the case of Edgar Allan Poe, which until that time had remained a mystery.

The basics of Poe's case were that he was found semiconscious on October 3, 1849, on a wooden plank that lay across two barrels located outside of Ryan's saloon on Lombard Street in Baltimore. He was wearing someone else's clothes, having been robbed of his suit. Poe had been traveling from Virginia to Baltimore on business. Finding him in this predicament was probably not a huge surprise, as he had had a history of alcohol and opiate abuse. He was taken to Washington College Hospital (later renamed Church Hospital), and his final four days were described in the medical record as follows:

- When Poe arrived at the hospital, he was unresponsive.
- At 3 A.M. he regained consciousness. He began to perspire heavily, was delirious, and had tremors and visual hallucinations for the next 28 hours.
- On the third day, he was calm, alert, and lucid. The tremors had disappeared.
- When queried, Poe said he had a headache, some abdominal discomfort, and felt terrible in general.
- He was transferred to a ward room because his condition had vastly improved.
- Physicians offered him alcohol (to relieve possible alcohol-withdrawal symptoms), but he refused to drink it. He was hydrophobic and swallowed a little bit of water with great difficulty.
- That evening Poe relapsed into a delirious state, becoming violent.
- He was restrained and lapsed into a coma until his death.
- Poe died on October 7, 1849, his fourth day of hospitalization. The Baltimore Commissioner of Health recorded "congestion of the brain" as his cause of death on the death certificate.
- There was no autopsy.

Based upon the historical evidence, Benitez concluded that rabies was the likely cause of Poe's death and that he may have contracted rabies from one of his many pets. Benitez had analyzed other possible causes for delirium, such as trauma, epilepsy, cancer, alcohol, and opiate withdrawal, but none of these maladies were consistent with Poe's symptoms, and there were accounts that Poe had not been drinking for six months prior to his death. At the conference Benitez commented, "It is also unusual for a patient to recover for a brief time and then worsen and die." Poe's symptoms were more consistent with a central nervous system (CNS) infection, such as that of rabies, rather than drug or alcohol abuse. The average survival after the onset of rabies symptoms at that period was four days—the same number of days Poe had been hospitalized before his death.

Benitez ruled out other potential reasons for Poe's delirium, such as metabolic, endocrine, nutritional, poisoning, or infectious diseases that could cause delirium (e.g., yellow fever or malaria). Poe's hydrophobic symptoms are a hallmark of this case. We may never know if this analysis is correct; however, Benitez's theory is plausible.

13.1   History of Rabies

Rabies, which was known as **hydrophobia** (fear of water) in the 1800s, is a terrifying disease. It affects the CNS, resulting in delirium and hydrophobia, and causes aggression or stupor.

French scientist Louis Pasteur (1822–1895) made numerous contributions to the field of microbiology. He was trained as a chemist and then applied his training to microbiology applications. He isolated and identified microorganisms responsible for the fermentation of wine, beer, and vinegar. His most important discovery, however, became the foundation for the science of microbiology. His "germ theory of disease," which proposes that infectious diseases are caused by germs, has become a cornerstone of modern medicine.

Pasteur's pioneering work regarding the development of vaccines against chicken cholera, anthrax, and swine erysipelas (a superficial bacterial infection that can spread to the lymphatics) allowed him to apply his concepts toward the treatment and prevention of rabies.

Pasteur and his colleague Emile Roux realized that conquering rabies would be a significant achievement for science and of great benefit to the public at large. They determined that the rabies agent existed in the spinal cord and began to make an attenuated vaccine by drying strips of spinal cords that were removed from rabid rabbits. After four years of intensive research, they created a vaccine consisting of dried spinal cord tissue injected under the skin of dogs that was used to induce immunity successfully in 1885. Fifty dogs vaccinated and challenged with rabies survived.

Pasteur was, however, cautious in using the rabies vaccine on humans, and insisted that additional years of research were needed before the treatment could be applied to humans. The press had picked up quickly on his successful vaccination of dogs, though, and on July 6, 1886, Pasteur's first human subject arrived at his laboratory.

Two days earlier, nine-year-old Joseph Meister had been mauled and bitten 14 times by a rabid dog. Meister's mother appealed to Pasteur for the rabies treatment. After consulting his colleagues Pasteur treated the boy inoculating him 13 times over a 15-day period with the dried spinal cord suspension. The child survived and remained in fine health. Months later, another victim showed up at Pasteur's lab, followed by still others.

Pasteur's success made him a hero and a legend. In 1887 the Pasteur Institute was founded to treat rabies victims. Today it is widely respected for its research in the field of microbiology. More recent discoveries at the Pasteur Institute include the discovery of HIV-1 and HIV-2 (1983 and 1985), a vaccine against *Helicobacter pylori,* the cause of many peptic ulcers and gastric cancers (1991), the complete genome sequence of *Mycobacterium tuberculosis*, the causative agent of tuberculosis (1998), and the discovery of the nicotine receptor responsible for the pain-relieving activity of nicotine (1999). The Institute's website is http://www.pasteur.fr/english.html.

13.2   Epidemiology

Rabies is one of the oldest known viral diseases. The word rabies originated in 3000 B.C. in Sanskrit, the official language of India. *Rabhas* ("rabies") means "to do violence." In Latin the word rabies is derived from *rabere*, which means "to rave." The Italian scholar Girolamo Fracastoro (1478–1553) first described the rabies disease in 1546 (350 years before Louis Pasteur and Emile Roux developed the rabies vaccine). His description of classic rabies symptoms was as follows:

■ **Figure 13-1**
This 1826 cartoon depicts citizens equipped with weapons to protect themselves and remove the rabid dog roaming the streets of London, England. A street peddler falls to avoid the dog while women run into hiding.

"The patient can neither stand nor lie down, like a mad man he flings himself hither and thither, tears his flesh with his hands, and feels intolerable thirst. This is the most distressing symptom, for he so shrinks from water and all liquids that he would rather die than drink or be brought near to water. It is then they bite other persons, foam at the mouth, their eyes look twisted, and finally they are exhausted and painfully breathe their last."

In the 19th century, canine or street rabies was a scourge everywhere, especially in Europe. Rabies victims killed themselves or were killed after being bit by a rabid dog. The image of the mad dog has symbolized man's fear of rabies for centuries (**Figure 13-1**). Even though there are vaccines available today, rabies remains a significant wildlife management and public health challenge. Education is essential in preventing this disease.

Rabies epidemiology is extremely complex and differs greatly from one continent to another. Rabies surveillance programs are used to address the following questions:

- What animals have rabies and in what regions of a country?
- How many people get rabies and from what animals did they contract it?
- What are the best strategies to prevent rabies in humans and animals?

■ Rabies in Animals

Rabies is a disease of mammals. Rabies in the United States is primarily a disease that affects wildlife populations. Worldwide, it is particularly a disease in wild dogs, coyotes, foxes, raccoons, skunks, mongooses, and bats. The disease is less frequent in domesticated dogs, cats, cows, horses, pigs, sheep, and goats. **Figure 13-2** is a composite showing the numbers of animal reservoirs in the world in 2003. Between 1000 and 5000 animal cases were reported in the former Soviet Union, parts of Asia, South America, and Europe in the year 2000.

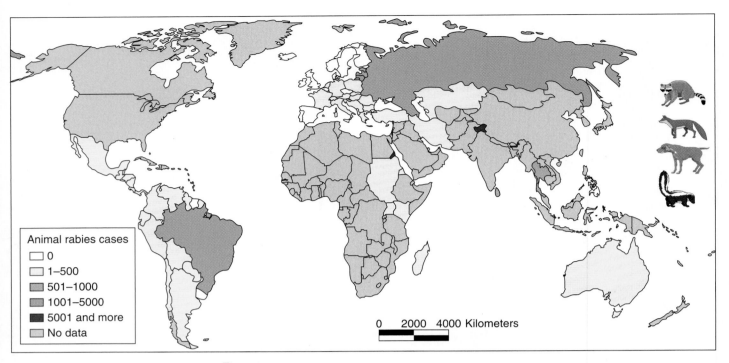

■ Figure 13-2
Rabies in animals: indicator status worldwide in 2003. Adapted from the World Health Organization, 2005.

Control of canine (dog) rabies in Asia, Africa, parts of South America, and Mexico has proved difficult. Foxes are an important rabies vector in Europe, Canada, Alaska, and the former Soviet Union. The raccoon dog, which is native from Siberia to Japan and in northern India, is also an important rabies reservoir in Europe. Raccoon dogs were introduced into Europe because of the commercial value of their long, thick fur and have now spread across Europe.

Mongooses, which were introduced into the Caribbean islands for rat control, are now an important rabies reservoir there as well as in their native southern Africa. The vampire bat is a threat to cattle and humans in Mexico and parts of South America. Insectivorous bats in North America are widely infected with the rabies virus.

Rabies has been extensively studied in Thailand. These studies have shown that dogs account for 95% of rabies cases, cats account for 3% of the cases, and rats, rabbits, civet cats, monkeys, tigers, squirrels, and other animals are responsible for the remaining 2% of cases—evidence that rabies virus is highly infectious among mammals.

Before 1992, Ontario, Canada, was known as the rabies capital of North America. Since the implementation of rabies control programs, though, the number of wildlife rabies cases has been reduced by 95%. The programs focused on the vaccination of arctic foxes and mid-Atlantic raccoons in addition to an educational focus regarding various bat strains.

The distribution of wild animal rabies in the United States is shown in **Figure 13-3**. Wildlife in the United States reported to be the most commonly infected with rabies are raccoons, skunks, foxes, coyotes, and bats. The spatial boundaries of wildlife rabies are temporally dynamic. Table 13-1 displays the breakdown of wildlife, domestic, and human rabies cases reported in the United States and Puerto Rico in 2001.

Rabies Management Programs in the United States

Vaccination and other rabies-control programs in the United States were implemented during the 1940s and 1950s. This caused a significant reduction in the number of domestic rabies cases, but by the 1960s it still had not succeeded in eliminating rabies virus in wild dogs. As a result programs were initiated to interrupt rabies in wild dogs. The programs continued through the 1970s and 1980s and did substantially reduce the spread of dog rabies.

A small but increasing number of rabies cases in human beings resulted from infection associated with bats, which are difficult to target for rabies control by conventional methods. Rabies in bats is widely distributed in the United States and accounted for 17% of all cases of rabies in animals reported to the Centers for Disease Control and Prevention (CDC) in 2001 (**Figure 13-4**).

The Wildlife Services (WS) program—part of the U.S. Department of Agriculture—is responsible for providing assistance in wildlife disease management (**Figure 13-5**). In 2004, there were 15 states distributing oral vaccines for raccoons; Texas distributes baits for gray fox and coyote as well.

Oral Rabies Vaccine

The oral vaccine used to vaccinate wildlife populations is combined with an outer bait matrix that is composed of fishmeal (for raccoons and coyotes) or dog food (for gray foxes). The vaccine is inserted inside of a small packet and waxed into the bait (**Figure 13-6**). The packet is punctured when the animal bites the bait, releasing 1.5 mL of the oral rabies vaccine. Animals mount an immune response against the rabies virus within 2 to 3 weeks.

Baits are distributed by hand in urban and suburban areas, but in rural areas planes are the most effective means for distributing baits over large vaccine zones. During flight, oral rabies vaccine for wildlife is dispensed from a bait dispenser chute that is located under the plane's wing. The dispenser is turned off when flying over a house or crossing a road to avoid human contact with the bait. In 2003, more than 10 million baits were distributed in the United States and Canada.

I3.3 Human Rabies

Human rabies has been reported in all parts of the world except Australia and Antarctica (**Figure 13-7**). The dog is the global reservoir of rabies, and as a result the majority of rabies cases outside of Canada and the United States occur in countries where dog rabies is not well controlled. The World Health Organization (WHO) estimates

■ Figure 13-3

Distribution of major terrestrial reservoirs of rabies in the United States in 2005. Adapted from the CDC, "Animals and Rabies," *Rabies: Just for Kids,* http://www.cdc.gov/ncidod/dvrd/kidsrabies/Animals/animals.htm.

TABLE 13-1	Cases of Rabies in the United States and Puerto Rico Reported to the CDC in 2006

Domestic Animals	Number of Rabies Cases
Dogs	79
Cats	318
Cattle	82
Horses/mules	53
Sheep/goats	11
Other domestics*	4
Total of all domestic animals	**547**
Wild Animals	**Number of Rabies Cases**
Skunks	1,494
Raccoons	2,615
Foxes	427
Bats	1,692
Rodents/lagomorphs**	44
Other wild animals***	121
Total wild animals	**6,393**
Humans	3

*Other domestics include ferrets and llamas.

**Rodents and lagomorphs include groundhogs, beavers, chipmunks, rabbits, badgers, bobcats, deer, opossums, mongooses, otters, coyotes, and ringtails.

***Other wild animals includes bobcats, cougars, deer, opossum, otters, coyotes, fishers, mongooses, and ringtails.

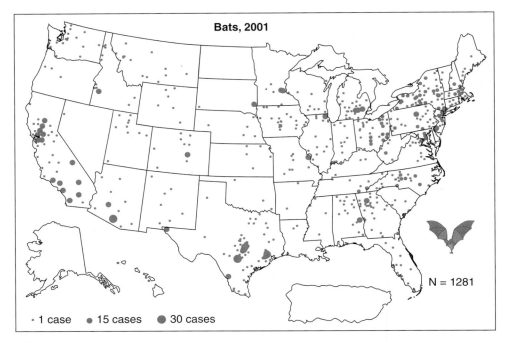

Bats, 2001

N = 1281

· 1 case   ● 15 cases   ● 30 cases

■ **Figure 13-4**
Distribution of bat rabies in the United States in 2001. Bat rabies has been reported in 47 of the 48 contiguous states. Adapted from the CDC, "Animals and Rabies," *Rabies: Just for Kids,* http://www.cdc.gov/ncidod/dvrd/kidsrabies/Animals/bats.htm.

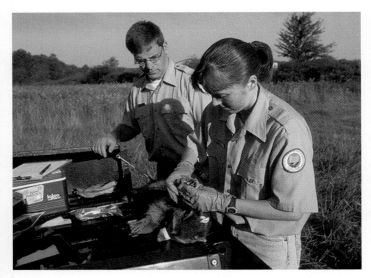

■ **Figure 13-5**
Biologists collect blood and other biological samples to evaluate the effectiveness of the oral rabies vaccine before releasing the animals back into the wild at the site of capture.

■ **Figure 13-6**
Merial Raboral V-RG rabies vaccine bait. The bait consists of a fishmeal polymer cube that is hollow. A plastic packet containing the vaccine is inserted into the hollow area of the bait and then sealed with wax. Planes are the most effective means for distributing baits over large-scale oral rabies vaccine zones. During flight, oral rabies vaccine for wildlife is dispensed from a chute located under the aircraft's wing.

that over 10 million humans are vaccinated postexposure to rabies annually and that there were more than 55,000 rabies-related human deaths in 2004. This number represents a fraction of the number of actual cases. Human rabies is most common in boys between the ages 5 and 14. In the United States the highest incidence of postexposure rabies vaccina-

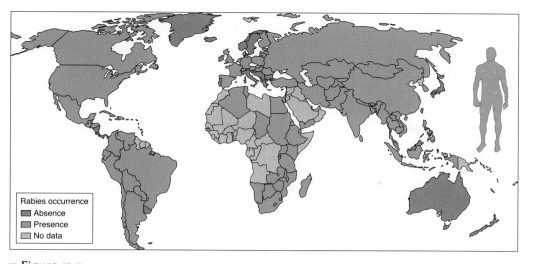

■ **Figure 13-7**
Total number of human rabies deaths worldwide in 2005 including imported cases in humans and animals. Adapted from
World Health Organization, 2005.

tion occurs among boys in rural areas, primarily during the summer months. Many baby-
boomers recall the 1957 Disney movie *Old Yeller*, which was based on a novel by Fredrick B.
Gipson. The story takes place in Texas in 1869. Two boys, Travis and Arliss Coates, live
on a remote homestead with their mother. The boys befriend a stray yellow mongrel dog
they name Old Yeller. The dog proves his loyalty by saving Mrs. Coates from a rabid wolf
but contracts rabies itself. The viewers watch the terrifying, raving transformation of the
boys' beloved pet. In the end, Travis is forced to shoot his dog (thus traumatizing several
generations of movie-watching children).

Since 1990 over 92% of human rabies cases in the United States were associated
with bat bites. Human-to-human transmission by bite is extremely rare. Besides bat bites,
there have been cases associated with direct implantation of infected organs during human
transplant surgery (such as corneal transplants; see Section 6.1). Infection by aerosol has
been suspected in caves heavily contaminated with bat guano and in laboratories.

■ Clinical Signs and Symptoms of Rabies

About 75% of humans contracting rabies experience encephalitis symptoms within the
first 20 to 60 days of exposure. The incubation period can vary, though, from as little as
4 days to as long as 6 years (1%–3% of cases).

Human rabies infections have been divided into two forms:

- **furious** (encephalitic) and
- **paralytic** (or dumb).

With either form, the average course of the disease runs from 2 to 14 days before coma
supervenes. Death occurs an average of 18 days after the onset of symptoms. Symptoms
during the primary or prodromal period of rabies are nonspecific and are similar to those
of other viral infections:

- headache
- malaise
- fever
- anorexia
- nausea
- vomiting

■ **Figure 13-8**
Two dogs afflicted with dumb rabies, which is manifested as depression and an attempt at self-imposed isolation. Domesticated animals afflicted with dumb rabies may become increasingly depressed and try to hide in isolated places, whereas wild animals seem to lose their fear of human beings, often appearing unusually friendly.

Secondary symptoms of furious rabies are:

- hydrophobia
- difficulty swallowing
- agitation
- anxiety
- hallucinations
- hypersalivation
- bizarre behavior
- biting
- jerky and violent contractions of the diaphragm

Secondary symptoms of paralytic rabies include:

- lack of hydrophobia
- lack of hyperactivity
- lack of seizures
- weakness and ascending paralysis

These symptoms also apply to animals. Animals that are predators show signs of furious rabies, whereas nonpredators display paralytic or dumb rabies symptoms (**Figure 13-8**).

■ Rabies Diagnosis: Rabies Diagnostic Testing in Animals

All individuals involved in rabies testing are required to receive preexposure immunization followed by regular serologic tests and booster immunizations when necessary. In addition, all laboratory workers must participate in national rabies proficiency testing, available through the Wisconsin State Laboratory of Hygiene in Madison, Wisconsin.

In the United States, direct fluorescent antibody test (dFA) is the gold standard for rabies diagnosis in animals. Animals that are behaving abnormally or show signs consistent with rabies should be tested when human or animal exposures have occurred. The test is performed postmortem.

Rabies virus is present in nervous tissues, thus the brain is the ideal test tissue (not blood, as is the case with many other viruses). Two or three areas of the animal's brain are tested: the brain stem (medulla), which merges with the spinal cord, and the cerebellum or the hippocampus. A piece of each tissue is removed and placed on an impression slide. The tissues are then air dried and fixed in acetone before being incubated with labeled antibodies (antirabies N protein labeled with a fluorescent dye [fluorescein-isothiocynate, or FITC]). After incubation, the slides are washed and viewed under a fluorescence micro-

Refresher What Is Encephalitis?

Encephalitis occurs when brain tissue becomes infected and inflamed. Viruses are often the cause. Encephalitic symptoms include fever, headache, stiff neck, nausea, and vomiting. Symptoms worsen to seizures, paralysis, blurred vision, delirium, and coma. Several different viruses can cause encephalitis, such as rabies, West Nile virus, and herpes simplex virus.

Differential diagnosis is a systematic method used by physicians to diagnose a disorder; for example, rabies symptoms are similar to other viral encephalitis disorders such as herpes simplex encephalitis. A physician must determine which virus is causing encephalitis (**Figure RB 13-1**).

■ **Figure RB 13-1**
CT scans of the human brain: a healthy vs. a brain with herpes encephalitis. Encephalitis results in the inflammation of the encephalon (the red spot).

scope in a dark room. dFA testing is rapid (30 minutes to less than 4 hours). The results may save a patient from the unnecessary physical, emotional, and financial burdens if the animal is not rabid.

■ Rabies Diagnosis in Humans

Laboratory tests for rabies are rarely conducted in developing countries. There are several routine tests performed in the United States on humans antemortem (before the death of the patient). Saliva, tears, and cerebral spinal fluid (CSF) samples are used for virus isolation in tissue culture or reverse-transcriptase polymerase chain reaction (RT-PCR) is used to detect viral RNA. Serum and CSF are immediately tested for antibodies to rabies virus in unvaccinated patients. Rabies antibodies usually appear during the second week of the illness. Skin punch biopsies at the nape of the neck are examined for rabies antigen that may be present in the cutaneous nerves at the base of the hair follicles.

Postmortem dFA tests are performed on the brain of the victim. Long-needle biopsies on two or more samples of the brain (e.g., the brain stem and cerebellum) are tested by RT-PCR, virus isolation in cell culture, or suckling-mouse inoculation. Further histologic, immunocytochemistry, and electron microscopic (**Figure 13-9**) examination of autopsy tissues may also be performed.

■ **Figure 13-9**
Rabies infection in the brain. This micrograph covers just part of the cytoplasm of an infected neuron. Two hallmarks of rabies virus infection are seen: There is minimal damage seen to the structure of infected neurons even though the extent of the infection is dramatic, and large numbers of bullet-shaped virions accumulate as a result of budding upon the endoplasmic reticulum membranes of these cells. Magnification approximately 25,000×.

■ Survivors

Only eight individuals have survived rabies. Seven of them had received pre- or postexposure rabies prophylaxis (passive antibody, immune globulin, or vaccine). Table 13-2 lists the individuals who have recovered from rabies encephalitis. Half of the survivors had severe, permanent neurological disorders.

Despite efforts to treat patients with steroids, interferon, and other antivirals, there is no therapy of proven value. Heavy sedation pain medication is used to relieve the patient of agonizing symptoms. Supportive care has prolonged life but there is no expectation of survival in unvaccinated patients (**Figure 13-10**). The first individual who survived rabies without receiving immune prophylaxis was a 15-year-old girl from Fond du Lac, Wisconsin, in 2004 (**Virus File 13-1**). She was treated with ketamine (brain protectant), midozolam (brain protectant), ribavirin (antiviral), and amantidine (antiviral). After 31 days she was removed from an isolation ward and was discharged to her home after 76 days. Five months after hospitalization, she was alert and communicative but with uncontrolled movements (choreothetosis), dysarthria (a speech condition), and an unsteady gait. Physicians who followed up on her progress after 27 months recorded some fluctuating gait and speech difficulties. She has had no problems with daily activities, including driving a car. She is currently attending college.

Pasteur described "spontaneous recovery" in a dog that showed signs of rabies, and there have been a few other reports of laboratory animals recovering from rabies infections; for example, in 1980, Fekadu and Baer reported the recovery of two beagles that had been infected with an Ethiopian strain of street (wild) rabies virus.

■ **Figure 13-10**
In 1958 this patient exhibited with early, though progressive, symptoms due to what was later confirmed as rabies.

TABLE 13-2 Human Rabies Survivors

Year	Age (yrs)	Gender/ Country	Exposure	Prophylaxis	Incubation Period	Symptoms	Recovery
1970	6	Male/ Ohio	Left thumb bite by rabid bat	Duck embryo vaccine the next day and 13 additional doses	20 days	Encephalitis, seizures, paralysis, coma	**Complete recovery** in 6 months
1972	45	Female/ Argentina	Bite by rabid dog	Suckling-mouse-brain rabies vaccine 10 days after bite	21 days	Headache, loss of motor strength, tremors, cerebellar dysfunction	**Complete recovery** 13 months after onset of rabies symptoms; relapsed twice after vaccine boosters
1977	32	Male/ New York	Inhaled aerosol of laboratory strain of rabies virus (SAD strain)	Preexposure duck-embryo rabies vaccine*	14 days	Fever, nausea, encephalitis, respiratory arrest	**Partial recovery**; dementia, personality disorder
1985	10	Male/India	Stray dog bite, lower left leg	Semple's vaccine (phenol-inactivated nerve tissue)	120 days	Fever, pain, hydrophobia, anxiety, photophobia, aerophobia	**Complete recovery**; case was severe, required 16 days of respiratory support
1986	18	Male/India	Stray dog bite, lower left leg	Semple's vaccine (phenol-inactivated nerve tissue)	60 days	Fever, pain, hydrophobia, anxiety, photophobia, aerophobia, alternating drowsiness with violent behavior	**Complete recovery**; patient also had cardiac irregularities and needed oxygen for 3 days
1992	9	Male/ Mexico	Bite on forehead, nose, and left cheek, by rabid dog	Vero-cell vaccine the next day and at days 3, 7, 14, and 30	15 days	Encephalitis, fever, convulsions, coma, paralysis	**Partial recovery**; blind and deaf, neurological dysfunction, died 34 months later
2000	6	Female/ India	Bites on hands and face by rabid dog	Three doses of purified chick embryo at days 0, 3, and 7; no wound treatment; 1 dose of human diploid cell vaccine on day 2 after hospital admission during symptoms	16 days	Encephalitis, fever, difficulty swallowing, photophobia, visual hallucinations, hypersalivation, frothing at the mouth, profuse sweating	**Partial recovery**; child was comatose for 3 months; responding to simple verbal commands and oral feeding at the end of 5 months; rigidity and tremors of limbs; discharged after 6 months with follow-ups every 3 months, which indicated little improvement
2004	15	Female/ Wisconsin	Bite by rabid bat	**No vaccine or immune globin;** instead patient was given ketamine, midazolam, ribavirin, and amantidine after onset of symptoms	21 days	Double vision, fatigue, tingling and numbness of left hand, nausea and vomiting, blurred vision, nerve palsy, muscular twitching, tremors, fever, hypersalivation	**Partial recovery**; was able to return to school. Some long-term effects.

*Six months prior to this episode, the individual had a neutralizing antibody titer of 1:32.

■ Pathogenesis

The most common way that rabies virus enters the body is through a break in the skin. The virus replicates in muscle cells surrounding the wound. At some point during the incubation period, the virus attaches to nicotinic acetylcholine receptors of the peripheral nerve cells of the neuromuscular junction. The virus journeys within the axons of the nerves at a rate of 0.5 to 15 inches per day by retrograde axonal transport (**Figure 13-11**). It may take days or weeks before the virus reaches the spinal cord motor neurons of the CNS. This is why postexposure prophylaxis is possible. Timely administration of antirabies immunoglobulin or vaccine prevents the spread of the virus to the CNS, thereby stopping the disease.

During the course of infection, the virus replicates in the motor neurons of the spinal cord as it makes its rapid ascent to the brain. While in the neurons, the virus is hidden from the body's immune surveillance. The virus spreads to many tissues via peripheral nerves (e.g., the cardiac muscle, adrenal gland, kidney retina, pancreas, cornea, nerves surrounding skin follicles, and salivary glands). Budding of infectious particles from infected cells takes place predominately in the salivary glands, excreting virus particles that are transmissible to other mammals.

| VIRUS FILE 13-1 | **Why Did Jeanna Giese Survive?** |

Fifteen-year-old Jeanna Giese was attending a church service in September, 2004, when a bat struck an interior window of the church. She picked up the bat and released it outside of the building. While handling the bat, she was bitten on her left middle index finger. The bite wound was washed with hydrogen peroxide, but she did not receive medical treatment. No rabies postexposure vaccine was administered.

About one month after the bat bite, she complained of fatigue and tingling in her left hand. Over the course of the next three days, she developed an unsteady gait, blurred and double vision, nausea, and vomiting. She was referred to a neurologist. A magnetic resonance image (MRI) of her brain was normal. By the fifth day, she had a fever. Her speech was slurred and she experienced tremors in her left arm. She was transferred to the Children's Hospital of Wisconsin in Milwaukee. Giese began salivating and became hydrophobic. A history of the bat bite was obtained. Samples of her serum, cerebral spinal fluid (CSF), skin biopsies, and saliva were sent to the CDC for the diagnosis of rabies. The CDC confirmed the presence of rabies-specific antibodies in her CSF and serum. A team of eight specialists developed a new protocol to treat Giese.

Jeanna Giese's parents were counseled about her diagnosis and prognosis (death). They offered hospice care and an aggressive treatment that had never been tested. The treatment was based on a combined strategy that uses **antiexcitatory** and antiviral drugs, along with supportive care. The parents opted for the latter treatment.

Geise was intubated and put into a drug-induced coma with aketamine and midazolam for seven days. She also received two antivirals: **ribavirin** and **amantadine**. (Neither rabies vaccine nor rabies immune globulin was administered to Giese because she had already developed an antibody response toward the rabies virus.) During her comatose state, she was continuously monitored for antirabies antibodies and detection of rabies nucleic acid in saliva. After seven days, her coma (antiexcitatory) drugs were tapered and the antivirals were discontinued. She became increasingly alert. She was removed from isolation on the thirty-first day of hospitalization because her titers of neutralizing antirabies antibodies from her CSF and blood were high. No virus or viral nucleic acids were detected in her saliva. It was assumed that she had cleared the virus.

■ **Figure VF 13-1**

(a) Jeanna Giese, the world's first survivor of rabies infection. **(b)** Timeline of Giese's hospital stay. It includes the incubation time after infection until two months after her discharge from the hospital. Adapted from Willoughby, R. E. Jr., et al., *N Engl. J. Med.* 352 (2005):2508–2514.

She was discharged from the hospital on the seventy-sixth day after rehabilitation (**Figure VF 13-1**). She was able to go back to school and graduated from high school in 2007. At the time of this writing, she was still experiencing some numbness of the bitten finger, an alteration in the tone of her left arm, and a wider gait when she runs.

Jeanna Giese made history as being the only survivor of rabies who did not receive any postexposure prophylaxis. We do not know why Jeanna Giese survived rabies. It is not known whether her recovery was related to an infection by an attenuated bat rabies variant or her therapy. This hypothesis is difficult to test because no virus was recovered from Jeanna Giese's bodily fluids. No attempt was made to isolate the virus itself from Giese.

Giese's recovery drew global interest. It prompted the use of the "Milwaukee protocol" to treat at least six other patients (located in Texas, Thailand, Germany, and India). Unfortunately these patients were unable to replicate Giese's recovery; all six died. On a global scale, about 55,000 cases of human rabies occur each year. It is the number one fatal infectious disease in China due to dog bites. The survival of Jeanna Giese has raised hope that an effective therapy may one day become a reality. Perhaps the best way to do follow-up research is to apply the Milwaukee protocol to rabid animals to systematically determine what parts of the protocol are critical in defeating rabies: the induced coma or the antivirals. Unfortunately, to date, veterinary schools have not permitted these studies because officials have raised concerns about treating rabies animals in their intensive care units.

References

Hemachudha, T. et al. 2006. "Failure of Therapeutic Coma and Ketamine for Therapy of Human Rabies." *J Neurovirol* 12:407–409.

Jackson, A. C. 2006. "Rabies: New Insights into Pathogenesis and Treatment." *Curr Opin Neurol* 19:267–270.

ProMED-mail: Rabies, human – USA (Texas). ProMED-mail 2006;13 May:20060513.1360.

ProMED-mail: Rabies, human—Canine—China (Hunan). ProMED-mail 2007;05 March:20070305.0782.

Willoughby, R. E. Jr. 2007. "A cure for rabies?" *Sci Am* April issue, 89–95.

Willoughby, R. E. Jr. et al. 2005. "Survival After Treatment of Rabies with Induction of Coma." *N Engl J Med* 35(24):2508-2514.

Willoughby, R. W. et al. 2007 "Long-Term Follow-Up after Treatment of Rabies by Induction of Coma." *N Engl J Med* 357(9):945–946.

■ **Figure 13-11**

(a) Sequential steps of rabies transmission and pathogenesis after a dog bite in a lower limb of a human. Adapted from Jackson, A. C. and W. H. Wunner. *Rabies*. Academic Press, 2002. **(b)** Rabies virus attaches to nicotinic acetylcholine receptors of nerve cells and journeys within the axons of the nerves.

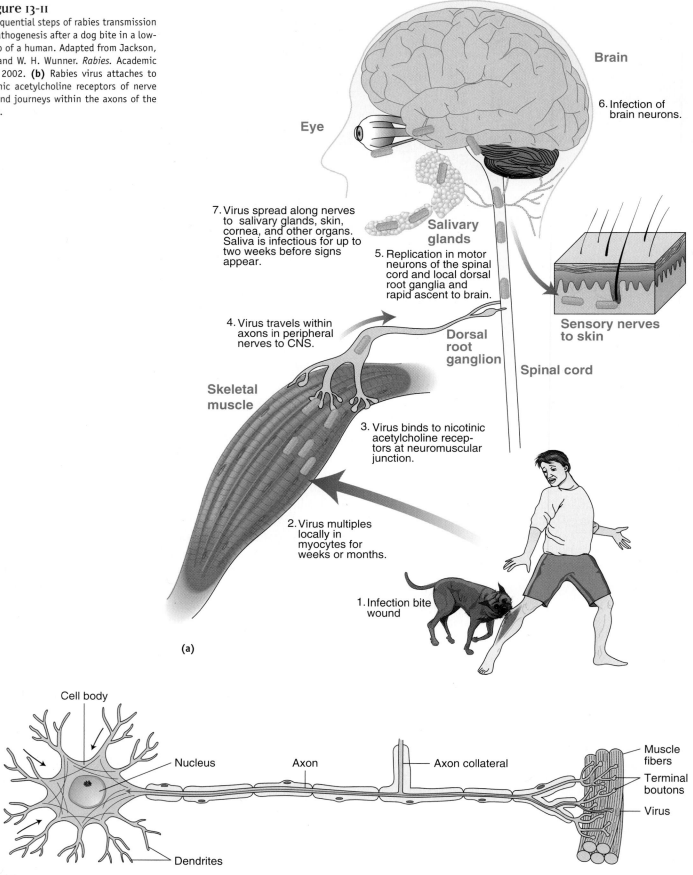

Brain

Eye

6. Infection of brain neurons.

7. Virus spread along nerves to salivary glands, skin, cornea, and other organs. Saliva is infectious for up to two weeks before signs appear.

Salivary glands

5. Replication in motor neurons of the spinal cord and local dorsal root ganglia and rapid ascent to brain.

4. Virus travels within axons in peripheral nerves to CNS.

Dorsal root ganglion

Sensory nerves to skin

Spinal cord

Skeletal muscle

3. Virus binds to nicotinic acetylcholine receptors at neuromuscular junction.

2. Virus multiples locally in myocytes for weeks or months.

1. Infection bite wound

(a)

Cell body

Nucleus   Axon   Axon collateral

Muscle fibers

Terminal boutons

Virus

Dendrites

(b)

Upon biopsy or autopsy, there is little evidence of brain damage even though fluorescent antibody labeling and electron microscopic analysis of brain tissues shows that almost all of the neurons are infected. The neural dysfunction of this disease may be mediated through the inhibition of neurotransmitters.

When fixed brain tissue is stained with various histological dyes, **Negri bodies** frequently appear in the cytoplasm of brain neurons. Dr. Adelchi Negri, an Italian pathologist, first reported these bodies in 1903 and believed that the Negri body was the etiological agent of rabies. Electron microscopic analysis of Negri bodies has shown that these inclusions contain virus particles. Negri bodies are only found in 50% of brain specimens, though, so their presence is not considered in the diagnosis of rabies (**Figure 13-12**).

■ **Figure 13-12**
Photomicrograph of hematoxylin- and eosin-stained brain tissue from a rabies encephalitis patient. Note the findings of Negri bodies within the neuronal cytoplasm.

■ Immunity

There are no antibody responses detected during the incubation period of rabies virus infection. Once neurological symptoms develop, antibodies appear in serum and later in the CSF. Thus the demonstration of antibodies is only useful during the late stages of the disease. Some patients mount a cell-mediated response. Those patients experience the encephalitic (furious) form of the disease. Rabies can also cause immune suppression.

13.4 Management of Human Rabies

■ Preexposure Prophylaxis

All high-risk individuals should be vaccinated against rabies virus. Approximately 40,000 individuals in the United States receive preexposure vaccinations. Examples of high-risk individuals are:

- veterinarians
- animal handlers, such as zookeepers
- dog catchers
- mail carriers
- speleologists
- trappers and hunters in areas where animal rabies is enzootic
- certain laboratory workers, such as researchers who work with live rabies virus or are involved in the production of rabies vaccines
- individuals who come in frequent contact with potentially rabid animals
- Peace Corps workers
- international travelers who go to countries that have endemic dog rabies and lack immediate access to medical care

The shot schedule for preexposure vaccination is given in three 1-mL shots injected intramuscularly into the forearm or shoulder on days 0, 7, and 21 or 28. Individuals who work with live rabies virus through research or vaccine production must be tested every six months for rabies antibodies. A booster will be administered if necessary. The vaccine usually takes 7 to 14 days to induce immunity, which lasts approximately two years.

■ Wound Care

It was common practice until the middle of the 20th century to cauterize wounds caused by rabid animals. Today wounds are washed thoroughly with a solution of 20% soap, 70% ethanol, or 2% benzalkonium chloride. and are irrigated with a virucidal agent such as povidone-iodine. All bite victims should seek medical attention and should supply the medical attendant with the following information:

- the animal involved
- whether the bite was provoked or unprovoked
- the vaccination status of the animal, if known
- whether or not the animal can be safely captured for rabies testing
- the geographic location of the incident

If the animal showed signs of rabies and can be captured, the animal is killed and the head is shipped to a qualified laboratory for testing.

■ Postexposure Prophylaxis

Immune Globulin

Unvaccinated individuals in the United States who have experienced a rabid animal bite are injected with human rabies immune globulin (HRIG, Hyperab) on day zero, along with a shot of vaccine. Rabies immune globin consists of antibodies from blood donors given rabies vaccine. It provides passive immunity until active antibodies are produced from the vaccine. It is injected at the bite site and in the buttocks. HRIG is expensive and is not available in all countries. Many countries use rabies immune globin of equine (horse) origin (ERIG). It is considerably cheaper and current preparations are highly purified and safe.

Postexposure Vaccination

There has been a pressing need for a safe and effective vaccine throughout history. Rabies vaccines can be divided into three different categories: nerve tissue vaccines, avian embryo vaccines, and cell culture vaccines. Table 13-3 lists important past and current vaccines for humans.

Early vaccines made from nerve tissues produced serious adverse side effects, such as Guillain Barré-like syndrome, paralysis, autoimmune CNS disease, and meningoencephalitis (inflammation of the brain and meninges). The incidence of neurological effects produced by the Semple-type vaccine is as high as 1 in 200 in recipients, with a lethality of up to 14%. Regrettably, nerve tissue vaccines are still being used for rabies prophylaxis in Asia, South America, and Africa.

Vaccines have been continuously improved over the years. Many people remember the 1950s human rabies vaccine made from duck embryos, which required 21 painful shots in the abdomen.

Three vaccines are currently available in the United States: HDCV, RVA, and PCECV. Unvaccinated individuals who are exposed to rabies receive one shot of HRIG along with the administration of one dose of an available vaccine immediately after exposure (day 0). Subsequently, the individual should receive additional vaccine injections at days 3, 7, 14, and 28. Injections must be administered intramuscularly in the deltoid area.

I3.5 The Rabies Virus Life Cycle

■ Classification of Virus

Rabies virus is classified as follows:

Order: Mononegavirales
Family: Rhabdoviridae
Genus: *Lyssavirus*

| TABLE 13-3 | Important Past and Current Rabies Vaccines for Humans |

Vaccine Name	Category	Type	Source	Where Used
Pasteur	Nerve tissue	Inactivated by drying	Rabbit spinal cord	No longer used
Fermi	Nerve tissue	Phenolized live virus	Sheep, goat, or rabbit brains	No longer used
Semple	Nerve tissue	Phenol-inactivated virus	Sheep, goat, or rabbit brains	Asia, Africa
Fuenzalida	Nerve tissue	Inactivated	Suckling-mouse brain	South America
PDEV	Avian	β-Propiolactone inactivated	Duck embryo	Primarily in Europe but available worldwide
DEV	Avian	Inactivated	Duck embryo	No longer used
HDCV	Cell culture	β-Propiolactone inactivated	Human-cultured fibroblasts	Primarily used in the United States and Europe but available worldwide
RVA	Cell culture	β-Propiolactone inactivated	Fetal rhesus lung cell culture	United States
PHK	Cell culture	Formalin inactivated	Primary Syrian hamster kidney cell culture	China, Russia
PCECV	Cell culture	β-Propiolactone inactivated	Chick embryo cell culture	Primarily used in Germany and the United States but available worldwide
PVRV	Cell culture	β-Propiolactone inactivated	Vero cell line	Primarily used in France but available worldwide

Abbreviations for vaccines: PDEV = purified duck embryo vaccine; DEV = duck embryo vaccine; HDCV = human diploid cell culture vaccine; RVA = rabies vaccine adsorbed; PHK = primary hamster kidney; PCECV = purified chick embryo cell culture vaccine; PVRV = purified Vero rabies vaccine.

The order Mononegavirales represents a group of viruses that contain nonsegmented single-stranded RNA (ssRNA) genomes of negative sense. **Rhabdo** is the Greek term for "rod-shaped;" **lyssa** in Greek means "frenzy or madness." Rabies was the first of seven *Lyssavirus* genotypes identified. All but one of them causes fatal encephalitis in humans. Most of these viruses have been found in bats; perhaps rabies virus is really a bat virus that has crossed species. New *Lyssaviruses* continue to be discovered.

■ Properties of the Rabies Virus Particle

Rabies virus particles and other members of the Rhabdovirus family have a unique bullet-shaped appearance, with one end flattened and the other rounded. The average length of infectious or mature rabies virus particles is 180 nm and the average diameter is 75 nm. The surface of the virus particle is covered with approximately 400 tightly arranged glycoprotein spikes. The spikes are an average 7 nm in length by 3 nm in diameter. They are composed of trimers of viral glycoprotein (G) (**Figure 13-13**). The glycoprotein is the primary surface antigen that induces and reacts with virus-neutralizing antibodies. It is also associated with receptor activities.

Internal to the glycoprotein spikes is a host-derived envelope or membrane bilayer. The envelope is lined with a **matrix (M) protein** and contains the helical-shaped ribonucleoprotein core (RNP). The RNP consists of the viral genomic RNA that

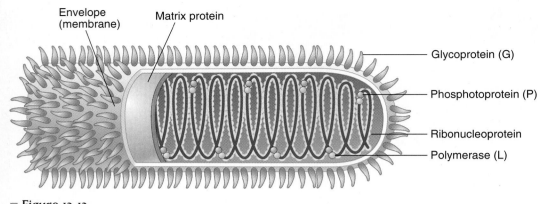

Figure 13-13
Longitudinal section of rabies virus. Adapted from the CDC.

is tightly encased with nucleocapsid (N) proteins. It also contains two additional proteins, the phosphoprotein (P) and the catalytic RNA-dependent RNA polymerase or large protein (**L protein**). The L protein has several functions, including RNA synthesis, capping, methylation, and polyadenylation of viral RNAs. The M protein is associated with both the envelope and the RNP.

The standard bullet-shaped rabies virus particles are designated **B particles**. Other shorter, often cone-shaped, particles are coproduced during infection. They are noninfectious **defective-interfering (DI)** particles. They contain shorter (defective) RNA genomes. DI particles can be separated from B particles by centrifugation in a sucrose density gradient. DI particles are readily generated in cell cultures infected with laboratory-adapted (fixed) strains of rabies virus. Rabies DI particles have been shown to be noninfectious in cell culture and in animals.

■ Viral Replication: Genome Organization

The rabies virus genome consists of an 11,932-nucleotide nonsegmented ssRNA genome of negative-sense polarity. The 3′ end of the genome contains a noncoding leader sequence. Downstream of the leader sequence are the five structural genes of the rabies virus genome: N, P, M, G, and L, followed by a noncoding trailer sequence at the 5′ end (**Figure 13-14**). The rabies virus gene functions are listed in Table 13-4. Each gene is separated by a short intergenic sequence. There are two nucleotides separating the N and P genes, five nucleotides separating the P and M genes, and five nucleotides separating the M and G genes. There is a larger intergenic sequence of 423 nucleotides between the G and L genes of rabies virus. It is long enough to represent a potential gene, but there is no detectable protein found that represents this coding region. It has been given the designation of a remnant gene or pseudogene (ψ).

Figure 13-14
Genome organization of rabies virus. Adapted from Flint, S.J., et al. *Principles of Virology: Molecular Biology, Pathogenesis, and Control of Animal Viruses,* Second Edition. ASM Press, 2003.

■ Entry

The rabies virus surface glycoprotein spikes mediate fusion to its target host cell by binding to nicotinic acetylcholine receptors present in neuromuscular junctions. Further studies on the glycoprotein have determined that it contains significant sequence homology to snake venom neurotoxins. Snake venom neurotoxins tightly bind nicotinic acetylcholine receptors and block their activity. The amino acid sequence of rabies virus glycoprotein that is similar to snake neurotoxins is the region correlated with receptor binding.

TABLE 13-4	Rabies Virus Gene Coding Assignments	
Gene	**Length**	**Function of Gene Product**
N	1424	Coat protein (nucleocapsid); part of the RNP core
P	991	Polymerase-associated phosphoprotein (NS); part of the RNP core
M	805	Matrix protein; part of the RNP core
G	1675	Glycoprotein (G-protein), receptor-binding protein, major surface antigen
L	6475	Polyprotein with RNA replicase, 5' capping, methylation, and 3' polyadenylation activity

There are variations in animal susceptibility to rabies virus infection; for example, when foxes are injected with rabies virus via an intramuscular inoculation, they are highly sensitive to rabies virus infection. Dogs, however, are less sensitive, and opossums are highly resistant to intramuscular injection with rabies virus. Presumably this striking difference has to do with the numbers of acetylcholine receptors present in muscles, because the red fox contains substantially higher numbers of acetylcholine receptors in its muscle content compared to opossums.

Mutations in the rabies virus glycoprotein play a critical role in viral pathogenesis. A single amino acid change at amino acid 333 of the 505 amino acid protein determines whether the virus will be highly virulent, less pathogenic, or avirulent. Virulent strains of virus contain an arginine or lysine at amino acid 333. The glycoprotein of rabies virus is of major importance immunologically and has been studied extensively for this reason. It is capable of inducing and reacting with virus-neutralizing antibodies.

After rabies virus glycoprotein spikes fuse with a host cell, the virus enters nerve terminals via low pH-dependent fusion with endosomal membranes. The viral membrane then fuses with an endosomal membrane and the glycoprotein undergoes a conformational change at a low pH. The acidic interior of the endosome allows the viral nucleocapsid to escape into the cytoplasm. The M-protein dissociates from the RNP during this uncoating step.

■ Transcription of Viral Genes

After uncoating, the viral L polymerase and P proteins (which were packaged inside of the particle and therefore brought into the cell via the virion) begin to transcribe the viral genomic RNA within the cytoplasm of the cell. Transcription begins at the 3' end of the viral RNA genome. It transcribes the RNA sequentially (e.g., the leader sequence, N, P, M, G, and L genes). A separate positive-sense RNA transcript is generated for each viral gene. Each viral transcript is capped and polyadenylated by the viral L-protein.

■ Viral Protein Synthesis

The viral messenger RNAs (mRNAs) resemble cellular mRNAs and are translated by cellular ribosomes. The N, P, M, and L viral mRNAs are translated by free ribosomes, whereas the G-mRNA is translated on membrane-bound ribosomes of the endoplasmic reticulum. The glycoprotein is posttranslationally modified (glycosylated) via the Golgi apparatus.

■ Viral Genome Replication

As soon as the viral N protein is synthesized in the cytoplasm, some of the N proteins bind to the leader region of the viral RNA genomes. In doing so, the N protein interferes with the initiation of internal transcription at the viral gene junctions. Consequently, a full-length complementary positive-sense copy of the viral genome is synthesized from

N-encapsidated viral RNAs. This is termed an antigenome or replicative intermediate RNA. Subsequently, the antigenome RNA serves as a template for progeny (negative-sense) genomic RNA, which will be packaged into the viral particle. During infection, an excessive amount of genome to antigenome is synthesized. Fifty copies of genomic RNAs are produced for each antigenome produced.

■ Virus Assembly and Exit

As soon as enough genomic negative-sense RNA, N, P, and L proteins have accumulated within the infected cells, rabies virus nucleocapsids are formed and virus assembly begins. The cytoplasmic M protein combines with the RNP complexes. The mature infectious bullet-shaped particles acquire the cellular lipid bilayer as the RNP-M buds through the host cell plasma membrane. See **Figure 13-15** for a complete rabies virus life cycle schematic diagram.

■ **Figure 13-15**
Life cycle of rabies virus. Adapted from Flint, S.J., et al. *Principles of Virology: Molecular Biology, Pathogenesis, and Control of Animal Viruses,* Second Edition. ASM Press, 2003.

13.6 Genetic Variation

■ Fixed versus Street Strains

The term *fixed* strain refers to rabies virus strains laboratory strains used in research. *Street* (wild) strains are those strains isolated from patients or animals that have experienced the disease via a bite from a rabid animal or other means (e.g., via infected organ during a transplantation procedure). The rabies virus virion-associated RNA replicase/transcriptase (L protein) does not possess RNA repair/proofreading capabilities. Consequently, it is error prone. Mutations are introduced at a relatively high frequency into the rabies virus RNA genome. The mutation rate has been estimated to be in the order of 10^{-4} to 10^{-5} per nucleotide per cycle. Mutations may affect the survival of the infected cell or mammalian host. L protein may affect the tropism of the virus for neurons and be involved in viral persistence.

■ Summary

Rabies is one of the oldest and most feared diseases. The disease is caused by the rabies virus. It is transmitted through the saliva of an infected mammal by an unprovoked bite. There are two forms of the disease: furious and dumb. The classic symptoms of furious rabies include hydrophobia, hypersalivation, delirium, tremors, and other encephalitis-like symptoms. The dumb form of rabies symptoms lack hydrophobia, seizures, and hyperactivity; instead, victims experience weakness and ascending paralysis.

Louis Pasteur and Emile Roux developed the first rabies vaccine during the late 1800s. It was prepared by drying the spinal cords of rabid rabbits. The vaccine was successfully tested on dogs; the first human to receive a postexposure vaccination was 9-year-old Joseph Meister in 1886. Meister had been severely bitten and mauled by a rabid dog. He made a full recovery after being inoculated with Pasteur's crude nerve tissue vaccine 13 times over a 15-day period. Today postexposure vaccination is a standard practice used to prevent rabies in individuals who have been bitten or scratched by a rabid mammal.

Rabies epidemiology is complex. The disease remains a significant wildlife management issue and public health challenge. Education plays a vital role in preventing this disease.

Rabies is a disease of both domestic and wild animals. Canine rabies continues to be a large problem in developing countries. Foxes and raccoon dogs are important rabies vectors in Europe. Wildlife most commonly infected in the United States are raccoons, skunks, foxes, coyotes, and bats. Wildlife vaccination and other rabies control measures implemented in the United States has substantially reduced rabies in wild dogs. The majority of human rabies cases in the United States today are caused by bat bites. Bats are difficult to target for rabies control by conventional methods.

Despite rapid medical advances, rabies remains a disease with an almost 100% fatality rate. Diagnosis of animals involves postmortem analysis of brain tissues via direct antibody fluorescent test. Diagnosis in humans antemortem is based on RT-PCR tests on saliva, tears, and cerebral spinal fluid. Rabies antibodies appear in unvaccinated patients during the second week of the illness and may aid diagnosis. Autopsies are performed on humans to confirm rabies cases.

There are no cures or antiviral drugs effective against this disease. Once symptoms begin, treatment is supportive. To date there is only one documented survivor of a rabies patient who was treated with a novel therapeutic regimen after the onset of rabies symptoms. This patient did not receive a postexposure vaccination. Preexposure vaccination of high-risk individuals and postexposure rabies vaccination and immune globulin are used today to prevent the disease. There are three categories of vaccines used: nerve tissue vaccines, avian embryo vaccines, and cell culture vaccines. Nerve tissue vaccines often cause vaccine complications. These vaccines are inexpensive to produce and are still used in developing countries.

Postexposure vaccination soon after infection is successful in preventing rabies because the virus infects muscle cells for weeks before it travels to the CNS. The vaccine elicits an immune response that prevents the virus from spreading throughout the CNS. Once the virus travels to the CNS, it spreads through the peripheral nerves to the salivary glands, skin, mucosal surfaces of the gut, and other organs. Saliva is infectious for several days and up to two weeks before symptoms occur.

The rabies virus is a unique enveloped, bullet-shaped rhabdovirus. It contains a single-stranded negative-sense RNA genome. The surface of the virus is covered with trimers of –glycoprotein (G) spikes. The virus contains a helical-shaped ribonucleoprotein core (RNP) that consists of the viral genomic RNA, which is tightly encased with nucleocapsid (N) proteins, a few copies of phosphoprotein (P), an RNA-dependent RNA transcriptase, and replicase (L) protein. A matrix (M) protein is also part of the RNP core. This lethal virus contains a mere five genes in this order: 3′ N, P, M, G, and L 5′.

Rabies virus infects nerve cells by binding to nicotinic acetylcholine receptors. The viral particle fuses with the host membrane via low pH-dependent fusion. The virus replicates solely in the cytoplasm of its host cell. After uncoating, the L protein transcribes the negative-sense RNA genome into five separate viral mRNAs. The viral mRNAs are translated by the hosts' protein synthesis machinery. As soon as enough N protein is produced, the L protein synthesizes a viral RNA intermediate or antigenome that is used as a template for the replication of full-length negative-sense viral RNA genomes that are packaged into the virus particle during assembly. Mature, infectious, bullet-shaped rabies particles acquire their cellular lipid bilayer as the RNP-M complex buds through the host cell plasma membrane.

Many aspects of the pathogenicity of rabies are still unknown. New patterns of rabies infection present a problem for both epidemiologists and virologists. The future of rabies control is a matter of continued research and prevention efforts. Pasteur said it best:

Let me tell you the secret that has led me to my goal: my strength lies solely in my tenacity.

Louis Pasteur (1822–1895)

▋ Resources

▋ Primary Literature and Reviews

Alverez, L. et al. 1994. "Partial Recovery from Rabies in a Nine-Year-Old Boy." *Pediatr Infect Dis J* 13(12):1154–1155.

Benitez, R. M. 1996. "A 39-Year-Old Man with Mental Status Change." *Md Med J* 45(9):765–769.

Centers for Disease Control and Prevention. (CDC). 1972. Human Rabies—Texas. *MMWR* 21(14):113–114.

Centers for Disease Control and Prevention. 1977 Rabies in a Laboratory Worker—New York. *MMWR* 26(21):182–183.

Centers for Disease Control and Prevention. 1977. Follow-up on Rabies—New York. *MMWR* 26(31):249–250.

Centers for Disease Control and Prevention. 1999. "Human Rabies Prevention—United States, 1999 Recommendations of the Advisory Committee on Immunization Practices (ACIP)." 48(RR-1):1–17.

Centers for Disease Control and Prevention. 2004. "Update: Investigation of Rabies Infections in Organ Donor Transplant Recipients—Alabama, Arkansas, Oklahoma, and Texas, 2004." *MMWR* 53(27):615–616.

Christenson, J. C. et al. 2007. "Human Rabies—Indiana and California, 2006." *MMWR* 56(15):361–365.

Cohen, J., and Powderly, W. G., eds. 2004. *Infectious Diseases*, 2nd ed. New York: Mosby.

Crepin, P. et al. 1998. "Intravitam Diagnosis of Human Rabies by PCR Using Saliva and Cerebrospinal Fluid." *J Clin Microbiol* 36(4):1117–1121.

Davis, A. D., Rudd, R. J., and Bowen, R. A. 2007. "Effects of Aerosolized Rabies Virus Exposure on Bats and Mice." *J Infect Dis* 195(8):1144–1150.

Dietzchold, B., and Koprowski, H. 2004. "Rabies Transmission from Organ Transplants in the USA." *Lancet* 364:648–649.

Dixon, B. 2007. "Watch your bats." *Lancet Infect Dis* 7(1):8.

Dutta, J. K. and Dutta, T. K. 1994. "Treatment of Clinical Rabies in Man: Drug Therapy and Other Measures." *Clin Pharmacol Ther* 32(11):594–597.

Emmons, W. et al. 1973. "A Case of Rabies with Prolonged Survival." *Intervirology*:60–72.

Fekadu, M. and Baer, G. M. 1980. "Recovery from Clinical Rabies of 2 Dogs Inoculated with a Rabies Virus Strain from Ethiopia." *Am J Vet Res* 41(10):1632–1634.

Fekadu, M. et al. 1996. "Possible Human-to-Human Transmission of Rabies in Ethiopia." *Ethiop Med J* 34:123–127.

Gautret, P. et al. 2007. "Rabies Preexposure Vaccination in Travelers." *J Travel Med* 14(2):136.

Gode, G. R. et al. 1988. "Treatment of 54 Clinically Diagnosed Rabies Patients with Two Survivals." *Indian J Med Res* 88:564–566.

Goldrick, B. A. 2005. "Human Rabies: Unusual Cases Shine the Spotlight on an Old Disease." *Am J Nursing* 105(5):31, 33–34.

Hemachudha, T. et al. 2006. "Failure of Therapeutic Coma and Ketamine for Therapy of Human Rabies." *J Neurovirol* 12:407–409.

Jackson, A. C. 2006. "Rabies: New Insights into Pathogenesis and Treatment." *Curr Opin Neurol* 19:267–270.

Jackson, A. C. and Wunner, W. H., eds. 2006. Rabies San Diego: Elsevier Science.

Knipe, D. M., and Howley, P. M., eds. 2001. *Fields Virology*, 4th ed. Philadelphia: Lippincott, Williams & Wilkins.

Lemos-Filho, L., and Fries, B. 2006. "An Encounter with Rabies in New York City." *Clin Infect Dis* 43(11):1492.

Madhusudana, S. N. et al. 2002. "Partial Recovery from Rabies in a Six-Year-Old Girl." *Int J Infect Dis* 6:85–86.

Mandell, G. L., Bennett, J. E., and Dolin, R., eds. 2000. *Mandell, Douglas, and Bennett's Principles and Practices of Infectious Diseases*, 5th ed. Philadelphia: Churchill Livingstone.

McColl, K. A. et al. 1993. "Polymerase Chain Reaction and Other Laboratory Techniques in the Diagnosis of Long Incubation Rabies in Australia." *Aust Vet J* 70(3):84–89.

McGuill, M. et al. 1999. "Mass Treatment of Humans Who Drank Unpasteurized Milk from Rabid Cows—Massachusetts, 1996–1998." *MMWR* 48(11):228–229.

Morgan, M., and Palmer, J. 2007. "Clinical Review: Dog Bites." *BMJ* 334:413–417.

Nicolle, L. 2002. "Rabies: Still With Us." *Can J Infect Dis* 13(2):83–84.

Plotkin, S. A. 2000. "Rabies." *Clin Infect Dis* 30:4–12.

Plotkin, S. A., and Orenstein, W. A., eds. 1999. *Vaccines,* 3rd ed. Philadelphia: W.B. Saunders.

Porras, C. et al. 1976. "Recovery from Rabies in Man." *Ann Intern Med* 85:44–48.

ProMED-mail: Rabies, human—USA (Texas). ProMED-mail 2006;13 May: 20060513.1360.

ProMED-mail: Rabies, human—Canine—China (Hunan). ProMED-mail 2007;05 March:20070305.0782.

Rupprecht, C. E., Willoughby, R., and Slate, D. 2006. "Current and Future Trends in the Prevention, Treatment and Control of Rabies." *Expert Rev Anti Infect Ther* 4(6):1021–1038.

Smith, J. S. Fishbein, D. B., and Rupprecht, C. E. 1991. "Unexplained Rabies in Three Immigrants in the United States." *N Engl J Med* 324(4):205–211.

University of Alabama at Birmingham Hospital, et al. 2004. "Investigation of Rabies Infections in Organ Donor Transplant Recipients—Alabama, Arkansas, Oklahoma, and Texas, 2004." *MMWR* 53(26):586–589.

Warrell, M. J., and Warrell, D. A. 2004. "Rabies and Other Lyssavirus Diseases." *Lancet* 363:959–969.

Wiktor, T. J. et al. 1977. "Induction and Biological Properties of Defective Interfering Particles of Rabies Virus." *Virology* 21(2):626–635.

Willoughby, R. E. et al. 2004. "Recovery of a Patient from Clinical Rabies—Wisconsin, 2004." *MMWR* 53(50):1171–1173.

Willoughby, R. E. Jr., et al. 2005. "Survival after Treatment of Rabies with Induction of Coma." *N Engl J Med* 352(24):2508–2514.

Winkler, W. G. et al. 1973. "Airborne Rabies Transmission in a Laboratory Worker." *JAMA* 226(10):1219–1221.

▪ Popular Press

Cockrum, E. L. 1997. *Rabies, Lyme Disease, Hanta Virus: And Other Animal-Borne Human Diseases in the United States and Canada,* Tucson: Fisher Books.

Finley, D. 1998. *Mad Dogs: The New Rabies Plague,* College Station, TX: Texas A & M University Press.

Gipson, F. and Poison, S. 2001. *Old Yeller,* New York: Harper Perennial Modern Classics, reissue edition.

Walsh, J. E. 2000. *Midnight Dreary: The Mysterious Death of Edgar Allan Poe,* New York: St. Martin's Minotaur.

Willoughby, R. E. Jr. 2007. "A cure for rabies?" *Sci Am,* April issue, 89–95.

▪ Video Productions

Old Yeller. 1957. Walt Disney Production.

Rabid. 1977. Film directed by David Cronenberg.

Rabies. 2006. The American Veterinary Medical Association.

Louis Pasteur. 2007. Films for the Humanities.

■ eLearning

http://biology.jbpub.com/book/virology

The site features eLearning, an online review area that provides quizzes and other tools to help you study for your class. You can also follow useful links for in-depth information, or just find out the latest virology and microbiology news.

ADDITIONAL CASE STUDY

James Welles is a 20-year-old college student who grew up on a dairy farm in Wisconsin. Every summer he returns home to work on the farm. One summer day, while walking through the cow pasture, James notices a raccoon scurrying in circles around an oak tree. Suddenly, he is distracted by his favorite Holstein cow Millie, who is standing alongside a fence. James was worried about Millie because lately she didn't have her usual appetite.

As Millie unsteadily stood next to the fence, she appeared to be in a stupor and foaming at the mouth. James was concerned and later discussed Millie's behavior with his father, who immediately called the local veterinarian. Based on Millie's loss of appetite, the veterinarian first thought that the cow had an intestinal obstruction. A few days later, though, the cow became aggressive and uncoordinated. Her health declined rapidly and she died. The veterinarian decided that a necropsy was needed to determine the cause of death.

1. What diagnostic tests should be performed to determine if Millie had rabies?
2. Should James and his parents receive postexposure rabies vaccines? Why or why not?

Millie had been milked 12 times during the week before her death. Her milk was pooled with the milk from the other dairy cows on the farm. A portion of the milk was not pasteurized and was distributed for human consumption.

3. Should individuals who drank the unpasteurized milk receive postexposure prophylaxis? Why or why not?
4. Speculate how Millie may have contracted rabies. How would you test your hypothesis?

Note: The CDC reported similar cases of cow rabies in *MMWR* March 26, 1999, Vol. 48, No. 11, pp. 228–229.

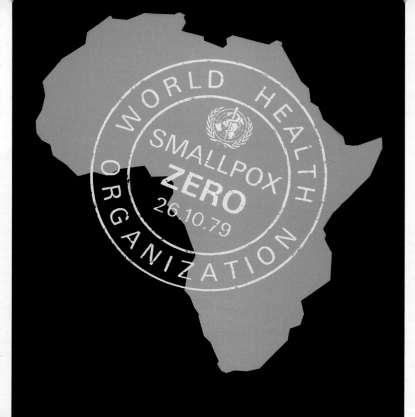

This poster was produced by the WHO in six different languages. The poster was created to celebrate the eradication of smallpox from the Horn of Africa on October 26, 1979, exactly two years after the last naturally occurring case that occurred in Somalia. Reproduced from F. Fenner, et al. *Smallpox and its Eradication*. World Health Organization, 1988.

CHAPTER

14

Poxviruses

66 *Could it not be contrived to send the Small Pox among those disaffected tribes of Indians? We must on this occasion use every stratagem in our power to reduce them.* 99

Lord Jeffrey Amherst, Commanding General of British forces in North America during the French and Indian War, July 1763

CASE STUDY

In 1985 Bob Miller, an 18-year-old National Guard member, received his first vaccination against smallpox at a U.S. Army facility. The vaccination gave him a lot of discomfort. His friend Jennifer applied compresses to the vaccination site on his arm to relieve some of the irritation and soreness caused by the inoculation. Two weeks later, Jennifer developed a slight fever and she felt very tired. A painful ulcer formed on her upper lip. It looked similar to Bob's vaccination lesion. The thought never crossed her mind that she could have contracted a poxvirus infection from Bob. Jennifer had been vaccinated against smallpox as a child even though she didn't have a scar on her arm from the inoculation. She assumed she was immune to a smallpox infection. Jennifer's mother encouraged her to go to the local clinic to determine what was causing the lesion. A physician at the clinic referred Jennifer to a dermatologist.

14.1   History

Smallpox is a human infectious disease caused by variola virus (family Poxviridae) and was a worldwide scourge for thousands of years. Dr. Michael T. Olsterholm of the University of Minnesota School of Public Health has called smallpox "the lion king of infectious diseases." Smallpox killed approximately 500 million people in the 20th century—more than the 320 million deaths caused by wars, the 1918 Spanish flu pandemic, and acquired immune deficiency syndrome (AIDS) combined. Those that survived smallpox were often left blind from corneal ulcerations and badly scarred by pockmarks. Famous victims and survivors of smallpox are listed in Table 14-1.

It has been speculated that smallpox emerged sometime after the first agricultural settlements, in about 10,000 B.C. The first evidence of smallpox comes from mummified remains of the Egyptian pharaoh Ramses V. Written descriptions of the disease appeared in China (340 A.D.) and southwestern Asia (910 A.D.). Smallpox was carried by explorers and traders from the Old World to the New World, where the population had no exposure or immunity to smallpox before the Europeans introduced it in the 16th century. In 1519, Spanish conquistador Hernando Cortez and his followers landed in Mexico, in the heart of

TABLE 14-1	Famous Individuals Who Suffered from Smallpox		
Individual	**Age Contracted**	**Year Contracted**	**Outcome**
Pharaoh Ramses V	35	1157 B.C.	Died (see Chapter 1)
Mary II of England	32	1694	Died
Peter II, Emperor of Russia	15	1730	Died
Louis XV, King of France	64	1774	Died
Wolfgang Amadeus Mozart	11	1767	Severe case, survived
George Washington	19	1751	Severe case, survived
Abraham Lincoln	54	1863	Mild case, survived

the Aztec empire, followed soon after by a second group of Spanish explorers. In the second group was an African slave who was afflicted with smallpox. In the ensuing months, smallpox spread throughout the Aztec empire. Over time, the Aztec and Inca empires, and eventually the Native American Indians, were devastated by outbreaks of smallpox. Smallpox ravaged Europe in the 17th and 18th centuries as well, afflicting up to 90% of the children in Britain alone. It was so pervasive that it was considered unusual if someone did not have **pox scars** on their face. In the United States, smallpox epidemics involving all age groups occurred frequently during the 18th century. Small hospitals referred to as "pesthouses" were used to isolate smallpox patients and their contacts during an outbreak.

14.2   Clinical Features of Human Poxviruses

■ Smallpox (Variola)

During the World Health Organization's (WHO's) eradication program, smallpox recognition cards were widely used by workers searching for cases in remote areas of India and Africa, where the last pockets of smallpox existed (**Figure 14-1**). Ultimately, the most effective method used to ensure prompt reporting was the offer of a reward, which was given to both the health worker who investigated the case and the person who reported it. At the beginning of 1974, a reward of 50 rupees (US$6.25) was offered per case in Indian states.

(a)

(b)

■ Figure 14-1
WHO Smallpox recognition card used in endemic countries in 1971.
(a) This photo is the front of the card. (b) These photos make up the
reverse side of the card.

By the end of 1974, the reward was increased to 100 rupees (US$12.50). By July 1975, the reward increased to 1000 rupees (US$125.00). Workers were sometimes paid as little 10 rupees or less per day by their employers, hence this reward was a significant amount. The reward system was also used in Bangladesh and Somalia. In 1978, the WHO increased the award to US$1000 for reporting a confirmed case.

Variola major and **variola minor** are two strains of the same virus (variola) but cause different diseases. Variola major is more common and causes a severe disease, with a more extensive rash and a higher fever. Variola minor causes a milder disease that has a 1% to 2% fatality rate in unvaccinated individuals. There are four types of variola major smallpox:

1. **ordinary** (the most frequent type, accounting for 89% or more of cases and with a 30% mortality rate);
2. **vaccine modified** (mild, occurring in 2.1% of previously vaccinated persons, and not lethal);
3. **flat or malignant pox** (rare—only 6.7% of cases—and very severe, with a 96% mortality rate);
4. and **hemorrhagic** (rare—2.4% of cases—and very severe, with a 96% mortality rate).

Historically, variola major has an overall fatality rate of about 30%; however, flat and hemorrhagic smallpox usually are fatal. Variola minor is a less common presentation of smallpox, and a much less severe disease, with death rates historically of 1% or less (**Figure 14-2**).

The average incubation period of smallpox is 12 to 14 days. During this time, people are not contagious. The first symptoms of smallpox include a fever of 101°F to 104 °F, a splitting headache, and a severe backache. Vomiting occurs in about half of all infected individuals and about 10% of individuals experience diarrhea. Delirium and convulsions may occur in a small percentage of individuals (7% to 15%), usually children. During this 2- to 4-day prodromal phase, the individual is too sick to carry on normal daily activities. The person may be contagious during this stage of infection. By the second or third day, the individual is feeling better. As the fever declines, a macular rash (small red spots) appears on the tongue and in the mouth (oral mucous membranes). The rash becomes papular (raised) and vesicular (blistery). It harbors large quantities of virus. As the vesicles rupture, large numbers of virus are liberated into the saliva. At this time, the person is most contagious. The lesions can also occur along the respiratory tract and some individuals may experience a sore throat. Around the same time that the vesicles break, a skin rash appears: first on the face, then spreading to the arms and legs, and finally to the hands and feet, all within a 24-hour period. This rash is described as being a **centrifugal** rash (it mainly covers the face and extremities as opposed to the entire body) and is important in the diagnosis of smallpox.

It is a raised rash that becomes vesicular, containing an opaque and turbid fluid by the fourth or fifth day. The vesicles mature into pustules by the seventh day. By the second week, the rash begins to crust over and the scabs separate by days 22 to 27. In fatal cases, death occurs between the tenth and sixteenth day of illness. The communicability of the disease extends from the onset of the rash to the complete separation of all scabs.

■ Monkeypox

Human monkeypox virus infections are rare. Before 1970, monkeypox was recognized as a disease of animals, normally occurring in the rainforests of central and western Africa. The monkeypox virus was first isolated from infected cynomolgus monkeys in 1958. Between 1970 and 1986, the first human cases of monkeypox were reported from western African and Congo Basin countries of Africa as smallpox disappeared. The smallpox vaccine protects or mitigates the clinical manifestations of monkeypox.

(a)

(b)

(c)

(d)

■ **Figure 14-2**

(a) This man is suffering from an ordinary variola smallpox infection. He is a patient at the Military Hospital No. 45, an isolation hospital at Gungalin, Australia. **(b)** The usual centrifugal pattern of smallpox maculopapular rash (less lesions on the trunk and more on his face and extremities) is revealed by this photograph of a Bangladesh boy (1973). Adapted from the CDC. *Health Information for International Travel 2008*. Elsevier, 2007. **(c)** The last known person in the world to have natural smallpox of any kind. This 23 year old, Ali Maow Maalin suffered from variola minor. He lived in Merka, Somalia (1977). **(d)** This Bangladesh man suffered from the most severe form of smallpox (hemorrhagic). He likely died from the viral illness (1975).

The first outbreaks of **human-to-human transmission** of monkeypox occurred in 13 villages in the Kasai Oriental, Zaire, from 1996 to 1997. The outbreaks were investigated by the Zaire Ministry of Health and the WHO. It has been postulated that lack of vaccination and a concurrent epidemic in a large number of animals allowed the monkeypox virus to cross the species barrier into humans. In June 2003, the first cases of monkeypox were reported among several people in a multistate outbreak in the United States who had had contact with infected pet prairie dogs and other exotic pets. The case-fatality rate of monkeypox ranges from 1% to 14%.

The signs and symptoms of monkeypox are similar to ordinary or modified smallpox but milder. Patients experience a fever, respiratory symptoms, and vesicular rash similar to smallpox victims (**Figure 14-3**). One difference is that **lymphadenopathy** (a chronic, abnormal enlargement of the lymph nodes) is more prominent in monkeypox cases during the early stages of the disease.

■ **Figure 14-3**
Crusted primary sites of monkeypox infection on the hands of a mother and daughter.

■ Molluscum Contagiosum

Molluscum contagiosum is a common poxvirus infection of worldwide distribution that can become a public health problem in areas of low sanitary and hygienic conditions. It represents 1% of all skin infections. The virus is transmitted by direct contact, including sexual contact or more commonly by a consequence of indirect contact through **fomites** such as sharing towels or from swimming pools. It can be transmitted rapidly among children in daycare centers and kindergartens. Today the disease is becoming a significant opportunistic infection in patients with human immunodeficiency virus (HIV) infections, especially those with severely depressed CD4+ T lymphocyte numbers. HIV patients may experience persistent and fulminating Molluscum contagiosum.

■ **Figure 14-4**
Molluscum contagiosum lesions.

The incubation period is two to eight weeks. The virus causes pink, pearl-like lesions (referred to as *molluscum*) on the face (especially eyelids), arms, and legs, which can be 1 to 5 mm in diameter (**Figure 14-4**). The molluscum often has a dimple in the center. If the infection is sexually transmitted, the lesions can be seen on the genitals, thighs, and the lower part of the stomach. Scratching can cause the lesions to spread. The infection is usually self-limiting. It can take between six months to five years for the lesions to disappear. There is continued debate about whether the lesions should be treated (e.g., by surgical removal, scraping, or freezing) or allowed to resolve spontaneously. Secondary bacterial infections are a complication of Molluscum contagiosum lesions. Molluscum contagiosum can serve as a marker for severe immunodeficiency.

■ Vaccinia Virus

Vaccination with **vaccinia virus** has been directly responsible for the successful eradication of smallpox (variola). Infection with this virus provides adequate cross-protective immunity against smallpox and monkeypox viruses. Although the exact origins of vaccinia virus are a mystery, genetically vaccinia virus is most similar to buffalopox. Inoculation with vaccinia virus produces a localized skin infection. In persons who are immunocompromised, vaccinia may disseminate and cause severe disease. Adverse reactions have been rare because routine childhood immunization was discontinued in the United States in 1972. Recent mysterious outbreaks of an emergent poxvirus from humans and cattle in Rio de Janeiro State, Brazil, may represent a persistent vaccinia-like virus infection in nature.

14.3   Laboratory Diagnosis of Poxvirus Infections

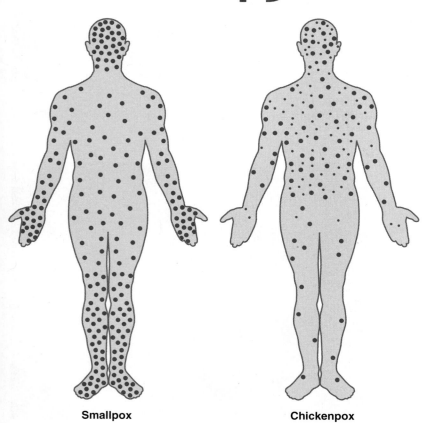

Smallpox   **Chickenpox**

■ **Figure 14-5**
Rash distribution of smallpox vs. chickenpox. Adapted from World Health Organization, *Diagnosis of Smallpox Slide Set,* http://www.who.int/emc/diseases/smallpox/slideset.

In the United States the last natural case of smallpox occurred in 1949 and routine smallpox vaccination of children was discontinued in 1972. Very few U.S. physicians have seen an actual case of smallpox. Variola major is a potential biological weapon today, though, so the Centers for Disease Control and Prevention (CDC) has prepared information and instructions for physicians in case of a smallpox emergency. The CDC has defined a smallpox clinical case definition as "an illness with acute onset of fever greater than or equal to 101°F (38.3°C) followed by a rash characterized by firm, deep-seated vesicles or pustules in the same stage of development without other apparent cause."

Typically, diagnosis of poxvirus infections is made based on the appearance of the lesions. Smallpox produces a centrifugal rash, as compared to a chickenpox rash that is more concentrated on the trunk of the body (**Figure 14-5**). Preliminary tests may be conducted on specimens that include scrapings of the pustules, blood, and scabs may be done by state health departmental laboratories. If smallpox or another poxvirus is suspected, scabs are also collected and analyzed by the CDC for definitive testing via electron microscopy to visualize poxvirus particles. Other methods such as virus isolation, histology, IgM and IgG enzyme-linked immunosorbent assay (ELISA), or polymerase chain reaction (PCR) techniques, followed by restriction fragment-length polymorphism (RFLP) or DNA sequencing analysis, may be used to detect the causative agent.

Electron microscopy has played a major role in viral diagnosis in the past. If available, it can be a first-line method for laboratory diagnosis of poxvirus infections and may provide one of the first clues to the cause of the unknown rash illness. PCR-RFLP analysis is the only way to accurately distinguish between variola, monkeypox, and vaccinia virus infections.

14.4   Cellular Pathogenesis

Despite the historical significance of smallpox, very little is known about the pathogenesis and virulence of variola virus. The knowledge we have comes from an era that predates modern advances in molecular virology and immunology. Virtually no modern molecular biology has been applied to the study of live variola virus. Today, variola virus is stored safely in two international repositories: the State Research Center of Virology and Biotechnology (Vector) near Novosibirsk in Russia and at the CDC in Atlanta, Georgia. The virus can only be safely worked with in a BSL-4 (Biosafety Level-4) maximum containment facility, sometimes referred to as a "hot lab." There is concern, though, that smallpox could reemerge in modern society through the use of variola virus as a bioweapon. To improve our understanding of variola pathogenesis, further research is needed to develop rapid diagnostics, antivirals, and a protective but less **reactogenic** and safer vaccine to treat those exposed to variola virus. To address these needs, research proposals with variola virus have been approved by the WHO. These proposals include the development of an animal model (e.g., the use of cynomolgus monkeys to attempt to repeat some of the pathologic features of human smallpox) because it is impractical and unethical to safely do smallpox experiments in humans. In nature, variola is uniquely restricted to humans, which is why surrogate primate models are needed to test vaccines and therapeutics.

14.5 Naming and Structure of Poxviruses

The name **variola** is derived from the Latin *varius* (spotted) or *varus* (pimple). The word *poc* or *pocca*—a bag or pouch—describes an **exanthematous** disease (a disease accompanied by skin eruption), such as smallpox, and English accounts began to use the word *pockes*. When syphilis appeared in Europe in the late 15th century, writers began to use the prefix *small* to distinguish variola, the smallpox, from syphilis, the great pox (which is caused by the spirochete bacterium *Treponema pallidum*). Vaccinia virus, the "vaccine virus," is a relative of variola virus. It is the prototype of poxviruses. Information regarding poxvirus structure and replication is based on laboratory experiments involving cell cultures infected with vaccinia virus.

Poxviruses are the largest of all animal viruses. They can be visualized by light microscopy. Virions are **enveloped** rectangular or "brick-shaped," ranging from 350 to 270 nm on average. They contain **linear double-stranded DNA (dsDNA)** genomes with *closed ends* that vary from 130 to 230 kilobase pairs (kbp) in length. Ends of the genome have inverted terminal repeat (ITR) sequences. Clinical specimens contain two different morphologies of virions: the intact M (or "mulberry") form mainly found in the vesicular fluid, and the C (or "capsule") form that is associated with dried scabs. Internally, poxviruses have a nucleoid and two **lateral bodies** surrounded by an outer membrane, as revealed by staining thin sections of infected cells using electron microscopy (**Figure 14-6**). The lateral bodies contain various enzymes essential for viral replication. Inside of the cell, the virion often has a double membrane.

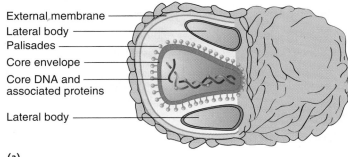

External membrane
Lateral body
Palisades
Core envelope
Core DNA and associated proteins
Lateral body

(a)

(b)

■ Figure 14-6
(a) Schematic drawing of a typical poxvirus virion. Adapted from an illustration by inDepthLearning, Ann Arbor, Michigan. **(b)** Electron micrograph of variola virus particles (310,000×, negative stain).

TABLE 14-2 Members of the Poxviridae Family That Infect Vertebrates (Subfamily Chordopoxvirinae)

Genus	Member Viruses
Avipoxvirus	Canarypox, fowlpox, pigeonpox, juncopox, quailpox, turkeypox, starlingpox, sparrowpox, peacockpox, penguinpox
Capripoxvirus	Goatpox, sheeppox, lumpy skin disease
Leporipoxvirus	Hare fibroma, myxoma, squirrel fibroma, rabbit fibroma
Molluscipoxvirus	**Molluscum contagiosum virus***
Orthopoxvirus	**Variola (smallpox),* vaccinia, monkeypox,*** buffalopox, camelpox, **cowpox***, ectromelia (mousepox), volepox, raccoonpox, skunkpox, elephantpox
Parapoxvirus	**Pseudocowpox*, orf*, bovine papular stomatitis virus***, sealpox, parapox of deer
Suipoxvirus	swinepox
Yatapoxvirus	**Tanapox*, Yaba monkey tumor***

*Human pathogens

Broad Host Range of Poxviruses

Naturally occurring poxvirus infections affect humans and many species of animals and insects. Most poxviruses were named after the animal from which they were originally isolated (e.g., cowpox and camelpox), but the main reservoirs for the viruses may be rodents or other species (Table 14-2). The one large Poxviridae family contains two subfamilies: Chordopoxvirinae, which infect vertebrates, and Entomopoxvirinae, which infect insect hosts. This chapter will focus on members of the Poxviridae family that infects humans: smallpox (variola major and minor), Molluscum contagiosum virus (MCV), monkeypox (a recently emerged virus in the United States in imported wild rodents from Africa), and vaccinia (the vaccine strain against smallpox). With the exceptions of the "extinct" variola virus and MCV, all other poxvirus infections of humans today are **zoonoses** (Table 14-3).

14.6 Vaccinia Virus Replication

Vaccinia virus is the prototype of poxviruses. It can be propagated in a wide host range of tissue culture cells (e.g., monkey, rabbit, hamster, and mouse). Vaccinia virus is like the *Escherichia coli* of a bacteriology laboratory: It can be grown to high titers in a short period of time. Within 12 to 24 hours,

TABLE 14-3 Human Poxvirus Pathogens and Their Natural Hosts

Virus	Natural Host*/Reservoir	Disease	Geographical Distribution
Variola major and minor viruses	Humans*	Smallpox, rash, generalized disease	Previously worldwide; eradication in humans in 1977
Monkeypox virus	Squirrels,* monkeys, rabbits, mice, rats, humans	Monkeypox rash, generalized disease	Western and central Africa
Molluscum contagiosum virus	Humans*	Molluscum contagiosum, skin nodules	Worldwide
Orf virus	Sheep,* dogs, goats, humans, chamois, reindeer, musk ox, Himalayan tahr, Steenbok, alpaca	Localized skin lesions	Worldwide
Pseudocowpox virus	European cattle,* humans	Milker's nodules	Worldwide
Bovine papular stomatitis virus	European cattle,* humans	Localized skin lesions	Worldwide
Cowpox virus	Rodents,* cats, cows, zoo animals, humans	Localized pustular lesions	Western Asia, Europe
Vaccinia virus	Natural host unknown (buffalo** and cattle?), humans	Buffalopox, localized pustular lesions	Asia, India, Brazil, and laboratory
Tanapox	Monkeys (?), rodents (?), humans	Tanapox, localized nodular lesions	Eastern and central Africa
Yaba monkey tumor poxvirus	Monkeys (?), humans	Localized nodular skin lesions	Western Africa

* Natural host.

**During the WHO smallpox eradication program, water buffalo in India and cattle in Brazil were infected with the local vaccine strain of vaccinia virus, which apparently persists in these animals and occasionally infects humans.

Table is adapted from White, D. O., and F. J. Fenner, *Medical Virology*, Fourth Edition, San Diego: Academic Press.

1×10^8 or 10^9 infectious viruses/ml of cell culture medium can be produced. Infectious vaccinia virus particles are large (300 to 400 nm in diameter) and brick-shaped. Lipoprotein membranes surround a complex core structure that contains a 200,000 base pair (bp) linear, dsDNA genome that encodes at least 200 genes. The ends of the

Figure 14-7

Typical poxvirus genome structure. Adapted from A. J. Cann, "Poxviruses," *MicrobiologyBytes: Virology,* http://www.microbiologybytes.com/virology/Poxviruses.html.

genome consist of a terminal hairpin loop (no free ends) with ITR sequences. The complete genome sequences of more than 40 poxviruses are available via the **Bioinformatics Resource Center** (http://www.poxvirus.org). Most of the **essential genes** are located in the central part of the genome, whereas **nonessential genes** (i.e., not essential for growth in cell cultures) are located at the ends of the genome (**Figure 14-7**). Approximately 90 essential genes are highly conserved among various poxviruses. Their functions are essential for viral replication and **morphogenesis**.

The entry of poxviruses into cells is complicated by the existence of multiple forms of infectious particles. One form contains two **extracellular enveloped virion** (**EEV**) membranes. The membranes of EEVs are obtained from the Golgi apparatus and the plasma membrane of the host cell. The second form is an **intracellular mature virion** (**IMV**), which only contains the inner membrane derived by a Golgi wrapping event. IMVs are released upon cell lysis. Each infectious form is thought to enter cells by different mechanisms. Vaccinia virus can enter almost every cell line tested. This means the receptor for vaccinia virus entry is highly conserved and ubiquitous in nature or that the virus can enter via more than one receptor. So far, some studies have shown that the A27L viron protein of vaccinia interacts with cell surface glycosaminoglycans (GAGs). GAGs are ubiquitously expressed on many different cell surfaces. The mechanism for cell entry and penetration is complex and may involve more than one mechanism.

During uncoating the outer membrane of the EEV is removed and the particle enters the cell, where it loses the second membrane and the viral core passes into the cytoplasm. *One of the unique hallmarks of poxviruses is that these viruses have acquired all of the functions necessary for genome replication in the cytoplasm even though they have DNA genomes.* Poxvirus gene expression and genome replication can occur in enucleated cells, but maturation of particles is blocked. Viral enzymes associated with the core carry out the three stages of gene expression: **early, intermediate**, and **late gene expression**. The three distinct classes of viral messenger RNAs (mRNAs) are transcribed from genes containing promoters and other sequence elements that provide the basis for their programmed order of expression. No splicing occurs in poxvirus mRNAs.

A complete early transcription system is synthesized late during infection and is packaged into the viral core. This viral transcriptional machinery consists of a DNA-dependent RNA polymerase, a transcription factor (VETF), capping and methylating enzymes, and a poly(A) polymerase. The machinery has the capability to synthesize mRNAs that are recognized and translated by the cell's protein synthesis machinery. The early mRNAs encode enzymes and factors needed for transcription of the intermediate class of genes that in turn encode enzymes for late gene expression. Late expression occurs after genome replication. The vaccinia virus D10 gene encodes a decapping enzyme that may accelerate viral mRNA turnover and help eliminate competing host mRNAs from being translated by the translational machinery. This would allow for stage-specific synthesis of viral proteins.

After the late structural proteins are synthesized, infectious progeny particles are assembled. Assembly involves interactions with the cytoskeleton (e.g., actin-binding proteins). The particles are wrapped with a Golgi-derived membrane and transported to the periphery of the cell. The EEV form picks up an additional membrane as it is released from the cell, completing the virus replication cycle. EEVs can initiate infection, mediating cell-to-cell spread. Refer to **Figure 14-8**.

14.7   Poxviruses and Immune Evasion

Poxviruses do not undergo a latent stage by integrating viral DNA into its host chromosome. Nor do they cause persistent infections that would make them invisible to the immune system. Instead, poxviruses use a number of viral proteins to *evade* host innate (nonspecific) immune responses. They produce **viroceptors** and **virokines**. Viroceptors

■ **Figure 14-8**
Life cycle of vaccinia virus. Adapted from G. McFadden, *Nat. Rev. Microbiol.* 3 (2005): 201–213.

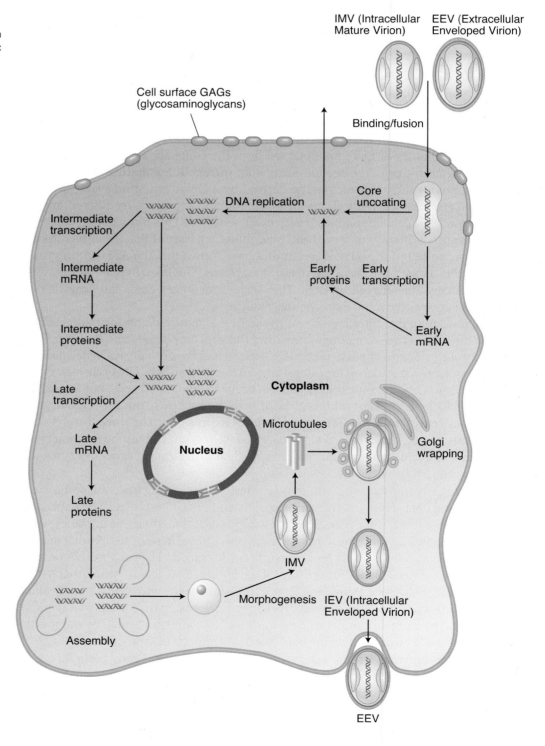

are altered cellular receptors that have lost their transmembrane anchor sequences. Consequently, these unanchored viral proteins are *secreted* from infected cells, where they sequester ligands onto the receptor portion of the protein. Virokines are secreted viral proteins that resemble host **cytokines**. The majority of poxvirus virokines and viroreceptors were discovered by investigators because of the deduced sequence homologies to their cellular counterparts. Besides secreted viral inhibitors, poxviruses also produce *intracellular proteins* that interfere with signaling pathways within the infected cell. Examples of these poxvirus inhibitors are:

- Secreted complement regulatory proteins
- Secreted proteins that bind to **interferons**
- Secreted **interleukin**-18 binding proteins
- Secreted **tumor necrosis factor** homologs (**apoptosis** inhibitors)
- Intracellular **serpins** (serine protease inhibitors)
- Intracellular inhibitors of **PKR** (interferon pathway; see Chapter 7)

The field of poxvirus-encoded immune modulators is nearly 20 years old and discoveries continue in this area. Even though no one specific poxvirus uses all of these collective strategies, all seem to target the immediate innate immune response (**Figure 14-9**).

14.8 Human Genetics and Smallpox Resistance

In order for an infectious disease to cause selective pressure on host genetics, it would need to have a significant effect on morbidity and mortality, before reproductive age, over a long time. Smallpox was endemic throughout much of the world for more than 2000 years. In populations where epidemics occurred frequently, smallpox was a childhood disease, killing as many as 30% of its victims. Since human populations were exposed to the virus for generations, resistant genes should be common in smallpox survivors. In 1965 and 1966, Vogel and Chakravartii conducted a comparative study of 415 unvaccinated Indian smallpox survivors and victims. They discovered that people who were Blood Type A were seven times more likely to contract smallpox, three times more likely to develop a severe case of the disease, and twice as likely to die of it.

A 2003 study by Galvani and Slatkin suggests that smallpox is responsible for the genetic selection of the CCR5-Δ32 deletion allele that confers resistance against HIV-1. CCR5 is a chemokine coreceptor required for HIV-1 infection (see Chapter 16). A homozygous CCR5-Δ32 deletion allele provides almost complete resistance to HIV-1 infection. Heterozygous CCR5-Δ32 deletion allele provides partial resistance and a slower disease progression. Since HIV is such a new disease, there have not been enough human generations or time for the selective rise of this resistance allele. Researchers have argued that other infectious agents are likely to have selected for this resistance allele. The most popular hypothesis suggests that this selective pressure was the result of bubonic plague (also referred to as the Black Death) pandemics in Europe. Galvani and Slatkin, however, argue that the plague outbreaks occurred in a shorter time frame—400 years—which is not enough time to generate the resistance allele. Smallpox, on the other hand, seems to be more consistent with selective pressure because the disease selection has been longer (more than 2000 years). The bottom line is that natural selection is a reality. The study of genetic susceptibility to infectious disease may contribute to the design of new therapeutics; for example, interference with the CCR5 chemokine receptor may have promise in the treatment of HIV.

■ Figure 14-9

Representation of poxvirus immune evasion proteins. Adapted from Moss, B., and J. L. Shisler, *Semin. Immunol.* 13 (2001): 59–66.

14.9   Smallpox Eradication

The word **eradicate** comes from the Latin word *eradicare*, which means "to tear out by the roots." Several diseases were candidates for a global eradication program, such as hookworm, yellow fever, and the eradication of mosquito vectors that carry the malarial parasite and other disease-causing organisms. Smallpox is the only human disease that has officially been eradicated.

There were several reasons why it was possible to eradicate smallpox:

* Smallpox has a narrow host range (variola only infects humans).
* There is no long-term carrier state in humans.
* There is no animal reservoir.
* highly effective and inexpensive freeze-dried vaccine was available.
* surveillance of the disease was easy (e.g., observation of centrifugal rash).
* The WHO created a program to eradicate it.

In 1967, the WHO launched a **mass-vaccination strategy** to vaccinate 100% of the human population. At that time, approximately 10 to 15 million cases of smallpox occurred annually and the disease was endemic in 30 countries. Over time, the strategy gradually changed to **containment vaccination** or **surveillance containment** around newly discovered cases or outbreaks. This new strategy evolved after countries like Nigeria and India experienced outbreaks originating in areas where religious groups resisted vaccination. To prevent spread of these outbreaks to populated areas, healthcare workers went on house-to-house searches to control local outbreaks. This was so successful in preventing spread of the disease that controlling outbreaks through variations of surveillance containment was adopted (**Figure 14-10**). Evaluation and assessment procedures constantly evolved in response to new experiences and lessons learned in the field. Important innovations, such as the use of **smallpox recognition cards** (Figure 14-1), **rewards**, the **bifurcated needle** (**Figure 14-11**), **rumor registers**, and **containment books** were used in the field. Every case of fever with rash was recorded, monitored, and treated as smallpox unless proven oth-

(a)

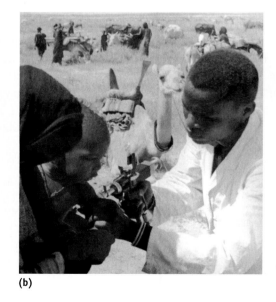

(b)

■ **Figure 14-10**
(a) WHO smallpox eradication workers faced rugged terrain as they rode four-wheel drive vehicles through Bangladesh countryside in an attempt to eradicate smallpox from the country. Off road Land Rovers enabled the country's eradication program to succeed, giving public health practitioners access to even the most inaccessible rural villages (1975). **(b)** Nigerian child being immunized during the Smallpox Eradication and Measles Control Program of West Africa (1960).

erwise. Four watch guards were placed at infected homes and all villages within ten miles of a case of known or suspected smallpox were searched and vaccinations were carried out. In 1977, the last natural case of smallpox was reported in Somalia. Smallpox was the first and only infectious disease to be eradicated.

14.10 Recombinant Vaccinia Viruses as Research Tools and Vaccines

Research on poxviruses did not languish after the eradication of smallpox. There was an explosion of interest in vaccinia virus, the prototype of poxviruses, in the 1980s. **Recombinant DNA technology** was applied to vaccinia virus. Inserting foreign genes into vaccinia virus has provided a way to study the expression of these foreign genes within the cytoplasm of mammalian cells. These new or **recombinant vaccinia viruses** have multiple applications in research, gene therapy, and vaccinology; for example, a successful recombinant vaccinia virus rabies vaccine has been used to eliminate rabies in western Europe and the United States (see Chapter 13). The construction of a recombinant vaccinia virus is illustrated in **Figure 14-12**. Briefly, the foreign gene of interest (e.g., rabies glycoprotein gene) is inserted into a **plasmid DNA** using restriction enzymes and T4 DNA ligase. The gene is inserted downstream of a vaccinia virus promoter and in the middle of a nonessential vaccinia virus gene such as the **thymidine kinase (TK) gene**. The presence of the TK gene allows for the homologous recombination incorporation of the foreign gene into the vaccinia genome. The engineered plasmid DNA is transfected into TK⁻ tissue culture cells (cells that do not contain a TK gene) simultaneously infected with vaccinia viruses. Absence of TK activity in host cells and disruption of the TK gene in vaccinia virus renders host cells resistant to toxic effects of 5-bromodeoxyuridine (BUdR). This selection enriches for cells that carry recombinant vaccinia virus.

Thymidine kinase is an essential *cellular* enzyme that is expressed during cell division activity. This enzyme allows a cell to utilize an alternate metabolic pathway for incorporating thymidine into DNA. BUdR is a mutagenic nucleoside that substitutes for thymidine in DNA, acting as a chain terminator. It causes breaks in the chromosomes of cells. It is used as an anticancer drug and is a potential antiviral drug. In the practice of creating vaccinia virus recombinants, a TK selection system has been developed. Only those cells and viruses that do not contain a functional TK gene can survive the effects of BUdR. Cells or viruses with an intact TK gene will incorporate BUdR, resulting in genetic mutations and likely cell death and/or viral inactivation.

One of the major advantages of using vaccinia virus is the fact that it has a large dsDNA virus that can package more than 200 genes, including foreign genes. RNA viruses have smaller genomes and a packaging size limit. RNA viruses are also more difficult to genetically engineer. Foreign genes can be introduced into nonessential parts (e.g., the TK gene) of the vaccinia genome via homologous recombination. Hence, vaccinia viruses are able to express one or more unrelated genes in a cell culture system. This makes it a very attractive tool for molecular biologists. One very important application of vaccinia virus is using its recombinants as new **live vaccines** against infectious agents of humans and animals.

A disadvantage of live vaccinia virus is the complications that can follow vaccination. To overcome this, attenuated strains of vaccinia virus have been generated. The modification of these attenuated strains will result in the production of safer live vaccines. It is

■ **Figure 14-11**

The **bifurcated needle** replaced the jet-injector to administer the smallpox vaccine. The jet injector could do over 1,000 vaccinations in an hour but its use was not practical and was too expensive to use for house-to-house vaccination. By 1970, the bifurcated needle replaced traditional methods and was used everywhere.

VIRUS FILE 14-1

Deliberate Use of Myxoma Poxviruses to Control Australian Wild Rabbits

Thomas Austin, a resident of Victoria in southern Australia, loved to hunt rabbits during his trips to England in the mid-1800s. To promote his hobby, he asked his brother in England to ship him some rabbits. In 1859, Austin released 24 wild European rabbits that had been trapped and shipped by his brother onto his farmland in southern Australia.

Rabbits, of course, are prolific breeders, and they quickly populated Austin's farm and his hunting tallies were published in the Victorian newspapers. In 1867, a newspaper reported he had killed 14,362 rabbits on his property for the year.

Austin didn't realize the rabbits were spreading throughout Australia. He had introduced a serious mammalian pest, an **invasive species**. The rabbits out-bred, out-ate, and out-competed other native Australian species. They multiplied so fast that two million rabbits could be shot or trapped each year without any noticeable effect on the population size. By 1900, the rabbit population was firmly established throughout all of Australia. Serious erosion problems occurred because the rabbits would consume native plants that would otherwise retain the soil. Some plant species became extinct. From 1901–1907, the western Australian government built a 1,833 kilometer-long rabbit-proof fence that ran between Cape Keraudren in the north and Starvation Boat Harbor in the south to prevent their spread. The rabbits managed to get past the fence because kangaroos, emus, and wombats made holes under the fences. Further complicating matters, storms and drifting sand damaged the fences, allowing the rabbits to penetrate the fence, and they were well beyond the fence-line before it was completed. By the 1940s, there were hundreds of millions of rabbits, causing massive agricultural and environmental damage wherever they were found (**Figure VF 14-1**). The invasion of Australia by rabbits remains one of the fastest recorded for any mammal species.

Conventional control measures such as hunting and poisoning were applied to reduce rabbit populations. Hunting was labor intensive and limited to certain geographic areas. The disadvantage of poisoning was that the rabbit could not be used as food for either humans or predators thereafter. Meanwhile, **myxomatosis** was causing mild benign lesions (myxomas) in the South American wild rabbit population. A poxvirus (**myxoma virus**) was isolated and determined to be the culprit of myxomatosis. This viral disease

■ Figure VF 14-1
High densities of rabbits surrounding a waterhole in Canberra, Australia, during the 1963 drought. It depicts the problem of rabbit control prior to the introduction of myxomatosis.

(continued)

was transmitted via a bite of an infected blood feeding flea or mosquito. When European rabbits were brought into a South American animal laboratory, the myxoma virus caused a highly lethal infection in the European rabbits. It was a vastly different disease than observed in the South American rabbits. The rabbits became bedraggled with eyes almost totally swollen shut and with lots of discharge coming out of its eyes and nose. The ears and head were swollen. Myxomatous nodules were found on the eyelids, face, ears, and sometimes the rest of the body. The myxoma virus was shed in discharges and the disease could be spread by close contact with infected rabbits. Myxomatosis killed 99.5% of the European rabbits about 10 to 12 days after infection.

Investigators in England began experiments in the 1930s to determine if myxoma virus infected any other common animals. They discovered the virus was species-specific. Fifteen years later (~1950), the virulent myxoma virus was introduced by Australian farmers via inoculation campaigns into wild rabbit populations. It was initially highly effective in controlling plague proportions of rabbits, but the impact was reduced when the virus and rabbit host adapted. The myxoma virus adapted into a benign strain and genetically resistant rabbits rebounded.

In 1993, the Australian government approved the genetic modification of myxoma virus. Scientists proposed to introduce genes that code for rabbit sperm and egg proteins into myxoma virus. In doing so, female rabbits infected with the recombinant virus would generate an antibody response toward the viral and sperm or egg antigens. The sperm and egg proteins would behave like foreign invaders, triggering an autoimmune response. This **immunocontraceptive vaccine** delivered by myxoma virus would neutralize the antigens, thereby inducing infertility in female rabbits. Recombinant myxoma viruses expressing reproductive rabbit antigens have been constructed. To date, the engineered viruses are being studied in the laboratory. This strategy for controlling wild rabbit populations is based on the control of fertility rather than mortality.

References

Fenner, F., and Fantini, B. 1999. *Biological Control of Vertebrate Pests: The History of Myxomatosis: An Experiment in Evolution.* Oxfordshire, England: CABI Publishing.

Gu, W. et al. 2004. "Immune Response in Rabbit Ovaries Following Infection of a Recombinant Myxoma Virus Expressing Rabbit Zona Pellucida Protein B." *Virology* 318(2):516–523.

Hayes, R. A., and Richardson, B. J. 2001. "Biological Control of the Rabbit in Australia: Lessons not Learned?" *Trends Microbiol* 9(9):459–460.

Holland, M. K., and Jackson, R. J. 1994. "Virus-Vectored Immunocontraception for Control of Wild Rabbits: Identification of Target Antigens and Construction of Recombinant Viruses." *Reprod Fertil Dev* 6:631–642.

Mackenzie, S. M. et al. 2005. "Immunocontraceptive Effects on Female Rabbits Infected with Recombinant Myxoma Virus Expressing Rabbit ZP2 or ZP3." *Biol Reprod* Nov 23rd Epub ahead of print.

Morell, V. 1993. "Australian Pest Control by Virus Causes Concern." *Science* 261:683–684.

recommended that laboratory workers who directly handle cultures or animals infected with vaccinia virus be vaccinated. Laboratory workers using highly attenuated strains of vaccinia virus, such as the modified vaccinia Ankara (MVA) virus, the New York vaccinia (NYVAC) virus, or avipox viruses such as ALVAC (attenuated canarypox) and TROVAC (attenuated fowlpox) do not require vaccination. These attenuated viruses are called **suicide vectors**. All of them undergo **abortive replication** in mammalian cells. In other words, these viruses can infect cells, but there is a block in their life cycle such that early viral proteins are produced but late proteins (and therefore full infectious particles) are not produced in mammalian cells. **These vectors can express high levels of a foreign antigen without being pathogenic to a host**. To engineer and work with these attenuated viruses, they can be propagated in chick embryo fibroblasts (CEF) or sometimes baby hamster kidney (BHK-21) cells. All of these attenuated poxviruses have a very restricted

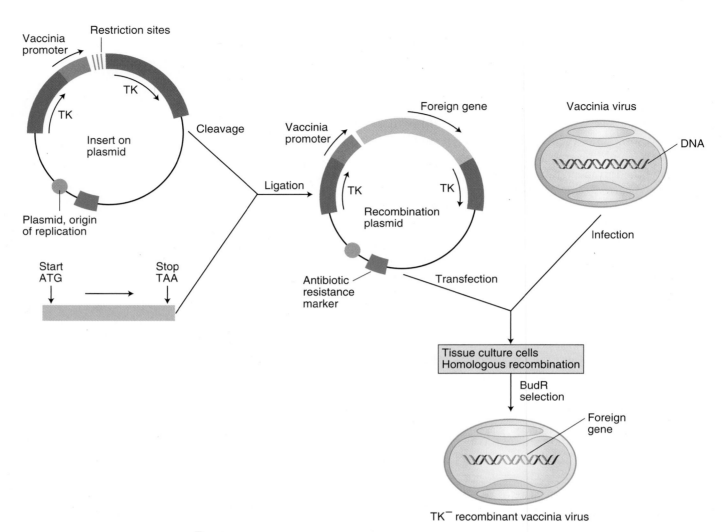

■ **Figure 14-12**
Flowchart depicting the creation of recombinant vaccinia viruses. Adapted from Mooney, H. A., and G. Bernardi. *Introduction of Genetically Modified Organisms into the Environment.* John Wiley & Sons, 1990.

host range. Recombinant vaccinia or other attenuated poxvirus vectors have been genetically engineered to contain genes from a wide variety of infectious agents including HIV and severe acute respiratory syndrome-coronavirus (SARS-CoV).

14.11   Prevention: Vaccines

■ Smallpox Vaccine History

Attempts to prevent the disease that caused "the speckled monster" date to practices in China beginning in the late 17th century. Two such practices were to inhale or plug the nose with powdered smallpox scabs, or to put the underwear of an infected child on a healthy child for several days. **Variolation** was practiced by Hindus in India during the 16th century. It is the intentional inoculation of dried smallpox scabs into the skin of an uninfected individual, causing a mild form of the disease and immunity against subsequent exposure to variola virus. The practice spread from central Asia, east to China, and then west to Africa and the Ottoman Empire. This practice involved the direct inoculation of smallpox into susceptible persons, so it is not surprising that 2% to 3% of variolated people died, as compared to 30% who died when they contracted smallpox naturally.

Lady Mary Wortley Montague (1689–1762), the wife of the British ambassador to Turkey, learned about variolation (referred to as *engrafting*) during her travels to Constantinople (now Istanbul) in 1717, when she observed Muslims using this technique. Montague expressed interest regarding this practice because she had survived smallpox in 1715. The disease left her without eyelashes and a badly pockmarked face; her brother had died from it. After returning to London, Montague had the embassy surgeon, Charles Maitland, engraft her 4-year-old daughter in 1721. Maitland gained permission to conduct a study in which six prisoners underwent the variolation procedure. The prisoners survived after exposure to two children with smallpox. They had a milder form of the disease and developed immunity. This study was witnessed by members of the Royal Society of London, and based on the results these inoculations began the acceptable medical practice of variolation in England.

Edward Jenner (1749–1823), a physician in England, is credited with **cowpox vaccination**, the first attempt to control smallpox without transmitting the disease. As mentioned in Chapter 1, Section 1.1, Jenner experimented with the folklore that milkmaids who contracted cowpox "did not take the smallpox," and in 1796 he variolated the 8-year-old son of a local farmer with fluid from the cowpox pustules from the hand of a local dairymaid. The boy developed a slight fever and a few lesions but remained unscathed for the most part. A few months later, the boy was injected with smallpox again and still failed to develop the disease. Jenner continued these experiments and published his findings in *Inquiry into the Cause and Effects of the Variolae Vaccinae* in 1798. The immediate reaction to Jenner's work was ridicule. Critics, especially the clergy, claimed it was repulsive and ungodly to inoculate someone with material from a diseased animal. A satirical cartoon of 1802 showed people who had been vaccinated sprouting cow's heads. Despite these initial reactions Jenner did go on to become famous, and the word **vaccination** was coined.

In the 1800s, **arm-to-arm passage** (or **arm-to-arm vaccination**) became a practice to prevent smallpox. The fluid or *lymph* taken from a vesicle or pustule from a previously vaccinated person was passaged arm-to-arm between humans. Occasionally, the vaccine was lost and further strains were obtained from cows or horses. Arm-to-arm passage was not a safe practice. Sometimes the vaccine became contaminated with variola major or minor, which sometimes resulted in the inadvertent transmission of other infectious diseases such as syphilis to tuberculosis. At least one recorded epidemic of hepatitis B was contributed to arm-to-arm passage. In 1898, the Vaccination Act banned arm-to-arm vaccination.

As early as 1876, the New York City health department constructed a laboratory to prepare smallpox vaccine. The laboratory was in a three-story building that included a stable on the ground floor containing stanchions to house heifers (**vaccinifers**) for vaccine production and an operating room and a sterilizing room on other floors. Cowpox lesions (referred to as **seed lymph**) from infected calves were smeared into superficial linear bloody incisions made with sharp knives on the shaved, washed, and sterilized skin of the belly or flank of uninfected calves. Vesicles appeared within the scarified incisions in a few days. Four days later after the appearance of lesions, the skin was scraped with a currette and the **vaccine (calf) pulp** was collected in a jar. Glycerin was added to prevent microbial contamination and act as a preservative. The pulp was emulsified and clarified via centrifugation to yield **vaccine lymph**. This early vaccine product was very crude and was contaminated with fragments of cells and bacteria.

By 1902, smallpox vaccination was practiced throughout industrialized countries. Little is known about the origins or history of the viruses present in the seed lymph used for vaccination until the 1960s. Vaccine technology was not consistent among manufacturers.

■ Figure 14-13

Two laboratory workers preparing smallpox vaccine (1980). The calf is bound to a grated table. Vaccinia virus was introduced into the scarified areas of skin.

Viruses were passed through a variety of vaccinifers such as cows, sheep, water buffalo, and sometimes rabbits, horses, and even humans. Seed lymph was obtained from "smallpox direct," cowpox, horsepox, sheeppox, goatpox, or even vaccinia in the human body. As protocols became standardized, vaccines produced in animal skin were tested for the presence of specific pathogenic microbes. These specifications allowed for the presence of a low concentration of nonpathogenic bacteria and fungi. National surveys in the United States revealed that 266 per million vaccinees experienced life-threatening complications after a primary vaccination.

By 1967, the WHO recommended the use of a seed lot containing the Lister or the New York City Board of Health strain (NYCBOH) grown by Wyeth Laboratories for vaccine production. These two were the least pathogenic of the effective vaccines. **Figure 14-13** shows the preparation of freeze-dried smallpox vaccine from virus grown on the skin of a calf around 1980.

Mass smallpox vaccination in the United States was discontinued in 1972. The country's current **stockpile of smallpox vaccine** available for biodefense consists of the Wyeth Dryvax produced from 1980–1982 and the Connaught (now Aventis-Pasteur) vaccine Wetvax produced in the 1950s. There is enough vaccine to vaccinate everyone in the country in the event of an emergency.

The vaccine stockpiles of the European Union and the WHO were also produced from calf-lymph. These vaccines have not been tested by modern methods for the presence of mycoplasma or bovine viruses. The WHO has agreed to develop safer, tissue culture-based vaccines that contain **attenuated** strains of vaccinia virus.

■ Smallpox Vaccination Today

Currently the only individuals in the United States vaccinated against smallpox are laboratory workers who do research with poxviruses, healthcare workers, and members of the military. After the events of September 11, 2001, the Bush administration called for a half-million healthcare workers to be vaccinated against smallpox. By 2004, only 40,000 had complied.

Vaccination Overview: Receiving the Vaccine

The smallpox vaccine available in the United States today is the Dryvax, live-attenuated preparation of vaccinia virus. It contains trace amounts of the antibiotics polymyxin B, streptomycin, tetracycline, and neomycin. The vaccine has been reconstituted in 50% glycerin and a small amount of phenol as a preservative. The vaccine is given with multiple punctures of a bifurcated (two-pronged) needle into the deltoid muscle of the arm: three times for a primary vaccination and 15 times for a revaccination. The virus is live, so it can spread to other parts of the body by inadvertent scratching or other contact. Thus the vaccination site is covered and the dressing changed every one to three days. Contaminated dressings are handled as infectious waste. **Figure 14-14** shows a typical smallpox reaction. Immunity lasts approximately three years.

Vaccine Complications

Data from the 1960s suggest that 1,000 of every 1 million vaccinees have a serious reaction to the vaccine. About one in 1 million of primary vaccinees will die and one in four million revaccinees will die. Rates of adverse reactions and deaths could vary considerably today. Serious side effects have occurred in people with skin conditions such as eczema or atopic dermatitis, as well as in people with weakened immune systems or people with

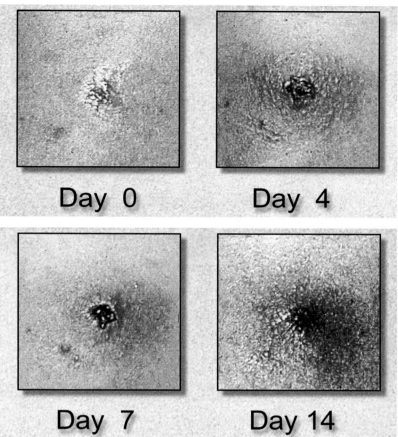

Day 0   Day 4

Day 7   Day 14

■ **Figure 14-14**
Expected vaccine site reaction and progression following a smallpox vaccination. The pustule dries from the center outward and forms a scab that separates 14 to 21 days after vaccination, leaving a pitted scar.

the following risk factors: heart disease, high blood pressure, diabetes, and high blood cholesterol. Severe complications that may follow a primary or revaccination include: **encephalitis, vaccinia necrosum (Figure 14-15a), eczema vaccinatum** (Figure 14-15b), **encephalomyelitis, encephalopathy,** and **myopericarditis (heart inflammation).** Adverse reactions may be treated with **vaccinia immunoglobulin** and **cidofovir.** Any one of these adverse effects may result in permanent disability and/or death. About two-thirds of complications after smallpox vaccination might have been preventable and avoided with better screening during the smallpox eradication era. Adverse reactions in the United States might be higher today than previous reports because there is a much higher proportion of people at risk for complications as a result of organ transplantation, cancer, cancer therapy, radiation, immune-modulating medications, eczema, atopic dermatitis, and other illnesses such as AIDS. The incidence of adverse cardiac events related to smallpox vaccinations administered during the National Smallpox Vaccination Program (NSVP) in 2002 received widespread attention. Safer vaccines are needed in case of an emergency bioterrorism event that would require mass-vaccination.

14.12 Orthopoxvirus Antivirals

The discontinued use of smallpox mass-vaccination with vaccinia virus has resulted in the lack of herd immunity against variola and monkeypox viruses. Infection with variola major is associated with an approximately 30% mortality rate. In an emergency today (e.g., intentional use of variola major in a bioterrorism event), immune-compromised individuals or other high-risk groups cannot be inoculated with vaccinia virus because of the

(a)

(b)

■ **Figure 14-15**
(a) This young child is suffering from a necrotic vaccination site. It is one of the most severe complications of the smallpox vaccine and is almost always life-threatening. This child required a skin graft to correct the necrosis. Those most susceptible to this condition are the immunocompromised. (b) This 8-month-old boy developed eczema vaccinatum after acquiring a vaccinia infection from a recently vaccinated sibling. Ezema vaccinatum occurs in people with atopic dermatitis who come in contact with vaccinia virus.

complications associated with the smallpox vaccine. There is no licensed drug treatment available for clinical smallpox, thus the focus has been on the development of antiviral strategies against variola as an alternative or additional strategy for the prevention or postexposure treatment of smallpox and/or monkeypox. **Cidofovir** (also called **HPMPC** or **Vistide**) has been used to treat Molluscum contagiosum in AIDS patients through intravenous injection. It has also been used as a topical treatment (1% cream) of orf infections. It causes the pox-induced lesions to regress after two to four months of therapy. Cidofovir has been licensed for the treatment of cytomegalovirus retinitis in AIDS patients as well. Cytomegalovirus is a large herpes virus that contains a dsDNA genome (see Chapter 15). Cidofovir is a nucleoside/nucleotide analog that interferes with virally encoded DNA polymerases during viral replication. It is currently being tested as an antiviral treatment after lethal monkeypox infection of cynomolgus monkeys. As described earlier in this chapter, monkeypox causes a disease similar to human smallpox and this animal model is being used to measure the effectiveness of cidofovir as a preventative or postexposure antiviral therapy.

An ideal antiorthopoxvirus drug has yet to be discovered. The best antiviral drugs target essential viral enzymes. Several viral gene candidates play essential roles in poxvirus replication. Potential targets include viral genes involved in DNA replication and recombination, mRNA synthesis and modification, and protein modification and virus assembly. Selected poxvirus enzyme targets are described in detail by Stephen C. Harrison and his colleagues (see References). Ultimately, the development of antiviral drugs against smallpox could deter terrorists from releasing variola because its affects would be diminished. Likewise, new antiorthopoxvirus therapies are likely to be useful in the treatment of other human orthopoxvirus infections.

14.13   Variola Virus in the Laboratory

There have been two fully documented laboratory-associated outbreaks of smallpox. Both outbreaks occurred in the United Kingdom after smallpox was no longer endemic there. The first outbreak occurred at the London School of Hygiene and Tropical Medicine in 1973. A 23-year-old female assistant in a mycology laboratory contracted smallpox after observing a friend inoculating chorioallantoic membranes of eggs with variola viruses at an open bench in a poxvirus laboratory in the same building. This laboratory accident resulted in four cases of smallpox, of which two were fatal. It was concluded that the young assistant inhaled aerosoled virus. At the time, variola was not studied within the setting of a Biosafety Laboratory Level-4 (BSL-4) built for dangerous pathogens.

The second laboratory-associated outbreak generated a great deal of publicity in the media. Janet Parker, a 40-year-old medical photographer in the Anatomy Department of the Medical School of the University of Birmingham, came down with smallpox in August 1978. After the appearance of the rash and a diagnosis was confirmed, she was placed in an isolation hospital. Health authorities identified 290 contacts with Mrs. Parker during her illness. These included her mother and other relatives and colleagues. All were vaccinated and placed under surveillance at home. It was concluded that Mrs. Parker contracted smallpox by an airborne route, either through a duct or telephone room while visiting the medical microbiology department where she regularly entered the animal pox room. Mrs. Parker died; her mother contracted smallpox but survived. The tragedy continued with the suicide of Professor Henry Bedson, the chief of the poxvirus laboratory. As a result of this outbreak, close attention was paid toward the handling of variola stocks in laboratories. As mentioned earlier in the chapter, today variola is a BSL-4 pathogen that is stored under high security at two repositories in the world. Any research studies using variola must be conducted in these two facilities.

14.14   The Variola Destruction Debate

Since the eradication of smallpox, it has been repeatedly proposed to destroy all of the last remaining stocks of variola virus that are stored in the two repositories. The destruction has been postponed indefinitely, though. New research proposals to develop diagnostics, safer vaccines, and antivirals against variola have been approved by the WHO's advisory committee. This research has been driven forward because of the concerns of bioterrorism. All approved research must be conducted at the two laboratories where the viruses are stored. These plans have been aggressively protested by at least two advocacy groups: the Sunshine Project of Austin, Texas, and the Third World Network, with headquarters in Penang, Malaysia. In 2005 the U.S. Congress passed an amendment, later signed into law by President Bush, which is part of the **Intelligence Reform and Terrorism Prevention Act**. The Act bans the synthesis of variola virus from scratch (e.g., using a DNA synthesizer and sequence information from a database such as the **Poxvirus Bioinformatics Resource Center**, which is available via the Internet) but does not prohibit researchers from engineering similar poxviruses to contain variola genes.

14.15   Bioterrorism and Biowarfare

The use of variola major as a biological weapon has a long history. The most documented incident was the intended use of variola major virus as germ warfare against the Native

Americans during the French and Indian Wars (1754–1763). In the 18th century, the British fought France and its Indian allies for possession of what was to become Canada during the French and Indian Wars. In 1763, while in Fort Pitt on the Pennsylvania frontier, British General Jeffery Amherst ordered that two blankets and a handkerchief be taken from smallpox patients in the fort's infirmary and given to the Delaware Indians surrounding the fort at a peace-making parley. It was Amherst's hope to induce a smallpox epidemic among the Indians and defeat them.

Another example of intentional transmission of variola major occurred much later, in the 1860s. Following the Civil War, there was an unprecedented increase in student enrollment in the medical colleges of Ohio, resulting in a high demand for cadavers. Physicians and their students needed to renew their own knowledge of anatomy or improve their surgical techniques. Professional grave robbers, which were also called body snatchers or resurrectionists, provided services to meet the demands. William Cunningham (1807–1871) was a professional grave robber for the Medical College of Ohio in Cincinnati when several anatomy students played a trick on him. In an act of revenge, he delivered a corpse of a recently buried smallpox victim to the anatomy dissecting room and a number of anatomy students were infected.

Smallpox as a bioterrorism weapon coincided with its declared eradication in 1980. The World Health Assembly recommended that all countries stop vaccination and that smallpox virus stocks be destroyed or transferred to one of the two specific reference laboratories. Countries complied; however, viral stocks in Russia were moved to a biological weapons development facility known as Vector. The Russians began producing upwards of 20 tons of variola virus for the use in bombs and intercontinental ballistic missiles. Much research focus was placed on optimizing virus viability during and after dissemination of a bioweaponized bomb or missile. Funding in the 1990s declined for the Russian laboratories and many scientists left to work in other laboratories. The fate of the viral stocks is uncertain.

The bottom line is that acts of bioterrorism occurred in the past and they will inevitably occur in the future. These types of acts are intended to generate panic and fear through their unpredictable manner.

Ordinary citizens are much more susceptible to bioweapons than are military targets. Military personnel are vaccinated against potential biological agents. In contrast, civilian populations will require rapid diagnosis and antimicrobial treatment and vaccination if available. Preparation is essential in order to protect ordinary citizens. This preparation takes two forms:

1. Intelligence and law enforcement activities.
2. Public health activities to prepare and respond to such acts to lessen their impact.

Is the use of variola major as a bioweapon a realistic threat today? What would happen if a terrorist infected him/herself intentionally with variola virus and walked through a crowded subway or shopping mall? Would this event cause a massive outbreak? In 1947, a situation somewhat like this happened in New York City. An American citizen, Eugene LeBar, contracted smallpox while in Mexico. Shortly after arriving in New York City, he developed a rash characteristic of hemorrhagic smallpox. He was hospitalized but not diagnosed until two more cases occurred. The new cases were individuals who had had contact with LeBar during his hospitalization. LeBar subsequently died. Within three weeks, 5.35 million New York City residents were vaccinated. The rapid vaccination response curbed this epidemic to a total of two deaths and twelve cases in less than a month.

What if a situation similar to what happened in 1947 occurred today? Smallpox has been eradicated globally and vaccination against variola ceased in the 1970s in most countries. As a result, today's human population is immunologically naive and susceptible to infection by variola virus.

The fact that smallpox has been eradicated with a vaccine is a good indication that we can contain and control this disease (via vaccination and isolation of patients). Other things to consider are that it requires a sophisticated biosafety laboratory to grow the virus. Terrorists who consider using the virus as a weapon would have to either intentionally infect him- or herself or produce large volumes of virus that would be aerosoled into the human population, a method that has never been done. If a terrorist did manage to inoculate him- or herself with variola major, it would be very difficult to disseminate the virus because the individual would be very ill during the most contagious time period of the disease. From the historical record, most individuals who contracted smallpox did so when they were caring for an infected person (i.e., they were in very close contact). It is also known that if a person is vaccinated within three to four days of exposure to the virus the disease will either be prevented or greatly ameliorated.

Preparing is the key to preventing the return of smallpox. There is currently a stockpile of vaccine to cover the entire U.S. population of healthy persons. Military staff members are vaccinated and healthcare and emergency workers may volunteer to be vaccinated. Unfortunately, the current vaccine cannot be given to immune-compromised or other high-risk individuals. At the time of this writing, 46% of all hospitals in the United States have written hospital terrorism preparedness emergency response plans. In addition, staged drills for biological attacks and severe epidemics are conducted at least once a year. Much work remains; however, through public education, surveillance, and continual national and international preparedness, the vulnerability to **weapons of mass destruction** will be significantly reduced.

Summary

. . . the confluent smallpox—invented perhaps as the cruelest remedy for human vanity. . .

Lawrence Durrell (1912–1990), playwright

Smallpox was one of the most devastating infectious diseases in human history and is the only human disease to be intentionally eradicated from the world's human population. It has contributed such words as variolation, inoculation, vaccination, immunity, and bioterrorism to our language.

Eradication of smallpox was possible for several reasons:

- Smallpox has a narrow host range (variola only infects humans).
- There is no long-term carrier state in humans.
- There is no animal reservoir.
- A highly effective and inexpensive freeze-dried vaccine was available.
- Surveillance of the disease was easy (e.g., by observation of centrifugal rash).
- The WHO created a coordinated program to eradicate it.

In addition to smallpox, there are other diseases caused by **poxviruses** that afflict many species of animals and insects (e.g., camelpox, canarypox, skunkpox). Poxviruses infect a diversity of hosts but each poxvirus is very species-specific; for example, rabbitpox only infects rabbits and smallpox only infects humans.

Smallpox is caused by variola major or variola minor, viruses that belong to the Poxviridae family. Variola major is the severe and most common form of smallpox. It can cause ordinary, vaccine-modified, flat, or malignant pox and hemorrhagic smallpox. The key clinical features used to diagnose smallpox are recognition of a high fever and the presence of a centrifugal rash. If a smallpox case was suspected today, pustules would be analyzed by experts at the CDC for definitive testing via electron microscopy and other molecular methods such as ELISAs or PCR techniques. Other human poxvirus infections are caused by monkeypox, Molluscum contagiosum, and vaccinia viruses.

Very little is known about the pathogenesis of smallpox because modern molecular biology has not been applied to the study of live variola virus. This has occurred because smallpox was eradicated before advanced molecular techniques were developed. Variola virus strains are stored under high security in two international repositories located in the United States and Russia. The WHO has approved research proposals that involve the development of an animal model to study variola pathogenesis. Poxvirus research is now focused on the development of rapid diagnostics, antivirals, and a safer vaccine against variola.

The majority of molecular biology we know regarding poxviruses comes from research on vaccinia virus. Vaccinia is the vaccine strain against smallpox and is the prototype of poxviruses. Genetically, its closest relative is buffalopox. Vaccinia virus readily grows in almost all cell lines tested. It is a large, brick-shaped virus that has at least two infectious forms produced during its life cycle. The extracellular enveloped virion (EEV) contains two membranes wrapped around its large linear dsDNA genome, whereas the intracellular mature virion (IMV) contains one membrane derived from Golgi wrapping. No specific host-cell receptors for viral entry have been identified. One of the unique hallmarks of poxviruses is that they have acquired all of the functions necessary for genome replication in the cytoplasm even though they possess DNA genomes. A complete early transcription system is synthesized late during infection and is packaged into the viral core. This viral transcriptional machinery consists of a DNA-dependent RNA polymerase, a transcription factor (VETF), capping and methylating enzymes, and a poly(A) polymerase. The virus has the capability to synthesize mRNAs that are recognized and translated by the cell's protein synthesis machinery. Poxvirus expression is sequential and temporally regulated (early, intermediate, and late mRNAs).

Poxviruses produce a number of immune evasion proteins such as viroceptors, virokines, interferon resistance proteins, and serpins. Even though no one specific poxvirus produces all of these collectively, all seem to target the nonspecific immune response.

Research on poxviruses did not languish after its eradication. Recombinant vaccinia viruses have been used as research tools and in the development of new live vaccines against a variety of infectious agents. Most notable is the successful use of a recombinant vaccinia rabies vaccine to eliminate rabies in wild raccoon and fox populations in western Europe and in the United States.

Mass vaccination against smallpox stopped in 1972. Today, some military and emergency healthcare workers have received the vaccine. This has been prompted by the threat of the use of variola as a bioterrorist agent. The current live vaccinia virus vaccine has caused complications in vaccinated individuals with skin conditions, weakened immune systems, heart disease, or other chronic conditions. Research is now focusing on the development of a safer, tissue culture-based vaccine that contains attenuated strains of vaccinia virus. A second focus has been placed on the development of rapid diagnostics and antiviral strategies as an alternative or additional strategy for the prevention or postexposure treatment of smallpox and/or monkeypox.

The anthrax attacks in the United States in the fall of 2001 called attention to the need for coordinated emergency planning and the stockpiling of antibiotics or antivirals and vaccines in case of a widespread bioterrorist attack. All levels of communities (national, state, county, city, neighborhood) are affected by these concerns and need to prepare. Public education and continual surveillance are needed to reduce the vulnerability to biological weapons such as that of a smallpox outbreak.

Resources

Primary Literature and Reviews

Bardell, D. 1976. "Smallpox During the American War of Independence." *ASM News* 42(9):526–530.

Besser, J. M., Crouch, N. A., and Sullivan, M. 2003. "Laboratory Diagnosis to Differentiate Smallpox, Vaccinia, and Other Vesicular/Pustular Illnesses." *J Lab Clin Med* 142:246–251.

Bhattacharjee, Y. 2006. "U.S. Panel Wants Security Rules Applied to Genomes, Not Pathogens." *Science* 314:743.

Bisht, H., et al. 2004. "Severe Acute Respiratory Syndrome Coronavirus Spike Protein Expressed by Attenuated Vaccinia Virus Protectively Immunizes Mice." *PNAS USA* 101:6641–6646.

Blenden R. J. et al. 2003. "The Public and the Smallpox Threat." *N Engl J Med* 348:426–432.

Block, S. M. 2001. "The Growing Threat of Biological Weapons." *Am Sci* 89:28–37.

Breman, J. G., Arita, M. D., and Fenner, F. 2003. "Preventing the Return of Smallpox." *N Engl J Med* 348(5):463–466.

Bugert, J. J., and Darai, G. 2000. "Poxvirus Homologues of Cellular Genes." *Virus Genes* 21(1–2):111–133.

Bugert, J. J., Melquiot, N., and Kehm, R. 2001. "Molluscum Contagiosum Virus Expresses Late Genes in Primary Human Fibroblasts but Does Not Produce Infectious Progeny." *Virus Genes* 22(1):27–33.

Buller, R. M., and Palumbo, G. J. 1991. "Poxvirus Pathogenesis." *Microbiol Rev* 55(1):80–122.

Bungum, T., and Day, C. 2006. "Smallpox-Related Knowledge and Beliefs Among Recent College Graduates." *J Am Coll Health* 55(3):181–183.

CDC. 1997. "Human Monkeypox- Kasai Oriental, Zaire, 1996-1997." *MMWR* 46(14):304–307.

CDC. 2003. "Update: Multistate Outbreak of Monkeypox—Illinois, Indianna, Kansas, Ohio, and Wisconsin, 2003." *MMWR* 52(27):642–646.

CDC. 2003. "Smallpox Vaccination and Adverse Reactions. Guidance for Clinicians." *MMWR* 2003(52):1–29.

Condit, R. C., Moussatche, N., and Traktman, P. 2006. "In a Nutshell: Structure and Assembly of the Vaccinia Virion." *Adv Virus Res* 66:31–124.

Damaso, C. R. et al. 2000. "An Emergent Poxvirus from Humans and Cattle in Rio de Janeiro State: Cantagalo Virus May Derive from Brazilian Smallpox Vaccine." *Virology* 277:439–449.

Davies, H. 2007. "Ethical Reflections on Edward Jenner's Experimental Treatment." *J Med Ethics* 33(3):174–176.

De Clercq, E., and Neyts, J. 2004. "Therapeutic Potential of Nucleoside/Nucleotide Analogues against Poxvirus Infections." *Rev Med Virol* 14:289–300.

DeWitt, S., Jr. 1978. "Victoria over Variola." *ASM News* 44(12):639–644.

Diamond, J. 1990. "A Pox Upon our Genes: Smallpox Vanished Twelve Years Ago, but its Genetic Legacy May Still Linger with Us." *Nat His* 2:26–30.

Enserink, M. 2005. "Unnoticed Amendment Bans Synthesis of Smallpox Virus." *Science* 307:1540–1541.

Enserink, M. 2005. "WHA Gives Yellow Light for Variola Studies." *Science* 308:1235.

Esposito, J. J. et al. 2006. "Genome Sequence Diversity and Clues to the Evolution of Variola (smallpox) Virus." *Science* 313(5788):807–812.

Fenner, F. et al. 1988. "Smallpox and its Eradication." WHO, Geneva, Switzerland.

Fenner, F. 2000. "Adventures with Poxviruses of Vertebrates." *FEMS Microbiol Rev* 24:123–133.

Flavio, G. et al. 2002. "Characterization of a Vaccinia-Like Virus Isolated in a Brazilian Forest." *J Gen Virol* 83:223–228.

Galvani, A. P., and Slatkin, M. 2003. "Evaluating Plague and Smallpox as Historical Selective Pressures for the CCR5-Δ32 HIV-Resistance Allele." *PNAS USA* 100(5):15276–15279.

Griffiths, P. D. 2002. "Benefits of Bioterrorism." *Rev Med Virol* 12:131–132.

Guarner, J. et al. 2003. "Monkeypox Transmission and Pathogenesis in Praire Dogs." *EID* 10(3):426–431.

Harrison, S. C. 2004. "Discovery of Antivirals Against Smallpox." *PNAS* 101(31):11178–11192.

Houston, C. S. and Houston, S. 2000. "The First Smallpox Epidemic on the Canadian Plains in the Fur-Traders' Words." *Can J Infect Dis* 11(2):112–115.

Huhn, G. D. 2005. "Clinical Characteristics of Human Monkeypox and Risk Factors for Severe Disease." *CID* 41:1742–1751.

Jahrling, P. B. et al. 2004. "Exploring the Potential of Variola Virus Infection of Cynomolgus Macaques as a Model for Human Smallpox." *PNAS USA* 101(42):15196–15200.

Lane, H. C., La Montagne, J., Fauci, A. S. 2001. "Bioterrorism: A Clear and Present Danger." *Nat Med* 7(12):1271–1273.

Langland, J. O. et al. 2006. "Suppression of Proinflammatory Signal Transduction and Gene Expression by the Dual Nucleic Acid Binding Domains of the Vaccinia Virus E3L Proteins." *Virology* 80(20):10083–10095.

Levine, R. S. et al. 2007. "Ecological Niche and Geographic Distribution of Human Monkeypox in Africa." PLoS ONE 1:e176. doi:10.1371/journal.pone.0000176.

Likos, A. M. et al. 2005. "A Tale of Two Clades: Monkeypox Viruses." *J Gen Virol* 86:2661–2672.

Maurer, D. M., and Harrington, B. 2003. "Smallpox Vaccine: Contraindications, Administration, and Adverse Reactions." *Amer Fam Phys* 68(5):889–896.

McFadden, G. 2004. "Smallpox: An Ancient Disease Enters the Modern Era of Virogenomics." *PNAS USA* 101(42):14994–14995.

McFadden, G. 2005. "Poxvirus Tropism." *Nat Rev Microbiol* 3(3):201–213.

Mcfee, R. B. Leikin, J. B., and Kiernan, K. 2004. "Preparing for an Era of Weapons of Mass Destruction (WMD)—Are We There Yet? Why Should All Be Concerned. Part II." *Vet Hum Toxicol* 46(6):347–351.

Moss, B. 1996. "Genetically Engineered Poxviruses for Recombinant Gene Expression, Vaccination and Safety." *PNAS USA* 93:11341–11348.

Moss, B., and Shisler, J. L. 2001. "Immunology 101 at Poxvirus U: Immune Evasion Genes." *Sem Immunol* 13:59–66.

Muraskin, W. 2007. "Expunging Variola: The Control and Eradication of Smallpox in India 1947-1977." *J Public Health Policy* 28(1):153–155.

Murphy, F. A., and Osburn, B. I. 2005. "Adventitious Agents and Smallpox Vaccine in Strategic National Stockpile." *EID* 11(7):1086–1089.

Parrino, J., and Graham, B. S. 2006. "Smallpox Vaccines: Past, Present and Future." *J Allergy Clin Immunol* 18(6):1320–1326.

Parrish, S. and Moss, B. 2006. "Characterization of a Vaccinia Virus Mutant with a Deletion of the D10R Gene Encoding a Putative Negative Regulator of Gene Expression." *J Virol* 80(2):553–561.

Parrish, S., Resch, W., and Moss, B. 2007. "Vaccinia Virus D10 Protein Has mRNA Decapping Activity, Providing a Mechanism for Control of Host and Viral Gene Expression." *PNAS USA* 104(7):2139–2144.

Perkus, M. E., Tartaglia, J., and Paoletti, E. 1995. "Poxvirus-Based Vaccine Candidates for Cancer, AIDS and Other Infectious Diseases." *J Leukocyte Biol* 58:1–13.

Pommerville, J. C. 2003."Integrating the Agents of Bioterrorism into the General Biology Curriculum. I. A Primer on Bioterrorism." *American Biology Teacher* 64(9):649–656.

Pommerville, J. C. 2003. "Integrating the Agents of Bioterrorism into the General Biology Curriculum. II Mode of Action of Biological Agents." *American Biology Teacher* 65(1):13–23.

ProMED-mail. 2003. "Cowpox, Bovine, Human—Brazil (Sao Paulo)." *ProMED mail* 2003;11 Jan;20030111.0095.

ProMED-mail. 2007. "Smallpox Vaccine, Eczema Vaccinatum–USA." *ProMED mail* 2007;18 Mar;20070318.0947.

Rubins, K. H. et al. 2004. "The Host Response to Smallpox: Analysis of the Gene Expression Program in Peripheral Blood Cells in a Nonhuman Primate Model." *PNAS USA* 101(42):15190–15195.

Ruef, C. 2006. "Five Years After 9/11—Fearing Smallpox, … and the Vaccine Against It." *Infection* 34(5):239–240.

Segal, S., and Hill, A. V. S. 2003. "Genetic Susceptibility to Infectious Disease." *Trends Microbiol* 11(9):445–448.

Sivapalasingam, S. et al. 2007. "Immunological Memory after Exposure to Variola Virus, Monkeypox Virus, and Vaccinia Virus." *J Infect Dis* 195(8):1151–1159.

Stittelaar, K. J. et al. 2005. "Antiviral Treatment Is More Effective than Smallpox Vaccination upon Lethal Monkeypox Virus Infection." *Nature.* Published online Dec. 11, 2005.

Sulaiman, I. M. et al. 2007. "Gene Chip Resequencing of the Smallpox Virus Genome Can Identify Novel Strains: A Biodefense Application." *J Clin Microbiol* 45(2):358–363.

Van Rijn, K. 2006. "Lo! The Poor Indian!" Colonial Responses to the 1862-63 Smallpox Epidemic in British Columbia and Vancouver Island." *Can Bull Hist* 23(2):541–560.

Vogel, F., Chakravartti, M. R. 1966. "ABO Blood Types and Smallpox in a Rural Population of West Bengal and Bihar (India)." *Humangenetik* 3(2):166–180.

Wiser, I., Balicer, R. D., and Cohen, D. 2007. "An Update on Smallpox Vaccine Candidates and Their Role in Bioterrorism Related Vaccination Strategies." *Vaccine* 25(6):976–984.

Xiao, Y. et al. 2007. "A Protein-Based Smallpox Vaccine Protects Mice from Vaccinia and Ectromelia Virus Challenges When Given As a Prime and Single Boost." *Vaccine* 25(7):1214–1224.

Zilinskas, R. A., 1997. "Iraq's Biological Weapons: The Past as Future?" *JAMA* 278:418–424.

■ Popular Press

Alibek, K., and Handelman, S. 1999. *Biohazard: The Chilling True Story of the Largest Covert Biological Weapons Program in the World—Told from the Inside by the Man Who Ran It,* New York: Random House.

Allen, A. 2007. *Vaccine: The Controversial Story of Medicine's Greatest Lifesaver,* New York: W. W. Norton.

Carrel, J. L. 2004. *The Speckled Monster: A Historical Tale of Battling Smallpox*, New York: Plume.

Fenn, E. A. 2002. *Pox Americana*, New York: Hill and Wang.

Glynn, I., and Glynn, J. 2004. *The Life and Death of Smallpox*, Cambridge, England: Cambridge University Press.

Henderson, D. A. 1976. "The Eradication of Smallpox." *Scientific American* 235(4):25–34.

The New York Times, Saturday, April 16, 1947. "Curb of Smallpox a 'Miracle' Says City Health Commissioner."

Hopkins, D. R. 1983. *Princes and Peasants: Smallpox in History*, Chicago: University of Chicago Press.

Hopkins, D. R. 2002. *The Greatest Killer: Smallpox in History*, Chicago: University of Chicago Press.

Munn & Co. eds., "Vaccine Virus—Its Preparation and Its Use." *Scientific American* January 19, 1901, pp. 41–42.

Preston, R. 2002. *The Demon in the Freezer*, New York: Random House.

Rodriguez, A. M. 2006. *Edward Jenner: Conqueror of Smallpox (Great Minds of Science)*, Berkley Heights, NJ: Enslow Publishers.

Stutzenberger, F. 1999. "Smallpox: Biological Weapon on the Frontier." *Muzzleloader Magazine* 70–73.

Tucker, J. B. 2002. *Scourge: The Once and Future Threat of Smallpox*, New York: Grove Press.

Zelicoff, A. P., and Bellomo, M. 2005. *Microbe: Are We Ready for the Next Plague?* New York: Amacom Books.

■ Video Productions

Germ Genie: The Threat of Biological Warfare. 1994. Films for the Humanities.

Plague War: A Report on the Biological Weapons Threat and How the Soviet Union Secretly Amassed an Arsenal of Bio-weapons. 1998. Frontline PBS.

History's Mysteries: Smallpox Deadly Again? 2001. The History Channel.

History Undercover: Clouds of Death. 2001. The History Channel.

Smallpox FX, made-for-TV movie. 2005.

Rx for Survival: A Global Health Challenge: Deadly Diseases, Smallpox, and the End of Smallpox: The Last Case. PBS. 2005.

Anthrax, Smallpox Vaccinations and the Mark of the Beast. 2005. UFO TV.

Insidious Killers: Chemical and Biological Weapons. 2006. The History Channel.

■ eLearning

http://biology.jbpub.com/book/virology

The site features eLearning, an online review area that provides quizzes and other tools to help you study for your class. You can also follow useful links for in-depth information, or just find out the latest virology and microbiology news.

CASE STUDY QUESTIONS

These questions relate to the Case Study presented at the beginning of the chapter.

1. What does the vaccine against smallpox consist of? Is it a live or killed vaccine?

2. Could Jennifer be suffering from a poxvirus infection? Explain your answer. How are poxvirus infections contracted?

3. What tests might the dermatologist use to determine the cause of Jennifer's lip ulcer?

4. Would an intramuscular shot of vaccinia immune globulin be considered a viable treatment of her skin lesion?

5. Are Bob and Jennifer contagious? Explain your answer.

6. Should an investigation be conducted to determine whether Jennifer or Bob had transmitted disease to further contacts, such as family members?

■ References

CDC. 1981. "Vaccinia Outbreak—Newfoundland." *MMWR* 30(36):453–455.

CDC. 1982. "Epidemiologic Notes and Reports Disseminated Vaccinia Infection in a College Student—Tennessee."*MMWR* 31(50):682–683.

CDC. 1983. "Vaccinia Outbreak—Nevada." *MMWR* 32(31):403–404.

CDC. 1984. "Contact Spread of Vaccinia from a Recently Vaccinated Marine—Louisiana." *MMWR* 33(3):37–38.

CDC. 1985. "Epidemiologic Notes and Reports Contact Spread of Vaccinia from a National Guard Vaccinee—Wisconsin." *MMWR* 34(13):182–183.

ADDITIONAL CASE STUDY

On March 31, 2003, a librarian at the College of Sante Fe's Fogelson Library discovered a small yellow envelope labeled "Scabs from vaccination of W. B. Yarrington's children." It was tucked inside of an 1888 Civil War medicine book that had been written by Dr. W. D. Kelly, a physician who had done work on childhood vaccinations during the late 1800s. The librarian decided not to open the envelope and contacted the Collections Manager of the National Museum of Civil War Medicine via email.

She queried whether the museum would want the envelope and if the scabs could be dangerous. This started a number of communications involving the museum director, the FBI, staff at Walter Reed Army Medical Center, and the CDC. The 115-year-old scabs were from smallpox victims or were used to vaccinate/inoculate healthy individuals. During the late 1800s pus or bits of scabs from smallpox patients who suffered from a mild case of smallpox were implanted into the skin of healthy individuals in order to cause a mild illness, resulting in protective immunity. Within two days, the FBI picked up the envelope of scabs and delivered it to the CDC for a battery of tests.

1. What biosafety precautions should be taken when handling this material?

2. Assuming that the scabs do not yield live infectious virus, what kind of viral characterization can be done on this material? What methods or techniques might be

used to analyze these scabs? What would these methods detect and tell us about the virus?

3. If the desiccated scabs did contain live viruses that could be grown in the laboratory, could this virus provide insight into the evolution of smallpox vaccines in the United States? Explain your answer.

Poxviruses in general are very hardy in the environment. Samples of variola virus freeze-dried in the laboratory have been revived after storage for 20 years. Study of the long-term survival of variola virus under natural conditions is lacking. Scientists have questioned how long variola virus is stable in victims' graves, clothing, and possessions or tissues. When the mummy of the Egyptian Pharaoh Ramses V was examined by Donald Hopkins in 1979, dried pustules covered mainly the face, neck, shoulders, and arms. There was no rash on the chest. The rash appeared to be characteristic of smallpox. Hopkins raised the issue of whether or not scabs and shrouds of smallpox victims posed an unrecognized threat to archaeologists and anthropologists in the field. Pieces of skin from the pharaoh were analyzed by electron microscopy but did not reveal virus particles. Another well-preserved mummy, this time of a two-year-old Italian boy who died from a severe form of smallpox, was discovered in 1986. The tissue remains of this 16th century mummy were examined by immuno-electron microscopy, which positively identified variola virus in the tissues. This was the first time that virus had been identified from such ancient tissues. Both of these mummies were preserved in a dry, cool crypt.

To determine the potential for transmission resulting from contact with old scabs, researchers conducted experiments in 1954 to study the survival of variola virus under normal conditions. Scabs were taken from three smallpox patients. The scabs were placed in unsealed envelopes and stored in a laboratory cupboard that was kept between 15°C and 30°C, with humidity varying from 35% to 98%. Over the next 12 years, scientists tested the scabs for live virus particles. The study was terminated after 13 years because they ran out of scabs for testing. They concluded that the virus does indeed survive under cool and dry environmental conditions.

4. As cities continue to grow, cemeteries are relocated. Are excavators involved in the relocation of smallpox victims in danger of being infected? (Refer to Joseph Kennedy's 1994 paper "The Archeological Recovery of Smallpox Victims in Hawaii: Scientific Investigation or Public Health Threat?" *Perspect Biol Med* 37(4):499–509.)

5. Smallpox has been eradicated worldwide and thus no herd immunity exists against this disease. Should it be recommended that archaeologists and excavators be vaccinated as a precaution in special circumstances where victims interred may be disturbed? Why or why not?

6. What physical factors are most directly related to the viability of variola major?

7. Would you predict smallpox victims buried in permafrost to be potentially infectious? Explain your answer.

8. What precautions, if any, would you take in exhuming interred smallpox victims?

References

Ambrose, C. T. 2005. "Osler and the Infected Letter." *EID* 11(5):689–693.

Fornaciari, G., and Marchetti, A. 1986. "Italian Smallpox of the Sixteenth Century." *Lancet* 2:1469–1470.

Fornaciari, G., and Marchetti, A. 1986. "Intact Smallpox Virus Particles in an Italian Mummy of Sixteenth Century." *Lancet* 2(857):625.

Maccallum, F. O., and McDonald, J. R. 1957. "Survival of Variola Virus in Raw Cotton." *Bull World Health Organ* 16(2):247–254.

Meers, P. D. 1985. "Smallpox Still Entombed?" *Lancet* 1(8437):1103.

ProMED-mail. 1997. "Smallpox, Human Remains, Likelihood." 1997; 11 Mar;19970311.0546.

ProMED-mail. 2004. "Smallpox, 115-Year Old Scabs Found, USA." *ProMED mail* 2004; 2 Jan;20040102.0016.

Stone, R. 2002. "Is Live Smallpox Lurking in the Arctic?" *Science* 295:2002.

Zuckerman, A. J. 1984. "Palaeontology of Smallpox." *Lancet* 22(29):1454.

This patient is suffering from a herpes lesion on his lower lip. Herpes simplex I (HSV-1) is the cause of oral lesions that are sometimes referred to as **cold sores** or **fever blisters**. The technical term is **recurrent oral herpes labialis**.

Herpesviruses

❝ *O'er ladies' lips, who straight on kisses dream,*

Which oft the angry Mab with blisters plagues,

Because their breaths with sweetmeats tainted are. **❞**

William Shakespeare, "Romeo and Juliet," Act 1, Scene IV

The blisters that Shakespeare refers to are in fact cold sores produced by the herpes simplex virus I (HSV-1).

CASE STUDY

During the summer of 1989, 175 male high school wrestlers attended a Minnesota wrestling camp. These young athletes participated in wrestling practices and competitions. During the final week of camp, many of the boys complained of sore throats, headaches, fever, and malaise. An inflamed skin rash that had the appearance of small, fluid-containing vesicles was observed on the head, neck, and arms of the wrestlers. It was particularly common in wrestlers who engaged in the lock-up position that places the face, neck, and arms of the opposing wrestlers in close contact. Some of the boys continued to wrestle for at least two days after the rash had appeared.

15.1 History

The Greek physician Hippocrates (570 B.C.–510 B.C.) documented herpesvirus infections as an assortment of cutaneous lesions compatible with herpes simplex or varicella zoster lesions. Greek scholars coined the term *herpes*, which means "to creep or crawl," in reference to the spreading nature of herpetic lesions. It came from the word *herpeton*, an animal that goes on all fours. In the first century A.D. the emperor of Rome, Tiberius Claudius Nero, banned kissing in public ceremonies after a herpes simplex virus epidemic. Herpesvirus infections have existed for centuries and evidence suggests that these viruses infect virtually all species of vertebrates and invertebrates. They are among the most persistent and common viruses found in humans. Once an individual has become infected by a herpesvirus, the infection remains in their body for life.

Herpesvirus lesions mysteriously appear and disappear because all herpesviruses are capable of establishing and maintaining a **latent state** of infection at a specific site within an immunocompetent host. Herpesviruses may remain silent for many years only to be reactivated later. An individual can be infected with more than one herpesvirus during their lifetime. Table 15-1 lists the eight common herpesvirus infections in humans and indicates

TABLE 15-1	Herpesvirus Nomenclature and Characteristics		
Acronym Name	Common Name	Seropositive Adults (%)	Disease
HHV-1	Human herpesvirus 1 or herpes simplex virus 1	75–95+	Cold sores (oral herpes), herpes keratitis (eye infection), mat herpes or herpes gladiatorum, herpes rugbeiorum, eczema herpeticum in children
HHV-2	Human herpesvirus 2 or herpes simplex virus 2	4–95	Genital herpes
HHV-3 or VZV	Varicella zoster virus	90–95	Chickenpox, shingles
HHV-4 or EBV	Epstein-Barr virus	40–95+	Mononucleosis, Burkitt's lymphoma, naso-pharyngeal carcinoma
HHV-5 or CMV	Human cytomegalovirus	70–95	Mononucleosis, congenital infection
HHV-6	Human herpesvirus 6	>85	Roseola in young children
HHV-7	Human herpesvirus 7	>85	Roseola or fever illness in infants and young children
HHV-8	Human herpesvirus 8	10–25	Kaposi's sarcoma

(HHV stands for human herpesvirus.)

the prevalence of these infections based on adult seroprevalence. **Seroprevalence** is the number of persons in a population who test herpesvirus-positive based on serology (blood serum) specimens; this is often presented as a percent of the total specimens tested or as a rate per 100,000 persons tested. Despite certain similarities, infection with one member of the Herpesviridae family does not confer protection against infection or disease with the other members of the Herpesviridae family.

15.2   Clinical Signs and Symptoms of Human Herpesviruses

■ Herpes Simplex Virus Type 1 (HSV-1) and Herpes Simplex Virus Type 2 (HSV-2)

HSV-1 and HSV-2 have preference for infected specific anatomic sites—usually the mouth or pharynx and genitals, respectively. Both are capable of causing latent infections. HSV-1 reactivation occurs most frequently above the waist, compared to HSV-2 reactivation that typically occurs below the waist. The lesions of HSV-1 and -2 initially look similar. Both start with a clear vesicle containing infectious virus with a base of red lesion at the base of the vesicle. The lesions may become encrusted and ulcers may develop. HSV-2 is associated with sexual transmission, whereas infections in children are usually associated with HSV-1.

HSV-1 can cause a number of herpetic diseases, including cold sores of the mouth, lesions on the lip, herpes keratitis of the eye (which is the leading cause of corneal blindness in the United States), herpes gladiatorum (transmitted during frequent contact in wrestling), and herpes rugbeiorum (seen in other contact sports like rugby). HSV-1 can cause genital herpes in about 10% of cases. HSV-1 reactivation is associated with the following factors:

- Immune suppression by cytotoxic drugs
- Sexual contact
- Physical and emotional stress
- Temperature changes (hot or cold, such as burning the mouth with hot coffee)
- Too much ultraviolet light (e.g., sunburn)
- Menstruation
- Pregnancy
- Lactation
- Malnutrition
- Excessive fatigue

HSV-2 is responsible for 90% of genital herpes cases. Approximately 45 million persons in the United States suffer from genital herpes infections (**Figure 15-1**). New infections occur at a rate of about one million new cases per year. The majority of infections are unrecognized and therefore undiagnosed. Individuals with HSV-2 infections can shed virus even during asymptomatic periods. Safe-sex practices such as the use of condoms in combination with valacyclovir therapy reduce the spreading of HSV-2 infection during heterosexual intercourse by 75%. A pregnant woman who has an active case of genital herpesvirus infection should deliver the infant by caesarean section because HSV-2 can be transmitted to the infant during a vaginal delivery.

■ Figure 15-1
This male has a herpetic rash caused by HSV-2 on the shaft of his penis. The blisters break, leaving tender ulcers that may take two to four weeks to heal after the first time they appear.

■ Varicella Zoster Virus (VZV)

VZV causes two different clinical diseases: **chickenpox** and **shingles**. Chickenpox is a mild disease that usually afflicts children but can be severe in infants, adults, and persons with impaired immune systems.

There are several explanations for the origin of the name chickenpox. One of the most accepted suggestions is that the name is derived from a scribal error for *cich-pease*, which was interpreted as chick peas, suggesting that the chickenpox vesicles resembled *chick peas*. Another idea is that the name came about because the rash looked as though the bill of a chicken had pecked the child.

Chickenpox is the only herpesvirus that spreads person to person by coughing or sneezing (airborne), making it highly contagious. Like other herpesviruses, it is also spread by close contact. Symptoms develop 10 to 21 days after contact with an infected person. When a person is initially infected with VZV, the virus infects the skin or mucosa of the respiratory tract and progresses through the blood and lymphatic system to the cells of the **reticulo-endothelial system**. The first sign of disease is often the itchy exanthematous rash that is characteristic of chickenpox (**Figure 15-2**). Some people experience a fever and malaise. The blisters dry and form scabs in four to five days. On average, a person has 300 to 400 lesions on their body during an attack. Adults are more susceptible to complications such as bacterial infection of the skin, swelling of the brain, and pneumonia. The Centers for Disease Control and Prevention's (CDC's) Advisory Committee on Immunization Practices recommends that all children be routinely vaccinated at 12 to 18 months of age and that all susceptible children receive the vaccine before their 13th birthday (see Section 15.6).

After a primary VZV infection, the virus remains dormant/latent in the dorsal root ganglia (neurons of the nerve roots) of all persons who had chickenpox. The virus can be reactivated later in life to cause an illness referred to as **shingles** or **herpes zoster**. VZV is most commonly reactivated after the age of 60 and the risk of reactivation increases with age. It is also more common and severe in immunocompromised patients (e.g., AIDS patients). The onset of shingles is characterized by severe pain, numbness, and itching, followed by a vesicular rash that forms in a three- to five-day period. The rash follows a nerve on one side of the body. In an otherwise healthy individual, the disease lasts 10 to 15 days, but it may take a month for the skin to return to normal. In an immunocompromised patient, lesion formation can take up to two weeks and scabbing may not take place until three to four weeks into the course of the disease. Chronic shingles may also occur in AIDS patients, in which new lesions form in the absence of healing of existing lesions. This can be particularly debilitating.

An individual suffering from shingles is contagious to individuals who have not had chickenpox; thus people who have not had chickenpox can be infected with VZV and contract chickenpox if they have close contact with the person who has shingles. One cannot, however, get shingles from someone afflicted with shingles. Shingles is caused only by VZV that has been dormant since an individual acquired chickenpox.

■ Cytomegalovirus (CMV)

CMV infections are common in all human populations, ranging from 50% to 85% adults in the United States and nearly 100% in some parts of Africa. Healthy individuals who become infected with CMV *after* birth experience few or no symptoms of the disease and no long-term health consequences of the disease. Once a person is infected, the virus is usually dormant within the person's body for life. For the majority of people, CMV is not a serious disease. CMV is, however, the most common **opportunistic pathogen** in the immunocompromised patient. It can cause a variety of diseases, such as:

- **congenital CMV syndrome** in **neonates** (newborn infants less than four weeks old)
- infectious mononucleosis with prolonged fever and hepatitis in young adults
- pneumonia in bone marrow transplant recipients
- disease syndromes in lung, liver, kidney, and heart transplant recipients
- **retinitis** (an infection of the eyes) in AIDS patients

■ Figure 15-2
This child has the characteristic chickenpox rash. The lesions are blister-like and contain pus. They appear on the face, scalp, or trunk of the body.

CMV is transmitted from person to person via close, intimate contact with a person excreting the virus in their saliva, urine, or other bodily fluids. It can be transmitted sexually or via breast milk, transplanted organs, and (rarely) from blood transfusions. CMV is the most important cause of **congenital viral infection** (during childbirth) in the United States, where approximately 1% to 3% of women are infected during pregnancy. Developing unborn babies are at highest risk for developing complications of CMV infection. These complications include hearing loss, visual impairment, varying degrees of mental retardation, and motor problems. When a pregnant woman who has never had CMV infection becomes infected with it, there is the potential risk that after birth the infant may have CMV-related complications. In contrast, infants and children who contract CMV after birth experience few, if any, symptoms or complications.

■ Epstein-Barr Virus (EBV)

It is estimated that EBV causes 79% of infectious mononucleosis cases and that CMV causes the remaining 21%. EBV is a common infection throughout the world. Most frequently it strikes students in high school or college in the United States. It is often called the kissing disease. Most people become infected with EBV during some time in their lives. In developing countries like Africa, EBV infection is associated with Burkitt's lymphoma in children (see Chapter 10).

EBV is transmitted via intimate contact with saliva of an infected person (e.g., kissing, sharing beverages, or eating utensils). The incubation period ranges from four to six weeks. Symptoms of infectious mononucleosis are:

- sore throat
- fever
- swollen lymph glands
- malaise
- enlarged spleen (sometimes)
- enlarged liver (sometimes)
- heart problems (rare)
- central nervous system (CNS) problems (rare)

These symptoms usually resolve within one or two months. EBV remains latent in the throat and blood for the rest of the infected person's life.

■ HHV-6, HHV-7, and HHV-8 (Kaposi's Sarcoma Virus)

HHV-6 was isolated from T-cell cultures derived from the blood of AIDS patients, whereas HHV-7 was isolated from CD4+ T cells of a healthy person. Like HIV, both viruses can infect and kill CD4+ T cells. HHV-6 infects nearly all humans by the age of 2. There are two distinctly different HHV-6 viruses: HHV-6A and HHV-6B. HHV-6B causes **sixth disease** (also referred to as **exanthum subitum**, **roseola infantum**, or **baby measles**). Sixth disease is a mild disease of children. It begins with a sudden fever followed by a red rash. The name sixth disease comes from the fact that when childhood rash diseases were enumerated, it was the sixth listed. The diseases are:

1. Measles
2. Scarlet fever
3. Rubella (German measles)
4. Duke's disease
5. Fifth disease
6. Sixth disease

HHV-6 may also play a role in multiple sclerosis (MS). HHV-6 reactivation may have the potential to trigger autoimmunity and tissue damage associated with MS lesion development (**Virus File 15-1**). To date, HHV-6A and HHV-7 are *orphan* **viruses**. In other words, these viruses have not been etiologically linked to any human disease. HHV-8 DNA sequences have been detected in all Kaposi's sarcoma tumors (see Chapter 10).

VIRUS FILE 15-1	**Do Herpesviruses Play a Role in Multiple Sclerosis, Alzheimer's Disease, or Epilepsy? Molecular Mimicry: Viruses Lie, Cheat, and Steal**

A key feature of herpesviruses is their close adaptation to their host and their ubiquity in nature. After a primary infection with herpesviruses, the infection becomes enigmatically silent in neurons or other cell types for the duration of one's life. Scientists have proposed that particular herpesviruses (e.g., HHV-6) may play a role in debilitating neurological diseases such as multiple sclerosis (MS), Alzheimer's disease, and mesial temporal lobe epilepsy (MTLE).

MS commonly affects people between the ages of 20 and 40, whereas Alzheimer's disease is usually a disease of aged brains (the majority of cases occurring in patients greater than 65 years old). In MTLE, seizures can begin as early as childhood or even later in adulthood. Remission can occur during childhood, lasting a few years, but then seizures resume in adulthood.

It is likely that all of these diseases may be triggered by multiple factors, including genetics, viral infection, autoimmune reactions, and environmental conditions. There is one theory that ties together some of these suspected triggers: the theory of **molecular mimicry molecules** (**Figure VF 15-1**). This theory proposes that molecules similar enough in protein structure "mimic" the structure of a "self" protein and

Induction of Autoimmunity in the CNS by Viral Mimicry

Lymph node · Viral peptide · T cell · Activation · Proliferation · Self peptide · Brain

■ **Figure VF 15-1**

Autoimmune diseases can be caused by molecular mimicry—that is, the amino acid sequence similarity between viral (or other types of pathogens) proteins and self-proteins. Adapted from K. W. Wucherpfennig, *Mechanism for the activation of self-reactive autoimmune diseases,* http://research.dfci.harvard.edu/tcell/discoveries.html.

(continued)

may be responsible for activating the autoimmune system. HHV-6 has pirated at least three host genes within its viral genome that produce proteins capable of interfering with the normal host immune defense. One of these genes, the U83 gene of HHV-6, encodes a functional **chemokine** that resembles the human chemokine CCR2.

Chemokines are small proteins that possess chemoattractant properties for a number of cell types. These proteins belong to four different families (C, CC, CXC, and CX3C) that are distinguished by the position of the cysteine residues near the N-terminal end of the protein. Chemokines of the CC family are mainly involved in the migration and activation of monocytes, lymphocytes, and macrophages. Most chemokines have broader functions, such as influencing angiogenesis, collagen production, and proliferation of blood precursor cells. Chemokines exert their effects through specific receptors that are expressed on cell populations of blood origin; for example, CCR2 binds to the CCR2 receptor.

Many inflammatory diseases such as rheumatoid arthritis and asthma been associated with increased CC-chemokine expression and the progression of these diseases have been related to the functions of the CC chemokines. CC-chemokines also play a role in traumatic injuries to the central nervous system through the recruitment and activation of macrophages. CCR2 specifically plays a role in the regeneration and recovery of function after traumatic muscle injury.

The function of viral chemokines is more difficult to predict. These proteins are expressed in infected cells, influencing the ability of the infected cells to respond to chemotactic signals. It has been postulated that the HHV-6 U83 protein may attract CCR2 expressing cells (e.g., macrophages), conceivably for the virus to infect and establish latency in. By this mechanism, the virus evades detection and destruction by the host immune system and creates an environment in which the virus survives. At the same time, we are offered a viral view of the host immune system. This new immune evasion knowledge might have therapeutic potential.

References

Alcami, A. 2003. "Viral Mimicry of Cytokines, Chemokines and Their Receptors." *Nature Immunol Rev* 3:36–50.

Campadelli-Flume, G. et al. 1999. "Human Herpesvirus 6: An Emerging Pathogen." *EID* 5(2):353–367.

Donati, D. et al. 2003. "Detection of Human Herpes-6 in Mesial Temporal Lobe Epilepsy Surgical Brain Resections." *Neurology* 61(10):1405–1411.

Fotheringham, J., and Jacobson, S. 2005. "Human Herpesvirus 6 and Multiple Sclerosis:Potential Mechanisms for Virus-Induced Disease." *HERPES* 12(1):4–9.

Fujimuro, M., Hayward, D. S., and Yokosawa, H. 2007. "Molecular Piracy: Manipulation of the Ubiquitin System by Kaposi's Sarcoma-Associated Herpesvirus." *Rev Med Virol* 2007 Aug 10;17688306 (E-Pub).

Wozniak, M. A. et al. 2005. "Productive Herpes Simplex Virus in Brain of Elderly Normal Subjects and Alzeimer's Disease Patients." *J Med Virol* 75:300–306.

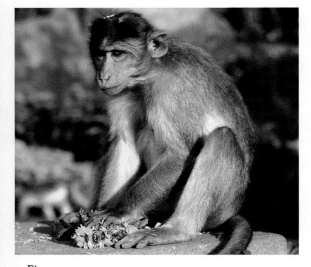

■ **Figure 15-3**

Photograph of a bonnet macaque (*Macaca radiata*). Herpes B infection is most commonly reported in the rhesus, cynomolgus, stumptail, pig-tailed, bonnet, Japanese, and Taiwan macaques.

■ Herpes B (Herpesvirus Simiae or Monkey B Virus)

Herpes B most commonly infects macaques (a type of monkey used extensively in biochemical research; see **Figure 15-3**). Most macaques carry herpes B virus with no signs of overt disease. Humans have contracted herpes B infections through direct contact with macaques, such as a bite or scratch or indirect contact with a contaminated **fomite** such as a cage scratch. The first documented case of human herpes B infection occurred in 1932 after a researcher was bitten by an apparently healthy rhesus macaque. The researcher died 15 days later of **encephalomyelitis** (inflammation of the brain and spinal cord).

The incubation period of herpes B in humans ranges from a few days to a month. Numbness and sometimes vesicles or ulcers occurs at the exposure site. The infection causes influenza-like symptoms such as fever, muscle aches, malaise, and headache. Other variable symptoms include nausea, vomiting, abdominal pain, and hiccups. Neurological symptoms begin when the infection spreads to the central nervous system. Spread of infection to the nervous system is ominous. Most patients who show neurological symptoms die, even with antiviral therapy and supportive

| VIRUS FILE 15-2 | **Can Herpesviruses Cause Chronic Atherosclerosis?** |

Fabricant and his colleagues were the first investigators to observe that pathogen-free chickens infected with Marek's disease herpesvirus (MDV) developed atherosclerotic plaques in their large coronary arteries, aortas, and major aortic branches of the heart. **Atherosclerosis** is a thickening of the artery walls that is mainly due to fatty diet high in cholesterol. This can result in clot formation or severe artery blockage, which may lead to heart attack.

When the MDV-infected chickens were fed a high-cholesterol diet, the rate and visibility of atherosclerosis increased. The plaques were not found in the arteries of uninfected chickens fed cholesterol-supplemented diets. In addition, when the pathogen-free chickens were vaccinated against MDV, the chickens did not develop atherosclerosis. Benditt's research team detected MDV genomic nucleic acid in the arteries of MDV-infected chickens. These experiments were conducted and reproduced in the late 1970s through the 1980s.

The plaques caused by MDV in chickens are very similar to those seen in atherosclerosis in humans. Chickens have been considered an important model organism for atherosclerosis research because herpesvirus infections are ubiquitous in chickens (**Figure VF 15-2**). This research suggested that human herpesviruses may play a role in similar plaques of human arteries. For this reason, researchers examined frozen sections of human arterial tissues from patients undergoing coronary artery bypass surgery for the presence of herpesvirus DNA genomes. Viral DNA sequences of human herpes simplex viruses were detected in some of the tissue samples by *in situ* **hybridization**.

When newer, more sensitive, nucleic acid detection methods became available in the 1990s researchers repeated these experiments. They examined more tissues from patients undergoing vascular surgery for the presence of cytomegalovirus (CMV) DNA. A study from a group of scientists from the Netherlands used polymerase chain reaction (PCR) to search for CMV nucleic acid in the artery tissues. They found 135 patients

(a)

■ **Figure VF 15-2**
(a) Scientists use chickens as a model to study atherosclerosis. **(b)** Photograph of a cross section of a human coronary artery autopsy specimen that contains atherosclerosis plaques in the lumen of the artery.

(continued)

(89%) with atherosclerosis had CMV DNA present in the arterial tissue. CMV DNA, but not infectious viruses, were found associated with the arterial plaques. Further studies conducted in the United States determined that high levels of antibodies against CMV were present in patients with atherosclerosis. More investigations are needed to determine the role of viruses in human atherosclerosis. Fundamentally, the potential exists that this disease could be controlled by vaccination or antiviral therapies. A CMV vaccine is in the pipeline. Even if CMV were responsible for only a small percentage of atherosclerosis cases, the benefits of its prevention would be high.

References

Benditt, E. P., Barrett, T., and McDougall, K. 1983. "Viruses in the Etiology of Atherosclerosis." *PNAS USA* 80:6386–6389.

Fabricant, C. G. et al. 1983. "Herpesvirus-Induced Atherosclerosis in Chickens." *Fed Proc* 42(8):2476–2479.

Fabricant, C. G., and Fabricant, J. 1999. "Atherosclerosis Induced by Infection with Marek's Disease Herpesvirus in Chickens." *Am Heart J* 138(5 Pt 2):S465–S468.

Melnick, J. L. et al. 1994. "Cytomegalovirus DNA in Arterial Walls of Patients with Atherosclerosis." *J Med Virol* 42:170–174.

Melnick, J. L. et al. 1998. "The Link between CMV and Atherosclerosis." *Infect Med* 15(7):479–486.

Minick, C. R. et al. 1979. "Atheroarteriosclerosis Induced by Infection with a Herpesvirus." *Am J Pathol* 96(3):673–706.

care. Symptoms vary depending upon what part of the spinal cord or brain is affected. As the virus spreads to the brain, ataxia (loss of coordination), agitations, seizures, confusion progressing to a coma, and progressive ascending paralysis occur. Deaths are often caused by respiratory failure associated with paralysis.

Only 40 cases of human herpes B infections have been reported. The majority of these cases occurred when large numbers of rhesus macaques were used in the production and test of poliovirus vaccines in the 1950s and '60s. Before available antiviral therapy, this virus was a serious *zoonotic threat* to people who came in contact with macaques. Full protective equipment is used when working with all macaques in a research setting. In 1989, the National Institute of Health's National Center for Research Resources began funding pathogen-free macaque colony development. This greatly reduced the numbers of cases of herpes B infections; however, herpes B virus is also prevalent in **free-ranging macaques** native to Southeast Asia. Free-ranging macaques are a tourist attraction and humans are at risk of contact with infected animals. Research has shown the risk of acquiring herpes B infections from macaques is low, but unfortunately the death rate is high.

15.3 Laboratory Diagnosis of Herpesvirus Infections

Herpesviruses have closely adapted to their host. When symptoms are observed, speed in using diagnostic procedures is important because the peak of shedding virus often occurs before the appearance of symptoms. The diagnostic method used varies for the different herpesvirus infections. The most definitive test is the presence of viable virus in a clinical specimen (e.g., oral and genital lesions, ocular samples, biopsies, and cerebrospinal fluid [CSF] see Table 15-2). HSV- and VZV-infected cells in tissue culture show the presence of multinucleated giant cells, along with intranuclear inclusion bodies (**Figure 15-4**).

| TABLE 15-2 | Most Common Diagnostic Tests of Herpesvirus Infections |

Virus	Test Specimen	Laboratory Tests
HSV-1	Skin lesions	Virus culture and DNA amplification
HSV-2	Genital lesions	Virus culture
VZV	Skin lesions	DNA amplification
CMV	Blood/serum	Serology to diagnose mononucleosis-like illness
	Urine	Virus culture, serology, and DNA amplification to diagnose neonatal disease
		DNA amplification to diagnose systemic infections in immune compromised
		DNA amplification to diagnose CNS infection
EBV	Blood/serum	Serology to diagnose mononucleosis-like illness
HHV-6	Blood/serum	Serology to diagnose Sixth disease
HHV-8	Kaposi's sarcoma lesions	DNA amplification
Herpes B	Wound culture	Virus culture from wound swab or biopsy or CNS fluid (BSL-4 facility required)
	CSF (cerebrospinal fluid)	DNA amplification, ELISA assay
	Blood/serum	

15.4 Herpesvirus Life Cycle

■ Virus Structure and Classes of Herpesviruses

Herpesviruses are large, enveloped, pleomorphic particles that are 150 to 300 nm in diameter when seen by electron microscopy. Herpesvirus virions comprise more than 30 virally encoded proteins and also contain cellular components. The viral envelope is obtained through a **double envelopment process**. The envelope is fragile and easily damaged by heat, desiccation (drying out), 70% alcohol, or disruption by soap or detergents. The envelope must be intact for herpesviruses to be infectious. The envelope is extremely sensitive to damage; thus the virus is usually transmitted through direct contact with mucosal surfaces or secretions of an infected person (such as the mouth or lips or on the genitals).

■ Figure 15-4
Photomicrograph showing intranuclear inclusions produced by VZV in tissue culture. Magnification 500×.

Herpesviruses dry out and become damaged when exposed to air so cannot be transmitted by toilet seats or other inanimate objects—a common misperception.

Virions contain linear double-stranded DNA (dsDNA) genomes that range from 125 to 230 kilobase pairs in length. An icosahedral capsid surrounds the DNA genome and an amorphous proteinaceous **tegument** surrounds the nucleocapsid. The tegument consists of at least eight different viral proteins (**Figure 15-5**). There are eight herpesviruses that naturally infect humans. Middle-aged adults usually have antibodies to most of these, with the exception of HHV-8 (which is common in HIV+ men).

The Herpesviridae family is divided into three subfamilies: Alphaherpesvirinae, Betaherpesvirinae, and Gammaherpesvirinae. The subfamilies are distinguished from each other based on such properties as the type of cells in which viral latency is established and the characteristics of their growth in cell cultures (Table 15-3). Viruses are named according

■ **Figure 15-5**

(a) Schematic of herpesvirus structure. There are more than a dozen different types of integral membrane proteins within the viral envelope. The tegument contains at least eight proteins that serve important functions after the virus has penetrated the host. **(b)** Electron micrographs of various viruses from the Herpesviridae family.

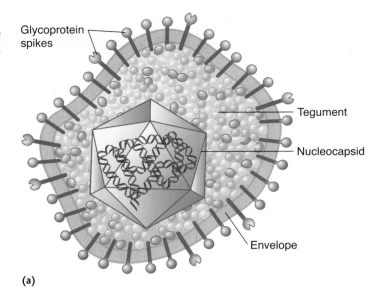

Glycoprotein spikes

Tegument

Nucleocapsid

Envelope

(a)

(b)

TABLE 15-3	Properties of the Subfamilies of the Herpesviridae Family		
Subfamily	**Examples**	**Growth in Cell Cultures**	**Latency**
Alphaherpesvirinae	HSV-1, HSV-2, VZV	Rapid growth and spread in cell cultures, short replication cycle, lytic infection in fibroblasts and epithelial cells	Established in sensory ganglia (neurons)
Betaherpesvirinae	CMV, HSV-6, HSV-7	Slow infection, long replication cycle, cells form enlarged (cytomegalic) cells	Established in lymphoid cells, kidneys, and other tissues
Gammaherpesvirinae	EBV, HHV-8	Limited to growth in lymphoblastoid cells	Established in B or T cells

TABLE 15-4	Herpesvirus Coreceptors		
Coreceptor	**Cellular Protein Family**	**Cellular Function**	**Cell Types Containing These Coreceptors**
HVEM	Tumor necrosis factor receptor	Tumor necrosis factor is a cytokine that binds to this receptor present on macrophages and T cells. In doing so, it exerts a toxic effect on cancer cells.	HVEM is mainly present on lymphoid cells
Nectin 1 and Nectin 2	Immunoglobulin superfamily (related to poliovirus receptor)	Function in specific immune system defenses.	Broadly expressed on skin, brain, and spinal ganglia

to their natural host species and numbered in the order in which they were first identified; for example, herpes virus simplex type 1 (HSV-1) was the first human herpesvirus identified. In the future, it is likely that the classification scheme of the Herpesviridae family members will be based on genetic organization, such as repetitive sequences, selected genes, and gene clusters.

■ Herpesvirus Entry and Uncoating

When herpesviruses are exposed to mucosal membranes or skin abrasions, the virus attaches to cells of the epidermis and dermis of the skin. Entry of herpesviruses into cells depends upon multiple cell-surface receptors and multiple proteins located on the surface of the virion. The viral envelope contains more than a dozen viral integral membrane glycoproteins, but only five have been shown to participate in HSV entry: gB, gC, gD, gH, and gL. Entry is achieved through a **binding receptor** and an **entry coreceptor**. The viral gB or gC envelope proteins of HSV attach or dock **to glycosaminoglycan chains** present on cell surface **proteoglycans**. **Heparin sulfate** is the most common kind of glycosaminoglycan and is the preferred binding receptor. This facilitates binding of the viral gD protein to an entry coreceptor that is one of two different types of cellular receptors that are structurally unrelated. The first type of coreceptor is the **herpes virus entry mediator (HVEM)**. The second contains two members: **nectin-1** and **nectin-2**. Descriptions of these entry coreceptors are listed in Table 15-4. Binding to any one of these three entry coreceptors triggers fusion of the viral envelope with the host cell's plasma membrane. This fusion activity requires the action of a gB, gD, gH-gL, and gD receptor. Glycoproteins gB, gH, and gL are structurally conserved among all herpesviruses and probably have similar essential roles in viral entry (**Figure 15-6**).

The nucleocapsids of herpesviruses are covered by a layer of tegument proteins (Figure 15-5). As the virus uncoats and the nucleocapsid is released in the cytoplasm of the cell, some of the tegument proteins remain in the cytoplasm (e.g., the **virion host shutoff protein, *vhs***) and other proteins such as the **VP16 protein** are transported to the nucleus. The

■ **Figure 15-6**
HSV gB and gC attaches to a cellular proteoglycan binding receptor. Subsequently the virion gD binds to HVEM entry coreceptors. This facilitates fusion of the viral and cellular membranes. Subsequently, the viral genome is uncoated and transported to the nucleus. Adapted from E. K. Wagner, *HSV Replication,* http://www.dbc.uci. edu/~faculty/wagner/hsv4f.html. Original illustration by Imagecyte.com.

viral *vhs* protein plays a role in the rapid degradation of cellular messenger RNAs (mRNAs) in the cytoplasm, causing the shut down or down regulation of host protein synthesis. Consequently, viral mRNAs accumulate in the cytoplasm and are preferentially translated. VP16 binds to DNA and is an activator of transcription.

The nucleocapsid docks with the nuclear membrane and delivers the genome to the nucleus, where the genome is transcribed and replicated. Herpesvirus genomes are composed of linear dsDNA. Under experimental conditions, the dsDNA is infectious. The length and complexity differ for each virus. The ends of the genomes consist of repetitive sequences. Some herpesvirus genomes contain internal large and small repetitive unique (U) sequences (**Figure 15-7**). These sequences encode over 50 distinct protein products such as DNA replication enzymes, glycoproteins important in viral host range, host defense proteins, and capsid proteins. The boxes regions of the genome represent repetitive sequences. Repetitive sequences located at the ends of the viral genome are involved in circularization and packaging of the DNA into the virion.

Box = repetitive sequences
U_S = short unique sequences
U_L = long repetitive sequences

■ **Figure 15-7**

Comparison of the genomes of herpesviruses. The genome contains unique (U) sequences and inverted repeat sequences (the boxes). Adapted from Murray, P. R., et al. *Medical Microbiology,* Third Edition. Mosby Elsevier Health Science, 1998.

■ Replication: Productive, Lytic Infection

Upon entry, the virus proceeds to a **productive, lytic infection** or establishes a **latent infection**. A productive infection occurs when the viral genome that has just entered the nucleus circularizes and is transcribed by the cellular DNA-dependent RNA polymerase and is regulated by viral- and cellular-encoded regulatory nuclear proteins. To initiate HSV DNA replication, the viral U_L9 protein binds to one of three possible origins of replication (ORI). U_L9 unwinds the DNA with the help of a viral single-stranded DNA binding protein designated ICP8. Next a helicase/primase complex that consists of U_L5, U_L8, and U_L52 binds to the single-stranded DNA and synthesizes RNA primers. A viral DNA polymerase, U_L30, with a bound U_L42 protein binds to the RNA primers and starts synthesis of DNA (**Figure 15-8**). At some point, the DNA replicates by a **rolling circle replication mechanism**, resulting in linear **concatemers** of DNA from a circular template (Figure 15-8).

A hallmark of herpesvirus genomes is that they encode most of the enzymes required to increase the pool of nucleotides in a cell (e.g., **thymidine kinase**, ribonucleotide reductase, uracil DNA glycosylase, and deoxyuridine triphosphatase) and to replicate the DNA genome. This feature allows the virus to replicate in slowly dividing or nondividing cells such as neurons. These enzymes are targets for antiviral drugs. Approximately 50% of HSV-1 and -2 genes are not required for replication in cell culture. About 50% of the HSV-1 and -2 genes may encode regulatory proteins involved in establishing latency and suppressing or evading the host immune system (e.g., virokines).

Like poxviruses, the transcription of herpesvirus occurs in a temporal and sequential manner that results in the transcription of three classes of viral genes expressed: immediate early (α), early (β), and late (γ) genes. The viral VP16 protein (the 16th viral protein to accumulate in cells after infection) activates the expression of the α genes. The α genes encode DNA binding proteins that play a role in viral transcription. The β genes encode DNA replication and additional viral transcription factors. The γ genes encode the late structural proteins that are produced after viral genome replication has begun (**Figure 15-9**).

After the γ proteins are synthesized, they are localized into the infected cell nucleus, where capsid assembly occurs. Viral genomic DNA concatemers are cleaved into monomers.

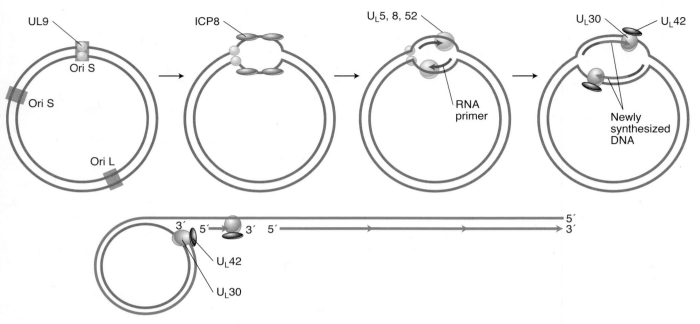

■ Figure 15-8

HSV replication initiates at one of three possible ORIs. Replication is bidirectional. RNA primers are created by a U$_L$5, U$_L$8, U$_L$52 complex. Newly synthesized DNA is generated by a viral DNA polymerase. U$_L$42 is bound to U$_L$30. U$_L$42 increases U$_L$30's ability to extend and detach from the growing strand of DNA from the template DNA. Adapted from N. H. Acheson. *Fundamentals of Molecular Virology*. John Wiley & Sons, Inc., 2006.

The monomers are packaged into the capsids and virion assembly proceeds. As the tegument proteins wrap around the nucleocapsid, viral glycoproteins present in the inner nuclear membrane promote the budding of the virion through the nuclear membrane. This is the first or primary budding event. New research suggests that viral membrane formation is a **double envelopment process**. The first envelopment of the virus by the nuclear membrane translocates the nucleocapsid to the cytoplasm of the cell. The nucleocapsid then buds through Golgi-derived vesicles. Mature virus particles are released after fusion with the Golgi-vesicle membrane and the cellular plasma membrane and **cell lysis** occurs. As a result, herpesviruses undergo a two-step envelope process: de-envelopment and re-envelopment (**Figure 15-10**). Death is a result of cellular injuries that occur as a result of viral replication and cellular responses to infection.

■ Viral Replication and Latency

Infected cells producing herpesvirus particles (a lytic infection) do not survive. Viruses benefit from their host cell remaining alive. HSV-1 and -2 have developed a survival strategy in immunocompetent hosts that centers on the establishment of lifelong **latency** in sensory neurons innervating the primary site of infection. After a productive primary infection, these herpesviruses enter sensory neuron axons and migrate along the axon to the cell body in a ganglion in the CNS (**Figure 15-11a**). In the sensory neuron cell body, the genome of the herpesvirus persists as an episome (not integrated) in the nucleus of the neuron. Episomes are circular DNAs that replicate independently of the cell's nucleus. During this latent stage, only a limited group of viral genes—the **latency associated transcripts (LATs)**—are expressed. The role of LATs is still under debate. Scientists have suggested that LATs may prevent expression of viral genes via an antisense mechanism and thus play a role in preventing apoptosis in neurons.

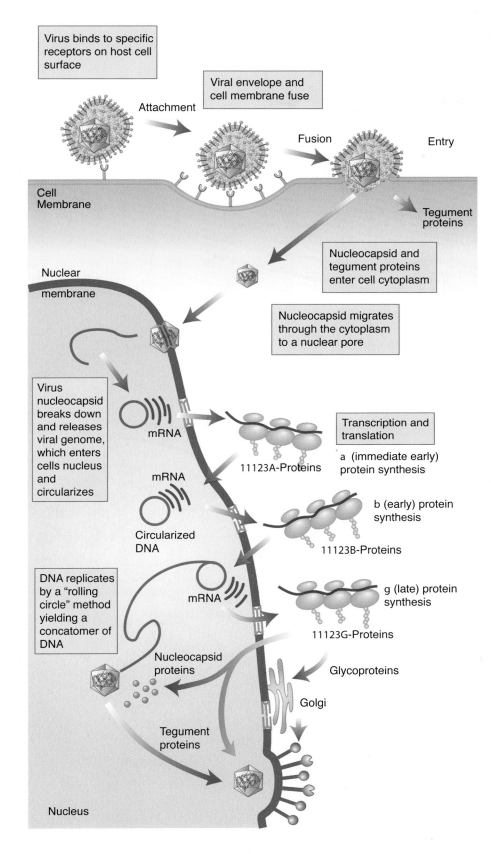

Virus binds to specific receptors on host cell surface

Attachment

Viral envelope and cell membrane fuse

Fusion

Entry

Cell Membrane

Tegument proteins

Nucleocapsid and tegument proteins enter cell cytoplasm

Nuclear membrane

Nucleocapsid migrates through the cytoplasm to a nuclear pore

Virus nucleocapsid breaks down and releases viral genome, which enters cells nucleus and circularizes

mRNA

Transcription and translation

11123A-Proteins

a (immediate early) protein synthesis

mRNA

Circularized DNA

b (early) protein synthesis

11123B-Proteins

DNA replicates by a "rolling circle" method yielding a concatomer of DNA

mRNA

g (late) protein synthesis

11123G-Proteins

Nucleocapsid proteins

Glycoproteins

Golgi

Tegument proteins

Nucleus

■ **Figure 15-9**
Upon entry, the genome circularizes and viral tegument proteins and cellular factors are involved in the transcription of the viral genome. Transcription and translation occurs in three phases: (α) immediate-early, (β) early, and (γ) late. Adapted from J. Cohen and W. G. Powderly. *Infectious Diseases,* Second Edition. Mosby, 2003.

■ **Figure 15-10**

Herpesvirus **morphogenesis** requires de-envelopment–re-envelopment processes. The virion is enveloped by the nuclear membrane that translocates the nucleocapsid to the cytoplasm where it matures. The majority of tegument proteins (e.g., aTIF, vhs) is added to the nucleocapsids and the final envelope is acquired by budding into the glycoprotein-containing Golgi-derived vesicles. Adapted from E. K. Wagner, *HSV Replication,* http://www.dbc.uci.edu/~faculty/wagner/hsv4f.html. Original illustration by Imagecyte.com.

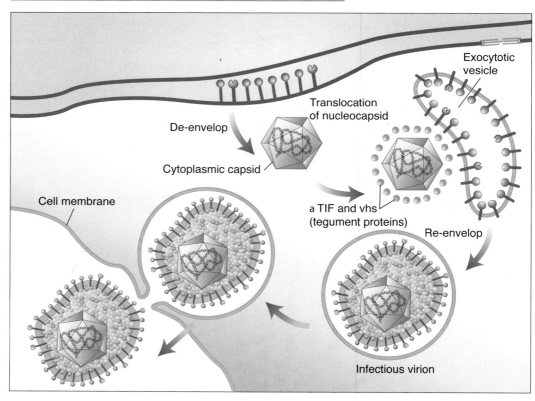

While latent, viral replication does not proceed further. No viral particles are detected. The virus hides from the immune system for months or even years until it is **reactivated** into a productive infection (Figure 15-11b). Once VZV, HSV-1, or HSV-2 is reactivated, it travels the nerve pathway to the surface of the skin (Figure 15-11c). The molecular details of latency and reactivation are different for each group of herpesvirus and it has proven difficult to dissect at the molecular level.

Lytic replication in epithelial cells

Latent HSV episome
Sensory neuron DNA
LATS

Retrograde transport moves capsid up axon

The sensory neuron is infected in the ganglia, which is the latency site

Sensory neuron

(a)

(a) Establishment of latency

Active HSV DNA
Sensory neuron DNA
HSV mRNAs

Anterograde transport moves capsid back down the axon

An appropriate stimulus reactivates the virus from its latent state in the neuron

Sensory neuron

(b)

Reinfection at site of original infection

(b) Reactivation from latency

Skin surface

Nerve fiber

Reactivated virus

Dormant virus

(c)

■ **Figure 15-11**

(a) HSV undergoes a productive infection in epithelial cells of the genital or oral mucosal surface. During latency, the virus travels up the axon to the neuronal cell body, where it remains dormant. Adapted from T. J. Taylor, et al., *Front. Biosci.* 7 (2002): d752–d764. **(b)** Once reactivated, the virus travels down the axon and establishes a productive, lytic infection. Adapted from T. J. Taylor, et al., *Front. Biosci.* 7 (2002): d752–d764. **(c)** Reactivation of VZV (chickenpox) in later years. A decrease in the body's immune system may contribute to an outbreak of shingles. In step (1) a cluster of small bumps begins to form and then (2) turns into blisters. The blisters will crust over (step 3) and eventually disappear (step 4). The typical course of shingles takes four to five weeks. Adapted from E. Zamula, *FDA Consumer Magazine* 35 (2001).

15.5 Antivirals/Treatment of Herpesvirus Infections

There are a number of antiviral drugs available for the treatment of active herpesvirus infections and prophylactic use (Table 15-5). Treatment is dependent upon the type, location of infection, and immune status of the patient. The most commonly prescribed anti-HSV drug is **acyclovir**. It is relatively nontoxic and has been used successfully for long-term prophylaxis. It can be administered topically to the skin, intravenously, orally, or topically to the eye. Most anti-HSV drugs are nucleotide analogs or inhibitors of the herpesvirus-encoded DNA polymerase.

Acyclovir, a guanosine analog (ACG), is converted 200 times more efficiently to ACG-monophosphate (ACG-P) by herpesvirus thymidine kinase (TK) than cellular thymidine kinases and other enzymes. After the viral TK converts ACG to ACG-P, a cellular guanosine monophosphate kinase phosphorylates (activates) ACG-P to ACG-triphosphate (ACG-PPP). Both the herpesvirus DNA polymerase and the cellular DNA polymerase α incorporate ACG-PPP into the growing strand of herpesvirus or cellular DNA instead of GTP. This results in a **chain termination** reaction, preventing the elongation of DNA. The herpesvirus DNA polymerase is ten times more inhibited than the cellular DNA polymerase by the incorporation of ACG-PPP. The mechanism of action for acyclovir is shown in **Figure 15-12**. **Drug resistance** occurs when mutations occur in the herpesvirus TK gene, reducing the conversion of ACG to its active form. Less frequently, the viral DNA polymerase is mutated, usually resulting in a less virulent form of herpesvirus.

Some research suggests that diet is an important factor in keeping herpesvirus outbreaks in remission. Foods high in l-arginine may cause herpesvirus outbreaks, whereas foods rich in L-lysine appears to reduce the occurrence, severity, and healing time for recurrent HSV infection. Supplements of L-lysine have been suggested as a useful therapeutic measure in controlling HSV outbreaks. Herpes simplex virus proteins synthesized in infected cells contain more arginine than lysine, methionine, phenylalanine, tyrosine, and isoleucine relative to leucine than proteins synthesized in uninfected cells. A favorable ratio of lysine to arginine suppresses viral replication and does not appear to cause harm to the host. Foods with a high lysine-to-arginine ratio are beef, chicken, fish, lamb, milk, cheese, beans, brewer's yeast, and most fruits and vegetables. Foods with a high arginine-to-lysine ratio are carob, chocolate, coconut, oats, whole wheat flour, white flour, gelatin, peanuts, soybeans, and wheat germ.

Varicella zoster immune globin and zoster immune plasma has been given to the immune-compromised or newborns at risk. It prevents the infection or minimizes the symptoms.

TABLE 15-5	FDA-Approved Antiherpesvirus Drugs	
Drug	**Chemical class**	**Target Herpesvirus/Disease**
Idoxuridine	Thymidine analog	Topical treatment of HSV-1 and HSV-2 keratoconjunctivitis
Vidarabine	Adenine arabinoside	Topical treatment of HSV-1 and HSV-2 keratoconjunctivitis
Trifluridine	Thymidine analog	Keratoconjunctivitis and keratitis caused by HSV-1 and HSV-2
Acyclovir	Guanosine analog	HSV-1, HSV-2 (oral form), VZV (intravenous or oral form)
Famciclovir	Guanosine analog	HSV-1, HSV-2, VZV (intravenous or oral)
Penciclovir	Guanosine analog	HSV-1 and HSV-2 (topical)
Valacyclovir	Guanosine analog	HSV-1, HSV-1, VZV
Foscarnet	Pyrophosphate analog	CMV, HSV-1, HSV-2
Cidofovir	Cytosine analog	HSV-1, HSV-2, CMV

Guanosine

Acyclovir

Deoxy-guanosine triphosphate (dGTP)

Acyclovir-TP

(a)

■ **Figure 15-12**

(a) Chemical structure of acyclovir and guanosine and their triphosphate forms. **(b)** Mechanism of action of the herpesvirus antiviral acyclovir (ACV). ACV has a high binding affinity for herpesvirus (but not the host) DNA polymerase. This leads to its enzyme inactivation. The incorporation of ACV-PPP into replicating DNA blocks chain elongation. Adapted from J. Cohen and W. G. Powderly. *Infectious Diseases,* Second Edition. Mosby, 2003.

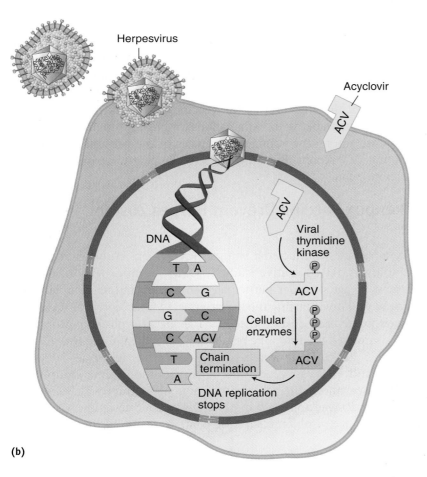

Herpesvirus

Acyclovir

DNA

Viral thymidine kinase

ACV

Cellular enzymes

ACV

Chain termination

DNA replication stops

(b)

15.6   Chickenpox and the Development of Other Herpesvirus Vaccines

VZV was isolated from vesicular fluid of both chickenpox and herpes zoster lesions via cell culture by Thomas Weller and colleagues in 1952. This led to the development of a chickenpox vaccine by Takahashi and colleagues at Osaka University, Japan, in 1974. An Oka VZV strain was isolated from an otherwise healthy three-year-old Japanese boy who had an acute case of chickenpox. The virus was attenuated by passaging it eleven times in human embryonic lung fibroblasts at 34°C, followed by twelve passages in guinea pig fibroblasts at 37°C and seven passages in human lung fibroblasts at 37°C. The entire genome of the Oka strain and its parent virus (P-Oka) has been sequenced. The Oka strain has 42 mutations, resulting in 20 amino acid changes or base changes in the origin of DNA replication region. The exact mechanism of attenuation is still unclear.

Vaccination studies using the live, attenuated Oka strain were carried out in Japan in the 1970s. Early participants were immune-compromised children who had undergone steroid therapy for leukemia. The chickenpox vaccine (Varivax Oka/Merck) was licensed by the FDA for use in the United States in March 1995. No other live attenuated vaccines had been approved for licensure in the United States from 1969 to 1995. Current CDC recommendations are one dose of the vaccine between 12 and 18 months of age and a catch-up vaccination at any age after that if the child has never had chickenpox. Healthy individuals that have not been vaccinated until 13 years of age or older should get two doses of the vaccine four to eight weeks apart.

Clinical trials continue after licensure. Since 1995, millions of children have been vaccinated and there has been a 75% decline in the number of hospitalizations related to VZV infection.

One of the unanticipated results of chickenpox vaccination among immunized children is the growing numbers of varicella outbreaks attributed to **breakthrough varicella,** a wildtype virus that causes a mild form of chickenpox (an average maximum number 50 lesions or less) in children who have been immunized at least 42 days prior to their illness (**Figure 15-13**). According to the manufacturer of the vaccine, the breakthrough rate observed is 0.3% to 3.8% of vaccinees per year. Explanations for breakthrough cases include a lessened immune response among the youngest vaccinees or the possibility of genetic variation among circulating VZV strains. Breakthrough cases appear to be more common in the United States than in Japan.

■ Will the Chickenpox Vaccine Prevent Herpes Zoster (Shingles)?

The Department of Veteran Affairs conducted a Shingles Prevention Study between 1998 and 2001 with a 3-year follow-up (Cooperative Study No. 403). A total of 38,546 immune-competent adults 60 years of age or older participated in a randomized, double-blind, placebo-controlled clinical trial investigating the live attenuated Oka/Merck VZV vaccine. The participants received a one-time dose of the VZV vaccine or a placebo. More than 95% of the participants completed the trial. The results were reported in the *New England Journal of Medicine* on June 2, 2005. There were 11.2 cases of herpes zoster per 1000 persons in the placebo group and 5.42 cases per 1000 persons in the vaccine group. Thus the incidence of shingles cases among the adult participants was reduced 51.3%. A new vaccine called Zostavax (Merck) was approved by the FDA in 2006 to reduce the risk of shingles in people 60 years of age or older. Each dose contains about 14 times more live attenuated VZV as Varivax.

(a)   **(b)**

■ **Figure 15-13**
(a) An eighteen-month-old child with mild breakthrough chickenpox. **(b)** Shingles rash caused by VZV.

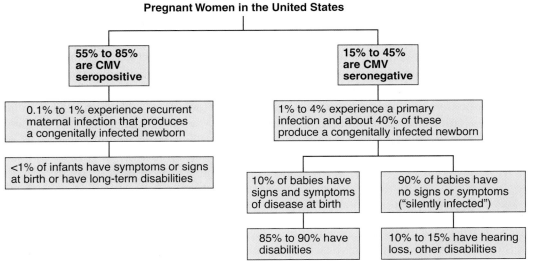

Pregnant Women in the United States

| 55% to 85% are CMV seropositive | | 15% to 45% are CMV seronegative |

0.1% to 1% experience recurrent maternal infection that produces a congenitally infected newborn

1% to 4% experience a primary infection and about 40% of these produce a congenitally infected newborn

<1% of infants have symptoms or signs at birth or have long-term disabilities

10% of babies have signs and symptoms of disease at birth

90% of babies have no signs or symptoms ("silently infected")

85% to 90% have disabilities

10% to 15% have hearing loss, other disabilities

■ **Figure 15-14**
Neonatal CMV statistics in the United States. Adapted from National Congenital CMV Disease Registry, *What Everyone Should Know About CMV,* http://www.bcm. edu/pedi/infect/cmv/cmvbroch.htm.

■ **Other Herpesvirus Vaccines in the Pipeline: Dream or Reality?**

CMV infection is a major disease of immune-compromised patients and is the leading cause of inner ear (cochlea) hearing loss and nervous system damage in children in the United States (**Figure 15-14**). Developing a vaccine against CMV has been a top priority for the prevention of congenital CMV infection but public awareness is still lacking. It is known that both cell-mediated immunity and antibodies are required to relieve the symptoms of CMV

■ Figure 15-15
Color-enhanced cerebral MRI showing a brain glioma.

infection. Studies have shown that maternal antibodies reduce the risk of congenital infection in future generations by 69%. A recombinant canarypox vaccine containing CMV genes has been generated and is being investigated in clinical trials. It has been proposed that this combined vaccine might generate the cellular and antibody mediated immunity needed for protection against CMV infections.

15.7 The Use of Genetically Engineered HSV to Treat Brain Tumors

Malignant **gliomas** affect 15 per 100,000 adults in the United States. Gliomas are tumors that originate from the brain or spinal cord. About 30% of CNS brain tumors are malignant gliomas. Brain gliomas are very aggressive and there is a lack of effective therapy. Current approaches include surgery, radiation, and chemotherapy. These methods extend the lives of patients an average of 14 weeks to one year. About 5.5% of individuals survive five years but often these methods fail to kill all of the tumor cells. Patients with brain gliomas are ideal candidates for novel molecular-based therapies for several reasons:

- metastases are rare
- Magnetic resonance imaging (MRI) studies are available to monitor the outcome (**Figure 15-15**)
- viruses provide a delivery technique that can target the tumor

Previous strategies involved the use of engineered recombinant adenoviruses and retroviruses to transfer the HSV thymidine kinase gene into tumor cells followed by treatment of the patient with acyclovir. These strategies have had limited success. Genetically engineered HSV is an attractive vehicle because it can replicate in neurons and glia and the HSV DNA can be easily manipulated. Wildtype HSV is neurovirulent. Hence the HSV vector must be engineered to be able to replicate in a dividing tumor but not in surrounding healthy cells of the CNS. Recombinant HSV's have been engineered that contain mutations in the viral thymidine kinase, DNA polymerase, ribonucleotide reductase, and the $\gamma_1 34.5$ gene. The $\gamma_1 34.5$ gene has been mapped to the neurovirulence phenotype of the virus. These mutations are necessary to create a replication defective, safe strain of HSV gene therapy vector for treatment of brain gliomas and other neurological applications. To date, replication defective HSV vectors have been optimized and plans are underway to carry out phase I clinical trials.

■ Summary

Herpesviruses are ubiquitous in nature and have existed for centuries. Once an individual has become infected with a herpesvirus the infection remains in their body for life. Herpesviruses have evolved an efficient survival strategy in which the virus can remain dormant (latent) for periods of time, hiding within the cells of the body by evading the host's immune system. While dormant the virus is protected from therapeutic agents. Latent infections occur in the cell body of neurons, where viral DNA remains dormant within the cytoplasm or nucleus until activated to replicate and migrate along the neural axis to an epithelial cell surface. A variety of stimuli may activate a herpesvirus infection:

- Immune suppression by cytotoxic drugs
- Sexual contact
- Physical and emotional stress

- Temperature changes (hot or cold, such as burning the mouth with hot coffee)
- Too much ultraviolet light (e.g., sunburn)
- Menstruation
- Pregnancy
- Lactation
- Malnutrition
- Excessive fatigue

Herpesviruses are large, linear dsDNA enveloped viruses that replicate in the nucleus of the host cell. The herpesvirus obtains its envelope from the inner membrane of the nucleus as it buds out of the host cell's nucleus. The envelope of herpesviruses is very fragile and must be intact in order for the virus to be infectious.

There are eight members of the human Herpesviridae family that naturally infect humans:

- Herpes simplex virus type 1 (HSV-1)
- Herpes simplex virus type 2 (HSV-2)
- Varicella zoster virus (VZV)
- Epstein-Barr virus
- Cytomegalovirus
- Human herpes virus 6
- Human herpes virus 7
- Human herpes virus 8 (Kaposi's sarcoma virus)

The Herpesviridae family is divided into three subfamilies (Alphaherpesvirinae, Betaherpesvirinae, and Gammaherpesvirinae), which are distinguished from each other based on the type of cells in which they establish latency.

HSV enters primarily through the break in the skin and intact mucous membranes. HSV-1 (oral herpes) occurs primarily above the waist, whereas HSV-2 (genital herpes) occurs primarily below the waist. HSV is lytic to human epithelial cells and latent in neural tissue. VZV causes a primary infection termed varicella (chickenpox) and is reactivated later in life as herpes zoster (shingles). Epstein-Barr virus has a tropism for B-lymphocytes. It causes infectious mononucleosis, Burkitt's lymphoma, and nasopharyngeal carcinoma. Cytomegalovirus infections usually occur early in childhood. A primary infection is usually mild or asymptomatic in people with normal immune systems. CMV causes a persistent, latent infection of T-lymphocytes. CMV infection is a major disease of immune-compromised patients and is the leading cause of inner ear (cochlea) hearing loss and nervous system damage in children in the United States. HHV-6 causes roseola, and HHV-8 is implicated in the development of Kaposi's sarcoma tumors. Other herpesviruses of interest are herpes gladiatorum, which is found among young wrestlers who pick up mat burns and other repeated abrasions. Herpes B (herpesvirus simiae) is a potential hazard to laboratory workers or zookeepers working with macaque monkeys.

The genomes of the human herpesviruses have been sequenced. Herpesvirus genomes vary remarkably in size and structure among the different herpesviruses. They have the second largest genome after the poxviruses. Hallmarks of herpesvirus replication include:

- Replication in the nucleus
- Sequential transcription and translation of immediate early (α), early (β), and late (γ) genes to produce α, β, and γ proteins
- The viral envelope is obtained by a double envelopment process
- A productive infection is cytocidal
- They are able to establish latent infections with the genome, thus persisting as an episome in the neurons or lymphocytes while only a subset of transcripts are expressed (LATs)
- Reactivation triggers replication and recurrent or continuous shedding of infectious virus

There are a number of antiviral drugs available to treat herpesvirus infections. The most commonly prescribed drug is acyclovir. Its mechanism of action is the inhibition of the herpesvirus-encoded DNA polymerase. Another focus has been placed on prevention of herpesvirus infections, which is the approach of the approved medication **Varivax**, a live, attenuated Oka/Merck chickenpox vaccine, and the development of a cytomegalovirus vaccine to prevent congenital neonatal infections. Other medical research includes the use of replication-defective HSV viruses as a vehicle to destroy brain gliomas.

Resources

Primary Literature and Reviews

Adler, S. P. 2005. "Congenital Cytomegalovirus Screening." *Ped Infect Dis J* 24(12):1105–1106.

Arvin, A. 2005. "Aging, Immunity, and Varicella-Zoster Virus." *New Engl J Med* 352(22):2266–2267.

Atanasiu, D. et al. 2006. "The Stable 2-kb LAT Intron of Herpes Simplex Stimulates the Expression of Heat Shock Proteins and Protects Cells from Stress." *Virology* 350(1):26–33.

Baines, J. D. et al. 2007. "Electron Tomography of Nascent Herpes Simplex Virus Virions." *Virology* 81(6):2726–2735.

Baker, M. L. et al. 2005. "Common Ancestry of Herpesvirus and Tailed DNA Bacteriophages." *Virology* 79(23):14967–14970.

Bernstein, D. I. et al. 2002. "Effect of Previous or Simultaneous Immunization with Canarypox Expressing Cytomegalovirus (CMV) Glycoprotein B (gB) on Response to Subunit gB Vaccine Plus MF59 in Healthy CMV-Seronegative Adults." *J Infect Dis* 85(5):686–690.

Burton, E. A., Fink, D. J., and Glorioso, J. C. 2005. "Replication-Defective Genomic HSV Gene Therapy Vectors: Design, Production and CNS Applications." *Curr Opin Mol Ther* 7(4):326–336.

Cullen, R. R. 2001. "Journey to the Center of the Cell." *Cell* 105:697–700.

Davenport, D. S. et al. 1994. "Diagnosis and Management of Human B Virus (Herpes-Virus Simiae) Infections in Michigan." *Clin Infect Dis* 19(1):33–41.

Deepak, S., and Spear, P. G. 2001. "Herpesvirus and Heparan Sulfate: An Intimate Relationship in Aid of Viral Entry." *J Clin Invest* 108:503–510.

Dove, A. 2006. "A Long Shot on Cytomegalovirus." *The Scientist,* December Issue 40–45.

Efstathiou, S., and Preston, C. M. 2005. "Towards an Understanding of the Molecular Basis of Herpes Simplex Virus Latency." *Virus Res* 111:108–119.

Fowler, K. B., Stagno, S., and Pass, R. F. 2003. "Maternal Immunity and Prevention of Congenital Cytomegalovirus Infection." *JAMA* 289(8):1008–1011.

Gogev, S. et al. 2003. "Biosafety of Herpesvirus Vectors." *Curr Gene Ther* 3:597–611.

Goins, W. F. et al. 2004. "Delivery Using Herpes Simplex Virus: An Overview." *Methods Mol Biol* 246:257–299.

Gomi, Y. et al. 2002. "Comparison of the Complete DNA Sequences of the Oka Varicella Vaccine and its Parental Virus." *Virology* 76(22)11447–11459.

Griffith, R. S. 1987. "Success of L-Lysine Therapy in Frequently Recurrent Herpes Simplex Infection." *Dermatologica* 175:183–190.

Grose, C. 2005. "Varicella Vaccination of Children in the United States: Assessment After the First Decade 1995-2005." *J Clin Virol* 33(2):89–95.

Grunewald, K. et al. 2003. "Three-Dimensional Structure of Herpes Simplex Virus from Cryo-Electron Tomography." *Science* 302:1396–1398.

Huff, J. L., and Barry, P. A. 2003. "B-Virus (*Cercopithecine herpesviridae* 1) Infection in Humans and Macaques: Potential for Zoonotic Disease." *EID* 9(2):246–250.

Jones, F. E., Smibert, C. A., and Smiley, J. R. 1995. "Mutational Analysis of the Herpes Simplex Virus Virion Host Shutoff Protein: Evidence that vhs Functions in the Absence of Other Viral Proteins." *Virology* 69(8):4863–4871.

Kent, J. R. et al. 2003. "Herpes Simplex Virus Latency-Associated Transcript Gene Function." *J Neurovirol* 9(2):285–290.

Khanna, R., and Diamond, D. J. 2006. "Human Cytomegalovirus Vaccine: Time to Look for Alternative Options." *Trends Mol Med* 12:27–33.

Mettenleiter, T. C. 2004. "Budding Events in Herpesvirus Morphogenesis." *Virus Res* 106(2):167–180.

Mettenleiter, T. C. 2006. "Intriguing Interplay between Viral Proteins during Herpesvirus Assembly or: The Herpesvirus Assembly Puzzle." *Vet Microbiol* 113(3–4):163–169.

Mettenleiter, T. C., Klupp, B. G., and Granzow, H. 2006. "Herpesvirus Assembly: A Tale of Two Mechanisms." *Curr Opin Microbiol* 9(4):423–429.

Oxman, M. N. et al. 2005. "A Vaccine to Prevent Herpes Zoster and Postherpetic Neuralgia in Older Adults." *N Engl J Med* 352(22):2271–2284.

Pfeffer, S. et al. 2005. "Identification of MicroRNAs of the Herpesvirus Family." *Nat Meth* 2(4):269–276.

Rainov, N. G., and Ren, H. 2003. "Gene Therapy for Human Malignant Brain Tumors." *Cancer J* 9(3):180–188.

Ramachandran, S., and Kinchington, P. R. 2007. "Potential Prophylactic and Therapeutic Vaccines for HSV infections." *Curr Pharm Des* 13(19):1965–1973.

Rouse, B. T., and Kaistha, S. D. 2006. "A Tale of Two a-herpesviruses: Lessons for Vaccinologists." *Clin Infect Dis* 42:810–817.

Samols, M., and Renne, R. 2006. "Virus-Encoded MicroRNAs: A New Chapter in Virus-Host Interactions." *Future Virol* 1(2):233–242.

Sanchez, V., and Spector, D. H. 2002. "CMV Makes a Timely Exit." *Science* 297:778–779.

Schleiss, M. 2005. "Progress in Cytomegalovirus Vaccine Development." *Herpes* 12(3):66–75.

Spear, P. G. 2004. "Herpes Simplex Virus: Receptors and Ligands for Cell Entry." *Cell Microbiol* 6(5):401–410.

Tang, Q., and Maul, G. G. 2006. "Mouse Cytomegalovirus Crosses the Species Barrier with Help from a Few Human Cytomegalovirus Proteins." *Virology* 80:7510–7521.

Thompson, R. L., and Sawtell, N. M. 2000. "HSV Latency-Associated Transcript and Neuronal Apoptosis." *Science* 289(5485):1651.

Vazquez, M. et al. 2004. "Effectiveness Over Time of Varicella Vaccine." *JAMA* 291(7):851–855.

Wagner, E. K., and Bloom, D. C. 1997. "Experimental Investigation of Herpes Simplex Virus Latency." *Clin Microbiol Rev* 10(3):419–443.

Weller, T. H., and Stoddard, M. B. 1952. "Intranuclear Inclusion Bodies of Human Tissue Inoculated with Varicella Vesicle Fluid." *J Immunol* 68(3):311–319.

Wills, E., Scholtes, L., and Baines, J. D. 2006. "Herpes Simplex Virus 1 DNA Packaging Proteins Encoded by UL6, UL15, UL28, and UL33 Are Located on the External Surface of the Viral Capsid." *Virology* 80(21):10894–10899.

■ Popular Press

Ewald, P. W. 2002. *Plague Time: The New Germ Theory of Disease*. New York: Anchor Books.

Regush, N. 2000. *The Virus Within, A Coming Epidemic: How Medical Detectives Are Tracking a Terrifying Virus that Hides in Almost All of Us*. New York: Dutton Books.

■ Video Productions

Hepatitis, Cytomegalovirus, and Epstein-Barr Virus. 1999. Films for the Humanities & Sciences.

Shingles: Treating Chronic Pain. 1999. Films for the Humanities & Sciences.

Genital Herpes. 2001. Films for the Humanities & Sciences.

■ eLearning

http://biology.jbpub.com/book/virology

The site features eLearning, an online review area that provides quizzes and other tools to help you study for your class. You can also follow useful links for in-depth information, or just find out the latest virology and microbiology news.

CASE STUDY QUESTIONS

These questions relate to the Case Study presented at the beginning of the chapter.

1. This outbreak was caused by a herpesvirus. Which one?
2. What tests were likely used to diagnose this infection?
3. How was the virus transmitted?
4. Speculate how the afflicted wrestlers were treated.
5. How can this viral disease be prevented?

■ Reference

Centers for Disease Control and Prevention. 1990. "Epidemiologic Notes and Reports Herpes Gladiatorum in a High School Wrestling Camp–Minnesota." *MMWR* 39(5):69–71.

ADDITIONAL CASE STUDY

Asian and African elephants were used in transportation, labor, and ritual for thousands of years. They are the world's largest mammals, weighing 11,000 to 13,200 pounds. These elephants are giant herbivores that can tear down huge tree limbs with their muscular trunks. Asian elephants are endangered, and both Asian and African elephants are difficult to breed in captivity. Today, some Asian and African elephants live in national zoos throughout the world. Zoo spectators enjoy observing the elephants using their versatile trunks to squirt water over their backs, manipulate tiny objects, or blow dirt onto their backs during dust baths. Between 1995 and 2003, approximately 32 Asian and African zoo elephants were infected with a highly virulent new herpesvirus in the United States and Canada.

1. The herpesvirus that infected these zoo elephants caused unique pathological effects. List them. (*Hint:* Refer to the references below.)

2. What parts of the elephant were found to contain herpesvirus-like particles? What cell type do these viruses infect?

3. How does the virus spread among the zoo elephants?

4. Are wild elephants susceptible to the infection?

5. Can elephant herpesvirus infect people?

■ References

Richman, L. K. et al. 1999. "Novel Endotheliotropic Herpesviruses Fatal for Asian and African Elephants." *Science* 283:1171–1176.

Richman, L. K. et al. 2000. "Clinical and Pathological Findings of a Newly Recognized Disease of Elephants Caused by Endotheliotropic herpesviruses." *J Wildl Dis* 36(1):1–12.

looped red ribbon is the universal symbol of AIDS awareness.

CHAPTER
16

> **"** *The AIDS epidemic is one of the greatest challenges to our society today. It is a fight that we cannot afford to lose.* **"**

—*Anthony S. Fauci, Director of the National Institutes of Allergies and Infectious Diseases*

Human Immunodeficiency Virus (HIV)

CASE STUDY

Former Los Angeles Lakers basketball star Earvin "Magic" Johnson announced at a press conference on November 7, 1991, that he had HIV and retired from professional basketball. He acquired his infection through heterosexual transmission. At the time of his announcement his wife was pregnant, and both she and the fetus had tested negative. In his book *My Life*, Johnson admitted to having casual, unprotected sex with many women. After winning five NBA championship rings, an Olympic gold medal, and an NCAA championship, one of our national sports icons was faced with a life-threatening HIV infection.

Johnson's announcement increased the public's awareness and concern about HIV and the behavioral changes that would lead to reduced risk. The nonprofit Magic Johnson Foundation, founded in December of 1991, was charged with educating the public about HIV and with providing supportive HIV programs to address the social needs of inner-city children and young adults throughout the United States.

Johnson attempted brief professional comebacks from 1992–1993 and 1995–1996. During the 1992–1993 season, several players voiced their concerns. Basketball is a highly physical sport, thus players may collide, crash, and inadvertently draw blood from one another while fighting for rebounds. Karl Malone of the Utah Jazz expressed his fears and opposition toward Johnson's first comeback. He pointed to the scars and scabs on his arms and said, "They can't tell me you're not at risk. And you can't tell me there's one guy in the NBA who hasn't thought about it." Other players, however, seemed very receptive to Johnson's return to basketball. Phoenix Suns player Charles Barkley added, "It's not like we are going to have unprotected sex with Magic on the floor." Later, Malone supported Magic's decision to come back for a second time in 1995.

As soon as Magic Johnson was diagnosed with HIV, he began antiretroviral therapy under the supervision of the Laker's team physician, Dr. Michael Mellman, and HIV expert Dr. David Ho. Within a few months, his viral load was reduced. In 1999, Johnson's wife, Cookie, said in an interview that her husband was healed. Johnson said there were no traces of virus in his bloodstream. Sixteen years after his announcement, Johnson is still alive and living normally. He remains a tireless crusader against acquired immunodeficiency syndrome (AIDS).

The December 2006 updated statistics report from the United Nations Program on HIV/AIDS (UNAIDS) included the following statements:

- By the end of 2006, 39.5 million people were living with HIV, including 17.7 million women and 2.3 million children under the age of 15.
- 4.3 million people became infected with HIV in 2006, including 530,000 children.
- In 2006 alone, a total of 2.9 million people died of AIDS-related causes.
- Worldwide, only 1 in 10 persons infected with HIV has been tested and knows his/her HIV status.
- In many regions of the world, new HIV infections are heavily concentrated among young people (15–24 years of age). *Young adults accounted for 40% of new HIV infections in 2006.*
- Two thirds (63%) of all people with HIV live in sub-Saharan Africa. Of these, one third (32%) live in Southern Africa.
- Thirty-four percent of all deaths due to AIDS in 2006 occurred in Southern Africa.
- In some African countries, three quarters of those infected are women—many of whom have not had more than one sexual partner.
- In 2005 and 2006, the number of people living with HIV increased in every region of the world. The most striking increases have occurred in Eastern Asia, Central Asia, and in Eastern Europe, where the number of people living with HIV in 2006 was over one fifth (21%) higher than in 2004.
- An estimated 5 to 6 million people in low- and middle-income countries will die in the next two years if they do not receive antiretroviral treatment (ART). At the end of 2005, only one in seven Asians and one in ten Africans who needed ART were receiving it.
- The U.S. government's commitment of $15 billion dollars over five years (2004–2008) has great promise to make a substantial contribution if fully funded.
- Top scientists from around the world are committed to vaccine development, which remains one of the greatest hopes the world has for preventing transmission of the virus. Clinical trials are now ongoing in several countries, including the United States.

16.1   The History of HIV

■ Gay Cancer, GRID, and AIDS (1980–1983)

During the early 1980s, physicians in New York and California made the first observations of a new infectious disease of viral origin. The following laboratory-confirmed infections were observed in young, homosexual men:

- The sudden appearance of a rare skin cancer called Kaposi's sarcoma, which became referred to as the **gay cancer**. Previously this cancer was only seen in elderly men of Mediterranean descent (**Figure 16-1a**).
- Atypical pneumonia caused by *Pneumocystis carinii*
- Cytomegalovirus infections
- Oral candidal mucosal infections (Figure 16-1b)

All of these observed **opportunistic infections** suggested that these individuals suffered from a type of cell-mediated immune suppression. In 1981, the Centers for Disease Control (CDC) named the syndrome **gay-related immune deficiency**, or **GRID**. As this gay men's health crisis was unraveled, physicians noted that many patients were also being treated for hepatitis B, herpes, and parasitic infections such as amebiasis and giardiasis. Other common trends among GRID patients included the use of drugs to heighten sex-

(a)   (b)

■ **Figure 16-1**
(a) These brown nodules represent Kaposi's sarcoma lesions commonly found in AIDS patients. **(b)** This AIDS patient has a chronic opportunistic oral candiasis infection.

ual experiences and unprotected, anonymous sex at bathhouses. The number of known deaths in the United States in 1981 was 234, and then climbed to 853 in 1982. At the same time, physicians reported that heterosexual individuals who received blood products or blood transfusions (e.g., hemophiliacs) began developing similar opportunistic infections. These latter cases were traced to the blood donors: homosexual men dying of GRID. In 1982, the CDC renamed GRID to **acquired immune deficiency syndrome**, or **AIDS**. In 1983, the CDC warned blood banks of a possible problem with the national blood supply. The number of known deaths in the United States during 1983 was 2304. In 1985, film star Rock Hudson died from the complications of AIDS. He was the first major American celebrity whose AIDS diagnosis became public knowledge. U.S. President Ronald Reagan mentioned the term "AIDS" in public for the first time that same year. Table 16-1 lists some of the famous people who are known to have or have had the virus known as HIV, including those who have died.

■ The Discovery of Human Immunodeficiency Virus (HIV)

The discovery of the cause of AIDS was published in the journal *Science* by two different research teams: Luc Montagnier's team at the Pasteur Institute in Paris (May 20, 1983) and Robert C. Gallo's group at the National Cancer Institute at the National Institute of Health (NIH) in Bethesda, Maryland (May 4, 1984). Both described a retrovirus isolated from cultured T lymphocytes derived from a lymph node biopsy of an AIDS patient with **lymphadenopathy** (swollen lymph nodes). Lymphadenopathy was considered a precursor syndrome to AIDS. The virus Gallo identified had originated from tissue samples sent to him by Montagnier, whose group suggested that the name of the virus be called Lymphadenopathy-Associated Virus (LAV). Gallo recommended the virus be named Human T-cell Lymphotrophic Virus Type III (HTLV III). In 1986, the name was changed from HTLV-III/LAV to the **human immunodeficiency virus** or **HIV**.

There has been controversy regarding which laboratory discovered HIV first. In 1990, the NIH's Office of Scientific Integrity began to investigate Gallo's HIV research program. The HIV discovery dispute was finally resolved in Washington, DC, in July 1994. At this time, it was acknowledged that the virus isolated at Gallo's laboratory was one of the first viruses isolated in 1983 at the Pasteur Institute. This dispute is the focus of John Crewdson's book *Science Fictions: A Scientific Mystery, a Massive Cover-up, and the Dark Legacy of Robert Gallo.*

TABLE 16-1	Famous HIV+ Individuals and Famous Individuals Who Have Died from AIDS-Related Causes	
Individual	**Occupation**	**HIV Status**
Arthur Ashe	Tennis player and social activist	Infected in 1983 via blood transfusion during heart surgery; passed away in 1993
John Curry	Figure skating champion	Died of AIDS-related illness in 1994
Earvin "Magic" Johnson	Former Los Angeles Lakers point guard	Announced his HIV+ status on November 7, 1991
Greg Louganis	Olympic diver	HIV+ in 1988; announced it in 1995
Tommy Morrison	Former world boxing champion	Tested HIV+ in 1996, automatically retiring him from boxing
Michael Bennett	Choreographer of the Broadway show *A Chorus Line*	Died in 1987
Rock Hudson	Movie star	First major American celebrity whose AIDS diagnosis became public knowledge; died in 1985
Liberace	Pianist	Died in 1987 of cytomegalovirus pneumonia due to AIDS.
Freddie Mercury	Lead singer of the band Queen	Died from AIDS-related causes in 1991
Anthony Perkins	Actor; famous for playing Norman Bates in the movie *Psycho*	Died of AIDS-related causes in 1992
Isaac Asimov	Science fiction author	Infected by a blood transfusion during heart surgery. Died in 1992.
Randy Shilts	American journalist and author of *And the Band Played On*	Died in 1994.
Ryan White	Teenager with hemophilia, AIDS activist.	Contracted AIDS via blood products; died in 1990 at the age of 18
Elizabeth Glazer	Wife of *Starsky and Hutch* actor Paul Michael Glazer	Infected via a blood transfusion. Her son and daughter were also infected. She started the Pediatric AIDS Foundation. She died in 1994; her daughter died in 1988. Her son, now a young adult, remains healthy.

■ HIV-1 versus HIV-2

The first HIV isolated by Montagnier's and Gallo's research teams were designated HIV-1. Shortly after the first HIV discovery, Montagnier's group isolated another strain, which they designated HIV-2. HIV-2 is rare in the United States but is endemic in Western Africa. HIV-2 is significantly less infectious and progresses more slowly to AIDS than HIV-1.

■ The Origin of HIV-1 and the AIDS Pandemic

Where did HIV originate? Has it been evolving for hundreds of years? The myths or controversial theories that have surfaced regarding the origin of HIV follow. The most widely accepted is the **hunter theory**, or extensions of it.

1. The house cat theory
2. The hunter theory (or crossing the species barrier theory)
3. The contaminated vaccine theory
4. The colonization theory (or Heart of Darkness theory)
5. The conspiracy theory

The House Cat Theory

Feline immunodeficiency virus (FIV) is a retrovirus that was discovered in 1987. It causes an infection of domestic cats that results in an immunodeficiency syndrome resembling HIV-1 infection in humans referred to as feline AIDS, or it may cause feline leukemia. FIV has not been shown to cause disease in humans; however, HIV-1 and FIV are related retroviruses. A 2005 study published in the journal *AIDS* showed that cats vaccinated with the p24 viral HIV-1 protein appeared to be at least as well-protected against FIV as those immunized with the FIV p24 protein currently used by veterinarians. This surprise finding suggests that the p24 protein of these two retroviruses is an important immunogen that is evolutionarily conserved. It may lead the way to the development of a protective vaccine against HIV-1 based on the cross-reactive regions of the p24 HIV-1 and FIV proteins.

The Hunter Theory

This is the most commonly accepted theory in the scientific community. This theory is based on the premise that the AIDS pandemic is a **viral zoonosis**. A virus related to HIV-1 has been isolated from the common chimpanzee (*Pan troglodytes troglodytes*, which are native to Cameroon, Gabon, and the Democratic Republic of Congo (**Figure 16-2**). The virus is referred to as simian immunodeficiency virus (SIV_{cpz}). The genetic sequence of SIV_{cpz} and the early strains of HIV-1 are nearly identical.

■ **Figure 16-2**
The oldest ancestor of HIV-1 to date is from the Democratic Republic of Congo. Kinshasa has the greatest genetic diversity of HIV-1 isolates, suggesting that the virus has been there longer than anywhere else. The initial HIV-2 epidemic is believed to have occurred during the war when Guinea Bissau gained its independence from Portugal (1963–1974). Shaded areas represent the geographical distribution of chimpanzees and sooty mangabeys.

The conclusion thus far is that the chimpanzee is the natural reservoir for HIV-1. The belief is that AIDS arose when chimpanzee-to-human transmission of SIV_{cpz} occurred. The naturally infected chimps were killed and eaten and their blood entered cuts or wounds on the hunter, and subsequently the SIV_{cpz} strain adapted in the human host to become HIV-1. A 2004 study has shown that retrovirus transmission from primates to hunters continues to occur today (see Chapter 10). These infections are likely acquired through the butchering and consumption of contaminated monkey or ape meat (**bushmeat**). There have been calls to ban bushmeat hunting to prevent the transmission of simian viruses to humans.

A serological study on plasma samples used for malarial studies in Africa between 1959 and 1982 was published in 1998 in the journal *Nature*. It reported that the oldest sample that contained HIV-1 antibodies dated to 1959. This seropositive sample also contained viral HIV-1 genetic material that was sequenced. It is currently the oldest known case of HIV-1 infection. The sample is from an adult Bantu-speaking male who lived in Kinshasa, Democratic Republic of Congo (Figure 16-2). It has been hypothesized that this person became infected in rural Cameroon and then traveled by river to Kinshasa.

The Contaminated Polio Vaccine Theory

This is an extension of the hunter theory proposed by virologist Preston A. Marx. His theory posits that the initial spread of HIV-1 occurred in Africa during the large-scale vaccination campaigns that began in the early 1950s. Disposable plastic syringes were introduced in the 1950s and were used to administer vaccines and medicines. This was a big change in medical practice; up until then, using huge quantities of traditional, metal syringes was too expensive in Africa. Multiple patients were inoculated with the same syringe without sterilization between patients. This allowed the rapid transfer of virus particles from one individual to another, creating the potential for the SIV_{cpz} virus to mutate and replicate in each new individual it entered.

Others believe in a slightly modified extension of this theory, suggesting that the oral polio vaccines were contaminated with SIV_{cpz} virus. Edward Hooper, author of *The River*, suggested that HIV could be traced to the oral polio vaccine referred to as Chat. The Chat vaccine was manufactured at the Wistar Institute in Philadelphia and tested in Africa. It was administered to a million people in the Democratic Republic of Congo and surrounding areas during the late 1950s. Hooper believed the vaccine was produced in kidney cells taken from chimpanzees that had been infected with SIV_{cpz}. Vaccinees received the contaminated vaccine and subsequently became infected with HIV-1. The Chat polio vaccines have since been exonerated. Original stocks prepared by the Wister Institute were tested for the presence of viral contamination. No HIV-1 or SIV_{cpz} or chimpanzee nucleic acid sequences were detected in the Chat vaccine. Furthermore, the vaccines made by the Wister Institute were created using the kidney cells of rhesus monkeys.

The Colonization Theory or Heart of Darkness Theory

In 2000 Jim Moore, a specialist in primate behavior, proposed another variant of the hunter theory. He pointed out that between 1880 and 1915 the colonial rule of French Equatorial Africa (also referred to as the Heart of Africa or the Heart of Darkness) was very harsh. Colonial authorities forced people to construct railroads or other projects. Many Africans were forced into labor camps and sent into the forest in search of valuable rubber for weeks at a time, year after year, and women were held hostage in unsanitary conditions and nearly starved. The physical demands were extreme. There was little time or energy left devoted to agriculture, leading to the increased reliance on bushmeat for food. These factors would have been sufficient to create poor health, including weakened immune systems. A stray and perhaps infected chimpanzee was likely a welcome source of food for laborers.

Moore believed that well-intentioned but undersupplied doctors routinely vaccinated the workers against smallpox with unsterile needles to keep them alive and working. A half a dozen syringes were used to draw blood to identify carriers and intravenously treat approximately 90,000 workers for sleeping sickness from 1917–1919. About 100,000 arm-to-arm passage smallpox inoculations were carried out prior to 1914 (refer to Chapter 14), and inoculation material with pox vesicles likely contained a high concentration of lymphocytes (the primary host cell of HIV-1). Many of the camps actively employed prostitutes, creating additional means of HIV/SIV_{cpz} transmission.

The transmission of pathogens was inevitable in the camps and disease was rampant. Anyone sick would not have stood out as being different because the laborers were present in an already disease-ridden population. It has been speculated that half of the labor workers died in the camps, and many of them would have died before the first symptoms of AIDS. No medical records for these camps exist.

The Conspiracy Theory

A significant number of individuals believe that HIV is a genetically engineered or man-made virus. During the 1980s, the Soviet press suggested that HIV was manufactured as part of an American biological warfare research program. Third World newspapers and publications run by Soviet front organizations picked up this disinformation. The Soviet reports were stopped in 1987.

Other individuals believe that HIV was genetically engineered to wipe out large numbers of black and homosexual people. Even though these theories cannot be proved without a doubt, the evidence they are based on is tenuous at best, as it ignores the clear link between SIV_{cpz} and HIV. It also ignores the fact that HIV antibodies have been detected in serum samples in people as far back as 1959—a time when genetic engineering technology was not available to "create" HIV. Genetic engineering didn't become a reality until 1977, when a man-made gene was used to manufacture human somatostatin in the bacterium *Escherichia coli*.

■ Where Did HIV-2 Originate?

Like HIV-1, HIV-2 entered the human population as the result of a zoonotic, or cross-species, transmission. It transferred from sooty mangabeys to humans during the first half of the 20th century in Western Africa. The sooty mangabey is an Old World monkey that is native to Guinea Bissau, Gabon, and Cameroon. Sooty mangabeys are naturally infected with SIV_{SM} that is genetically similar to HIV-2. They are commonly hunted for food and kept as pets in this region of the world. It is believed that the initial HIV-2 epidemic coincided with the independence war (1963–1974) in Guinea Bissau, a former Portuguese colony. The war caused social disruption and a mass vaccination effort that may have brought forth a regional HIV-2 epidemic by increasing the number of people who were administered (HIV-2-contaminated) vaccine injections through unsterile reusable needles at the Canchungo clinic in Guinea Bissau. HIV-tainted blood transfusions also occurred. Social disruption resulted in the increased movement of people and sexual activity such as rape and prostitution. The first reported cases of HIV-2 in Europe occurred among Portuguese soldiers returned from the independence war. Today, up to 10% of the general population in Guinea Bissau is HIV-2 sero-positive.

■ The AIDS Pandemic: Patient Zero versus the Earliest AIDS Cases

The AIDS epidemic appeared suddenly and nearly simultaneously in several metropolitan areas of the United States. The greatest number of cases occurred among homosexual men living in Los Angeles, San Francisco, and New York City. In 1981, the CDC began an investigation of this epidemic, led by Dr. William Darrow and colleagues, to determine the risk factors involved in AIDS. The term **patient zero** refers to the first infected patient in an epidemiological investigation that is likely responsible for the spread of a particular infectious disease.

Randy Shilts, author of *And the Band Played On*, chronicled Darrow's investigation. It was Shilts who proposed that a homosexual Canadian flight attendant was likely patient zero. The flight attendant admitted to anonymous, unprotected sex with as many as 2,500 partners, even after he developed Kaposi's sarcoma. As research continued, though, earlier cases of AIDS were reported (Table 16-2), disproving the patient zero theory.

TABLE 16-2	Earliest Cases of AIDS		
Year of Death	**Case**	**Location**	**Evidence**
1959	Preserved blood sample from a male	Kinshasa, Democratic Republic of Congo, Africa	HIV and antibodies in blood sample of this individual who died in 1959
1959	25-year-old male, former naval seaman	Manchester, England	Unexplained immunodeficiency, pneumocystis, cytomegalovirus infection. PCR detected HIV proviral DNA. Findings were controversial.
1969	15-year-old male prostitute	St. Louis, Missouri	Frozen tissue and serum samples contained HIV antibodies. Patient died of aggressive Kaposi's sarcoma.
1977	47-year-old female Danish surgeon who had worked in a primitive hospital in Zaire from 1972–1975	Europe/Denmark	Died of AIDS-like illness, no obvious risk factors
1984	31-year-old homosexual French-Canadian flight attendant	Quebec City, Canada	Kaposi's sarcoma; died of kidney failure caused by AIDS-related infections

16.2   HIV Transmission

HIV is present in blood, semen, vaginal fluids, breast milk, and in very low levels in saliva and tears. The most common ways that HIV is transmitted are by means of

- anal or vaginal intercourse
- sharing of HIV-contaminated needles (e.g., by injection drug users)
- blood transfusions using infected blood or blood-clotting factors (this is rare in the United States)
- accidental needlestick injuries (healthcare workers are at risk while working with HIV-positive patients)
- congenital AIDS (before or during birth or through breast-feeding)
- sharing of HIV-contaminated tattoo needles, razors, acupuncture needles, or ear-piercing implements.

■ Can Kissing and Oral Sex Transmit HIV?

Social kissing is not a high-risk behavior. The risk increases, though, with open-mouthed or "French" kissing because considerable amounts of saliva are exchanged. The risk increases if the uninfected person has canker sores or other lesions in his/her mouth. Oral sex also poses a similar risk to uninfected individuals, as HIV-infected T lymphocytes from semen may enter abrasions or lesions in the mouth.

■ Ways That HIV Is *Not* Transmitted: The Fragility of HIV in the Environment

HIV is an enveloped virus. Soap easily disrupts the virus, which also is highly susceptible to disruption through drying in the environment. It is important to understand that finding a small amount of HIV in a body fluid does not necessarily mean that HIV can be *transmitted* by that body fluid; for example, HIV has not been recovered from the sweat of HIV-infected persons. Contact with saliva, tears, or sweat has never been shown to result

| VIRUS FILE 16-1 | **Transmission of HIV by Dental Procedure** |

In 1990, a young woman who had no risk factors for HIV infection tested seropositive. The patient's family and friends were interviewed extensively and it was determined that she was not an intravenous (IV) drug user. She did not have any tattoo procedures, body piercings, acupuncture treatments, or artificial insemination procedures. She did not have sex with an HIV-infected person or receive a blood transfusion or other blood factors. She had never been pregnant and did not have a history of acquiring sexually transmitted diseases. Both of her prior boyfriends were seronegative for HIV infection. She had never worked in a health care or any other setting where she could have been exposed to HIV-infected blood or other body fluids. She had no risk for HIV transmission.

In 1988, though, she had two teeth extracted by dentist Dr. David Acer. About three months prior to this, Dr. Acer was diagnosed with HIV and a T-cell count that was less than 200. He had developed AIDS-related symptoms and continued to treat patients after his HIV status was known. The CDC began an epidemiologic investigation that involved the review of medical records of the dentist, interviews of staff at the dental practice, including review of the infection-control procedures at Dr. Acer's dental practice. Dr. Acer sent letters to his patients recommending them to be tested for HIV. Florida Department of Health and Rehabilitative Services (HRS) tested about 1,100 patients for HIV infection. The CDC investigation revealed that four additional patients were likely infected while undergoing tooth extractions or other invasive dental procedures performed by Dr. Acer.

How did scientists prove that Dr. Acer transmitted HIV to his patients? The advent of techniques used to analyze viral genetic sequences proved to be the valuable tools needed to answer this question. Even though HIV has a high mutation rate, genomic sequencing was able to determine that the HIV strains from different individuals are genetically distinct. In this case, this technique was used to resolve whether Dr. Acer was responsible for the HIV transmission event to five of his patients. In this study, sequences of the HIV proviral envelope gene from the dentist, seven of his patients, and 35 HIV-positive individuals located in the same geographical area as the dental practice were amplified by polymerase chain reaction and sequenced. The proviral envelope gene (*env*) codes for gp120.

The sequences were analyzed by computer-based methods for genetic variation. The greater the variation, the easier it is to distinguish different strains of the virus. The study conducted showed that there was a high degree of **genetic relatedness or similarity** (within 3% variation) between the HIV strains of the five infected dental patients and Dr. Acer, suggesting that they became infected while undergoing care from a dentist with AIDS. Two other patients had high-risk behavioral exposures to HIV and genetically distant strains (varying by more than 13%), suggesting they contracted their HIV infections from other sources. The actual mode of transmission of the virus is still uncertain but that does not mean that it did not occur. What are some possibilities? What precautions are used in dental practices to prevent transmission of infectious diseases? Discuss potential injuries that may occur during invasive dental procedures.

References

Centers for Disease Control and Prevention. 1991. "Epidemiologic Notes and Reports Update: Transmission of HIV Infection During Invasive Dental Procedure—Florida." *MMWR* 40(2):21–27, 33.

Ciesielski, C. A. et al. 1994. "The 1990 Florida Dental Investigation: The Press and the Science." *Ann Intern Med* 121(11):886–888.

Hillis, D. M., and Huelsenbeck, J. P. 1994. "Support for Dental HIV Transmission." *Nature* 369:1994.

Myers, G. 1994. "Molecular Investigation of HIV Transmission." *Ann Inter Med* 121(11):889–890.

Ou, C.-Y. et al. 1992. "Molecular Epidemiology of HIV Transmission in a Dental Practice." *Science* 256:1165–1171.

Rom, M. Carol. 1997. *Fatal Extraction: The Story Behind the Florida Dentist Accused of Infecting His Patients with HIV and Poisoning Public Health.* San Francisco: Jossey-Bass.

in transmission of HIV. HIV cannot be acquired via sharing a toilet seat used by an AIDS patient, nor can it be transmitted by hugging, handshaking, or contact with the sweat or mucus (e.g., coughing and sneezing) of an infected individual.

Mosquitoes or other insects cannot transmit HIV, and it is not expected that an HIV–mosquito connection will occur. Pathogens that are transmitted by mosquitoes multiply in high numbers in the mosquito or other blood-sucking host and then concentrate in its salivary glands. When the mosquito takes a blood meal, it passes the pathogen into the victim's blood via its saliva. HIV cannot replicate in mosquitoes nor can it concentrate in any part of the mosquito so that it could leave the mosquito.

16.3   Prevention of HIV Infection

There is no "silver bullet" method to prevent HIV infection; however, there are a variety of practices and methods in development that have the potential to stem the HIV epidemic. The following practices are being used to prevent HIV transmission; preventative HIV vaccines will be discussed later in this chapter.

- Abstinence from sex
- Barrier methods (e.g., condoms)
- Microbiocides
- Preexposure prophylaxis (PREP)
- Postexposure prophylaxis (PEP)

Abstinence from sexual activity eliminates the risk of acquiring HIV. The use of male and female condoms effectively reduces the risk of HIV transmission. The Roman Catholic Church, which has banned contraceptives, has been considering the issue of using condoms as a barrier to infection among married couples when one of the partners is infected with HIV. Some priests hold the view that it would be a sin for an HIV-seropositive person to engage in sex without the use of a condom because the act would ultimately kill the partner. Driving this debate is the fact that 165 million Roman Catholics live in Africa, the continent most affected by HIV and AIDS. If condom use is approved by the Roman Catholic Church, the approval offers a sign of hope for those suffering from AIDS, especially in Africa, where about 6,600 people die every day of the disease.

Microbiocides are being developed to reduce sexual transmission of HIV to women. Formulations may be a gel, cream, suppository, or slow-release vaginal sponge that would be applied prior to sexual intercourse. The microbiocides could prevent HIV transmission through several different mechanisms of action, such as:

- **Surfactants** (which disrupt the envelope of HIV)
- Fusion inhibitors (which block attachment of HIV to the host-cell receptors and coreceptors)
- Replication inhibitors (which inhibit HIV reverse transcriptase)

Microbiocides with only one mechanism of action will likely not offer complete protection against viral infection. As a result, a combination of microbiocides will increase their efficacy. There are nearly 30 microbiocide candidate products undergoing preclinical or early-phase clinical trials. An intriguing approach is the use of genetically engineered probiotic strains of *Lactobacillus*. These strains are involved in the production of yogurt and cheese. *Lactobacillus lactis* has been engineered to produce the antiviral agent **cyanovirin**. Cyanovirin is a HIV cell fusion inhibitor that was isolated from cultures of the blue green algae (cyanobacterium). *Lactobacillus jensenii* has been engineered to secrete CD4 proteins that bind to HIV gp120 that could inhibit viral entry. The idea is to use these bacteria to prevent vaginal and oral transmission. Will anti-HIV yogurt be a future microbiocide?

Preexposure prophylaxis (PREP) is the use of antiretroviral drugs by high-risk individuals prior to HIV exposure to reduce the risk of becoming infected. For this method to be desirable, the antiviral drugs must be effective, nontoxic, and not cause resistant strains of HIV to develop. PREP trials testing tenofovir were provided to prostitutes in Cambodia, Cameroon, Malawi, and Nigeria, but local governments stoppe d the studies due to activist protests. Tenofovir is an HIV reverse transcriptase inhibitor. In PREP, its use is as an oral, once-daily, single-tablet regimen. New trials using truvada are underway in Peru, Thailand, Ghana, Botswana, and the United States. Truvada is a single-pill therapy that combines tenovir and emtricitabine reverse transcriptase inhibitors.

Postexposure prophylaxis (PEP) is providing antiretroviral drugs to lower the risk of HIV infection after an individual has had a possible exposure to the virus (e.g., through occupational, accidental needlestick injuries). PEP should be administered within 48 hours (not to exceed 72 hours) of a high-risk exposure to HIV. The sooner PEP is administered, the more effective it is. It is a four-week program in which two or three antiviral medications are provided several times per day. Some individuals may not be able to adhere to the regime due to serious side effects of the drugs.

16.4   AIDS in Africa

A world map representing the average number of adults and children estimated to be living with HIV as of the end of 2005 is shown in **Figure 16-3**. Africa, the world's second largest continent, has been hit harder by HIV/AIDS than any other region of the world. The future of Africa is threatened by a combination of ongoing crises that keep its people poor and its nation weak. The countries of Africa are suffering from unpayable debt, the AIDS epidemic, and trade policies that limit Africans from being able to sell their products at world prices in order to reduce their poverty status. Sub-Saharan Africa is the world's poorest region: 70% of its population lives on less than $2.00 per day. Approximately 200 million of the people in this region go hungry every day. Each day in Africa:

- 6600 people die of AIDS
- 8800 people are infected with the HIV virus
- 1400 newborn babies are infected with the HIV virus during birth or through breast-feeding

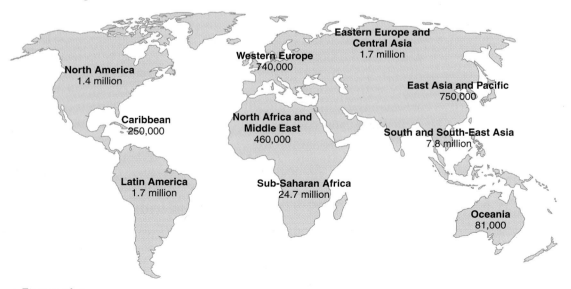

■ Figure 16-3
Average estimates of adults and children believed to be living with HIV at the end of 2005. Data from United National program on HIV/AIDS.

At least 12 million African children have lost one or both parents to AIDS. AIDS prevention campaigns can help to stop the spread of HIV, but access to antiretroviral drugs is a significant problem in Africa. Only a half a million of the 40.3 million HIV-seropositive people have access to antiretroviral drugs. This is because the drugs are too expensive and a sufficient number of trained healthcare workers to monitor and administer treatment are not available. Resources must be raised, treatment provided, and educational programs (including testing and support for those who are infected with the HIV virus) are necessary to further stop this global pandemic.

16.5 General Epidemiology: HIV/AIDS in the United States Today

The number of individuals living with AIDS and the number of AIDS-related deaths in the United States has been declining since 1993 (**Figure 16-4a**). Highly active antiretroviral therapy (HAART) has slowed down the progression of HIV in many infected individuals, resulting in a decline in the number of AIDS cases and AIDS-related deaths. (Trends in HIV diagnosis and deaths are discussed in Section 16.10)

A map of the United States that includes the estimated rates (per 100,000) for adolescents and adults (individuals 13 or older) living with HIV infection (not AIDS) or with AIDS in 2005 is shown in Figure 16-4b. At the end of 2005, there were 214,733 individuals (all ages) living with HIV infection (not AIDS) and 425,910 living with AIDS. It is estimated that about 40,000 individuals become infected with HIV each year. The following is a list of U.S. HIV/AIDS statistics as of 2005 (see the UNAIDS website, http://www.unaids .org/en/, for the latest statistics):

- The largest proportion of HIV-positive individuals were homosexual men, followed by adults and adolescents infected through heterosexual contact.
- By age group, the most cases of individuals living with HIV/AIDS, HIV infection (not AIDS), or AIDS were persons aged 40–44 (21% of cases). (HIV/AIDS means the proportion of adults and adolescents living with HIV infection regardless of whether they have progressed to AIDS at the time of diagnosis.)
- Overall, 77% of adults and adolescents living with AIDS were male and 23% were female. This is further broken down into the transmission categories shown in Figure 16-4c.

Accurate surveillance is needed to monitor and assess the AIDS epidemic in the United States, where the statistics are collected by the CDC from each state. Not all states collect data in the same way, though. Most states use **confidential name-based reporting**, whereas some use other methods. In name-based reporting of AIDS cases, patient names are forwarded to the Health Department by healthcare providers when AIDS is diagnosed. Patient names are kept secure and confidential at the state health department, and no patient names are forwarded to the federal government. Name-based reporting for HIV infection is similar to name-based reporting for AIDS cases. The different methods in data collection pose a challenge when compiling national data.

■ A Risky Workplace? AIDS in the Adult Film Industry

There are over 200 pornographic film production companies in Los Angeles County, California, alone that employ at least 1200 workers who engage in work-related sexual contact. Production companies of heterosexual segments in general do not require condom use for any sexual act. Workers participate in voluntary programs that screen for HIV and other sexually transmitted diseases. At least 62 male and 6 female pornographic film performers died of AIDS-related illness from 1985–2002. It claimed the life of John Holmes, the most

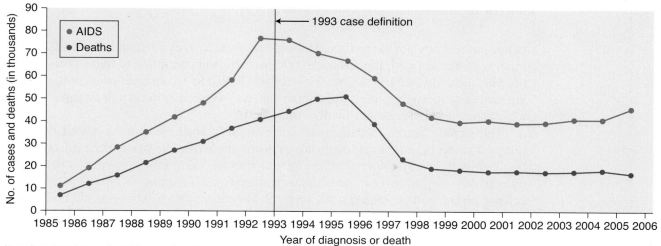

(a)

Note: Data have been adjusted for reporting delays.

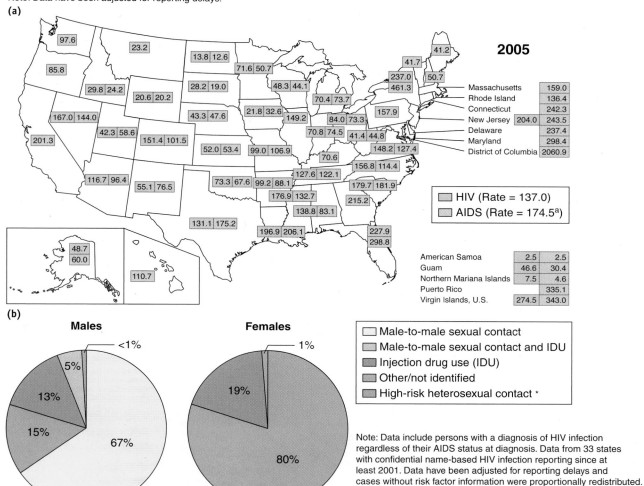

2005

Massachusetts	159.0
Rhode Island	136.4
Connecticut	242.3
New Jersey	204.0	243.5
Delaware	237.4
Maryland	298.4
District of Columbia	2060.9

HIV (Rate = 137.0)
AIDS (Rate = 174.5ª)

American Samoa	2.5	2.5
Guam	46.6	30.4
Northern Mariana Islands	7.5	4.6
Puerto Rico		335.1
Virgin Islands, U.S.	274.5	343.0

(b)

Males

<1%
5%
13%
15%
67%

Females

1%
19%
80%

☐ Male-to-male sexual contact
☐ Male-to-male sexual contact and IDU
☐ Injection drug use (IDU)
☐ Other/not identified
☐ High-risk heterosexual contact *

Note: Data include persons with a diagnosis of HIV infection regardless of their AIDS status at diagnosis. Data from 33 states with confidential name-based HIV infection reporting since at least 2001. Data have been adjusted for reporting delays and cases without risk factor information were proportionally redistributed.
*Heterosexual contact with a person known to have or to be at high risk for HIV infection.

(c)

■ Figure 16-4

(a) Estimated HIV cases and deaths among adults and adolescents diagnosed with AIDS in the United States from 1985–2005. Data from Joint United National Programme on *HIV/AIDS, AIDS Epidemic Update:* December 2006, http://www.unaids.org/en/KnowledgeCentre/HIVData. **(b)** Estimated prevalence rates (per 100,000) for adults and adolescents living with HIV infection (not AIDS) or with AIDS in the United States in 2005. Adapted from the Centers for Disease Control, *HIV/AIDS Surveillance Report* 17 (2007): p. 20. **(c)** Proportion of HIV/AIDS cases among adults and adolescents by sex and trans-mission category in 2005. Data is from 33 states, representing approximately 63% of the epidemic in the United States. High-risk sexual contact means sexual contact with a person known to have or to be at high risk for HIV infection. Data from Joint United National Programme on *HIV/AIDS, AIDS Epidemic Update:* December 2006, http://www.unaids.org/en/KnowledgeCentre/HIVData.

famous male porn star at the time. Holmes tested positive in 1985 and died in 1988. He reportedly had sex with more than 10,000 partners and continued to make porn movies until his death. In 2004, an outbreak of HIV was linked to a male actor who contracted the virus while working unprotected in Brazil. He then went on to infect at least three women who were working for an adult video company.

Testing programs cannot adequately prevent HIV transmission or other sexually transmitted diseases because individuals may transmit these diseases before their infection can be diagnosed. For HIV infection, the period after infection until the virus is detectable by methods such as reverse transcriptase-polymer chain reaction (RT-PCR) is called the **eclipse phase**, and the period until antibodies are detectable by serologic methods (such as enzyme-linked immunosorbent assay [ELISA]) is called the **window period**. The average eclipse phase is estimated to last 10 to 15 days but can be longer. Regulators and lawmakers have urged the industry to require that actors in adult films use condoms.

◾ HIV/AIDS in U.S. Correctional Facilities

In 2004, 724,000 to 100,000 individuals were imprisoned in the U.S. correctional system. HIV infection is five to seven times higher among prisoners than for the general population. Many prisoners are illegal drug users (e.g., in 2001, 57% of federal prisoners were incarcerated for drug-related offenses). The National Commission on AIDS stated in its 1991 report: "By choosing mass imprisonment as the federal and state governments' response to the use of drugs, we have created a de facto policy of incarcerating more and more individuals with HIV infection." Current epidemiology of HIV infection in state correctional institutions is shown in **Figure 16-5**. At the end of 2001, 3.2% of all female state prison inmates were HIV positive, compared to 2.0% of males.

There are numerous activities known to occur among prisoners that pose a risk for HIV transmission. These activities include:

- **Homosexual activity**—consensual sex and rape among male inmates without access to condoms. Many institutions object to condom distribution because the condoms can be used to hide contraband such as drugs. Some prisoners use ineffective makeshift devices such as the fingers from latex gloves and Saran Wrap to practice safer sex.
- **Intravenous drug use** with used syringes, pieces of pens, and lightbulbs.
- **Tattooing** and **body piercing** with recycled sharpened and altered objects like staples, paper clips, and ballpoint pens.

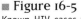
Figure 16-5
Known HIV cases in state correctional facilities shown as a percent of the total custody population in state prisons in 2002. These statistics are from *The Bureau of Justice Statistics Bulletin*, December 2004, NCJ 205333. Data from U.S. Department of Justice, "HIV in Prisons and Jails, 2002," *Bureau of Justice Statistics Bulletin* (December 2004).

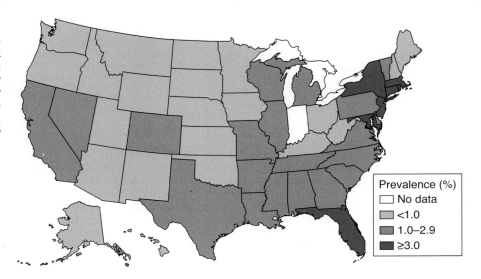

Prevalence (%)
☐ No data
◻ <1.0
◼ 1.0–2.9
◼ ≥3.0

- **Sharing of toothbrushes and shaving equipment** in facilities where these items are not adequately provided.
- **Incidents of violence**—fights that involve bites, lacerations, and bleeding of the participants.

HIV testing in U.S. prisons can be mandatory, routine, voluntary but encouraged, or only on demand. The courts have prevented local correctional facility policies on this issue. Prison inmates do have access to health care as a protected right. Treatment of HIV seropositive prisoners has been criticized for years, though. In 1995, 34% of all deaths in state prisons were AIDS-related. HAART and directly observed therapy (DOT) are available in some prison systems. Antiretrovirals account for a large portion of prison pharmaceutical budgets, hence DOT (also known as "watch-take medication") assures that the patient ingests every dose dispensed to reduce costs. Some prisons attempt to segregate known HIV-infected inmates to "contain" the epidemic. This approach allows staff to be more careful around HIV-positive persons and to educate and provide expert care to HIV-infected inmates.

Jails and prisons bear a disproportionate share of the HIV burden in the United States. Approximately 25% of HIV-infected individuals in the United States have spent time in the correctional system. Educational, counseling, and care programs in the community are important to ensure that the HIV-infected patient has care both inside prison and after release. The "epidemic of imprisonment" contributes to the HIV epidemic in the United States.

■ AIDS and Seniors

AIDS among seniors is a growing problem. Approximately 11% to 17% of people living with HIV in the United States are over 50 years of age. Between 1990 and 2001 cases in seniors quintupled to 90,513 from 16,288. About 2.4% of these adults were infected with HIV by blood transfusions during surgeries from 1979 to 1985.

Surveys have shown that 24% to 30% of men and women ages 60–74 report that they are sexually active. This generation of individuals is living longer, healthier lives, but it has as not been targeted for sex education. Older women are more susceptible to HIV infection due to physical changes that occur with menopause, such as vaginal dryness and thinning of vaginal walls. This can lead to abrasions and tears that increase the risk of infection during unprotected sex. Older adults have not felt comfortable discussing their sexual histories and safe sex practices with partners and medical professionals, and they now represent a significant percentage of AIDS cases. Erectile dysfunction drugs, such as sildenafil (Viagra), tadalafil (Cialis), and vardenafil (Levitra), used by older adults, have been associated with higher risk of STDs, especially HIV transmission. **Figure 16-6** shows the 2005 statistics of persons by age group. In 2005, 15% of U.S. individuals over the age

■ **Figure 16-6**
Estimated HIV and AIDS cases and deaths by age in United States for the year 2005. Data from Avert, *United States Statistics Summary,* http://www.avert.org/statsum.htm.

of 50 were diagnosed with HIV and 19% were diagnosed with AIDS. Thirty-five percent of the deaths in this age group were attributable to AIDS (Figure 16-6).

There are several barriers to diagnosis of HIV infection in older adults. The symptoms of other chronic illnesses resemble those of AIDS, such as:

- night sweats and hot flashes
- weight loss or fatigue
- respiratory problems
- skin rashes
- flulike symptoms or diarrhea
- chronic pain or numbness
- early signs of dementia

Healthcare providers rarely think to test for HIV in older adults. Many times the older adults are often further along in the disease before they are diagnosed. There are treatment barriers. In some cases, older patients have been told they "have lived a long life" and will not be offered aggressive treatment for AIDS-related illnesses. This same age group usually has a marked decrease in income since diagnosis and may not have enough money to live on if they must give up work due to HIV.

The AIDS crisis among older adults needs specific outreach programs devoted to HIV information in general, safe sex practices, and testing. New media and marketing campaigns can raise awareness in older people while promoting respect and validation for the elderly as a group.

16.6   Clinical Symptoms

There are three phases of HIV-1 infection:

1. Primary HIV-1 infection
2. Chronic asymptomatic phase
3. AIDS

■ Primary HIV-1 Infection

Primary HIV infection is the period after infection but before the development of detectable antibodies against HIV-1 (**Figure 16-7**). The virus replicates rapidly during this window, which lasts a few weeks or months. The virus is present in high numbers in the blood, central nervous system, and lymphatic system and invades other tissues. The severity of a primary infection differs for each individual. About 50% of individuals do not experience any symptoms. Table 16-3 contains a list of the signs and symptoms of primary HIV-1 infection for those people who do experience them. Their illness resembles an infection such as mononucleosis or influenza. These symptoms are generally referred to as acute retroviral syndrome (ARS). They typically occur two to six weeks after infection and last two to three weeks.

■ The Chronic Asymptomatic Phase of Infection

During this phase, neither signs nor symptoms of the disease are present. This phase typically lasts an average of ten years. These HIV-1 infected persons are defined as **typical progressors**. The virus continues to replicate in the individual. As the

■ Figure 16-7
Typical course of a primary HIV-1 infection.

levels of virus increase in the bloodstream, CD4+ T cell counts drop. When these counts get below 200 cells/μl, the development of AIDS opportunistic infections occurs.

About 10% to 20% of HIV-1 infected individuals develop AIDS within five years of infection. These patients are called **rapid progressors**. About 5% to 15% of HIV-infected individuals remain free of AIDS for more than 15 years and are termed **slow progressors**. There is a subgroup of HIV-1 infected individuals who are **long-term nonprogressors (Figure 16-8)**. This 1% subgroup of individuals have not previously taken or received antiretroviral therapy and show no sign of disease [e.g., normal CD4+ T cell counts and low levels of virus (500–1000 copies of RNA genomes/ml or <50 viruses/ml of plasma)]. The disease course of long-term nonprogressors is different due to genetic, immunologic, or other driving factors.

■ AIDS

Full-blown AIDS is the last phase of HIV-1 infection. Without antiretroviral therapy, the patient will die within two to three years. HIV doesn't kill the individual directly. Instead, it weakens the body's ability to fight other infections. As CD4+ T cell counts decrease below 50 cells/μl, the number of

TABLE 16-3	Signs and Symptoms of Primary HIV-1 Infection	
Signs and Symptoms	**Frequency**
Fever	Experienced by more than 50% of infected individuals
Fatigue	
Rash	
Muscle pain	
Sore throat	
Swelling of lymph nodes	
Headache	Experienced by 5% to 32% of infected individuals
Diarrhea	
Nausea and vomiting	
Night sweats	
Weight loss	
Thrush (oral candidiasis)	
Neurological symptoms (depression, dizziness, photophobia)	
Oral and genital ulcers	
Cough	
Enlargement of the spleen and liver	

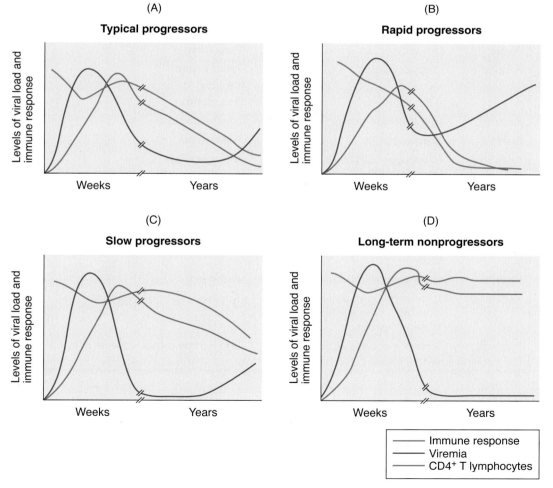

■ **Figure 16-8**
Graphs depicting the different types of progressors based on changes in viral load, CD4+ T cell counts, and antibody response during the natural course of HIV-1 infection. Adapted from J. Cohen and W. G. Powderly. *Infectious Diseases,* Second Edition. Mosby, 2003.

TABLE 16-4 Examples of Opportunistic Infections Commonly Associated with AIDS

Type of Pathogen	Name of Pathogen	Disease/Disorder
Viral	Cytomegalovirus	Retinitis Enterocolitis Pneumonitis
Viral	Varicella zoster virus	Shingles Encephalitis Penumonitis
Viral	Herpes simplex virus Types 1 and 2	Genital ulceration Herpetic whitlow Encephalitis
Viral	Papillomavirus	Common and genital warts Cervical and anal cancer
Viral	Hepatitis B	Hepatitis, chronic cirrhosis, liver cancer
Viral	Hepatitis C	Hepatitis, chronic cirrhosis, liver cancer
Viral	Molluscum contagiosum virus	Molluscum contagiosum
Fungal	*Candida albicans*	Candidiasis (thrush, yeast infection)
Fungal	*Histoplasma capsulatum*	Histoplasmosis
Fungal	*Penicillium marneffei*	Penicilliosis
Fungal	*Coccidioides immitis*	Coccidioidomycosis
Fungal	*Aspergillus* spp.	Aspergillosis
Fungal	*Pneumocystis carinii*	Pneumonia
Parasitic	*Toxoplasma gondii*	Toxoplasmosis Retinitis Pneumonitis
Parasitic	*Cryptosporidium parvum*	Cryptosporidiosis
Parasitic	*Isopora belli*	Isosporiasis
Parasitic	*Enterocytozoon, Encephalitozoon, Septata, Pleistophora, Nosema* spp.	Microsporidiosis
Bacterial	*Mycobacterium tuberculosis*	Tuberculosis
Bacterial	*Mycobacterium avium*	*Mycobacterium avium* complex
Bacterial	*Salmonella* sp., *Shigella flexneri, Clostridium difficile, Shigella, Campylobacter* sp.	Enterocolitis
Bacterial	*Rhodococcus equii, Haemophilus* sp.	Pneumonia
Bacterial	*Streptococcus pneumoniae, Moraxella catarrhaliz, Haemophilus* sp., *Pseudomonas aeruginosa*	Sinusitis
Bacterial	*Bartonella henselae* and *Bartonella quintana*	Skin infections (subcutaneous nodules)

opportunistic infections increases and there is a higher risk for death. HAART slows the rate of progression of this disease. Infections that rarely occur in people with competent immune systems are deadly to those with HIV. Table 16-4 lists opportunistic infections commonly associated with AIDS. In addition to microbial infections and Kaposi's sarcoma, AIDS patients often suffer from **malignancies** such as systematic non-Hodgkin's lymphoma.

Wasting syndrome, a loss of more than 10% of body weight due to fever or diarrhea for more than 30 days, is a common problem in many AIDS patients as well.

AIDS patients that are severely immune-compromised are managed with antimicrobial prophylactic regimens. Together with the use of antiretroviral therapy, this has led to longer survivorship and decreased mortality of patients. The development of drug resistance to the most commonly used antimicrobial agents is of major concern when long-term prophylaxis is used to manage patients. The U.S. Public Health Services and the Infectious Diseases Society of America have made recommendations for the prevention of opportunistic infections in AIDS patients. They recommend prophylaxis against the following disease specific pathogens: *Pneumocystis carinii*, *Toxoplasma gondii*, *Mycobacterium tuberculosis*, *Mycobacterium avium*, *Streptococcus pneumoniae*, and cytomegalovirus.

16.7   Laboratory Diagnosis of HIV

HIV tests are based on the detection of antibodies against HIV. HIV was isolated in 1983 and the first commercial antibody detection tests were available in 1985. Serologic assays are used to detect HIV antibodies in serum, whole blood, saliva, urine, and dried blood collected on filter paper. Most clinical laboratories screen for HIV-1 and HIV-2 antibodies by means of an ELISA, an assay that is widely used throughout the world. Initial tests were only able to detect IgG anti-HIV antibodies. Today all classes of anti-HIV antibodies can be detected with these assays. Positive ELISA test results should be confirmed by Western blot.

An ELISA test requires the drawing of a blood sample from a vein. It also requires two doctor visits: the first is for blood drawing and pretest counseling and the second is to receive the test results and additional counseling if needed. Healthcare workers may perform **rapid HIV tests**, which produce results within 5 to 30 minutes. Testing, counseling, and referrals can be done in one visit. Typically rapid tests are used for the diagnosis of HIV infection in women during labor and delivery and to determine the infection status of patients following an accidental occupational needlestick injury. As for positive ELISA test results, positive rapid test results should be confirmed by Western blot.

The Federal Drug Administration (FDA) approved **HIV home testing systems** in 1996. These home tests refer to "home collection" that uses a simple "finger prick" of blood sample that has been applied to a filter paper and mailed in for laboratory testing. The confidential test results are obtained through a toll-free phone number and posttest counseling is provided by telephone when results are obtained. Consumers should be aware that there are several HIV home testing centers that are not approved and fraudulently marketed for home-use HIV testing. The only FDA approved home test system is sold as "The Home Access HIV-1 Test System" or "The Home Access Express HIV-1 Test System."

The **Western blot** is the confirmatory test essential to exclude false-positive results. HIV proteins are separated by sodium dodecyl sulfate-polyacrylamide gel electrophoresis (SDS-PAGE) and transferred to a nitrocellulose membrane. The membrane is then reacted with test serum to determine which, if any, HIV proteins are recognized by patient antibodies (**Figure 16-9**; see Chapter 5 for more details regarding Western blot testing).

The CDC proposed guidelines for voluntary testing that would apply to every American ages 13–64. Approximately one fourth of the one million Americans infected with HIV don't know they are infected. This group is most responsible for HIV's spread. The CDC's plan was released in 2006 and is supported by the American Medical Association.

■ Genetic Variation/Groups

HIV mutates very readily. Hence it is a highly variable virus that consists of many different strains. Researchers have divided HIV-1 into three distinct groups based on genetic similarities: the major group (M), the outlier group (O), and the new group (N). The three

Figure 16-9
CDC technician filling out an AIDS diagnostic report based on Western blot results.

Figure 16-10
Schematic illustrating the classification of HIV strains into groups and further subtypes.

different groups may represent three different introductions of SIV into humans. The O group is restricted to west-central Africa and the N group was discovered in Cameroon in 1994. The first case of HIV-1 group O in the United States was identified in California. The patient was a native of Africa who came to the United States in 1994. Standard tests did not detect HIV infection during her initial evaluation by physicians.

The M group has been further divided into **clades** or **subtypes**: A, B, C, D, F, G, H, and K. Periodically, two viruses of different subtypes can infect the same cell in an individual, resulting in new progeny hybrid viruses with recombined genomes. These hybrid viruses often do not survive very long but if they do infect more than one individual, they are referred to as **circulating recombinant forms** or **CRFs**. **Figure 16-10** is a diagram depicting the different classifications of HIV strains. It is almost certain that new genetic subtypes and CRFs will be discovered in the future. ELISA screening detects both HIV-1 and HIV-2. Routine ELISA screening and rapid tests detect all of the group M subtypes. Anyone who thinks they may have contracted the rare O subtype should seek expert medical advice.

16.8 HIV Virus Life Cycle

■ HIV Classification and Virion Structure

HIV is a member of the *Retroviridae* family and is placed in the *Lentivirus* genus (from the Latin word *lenti*, for "slow"). Lentiviruses have been implicated in slowly progressive, inflammatory diseases. They undergo long incubation periods and persistently infect monkeys or chimpanzees (e.g., SIV), sheep (e.g., Visna), cattle (e.g., bovine leukemia virus), cats (e.g., feline immunodeficiency virus), and goats (e.g., caprine arthritis-encephalitis virus).

HIV particles are 100 to 120 nm icosahedron-shaped spheres surrounded by a membrane (**Figure 16-11a**). The membrane consists of protruding glycoproteins gp120 (the head) and gp41 (the spike). A matrix protein termed p17 is located underneath the bilipid layer. The capsid protein, p24, covers the two copies of the (+) single-stranded RNA (+ssRNA) viral genome. The HIV-1 genome is 9749 nucleotides in length. Reverse transcriptase (p64) and an integrase (p32) are bound to the viral genome (Figure 16-11b). A cellular tRNA^{lys} is bound to the RNA genome that serves as a primer for the HIV reverse transcriptase. A nonbound protease, p10, is also found within the nucleocapsid of the virus particle).

■ HIV-1 Replication

HIV infects CD4+ T lymphocytes and will lyse them during a productive infection. Other cells harbor, replicate, and bud HIV without lysis, such as:

- natural killer cells
- CD8+ killer T cells
- macrophages
- cells of the nervous system (e.g., astrocytes, neurons, glial cells and brain macrophages)
- dendritic cells (HIV concentrates on the cell surface)

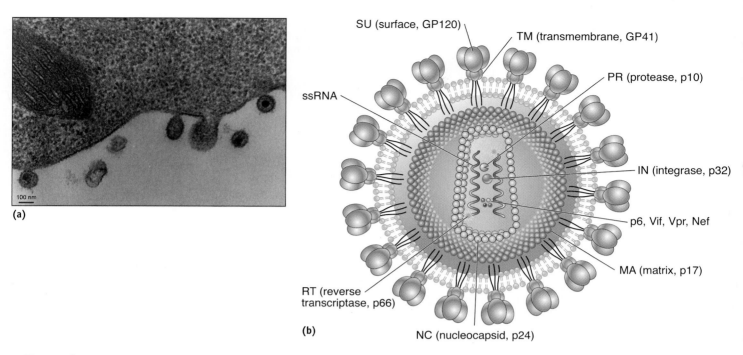

■ Figure 16-11
(a) Electron micrograph showing the presence of mature HIV virions in a tissue sample. (b) Schematic of a mature HIV virion.

During the early course of infection, HIV is macrophage tropic. Later during the course of infection, HIV is T-lymphocyte trophic. HIV enters cells via a cellular receptor and coreceptor. The major cellular receptor is CD4 that is abundantly present on T lymphocytes. The T lymphocyte coreceptor is **CXCR4** (also known as **fusin**). The macrophages' (often found in the skin and mucous membranes) coreceptor is **CCR5**. CD4 is present at low concentrations on macrophages. The rapid progression to AIDS has been associated with a switch in coreceptor preference from CCR5 to CXCR4. When the HIV virus attaches to a cell, the gp120 portion of the virus interacts with CD4. Subsequently, gp120 and gp41 undergo a conformational change, exposing new binding regions on these proteins, thus causing a coreceptor reaction. Subsequently, the virus anchors or embeds into the membrane of the CD4+ cell. The HIV gp41 protein changes into a coiled or hairpin-like shape that causes the virus and cell membrane to come together in proximity, allowing the membrane of the virus and host cell to fuse, resulting in entry and uncoating (**Figure 16-12**).

In the cytoplasm, the viral RNA is converted to DNA by the HIV-encoded reverse transcriptase (RT). Reverse transcriptase binds to the tRNA^{lys} present on the viral genome and initiates DNA synthesis (see Chapter 10 for more information on retroviral genome replication and the functions of reverse transcriptase). When reverse transcription is completed, the final product consists of double-stranded DNA (dsDNA) that contains long terminal repeats (LTRs) located at the ends of the viral genome. The viral DNA is transported to the nucleus of the cell where the viral genome may be integrated into the host cell's chromosomal DNA. Proviral genome integration is catalyzed by the integrase (p32) protein that was packaged into the original HIV particle. The HIV viral genome is more complicated than a typical retrovirus genome that consists of *gag*, *pol*, and *env* and that may also contain an *onc* gene (**Figure 16-13** and Tables 16-5 through 16-7).

HIV-1 can **latently** infect cells. These latent HIV reservoirs are one of the main barriers to the elimination of HIV infection. During a productive infection, HIV-1 is reactivated and the completion of a lytic cell cycle occurs. HIV-1 utilizes the host cell's transcription and translational machinery. The proviral DNA is transcribed from a single promoter in

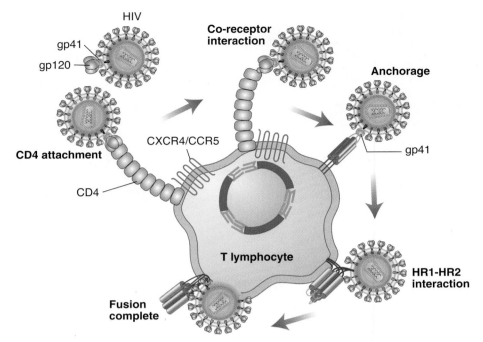

■ **Figure 16-12**

HIV enters cells by attaching to host cell CD4 receptors at a chemokine coreceptor such as CXCR4 or CCR5. Adapted from F. Hoffmann-La Roche Ltd., "Blockade of viral peptide helices prevents HIV from fusing with the host cell," *Roche Facets Clinical Trials,* http://www.roche.com/pages/facets/16/fusinh.htm.

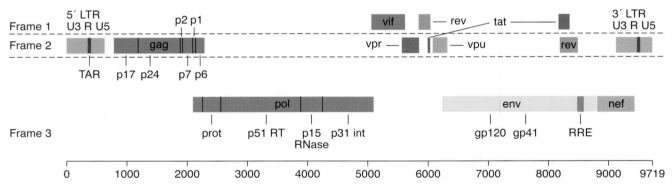

■ **Figure 16-13**

HIV-1 genome organization depicting open reading frames. The genome has extra open reading frames. A total of nine proteins are derived from *gag, pol,* and *env.* HIV makes six other proteins. HIV-2 contains a virion protein termed *vpx* that is not found in HIV-1 and SIVs. It is a 12-kd protein that is a gene homolog of HIV-1 *vpr.* The function of *vpx* is unknown. Modified from http://www.hiv.lanl.gov/content/sequence/HIV/MAP/landmark.html. Adapted from R. S. Sala, "Evolució I Mutació del Virus," *HIV,* http://bioinformatica.uab.es/biocomputacio/treballs02-03.

the 5′ LTR into a 9 kb viral RNA primary transcript by the cellular RNA polymerase II. Tat and Rev are involved in the regulation of viral gene expression. RNA elements vital to replication and transcription are listed in Table 16-8. *tat* is a transcriptional transactivator that is essential for HIV-1 replication. It interacts with TAR. TAR is located at the 5′ end of all HIV RNAs. The binding of *tat* to TAR increases the transcription rate from the HIV LTR at least 1000-fold. *Rev* binds to the RRE to facilitate export of unspliced and incompletely spliced viral RNAs from the nucleus to the cytoplasm. The accessory proteins of HIV-1: *nef, vif, vpu,* and *vpr* play a role in HIV virulence. Some full-length viral messenger RNAs (mRNAs) are packaged into virions following transport to the cytoplasm whereas other viral mRNAs are spliced within the nucleus to form mRNAs that are translated into the different viral proteins.

TABLE 16-5 | HIV-1 Structural Gene Products and Their Functions

Structural Gene	Gene Product(s)	Function of Gene Product
Gag	p17	Matrix protein
	p24	Capsid protein
	p9	RNA-binding nucleocapsid protein
	p7	RNA-binding nucleocapsid protein
Pol	p10	Protease
	p15, 51	Reverse transcriptase RNase activity
	p32	Integrase
Env	gp120	Envelope glycoprotein (external), receptor binding
	gp41	Envelope glycoprotein (spike, transmembrane), receptor binding

TABLE 16-6 | HIV-1 Regulatory Gene Products and Their Functions

Regulatory Gene Product	Function of Gene Product
Tat Trans-activator of transcription	RNA binding transactivating protein/enhances transcription of HIV full-length transcripts
Rev Regulator of virion protein expression	Facilitates the export of unspliced and incompletely spliced viral RNAs from the nucleus to the cytoplasm

TABLE 16-7 | HIV-1 Accessory Gene Products and Their Functions

Regulatory Gene Product	Function of Gene Product
Tat Trans-activator of transcription	RNA binding transactivating protein/enhances transcription of HIV full-length transcripts
Rev Regulator of virion protein expression	Facilitates the export of unspliced and incompletely spliced viral RNAs from the nucleus to the cytoplasm

TABLE 16-8 | HIV-1 RNA Cis-Acting Elements

RNA Element	Function
LTR	Long terminal repeat, contains promoter region, integration of proviral genome, binding site for cellular transcription factors
U3	Unique 3' region, contains promoter region, binding site for cellular transcription factors
R	Terminal redundancy, contains promoter region, binding site for cellular transcription factors
U5	Unique 5' region, contains promoter region, binding site for cellular transcription factors
TAR	Transactivation response element, activates transcription from LTR
RRE	Rev response element, involved in export of viral RNAs

The ribosomes of the host cellular machinery translate the proviral mRNA into viral proteins. The *gag* gene and the *gag* and *pol* genes together are translated into large precursor polyproteins that are cleaved by a virus encoded protease. The full-length *env* protein, gp160, is transported through the trans-Golgi network where it is glycosylated and cleaved by a cellular protease into gp120 and gp41 to form mature envelope proteins that are targeted to the surface of the infected cell. The gp120 protein is attached to gp41 by noncovalent bonds. The genes of the smaller HIV proteins like *tat* overlap with the structural genes but are in different open reading frames. Their mRNAs are derived by alternative splicing of the structural gene mRNAs and translated accordingly.

The virion components of HIV-1 (e.g., the viral RNA, *gag*, *pol*, and *env* proteins) are assembled at budding sites located at the cellular plasma membrane. Two copies of full-length viral genomes that contain the cellular replication primer tRNA^{lys} are packed into the virus particles. Other cellular factors may assist assembly of infectious viral particles. The *gag* and *gag-pol* proteins are cleaved by a HIV-specific protease to form mature virus particles. Our understanding of HIV-1 assembly, maturation and release are just beginning to be characterized. Inhibitors are targeted at this HIV protease as anti-HIV chemotherapy. The life cycle of HIV-1 is shown in **Figure 16-14**.

■ HIV Cellular Pathogenesis

Ultimately, HIV causes AIDS by depleting the number of CD4+ T helper lymphocytes. This in turn results in the weakening of the immune system, allowing opportunistic infections to occur. Without T lymphocytes, essentially no immune response can occur. The body is unable to stop infections caused by other microbes or remove cancer cells. HIV causes **syncytia**, giant cells formed through the fusion of host cells (**Figure 16-15**). Viral *env* pro-

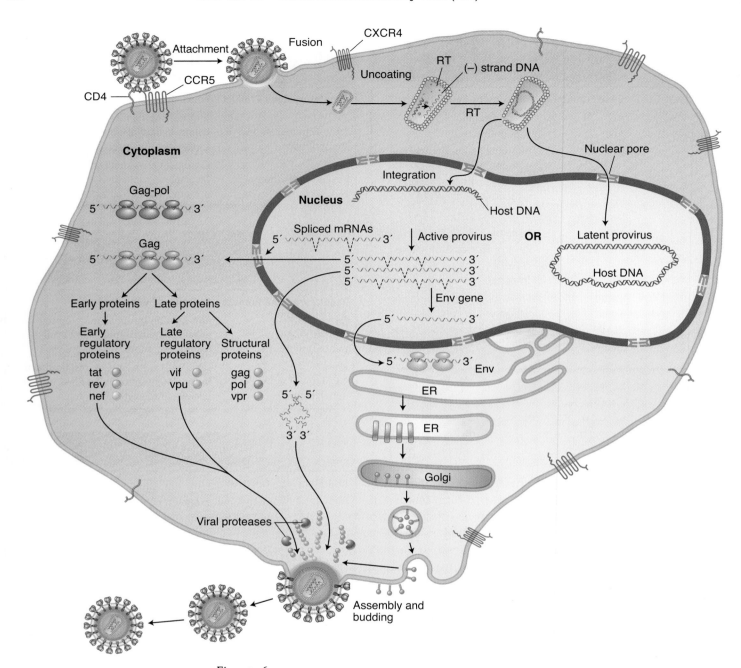

■ **Figure 16-14**
Life cycle of HIV-1. Adapted from S. J. Flint, et al. *Principles of Virology: Molecular Biology, Pathogenesis, and Control of Animal Viruses,* Second Edition. ASM Press, 2003.

teins are expressed on the surface of infected cells. These bind to uninfected cells, causing the plasma membrane to fuse resulting in syncytial formation. Ultimately, these cells die prematurely.

AIDS dementia complex is a serious neurological complication that occurs in as many as 20% of infected individuals. Symptoms may affect cognitive reasoning (e.g., impaired short-term memory and concentration), behavior (e.g., apathy, withdrawal, irritability, depression, and personality changes) or motor performance (clumsiness, tremors, and leg weakness). When HIV infects monocytes and macrophages, they may travel to other organs, especially to the lungs and past the blood-brain barrier to the brain, triggering a cytokine and chemokine response that results in inflammation leading to neuronal

■ Figure 16-15
Lymph node of a patient who died of AIDS. Note the syncytial formation/multinucleated lymphyocytes in the center of the photograph.

injuries. Brain microglial nodules are nonspecific microscopic brain lesions often associated with fatal HIV infection. Current research is underway that looks at the roles of both viral and host factors in mediating HIV-induced neurological disease. Understanding HIV pathogenesis is essential to developing new approaches to AIDS therapy. What we know about HIV-1 biology and pathogenesis represents only a thin veneer on the surface of what needs to be known.

16.9   HIV Human Genetics/Resistance: The Smallpox Hypothesis

There are individuals who have had repeated exposures to HIV but either remain uninfected or if infected, progress more slowly to full-blown AIDS. Recent studies have shown that there is a genetic component involved in host resistance. Individuals who are homozygous for a defective CCR5 gene are virtually completely resistant to HIV infection (two defective copies are inherited, one from each parent). Individuals who are heterozygous for the defective CCR5 gene progress more slowly to AIDS (only one defective CCR5 inherited). In European populations about 5% to 14% of individuals are heterozygous and 1% are homozygous in some populations such as Caucasian North Americans. The allele is almost absent in African, Asian, Native American Indian, and Middle Eastern populations.

The CCR5 chemokine coreceptor is fundamental to establishing HIV infection. In the human host, secreted chemokines involved in inflammatory responses bind to chemokine receptors; for example, the following chemokines bind to the CCR5 receptor: RANTES, MIP-1α, and MIP-1b. These chemokines can block HIV infection if they are bound to

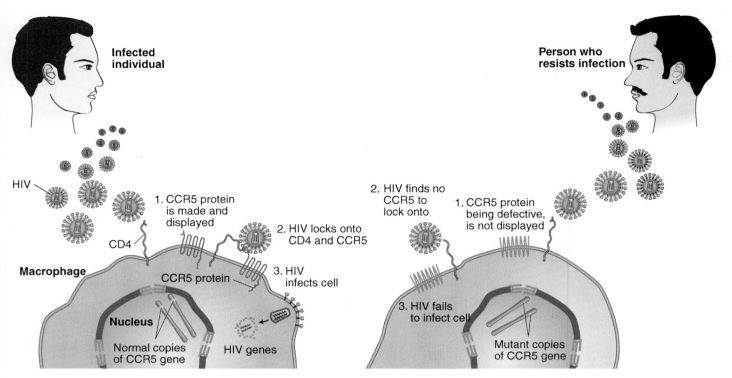

■ Figure 16-16
CCR5Δ32 mechanism for HIV resistance in humans. There are likely other genetic mutations that are also involved in resistance to HIV infection. Adapted from F. Coleman, "HIV," *Chem101: Chemistry*, http://www.wellesley.edu/Chemistry/Chem101/hiv/resist.gif.

CCR5. A defective CCR5 gene that is missing 32 basepairs is a genetic **polymorphism** named CCR5Δ32. It codes for a protein that is severely truncated and cannot be detected at the cell surface. It blocks HIV entry because the viral gp120/gp41 cannot attach to it to infect cells. This defective coreceptor has been linked to the resistance to HIV infection (**Figure 16-16**).

The HIV resistance gene (CCR5Δ32) existed when the HIV pandemic began. Where did the gene come from? When did it arise? HIV is likely less than 100 years old. One hundred years is not sufficient enough time for **natural selection** to increase the frequency of a rare allele. In addition, the selective pressures caused by HIV should be much higher in Africa than in Europe and this is not the case. Scientists have estimated that selective pressures occurred in our history when deadly pathogens such as *Yersinia pestis* (causative agent of the bubonic plague or Black Death), variola major (smallpox), *Treponema pallidium* (syphilis), or *M. tuberculosis* killed millions of individuals approximately 600 to 700 years ago. Chemokine receptors play a central role in the immune response against many pathogens, particularly in the inflammatory response. Individuals who are CCR5Δ32 homozygous survive without immune system problems because of genomic redundancy of chemokine receptor functions; for example, CXCR4 or CCR2 compensate for CCR5.

The most popular theory among the genetic and medical literature is that the CCR5Δ32 allele led to increased survival during smallpox outbreaks that occurred in 14th century Europe. During this time, smallpox epidemics were ongoing, allowing for continuous natural selection. The defective allele was an unintended but welcomed consequence of HIV resistance. The frequency of the CCR5Δ32 variant in Europe is consistent with this scenario. Others speculated that the allele arose when the Black Death killed 25% to 40% of Europeans of all ages from 1346–1352 and 15% to 20% of Europe's population from 1665–1666. These were intermittent epidemics, though, and the bubonic plague virtually disappeared from Europe by 1750. Hence there were no selective pressures to retain the rare allele. For this reason, the selective pressure of variola major epidemics more likely contributed to the higher frequency of CCR5Δ32 alleles. How would a CCR5Δ32 allele protect against variola infection?

Variola virus encodes a 35 kd secretory protein that binds to several CC-chemokine receptors. The variola C-terminal of the protein contains chemokine binding activity termed the smallpox virus-encoded chemokine receptor (SECRET) domain. During infection, the chemokine-binding protein is secreted and may act as a chemokine inhibitor, allowing the virus to evade the immune system, influencing smallpox pathogenesis. In turn, fortuitously, individuals who possess defective chemokine receptors would have been resistant to these effects by variola and HIV.

16.10 Managing HIV Patients: Antiviral Therapy

CD4+ T lymphocyte counts and HIV-1 RNA assays are used to track the progression of HIV infection. *A CD4+T lymphocyte count of less than 200 per μl in an HIV infected individual defines clinical AIDS.* **Virus load monitoring** is measured by the number of HIV-1 RNA genome copies per ml of plasma. The level of viral RNA is a powerful predictor of the disease progression to AIDS. Greater than 100,000 copies per ml of plasma will have clinical AIDS at that time. Viral load monitoring is used to make recommendations for antiviral treatment of patients; for example, a rise in plasma HIV-1 RNA levels suggests a failure of the treatment regimen to suppress replication of the virus. Conversely, an absence of detectable HIV-1 RNA suggests a slower progression to AIDS.

The first antiviral drug approved for HIV-1 treatment was zidovudine (AZT), a thymidine analog that inhibits reverse transcription of viral genomes. The benefits of this monotherapy were limited, though, because drug-resistant strains of the virus rapidly emerged. In 1996, virologist David Ho presented a mathematical model at the 12th World AIDS Conference in Vancouver. He postulated that highly active antiretroviral therapy might cure HIV infection within several years of treatment. HAART is based on administrating at least three different compounds to jointly block viral replication by inhibiting the viral protease/and or reverse transcriptase of the virus. It was hoped that the virus would be eliminated from the patient altogether. Unfortunately, there is a minority of cells that cannot be eliminated by chemotherapy.

Currently there are five classes of HIV inhibitors:

1. Nonnucleoside or nucleoside **reverse transcriptase inhibitors** of the HIV reverse transcriptase.
2. **Protease inhibitors** that inhibit HIV maturation by blocking an HIV-specific protease, resulting in noninfectious virus.
3. **Fusion inhibitors** that block entry of HIV virions into a new host cell by blocking fusion of the viral gp41 envelope protein and host membrane.
4. **Integrase inhibitors** that block the HIV integrase activity, abolishing the integration of a DNA copy of the viral RNA genome into the host cell chromosome.
5. **CCR5-blocking inhibitor**

The five classes of drugs are targeted at entry (blocking HIV gp41 or the CCR5 coreceptor), reverse transcription of viral genomes by the HIV reverse transcriptase, integration of the viral genome, and at the end of the virus life cycle (**Figure 16-17**). From 1996 to 1997, the benefits of HAART were observed, but this therapy is not a cure. More drugs are commercially available to treat HIV (Table 16-9). The major problem with long-term antiretroviral therapy is the development of drug resistance and serious side effects that limit their usefulness. At least 15% of patients do not respond to protease inhibitors and experience severe side effects. Drug resistance is related to the high mutation rate of the HIV reverse transcriptase. HAART in combination with the treatment of opportunistic infections has greatly extended the average lifespan of HIV-infected individuals since its

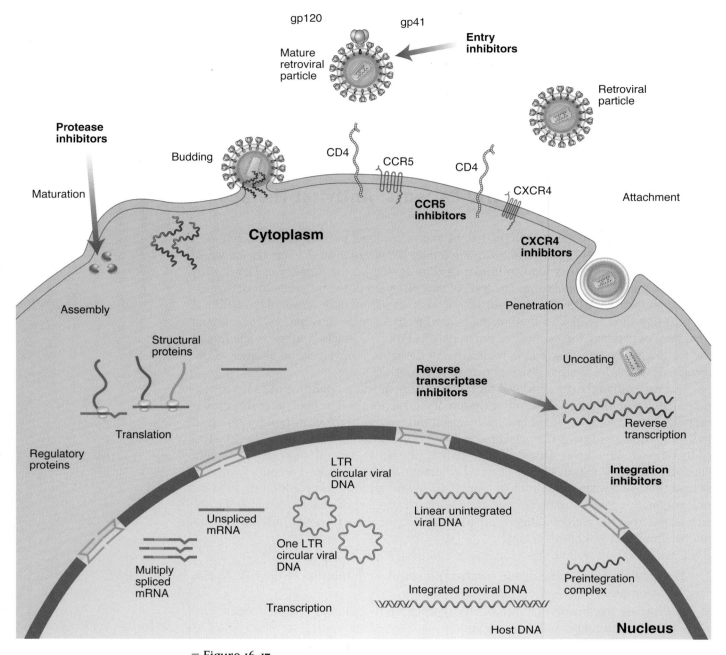

■ Figure 16-17
Antiviral drugs target different stages of the HIV-1 life cycle. Adapted from "Battling AIDS," *Nat. Struct. Biol.* 6 (1999): 895–896.

TABLE 16-9	Approved Antiretroviral Therapy (2007)

Abbreviation	Generic Name	Trade Name	Drug Class*	Year FDA Approval
AZT, ZDV	Zidovudine, Lamivudine	Retrovir, Combivir	RTNI	1987
ddI	Didanosine	Videx	RTNI	1991
ddC	Zalcitabine	Hivid	RTNI	1992
d4T	Stavudine	Zerit	RTNI	1994
3TC	Lamivudine	Epivir	RTNI	1995
SQV	Saquinavir	Invirase, Fortovase	PI	1995
NVP	Nevirapine	Viramune	RTNNI	1996
RTV	Rionavir	Norvir	PI	1996
IDV	Indinavir	Crixivan	PI	1996
DLV	Delavirdine	Rescriptor	RTNNI	1997
NFV	Nelfinavir	Viracept	PI	1997
	One pill combines zidovudine and lamivudine	Combovir	RTNI + RTNI	1997
EFV	Efavirenz	Sustiva	RTNNI	1998
ABC	Abacavir	Ziagen	RTNI	1998
APV	Amprenavir	Agenerase	PI	1999
LPV/r	Lopinavir/Ritonavir	Kaletra	PI	2000
	One pill combines Abacavir, Lamivudine, and Zidovudine	Trizivir	RTNI+RTNI+RTNI	2000
TDF	Tenovir	Viread	RTNI	2001
ATV	Atazanavir	Reyataz	PI	2003
FPV	Fosamprenavir	Lexiva	PI	2003
FTC	Emtricitabine	Emtriva	RTNI	2003
ENF, T-20	Enfuvirtide	Fuzeon	EI (gp41)	2003
	Maraviroc	Selzentry	EI (CCR5)	2007
	Raltegravir	Isentress	II	2007
	One pill combines abacavir and lamivudine	Epzicom	RTNI + RTNI	2004
	Tipranavir	Aptivus®	PI	2005
	One pill combines emtricitabine and tenofovir	Truvada	RTNI + RTNI	2005
	Darunavir	Prezita	PI	2005
	One pill combines Sustiva, Emtriva, and Viread	Atripla	RTNNI+RTNI+RTNI	2006

*Reverse transcriptase nucleoside inhibitors (RTNI); reverse transcriptase non-nucleoside inhibitors (RTNNI); protease inhibitors (PI); entry inhibitors (EI); integrase inhibitor (II).

■ **Figure 16-18**

The progression of HIV infection based on T-cell counts and viral load. AIDS is defined as the stage when opportunistic infections and HIV-associated cancers occur. Note that as the infection proceeds, genetic diversity of HIV increases due to the error-prone reverse transcriptase. This situation challenges treatment of the patient. Adapted from V. Simon and D. D. Ho, *Nat. Rev. Microbiol.* 1 (2003): 181–190.

inception. Ultimately, as viral loads increase, T cells are depleted and the individual will succumb to the disease (**Figure 16-18**). Lastly, the pricing strategy used by drug companies makes it nearly impossible for the developing world to be able to afford HIV drugs; for example, Roche announced in 2003 that the cost of Fuzeon would be $20,963/year per patient. HIV/AIDS advocacy groups are protesting these costs. The first CCR-5 blocking drug, Selzentry, was approved by the FDA for use in adult HIV patients in August, 2007.

| VIRUS FILE 16-2 | **Five Reasons Why HIV Is Invincible** |

At the time of this writing, more than 215,000 journal articles were published on HIV research since the beginning of the AIDS pandemic. John M. Coffin authored "HIV Population Dynamics *In Vivo*: Implications for Genetic Variation, Pathogenesis, and Therapy" (*Science*, January 27, 1995). This highly cited paper outlines the reasons why HIV infection has been so challenging in the consideration of therapeutic strategies. Briefly listed below are Coffin's theoretical insights into why HIV infection remains incurable and only modestly treatable despite international research efforts.

1. HIV replicates very rapidly throughout the whole course of infection. The latency period is not a period of viral inactivity, but an active process in which *cells are infected and dying at a high rate and in high numbers.* This is referred to as a **steady-state model** of viral population dynamics.

2. The virus *replicates at an amazingly rapid speed.* An individual who has been infected for ten years has viral genomes present in the body that are 3,000 generations from the virus that initiated the infection. On average, the virus that is transmitted to someone else will be over 1,000 generations removed from the initial infection.

3. *HIV has an extraordinary mutation rate.* Reverse transcriptase does not have proof reading/error correcting functions. *Greater than 50% of viral genomes contain at least one error.* Since thousands of viral generations of virus are present in an individual, this mutation rate may allow the virus to escape detection by the immune system and response to antiviral therapies.

4. The rapid mutation rate of the virus results in drug-resistant strains. *Antiviral drug resistance has been found for all compounds used as a therapy for HIV infection.* Hence, drug therapies only work for a short period of time due to the genetic diversity of HIV.

5. *Immunodeficiency is the result of the direct killing of infected cells either by HIV or the immune system.* Massive viral replication drives the pathogenic process that leads to immune degradation.

Reference

Coffin, J. M. 1995. "HIV Population Dynamics *In Vivo*: Implications for Genetic Variation, Pathogenesis, and Therapy." *Science* 267:483–489.

16.11 Is an HIV Vaccine Possible?

Twenty-five years after the discovery of HIV, there is still no vaccine. An asymptomatic HIV patient harbors at least one million genetically distinct variants of HIV. An AIDS patient harbors 100 million genetically distinct variants of HIV. HIV variants can escape both antibody and T-cell immune responses. Will a vaccine ever be able to cope with HIV variability?

HIV causes a chronic infection in which there are reservoirs of virus in T cells, macrophages, and monocytes, where it may be integrated as a silent provirus. A vaccine needs to be able to prevent subsequent attacks by the same virus. To date, more than 65 million people worldwide contracted HIV, of which 25 million have died. More than 95% of today's infections and deaths occur in developing countries where significant health challenges continue to be a burden. HIV/AIDS threatens human welfare, social, political, and economic stability. Despite advances in HIV/AIDS research, the pandemic continues.

For the sake of simplicity, textbooks portray the HIV virion with a perfectly shaped enveloped virus containing gp120/gp41 spikes on its surface. The immune system faces a vastly different virus. About one in 1000 to 10,000 HIV particles are not defective and can reproduce in host cells. HIV particles carry numerous host cell-derived proteins within the HIV envelope. Many different serum proteins are found bound to the virion. Many of the original spikes have lost the gp120 subunits, leaving only the gp41 portion of gp160 remaining. Any remaining intact spikes may differ as much as 10% of amino acids between different HIV virions. This interferes with the affinity and neutralization of antibodies produced by the immune system to combat HIV (**Figure 16-19**). It makes the development of an HIV vaccine a complex research challenge. Promising vaccine candidates are advancing to clinical trials. Overall, a collective effort will be needed to slow the scourge of HIV/AIDS worldwide.

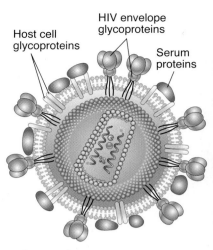

■ Figure 16-19
Schematic portrayal of a more realistic view of HIV virions found in an infected cell. The surface of HIV virions are not uniform, making it an even greater challenge for the immune system to clear the virus compared to other human viruses.

Summary

The AIDS pandemic began in the United States during the early 1980s. The first HIV-1 isolate was cultured in 1983 from the lymph node tissues of a patient. More than 199,000 medical research studies have been published since the first reported cases of what we now know as the acquired immunodeficiency syndrome (AIDS). AIDS affects men, women, and children in nearly every country in the world.

Several theories about the origin of HIV exist. The most widely accepted is the hunter theory or extensions of it. This theory is based on the premise that the AIDS pandemic is a viral zoonosis. A virus related to HIV-1 has been isolated from the common chimpanzee (*Pan troglodytes troglodytes*), which is native to Cameroon, Gabon, and the Democratic Republic of Congo. The virus is referred to as simian immunodeficiency virus (SIV_{cpz}). The genetic sequence of SIV_{cpz} and the early strains of HIV-1 are nearly identical. The belief is that AIDS arose when naturally infected chimps with SIV_{cpz} were killed and eaten and their blood entered cuts or wounds on the hunter. The SIV_{cpz} strain adapted in the human host to become HIV-1. Like HIV-1, HIV-2 entered the human population as the result of a zoonotic or cross-species transmission. It transferred from sooty mangabeys to humans during the first half of the 20th century in Western Africa.

Africa has been hit harder by the HIV/AIDS crisis than any other region in the world. Access to antiretroviral drugs is a significant problem in Africa. Treatment and educational programs that include testing and support for those infected with HIV are especially needed in developing countries to stop this global pandemic.

HIV is present in blood, semen, vaginal fluids, breast milk, and in very low levels in saliva and tears. HIV is transmitted by:

- anal or vaginal intercourse
- sharing of HIV-contaminated needles (e.g., by injection drug users)
- blood transfusions using infected blood or blood-clotting factors (this is rare in the United States)
- accidental needlestick injuries (healthcare workers are at risk while working with HIV-positive patients)
- congenital AIDS (before, or during birth or through breastfeeding)
- sharing of HIV-contaminated tattoo needles, razors, acupuncture needles, or ear-piercing implements.

There is no "silver bullet" method to prevent HIV infection. Abstinence from sex, barrier methods, microbiocides, and pre- and postexposure prophylaxis have the potential to stem HIV transmission. In the United States HIV infection has hit the adult film industry, correctional facilities, and an increasing number of aging adults.

The clinical symptoms of HIV are divided into three phases:

1. Primary HIV-1 infection
2. Chronic asymptomatic phase
3. AIDS

Full-blown AIDS is the last phase of infection in which opportunistic infections increase and there is a higher risk for death. AIDS patients that are severely immune-compromised are managed with antimicrobial prophylactic regimens. Ultimately, HIV causes AIDS by depleting the number of CD4+ T helper lymphocytes. This results in the weakening of the immune system, which then is unable to combat infections and cancers associated with HIV infection. AIDS dementia is a serious neurological complication that occurs in as many as 20% of infected individuals.

HIV infection is diagnosed by serologic assays such as the ELISA, rapid HIV tests, and HIV home-testing systems. A Western blot must be used to confirm all positive test results. Commercial tests need to be updated on a continual basis to detect variant strains of HIV. HIV patients are managed with highly active antiretroviral therapy (HAART). Viral load testing and CD4+ T cell counts are used to make recommendations for antiviral treatment of patients. There are five classes of HIV inhibitors:

1. Nonnucleoside or nucleoside reverse transcriptase inhibitors.
2. Protease inhibitors that inhibit HIV maturation, resulting in noninfectious virus.
3. Fusion inhibitors that bind gp41, blocking entry of HIV virions into a new host cell.
4. Integrase inhibitors that block the HIV integrase activity, abolishing the integration of a DNA copy of the viral RNA genome into the host cell chromosome.
5. CCR5-blocking inhibitor

HIV is a member of the *Retroviridae* family and is placed in the *Lentivirus* genus. HIV virions are enveloped with protruding glycoproteins gp120 (the head) and gp41 (the spike). Each virion contains two copies of +ssRNA genome that has a cellular tRNA^{lys} bound to it, in addition to other bound viral proteins such as reverse transcriptase.

Viral entry is accomplished by binding CD4, a major cellular receptor present on the surface of T lymphocytes and a chemokine coreceptor (CXCR4 or fusin present on T cells and CCR5 present on macrophages). The rapid progression to AIDS has been associated with the switch in coreceptor preference from CCR5 to CXCR4. In the cytoplasm, the viral RNA genome is converted to DNA by the HIV encoded reverse transcriptase. The viral DNA is transported to the nucleus where the viral genome may be integrated into the host cell's chromosome. The integrated HIV DNA is termed a provirus. The HIV viral genome is more complicated than that of a typical retrovirus. It codes for 15 proteins that serve as structural, regulatory, or accessory proteins during the life cycle of the virus.

HIV is an extraordinary virus. It replicates at an amazingly rapid speed and possesses a high mutation rate. The rapid mutation rate of the virus results in drug-resistant strains and strains that can evade the immune system. A very small percentage of individuals are resistant to HIV infection. It has been determined that individuals who are homozygous for a defective CCR5 gene are virtually completely resistant to HIV infection. There are likely other genetic mutations that may also account for resistance to HIV infection. Despite over 25 years of medical research efforts, there is still no cure or vaccine for AIDS. Challenges remain in the area of therapeutic research. Continuous commitment and collaborative efforts may one day slow the scourge of HIV/AIDS in the world. Research efforts may shift toward long-term management of HIV infection rather than eradication of HIV from the body.

Resources

Primary Literature and Reviews

Abbott, A. 2004. "Gut Reaction. Consumers Are Stocking up on Live Yoghurts and Fermented Drinks that Claim to Improve Health. But Is There Any Science Behind the Marketing of These 'Probiotic' Products?" *Nature* 427:284–286.

Alejo, A. et al. 2006. "A Chemokine-Binding Domain in the Tumor Necrosis Factor Receptor from Variola (smallpox) Virus." *PNAS USA* 103(15):5995–6000.

Bailies, E. et al. 2003. "Hybrid Origin of SIV in Chimpanzees." *Science* 300:1713.

Barre-Sinoussi, F. et al. 1983. "Isolation of a T-Lymphotropic Retrovirus from a Patient at a Risk for Acquired Immune Deficiency Syndrome (AIDS)." *Science* 220(4599):868–871.

Berry, N. et al. 2001. "Analysis of Oral Polio Vaccine CHAT Stocks." *Nature* 410:1046–1047.

Blanchard, A. et al. 1998. "Molecular Evidence for Nosocomial Transmission of Human Immunodeficiency Virus from a Surgeon to One of His Patients." *Virology* 72(5):4537–4540.

Blancou, P. et al. 2001. "Polio Vaccine Samples not Linked to AIDS." *Nature* 410:1045–1046.

Boyd, M. R. et al. 1997. "Discovery of Cyanovirin-N, a Novel Human Immunodeficiency Virus-Inactivating Protein that Binds Viral Surface Envelope Glycoprotein gp120: Potential Applications to Microbiocide Development." *Antimicrob Agents Chemother* 41(7):1521–530.

Britvan, L. et al. 1996. "Identification of HIV-1 Group O Infection—Los Angeles County, California, 1996." *MMWR* 45(26):561–565.

Buckhard, M., and Dean, G. A. 2003. "Transmission and Immunopathogenesis of FIV in Cats As a Model for HIV." *Curr HIV Res* 1:15–29.

Bukrinskaya, A. G. 2004. "HIV-1 Assembly and Maturation." *Arch Virol* 149(6):1067–1082.

Busch, M. P., and Kleinman, S. H. 2000. "Nucleic Acid Amplification Testing of Blood Donors for Transfusion-Transmitted Infectious Diseases." *Transfusion* 40:143–159.

CDC. 2001. "Updated U.S. Public Health Service Guidelines for the Management of Occupational Exposures to HBV, HCV, and HIV and Recommendations for Postexposure Prophylaxis." *MMWR* 50(RR11):1–42.

Chang, T. L.-Y. et al. 2003. "Inhibition of HIV Infectivity by a Natural Human Isolate of *Lactobacillus jensenii* Engineered to Express Functional Two-Domain CD4." *PNAS USA* 100:11672–11677.

Chitnis, A., Rawls, D., and Moore, J. 2000. "Origin of HIV Type 1 in Colonial French Equatorial Africa?" *AIDS Res Hum Retroviruses* 16(1):5–8.

Citterio, P., and Rusconi, S. 2007. "Novel Inhibitors of the Early Steps of the HIV-1 Life Cycle." *Expert Opin Investig Drugs.*" 16(1):11–23.

Coffin, J. M. 1995. "HIV Population Dynamics *In Vivo*: Implications for Genetic Variation, Pathogenesis, and Therapy." *Science* 267:483–489.

Cohen, J. 2006. "Novel Attacks on HIV Move Closer to Reality." *Science* 311:943.

Coleman, J. K. et al. 2005. "HIV-1 p24 Vaccine Protects Cats Against Feline Immunodeficiency Virus Infection." *AIDS* 19(14):1457–1466.

Deng, J. et al. 2007. "Design of Second Generation HIV-1 Integrase Inhibitors." *Curr Pharm Des* 13(2):129–141.

Dicko, M. et al. 2000. "Safety of Immunization Injections in Africa: Not Simply a Problem of Logistics." *Bull World Health Organ* 178:163–169.

Douglas, J. M. et al. 1997. "Contraceptive Practices Before and After an Intervention Promoting Condom Use to Prevent HIV Infection and Other Sexually Transmitted Diseases among Women—Selected U.S. Sites, 1993-1995." *MMWR* 46(17):373–377.

Drucker, E., Alcabes, P. G., and Marx, P. A., 2001. "The Injection Century: Massive Unsterile Injections and the Emergence of Human Pathogens." *Lancet* 358:1989–1992.

Fiebig, E. W. et al. 2003. "Dynamics of HIV Viremia and Antibody Seroconversion in Plasma Donors: Implications for Diagnosis and Staging of Primary Infection." *AIDS* 17:1871–1879.

Freed, E. O., and Mouland, A. J. 2006. "The Cell Biology of HIV-1 and Other Retroviruses." *Retrovirology* 3:77.

Gallo, R. C. 2002. "The Early Years of HIV/AIDS." *Science* 298:1728–1730.

Gallo, R. C., and Montagnier, L. 2003. "The Discovery of HIV As the Cause of AIDS." *N Engl J Med* 349(24):2283–2285.

Gallo, R. C. et al. 1984. "Frequent Detection and Isolation of Cytopathic Retroviruses (HTLV-III) from Patients with AIDS and at Risk for AIDS." *Science* 224(4648):500–503.

Galvani, A. P., and Novembre, J. 2005. "The Evolutionary History of the CCR5-Δ32 HIV-Resistance Mutation." *Microbes and Infection* 7:302–309.

Galvani, A. P., and Slatkin, M. 2003. "Evaluating Plague and Smallpox as Historical Selective Pressures for the CCR5-Δ32 HIV-Resistance Allele." *PNAS USA* 100(25):15276–15279.

Gao, F. et al. 1999. "Origin of HIV-1 in the Chimpanzee *Pan troglodytes troglodytes.*" *Nature* 387:436–444.

Gottlieb, M.S. et al. 1981. "*Pneumocystis* pneumonia—Los Angeles." *MMWR* 30(21):250–252.

Hahn, B. H. et al. 2000. "AIDS as a Zoonosis: Scientific and Public Health Implications." *Science* 287:607–614.

Hedrick, P. W., and Verrelli, B. C. 2006. "Ground Truth for Selection on CCR5-Delta32." *Trends Genet* 22(6):293–296.

Holden, C. 1988. "Curbing Soviet Disinformation." *Science* 242:665.

Keele, B. F. et al. 2006. "Chimpanzee Reservoirs of Pandemic and Nonpandemic HIV-1." *Science Express* E-Pub May 25, 2006.

Kourtis, A. P. 2006. "Prevention of Sexually Transmitted Human Immunodeficiency Virus (HIV) Infection in Adolescents." *Curr HIV Res* 4(2):209–219.

Lalani, A. S. et al. 1999. "Use of Chemokine Receptors by Poxviruses." *Science* 286:1968–1971.

Laurent, C., et al. 2006. "Antiretroviral Drug Resistance and Routine Therapy, Cameroon." *EID* 12(6):1001–1004.

Lemey, P. et al. 2003. "Tracing the Origin and History of the HIV-2 Epidemic." *PNAS USA* 100(11):6588–6592.

Leonard, J. T., and Roy, K. 2006. "The HIV Entry Inhibitors Revisited." *Curr Med Chem* 13(8):911–934.

Liu, R. et al. 1996. "Homozygous Defect in HIV-1 Coreceptor Accounts for Resistance of Some Multiply-Exposed Individuals to HIV Infection." *Cell* 86(3):367–377.

Maruschak, L. M. 2004. "HIV in Prisons and Jails, 2002." *Bureau of Justice Statistics Bulletin*, Document NCJ 205333.

Marx, P. A., Alcabes, P. G., and Drucker, E. 2001. "Serial Human Passage of Simian Immunodeficiency Virus by Unsterile Injections and the Emergence of Epidemic Human Immunodeficiency Virus in Africa." *Philos Trans R Soc B Biol Sci* 356(1410):911–920.

McMichael, A. J., and Hanke, T. 2003. "HIV Vaccines 1983-2003." *Nat Med* 9(7):874–880.

Miedema, F. 2002. "Review of Science Fictions: A Scientific Mystery, a Massive Coverup, and the Dark Legacy of Robert Gallo." *Nat Med* 8(7):655.

Montagnier, L. 2003. "A History of HIV Discovery." *Science* 298:1727–1728.

Novembre, J., Galvani, A. P., and Slatkin, M. 2005. "The Geographic Spread of the CCR5 Δ32 HIV-Resistance Allele." *PLoS Biology* 3(11):1954–1962.

Paul, S. M. et al. 1998. "Emerging Issues in AIDS: Variant Strains of Human Immunodeficiency virus and its Subtypes." *Med Lab Obs* 30(2):32–36.

Piedade, J. et al. 2000. "Longstanding Presence of HIV-2 Infection in Guinea-Bissau (West Africa)." *Acta Tropica* 76:119–124.

Poulsen, A. G., Aaby, P., Jensen, H., and Dias, F. 2000. "Risk Factors for HIV-2 Seropositivity among Older People in Guinea-Bissau, a Search for the Early History of HIV-2 Infection." *Scand J Infect Dis* 32(2):169–175.

Pusch, O. et al. 2005. "Bioengineering Lactic Acid Bacteria to Secrete the HIV-1 Virucide Cyanovirin." *J Acquir Immune Defic Syndr Hum Retrovirol* 40(5):512–520.

Rambeau, A. et al. 2001. "Phylogeny and the Origin of HIV-1." *Nature* 410:1047–1048.

Rotblatt, H. et al. 2005. "HIV Transmission in the Adult Film Industry—Los Angeles, California, 2004." *MMWR* 54(37):923–926.

Schim, M. F. et al. 2001. "HIV-2 Does Not Protect Against HIV-1 Infection in a Rural Community in Guinea-Bissau." *AIDS* 15:2303–2310.

Simon, V., and Ho, D. D. 2003. "HIV-1 Dynamics *in vivo*: Implications for Therapy." *Nat Rev Microbiol* 1(3):181–190.

Spaulding, A. et al. 2002. "Human Immunodeficiency Virus in Correctional Facilities: A Review." *Clin Infect Dis* 35:305–312.

Stephens, J. C. et al. 1998. "Dating the Origin of the CCR5-Δ32 AIDS-Resistance Allele by Coalescence of Haplotypes." *Am J Hum Genet* 62:1507–1515.

Stevenson, M. 2003. "HIV-1 Pathogenesis." *Nat Med* 9:853–860.

Stremlau, M. et al. 2004. "The Cytoplasmic Body Component TRIMa Restricts HIV-1 Infection in Old World Monkeys." *Nature* 427:848–852.

Taussig, J. et al. 2006. "HIV Transmission among Male Inmates in a State Prison System—Georgia, 1992–2005." *MMWR* 55(15):421–426.

Vandamme, A.-M. 2006. "Anti-HIV Yoghurt?" *AIDS Reviews* 8:44.

Weiss, R. A. 2001. "Polio Vaccines Exonerated." *Nature* 410:1035–1036.

Zhu, T. et al. 1998. "An African HIV-1 Sequence from 1959 and Implications for the Origin of the Epidemic." *Nature* 391:594–597.

■ Popular Press

Crewdson, J. 2003. *Science Fictions: A Scientific Mystery, a Massive Cover-up and the Dark Legacy of Robert Gallo.* Boston: Back Bay Books.

Culshaw, R. 2007. *Science Sold Out: Does HIV Really Cause AIDS?* Berkeley, CA: North Atlantic Books.

Curtis, T. 1992. "The Origin of AIDS." *Rolling Stone Magazine,* pp. 54–59, 61, 106, 108.

Duesberg, P. H. 1997. *Inventing the AIDS Virus.* Washington, DC: Regnery Publishing.

Farber, C. 2006. *Serious Adverse Events: An Uncensured History of AIDS.* Hoboken, NJ: Melville House.

Hooper, E. 1999. *The River: A Journey to the Source of HIV and AIDS.* London: Penguin.

Jefferson, D. 2006. "How AIDS Changed America." *Newsweek,* May 15, 2006, pp. 36–53.

Johnson, E. "Magic," and Novak, William. 1992. *My Life.* New York: Random House.

Markel, H. 2004. *When Germs Travel: Six Major Epidemics That Have Invaded America Since 1900 and the Fears They Have Unleashed.* New York: Pantheon.

Rom, M. 1997. *Fatal Extraction: The Story Behind the Florida Dentist Accused of Infecting His Patients with HIV and Poisoning Public Health.* Hoboken, NJ: John Wiley & Sons.

Sherman, I. W. 2007. *Twelve Diseases That Changed Our World.* Washington DC: ASM Press.

Shilts, R.1987. *And the Band Played On: Politics, People and the AIDS Epidemic.* New York: St. Martin's Press.

■ Video Productions

AIDS in America History. 1998. Films for the Humanities.

Surviving AIDS. 1999. NOVA Production, PBS.

Changing Faces. 2000. Films for the Humanities.

Exposed: The Continuing Story of AIDS. 2001. Films for the Humanities.

And the Band Played On. 2001. HBO Home Video.

Longtime Companion. 2001. MGM.

AIDS: A Global Crisis. 2002. Films for the Humanities.

The Bottom Line: Privatizing the World. 2002. Films for the Humanities.

New Blood. 2002. Films for the Humanities.

Pediatric AIDS. 2002. Films for the Humanities.

Breaking the Silence: Lifting the Stigma of HIV/AIDS in Ethiopia. 2003. Films for the Humanities.

Deadly Desires. 2003. Films for the Humanities.

Pandemic: Facing AIDS. 2003. HBO.

AIDS and other Epidemics. 2004. Films for the Humanities.

Three Girls I Know: Intimate Stories of Personal Responsibility. 2004. Films for the Humanities.

The United Nations: Working for All of Us. 2004. Films for the Humanities.

Absolutely Positive. 2004. New Video Group.

RX For Survival: A Global Health Challenge. 2005. PBS.

Fighting AIDS. 2006. CBS. 60 Minutes.

Helping the Youngest Victims of AIDS: Spotlight on South Africa. 2006. Films for the Humanities.

Out of Control: AIDS in Black America. 2006. Films for the Humanities.

Yesterday. 2006. HBO Home Video.

Portraits in Human Sexuality: Sexual Orientation. 2006. Films for the Humanities.

Age of AIDS. 2006. PBS, Frontline.

NOVA: Epidemic—Ebola, AIDS, Bird Flu and Typhoid. 2007. WGBH Boston.

■ eLearning

http://biology.jbpub.com/book/virology

The site features eLearning, an online review area that provides quizzes and other tools to help you study for your class. You can also follow useful links for in-depth information, or just find out the latest virology and microbiology news.

CASE STUDY QUESTIONS

These questions relate to the Case Study presented at the beginning of the chapter.

1. Magic Johnson's viral loads are undetectable. Is he cured, or can he be considered "virus-free"? Explain your answer.

2. If Magic Johnson were to discontinue HAART today, make a prediction as to what would happen to his viral loads and his CD4+ T cell counts. Explain your answer.

3. How could Magic Johnson have prevented his HIV infection?

4. List and explain the major routes of HIV transmission.

5. What is the difference between HIV and AIDS?

6. What does seropositive mean and how is a person tested for HIV?

7. What are some symptoms associated with the primary phase of HIV infection? What are the symptoms of AIDS?

8. The NBA has instituted safeguards for trainers and players. What are the precautions that are aimed to reduce the risk of contracting an HIV infection when treating open wounds on the basketball court?

9. If Magic Johnson were a less talented or charismatic NBA player, do you think the press and general public would have embraced his announcement and statements about HIV/AIDS in the same way? Discuss your answer.

■ References

Centers for Disease Control and Prevention. 1993. "Sexual Risk Behaviors of STD Clinic Patients Before and After Earvin "Magic" Johnson's HIV-Infection Announcement—Maryland, 1991–1992." *MMWR* 42(3):45–48.

Johnson, Earvin "Magic" and William Novak. 1992. *My Life.* New York: Random House.

Langer, L. M. et al. 1992. "Effect of Magic Johnson's HIV Status on HIV-Related Attitudes and Behaviors of an STD Clinic Population." *AIDS Educ Prev* 4(4):295–307.

Sigelman, C. K., Miller, A. B., and Derenowski, E. B. 1993. "Do You Believe in Magic? The Impact of "Magic" Johnson on Adolescents' AIDS Knowledge and Attitudes." *AIDS Educ Prev* 5:2153–161.

Whalen, C. K. et al. 1994. "Preadolescents' Perceptions of AIDS Before and After Earvin Magic Johnson's Announcement." *J Pediatr Psychol* 19(1):3–17; discussion 19–26.

CHAPTER

17

> ❝*Love is like a virus. It can happen to anybody at any time.*❞
>
> Maya Angelou, American Poet

Hepatitis Viruses

OUTLINE

CASE STUDY

In 2003, over 600 individuals who dined at a Mexican restaurant in Monaca, Pennsylvania, fell ill with hepatitis A. At least 13 of the food service workers also became ill. Three individuals died and over 100 were hospitalized. Epidemiologists from the Centers for Disease Control and Prevention (CDC) were charged with determining the cause of the outbreak, which was determined to be the largest of its kind in the United States. Their ongoing investigation tested foods prepared at the restaurant and stool samples from staff and restaurant customers. The CDC determined that restaurant workers were not the source of the outbreak; it was the uncooked green onions that were used in making salsa.

17.1   The History of Viral Hepatitis

Hepatitis means "inflammation of the liver." The classic symptom of hepatitis is **jaundice**, a yellowing of the skin and eyes caused by too much **bilirubin** in the blood (refer to the clinical features of the virus for further explanation). Hepatitis is caused by a number of viruses and on occasion is caused by alcohol or prescription drugs. Viral hepatitis is one of the most important public health threats worldwide. One of the most notorious cases of viral hepatitis is that of the popular American stunt performer Robert Craig "Evel" Knievel, Jr. Knievel was diagnosed with a hepatitis C infection in 1993. He contracted hepatitis C from contaminated blood received during one of his fourteen reconstructive surgeries used to repair broken bones acquired during a stunt. He received a liver transplant in 1999. Knievel died November 30, 2007, of pulmonary fibrosis at the age of 69. In 2002, actress from the television series "Baywatch" and former Playboy model Pamela Anderson claimed she contracted hepatitis C from sharing a tattoo needle with her exhusband, rock musician Tommy Lee.

Epidemics of **jaundice** or hepatitis have been recorded throughout history, especially during times of war; for example, outbreaks occurred among Napoleon's troops during the Egyptian and Russian campaigns that took place in the early 1800s. The crowding and unsanitary conditions of military encampments created an ideal environment for hepatitis A viruses to be transmitted. In 1821, Napoleon Bonaparte died in exile on the Island of St. Helena. There are numerous theories about his cause of death, including stomach cancer, arsenic poisoning, inappropriate medical treatment, and hepatitis—an endemic disease at St. Helena.

Approximately 70,000 troops fell ill with hepatitis during the U.S. Civil War. Hepatitis was referred to as "camp jaundice" during the trench warfare battles in the Mediterranean theater in World War I (**Figure 17-1**). During World War II, there were at least two significant outbreaks of hepatitis. The first occurred in 1942, when approximately 330,000 soldiers were vaccinated against yellow fever virus. Of these vaccinees, 50,000 experienced jaundice and 62 died. It was believed that a virus was present in the

■ **Figure 17-1**

Many soldiers fighting in World War I contracted viral hepatitis during trench warfare, where infectious hepatitis infection was common. Field sanitation during heavy combat was inadequate, and hepatitis spread by a fecal–oral mode of transmission.

serum used to manufacture the vaccine. After those lots of vaccines were destroyed and a human serum-free vaccine was manufactured, the cases of jaundice stopped. Years later it was confirmed that these soldiers had **serum hepatitis** caused by hepatitis B virus.

Later jaundice epidemics during World War II occurred during the invasion of North Africa and subsequent invasion of the Italian mainland in the Mediterranean theater of operations (MTO). Even though the antibiotic penicillin was available at this time to treat bacterial infections and medicine in general had improved, diseases still proliferated in combat situations, making treatment of the troops difficult. Malaria and hepatitis epidemics incapacitated 55,000 American assault troops, thus delaying D-Day. The viral hepatitis outbreaks were caused by **infectious hepatitis** (hepatitis A virus) during the occupation of recaptured land, amid battlefields that were littered with human excrement and corpses. Hepatitis A virus is found in the feces of people infected with hepatitis A virus and is spread by fecal–oral transmission. Unsanitary conditions were common at the frontlines of war. There were no bathroom facilities at the battle lines and thus troops could not move behind the lines when they needed to go to the bathroom. Hence, feces got on their boots and clothing and into the bottom of the next shell hole or foxhole they dashed into. Soldiers detected the proximity of the frontlines because of the increasing intensity of odors. Infectious hepatitis was the greatest cause of disabling disease among U.S. and British forces in the MTO.

Today hepatitis C is a major problem in U.S. military veterans. Approximately 8% to 9% of Veteran Affairs (VA) medical center patients are positive for hepatitis C antibodies. Some VA hospitals have had as high as 10% to 20% of patients with hepatitis C antibodies.

Hepatitis C in Vietnam-era veterans, who are at the front lines of the hepatitis C epidemic, is on an ongoing problem, and most studies have focused on this group. There are multiple risk factors for hepatitis C virus transmission among veterans in this time period, including:

- combat casualties who survived multiple blood transfusions in an era prior to hepatitis C virus screening of the blood supply
- intravenous drug experimentation (heroin use)
- blood exposure through sharing of razors or other nonsterile instruments
- history of tattooing
- history of prostitution (or more than 15 sexual partners)
- blood/body fluid exposure to healthcare and combat personnel
- receipt of immune globulin for hepatitis A prophylaxis in an era prior to hepatitis C virus screening of the blood supply.

Challenges remain in the treatment of hepatitis C infection and prevention. Testing and improved treatments will benefit all individuals who suffer from hepatitis C infection.

17.2   Epidemiology

Hepatitis can be caused by viral infections, trauma, alcohol abuse, or drug-induced toxicity. Viral hepatitis is the most important cause of hepatitis on a global scale. Yellow fever virus, herpes simplex viruses, cytomegaloviruses, and Epstein-Barr virus can cause hepatitis, but a range of unrelated human pathogens termed the "**hepatitis viruses**" cause the vast majority of virally induced hepatitis cases. This chapter focuses on the hepatitis viruses.

Each hepatitis virus is named with a letter of the alphabet with the exception of the newly identified transfusion transmission virus (TTV) and SEN viruses. Although the hepatitis viruses cause similar disease, they are widely varied in their origin and are evolutionarily distinct (Table 17-1).

For years there were three main hepatitis viruses: hepatitis A virus, the cause of infectious hepatitis; hepatitis B virus, the cause of serum hepatitis; and hepatitis "non-A, non-B"

TABLE 17-1	Human Hepatitis Viruses Nomenclature and Characteristics			
Virus Member	**Abbreviation**	**Enveloped or Naked**	**Genome**	**Family**
Hepatitis A virus	HAV	Naked	+ssRNA	*Picornaviridae*
Hepatitis B virus	HBV	Enveloped	DNA (partially double-stranded)	*Hepadnaviridae*
Hepatitis C virus	HCV	Enveloped	+ssRNA	*Flaviviridae*
Hepatitis D (δ) virus	HDV	Enveloped	−ssRNA	Not assigned (defective virus, requires HBV to replicate)
Hepatitis E virus	HEV	Naked	+ssRNA	*Hepeviridae*
Hepatitis G virus	HGV	Enveloped	+ssRNA	*Flaviviridae*
Transfusion transmission virus or torque teno virus	TTV	Naked	ssDNA	*Circoviridae*
SEN virus	SENV	Naked	ssDNA (circular)	*Circoviridae*

viruses. Diagnostic tests were developed to identify hepatitis A and B viruses in the 1970s. Hepatitis non-A, non-B viruses were considered the cause of all other not identified viral causes of hepatitis. In 1989, hepatitis C, the agent that caused non-A, non-B hepatitis, was discovered using modern molecular techniques. Since that time, additional non-A, non-B hepatitis viruses have been discovered: hepatitis D, E, G, and TTV. Hepatitis A, B, and C viruses cause over 90% of acute viral hepatitis in the United States. Table 17-2 lists these hepatitis viruses and their modes of transmission. The human hepatitis viruses represent a group of diverse pathogens that share an ability to cause inflammation and necrosis of the liver (Table 17-2). The geographical distribution of hepatitis viruses A–E is shown in **Figures 17-2a–e**.

Hepatitis A commonly occurs in developing parts of the world where sewage disposal and food hygiene are unsatisfactory. Hepatitis B is spread via a **parenteral** (blood-to-blood) mode of transmission, such as through tattooing, body piercing, and drug abuse. Transmission can also occur sexually and via fomites (e.g., sharing contaminated razors). High to intermediate prevalence of hepatitis B viruses also occurs in developing countries, Western Europe, newly independent states of the former Soviet Union, Central America, and the Caribbean. Variants of hepatitis B virus have been described, and the current hepatitis B vaccine does not protect immunized individuals against these variant hepatitis B viruses.

TABLE 17-2	Transmission of Human Hepatitis Viruses
Virus Member	**Mode of Transmission**
Hepatitis A virus	Fecal–oral
Hepatitis B virus	Blood-to-blood contact Sexual Sweating?*
Hepatitis C virus	Blood-to-blood contact Sexual
Hepatitis D (δ) virus	Blood-to-blood contact
Hepatitis E virus	Fecal–oral
Hepatitis G virus	Blood-to-blood contact Sexual
Transfusion transmission virus	Blood-to-blood contact
SEN virus	Post-transfusion hepatitis

*New study by Selda Bereket-Yucel. 2007. "Risk of Hepatitis B Infections in Olympic Wrestling." *Br J Sports Med,* doi:10.1136/bjsm.2006.032847.

■ Figure 17-2

Geographical prevalence of human hepatitis viruses A–E. **(a)** Global prevalence of hepatitis A (based on 2005 data, WHO). Adapted from CDC. *Health Information for International Travel 2008*. Elsevier, 2007. **(b)** Global prevalence of hepatitis B (based on 2005 data, WHO). **(c)** Global prevalence of hepatitis C (based on 2003 data, WHO). Adapted from World Health Organization. *International Travel and Health 2007*. WHO, 2007.

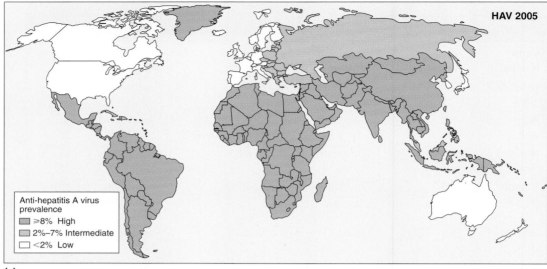

HAV 2005

Anti-hepatitis A virus prevalence
≥8% High
2%–7% Intermediate
<2% Low

(a)

HBV 2005

Hepatitis B surface antigen prevalence
≥8% High
2%–7% Intermediate
<2% Low

(b)

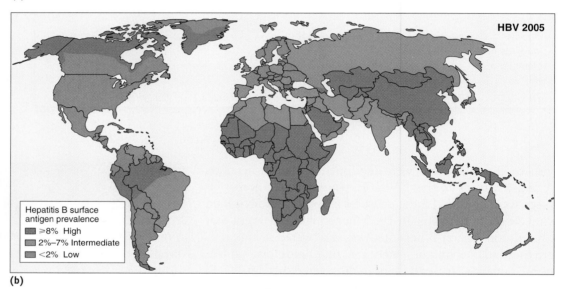

HCV 2003

Hepatitis C global prevalence, June 2003
>10%
2.5%–10%
1%–2.5%
No data

(c)

(d)

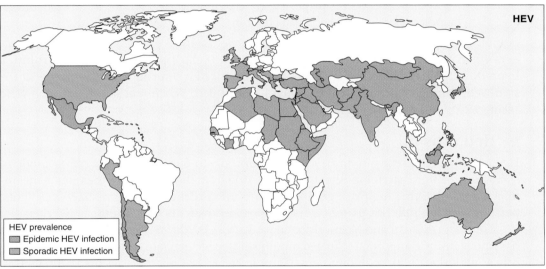

(e)

■ **Figure 17-2 (Continued)**

(d) Global prevalence of hepatitis D (CDC data). Adapted from the Centers for Disease Control, *Epidemiology and Prevention of Viral Hepatitis A to E: Hepatitis D Virus*: Slide 6. **(e)** Global prevalence of hepatitis E (CDC data). Adapted from Panda, S. K., Thakral, D., and S. Rehman, *Rev. Med. Virol.* 17 (2006): 151–180.

Hepatitis C virus is spread primarily by direct contact with human blood. There is a higher prevalence of hepatitis C infection among blood donors in the Eastern Mediterranean, Western Pacific, and Southeast Asia compared to some countries in North America and Europe. Reporting of data is lacking from African countries.

Hepatitis D virus requires the presence of hepatitis B virus in order to replicate. In general, then, the global pattern of hepatitis D infection corresponds to the prevalence of hepatitis B virus infection; for example, in countries where chronic hepatitis B cases are low, there is a low prevalence of hepatitis D virus. Hepatitis E is spread by the fecal–oral mode of transmission, often through contaminated water. It is endemic and sometimes epidemic in the developing world.

■ Figure 17-3
This person has jaundice of the conjunctiva and facial skin that manifested after a hepatitis A infection.

I7.3   Clinical Features

■ Hepatitis A

Most hepatitis A outbreaks are sporadic and associated with contaminated food or water supplies. Shellfish may become contaminated with sewage and represent a problem because they are able to retain and concentrate viruses from the water. The major mode of transmission is fecal–oral. The average incubation period for hepatitis A is 30 days. Adults experience signs and symptoms more often than children. The onset of symptoms include:

- fatigue
- abdominal pain
- loss of appetite
- nausea and vomiting
- dark urine
- jaundice, which occurs in 70% to 80% of individuals older than 14 years of age. Jaundice is less likely to occur in children.

Jaundice is a yellow color in the skin, mucous membranes, or eyes (**Figure 17-3**) and occurs when the liver is not functioning properly. The yellow pigment is from **bilirubin**, a byproduct of old red blood cells. (You may have noticed when you've had a bruise that the skin went through a series of color changes as it healed. When you saw yellow you were seeing bilirubin.)

■ Hepatitis B

Hepatitis B is relatively rare in developed countries. In endemic areas, a major mode of spread occurs from **carrier** mother to infant (blood from the infected mother enters the uninfected fetus). Other high-risk groups are intravenous drug users, hemodialysis patients, persons with multiple sex partners, institutionalized patients, and healthcare workers.

The average incubation period for hepatitis B is 80 days. About 30% of individuals have no signs or symptoms. When symptoms do occur they are similar to those of hepatitis A, with the addition of joint pain. Chronic hepatitis B infection occurs in 5% to 10% of individuals infected after the age of 5. Chronic infection can lead to cirrhosis of the liver and **hepatocellular (liver) cancer**, or **HCC** (refer to Chapter 10, Viruses and Cancer). Hepatitis B viral DNA sequences can be detected in the chromosomes of hepatocellular tumors associated with hepatitis B infection. Integration of hepatitis B DNA occurs where there are breaks in the cellular DNA of liver cells. In humans, chronic hepatitis B infections cause an ongoing inflammatory response that results in oxidative damage to the DNA, such as double-stranded breaks in the DNA of liver cells. Death from chronic liver disease occurs in 15% to 25% of chronically infected individuals.

■ Hepatitis C

Prior to 1989 there were cases of hepatitis after blood transfusions that were not caused by hepatitis A or B virus, and investigators found that identifying the cause of these "hepatitis non-A, non-B" viruses was difficult. In 1989, a direct molecular biology approach by Michael Houghton and colleagues provided the tools to identify and characterize the cause of hepatitis non-A, non-B. Their approach involved the cloning of the new viral genome present in infectious plasma, which they termed hepatitis C virus. This important new pathogen was identified without the ability to grow, visualize, or detect the viral agent. Substantial progress has been made in the last decade of research to isolate, grow, and visualize hepatitis C virus, which is now a major public health problem. It causes a "silent

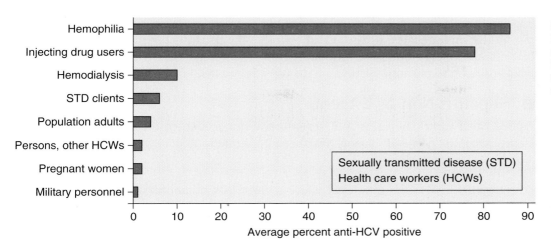

■ **Figure 17-4**
Hepatitis C virus prevalence by selected groups in the United States. Adapted from the Centers for Disease Control, *Epidemiology and Prevention of Viral Hepatitis A to E: Hepatitis C Virus*: Slide 24.

epidemic," as many victims show few or no signs of disease for years and even decades. Early assessments of the total number of infected individuals were underestimated.

Unlike hepatitis B infection, hepatitis C infection is common in the developed world. Approximately four million people in the United States (1.8% of the population) are infected. Hepatitis C virus spread is almost exclusively through blood contact (**Figure 17-4**). Sexual transmission is rare. Individuals who received blood transfusions or blood products, had long-term kidney dialysis or a solid organ transplant before 1992 (when screening donated blood for hepatitis C virus was not available) are at risk for contracting hepatitis C. About 80% of infected individuals have no signs or symptoms. If present, signs and symptoms are similar to other hepatitis infections. Between 55% and 85% of infected persons experience a chronic infection, resulting in chronic liver disease. Chronic infection can lead to cirrhosis of the liver and HCC in 5% to 20% of persons (refer to Chapter 10, Viruses and Cancer). The average incubation period is six to seven weeks.

■ Hepatitis D

Hepatitis D virus requires the presence of hepatitis B virus in order to replicate. Symptoms of hepatitis D infection are indistinguishable from those of hepatitis B infection. The hepatitis D virus can be contracted as a coinfection with hepatitis B virus. The highest risk factor for hepatitis D infection in the Western world is intravenous drug use (17% to 90% of addicts test positive for hepatitis D virus).

■ Hepatitis E

Hepatitis E virus is endemic in the developing countries of Asia and Africa and rare in industrialized nations. Sporadic cases in the developed world almost always occur in travelers returning from endemic areas. The mode of transmission and symptoms are similar to hepatitis A virus (i.e., through fecal–oral transmission). Person-to-person transmission is rare. The average incubation period is 40 days. Outbreaks are often associated with fecally contaminated water supplies. Prevention strategies include the avoidance of drinking water and beverages with ice of unknown purity, uncooked shellfish, and uncooked vegetables not peeled or prepared by the traveler.

Infection with hepatitis E virus causes a more severe illness than hepatitis A virus. It causes mortality in 1% to 3% of persons and in 15% to 25% of infected pregnant women. Even though hepatitis E is rarely diagnosed in industrialized nations, however, antihepatitis E virus antibodies have been found in a significant proportion (up to 28% in some areas) of healthy individuals. Sporadic cases have been reported in the United States, northern England, Italy, and France. Considerable evidence suggests that hepatitis E may be a **zoonotic disease** (e.g., transmitted from animals to people). Human hepatitis E virus, for which isolates are genetically similar to pig hepatitis E strains, has been isolated from pigs in the United States. It has been shown that pig hepatitis E viruses can cross species barriers and infect nonhuman primates. Human antihepatitis E virus antibodies cross-react and bind to pig antihepatitis E virus capsid proteins.

■ Hepatitis Non-A–E Agents

As described earlier, hepatitis A–E viruses have not accounted for all cases of hepatitis. Hence hepatitis "non-A–E" agents have been implicated.

Hepatitis F

Hepatitis F virus does not exist. During the 1990s, a handful of cases were reported from France. Experiments demonstrated that monkeys could be infected with the isolated hepatitis F virus from patient stools. This research was not reproducible and the scientific community no longer lists hepatitis F as a cause for infectious hepatitis.

Hepatitis G

Hepatitis G virus was first identified and characterized in 1996 from the plasma of a patient with chronic hepatitis. Hepatitis G virus, which is transmitted parenterally, is a flavivirus and is a distant relative of hepatitis C virus. The prevalence of hepatitis G virus antibodies in blood donors ranges from 1% to 10%, so is considered rare. The clinical significance of hepatitis G virus is debatable.

Transfusion Transmission Virus or Torque Teno Virus (TTV)

In 1997, TTV was found using **representational difference analysis (RDA)** in Japanese patients who had posttransfusion hepatitis of unknown etiology (hepatitis non-A–G). RDA was used to compare the DNA from sera of hepatitis patients before and after they experienced elevated levels of **alanine aminotransferase (ALT)**. Elevated ALT levels are an indicator of liver inflammation that can be the result of viral hepatitis. The procedure detected extraneous viral DNA that was amplified by polymerase chain reaction (PCR) and sequenced and reported to be a new candidate hepatitis virus. To date, there is no conclusive evidence that TTV causes human disease.

SEN virus

About 10% of transfusion-associated hepatitis and 20% community-acquired cases of hepatitis are of unknown origin, suggesting the existence of additional causative agents. In 2000, a new virus, called SEN was identified as a hepatitis non-A–E viral agent. It was thought to be associated with post-transfusion hepatitis. Little is known about the clinical significance of SEN virus.

I7.4 Laboratory Diagnosis of Viral Hepatitis Infections

Diagnosis of viral hepatitis is based on:
- symptoms
- blood tests for liver enzymes
- viral antibodies (e.g., IgM)
- viral genetic material (e.g., reverse transcriptase PCR [RT-PCR] or PCR)

Patient symptoms of **acute hepatitis** are fatigue, abdominal pain, loss of appetite, nausea and vomiting, and darkening of urine, followed by jaundice. Serology (enzyme-linked immunosorbent assay [ELISA] tests detecting viral antibodies or antigens), liver enzyme tests, and molecular techniques to detect viral genomes (e.g., RT-PCR or PCR) are used to confirm diagnosis of acute viral hepatitis. Blood samples are tested for the presence of

■ **Figure 17-5**

(a) Events in hepatitis A virus infection. Adapted from the Centers for Disease Control, *Epidemiology and Prevention of Viral Hepatitis A to E: Hepatitis A Virus*: Slide 6. **(b)** Events in hepatitis E virus infection. "ALT" represents levels of alanine aminotransferase activity. Adapted from the Centers for Disease Control, *Epidemiology and Prevention of Viral Hepatitis A to E: Hepatitis E Virus*: Slide 3.

elevated levels of two liver enzymes: **aspartate aminotransferase (AST)** and ALT. These enzymes are normally found in the liver but spill into the blood if the liver is damaged, thus raising the enzyme levels in the blood. Nucleic acid tests to detect viral genomes are only available in specialized laboratories. Patients with **chronic hepatitis** are harder to diagnose because these patients do not have nausea or jaundice until liver damage is quite advanced.

Hepatitis A infections are reliably diagnosed by the presence of anti-HAV IgM. Hepatitis E infections are clinically indistinguishable from hepatitis A infections. Diagnosis of hepatitis E infections is made by serology tests that test for anti-HEV IgM or by RT-PCR. Tests for hepatitis E virus are not widely available. Hepatitis A and E viruses do not persist in the liver and there is no evidence of progression to chronic liver damage. The courses of hepatitis A and hepatitis E infections are shown in **Figures 17-5a** and **b**.

Hepatitis B infections are diagnosed by the level of IgM antibodies produced toward the hepatitis B surface antigen (anti-**HBsAg**) and hepatitis B anticore-antigen (anti-**HBcAg**). Levels of antibodies will vary depending upon whether or not the patient has an acute or chronic hepatitis infection (Table 17-3). A patient is a **chronic hepatitis B virus carrier** when the anti-HBsAg test is found to be positive for six months, but the diagnosis is often suspected much earlier (Figure 17-6).

TABLE 17-3	Diagnostic Testing for Hepatitis Viruses A–C Infection
Type of Viral Infection	**Diagnostic Tests**
Acute hepatitis A	IgM anti-HAV positive result
Acute hepatitis B	IgM anti-HBcAg positive, anti-HBsAg positive
Chronic hepatitis B	Anti-HBsAg positive, IgM and IgG anti-HBcAg positive, IgM anti-HBeAg negative
Acute hepatitis C	High serum alanine aminotransferase levels (7× normal limit), nucleic acid testing for HCV-RNA
Chronic hepatitis C	Anti-HCV positive, HCV RNA ≧ 6 months apart

■ **Figure 17-6**
(a) Events in hepatitis B virus chronic infection. Adapted from the Centers for Disease Control, *Epidemiology and Prevention of Viral Hepatitis A to E: Hepatitis B Virus*: Slide 10. **(b)** Events in hepatitis C virus chronic infection. Adapted from the Centers for Disease Control, *Epidemiology and Prevention of Viral Hepatitis A to E: Hepatitis C Virus*: Slide 9. **(c)** Natural history of hepatitis B and C virus infections.

(a)

(b)

(c)

VIRUS FILE 17-1

A Breakthrough for Hepatitis C Virus Research: Growing Hepatitis C Viruses in Cell Cultures

Approximately 170 million people worldwide are chronically infected with hepatitis C virus, which exclusively infects humans and chimpanzees. The only therapy available to treat hepatitis C virus infections is a combination of ribavirin and interferon α (**Figure VF 17-1**). Interferon therapy is effective in just a fraction of patients due to the adverse side effects associated with interferon treatment. There is no vaccine for hepatitis C virus. Hepatitis C virus-associated end-stage liver disease is now the leading cause for liver transplantation in the United States.

■ **Figure VF 17-1**
Interferon α is used to treat hepatitis C infections. Unfortunately, it has only limited success.

The hepatitis C virus was discovered in 1989. It was difficult to study hepatitis C viruses because cell culture and small animal models to propagate and research the virus in the laboratory were not available at that time; thus understanding the virus life cycle and how the virus damages the liver was hampered. Testing potentially useful drugs or development of a vaccine against these infections was not possible.

In 2005, major breakthroughs by three different research groups made it possible to grow hepatitis C viruses in cell culture, paving the way for the development of new antiviral therapies and vaccines. A critical advance in this breakthrough was the isolation of the entire viral genome from an infected individual who was suffering from fulminant hepatitis C. The genome was cloned and sequenced and designated JFH1. RNA transcripts from this genome were transfected into a human liver hepatoma cell line (Huh-7.5 cells). With this method, infectious particles of hepatitis C virus were generated at relatively high titers. Chimpanzees were intravenously inoculated with the viruses produced in the Huh-7.5 cells and proved to be infectious (**Figure VF 17-2**). The development of this tissue-culture system has accelerated the pace of hepatitis C research.

References

Bukh, J., and Purcell, R. H. 2006. "A Milestone for Hepatitis C Research: A Virus Generated in Cell Culture Is Fully Viable *in vivo*." *PNAS USA* 103(10):3500–3501.

Lindenbach, B. D. et al. 2005. "Complete Replication of Hepatitis C Virus in Cell Culture." *Science* 309:623–626.

Wakita, T. et al. 2005. "Production of Infectious Hepatitis C Virus in Tissue Culture from a Cloned Viral Genome." *Nat Med* 11:791–796.

Zhong, J. et al. "Robust Hepatitis C Virus Infection *in vitro*." *PNAS USA* 102:9294–9299.

■ **Figure VF 17-2**
RNA transcripts of the JFH1 virus were transfected into Huh-7.5 cells. New viruses from the infected Huh-7.5 cells were present in the supernatant of the cell cultures. The supernatant was filtered and used to infect naïve (uninfected) Huh-7.5 cells in order to generate a stock of virus. The virus stock was then used to infect chimpanzees and SCID mice that contained human liver grafts. Viruses were recovered from the infected chimpanzees and mice and efficiently were able to infect naïve Huh-7.5 cells. NCR = noncoding region, * = HCV. Adapted from Bukh, J., and R. H. Purcell, *Proc. Natl. Acad. Sci. USA* 103 (2006): 3500–3501.

Acute hepatitis C cannot be reliably diagnosed by serology tests because patients usually take up to three months to become positive. Acute hepatitis C is diagnosed by blood tests detecting serum ALT levels that are seven times higher than the normal upper limit of liver enzyme levels. In addition, nucleic acid testing for hepatitis C virus RNA in serum is also an indicator of infection. Early diagnosis is beneficial because it is believed that early treatment can prevent chronic infection with hepatitis C virus. Chronic Hepatitis C virus infection can occur in as high as 80% of untreated patients (Figure 17-6c). Diagnosis is based on antihepatitis C virus antibodies and hepatitis C virus RNA levels (Table 17-3 and Figure 17-6b).

17.5 Screening the Blood Supply for Viral Hepatitis Agents

The American Red Cross has been screening for hepatitis B surface antigen since 1971. In 1987, a test for anti-HBcAg was added to the screening protocol. From 1986–2003, the U.S. blood supply was also screened for elevated levels of ALT. In 1990, testing began for antihepatitis C virus, and in 1999 a nucleic acid test for hepatitis C virus-RNA was added to blood donation screening in order to reduce the risk of disease transmission. Blood is not screened for other hepatitis viruses and is not entirely risk-free, but it is very safe. The U.S. blood supply in particular is among the safest in the world.

17.6 Pathogenesis: Chronic Hepatitis

Chronic hepatitis occurs when the inflammation of the liver is active, persists for more than six months, and is detectable by increased ALT levels in serum. Hepatitis B, C, D, and G viruses can cause chronic hepatitis infections. A patient who is **viremic** and has an abnormal ALT level should have a liver biopsy, which is the only way to assess the degree of inflammation of the liver and the stage of liver disease. Chronic liver damage may result in **cirrhosis**, which is characterized by the formation of fibrous tissues, nodules, and scarring that interfere with liver cell function and blood circulation (**Figure 17-7**). A late complication of cirrhosis is hepatocellular carcinoma, which takes many years to develop.

17.7 Hepatitis Virus Life Cycles

The hepatitis viruses belong to five different families, designated by terms with the suffix *viridae* (Table 17-1). Families are groups of viruses that share common characteristics. Although there are five families listed in the right-hand column of Table 17-1, two of the viruses are unassigned. Five of eight hepatotropic viruses (hepatitis viruses A–E) discussed in this chapter have been well characterized.

■ Virus Structure

Hepatitis viruses A–E have a spherical shape and icosahedral capsid symmetry ranging from 28 to 50 nm in diameter. Virus particles are either enveloped or nonenveloped. Electron micrographs of hepatitis A–D viruses are shown in **Figure 17-8**. Hepatitis B, C, and D are enveloped and relatively sensitive to many physical and chemical agents, whereas hepatitis A is not enveloped and can remain infectious on inanimate surfaces in the environment for a month. Hepatitis A viruses can also retain their infectivity in the hostile environment of the gastrointestinal tract, as they are acid and bile resistant.

(a)

■ Figure 17-7
(a) A healthy human liver. **(b)** A human liver diseased by viral hepatitis and cirrhosis.

(b)

(b)

■ Figure 17-8
Electron micrographs of hepatitis viruses.
(a) Hepatitis A virus. **(b)** Hepatitis B virus.
(c) Hepatitis C virus.

(a)

(c)

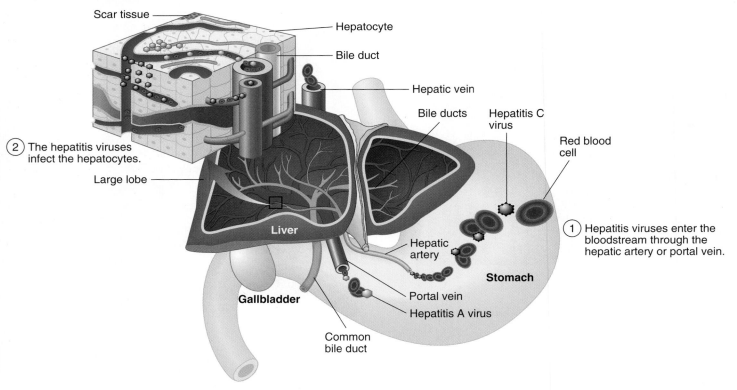

③ As the hepatitis viruses spread, the viral infection or the body's immune response to it, may cause damage to the liver such as scarring (cirrhosis). Damage impairs liver function and a rise in ALT levels in the bloodstream.

Scar tissue

Hepatocyte

Bile duct

Hepatic vein

Bile ducts

Hepatitis C virus

Red blood cell

② The hepatitis viruses infect the hepatocytes.

Large lobe

Liver

Hepatic artery

Stomach

① Hepatitis viruses enter the bloodstream through the hepatic artery or portal vein.

Gallbladder

Portal vein

Hepatitis A virus

Common bile duct

■ **Figure 17-9**
Hepatitis A and E viruses are ingested and gain entry into liver cells by way of the bloodstream via the hepatic artery or the portal vein. The portal vein carries blood containing digested food from the small intestine to the liver, thus facilitating the entry of hepatitis A virus into the liver. Bloodborne hepatitis viruses such as hepatitis C virus enter the liver via the hepatic artery. Adapted from the American Medical Association. *Complete Medical Encyclopedia*. Random House Reference, 2003.

■ Virus Replication

Hepatitis viruses enter the bloodstream and are carried to the liver, where they infect the **hepatocytes** of the liver. As the viruses spread and replicate in the liver, hepatocytes may become damaged. The damage may result in cirrhosis, impairing liver function (**Figure 17-9**). The liver has many functions, such as playing a role in metabolism and the filtering of toxins and waste products in the blood. The liver produces **bile**, which aids in digestion.

The clinical importance of hepatitis F and G viruses and TTV is uncertain and poorly understood; thus the remainder of this chapter will summarize the life cycles of hepatitis viruses A–E.

Hepatitis A Virus

Hepatitis A virus is a very stable, naked picornavirus that contains a +ssRNA genome that is 7.5 kb in length. The viral genome contains a small protein, VPg, that is covalently linked to the 5′ end of the genome and a poly-(A) tail at the 3′ terminus of the genome. The 5′ terminus also contains a nontranslated region that contains **hairpins** and **pseudoknots**. The pseudoknots may function in the recognition of the genome by the viral RNA replicase. The hairpin secondary structures act as an **internal ribosome entry site** (IRES) that is necessary for cap-independent translation of the viral RNA (**Figure 17-10a**).

(a)

(b)

■ **Figure 17-10**

(a) Secondary structure of the 5′ noncoding region of hepatitis A virus genome. The pseudoknots are involved in the recognition of the viral RNA-dependent RNA polymerase or replicase, whereas the internal ribosome entry site allows for cap-independent translation of the viral mRNA transcripts into a polyprotein product. The function of the polypyrimidine tract is unknown. Adapted from Thomas, H. C., Lemon, S., and Zuckerman, A. J. *Viral Hepatitis,* Third Edition. Blackwell Publishing, 2005. (b) Organization of the hepatitis A virus genome. Genes are listed within the genome and the gene product names are listed above the genes. The genome is translated into a large polyprotein that is processed by the viral 3C protease into three distinct precursors that are proteolytically processed to yield smaller precursors and mature viral proteins, etc. Adapted from Thomas, H. C., Lemon, S., and Zuckerman, A. J. *Viral Hepatitis,* Third Edition. Blackwell Publishing, 2005.

Hepatitis A viruses bind receptors located on the outside of hepatocytes. A candidate cellular receptor that interacts with the virus particle has been identified. It is a mucin-like glycoprotein referred to as the **hepatitis A virus cellular receptor 1** (huHAVcr-1). After entry, the virus particles undergo penetration and uncoating with the release of viral RNA into the cytoplasm of the cell. The +ssRNA viral genome acts directly as an mRNA for the synthesis of a large polyprotein. The polyprotein is processed by a viral 3C protease into structural and nonstructural proteins of the virus. A viral RNA dependent RNA polymerase encoded by 3D synthesizes new −ssRNA intermediates that are used to create new progeny genomic +ssRNAs that will be packaged into new virus particles. Newly assembled particles are transported to the surface of hepatocytes and exported (Figure 17-10b).

Hepatitis B virus

Dr. Baruch Blumberg and colleagues began characterizing and comparing serum proteins from **hemophiliacs** and nonhemophiliacs in the 1950s. They collected blood samples from native populations in remote parts of the world with the goal of learning about the genetics of disease susceptibility. They reasoned that hemophiliacs who received multiple blood transfusions would be exposed to serum proteins they had not inherited genetically but instead may have "inherited" from their donors. As a result, the hemophiliacs would produce antibodies against the inherited donor proteins. In 1963, Blumberg's team discovered an antibody present in the serum of a New York hemophiliac that reacted with an antigen present in the blood of an Australian aborigine infected with hepatitis. Later, they determined that the new unknown **Australia antigen** was **hepatitis B surface antigen (HBsAg)**. Further experiments by British virologist David M.S. Dane led to the discovery of the complete hepatitis B virus known as the **Dane particle**, which is now recognized as the agent responsible for serum hepatitis.

Through research and clinical observations, it is known that three types of virus-associated particles are present in the blood of individuals suffering from hepatitis B. The most abundant hepatitis B-like particle present in highly viremic carriers of hepatitis B virus is a spherical particle that is approximately 17 to 25 nm in diameter. These particles appear as small vesicles that contain **small HBsAg proteins** (**Figure 17-11**). Less numerous are filamentous particles that are approximately 17 to 20 nm in diameter and up to 200 nm in length (Figure 17-11). The filamentous particles contain small, **medium**, and **large HBsAg proteins** and are not infectious. The large amounts of free HBsAg present in the serum of hepatitis patients correlates with viremia and in many cases indicate chronic infection.

Dane particles are infectious. These enveloped particles measure 42 nm in diameter and contain small, medium, and large HBsAg proteins. In addition to the HBsAg proteins, a DNA-based core that is 27 nm in diameter is located within the virus particle (Figure 17-11). The core that surrounds the DNA genome contains two proteins: HBcAg and HBeAg. Most of HBeAg is secreted and not actually incorpo-

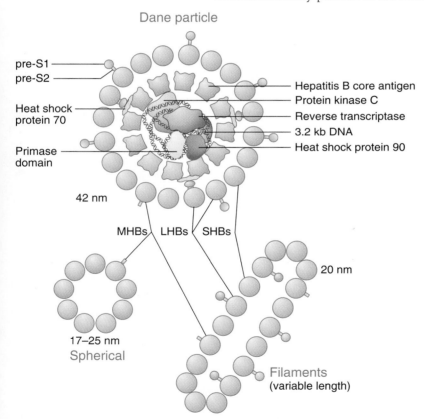

■ **Figure 17-11**

Structure of hepatitis B virus particles. Only the Dane particle is infectious. Classic HBsAg, which contains the S domain only, is also called the S-protein. Two other proteins share the C-terminal S domain but differ by length and structure of their N-terminal (pre-S) extensions. The large L protein contains the pre-S1, the pre-S2 region, and the S region, whereas the medium M protein contains the pre-S2 and the S region only. HBsAg is the most abundant of the S-related antigens. The L and M proteins are expressed at levels of about 5% to 15% and 1% to 2% compared with S protein. Adapted from Thomas, H. C., Lemon, S., and Zuckerman, A. J. *Viral Hepatitis*, Third Edition. Blackwell Publishing, 2005.

rated into the particle. The viral DNA polymerase (reverse transcriptase) protein kinase C and heat shock protein 90 are associated with the genome within the core of the particle. Hepatitis B viruses are amazingly stable in the environment. They are resistant to organic solvents, heat, and pH changes. Hepatitis B viruses present in blood can withstand drying on a surface for at least a week.

Hepatitis B virus is a **hepadnavirus** (*hepa* from hepatotropic and *dna* from their DNA genome). The circular genome of hepatitis B virus is composed of partially double-stranded DNA. The completed full-length strand is approximately 3.2 kb in length and the shorter strand is approximately 1.7 kb in length (**Figure 17-12**). One of the molecular biology hallmarks of hepadnaviruses is that they use a replication strategy common to retroviruses: they replicate through an RNA intermediate, sometimes referred to as a pregenomic RNA by **reverse transcription**.

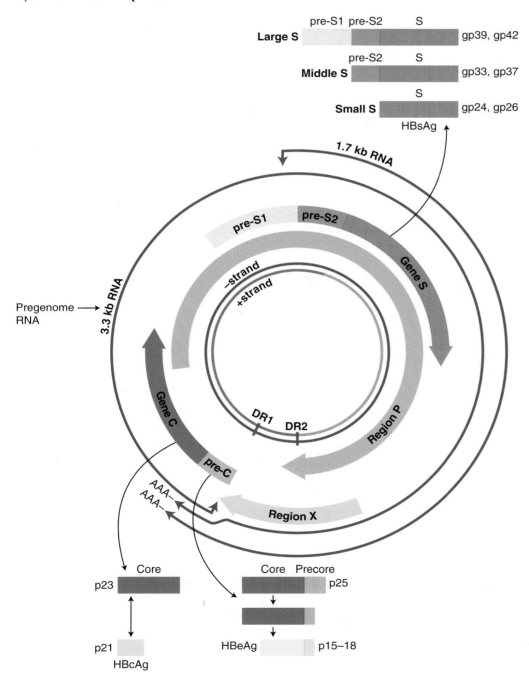

■ **Figure 17-12**
Genomic organization of the hepatitis B virus. Adapted from J. Cohen and W. G. Powderly. *Infectious Diseases,* Second Edition. Mosby, 2003.

TABLE 17-4	Hepatitis B Virus ORFs and Their Gene Products

ORF	Gene Products
1 (S)	Large, middle, and small hepatitis B surface (envelope) antigens (HBsAg)
2 (C)	Hepatitis B secreted precore antigen (HBeAg) and hepatitis B core (capsid) antigen (HBcAg)
3 (P)	Viral polymerase (DNA-dependent DNA polymerase, reverse transcriptase, with RNase H activity)
4 (X)	Transcriptional transactivating protein kinase

The host cell receptor used for the attachment and entry of hepatitis B viruses into hepatocytes is unknown. A few potential receptors have been shown to interact with HBsAg, such as the transferrin receptor, human liver endonexin, and the asialoglycoprotein receptor molecule, but there is no convincing evidence of their connection to infectivity. Hepatitis B viruses replicate poorly in cell cultures, making it difficult to fully understand the early steps of viral infection. After fusion and entry with the host cell, the viral cores are released into the cytoplasm where the genome uncoats and enters the nucleus through the nuclear pores.

In the nucleus, host enzymes ligate the ends of the genome. DNA synthesis is completed and gaps in both DNA strands are repaired, resulting in a completed covalently closed circular plasmid-like DNA molecule called an **episome**. The episome replicates independently of the host chromosome in contrast to being integrated into the cellular DNA, as is the case with retroviruses. This is because hepatitis B viruses *do not* possess integrase activity.

The episome acts as a template for two classes of viral transcripts: viral **pregenomic** RNA transcripts and **genomic** RNAs that are transcribed by the host's RNA polymerase II. Hepatitis B virus DNA has a very compact coding organization with four partially overlapping open reading frames (ORFs) that are translated into seven known proteins (Figure 17-12). There are at least four promoters, two enhancers, and several binding sites recognized by transcription factors identified in the hepatitis B virus genome. Noncoding regions are not present on the genome. Table 17-4 lists the ORFs and their gene products.

The full-length, pregenomic +ssRNA is synthesized and complexed with the viral polymerase and protein kinase C protein into core particles. Host-cell heat shock proteins associate with the viral reverse transcriptase, allowing it to fold into an active conformation. The active viral reverse transcriptase converts this pregenomic RNA into DNA *inside* the particles. Unlike retroviruses, the HBV reverse transcriptase activity occurs by **protein-priming** as opposed to RNA-priming. Precise replication can only occur in the specialized environment of the intact nucleocapsids.

The nucleocapsid cores reach the endoplasmic reticulum (ER), where they associate with the viral surface glycoproteins and bud into the lumen of the ER and/or the Golgi apparatus out of the cell (**Figure 17-13**). Empty envelopes containing viral surface proteins embedded in the host cell's lipid bilayer are continually being shed along with mature, infectious particles.

Coinfection of Hepatitis B Virus and Hepatitis D Virus. As described earlier, hepatitis D virus is a defective virus that requires the presence of hepatitis B "helper" virus to replicate. Hepatitis D virus is frequently associated with severe acute or chronic hepatitis. A hepatitis D virus infection can occur as a coinfection at the time of a hepatitis B virus infection or as a **superinfection** in individuals who are carriers of hepatitis B virus. In the latter scenario, a superinfection is defined as a hepatitis D virus infection following a previous infection by hepatitis B virus. Hepatitis D virus probably makes use of the same cellular receptor as hepatitis B virus in order to attach to and enter hepatocytes.

Hepatitis D virus is a spherical particle that is approximately 36 nm in diameter. The surface or outer coat of the virus consists of a lipid bilayer that contains small, medium, and large HBsAgs and which envelopes the −ssRNA circular genome and the delta antigen. Hepatitis D virus can only form infectious particles in a cell coinfected with hepatitis B virus because hepatitis B virus provides the HBsAg that is required for reinfection into another cell. Once inside the cell, hepatitis D virus can replicate in the absence of hepatitis B virus.

The genome is 1.7 kb in length, which is similar to plant viral satellites and viroids (see Chapter 19). It codes for two different types of the same protein (the **delta antigen**) that

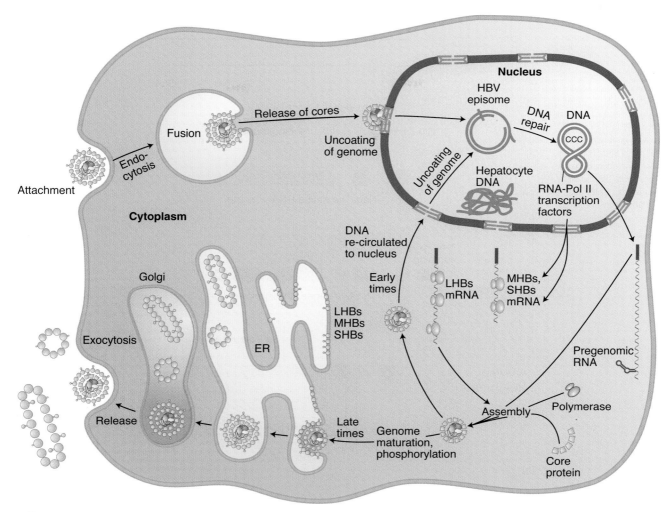

■ Figure 17-13

Life cycle of hepatitis B virus. The HBeAg and HBxAg synthesis are omitted for the sake of simplicity. HBsAg proteins are inserted into the host's endoplasmic reticulum membrane. Adapted from Thomas, H. C., Lemon, S., and Zuckerman, A. J. *Viral Hepatitis,* Third Edition. Blackwell Publishing, 2005.

are 195 or 214 amino acids in length. About 70 molecules of delta antigen surround and stabilize the viral RNA genome. The large delta antigen contains four different functional domains: an RNA binding domain, a nuclear localization signal, a virus assembly signal, and a coiled-coil sequence that is responsible for oligomerization of the protein. The delta antigen can form either a homo- or heterodimer. The small form of the delta antigen is required for hepatitis D virus RNA replication, whereas the large form is required for the suppression of hepatitis D virus RNA replication and the assembly and export of virion particles. The small delta antigen is missing the virus assembly signal (**Figure 17-14a**).

The genome has a high degree of intramolecular base-pairing, giving it a double-stranded property similar to that found in plant viroids under natural conditions. When the envelope of the virus is removed inside of an infected cell, the viral genome is targeted to the nucleus. Unlike most RNA viruses, though, it does not encode its own RNA-dependent RNA polymerase for genome replication. Instead, it is dependent upon the cellular RNA polymerase II and other host factors to replicate its genome. The hepatitis D virus genomic RNA is a **ribozyme** that cleaves itself, and ribozyme activity is necessary for hepatitis D virus replication. HDV genome replication is believed to occur via a **rolling circle mechanism** similar to that of viroids (see Chapter 19). Figure 17-14b shows the structure of hepatitis D virus RNAs, and a model for the hepatitis D virus replication

■ **Figure 17-14**
(a) Hepatitis D virus functional domains of the small and large forms of the delta antigen. RBD = RNA-binding domain, CCS = coiled-coil sequence, NLS = nuclear lo-calization sequence, VAS = virus assembly signal. Adapted from Thomas, H. C., Lemon, S., and Zuckerman, A. J. *Viral Hepatitis*, Third Edition. Blackwell Publishing, 2005. (b) Structure of hepatitis D virus RNAs. Adapted from University of South Carolina, School of Medicine. "Virology: Hepatitis Viruses." *Microbiology and Immunology.* University of South Carolina, 2008. http://pathmicro.med.sc.edu/virol/hepatitis-virus.htm.

cycle is shown in **Figure 17-15**. The hepatitis D RNA –sense (negative-sense) genome acts as a template for synthesis of antigenomic RNA (+sense, or positive-sense) and the vi-ral mRNAs. The antigenomic RNA multimers are self-cleaved (step 2 in Figure 17-15) and recirculaize, serving as a template for multimers of genomic RNAs, which are self-cleaved and circularized (step 4 in the figure). The single mRNA transcribed from the viral genome exits the nucleus to produce the small and large forms of the delta anti-gen (step 7 in the figure). The ribonucleoprotein complexes (RNPs) assemble and are exported to the ER located in the cytoplasm of the cell, where they associate with the HBsAgs (steps 8 and 9 in the figure). The HBsAgs are required for the packaging of the hepatitis D virions. Mature hepatitis D viruses are produced and secreted outside of the cell.

Hepatitis C Virus

Hepatitis C virus is an icosahedral-shaped, enveloped +ssRNA flavivirus that causes hepatitis non-A, non-B. Little is known about the ultrastructure of hepatitis C virus be-cause it has been extremely difficult to visualize the virus particles directly from infected serum and tissues. The hypothetical structure of hepatitis C virus is shown in **Figure 17-16**. It is the only flavivirus that is not transmitted by arthropod vectors (e.g., mosquitoes). Yellow fever virus is the prototype of viruses in the *Flaviviridae* family. Hepatitis C viruses are also similar to picornaviruses (e.g., poliovirus), with the main exception that they are enveloped. Since the cloning of the viral nucleic acid in 1989, considerable progress has been made in characterizing the virus genome and proteins.

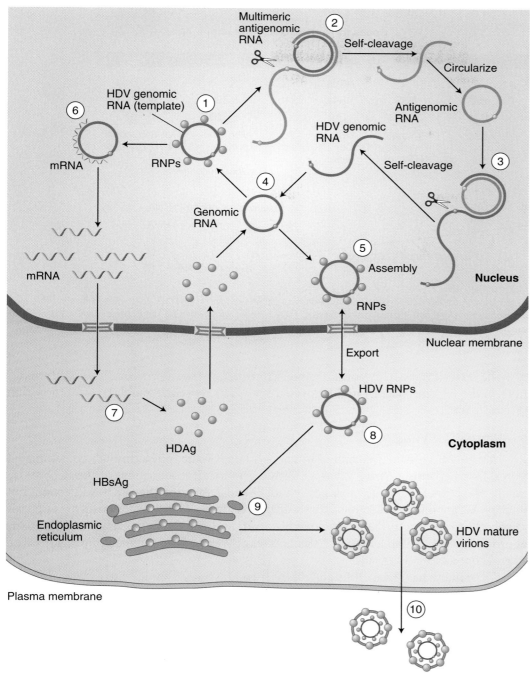

■ **Figure 17-15**
Proposed model for hepatitis D virus life cycle. Adapted from Cunha, C., Freitas, N., Mota, S., "Developments in Hepatitis Delta Research," *The Internet Journal in Tropical Medicine* 1 (2003).

The hepatitis C virus genome is about 9.2 kb in length and contains an IRES and one long ORF that encodes a polyprotein precursor. The viral RNA is translated by host ribosomes by cap-independent translation. The polyprotein precursor is cleaved into structural and nonstructural proteins by cellular and viral proteases. Hepatitis C virus NS5b gene encodes its own RNA-dependent RNA polymerase. There is substantial sequence variation in the hepatitis C virus genome because NS5b lacks proofreading capability.

A better understanding of the viral life cycle, especially the entry process into host cells is needed. Viral entry requires clathrin and more than one receptor. CD81, an integral membrane protein belonging to a family of **tetraspanins**, scavenger receptor class B type 1 (SR-B1) and claudin-1 have recently been identified as co-receptors based on their interaction with hepatitis C viral structural E2 or E1 proteins.

■ **Figure 17-16**

Hypothetical structure of the hepatitis C virus. Nonstructural proteins are labeled "NS" followed by a number. They have diverse functions and form the replication complex. There is no known function for the p7 protein and it has not been classified as structural or nonstructural. Adapted from P. Roingeard, *Biol. Cell* 96 (2004): 103–108.

The lack of patient response to interferon therapy has been correlated with muta-tions in the E2 gene. The E1 and E2 proteins presumably self-assemble to form the virion (Figure 17-16).

Hepatitis E Virus

Hepatitis E virus is transmitted by the fecal–oral route, often through contaminated water. Like hepatitis A virus, it has a +ssRNA genome. It is a member of the *Hepeviridae* family. Hepatitis E infection is clinically indistinguishable from hepatitis A infection, but its particles are much less stable than those of hepatitis A. Hepatitis E viruses are approxi-mately 32 to 34 nm in diameter, nonenveloped, and icosahedral-shaped. Its genome is approximately 7.2 kb in length and contains short 5′- and 3′-end noncoding regions. The 3′ end contains a poly (A) tail.

The genome has three ORFs and all three coding frames are used to express different proteins. ORF1 codes for nonstructural proteins that possess methyltransferase, protease, RNA helicase, and RNA-dependent RNA polymerase (replicase) motifs. ORF2 does not overlap with ORF1 and is located at the 3′ end of the genome and presumably codes for the only capsid (structural) protein. ORF3 begins at the end of ORF1. It overlaps with ORF2 and codes for a small phosphoprotein of undefined function (**Figure 17-17**). Presumably hepatitis E virus replicates solely in the cytoplasm of the cell. Overall, our knowledge of hepatitis E virus replication is poor. The lack of a suitable cell culture system to propagate the virus is an obstacle in deciphering its molecular biology.

17.8 A Quick Note about the Pathophysiology of Chronic Hepatitis Virus Infections

The biggest difference between enveloped and naked hepatitis viruses is that the enveloped viruses (hepatitises B, C, D, and G) cause persistent and chronic infections. These viruses have devised a strategy to escape detection and elimination following natural infection and thus can hide from the host's immune system. For example, reports have described

■ Figure 17-17
Genome organization of hepatitis E virus. Three ORFs encode the viral proteins: ORF1 (a nonstructural, replicative polyprotein), ORF2 (a capsid protein), and ORF3 (unknown function). Adapted from S. Jameel, *Expert Rev. Mol. Med.* 6 (1999): 1–16.

reactivation of hepatitis B virus after liver transplantation with donor livers from hepatitis B virus-immune individuals. In other words, hepatitis B virus DNA was recovered from "immune" patients and donors. This suggests that hepatitis B virus may exist in the hepatocytes in a latent form for a long time. It has been shown that hepatotropic viral clearance is associated with a strong virus-specific cytotoxic T cell and T helper cell response. Antibody-mediated responses have been inadequate in clearing the infection.

Evidence is accumulating that the liver damage caused by hepatitis B and C viruses during the course of infection may result from the **autoimmune reaction** directed against hepatocyte membrane antigens that is initiated by viral infection. Damage to the liver is mediated by inflammatory cytokines, which are small proteins that communicate between cells and may play a role in the liver. They play an important role in the defense against viral infections. Both hepatitis B and C viruses may have the capacity to modulate cytokine gene expression and responses. The chronic infections caused by these viruses may result in an ongoing inflammatory response that activates the process of liver fibrosis. More studies are needed to develop strategies useful in combating the effects of hepatitis B and C infections on the liver.

17.9 Genetic Diversity among the Hepatitis Viruses

There is only one known **serotype** of hepatitis A viruses but there are at least seven different **genotypes** worldwide. Individuals who are infected by hepatitis A virus in one part of the world are not susceptible to reinfection by a different hepatitis A virus genotype in another part of the world. Immune globulin and vaccine prepared in a variety of countries protect travelers from hepatitis A irrespective of their destination.

The majority of hepatitis E virus genomic isolates have only been partially sequenced. Based on what genomic sequence is available, there are four major genotypes. Hepatitis E viral genomes are present in sewage from pig slaughterhouses. This suggests that they are widespread in the general swine population. There are reports of hepatitis E virus antibodies among farmers working in close contact with pigs, raising the possibility that pig hepatitis E viruses could infect humans.

A common theme between the chronic hepatitis B and C viruses is that they synthesize many **variants** during the course of infection. Individuals with chronic hepatitis B or C infection produce 10^{10} to 10^{11} virus particles daily, which indicates that the viruses are actively replicating. This high replication activity by the viral RNA-dependent RNA polymerases that lack proofreading function explains, in part, the rapid emergence of viral variants. It also may explain the frequent immune escape phenomena. Mutations in the hepatitis B virus promoter of the core gene or in the precore region of the core gene are frequently found in patients with chronic hepatitis B infection.

17.10 Management and Prevention of Hepatitis A–E Viruses

■ Hepatitis A

No specific treatment for hepatitis A infections is available and management is supportive. Spread of hepatitis A infections can be reduced by handwashing and proper sanitary disposal of human feces. Prevention by passive immunization of individuals who likely had been exposed to or in close contact with a person with hepatitis A is achieved by intramuscular injection of human immunoglobulin that contains hepatitis A antibodies. In general, if administered before exposure or within two weeks after exposure, immunoglobulin is 85% effective in preventing hepatitis A.

Hepatitis A vaccines were developed in a manner similar for that of poliovirus vaccines. Formalin-inactivated, cell culture-produced whole-virus vaccines such as Havrix, Vaqta, and Avaxim are now approved in much of the world. The viruses are propagated in MRC-5 cells (a line of human lung fibroblast cells). Injections are typically administered at 0, 6, and 12 months in individuals who are 2 years of age or older. (In the United States the vaccine is not licensed for children under the age of 1.) In addition to high-risk persons, those who travel to or work in countries with a high prevalence of hepatitis A (e.g., Mexico, Central or South America, Asia, Africa, and Eastern Europe) should be vaccinated. Live attenuated vaccines (like the Sabin-type of oral vaccine) have been developed and tested in animals and humans but are not yet available, as they have not been able to induce a satisfactory immune response when administered orally.

■ Hepatitis B

The basic aim of treating hepatitis B patients is to stop viral replication and prevent end-stage liver disease. There are three licensed drug therapies used against hepatitis B infections: **interferon α-2b**, **lamivudine**, and **adefovir dipivoxil** therapy. Interferon is an **immune modulator** and is administered as an injection. About 46% of patients respond to interferon α-2b (Intron A) in the first year of treatment. (A response is the cessation of viral replication.) There are three drawbacks to interferon α-2b treatment: it has a large number of side effects (see Chapter 7), is expensive, and is not effective in a high percentage of patients.

Lamivudine (Epivir) and adefovir dipivoxil (Hepsera) are nucleoside analogs that are potent inhibitors of DNA replication. Lamivudine was approved for treatment in 1999 and was first used to treat HIV patients, its mechanism of action being the inhibition of reverse transcriptase. Advantages of lamivudine are that it has few side effects compared to interferon α-2b and has been shown to dramatically inhibit hepatitis B virus DNA replication. The disadvantage is that replication rapidly returns when therapy is stopped. Lamivudine-resistant strains of hepatitis B virus develop at a rate of 15% to 20% per year of therapy.

Adefovir dipivoxil therapy has been used since 2002 as a first-line monotherapy, combination therapy, or a therapy in patients who have lamivudine-resistant infections. It can be administered orally and patients tolerate it well.

Antibodies against HBsAg protect individuals from acute and chronic hepatitis B infection if used shortly after exposure to hepatitis B virus. Today immune-globulin is used as an adjunct to hepatitis B vaccine in preventing hepatitis B virus transmission from an infected mother to fetus. If untreated, 70% to 90% of infants born to HBeAg-positive mothers become infected at birth and develop a chronic hepatitis B infection. Hepatitis B immuneglobulin is also used for postexposure prophylaxis after accidental needlestick or other medical-related injuries in persons who work with infectious body fluids that contain HBsAg.

Early **hepatitis B vaccines** were prepared by harvesting the 17 to 25 nm particles from the plasma of chronically infected individuals. The particles were purified and inactivated by heat, formaldehyde, urea, or pepsin. These **plasma-derived vaccines** have been available since 1982. Subsequently, vaccine manufacturers used genetic engineering to express HBsAg in yeast (*Saccharomyces cerevisiae*) and mammalian cells. This led to the development of **recombinant DNA vaccines**.

Recombinant DNA vaccines were produced by inserting the S gene that codes for the HBsAg into a DNA plasmid. The plasmids were then transformed into yeast or transfected into mammalian cells. The HBsAg was expressed and purified by chromatography and filtration (**Figure 17-18**). Under these conditions, purified HBsAg self-assembles into the spherical particles closely resembling the 17 to 25 nm particles found in the serum of people with chronic hepatitis. This vaccine is not an infectious particle, making this a very safe vaccine.

The CDC recommends that all newborns receive a birth dose of hepatitis B vaccine before leaving the hospital unless a physician provides a written order to defer the birth dose. The CDC also recommends that all children age 19 and younger receive the vaccine series. Hepatitis B can cause liver cancer; thus an added benefit of the vaccine is that it prevents hepatitis B-related liver cancer. (This vaccine was the first to prevent a cancer.) From 1990 to 2002 the incidence of hepatitis B decreased 67% in the United States. Hepatitis B vaccination programs have been implemented with considerable success. Unfortunately, the recombinant hepatitis B vaccine is expensive to purchase, which restricts its availability in developing nations. For this reason, oral hepatitis B vaccine candidates are being produced and delivered in plants such as potatoes and soybeans. A number of candidates are suitable for early stage clinical trials.

■ Hepatitis C

Hepatitis C infections progress to liver disease in up to 85% of patients. There are no vaccines available to prevent hepatitis C infection. The therapies available for treatment are: **pegylated interferon α-2a** or **pegylated interferon α-2b** and/or **ribavirin**.

Pegylation involves the attachment of a polyethylene glycol molecule to the active interferon molecule. Interferon is a glycoprotein produced by the body as part of the immune system response toward viral infection (see Chapter 7). Hence interferon treatment may prevent hepatitis C virus replication and the production of new viral particles in infected individuals. Response to therapy is measured by determining the levels of serum transaminases and the detection of hepatitis C virus RNA in serum. About 20% of

■ Figure 17-18
Flowchart showing the steps involved in preparing a recombinant DNA hepatitis B vaccine in yeast. Adapted from Marks, D. B., Marks, A. D., and C. M. Smith. *Basic Medical Biochemistry: A Clinical Approach.* Lippincott Williams & Wilkins, 1996.

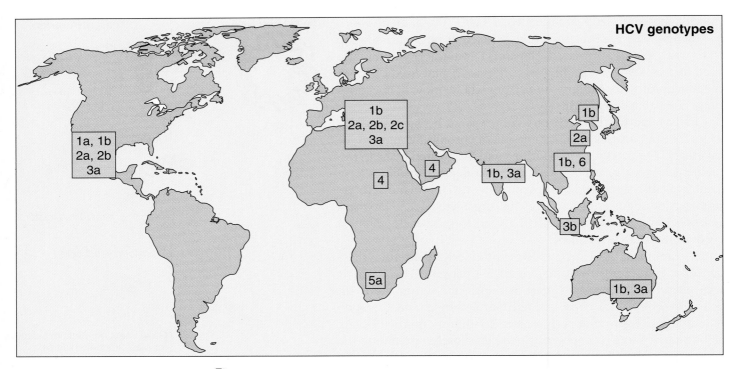

Figure 17-19
Hepatitis C virus genotype geographic distribution. Reproduced from *Clin. Liver Dis.,* vol. 1, Fang, J. W. S., Chow, V., and J. Y. N. Lau, *Virology of Hepatitis C Virus*, pp. 493–514, Copyright 1997, with permission from Elsevier.

individuals experience a sustained reduction in serum transaminases or hepatitis C virus RNA levels after stopping therapy.

Ribavirin is an oral nucleoside analog that inhibits replication of a number of viruses. A combination of ribavirin/pegylated interferon α-2b treatment over a 6- to 12-month period has increased overall cure rates from 20% to 35%–40%. This therapy is challenging because of the side effects caused by interferon and ribavirin. Ribavirin is **teratogenic** (i.e., it interferes with normal embryonic development) and therefore cannot be taken by patients who are pregnant. Patients with genotypes 2 or 3 respond better to this combination treatment than those with genotypes 1 and 4. (Genotype refers to the genetic make-up of the virus.) Like other RNA viruses, hepatitis C has a high mutation rate, resulting in genetic diversity. There are six main genotypes of hepatitis C virus. Recently new variants, assigned as types 7–11, have been recognized. Genotypes are further broken down into subtypes designated by a lowercase letter. For example, there are three subtypes of hepatitis C type 1 viruses, which are designated 1a, 1b, and 1c. There are general global patterns of genotypes. Genotype 1, 2, and 3 are the most common genotypes seen in the United States. (**Figure 17-19**). Patients need to be monitored closely for complications or symptoms of adverse reactions of combination therapy.

■ Hepatitis D

Hepatitis D infections are maintained by reducing hepatitis B virus replication (e.g., interferon α-2b, lamivudine, and adefovir dipivoxil therapy). There is no immunoglobulin or vaccine available against hepatitis D virus.

■ Hepatitis E

There is no immunoglobulin available for pre- or postexposure prophylaxis. Hepatitis E infections are usually self-limited and hospitalization is generally not required. Prevention is the most effective approach against the disease and treatment is supportive. There is no vaccine available against hepatitis E virus.

 ## Summary

Viral hepatitis is a major global health problem and the clinical significance and economic costs of it have made it one of the most important of all infectious diseases. Epidemics of infectious and serum hepatitis have been recorded throughout history, especially during times of war. **Infectious hepatitis** is caused by the fecal–oral mode of transmission, whereas **serum hepatitis** is an infection of the liver caused by a bloodborne virus. In general, the signs and symptoms of hepatitis are:

- fatigue
- abdominal pain
- loss of appetite
- nausea and vomiting
- dark urine
- jaundice

Viral hepatitis occurs endemically in all parts of the world. Epidemics of enterically transmitted hepatitis often occur in countries in Asia and Africa where sanitation is suboptimal. The nomenclature of hepatitis viruses is based on the order of discovery of new agents that cause hepatitis rather than modes of transmission or clinical problems associated with that viral agent. The hepatitis viruses belong to five different families. There are eight hepatitis viruses: hepatitises A–G and TTV. Five of eight hepatotropic viruses (hepatitis viruses A–E) account for 90% of viral hepatitis cases and are well characterized. There are still other hepatitis viruses awaiting discovery, but it appears that other non-A–E viruses play a minor role in pathogenicity.

Hepatitis viruses enter the bloodstream and are carried to the liver where they infect the hepatocytes of the liver. As the viruses spread and replicate in the liver, hepatocytes may become damaged. The damage may result in cirrhosis, which is an impairing of liver function. The liver has many functions, such as playing a role in metabolism and the filtering of toxins and waste products in the blood. It produces bile, which aids in digestion. The biggest difference between enveloped and naked hepatitis viruses is that enveloped viruses (hepatitises B, C, D, and G) cause persistent and chronic infections. These viruses have devised a strategy to escape detection and elimination following natural infection and can hide from the host's immune system. In contrast, hepatitis A and E viruses are both self-limited, fecally spread diseases.

Proper sanitation practices are the best way to prevent outbreaks of hepatitis A and E viruses. Once an individual is infected treatment is supportive. Passive immunization and a vaccine are available for hepatitis A virus.

Hepatitis B and C viruses are well-recognized causes of chronic hepatitis, cirrhosis, and hepatocellular carcinoma and are capable of triggering autoimmune reactions. Treatments for these two viruses consist of two classes of drugs: immune modulators (such as interferon) and nucleoside analogs that block viral RNA or DNA replication. The side effects of these drugs make it a challenging therapy for patients.

DNA technology has made the development and production of a safe hepatitis B vaccine possible. It is the first anticancer vaccine because it prevents hepatitis B and thus hepatocellular carcinoma. Infant vaccination against hepatitis B virus is having a huge impact on carrier rates of hepatitis B in adolescents and young adults. Only modest progress has been made toward the development of a hepatitis C vaccine.

Resources

Reviews and Primary Literature

Abraham, P. 2005. "TT viruses: How much do we know?" *Indian J Med Res* 122:7–10.

Andenaes, S., Lie, A., and Degre, M. 2000. "Prevalence of Hepatitis A, B, C, and E Antibody in Flying Airline Personnel." *Aviat Space Environ Med* 71(12):1178–1180.

Beck, J., and Nassal, M. 2007. "Hepatitis B Replication." *World J Gasteroenterol* 13(1):48–64.

Bereket-Yucel, S. 2007. "Risk of Hepatitis B Infections in Olympic Wrestling." *Br J Sports Med.* doi:10.1136/bjsm.2006.032847.

Bill, C. A., and Summers, J. 2004. "Genomic DNA Double-Strand Breaks Are Targets for Hepadnaviral DNA Integration." *PNAS USA* 101(30):11135–11140.

Bourliere, M. et al. 2000. "Covert Transmission of Hepatitis C Virus During Bloody Fisticuffs." *Gastroenterology* 119(2)507–511.

Briggs, M. E. et al. 2001. "Prevalence and Risk Factors for Hepatitis C Virus Infection at an Urban Veterans Administration Medical Center." *Hepatology* 34(6):1200–1205.

Bukh, J., and Purcell, R. H. 2006. "A Milestone for Hepatitis C Research: A Virus Generated in Cell Culture Is Fully Viable *in vivo*." *PNAS USA* 103(10):3500–3501.

CDC. 2005. "A Comprehensive Immunization Strategy to Eliminate Transmission of Hepatitis B Virus Infection in the United States." *MMWR* 54(RR16):1–23.

Chau, T. N. et al. 2006. "Epidemiology and Clinical Features of Sporadic Hepatitis E as Compared with Hepatitis A." *Am J Gastroenterol* 101(2):292–296.

Cheung, R. C. 2000. "Epidemiology of Hepatitis C Virus Infection in American Veterans." *Am J Gastroenterol* 95(3):740–747.

Cheung, R. C. et al. 1997. "Hepatitis G Virus Is it a Hepatitis Virus?" *West J Med* 167(1):23–33.

Choo, Q. L. et al. 1989. "Isolation of a cDNA Clone Derived from a Blood-Borne Non-A, Non-B Viral Hepatitis Genome." *Science* 244(4902):359–362.

Cormier, E. G. et al. 2004. "CD81 Is an Entry Coreceptor for Hepatitis C Virus." *PNAS USA* 101(19):7270–7274.

Deka, N., Sharma, M. D., and Mukerjee, R. 1994. "Isolation of the Novel Agent from Human Stool Samples That Is Associated with Sporadic Non-A, Non-B Hepatitis." *J Virol* 68(12):7810–7815.

Dooley, D. P. 2005. "History of U.S. Military Contributions to the Study of Viral Hepatitis." *Mil Sci* 170(4):71–76.

Evans, M. J. et al. 2007. "Claudin-1 Is a Hepatitis C Virus Co-Receptor Required for a Late Step in Entry." *Nature* 446:801–805.

Fang, J., Chow, V., and Law, J. 1997. "HCV Infection: Worldwide Genotype Distribution." *Clin Liver Dis* 1:503.

Freeman, G. 1946. "Epidemiology and Incubation Period of Jaundice Following Yellow Fever Vaccinations." *Am J Trop Med* 26:15–32.

Green, R. C. 1987. "The Epidemics That Delayed D-Day." *Nurs RSA* 2:24–25.

Guha, C. et al. 2005. "Cell Culture Models and Animal Models of Viral Hepatitis. Part II: Hepatitis C." *Lab Anim* 34(2):39–47.

Hilleman, M. R. et al. 1983. "The Preparation and Safety of Hepatitis B Vaccine." *J Infect* 7(Suppl 1):3–8.

Hollinger, F. B. 1998. "Overview of Viral Hepatitis." *Circumpolar Health* 96:276–279.

Hyams, K. C. et al. 2001. "Prevalence and Incidence of Hepatitis C Virus Infection in the U.S. Military: A Seroepidemiologic Survey of 21,000 Troops." *Am J Epidem* 153(8):764–770.

Huang, Z. et al. 2005. "Virus-Like Particle Expression and Assembly in Plants: Hepatitis B and Norwalk Viruses." *Vaccine* 23(15):1851–1858.

Kobayashi, N. et al. 2003. "Clinical Significance of SEN Virus Infection in Patients on Maintenance Haemodialysis." *Nephrol Dial Transplant* 18:343–352.

Koutsoudakis, G. et al. 2006. "Characterization of the Early Steps of Hepatitis C Virus Infection by Using Luciferase Reporter Viruses." *Virol* 80(11):5308–5320.

Koziel, J. M. 1999. "Cytokines in Viral Hepatitis." *Semin Liver Dis* 19(2):157–169.

Lemon, S. M. et al. 1992. "Why Do Human Hepatitis Viruses Replicate So Poorly in Cell Cultures?" *FEMS Microbiol Lett* 79(1–3):455–459.

Lin, K. W., and Kirchner, J. T. 2004. "Hepatitis B." *Amer Fam Phys* 69(1):76–82.

Lindenbach, B. D. et al. 2005. "Complete Replication of Hepatitis C Virus in Cell Culture." *Science* 309:623–626.

Linnen, J. et al. 1996. "Molecular Cloning and Disease Association of Hepatitis G Virus: A Transfusion-Transmissible Agent." *Science* 271:505–508.

Matsuo, E. et al. 2006. "Characterization of HCV-Like Particles Produced in a Human Hepatoma Cell Line by a Recombinant Baculovirus." *Biochem Biophys Res Comm* 340(1):200–208.

Meng, X.-J. et al. 1997. "A Novel Virus in Swine Is Closely Related to the Human Hepatitis E Virus." *PNAS USA* 94:9860–9865.

Meng, X.-J. et al. 1998. "Genetic and Experimental Evidence for Cross-Species Infection by Swine Hepatitis E Virus." *J Virol* 72(12):9714–9721.

Nainan, O. V. et al. 2006. "Hepatitis C Virus Genotypes and Viral Concentrations in Participants of a General Population Survey in the United States." *Gastroenterology* 131(2):478–484.

Nishizawa, T. et al. 1997. "A Novel DNA Virus (TTV) Associated with Elevated Transaminase Levels in Post-Transfusion Hepatitis of Unknown Etiology." *Biochem Biophys Res Commun* 242:92–97.

Norman, J. E. et al. 1993. "Mortality Follow-Up of the 1942 Epidemic of Hepatitis B in the U.S. Army." *Hepatology* 18(4):790–797.

Panda, S. K., Thakral, D., and Rehman, S. 2007. "Hepatitis E Virus." *Rev Med Virol* 17(3):151–180.

ProMED-mail. 2007. "Hepatitis E, Porcine Carriers—United Kingdom (England)." *ProMED mail* 2007 18 Feb, 20070218.0615.

Roingeard, P. et al. 2004. "Hepatitis C Virus Ultrastructure and Morphogenesis." *Biol Cell* 96(2):103–108.

Roome, A. J et al. 2000. "Hepatitis C Virus Infection Among Firefighters, Emergency Medical Technicians, and Paramedics—Selected Locations, United States, 1991–2000." *MMWR* 49(29):660–665.

Roque-Afonso, A. M. et al. 2002. "Antibodies to Hepatitis B Surface Antigen Prevent Viral Reactivation in Recipients of Liver Grafts from Anti-HBC Positive Donors." *Gut* 50(1):95–99.

Sadler, G. J. et al. 2006. "UK Acquired Hepatitis E—Emerging Problem?" *J Med Virol* 78:473–475.

Sagir, A. et al. 2004. "SEN Virus Infection." *Rev Med Virol* 14(3):141–148.

Springfeld, C. et al. 2000. "TT Virus as a Human Pathogen: Significance and Problems." *Virus Genes* 20(1):35–45.

Streatfield, S. J. 2005. "Oral Hepatitis B Vaccine Candidates Produced and Delivered in Plant Material." *Immunol Cell Biol* 83(3):257–262.

Tavanez, J. P. et al. 2002. "Hepatitis Delta Virus Ribonucleoproteins Shuttle Between the Nucleus and the Cytoplasm." *RNA* 8:637–634.

Taylor, J. M. 2003. "Replication of Human Hepatitis Delta Virus: Recent Developments." *Trends Microbiol* 11(4):185–190.

Wakita, T. et al. 2005. "Production of Infectious Hepatitis C Virus in Tissue Culture from a Cloned Viral Genome." *Nat Med* 11:791–796.

Wim, H. M. et al. 2001. "Hepatitis E Virus Sequences in Swine Related to Sequences in Humans, the Netherlands." *EID* 7(6):970–976.

Zhong, J. et al. "Robust Hepatitis C Virus Infection *in vitro*." *PNAS USA* 102:9294–9299.

■ Popular Press

Blumberg, B. S. 2003. *Hepatitis B: The Hunt for a Killer Virus.* Princeton, NJ: Princeton University Press.

Pierce, J. R., and Writer, Jim. 2005. *Yellow Jack: How Yellow Fever Ravaged America and Walter Reed Discovered Its Deadly Secrets.* New York: John Wiley & Sons.

Sledge, E. B. 1981. "The Stench of Battle." In *Classics of Naval Literature: With the Old Breed at Peleliu and Okinawa.* Annapolis, MD: Naval Institute Press.

Tiollais, P., and Buendia, M.-A. 1991. "Hepatitis B virus." *Scientific American*, April, 1991, pp. 116–123.

Turkington, C. 1998. *Hepatitis C: The Silent Killer.* Columbus, OH: McGraw-Hill/Contemporary.

Wills, C. 1996. *Yellow Fever Black Goddess: The Coevolution of People and Plagues.* Reading, MA: Helix Books, Addison-Wesley.

■ Video Productions

Fighting Hepatitis C. 2001. Films for the Humanities & Sciences.

Blood and War. 2002. Films for the Humanities & Sciences.

New Blood. 2002. Films for the Humanities & Sciences.

Tainted Blood. 2002. Films for the Humanities & Sciences.

Old Foes, A New Threat. 2004. Films for the Humanities & Sciences.

Food-Borne Illness. 2006. Films for the Humanities & Sciences.

Understanding Hepatitis. 2006. Information Television Network.

Understanding Hepatitis: 3-part Series Covering Hepatitis A–C. 2007. Films for the Humanities & Sciences.

■ eLearning

http://biology.jbpub.com/book/virology
The site features eLearning, an online review area that provides quizzes and other tools to help you study for your class. You can also follow useful links for in-depth information, or just find out the latest virology and microbiology news.

CASE STUDY QUESTIONS

These questions relate to the Case Study presented at the beginning of the chapter.

1. What is the incubation period of hepatitis A?
2. What are the signs and symptoms of hepatitis A?
3. How did CDC epidemiologists eliminate restaurant workers as the cause of this outbreak?
4. How is hepatitis A virus transmitted? How is it prevented?
5. In this instance, would health officials recommend that consumers of green onions obtain postexposure prophylaxis? Why or why not?
6. Trace-back investigations determined that one or more farms in Mexico were the source of the green onions. Hypothesize how this fresh produce became contaminated. Be sure to address the cultivation and harvesting practices of fresh fruits and vegetables.
7. Compare and contrast hepatitis A and E infections.

■ References

CDC. 1999. "Prevention of Hepatitis A Through Active or Passive Immunization: Recommendations of the Advisory Committee on Immunization Practices (ACIP)." *MMWR* 48(RR12):1–37.

Dato, V. et al. 2003. "Hepatitis A outbreak associated with green onions at a restaurant—Monaca, Pennsylvania, 2003." *MMWR* 52(47):1155–1157.

Pugh, J. 2004. "Learning about Food Safety from Deadly Hepatitis A Virus Outbreak." *ASM News* 70(2):51–52.

US FDA/CFSAN. 1998. *Guide to Minimize Microbial Food Safety Hazards for Fresh Fruits and Vegetables.* Washington, DC.

Wasley, A., Fiore, A., Bell, B. P. 2006. "Hepatitis A in the Era of Vaccination." *Epidemiol Rev* 28:101–111.

Wheeler, C. et al. 2005. "An Outbreak of Hepatitis A Associated with Green Onions." *New Engl J Med* 353(9):890–897.

ADDITIONAL CASE STUDIES AND QUESTIONS

Additional Case Study 1

Bob Massie, a hemophiliac, was used to daily blood transfusions and frequent trips to the hospital. Despite his physical illness, he went on to earn degrees at Princeton University and Yale University's Divinity School and led an active and full life as an Episcopal priest, scholar, writer, and political activist.

At the beginning of his first semester at Yale in the fall of 1978 Massie fell ill with an undiagnosable illness that was so severe he withdrew from school and went home for the rest of the year. Years later, in 1984, he was diagnosed as being HIV-positive while participating in a hemophilia research study.

Massie had contracted HIV when receiving contaminated Factor VIII blood clotting factors. At the time of his diagnosis doctors told him that his life expectancy was 1–5 years. As the years passed, though, it was clear that Massie's case was unusual because his viral loads remained nearly undetectable. Scientists studied his immune response as they tried to determine why he was resistant to the effects of HIV infection. In 1999, PBS broadcasted a NOVA program called "Surviving AIDS" that featured Bob Massie. Massie had never shown any symptoms of AIDS and for years lived a full and vigorous life.

Unfortunatelly Bob Massie contracted another bloodborne pathogen, hepatitis C virus, which caused a chronic hepatitis infection. He likely contracted the infection when he received large-pool clotting factor from plasma donors during a time when it was not virucidally treated (the 1980s through the mid-1990s). Today he is on a waiting list for a liver transplant.

1. What virus(es) cause chronic hepatitis?
2. What are the symptoms of chronic hepatitis?
3. What diagnostic tests are used to detect viral hepatitis?
4. How is chronic hepatitis C managed?

■ References

Bob Massie, http://www.bobmassie.org/.

Surviving AIDS. 1999. NOVA. http://www.pbs.org/wgbh/nova/aids/.

Additional Case Study 2

Outbreaks of viral hepatitis E have been plaguing the African country of Chad in recent years. Villages in Chad have few roads and during the rainy season floodwaters create huge seasonal muddy rivers called **wadis**, making travel even more difficult. There are no boats or horses to help people cross wadis. People have to swim to cross them. There are overcrowded refugee camps in Chad that struggle to accommodate the stressed civilians. Clean drinking water and good hygiene practices are lacking.

1. How is hepatitis E virus transmitted? What is the likely hepatitis E virus contaminated source in Chad?

2. How is hepatitis E diagnosed?

3. How is hepatitis E treated? How is it prevented?

4. Outbreaks of hepatitis E in Hong Kong have been traced to contaminated shellfish. Why are shellfish a common reservoir of hepatitis A and E viruses? Explain your answer.

5. There is evidence that hepatitis E virus is a zoonosis. Hepatitis E virus has been isolated from what animal(s) and how would the virus be transmitted to humans?

■ References

ProMED archive number 20050822.2477. Published 22-August-2005. "Hepatitis E—Chad (Eastern)."

Chau, T. N. et al. 2006. "Epidemiology and Clinical Features of Sporadic Hepatitis E As Compared with Hepatitis A." *Am J Gastroent* 101(2):292–296.

Sadler, G. J. et al. 2006. "UK Acquired Hepatitis E—An Emerging Problem?" *J Med Virol* 78:473–475.

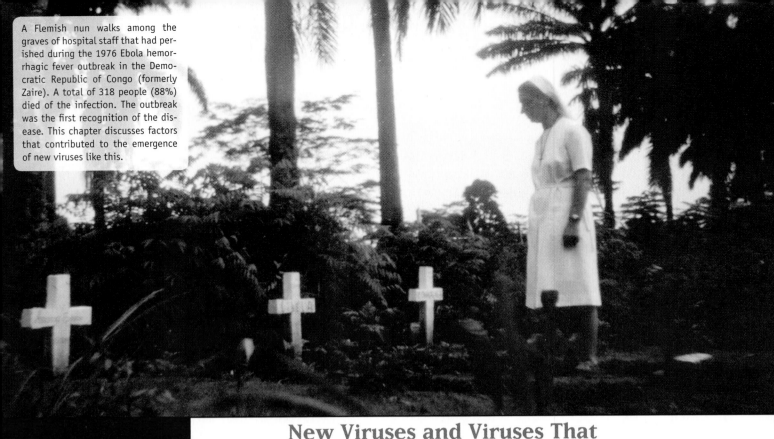

A Flemish nun walks among the graves of hospital staff that had perished during the 1976 Ebola hemorrhagic fever outbreak in the Democratic Republic of Congo (formerly Zaire). A total of 318 people (88%) died of the infection. The outbreak was the first recognition of the disease. This chapter discusses factors that contributed to the emergence of new viruses like this.

New Viruses and Viruses That Are Reemerging

❝*It's the perfect setup. Then you put air travel in and it could be around the world overnight.* **❞**

Michael T. Osterholm, Director of the Center for Infectious Disease Research and Policy (CIDRAP), Associate Director of the Department of Homeland Security's National Center for Food Protection and Defense (NCFPD), and Professor in the School of Public Health at the University of Minnesota

CASE STUDY

Borna disease was first described as a neurological illness of horses and sheep more than 200 years ago. It was named after the town of Borna in Saxony, Germany, where a large number of horses of a German cavalry regiment died in an 1885 epidemic. The diseased horses exhibited the following abnormal behaviors: running about excitedly, walking into walls, being unable to chew food, and standing with their heads and necks strained forward and down.

In later years, the Borna disease virus was isolated from the brains of infected horses. Brain homogenates from infected horses reproduced the disease in experimental naïve (uninfected) animals. Current research suggests a possible link between Borna disease virus and human neuropsychiatric disorders. Antibodies reactive with this virus were found in the sera of patients with psychiatric disorders such as schizophrenia. In 1996, researchers at the Robert Koch-Institut and Free University in Berlin, Germany, isolated Borna disease virus from patients with mood disorders.

W hat are the odds that a natural pandemic could kill a million people in the United States? What kind of viral outbreaks will we see in the future? Will there continue to be **emerging** and **reemerging** viruses? Emerging can be defined as new or recently identified viruses to humans. Reemerging viruses are viruses once thought to be under control from a public health perspective but that are making a "comeback" or reappearing and causing increased incidence or geographic range of infections in exposed human populations. In developed countries, public health measures such as sanitation, sewage treatments, vaccination programs, and access to good medical care have virtually eliminated "traditional" viral diseases such as smallpox, yellow fever, measles, and poliomyelitis. During 2006, the following viral outbreaks were the focus of attention by the news media:

- **Avian influenza H5N1** was killing millions of birds and some people in Indonesia, China, Azerbaijan, Cambodia, Egypt, Iraq, Thailand, Turkey, and Vietnam.
- A multistate, record-breaking outbreak of **mump**s occurred in the midwestern United States.
- **Chikungunya fever virus** caused extensive outbreaks in several islands in the southwest Indian Ocean including the Reunion Islands, the Seychelles, Mauritius, Mayetta, and Madagascar. Island travelers returned with Chikungunya infections to France, Germany, Italy, Norway, Switzerland, and Canada.
- An Amish community in Minnesota had several cases of **poliomyelitis**.
- Various outbreaks of **norovirus** on cruise ships, in hospitals and hotels, and at public gatherings occurred.

- **Bluetongue virus**, an insect-borne infection of ruminants such as cows, sheep, goats, and deer, spread from Africa to Northern European farms.

Human behavior plays a key role in influencing disease emergence and patterns. Moreover, there are three different general types of factors that contribute to the emergence or reemergence of viral diseases:

- viral
- human
- ecological

18.1 Viral Factors: Evolution and Adaptation

Table 18-1 lists emerging and reemerging viruses, the majority of which contain RNA genomes. Viruses evolve by rapidly ongoing processes. Some genes in viruses mutate rapidly, whereas others may mutate but you do not see the product because the mutations are lethal; for example, a gene that codes for a viral polymerase (*pol*) has a very specific shape that is related to its function. A regular mutation in the *pol* gene is not tolerable, whereas in the case of a gene that encodes a capsid protein, it could be tolerated and not lethal to the virus.

The RNA viruses possess high mutation rates due to the lack of proofreading capability of the viral RNA-dependent RNA polymerases used to transcribe or replicate the viral genomes. In general, the **point mutation** rate of a RNA virus is one mutation per every 10^4 to 10^5 nucleotides. In contrast, the mutation rate of DNA viruses is one mutation per every 10^8 to 10^{11} nucleotides. The mutation rate of the human immunodeficiency virus (HIV) is two mutations per every five genomes. The mutation rate for severe acute respiratory syndrome coronavirus (SARS-CoV) was estimated to be three mutations per every RNA genome in every round of replication. Point mutations in the genome may result in amino acid changes in the encoded protein products, affecting its function. Mutations in genes can result in drug resistance (e.g., changes in the viral reverse transcriptase or polymerases, proteases, etc.) or changes that prevent host antibodies from binding to the surface proteins of the virus, thereby evading the host's immune system (e.g., **antigenic drift** occurring in influenza viruses).

In addition to point mutations during replication, there are two other mechanisms of genetic variation that play a role in the evolution of viruses: **recombination** and **reassortment**. Recombination occurs when two viruses infect the same cell and a new chimeric or *hybrid* genome is formed via a process of intermolecular exchange of the viral genomes (**Figure 18-1a**). Recombination can occur in either segmented or nonsegmented viruses. A model regarding the recombination of RNA virus genomes is based on the premise that hybrid RNAs are formed when the viral RNA-dependent RNA polymerase complex switches, mid-replication, from one RNA molecule to another. Examples of RNA viruses with high recombination rates are SARS-CoV and other coronaviruses, such as Eastern equine encephalitis virus and Western equine encephaltitis virus. Recombination can significantly contribute to the establishment of new virus families. Viruses can steal genes from their hosts through a recombination process with the cellular chromosome. These cellular genes may be used or sometimes the virus does not utilize the genes. Retroviruses are notorious for pirating cellular genes (refer to Chapter 10, Viruses and Cancer).

Gene swapping or reassortment occurs when viruses that contain segmented genomes coinfect the same cell (Figure 18-1b). Influenza A viruses are notorious for this type of genetic adaptation. The genome of influenza A consists of eight single-stranded RNA

TABLE 18-1	Emerging or Reemerging* Human Viruses Since 1970

Year	Virus
1972	Norwalk virus (now known as norovirus)
1973	Rotavirus
1975	Parvovirus B-19
1975	Enterovirus 71
1976	Ebola
1977	Hantavirus
1980 (southern Texas)	Dengue fever virus*
1980	Human T cell leukemia virus I
1982	Human T cell leukemia virus II
1983	Human immunodeficiency virus
1988	Human herpes virus type 6
1988	Hepatitis E virus
1989	Hepatitis C virus
1989	Guanarito virus (Venezuelan hemorrhagic fever virus)
1989 (United States)	Measles virus*
1990	Sabia virus
1993	*Sin nombre* virus
1994	Hendra virus
1995	Human herpes virus type 8
1996	Hepatitis G virus
1996 (Uganda)	O'nyong'nyong fever virus*
1997	Transfusion transmission virus or torque teno virus (TTV)
1997 (Hong Kong)	Avian influenza A H5N1*
1999 (New York City)	West Nile virus*
1999	Nipah virus
2001	Human metapneumonia virus (hMPV)
2003	SARS-CoV
2003 (multistate outbreak in the United States)	Monkeypox*
2005	Human T cell lymphotropic virus III
2005	Bocavirus
2005 (Amish community in Minnesota)	Poliovirus*
2006 (midwestern United States)	Mumps virus*
2006 (La Reunion Island, France)	Chikungunya virus
2007 (United States)	Adenovirus 14 variant

*Reemerging viruses are indicated with an asterisk. All other viruses listed are new or emerging.

(A)
Corona virus

(B)
Influenza A

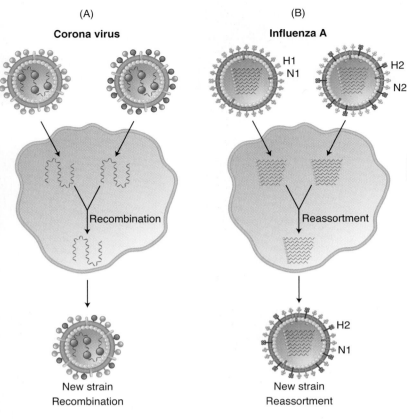

■ **Figure 18-1**
(a) Two coronaviruses coinfect the same cell in which the viral genomes undergo recombination. This results in the genome of a new strain. **(b)** Two different strains of influenza A viruses (H1N1 and H2N2, in this case) coinfect the same host animal or bird. The H or N genes are swapped to form a new strain. Adapted from Ka-Wai Hui, E., *Microbes and Infection* 8 (2006): 905–916.

(ssRNA) segments. When the virus surface glycoprotein gene coding for hemagglutinin (H) or neuraminidase (N) undergo reassortment, a new strain is formed. Progeny viruses contain a genome that has gene(s) from both or multiple parent viruses. When this gene swapping occurs, it is referred to as **antigenic shift** (refer to Chapter 12, Influenza Viruses).

18.2   Human Factors

The genetic adaptation of viruses does not appear to be the major driving force that causes viral emergence. Human demographics drive viral disease emergence more than virus evolution or ecological factors. **Human demographics** means "physical population characteristics." Demographics includes such characteristics as:

- sex/gender
- race/ethnicity
- age
- mobility/travel
- occupation
- sexual behavior
- socioeconomic status (the economic, social, and physical environments in which individuals live and work)
- geographic location
- family size

■ Population Growth: Density and Crowding

A virus emerges when it reaches a new population and then disseminates to new places. The dramatic increase in the human population on the planet is correlated with higher human densities in a given area. The world human population growth curve is shown in **Figure 18-2a**. Human populations lead to **urbanization**—the migration of people from the countryside to cities. In 2005, there were at least 25 **megacities** in the world, which contained at least 10 million inhabitants. Figure 18-2b illustrates the geographic distribution of humans in the world in 2005. China, India, other parts of Asia, and Africa are the most populated. The largest megacity is the greater Toyko area, which has a population of 33 million. The eight largest megacities after Tokyo are, in decreasing order of population:

- Mexico City, Mexico (22,800,000)
- Seoul, South Korea (22,300,000)
- New York City, United States (21,900,000)
- São Paulo, Brazil (20,200,000)
- Mumbai (Bombay), India (19,850,000)
- Delhi, India (19,700,000)
- Shanghai, China (18,150,000)
- Los Angeles, United States (18,000,000)

Higher population densities favor the spread of viral diseases; for example, dense populations result in problems of:

- crowding,
- sanitation,

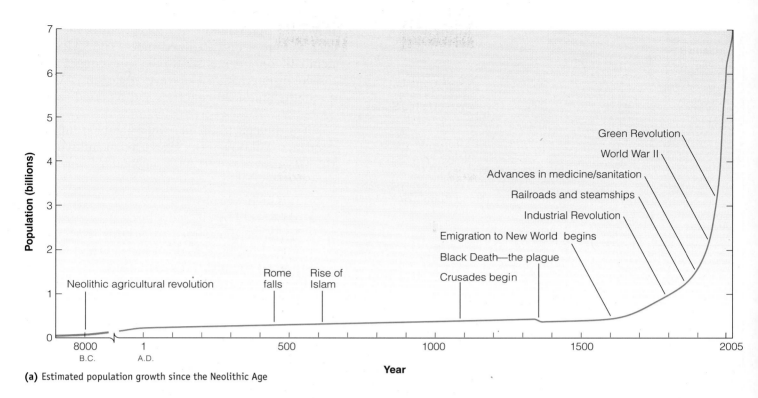

(a) Estimated population growth since the Neolithic Age

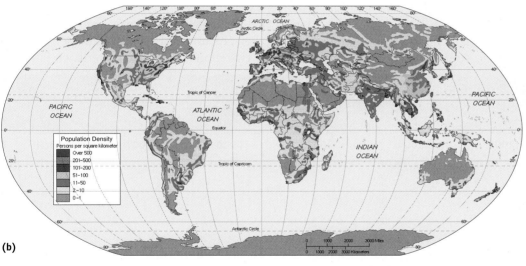

(b)

■ **Figure 18-2**
(a) World population over time (8000 B.C. to 2005 A.D.). (Source: U.S. Census Bureau, International Programs Center, 2001.) Global population is rising at an exponential rate. **(b)** Distribution of world population in 2005.

- drinking water,
- pollution, and
- healthcare facilities.

When sanitary conditions are poor, people are more susceptible to respiratory and gastrointestinal infections.

■ Human Movement (Travel and Migration): Viruses Live in a World without Borders

Humans are constantly on the move either for planned migration (e.g., for leisure, work, and commerce) or unplanned migration (e.g., because of war or natural disasters). The speed of air travel allows infected travelers to reach any part of the world in less than 24 hours, possibly starting a global pandemic. The spread of viral diseases to new areas can happen at any time. Viruses present in rural populations of the world such as Africa or Asia

■ **Figure 18-3**
Spread of SARS-CoV from the Metropole Hotel in Hong Kong as of March 28, 2003. Adapted from National Intelligence Council, "SARS Down But Still a Threat," *Intelligence Community Assessment,* http://www.dni.gov/nic/special_sarsthreat.html.

may show up in a more developed part of the world such as Europe or the United States. The **SARS pandemic** of 2003 demonstrates the spreading of a viral disease by international air travel (**Figure 18-3**). Within a month, almost 20 countries had reported cases of SARS.

It is difficult to predict when the next influenza pandemic will occur. The **H5N1 avian influenza virus** has raised concerns about a potential human pandemic for several reasons:

- It is highly virulent.
- It is spread by migratory birds.
- It can be transmitted from birds to mammals (e.g., from birds to domestic cats) and in some limited circumstances to humans.
- It continues to evolve (i.e., due to antigenic shift and drift).

Since 2003, human cases of H5N1 avian influenza have been reported in 12 countries (Table 18-2 and **Figure 18-4**). Avian influenza occurs naturally among wild waterfowl, which usually do not get sick from it. The virus is shed in bird feces, saliva, and nasal secretions. H5N1 avian influenza is highly contagious and nearly 100% fatal in domesticated birds such as chickens, turkeys, and ducks, often within 48 hours. Persons in direct contact with sick birds or surfaces contaminated with secretions and/or excretions from infected birds on farms or

TABLE 18-2	The World Health Organization's (WHO) Report of Human Cases and Deaths of Avian Influenza (2003–October 12, 2007)										
	2003		**2004**		**2005**		**2006**		**2007**		**Total**	
Country	**Cases**	**Deaths**	**Cases**	**Deaths**	**Cases**	**Deaths**	**Cases**	**Deaths**	**Cases**	**Deaths**	**Cases**	**Deaths**
Azerbaijan	0	0	0	0	0	0	8	5	0	0	8	5
Cambodia	0	0	0	0	4	4	2	2	1	1	7	7
China	1	1	0	0	8	5	13	8	3	2	25	16
Djibouti	0	0	0	0	0	0	1	0	0	0	1	0
Egypt	0	0	0	0	0	0	18	10	20	5	38	15
Indonesia	0	0	0	0	20	13	55	45	33	29	108	87
Iraq	0	0	0	0	0	0	3	2	0	0	3	2
Lao People's Democratic Republic	0	0	0	0	0	0	0	0	2	2	2	2
Nigeria	0	0	0	0	0	0	0	0	1	1	1	1
Thailand	0	0	17	12	5	2	3	3	0	0	25	17
Turkey	0	0	0	0	0	0	12	4	0	0	12	4
Viet Nam	3	3	29	20	61	19	0	0	7	4	100	46
Total	4	4	46	32	98	43	115	79	67	44	330	202

Total number of cases includes number of deaths.

All dates refer to onset of illness.

Data from the World Health Organization. WHO reports only laboratory-confirmed cases.

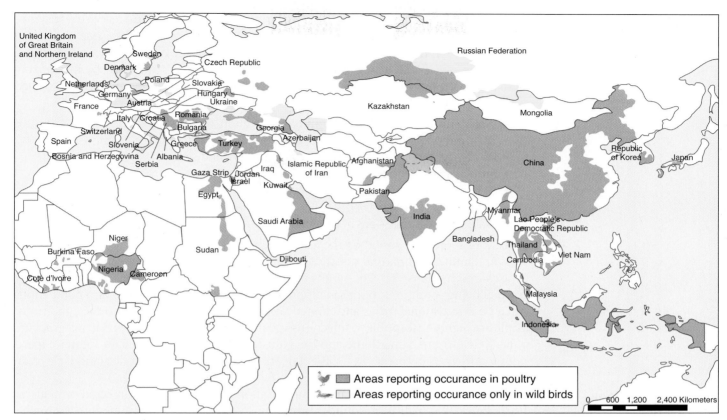

■ Figure 18-4
Nations with confirmed cases of H5N1 avian influenza in poultry and wild birds as of April 12, 2007. Courtesy of the World Health Organization/CDC.

live animal markets are most susceptible to the virus. At the time of this writing, the virus did not efficiently spread from person to person. Half of the humans infected with the H5N1 influenza strain, however, have died. To date, the risk of avian influenza to travelers is very low.

The U.S. Geological Survey's National Wildlife Health Center located in Madison, Wisconsin, monitors samples taken from migratory waterfowl for avian influenza viruses. They speculate that the H5N1 influenza strain will enter North America through migratory birds in the Pacific flyway, which follows the eastern Pacific coastline from the western Arctic, including Alaska and the Aleutian Islands, down the Rocky Mountain and Pacific coastal regions of Canada, the United States, and Mexico, to where it blends with other flyways in Central and South America. This monitoring can provide an early warning to agriculture, public health, and wildlife communities if the virus is detected among migratory birds. There are still other possible routes of the virus entering North America, such as through illegal importation of infected domestic birds or by an infected traveler.

Cruise vacations are an increasingly popular leisure activity. From 1993 to 1998, the number of cruise ship passengers in the United States increased by 50%. In North America alone, about 6.8 million passengers board cruise ships each year. In recent years, there has been an increase in gastrointestinal illness caused by **norovirus** on cruise ships, which in essence are floating minicities with a constantly changing population of hundreds of thousands of people in a confined space. Between 2001 and 2004, the number of norovirus outbreaks on cruise ships increased tenfold. In 2002 a new norovirus variant emerged in hospitals in the United Kingdom and Ireland and on U.S. cruise ships, and two new variants emerged in 2006 in the Netherlands. Noroviruses cannot be cultured in the laboratory and there is no animal model available to study these viruses, thus making it difficult to determine what genetic changes in a virus trigger outbreaks or cause more severe symptoms. The Centers for Disease Control and Prevention (CDC) started the Vessel Sanitation Program (VSP) in the early 1970s as a result of several disease outbreaks on cruise ships. The mission of the VSP was to protect the health of passengers and crew by minimizing the risk of gastrointestinal illness on cruise ships. Routine inspections are now performed on the following:

- Water supply—storage, distribution, protection, and disinfection
- Spas and pools—filtration and disinfection
- Food—protection during storage, preparation, and service
- Employee hygiene practices
- General cleanliness and physical condition of the ship—cleanliness and absence of insects and rodents
- Training programs—environmental and public health practices

Inspections scores are posted on the CDC's Website.

War, famine, and natural disasters have played a large part in introducing infectious diseases into humans. Refugee camps and temporary shelters are often characterized by crowded living conditions, poor sanitation, a lack of access to clean water, and populations with a poor nutritional status and limited access to medical care. Under these conditions, people are highly susceptible to infectious agents; for example, hurricane Katrina evacuees in the New Orleans Superdome and the Houston Astrodome and Reliant Center experienced a norovirus outbreak. For some time, there were no working toilets and little clean water in these facilities (**Figure 18-5**).

Aircrafts are a potential means of unintentionally moving virus-infected animals or arthropod vectors such as mosquitoes from country to country and continent to continent. Researchers have demonstrated that mosquitoes, houseflies, and flour beetles can survive in the wheel bays of Boeing 747B airplanes. The insects were able to withstand the extreme

(a)

(b)

■ **Figure 18-5**
(a) This photograph depicts New Orleans, Louisiana, on September 5, 2005. These homes and streets remain flooded seven days after hurricane Katrina hit the city. Much of the city was underwater and without electricity. **(b)** Many injured individuals were rescued from their flooded homes and evacuated following hurricane Katrina. This photograph depicts families evacuated to the Astrodome in Houston, Texas. The conditions in these large rescue centers became overcrowded and filthy.

temperatures in one-way and round-trip flights. The leading theory is that the 1999 **West Nile virus (WNV) outbreak** in New York was attributed to airplanes carrying West Nile virus-infected *Culex pipiens* mosquitoes when they flew across the Atlantic Ocean from Israel. At the time, aircraft cabin spaces were not routinely sprayed with insecticides on intercontinental flights entering the United States.

Prior to 1999 West Nile encephalitis had never been reported in the Western hemisphere and no one had considered that it could be introduced. The outbreak was originally thought to be caused by St. Louis encephalitis virus, a mosquito-borne illness endemic to the United States. A correct diagnosis was made after a veterinarian at the Bronx Zoo correlated the death of native birds with human cases of encephalitis. (St. Louis encephalitis virus does not infect birds.) The WNV quickly spread across the contiguous states of the United States and into Canada, the Caribbean, and Mexico (**Figures 18-6a** and 18-6b). The main reservoir of the West Nile virus is birds. Mosquitoes pick up the virus while taking a blood meal from infected birds. From there, the virus moves to horses and humans through a mosquito bite. Humans and horses are "**dead-end hosts**" that cannot transmit the virus to further species (Figure 18-6c). Between 2003 and 2004 there were over 12,000 human encephalitis cases and 362 human deaths in the United States, and by 2004 15,000 horses had died of West Nile encephalitis.

Investigation of a new reservoir of WNV began in 2007. Stable flies were suspected of being involved in the West Nile virus deaths of hundreds of pelican chicks at the Medicine Lake National Wildlife Refuge in northeast Montana. Montana State University entomologist Greg Johnson observed stable flies feeding on the blood of sick and dying pelicans. Stable flies look like house flies, but they have a painful bite. Johnson captured 1,300 stable flies and divided them into 60 groups. Eighteen of those groups tested positive for West Nile virus. This was the first evidence to suggest that stable flies might transmit West Nile virus at the pelican colony.

In 2002, four novel routes of West Nile Virus transmission to humans were reported:

- blood transfusion
- organ transplantation
- transplacental transfer
- breastfeeding

Twenty-three people in the United States were reported to have acquired WNV infection after receiving blood components from 16 West Nile Virus–infected blood donors in 2002. Per the recommendation of the Food and Drug Administration (FDA), blood-collection agencies have since implemented West Nile virus nucleic acid amplification tests to screen all blood donations in order to prevent transmission of the virus through contaminated blood products.

Human Exposure to Zoonotic Diseases: Pasture, Hunting, and Fishing Practices

Zoonoses are infectious diseases that are transmissible from animals to humans or from humans to animals. The word is derived from the Greek words *zoon* (animal) and *nosos* (disease). There are approximately 208 human pathogenic viruses or prions (prions will be discussed in Chapter 19). Of these human pathogens, 77 (37%) are considered emerging or reemerging, and about 73% of the emerging or reemerging viral or prion pathogens are known to be zoonotic. In many parts of the world, the close proximity of wildlife to humans is not uncommon. Under these conditions, viruses may cross the **species barrier**.

An example of a reemerging virus crossing the species barrier is the 2003 **monkeypox outbreak** in the United States. The first human cases of monkeypox were reported in 1970. It is a rare viral disease endemic in monkeys in the rainforests of Central and West Africa. Rodents are the reservoir of the monkeypox virus; humans and monkeys are

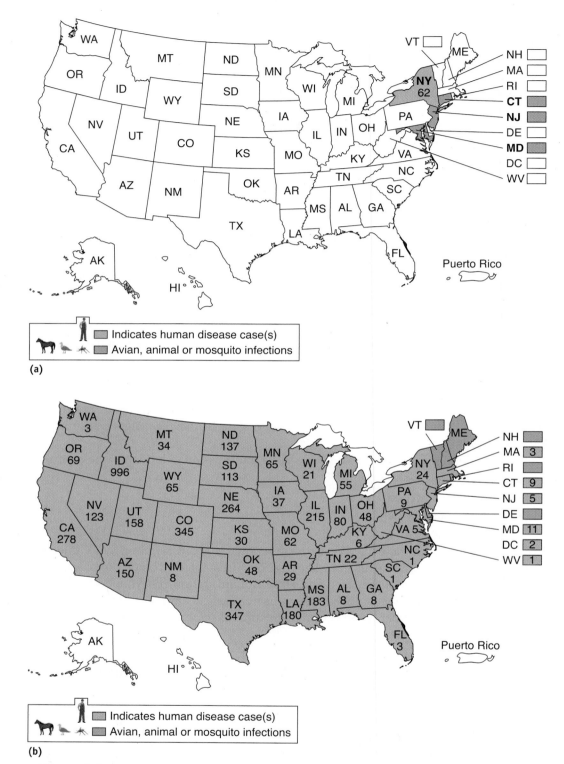

■ Figure 18-6

(a) Map of human West Nile encephalitis cases and avian, animal, or mosquito infections in 1999, the first year of the outbreak in the United States. (b) Map of human West Nile encephalitis cases and avian, animal, or mosquito infections in 2006. The virus spread quickly across the United States. Data courtesy of the Division of Vector-Borne Infectious Diseases/CDC.

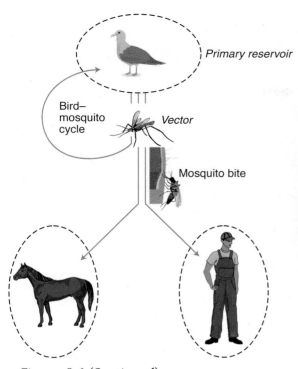

Primary reservoir

Bird–mosquito cycle

Vector

Mosquito bite

■ **Figure 18-6 (Continued)**
(c) West Nile Virus transmission cycle. Data courtesy of the Division of Vector-Borne Infectious Diseases/CDC.

■ **Figure 18-7**
Prairie dogs spread monkeypox, a rare zoonotic disease, in 2003. It was the first occurrence of monkeypox in the United States.

incidental hosts. In 2003, 762 rodents, including Giant Gambian pouched rats, were legally imported from Ghana in West Africa to Texas. The Gambian rats were infected with monkeypox and were housed in close proximity to native pet prairie dogs (**Figure 18-7**) in a pet distributor's premises in Illinois. The prairie dogs became infected with monkeypox before being purchased at an exotic pet swap meet. The virus spread from the infected prairie dogs to 71 people through bites or through close contact with the rodents' blood, body fluids, or rash. To prevent further transmission of monkeypox, the U.S. government banned the importation of all rodents from West Africa and banned the transport, sale, or release of pet prairie dogs. The smallpox vaccine can prevent people from getting monkeypox as well as smallpox.

Since the beginning of human history people have lived in close contact with animals—usually as hunters and as farmers. This practice is most common in developing countries where **free-range** farming—a method of farming in which the animals or birds are allowed to roam freely instead of contained in any manner (**Figure 18-8a**)—is used. There are 40 million small rural farms in Asia alone.

In southern China, especially the Guangdong province, wild animals are captured and sold in live markets or kept in cages in restaurants waiting for consumption. In the Chinese culture, fresh foods made from wild animals are considered a delicacy called "wild taste." The most common wild animals sold are beavers, badgers, civet cats, domestic cats, hares, raccoon dogs, snakes, and pangolin. The captured animals are kept in the same cage or in stacked cages where the animals—included those that are infected—often fight. These animals' blood, secretions, feces, and urine contaminate the cages, and the food handlers who subsequently butcher the animals have direct contact with the fluids.

The **SARS outbreak** of 2003 was an example of a virus that was transmitted from live-market animal to a human. An infected masked palm civet cat at a restaurant infected chefs, food handlers, and others who lived near the live-animal market. Further research suggested the natural reservoir of SARS-CoV, which has killed 774 people worldwide, is

(a)

(b)

■ **Figure 18-8**

(a) These egg-laying chickens are allowed to free-range. The poultry house is located behind the chickens. **(b)** Ducks loaded onto a weighing-scale at a wholesale, live poultry market in the Hatay province located 15.5 miles outside of Hanoi, Viet Nam. Viet Nam has experienced avian influenza outbreaks in poultry since 2004. Human cases of avian flu were first reported in Viet Nam in 2004 as well.

the Chinese horseshoe bat. These bats are commonly found at markets in southern China. Live poultry are also housed in crowded and unhygienic conditions at traditional markets (Figure 18-8b). Under these conditions **avian influenza** may spread from poultry to humans.

In Africa, bushmen live in temporary shelters and hunt animals for food. Sometimes they slaughter pathogen-infected nonhuman primates. During slaughter, they come in contact with raw bushmeat, blood, and bodily fluids of the butchered animal. Simian immunodeficiency virus (SIV) is found in nonhuman primates (such as SIV_{cpz} in chimpanzees). It crossed the species barrier into humans in the form of HIV. **HIV-1** is most closely related to SIV_{cpz}, whereas **HIV-2** is most similar to SIV_{sm}, which is found in the sooty mangabey (recall the theories of the origin of HIV, which were described in Chapter 16).

Media reports about a deadly Ebola-like virus that kills at least 15 different fish species made the headlines of U.S. newspapers from 2006 to 2007. **Viral hemorrhagic septicemia** (VHS) virus is a serious pathogen of fresh and saltwater fish and is causing an emerging disease in the Great Lakes region of the United States and Canada. Infected fish show signs that include bulging eyes, hemorrhaging in the eyes, gills, skin, and at the base of the fins, bloated abdomens, and inactive or overactive behavior. Genetic tests how that the strain of VHS found in the Great Lakes probably originated in Atlantic Ocean fish located near New Brunswick, Canada. This places the origin of the new strain near the start of the St. Lawrence Rivers shipping route that leads to the Great Lakes. Besides the Great Lakes, at the time of this writing, this highly contagious fish pathogen has been found in fish populations in the Niagara River and inland lakes in New York such as Lakes Skaneateles, and Winnebago and Little Lake Buttes des Morts near Oshkosh, Wisconsin.

On October 24, 2006, the United States Department of Agriculture's Animal and Health Inspection Service (APHIS) issued a federal emergency ordering the banning of importation of 37 species of live fish from two Canadian provinces into the country and the interstate movement of the same species from the eight states bordering the Great Lakes. This is a major fish health crisis. Sport fisherman and recreational boaters were being asked to adhere to good biosecurity practices of fishing or boating in waters where VHS has been found. Examples of some biosecurity and preventative measures encouraged include:

- Rinsing boats and any other equipment that have been in VHS waters with hot water or drying it for at least five days.

VIRUS FILE 18-1

Retroviruses Crossing the Species Barrier in Nature: Hunters in Africa Infected with Retroviruses via Bushmeat

The origin of HIV has been debated. Genetic studies have traced the virus to its relative SIV. Scientists proposed that HIV arose from SIV in chimpanzees. Presumably, this crossing-over occurred in humans living in African communities where people hunted chimpanzees for food. The virus was transmitted to humans via contact with blood and body fluids of animals during hunting or butchering (**Figure VF 18-1a**). At first this theory was not proved and there was no documentation of transmission of SIV to laboratory and zoo workers who had close contact with nonhuman primates. Now, however, this theory has been backed up by a recent study carried out by U.S. and Cameroonian researchers who collected blood samples from 1800 volunteer participants of a community-based HIV-prevention campaign in Cameroon (Figure VF 18-1b). Sixty-one percent (1099) of the participants had exposure to nonhuman primates (monkeys, chimpanzees, or gorillas) through hunting, butchering, or as pets and reported exposure to fresh primate blood and body fluids. Hands, guns, bow and arrows, wire snares, and machetes were used to hunt the primates.

Blood samples were screened for antibodies against simian foamy virus (SFV), which is also known as spumaretrovirus. SFV is transmitted at a higher rate (2.5%) than normal primate retroviruses to zoo workers and researchers. SFV is also endemic in most Old World nonhuman primates. Thus far, though, no humans have gotten ill from SFV, and the virus doesn't make nonhuman primates sick (as is the case with SIV).

SFV antibodies were detected in 10 of the 1099 blood samples (a 1% transmission rate). Via polymerase chain reaction (PCR) analysis, it was determined that the ten SFV infected individuals had been infected via three different primates: De Brazza's guenon, mandrill, and gorilla. The De Brazza's guenon and mandrill are also naturally infected with SIV.

These results show that retroviruses actively cross into human populations and that people in west Central Africa are currently infected with SFV. Contact with nonhuman primates during hunting and butchering can play a partial role in the emergence of human retroviruses. The urban demand for bushmeat and greater access to primate habitats by logging roads has increased the frequency of human exposure to primate retroviruses and other disease-causing pathogens. In addition to preserving endangered old world primates, reducing hunting activities will reduce the frequency of cross-species transmission of retroviruses and other biological agents.

(a)

References

Wolfe, N.D. et al. 2004. "Naturally Acquired Simian Retrovirus Infections in Central Africa." *Lancet* 363:932–937.

■ **Figure VF 18-1**
(a) Child carrying the head of a gorilla from a recent bushmeat hunt. **(b)** The gorilla head is removed during prepration of the meat. Bushmeat hunting is common in sub-Saharan African forests.

(b)

- Never moving fish eggs or live fish to other waters.
- Reporting fish dieoffs to the local Department of Natural Resources (DNR) representative or conservation warden.
- Cleaning and disinfecting all fishing gear.

■ Agricultural Practices, Deforestation, and Dam Construction

The extension of farmland into unused land exposes farmers to zoonotic diseases (especially rodents that carry viruses), new animal species (and their viruses), and disease-carrying arthropods; for example, there was a fivefold increase in **Argentine hemorrhagic fever** cases occurring at the forest-farmland margins in the northwest province of Buenos Aires, South America, from 1958 to 1974. This region is the richest farmland in Argentina and farmers soon began to clear plains (called pampas) and plant maize. During the clearing practices, rodents that carry the **Junin virus**—the causative agent of Argentine hemorrhagic fever—began to flourish. The Junin virus was shed in the urine of the rodents and aerosolized by agricultural machinery. In similar agricultural situations, increases in Bolivian hemorrhagic fever and Lassa fever cases caused by the Machupo virus and Lassa fever virus, respectively, via their natural rodent hosts, were recorded.

Deforestation is the removal of trees in forested areas without sufficient reforestation. There are many causes, ranging from natural wildfires or animal grazing to human activity. Forestry practices such as logging, mining, dam construction, and petroleum exploration all contribute to human-caused deforestation. In 2005, outbreaks of vampire bat-related human rabies in the rural parts of the states of Para and Maranhao were correlated with the deforestation of the Amazon rainforests in Brazil (**Figure 18-9**). The deforestation of the Amazon region caused thousands of the common vampire bats (*Desmodus* sp.) carrying rabies to move across northern Brazil.

Vampire bats, which are native to the Americas, and in particular Brazil, Chile, and Argentina, feed on blood. The common vampire bat, which is **nocturnal**, rarely bites humans, instead feeding on sleeping cattle and horses. Vampire bats live almost exclusively in dark places such as caves, old wells, and hollow trees, and are common carriers of rabies virus. The abandoned gold mines in Maranhao provided a favorable habitat for the vampire bat populations. During the 2005 outbreak, there was a failure of a generator that left people without electricity for six weeks. Many homes in the marshlands did not have screening in windows and had large gaps in the floor and ceiling, making it easy for vampire bats to gain access. The vampire bats carrying rabies may behave abnormally, which could explain in part the uncharacteristic behavior of biting humans during these Brazilian outbreaks. It was speculated that the vampire bats bit several hundred people and that at least 23 human rabies deaths were reported. Over 1350 people received postexposure rabies vaccine.

Another example of an outbreak resulting from deforestation activity is the **Nipah virus outbreak** that occurred in the north peninsula of Malaysia from 1998 to 1999. The virus caused severe fever and encephalitis in 265 patients, killing 104 (40%). The Nipah virus infects humans, pigs, dogs, and cats. Most patients in Malaysia were pig farmers and the infections were linked to exposure to sick pigs. The Nipah virus was transmitted to the pigs via bat droppings from infected Malayan flying fox and variable flying fox fruit bats, which feed on fruit and nectar. They play an important role in the rainforest as seed dispersers and pollinators. Both types of bats carry the Nipah virus. Many pig farms were located next to orchards, where the fruit trees were a natural attraction for Malayan flying fox and variable flying fox bats. The pig pens were likely contaminated with bat droppings that contained the Nipah virus, providing a means for transmission to the pigs. The virus spread quickly because the farm was overcrowded with sick domestic pigs that ultimately spread to humans and other animals by aerosolizing the virus (**Figure 18-10a**). Nearly a million pigs were culled as a measure to stop the outbreak (Figure 18-10b).

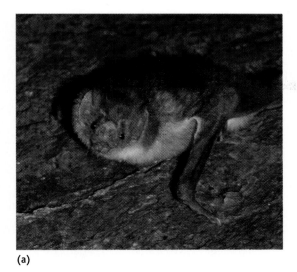

(a)

■ Figure 18-9

(a) The common vampire bat (*Desmodus* sp.) was responsible for at least 23 human rabies deaths in Brazil in 2005. **(b)** Map of South America showing the Amazon region in relationship to human rabies transmitted by displaced vampire bats carrying the rabies virus.

(b)

A similar situation to the Nipah virus outbreak occurred in Australia from 1994 to 1995. A virus relative of Nipah virus, termed the **Hendra virus (formerly called equine morbillivirus)** was infecting racehorses, horse trainers, and stablehands. (The name Hendra comes from the location of the outbreak: Hendra, a suburb of Brisbane, Australia.) Hendra virus causes severe flulike symptoms and neurologic disease in horses and humans. The natural reservoir of the Hendra virus is the flying fox fruit bat (*Pteropus* sp.). Humans became infected when exposed to tissues and secretions from infected horses (**Figure 18-11**), which had been infected with Hendra virus from bat placental fluid. Two of three humans infected and at least 14 horses died during this outbreak. A subsequent outbreak occurred in 2004.

Severe outbreaks of **porcine reproductive and respiratory syndrome** (PRRS) in China began causing severe outbreaks in domestic pigs during the summer of 2006. An arterovirus virus causes PRRS. PRRS is sometimes referred to as "blue-ear pig disease." The virus attacks macrophages, crippling the immune system of pigs. The pigs are susceptible to secondary infections. Adult pigs (sows) usually recover and develop immunity. Symptoms of PRRS include reproductive failure (e.g., weak or stillborn piglets) in breeding stock and a respiratory illness (pneumonia) in piglets. The virus and secondary infections can kill piglets, whose ears turn blue due to **cyanosis**. Cyanosis is a bluish discoloration of the skin that is caused by a circulatory or lung problem that occurs when there is a lack of oxygen in the blood of the lungs or skin blood vessels (in this case the vessels of the pigs' ears). Cyanosis occurs in PRRS infected piglets suffering from secondary infections. The virus spreads rapidly from farm to farm. The PRRS virus is spread by pig-to-pig contact through contaminated mucus, manure, urine, and semen (artificial and natural) and possibly by airborne transmission. Infected live pigs are the major source of transmission to healthy pigs.

■ **Figure 18-10**

(a) Routes of transmission for Nipah virus. Adapted from Ka-Wai Hui, E., *Microbes and Infection* 8 (2006): 905–916. **(b)** Pigs were buried alive in mass graves to curb the Nipah virus outbreak.

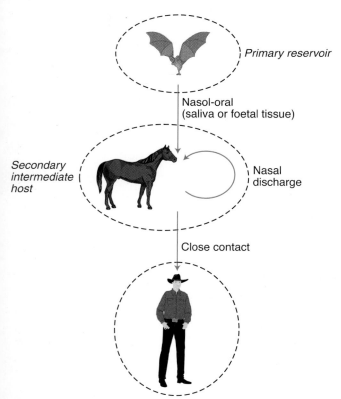

(A)

Naso-oral (saliva)

Primary reservoir

Close contact

Secondary intermediate host

Close contact

(a)

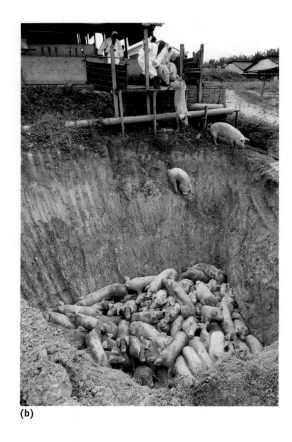

(b)

PRRS is becoming one of the most economically significant diseases, reducing the number of live pigs and prompting pork shortages and inflation of pork prices. The outbreak in China caused the pork economy to sizzle. The prices of pork and other food products containing pork skyrocketed over 85%. The country's consumer price index increased to 6.5% during August, 2007, after it rose to a 10-year high of 5.6% in July, 2007. China is one of the largest exporters of pork and pork products in the world. In 2007, Chinese officials received criticism for the safety of its food and other exports.

The PRRS virus began causing outbreaks in the United States during the late 1980s, when it was known as "mystery swine disease." PRRS first appeared in Europe in 1990. It is now present in almost all pig-breeding countries. At the time of this writing, the strain of PRRS virus circulating in China evolved into a highly pathogenic and lethal virus, killing sows and piglets. Millions of pigs were killed by the virus or culled in an effort to prevent spread of PRRS. These outbreaks were considered a threat to the global industry. Chinese officials were criticized for the lack of information made available to the public, comparing this to the 2003 SARS outbreak. Besides being a threat to the food supply, virologists raised concerns that this virus may cross the species barrier from pigs to humans. Central to containing these outbreaks is monitoring the evolution of PRRS virus for its ability to replicate in alternate hosts.

Primary reservoir

Nasol-oral (saliva or foetal tissue)

Secondary intermediate host

Nasal discharge

Close contact

■ **Figure 18-11**

Routes of transmission for the Hendra virus. Adapted from Ka-Wai Hui, E., *Microbes and Infection* 8 (2006): 905–916.

Dam Construction

Most of the world's dams for irrigation and flood control were constructed in the 1930s, and nearly every large river worldwide has at least one dam. Several mosquito-borne outbreaks of viral diseases have occurred following dam construction. In 1987, an outbreak of **Rift Valley fever** in Mauritania occurred during construction of a dam on the Senegal River (West Africa). Rift Valley fever causes serious complications: meningoen-cephalitis (an inflammation of the brain) and lesions of the retina, which leave victims with at least some permanent loss of vision. About 1% to 3% of infected individuals experience hemorrhagic symptoms and kidney failure.

In the case of the outbreak in Mauritania, which resulted in 200 deaths, the dam caused flooding in the lower Senegal River area. In 1993, another Rift Valley fever outbreak occurred during the construction of the Aswan dam in Egypt, when approximately 600 to 1500 human cases of Rift Valley Fever were recorded.

More than 40 different species of mosquitoes carry Rift Valley fever virus. Floods and heavy rainfall contributed to the spread of Rift Valley fever virus because mosquito populations increase dramatically during these periods. Dam construction results in a large amount of standing water that provides a breeding ground for mosquitoes. These arthropods serve as vectors that catalyze the spread of the virus.

■ Global Commerce

Today the buying and selling of foods, especially on a large scale, occurs between nations. People no longer depend upon food produced locally. Imported fruits and vegetables from developing countries may contain viral contaminants through the use of raw human sewage as fertilizers. Studies have shown that viruses may persist for weeks or even months on vegetable crops and in soils that have been irrigated or fertilized with human sewage wastes. Hepatitis A viruses, noroviruses, enteroviruses, astroviruses, rotaviruses, and coronaviruses have caused foodborne disease outbreaks associated with the consumption of raw fruits and vegetables. The most commonly contaminated foods associated with foodborne viral outbreaks are iceberg lettuce, strawberries, raspberries, green onions, diced tomatoes, shredded cabbage, and raw oysters from contaminated bays (**Figure 18-12a**).

At the time of this writing, honey bees in the United States are mysteriously dying of colony collapse disorder (CCD). Beekeepers are baffled by the cause of CCD. Approximately 23% of beekeeping operations in the United States suffered from CCD in 2006 to 2007. It has resulted in an average loss of 45% of each affected business. One hypothesis is that CCD is caused by a novel infectious agent.

To test the novel-infectious-agent hypothesis, a team of beekeepers, entomologists, and molecular biologists analyzed nucleic acids from pooled samples of bees from healthy colonies and samples of bees with CCD using a **metagenomic survey**. This survey analyzed genomes of microflora present in normal hives and CCD hives. Both DNA and RNA was extracted from the bees to determine if RNA viruses or other pathogens were present in the samples. All of the bee hives contained a rogues gallery of pathogens. Israeli acute paralysis virus (IAPV), however, was found in 25 of the 30 CCD hives and in only one of the healthy hives. These results suggest that IAPV is strongly associated with CCD. Where did IAPV come from?

Since 2004, beekeepers have struggled to keep up with the demand for almond pollination in California. To meet this need, millions of dollars worth of bees from Australia were imported into the United States. Hives with CCD contained imported bees from Australia or were located near operations with Australian bees. Bees imported from Australia also tested IAPV-positive. The sudden loss of honey bees, particularly among imported hives, was linked to IAPV that may have arrived with bees from Australia.

■ **Figure 18-12**
(a) This man is shopping for fresh produce in a supermarket. Some of the produce is likely imported from other countries and may serve as a vehicle for human disease. **(b)** This African green monkey is the same species that was involved in the 1967 Marburg hemorrhagic fever outbreak in Marburg, Germany, and Belgrade, Yugoslavia.

(a)

(b)

Importing animals for biomedical research or for exotic pet trading has been a cause for concern. In 1967, African green monkeys were imported simultaneously to Marburg, Germany and Belgrade, Yugoslavia, for research and preparation of poliovirus vaccine (Figure 18-12b). The monkeys were infected with **Marburg virus**, which causes a hemorrhagic fever in humans and has a high mortality rate. The first people infected were laboratory workers who had contact with monkey blood or organs or with prepared cell cultures.

With a few exceptions, the import of exotic species from around the world into the United States has been a largely unregulated industry. The **monkeypox outbreak** in the United States in 2003 discussed previously demonstrates how quickly an unusual virus can spread through the exotic-pet trade. The outbreak made many people consider the potential for human health risks related to importing exotic species.

■ Human Social Behavior: Sex, Intravenous Drugs, Cultural Traditions, and Research Laboratories

Having multiple sex partners increases the risk of acquiring sexually transmitted viral diseases such as HIV, hepatitis B and C, and human papillomaviruses. As discussed earlier, HIV originated during a cross-species transmission of SIV from nonhuman primates to humans. The HIV pandemic began when the virus began to spread from human to human, primarily via homosexual contact or by sharing contaminated needles used for **intravenous drug use**. Sub-Saharan Africa is home to about 64% of the world population living with HIV and South Africa is the epicenter of the AIDS epidemic. Transmission is primarily through heterosexual contact and more women than men are infected with HIV. The Caribbean is the second-most HIV-affected region of the world. Transmission there is also primarily heterosexual.

Cultural traditions can have a role in spreading viruses. Consider, for example, how many traditions involve physical contact or the sharing of a cup or other drinking and eating vessels. An example of this is a traditional belief that led to the 2005 Marburg hemorrhagic fever outbreak in the Angolan province of Uige, which is the deadliest one on record. The outbreak in Uige, which is located in northeastern Angola (**Figure 18-13**), lasted from March through August. According to information collected by health officials, the first cases appeared among Itoumbi villagers who had gone elephant hunting in the bush. "All the victims were great hunters. They touched a monkey they found dead in the forest and then ate it." Main symptoms of the infection were fever, hemorrhage (bleeding), vomiting, cough, diarrhea, and jaundice (yellow skin and eyes).

There were a total of 374 cases and 329 deaths (88% mortality). The majority of deaths occurred in the main hospital in Uige, and in fact the hospital was the source of the infection for many peoples. Hospital workers were administering medicine to patients by injection, using shared/contaminated syringes. Family members adhered to traditional funeral rites. They washed bodies of the deceased loved ones, and kissed the body to show respect and love for the deceased and to keep vengeful spirits away. This custom allowed the rapid spread of the virus from blood-to-blood contact. Safety protocols (e.g., barrier techniques for infection control) were breached. Relatives of the deceased asked doctors and nurses to respect these customs while doing what was necessary to prevent further infections.

The country had been ravaged by a 27-year civil war, and thus hospitals lacked the basic equipment, supplies, transportation means, and infrastructure. At the beginning of the outbreak, at least 16 doctors, nurses, and traditional healers died from the disease after caring for sick patients. Officials from the CDC, World Health Organization (WHO), Health Canada, and Medecins sans Frontieres (MSF, or Doctors Without Borders) rushed in with medicines and protective gear to stem the epidemic, but convincing some communities to change their traditions in order to protect themselves from the communicable disease proved difficult. The locals feared the isolation wards because infected people in hospitals had died there. The families cared for the sick at home and then hid the bodies from the officials sent in to help. On at least three occasions, relief workers were stoned and their vehicles damaged by hostile residents who blamed them for the spread of the disease. Building trust was central to being able to collect and bury corpses appropriately. Religious leaders in Uige joined the public information campaign to stop the use of unsafe injections, an important component in the spread of the Marburg virus. Eventually trust was secured between the community and a collaborative effort brought the outbreak under control.

Applied biomedical and biodefense research on dangerous viral pathogens takes place in specialized Biosafety Level 3 and 4 (BSL-3 and 4) laboratories. These laboratories have the most stringent safety and security requirements (**Figure 18-14**). There are currently only four operational BSL-4 laboratories in the United States, which are located at the following institutions:

- CDC in Atlanta, Georgia
- U.S. Army Medical Research Institute for Infectious Diseases at Fort Detrick in Frederick, Maryland
- Southwest Foundation for Biomedical Research in San Antonio, Texas
- University of Texas at Galveston

Georgia State University in Atlanta has a small BSL-3/BSL-4 glove box facility. In addition, a small BSL-4 facility exists on the National Institutees of Health (NIH) campus in Bethesda, Maryland, but it is currently being operated only at a BSL-3 level for research on important emerging infectious disease pathogens.

The chances of a viral pathogen "escaping" from a BSL-3 or BSL-4 laboratory are remote. In 2005, though, a serious mistake occurred when a H2N2 influenza A virus present in diagnostic test kits was sent to thousands of laboratories in 19 different countries. This Asian strain killed millions of people in a pandemic of 1957–1958, and any person born after 1968 would have little or no immunity to this virus. Within days, all packages containing the deadly strain

■ **Figure 18-13**
A map of Angola showing the location of the 2005 Marburg outbreak. The province of Uige was the epicenter of this epidemic.

■ **Figure 18-14**
Biomedical research laboratories contain some of the deadliest human pathogens on this earth. The viruses are stored in secured freezers like the one shown in this photograph.

were recovered and destroyed and no one was infected by the virus during this mishap. This serious mistake created a heightened awareness of the management and operation of laboratories that contain viral pathogens that are potential bioweapons. Well-established guidelines aimed to protect laboratory workers and the surrounding community were updated and implemented.

■ Human Medicine and Susceptibility to Infection

Health-related infections can occur in a number of ways, such as:

- unsafe medical practices (e.g., reusing syringes and the overuse of antimicrobials)
- blood transfusions
- poor hospital practices
- immunosuppression
- xenotransplantation (see Chapter 9)
- breakdown in public health measures including lack of vaccination programs at local, state, national, and global levels; problems with basic sanitation and infection-control procedures

Typically one thinks of poor hospital practices in developing countries regarding the spread of bloodborne pathogens. Health care in the United States, however, is not without problems. In 2006 CDC viral hepatitis expert Dr. Joseph Perz presented the challenges that exist today in outpatient and long-term care facilities in the United States at an international conference on emerging and infectious diseases. A disturbing trend in the last five years involving patient-to-patient spread of bloodborne diseases is being recognized. According to Perz, a common theme is that unsafe injection practices and failure to adhere to aseptic technique has resulted in the investigation of several outbreaks of bloodborne illnesses in outpatient settings. Bloodborne infections are not just a problem of the developing world. This represents an element of patient safety in the United States that must be remedied as soon as possible.

The good news is that blood supply safety in the United States is excellent, but the poor hospital practices and the blood supply of developing countries is still a very efficient way of transmitting bloodborne viruses. Most notably, HIV and hepatitis C virus infections are now prevalent in Chinese communities. The origin of the HIV and hepatitis C epidemic in central China began in the late 1980s and early 1990s through a contaminated blood supply. The Chinese have a cultural belief that losing blood is unhealthy; for this reason, the blood supply is often short due to the lack of blood donors. As a means to supplement their income, Chinese villagers sell their blood for plasma. It was standard practice to pool the blood from dozens of sellers. The plasma was separated and red blood cells were reinfused into sellers. No HIV or hepatitis C virus screening was performed on the red blood cells. About one million paid blood donors contracted HIV and/or hepatitis C virus through this procedure as well as through the reuse of syringes and nonsterilzed equipment. China has since taken steps to halt illegal plasma collection and to improve blood-banking methods.

The population of individuals who are immune-compromised is on the rise. In the United States alone there were about 10 to 20 million immune-compromised people in 2006. This was the direct result of the use of immune-suppressive drugs used during organ or bone marrow transplants, kidney dialysis, chronic corticosteroid treatment, and chemotherapy. That being said, the number of opportunistic infections is on the rise. Immune suppressants encourage the following viral infections:

- human cytomegalovirus
- varicella zoster
- herpes simplex I
- Epstein-Barr virus
- human herpes virus type 6

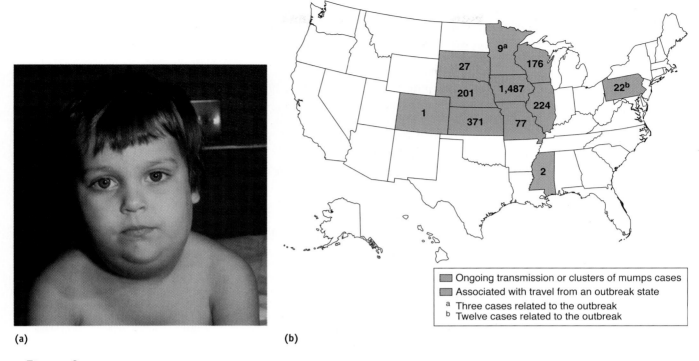

■ Figure 18-15
(a) A child with mumps. Note the swelling in his neck due to lymphatic build-up caused by mumps virus infection of the parotid salivary glands. Reproduced from Centers for Disease Control and Prevention, *MMWR* 55 (2006):559–563.
(b) Mumps cases (2,597) linked to multistate outbreak in 2006.

- human herpes virus type 7
- adenoviruses
- hepatitis viruses

The large-scale use of drugs to treat these opportunistic infections led to the emergence of drug-resistant strains and other phenotypes of new strains that dominate the population. In turn, transmission of drug-resistant and new viral strains can occur.

Vaccine-preventable diseases such as measles and mumps are reemerging on college campuses. The safety of vaccines has been questioned and some parents are not allowing their children to be vaccinated. The first cases of outbreaks were in unvaccinated or immune-compromised individuals. In 2006 there was a multistate mumps outbreak in the Midwest. From January to May of that year there were 2597 reported cases of mumps in eight different states. (**Figure 18-15a**). No deaths were reported. The majority of cases were in Iowa (Figure 18-15b). Eleven of the infected individuals traveled by aircraft on 33 commercial flights that were operated by eight different airlines. At least two persons acquired mumps during air travel.

A 2005 measles outbreak occurred in Indiana after an unvaccinated 17-year-old Indiana resident working as a missionary in an orphanage and hospital in Romania contracted measles. The 17-year-old returned to the United States with symptoms of the measles. Subsequently, the largest measles outbreak occurred at the Romanian orphanage. Upon her return, the teenager (patient zero) attended a church function in which unvaccinated individuals were present. A total of 34 persons contracted measles through direct contact with the teenager. Vaccination and isolation measures were undertaken to prevent further measles transmission.

The first outbreak of poliomyelitis in the United States in 26 years occurred in a central Minnesota Amish community in 2005. For religious or social reasons, Amish avoid immunizations. The Amish live as isolated communities with little risk of passing on or being exposed to infectious diseases outside of the community. In this instance, an unvaccinated

VIRUS FILE 18-2   **Human Bocavirus (HBoV)—An Emerging Viral Pathogen?**

Lower respiratory tract infections are the leading cause for hospitalization of infants and young children (**Figure VF 18-2**) and account for approximately 250,000 hospitalizations annually in the United States. Respiratory syncytial virus (RSV) is a leading viral agent in this group of patients. In about 12% to 39% of cases, though, no known agent has been identified as the cause of the lower respiratory tract infection.

In 2005 a group of researchers in Sweden identified a new virus present in respiratory secretions of children with lower respiratory tract infections. The new virus was named **human bocavirus (HBoV)**. Bocaviruses belong to the family *Parvoviridae*, which includes the smallest known viruses at a mere 18 to 26 nm in diameter. The viruses are nonenveloped and icosahedral-shaped with ssDNA genomes and are very resistant to environmental forces.

The HBoV DNA was amplified from pooled samples of respiratory tract se-

■ **Figure VF 18-2**
Child hospitalized with a lower respiratory tract infection. Respiratory tract infections are among the leading causes of death in children under 5 years of age.

TABLE VF18-1	HBoV Detection in Children Suffering from Lower Respiratory Tract Infections	
Country	**Patient Sample Size**	**% HBoV positive by PCR**
Canada	1,209	1.5%
France	589	4.4%
Germany	835	10.3%
Japan	318	5.7%
Korea	515	11.3%
United States (California)	1474	5.6%

cretions collected from Swedish patients. This type of molecular screening is improving the speed at which new viruses can be identified since these viruses have not yet been cultivated in the laboratory. Follow-up studies screening for the presence of HBoV in children suffering from lower respiratory tract infections in other countries is ongoing (Table VF 18-1).

These studies affirm that viral sequences from other viral respiratory pathogens (coinfections) have also been found in up to 39% of HBoV-positive samples. As a result of the high rates of coinfections with HBoV and other respiratory tract pathogens, the clinical significance of HBoV is unknown.

References
Allander, T. et al. 2005. "Cloning of a Human Parvovirus by Molecular Screening of Respiratory Tract Samples." *PNAS USA* 102(36):12891–12896.
Arnold, J. C. et al. 2006. "Human Bocavirus: Prevalence and Clinical Spectrum at a Children's Hospital." *Clin Infect Dis* 43(3):283–288.
Choi, E. H. et al. 2006. "The Association of Newly Identified Respiratory Viruses with Lower Respiratory Tract Infections in Korean Children, 2000–2006." *Clin Infect Dis* 43(5):585–592.
Foulongne, V. et al. 2006. "Human Bocavirus in French Children." *EID* 12(8):1251–1253.
Vicente, D. et al. 2007. "Human Bocavirus, a Respiratory and Enteric Virus." *EID* 13(4):636–637.
Weissbrich, B. et al. 2006. "Frequent Detection of Bocavirus in German Children with Respiratory Tract Infections." *BMC Infect Dis* 6:109.

immune-suppressed Amish infant contracted an oral vaccine-derived poliovirus strain. Three additional children in the Amish community were infected. The original source of the poliovirus was likely a person who received the live oral poliovirus vaccine in another country. A WHO global initiative to eradicate polio continues. Countries like Sudan that were once declared polio-free are experiencing outbreaks. The distrust of Western vaccines hampers the efforts by healthcare workers to immunize children most susceptible to the virus.

18.3 Ecological Factors: Climate Variability

Many emerging infectious disease outbreaks occur after environmental disruptions such as hurricanes, tsunamis, extreme floods, increased rainfall, and droughts. Global climate changes are expected to increase, which likely will broaden the range of many diseases, especially those that are vectorborne. Mosquitoes, mice, and other carriers of viruses are surviving warmer winters and expanding their range, bringing their viruses with them (**Figure 18-16**). When pathogens adapt to new environments, the diseases they cause pose a serious threat to international health. What is one nation's problem will become every nation's problem.

El Niño is an abnormal warming of the surface ocean waters that causes weather changes (e.g., heavy rains) around the globe. From 1991 to 1993, the southern United States experienced an increase in rainfall caused by El Niño, particularly in the Four Corners area, which consists of Utah, Colorado, Arizona, and New Mexico. Rodents must forage large areas to obtain food and shelter. These states contain areas that are normally very dry, but when the El Niño rains hit this area at the beginning of 1991 there was increased production of piñon nuts, a major source of food for rodents such as deer mice.

The deer mouse population increased from less than one mouse per 2.5 acres during dry years to over five per 2.5 acres within eight months of the first rains. By the spring of 1993, there were 20 to 30 deer mice per 2.5 acres. Some of these rodents carried the *sin nombre* **hantavirus**. As the deer mouse population densities increased, the virus was transmitted from mouse to mouse. In 1993 about 30% of the deer mice carried the *sin nombre* hantavirus, the cause of hantavirus pulmonary syndrome. In May of 1993, young healthy human adults suddenly developed acute respiratory symptoms and died. They had acquired the *sin nombre* hantavirus infection by breathing aerosolized deer mice saliva,

(a)   (b)

■ Figure 18-16
Mosquito and rodent populations fluctuate during climate changes. **(a)** Culex tarsalis mosquito that is about to feed on its human host. This mosquito is currently the main vector of West Nile virus in the United States. **(b)** Deer mouse (*Peromyscus maniculatus*), which is the carrier of *sin nombre* hantavirus, the causative agent of hantavirus pulmonary syndrome.

urine, or droppings that contained the excreted viruses. The deer mice were infesting their homes, contaminating floors and blankets.

Insect populations such as mosquitoes thrive during warming trends. Droughts reduce populations of predators of mosquitoes such as frogs, dragonflies, ladybugs, and lacewings. New York experienced a mild winter in 1998–1999, allowing mosquitoes to survive in hibernation. The dry spring and the summer heat waves of 1999 decreased mosquito predators and evaporated mosquito larvae breeding sites. The mosquitoes thrived in drainpipes and sewer puddles that contained concentrated organic compounds that attracted birds in search of water. This provided an opportunity for mosquitoes to thrive and become infected with WNV when feeding on sick birds. Infected mosquites can then transmit WNV to humans and animals while biting to take blood.

It is expected that extreme floods, droughts, and warming trends will be more common over the next 200 years. Viral pathogens will adapt to new environments in developing and industrialized countries. Global warming and air travel between continents will spread vectorborne diseases. It will take an international effort to control the impact resulting from these climate changes and disease epidemics.

Summary

In the past three decades, humans have faced many new and reemerging infectious diseases of viral origin. There are many reasons for the emergence of new viral diseases (Table 18-3). It is necessary to prepare to confront the unexpected. Viral, human, and ecological factors contribute to their emergence. Of these three factors, human behavior plays the most important role in influencing disease emergence and patterns. The three main factors have been dissected into further individual causes:

- Viral factors:
  - point mutations
  - certain genes mutate more rapidly
  - antigenic drift and shift
  - recombination
  - reassortment of viral genomes

TABLE 18-3	Reasons for the Emergence or Reemergence of Viral Diseases										
Viral Pathogen Factor	HIV	Monkeypox	Chikungunya Virus	West Nile Virus	Norovirus	Nipah Virus	*Sin Nombre* Hantavirus	Avian Influenza	SARS-CoV	Mumps	Marburg Virus
Viral mutation	X		X				X	X			
Human travel and migration	X	X	X	X	X			X	X	X	
Human population growth and urbanization					X		X	X	X		
Humans and deforestation											
Humans and agriculture						X					
Human exposure to zoonotic diseases via hunting and pasturing	X					X	X	X	X		X
Humans and commerce		X						X			X

TABLE 18-3 | Reasons for the Emergence or Reemergence of Viral Diseases (Continued)

Viral Pathogen	HIV	Monkeypox	Chikungunya Virus	West Nile Virus	Norovirus	Nipah Virus	Sin Nombre Hantavirus	Avian Influenza	SARS-CoV	Mumps	Marburg Virus
Human social behavior: Sex and drugs	X										
Human social behavior: Cultural traditions											X
Humans and modern medicine and unsafe practices	X										X
Humans and breakdown in public health measures	X		X					X	X		X
Ecological factors: Rain			X			X					
Ecological factors: Drought				X			X				

- Human factors:
  - population growth and megacities (density/overcrowding)
  - human movement (travel and migration)
  - human exposure to zoonotic diseases (pasture and hunting practices)
  - human agricultural practices, deforestation, and dam construction
  - humans and global commerce
  - human social behavior (sex, intravenous drugs, cultural traditions, and research)
  - human medicine and susceptibility to infection
- Ecological factors:
  - Climate variability (El Niño rains, droughts)

A combination of factors contributes to emerging viral disease outbreaks. The future is hard to predict but we can be certain that we are going to continue be challenged by new and reemerging viral diseases.

Viruses live in a world without borders. Organized community efforts will be needed to recognize, prevent, and control the future viruses that will challenge us.

Resources

Primary Literature and Reviews

Arthur, R. R. et al. 1993. "Recurrence of Rift Valley Fever in Egypt." *Lancet* 342(8880):1149–1150.

Bahta, L. et al. 2005. "Poliovirus Infections in Four Unvaccinated Children— Minnesota, August–October, 2005." *MMWR* 54(Dispatch):1–3.

Beasely, D. W. C. 2005. "Recent Advances in the Molecular Biology of West Nile Virus." *Curr Mol Med* 5:835–850.

Busch, M. et al. 2003. "Update: Detection of West Nile Virus in Blood Donations— United States, 2003." *MMWR* 52:916–919. [Erratum, *MMWR Morb Mortal Wkly Rep.* 2003. 52:942.]

Centers for Disease Control and Prevention (CDC). 1999. "Update: Outbreak of Nipah Virus—Malaysia and Singapore, 1999." *MMWR* 48(16):335–337.

Chang, C. C. et al. 2002. "Evolution of Porcine Reproductive and Respiratory Syndrome Virus During Sequential Passages in Pigs. *J Virol* 76(10):4750–4763.

Chironna, M. et al. 2003. "Prevalence Rates of Viral Hepatitis Infections in Refugee Kurds from Iraq and Turkey." *Infection* 31:70–74.

Cox-Foster, D. L. et al. 2007. "A Metagenomic Survey of Microbes in Honey Bee Collapse Disorder." *Science* 318(5848):283–287.

Cramer, E. H., Gu, D. X., and Durbin, R. E. 2003. "Diarrheal Disease on Cruise Ships, 1990–2000." *Am J Prev Med* 24:227–233.

Dato, V. et al. 2003. "Hepatitis A Outbreak Associated with Green Onions at a Restaurant—Monaca, Pennsylvania, 2003." *MMWR* 52(47):1155–1157.

Fauci, A. S., Touchette, N. A., and Folkers, G. K. 2005. "Emerging Infectious Diseases: A 10-year Perspective from the National Institute of Allergy and Infectious Diseases." *EID* 11(4):519–525.

Gaidet, N. et al. 2007. "Avian Influenza Viruses in Water Birds, Africa." *EID* 13(4):626–629.

Gershman, K. 2006. "Update: Multistate Outbreak of Mumps—United States, January 1–May 2, 2006." *MMWR* 55(Dispatch):1–5.

Gibbs, E. P. J. 2005. "Emerging Zoonotic Epidemics in the Interconnected Global Community." *Vet Rec* 157:673–679.

Giladi, M. et al. 2001. "West Nile Encephalitis Virus in Israel, 1999: The New York Connection." *EID* 7(4):659–661.

Gupta, R. 2005. "Recent Outbreak of Rabies Infections in Brazil Transmitted by Vampire Bats." *Eurosurveillance* 10:11.

Hernandez, F. et al. 1997. "Rotavirus and Hepatitis A Virus in Market Lettuce (*Latuca sativa*) in Costa Rica." *Int J Food Microbiol* 37(2–3):221–223.

Holland, R. A., Wikelski, M., and Wilcove, D. S. 2006. "How and Why Insects Migrate?" *Science* 313:794–796.

Holmes, E. C., and Rambaut, A. 2004. "Viral Evolution and the Emergence of SARS Coronavirus." *Philos Trans Soc Lond B Biol Sci* 359(1447):1059–1065.

Hughes, J. M. 2001 "Emerging Infectious Diseases: A CDC Perspective." *EID* 7(3 Suppl):494–496.

Kamugisha, C., Cairns, K. L., and Akim, C. 2003. "An Outbreak of Measles in Tanzanian Refugee Camps." *J Infect Dis* 187:S58–S62.

Ka-Wai Hui, E., 2006. "Reasons for the Increase in Emerging and Re-emerging Viral Infectious Diseases." *Microbes and Infect* 8:905–916.

Leroy, E. M. et al. 2005. "Fruit Bats Are Reservoirs of Ebola Virus." *Nature* 438:575–576.

Kumar, D., and Humar, A. 2005. "Emerging Viral Infections in Transplant Recipients." *Curr Opin Infect Dis* 18(4):337–341.

Lopman, B. et al. 2004. "Increase in Viral Gastroenteritis Outbreaks in Europe and Epidemic Spread of New Norovirus Variant." *Lancet* 363:682–688.

Lu, Y. et al. 2005. "The Needs of AIDS-Infected Individuals in Rural China." *Qual Health Res* 15(9):1149–1163.

Maiztegui, J. T. 1975. "Clinical and Epidemiological Patterns of Argentine Haemorrhagic Fever." *Bull WHO* 52:567–575.

Morse, S. S. 1995. "Factors in the Emergence of Infectious Diseases." *EID* 1(1):7–15.

Murray, K. et al. 1995. "A Morbillivirus That Caused Fatal Disease in Horses and Humans." *Science* 268(5207):94–97.

Nabeth, P. et al. 2001. "Rift Valley Fever Outbreak, Mauritania, 1998: Seroepidemiologic, Virologic, Entomologic, and Zoologic Investigations." *EID* 7(6):1052–1054.

Oregon Dept. of Health Services et al., 2007. "Acute Respiratory Disease Associated with Adenovirus Serotype 14—Four States, 2006–2007." *MMWR* 56(45):1181–1184.

Pealer L. N., Marfin, A. A., Petersen, L. R., et al. 2003. "Transmission of West Nile Virus Through Blood Transfusion in the United States in 2002." *N Engl J Med* 349:1236–1245.

Petersen, L. R., and Roehrig, J. T. 2001. "West Nile Virus: A Reemerging Global Pathogen." *EID* 7:611–614.

ProMED-mail. 2004. "Poliomyelitis—Africa: Sudan." ProMED-mail 2004;16 Dec: 2004, 1216.3324.

ProMED-mail. 2005. Marburg Hemorrhagic Fever—Angola. ProMED-mail 2005; 26 May: 2005. 0526.1458.

ProMED-mail. 2005. "Norovirus, Post-Hurricane—USA (Louisiana)." ProMED-mail 2005;11 Sep: 2005. 0911.2693.

ProMED-mail. 2005. "Rabies, Human, Vampire Bats—Brazil (Maranhao)." ProMED-mail 2005; 2 Nov: 2005. 1102.3203.

ProMED-mail. 2005. "Rabies, Human, Vampire Bats—Brazil (Maranhao)." ProMED-mail 2005; 10 Nov: 2005. 1110.3287.

Qian, H.-Z. et al. 2006. "Co-infection with HIV and Hepatitis C Virus in Former Plasma/Blood Donors: Challenge for Patient Care in China." *AIDS* 20:1429–1435.

Reid, T. M., and Robinson, H. G. 1987. "Frozen Raspberries and Hepatitis A." *Epidemiol Infect* 98(1):109–112.

Rodas, J. D., and Salvato, M. S. 2006. "Tales of Mice and Men: Natural History of Arenaviruses." *Rev Col Cienc Pec* 19(4):382–400.

Roehrig, J. T., Layton, M., Smith, P., et al. 2002. "The Emergence of West Nile Virus in North America: Ecology, Epidemiology, and Surveillance." *Curr Top Microbiol Immunol* 267:223–240.

Rosenblum, L. S. et al. 1990. "A Multifocal Outbreak of Hepatitis A Traced to Commercially Distributed Lettuce." *Amer J Pub Health* 80(9):1075–1079.

Rosenthal, M. 2006. "Transmission of Bloodborne Infections Also Occurs in the U.S." *Infect Dis News,* August/2006.

Russel, R. C. 1987. "Survival of Insects in the Wheel Bays of a Boeing 747B Aircraft on Flights Between Tropical and Temperate Airports." *Bull WHO* 65(5):659–662.

Staggs, W. et al. 2005. "Import-Associated Measles Outbreak—Indiana, May–June 2005." *MMWR* 54(42):1073–1076.

Stokstad, E. 2007. "Genomics: Puzzling Decline of U.S. Bees Linked to Virus from Australia." *Science* 317(5843):1304–1305.

Sutherst, R. W. 2004. "Global Change and Human Vulnerability to Vector-Borne Diseases." *Clin Microbiol Rev* 17(1):136–173.

Tian, K. et al. 2007. "Emergence of Fatal PRRSV Variants: Unparalleled Outbreaks of Atypical PRRS in China and Molecular Dissection of the Unique Hallmark." *PLoS ONE* 2(6):e526. DOI:10.1371/journal.pone.0000526.

Wendong, L. 2005. "Bats Are Natural Reservoirs of SARS-like Coronaviruses." *Science* 310:676–679.

Widdowson, M.-A., Monroe, S. S., and Glass, R. L. 2005. "Are Noroviruses Emerging?" *EID* 11(5):735–737.

Wolfe, N.D. et al. 2007. "Origins of Major Human Infectious Diseases." *Nature* 447: DOI10.1038/nature05775.

World Health Organization et al. 2006. "The Global HIV/AIDS Pandemic, 2006." *MMWR* 55(31):841–844.

■ Popular Press

Abraham, T. 2007. *Twenty-First Century Plague: The Story of SARS.* Baltimore: The Johns Hopkins University Press.

Carborne, K. M. Ed. 2002. *Borna Disease Virus and Its Role in Neurobehavioral Disease.* Washington, DC: ASM Press.

Close, W. T. 2002. *Ebola Through the Eyes of the People.* Marbleton, WY: Meadowlark Springs Productions.

Crosby, M. C. 2006. *The American Plague: The Untold Story of Yellow Fever, the Epidemic That Shaped Our History.* New York: Berkley Publishing Group.

Dickerson, J. L. 2006. *Yellow Fever: A Deadly Disease Poised to Kill Again.* Amherst, New York: Prometheus Books.

Garrett, L. 2000. *Betrayal of Trust: The Collapse of Global Public Health.* New York: Hyperion.

Goudsmit, J. 2004. *Viral Fitness: The Next SARS and West Nile in the Making.* New York: Oxford Press.

Greenblatt, C. and Spigelman, M. Eds. 2003. *Emerging Pathogens: Archaeology, Ecology & Evolution of Infectious Diseases.* Oxford, England: Oxford University Press.

Harper, D. R., and Meyer, A. S. 1999. *Of Mice, Men, and Microbes: Hantavirus.* San Diego: Academic Press.

Krauss, H., et al. Eds. 2003. *Zoonoses: Infectious Diseases Transmissible from Animals to Humans.* 3rd ed. Washington, DC: ASM Press.

Krause, R. M., Gallin, J. I., and Fauci, A. Eds. 2000. *Emerging Infections: Biomedical Research Reports.* San Diego: Academic Press.

Loh, C. and Civic Exchange. Eds. 2004. *At the Epicentre: Hong Kong and the SARS Outbreak.* Hong Kong: Hong Kong University Press.

McKenna, M. 2004. *Beating Back the Devil: On the Front Lines with the Disease Detectives of the Epidemic Intelligence Service.* New York: Free Press.

McNeill, W. H. 1977. *Plagues and Peoples.* New York: Anchor Books Doubleday.

Morse, S. S. 1996. *Emerging Viruses.* Reprint Edition. Oxford, England: Oxford University Press.

Osterholm, M. T. and Swartz, John. 2000. *Living Terrors: What America Needs to Know to Survive the Coming Bioterrorist Catastrophe.* New York: Delacorte Press.

Peters, C. J., and Olshaker, M. 1997. *Virus Hunter: Thirty Years of Battling Hot Viruses Around the World.* New York: Anchor Books.

Quammen, D. October, 2007. "Deadly Contact: How Animals and Humans Exchange Disease." *National Geographic* 79–105.

Scheld, W. M., Murray, B. E., and Hughes, J. H., Eds. 2004. *Emerging Infections.* Washington, DC: ASM Press.

Schlossberg, D. Ed. 2004. *Infections of Leisure.* 3rd ed. Washington, DC: ASM Press.

Snodgrass, M. E. 2003. *World Epidemics: A Cultural Chronology of Disease from Prehistory to the Era of SARS.* Jefferson, NC: McFarland.

Villarreal, L. P. 2005. *Viruses and the Evolution of Life.* Washington, DC: ASM Press.

Walters, M. J. 2003. *Six Modern Plagues and How We Are Causing Them.* Washington, DC: Shearwater Books.

Wheelis, M., Rozsa, Lajos, and Dando, Malcolm, Eds. 2006. *Deadly Cultures: Biological Weapons Since 1945.* Cambridge, MA: Harvard University Press.

Zelicoff, A. P., and Bellomo, M. 2005. *Microbe: Are We Ready for the Next Plague?* New York: Amacom American Management Association.

■ **Video Productions**

The Next Plague: The Nipah Virus. 1998. Films for the Humanities.

The New Explorers: On the Trail of a Killer Virus. 2001. A&E Production.

Outbreak: Stopping SARS. 2003. Films for the Humanities.

SARS: The True Story. 2003. Films for the Humanities.
Emerging Diseases. 2004. Films for the Humanities
Infectious Diseases: More Mobility, Greater Danger. 2004. Films for the Humanities.
The Age of Viruses. 2005 Films for the Humantities.
H5N1: Killer Flu. 2005. Films for the Humanities.
Influenza. 2005. Films for the Humanities.
Ready or Not: Avian Flu. Aired 4/10/2006. ABC News Primetime.
RX for Survival: A Global Health Challenge. 2006. PBS.
NOVA: Epidemic—Ebola, AIDS, Bird Flu and Typhoid. 2007. WGBH. Boston.
Mega Disasters: Alien Infection. 2007. A&E Productions.

■ eLearning

http://biology.jbpub.com/book/virology
The site features eLearning, an online review area that provides quizzes and other tools to help you study for your class. You can also follow useful links for in-depth information, or just find out the latest virology and microbiology news.

CASE STUDY QUESTIONS

These questions relate to the Case Study presented at the beginning of the chapter.

1. Could Borna disease virus be an emerging zoonotic pathogen? Discuss your answer.

2. What population of people would you expect to be most vulnerable to this viral pathogen?

3. The field of Borna disease virus research is still fairly new and controversial. Perform a literature search and write an up-to-date summary of modern Borna disease virus research.

Additional Case Study
Access to proper sanitation in some parts of India does not exist. About 88% of the population of India has access to safe water and 31% has access to safe sanitation. Members of one Hindu caste known as *untouchables* are pig owners in charge of cleaning up the slums of some cities. They allow the pigs to roam and consume household garbage, including human waste. In February of 2005, there were reports of 20 to 25 pigs dying each day in a slum of Agra as a result of an illness the *untouchables* called "pig flu." Officials stated that the pigs died of "cold and viral fever." There were over 100 rotting pig carcasses in the city slum at the time of the report.

1. If you were hired to investigate this outbreak, how would you rule whether or not an infectious agent caused this mysterious pig disease?

2. What types of specimens would you collect during the investigation and what would you test them for?

3. What factors in this instance may be contributing to the emergence of a viral pathogen?

4. What efforts would you use to improve sanitation?

5. How should carcass disposal be handled?

■ Reference

ProMED-mail. Unexplained deaths, pigs—India (Kerala) 2005;15 Feb:20050215.0506.

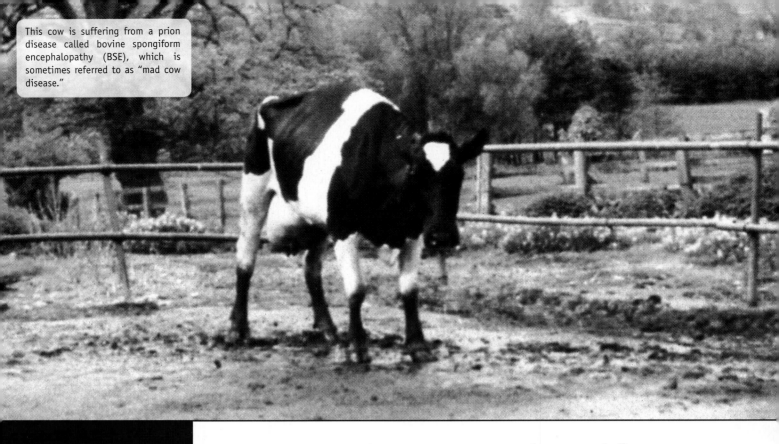

This cow is suffering from a prion disease called bovine spongiform encephalopathy (BSE), which is sometimes referred to as "mad cow disease."

CHAPTER

19

" *It has just stopped me cold from eating another burger!* **"**

Oprah Winfrey, during a segment on mad cow disease on her April 16, 1996 show

What About Prions and Viroids?

CASE STUDY

In 1990 the first cases of feline spongiform encephalopathy (FSE) were reported in the United Kingdom. In Italy in 1993, a cat owner and his cat suffered from simultaneous transmissible spongiform encephalopathies (TSEs). The 7-year-old short-haired, spayed female cat was usually fed canned food and slept under its owner's bed. In November of 1993, the cat became **ataxic** (lost its coordination) and suffered from bouts of frenzy and twitches. The cat was euthanized in mid-January, 1994. The clinical presentation of symptoms of the cat was different from previously reported feline spongiform encephalopathies.

The 60-year-old cat owner was admitted to a hospital in November of 1993. He suffered from an unsteady ataxic gait, jerky movements, loss of speech, and was unable to swallow. He died in January of 1994. There was no recollection of the cat biting her owner and the owner had no unusual dietary habits. The *PRNP* genes of the cat and owner were analyzed but no mutations were found. Both the cat and the owner were methionine homozygous at codon 129. Researchers have usually found clinical disease only occurs in patients homozygous for methionine at codon 129 of the *PRNP* gene. The brains of the cat and owner were analyzed. Both brains shared similar pathology: spongiosis.

Prions and **viroids** are **unconventional infectious agents**. They are not viruses, bacteria, or parasites, but instead are molecules that cause fatal diseases in humans and animals or cause a variety of effects in plants. Given their simple nature, these molecules find a home in virology textbooks. **Prions are proteins** that cause a group of diseases of the brain and nervous system called **transmissible spongiform encephalopathies** (TSEs). These diseases affect humans, sheep, goats, mink, deer, elk, antelope, and cats (Tables 19-1 and 19-2). *None of the TSEs evoke a host immune response.* Instead, they cause a noninflammatory process that results in the vacuolation or **spongiosis** in the gray matter of the brain. The observation that there is no inflammation or immune defense associated with prion diseases is fundamentally important for understanding the prion model of disease. **Viroids are small pathogenic RNAs** that cause viruslike diseases in plants. They do not code for proteins and thus depend on plant host enzymes for their replication and other functions.

TABLE 19-1 — Human Prion Diseases

Disease	Cause	Life Span After Symptoms Occur
Kuru	Cannibalism	3–6 months
Variant Creutzfeldt-Jakob disease (vCJD)	Consumption of contaminated beef (bovine prions)	13–14 months
Creutzfeldt-Jakob disease	Inherited germline mutation in PrP gene, sporadic (unknown cause), or iatrogenic	4–5 months
Gerstmann-Straussler-Scheinker disease (GSS)	Inherited germline mutation in PrP gene	2–6 years
Fatal familial insomnia (FFI)	Inherited germline mutation in PrP gene	12 months

TABLE 19-2 — Animal Prion Diseases

Disease	Animal Host
Scrapie	Sheep and goats
Chronic wasting disease (CWD)	Deer and elk
Feline spongiform encephalopathy (FSE)	Cats
Bovine spongiform encephalopathy (BSE)	Cattle
Exotic ungulate encephalopathy (EUE)	Nyala and Greater Kudu (antelope in South Africa)
Transmissible mink encephalopathy (TME)	Mink

19.1 The "Mad" Diseases, Transmissible Spongiform Encephalopathies (TSEs): Kuru and Cannibalism

■ Figure 19-1
A Fore child with symptoms of the ambulant stage of Kuru.

Deadly Feasts by Richard Rhodes is a compelling account of prion diseases. The author begins the book by describing **Kuru**, a fatal brain disorder that occurred among the South Fore people of the highlands of Papua New Guinea at epidemic levels during the 1950s and '60s. Kuru was known as "laughing sickness" because patients suffered from outbursts of laughter during the second stage of the disease. In the 1950s scholars Vin Zigas, Shirley Lindenbaum, and Daniel Carleton Gadjusek traveled to New Guinea to study this mysterious disease. Gadjusek's first impressions and observations of the Kuru epidemic were that the disease appeared to be "classical advancing Parkinsonism involving every age, overwhelming in females. . . ." As field work progressed, Lindenbaum reported that in the early 1960s fewer than 10% females survived past child-bearing age, whereas males only had a 20% chance of dying of the disease. Gadjusek reported that Kuru victims suffered from three distinct stages of symptoms:

1. The **ambulant stage**: patients suffered from an unsteady gait, voice, hands, and eyes; tremors and shivering; slurred and deteriorating speech; loss of coordination in the lower extremities that slowly moved upward (**Figure 19-1**).

2. The **sedentary stage**: patients could no longer walk without support; experienced tremors and coordination problems with increased severity; suffered from jerky muscular movements, outbursts of laughter, depression, and mental slowing.

3. The **terminal stage**: patients could not sit without support; tremors and slurring of speech continued in severity. Patients suffered from incontinence, difficulty swallowing, and deep ulcerations.

The Fore people of Papua New Guinea began eating their dead relatives (**endocannibalism**) during the early 1900s. Endocannibalism is a form of cannibalism in which the Fore ate their relatives as a sign of love and respect, as part of their funeral rites, and everyone who died in the community was eaten. Human flesh was regarded as meat. The adult males preferred to eat domestic pigs or wild boars and Kuru victims were considered excellent sources of food because the fat of the victims resembled pork.

Lindenbaum's description (in *Kuru Sorcery: Disease and Danger in the New Guinea Highlands*, 1978) of this practice is as follows:

> *After a person's death, the maternal next of kin would dismember the corpse. She removed the arms and feet and stripped the muscle from the limbs. Subsequently, the chest was cut open and the internal organs were removed. The head was severed from the skull and broken open. The brain was scooped out of the skull. Bones were broken and marrow was sucked out. The wife was expected to eat the penis of her dead husband. The entire body was eaten, even the feces. Care was taken not to rupture the gallbladder because gallbladder contents seemed to spoil or ruin the taste of the body parts. A man's brain was eaten by his sister. A woman's brain was given to her son's wife or her brother's wife. Children under the age of ten and the elderly ate whatever the mothers ate and what was given to them: morsels of the brain or other internal organs. After the age of ten, the male children lived with the adult males. Males never ate the meat of females.*

Scientists came up with two main hypotheses to explain the cause of Kuru:

1. Kuru was a hereditary disease.
2. A biological agent transmitted by endocannibalism caused Kuru.

Heredity was considered unlikely rather quickly because the disease appeared recently in the Fore population (between 1900 and 1920). It quickly spread through a population of 40,000 that could not have all descended from a single individual. During the early 1960s it reached epidemic numbers. About 1% of the South Fore people were dying of Kuru each year. Eight times more females than males contracted the disease. Females of all ages got the disease; old men and young boys got the disease as well. It was determined that the practice of endocannibalism began about ten years before the first appearance of Kuru.

James McConnell published a controversial paper regarding cannibalism in 1962. Mc-Connell concluded that untrained flatworms (planaria) that were fed chopped up trained flatworms retained some of the memories of the flatworms they ate. This research pointed Kuru researchers to the idea that cannibalism can affect the brain and raised the question of whether Kuru and cannibalism could be connected. Gajdusek's team inoculated the brains of healthy chimpanzees with brain suspensions made from Kuru patients. The chimpanzees were held in isolation and observed for up to five years. Three chimpanzees developed Kuru-like syndromes similar to that seen in human patients. The average time it took for the chimpanzees to become sick was between 18 and 21 months (this is considered a very long incubation period). These experiments lead to the conclusion that a transmissible agent caused the Kuru-like disease, and that the agent was either a dormant or slow virus. In 1976, Gajdusek shared the Nobel Prize for Physiology or Medicine with Baruch S. Blumberg for their research on the origin and dissemination of infectious diseases. Blumberg gained notoriety for his work on the Australian antigen and the discovery of Hepatitis B virus, whereas Gajdusek was awarded for work on the origin of a class of diseases now called TSEs.

In 1972, Stanley Prusiner initiated research to isolate the infectious agent that caused Kuru and similar diseases such as Creutzfeldt-Jakob disease (CJD) and scrapie, a disease affecting sheep. Ten years later, Prusiner and his colleagues isolated a single infectious protein from diseased hamster brains that they named a "prion," which stands for "proteinaceous infectious particle." The scientific community was very skeptical about this research because the infectious agent did not contain any nucleic acid or hereditary DNA or RNA. In 1984, Prusiner's team showed that the gene encoding the prion was found in the brains of all animals tested, including humans. It later became clear that there were two forms of the prion: the normal PrP^C proteins and the other prion that caused disease—the prion that causes scrapie—termed PrP^{SC}.

Another pioneer of prion research, Reed B. Wickner of the National Institutes of Health, reported in 1994 that a yeast prion called Ure2p could change shape and propagate that shape to change other yeast proteins. The Ure2p protein shared no sequence homology between the yeast and human protein. Wickner's group continues to contribute to the field of prion research using yeast as a model. His work was critical in the acceptance of Prusiner's work. In 1997 Prusiner was awarded the Nobel Prize in Physiology or Medicine for his "discovery of prions—a new principle of infection."

19.2 PrP and the "Protein Only" Hypothesis

Prions are infectious proteins that are highly resistant to routinely used methods of decontamination and steam sterilization. They are not inactivated by proteases, organic solvents, alkaline cleaners, ultraviolet light radiation, ethanol, formaldehyde, or extremely high temperatures (e.g., greater than 100°C; sterilization for one hour at 121°C in an autoclave does not kill prions). Researchers working with tissues, infectious waste, and instruments used in the processing of prion-contaminated samples decontaminate them in 1 N NaOH or undiluted fresh household bleach followed by autoclaving at 132°C for 4.5 hours.

PrP^C PrP^{res}

■ α helix
■ β sheet
□ Loop

■ **Figure 19-2**
Tertiary structure of PrP^C and PrP^{res} proteins. The blue regions represent β sheets, the yellow regions are loops, and the green regions are α helices. The β sheets are thought to cause the amyloid clumping or aggregates in the brain.

There are two distinct conformations of the prion protein, PrP. PrP^C is found throughout tissues of the body in healthy people and animals (**Figure 19-2**). The normal cellular form of PrP, designated **PrP^C**, is sensitive to denaturing agents. The "**protein only**" **hypothesis** proposes that the abnormal, misfolded infectious form of PrP is able to initiate a reaction that causes the PrP^C to convert to the highly pathogenic and **resistant** or stable form termed **PrP^{res}**. Over time the PrP^{res} accumulates into clumps that damage or destroy nerve cells in the brain.

Purifying the infectious scrapie agent from hamster brains led to the amino acid sequence of the PrP^{SC} (or PrP^{res}) and, subsequently, to the identity of the encoding gene, PRNP. The PRNP gene is located on the short arm of chromosome 20 of humans. It codes for a protein of about 254 amino acids in length (**Figure 19-3**). It is unique, with no other proteins of similar homology to it in the database. Sequence analysis indicates that the prion protein is targeted via a secretory pathway to the cell surface of neurons and other cell types. A glycosylinositol phospholipid anchors it into the membrane. While in the membrane it may bind copper, and then is cycled back into the cell via endocytic vesicles where it may be degraded in lysozymes (**Figure 19-4**). Experiments suggest that the infectious prion finds its way to the endocytic vesicles, where it interacts with and changes the conformation of the wild type noninfectious prion into the resistant form. These prions are resistant to degradation by the lysozymes. They accumulate, causing neurotoxicity.

Weak binding
Cu^{++}
Cu^{++} Cu^{++} **Strong binding**
Cu^{++} Cu^{++}

178   213
S   S

1   23   51   90   231   254

Signal peptide   Hydrophobic/toxic
        Octarepeats

■ **Figure 19-3**
Biochemical analysis of the prion amino acid sequence. It contains a signal peptide that targets it to the surface of cells, a hydrophobic region that binds copper with a high affinity, and an octarepeat motif that contains amino acid residues that have low affinity for metals, especially copper. It is held together by a single disulfide bond. Adapted from I. Jones. "Prions Show Their Metal." *Chembytes E-Zine*. The Royal Society of Chemistry, 2008. http://www.chemsoc.org/chembytes/ezine/2002/jones_apr02.htm.

Some researchers have hypothesized that other cellular factors stimulate the conversion of PrP^C to PrP^{res}. It has been shown that vertebrate host ssRNAs are required for the *in vitro* propagation of PrP^{res}. It is proposed that these specific ssRNAs bind avidly to and promote the conformational change in PrP^C to PrP^{res}.

Normal PrP^C is highly conserved in mammals and expressed predominantly in the brain. The exact function of PrP^C is unknown. Substantial scientific evidence suggests that it is a copper-binding protein. In the conversion to the aberrant form of the protein, copper-binding is lost. Other studies suggest that PrP^C can bind other metals such as manganese or zinc. Possible functions for PrP^C are roles in:

- signal transduction
- cellular differentiation
- cell adhesion
- copper transport
- resistance to the accumulation of destructive free radicals that can result in neuronal death

■ The Three Ways That TSEs Can Arise: Infection, Inherited, and Sporadic Forms

Sporadic CJD is the most frequent form of a human TSE. Its cause is unknown and patients usually die between the ages of 60 and 70 years old. Other forms of TSEs are inherited. Examples of genetic forms are genetic CJD, Gerstmann-Straussler-Scheinker disease and

■ Figure 19-4

Hypothetical model showing PrP^C involved in the secretory pathway of cells. PrP^{res} causes a conformational change in PrP^C, resulting in the accumulation of prions resistant to lysozomal degradation. Adapted from I. Jones. "Prions Show Their Metal." *Chembytes E-Zine*. The Royal Society of Chemistry, 2008. http://www.chemsoc.org/chembytes/ezine/2002/jones_apr02.htm.

fatal familial insomnia (Table 19-1). In 5% to 15% of TSE cases, mutations or insertions of nucleotides in the PRNP gene are found. A history of TSE or dementia is recorded in less than 50% of cases.

Creutzfeldt-Jakob disease can be inherited, sporadic, or infectious via diet (variant CJD) or acquired by iatrogenic means such as surgery, contaminated growth hormone injections, and corneal transplants. Kuru is an infectious form of TSE.

19.3 Oral Transmission: How Do "Eaten" Prions Travel to the Brain to Cause Disease? Why Isn't Variant CJD More Common?

The majority of experiments designed to study transmission of bovine spongiform encephalopathy (BSE) and other TSEs are with animals of the same species or across different species using the intracranial route of transmission. It is known that oral transmission of TSE diseases is very inefficient compared with intracerebral inoculations. Prion ingestion leads to infection of the gastrointestinal tract. Neuroinvasion of the prions occurs via the splanchnic and vagus nerves (the sympathetic peripheral nervous system) present in the abdominal region of the body that extends to the brain. New research suggests that prions may also invade the brain via the **hypoglossal nerve of the tongue**. Food products that contain tongue may be a potential source of prion infection for humans.

The **infectious dose** through ingestion of prion-contaminated food is unknown. A 2001 study by Gunn estimated the human oral infectious dose (ID_{50}) to be 10^{13} BSE prion molecules. This is a very large infectious dose compared to known bacterial and viral pathogens. It was mistakenly believed that the minimum infectious dose for cattle was the ingestion of 1 gram of infected brain. This estimate caused concern with regard to the potential risks of recycling BSE to cattle through the application of sewage sludge to agricultural land. A 4 mm mesh screen was placed over drains of slaughterhouses in the United Kingdom to prevent particles bigger than 0.1 g from entering the sewage system. A 2005 study by Lasmezas, though, showed that cattle are infected by oral doses as small as 0.01 to 0.001 g of brain.

Some studies suggest that very low doses through diet may be enough to cause a sub-clinical infection in humans. These individuals would be carriers without symptoms of the disease. The scale of the variant CJD epidemic was calculated to be a few thousand cases as an upper limit but carriers might pose risk for contamination of blood products, surgical instruments, and tissue transplants. The variant CJD epidemic in the United Kingdom remains a public health concern and a subject of speculation.

19.4 Other Routes of Transmission: Iatrogenic Transmission, Including Prions in Blood

An **iatrogenic disease** is one that may be inadvertently caused by a physician or surgeon or by a contaminated medical or surgical instrument or diagnostic procedure. Iatrogenic transmission of CJD, which is rare, has been reported since the late 1970s. The following incidents have been associated with iatrogenic transmission of CJD:

- recipients of a corneal graft acquired from donors who developed CJD
- patients acquired CJD from contaminated depth electroencephalography (EEG) electrodes implanted into their brains
- patients acquired CJD from contaminated neurosurgical instruments
- patients acquired CJD after acquiring human growth hormone from donors who developed CJD
- patients who received dura mater grafts from donors who developed CJD

The bloodborne transmission of variant CJD has long been suspected as possible for two reasons:

1. The variant CJD agent can be detected in lymphoid tissues, raising the possibility that it could also be found in circulating lymphocytes present in blood.
2. The prions may exist in the blood as it travels from the original site of infection of the gut to the brain.

Experimental studies have demonstrated the transmission of BSE to sheep by blood transfusion from asymptomatic infected sheep to healthy sheep, which means that the BSE agent is infectious in blood during the incubation period. Two highly probable bloodborne, person-to-person cases of transmission of variant CJD were reported in the United Kingdom. All cases of probable or definite variant CJD are reported to United Kingdom blood services by the national CJD surveillance unit. At least 48 individuals who received blood components from a total of 15 donors who later become variant CJD cases are being monitored as a precautionary step for their "at risk" status. Recipients of United Kingdom plasma products in the 1980s and early 1990s might also be at increased risk of variant CJD infection. For this reason, hemophiliacs in the United Kingdom have been notified

TABLE 19-3	UK Measures to Reduce the Spread of Variant CJD Associated with Blood or Blood Products

Year	Measure/Precautionary Step
1997	Blood components, plasma products, or tissues from an individual who contracted variant CJD were withdrawn or recalled
1998	Plasma imported from the U.S. for fractionation (extracting and purifying proteins in plasma for patients)
1998–1999	Leukodepletion of all blood used for transfusion
2002	Importation of fresh plasma from the U.S. for patients born after January 1, 1996
2004	Blood donation is not accepted from people who have received a blood transfusion in the UK since 1980
2005	Donors of blood to patients who have developed variant CJD following transfusion have been advised that they are "at risk" for variant CJD.

that they are at an increased risk of variant CJD. Table 19-3 lists the precautionary steps introduced in the United Kingdom to reduce the risk of variant CJD transmission by blood and blood products. Surveillance systems record the actual chain of exposure to blood.

19.5 Clinical Signs and Symptoms of Variant Creutzfeldt-Jakob Disease (Variant CJD)

Over 50% of variant CJD patients die before the age of 30 (the average age of death is 28). Patients suffering from sporadic or classic CJD die at an average of 68 years of age. The symptoms of variant CJD begin with anxiety, memory loss, mood changes, depression, and withdrawal, followed by obvious neurologic signs that include muscle twitching or spasms (jerky movements) and posture and gait abnormalities (motor difficulties). Final symptoms are loss of speech, stupor, and a persistent vegetative state (coma) before death 14 months after symptoms appear.

19.6 Diagnosis of Variant CJD

Most patients with variant CJD are often referred to a psychiatrist because of the behavioral changes associated with the disease. A definite diagnosis of variant CJD can be made via prion positive immunostaining of biopsy material from tonsil, spleen, or lymph nodes to detect prion accumulation. Other methods to aid diagnosis in conjunction with clinical symptoms are EEG (looking for slow or negative brain wave activity), magnetic resonance imaging (MRI, looking for brain lesions), and testing cerebral spinal fluid (CSF) for elevated levels of neuronal, astrocytic, and glial proteins. Elevated levels of CSF proteins reflect a change in blood–brain barrier function. The CSF proteins are released into the CSF as a consequence of extensive brain tissue damage.

There is no detectable immune response to infection, and as a result no routine test is available to diagnose asymptomatic individuals or patients experiencing symptoms. This rare but significant disease is difficult to diagnose with accuracy before death.

The gold standard of diagnosis is the **postmortem examination of brain tissues** via the demonstration of abnormal protease resistant prion proteins by Western blot analysis

Normal brain   Sporadic CJD brain   vCJD brain

(a)   (b)

■ **Figure 19-5**

(a) Detection of PrP^res by Western blot analysis. Brain homogenates are treated with proteinase K. Proteinase K will digest PrP^c but not PrP^res. Digests are electrophoretically separated on a polyacrylamide gel and then blotted onto a membrane that is probed with tagged anti-PrP antibodies. The arrows indicate PrP^c or PrP^res. The sporadic CJD brain contains a nonglycosylated PrP^res protein (resulting in a double band). **(b)** Samples of human brain tissues from a diseased individual suspected of variant CJD.

and immunocytochemistry of PrP^res accumulation in brain tissues (**Figure 19-5**). Genetic studies may also be performed to examine whether the patient is homozygous for methionine at codon 129 of the prion protein.

19.7 Pathogenesis of TSEs

The incubation period of TSEs is long (20 to 56 years). Individuals who lived in the South Fore in Papua New Guinea that were exposed to mortuary feasts are still dying of Kuru today, some 39 to 56 years after the cessation of cannibalism.

The brain, spinal cord, and retina are heavily infected before symptoms or clinical signs of infection appear. The term **spongiform**, which is sometimes referred to as **spongiosis**, comes from the microscopic observation of infected brains. Upon autopsy, slices of the brain contain vacuoles (clear zones) similar to a sponge (**Figure 19-6a**). Other classic histological changes of the brain are **neuronal loss**, **astrocytosis** (the spread of astrocytes to damaged tissues in the brain), and the formation of PrP threadlike structures that aggregate into **amyloid plaques**. The amyloid plaques accumulate in different regions of the brain (**Figure 19-6b**).

Depending upon what region of the brain is affected, different symptoms that are typical for the particular type of disease are evident; for example, memory is affected when the cerebral cortex is infected. The precise mechanisms that lead to brain damage are not known; however, evidence suggests that apoptosis causes neuronal death. No inflammation or immune defenses against prions exist, presumably because they are natural proteins (i.e., the body does not recognize prions as being foreign). The prion proteins become harmful only when they are converted to PrP^res.

19.8 Genetic Research and the Function of PrP^c

If the protein only hypothesis holds true, then animals that lack the *PRNP* gene would be resistant to scrapie infection. Charles Weissman's team of researchers created knock-out mice that do not express PrP^c. When they were injected with scrapie, the mice failed to develop symptoms of scrapie, an indication that the cellular form of PrP is required for propagation of the infectious from of PrP^res.

■ Figure 19-6

(a) Brain tissues showing histopathologic changes found in bovine spongiform encephalopathy. Note the presence of vacuoles or spongiosis. **(b)** Diagram showing the major regions of the human brain affected by the different TSEs. Adapted from University of Illinois at Urbana-Champaign, *BSE Slide Show,* http://w3.aces.uiuc.edu/AnSci/BSE.

The idea that prions act as copper-binding proteins has been enticing to scientists. Some neurological disorders such as Menkes syndrome and Wilson's disease are caused by altered copper metabolism. Could a change in copper binding be associated with the change to the pathogenic prion that is directly linked to TSEs? Weissman's group answered this question by introducing a *PRNP* gene that lacked the **octarepeat copper binding motif** into the prion knock-out mice (the gene that encodes the PrP protein has been disrupted in knock-out mice), the mice became susceptible to scrapie infection. This suggests that copper-binding octarepeat motif is not necessary for the pathogenic effects of prions. Does this mean copper binding is not important in pathogenesis?

Researchers have found a different site on PrP^C that is outside of the octarepeat region. It lies within the hydrophobic region of PrP^C and binds copper strongly. This region is essential for disease propagation (see Figure 19-3). Rather than PrP^C copper binding being involved in transport, it may be involved in chelating free copper. Free copper radicals are toxic to cells and are usually quickly scavenged. Experiments in which radioactive copper was added to cells expressing *PRNP in vitro* showed that PrP^C bound the radioactive copper at the cell surface and internalized it. These cells were more resistant to copper toxicity and oxidative stress compared to cells that did not express PRNP. Hence PrP^C may play a role in cleaning up free radicals similar to other **cellular scavenging mechanisms**. The loss of PrP^C function may change in copper balance in the brain and other organs and cause oxidative damage throughout the brain. Further research is needed to determine if oxidative stress and copper activity are involved the pathogenesis of TSEs.

■ Human Genetics: Codon 129

At least 50 known mutations in the *PRNP* gene that result in spontaneous PRP^res formation have been identified in people who suffer from inherited TSEs such as classic Creutzfeldt-Jakob disease, fatal familial insomnia, or Gerstmann-Straussler-Scheinker syndrome. A few of these mutations or common variations, referred to as **polymorphisms** in the *PRNP* gene, are recognized as increasing the susceptibility to TSEs (Table 19-4).

Point-Counterpoint: Is *Spiroplasma* Involved in TSEs? The Scientific Debate Continues

The beauty of science is that knowledge in the field is cumulative. The scientific method allows researchers to explain natural phenomena through the testing of hypothesis-driven experiments. As technology improves, the same questions asked 20 or 30 years ago can be revisited with new methods of experimentation in order to gain further knowledge.

In 1982 Prusiner's team showed that TSEs are caused by an infectious proteinaceous particle. These findings were unexpected: the idea that a protein can act as an infectious pathogen and cause the rapid deterioration of the central nervous system was only accepted after a long and grueling scientific debate.

A conventional pathogen, *Spiroplasma* sp., was postulated in the late 1970s to be associated with TSEs. *Spiroplasma* is a wall-less, fastidious bacterium that can pass through a 0.05 µM filter and has an affinity for mammalian membranes. Spiroplasmas can evade the host immune system and "enter" cells, thus making their detection difficult. Pathologist Frank O. Bastian examined brain biopsies from CJD patients using electron microscopy in 1976. He observed spiral structures foreign to the tissue that had features of a newly reported *Spiroplasma*.

Subsequently researchers found a fibril protein in scrapie-infected brain tissues that was named scrapie-associated fibril (SAF). SAF proteins were identical in shape to the internal fibrils of spiroplasmas (**Figure VF 19-1**). Antibodies to SAF reacted with the fibrillar proteins from *Spiroplasma* in Bastian's experiments. Hence the spiroplasmas contained fibrillar proteins that were morphologically and immunologically similar to the CJD and scrapie fibrillar proteins observed in diseased brain tissues. Bastian's team inoculated *Spiroplasma* proteins into rodents and was able to show a similar neuropathology to TSEs.

In 1983 a group of researchers was unable to confirm Bastian's findings. Dr. R. H. Leach's team was unable to culture spiroplasmas from the brain tissue of CJD patients, and the team also determined that antibodies that recognize *Spiroplasma* sp. were not detected in the sera of CJD patients. These negative results did not support Bastian's claims of CJD brains containing *Spiroplasma* structures.

In 2003 a group of Japanese researchers showed that the normal cellular form of PrP could serve as a receptor for the bacterium *Brucella*. The team implied that the abnormal, resistant form of PrP was a byproduct of infection rather than the cause. A prior study by Tremblay in 1998 showed that rodents infected with the scrapie prions that were treated with tetracycline did not develop scrapie, which supports the idea that the prion may serve as a receptor for a bacterial infection. Presumably in these experiments, the antibiotic tetracycline inhibited the bacterial infection, thus preventing scrapie.

In 2001 Bastian's team was able to demonstrate via polymerase chain reaction (PCR) the presence of *Spiroplasma* 16S rDNA in TSE-infected brain tissues (13 of 13 CJD cases and 5 of 9 scrapie cases), thus suggesting that *Spiroplasma* is not necessarily the causative agent of TSEs but is a factor involved in the pathogenesis of TSEs. A team of researchers countered with a 2005 blind study in which the

■ Figure VF 19-1
Scanning electron micrograph of a *Spiroplasma* (15,000×). They look similar to TSE fibrils.

DNA samples prepared from the brains of scrapie-infected or uninfected hamster brains were screened via PCR for *Spiroplasma* 16S rDNA sequences. No samples were positive for the bacterial *Spiroplasma* DNA. Alexeeva points out that PCR is an extremely sensitive method. Autopsy and field material are vulnerable to contamination with environmental DNAs that may interfere with the validation of the results obtained by researchers.

Is *Spiroplasma* involved in the pathogenesis of TSEs? Could bacteria cause TSEs by either triggering autoimmunity by molecular mimicry with bacterial antigens or as a source of chronic infection? How would you prove or disprove that *Spiroplasma* is responsible for the cytopathic effects such as spongiosis observed in the TSE-infected brains? This scientific investigation continues.

References

Alexeeva, I. et al. 2006. "Absence of Spiroplasma or Other Bacterial 16S rRNA Genes in the Brain Tissue of Hamsters with Scrapie." *J Clin Microbiol* 44(1):91–97.

Bastian, F. O. 1979. "Spiroplasma-like Inclusions in Creutzfeldt-Jakob Disease." *Arch Pathol Lab Med* 103(13):665–669.

Bastian, F. O., Dash, S., and Garry, R. F. 2004. "Linking Wasting Disease to Scrapie by Comparison of *Spiroplasma mirum* ribosomal DNA Sequences." *Exp Mol Pathol* 77(1):49–56.

Bastian, F. O., and Fermin, C. D. 2005. "Slow Virus Disease: Deciphering Conflicting Data on the Transmissible Spongiform Encephalopathies (TSE) Also Called Prion Diseases." *Micro Res and Tech* 66:239–246.

Bastian, F. O., and Foster, J. W. 2001. "*Spiroplasma* sp. 16S rDNA in Creutzfeldt-Jakob Disease and Scrapie As Shown by PCR and DNA Sequence Analysis." *J Neuropath Exp Neuro* 60(6):613–620.

Bastian, F. O., Jennings, R. A., and Gardner, W. A. 1987a. "Antiserum to Scrapie-Associated Fibril Protein Cross-Reacts with *Spiroplasma mirum* Fibril Protein." *J Clin Microbiol* 25:2430–2431.

Bastian, F. O., Jennings, R. A., and Hoff, C. J. 1987b. "Neurotropic Response of *Spiroplasma mirum* Following Peripheral Inoculation in the Rat." *Ann Inst Pasteur Microbiol* 138:651–655.

Leah, R. H., Mathews, W. B., and Will, R. 1983. "Creutzfeldt-Jakob Disease. Failure to Detect Spiroplasmas by Cultivation and Serological Tests." *J Neurol Sci* 59(3):349–353.

Tremblay, P. et al. 1998. "Doxycycline Control of Prion Protein Transgene Expression Modulates Prion Disease in Mice." *PNAS USA* 95:12580–12585.

Watarai, M. et al. 2003. "Cellular Prion Protein Promotes *Brucella* Infection into Macrophages." *J Exp Med* 198(1):5–17.

A common polymorphism at codon 129 of PRNP appears to act as a genetic susceptibility factor. Either methionine or valine is encoded at this position. All people suffering from variant CJD acquired through the consumption of prion-contaminated beef products have been homozygous for methionine. Methionine homozygosity is generally associated with a rapidly progressive dementing disease, whereas a more prolonged course with an onset of ataxia (loss of motor coordination) is most often associated with the valine/valine genotype.

19.9 Steps Toward Treatment and Vaccination

The following compounds were tested in cell lines and animal models: amphotericin B derivatives, Congo red, the spice curcumin, anthracyclines, polyanions, porphyrins, polyamines, β-sheet breakers, and even small interfering RNAs. There have been promising prion therapy approaches *in vitro*, but none of these treatments has been successful in human clinical trials due to toxicity or moderate untoward effects.

Anti-PrP antibodies can inhibit prion replication in cultured cells. Passive immunity experiments in which infected mice were injected with anti-PrP antibodies produced a delay in the onset of symptoms. Any active vaccination experiments, however, have met without success because the mammalian system is tolerant to PrP^C. Studies in which antibodies against PrP^C were injected into the brains of mice caused neurotoxicity. Vaccination efforts therefore should proceed through exhaustive safety trials in animals prior to application in humans.

19.10 Species Barrier: Bovine Spongiform Encephalopathy (BSE) and Variant Creutzfeldt-Jakob Disease

Transmissibility of TSEs is easy among the same species. A high degree of homology in the amino acid sequence of the prion protein between two species increases the efficiency of transmission. It is also possible, though, for transmission to occur between different species.

The origin of BSE is unclear. It has been hypothesized that it likely came from scrapie-infected sheep. The disease was spread to cattle by the ingestion of scrapie-contaminated bone meal derived from sheep **offal** fed to young calves. (Offal consists of brain, spleen, thymus, tonsil, and guts—parts of the animal normally discarded.) When bone meal of rendered bovine protein from infected cattle was fed to cattle in order to increase their milk yield, a new disease was further amplified among cattle.

Scrapie was considered a rare disease of sheep that did not infect humans. It has been recognized as a disease of sheep and goats in Great Britain and other countries in Western Europe for more than 250 years. The first case of scrapie in the United States was diagnosed in 1947 in a Michigan flock of sheep. The sheep owner had imported sheep of British origin through Canada for several years. Today, only Australia and New Zealand are free of scrapie.

BSE was first diagnosed in 1985. A dairy farmer in England noticed several cows with abnormal behavior: unsteady gait, kicking unexpectedly during milking, and aggressiveness—hence the term "raging" or "mad cow" disease. Other signs of the disease are:

- difficulty in rising from a lying position
- itching
- heightened sensory perception
- anorexia
- excessive licking
- decreased milk production

The symptoms last for two to six months before the animal dies. In 1986 an official diagnosis of BSE was made after brain tissues of slaughtered sick cows were similar to those of sheep suffering from scrapie. More BSE cases were diagnosed, and by June of 1990 14,324 cases of BSE were confirmed out of an estimated population of 10 million cattle in Great Britain. Since 1986 over 200,000 cattle in the United Kingdom have developed mad cow disease and one to three million were likely to have been infected with the BSE agent, most of which were slaughtered for human consumption before developing signs of the disease. Cattle and feed exported from the United Kingdom seeded smaller epidemics in

TABLE 19-4	Polymorphisms of the Human *PRNP* Gene
Polymorphism	**Disease Phenotype**
Point mutation: 129 methionine or valine	Increases susceptibility to vCJD but does not cause disease directly
Double point mutations: 171 asparagine or serine coupled and 129 methionine or valine	Increases susceptibility to vCJD but does not cause disease directly
Point mutation: D178N (aspartic acid → asparagine) and 129 methionine	Fatal familial insomnia
Point mutation: V180I (valine → isoleucine)	Creutzfeldt-Jakob disease
Point mutation: T183A (threonine → alanine)	Creutzfeldt-Jakob disease
Point mutation: E200K (glutamic acid → lysine)	Creutzfeldt-Jakob disease
Point mutation: R208H (arginine to histidine)	Creutzfeldt-Jakob disease
Point mutation: V210I (valine → isoleucine)	Creutzfeldt-Jakob disease
Point mutation: M232R (methionine → arginine)	Creutzfeldt-Jakob disease
Point mutation: P102L (proline → leucine) and 129 methionine	Gerstmann-Straussler-Scheinker disease
Point mutation: P105L (proline → leucine)	Gerstmann-Straussler-Scheinker disease
Point mutation: A117V (alanine → valine) and 129 methionine	Gerstmann-Straussler-Scheinker disease
48 base pair insertion	Creutzfeldt-Jakob disease
96 base pair insertion	Creutzfeldt-Jakob disease
120 base pair insertion	Creutzfeldt-Jakob disease
192 base pair insertion	Gerstmann-Straussler-Scheinker disease
216 base pair insertion	Gerstmann-Straussler-Scheinker disease

19.11 Plant Viroids: The Smallest Living Fossils of a Former RNA World?

551

other European countries. In 1989 the United Kingdom implemented control measures that included the culling of all sick animals and the banning of all bovine materials from entering food that was fed to cattle.

In humans, variant CJD was first described in the United Kingdom in 1996. The British Minister of Health declared that ten people had died from a new form of CJD, a variant form. Transmission of variant CJD was (and is) believed to be caused by the ingestion of cattle products contaminated with the BSE agent. As of October 2nd, 2007, 161 deaths of variant CJD patients were reported in the United Kingdom since the start of the epidemic. The epidemic in cattle is largely under control and any remaining risk to humans through the consumption of beef should be very small.

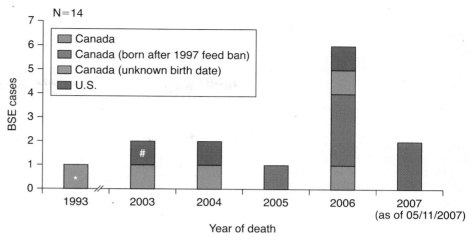

* Cow imported from the United Kingdom into Canada
# Cow imported from Canada into the United States

■ **Figure 19-7**

BSE cases in North America, 1993–May 11, 2007. Adapted from Division of Viral and Rickettsial Diseases, Centers for Disease Control and Prevention, *BSE,* http://www.cdc.gov/ncidod/dvrd/bse.

Cases of BSE are diminishing in the United Kingdom, and only two cases of BSE originating in the United States have occurred. Eight other BSE cases in the United States were cows imported from the United Kingdom into Canada or Canada into the United States (**Figure 19-7**). In 2006, the United State Department of Agriculture (USDA) announced the confirmation of a BSE-infected, 10-year-old cow in Alabama. The herd of origin of the cow is unknown.

19.11 Plant Viroids: The Smallest Living Fossils of a Former RNA World?

Viroids are small RNA molecules that infect plants in the same manner as conventional plant viruses (see Chapter 20), but they are smaller in genome size (ranging from 246 to 401 nucleotides in length) and are not encapsidated in a protein coat. Viroid RNAs are positive sense, single-stranded, covalently closed circular pathogenic molecules. Short helical regions are interrupted by internal and bulging loops. There are several regions in which base-pairing occurs across adjacent portions of the RNA molecule, a process sometimes referred to as **internal-basing**. In nature, viroids assume a rodlike conformation (~37 nm) that is very stable against ribonucleases. Viroids do not code for any proteins, and some viriod RNAs even lack the AUG initiation codon. Viroid RNAs are classified as noncoding RNAs. As a result, viroids depend upon the plant host enzymes for their replication and other functions.

There are two families of viroids: Avsunviroidae and Pospiviroidae. Members of the Avsunviroidae family have a branched or "quasi" rodlike secondary structure, whereas members of the Pospiviroidae family possess a true rodlike secondary structure (**Figures 19-8a–c**). Viroids contain five structural or functional domains: central (C), pathogenicity (P), variable (V), and two terminal domains (T1 and T2; Figure 19-8d). Viroids of the Avsunviroidae family lack a C region but possess hammerhead **ribozyme** structures with self-cleaving properties. The C domain consists of conserved nucleotides in the upper and lower strands of the molecule. A secondary structure—the bulges—in the conserved C domain are critical for viroid replication and processing. The P domain is associated with symptoms of viroid-infected plants. The V domains contain the highest variability in

■ **Figure 19-8**

Models of viroid structures. **(a)** Rodlike secondary structure of a member of the Pospiviroidae family. **(b)** "Quasi" rodlike secondary structure of the Avsunviroidae family member that has two terminal hairpins in the left part of the RNA molecule. **(c)** A member of the Avsunviroidae family with a complex branched structures. (a)–(c) Adapted from A. Gora-Sochacka, *Acta Biochim. Pol.* 51 (2004): 587–607. **(d)** Typical regions of a viroid: Terminal ends (T1 and T2), pathogenicity (P), conserved central region (C), and a variable domain (V). Adapted from an illustration by W. Rohde and J. W. Randles, Max Planck Institute for Plant Breeding Research.

(A)

(B)

(C)

| T1 | P | C | V | T2 |

Oligo - (A)

Left terminal domain

Pathogenic domain

Conserved central domain

Variable domain

Right terminal domain

(d)

(A)

Rolling circle ("toilet paper") mechanism of replication

Genome +

(−)

+

(B)

Positive-strand synthesis

(−)   (−)   (−)

↓

(+)   (+)   (+)

(C)

Self-cleavage reaction

(+)   (+)   (+)

(+)   (+)   (+)

(D)

Circularization

+   +   +

■ **Figure 19-9**

Rolling circle mechanism ("toilet paper" mechanism) of viroid RNA replication. The host cell RNA polymerase begins making multiple copies of the viroid genome much like toilet paper being unraveled from a dispenser. Adapted from J. Komoto, "The Hammerhead Ribozyme," *Introduction to the RNA World*, http://rnaworld.bio.ku.edu/class/RNA/RNA00/RNA_World_3.html.

nucleotide sequences between closely related viroids. The T domains are interchangeable between viroids and may play a role in viral movement.

Viroids do not replicate in the cytoplasm of cells like conventional plant RNA viruses. They instead traffic within the cell through the nuclear pores using a host nuclear localization protein that binds to viroid RNA. The viroids traffic from cell-to-cell through the plasmodesmata of the plant, traveling long distances through the phloem. All of these processes are associated with host proteins (refer to Chapter 20).

Viroids replicate in either the nucleus or the chloroplast of the plant. In the nucleus, the cellular DNA-dependent RNA polymerase III synthesizes the viroid RNA. The secondary structure of the viroid might provide binding signals to host factors directly or indirectly involved in the life cycle of the infectious agent. Members of the Avunsviroidae family accumulate and replicate in·chloraplasts, whereas members of the Pospiviroidae family have a nuclear localization. It is proposed the viroid replication occurs by the **rolling-circle mechanism of replication**. The host cell RNA polymerase synthesizes multiple copies of a linear complementary minus strand using the positive single-stranded RNA (ssRNA) viroid genome as a template. The new, longer plus-strand RNA is then synthesized by the host cell RNA polymerase. The multiunit +ssRNAs are cleaved via the **enzymatic self-cleavage** properties of the **hammerhead motifs** of the viroid RNAs. A host RNA ligase may cause circularization of the plus strands (**Figure 19-9**). Viroid strands of positive polarity localize to the nucleolus and nucleoplasm of host cells. Viroid strands of negative polarity are localized only to the nucleoplasm.

More than 40 viroid species and variants have been characterized (Table 19-5) and they cause at least 15 crop diseases. "Classical" viroids have been found only in plants. Human hepatitis delta virus RNA contains a viroid-like region with secondary structure that has similar properties to viroid RNAs; it also appears to replicate by some type of rolling-circle mechanism. The RNA is larger (1.7 kb), though, is encapsidated, and encodes a virion-associated protein (hepatitis delta antigen; see Chapter 17).

Viroids spread by mechanical transmission, vegetative propagation, and through pollen and seed (refer to Chapter 20). As a group, nothing distinguishes the disease symptoms produced by viroids from those caused by plant viruses. Infections from any type results in stunting, mottling, leaf distortion, and necrosis. Viroid diseases can cause a range of symptoms, from a slowly developing lethal disease to more mild and symptomless infections. Viroids cause a number of serious diseases in economically important plants including potato, tomato, coconut palm, grapevine, avocado, peach, apple, pear, citrus, coleus, and chrysanthemums.

Potato spindle tuber viroid (PSTVd) was the first viroid characterized. Theodor O. Diener, a plant pathologist at the U.S. Agricultural Research Service, discovered it in 1971. Tubers from diseased plants are long and narrow, with smooth skin and more eyes than are typically found in potatoes (**Figure 19-10**). The disease is spread easily by contact of healthy plants with diseased plants, by contaminated cultivating equipment, and through seed and pollen. All potatoes and tomatoes are susceptible to PSTVd.

Chrysanthemum stunt disease crippled and nearly destroyed the chrysanthemum industry prior to 1950. It was prevalent in U.S. and Canadian greenhouses with infections rates as high as 50% to 100%. **Chrysanthemum stunt viroid (CSVd)** is difficult to detect. It can be spread plant to plant by infected plant material that does not show symptoms and it takes weeks for symptoms to appear after an infection. Symptoms of chrysanthemum stunt include shortened stems, uneven flowering (such as faded or irregular color), smaller than normal foliage, irregular flower sizes, and uneven maturation of parts within single flowers (**Figure 19-11**). Chrysanthemums are now grown in "clean" rooms using stringent precautions to prevent infection by CSVd.

19.12 Viroid Pathogenesis

The various effects of viroid infection are likely caused by more than one mechanism. Recent evidence suggests that pathogenic viroids activate a plant RNA-activated protein kinase, termed PKR. The plant PKR is analogous to the mammalian PKR that is activated by viral RNAs, which leads to the induction of the interferon pathway (see Chapter 7).

TABLE 19-5	Examples of Plant Viroid Diseases

Viroid	Abbreviation
Apple dimple fruit viroid	ADFVd
Apple scar skin viroid	ASSVd
Australian grapevine viroid	AGVd
Avocado sunblotch viroid	ASBVd
Chrysanthemum stunt viroid	CSVd
Citrus bent leaf viroid	CBLVd
Citrus viroid species III	CVd-III
Citrus viroid species IV	CVd-IV
Citrus exocortis viroid	CEVd
Coconut cadang-cadang viroid	CCCVd
Coconut tinangaja viroid	CTiVd
Coleus blumei viroids I, II, and III	CBVd I, II and III
Columnea latent viroid	CLVd
Grapevine yellow speckle viroids 1 and 2	GYSVd 1 and 2
Hop latent viroid	HLVd
Hop stunt viroid	HSVd
Iresine viroid	IRVd
Mexican papita viroid	MPVd
Peach latent mosaic viroid	PLMVd
Pear blister canker viroid	PBCVd
Potato spindle tuber viroid	PSTVd
Tomato apical stunt viroid	TASVd
Tomato planta macho viroid	TPMVd

■ **Figure 19-11**
Chrysanthemums in the foreground of this photograph show symptoms of stunting and premature opening and color break caused by CSVd infection.

■ **Figure 19-10**
Healthy tuber (top row) and diseased tubers caused by PSTVd (bottom row).

Summary

Prions and viroids are simple pathogenic molecules. Some scientists propose that they are the smallest living fossils. Could either one be related to the emergence of early life? Both types of molecules are very stable in the environment. Prions are proteinaceous proteins, whereas viroids are circular +ssRNAs that contain a lot of secondary structure. Neither one codes for proteins and both have self-replicating properties.

Prions cause transmissible spongiform encephalopathies (TSEs) in animal and human hosts. TSEs are rare, incurable neurodegenerative fatal diseases. They do not induce an immune response. Creutzfeldt-Jakob disease (CJD) and variant CJD (caused by eating prion-contaminated beef products) are the most common TSEs in humans. The incubation period of TSEs is long (20–56 years). The brain, spinal cord, and retina are heavily infected before symptoms or clinical signs of infection appear. The term spongiform (sometimes referred to as spongiosis) comes from the microscopic observation of infected brains. Upon autopsy, slices of the brain contain vacuoles (clear zones), similar to a sponge. Other classic histological changes of the brain are neuronal loss, astrocytosis, and the formation of PrP threadlike structures that aggregate into amyloid plaques.

Prions are highly resistant to routinely used methods of decontamination and steam sterilization. There are two distinct conformations of the prion protein, PrP. PrP^C is found throughout tissues of the body in healthy people and animals. The normal cellular form of PrP, designated PrP^C, is sensitive to denaturing agents. Its exact function is unknown. The "protein only" hypothesis proposes that the abnormal, misfolded infectious form of PrP is able to initiate a reaction that causes the PrP^C to convert to the highly pathogenic and resistant or stable form termed PrP^{res}. Over time the PrP^{res} accumulates into clumps that damage or destroy nerve cells in the brain. At least 50 known mutations in the *PRNP* gene that result in spontaneous PRP^{res} formation have been identified in people who suffer from inherited TSEs such as classic Creutzfeldt-Jakob disease, fatal familial insomnia, or Gerstmann-Straussler-Scheinker syndrome.

Bovine spongiform encephalopathy (BSE), a disease in cattle, evolved into a mass epidemic in Great Britain, causing the death of more than 200,000 cattle during the 1980s to early 1990s. The BSE agent has been shown to cause variant CJD in humans. Symptoms of TSEs in humans vary, but they commonly include personality changes, psychiatric problems such as depression, lack of coordination, and/or an unsteady gait. Patients may experience involuntary jerking movements called myoclonus, unusual sensations, insomnia, confusion, or memory problems. In the later stages of the disease, patients have severe mental impairment and lose the ability to move or speak. Death occurs within a few months to a few years. There is no treatment that can halt the progression of TSEs.

Viroids are small (about 300 nucleotides), infectious, nonencapsidated +ssRNAs that infect plants of economic importance. They reproduce by a process called the rolling circle model of replication. Viroids do not code for any proteins and are totally dependent upon and interact with host cell proteins for their replication and movement from cell to cell. They do have self-cleavage ribozyme activity. Nothing distinguishes plant infections caused by viroids from those caused by viruses. Despite their simplicity, viroids can cause varied symptoms such as stunting, mottling, necrosis and leaf distortion, or no symptoms at all. These pathogens are difficult to control and can be catastrophic where large areas of planted food crops are destroyed by disease, thus threatening our food supplies.

Resources

Primary Literature and Reviews

Aguzzi, A. et al. 2004. "Progress and Problems in the Biology, Diagnostics, and Therapeutics of Prion Diseases." *J Clin Invest* 114:153–160.

Aguzzi, A., and Glatzel, M. 2006. "Prion Infections, Blood and Transfusions." *Nat Clin Pract Neurol* 2(6):321–329.

Almond, J., and Pattison, J. 1997. "Human BSE." *Nature* 389:437–438.

Alper, T. et al. 1967. "Does the Agent of Scrapie Replicate without Nucleic Acid?" *Nature* 214:764–765.

Animal and Plant Health Inspection Ser. et al. 2004. "Bovine Spongiform Encephalopathy in a Dairy Cow—Washington State, 2003." *MMWR* 52:1280–1285.

Baier, M. et al. 2003. "Prion Diseases: Infectious and Lethal Doses Following Oral Challenge." *J Gen Virol* 84:1927–1929.

Balter, M. 2000. "Epidemiology: Tracking the Human Fallout from 'mad cow disease.'" *Science* 289(5484):1452–1454.

Barnaby, C. H. et al. 2006. "Developing Therapeutics for the Diseases of Protein Misfolding." *Neurology* 66(Suppl 1):S118–S122.

Bartz, J. C. et al. 2003. "Rapid Prion Neuroinvasion Following Tongue Infection." *J Virol* 77(1):583–591.

Belay, E. D. et al. 2001. "Creutzfeldt-Jakob Disease in Unusually Young Patients Who Consumed Venison." *Arch Neurol* 58:1673–1678.

Belay, E. D. et al. 2004. "Chronic Wasting Disease and Potential Transmission to Humans." *EID* 10(6):977–984.

Belay, E. D., and Schonberger, L. B. 2005. "The Public Health Impact of Prion Diseases." *Annu Rev Public Health* 26:191–212.

Berger, J. R. et al. 1997. "Creutzfeldt-Jakob Disease and Eating Squirrel Brains." *Lancet* 350:642.

Bratosiewicz, J. et al. 2001. "Codon 129 Polymorphism of the PRNP Gene in Normal Polish Population and in Creutzfeldt-Jakob Disease, and the Search for New Mutations in PRNP Gene." *Acta Neurobiol Exp* 61:151–156.

Brown, D. R. 2004. "Metallic Prions." *Biochem Soc Symp* 71:193–202.

Brown, D. R. et al. 1999. "Normal Prion Protein Has an Activity Like That of Superoxide Dismutase." *Biochem J* 344:1–5.

Brown, P. 2004. "Mad-Cow Disease in Cattle and Human Beings." *Am Sci* 92:334–341.

Caughey, B., and Baron, G. S. 2006. "Prions and Their Partners in Crime." *Nature* 443:803–810.

Caughey, B., and Kocisko, D. A. 2003. "A Nucleic-Acid Accomplice?" *Nature* 425(6959):673–674.

Choi, C. J. et al. 2006. "Interaction of Metals with Prion Protein: Possible Role of Divalent Cations in the Pathogenesis of Prion Diseases." *Neurotoxicology* 27(5):777–787.

Collinge, J. et al. 2006. "Kuru in the 21st Century—An Acquired Human Prion Disease with Very Long Incubation Periods." *Lancet* 367(9528):2068–2074.

Dabaghian, R. H. et al. 2004. "Prospects for the Development of Pre-Mortem Laboratory Diagnostics for Creutzfeldt-Jakob Disease." *Rev Med Virol* 14:345–361.

Davis, J. P. et al. 2003. "Fatal Degenerative Neurologic Illnesses in Men Who Participated in Wild Game Feasts—Wisconsin, 2002." *MMWR* 52(7):125–127.

Deleault, N. R. et al. 2003. "RNA Molecules Stimulate Prion Protein Conversion." *Nature* 425:717–720.

Dormant, D. 2002. "Prion Diseases: Pathogenesis and Public Health Concerns." *FEBS Letters* 529:17–21.

Farquhar, J., and Gajdusek, D. C. Eds. 1981. *Kuru: Early Letters and Field-Notes from the Collection of D. Carleton Gajdusek.* New York: Raven Press.

Flores, R. et al. 2005. "Viroids and Viroid-Host Interactions" *Ann Rev Phytopath* 43:117–139.

Gajdusek, D. C. 1977. "Unconventional Viruses and the Origin and Disappearance of Kuru." *Science* 197(4307):943–960.

Gale, P. 2006. "BSE Risk Assessments in the UK: A Risk Tradeoff?" *J App Micro* 100:417–427.

Griffith, J. S. 1967. "Self-Replication and Scrapie." *Nature* 215:1043–1044.

Guillaume, E. et al. 2003. "A Potential Cerebrospinal Fluid and Plasmatic Marker for the Diagnosis of Creutzfeldt-Jakob Disease." *Proteomics* 3:1495–1499.

Hartry, A. L. et al. 1964. "Planaria: Memory Transfer through Cannibalism Re-examined." *Science* 146:274–275.

Hill, A. F. et al. 1997. "Diagnosis of New Variant Creutzfeldt-Jakob by Tonsil Biopsy." *Lancet* 349:99–100.

Horonchik, L. et al. 2005. "Heparan Sulfate Is a Cellular Receptor for Purified Infectious Prions." *J Biol Chem* 280(17):17062–17067.

Houston, F. et al. 2000. "Transmission of BSE by Blood Transfusion in Sheep." *Lancet* 356(9234):999–1000.

Huillard d'Aignaux, J. N. et al. 2001. "Predictability of the UK variant Creutzfeldt-Jakob Disease Epidemic." *Science* 294:1729–1731.

Hunter, N., and Houston, F. 2002. "Can Prion Diseases be Transmitted Between Individuals Via Blood Transfusion: Evidence from Sheep Experiments." *Adv Transf Safety Dev Biol Basel, Karger* 108:93–99.

Kamin, M., and Patten, B. M. 1984. "Creutzfeldt-Jakob Disease: Possible Transmission to Humans by Consumption of Wild Animal Brains." *Am J Med* 76:142–145.

Ladogana, A. et al. 2005. "High Incidence of Genetic Human Transmissible Spongiform Encephalopathies in Italy." *Neurology* 64:1592–1597.

Llewelyn, C. A. et al. 2004. "Possible Transmission of variant Creutzfeldt-Jakob Disease by Blood Transfusion." *Lancet* 363(9407):417–421.

Lupi, O. et al. 2006. "Are Prions Related to the Emergence of Early Life?" *Med Hypotheses* 67:1027–1033.

Masison, D. C., and Wickner, R. B. 1995. "Prion-inducing Domain of Yeast Ure2p and Protease Resistance of Ure2p in Prion-containing Cells." *Science* 270(5233):93–95.

Mathiason, C. K. et al. 2006. "Infectious Prions in the Saliva and Blood of Deer with Chronic Wasting Disease." *Science* 314:133–136.

MaWhinney, S. et al. 2006. "Human Prion Disease and Relative Risk Associated with Chronic Wasting Disease." *EID* 12(10):1527–1535.

McConnell, J. V. 1962. "Memory Transfer Through Cannibalism in Planarians." *J Neuropsychiatry* 3:42–48.

McDonnell, G., and Burke, P. 2003. "The Challenge of Prion Decontamination." *CID* 36:1152–1154.

Miller, M. W. et al. 2004. "Environmental Sources of Prion Transmission in Mule Deer." *EID* 10(6):1003–1006.

Minor, P. et al. 2004. "Standards for the Assay of Creutzfeldt-Jakob Disease Specimens." *J Gen Virol* 85:1777–1784.

Oomkes, C., and van Knapen, F. 2001. "Cows, Cats, and FSE: Death Penalty Justified?" *Vet Q* 23(1):51–52.

Pattison, J. 1998. "The Emergence of Bovine Spongiform Encephalopathy and Related Diseases." *EID* 4(3):300–304.

Pearson, G. R. et al. 1993. "Feline Spongiform Encephalopathy: A Review." *Vet Q* 33:1–10.

Peden, A. H. et al. 2004. "Preclinical vCJD After Blood Transfusion in a PRNP Codon 129 Heterozygous Patient." *Lancet* 364(9433):527–529.

Peden, A. H., Ritchie, D. L., and Ironside, J. W. 2005. "Risks of Transmission of variant Creutzfeldt-Jakob Disease by Blood Transfusion." *Folia Neuropathol* 43(4): 271–278.

Priola, S. A., Chesebro, B., and Caughey, B. 2003. "Biomedicine: A View from the Top-Prion Diseases at 10,000 feet." *Science* 300:917–919.

Priola, S. A., Rianes, A., and Caughey, W. S. 2000. "Porphyrin and Phthalocyanine Antiscrapie Compounds." *Science* 287:1503–1506.

ProMED-mail. 1997. "Prion Research Safety Guidelines—USA." *ProMED-mail* 1997; 03 Jun: 199770603.1151.

Prusiner, S. B. 1994. "Inherited Prion Diseases." *PNAS USA* 91:4611–4614.

Prusiner, S. B. 2001. "Shattuck Lecture—Neurodegenerative Diseases and Prions." *N Engl J Med* 344(20):1516–1526.

Raeber, A. J., and Oesch, B. 2006. "Diagnostics for TSE agents." *Dev Biol (Basel)* 123:313–323.

Roma, A. A., and Prayson, R. A. 2005. "Bovine Spongiform Encephalopathy and variant Creutzfeldt-Jakob Disease: How Safe Is Eating Beef?" *Cleveland Clin J Med* 72(3):185–194.

Solforosi, L. et al. 2004. "Cross-linking Cellular Prion Protein Triggers Neuronal Apoptosis in vivo." *Science* 303:1514–1516.

Tabler, M., and Tsagris, M. 2004. "Viroids: Petite RNA Pathogens with Distinguished Talents." *Trends Plant Sci* 9(7):339–348.

Thackray, A. M. et al. 2003. "Subclinical Prion Disease Induced by Oral Inoculation." *J Virol* 77(14):7991–7998.

Trifilo, M. J. et al. 2006. "Prion-induced Amyloid Heart Disease with High Blood Infectivity in Transgenic Mice." *Science* 313:94–97.

Valleron, A.-J. et al. 2001. "Estimation of Epidemic Size and Incubation Time Based on Age Characteristics of vCJD in the United Kingdom." *Science* 294:1726–1728.

Weissmann, C., and Flechsig, E. 2003. "PrP Knock-Out and PrP Transgenic Mice in Prion Research." *Br Med Bull* 66:43–60.

Wickner, R. B. 1994. "[URE3] As an Altered URE2 Protein: Evidence for a Prion Analog in *Saccharomyces*." *Science* 264(5158):566–569.

Will, R. G. et al. 1996. "A New Variant of Creutzfeldt-Jakob Disease UK." *Lancet* 347:921–925.

Wong, B.-S. et al. 2001. "Oxidative Impairment in Scrapie-Infected Mice Is Associated with Brain Metals Perturbations and Altered Antioxidant Activities." *J Neurochem* 79:689–698.

Zanusso, G. et al. 1998. "Simultaneous Occurance of Spongiform Encephalopathy in a Man and in His Cat in Italy." *Lancet* 352:1116–1117.

Zeidler, M. et al. 1997. "New variant Creutzfeldt-Jakob Disease: Neurological Features and Diagnostic Tests." *Lancet* 350:903–910.

■ Popular Press

Cowley, G. 2001. "Cannibals to Cows: The Path of a Deadly Disease."*Discover Magazine,* March 12, 2001.

Kelleher, C. A. 2004. *Brain Trust: The Hidden Connection Between Mad Cow and Misdiagnosed Alzheimer's Disease.* New York: Paraview Pocket Books.

Klitzman, R. 2001. *The Trembling Mountain: A Personal Account of Kuru, Cannibals, and Mad Cow Disease.* New York: Perseus Publishing

Lindenbaum, S. 1978. *Kuru Sorcery: Disease and Danger in the New Guinea Highlands.* New York: McGraw-Hill.

Prusiner, S. 1995. "The Prion Diseases." *Scientific American,* January, 1995.

Prusiner, S. B. 1991. "The Molecular Biology of Prion Diseases." *Scientific American,* June 1991.

Rhodes, R. 1997. *Deadly Feasts: Tracking the Secrets of a Terrifying New Plague.* New York: Simon and Schuster.

Sacks, O. 1997. "Eat, Drink, and Be Wary." *The New Yorker,* April 14, 1997.

Schwartz, M. 2003. *How the Cows Turned Mad.* Berkeley, California: University of California Press.

Shell, E. R. 1998. "Could Mad-Cow Disease Happen Here?" *Atlantic Monthly,* September, 1998.

Thornton, J. 2007. "Special Feature: The Quiet Spread of CWD." *Field & Stream,* May 10, 2007.

■ Videos

"Our Town" *(The X-Files),* Season 2, Episode 24. Original airdate: May 12, 1995. Fox Television.

Foreign Body: Mad Cow Disease. 1998. Films for the Humanities.

The Brain Eaters. 1998. NOVA PBS.

New Killers. 2002. Films for the Humanities.

■ eLearning

http://biology.jbpub.com/book/virology

The site features eLearning, an online review area that provides quizzes and other tools to help you study for your class. You can also follow useful links for in-depth information, or just find out the latest virology and microbiology news.

CASE STUDY QUESTIONS

These questions relate to the Case Study presented at the beginning of the chapter.

1. Is it possible that the cat and its owner contracted the same TSE agent strain? How could you test for this in the laboratory?

2. List common sources of prion disease agents.

■ Reference

Zanusso, G. et al. 1998. "Simultaneous Occurrence of Spongiform Encephalopathy in a Man and His Cat in Italy." *Lancet* 352:1116–1117.

ADDITIONAL CASE STUDIES

Case Study 2

In 1997 five unrelated individuals from different towns who were suffering from a CJD-like disease attended a clinic in western Kentucky. The patients, two of whom were female, ranged in age from 56–78. All five of the patients had a history of eating squirrel brains. The neurologist who observed these patients suggested a possible association between eating squirrel brains and CJD in the British medical journal *The Lancet*.

Eating wild squirrels is common in rural Kentucky. The people usually eat squirrel brains or the meat, but not both. **Burgoo** is a vegetable stew that contains chopped squirrel meat. There are two different ways in which squirrel brains are eaten. One popular way is to scramble the squirrel brains in white gravy with eggs. Squirrel brains are also eaten during a gift-giving ritual in which someone brings the head of a squirrel to the home of a family. The fur is shaved off the head and the entire head is fried, the skull is cracked open at the dinner table, and the brains are scooped out and eaten.

1. Could these patients have contracted a CJD-like disease from eating beef and not squirrels? Explain your answer.
2. Typically, one CJD case is reported in Kentucky every ten years, so it was unusual to have a cluster of cases all in the same given year. In cases such as this, should doctors issue a warning that people should not eat squirrel brains? Why or why not?
3. Do a literature search to determine if there are reports of squirrels or other small mammals contracting transmissible spongiform encephalopathies.

■ References

Berger, J. R., Weisman, E., and Weisman, B. 1997. "Creutzfeldt-Jakob Disease and Eating Squirrel Brains." *Lancet* 350:642.

Bilger, B. 2000. "Squirrel and Man: Is Local Custom Worth Dying For? *The New Yorker,* July 17, 2000.

Kamin, M., and Patten, B. M. 1984. "Creutzfeldt-Jakob Disease: Possible Transmission to Humans by Consumption of Wild Animal Brains." *Am J Med* 76:142–145.

Case Study 3

From 1976 to 2002 a group of hunters from the midwest met at a cabin in northern Wisconsin to participate in wild game feasts. Elk, deer, antelope, and other game were eaten during these gatherings. Three of the hunters attending these feasts died of degenerative neurological diseases during 1993 to 1999. The deaths were later investigated because of the increasing public health concerns about the possible transmission of TSEs to humans from deer and elk that suffer from chronic wasting syndrome. All three hunters ate venison frequently.

1. What did the investigators conclude in their report (refer to the *MMWR* reference)?
2. Another cluster of young male hunters (aged 28–30 years) from the United States who consumed deer or elk meat regularly died of fatal neurodegenerative diseases from 1997–1998. What did investigators conclude in this instance (refer to the *Archives of Neurology* reference below)?

■ References

Belay, E. D. et al. 2001. "Creutzfeldt-Jakob Disease in Unusually Young Patients Who Consumed Venison." *Arch Neurol* 58:1673–1678.

Davis, J.P. et al. 2003. "Fatal Degenerative Neurologic Illnesses in Men Who Participated in Wild Game Feasts—Wisconsin, 2002." *MMWR* 52(7):125–127.

Case Study 4

Sporadic CJD occurs at a rate of about one case per million people. In 1985, a 52-year-old man began showing symptoms of a CJD, and he passed away in 1987. Five years later, his then-55-year-old widow experienced a sudden onset of confusion. Her condition deteriorated rapidly and she died one month after the onset of her symptoms. The brains of the husband and wife both contained the resistance prion protein, PrP^{res}. Neither one had a family history of neurological illnesses. The *PRNP* genes were normal.

1. Could this be a case of human-to-human transmission?

2. Were there any surgical or dietary risks identified?

3. What is the probability that married couples would both die of CJD within years of one another?

■ Reference

Brown, P. et al. 1998. "Creutzfeldt-Jakob Disease in a Husband and Wife." *Neurology* 50:684–688.

Case Study 5

On December 14, 2007, Froedtert Memorial Hospital located in the Milwaukee, Wisconsin, area suspended surgery after learning that an operation was performed on a patient who had Creutzfeldt-Jakob disease. About 100 patients had been operated on after this patient. Authorities contacted all of them. The hospital officials collected all potentially contaminated surgical instruments and cleaned them using special sterilization methods. Iatrogenic transmission of prion diseases by medical devices poses a serious infection control challenge to health-care facilities.

1. Surface contamination of reusable medical devices is a concern. What are some classic decontamination procedures used in hospitals to ensure safety of medical and surgical instruments?

2. How should individuals treat skin contact with possible infectious prion material?

■ References

ProMed-mail. 1997. "Prion Research Safety Guidelines—USA." ProMED-mail 1997; 3 Jun:1997. 70603.1151.

Fichet, G. et al. 2004. "Novel Methods for Disinfection of Prion-Contaminated Medical Devices." *Lancet* 364(9433):521–526.

Fichet, G. et al. 2007. "Investigation of a Prion Infectivity Assay to Evaluate Methods of Decontamination." *J Microbiol Methods* 70(3):511–518.

Lawson, V. A. et al. 2007. "Enzymatic Detergent Treatment Protocol that Reduces Protease-Resistant Prion Protein Load and Infectivity from Surgical-Steel Monofilaments Contaminated with a Human-Derived Prion Strain." *J Gen Virol* 88(Pt 10):2905–2914.

Lipscomb, I. P. et al. 2007. "Effect of Drying Time, Ambient Temperature and Pre-Soaks on Prion-Infected Tissue Contamination Levels on Surgical Stainless Steel: Concerns over Prolonged Transportation of Instruments from Theatre to Central Sterile Service Departments." *J Hosp Infect* 65(1):72–77.

Case Study 6

The deer population is plagued by a new disease. Symptoms of the disease were first observed in mule deer grazing on northern Colorado wildlife research land in 1967. Symptoms were chronic weight loss (ribs showing), blank facial expression, excessive drooling and thirst, frequent urination, teeth grinding, holding head in a lowered position, nervousness, sluggish behavior, and isolation from the herd. In 1978, researchers named it chronic wasting disease (CWD) and classified it as a transmissible spongiform encephalopathy (TSE). In the mid-1980s, CWD was observed in free-range elk and deer in northern Colorado and adjacent parts of southern Wyoming. In 1997, it was observed in a farmed herd of elk in South Dakota. Since 1999, the Wisconsin Department of Natural Resources has been routinely testing the state's deer herd for CWD. In 2002, Wisconsin's first cases of CWD were reported. A map of CWD in North America is shown in **Figure CS 19-1**.

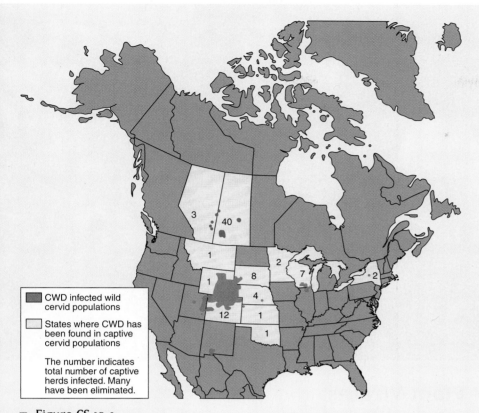

CWD infected wild
cervid populations

States where CWD has
been found in captive
cervid populations

The number indicates
total number of captive
herds infected. Many
have been eliminated.

■ **Figure CS 19-1**
CWD in North America as of 2/08/2006. Adapted from Chronic Wasting Disease Alliance.

Hunting season typically occurs in the fall. The deer hunt plays an important role in wildlife management. Deer cause agricultural damage, deer-vehicle collisions, forest damage by overgrazing, damage to ornamental plants and landscaping, airport runway safety issues, and decreased food supply and cover for other species. There are now CWD surveillance programs, which identify CWD management zones.

1. The first step to disease control is understanding CWD. Deer hunting is a tradition that needs to continue. What precautions should deer hunters follow when handling deer?

2. The Department of Agriculture, Trade and Consumer Protection has issued an emergency rule aimed at preventing CWD on Wisconsin's deer and elk farms. What is this rule and its provisions?

3. What special measures are used to collect and kill deer in the eradication zones?

4. Has CWD been linked to human disease?

5. In 2005, a single case of CWD in a moose was discovered in Colorado. Wildlife veterinarians believe that it is unlikely that there will be large numbers of moose contracting CWD, why? (Hint: What are the social habits of moose?)

■ **References**

Canadian Food Inspection Agency—Animal Health—Disease Information—Chronic Wasting Disease (CWD) of Deer and Elk.http://www.inspection.gc.ca/english/anima/heasan/disemala/cwdmdc/cwdmdce.shtml.

Chronic Wasting Disease Alliance. http://www.cwd-info.org/.

CWD Info & Testing—Colorado Division of Wildlife. http://wildlife.state.co.us/Hunting/BigGame/CWD/.

WDNR—Chronic Wasting Disease in Wisconsin. http://www.dnr.state.wi.us/org/land/wildlife/whealth/issues/CWD/index.htm.

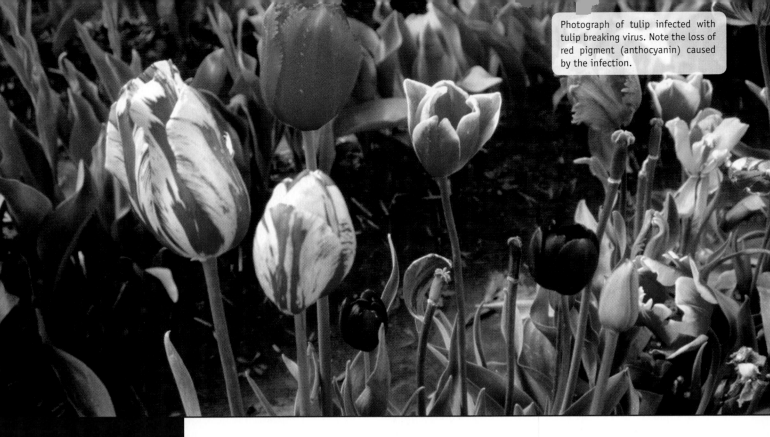

Photograph of tulip infected with tulip breaking virus. Note the loss of red pigment (anthocyanin) caused by the infection.

CHAPTER

20

Plant Viruses

"Nature's bioterrorism is far more fearsome than man-made bioterrorism."

Stanley Falkow, Professor of Molecular Microbial Pathogenesis, Stanford University

CASE STUDY

Pennsylvania is the leading producer of **stone fruits** in the United States. Stone fruits are fleshy fruits that contain a single seed or pit such as peaches, apricots, nectarines, plums, and cherries. In 1999, peach trees located on a commercial grove in Adams County, Pennsylvania, were infected with **plum pox virus**, which is also known as **Sharka virus**. The first symptoms appeared on the leaves of fruit of the fruit trees in the form of chlorotic (yellowing) and necrotic (browning) ring patterns. Infected fruits became fibrous and gummy with irregular brown and reddish spots. The fruit was low in sugar and not tasty. Fruits dropped prematurely (about three to four weeks before ripening), making them unsuitable for eating and processing.

Plum pox virus was first discovered in Bulgaria some time between 1915 and 1918. Within 30 years, it spread throughout most eastern European countries and the former U.S.S.R. Following World War II, it spread to Western European countries, Egypt, Syria, and Cyprus; it was found in New Zealand and Chile in 1992 and in India in 1994. The virus was first detected in North America in 1998 and since 1999 has been detected in Michigan and New York and in orchards in Ontario, Canada. The strain of the virus found in Canada was identical to the strain found in Pennsylvania. Researchers and growers believe that plum pox virus may be the most damaging virus in fruit production.

20.1   History of Plant Viruses

Many still-life paintings and drawings created in Western Europe from 1600 to 1660 contained tulips that portrayed flower symptoms of a viral disease. These tulips had striped or variegated patterns that were considered prized as special varieties. It led to a craze called *tulipomania* in which bulbs of the infected tulips were traded for large amounts of money or goods (Table 20-1). These tulips were likely infected with tulip breaking virus, an infection that interferes with the pigmentation of the flower and results in a "breaking" or loss of pigment that causes the flower to appear marbled.

By the end of the 1900s, the idea that infectious disease was caused by microorganisms was well accepted. Martinus Beijerinck's 1898 discovery of a plant virus that infected tobacco (refer to Chapter 1) was considered to be the birth of virology. Between 1900 and 1935, many plant diseases were thought to be caused by viral agents that could pass through porcelain filters that would normally trap bacterial pathogens.

Later it was discovered that some plants displayed virus-like symptoms that could not be transmitted to healthy plants by **mechanical transmission**, which is the most common technique for experimental infection of plants. It is usually performed by inoculating or rubbing virus-containing preparations into the leaves of healthy susceptible plants. In 1922, Kunkel published the first paper to recognize that insects transmitted some plant viruses by showing that yellow stripe disease virus was transmitted to corn by a leafhopper. Within ten years, many insects were reported to be virus vectors of plant diseases. In 1939, Holmes published the *Handbook of Phytopathogenic Viruses*, a list of 129 known viral diseases of plants.

TABLE 20-1	Examples of the Goods Exchanged for One Bulb of Viceroy Tulip Variety During Tulipomania
Two lasts (four tons) of wheat	
Four lasts (eight tons) of rye	
Four fat oxen	
Eight fat pigs	
Twelve fat sheep	
Two hogsheads of wine (126 gallons)	
Four barrels of beer (252 gallons or 15 kegs)	
1000 pounds of cheese	
A bed with accessories	
A full dress suit	
A silver goblet (drinking cup)	

Many advances were made toward virology research during the 1930s through the 1950s and much of the attention focused on tobacco mosaic virus (TMV). Serological, electron microscopic, and X-ray crystallography were the major techniques used to distinguish different strains of virus and to explore virus structure. During the 1980s research in plant virology focused on the diagnosis of virus diseases, especially using enzyme-linked immunosorbent assays (ELISA; refer to Chapter 7) and the application of molecular biology techniques to study the organization of viral genomes and viral replication strategies. Today there are approximately 900 plant virus species recognized by the **International Committee on Taxonomy of Viruses** (**ICTV**) and plant virology research is focused on the manipulation of plant virus genomes in order to understand viral resistance for commercial gain in the agriculture business. Plant viruses are of considerable importance: At least 10% of global food production is lost to plant disease each year. In the United States alone over $60 billion in crop losses occur each year.

20.2 Transmission of Plant Viruses

The infection of plant cells is not achieved by surface receptors; this is a major difference between viral infections of animals and those of plants. Infection of plants requires cell wounding or the transfer of extracellular fluid (e.g., sap). Viruses infect plants by **horizontal** or **vertical transfer**. **Vertical transfer** occurs from plant to plant (within generations), such as when plants are touching each other. **Horizontal transfer** is from parent to offspring such as infected seeds (between generations). Plant viruses are transmitted in a number of different ways, such as:

- mechanical means (human and environmental damage)
- soil transmission
- vegetative propagation (grafting)
- piercing and chewing insects and other vectors
- seed transmission
- pollen transmission

Plant viruses depend upon a break in the cell wall for entry. Mechanical transmission is a common way to experimentally infect plants by wounding the leaves with virus-containing preparation (inoculum). It is a valuable method for plant virologists; however, not all viruses are mechanically transmissible and in general mechanical inoculation is very inefficient (at least 500 virus particles are needed to give rise to a visible infection).

In addition to human intervention, physical damage to plants can also occur through wind damage. Leaves of healthy and infected plants may rub together in the wind, allowing natural transmission to occur. Viruses present in the soil may be transmitted to leaves of new plants as wind-blown dust or rain-splashed mud strikes the leaves. Soil acts as an abrasive, causing damage that will give the virus access to the plant cells. **Soilborne** and **waterborne viruses** may also infect plants through slightly damaged rootlets.

Grafting, a process in which two young plants are joined together, is a form of vegetative propagation that also provides an opportunity for virus transmission. Typically a twig or bud (called a **scion**) is grafted onto a rootstock (**Figure 20-1**). The scion eventually develops into a new shoot. Grafting allows greenhouse workers to combine the best features of two different plants into one plant. For a long time, grafting was the only experimental method available to create virus infections in plants. It was a way for researchers to graft an infected scion onto a healthy plant's rootstock.

Due to the rigidity of the plant cell walls, most plant viruses have to be introduced into cells with the help of **vector organisms**. Many different organisms can act as vectors and spread plant viruses such as bacteria, fungi, nematodes, parasitic plants, and

Grafting

Scion

Cambium

Stock

Cambium

(a)

(b)

■ **Figure 20-1**
(a) Grafting. Adapted from V. G. James. "SparkNote on The Life Cycle of Plants." *Biology Study Guides*. SparkNotes, LLC. http://www.sparknotes.com/biology/plants/lifecycle. **(b)** Photograph of grafting showing a chip bud being joined to a rootstock.

(a)

(b)

(c)

■ **Figure 20-2**
Insects form the largest and most significant vector group. Most notably this group includes **(a)** aphid, **(b)** hopper, and **(c)** thrips.

insects (e.g., aphids, leafhoppers, planthoppers, beetles, mites, mealybugs, whiteflies, and thrips). Several soilborne viruses are transmitted by fungi. Most plant viruses are transmitted by vectors, the majority of which are insects (**Figure 20-2**). The viruses are transmitted directly into cells when the mouthparts of an insect such as a beetle directly injure the plant through chewing or when injected into the plant through the piercing of mouthparts of a sap-sucking insect or a root-feeding nematode.

Viruses transmitted through seed are also transmitted through pollen grains. When a virus is transmitted by pollen, it may infect the seed and the seedling that will grow from that seed, or it may infect the plant through the fertilized flower. Sometimes, insects play an important role in pollen-mediated transmission. Plant-to-plant transmission of a virus by pollen is known to occur in fruit trees. Seeds may be contaminated by viruses adhering to the outside of the seed or due to infection of the living tissues of the plant embryo.

20.3   Symptoms of Plant Diseases Caused by Viruses

Some infected plants exhibit no symptoms. Plants infected by viruses can lead to the following symptoms, among others:

- dwarfing or stunting of plants
- leaf curling
- reduced yield
- fruit distortion
- chlorosis (yellowing)
- other color deviations (e.g., variegation of flower petals)
- "mosaic" patterns on leaves
- ring-shaped spots on leaves
- wilting and withering
- necrosis (black or grayish brown discoloration due to the death of cells and tissues)
- bark scaling

All of these symptoms mimic other problems of the plant, such as nutrient deficiencies or toxicities and infection by other pathogens (e.g., fungi, bacteria).

Viral infections rarely kill the plant. Most plant viruses multiply at the site of infection, giving rise to localized symptoms such as necrotic lesions on leaves. Viruses must pass various tissue barriers in order to cause systemic infections. Virus **movement proteins** must be compatible with the host in order for the virus to move systemically (refer to Section 20.8, Plant Virus Life Cycles). Once a virus infects a plant, the plant usually remains infected during its life. Examples showing viral disease symptoms are shown in **Figure 20-3**.

(a)

(b)

(c)

■ Figure 20-3
(a) Viral necrosis to corn. **(b)** Yellowing of lettuce by closterovirus. **(c)** Ring and band mosaics due to plum pox potyvirus.

20.4 Diagnosis and Detection of Plant Viruses

In addition to observing and recording plant symptoms, there are several considerations or questions that need to be asked to determine what diagnostic approach should be applied to a particular plant disease. For example, is it important to know if the plant is infected with a virus or what virus is infecting the plant? Or what virus strain is infecting the plant? Costs and the sophistication of the technique must also be considered, particularly in the developing countries of the tropics. Most methods used are similar to those used in detecting animal and human viruses such as:

- Detection of inclusion bodies in infected cells by light microscopy
- Direct observation of virus particles by electron microscopy
- Infectivity assays (e.g., inoculation of healthy plants with sap from a symptomatic plant—this is time consuming)
- Use of serological probes (e.g., ELISA)
- DNA or RNA probes (e.g., PCR)

20.5 Prevention and Control of Plant Virus Diseases

Plant viruses cause important plant diseases that cause huge losses in crop production and quality in all parts of the world. Infected plants may show a range of disease symptoms. Plant viruses cannot be directly controlled by chemical application. The major means of control (depending on the disease) include:

- Control of insect vectors (chemical or biological control)
- Removal of alternate hosts (e.g., weeds)
- Sanitation techniques (e.g., cleaning of farm implements, proper grafting techniques)
- Use of certified virus-free seed or stock
- Growing resistant crop varieties
- Plant quarantines to prevent disease establishment in areas where it does not occur (material is grown or kept isolated for longer periods for observation—absence of disease or pest) and testing. These procedures are time-consuming, costly and require skilled professionals.

20.6 Morphology of Plant Viruses

An envelope is a typical feature in animal viruses but is uncommon in plant viruses; for plant viruses, the typical feature is a naked helical rod. The rods may be

- naked, long, helical flexuous rods (full of bends or curves) that are typically 10 nm wide by 480 to 2000 nm in length
- rigid helical rods of 15 nm by 300 nm in length
- short (bacillus-like) rods

Polyhedron-shaped plant viruses also exist that are 17 to 60 nm in diameter in addition to multipartite viruses that may contain the same component proteins but often differ in size depending on the length of the genome segment packaged. The only plant viruses that contain membranes are the plant rhabdoviruses and tospoviruses. Examples of these morphologies are shown in **Figure 20-4**.

■ **Figure 20-4**
(a) Transmission electron micrograph (TEM) of a potyvirus flexuous rods (turnip mosaic virus). **(b)** TEM of a zucchini squash infected with an isolate of Papaya ringspot virus with the characteristic pinwheel configuration of the flexuous potyvirus rods. **(c)** TEM of melilotus (white clover rhabdovirus). V stands for mature enveloped particles. **(d)** TEM of a Brazilian rhabdovirus isolate (maize mosaic virus) infecting parenchymal cells of maize.

(a)

(b)

(c)

(d)

20.7   Types of Plant Virus Genomes

(a)

(b)

■ **Figure 20-5**
(a) Segmented influenza virus particle. Each influenza particle contains eight molecules of negative sense ssRNA of different sizes and sequence. **(b)** Bipartite plant Gemini virus. Gemini (twin) viruses are usually found as two joined incomplete icosahedral particles. Their genome consists of two molecules of circular ssDNA of almost equal size but of different sequence.

The majority of all known plant viruses contain their genetic information encoded in positive-sense single-stranded RNA (ssRNA). Like animal viruses, there are also genomes of negative sense ssRNA, double-stranded RNA (dsRNA), ssDNA, and dsDNA (dsDNA is the rarest genome type in plant viruses). Plant viruses of segmented genomes (genomes that comprise more than one molecule of nucleic acid) also exist. They are referred to as **multipartite genomes** that are either quadra-, tri, or bipartite (i.e., four, three, or two molecules comprise the total genome of the virus).

Animal viruses with segmented genomes contain all of the nucleic acid molecules or segments within the same viral particle. *Unlike animal viruses, multipartite plant viruses package each nucleic acid molecule into a separate virus particle* (**Figure 20-5**). As a result, the sizes of each virus particle can also differ if the lengths of the segments differ.

■ What Are the Advantages and Disadvantages of Multipartite Genomes of Plant Viruses?

The advantage of this multipartite strategy is that it reduces the probability of losing the coding capacity of the genome if breakages of the genome occur. It also removes the requirement for accurate sorting or packaging of genomes into one virus particle.

■ **Figure 20-6**

The sizes of some plant viruses compared to the plasmodesmata. Citrus tristeza virus (CTV; 2 μM 10 nm), tobacco mosaic virus (TMV; 300 nm × 18 nm), cowpea mosaic virus (CPMV; 28 nm), potato virus Y (PVY; 750 nm × 11 nm), lettuce necrosis yellow virus (LNYV; 220 nm × 80 nm), tomato spotted wilt virus (TSWV; 80 nm), clover wound tumor virus (CWTV; 70 nm), cauliflower mosaic virus (CaMV; 50 nm). Adapted from R. Hull. Matthews' *Plant Virology,* Fourth Edition. Academic Press, 2001.

The disadvantage of this multipartite strategy is that all the individual genome segments must be packaged into a separate virus particle. All of the discrete virus particles must be taken up by a single cell to establish a productive infection or the virus will be defective as a result of loss of genetic information. This may be why multipartite viruses are only found in plants. Large inoculums are necessary to provide opportunities for infection of a cell by more than one particle.

20.8 Plant Virus Life Cycles

All plant cells contain an impermeable cell wall composed of cellulose that blocks viral entry. Viruses can only enter through a break in the cell wall by a wound in the plant or by vector transmission, especially by insects. Communication between plant cell walls is achieved through microchannels called **plasmodesmata**. The plasmodesmata allows the passage of molecules (e.g., diffusible plant metabolites) between cells; however, they are too small for virus particles or viral genomes to pass through them unaided (**Figure 20-6**). Plant viruses have evolved to carry genes that code for specialized **movement proteins** that enable their movement from one infected cell to neighboring cells. The movement proteins function by

- associating with or coating the RNA or DNA genomic nucleic acid of the virus to form nucleoprotein complexes. These nucleoprotein complexes cause the plasmodesmata microchannels to dilate and a host translocation system allows the complex to be delivered in the cytoplasm of the neighboring cell.
- forming a tubular transport structure that is inserted into a plasmodesmata pore, allowing the passage of virus particles from one cell to another through the modified plasmodesmata (**Figure 20-7**).

■ Figure 20-7
Tubule strategy for cell-to-cell movement of plant viruses. Adapted from R. Hull. Matthews' *Plant Virology,* Fourth Edition. Academic Press, 2001.

Movement proteins appear to be derived from host plant genes that encode for **chaperonins** and plasmodesmata-associated proteins. Most plant viruses multiply at the site of infection, causing localized symptoms such as necrotic spots on leaves. A systematic (long distance) infection of the plant may occur if plant viruses can be transported longer distances through the vascular system via the **phloem**. The phloem consists of specialized living cells that transport sap. One type of specialized cell within the phloem is a sieve-tube cell. Sieve-tube cells lack a nucleus but contain other organelles and ribosomes. These cells conduct food materials throughout the plant. The end walls of the sieve tube cells have many smaller pores and enlarged plasmodesmata (**Figure 20-8**). Plant viruses "channel" through the plant cell wall via movement proteins without causing cellular lysis. As a result all plant viruses spread directly from cell to cell within a leaf without an extracellular phase. Viral movement is localized.

Once viral particles have reached the cytoplasm the genome is uncoated, exposing the viral genome to the replication processes. The uncoating step of the plant virus genome is not well understood. Studies suggest that low Ca^{2+} concentrations may facilitate uncoating of some plant viruses.

About 90% of all plant viruses contain positive sense ssRNA genomes (+ssRNAs); see **Figure 20-9** for a list of plant virus genomes and taxonomy. The +ssRNA plant viruses take advantage of the host cell mRNA processing and translational machinery. In contrast to the 5' capped host messenger RNAs (mRNAs), the 5' end of plant viral +ssRNAs can take one of several forms:

- a 5' phosphate group
- a 5' cap
- a virus-encoded polypeptide called VPg (viral protein genome-linked) that is covalently attached to the first nucleotide of the RNA.

The 5' untranslated regions (UTRs) of the viral RNAs different significantly from cellular mRNAs by length and secondary structure. Some contain **internal ribosomal entry sites (IRES)** that allows for **cap-independent translation**. The 3' end of viral RNAs may contain a poly(A) tail, tRNA-like structure, or simply a 3' hydroxyl (OH) group.

The +ssRNA plant viruses encode their own RNA-dependent RNA polymerases for genome replication. They also need host factors for the formation of the replicase complex. During replication, the +ssRNA genome is copied into a –ssRNA intermediate that serves as a template for the production of genomic +ssRNAs. These genomic RNAs are used for translation, replication, or as genomic RNA in new virions.

The number of genes that plant viruses have varies considerably. Most plant viruses have at least three genes:

1. One or more involved with the replication of the viral genome.
2. One or more concerned with cell-to-cell movement of the virus.
3. One or more encoding a structural protein that makes up the coat or capsid protein of the virus.

The identification of the role(s) played by host factors in the virus life cycle remains a major unknown in plant virology. Plant molecular virologists are currently documenting the complex interactions between virus and host factors necessary for infection. Plant viruses exit the cell through the modified plasmodesmata without cell lysis. This differs from animal viruses that lyse cells or bud through the plasma membrane of cells.

(A)

Xylem vessel

- One-way only
- Water and minerals
- No end walls between cells
- Thick walls stiffened with lignin

Phloem vessel

- Cells have end walls with perforations
- Water and food
- Two-way flow

(a)

Vascular bundle

Phloem

Xylem

Cambium

Cortex

Epidermis

(b)

3 days

4 days

5 days

Initial viral infection

10 days

18 days

25 days

(c)

■ Figure 20-8

(a) The vascular plant anatomy, which delivers water and nutrients to the plant. It is composed of two main tissue types: the phloem and the xylem. Adapted from BBC, *Schools: Learning Resources for Home and School,* http://www.bbc.co.uk/schools/gcsebitesize/img/bixylemphloem.gif. **(b)** The xylem is made up of nonliving cells that are responsible for water movement in the plant. The phloem contains living cells that conduct nutrient movement. Viruses can cause a systematic infection of the plant via the phloem. Adapted from R. Hull. Matthews' *Plant Virology,* Fourth Edition. Academic Press, 2001. **(c)** Systematic spread of a virally infected plant. Note the viral spread (shaded areas) after the initial infection of the plant through the tissues of the phloem. Adapted from Fairchild Tropical Botanic Garden, *Teaching Resources,* http://www.fairchildgarden.org/index.cfm?section=education&page=teacherprofessionaldevelopment.

Families and genera of viruses infecting plants

■ Figure 20-9

Morphology and genomes of plant viruses shown by genera and family. Adapted from C. M. Fauquet, et al., eds. *Virus Taxonomy: VIIIth Report on the International Committee on Taxonomy of Viruses.* Academic Press, 2005.

20.9 Plant Satellite Viruses and Satellite Nucleic Acid

Satellites are often associated with plant viruses. **Satellite viruses** encode their own coat protein but lack the genes that would encode the enzymes necessary for replication. As a result of this they are completely dependent upon **helper viruses** for replication. Satellite RNAs or DNAs, on the other hand, become packaged in a protein capsid from the helper virus.

Satellite viruses and nucleic acids share the following properties:

- Their genetic material is small in size (200 to 1500 nucleotides in length), with little sequence similarity to the helper virus genome (**satellites are not defective interfering particles, RNAs, or DNAs**).
- Their replication requires a helper virus.
- They may have a dramatic affect on disease symptoms of the plant in most hosts.
- Replication of the satellite interferes to some extent with replication of the helper virus.
- Satellites are replicated on their own nucleic acid template.

How did satellite agents evolve? What is their function? The most popular theory is that satellite viruses arose from an independent virus. During the course of infection satellite viruses lose genetic material, making them dependent upon a helper virus for their replication. Satellite nucleic acids may be a renegade nucleic acid that originated as plant genomic nucleic acid. Overall, there appears to be selective pressures to maintain these virus variants.

20.10 Plants and RNA Silencing: Plants Possess an Immune System of Their Genomes

Compared to animals, plants do not make very good hosts. They are not, however, defenseless toward foreign invaders. In a broad sense plants possess nonspecific barriers to viral infection. For example, woody plants contain bark that protects the delicate tissues of the plant from biting insects and foreign agents. Plants secrete **saponins** and contain **bioflavenoids** that possess antibacterial and antiviral properties. Some plants accumulate heavy metals or other toxic substances from soil in the vacuoles of cells, making them more resistant to microbial infection.

Plants do not have an "active" immune system analogous to humans, such as the production of antibodies, complement, phagocytes, and interferon to combat pathogens. They do, however, possess an "immune system of the genome." Rich Jorgensen and other plant geneticists at a biotechnology company first observed this defense mechanism during the late 1980s. They introduced an extra chalcone synthetase **transgene** into petunias in order to create a more purple petunia. (A transgene is a cloned gene incorporated into the genome.) Instead, white petunias were produced (**Figure 20-10a**) because pigmentation was lost or suppressed completely. It took another decade of research on organisms like fruit flies, petunias, and roundworms in order to discover the phenomena called **RNA interference** or **RNAi** (**also referred to as RNA silencing**).

RNAi is a form of **genomic immunity** that responds to invading nucleic acid. It represents a sequence-specific antiviral defense mechanism in plants. Plant cells use RNA silencing to bind and cut any nucleotide sequence that may be harmful to the plant cell or produces a product that may inhibit plant cell activities. The discovery was hailed by

| **Silencing Genes**

All genomes are targets for invading viruses and **transposons**. Transposons are sequences of DNA that can move around to different positions within the genome of a single cell, a process called transposition. About 45% of the human genome consists of remnant sequences of previous transposon and virus invasions. As a result, it is expected that organisms need to fight off invading nucleic acids so that it is not completely taken over by these molecular invaders. The immune system of vertebrates fights off invaders by antibody-mediated responses. In addition to the immune system, the genome defense mechanism protects the genome of the organism. This mechanism appears to be an ancient defense against viral invaders.

RNAi gene-silencing is conserved in plants, fungi worms, flies, and mammals. It has become an extremely powerful tool for silencing gene expression *in vitro*. It promises to revolutionize experimental biology and may have many important therapeutic applications.

RNAi technology can be applied to the following areas:

- as an applied experimental technique to "knock out" genes
- in functional genomic studies
- in studies to identify genomic regulators
- for determining the importance of a gene in a process (e.g., cell development and cell division)
- as therapeutic tools (especially in the areas of genetic disorders, cancer, and viral infection)
- in engineering disease-resistant crops
- in engineering improved nutritional and handling characteristics of fruits

RNAi technology has the potential to target any gene unique to a specific disease or viral infection, thus reducing host cell toxicity problems. The siRNAs can be synthesized chemically in the laboratory and then introduced into cells, opening up many opportunities for siRNAs as potential drug candidates. Studies to date have shown that siRNAs can inhibit infection by HIV-1, SARS-CoV, respiratory syncytial virus (RSV), parainfluenza virus (PIV), herpes simplex 2, poliovirus, and hepatitis C viruses (**Figure VF 20-1**).

In 2005, a Phase I clinical trial used an RNAi therapeutic to treat 26 patients for **age-related macular degeneration**. Macular degeneration is the leading cause of adult blindness. It is caused by the overexpression of vascular endothelial growth factor (VEGF). VEGF is a protein that induces the growth of leaky and inflamed blood vessels underneath the retina, resulting in the slow progression of vision loss (**Figure VF 20-2**). The new RNAi drug (Sirna-027) was directly injected into the eye of patients as a means to shut down VEGF genes. Patients received 100 to 1600 μg of Sirna-027. After three months of a single injection, 24 of 26 patients showed visual stabilization and four patients experienced significant improvement in vision. Only two patients experienced vision loss. Sirna-027 studies have proceeded to Phase II clinical trials.

In 2006, clinical trials to use RNAi to treat asthma and Huntington's disease began. Huntington's disease is a neurodegenerative disease caused by the accumulation of mutated proteins that contain polyglutamine repeats (up to about 37 to 40 glutamines in the mutated protein, whereas normal proteins contain about 35 glutamines). Patients with Huntington's disease gradually lose their ability to think, speak, or care for themselves. There is no cure or treatment. Other applications of RNAi technology include the treatment of HIV infection and AIDS lymphomas.

Is RNAi technology really that magical? Are there any technological hurdles? Initial experiments using RNAi technology to combat viral infections resulted in the activation of genes in the **interferon pathway**, causing cells to undergo **apoptosis** (cellular suicide). Interferons are cytokines that function as the host's first line of defense against viral infection in mammals. This problem was overcome by using shorter siRNA molecules that no longer induce the interferon response. Another obstacle is addressing viral sequence diversity. Viruses like HIV mutate so rapidly that they will escape RNA silencing. This has been addressed by targeting genes required for viral entry or replication. These sequences of these genes contain fewer mutations. Delivering the siRNA molecules to where they are needed most remains a challenge. The siRNAs are rapidly degraded in the bloodstream and they do not home only on the diseased or infected cells. The solutions to these problems may make or break the field.

■ **Figure VF 20-1**

siRNA therapy to treat viral infections in different animal models. **(a)** Intravaginal application of siRNAs to inhibit sexual transmission of herpes simplex virus 2 in mice. **(b)** Intranasal admininstration of siRNAs to protect against RSV in mice. **(c)** Intranasal administration of siRNAs in rhesus monkeys to protect against SARS CoV infection. **(d)** Intravenous injection of siRNAs to inhibit hepatitis B and C viruses. **(e)** Intracerebral injection of siRNAs to protect against Dengue fever and Japanese encephalitis viruses. (a)–(e) Adapted from D. M. Dykxhoorn and J. Lieberman, *PLoS Med.* 3 (2006): 1000–1004.

■ **Figure VF 20-2**

Eyeball showing the neovascularization that occurs in age-related macular degeneration.

References

Adams, A. 2004. "RNAi Inches Toward the Clinic." *Scientist* 18(6):32.

Bitko, V. et al. 2005. "Inhibition of Respiratory Viruses by Nasally Administered siRNA." *Nat Med* 11:50–55.

Check, E. 2005. "A Crucial Test." *Nat Med* 11(3):244–245.

Constans, A. 2006. "RNAi: Five Tips to Better Silencing." *Scientist* 20(1):71–72.

Dykxhoorn, D. M., and Lieberman, J. 2006. "Silencing Viral Infection." *PLOS Medicine* 3(7):1000–1004.

Grimm, D. et al. 2006. "Fatality in Mice Due to Oversaturation of Cellular microRNA/short Hairpin RNA Pathways." *Nature* 441:537–541.

Howard, K. 2003. "Unlocking the Money-Making Potential of RNAi." *Nat Biotechnol* 21:1441–1446.

Palliser, D. et al. 2006. "An siRNA-based Microbicide Protects Mice From Lethal Herpes Simplex Virus 2 Infection." *Nature* 439:89–94.

Plasterk, R. H. A. 2002. "RNA Silencing: The Genome's Immune System." *Science* 296:1263–265.

Shen, J. et al. 2006. "Suppression of Ocular Neovascularization with siRNA Targeting VEGF Receptor 1." *Nat Gene Ther* 13:225–234.

Sledz, C. A. et al. 2003. "Activation of the Interferon System by short-interfering RNAs." *Nat Cell Biol* 5(9):834–839.

(a)

(b)

■ **Figure 20-10**

(a) The effects of the RNA silencing pathway were first observed when transgenes introduced into petunias to enhance their purple color resulted in white or variegated petunia flowers. The pigmentation genes of the petunia were suppressed. Adapted from C. Antler, "Antisense RNA," *The Science Creative Quarterly,* 2003, http://www.scq.ubc.ca/antisense-rna. **(b)** RNA silencing pathway of plants. This defense system protects the genome from invading viral nucleic acid. It can also protect the plant from other foreign nucleic acids such as transposons and transgenes introduced into plant cells by biotechnologists attempting to genetically modify plants. Adapted from Roth, B. M., G. J. Pruss, and V. B. Vance, *Virus Res.* 102 (2004): 97–108.

Science as the "breakthrough of the year" in 2002. Craig C. Mello and Andrew Z. Fire shared the Nobel Prize in Physiology or Medicine in 2006 for their discovery of the mechanism of RNAi in *Clostridium elegans*.

The RNAi defense system is triggered by **dsRNA molecules**. Most plant viruses contain RNA genomes and during the replication of RNA viruses by RNA-dependent-RNA polymerase dsRNA is a replicative intermediate during the viral infection. The viral dsRNA intermediate triggers a cascade of events. Specifically, it causes a host cell RNase III-like enzyme termed **dicer** (because it chops or "dices" the dsRNA) into 21- to 24-nucleotide dsRNA molecules called **short-interfering RNAs (siRNAs)**. This is an adenosine triphosphate (ATP)-dependent step that likely requires additional proteins that have dsRNA binding and RNA helicase activity.

Subsequently, in another ATP-dependent step, the siRNAs are denatured and incorporated into an endonuclease silencing complex called **RNA-induced silencing complex (RISC)**. The siRNAs act as a guide to bring the RISC into contact with complementary mRNAs, causing their degradation and silencing the expression of the protein it encodes. Plant viruses have evolved to carry genes that code for proteins that suppress or counter RNA silencing (Figure 20-10b). Many suppressors prevent silencing by blocking the production of siRNAs that provide the sequence specificity of the process.

1886	Adolf Mayer report describes a transmissible tobacco plant disease
1892	Dmitri Ivanoski demonstrates the infectious agent passes through a Chamberland filter candle (bacteria are trapped by such filters)
1898	Martinus Beijerinck was the first to call TMV a 'contagium vivum fluidum' or a "virus"
1935	Wendell Stanley crystallized TMV for electron microscopy
1946	Stanley shares the Nobel Prize in Chemistry for his work
1955	Heinz Fraenkel-Congrat and Robley Williams demonstrated that TMV "self-assembles" *in vitro*
1956	Rosalind Franklin *Nature* paper describes RNA in TMV particle
1958	Rosalind Franklin (working with Stanley) builds a TMV model for the World's Fair at Brussels
1972	Complete amino acid sequence of TMV's coat protein published in *American Chemical Society's Chemical Abstracts*
1982	Entire genome of TMV genome sequenced by Goelet et al.
1986	Dawson and Okada's group: Create genomic cDNA library of TMV sequences and production of infectious mRNA transcripts
1986	Powell-Abel's group demonstrated the coat protein gene of TMV confers virus-derived resistance in transgenic plants
1987	Doem's group determines 30K protein of TMV responsible for virus movement
1987	Takamatus et al. inserted foreign gene into the TMV viral genome to develop TMV as a gene vector
1990	Golemboski's group demonstrates plants transformed with the nonstructural gene coding for a 54 kDa protein are resistant to virus infection
1995	Advanced TMV vectors express malarial or animal viral epitopes
1999	Song's group shows that transgenic plants containing the TMV 126 kDa protein gene are completely resistant to viral infection
2004	Ding's group discovers the 126 kDa protein of TMV suppresses RNA silencing

■ **Figure 20-11**
Timeline of the history of tobacco mosaic virus.

20.11 Tobacco Mosaic Virus (TMV)

Plant viruses, as a rule, are named after the first plant on which they are found—hence TMV infects tobacco. Most plant viruses have wide host ranges, which allows them to be used with well-characterized model plants such as tobacco (*Nicotinia* spp.) and *Arabidopsis*. A chapter on plant viruses would not be complete without discussing the first virus to be discovered, TMV. TMV is the most studied plant virus, having been examined for over 100 years. It has served a model system for virology and molecular biology. A timeline of the history of TMV is shown in **Figure 20-11**. Martinus Beijerinck (1851–1931), a young botanist trained in agricultural chemistry, is given credit for his TMV experiments and coining the term "virus." Like many early discoveries in the field of microbiology, Beijerinck's 1898 vision of viruses was not appreciated or confirmed during his lifetime. Another player in TMV's history is Rosalind Franklin (1920–1958), who hypothesized that the TMV particle was hollow and that its RNA genome was single-stranded. Franklin's scientific work on viruses and the structure of DNA contributed toward research resulting in two Nobel Prizes (**Figure 20-12**).

■ TMV Structure

TMV particles are typically helical shaped with dimensions of 300 nm in length by 18 nm in diameter. TMV is one of the most stable viruses. It is resistant to chemical and physical agents that inactivate many other viruses. The coat protein (CP) of TMV is extraordinarily resistant to most proteases. Its stability is likely why the virus was the first one to be

■ **Figure 20-12**
Rosalind Franklin. Her gravestone reads, *"Scientist. Her work on viruses was of lasting benefit to mankind."*

■ **Figure 20-13**
(a) Drawing of the structure of TMV.
(b) Electron micrograph of TMV. Adapted from University of South Carolina, School of Medicine. "Virology: Basic Virology." Microbiology and Immunology. University of South Carolina, 2008. http://pathmicro.med.sc.edu/mhunt/intro-vir.htm.

Nucleic acid

Protein

(a)

(b)

identified and purified to homogeneity. The exact structure of TMV has been worked out: the capsid contains 2130 identical CP subunits. Particles contain a single +ssRNA that is approximately 6400 to 6600 nucleotides in length. The protein:RNA ratio is 95%:5% (**Figure 20-13**). TMV virions can **self-assemble**. In other words, purified TMV RNA and coat protein will self-assemble into stable rodlike helical virus particles. This self-assembly process takes little free energy to occur.

■ Host Range and Transmission

TMV has a broad host range; over 550 species of flowering plants can be infected by TMV. Natural hosts that are important commercially include several tobacco species, peppers, tomatoes, and potatoes. There are high concentrations of TMV in cells of tobacco and solanaceous plants (potato family).

TMV is easily transmissible from crop to crop primarily by **mechanical transmission** or in the roots/soil from infected plants but is not known to spread by insect vector transmission. TMV is so stable that its infectivity can be maintained for about two years in soil that is not exposed to freezing and drying. The virions are stable in plant residues in the soil and in the composts of tomato plants. Tobacco mosaic is one of the most persistent diseases of tomatoes because the virus can remain infectious without a host for many years and is able to withstand high heat. The hands and clothing of smokers who come in contact with TMV-infected tobacco, particularly when rolling cigarettes, easily transmit TMV to susceptible plants while working in the fields. Cigarettes and other tobacco products such as chewing tobacco or snuff can be important sources of TMV and contribute to its spread, which is why smoking should not be permitted in greenhouses, especially propagation houses.

■ Symptoms and Diagnosis

Compared to other plant viruses, the symptoms of TMV-infected plants are not that distinct. They vary depending upon virus strains, plant age, and growing conditions. A common characteristic is yellow or light green coloration between the veins of young leaves followed by a "mosaic" or mottled pattern of light and dark green areas in the leaves (**Figure 20-14a**). Lower leaves are subjected to "mosaic burn," especially during hot and dry weather (Figure 20-14b). The virus almost never kills plants, but infection does lower the quality and quantity of the crop.

(a)

(b)

■ **Figure 20-14**
(a) Early symptoms of TMV-infected tobacco plants. **(b)** Later symptoms of TMV-infected tobacco plants.

TMV-infected plants can easily be confused with plants affected by herbicides, mineral deficiencies, and other plant diseases. A plant pathologist and the use of electron microscopy are required for a positive identification of tobacco mosaic virus in infected plants.

■ TMV Life Cycle

TMV enters the cell by mechanical transmission. Upon entry, after a few CP subunits are removed, the 5′ end of the genome appears and is exposed to the cytoplasm. This initiates uncoating. The Ca^{2+} concentrations in the cell may alter the CP subunits, causing a conformational change that results in the uncoating of the viral genome. TMV replicates in the cytoplasm of the host plant cell. The genome +ssRNA genome of TMV contains a 5′ terminal cap (m7GpppG) followed by an AU-rich UTR of about 70 nucleotides. The 3′ end of genome contains a UTR that can fold into a transfer-RNA–like (tRNA-like) structure that can accept histidine *in vitro*. The tRNA-like structure is important for −ssRNA synthesis during genomic replication. The TMV genome contains four open reading frames (ORFs; **Figure 20-15**). The first ORF codes for an **RNA-dependent RNA polymerase (RdRp)** that has helicase and methyltransferase activity. The RdRp is made up of two proteins of 126 kd or 183 kd, respectively. The 183 kd protein is produced as a readthrough of the UAG during translation. About 5% to 10% of the time, the 126 kd protein is produced because the ribosome stops translation at the UAG.

The remaining two ORFs code for a 30 kd **movement protein (MP)** and a 17.5 kd CP. Viral RNA is infectious and acts as a mRNA that is translated by the host machinery. After the viral RdRp is synthesized, it begins to replicate full-length −ssRNAs or three additional shorter −ssRNAs, termed **subgenomic RNAs**, which function as monocistronic RNAs. The smallest subgenomic RNA is the most abundant and translated into the viral CP. The middle-sized subgenomic RNA is translated at lower levels and expresses MP that is responsible for viral cell-to-cell spread. The largest subgenomic RNA codes for a 54 kd protein that has not been detected in infected cells or protoplasts. Plants that contain the transgene of the 54 kd protein, however, are resistant to TMV infection even though there were not any detectable levels of the 54 kd protein expressed in the transgenic plants. As a result of this, the 54 kd protein remains enigmatic.

■ **Figure 20-15**

TMV viral genome and subgenomic RNAs and their translated products. Adapted from D. M. Knipe and P. M. Howley, eds. *Fundamental Virology*, Fourth Edition. Lippincott Williams & Wilkins, 2001.

■ **Figure 20-16**

The life cycle and rapid cell-to-cell spread of TMV. Adapted from Kawakami, S., Y. Watanabe, and R. N. Beachy, *Proc. Natl. Acad. Sci. USA* 101 (2004): 6291–6296.

It was recently proposed that TMV infection is spread quickly from cell to cell via intact **viral replication complexes (VRCs)**. The VRCs increase in size on the endoplasmic reticulum and in association with the protein cytoskeleton. The VRCs move along microtubules of filamentous actin and myosin and through the plasmodesmata as large bodies (**Figure 20-16**). Movement through the plasmodesmata is facilitated by the action of the viral MPs or VRCs or by the β 1.3 glucanase of the host cell. The VRCs spread to neighboring cells as VMCs (VRCs that move to adjacent cells are referred to as VMCs).

■ Control

It is nearly impossible to prevent TMV infection in nature because of the stability of the virus. TMV occurs wherever tobacco is grown (**Figure 20-17**). On average, TMV reduces crop yield by 30% to 35%, reducing the market value. As mentioned earlier in the chapter, the virus remains stable in dead plant matter in the soil and on contaminated seeds. In addition, TMV can exist for years in cigars and cigarettes made from TMV-infected leaves. The following control measures are recommended to prevent the spread of TMV when maintaining and transplanting seedlings in the greenhouse or field:

- Use only uncontaminated soils for seedling production in flowerbeds and greenhouses.
- Prohibit smoking during work.
- Ask workers to wash hands regularly.
- Remove and destroy all infected or suspected plants from nurseries.
- When transplanting in fields, transplant seedlings into soils free of tobacco, tomato, and pepper plant residues.
- Do not plant tomato or pepper seedlings in the same flower beds.
- Spray plants with skim milk or buttermilk to reduce mechanical spread of TMV (milk changes the pH of the surface of the leaves so that they are less susceptible to mildew and viral infection).
- Destroy all weed hosts of TMV in tobacco and nearby fields.
- Rotate crops every three years with maize and corn (avoiding tomato and pepper crops).
- Plant TMV-resistant varieties.

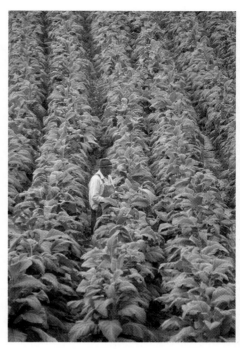

■ **Figure 20-17**
A farmer checks his tobacco plants on his farm in Virginia.

20.12   Citrus Tristeza Virus (CTV): Significance, Transmission, Symptoms, Detection, and Control

CTV occurs wherever citrus is grown. It is the most important pathogen affecting citrus worldwide (**Figure 20-18a**). Tens of millions of trees have been destroyed by the disease, mainly in South America and some Mediterranean countries. It infects nearly all citrus species, especially sweet oranges, mandarins, lemons, limes, and grapefruit. The word **tristeza** means sadness in Portuguese and Spanish. Farmers in South America coined this word in the 1930s, a time when devastating epidemics of CTV occurred in Brazil and Argentina. CTV is efficiently transmitted by aphids and by grafting. CTV was introduced into new geographic areas by importation of infected living citrus material (e.g., infected budwood) or fruits that may also carry aphid vectors. Aphids acquire the virus after feeding upon infected plants. Feedings as brief as ten minutes are long enough to bring in the virus from infected plants. Aphids are capable of transmitting the virus for 24 hours after leaving the plant.

Depending on viral strain, citrus plants will exhibit a variety of symptoms from mild to severe based on the host and the environment. Severe strains cause one or more of the following symptoms: dieback, **defoliation** (loss of leaves), stem pitting, small or poor fruit quality, stunting, and overall decline and death of the tree (Figure 20-18b). Symptoms are caused by starvation of the roots.

CTV is detected and identified using a biological assay in which buds or patches from trees thought to be infected are grafted onto healthy lime seedlings, which then are grown

(a)

(b)

■ Figure 20-18

(a) Global distribution of CTV. Adapted from European and Mediterranean Plant Protection Organization, "Citrus tristeza closterovirus," *Distribution Maps of Quarantine Pests for Europe,* http://www.eppo.org/QUARANTINE/virus/Citrus_tristeza/ CTV000_map.htm. **(b)** The navel, sweet orange tree was grafted with a CTV-infected sour orange rootstock. Note the quick decline in which the limbs die back and the tree gradually dies. (August, 1999, near Lindsay, California.)

in a temperature-controlled greenhouse. Within two to six months infected lime seedlings will show symptoms of citrus tristeza, a process that is both time-consuming and expensive. Commercial ELISA tests are now available and used routinely for large-scale testing in several countries.

Infected trees must be removed and destroyed from established citrus orchards. When replanting, tristeza-tolerant rootstocks should be used during grafting for propagation to control the disease. Strict quarantine measures are necessary to avoid the introduction of CTV into countries that are tristeza-free or in which only mild strains of CTV are present. The European and Mediterranean Plant Protection Organization (EPPO) recommends that citrus-growing countries prohibit the importation of host plants from countries where CTV epidemics occur.

■ **Figure 20-19**
Electron micrograph of filamentous-shaped CTV isolated from an infected plant. The particles are approximately 2000 nm in length.

■ Virus Structure and Genome

CTV is especially difficult for researchers to work with because the work must be done with citrus trees. Growing citrus seedlings is time-consuming; therefore, the molecular biology of CTV has progressed slowly. CTV has been observed to be the largest known plant virus via electron microscopy (**Figure 20-19**). Particles are nonenveloped, long, flexuous or threadlike helical rods that are 2000 nm by 11 nm in diameter. Virions contain +ssRNA that is approximately 19,300 nucleotides in length. The entire genomes of several strains have been sequenced to date. The first CTV isolate sequence from Florida encodes 12 ORFs that potentially code for 17 protein products, including two papain-like proteases, a methyltransferase, and a helicase. Research to isolate, identify, and characterize CTV isolates with respect to pathogenicity, molecular structure, and genome organization is in progress. There is a need to adapt and develop new biological, serological, and molecular-based methods to detect CTV strains in the field.

20.13   The Next Target: Anti-Crop Bioterrorism

Plum pox, citrus tristeza, sugarcane mosaic, sugar beet yellow, and cacao swollen shoot viruses have been responsible for heavy crop losses, famine, and massive economic losses. These disease epidemics resulted from human activity. It is not surprising that crops would be good targets for biological agents. Most crops are planted using varieties that are genetically identical or almost identical. If one plant is susceptible to disease, all plants in the same field or grove will be susceptible to disease. Developing countries with millions of people dependent upon such staples as rice or wheat could experience famine, starvation, and severe malnutrition if these crops were severely damaged by a deliberate anti-crop attack.

Anti-crop warfare research and development programs existed in the United Kingdom, France, Germany, and Japan before World War II. From 1946 to 1973, the United States maintained an active biological weapons program that included anti-crop agents. The former Soviet Union maintained an active anti-crop program until its dissolution in 1991. At the time of the Gulf War, Iraq had an anti-crop component as part of its comprehensive biological weapons program.

All of these programs have focused on mainly fungal and bacterial pathogens. Only a couple of plant viruses are listed as important anti-crop pathogens. Even though extensive research has been done regarding current anti-crop agents, no one seems to use them. Many scientists and governments view anti-crop bioterrorism as an inevitable event for which countries must be prepared.

Summary

Martinus Beijerinck, a botanist, is credited with coining the term *virus* while studying TMV-infected plants during the late 1800s. Even though the first virus to be discovered was tobacco mosaic virus (TMV), plant viruses are not nearly as well understood as their animal counterparts. Plant viruses continue to be a major threat in the production of vegetable and ornamental crops worldwide. Their control remains a major challenge in the twenty-first century.

The infection of plant cells is not achieved by surface receptors—a major difference between viral infections of plants as opposed to animals. Plant viruses depend upon a break in the cell wall for entry and are transmitted in a number of different ways, including:

- mechanical means (human and environmental damage)
- soil transmission
- vegetative propagation (grafting)
- piercing and chewing insects and other vectors
- seed transmission
- pollen transmission

The majority of plant viruses are transmitted by insect vectors (e.g., aphids, leafhoppers, planthoppers, beetles, mites, mealybugs, whiteflies, and thrips). Symptoms of viral plant diseases vary from mild to severe but rarely kill the plant. Examples of symptoms are:

- dwarfing or stunting of plants
- leaf curling
- reduced yield
- fruit distortion
- chlorosis (yellowing)
- other color deviations (e.g., variegation of flower petals)
- "mosaic" patterns on leaves
- ring-shaped spots on leaves
- wilting and withering
- necrosis (black or grayish brown discoloration due to the death of cells and tissues)
- bark scaling

In addition to symptomatic observations, methods used to detect and identify plant viruses are similar in those detecting animal viruses: Infectivity assays, ELISAs, electron microscopy, and PCR are used to diagnose diseases caused by plant viruses. The major means of control (depending on the disease) include:

- control of insect vectors (chemical or biological control)
- removal of alternate hosts (e.g., weeds)
- sanitation techniques (e.g., cleaning of farm implements and proper grafting techniques)
- use of certified virus-free seed or stock
- growing resistant crop varieties
- plant quarantines to prevent disease establishment in areas where it does not occur (material is grown or kept isolated for longer periods for observation-absence of disease or pest) and testing. These procedures are time-consuming, costly, and require skilled professionals.

Advances in control of viral plant diseases are focused on creating natural (breeding) and engineered resistance to plant viruses.

The majority of plant viruses are naked, helical-shaped +ssRNA viruses. Instead of having segmented genomes like influenza virus, some plant viruses have multipartite genomes in which the genome consists of more than one molecule of nucleic acid, but each genome molecule is packed into a separate virus particle. Thus all discrete virus particles must enter the cell to establish a productive infection.

Viruses spread short distances (from cell to cell) with the aid of movement proteins that "channel" them through the plasmodesmata. This channeling is done without causing cellular lysis. A systematic (long distance) infection of the plant may occur if plant viruses can be transported longer distances through the vascular system via the phloem.

Plants do not have an "active" immune system analogous to humans, such as the production of antibodies to combat pathogens. Plants do, however, possess an "immune system of the genome" that is known as RNA interference (RNAi) or RNA silencing. This system is a sequence-specific antiviral defense mechanism. Plant cells use RNA silencing to bind and cut any nucleotide sequence that may be harmful to the plant cell or produces a product that may inhibit plant cell activities. The players involved in this pathway of defense are dsRNA, RNA-dependent RNA polymerase, a DICER protein, and siRNAs. The discovery of this new mechanism of gene regulation has revitalized interest in the development of nucleic acid-based technologies as therapeutic tools (especially in the areas of genetic disorders, cancer, and viral infection).

TMV and citrus tristeza virus represent two important viral plant pathogens. Both are naked, helical-shaped +ssRNA viruses. Over 100 years of research has been conducted on TMV. TMV's stability in nature, the fact that it can easily be grown in large quantities in infected plants in a greenhouse, and the fact that it does not infect humans or animals has made it an attractive virus to investigate.

Resources

Primary Literature and Reviews

Ahlquist, P. 2002. "RNA-dependent RNA Polymerases, Viruses, and RNA Silencing." *Science* 296:1270–1273.

Aaziz, R. et al. 2001. "Plasmodesmata and Plant Cytoskeleton." *Trends Plant Sci* 6:326–330.

Bagasra, O., and Prilliman, K. R. 2004. "RNA Interference: The Molecular Immune System." *J Mol Histol* 35:545–553.

Baulcombe, D. 2004. "RNA Silencing in Plants." *Nature* 431:356–363.

Behlke, M. A. 2006. "Progress Towards *in vivo* Use of siRNAs." *Mol Ther* 13(4):644–670.

Beijerinck, M. W. 1898. "Over Een Contagium Vivum Fluidum Als Oorzaak van de Vlekziekte der Tabaksbladen." *Versl Gewone Vergad Wis Natuurkd Afd K Akad Wet Amsterdam* 7:229–235.

Bos, L. 1999. "Beijerinck's Work on Tobacco Mosaic Virus: Historical Context and Legacy." *Phil Trans R Soc Lond B* 354:675–685.

Bustamante, P. I., and Hull, R. 1998. "Plant Virus Gene Expression Strategies." *EJB* 1(2):1–18.

Cousins, N. 2000. "The Next Target of Bioterrrism: Your Food." *Environ Health Perspect* 108(3):A126–A129.

Couzin, J. 2002. "Breakthrough of the Year: Small RNAs Make a Big Splash." *Science* 5602:2296–2297.

Deteris, A. et al. 2006. "Hierarchical Action and Inhibition of Plant Dicer-like Proteins in Antiviral Defense." *Science* 313:68–71.

Dry, I. B. et al. 1997. "A Novel Subviral Agent Associated with a Geminivirus: The First Report of a DNA Satellite." *PNAS USA* 94:7088–7093.

Fire, A. et al. 1998. "Potent and Specific Genetic Interference by Double-Stranded RNA in *Caenorhabditis elegans*." *Nature* 391:806–811.

Jones, J. D. G., and Dang, J. L. 2006. "The Plant Immune System." *Nature* 444:323–329.

Karasev, A. V. et al. 1995. "Complete Sequence of the Citrus Tristeza Virus RNA Genome." *Virology* 208:511–520.

Kawakami, S. et al. 2004. "Tobacco Mosaic Virus Infection Spreads Cell to Cell As Intact Replication Complexes." *PNAS USA* 101:6291–6296.

Kunkel, L. O. 1922. "Insect Transmission of Yellow Stripe Disease Virus." *Hawaii Plant Rec* 26:58–64.

Lazarowitz, S. G., and Beachy, R. N. 1999. "Viral Movement Proteins As Probes for Intracellular and Intercellular Trafficking in Plants." *The Plant Cell* 11:535–548.

Lee, S. K. et al. 2005. "Lentiviral Delivery of Short Hairpin RNAs Protects CD4 T Cells from Multiple Clades and Primary Isolates of HIV." *Blood* 106:818–826.

Lucas, W. J. 2006. "Plant Viral Movement Proteins: Agents for Cell-to-Cell Trafficking of Viral Genomes." *Virology* 344(1):169–184.

Mayer, A. 1886. "Ueber die Mosaikkrankheit des Tabaka." (English Translation: Concerning the Mosaic Disease of Tobacco.) *Phytopathol Classics* 7:11–24.

Mello, C. C., and Conte, Jr., D. 2004. "Revealing the World of RNA Interference." *Nature* 431:338–342.

Nelson, R. S., and Citovsky, V. 2005. "Plant Viruses: Invaders of Cells and Pirates of Cellular Pathways." *Plant Physiol* 138:1809–1814.

Okada, Y. 1999. "Historical Overview of Research on the Tobacco Virus Genome: Genome Organization, Infectivity and Gene Manipulations." *Phil Trans Soc Lond B* 354:569–582.

Plasterk, R. H. A. 2002. "RNA Silencing: The Genome's Immune System." *Science* 296:1263–1265.

Power, A. G. 2000. "Insect Transmission of Plant Viruses: A Constraint on Virus Variability." *Curr Opin Plant Biotech* 3:336–340.

Ritzenthaler, C. 2005. "Resistance to Plant Viruses: Old Issue, New Answers?" *Curr Opin Biotech* 16:118–122.

Rocheleau, C. E. et al. 1997. "Wnt Signaling and an APC-related Gene Specify Endoderm in Early *C. elegans* Embryos." *Cell* 90:707–716.

Roossinck, M. et al. 1992. "Satellite RNAs of Plant Viruses: Structures and Biological Effects." *Microbiol Rev* 56(2):265–279.

Roth, B. M. et al. 2004. "Plant Viral Suppressors of RNA Silencing." *Virus Res* 102:97–108.

Ruiz-Ruiz S. et al. 2006. "The Complete Nucleotide Sequence of a Severe Stem Pitting Isolate of Citrus Tristeza Virus from Spain: Comparison with Isolates from Different Origins." *Arch Virol* 151(2):387–398.

Silhavy, D., and Burgyan, J. 2002. "Effects and Side-Effects of Viral RNA Silencing Suppressors on Short RNAs." *Trends Plant Sci* 296:1263–1265.

Thivierge, K. et al. 2005. "Update on What Makes Virus RNAs Different from Host mRNAs: Plant Virus RNAs. Coordinated Recruitment of Conserved Host Functions by (+) ssRNA Viruses During Early Infection Events." *Plant Physiol* 138:1822–1827.

Tompkins, S. M. et al. 2004. "Protection Against Lethal Influenza Virus Challenge by RNA Interference *in vivo*." *PNAS USA* 101: 8682–8686.

Uprichard, S. L. 2005. "The Therapeutic Potential of RNA Interference." *FEBS Lett* 579:5996–6007.

van der Want, J. P., and Dijkstra, J. 2006. "A History of Plant Virology." *Arch Virol* 151(8):1467–1498.

Waterhouse, P.M. et al. 2001. "Gene Silencing As an Adaptive Defence Against Viruses." *Nature* 411:834–842.

Whitby, S., and Rogers, P. 1997. "Anti-crop Biological Warfare—Implications of the Iraqi and US Programs." *Def Anal* 13(3):303–318.

Whitby, S. M. 2002. *Biological Warfare Against Crops*. Chippenham, England: Palgrave Publishers.

Xie, F. Y. et al. 2006. "Harnessing *in vivo* siRNA Delivery for Drug Discovery and Therapeutic Development." *Drug Discov Today* 11:67–73.

■ Popular Press

Creager, A. N. 2002. *The Life of a Virus: Tobacco Mosaic Virus as an Experimental Model, 1930–1965*. Chicago: University of Chicago Press.

Khan, J. A., and Dijkstra, J. Eds. 2006. *Handbook of Plant Virology*. New York: Food Products Press.

Rogers, P., Whitby, S., and Dando, M. 1999. "Biological Warfare Against Crops." *Scientific American,* June 1999.

Scholthof, K.-B. G., Shaw, J. G., and Zaitlin, M. Eds. 1999. *Tobacco Mosaic Virus: One Hundred Years of Contributions to Virology*. St. Paul, MN: APS Press.

Sutic, D. D., Ford, R. E., and Tosic, M. T. Eds. 1999. *Handbook of Plant Virus Diseases*. New York: CRC Press.

■ Video Productions

The Seeds of a New Era. 2003. Films for the Humantities.

■ eLearning

http://biology.jbpub.com/book/virology

The site features eLearning, an online review area that provides quizzes and other tools to help you study for your class. You can also follow useful links for in-depth information, or just find out the latest virology and microbiology news.

CASE STUDY QUESTIONS

These questions relate to the Case Study presented at the beginning of the chapter.

1. Speculate as to how plum pox virus is spread over short distances (within the same grove) and longer distances (e.g., to states outside of Pennsylvania and to Canada).

2. Infected trees must be destroyed to prevent the spread of disease. What other control measures do growers and agricultural officials put in place in order to prevent its spread?

3. Can plum pox virus be transmitted to humans?

■ References

ProMED-mail. 1999. "Plum Pox Virus, Peaches—USA (Pennsylvania)." *ProMED-mail* 1999; 24, Oct;19991024.1912.

ProMED-mail. 2000. "Plum Pox Virus, Nectarines—Canada (Ontario)." *ProMED-mail* 2000; 26, June; 20000626.1057.

ProMED-mail. 2006. "Plum Pox Virus, Plum—USA (Michigan): First Report." *ProMED-mail* 2006; 14, Aug; 20060814.2277.

ProMED-mail. 2006. "Plum Pox Virus, Plum—USA (New York): First Report." *ProMED-mail* 2006; 06, Aug; 20060806.2181.

Electron micrograph of bacterio-phages attached to a bacterium.

The Best for Last: Bacteriophages

> "*Do you mean to say you think you've discovered an infectious disease of bacteria, and you haven't told me about it? My dear boy, I don't believe you quite realize that you may have hit on the supreme way to kill pathogenic bacteria . . . And you didn't tell me!*"
>
> *Sinclair Lewis, Arrowsmith, 1924.*

CASE STUDY

Had it not been for the elegant experiments done by H. Williams Smith and his colleagues during the 1980s, phage therapy would not be in the headlines today. Smith reported successful veterinary applications of treating *Escherichia coli* infections in calves with bacteriophages. Use these publications to answer the questions that follow:

> Smith, H. W., and Huggins, M.B. 1983. "Effectiveness of Phages in Treating Experimental *Escherichia coli* Diarrhoea in Calves, Piglets and Lambs." *J Gen Microbiol* 129:2659–2675.

> Smith, H. W., Huggins, M. B., Shaw, K. M. 1987. "The Control of Experimental *Escherichia coli* Diarrhoea in Calves by Means of Bacteriophages." *J Gen Microbiol* 133:1111–1126.

> Smith, H. W., Huggins, M. B., and Shaw, K. M. 1987. "Factors Influencing the Survival and Multiplication of Bacteriophages in Calves and in Their Environment." *J Gen Microbiol* 133:1127–1135.

1. Choose one of the preceding papers and outline the experiments performed by Smith and his colleagues.
2. How were the cattle treated for *E. coli* infections? What was the success rate?
3. Was phage therapy more successful than multiple doses of antibiotic therapy in Smith's experiments? Discuss your answer.
4. Were phage-resistant mutants of *E. coli* strains isolated from the animals used in these studies? Discuss your answer.

21.1 Bacteriophage Research History

Bacteriophages are viruses that infect bacteria. The term *bacteriophage* is a combination of the word bacteria and the Greek word *phagein*, meaning "to eat." They were discovered after the recognition of bacterial hosts in the 1880s, a time known as the golden age of microbiology. British bacteriologist **Frederick W. Twort** authored a paper published in 1915 that is considered to be the birth of modern bacteriophage research. He reported an observation termed *glassy transformation*. At the time, Twort was trying to grow vaccinia viruses on agar medium in the absence of host cells. He inoculated the solid medium with unfiltered pustule fluid used in smallpox vaccinations. Rather than vaccinia virus, though, micrococci colonies grew on the solid medium, where they appeared watery or *glassy* in some areas. Twort collected the watery colonies, which could not be grown on new medium, and filtered them with a **Chamberland filter**. The filtrate was added to fresh cultures of micrococci, causing them to undergo *glassy transformation*. He concluded that a filterable infectious agent killed the bacteria, and that in the process the agent multiplied itself, thus causing the glassy transformation. Twort did not state that it was a bacterial virus despite the fact that it was known that filterable agents infected plants and animals. The scientific community did not acknowledge Twort's paper for five years.

French-Canadian **Felix d'Herelle** is credited as the sole discoverer of bacteriophages (**Figure 21-1**). In a 1917 paper, he described the lysis of dysentery-causing bacteria grown in liquid medium. He hypothesized that "an invisible antagonist"—a **bacteriophage**—of the dysentery bacteria that could pass through a Chamberland filter caused the lysis. d'Herelle did not cite Twort's research in his publication. He continued research in two directions: determining the biological nature of bacteriophages and exploring the use of bacteriophages as a therapy to treat bacterial infections in a preantibiotic era.

■ **Figure 21-1**

Felix d'Herelle (1873–1949) is credited with the discovery of bacteriophages and is considered the father of bacteriophage therapy.

d'Herelle believed that bacteriophages were an agent of immunity in fighting infectious diseases, a conclusion he reached by observing that the numbers of bacteriophages increased in patients recovering from bacterial dysentery and typhoid. He speculated that the lysis of pathogens by specific bacteriophages formed the mechanism of recovery. This idea supported his efforts to use bacteriophage therapy to treat a wide variety of bacterial diseases. The majority of the scientific world failed to accept the fact that bacteriophages were filterable viruses of bacteria. Instead, the leading theory regarding bacterial lysis was based on Jules Bordet's view that endogenous autolytic enzymes caused bacteria to be lysed during infection. Not until the early 1940s did d'Herelle's bacteriophage theory become universally accepted.

d'Herelle was quick to realize the therapeutic potential of bacteriophages. During the summer of 1919 in France, he attempted to use bacteriophages in field trials to control an epidemic of chicken typhoid caused by the bacterium *Salmonella gallinarum*. He inoculated chickens either orally or by injection with bacteriophages, and the overall results suggested that bacteriophage-treated flocks suffered fewer deaths and shorter epidemics that did not reoccur. He also conducted field trials in Indochina during an outbreak of highly fatal water buffalo pasteurellosis (sometimes referred to in French as *barbone* disease). Once again inoculations appeared successful. These positive results motivated d'Herelle to conduct human trials in the 1920s, a time when human trials were scientifically and ethically crude and not very safe by today's standards.

To prove that bacteriophage preparations (Shiga-bacteriophage **lysates**) were safe for human experiments, d'Herelle injected himself, his family members, and his coworkers. No harmful effects were observed. He applied this treatment to a 12-year old boy suffering from a confirmed case of bacterial dysentery. The boy's symptoms disappeared after one dose and he fully recovered after a few days. Based on this success, three additional dysentery patients received similar treatment. All of them were cured.

The most notorious bacteriophage therapy experiments occurred when d'Herelle worked at the League of Nations quarantine station in Alexandria, Egypt. Four patients on a ship passing through the Suez Canal were suffering from laboratory-confirmed **bubonic plague**. d'Herelle injected all four individuals with antiplague bacteriophages into the bubos present in their lymph nodes and all four patients recovered rapidly. This extraordinary result was reported in 1925 in the French medical journal *Presse Medicale*. After this report, the British government invited d'Herelle to work at the Haffkine Institute in Bombay on bacteriophage therapies for plague and cholera in India. Cholera epidemics posed a major concern because they occurred regularly during religious festivals and pilgrimages in India. Reports from India during the 1920s and 1930s were positive regarding the oral administration of cholera-specific bacteriophages in patients. This treatment reduced the overall severity of symptoms and mortality from the disease.

d'Herelle traveled the world continuing bacteriophage therapy as a means of controlling cholera outbreaks. He accepted an appointment as a professor of protobiology at Yale University in 1928 and went on to play a vital role in the establishment of a bacteriophage institute in Tbilisi, Soviet Georgia (the current Republic of Georgia) in 1934. This institute exists today as the **Georgia Eliava Institute of Bacteriophage, Microbiology and Virology**.

Bacteriophage therapy was popularized by Sinclair Lewis's Pulitzer Prize-winning 1924 novel *Arrowsmith*. The main character, a young physician named Martin Arrowsmith, travels to the West Indies to use bacteriophages as a therapy against bubonic plague.

For several reasons nearly all bacteriologists abandoned bacteriophage therapy in the 1930s. For one, published reports on bacteriophage therapy contained both negative and positive conclusions. It appeared to be a "hit or miss" therapy and the biological nature of bacteriophages was poorly understood. The main reason, though, for the abandonment of bacteriophage therapy was the development of antibiotics. Today, the Western world has a renewed interest in bacteriophage therapy as a treatment to combat antibiotic-resistant strains of pathogenic bacteria.

The History of the Georgia Eliava Institute of Bacteriophage, Microbiology and Virology

The Tibilisi Institute, founded by Professor Giorgyi Eliava, opened its doors as a bacteriology laboratory in 1923. Professor Eliava met Felix d'Herelle in 1926 during a visit to the Pasteur Institute in Paris. After meeting at the Institute, d'Herrelle and Eliava exchanged information about bacteriophage therapy. As a result of these exchanges, d'Herelle visited the Institute during 1934–1935. Josef Stalin (the dictator of the Soviet Union from roughly 1928–1953) invited d'Herelle to the Institute to explore the possibility of bacteriophage therapy for military use. d'Herelle worked at the Institute off and on for the year, hoping to form a great collaboration with Eliava. Unfortunately, the KGB executed Eliava in 1937.[1] d'Herelle did not return to Tbilisi.

Even after Eliava's death, the Institute continued activities in bacteriological and bacteriophage research. In the 1940s, Institute researchers isolated bacteriophages to combat gas gangrene caused by *Clostridium perfringens*. The Institute merged with other research institutes and became the Institute of Vaccine and Sera in 1952. In 1988, the Institute was once again reorganized and was renamed the George Eliava Research Institute of Bacteriophage and included such notable researchers as Zemphira Alavidze and Amiran Meipariani. The Institute manufactured bacteriophage sprays, salves, ointments, pills, and patches and supplied these therapies to the entire Soviet Union—especially the Soviet military, which was, and continues to be, a major consumer of bacteriophage preparations. Bacteriophage therapy was and continues to be a routine part of treatments in clinics and hospitals in Eastern Europe. These preparations are sold at pharmacies at incredibly low prices and are available without a doctor's prescription. The Institute has sole governing power over licensing and quality control of bacteriophage production.

The Eliava Institute facilities were damaged during the Georgian civil war. When the Soviet Union collapsed in 1991, thousands of bacteriophage samples that were identified and catalogued were lost. Electrical outages ruined many refrigerated bacteriophage libraries, and the Institute nearly closed. A 1997 BBC broadcast, *The Virus That Cures*, inspired energetic entrepreneurs from around the world to help save the Institute and its stocks. At the time of this writing, many companies around the world are avidly pursuing bacteriophage therapy as an inexpensive, effective remedy to counter antibiotic resistance and hard-to-treat bacterial infections.

The American Phage Group

During the 1940s scientists from universities throughout the United States that were studying bacteria and bacteriophages formed the "Phage Group." Among the members of the group were Max Delbruck, Salvador Luria, and Alfred Hershey. These key members were educated as theoretical physicists or biologists, applying their approaches to the study of the physical nature of the gene. The Phage Group spent summers doing research experiments at Cold Spring Harbor Laboratory (in Long Island, New York) and designed an annual course to improve laboratory instruction in the techniques of bacteriophage research.

Their experiments centered upon studying the basic biology of bacteriophages, including the optimization of **one-step growth experiments** (see Chapter 5). The development

---

[1] Eliava had become romantically involved with the same woman that the head of Stalin's police was in love with. Reports out of the Soviet Union suggested that the KGB assassinated Eliava, denouncing him as an enemy of the people.

VIRUS FILE 21-1

Bacteriophage Therapy Makes a Comeback

On a frigid day in December 2001, three men gathering wood in the Republic of Georgia found some canisters the size of paint pails that were so hot to the touch that they melted the surrounding snow. The men hauled them to their campsites where they used the canisters to warm themselves during a bitterly cold night. Unfortunately, the heat of the canisters was so intense that it caused severe deep burns on the backs of two of the men. The containers were old Soviet-era makeshift heaters packed with strontium 90, a powerful chemical that was used to power remote generators.

Within hours the two men began suffering from radiation poisoning. They were dizzy and started vomiting. And their skin started to peel. The bacterium *Staphylococcus aureus* infected their wounds. Antibiotics failed to prevent the pathogenic bacteria from invading deeply into the wounds and the two men were near septic shock. They were rushed to a hospital in Tbilisi where doctors placed patches containing bacteriophages on the wounds. The infections cleared up within a few weeks and the men were stable enough to undergo skin grafting abroad.

Bacteriophage therapy is making a comeback because of the accelerating crisis of antibiotic resistance. Several hurdles have confronted bacteriophage therapy, such as:

■ **Figure VF 21-1**
These wounds were treated with the bacteriophage powder PhagoBioDerm. There is rekindled interest in bacteriophage applications against antibiotic resistant bacteria.

- contamination of bacteriophage stocks with bacterial toxins and bacterial debris that causes symptoms ranging from mild fever to death in patients.
- the narrow host range of bacteriophages.
- the elimination of bacteriophages by the host's immune system (antibodies).
- bacterial host resistance to bacteriophage infection.
- **lytic** bacteriophages are ideal for therapy, but half of all bacteriophages are **temperate** (their DNA is integrated into the host genome, leaving the host intact and alive).

In the 1990s, U.S. scientists began laboratory experiments to successfully address these hurdles. Pure preparations that remove toxins and bacterial debris from bacteriophage stocks can now be produced. Methods have been developed to isolate bacteriophage mutants that are hardier and have broader host ranges. The hardy strains possess the ability to avoid rapid elimination by the host's immune system. Since 1993, at least 13 companies located in the United States, Canada, Germany, and the United Kingdom were founded to develop bacteriophage therapeutics. Some of these companies are creating bacteriophage cocktails, whereas others are isolating specific bacteriophage components such as lytic enzymes aimed to target pathogenic bacteria. For therapeutic purposes, the Federal Drug Administration (FDA) would approve bacteriophages that are stably lytic. Experts believe that bacteriophage therapy that was once scorned may ultimately find a niche in Western medicine. It has the potential to save lives.

References

Carlton, R. M. 1999. "Phage Therapy: Past History and Future Prospects." *Archivum Immunologiae et Therapiae Experimentalis* 47:267–274.

Koerner, B. I. 1998. "Return of a Killer: Phages May Once Again Fight Tough Bacterial Infections." *U.S. News & World Report,* November 2, 1998.

Merril, C. R. et al. 1996. "Long-circulating Bacteriophage As Antibacterial Agents." *PNAS USA* 93:3188–3192.

Stone, R. 2002. "Stalin's Forgotten Cure." *Science* 298:728–731.

Thiel, K. 2004. "Old Dogma, New Tricks—21st Century Phage Therapy." *Nat Biotech* 22:31–36.

(a)

(b)

■ **Figure 21-2**
(a) Bacterial cells growing in log phase (left) and being lysed by bacteriophages (right). **(b)** Bacteriophage plaque assays from one-step growth experiments. The circular clearings present on the lawn of bacteria represent plaques or regions where the bacteriophage infected the bacterium and lysed the cells. Each plaque arises from a single infectious bacteriophage. The infectious particle that gives rise to a plaque is called a PFU (plaque-forming unit).

of bacteriophage **plaque assays** contributed to the foundations of modern animal virology (**Figure 21-2**). By 1952, the Phage Group consisted of about 50 members. Important problems of bacteriophage research were tackled because researchers focused on a selected group of "authorized" phages, such as the Type (T) phages. During the 1950s Hershey and Chase showed by radiolabeling that the phosphorous (DNA) entered bacterial cells during T2 bacteriophage infection but that most of the sulfur (protein) did not (refer to Chapter 1). Delbruck, Luria, and Hershey shared the 1969 Nobel Prize in Physiology or Medicine for "their discoveries concerning the replication mechanism and the genetic structure of viruses."

21.2 Bacteriophage Ecology

Most bacteria live in the subsurfaces of soil and sediment and the open ocean, and are essential components of Earth's biota. Scientists at the University of Georgia (in Athens, Georgia) estimated the total number of bacteria on Earth to be 4–6×10^{30} cells. The scientific community agrees that there is a global population of about 1×10^{31} bacteriophages. Both values come from bacteriophage estimates in aquatic environments. These marine viruses are the best characterized of the phage ecology system. Marine bacteriophages infect and lyse bacteria in aquatic microbial communities. This is now recognized as the most important mechanism of recycling bacterial carbon in the marine environment. The dissolved organic carbon released by viral lysis of a bacterial population stimulates the growth of new bacterial populations that are part of the microbial food web in marine systems (refer to Chapter 1). Marine microbial ecology is a rapidly developing field.

21.3 The Biology of Bacteriophages: Composition and Structure

To date over 5,100 bacteriophages have been examined by means of electron microscope. The International Committee on the Taxonomy of Viruses (ICTV) recognizes one order, 13 families, and 31 genera of bacteriophages. There are four basic shapes or symmetries of bacteriophages: binary (phages that have a head and tail structure), icosahedral (also referred to as cubic), helical (filamentous), and pleomorphic (**Figure 21-3**). All bacteriophages contain a head or capsid structure that varies in size or shape. The majority of bacteriophages contain a tail structure (**Figure 21-4**) that varies in size and length. The tail structure is a helical, hollow tube. The genome of the bacteriophage passes through the tail and into

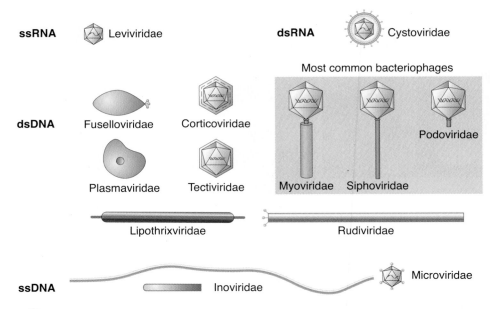

■ Figure 21-3
Diagram depicting the 13 different bacteriophage families grouped by their types of nucleic acid genomes. Tailed bacteriophages are the most prevalent worldwide and infect eubacteria and the archeabacteria. Adapted from H. -W. Ackermann, *Arch. Virol.* 146 (2001): 843–857.

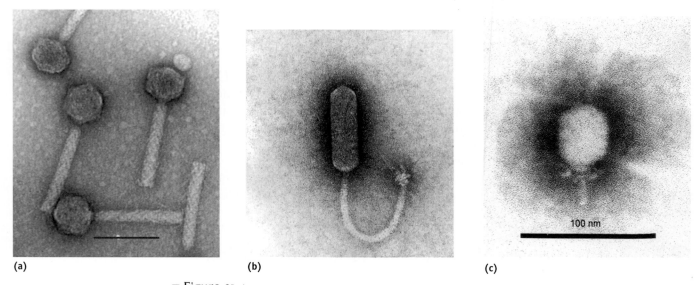

■ Figure 21-4
Images of tailed bacteriophages. **(a)** *Enterobacter* virus P2, Myoviridae family. **(b)** *Bacillus licheniformis* virus, Siphoviridae family. **(c)** Bacteriophage 3/K26 (infects *Kurthia zopfii*), Podoviridae family.

the bacterial host during the initiation of infection. The length of binary bacteriophages varies between 17 and 500 kb and their tail lengths range from 10 to 800 nm.

Three families contain viruses that are enveloped. About 96% of all bacteriophages contain a double-stranded DNA (dsDNA) genome. The remaining 4% of bacteriophages contain genomes of single-stranded DNA (ssDNA), ssRNA, and dsRNA. Genomes may code for as few as three to five gene products or as many as 100. The genomes of bacteriophages contain unusual or modified bases that protect them from degradation by host nucleases during phage infection. The most famous group is the T-Type bacteriophages that are numbered T1 to T7. The best known individual bacteriophages are T4 and λ. With respect to bacteriophages, much research has focused on new viruses and thus the 5000 others that are known have been neglected. It is inevitable that new bacteriophage families are likely to be discovered in unusual habitats, such as hypersaline lagoons, volcanic hot springs, and the mammalian rumen.

21.4 Overview of Bacteriophage Infection: Bacteriophages Possess Alternative Lifestyles: Lytic versus Temperate Phages

Bacteriophages adsorb to the surface receptor molecules of bacterial cells during the first step of the infection. Receptors may be host pili, proteins, oligosaccharides, or lipopolysaccharides (LPS). **Adsorption** is mediated by specialized structures such as tail fibers. The tailed T4 bacteriophage anchors its tail fibers onto the LPS receptors of its host. This causes a comformational change resulting in a contraction of the tail sheath and penetration of the cell membrane and the bacteriophage. The DNA is subsequently injected into the host cell through the tail tube (**Figure 21-5**).

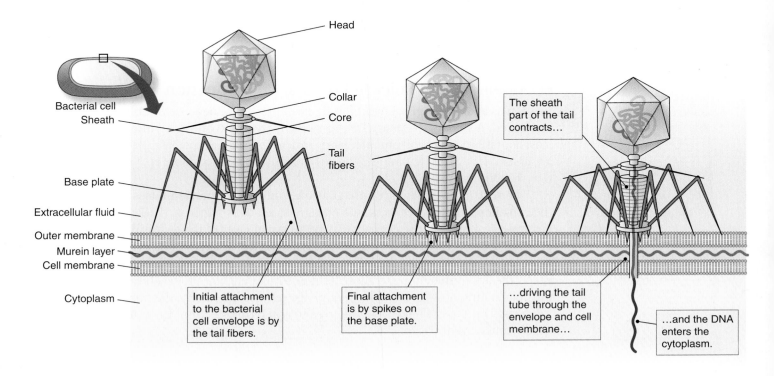

■ **Figure 21-5**
Bacteriophage T4 penetrating through the *E. coli K-12* Omp C outer membrane protein receptor.

Other bacteriophages may bind to a second receptor. Bacteriophages that do not have tails penetrate the host bacterium by producing polysaccharide-degrading enzymes that digest components of the bacterial envelope or cell wall. Bacteria develop resistance to bacteriophage infection when the host cell receptors are altered by a mutation. Losing some receptors offers no protection against infection by bacteriophages that bind to other host receptors. There is much interest in engineering new receptor-recognition elements into the tail fibers of well-characterized bacteriophages so that they can infect taxonomically distant hosts.

The bacteriophage genome **penetrates** through the tail tube into the host cell. This is not an injection process, as it has often been portrayed. Bacteriophage T4 packages lysozyme in the base of its tail from a prior infection and uses the enzyme to degrade a portion of the peptidoglycan of the bacterial cell wall. The DNA is drawn into the cell by a process that is not well understood for most bacteriophages. Once inside the host cell, the bacteriophage circularizes its DNA rapidly by means of sticky ends or termini, or the linear ends are modified and protected from the bacterial nucleases (Figure 21-5).

As soon a bacteriophage DNA genome enters the cell, the host RNA polymerase recognizes the viral DNA promoters and transcription of the early genes begins. Translation of these **early genes** is coupled with transcription. Examples of early proteins produced are repair enzymes (to repair the hole in the bacterial cell wall created during genomic penetration) and proteins that deactivate host proteases and block restriction enzymes (nucleases) that could degrade the bacteriophage DNA. During this time period, copies of the bacteriophage genome are replicated. Subsequently, a set of **late genes** are transcribed and translated. Examples of late gene products are structural proteins that make up the capsomers of the head and tail of the bacteriophage and lysozyme, which is used by the bacteriophage to escape the host during a **lytic infection**. **Lysozyme** is packaged into the tail of some bacteriophage in order to initiate a new infection.

How do the RNA bacteriophages regulate the amount of each protein synthesized during their replication? The secondary structure of the ssRNA phage genomes of phages such as **MS2** and **Q-beta** regulates both the quantities of different phage proteins that are translated, but in addition it also operates temporal control of a switch in the ratios between the different proteins produced in infected cells.

■ Assembly and Release Process: Lytic Infection

As soon as all bacteriophage "parts" have been produced, new bacteriophage particles are assembled. A copy of the phage DNA genome is packaged or "reeled into" a preassembled icosahedral head. The tail and accessory structures (such as the base plate and tail fibers) are assembled, and a few molecules of lysozyme or a comparable enzyme are packaged into the tail base plate.

The remaining lysozyme or **phage lysin**, **endolysins**, **muramidases**, or **virolysins** in the cell allows the viruses to escape or be released from the host. These enzymes hydrolyze specific bonds in the murein or peptidoglycan layer of the cell wall. This part of the cell wall is responsible for the rigidity and mechanical strength of bacterial cells. Another key enzyme, **holin**, is used by phages to create pores in the inner membrane of the host cell at the appropriate time to allow lysin or similar enzymes to reach the peptidoglycan, thus facilitating host lysis and bacteriophage release. Ultimately, the host cell is killed by cell lysis. This type of infection is referred to as a **lytic infection**. Lysis of the host cell is a tightly timed event (**Figure 21-6**).

■ Lysogenic (Temperate) Infections

Lysogenic or **temperate bacteriophages** infect their hosts, but instead of killing the host during a lytic infection their genome becomes integrated into a specific region of the host

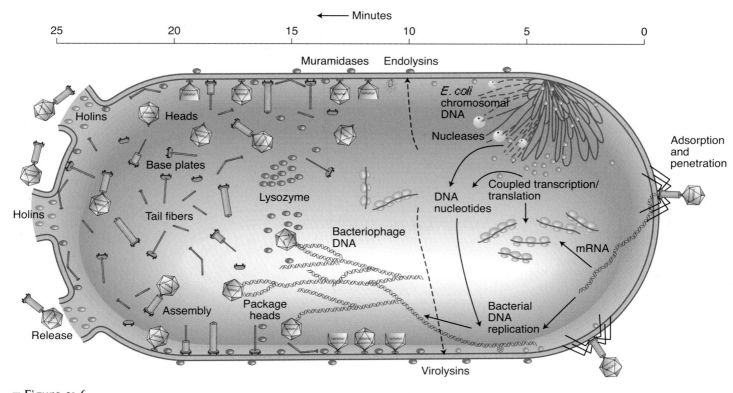

■ **Figure 21-6**
E. coli bacteriophage T4 lytic infection cycle. Adapted from S. T. Abedon and R. L. Calendar, ed. *The Bacteriophages,* Second Edition. Oxford University Press, 2005.

chromosome. After penetration, the viral DNA integrates into the host chromosome and replicates every time the cell copies its chromosomal DNA during cell division. Lysogenic cells divide, giving rise to lysogenic progeny. When the phage genome is integrated into a site in the bacterial chromsome it is called a **prophage**. Some temperate bacteriophages encode **transposase**, which allows the phage to insert randomly into the chromosome. Other bacteriophages integrate into specific locations within the chromosome. During the prophage state, all of the bacteriophage genes are repressed except a gene encoding a **repressor** protein. The repressor protein prevents the synthesis of enzymes and proteins required for the lytic cycle.

If the repressor becomes inactivated (loses function), viral DNA is excised from the bacterial chromosome. The excised DNA (bacteriophage genome) acts like a lytic virus that is able to produce new viral particles that are released during cell lysis. This spontaneous **derepression or induction** happens about once in every 10,000 cell divisions (**Figure 21-7**). Temperate bacteriophages can carry host genes from one bacterial cell to another in a process called **transduction**.

21.5 Bacteriophages Create Pathogenic Bacteria in Nature

Bacteriophages have contributed to virulence of pathogenic bacteria. Sometimes a prophage may carry genes that alter the phenotype of a lysogenic bacterium in a process called **lysogenic conversion**. For example, the pathogen *Corynebacterium diphtheriae* produces a toxin responsible for diphtheria only if it carries the temperate bacteriophage called β. The

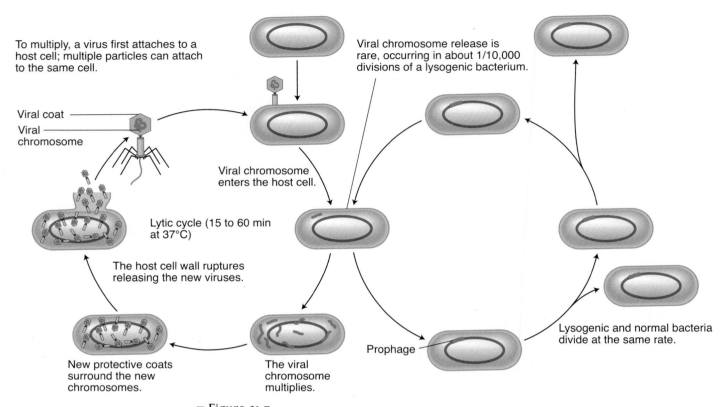

To multiply, a virus first attaches to a host cell; multiple particles can attach to the same cell.

Viral chromosome release is rare, occurring in about 1/10,000 divisions of a lysogenic bacterium.

Viral coat

Viral chromosome

Viral chromosome enters the host cell.

Lytic cycle (15 to 60 min at 37°C)

The host cell wall ruptures releasing the new viruses.

New protective coats surround the new chromosomes.

The viral chromosome multiplies.

Prophage

Lysogenic and normal bacteria divide at the same rate.

■ **Figure** 21-7

Infection cycle of a temperate bacteriophage. Adapted from K. Todar. "Introduction to Viruses: Bacteriophage." *The Microbial World*. University of Wisconsin-Madison, Department of Bacteriology, 2006. http://www.bact.wisc.edu/ themicrobialworld/Phage.html.

■ **Figure** 21-8

This child has the scarlet fever rash caused by a lysogenic *Streptococcus pyogenes* bacterium.

tox gene is located near one end of the phage genome. Diphtheria is a very contagious and potentially life-threatening disease that usually attacks the mucous membranes of the throat and nose. The hallmark sign of this disease is a thick, gray covering in the back of the throat that can make breathing difficult. It is very rare today because of widespread vaccination. The diphtheria vaccine is produced by growing the lysogenic *C. diphtheria* in a liquid medium. The bacterial culture is filtered and the filtrate is treated with formaldehyde, converting the β phage toxin to a **toxoid**. (Single antigen diphtheria toxoid is not available.) The toxoid is available when it is combined with both tetanus toxoid and acellular pertussis vaccine as DTaP.

The infection of *Streptococcus pyogenes* with the temperate bacteriophage T12 results in the lysogenic conversion of a nontoxigenic strain to a pyrogenic- or **erythrogenic exotoxin**-producing bacterium. This type of toxin causes the rash of scarlet fever that sometimes occurs in people who have strep throat (**Figure 21-8**). The loss of the bacteriophage may render the bacterium nonpathogenic. The majority of bacteriophages possessing **virulence genes**, however, are temperate phages that form stable **lysogens**.

The evolution of toxigenic pathogens has depended extensively on bacteriophage infections and exchanges of genetic information. Due to the lack of genetic and bacteriophage systems available to study the mechanisms of toxin gene transfer, scientists have barely scratched the surface in advancing knowledge of bacteriophage molecular biology and evolution. Table 21-1 lists examples of virulence factors carried by bacteriophages.

TABLE 21-1	Examples of Virulence Factors Carried on Bacteriophages		
Bacterium	**Bacteriophage**	**Toxin or Other Gene Product**	**Phenotype**
Corynebacterium diphtheriae	β	Diphtheria toxin	Diphtheria
Streptococcus pyogenes	T12	Erythrogenic toxins	Scarlet fever
Clostridium botulinum	Clostridial phages (e.g., CE β)	Botulinum toxin	Botulism (food poisoning)
Vibrio cholerae	CTX	Chlorerae toxin	Cholera
Escherichia coli	H-19B	Shigalike toxins	Hemorrhagic diarrhea
Staphylococcus aureus	φ315, φ13, φMu50A	Enterotoxins P and A	Food poisoning
Mycoplasma arthritidis	MAV1	Outer membrane protein (*vir* gene)	Arthritis involving two or more joints?

21.6 Control of Bacteriophages in Industrial Fermentations

Bacteria are used in a variety of food fermentation processes because they are able to break down complex organic substances into simpler ones. Examples of commercial food fermentation products are yogurt, cheese, sauerkraut, and soy sauce. The pharmaceutical and biotechnology industries use bacteria on a large scale to produce products such as alcohols, vitamins, amino acids, enzymes, hormones, biopolymers, antibiotics, and other therapeutics (**Figure 21-9**).

Bacteriophages are ubiquitous in nature. Any bacterial strain can be infected by virulent bacteriophages or harbor one or more prophages. All industries that utilize bacteria to produce food or commodity chemicals are vulnerable to bacteriophage infections. Bacteriophage researcher Roger Hendrix provides us with the following analogy: *"If a bacteriophage were the size of a cockroach—these cockroaches would cover the surface of the earth in a layer that is 31,071 miles or 50,000 km deep!"* This is a nightmare statistic to laboratory staff working in a commercial fermentation factory, where bacteriophages really are considered to threaten production.

Attacks by bacteriophages can cause serious problems in the production process and result in considerable economic losses. An entire fermentation batch may be lost due to bacteriophage contamination. Examples of common products and their bacterial hosts in fermentation-based industries are listed in Table 21-2. Approximately 1% to 10% of dairy product fermentation batches are lost to bacteriophage infection. This usually happens because the raw starting materials can be contaminated with undetectable numbers of bacteriophages.

Laboratory staff at fermentation facilities should be trained to expect and respond to bacteriophage outbreaks, as the problem is unavoidable. Effective cleaning and monitoring procedures, especially during the bacteriophage "seasons" of January to March and October to November is warranted. Measures used to control bacteriophages in the dairy

■ **Figure 21-9**
Microbe fermentation vessel used to make enzymes for medical and industrial use.

TABLE 21-2	Common Products and Their Bacterial Hosts in Fermentation-Based Industries

Product	Bacterial Host
Yogurt	*Lactobacillus delbrueckii* subspecies *bulgaricus*
	Streptococcus thermophilus
Cheese	*Lactobacillus delbrueckii* subspecies *lactis*
	Lactobacillus helveticus
	Lactobacillus lactis
	Propionibacterium freudenreichii
	Streptococcus thermophilus
Sourdough bread	*Lactobacillus fermentum*
Sauerkraut	*Leuconostoc mesenteroides*
	Leuconostoc fallax
	Lactobacillus plantarum
Vinegar	*Acetobacter* sp.
Soy sauce	*Tetragenococcus halophila*
Chloramphenicol	*Streptomyces venezuelae*
Streptomycin	*Streptomyces griseus*
Tetracycline	*Streptomyces aureofaciens*
L-glutamic acid	*Brevibacterium lactofermentum*
Insecticide (BT)	*Bacillus thuringiensis*
Silage	*Lactobacillus plantarum*
Hormones, enzymes, and other biotechnology products	*Escherichia coli*
Butanol	*Clostridium beijerinckii*
Acetone	*Clostridium* sp.

TABLE 21-3	Bacteriophage Control Measures in the Dairy Food Industry

- Rotation of bacterial starter cultures
- Use of starter cultures that do not contain strains of similar bacteriophage sensitivity patterns
- Air filtration (HEPA)
- Preparation of starter cultures in a positively pressured room
- Cleaning and chlorinating vessels between fills
- Performing daily tests for bacteriophage detection
- Regular inspections of equipment surfaces to remove biofilms
- Spraying the environment with adequate disinfecting agents
- Rotation of manufacturing processes

industry are listed in Table 21-3. Dairy plants typically harbor 10^5 plaque-forming units per cubic meter of air. Effective control measures are needed to minimize bacteriophage infection.

21.7 Biofilms and Bacteriophages

Bacteria can adhere to solid surfaces to form a slimy, slippery coat called a **biofilm**. Biofilms are found on most wet surfaces in nature, such as river rocks, the walls of limestone caves, pipes, industrial equipment, the hulls of ships, on teeth, lining the colon, on sutures, the lungs of cystic fibrosis patients, and on medical devices such as catheters, heart valves and surrounding tissues of the heart, orthopedic devices, or facial implants. Biofilms are complex sessile (permanently attached) communities of bacteria that may consist of a single bacterial species to hundreds or even thousands of them. The biofilm bacteria produce extracellular polysaccharide polymers that surround and encase the microbes, facilitating their adhesion to surfaces (**Figure 21-10**). Biofilms can cause environmental problems or chronic bacterial infections in humans.

Biofilms present an important challenge to patient medical care. Bacteria commonly isolated from medical devices are *Enterococcus faecalis*, *S. aureus*, *S. epidermidis*, *Streptococcus viridans*, *E. coli*, *Klebsiella pneumoniae*, *Proteus mirabilis*, and *Pseudomonas aeruginosa*.

These bacteria originate from either the skin of the patient or healthcare workers, tap water (e.g., when entry ports of catheters are exposed to tap water), or other sources in the environment. Biofilms are tenacious and highly resistant to antimicrobial treatment, making these infections difficult or impossible to treat.

Preventative strategies and treatment of biofilms on medical implants include using silver-impregnated catheters and cuffs, incorporating inline filters into catheters, coating devices with antibiotics, and disinfection at the surface site. Interest is growing in the role of bacteriophages in disrupting or reducing the formation of biofilms on medical implants. Studies by Curtin and Donlan attempting to pretreat catheter surfaces with bacteriophages to control biofilms are promising. Further research in this area is needed, particularly as the problem of antibiotic resistance continues to grow and traditional antibiotic treatment becomes less effective.

■ **Figure 21-10**

Electron micrograph of *Staphylococcus aureus* bacteria found on the surface of a patient's catheter. The sticky-looking substance woven between the bacteria is composed of polysaccharides and is the biofilm that protects the bacteria from antimicrobial agents such as antibiotics. Magnified 2363×.

21.8 FDA-Approved *Listeria*-Specific Bacteriophage Preparation on Ready-to-Eat Meats

Hot dogs, luncheon meats, and cheeses such as feta, Brie, Camembert, blue-veined cheeses, or Mexican-style cheeses such as queso blancho that are not made with pasteurized milk may contain *Listeria monocytogenes*. Luncheon meats are especially prone to contamination with *L. monocytogenes* during slicing and packaging at food processing plants. *L. monocytogenes* is a foodborne pathogen that is harmless in most healthy people but can cause **listeriosis** in pregnant women, newborns, and individuals with weakened immune systems.

Infections during pregnancy can lead to a miscarriage or stillbirth, premature delivery, or infection of the newborn. The symptoms of listeriosis include flulike symptoms such as nausea and diarrhea. If the bacterial infection spreads to the nervous system, individuals experience a headache, stiff neck, confusion, loss of balance, and possibly convulsions. Listeriosis is 30% fatal in high-risk groups.

In 2006 the FDA recognized the use of a cocktail of six bacteriophages in the form of an application spray as GRAS (Generally Recognized as Safe). The product is marketed as LISTEX™ P100 and is produced by the Phage Technology Center in the Netherlands.

LISTEX will be used in the clean rooms of cheese, meat, and poultry processing plants to inhibit the growth of *Listeria* on products such as lunch meat and hot dogs. The phage preparation will not be declared as an ingredient on the label of a treated product.

■ Summary

No virology textbook should be without a chapter on bacteriophages. Bacteriophages—viruses that infect bacteria—have been an attractive "model" organism for scientists to learn about the basic biology of life. Bacteriophages are inexpensive and easy to work with in the laboratory. They have small genomes and reproduce rapidly, making them amenable to obtaining mutants identified by rapid screening techniques.

The field of bacteriophage biology began during what is sometimes called the golden age of microbiology (~1870–1920) and then languished for decades. Today it is once again thriving due to the use of phages to combat drug-resistant pathogens. Phage ecology is also a rapidly developing field. There are over 5,100 bacteriophages that have been characterized by electron microscopy. The majority of bacteriophages are binary, in that they contain head and tail structures. About 96% of bacteriophages contain dsDNA genomes and the remaining 4% contain ssDNA, ssRNA, or dsRNA genomes. Bacteriophages may undergo a lytic or lysogenic infection. The host is killed (lysed) during a lytic infection and progeny phages are released. Lysogenic or temperate bacteriophages infect their hosts, but instead of killing the host their genome becomes integrated into a specific region of the host chromosome. The integrated viral genome is called a prophage. A prophage may carry genes that alter the phenotype of its host in a process called lysogenic conversion. Specifically, the evolution of several toxinogenic pathogens has depended extensively on bacteriophage infections and exchanges of genetic material. Examples include the following pathogenic bacteria: *C. diphtheriae* (causes diphtheria), *S. pyogenes* (causes strep throat and scarlet fever), and *C. botulinum* (causes food poisoning or botulism).

Felix d'Herrelle is credited with discovering bacteriophages and with the idea of bacteriophage therapy to treat bacterial diseases. He played a significant role in the establishment of the Georgia Eliava Institute of Bacteriophage, Microbiology and Virology in Tbilisi in the Republic of Georgia. Bacteriophage therapy has been used by the Soviet Union since the 1920s. Bacteriophage sprays, salves, ointments, patches, and pills are still prepared and used in clinics and hospitals in the former Soviet Union and Eastern Europe. Today bacteriophage therapy is being investigated in the Western world as a potential therapy to defeat multidrug resistant bacteria. Other applications of bacteriophages are to eliminate superbugs that form biofilms present on implanted medical devices and to treat ready-to-eat meats and soft cheeses with bacteriophages in order to eliminate the foodborne pathogen *L. monocytogenes*.

Bacteriophages are ubiquitous in nature. Bacteriophage outbreaks occur in the food fermentation, biotechnology, and pharmaceutical industries that use bacteria on a large scale to produce fermented foods, chemicals, enzymes, hormones, biopolymers, antibiotics, and therapeutics. Effective control measures are needed to minimize bacteriophage infections during the large-scale production of bacteria in these industries.

Resources

■ Primary Literature and Reviews

Ackermann, H.-W. 2001. "Frequency of Morphological Phage Descriptions in the Year 2000." *Arch Virol* 146:843–857.

Beher, M. G., and Pugsley, A. P. 1981. "Coliphage Which Requires Either the lamB Protein or the ompC Protein for Adsorption to *Escherichia coli* K-12." *J Virol* 38(1):372–375.

Bernhardt, T. et al. 2002. "A Protein Antibiotic in the Phage Qb Virion: Diversity in Lysis Targets." *Science* 292:2326–2329.

Brussow, H. 2005. "Phage Therapy: The *Escherichia coli* experience." *Microbiology* 151:2133–2140.

Costerton, J. W., Stewart, P. S., and Greenberg, E. P. 1999. "Bacterial Biofilms: A Common Cause of Persistent Infections." *Science* 284:1318–1322.

Curtin, J. J., and Donlan, R. M. 2006. "Using Bacteriophages to Reduce Formation of Catheter-Associated Biofilms by *Staphylococcus epidermidis*." *Antimicrob Agents Chemother* 50(4):1268–1275.

Danovaro, R., and Serresi, M. 2000. "Viral Density and Virus-to-Bacterium Ratio in Deep-Sea Sediments of the Eastern Mediterranean." *Applied Environ Microbiol* 66(5):1857–1861.

d'Herelle, F. 1917. "Sur un Microbe Invisible Antagonistic des Bacilles Dysenterique. (On an invisible microbe antagonistic to dysentery bacteria.)" *C R Acad Sci Paris* 165:373–375.

d'Herelle, F. 1925. "Essai de Traitement de la Pest Bubonique par le Bacteriophage. (Test of processing of the bubonic pest by the bacteriophage)." *Presse Med* 33:1393–1394.

d'Herelle, F., Malone, R. H., and Lahiri, M. 1930. "Studies on Asiatic Cholera." *Indian Med Res Memoirs* 14:1–161.

Donlan, R. M. 2001. "Biofilms and Device-Associated Infections." *EID* 7(2):277–281.

Duckworth, D. H. 1976. "Who Discovered Bacteriophage?" *Bacteriol Rev* 40(4): 793–802.

Furhrman, J. A. 1999. "Marine Viruses and Their Biogeochemical and Ecological Effects." *Nature* 399:541–548.

Greer, G. G. 2005. "Bacteriophage Control of Foodborne Bacteriat." *J Food Prot* 68(5):1102–1111.

Hudson, J. A. et al. 2005. "Bacteriophages As Biocontrol Agents in Food." *J Food Prot* 68(2):426–437.

Jones, D. T. et al. 2000. "Bacteriophage Infections in the Industrial Acetone Butanol (AB) Fermentation Process." *J Mol Microbiol Biotechnol* 2(1):21–26.

Letellier, L. et al. 2004. "Main Features on Tailed Phage, Host Recognition and DNA Uptake." *Bioscience* 9:1228–1239.

Kanamaru, S. et al. 2002. "Structure of the Cell-Puncturing Device of Bacteriophage T4." *Nature* 415:553–557.

Maki, D. G., and Tambyah, P. A. 2001. "Engineering Out the Risk of Infection with Urinary Catheters." *EID* 7(2):1–6.

Miedzybrodzki, R. et al. 2007. "Phage Therapy of Staphylococcal Infections (including MRSA) May Be Less Expensive than Antibiotic Treatment." *Postepy Hig Med Dosw* (61):461–465.

Miller, E. S. et al. 2003. "Bacteriophage T4 Genome." *Microbiol and Mol Biol Rev* 67(1):86–156.

Pennazio, S. 2006. "The Origin of Phage Virology." *Rivista di Biologia/Biology Forum* 99:103–130.

Shen, Y. et al. 2006. "Isolation and Characterization of *Listeria monocytogenes* Isolates from Ready-to-Eat Foods in Florida." *App Environ Microbiol* 72(7):5073–5076.

Summers, W. C. 1993. "Plague and Cholera in India: The Bacteriophage Inquiry of 1928–1936." *J Hist Med Allied Sci* 48:275–301.

Sutherland, I. W. et al. 2004. "The Interaction of Phage and Biofilms." *FEMS Microbiol Lett* 232:1–6.

Twort, F. W. 1915. "An Investigation on the Nature of Ultra-Microscopic Viruses." *Lancet* 2:1241–1243.

Weeks, C. R., and Ferretti, J. 1984. "The Gene for Type A Streptococcal Exotoxin (erythrogenic toxin) Is Located in Bacteriophage T12." *Infection and Immunity* 46(2):531–536.

Whitman, W. B., Coleman, D. C., and Wiebe, W. J. 1998. "Prokaryotes: The Unseen Majority." *PNAS USA* 95:6578–6583.

Wunsche, L. 1989. "Importance of Bacteriophages in Fermentation Processes." *Acta Biotechnol* 9(5):395–419.

Wurtz, M. 1992. "Bacteriophage Structure." *Microscop Rev* 5:283–309.

■ Popular Press

Blakely, P. 1996. "The Good Virus." *Discover Magazine*, November issue, pp. 50–58.

Calendar, R., and Abedon, S. T. Eds. 2006. *The Bacteriophages*. 2nd ed. Oxford and New York: University Press.

Cairns, J., Stent, G. S., and Watson, J. D., Eds. 1992. *Phage and the Origins of Molecular Biology*. Expanded Edition. Cold Spring Harbor, NY: Cold Spring Harbor Press.

Hausler, T. 2006. *Viruses vs. Superbugs*. New York: Macmillan.

Koerner, B. 1998. "Return of a Killer: Phages May Once Again Fight Tough Bacterial Infections." *U.S. News & World Report*, November issue, pp. 51–52.

Kutter, E., and Sulakvelidze, A. *Bacteriophages: Biology and Applications*. New York: CRC Press.

Lewis, S. 1998. *Arrowsmith,* with a new afterword by E. L. Doctarow, revised edition. New York: Signet Classics.

Stahl, F. W., and Hershey, A. D., Eds. 2000. *We Can Sleep Later: Alfred D. Hershey and the Origins of Molecular Biology*. Cold Spring Harbor, NY: Cold Spring Harbor Press.

Shnayerson, M., and Plotkin, M. J. 2003. *The Killers Within: The Deadly Rise of Drug-Resistant Bacteria.* New York: Back Bay Books.

Waldor, M. K. et al. Eds. 2005. *Phages: Their Role in Bacterial Pathogenesis and Biotechnology.* Washington, DC: ASM Press.

Young, R. 1992. "Bacteriophage Lysis: Mechanisms and Regulation." *Microbiol Rev* 56(3):430–481.

■ Video Productions

The Virus That Cures. 1998. Films for the Humanities.

Arrowsmith (1931). 2005. MGM.

■ eLearning

http://biology.jbpub.com/book/virology

The site features eLearning, an online review area that provides quizzes and other tools to help you study for your class. You can also follow useful links for in-depth information, or just find out the latest virology and microbiology news.

Glossary

(–) sense   Describes viral RNA that is complementary to the viral mRNA and, therefore, must be changed into (+) sense RNA before it can begin to translate itself into proteins within the host cell

(+) sense   Describes viral RNA that, upon entering the host cell, can begin to translate into proteins; it is of the same form as mRNA.

2′5′oligo (A) synthetase   An antiviral protein that activates latent RNAse L.

5′m⁷G mRNA cap structure   A methylated guanine nucleotide that is a "cap" located on the 5′ end of mRNA; during transcription it is recognized by cellular ribosomes and thus plays an important role in the initiation of translation; the 5′m⁷g cap helps protect the mRNA from degradation.

β galactosidase   An enzyme that cleaves the chromogenic substrate X-gal, resulting in a blue color; useful in quantifying viruses in a plaque assay.

β propiolactone   A chemical that inactivates viruses to use in vaccines.

A

Aborted life cycle   In viruses, a life cycle in which only the early viral genes are expressed.

Abortive replication   A block in the life cycle of viruses that can infect cells such that early viral proteins are produced, but late proteins are not, and, therefore, full infectious particles are not produced in mammalian cells.

Acquired immunity   A response to a specific immune stimulus that involves immune defensive cells and frequently leads to the establishment of host immunity.

Acquired immunodeficiency syndrome (AIDS)   A serious viral disease caused by the human immunodeficiency virus (HIV) in which the T (CD4) lymphocytes are destroyed and opportunistic illnesses occur in the patient.

Active immunity   The immune system responds to antigen by producing antibodies and specific **lymphocytes.**

Acute disease   A disease that develops rapidly, exhibits substantial symptoms, and lasts only a short time.

Acute hepatitis   A case of hepatitis in which symptoms are severe and worsen quickly.

Acute infections   Infections that have symptoms of sudden onset or last a short time.

Acute vascular rejection   When the human immune system causes a rapid vascular injury in a transplanted organ within a few days

to several weeks of the transplant; triggered by complement and antibody response toward the organ tissues.

ADA deficiency   A deficiency in the enzyme adenosine deaminase; a condition that severely compromises the immune system by destroying immature lymphocytes so they fail to reach maturity.

Adenosine deaminase (ADA) genes   Genes located on chromosome 20 that produce the enzyme adenosine deaminase, which is required for metabolic function of a variety of cells, especially T lymphocytes.

AIDS dementia complex   A neurological complication of AIDS that may impair cognitive reasoning, behavior, or motor performance.

Alanine aminotransferase (ALT)   An enzyme in the body that, when at elevated levels, indicates liver inflammation that can be the result of viral hepatitis.

Alveolar sacs   Tiny subdivisions at the ends of the bronchioles in the lungs that are lined with immune cells called macrophages.

Amantidine   An antiviral drug that blocks the M2 ion channel function, resulting in the incomplete release of the viral ribonuclear proteins, thus interfering with uncoating during influenza virus infections.

Ambisense   Describes ssRNA that is both + and – sense on the same ssRNA segment.

Amyloid plaques   Cluster of dead and dying protein fragments that accumulate in different regions in the brain; characteristic of Alzheimer's patients and those suffering from prion diseases.

Analytical epidemiology   Determines the why and how of an epidemic in a given population.

Antibody   A highly specific protein produced by the body in response to a foreign substance, such as a bacterium or virus, and capable of binding to the substance.

Antibody-dependent cell-mediated cytotoxicity (ADCC)   A type of cytotoxicity in which NK cells, monocytes, macrophages, or neutrophils bind to target cells containing bound antibodies to kill them.

Antibody-dependent enhancement   The rare condition in which certain antibodies can be beneficial to a virus.

Antigen   A chemical substance that stimulates the production of antibodies by the body's immune system; also called immunogen.

Antigen-presenting cell (APC)   A macrophage or dendritic cell that on its surface expresses MHC II and exposes antigen peptide fragments to T_H cells.

Antigenic drift   A minor variation over time in the antigenic composition of influenza viruses.

Antigenic shift A major change in the antigenic composition of influenza viruses such as reassortments between human and bird influenza. The result can be a potentially pandemic strain of influenza A virus.

Antitoxin An antibody produced by the body that circulates in the bloodstream to provide protection against toxins by neutralizing them.

Antiviral state The cellular state occurring when host cells have secreted interferons in response to a viral invasion and interferons have bound to receptors on neighboring cells, signaling other cells to produce antiviral proteins.

Apoptosis A genetically programmed form of cell death. Apoptosis may be induced during viral infection, allowing for the removal of infected cells in the body.

Artificially acquired active immunity The production of antibodies by the body in response to antigens in a vaccination.

Artificially acquired passive immunity The transfer of antibodies formed in one individual or animal to another susceptible person.

Assembly The process in which the immature virus particle is formed.

Astrocytosis The spread of astrocytes (star-shaped nerve cells) to damaged tissues in the brain.

Atherosclerosis A thickening of the artery walls that is mainly due to a fatty diet that is high in cholesterol.

Attenuate To reduce the ability of a virus to do damage to the exposed individual. Attenuated virus strains may be used to vaccinate individuals against wild-type viral pathogens.

Australia antigen The original name for the hepatitis B surface antigen (hbsAg).

Autocleavage The process of a protein cleaving itself.

B

B lymphocyte (B cell) A white blood cell that matures into memory cells and plasma cells that secrete antibody.

Bacteriophage (phage) A virus that infects and replicates within bacterial cells.

Bacteriophage therapy Bacteriophages used in the curing of bacterial infections in humans.

Barrier technique A method of containing infection in which an impenetrable object or surface is placed between the infected and the uninfected substance or body (e.g., gloves and gowns are worn to prevent the spread of infection).

Bifurcated needle A two-pronged needle used in mass vaccination against the smallpox virus.

Bile A digestive fluid produced by the liver that aids in digestion of fats and gets rid of wastes in the body.

Bilirubin A yellow-pigmented byproduct of old red blood cells that causes jaundice.

Biofilm A complex community of microorganisms that form a protective and adhesive matrix that attaches to a surface, such as a catheter or industrial pipeline.

Bioflavenoids Brightly colored, water-soluble compounds with antibacterial and antiviral properties that are secreted by plants.

Biosafety level 4 (BSL-4) Indicates that the strictest containment and safety measures possible are in place for facilities that work with and study dangerous microorganisms that pose a high risk of life-threatening disease and for which there is no cure, treatment, or vaccine available (e.g., the ebola virus).

Bioterrorism The intentional or threatened use of biological agents to cause fear in or actually inflict death or disease upon a large population.

Bloodborne pathogen A disease-causing microorganism that is carried in the bloodstream and can be transmitted to others if proper precautions are not taken in handling the infected blood.

Blood–brain barrier A semipermeable interface between the bloodstream and CNS tissues that protects the brain from potentially toxic substances or microbes.

Breakthrough virus Wild-type virus that causes a mild form of disease.

BUdR (5-bromodeoxyuridine) A toxic analog to thymidine in DNA; the vaccinia virus (smallpox vaccine) disrupts the activity of the thymidine kinase gene and renders host cells resistant to the effects of BudR; also an anticancer drug and a potential antiviral drug.

Bulbar polio Less common than spinal polio; results in weakness of muscles, thus impairing the ability to talk or swallow and requiring the need for an iron lung or respirator.

Bulbospinal polio A combination of bulbar and spinal paralysis.

Burgoo Thick spicy stew that contains whatever meat (e.g., squirrel brains) and vegetables available; often served in the southern United States.

Bushmeat The meat of wild animals, often used in reference to monkey or ape meat.

C

Cancer A disease characterized by the radiating spread of malignant cells that reproduce at an uncontrolled rate.

Cap-dependent translation Refers to the fact that with some rare exceptions, all eukaryotic initiation of translation requires the 5′ cap of the cellular mRNA to be present.

Cap-independent translation The phenomenon in which some viruses bypass the cap recognition requirement.

Capsid The protein shell that encloses and protects the nucleic acid genome of a virus.

Capsomere Many viral structural proteins that come together to form identical subunits, forming the capsid of a virus.

Carcinogen Any physical or chemical substance that causes cancer.

Carcinoma Malignant tumor (cancer).

Carrier An individual who has recovered from a disease but retains the infectious agent in the body and continues to shed them.

Case-control method A method of experimentation in which two subject groups—one exposed to the tested factor and one not—are compared with each other.

Case definition A standard set of criteria that is used to identify who has the disease being studied.

CCR5 A coreceptor present on macrophages that helps HIV to enter cells.

CCR5-Δ32 A genetic polymorphism of the CCR5 gene that codes for a protein that is severely truncated and blocks HIV entry because the viral gp120/gp41 cannot attach to it to infect cells; it has been linked to the resistance to HIV infection.

CD4   A type of receptor expressed on the surface of T_H cells in association with the T cell receptor (TCR) on their surface in order to recognize antigen bound to MHC II molecules.

Cell cycle   The life cycle of a cell from formation to division.

Cell-mediated immune response   The body's ability to resist infection through the activity of T lymphocyte recognition of antigen peptides presented on macrophages and dendritic cells and on infected cells.

Cell tropism   The affinity a virus has to target and infect a particular cell type.

Cellular oncogene   Mutated form of proto-oncogenes that cause tumors.

Cellular scavenging mechanism   Cellular molecules that remove harmful free radicals in order to detoxify their effects on the cell; it helps to protect the cell from DNA damage.

Cellular surface receptors   Usually proteins, glycoproteins, carbohydrates, or lipids that allow the attachment proteins on a virus to infect cells.

Central nervous system (CNS)   Refers to the brain and spinal cord.

Centrifugal rash   A rash mainly covering the face and extremities as opposed to the entire body.

Chain of infection   A term regarding the practices used to control and prevent infectious diseases (e.g., proper sanitation, handwashing, and recognizing high-risk individuals)

Chain of transmission   How infectious diseases can be spread from human to human (or animal to human).

Chain termination   The end effect of nucleoside and nonnucleoside analogs that prevent the elongation of viral DNA of an infected cell, halting their replication.

Chamberland filter   A porcelain filter that removes microorganisms from a liquid.

Chemokine   A small protein that prompts specific white blood cells to migrate to an infection site and carry out their immune system functions.

Chickenpox   A mild infectious disease caused by the varicella zoster virus that usually afflicts children but may be severe in infants, adults, and persons with impaired immune systems.

Chorioallantoic membrane   An extensively vascularized membrane covering the embryos of birds and fishes.

Chronic hepatitis   Hepatitis lasting longer than six months that often does not show any symptoms until the late stages of the disease.

Chronic infection   An infection lasting more than six months.

Chronic rejection   When the human immune system rejects an organ within months to years following transplantation; probably the result of continued, prolonged multiple acute rejections.

Cidofovir   An antiviral medication used for patients with AIDS and HIV and for treating adverse reactions associated with the smallpox vaccine; also known as HPMPC or Vistide.

Ciliary action   The sweeping motion of hairlike cilia of respiratory cells that helps to move particles.

Circulating recombinant forms (CRF)   Two HIV viruses of different subtypes can infect the same cell in an individual, resulting in new HIV progeny hybrid viruses with recombined genomes. These HIV hybrid viruses often do not survive very long but if

they do infect more than one individual, they are referred to as CRFs.

Cirrhosis   The formation of fibrous tissues, nodules, and scarring on the liver that interfere with its cell function and blood circulation.

Clade   A group of organisms that have a common ancestor; also referred to as subtypes.

Clathrin   A large, fibrous protein that forms a basketlike network around vesicles.

Clathrin-coated pits   Specialized regions of the cell membrane that appear as invaginations that are coated on the cytoplasmic side of the membrane with dark material.

Clathrin-coated vesicles   Transport vesicles coated with a latticelike network of the protein clathrin.

Cohort method   A method of experimentation in which two similar populations are studied; members are grouped by common characteristics.

Commerce   Large-scale buying and selling of goods between cities and countries; food commerce today is a major cause of viral spread.

Common name   A nickname by which a virus may be known that isn't as scientific as its taxonomic name.

Communicable disease   A disease that is readily transmissible between hosts.

Communicable period   The time period when an infected individual or animal is contagious and he/she can directly or indirectly infect another person, animal, or arthropod.

Complement system   Over 30 different serum- and membrane-bound glycoproteins that act in sequence when activated by a viral infection to form a membrane attack complex that ultimately causes the destruction of the invading viruses and infected cells; there are three complement system pathways: the classical, the lectin, and the alternative.

Complex   The shape used to describe viruses that do not fit the typical icosahedral or helical design.

Confidential name-based reporting   A method of assessing and monitoring the AIDS epidemic. Patient names are forwarded to the local health department by healthcare providers when AIDS or HIV is diagnosed. Patient names are kept secure and confidential at the state health department.

Congenital effects   Also called teratogenic effects, these are severe congenital malformations in a fetus caused when some blood-borne viruses cross the placenta to reach the fetal circulation.

Conjunctiva   The thin, transparent tissue that covers the outer surface of the eye.

Conjunctivitis   A general term for disease of the conjunctiva, the thin mucous membrane that covers the cornea and forms the inner eyelid; also called pinkeye.

Contact inhibition   When normal cells stop replicating because they come in contact with another cell; in cancers, abnormal cells continue to divide and pile up on top of each other into a focus.

Contagious   A disease whose agent passes with particular ease among hosts.

Containment books   Record-keeping for smallpox outbreak investigations. The books would provide basic data that included cases of smallpox and corresponding dates that would allow field workers to plot the spread of smallpox from person to person by containment teams.

Containment vaccination   Vaccination of a population in a certain area around an outbreak of a disease.

Control group   A group of subjects in an experiment that are not subject to the factor being tested.

Convalescence   The recovery period after an illness.

Convalescent serum   Antibody-rich serum obtained from a convalescing patient.

Coreceptor   A second cellular receptor necessary for viral entry into a cell.

Cross-sectional study   A study that looks at its subject at a single point in time.

Crusades   A time period of religious expeditions and wars. It was a controversial time in the history of Christianity (1095–1270 A.D.).

CXCR4   Also known as fusin; the T lymphocyte coreceptor that helps to allow HIV to enter cells.

Cyanosis   Bluish discoloration of the skin and mucous membranes caused by a lack of oxygen in the blood. It can be associated with certain viral diseases (e.g., blue ear pig disease).

Cyanovirin   A HIV cell fusion inhibitor that was isolated from cultures of blue green algae (cyanobacterium).

Cyclosporin   A drug that suppresses the body's immune system and is used to prevent organ rejection.

Cytokine   Small proteins released by immune defensive cells that affects other cells and the immune response to an infectious agent.

Cytokine storm   An immune system that is overreacting toward the pathogen; cytokine-signaling immune cells such as macrophages and T cells travel to the site of infection causing damage to the body and resulting in failure of multiple organs; also known as systemic inflammatory response syndrome (SIRS).

Cytopathic effects (CPEs)   The visible changes in a host cell that take place because of a viral infection.

Cytoplasm   The part of a eukaryotic cell in which processed mRNAs exit the nucleus and are translated

Cytotoxic T cells   T lympocytic cells that express CD8 in association with TCR on their surfaces; they also recognize and destroy antigens that are associated with MHC I molecules present on infected cells.

D

Dane particle   A 42-to-47-nm mature spherical hepatitis B virus particle.

Dead-end hosts   Virus hosts that cannot transmit the virus to further species.

Defective interfering particles   Noninfectious virus particles coproduced with infectious viruses during infection. These particles contain defective genomes and may interfere with subsequent infections.

Defoliation   Loss of leaves; a characteristic of viral infections in plants.

Dendritic cells   Immune cells present in tissues that have contact with the environment and identify foreign invaders such as viruses and bacteria; once dendritic cells find foreign invaders they migrate to the nearest lymph node via the lymphatics, where they will come in near proximity to other immune cells to eliminate the pathogen.

Deoxyribonucleic acid (DNA)   The genetic material of all cells and many viruses.

Descriptive studies   "After the fact" studies used to generate a testable hypothesis or enough evidence to indicate sufficient cause for conducting lengthier and more costly analytical studies.

DICER   A host cell RNAse III-like enzyme that chops or "dices" dsRNA.

Differential diagnosis   A systematic method used by physicians to distinguish between two or more diseases with similar symptoms.

Dilated cardiomyopathy (DCM)   Disease of the heart muscle that causes the heart to become enlarged and to pump less strongly. As a result the heart becomes thin, weak, or floppy and unable to pump blood efficiently around the body. This causes fluid to build up in the lungs, causing congestion and the feeling of breathlessness.

Direct contact   The form of disease transmission involving close association between hosts; *see also* indirect contact.

Direct detection   A method to diagnose viral infections that directly visualizes virus particles contained in a clinical specimen (e.g., electron microscopy).

Disease   Any change from the general state of good health.

DNA ligase   An enzyme that binds together DNA fragments; it creates an ester bond between adjacent $3'OH$ and $5'PO_4$ ends on cleaved DNA.

DNA microarray   A tool consisting of a chip that contains an array of nucleic acids for use in probing a biological sample to determine gene expression. It can be used to assess and classify large numbers of genes such as the genes present in tumors of cancer patients; the risk for developing certain cancers can be assessed and a prognosis made based on microarray test results. It can also be used to identify pathogens causing a particular infection such as the quickly identifying or screening for types of influenza, SARS-CoV, respiratory syncytial virus (RSV), and other airborne bioterrorist pathogens.

DNA polymerase   An enzyme that catalyzes DNA replication by combining complementary nucleotides to an existing strand.

DNA template   The original strand of DNA to be replicated.

DNA vaccine   A vaccine consisting of plasmid DNAs that have been manipulated to contain a gene encoding a viral antigen of interest and raises an immune response to the expressed antigen carried on the plasmid DNA.

Donor   One who supplies pieces of bodily tissue for use in another person's body.

Downstream DNA element   A region of DNA that is located further in the direction of transcription.

dsRNA   RNA with two complementary strands that trigger the RNAi defense system.

E

Eclipse phase   The period after the infection in which the input, or inoculated virus, disappears. No virus particles are detected at this time.

Eczema vaccinatum   A rare and severe side effect of smallpox vaccination that can occur in people with eczema.

El niño   An abnormal warming of the surface ocean waters that causes weather changes around the globe.

Emerging infectious disease   A new disease or changing disease that is seen for the first time; *see also* reemerging infectious disease.

Emerging virus   A new or recently identified virus.

Emigration   The movement of a population from the native land to settle another.

Enanthem   A rash that affects mucous membranes; accompanies some viral infections.

Encephalitis   Inflammation of the tissue of the brain or infection of the brain.

Encephalomyelitis   Inflammation of the brain and spinal cord.

Encephalopathy   General term for disease of the brain.

Endemic   Refers to a disease that is constantly present in a specific area or region.

Endocannibalism   A form of cannibalism in which the dead members of a group or tribe are eaten by their relatives as a sign of love and respect as part of their funeral rites.

Endogenous infection   A disorder that starts with a microbe or virus that already was in or on the body as part of the microbiota; *see also* exogenous infection.

Endogenous retroviruses   A retrovirus formed when the retroviral DNA is inherited from parent to offspring of the infected host if germline cells (sperm and egg) contain the integrated viral genome; also called proviruses.

Endolysin   An enzyme that allows viruses to escape or be released from the host and hydrolyzes specific bonds in the murein or peptidoglycan layer of the cell wall.

Endosome   A clathrin-coated vesicle shortly after formation, when its clathrin coat has been removed.

Enhancers   DNA elements outside of the promoter region that stimulate the frequency of transcription of genes by RNA polymerase II.

env   A retrovirus gene that encodes a protein that is embedded within a lipid bilayer and surrounds the nucleoprotein core particle of the virus; these proteins are the "spikes" that bind to host cell receptors.

Envelope   The flexible membrane of protein and lipid that surrounds many types of viruses.

Enveloped virus   A human or animal virus with an additional lipid bilayer membrane that has been stolen from the host cell wrapped around the capsid of the virus particle.

Enzyme   A reusable protein that while remaining unchanged itself brings about a chemical change.

Enzyme-linked immunosorbent assay (ELISA)   A serological test in which an enzyme system is used to detect an individual's exposure to a pathogen.

Epidemic   An unusually high number of cases in excess of normal expectation of a similar illness in a population, community, or region.

Epidemiological triad   Shows the interactions among the host, agent, and environment that produce disease.

Epidemiology   The study of how diseases affect whole communities; the scientific field linked to virology.

Episome   A viral genome that is maintained in cells by autonomous replication.

Epitope   A section of an antigen molecule that stimulates a specific response and to which the response is directed; often consists of several amino acids or monosaccharides. Also called an antigenic determinant.

Eradication   To destroy or remove a pathogen after a disease has been established; for example, smallpox eradication.

Essential genes   Genes essential for growth in cell cultures; they are located in the central part of the genome of poxviruses.

Etiological agent   The disease-causing agent.

Etiology   The assignment of the cause or origins of a disease.

Eukaryotic   Refers to a cell or organism containing a cell nucleus with multiple chromosomes, a nuclear envelope, and membrane-bound compartments.

European Medicines Evaluation Agency (EMEA)   A decentralized agency of the European Union that evaluates and supervises any medicines used for humans and animals.

Exanthema   A maculopapular rash occurring on the skin surface.

Exanthematous   Describes a disease accompanied by skin eruption.

Exhuming variola victims   Disinterring the bodies of dead smallpox victims in order to study the variola virus.

Exogenous infection   A disorder that starts with a microbe or viruses that enter the body from the environment; *see also* endogenous infection.

Exotic pet trade   The import of exotic species from around the world to be sold as pets.

F

Family   The second broadest classification in the taxonomy of viruses.

Fc fragment   The portion of an antibody molecule that combines with phagocytes, mast cells, or complement. Fc stands for the "fragment crystallizable" portion of an antibody binding site.

Febrile response   A rise in body temperature (fever); a defense mechanism against some invading viruses and other microbes.

Fixed strains   Virus strains used in laboratory research as opposed to strains isolated directly from infected humans or animals; for example, rabies fixed strains.

Flaccid paralysis   A loss of voluntary movement or paralysis because weakness or loss of muscle tone has caused damage to the nerves in the muscle; for example, as a result of poliovirus infections.

Flavivirus   A virus genus that includes the human pathogens West Nile virus, Dengue fever virus and, yellow fever virus.

Fluor   A fluorescent compound, as a dye that is fluorescent in ultraviolet light and used in a method of viral study and isolation utilizing real-time PCR and fluorescence resonance energy transfer (FRET).

Fluorescence   The emission of one color of light after being exposed to light of another wavelength.

Fluorescence resonance energy transfer (FRET)   When used in combination with real-time PCR, part of a virus detection method that emits a fluorescent signal proportional to the amount of PCR product.

Fomite   An inanimate object, such as clothing or a utensil, that carries disease organisms.

Formalin   A 37% to 40% solution of formaldehyde used as embalming fluid, in the inactivation of viruses, and as a disinfectant.

Free-ranging animals   Animals or birds on farms that are allowed to roam freely instead of being contained in any manner.

FRET technology   Fluorescence resonance energy transfer technology; used in combination with real-time PCR for viral detection, viral-load monitoring, and detection of nucleic acids in pathogens.

Fusion protein   A protein created by "fusing" (joining) two genes together. Fusion proteins can be created in the laboratory for research but can also occur naturally.

G

gag   An acronym for a group-specific antigen gene that encodes the internal structural proteins of retroviruses such as HIV.

Gastroenteritis   An infection of the stomach and intestinal tract, often due to a virus.

Gay cancer   Another name in the early 1980s for Kaposi's sarcoma, a rare skin cancer that had begun to appear in many young homosexual men.

Gene   A segment of a DNA molecule that provides the biochemical information for a function product.

Gene therapy   An experimental treatment that involves the introduction of genes into a person's cells to replace or compensate for defective genes in a person's body that are responsible for a disease or medical problem; genes can be carried and delivered by customized vectors such as viruses.

Genetic code   The specific order of nucleotide sequences in DNA or RNA that encode specific amino acids for protein synthesis.

Genetic engineering   The use of bacterial and microbial genetics to isolate, manipulate, recombine, and express genes.

Genetic recombination   The process of bringing together different segments of DNA.

Genetically modified organism (GMO)   An organism produced by genetic engineering.

Genome   The complete set of genes in a virus or an organism.

Genus   The second smallest classification in the taxonomy of viruses.

Germ theory   The principle formulated by Pasteur and proven by Koch that microorganisms are responsible for infectious diseases.

Germline cells   Sperm and egg cells.

Glassy transformation   An important observation made by Frederick Twort in the discovery of bacteriophages; the transformation to a watery or glassy appearance undergone by micrococci when filtrate from other watery-appearing micrococci was applied to them.

Glioma   Tumors that originate from the brain or spinal cord.

Glycan microarray   A new technology that focuses on detecting the virus–receptor specificity of new influenza strains, especially H5N1 viruses.

Glycosaminoglycans (GAGs)   Long, chained molecules of disaccharides on the surfaces of cells to which the viral gb or gc envelope proteins of HSV attach or dock. The vaccinia virus A27L virion protein also interacts with GAGs.

Glycosylation   The process of adding saccharide molecules to protein molecules

Grafting   A form of vegetative propagation in which two young plants are joined together; provides an opportunity for virus transmission.

Green Revolution   A time period when agricultural productivity increased significantly due to the development of hybrid seeds, use of pesticides, and mechanization that allowed for scaled-up production of crops (these developments began in the early 1960s).

GRID (gay-related immune deficiency)   The original name given to AIDS by the Centers for Disease Control in 1981.

H

HAART   (highly active antiretroviral therapy)   The administration of at least three different compounds to jointly block viral replication by inhibiting the viral protease/and or reverse transcriptase of the HIV virus; was a possible approach to eliminate the virus from the body altogether.

Hairpins   The structure on a viral genome that acts as an internal ribosome entry site (IRES), which is necessary for cap-independent translation of the viral RNA; heptatitis A and poliovirus contain hairpin structures in their genome.

Hammerhead motif   A unit of plant viroid RNAs with enzymatic self-cleaving properties.

Hand, foot, and mouth disease   A virulent disease often caused by enterovirus 71 and Coxsackie viruses. It is common in infants and children; symptoms are fever, sores in the mouth, and blisters on the hands and the bottom of toes.

HBsAg   Hepatitis B surface antigen (hbsag)

Helicase   The enzyme that separates double-stranded DNA into single strands for replication.

Helper viruses   Viruses that enable satellite viruses to replicate.

Hemadsorption test   A test used to detect the presence of viruses that bind to red blood cells.

Hemagglutination   The process in which there is a virus in solution and red blood cells are added to the solution; subsequently the virus can interact with the red blood cells to form a lattice-like structure, resulting in agglutination of red blood cells.

Hemagglutination   The formation of clumps of red blood cells.

Hemagglutinin   An enzyme composing one type of surface spike on influenza viruses that enables the viruses to bind to the host cell.

Hemagglutinin   An agent such as a virus or an antibody that causes red blood cells to clump together.

Hemophilia   A congenital disorder in which blood cannot clot normally. The most common form of hemophilia is caused by a defective clotting factor known as factor viii.

Hepadnavirus   Virus capable of causing hepatitis B in humans and that replicates through an RNA intermediate, sometimes referred to as a pregenomic RNA by reverse transcription.

Heparin sulfate   The most common kind of glycosaminoglycan; the preferred binding receptor for viral gb or gc envelope proteins of HSV.

Hepatitis   Inflammation of the liver caused by a number of viruses or by alcohol or prescription drugs.

Hepatitis non-A, non-B   The hepatitis C virus, which causes chronic hepatitis in 80% of infected individuals.

Hepatocellular cancer (HCC)   Liver cancer; it may be associated with hepatitis B or C infections.

Hepatocyte   A liver cell.

Herd immunity   The premise that if the majority of the population is protected from a disease through immunizations or genetic resistance, the chance of a major epidemic is highly unlikely; the proportion of a population that is immune to a disease.

Heterozygous   Containing two different alleles for the same gene, one from each parent.

High efficiency particulate (HEP) filter   A filter that removes 99.97% of particles of 0.3 μm or higher from the air.

HIV home testing systems   Home tests to detect HIV that use a simple "finger prick" blood sample that has been applied to a filter paper and mailed to a laboratory for testing.

Holin   An enzyme used by bacteriophages to create pores in the inner membrane of the host cell to facilitate host lysis and bacteriophage release.

Homolog   A gene sequence that is similar to a gene sequence in another species both structurally and in evolutionary origin.

Homozygous   Having two identical alleles for a gene.

Hormone   A chemical substance synthesized by one type of cell that travels through the bloodstream to affect and/or direct the function of another type of cell.

Host   An organism on or in which a microorganism lives and grows or in which a virus replicates.

Host range   The variety of species and types of cells that a disease-causing microorganism or virus can infect.

Human immunodeficiency virus (HIV)   The virus that causes AIDS by attacking and compromising the body's immune system.

Hunter theory   The theory that HIV was originally transmitted to human beings via infected chimpanzees that were killed and eaten by African hunters.

Hydrophobia   An emotional condition ("fear of water") arising from the inability to swallow as a consequence of rabies.

Hyperacute rejection   When the immune system quickly kills a transplanted organ and thus kills the recipient.

Hypocomplementemia   A rare condition in which components of the complement system are lacking or reduced in concentration.

Hypoglossal nerve   The nerve that innervates the muscles in the tongue.

Hypovolemic shock   A type of shock in which severe loss of blood and fluid from the body makes the heart unable to pump enough blood to the body's organs.

I

Iatrogenic disease   Physician-induced disease introduced during a medical treatment or procedure.

Icosahedron   A symmetrical figure composed of 20 triangular faces and 12 points; one of the major shapes of some viral capsids.

IgA   A class of antibody found in bodily secretions, especially the mucous membranes of the respiratory tract, the gastrointestinal tract, and other mucous surfaces, that help neutralize pathogens.

IgG   The most abundant class of antibody present in serum, produced for very long periods of time, offering long-term protection against encounters with prior pathogens.

IgM   A class of antibody that is the first immunoglobin to respond to a viral or other microbial antigen.

Immune modulator   A substance that changes the immune system to boost immunity.

Immune–contraceptive vaccine   A vaccine that causes the body of the female of a species to produce an immune reaction to sperm and egg proteins, thus causing infertility.

Immunofluorescence   A method of detecting viral antigens within a cell or on its surface. The virus-specific antibodies containing a fluorescent tag bound to the Fc region of the antibody are allowed to react with the specimen that contains the virus and any unbound antibody is washed away and the specimen is observed under a fluorescent microscope.

Immunogenic   Capable of generating an immune response.

Immunoglobulin (Ig)   The class of immunological proteins that react with an antigen; an alternate term for antibody.

Immunological memory   The long-term ability of the immune system to remember past pathogen exposures.

Immunology   The scientific study of how the immune system works and responds to nonself agents.

Immunomodulation   The modification of some aspect of the immune system as part of a treatment, especially the suppression of an overactive inflammatory response.

Immunotherapy   Treatment of a disease by enhancing or suppressing the actions of the body's immune system.

In situ **hybridization**   A method of locating nucleic acids in the place where they naturally occur.

In vitro   In an artificial environment.

Inactivation protocols   Methods of killing but not destroying a virus so it is no longer able to infect cells; developed to determine what procedures are necessary to decontaminate or completely disinfect surfaces where viruses are present.

Incidence   A measurement of morbidity; the number of new cases of a disease that occurs in a specified period of time in a susceptible population, expressed per 1,000 persons.

Incidental host   A host that becomes infected but is not required for the maintenance of a pathogen. For example, humans are incidental hosts for West Nile virus.

Incineration   To burn to ashes or cause something to burn to ashes.

Inclusion bodies   Subtle intracellular abnormalities that only occur in virus-infected cells.

Incubation period   The time that elapses between the entry of a pathogen into the host and the appearance of signs and symptoms of disease.

Indirect contact   The mode of disease transmission involving non-living objects; *see also* direct contact.

Infectious disease   A disorder arising from a pathogen invading a susceptible host and inducing medically significant symptoms.

Infectious dose   The number of microorganisms or viruses needed to bring about infection.

Infectious hepatitis   A hepatitis A virus infection; can cause symptoms such as fever, nausea, and jaundice.

Infectious mononucleosis   A virus infection causing a sore throat, fever, and enlarged and tender glands. It frequently causes a prolonged period of tiredness.

Innate immunity   An inborn set of the preexisting defenses against infectious agents; includes the skin, mucous membranes, and secretions; another term for nonspecific immunity; protects us against any pathogen, regardless of the species or type of microbe, but is not improved by repeated exposure to the pathogen.

Insertional activation   The increase in expression of a *c-onc* due to the insertion of a viral promoter or enhancer element into the host's chromosome upon infection.

Interference assays   A method of virus detection in which the assays' ability to interfere with the growth of a second virus added to the same cell culture is examined.

Interferon   An antiviral protein produced by body cells on exposure to viruses and that trigger the synthesis of antiviral proteins.

Interferon (pegylated)   An active interferon molecule that has an attached polyethylene glycol molecule fused to it; an antiviral used to treat hepatitis C infections.

Interferons   Proteins that are the first line of defense against all viral infections; induce nonspecific immune responses before specific ones begin.

Integrase activity   Enzyme that facilitates the integration of viral into cellular DNA; HIV and hepatitis B viruses possess integrase activity.

Interleukin   A chemical cytokine produced by white blood cells that causes other white blood cells to divide; *see also* cytokine.

Internal base-pairing   Base-pairing that occurs across adjacent portions of a nucleic acid molecule.

Internal ribosomal entry sites (IRES)   Sites that allow the ribosome to enter the 5′ end of the viral RNA independently of a cap structure at the 5′ end and cause translation.

Invasive species   A species that is not native to its environment, reproduces quickly, and often has adverse environmental and economic effects.

Iron lung   An artificial respirator in the shape of a cylindrical steel chamber or tank and containing pumped air, causing the lungs of a patient to expand; used from the 1930s to the 1950s to help victims of poliomyelitis in breathing.

Isolation   A method to diagnose viral infections in which various methods and host systems are used to isolate viruses from clinical specimens; also the separation of ill/infected individuals from healthy individuals.

J

Jaundice   Yellowing of the skin and eyes caused by too much bilirubin in the blood.

Jaundice   A condition in which bile seeps into the circulatory system, causing the complexion to have a dull yellow color.

K

Kaposi's sarcoma   A type of cancer in immunocompromised individuals, such as AIDS patients, where cancer cells and an abnormal growth of blood vessels form solid lesions in connective tissue.

Killed vaccine   A vaccine in which whole-virus particles have been inactivated.

Koch's postulates   A set of procedures by which a specific organism or virus can be related to a specific disease.

Kozak's rules   Marilyn Kozak's hypothesis that the 40S ribosome will scan along the mRNA until it encounters an AUG in the best consensus sequence (usually, but not always, the first AUG); the consensus sequence is GCC A/G CCAUG(G).

Kuru   A fatal brain disorder that occurred among the South Fore tribe of the highlands of Papua New Guinea at epidemic levels during the 1950s to 1960s; it was caused by the eating of infected human tissues by members of the tribe.

L

Laminar vertical flow biosafety hood   A piece of equipment used in virology laboratories that provides clean/sterile air to the working area and provides a constant flow of air out of the work area to prevent room air from entering it.

Langerhans cells   Dendritic cells in the skin.

Latency   A process in which the viral DNA (provirus) becomes inserted into the host's DNA and the proviral DNA replicates "silently" along with the cellular DNA without immediately causing disease.

Lateral bodies   Part of the structure of poxviruses containing various enzymes essential for viral replication.

LATs   Latency associated transcripts of herpesviruses; a limited group of viral genes expressed in the latent stage.

Leaky scanning   In which the ribosome may inefficiently initiate translation at the first AUG, but more often the 40S ribosome will bypass that first AUG and initiate translation farther downstream at an AUG in better context; allows multiple viral proteins to be synthesized from a single mRNA.

Ligand   A molecule that binds to another to form a larger molecule.

Ligand-mediated fusion   Fusion in which viral ligand rather than the host receptor mediates the event.

Ligase   An enzyme that joins DNA molecules together by creating a phosphodiester bond between the two molecules.

Listeriosis   An infection caused by a foodborne listeria bacteria that primarily affects pregnant women.

Live attenuated vaccine   A traditional vaccine that stimulates the host to produce antibodies with highly weakened, but still live, viruses.

Localized infection   An infection that, for one or more reasons, is restricted to a confined location.

Long-term nonprogressors   A 1% subgroup of HIV-1 infected individuals who have not previously taken or received antiretroviral therapy and show no sign of disease.

LTR   Long terminal repetitive sequences of DNA or RNA; located at the ends of the retrovirus genome.

Lymph   A watery fluid that consists of water, salts, glucose, urea, proteins, and some immune cells such as lymphocytes and macrophages.

Lymph node   A bean-shaped organ located along lymph vessels that is involved in the immune response and contains phagocytes and lymphocytes.

Lymphadenopathy   Swollen lymph nodes.

Lymphatic system   Returns fluids from body tissues to the blood.

Lymphocytes   White blood cells that are formed in the lymphoid organs and tissues and that make up 25% to 33% of all white blood cells in adult peripheral blood; lymphocytes exhibit exquisite recognition in distinguishing pathogens from host cells.

Lymphoma   Cancer that arises from the lymphatic system.

Lysine   One of the 20 essential amino acids present in many proteins.

Lysis   The rupture of a cell and the loss of its contents.

Lysogenic conversion   When a prophage carries genes that alter the phenotype of a lysogenic bacterium.

Lysogenic cycle   The events of a bacterial virus that integrate its DNA into the bacterial chromosome.

Lysogenic virus   A bacteriophage that, when it infects its host, integrates its genome into a specific region of the host chromosome and replicates every time the cell copies its chromosomal DNA during cell division.

Lysozyme   An enzyme found in tears and saliva that digests the peptidoglycan of gram-positive bacterial cell walls.

Lytic cycle   A process by which a bacterial virus replicates within a host cell and ultimately destroys the host cell.

M

Macrophage   A large cell derived from monocytes that is found within various tissues; macrophages are five to ten times larger than monocytes and contain more lysosomes; they can ingest viruses and other foreign invaders, dead cells, cell debris, and other cellular matter.

Macule   A patch of skin that is pink-red but not usually elevated; associated with infectious disease.

Maculopapular rash   In general, a large area that is red and has small, confluent bumps.

Major histocompatibility complex (MHC)   A set of genes that controls the expression of MHC proteins; involved in transplant rejection.

Major histocompatibility complex (MHC) protein   Any of a set of proteins at the surface of all body cells that identify the uniqueness of the individual.

Malaise   A vague feeling of bodily discomfort, as at the beginning of an illness.

Malignancies   Cancerous tumors that have the potential to spread to other parts of the body and invade and destroy tissue.

Mass vaccination   The vaccination of great numbers of people at one time.

Matrix protein   A protein shell between the genome and capsid that is found in some viruses.

Maturation   The stage of the virus life cycle in which the virus becomes infectious.

Mechanical vector   A living organism, or an object, that transmits disease agents on its surface; *see also* biological vector.

Megacity   Cities that contain at least ten million inhabitants

Membrane attack complex   The end result of complement activation that inserts into lipid membranes of bacteria eukaryotic cells or viruses and causes osmotic lysis.

Memory cell   A cell derived from B lymphocytes or T lymphocytes that reacts rapidly upon reexposure to antigen.

Meninges   The covering layers of the brain and spinal cord.

Meningitis   A general term for inflammation of the covering layers of the brain and spinal cord due to any of several bacteria, fungi, viruses, or protozoa.

Messenger RNA (mRNA)   An RNA transcript containing the information for synthesizing a specific polypeptide.

Metagenomics   A relatively new genetic strategy based on technical advances in sequencing protocols used to analyze the large genomic DNA fragments recovered from environmental samples.

Metastasis   When a cell or clump of cells separates from a tumor and spreads to another location.

Miasmatic theory   A popular theory of disease in the 19th century that holds that disease is caused by *miasma* or polluted gases that rise from swamps and decaying or putrid matter.

Microbiocide   Any agent that kills microbe.

Microorganism (microbe)   A microscopic form of life including bacterial, archaeal, fungal, and protozoal cells.

Mode of transmission   Defines how an infectious disease is spread or passed on; can be direct or indirect.

Molecular epidemiology   The study of the sources, causes, and mode of transmission of diseases by using molecular diagnostic techniques.

Molecular mimicry   The occurrence of latent viruses producing antigens that are similar to host antigens.

Molluscum   Pink, pearl-like lesions, often with a dimple in the center, that are a sign of molluscum contagiosum, a common poxvirus infection; a marker for severe immunodeficiency.

Monoclonal antibodies   Clones of a single antibody produced by one parent immune cell; "pure" antibodies. A monoclonal antibody recognizes only one antigen.

Monoclonal antibody   A type of antibody produced by a clone of hybridoma cells that consists of antigen-stimulated B cells fused to myeloma cells.

Monocyte   Precursors to macrophages; large white blood cells that circulate in the bloodstream, during which time they enlarge, migrate to tissues, and differentiate into macrophages.

Monolayers   A confluent, single layer of cells in culture growing side by side on the bottom of a dish.

Monopartite   A configuration in which the entire genome occupies one nucleic acid molecule; also known as a linear genome.

Monotherapy   Treating a disease using only one drug.

Morbidity   Refers to the illness or disease state.

Morphogenesis   The process of creating form and structure during growth and development; the formation of virus particles.

Mortality   Refers to numbers of deaths correlated with a particular disease.

Mosaic patterns on plants   A symptom of a viral infection in plants characterized by a pattern of parallel, discontinuous streaks.

Movement proteins   Proteins in plant viruses that enable their movement from one infected cell to neighboring cells.

Multipartite genomes   A situation in which the entire genome occupies several nucleic acid molecules.

Multiplicity of infection (MOI)   The average number of viruses that infect a single cell in a specific experiment.

Muramidase   An enzyme that allows viruses to escape or be released from the host and hydrolyzes specific bonds in the murein or peptidoglycan layer of the cell wall; produced by some bacteriophages.

Mutation   A change in the characteristic of an organism or virus arising from a permanent alteration of a DNA or RNA sequence.

Myalgia   Pain in muscles.

Myocarditis   The inflammation or degeneration of the myocardium.

Myocarditis   Infection of the heart muscle, often due to Coxsackie virus.

Myocarditis and dilated cardiomyopathy (DCM)   A disease of the heart muscle that causes the heart to become enlarged and to pump less strongly; as a result the heart becomes thin, weak, or floppy and unable to pump blood efficiently.

Myocardium   The muscular tissue of the heart.

Myopericarditis   Inflammation of the heart.

Myxomatosis   A disease caused by a species-specific pox virus used to control the rabbit population in Australia.

N

Naïve T cell   An immature T cell.

Naked virus   A virus without a lipid bilayer membrane envelope around the capsid of the virus particle.

Natural killer (NK) cell   A type of defensive body cell that attacks and destroys cancer cells and infected cells without the involvement of the immune system.

Natural selection   The Darwinian theory of evolution, which holds that the organisms best adapted to their environment are the most likely to survive and produce the most offspring.

Naturally acquired active immunity   A host response resulting in antibody production as a result of experiencing the disease agent.

Naturally acquired passive immunity   A process resulting from the passage of antibodies to the fetus via the placenta or the milk of a nursing mother.

Necrosis   The death of an area of live tissue or cells.

Negative strand   Refers to RNA viruses whose genome cannot be directly transcribed into protein; also known as negative sense.

Negri bodies   Round or oval bodies commonly found in the cytoplasm of brain neurons of a rabies-infected subject.

Neolithic agricultural revolution   The change from nomadic hunting and gathering communities to settlement and the agricultural practice of using wild and domestic crops and animals (8000 B.C.).

Neuraminidase   A protein that cleaves the sialic acid receptors on the outside of cells as the infectious influenza viruses are released, thus preventing the viruses from aggregating at the cell surface and releasing.

Neuraminidase inhibitor   A compound that inhibits neuraminidase, thus preventing the release of influenza viruses from an infected cell.

Neuron   The cell of the nervous system that transmits impulses in the body; main actors of the brain.

Neurotoxin   A substance that is toxic to nerve tissue.

Neurotropic   Describes viruses that infect the nervous system.

Neurovirulence   The ability of viruses to cause disease in the nervous system.

Neutralization   A type of antigen–antibody reaction in which the activity of a toxin is inactivated.

Neutralizing antibody   An antibody that interferes with the infectivity of viruses or other pathogens.

Neutrophil   The most common type of white blood cell; originates in the bone marrow and contains specialized granules that possess peroxidases, lysozyme, hydrolytic enzymes, collagenase, and lactoferrins that aid in their phagocytic activity in order to engulf and destroy foreign material, including bacteria and viruses that have entered the body.

Newer-generation vaccines   Vaccines that incorporate advances based on recombinant DNA technology, thus providing advantages over traditional vaccines.

Nocturnal   Describes species that are active at night.

Nonessential genes   Genes not essential for growth in cell cultures; they are located at the ends of the genome.

Nonneutralizing antibody   An antibody that binds to viral antigens but does not interfere with infectivity; in some cases a nonneutralizing antibody can enhance infectivity.

Nonsegmented genome   A type of viral genome that determines how the virus replicates; examples are rabies, herpes, and influenza viruses.

Nonspecific immunity   Immunity that protects against any pathogen regardless of the species or type of microbe.

Nosocomial infection   A disorder acquired during an individual's stay at a hospital.

Nuclease   An enzyme that breaks the phosphodiester bonds of nucleic acids.

Nucleic acid   A high-molecular-weight molecule consisting of nucleotide chains that convey genetic information and are found in all living cells and viruses; *see* DNA and RNA.

Nucleocapsid   A viral capsid and its associated genome.

Nucleoid   The chromosomal region of a prokaryotic cell.

Nucleoside analogs   Artificial molecules that resemble nucleosides and when incorporated into the RNA or DNA of viruses inhibit viral replication.

Nucleotide   A component of a nucleic acid consisting of a carbohydrate molecule, a phosphate group, and a nitrogenous base.

Nucleus   The part of a eukaryotic cell in which DNA replication and RNA transcription occurs.

O

Okazaki fragment   A segment of DNA resulting from discontinuous DNA replication.

Oncogene   A segment of DNA that can induce uncontrolled growth of a cell if permitted to function.

Oncogenesis   The growth and development of a tumor.

Oncogenic   Refers to any agent, such as a virus, that can cause tumors.

Oncology   The scientific study of tumors and cancers.

One-step growth experiments   Experiments used to study a single replication cycle of viruses.

Open reading frame (ORF)   A section of DNA that begins with an *atg* codon and ends with a stop codon (*taa*, *tag*, or *tga*) and that has the potential to be translated into an amino acid.

Opportunist   A microorganism that invades the tissues when body defenses are suppressed.

Opportunistic infection   A disorder caused by a microorganism or virus that does not cause disease but that can become pathogenic or life-threatening if the host has a low level of immunity.

Oral herpes labialis   Oral lesions caused by a herpes virus; sometimes referred to as cold sores or fever blisters.

Oral rehydration solution   A mixture of blood salts and glucose in water.

Oral–fecal route of transmission   The means of viral infection in which viruses shed in feces are transferred into someone's mouth and are ingested with swallowed materials (e.g., food or drink) and then carried to the intestinal tract.

Orchitis   A condition caused by the mumps virus in which the virus damages the testes.

Order   The broadest classification in the taxonomy of viruses.

Ornithine transcarbamylase (OTC) deficiency   A genetic disorder of the liver in which there is a lack of the ornithine transcarbamoylase enzyme that is needed to help break down ammonia in the body.

Orphan virus   A virus that has not been etiologically linked to any human disease.

OTC deficiency; *See* **ornithine transcarbamylase (OTC) deficiency**   Ornithine transcarbamylase deficiency, a rare liver disease; gene therapy using adenoviruses was being studied as a possible treatment for the disease until the 1999 death of Jesse Gelsinger.

Outbreak   A small, localized epidemic.

P

Pandemic   A worldwide epidemic.

Panspermia hypothesis   A hypothesis that asserts viruses or other microorganisms are raining down upon Earth and contaminating it.

Papilloma   A wart.

Papule   Small, solid, usually inflammatory (red) elevations of the skin that do not contain pus; a pink pimple on the skin.

Parenteral mode of transmission   Blood-to-blood mode of transmission.

Parotid salivary glands   The largest of the three sets of the glands that produce saliva that are located on either side of the head, above the jaw, and in front of the ear; the mumps virus commonly infects the parotid salivary glands.

Paroxysm   A sudden intensification of symptoms, such as a severe bout of coughing.

Passive immunity   The temporary immunity that comes from receiving antibodies from another source.

Pathogen   A microorganism or virus that causes disease in a host organism.

Pathogenicity   The ability of a disease-causing agent to gain entry to a host and bring about a physiological or anatomical change interpreted as disease.

Patient zero   The first infected patient in an epidemiological investigation that is likely responsible for the spread of a particular infectious disease.

PCR   Polymerase chain reaction, a method of quickly replicating a piece of DNA a great number of times using a thermostable DNA polymerase in a test tube; can be used to detect the presence of viral nucleic acids.

Peptide vaccine   A vaccine that uses chemically synthesized viral peptides to induce a protective immune response via using a specific domain of a protein that contains a single epitope or antigenic determinant.

Period of convalescence   The phase of a disease during which the body's systems return to normal.

Period of decline   The phase of a disease during which symptoms subside.

Peripheral nervous system   The nerves and neurons outside the central nervous system (i.e., the brain and spinal cord).

Persistent infection   A continuing state of infection.

PERV   Porcine endogenous retrovirus; pigs harbor the sequences for this virus in their genomes, and it may potentially cause disease in humans; thus, it is a safety concern in xenotransplantation from pigs.

PFU   Plaque forming unit; the measure of viruses that can form a plaque on a monolayer of the cells.

pH-dependent fusion   A mode of viral penetration that depends on an acidic pH for fusion between the viral envelope and the host cell membrane to occur.

pH-independent fusion   A mode of viral penetration that does not depend on an acid pH for fusion between the viral envelope and the host cell membrane to occur; the remaining viral envelope remains as a "patch" on the cellular plasma membrane.

pH scale   A scale from 1 to 14 that indicates the degree of acidity or alkalinity of a solution, with 1 representing the highest degree of acidity and 14 representing the highest degree of alkalinity.

Phage   *See* bacteriophage.

Phage typing   A procedure of using specific bacterial viruses to identify a particular strain of a bacterium.

Phagocyte   A white blood cell capable of engulfing and destroying foreign materials or cells, including bacteria and viruses.

Phagocytosis   The engulfment and ingestion of foreign material (e.g., viruses and bacteria) by phagocytes.

Phenol   A chemical derivative of benzene used in antiseptics and disinfectants to kill germs and to inactivate viruses for use in vaccines; also called carbolic acid.

Phloem   Specialized living cells that transport sap in plants.

Phosphodiester bond   A chemical bond that forms the sugar-phosphate-sugar backbone of DNA and RNA.

Phosphorylation   A mechanism of adding a phosphate molecule to a protein.

Phytoplankton   Microscopic free-floating communities of cyanobacteria and unicellular algae.

PKR   dsRNA-dependent serine/threonine kinase; functions as a kinase to phosphorylate serine or threonine residues on itself or on amino acid residues of other protein targets; involved in the interferon response.

Placard   A notice from a state's board of health posted on entrances of the homes or dwellings of infected individuals.

Plaque   A clear area on a lawn of bacteria or a monolayer of cells where viruses have destroyed the cells.

Plaque assay   Used to quantitate the number of intracellular or extracellular virus particles present during a point of time in an infection by examining the plaques made by viruses *in vitro*.

Plaque reduction assays   A method for directly measuring the extent to which an antiviral drug inhibits the effects of viral infection in tissue culture in which cells infected with the virus are incubated in the presence of the antiviral compound.

Plasmid   A small, closed-loop molecule of DNA apart from the chromosome that replicates independently and carries nonessential genetic information.

Plasmodesmata   Microchannels in plant cell walls that allow the passage of molecules between cells, but that are too small for viruses to pass through unaided.

Pneumonia   Infection of the alveoli and surrounding lung tissue.

Point mutation   The replacement of one base in a DNA strand with another base.

pol   A retrovirus gene that encodes reverse transcriptase and performs the conversion of RNA into DNA.

Poliomyelitis   A disease caused by an enterovirus that, in severe cases, can weaken or paralyze its victims; poliomyelitis is rare today because of vaccination efforts.

Poliovirus receptor (PVR)   A cell surface integral membrane protein and a member of the immunoglobin (Ig) superfamily of proteins; functions as an activating ligand that stimulates natural killer cells.

Poly(A) tail   A series of adenine nucleotides that is added to the end of mRNA after transcription that may help protect the mRNA from degradation and affects the stability of some mRNAs.

Polyadenylated   Describes an mRNA molecule with a poly(A) tail attached.

Polycistronic mRNA   Messenger RNA that codes for more than one protein.

Polymorphisms   Common mutations in DNA.

Polyprotein   A protein generated by a viral mRNA encompassing several genes, which is then cleaved into individual proteins via viral or cellular proteases

Polythetic class   A class whose members share several common properties but for which no individual members possess all properties.

Portals of entry   The points on the body where viruses can enter to cause infection; usually body openings or surfaces.

Portals of exit   The points on the body from which viruses shed themselves to infect new hosts; usually body openings (e.g., oral or fecal exit) or surfaces.

Positive strand   Refers to the RNA viruses whose genome consists of an mRNA molecule; + sense RNA.

Postexposure immunization   The receiving of a vaccine after contracting the pathogen; used after a bite by a rabid animal.

Postexposure prophylaxis   The provision of antiretroviral drugs to lower the risk of HIV infection after an individual has had a possible exposure to the virus.

Postherpetic neuralgia   Pain that persists for months and sometimes years after a bout of shingles.

Post-polio syndrome   A condition that affects polio survivors years after recovery from an initial acute attack by the polio virus.

Posttranslational modifications   Modifications to eukaryotic proteins following translation, such as phosphorylation and glycosylation.

Pox   A disease such as syphilis, chickenpox, or smallpox that is characterized by a rash that forms eruptive skin pustules that may leave pockmarks (a pitlike scar).

Prevalence   Refers to the number of disease cases existing in a population at a specified time; does not take into account the duration of the disease.

Primary antibody response   The first contact between an antigen and the immune system, characterized by the synthesis of IgM and then IgG antibodies; *see also* secondary antibody response.

Primary viremia   The stage of a viral infection in which the virus is still localized in the bloodstream.

Primase   Cellular proteins that synthesize RNA primers.

Prion   An infectious, self-replicating protein containing no genetic material that is responsible for a number of neurodegenerative brain diseases (*see* transmissible spongiform encephalopathy in both humans and animals.

Prodromal period   Refers to the first appearance of mild or nonspecific signs and symptoms of an illness.

Promoter   Region on DNA to which RNA polymerase binds before initiating transcription of DNA into RNA.

Proofreading ability   The ability of virus polymerases (or replicases) to correct errors or point mutations during the replication of their genomes.

Prophage   The viral DNA of a bacterial virus that is inserted into the bacterial DNA and is passed from one generation to the next during binary fission.

Prophylaxis   Measures taken to prevent the development of a disease.

Prospective study   A study that looks at its subject forward in time.

Prostaglandins   The substance produced by the brain's hypothalamus that raises the body's temperature, resulting in fever.

Protease   An enzyme that cleaves the peptide bonds in proteins.

Protease inhibitor   A compound that blocks the activity of the enzyme protease, thus inhibiting the replication of some viruses such as HIV.

Protein   A chain or chains of linked amino acids used as a structural material or enzyme in living cells.

Protein array   A spin-off of the DNA chip used in viral diagnostics in which proteins produced by an infectious microorganism are immobilized on DNA chips and subsequently scanned and interpreted by a microarray reader instrument.

Protein synthesis   The process of forming a polypeptide or protein through a series of chemical reactions involving amino acids; also referred to as translation.

Proteoglycans   Large molecules on cell surfaces consisting of protein and glycosaminoglycan.

Proto-oncogene   Cellular genes that promote normal growth and division of cells.

Provirus   A retrovirus formed when the retroviral DNA is inherited from parent to offspring of the infected host if germline cells (sperm and egg) contain the integrated viral genome; also called an endogenous virus.

PrP^C   The normal cellular form of the prion protein.

PrP^{res}   The highly pathogenic and resistant or stable form of PrP^C, termed PrP^{res}.

PrP^{SC}   The infectious PrP (prion) that causes scrapie.

Pseudoknots   Structures on the genome of the hepatitis A virus that function in the recognition of the genome by the viral RNA replicase.

Pustule   Elevation on the skin containing pus.

Pyrogen   Fever-inducing substance.

Q

Quantitative assay   An assay used to determine the number of viruses in a given sample.

Quarantine   The segregation from the general population of healthy persons who are not ill but have been exposed to an individual who suffers from a communicable disease.

R

Rabies vaccine   A vaccine against the rabies virus that is used either pre- or postexposure to the virus.

Rapid progressors   Individuals infected with HIV-1 who develop AIDS within five years of infection.

Rash (exanthem) A change in the skin's appearance or texture, often produced after viruses have invaded the skin via blood vessels.

Reactivation Becoming infectious again; such as the reactivation of latent herpes simplex viruses.

Reactogenic Capable of causing a reaction, especially an immune reaction.

Real-time PCR A variation of PCR that bypasses the need for gel electrophoresis because fluorescence in the PCR reaction tube of amplified DNA can be measured instead of visualizing DNA fragments in a gel.

Reassortment A virus containing segmented genomes from two parent viruses, created after two viruses containing segmented genomes have infected the same cell.

Receptors On the surface of cells, they allow the receptor-binding protein or viral attachment protein particles on viruses to adhere to a cell.

Receptor-mediated endocytotic entry Occurs when an enveloped virus attaches to a receptor on the plasma membrane of the cell and the cell is stimulated to engulf the entire virus, forming an endocytotic vesicle.

Recombinant DNA technology Genetic engineering; the insertion of foreign genes into a virus in order to study the expression of these foreign genes within the cytoplasm of mammalian cells.

Recombinant subunit vaccine Vaccines consisting of purified antigenic components of viruses or other pathogens; these vaccines are safer than live vaccines.

Recombination A process that occurs when two viruses infect the same cell and a new chimeric or hybrid genome is formed via a process of intermolecular exchange of the viral genomes.

Reemerging viral diseases Diseases caused by viruses that are making a "comeback" or are reappearing and causing increased incidence or geographic range of infections in exposed human populations.

Replicase Describes RNA-dependent RNA polymerase whose second function is to synthesize the viral/progeny genome using the +ssRNA as a template.

Replication The process in which genetic material copies itself.

Replication fork The point where complementary strands of DNA separate and new complementary strands are synthesized.

Representational difference analysis A method to analyze differences between two given sets of DNA.

Reservoir Where the etiological agent lives, grows, and multiplies.

Restriction fragment length polymorphisms (RFLP) Technique used to detect the differences between two very similar but not identical viral nucleic acid sequences in which the DNA is digested with restriction enzymes and the digested fragments are analyzed for their electrophoretic pattern; based on the concept that restriction enzymes recognize very specific sequences.

Reticulo-endothelial system Phagocytic cells constituting part of the immune system that accumulate in the lymph nodes and spleen.

Retinitis An infection in the eyes.

Retrospective study A study that looks at its subject backward in time.

Retrovirus A virus that contains an RNA genome and reverse transcriptase; e.g., HIV and HTLV.

Reverse genetics An experimental procedure that starts with cloned segments of DNA and uses this knowledge to introduce programmed mutations or gene sequences back into the genome in order to determine gene and protein function; used to systematically create candidate influenza vaccine against pandemic influenza strains.

Reverse transcriptase An enzyme that synthesizes a DNA molecule from the code supplied by an RNA molecule.

Reverse transcriptase inhibitor A compound that inhibits the action of reverse transcriptase, thus preventing the viral genome from being replicated.

Reye's syndrome A complication of influenza and chickenpox, characterized by vomiting and convulsions as well as liver and brain damage. It is associated with aspirin consumption by children for flu symptoms.

Rhinorrhea Nasal discharge.

Ribonucleic acid (RNA) The nucleic acid involved in protein synthesis and gene control; also the genetic information in some viruses.

Ribosomal frameshifting Occurs when the ribosome shifts into another reading frame and then continues translating the mRNA into protein in that new frame.

Ribosomal RNA (rRNA) An RNA transcript that forms part of the ribosome's structure.

Ribosome A cellular component of RNA and protein that participates in protein synthesis.

Ribozyme A segment of RNA that can catalyze the breakage and formation of RNA bonds at certain sites.

Rimantidine An antiviral drug that blocks the M2 ion channel function of influenza viruses, resulting in the incomplete release of the viral RNPs, thus interfering with uncoating.

RISC siRNAs that are denatured and incorporated into an endonuclease-silencing complex.

Rivers' postulates A set of procedures, modifying Koch's postulates, by which a specific virus can be associated with a specific disease.

RNA interference (RNAi or RNA silencing) A form of genomic immunity that responds to invading nucleic acid; double-stranded RNA inhibits gene expression in a sequence-specific manner.

RNA interference systems The application of RNA interference that uses double-stranded RNA to inhibit gene expression in a sequence-specific manner. It is useful in research and therapy development.

RNA polymerase The enzyme that synthesizes an RNA polynucleotide from a DNA template.

RNA polymerase II Eukaryotic enzyme synthesizes messenger RNA (mRNA) and some small nuclear RNAs (snRNA).

RNase Ribonuclease, an enzyme that degrades RNA.

RNase H A ribonuclease that breaks down the bonds in an RNA/DNA complex; an example is the pregenome in retroviruses that use reverse transcriptase to replicate.

RNase L An antiviral protein activated by 2'5' oligo(A) synthetase to catalyze the degradation of both viral and host cellular RNAs, resulting in the shut down of viral and host protein synthesis, a cellular altruistic event.

Rolling circle model of replication A method of DNA replication resulting in linear concatemers of DNA from a circular template.

Rous sarcoma virus A retrovirus capable of causing sarcomas in chickens.

RT-PCR Reverse-transcriptase PCR, in which a cDNA is made from RNA by reverse transcription; the cDNA is then amplified by standard PCR protocols. Used in tests to measure HIV viral load and other diagnostic testing of viruses with RNA genomes.

Rumor registers In 1975, when smallpox cases decreased to very low levels globally, hospitals and health centers were asked to enter the names of suspected smallpox cases into a "rumor register" so that these cases could be checked by surveillance teams.

S

Sabin vaccine A type of polio vaccine prepared with attenuated viruses and taken orally.

Salk vaccine A type of polio vaccine prepared with inactivated viruses and injected into the body.

Saponins A substance secreted by plants that has antibacterial and antiviral properties.

Sarcoma A slow-growing solid tumor of the connective tissue.

Satellite viruses Viruses that encode their own coat protein but lack the genes that would encode the enzymes necessary for replication; as a result they are dependent upon helper viruses.

Scion A twig containing buds from a woody plant, used in grafting.

Secondary antibody response A second or ensuing response triggered by memory cells to an antigen and characterized by substantial production of IgG antibodies; *see also* primary antibody response.

Seed lymph Cowpox lesions from infected calves used to make an early smallpox vaccine.

Segmented genome A viral genome that consists of two or more physically separate nucleic acid molecules that is usually packaged into a single virion.

Self-assembly Spontaneous assembly; some viral particles such as tobacco mosaic virus can self-assemble in a test tube.

Sentinel chickens A surveillance program used to identify the presence of West Nile virus in susceptible birds before the disease is detected in humans, in which chickens are tested for the presence of antibodies against West Nile virus on a weekly basis.

Sentinel physician A doctor who conducts surveillances for influenza-like illness (ILI) in collaboration with a state's health department and the CDC, helping to provide a national picture of influenza virus and ILI activity in the United States.

Serological epidemiology A form of epidemiology that investigates for the presence of virus antibodies in the serum of a population.

Serology A branch of immunology that studies serological reactions.

Seroprevalence The number of persons in a population who test positive for a virus based on serology (blood serum) specimens; often presented as a percent of the total specimens tested or as a rate per 100,000 persons tested.

Serpins Serine protease inhibitors; these are produced by some poxviruses.

Serum (pl. sera) The fluid portion of the blood consisting of water, minerals, salts, proteins, and other organic substances, including antibodies; contains no clotting agents.

Serum hepatitis A type of hepatitis caused by the hepatitis B virus present in a human serum vaccine against the yellow fever virus.

Serum sickness A hypersensitivity reaction in which the body reacts toward antigens of nonhuman species present in antiserum.

Sexually transmitted disease (STD) An infection that can be transferred from one person to another through sexual contact.

Shell vial technique A method for rapid diagnosis of viral infections used in clinical labs using a combination of cell culture and centrifugation to detect viral antigens before cytopathic effects are present in a given clinical specimen.

Shingles A disease caused by the reactivation of the previously dormant varicella zoster virus during a period when the immune system is weakened.

Sialic acid A chemical found in receptors on cell surfaces that binds to viral H glycoprotein in influenza viruses, anchoring the virus to the cell; it is then removed by the viral N glycoprotein to prevent the viral particles from aggregating, preventing the clumping or aggregation of viruses to the cell surface.

Sign An indication of the presence of a disease, especially one observed by a doctor but not apparent to the patient; *see also* symptom.

Single-dose vaccine The combination of several vaccines into one measured quantity.

siRNA Short-interfering RNAs; 21 to 24 nucleotide dsRNA molecules chopped by DICER molecules.

Slow infections Infections that have long incubation periods (measured in years); these types of infections lead to slow, progressive diseases.

Slow progressors HIV-1 infected individuals who remain free of AIDS for more than 15 years.

Smallpox recognition cards Cards featuring pictures of a case of smallpox that are distributed among populations in endemic countries to facilitate diagnosis and surveillance of the disease.

Species A polythetic class of viruses that share the same replicating lineage and occupy a particular niche.

Species barrier The differences between species that make it impossible for an infectious disease to cross from one species to another.

Spike A protein projecting from the viral envelope or capsid that aids in attachment and penetration of a host cell.

Spinal polio Polio characterized by asymmetric paralysis.

Spontaneous mutation A mutation that arises from natural phenomena in the environment.

Sporadic Describes disease outbreaks that have no pattern of occurrence in time or location.

ssDNA Single strand DNA.

ssRNA Single strand RNA.

Stone fruits Fleshy fruits that contain a single seed or pit such as peaches, apricots, nectarines, plums, and cherries.

Strain Different isolates of the same virus that come from different geographical locations.

Street strains Rabies strains isolated from patients or animals that have experienced the disease via a bite from a rabid animal or other means.

Structural protein Proteins that make up the virus particle both inside and outside.

Subclinical disease A disease in which there are few or inapparent symptoms.

Subfamily   The third broadest classification in the taxonomy of viruses.

Subgenomic RNAs   Short ssRNAs that function as monocistronic RNAs.

Subtypes or clades   A taxonomic group of viruses that evolve from a single common viral ancestor.

Surfactant   A synthetic chemical, such as a detergent, that emulsifies and solubilizes particles attached to surfaces by reducing the surface tension.

Surveillance   Close observation of infection patterns of infectious diseases by experts in the field; systematic collection, analysis, and interpretation of health data to assist in the planning of prevention programs (e.g., vaccination).

Symptom   An indication of some disease or other disorder that is experienced by the patient; *see also* sign.

Syncytia   Giant cells formed through the fusion of host cells; cytopathic effect of certain viral infections.

Syndrome   A collection of signs or symptoms that together are characteristic of a disease.

Systemic infection   An infection that disseminates to the deeper organs and systems of the body.

T

T lymphocyte (T cell)   A type of white blood cell that matures in the thymus gland and is associated with cell-mediated immunity.

T lymphocyte helper cells   A type of immune cell that contains CD4 receptor molecules on its surface and is infected and destroyed by HIV.

TATA box   A eukaryotic promoter sequence that defines the transcription start site.

Telomerase   An enzyme that creates and relengthens telomeres on the ends of eukaryotic chromosomes.

Telomere   DNA structures present at the ends of eukaryotic chromosomes that are not included in DNA replication and protect the chromosome from fusion to other chromosomes and degradation by nucleases.

Temperate   Refers to a bacterial virus that enters a bacterial cell and then the viral DNA integrates into the bacterial cell's chromosome.

Teratogenic effects   Severe congenital malformations, including deafness, blindness, and congenital heart and brain defects.

Tetraspanin   A family of membrane proteins found in all multicellular eukaryotes. CD81 is a tetraspanin that has recently been identified as a coreceptor for hepatitis C virus.

T_H cells   Cells that promote immune responses via a T_{H1} response or a T_{H2} response.

T_{H1} response   Part of the T_H cells' immune response that is involved in inflammation and cell-mediated immunity.

T_{H2} response   Part of the T_H cells' immune response that activates immune responses dependent on antibodies.

Thymidine kinase (cellular)   Essential *cellular* enzyme that is expressed during cell division activity. This enzyme allows a cell to utilize an alternate metabolic pathway for incorporating thymidine into DNA. 5-bromodeoxyuridine (BudR) is a mutagenic nucleoside that substitutes for thymidine in DNA, acting as a chain terminator. It causes breaks in the chromosomes of cells.

Thymidine kinase gene (vaccinia)   Nonessential gene present in the vaccinia virus genome; absence of thymidine kinase activity in host cells and disruption of the thymidine kinase gene in vaccinia virus renders host cells resistant to toxic effects of 5-bromodeoxyuridine (BudR). This selection enriches for cells that carry recombinant vaccinia virus.

Tissue culture infectious dose (TCID)   A method used to study viruses in which cell monolayers are infected in replicates with serial dilutions of virus. After incubation, the infected cells are observed for cytopathic effects and are scored + (positive or infected) or – (negative or uninfected).

Tissue tropism   Refers to the specific tissues within a host that a virus infects.

Titer   Quantitation of the number of viruses in a given sample.

Titer   The amount of antibody in a sample of serum that is determined by the most dilute concentration of antibody that will yield a positive reaction with a specific antigen.

Toxemia   The presence of toxins in the blood.

Toxins   Poisonous substances.

Toxoid   A toxin whose harmful properties have been destroyed but still retains the capacity to produce an immune response; toxoids are used as vaccines.

Traditional vaccines   Live or inactivated whole vaccines; vaccines not made via recombinant DNA technology.

Transcriptase   Describes RNA-dependent RNA polymerases that transcribe its −ssRNA genome into several different viral monocistronic +ssmRNAs that can be recognized by the host cell machinery.

Transcription   The biochemical process in which RNA is synthesized according to a code supplied by the bases of a gene in the DNA molecule; the creation of complementary RNA from a DNA template.

Transcription factors   Cellular proteins that facilitate the binding of RNA polymerase II to a gene promoter and determine the starting point of transcription.

Transfection   A method that introduces the genome of a virus or viral gene into cultured cells.

Transfer RNA (tRNA)   A molecule of RNA that unites with amino acids and transports them to the ribosome in protein synthesis.

Transformation   The conversion of a normal cell into a malignant cell due to the action of a carcinogen or virus.

Transformation or focus assays   An assay used to determine if a virus is capable of "transforming" or immortalizing cells rather than killing them.

Transgene   A cloned gene incorporated into the genome.

Translation   The biochemical process in which the code on the mRNA molecule is translated into a sequence of amino acids in a polypeptide.

Translational readthrough   A strategy that viruses can use to control gene expression in which a stop translation signal may be ignored; a variation of frameshifting.

Transmissible spongiform encephalopathy   A group of slow infection diseases caused by prions, including bovine spongiform encephalopathy and new variant Creutzfeldt-Jakob disease.

Transposable genetic element   Fragments of DNA called insertion sequences or transposons that can cause mutations.

Transposase An enzyme that is involved in the transfer of transposons randomly into the host chromosome; transposase genes are carried by some phages.

Transposon A segment of DNA that moves from one site on a DNA molecule to another, carrying information for protein synthesis; also called jumping gene or transposable element.

Tulipomania A fad in Western Europe from 1600 to 1660 in which bulbs of tulips infected with a virus that made their petals striped were traded for large amounts of money or goods.

Tumor An abnormal uncontrolled growth of cells that has no physiological function.

Tumor-associated carbohydrate antigens A type of antigen that appears on the cell membranes of cancer cells.

Tumor necrosis factor A superfamily of proteins that induces necrosis of tumors cells and may cause inflammatory actions; blocking tumor necrosis factor in cells has shown to be beneficial in reducing inflammatory responses.

Tumor suppressor genes Genes that suppress or inhibit the conversion of a normal cell into a cancer cell.

Tumor virus A virus capable of inducing a tumor in its host.

Tumorigenicity The ability to form tumors if injected into an animal model.

Type (T) phages A group of dsDNA bacteriophages.

Type-species Different serotypes of the same species.

Typical progressors Persons infected with HIV-1 who display neither signs nor symptoms of AIDS for approximately ten years.

U

Ultrastructure The detailed structure of a cell, virus, or other object when viewed with an electron microscope.

Ultraviolet (UV) light A type of electromagnetic radiation of short wavelengths that damages DNA.

Uncoating Refers to the separation of viral nucleic acid from the capsid inside the infected eukaryotic host cell.

Universal precautions Measures taken to avoid contact with a patient's bodily fluids; examples include wearing gloves, goggles, and proper disposal of used hypodermic needles.

Universal vaccine Refers to a potential vaccine that would protect effectively against all strains of influenza viruses affecting humans.

Untranslated region (UTR) A region on a viral mRNA that is not translated by cellular ribosomes; in the poliovirus, it is located downsteam of the clover-leaf structure.

Upstream DNA element In DNA sequences that regulate transcription; located in the direction from which the polymerase has come.

Urbanization The migration of people from rural locations to cities.

V

Vaccination Inoculation with weakened or dead microbes or viruses in order to generate immunity; *see also* immunization.

Vaccine A preparation containing weakened or dead microorganisms or viruses, treated toxins, or parts of microorganisms or viruses to stimulate immune resistance.

Vaccine adverse events reporting system (VAERS) A reporting system designed to identify any serious adverse reactions to a vaccination.

Vaccine-associated paralytic polio (VAPP) The rare occurrence of poliomyelitis in a person who received the oral polio vaccine.

Vaccine lymph An early smallpox vaccine that was made by mixing vaccine pulp with glycerin and then emulsifying and clarifying the mixture via centrifugation.

Vaccine pulp Cowpox lesions scraped from the skin of calves and used to make an early smallpox vaccine.

Vaccinee One who has been vaccinated.

Vaccinia The prototype of poxviruses and the virus used in smallpox vaccines.

Vaccinia immunoglobulin Antiserum used to treat the adverse effects of the smallpox virus.

Vaccinia necrosum A severe reaction following a smallpox vaccination; progressive necrosis at the vaccination site.

Vaccinifer Heifers used in the late 1800s for production of an early smallpox vaccine.

Vagus nerve The longest of the cranial nerves, stretching from the brain stem to the abdomen.

Variant A virus whose phenotype differs from the original wild-type strain but where the genetic basis is not known.

Variolation An 18th century method to inoculate someone with the smallpox virus to render that person resistant to infection; the intentional inoculation of dried smallpox scabs into the skin of an uninfected individual, causing a mild form of the disease and immunity against subsequent exposure to variola virus.

Vector An arthropod that transmits the agents of disease from an infected host to a susceptible host.

Vector A plasmid used in genetic engineering to carry a DNA segment into a bacterium or other cell.

Vesicle A fluid-filled skin lesion ranging up to one centimeter in size, such as that occurring in chickenpox.

Vesicle A small, membrane-enclosed compartment found in many eukaryotic cells.

Viral dsRNA A replication intermediate produced within cells during genome replication of RNA viruses.

Viral oncogene A viral gene responsible for causing cancer or the transformation of cells.

Viral replication complexes (VRCs) Viral complexes move along microtubules of filamentous actin and myosin and through the plasmodesmata as large bodies; they help spread tobacco mosaic virus quickly through a plant.

Viral zoonosis A viral disease transmittable between animals and human beings.

Viral-load monitoring The measure of the number of HIV-1 RNA genome copies per mL of plasma; a predictor of the disease progression to AIDS.

Viremia The presence and spread of viruses through the blood.

Virion A completely assembled virus outside its host cell.

Viroceptor Altered cellular receptors that have lost their transmembrane anchor sequences; consequently, these unanchored viral proteins are *secreted* from infected cells where they sequester ligands into the receptor portion of the protein.

Viroid An infectious RNA segment associated with certain plant diseases.

Virokine Secreted viral proteins that resemble host cytokines.

Virology The scientific study of viruses.

Virucide A drug or chemical that inactivates viruses.

Virulence   The degree to which a pathogen is capable of causing a disease.

Virulence factor   A molecule possessed by a pathogen that increases its ability to invade or cause disease to a host.

Virulent   Refers to a virus or microorganism that can be extremely damaging when in the host.

Virus   An infectious agent consisting of DNA or RNA and surrounded by a protein sheath; in some cases, a membranous envelope surrounds the coat.

VLP   Virus-like particles.

W

Wart   A small, usually benign, skin growth commonly due to a virus.

Wasting syndrome   A loss of more than 10% of body weight due to fever or diarrhea for more than 30 days; a common problem in many AIDS patients.

Weapons of mass destruction   Weapons with the potential to kill an extremely high number of people.

Western blot   Method used to detect proteins in a given sample of tissue homogenate or extract. The Western blot method uses electrophoresis to separate the proteins; proteins are then transferred to nitrocellose and probed with antibodies. This allows for the detection of a specific protein out of many thousands of different proteins. The confirmatory test essential to exclude false-positive HIV test results.

Wild-type   The form of an organism, virus, or gene isolated from nature; the typical infectious form of virus in nature that causes disease as distinguished from a mutant form that may cause a milder form or no disease in its host.

Window period   The period after infection until antibodies are detectable by serologic methods.

X

Xenotransplantation   Any procedure that involves the use of live cells, tissues, or organs from a nonhuman animal source, transplanted or implanted into humans or used for clinical *ex vivo* perfusion.

Xenozoonosis   A disease transmitted from an animal to a human recipient after transplantation of an animal organ.

X-gal   A chemical (5-bromo-4-chloro-3-indolyl-b-D-galactopyranoside) used in biological assays such as plaque assays that when cleaved by the enzyme β-galactosidase turns blue; useful in quantifying viruses.

Xylem   Water-conducting tissue that consists of mainly nonliving cells in higher plants.

Z

Zoonosis   Refers to a disease being transmitted from an animal to a human.

Index

Note: Page numbers containing a *b, f,* or *t* refer to pages on which a box, figure, or table, respectively, appears.

Photo Credits

Note: Unless otherwise indicated, photographs are under copyright of Jones and Bartlett Publishers, LLC, or have been kindly provided by the authors.

Front Matter
Page iv: Courtesy of James Hicks/CDC. **Page vi:** Courtesy of CDC. **Page vii (top):** © National Archives and Records Administration. **Page vii (bottom):** © Jaimie Duplass/ShutterStock, Inc. **Page viii (top):** © National Library of Medicine. **Page viii (bottom):** © National Library of Medicine. **Page ix (bottom):** Courtesy of Dr. Erskine Palmer/CDC. **Page x:** Courtesy of James Gathany/CDC. **Page xi:** © Francois Etienne du Plessis/ShutterStock, Inc. **Page xiii:** © Olivier Le Queinec/ShutterStock, Inc. **Page xiv:** Courtesy of James Gathany/CDC. **Image of Dr. Teri Shors:** Photographed by Dylan Stolley. **Timeline 1:** © National Library of Medicine. **Timeline 2:** © National Library of Medicine. **Timeline 3:** Courtesy of Dr. Lyle Conrad/CDC. **Timeline 4:** Courtesy of CDC. **Timeline 5:** Courtesy of Frank Collins, Ph.D./CDC. **Timeline 6:** © AbleStock. **Timeline 7:** © AbleStock.

Chapter 1
Opener: Courtesy of Cynthia Goldsmith/CDC. **1.1:** © Oliver Meckes/E.O.S./MPI Tubingen/Photo Researchers, Inc. **1.5a:** Courtesy of James Hicks/CDC. **1.5b:** © nazira_g/ShutterStock, Inc. **1.9a:** Courtesy of Dr. Frederick Murphy/CDC. **1.9b:** Courtesy of James Gathany/CDC. **1.10:** © SPL/Photo Researchers, Inc. **Virus File 1:** Courtesy of NCBI/NLM. **1.12a:** Courtesy of the City of Milwaukee Health Department. **1.12b:** © National Archives and Records Administration. **1.13:** Courtesy of LADHS. **1.14a–b:** Courtesy of Franklin D. Roosevelt Presidential Library and Museum. **1.16a:** © Simon Fraser/Photo Researchers, Inc. **1.16b:** © Barry Batchelor/PA Photos/Landov. **1.17:** Courtesy of CDC.

Chapter 2
Opener: Courtesy of Cynthia Goldsmith, Jacqueline Katz, and Sherif R. Zaki/CDC. **Virus File 1:** Courtesy of Gary P. Williams, M.D., University of Wisconsin Medical School, Department of Pediatrics.

Chapter 3
Opener: Courtesy of Cynthia Goldsmith/CDC. **3.3c:** Micrograph from F.A. Murphy, School of Veterinary Medicine, University of California, Davis. **3.7a:** Courtesy of CDC. **3.15:** Courtesy of Shmuel Rozenblatt, Tel Aviv University, Israel. **3.16:** © Richard Vogel/AP Photos.

Chapter 4
Case Study 1: Courtesy of Didier Raoult, Rickettsia Laboratory, La Timone, Marseille, France. **4.2:** Courtesy of Dr. Fred Murphy, Sylvia Whitfield/CDC. **4.3a:** Courtesy of David Bhella, Medical Research Council Virology Unit, University of Glasgow. **4.3b:** Courtesy of Dr. Eric Blair, Biochemistry and Molecular Biology, University of Leeds. **4.7a:** Courtesy of CDC. **4.7b–c:** Micrograph from F.A. Murphy, School of Veterinary Medicine, University of California, Davis. **4.9:** Courtesy Dr. Ng Mah Lee, Mary, Department of Microbiology, National University of Singapore. **Virus File 1:** © Guido Picchio/AP Photos. **4.10:** Reprinted from *Trends in Biochemical Sciences*, Vol. 12, Hurst, C. J., W. H. Benton, and J. M. Enneking, Three-dimensional model of human rhinovirus type 14, p. 460, 1987, with permission from Elsevier. Courtesy of Christon Hurst, Xavier University.

Chapter 5
Opener: Courtesy of CDC. **Case Study 1:** © Reuters/Romeo Ranoco/Landov. **5.1a–b:** Reproduced from *The Lancet*, Vol. 362, T. W. Geisbert et al, Treatment of Ebola virus infection with a recombinant inhibitor of factor VIIa/tissue factor: a study in rhesus monkeys, pp. 1953–1958, Copyright 2003, with permission from Elsevier. Photograph courtesy of Thomas W. Geisbert. **5.4a–b:** Courtesy of Shmuel Rozenblatt, Tel Aviv University, Israel. **5.6:** Courtesy of Dharam Ramnani, Virginia Urology Center Pathology Laboratory. **5.7:** Courtesy of Shmuel Rozenblatt, Tel Aviv University, Israel. **5.10:** Courtesy of Dr. Linda Cameron, University of Manitoba. **5.12:** Reproduced from P. R. Hazelton and H. R. Gelderblom, *Emerg. Infect. Dis.* 9 (2003): 294–303. **5.13:** Reproduced from P. R. Hazelton and H. R. Gelderblom, *Emerg. Infect. Dis.* 9 (2003): 294–303. **5.14:** Courtesy of John Strous, Medical Technology, UW-Oshkosh. **5.17b:** Reproduced from Athmanathan, S., S. R. Bandlapally, and G. N. Rao, *BMC Clin. Pathol.* 2 (2002): 1–5. **5.20:** © Hank Morgan/Science Photo Library/Photo Researchers, Inc. **5.21c:** Image courtesy of Bio-Rad Laboratories. **Virus File 1:** Courtesy of Dr. Fred Murphy/CDC. **5.25a:** Courtesy of James Gathany/CDC. **5.25b–c:** Courtesy of CDC.

Chapter 6
Opener: © National Museum of Health and Medicine, Armed Forces Institute of Pathology, (Reeve 32486). **6.b insert:** © Phototake, Inc./Alamy Images. **6.5a:** © J. Helgason/ShutterStock, Inc. **6.5b:** Courtesy of Dr. Joseph Sowka, Nova Southeastern University. **Virus File 1a:** © Lyn Alweis, The Denver Post/AP Photos. **Virus File 1b:** © Gilbert S. Grant/Photo Researchers, Inc. **6.7:** © PhotoSpin/age fotostock. **6.10:** Courtesy of CDC. **6.11:** Courtesy of Dr. Herrmann/CDC.

Chapter 7
Opener: Reproduced from F. D. A. Fenner, et al, eds. *Smallpox and Its Eradication.* World Health Organization, 1988. **Case Study 1:** © Feng Yu/ShutterStock, Inc. **7.2:** © Stephen VanHorn/ShutterStock, Inc. **7.6:** Reproduced from K. Cantell. *The Story of Interferon: The Ups and Downs in the Life of a Scientist.* World Scientific Publishing Company, 1998. **7.7:** © Phototake, Inc./Alamy Images. **7.9:** Courtesy of Drs. Patrizia Stoitzner and Kristian Pfaller, Innsbruck Medical University. **Virus File 1a:** Courtesy Dr. Erskine Palmer, Russell Regnery, Ph.D./CDC. **Virus File 1c:** Courtesy of CDC. **7.24:** Courtesy of CDC. **7.25:** © Jaimie Duplass/ShutterStock, Inc. **7.30:** Courtesy of APHIS/USDA. **7.36:** Courtesy of CDC.

Chapter 8
Opener: Courtesy of CDC. **8.4:** Courtesy of the University of Michigan Health System, Gift of Pfizer, Inc. UMHS.23. **8.5 insert:** © National Library of Medicine. **8.6 insert:** © National Library of Medicine. **Virus File 1:** Reproduced from Centers for Disease Control and Prevention, *MMWR* 5 (1981): 250–252. **Virus File 2:** Courtesy of CDC. **8.12:** © National Library of Medicine. **8.14:** © David P. Lewis/ShutterStock, Inc. **8.15:** Courtesy of INTREPID, NOAA, AVHRR/NASA.

Chapter 9
Opener: Courtesy of Department of Historical Collections, Health Sciences Library, SUNY Upstate Medical University. **9.1:** © National Library of Medicine. **9.2:** © National Library of Medicine. **9.3:** © National Library of Medicine. **9.4a:** © National Library of Medicine. **9.4b:** Courtesy of the Archives of Ontario [ACC13993–8]. **9.5:** Courtesy of Upjohn Company. Used with permission from Pfizer, Inc. **9.8:** © M. English, M.D./Custom Medical Stock Photo.

Chapter 10

Opener: Photo courtesy of the U.S. Department of Energy. **10.1:** Used with permission from Stars and Stripes. © 1965, 2008 Stars and Stripes. **Refresher Box 1b:** Courtesy of Robert Moyzis, University of California, Irvine, CA/U.S. Department of Energy Human Genome Program (http://genomics.energy.gov). **Virus File 2:** © Wendy Nero/ShutterStock, Inc. **Virus File 3:** Courtesy of Charles N. Farmer/CDC. **10.11:** Courtesy of Rober S. Craig/CDC. **10.12:** Courtesy of Dr. Steve Kraus/CDC. **10.13:** Courtesy of CDC. Used with permission of Patricia F. Walker, M.D., D.T.M. & H., Center for International Health & International Travel Clinic, HealthPartners. **10.14a:** Courtesy Dr. Wiesner/CDC. **10.14b:** Courtesy of Susan Lindsley/CDC. **10.15:** Reproduced from B. L. Trus, et al., *Nat. Struct. Mol. Biol.* 4 (1997): 413–420. Photo courtesy of Benes L. Trus, National Institutes of Health. **10.20:** Courtesy of David Bhella, Medical Research Council Virology Unit, University of Glasgow. **10.22a:** Courtesy of Dr. Erskine Palmer/CDC.

Chapter 11

Opener: Courtesy of Mr. Stafford Smith/CDC. **11.2:** © March of Dimes Birth Defects Foundation. **11.4a:** Courtesy of Post-Polio Health International. **Virus File 1:** Courtesy of Dr. Joseph J. Esposito/CDC. **11.9:** © Minnesota Historical Society. **11.10:** © AP Photos. **11.13:** © Dr. P. Marazzi/Photo Researchers, Inc.

Chapter 12

Chapter 12.6a: Courtesy of Dr. Erskine Palmer/CDC. **12.6b:** Courtesy of Dr. Erskine Palmer/CDC. **12.5a–b:** © Bjorn Svensson/Alamy Images. **12.16:** Courtesy of the National Museum of Health and Medicine, Armed Forces Institute of Pathology, Washington, D.C., NCP 1603. **12.17:** Courtesy of Johan Hultin. **12.18:** Courtesy of James Gathany/CDC. **12.19:** © Vincent Yu/AP Photos. **12.22:** © Huang Benqiang, Xinhua/AP Photos. **Virus File 1b:** Courtesy of Seth Dixon, St. Jude Children's Research Hospital. **Case Study 1:** Courtesy and © Becton, Dickinson and Company.

Chapter 13

Opener: Courtesy of Library of Congress, Prints & Photographs Division, [reproduction number LC–USZ62–10610]. **13.1:** © National Library of Medicine. **13.5:** Courtesy of APHIS/USDA. **13.6:** Courtesy of APHIS/USDA. **13.8:** Courtesy of CDC. **Refresher Box 1a:** © ZTS/ShutterStock, Inc. Refresher Box 1b: © Airelle-Joubert/Photo Researchers, Inc. **13.9:** Micrograph from F.A. Murphy, School of Veterinary Medicine, University of California, Davis. **13.10:** Courtesy of CDC. **Virus File 1a:** © Morry Gash/AP Photos. **13.12:** Courtesy of CDC.

Chapter 14

Opener: Reproduced from F. Fenner, et al. *Smallpox and its Eradication.* World Health Organization, 1988. **14.1a–b:** Reproduced from F. Fenner, et al. *Smallpox and its Eradication.* World Health Organization, 1988. **14.2a:** Courtesy of Barbara Rice/NIP/CDC. **14.2b:** Courtesy of James Hicks/CDC. **14.2c:** Courtesy of the World Health Organization. **14.2d:** Courtesy of Stanley O. Foster, M.D., M.P.H./World Health Organization/CDC. **14.3:** Courtesy of Marshfield Clinic. **14.4:** Courtesy of UK Clinical Virology Network, Gartnavel General Hospital. **14.6b:** Courtesy of CDC. **14.10a:** Courtesy of the WHO, Stanley O. Foster M.D., M.P.H./CDC. **14.10b:** Courtesy of Dr. J.D. Millar/CDC. **14.11:** Courtesy of James Gathany/CDC. **Virus File 1:** Courtesy of the National Archives of Australia: A1200, L44186. **14.13:** © National Library of Medicine. **14.14:** Courtesy of John D. Millar/CDC. **14.15a:** Courtesy of Allen W. Mathies, MD/ California Emergency Preparedness Office (Calif/EPO), Immunization Branch/CDC. **14.15b:** Courtesy of Arthur E. Kaye/CDC.

Chapter 15

Opener: Courtesy of Dr. Hermann/CDC. **15.1:** Courtesy of Dr. N.J. Flumara and Dr. Gavin Hart/CDC. **15.2:** Courtesy of CDC. **Virus File 2a:** Courtesy of Stephen Ausmus/USDA ARS. **Virus File 2b:** © Phototake/Alamy Images. **15.3:** © Mikhail Nekrasov/ShutterStock, Inc. **15.4:** Courtesy of Dr. Phillip Brunell/CDC. **15.5b:** Courtesy of E. L. Palmer/CDC. **15.13a:** © Dagfrida/ShutterStock, Inc. **15.13b:** © Stephen VanHorn/ShutterStock, Inc. **15.15:** © Scott Camazine/Alamy Images.

Chapter 16

Opener: © Gary Woodard/ShutterStock, Inc. **16.1a:** Courtesy of National Cancer Institute. **16.1b:** Courtesy of CDC. **16.9:** Courtesy of

CDC. **16.11a:** Courtesy of Louisa Howard, Dartmouth College, Electron Microscope Facility. **16.15:** Courtesy of Dr. Edwin P. Ewing, Jr./CDC.

Chapter 17

Opener: © Laurie K/ShutterStock, Inc. **17.1:** © National Library of Medicine. **17.3:** Courtesy of Dr. Thomas F. Sellers/Emory University/CDC. **Virus File 1:** © Michelle Marsan/ShutterStock, Inc. **17.7a:** © Southern Illinois University/Photo Researchers, Inc. **17.7b:** © Medical-on-Line/Alamy Images. **17.8a:** Courtesy of Betty Partin/CDC. **17.8b:** Courtesy of CDC. **17.8c:** © James Cavallini/Photo Researchers, Inc.

Chapter 18

Opener: Courtesy of Dr. Lyle Conrad/CDC. **18.5a:** Courtesy of Petty Officer 2nd Class Kyle Niemi/U.S. Coast Guard. Photo courtesy of U.S. Army. **18.5b:** Courtesy of Andrea Booher/FEMA. **18.7:** Courtesy of Susan Mercado/CDC. **18.8a:** © CoolR/ShutterStock, Inc. **18.8b:** © Reuters/Kham/Landov. **Virus File 1a–b:** © Karl Ammann. **18.9a:** Courtesy of Alessandro Catenazzi. **18.10b:** © Andy Wong/AP Photos. **18.12a:** © Photos.com. **18.12b:** © Francois Etienne du Plessis/ShutterStock, Inc. **18.14:** © Olivier Le Queinec/ShutterStock, Inc. **18.15a:** Courtesy of CDC. **Virus File 2:** © Adam Borkowski/ShutterStock, Inc. **18.16a–b:** Courtesy of James Gathany/CDC.

Chapter 19

Opener: Courtesy of Dr. Art Davis, U.S. Dept. of Agriculture—Animal and Plant Health Inspection Service, APHIS/CDC. **19.1:** © National Library of Medicine. **19.5a:** Reproduced from P. Minor., *J. Gen. Virol.* 85 (2004): pp. 1777–1784. Image courtesy of P. Minor. **19.5b:** © vario images GmbH & Co.KG/Alamy Images. **19.6a:** Courtesy of Dr. Al Jenny, APHIS, USDA/CDC. **Virus File 1:** © David M. Phillips/Photo Researchers, Inc. **19.10:** Courtesy of ARS Archive, USDA. **19.11:** © Crown/Courtesy of Central Science Laboratory Photographic Services Unit.

Chapter 20

Opener: © Photos.com. **20.1b:** Courtesy of Peggy Greb/USDA ARS. **20.2a:** Courtesy of Whitney Cranshaw, Colorado State University, Bugwood.org. **2.2b:** Courtesy of Larry R. Barber, USDA Forest Service, Bugwood.org. **2.2c:** Courtesy of Alton N. Sparks, Jr., University of Georgia, Bugwood.org. **20.3a:** Courtesy of Clemson University—USDA Cooperative Extension Slide Series, Bugwood.org. **20.3b:** Courtesy of J.K. Brown, University of Arizona, Bugwood.org. **20.3c:** Courtesy of the Canadian Food Inspection Agency. **20.4a–b:** Courtesy of Elliot W. Kitajima, Ph.D., University of São Paulo, Brazil. **20.4c:** Reproduced from *J. Ultstruct. Res.* Vol. 29, Kitajima, E.W., Lauritis, J.A. and H. Swift, Morphology and intracellular localization of a bacilliform latent virus in sweet clover, p. 141, Copyright 1969, with permission from Elsevier. Image courtesy of Elliot W. Kitajima, Ph.D., University of São Paulo, Brazil. **20.4d:** Reproduced from E. W. Kitajima, *Fitopatol. Bras.* 1 (1976): 34. **Virus File 2:** © Phototake/Alamy Images. **20.12:** © Science Source/Photo Researchers, Inc. **20.13b:** Photo courtesy of the ATCC. **20.14a:** Courtesy of R.J. Reynolds Tobacco Company Slide Set, R.J. Reynolds Tobacco Company, Bugwood.org. **20.14b:** Courtesy of Clemson University—USDA Cooperative Extension Slide Series, Bugwood.org. **20.17:** Courtesy of Ken Hammond/USDA ARS. **20.18b:** Courtesy of Raymond K. Yokomi, Ph.D., USDA, Agricultural Research Service, Crop Diseases, Pests & Genetics Research Unit. **20.19:** Courtesy of Dr. Ronald H. Brlansky, University of Florida, CREC.

Chapter 21

Opener: Courtesy of Dr. Graham Beards. **21.1:** © SPL/Photo Researchers, Inc. **Virus File 1:** Courtesy Dr. Ramaz Katsarava, Center for Medical Polymers & Biomaterials and Georgian Technical University. **21.2a–b:** © David B. Fankhauser, PhD, University of Cincinnati Clermont College. **21.4a:** Courtesy of Maria Schnos and used with permission of Ross Inman, Department of Molecular Virology, Bock Laboratories, University of Wisconsin–Madisonx. **21.4b–c:** Photo courtesy of ICTVdB Picture Gallery. Used with permission from Hans W. Ackermann, Department of Medical Biology, Laval University. **21.8:** © Medical-on-Line/Alamy Images. **21.9:** Courtesy of Shawn Walshaw-Wertz, Cherokee Pharmaceuticals LLC. **21.10:** Courtesy of Rodney M. Donlan, Ph.D. and Janice Carr/CDC.